★

THE EIGHTH LIFE

(FOR BRILKA)

★

NINO HARATISCHVILI

Translated by
Charlotte Collins
and
Ruth Martin

HarperVia

An Imprint of HarperCollinsPublishers

Excerpt from "In a Shattered Mirror" by Anna Akhmatova from *The Poetry of Anna Akhmatova: Living in Different Mirrors* by Alexandra Harrington quoted by kind permission of Anthem Press.

Excerpts from *The Complete Poems of Anna Akhmatova* by Anna Akhmatova translated by Judith Hemschemeyer reprinted by kind permission of Canongate Books.

Excerpt from untitled poem by Anna Akhmatova translated by Graham Harrison reprinted by kind permission of the translator.

Excerpt from *Lolita* by Vladimir Nabokov. Copyright © 1955, Vladimir Nabokov, used by permission of The Wylie Agency (UK) Limited.

Excerpt(s) from *A RUSSIAN JOURNAL* by John Steinbeck, photographs by Robert Capa, copyright © 1948 by John Steinbeck, copyright renewed © 1976 by Elaine Steinbeck, Thom Steinbeck, and John Steinbeck IV. Used by permission of Viking Books, an imprint of Penguin Publishing Group, a division of Penguin Random House LLC. All rights reserved.

Every effort has been made to acknowledge and contact the copyright holders for permission to reproduce material contained in this book. Any copyright holders who have been inadvertently omitted from the acknowledgements and credits should contact the publisher so that omissions may be rectified in subsequent editions.

Without limiting the exclusive rights of any author, contributor, or the publisher of this publication, any unauthorized use of this publication to train generative artificial intelligence (AI) technologies is expressly prohibited. HarperCollins also exercise their rights under Article 4(3) of the Digital Single Market Directive 2019/790 and expressly reserve this publication from the text and data mining exception.

This is a work of fiction. Names, characters, places, and incidents are products of the author's imagination or are used fictitiously and are not to be construed as real. Any resemblance to actual events, locales, organizations, or persons, living or dead, is entirely coincidental.

THE EIGHTH LIFE (FOR BRILKA). Copyright © 2014 by Frankfurter Verlagsanstalt GmbH, Frankfurt am Main. English translation copyright © 2018 by Charlotte Collins and Ruth Martin. All rights reserved. Printed in Canada. No part of this book may be used or reproduced in any manner whatsoever without written permission except in the case of brief quotations embodied in critical articles and reviews. For information, address HarperCollins Publishers, 195 Broadway, New York, NY 10007. In Europe, HarperCollins Publishers, Macken House, 39/40 Mayor Street Upper, Dublin 1, D01 C9W8, Ireland.

HarperCollins books may be purchased for educational, business, or sales promotional use. For information, please email the Special Markets Department at SPsales@harpercollins.com.

harpercollins.com

Originally published as *Das achte Leben (Für Brilka)* in Germany in 2014 by Frankfurter Verlagsanstalt GmbH.

FIRST HARPERVIA PAPERBACK EDITION PUBLISHED IN 2026

Library of Congress Cataloging-in-Publication Data is available upon request.

ISBN 978-0-06-348585-3

26 27 28 29 30 TC 10 9 8 7 6 5 4 3 2 1

LONGLISTED FOR THE INTERNATIONAL BOOKER PRIZE
WINNER OF THE 2020 WARWICK PRIZE FOR WOMEN IN TRANSLATION

★

PRAISE FOR NINO HARATISCHWILI'S
THE EIGHTH LIFE (FOR BRILKA)

"The world fell away and I fell, wholly, happily, into the book. . . . My breath caught in my throat, tears nestled in my lashes . . . poignant, heart-stopping, sublime." —*New York Times Book Review*

"A harrowing, heartening, and utterly engrossing epic novel . . . astonishing." —*The Guardian*

"This multigenerational epic . . . offers not only a critique of Soviet and Russian imperial ambitions but a necessary reappraisal of Georgian history." —*The New Yorker*

"An exceptional, deeply evocative saga of an elite Georgian family as they endure the 20th century's political upheavals, from before the Bolshevik Revolution through the post-Soviet era. . . . In heartfelt prose, Haratischwili seamlessly weaves the political upheaval around the characters into the love and loss in their lives. Haratischwili's epic portrait of a close-knit family doubles as a stunning tribute to the power of resilience." —*Publishers Weekly* (starred review)

"A lavish banquet of family stories that can, for all their sorrows, be devoured with gluttonous delight. . . . [*The Eighth Life*] shows a double face, its crushing pain and loss nonetheless conveyed with an artful storyteller's sheer joy in her craft." —*Financial Times*

"This novel has generated substantial industry buzz and international critical praise. Both are justified . . . *The Eighth Life*—the story of a family, a country, a century—is an imaginative, expansive, and important read." —*Booklist* (starred review)

"If it's a family saga you're seeking, look no further than this grand tale . . . heartily recommended." —*Library Journal* (starred review)

For my grandmother,
who gifted me 1,000 stories and a poem.

For my father,
who left me with a bag full of questions.

And for my mother,
who told me where to seek the answers.

PROLOGUE
or
THE SCORE OF FORGETTING

2006

This story actually has many beginnings. It's hard for me to choose one, because all of them constitute *the beginning*.

You could start this story in an old, high-ceilinged flat in Berlin, quite undramatically, with two naked bodies in bed. With a twenty-eight-year-old man, a fiercely talented musician in the process of squandering his gift on impulse, alcohol, and an insatiable longing for intimacy. But you could also start this story with a twelve-year-old girl who decides to say NO! to the world in which she lives and set off in search of another beginning for herself, for her story.

Or you start the story with all the beginnings at once.

*

At the moment when Aman Baron, whom most people knew as 'the Baron', was confessing that he loved me — with heartbreaking intensity and unbearable lightness, but a love that was unhealthy, enfeebled, disillusioned — my twelve-year-old niece Brilka was leaving her hotel in Amsterdam on her way to the train station. She had with her a small bag, hardly any money, and a tuna sandwich. She was heading for Vienna, and bought herself a cheap weekend ticket, valid only on local trains. A handwritten note left at reception said she did not intend to return to her homeland with the dance troupe and that there was no point in looking for her.

At this precise moment, I was lighting a cigarette and succumbing to a coughing fit, partly because I was overwhelmed by what I was hearing, and partly because the smoke went down the wrong way. Aman (whom I personally never called 'the Baron') immediately came over, slapped me on the back so hard I couldn't breathe, and stared at me in bewilderment. He was only four years younger than me, but I felt decades older; besides, at this point I was well on my way to becoming a tragic figure — without anyone really noticing, because by now I was a master of deception.

I read the disappointment in his face. My reaction to his confession was not what he'd anticipated. Especially after he'd invited me to accompany him on tour in two weeks' time.

Outside, a light rain began to fall. It was June, a warm evening with weightless clouds that decorated the sky like little balls of cotton wool.

When I had recovered from my coughing fit, and Brilka had boarded the first train of her odyssey, I flung open the balcony door and collapsed on the sofa. I felt as if I were suffocating.

I was living in a foreign country; I had cut myself off from most of the people I'd once loved, those who used to mean something to me, and had accepted a visiting professorship that, though it guaranteed me a livelihood, had absolutely nothing to do with who I really was.

The evening Aman told me he wanted to *grow normal with me*, Brilka, my dead sister's daughter and my only niece, set off for Vienna, a place she had conceived of as her home, her personal utopia, all because of the solidarity she felt with a dead woman. In her imagination, this dead woman — my great-aunt, Brilka's great-great-aunt — had become her heroine. Her plan was to go to Vienna and obtain the rights to her great-great-aunt's songs.

And, in tracing the path of this ghost, she hoped to find redemption, and the definitive answer to the yawning emptiness inside her.

But I suspected none of this then.

After sitting on the sofa and putting my face in my hands, after rubbing my eyes and avoiding Aman's gaze for as long as possible, I knew I would have to weep again, but not now, not at this moment, while Brilka was watching old, new Europe slipping past her outside the train window and smiling for the first time since her arrival on this continent of indifference. I don't know what she saw that made her smile as she left the city of miniature bridges, but that doesn't matter anymore. The main thing is, she was smiling.

At that moment, I was thinking that I would have to weep. In order not to, I turned, went into the bedroom, and lay down. I didn't have to wait long for Aman. Grief like his is very quickly healed if you offer to heal it with your body, especially when the patient is twenty-eight years old.

I kissed myself out of my enchanted sleep.

As Aman laid his head on my belly, my twelve-year-old niece was leaving the Netherlands, crossing the German border in her compartment that stank of beer and loneliness, while several hundred kilometres away her unsuspecting aunt feigned love with a twenty-eight-year-old shadow. All the way across Germany she travelled, in the hope it would get her somewhere.

After Aman fell asleep, I got up, went to the bathroom, sat on the edge of the bath, and started to cry. I wept a century's worth of tears over the feigning of love, the longing to believe in words that once defined my life. I went into the kitchen, smoked a cigarette, stared out of the window. It had stopped raining, and somehow I knew that it was happening, something had been set in motion, something beyond this apartment with the high ceilings and the orphaned books; with the many lamps I had collected so eagerly, a substitute for the sky, an illusion of true light.

Perhaps it should be mentioned that Brilka was a very tall girl, almost two heads taller than me (which, at my height, isn't that difficult); that she had buzz-cut hair and John Lennon glasses, was wearing old jeans and a lumberjack shirt, had perfectly round cocoa-bean eyes that were constantly searching for stars, and an immensely high forehead that concealed a great deal of sorrow. She had just run away from her dance troupe, which was performing in Amsterdam; she danced the male roles, because she was too extravagant, too tall, too melancholy for the gentle, folkloristic women's dances of our homeland. After much pleading, she was finally allowed to perform dressed as a man and dance the wild dances; her long plait had fallen victim to this concession the previous year.

She was allowed to do leaps and to fence, and was always better at these than at the female dancers' wavelike, dreamy movements. She danced and danced with a passion, and after being given a solo for the Dutch audience — because she was so good, so much better than the young men who had sneered at her in the beginning — she left the troupe in search of answers that dancing, too, was unable to give her.

★

The following evening, I received a call from my mother, who was always threatening to die if I didn't return soon to the homeland I had fled all those years ago. Her voice trembled as she informed me that 'the child' had disappeared. It took me a while to work out which child she was talking about, and what it all had to do with me.

'So tell me again: where exactly was she?'

'In Amsterdam, for goodness' sake, what's the matter with you? Aren't you listening to me? She ran away yesterday and left a message. I got a call from the group leader. They've looked everywhere for her, and —'

'Wait, wait, wait. How can an eleven-year-old girl disappear from a hotel, especially if she —'

'She's twelve. She turned twelve in November. You forgot, of course. But that was only to be expected.'

I took a deep drag on my cigarette and prepared myself for the impending disaster. Because if my mother's voice was anything to go by, it would be no easy matter just to wash my hands of this and disappear: my favourite pastime in recent years. I armed myself for the obligatory reproaches, all of them intended to make clear to me what a bad daughter and failed human being I was. Things I was only too well aware of without my mother's intervention.

'Okay, she turned twelve, and I forgot, but that won't get us anywhere right now. Have they informed the police?'

'Yes, what do you think? They're looking for her.'

'Then they'll find her. She's a spoilt little girl with a tourist visa, I presume, and she —'

'Do you have even a spark of humanity left in you?'

'Sorry. I'm just trying to think aloud.'

'So much the worse, if those are your thoughts.'

'Mama!'

'They're going to call me. In an hour at most, they said, and I'm praying that they find her, and find her fast. And then I want you to go to wherever she is — she won't have got all that far — and I want you to fetch her.'

'I —'

'She's your sister's daughter. And you will fetch her. Promise me!'

'But —'

'Do it!'

'Oh God. All right, fine.'

'And don't take the Lord's name in vain.'

'Aren't I even allowed to say "Oh God" now?'

'You're going to fetch her and bring her back with you. And then you'll put her on the plane.'

They found her that same night, in a small town just outside Vienna, waiting for a connecting train. She was picked up by the Austrian police and taken to the police station. My mother woke me and told me I had to go to Mödling.

'Where?'

'Mödling, the town's called. Write it down.'

'Fine.'

'You don't even know what day it is today.'

'I'm writing it down! Where the hell is that?'

'Near Vienna.'

'What on earth was she doing there?'

'She wanted to go to Vienna.'

'Vienna?'

'Yes, Vienna. You must have heard of it.'

'All right! I've got it.'

'And take your passport with you. They know the child's aunt is picking her up. They made a note of your name.'

'Can't they just put her on a plane?'

'Niza!'

'Okay, I'm getting dressed. It's all right.'

'And call me as soon as you've got her.'

She slammed down the phone.

That's how this story begins.

Why Vienna? Why this, after the night of fleeing from my tears? There were reasons for it all, but for that I'd have to start the story somewhere else entirely.

★

My name is Niza. It contains a word: a word that, in our mother tongue, signifies 'heaven'. *Za*. Perhaps my life up till now has been a search for this particular heaven, given to me as a promise that has accompanied me since birth. My sister's name was Daria. Her name contains the word 'chaos'. *Aria*. Churning up, stirring up; the messing up and the not putting right. I am duty bound to her. I am duty bound to her chaos. I have always been duty bound to seek my heaven in her chaos. But perhaps it's just about Brilka. Brilka, whose name has no meaning in the language of my childhood. Whose name bears no label and no stigma. Brilka, who gave herself this name, and kept on insisting she be called this until others forgot what her real name was.

And, even if I've never told you, I would so like to help you, Brilka, so very much; to write your story differently, to write it anew. So as not just to say this, but to prove it as well, I'm writing all of this down. That's the only reason.

I owe these lines to a century that cheated and deceived everyone, all those who hoped. I owe these lines to an enduring betrayal that settled over my family like a curse. I owe these lines to my sister, whom I could never forgive for flying away that night without wings; to my grandfather, whose heart my sister tore out; to my great-grandmother, who danced a *pas de deux* with me at the age of eighty-three; to my mother, who went off in search of God … I owe these lines to Miro, who infected me with love as if it were poison; I owe these lines to my father, whom I never really got to know; I owe these lines to a chocolate-maker and a White-Red Lieutenant; to a prison cell; to an operating table in the middle of a classroom; to a book I would never have written, if … I owe these lines to an infinite number of fallen tears; I owe these lines to myself, a woman who left home to find herself and gradually lost herself instead; but, above all, I owe these lines to you, Brilka.

I owe them to you because you deserve the eighth life. Because they say the number eight represents infinity, constant recurrence. I am giving my eight to you.

A century connects us. A red century. Forever and eight. Your turn, Brilka. I've adopted your heart. I've cast mine away.

You are the miracle child. You are. Break through heaven and chaos, break through us all, break through these lines, break through the ghost world and the real world, break through the inversion of love, of faith, shorten the centimetres that always separated us from happiness, break through the destiny that never was.

Break through me and you.

Live through all wars. Cross all borders. To you I dedicate all gods and all rosaries, all burnings, all decapitated hopes, all stories. Break through them. Because you have the means to do it, Brilka. The eight — remember it. All of us will always be interwoven in this number and will always be able to listen to each other, down through the centuries.

You will be able to do it.

Be everything we were and were not. Be a lieutenant, a tightrope walker, a sailor, an actress, a filmmaker, a pianist, a lover, a mother, a nurse, a writer; be red and white, or blue; be chaos and heaven; and be them and me, and don't be any of it. Above all, dance countless *pas de deux*.

Break through this story and leave it behind you.

★

I was born on 8 November 1974, in an otherwise insignificant village clinic near Tbilisi, Georgia.

Georgia is a small country. It's beautiful, too — I can't argue with that; even you will agree with me, Brilka — with mountains and a rocky coastline along the Black Sea. The coastline has shrunk somewhat over the course of the past century, thanks to a multitude of civil wars, stupid political decisions, and hate-filled conflicts, but a part of it is still there.

You know the legend only too well, Brilka, but I'd like to mention it here anyway, to make clear to you what it is I'm trying to say — the legend that tells how our country came into being. Like this:

One beautiful, sunny day, God took the globe he had created, divided it up into countries (this must have been long before they built the tower at Babel), and held a fair, where all the people tried to outdo one another, shouting at the tops of their voices, vying for God's favour in the hope of snaffling the best patch of earth (I suspect the Italians were the most effective in the art of making an impression, whereas the Chukchi hadn't quite got the hang of it). It was a long day, and at the end of it the world had been divided up into many countries and God was tired. However, God — wise as ever — had, of course, kept back a sort of holiday residence for himself: the most beautiful place on earth, rich in rivers, waterfalls, succulent fruits, and — he must have known — the best wine in the world. When all the people had set off, excited, for their new homelands, God was just about to take a rest beneath a shady tree when he spotted a man (doubtless with a moustache and a comfortable paunch, at least that's how I've always imagined him), snoring. He hadn't been present at the distribution, and God was surprised. He woke him up and asked what he was doing here and why he wasn't interested in having a homeland of his own. The man smiled amiably (perhaps he had already permitted himself a glass or two of red wine) and said (here there are different versions of the legend, but let's agree on this one) that he was quite content as he was, the sun was shining, it was a gorgeous day, and he would settle for whatever God had left over for him. And God, gracious as ever, impressed by the man's nonchalance and utter lack of ambition, gave him his very own holiday paradise, which is to say: Georgia, the country you, Brilka, and I, and most of the people I will tell of in our story, are from.

What I'm trying to say is this: bear in mind that, in our country, this nonchalance (that is, laziness) and lack of ambition (lack of arguments) are considered truly noble characteristics. Bear in mind also that a profound identification with God (the Orthodox God, of course, and no other) does not prevent the people of our country from believing in everything that has even the slightest hint of the mysterious, legendary, or fairytale about it — and this is by no means restricted to the Bible. Giants in the mountains, house spirits, the evil eye that can plunge a man into misfortune, black cats and the curse that goes with them, the power of coffee grounds, the truth that only the cards reveal (you said that nowadays people even sprinkle new cars with holy water in the hope it will keep them accident-free).

The country, once golden Colchis, that had to surrender the secret of love to the Greeks in the shape of the Golden Fleece because the king's wayward daughter, Medea, so lovestruck she had lost her mind, commanded it.

The country that encourages in its inhabitants endearing traits like the sacred virtue of hospitality, and less endearing traits, like laziness, opportunism, and conformism (this is certainly not the perception of the majority — you and I agree on this, too).

The country in whose language there is no gender (which certainly does not equate to equal rights).

The country that, in the last century, after a hundred and thirty-five years of tsarist Russian patronage, managed to establish a democracy for precisely four years before it was toppled again by the mostly Russian but also Georgian Bolsheviks, and proclaimed the Socialist Republic of Georgia and thus a constituent republic of the Soviet Union.

The country that then remained in this *union* for the next seventy years. There followed numerous upheavals, bloodily suppressed demonstrations, several civil wars, and, finally, the long-awaited democracy — though that designation has remained a question of perspective and interpretation.

I think that our country can really be very funny (by which I mean not only tragic). That in our country forgetfulness, too, is very possible, in combination with repression. Repression of our own wounds, our own mistakes, but also of unjustly inflicted pain, oppression, losses. In spite of these, we raise our glasses and laugh. I think that's impressive, I really do, in view of the not very pleasant things the past century brought with it, the consequences of which people still suffer today (though I can already hear you contradict me!).

It's a country from which, in addition to the great executioners of the twentieth century, many wonderful people also come, people I personally have loved and still love very much. A country that is still mourning its Golden Age, from the tenth to the thirteenth century, and hopes one day to recover its former glory (yes, in our country progress is always simultaneously retrogression).

Traditions seem a pale reflection of what they once were. The pursuit of freedom is like a senseless quest for uncertain shores because, these past twenty years especially, we haven't even been able to agree on what exactly it is we mean by freedom. And so, today, the country where I came into the world thirty-two years ago is like a king who still sits in a glittering crown and magnificent robe, issuing commands, presiding over his realm, not realising that his entire court has long since fled and he is alone.

Don't cause any trouble — that's the first commandment in this country. You said this to me once, on our journey, and I made a note of it (I made a note of everything you said to me on our journey, Brilka).

To which I'll add:

Live as your parents lived; be seldom — better, never — alone. Being alone is dangerous and unprofitable. This country idolises community and mistrusts loners. Appear in cliques, with friends, in family or interest groups — you're worth very little on your own.

Procreate. We're a small country and we have to survive. (This commandment ranks alongside the first commandment.)

Always be proud of your country, never forget your language, find foreign countries, whichever they may be, beautiful, exciting, and interesting, but never, never, never better than your home.

Always find quirks and characteristics among the people of other nations that in Georgia would be, to say the least, disgraceful, and get worked up about them: general stinginess (that is, the reluctance to spend all your money for the benefit of the community); lack of hospitality (that is, the reluctance to reorganise your entire life whenever anyone comes to visit); insufficient willingness to drink and eat (that is, the inability to drink to the point of unconsciousness); lack of musical talent — characteristics like these.

Let your behaviour tend towards openness, tolerance, understanding, and interest in other cultures, provided they respect and always affirm the specialness and uniqueness of your homeland.

Be religious, go to church, don't question anything related to the Orthodox Church, don't think for yourself, cross yourself every time you see a church (very *en vogue*, you said!) — so about ten thousand times a day if you're in the capital. Don't criticise anything sacred, which is pretty much everything that has anything to do with our country.

Be bright and cheerful, because that's this country's mentality, and we don't like gloomy people in our sunny Georgia. You'll be all too familiar with that, too.

Never be unfaithful to your man, and if your man is unfaithful to you, forgive him, for he is a man. Live first and foremost for others. Because, in any case, others always know better than you what's good for you.

Finally, I want to add that, despite my years of struggling both for and with this country, I have not managed to replace it, to drive it out of me like an evil spirit that beset me. No ritual purification, no repression mechanism has yet been of any assistance. Because everywhere I went, travelling further and further from my country, I was searching for the squandered, scattered, wasted, unused love I'd left behind.

Yes — it's a country that doesn't want to show any ambition, that would ideally like to have everything handed to it on a plate because its people are so lovely, so nice, so happy and cheerful, and capable (on a good day) of putting a smile on the face of the world.

★

In this country, then, I came into the world, on 8 November 1974. A world that was too busy with other things to pay much attention to my arrival. The Watergate scandal, the anti-Vietnam-War campaigns, the military coup in Greece, the oil crisis, and Elvis were keeping the western world on its toes, while the eastern world was mired in dull stagnation under Brezhnev and the Soviet *nomenklatura*. A stagnation that consisted of people preserving power by all possible means, thereby rejecting any kind of reform, while increasingly closing their eyes to the black market and the burgeoning corruption.

Either way, people in both parts of the world were listening to Pink Floyd's 'The Great Gig in the Sky' for the first time. In the West, openly; secretly in the East.

And Vysotsky was to sing about those times:

> The eternal circus
> where promises burst
> like soap bubbles:

rejoice, if you can.
Great changes?
Nothing but words.
I don't like any of this,
it makes me sick.

Apart from my birth, and my sister's fall, nothing special happened that day. Except, perhaps, for the fact that, on this day, my mother finally lost her patience in the eternal battle with her father and her eternal hope for the understanding of her female relatives, and started screaming.

'Are you a whore?' my grandfather is said to have yelled at her; and my mother, weeping, is said to have screamed back, 'I might as well be, the way you treat me!'

Two hours later, she went into labour.

Parties to the conflict: my domineering grandfather, my infantile grandmother, and my mother, increasingly losing control of her own life.

The other unusual event that day, right before the contractions began, was my three-and-a-half-year-old sister's concussion.

A few days earlier, she had visited the nearby stud farm with our grandfather and fallen in love with the Arab horses and Dagestani ponies there; so on the day I was born, my grandfather had sat her on a pony and was just holding her lightly by the waist when the pony suddenly broke free and threw the little girl off. It happened so fast that my grandfather failed to catch her.

She fell, and crashed like a heavy pumpkin to the ground, which was lined with straw, but hard enough for my soft and rosy sister.

As my grandfather was throwing himself on his granddaughter in desperation, blaming the horse breeders and threatening to close 'the whole organisation' down, my mother — upset by the fight and by the hurtful words that would echo for a long time in the 'Green House', my childhood home — was starting to groan. My grandmother, who during this kind of noisy argument — and there were many — between her husband and her daughter would make a show of acting as a kind of umpire, but only inflamed both parties' anger by refusing to take sides, immediately ran into the kitchen where my mother was sitting and reached, without a word, for the massive telephone that hung on the kitchen wall.

The labour lasted precisely eight hours.

At the same moment that my mother, accompanied by her corpulent mother, was heading for the hospital in the village, my sister Daria, usually called Daro, Dari, or Dariko, was also being rushed to hospital.

My grandfather leapt into his daughter's white Lada — because his beloved Chaika (the 'Seagull', officially a GAZ-13 reserved for the Soviet elite) was too slow for the country roads — and raced to the best Tbilisi hospital, where it was certified that Daria had a slight concussion. And, a few kilometres away and a few hours later, that I had come into the world.

My noisy crying compelled my exhausted mother to raise her head, look at me, and realise that I didn't resemble anyone, before falling back again on what appeared to be a rather makeshift birthing stool.

My grandmother was the first person to hold me while fully conscious. I was, she declared, 'a baby with a preternaturally developed need for harmony': after all, I had come into the world in the middle of an argument.

As far as the need for harmony was concerned, she couldn't have been more wrong.

My grandfather, who had transported my sister home again from the hospital — she had been prescribed bed rest — received by telephone the news that I, 'scrawny and dark-haired', had now arrived and was blessed with 'robust health'. He sat down on the terrace, wrapped himself in his old sailor's jacket, which my sister and I were to squabble over so often, and shook his head.

While his mother baked a welcoming cake, fetched her favourite sour cherry liqueur from the cellar, and planned a birthday party, my grandfather sat there, not moving, stunned by his daughter's fresh disgrace, unable to do anything but shake his head repeatedly. My birth forced him once again to bestow his own family name — Jashi — upon a granddaughter, because I was conceived out of wedlock. And this time not just with a deserter and traitor, like my sister's progenitor, but with a man who was, quite simply, a criminal, in prison at the time of my birth.

'This child is a product of Elene's shamelessness and depravity, sealing my conclusive defeat in the battle for her honour, so I have absolutely no reason to be happy, or to celebrate anything at all. Even if it's not her fault, the girl is the embodiment of all the ills her mother has brought down upon us.' This was his first sentence, uttered with governmental finality after repeated demands from his mother — my great-grandmother — to please show some reaction to the arrival of his second grandchild.

Well, in this he wasn't too far wrong, and, given the circumstances into which I was born, I can't hold his words against him.

During the five days I spent in hospital with my mother, where my grandmother visited her daughter every day bringing chicken soup and pickled vegetables, my grandfather stayed at home and kept watch at Daria's bedside. She couldn't understand why she wasn't allowed to get up, so he kept her entertained with all sorts of stories, games, cartoons (he put a television set in her room specially); and Daria knew nothing of my existence, while my mother knew nothing of her first-born's concussion.

★

Daria was the idolised, adored child in our powerful grandfather's kingdom, destined to be worshipped and looked upon with wonder. Until she … But I'm getting ahead of myself. Before then, many years were to pass in which she performed brilliantly in the role of universally admired jewel.

Yet despite these circumstances — the extreme contrast in the division of roles that our grandfather, the head of the family, assigned to us from the very beginning — I had secured one advantage forever the day I was brought home from the village hospital: I had the crazy, unconditional love of my great-grandmother Stasia all to myself. She belonged to me and me alone. Great-Grandmother gave me the love she'd denied everyone else for decades; had given only frugally, in small doses, covertly, almost hesitantly, and, above all, not to her own son. But she gave it to me now: belligerently, loudly, almost obsessively, childishly, extravagantly. As if for all these years she had just been waiting for my arrival; as if she had been saving herself for me.

The day they brought me home, scrawny, shrivelled, and not the slightest bit sweet, was the day Anastasia, to give her full name, left her soundproof castle and emerged into the daylight to greet my ugly, humble self. No longer was she half-hearted and unworldly, as had been her way for so many years; something changed abruptly the minute she took me in her arms and closed her eyes.

And when she awoke from this somnambulistic state and finally inspected her great-granddaughter, she said: 'This is a different child. A special one. She needs a lot of protection and a lot of freedom.'

And everyone slapped their palms to their foreheads and groaned. The mad old lady had come back to life, and they weren't really sure whether this was a good thing or a disaster.

★

Initially, I, too, was permitted to idolise my older sister.

In my former life, I was often asked whether I suffered because of her beauty, her popularity, the general admiration she received. But it wasn't like that. Despite all the difficulties that accompanied Daria and me in our childhood and adolescence; although we tormented, almost tortured, one another, and found it very hard to forgive each other's failings, all this was only because of our incandescent love for one another.

When I was little, I always fell silent as soon as Daria approached, as soon as she contemplated touching my head or tickling my nose. I couldn't have done anything but idolise Daria, just like everyone else around us. Perhaps at this point I ought to try to explain her cruel, evident allure by saying that Daria had golden hair. And I mean really golden. Or perhaps that Daria had different-coloured eyes, incredibly different and incredibly fascinating, one a crystalline blue, the other hazelnut brown. That she had a captivating smile and an unusually deep, throaty voice for such a golden child, like that of a pudgy, sulky little boy. But that would make it all too easy; it wouldn't be enough.

Although my grandfather loved Daria so very much and saw my birth as a kind of effrontery because it threatened Daria's dominion, and although I, too, sensed this, right from the beginning, it made no difference: I sought and needed Daria's company.

★

I was an ugly child (and as such you quickly learn to fight to acquire beauty).

Stasia, as Anastasia was always called, had been a striking woman; not as unusually and dizzyingly beautiful as her younger sister Christine, but by the time I was born my great-grandmother's beauty had transformed into something surreal, dreamy. She had started to rediscover ballet, and, in doing so, to become young again.

We made a really great couple.

Stasia … I owe her so much, even if there were certainly moments in my childhood when I would have liked to reverse her awakening. When her love felt like a curse, and I often wished not to receive this love as strange compensation for the many other deprivations of my childhood. But, all in all, she taught me to live, to dance on a tightrope when everything around me was going up in flames, on a tightrope stretched taut, higher than any tower, poised and fearless — because, when you fall, all you do is stretch out your arms and you're flying. Thanks to her, I learned to curse (a very underappreciated skill: the ability to curse well in times when the world around you is falling apart). Thanks to her, I learned to look for ways of escaping when there is no escape, to climb the walls when bridges are collapsing, and to laugh *like a soldier*. Always, and especially when there's nothing to laugh about.

Thanks to her, I was able to slough off many curses like inconvenient clothes, and thanks to her I was able to see through hypocritical haloes. I owe all this, and much more, to Stasia, with whom everything really began …

One thing Stasia gave me, the thing that perhaps made the most lasting impression on me, is the story of the carpet.

One rainy morning — I was in the second or third year at school — when I'd stayed at home at the Green House because I'd caught a cold, I came across Stasia in the attic, the conversion of which had never been finished. There was an open balcony — wide as a terrace, but without a railing — where we children were always forbidden to set foot, but which was nonetheless our favourite place to spend time, as we often did in secret. Now Stasia was standing on this balcony beating out a moth-eaten carpet, beautifully patterned in various shades of pomegranate red. I'd never seen the carpet before.

'Stay there. Don't come any closer!' she commanded when she saw me.

'What are you doing?'

'I've decided to have this carpet restored.'

'What does restored mean?' I asked. I stopped in front of her, fascinated.

'I'm going to make the old carpet new again and hang it on the wall. The carpet belonged to our grandmother, and Christine inherited it. She never liked it, so she gave it to me, but I never appreciated it either, not until I was old. It's a very ancient, very valuable tapestry.'

'You can't do that, can you, make something old new?'

'Of course you can. The old thing will become new, so it'll be different, never quite what it used to be, but that's not the point of the exercise. It's better and more interesting when something transforms itself. We'll make it new, hang it up, and see what happens.'

'But what for?' I wanted to know.

'A carpet is a story. And hidden within it are countless other stories. Come here; be careful, take my hand, yes, that's it. Now look: do you see the pattern?'

I stared at the colourful ornamentation on the red background.

'Those are all individual threads. And each individual thread is an individual story. Do you understand what I'm saying?'

I nodded, spellbound, although I wasn't sure I did understand.

'You're a thread, I'm a thread; together we make a little ornamentation, and together with lots of other threads we make a pattern. The threads are all different, differently thick or thin, dyed different colours. The patterns are hard to make out if you look at just one individual thread, but if you look at them together you start to see all sorts of amazing things. Look here, for example. Isn't that gorgeous? This ornamentation — absolutely marvellous! Then there's the density and number of knots, the different colour structures — all that creates the texture. I think it's a very good metaphor. I've been thinking about it a lot lately. Carpets are woven from stories. So we have to preserve and take care of them. Even if this one has spent years packed away somewhere for moths to feast on, it must now come to life again and tell us its stories. I'm sure we're woven in there, too, even if we never suspected it.'

And Stasia beat away at the heavy carpet with all her might.

It's a lesson I've never forgotten.

I don't know whether I should thank Stasia at this point because, with this knowledge, she more or less condemned me to become addicted to stories and spend years looking obsessively for the stories *behind* the stories, like the different patterns in a precious carpet.

So I'll begin here, comforting myself a little, like a fearful child hugging her favourite toy as tightly as she can. Because I am afraid. I don't know whether I can do myself justice with what I want to try to tell you — whether I can do you justice, Brilka.

And I'm afraid of these stories. These stories that constantly run in parallel, chaotically; that appear in the foreground, conceal themselves, interrupt one another. Because they connect and break through each other, they betray and mislead, they lay tracks, cover them up, and most of all they contain within them hundreds of thousands of other stories.

I don't know whether I myself have understood everything and recognised the connections, but I have to hope, and — if I must, if the ropes fail and all the bridges collapse — stretch out my arms once again; I have to hope that, if the worst comes to the worst, I will, somehow, fly.

I'll start with Stasia in order to make my way to you, Brilka.

★

She came into the world — so I was told — in the coldest winter at the dawn of the twentieth century. She had a headful of hair; you could have plaited it, they said. And with her first cry she was, in fact, already dancing. They said she laughed as she cried, as if she were crying more to reassure the adults, her parents, the midwives, the country doctor, not because she had to.

And they said that with her first steps she was already describing a *pas de deux*. And that she loved chocolate, always. And that before she was able to say 'Father' she was babbling *Madame Butterfly*. And that she discovered the gramophone at an early age and played the latest records before she could write and read properly, singing and dancing along. And that Eleonora Duse was her favourite. And that she was more nimble and eloquent than either of her sisters. And the cleverest and the most cheerful.

But people say all kinds of things when they tell stories like these.

She loved books and the fine arts, they said, but above all it was in dancing that she spent her days. And they said it was in dancing that she turned the head of the White Guard lieutenant, at the mayor's New Year ball, her first ball; impudent, gamine she seemed then, they said, you might have thought almost provocative. And the plaits: she had braided her long plaits around her head, they shone round her narrow head like a halo, around her porcelain brow. She shone, they said, so brightly that he fell in love with her light. Undying love, of course; forever, of course.

And they say that, of all the women, she was the best at riding astride, and that this impressed the lieutenant. Considerably. And that she was interested in the bluestockings and wanted to train as a dancer, in Paris, at the *Ballets Russes*. She was seventeen then; he asked for her hand, then the Revolution came and threatened to tear them apart. Shortly before he left for Russia, she grew afraid and forgot the *Ballets Russes* and the bluestockings, and married him. In the little church, in the presence of two of her sisters and the priest Seraphim. They spent the wedding night in a guesthouse on the edge of the steppe, near the cave monastery: just the two of them, the night, the cave, the stones. That's how it was, they said.

Of course, she should have fallen pregnant immediately, that's what usually happens in stories like these, but not in this one.

Before this, they said, she had repeatedly asked her father, the chocolate-maker, to give her permission to go to Paris and study the fine art of dance. He had always replied that it was improper to ride astride, and most certainly improper to perform vulgar bodily contortions in a foreign city.

So she travelled to Petrograd, to her husband, and not to Paris.

And it was only much later, they said, after many peregrinations and much suffering, that she returned to the warmth of her homeland.

To the land where, decades later, I, too, would be born; and you, Brilka.

And this is where, for now, legend ends and facts begin. Their child, the eldest child she bore, grew to manhood and fathered a daughter. The daughter grew to womanhood and bore Daria and me. And Daria had you, Brilka. The women, the lieutenants, the daughters and sons are dead, and the legend, you, and I are alive. So we must try to make something of this.

BOOK I
★
STASIA

> No, not under the vault of alien skies
> And not under the shelter of alien wings —
> I was with my people then,
> There, where my people, unfortunately, were.
>
> ANNA AKHMATOVA

The doorbell was ringing and none of her sisters were answering. Someone kept yanking at the bell-pull and she continued to sit, motionless, looking out at the garden. It had been raining all morning; her mood rendered visible. The rain, the grey sky, the damp earth: they exposed her, giving the whole world an insight into her wounds.

Her father was not yet home, and her stepmother had taken the little one out to buy fabric in Papa's magnificent new carriage. She called her sisters. No one answered, so she slowly stood up and forced herself to go downstairs and open the door.

A young man in a white uniform was standing outside. She had never seen him before, and she stepped back from the heavy oak door, slightly confused.

'Good morning. You must be Anastasia? Allow me to introduce myself: Simon Jashi, lieutenant of the White Guard and a friend of your father's. We have an appointment. May I come in?'

No ordinary soldier, then; a lieutenant, an officer. She merely nodded silently and proffered her hand. He was well built, tall and broad-shouldered, with slender limbs and bony hands: the latter were rather hairy, which seemed incongruous in such a dapper gentleman; it was as if Nature were forcing its way through the uniform.

He removed his perfectly angled headgear, which she found ever so slightly ridiculous, and stepped inside. She wondered where all the others were; it was only now that she noticed that the whole house was silent as the grave.

The smell of coffee and cake wafted from the kitchen, but no one was there. She took the guest through to the reception room, where the door to the garden stood open. Rain was blowing into the room, the white curtains flapping in the damp wind. She quickly ran to the door and closed it. The rain was a threat to her: seeing it, she felt the urge to cry again, which in the presence of this strange man was inconceivable.

It occurred to her that he had recognised her and addressed her by name, although they were four sisters. Yet he had never been to their house before; she could tell that from the way his eyes kept darting curiously about. It was a trap. Yes, that was what it was. Now she understood the sudden emptiness of the house. So it was him. He was the one. He was the wrathful God who was to mete out her punishment. He was the guarantor of her future. He was the slaughterer, the executioner. She turned pale and stumbled out of the room.

'Is everything all right?' he called after her.

'Oh yes, yes. I'll just fetch us some coffee and cake. You do like coffee?' she called from the kitchen, leaning against the wall and wiping away her tears with her sleeves.

Nothing would ever again be as it was. Suddenly, she had understood this; she had received confirmation that her childhood was over. That her life would, at a stroke, become another; that everything — all her dreams, desires, visions — would be reduced to this one man in the white Russian uniform, probably a subordinate of the fat, uneducated governor of Kutaisi — how frightful!

She felt like throwing up, but the coffee was steaming in its pot and the chocolate gateau from Papa's patisserie, symmetrically cut, was waiting to be offered to the guest.

And so the chocolate gateau was her first offering to her executioner. Just as she would have to offer up to him all the promises of a future that Life itself had whispered into her ear night after night: offer them up for him to kill, in that she would start to live his life, where she would not find her place, where she would be an outsider, where she would never be at home. She bit her lip and stifled the pain.

She carried out the silver tray with the steaming coffee and the porcelain cups and saucers. The man was sitting in Papa's armchair, legs crossed, staring at the green lawn that was being drowned and buried by the heavy rain, along with the little spring flowers that had forced their way up through the earth, greedy for life and warmth.

'Oh, that's delicious. Your father is a true genius. And such a good man. So modest: a man of humility. One seldom finds such men nowadays. Someone plants a tree and the whole parish has to hear about it. Nobody does good deeds any more nowadays, at least, not without shouting them from the rooftops. Your father's not like that. I'm very proud to be able to count myself one of his circle. And your *maman*. She is enchanting.'

'She's my stepmother.'

'Oh.'

'Do take a slice. We have plenty more cake. There's never a shortage of sweets in this house.'

'Yes, I'm familiar with your father's creations. Those delicious little almond tarts — and his plum mousse is magnificent! An absolute dream.'

'And how do you know Papa, may I ask?'

'I ... I did him a favour once, if I might put it that way.'

'You said just now that, when one has done something good, one should not speak of it. That, if I understood you correctly, is true greatness.'

'You're very precise.'

'I am indeed.'

'The cake is divine. Why don't you try some?'

'I eat enough of it every day. Thank you.'

'I did him a favour, that's all. I didn't say it was a good deed that I did.'

'It's in the nature of a favour that it should be good.'

'That depends entirely on how you look at it, wouldn't you agree? Everyone sees things from their own perspective, which is not necessarily shared by others.'

'That's not what I meant. There are some things about which all people should feel the same. And see in the same way.'

'And what would those things be?'

'For example, that the sun is wonderful, and that spring can work miracles; that the sea is deep, and water soft. That music is magical when it is well played. That toothache is a dreadful business, and ballet the most beautiful thing in the world.'

'I understand. You love to dance, don't you?'

'Yes, I do.'

'And you don't like me because you think I don't share this view?'

'How should I know?'

'It's what you think. It's what you suppose.'

'I don't suppose anything at all.'

'That I don't believe.'

'All right, I admit it: no, I don't believe you share many of my opinions, not least because you're serving in the army and I am not fond of the army.

Why are you laughing?'

'I'm sorry. You amuse me.'

'Oh, splendid. At least one of us is in a good mood.'

'Do you ride?'

'What?'

'I said: do you ride?'

'Yes, of course I ride.'

'Side-saddle, I presume?'

'I prefer astride.'

'Excellent! Would you venture on a ride across the steppe with me tomorrow?'

'I have a ballet lesson tomorrow.'

'I can wait for you.'

'I don't know.'

'Or are you afraid?'

'What would I be afraid of? Certainly not of you.'

'It's agreed, then?'

'Listen: I don't know what my father has told you about me. But it's bound to be untrue. I don't know what he's promised you, but I'm certain I am unable to give you that, either. I will happily risk your anger, and my father's, but I have no intention of deceiving you. I will not love you. Why are you laughing again?'

'You're even better than your father's description of you.'

'What has he promised you?'

'Nothing. He just said that I might visit you from time to time.'

'So that later on I'll marry you and won't be permitted to dance any more?'

'So that we can get to know each other.'

'You're much older. It's inappropriate.'

'I'm twenty-nine.'

'You're still much older. Twelve years is a big age gap.'

'I look very young.'

'You know nothing whatsoever about ballet.'

'I saw you dance at the private performance at Mikeladze's.'

'Really?'

'Yes.'

'And?'

'You were quite good.'

'*Quite* good? I was *very* good.'

'Perhaps. After all, you just said I know nothing about it.'
'Well, every layman has the right to an opinion.'
'Oh, how generous of you.'
'You don't have a moustache.'
'And what does that mean?'
'It's not the done thing.'
'According to the latest fashion, it is.'
'I'm very conservative.'
'That's not my impression.'
'You don't know me.'

'I saw you when you were fourteen, listening to the Maxim brothers' violin concert. We sat side by side, and you were so moved that you wept, and you wiped away your tears with the sleeves of your dress. You didn't use a silk handkerchief. I liked that. And then you stormed out of the concert hall. And, months later, I saw you at the circus that pitched its big top up there in the hills. And you were eating a baked apple and licking your fingers. You didn't use a silk handkerchief. *Which is the done thing.* And later I saw you at the New Year's ball, your first ball, given by the mayor. You were enchanting, dancing your first dance, but your partner was an idiot, incapable of leading you. He kept treading on your feet, and every time he did you pulled a face. You came out and wiped the little pearls of sweat from your brow with the edge of your dress. No silk handkerchief. Then you sat down on the stone steps and looked up at the sky. And I decided it was time I got to know you.'

'Why should I want to get to know *you*?'
'Because I'm another one who never uses a handkerchief.'
'What's that supposed to mean?'
'Someone who needs a veil, an object, even one made of silk, between themselves and the world is afraid of life. They're afraid to experience things, to really feel them. And I think life is far too short and far too wonderful not to really look at it, not to really grab it, not to really live it.'
'By which you're trying to say that we are similar?'
'No, I just think that we have a similar attitude to life.'
'Nonetheless, I am not going to marry you and move with you to Moscow.'
'I'm not in Moscow. I'm here.'
'You serve the Russians, and I don't like Russians. They say that soon there will be uprisings. That things are unsettled in Russia. There are rumours. Anyway, Papa went to Russia, too, and brought his wife back here with him when he married the second time. I know how things work in this world.'

'And how do they work?'

'Not exactly to the advantage of us women, shall we say?'

'A real bluestocking, then.'

'Now what are you talking about?'

'In Europe, there are women who believe they are equal to men. And who fight for these rights. Bluestockings, they're called.'

'And they're right to fight. But it's a very stupid name, in my opinion.'

'In that case, we can go on a proper ride across the steppe. Then we can see just how equal men and women are.'

'I don't believe they are equal. I believe women are better.'

'Better still. I'll see you tomorrow, then.'

'Wait ... You don't even know where I take my ballet classes.'

'I'll find you. And send my best wishes to your father. No need to see me out. A truly emancipated lady should always remain seated.'

'A what lady?'

'One who fights for her rights.'

He left the room, with quick, light steps and a mischievous grin. Stasia remained seated, as if turned to stone, unable to believe what had just occurred. It wasn't permitted to like your executioner; it wasn't permitted to flirt with him. It wasn't permitted to offer him more sacrifices than were necessary. It wasn't permitted to go riding with him. And then she laughed aloud. The rain had stopped and the flowers were springing up out of the earth. Life was everywhere again, with its sweet multitude of promises. Stasia opened the door to the garden and ran out. The earth was damp and her feet got stuck in the mud, but that didn't stop her from dancing a *pas de deux* in the sodden garden.

★

They met and rode across the steppe, both of them astride. I'm sure she looked incredibly graceful and self-assured. She had started learning to ride when she was a little girl, and she loved to take the thoroughbred Kabardins out and ride them bareback. She liked to linger in the barren landscape of the steppe. The old cave city was a place she knew like the back of her hand. People were always going missing in this mysterious labyrinth of stone steps, interconnected rooms, and crannies, but Stasia always found her way back: the way out of the cave city, which had been cut into the huge mountain centuries ago at the command of the country's powerful queen, and had now become a desolate landscape where the ghosts sang. Yes, you could hear them, if you closed your eyes tightly enough and silenced the thoughts in your own head. And I'm sure the lieutenant was even more impressed by her skill. They are sure to have talked about all kinds of things, and Stasia often challenged him to race her.

They started making plans to go riding together every day. Soon, Stasia was so enthralled by the hours they spent together on the steppe that some days she even forgot about dancing.

Of course, our seventeen-year-old Stasia had to fall in love. The White Lieutenant was delighted by Stasia's trust, which grew day by day, ride by ride. And it was his firm belief that they would be good for each other; that he needed just such a headstrong wife — and this firm belief inevitably impressed Stasia.

Simon Jashi also admired the chocolate-maker's family, and his affection was returned by his beloved's father. Anastasia was to experience no resistance to her choice of husband — unlike her second-eldest sister, who, whenever she fell for a man, could always count on her father's disapproval. The White Lieutenant, by contrast, seemed to be Papa's first choice.

And since these were troubled times, and one never knew which way the wind would blow, one had to act quickly. Even in matters of the heart.

★

The White Lieutenant had attended a cadet school in St Petersburg, when the St Petersburg of delightful balls and sweet French accents still existed. He had fought only briefly in Russia's war with Japan, where he was wounded, promoted to lieutenant, and sent back to his homeland. This wound saved him from being sent to fight in the First World War. After his recovery, he was assigned to administrative duties in his sleepy little hometown, where he analysed war correspondence.

Simon did not rush to request a transfer. The political situation was unfathomable, and he was insufficiently resolute; never in his life had he been able to feel at home with an ideology that would determine his onward path.

At that time, innumerable ideologies and political groups were springing up out of the ground every day like mushrooms, in little attic rooms, canteen cellars, and flats overlooking dingy courtyards, and all of them believed they had discovered the solution to every problem, or knew precisely how to guarantee a rosy future for the downtrodden Russian people.

Simon came from a good middle-class family: his father, a respected doctor, had made sure his son received a good education. Influenced at an early age by liberal, democratic ideas, as a young man he had made contact with the liberals in the military circles of his cadet school, and had even been to a few meetings. But at the same time he had realised that, if it were to come to the crunch, the liberals seemed too weak and not nearly purposeful enough to withstand a serious threat, such as that represented by socialism. And Simon could also see that the socialists were always louder, always more demanding and fearless. All kinds of conspiracy theories and legends circulated about the party's ringleaders, the majority of whom had already been imprisoned or had moved abroad.

Simon had little sympathy with the socialists; they were too primitive, too unrefined, too loud for his middle-class ears, but at the same time he didn't want to end up on the wrong side. He had to act. He had to decide, but he was still too hesitant: events were not transparent enough, there were still too many possibilities.

He had already come into contact with a few ideas at the front, and, having been wounded and ordered back to his hometown, he started a circle for 'the study of the philosophical writings of the Ancient Greeks' in the hope that, together with others who were confused and searching for answers, he would find some knowledge that would take him further. Simon Jashi felt himself to be neither a reformer nor a revolutionary. As a soldier loyal to the authorities, he served the military unquestioningly, along with its clear hierarchies, discipline, and division of duties. He loved clear structures and regulated relationships, in which everyone knew exactly where they stood. Simon was a rational man. He was gallant, tractable, rather morose, and thoughtful by nature, not a man of burning ideas and deeds. He also had nothing against the tsars, though he might have had a little sympathy for the peasants, as was proper for the authorities at that time.

But one notable characteristic may have recommended him to the chocolate-maker as a good match for his daughter: Simon was a sentimental man, and a great devotee of the past. He loved Pushkin's Russia; he dreamed of the great Napoleonic balls, grew downright maudlin at *Swan Lake*. In my great-great-grandfather's eyes, his heart was warmed by everything connected to the divinely appointed king, the tsar, and thus to a clearly structured world.

This must have been a very idiosyncratic and peculiar attitude for such a young man at the time, but it chimed perfectly with my great-great-grandfather's worldview. Simon's heart belonged to Old Russia, to the European elite, and the lovely, glittering life of the *good old days* — or rather, what he imagined these to be.

★

To my great-great-grandfather, being conscious of tradition meant living according to the values of the elite: displaying modesty and excellent manners, and being neither too hedonistic nor too puritanical. And knowing exactly which layer of society was created for which purpose, and which people in society had to occupy which places. Great-Great-Grandfather stemmed from the impoverished minor Georgian nobility. He had completed a confectionary apprenticeship at a high-class spa hotel in the Crimea, rising quickly from apprentice to head of the *chocolaterie*. His skill had enabled him to attract the regular custom of a lot of rich aristocrats, whose patronage he enjoyed, and, thanks to their support, he was eventually able to spend two years in Budapest with a master *chocolatier*, who had previously worked for the royal household in Vienna.

My great-great-grandfather gathered experiences from all over Europe. He toured some excellent patisseries in western Europe, and yet, contrary to his employers' expectations, he decided to return to his homeland and start a business of his own.

He had — and unfortunately I am not in possession of any verifiable information about where exactly he developed his incomparable chocolate — discovered a magical secret formula, and had a recipe in his pocket that would revolutionise the taste of hot chocolate.

★

At this point, the recipe — or rather, the hot chocolate resulting from it — should be introduced as one of the principal characters in our story, Brilka.

As, unfortunately, I may not reveal the ingredients of the drink (under no circumstances, no way, never, never, never), I have to find words to describe the indescribable. And, unfortunately, I also don't know whether my great-great-grandfather derived this recipe from somebody else or developed it himself. He guarded it like a secret of war. But one thing is certain: on his return home, he already had the guarantee for his future success in his pocket (at that point, nothing was known of the side-effects of his magic chocolate).

For now, it was a recipe for a simple Viennese-style hot chocolate. This meant that the base was chocolate, not cocoa. First the chocolate was manufactured, then it was melted and mixed with other ingredients.

But something in the mixture and the preparation made this chocolate special, unique, irresistible, startling. The very scent of it was so enticing and so intense that one couldn't help hurrying towards its source.

The chocolate was thick, syrupy, and black as the night before a heavy storm. It was consumed in small portions, hot, but not too hot, in small cups, and — ideally — with silver spoons.

The taste was incomparable: savouring it was like a spiritual ecstasy, a supernatural experience. You melted into the sweet mass, you became one with this delicious discovery, you forgot the world around you, and felt a unique sense of bliss. As soon as you tasted this chocolate, everything was exactly as it should be.

My great-great-grandfather returned home from Budapest with this secret recipe in his pocket. He was proud of what he had achieved, and he believed it was possible to bring the gallantry and exquisite tastes of Paris or Vienna to the Georgian provinces, and change the tastes of the people there.

Following his return, he married a pupil from the Holy Mother of God convent school, a pious and taciturn woman named Ketevan, who had what one might call melancholic tendencies. She didn't care two figs for the Russian Empire, thought Russia's annexation of Georgia the most disastrous mistake in the whole of Georgian history, and all her life refused to speak Russian. He had fallen in love with her; it was not an arranged marriage, but unfortunately it was not a happy one, either. She espoused different values; she saw Russia as the origin of all evil, while my great-great-grandfather viewed Russia as an opportunity for Georgia, and believed it was the Russians who had first given the Caucasus access to world culture, combating the illiteracy among Georgia's population and the greed of its minor aristocracy. He was pro-tsarist, and enjoyed all the privileges that his *collaborateur* lifestyle afforded. His wife, however, never tired of claiming that Georgia was nothing more than a colony, and that the Slavic culture was the downfall of the Caucasian.

'We ourselves called on our great neighbour — we invited him here,' my great-great-grandfather told his wife in the first months of their marriage, in an attempt to change her mind.

'We invited them as helpers, not occupiers,' Ketevan retorted. 'Our king was exhausted by all the occupations and raids by our Muslim neighbours. He couldn't see any other way out, and when he asked the tsar to sign a protection treaty he was choosing what, in his view, was the lesser of two evils. A protection treaty, with the emphasis on protection. If I might remind you.'

'Yes, but, my love, in practice it still meant that, from then on, we were subject to the great Russian Empire, and our king knew that when he brought the Russians into the country.'

'Certainly, my dear, but he probably didn't know that our northern neighbour would accept this invitation not for a few years, but for a few centuries.'

Ketevan refused to be beaten.

'I think it is wrong, my love, always to take the image of David and Goliath and use it as a parable for our country. I think that, in so doing, we make it very easy for ourselves. Too many Georgians have benefited from it, Ketevan; you surely must agree with that!'

'In this country, assimilation is always feigned, and at the core of this assimilation you always find a longing for what belongs to us alone. I speak of true Georgians and not of traitors,' replied Ketevan, casting a scornful glance at her husband.

Ketevan barely involved herself in my great-great-grandfather's business. She was good at managing the household and knew how to present herself in society, and she bore him two daughters. But the couple's love and affection for each other was extinguished, at the latest, after the birth of their second daughter. Ketevan dedicated herself to piety, praying, and maintaining good relationships with the Church and the priests, while her husband opened his shop, The Chocolaterie, which everyone always called 'the chocolate factory', with my great-great-grandfather known only as the 'chocolate-maker'. The business flourished, sales rose from one year to the next, and the chocolate-maker's reputation was established.

He was disappointed that his wife didn't value his success and seemed to make no use at all of the family's social and financial privileges, or to enjoy their increasing prosperity. He had looked for the same support and encouragement from her that he got from others. Five years after his return, he was running a patisserie that was famed throughout the town, and planning branches all over the country; later, he hoped, at the pinnacle of his success, he would be able to supply the whole of the tsar's empire with the very best chocolate products.

He produced divine gateaux and cakes of every description. Truffles, bitter chocolate, milk chocolate with apricot jelly, with walnuts, or raisins, and more exotic items like chocolate tarts with black pepper, cherry liqueur centres coated with mint chocolate, chocolate biscuits filled with fig cream, or chocolate nougat with watermelon jelly. The Chocolaterie managed to unite the French art of patisserie and traditional Austrian baking with Eastern European opulence.

At six o'clock every morning he went to the shop and added his own ingredients to the huge mixtures of chocolate prepared by his employees for each product in his range, giving them their special flavour. Nobody could work out the formula, and it was this that made his chocolate so irresistible.

So far, he had added only a very small amount of the special mixture to all his chocolate products — a finishing touch to the flavour, as it were — but it was in the hot chocolate that its magic was at its most potent.

Encouraged by the tremendous success of his magic formula, which made him flirt with ambitious plans for expansion, he planned to unveil the *crème de la crème* of his creation — the hot chocolate — only at the very pinnacle of his fame and success, in Tbilisi, Moscow, or St Petersburg. It would make everybody swoon. In spite, or perhaps because of his success, the chocolate-maker, who was hoping for an heir, had sworn to keep his recipe in the family, and to keep it secret for the time being.

According to Stasia, this decision saved our family, if not our whole country, from total ruin.

Alongside his work, my great-great-grandfather was a freeman of the town, and took part in its social and cultural life, moving in elevated circles in local politics, founding the town's only gentlemen's club (in the European style), and becoming the patron of several literature, theatre, and philosophy circles. He sat on the committee of the 'Society for Tradition and Honour' and was also, incidentally, one of the richest inhabitants of the little town, which he wanted to transform into the 'Nice of the Caucasus', since Tbilisi already enjoyed a reputation as the Caucasian Paris.

His wife cared little for these outward appearances, preferring to occupy her time with Bible study and the strict upbringing of their two daughters. She had to be persuaded to take part in any kind of social event, and was not particularly keen on travelling, either, which didn't please the chocolate-maker at all. Her exaggerated piety also vexed him. He sensed that, because of it, he had lost all connection with his children, who were also, under the strict eye of their mother and a religious governess, growing into pious, timid, un-European girls.

The battle on the female front in his own house seemed to be one he was losing, with grave consequences.

He had to have a son! The female majority in his house had simply become too threatening. He needed an heir, a man to fight by his side in the battle against the opposite sex. It was a long time since the couple had shared a marital bed, and he knew it would require a lot of time and all his powers of persuasion. The two births had been very difficult for Ketevan, and she wasn't in the best of health. It wouldn't be easy to convince her to go through another pregnancy.

Several times he explained to his wife that it was purely a matter of inheritance because, after all, the chocolate factory needed a male heir — but she remained unimpressed, and consoled him with the thought that his two daughters would marry, and a shrewd son-in-law was a good alternative solution to the problem.

He therefore had to employ other means to convince his wife to bear him a successor. And so he decided to make his finest creation for her — the hot chocolate — because the more concentrated the ingredients, the greater the effect of the recipe.

He arranged for a little string quartet to play, just for her, in the chocolate factory, which was already closed to visitors; and, by candlelight, enveloped in the intoxicating aroma of his own concoction, he set in front of her the most beautiful porcelain cup he had been able to find in his shop. As she spooned up the chocolate, he spoke honeyed words to her, convincing her of how essential it was for him to have a male heir.

Like so many people after her, Ketevan was overcome by an unbridled craving for more, and, in the days that followed, she begged her husband to make the hot chocolate for her again. And so my great-great-grandfather was finally able to give her an ultimatum: if she would undergo another pregnancy, he would prepare the hot chocolate for her every day for the following nine months. Her resistance was broken, and her longing for the most delicious taste in the world gave her no choice but reluctantly to give in and agree to his offer.

And so it was that, nine months later, she found herself in labour in her bedroom once again, attended by a country doctor and two midwives. It was several hours before they got a healthy, well-formed girl out of her (the mother just gave a disappointed sigh). She thought she had come through it all successfully, until the worried doctor called out that the labour was still progressing. A second one was on the way. After more pushing and screaming, another girl finally saw the light of day.

But the second child refused to cry. Something wasn't right with her lungs, the doctor declared; the child was turning blue, she wasn't getting any air, and he slapped her hard on the back. A few minutes after the birth, the second baby had to be pronounced dead (they had been identical twins).

But the first, who was baptised Anastasia, seemed healthy and cheerful, and screamed lustily for her mother's milk.

A short while later, Ketevan died of pneumonia contracted during her confinement. She went quickly, without any great torment, after giving Anastasia the breast for the last time.

These two tragedies were the first in my great-great-grandfather's life: they came in such quick succession, and were so definitive, so immense, that for months afterwards he handed the whole of the business over to his chief secretary, as he was in no condition to leave the house. Only in the mornings did he walk to the shop, with sluggish, shuffling steps, to prepare the mixture that went into every batch of chocolate.

His love for his wife may not have been as fresh and radiant over the preceding years as at the start of their marriage, but she had remained an important part of his life. The loss of the mother of his children weighed heavily upon him, and, left alone, he had no idea what to do with the three girls.

During this time, he began to be haunted by peculiar thoughts. He couldn't shake the feeling that he had been responsible for his wife's death. If he hadn't coerced her into another pregnancy, she might have been alive, and he would also have been spared the tragedy of the baby's death.

Could it be that there was a fatal aspect to his bewitching creation? Had the chocolate he had so enthusiastically prepared for her through all those months set the catastrophe in motion? Was it simply too delicious to be consumed without paying a high price? Did it make those who tasted it so happy and carefree that reality then had to avenge itself upon them all the more mercilessly? Could it even be cursed? Could he have discovered something that was too *good* for mankind? Was his plan to offer the hot chocolate for sale only at the pinnacle of his success not, in fact, a calculated strategy, as he had first thought, but a premonition that had made him mix the recipe into his products only in small amounts?

At the same time, there was a nagging doubt in his mind: he thought it childish to believe something so irrational. He wasn't a God-fearing man: he even had his doubts about the Church, let alone superstitions, which he held to be a religion for the poor.

In an attempt to bring himself to his senses, he decided to bequeath the most valuable thing he possessed to Anastasia. Anastasia should inherit the recipe for his hot chocolate. And he swore to himself that he would pass on the recipe to her when she married, as the most precious dowry he was able to bestow.

Little by little, the chocolate-maker awoke from his stupor and employed a peasant woman, herself newly delivered of a baby, to nurse Anastasia. He finally dismissed the strict, religious governess and found a young nanny, who cared for the girls with patience and a warm heart.

The oldest of the three girls, Lida, was already six, and was probably the one most affected by her mother's death. She had been her mother's favourite, and had always tried to please her. She was therefore excessively shy, taciturn, and God-fearing, more like a grown woman than a child. Her father was even a little afraid of her, with her stern gaze, her highly developed sense of morality, and her gloomy disposition.

The second child, five-year-old Meri, did not yet display any revealing characteristics, but she was often sickly, and had an innate dissatisfaction for which her father could find no remedy.

Both of them missed their mother, and their father was a stranger to them. Before their mother's death he had always been at work, or fulfilling social duties. He smoked a pipe, talked loudly, liked to drink cognac with friends in his study, and spoke about things that didn't interest little girls.

But the youngest, Anastasia, who quickly became known to everyone as Stasia, was influenced by none of this. She was much too young to be conscious of losing her mother; she had no memory of her. Despite the difficult circumstances of her birth, she was a cheerful child, with an impressive head of hair. Even when she was a baby, you could have plaited it — as I've said already — and she revealed a dominant disposition early on.

The chocolate-maker decided to do everything right with her. He wouldn't allow her to become estranged from him like her sisters, and grow up far removed from his philosophy of life.

After the first and most oppressive year of mourning had elapsed, the chocolate-maker summoned his courage and decided to give his family a new start.

Over the following four years, my great-great-grandfather made a real effort to win his girls' affection. He spoiled them, introducing them to the good things in life that their mother had denied them: they were permitted to stuff themselves with food and stay up late; they were permitted to go to the bazaar and the travelling circus; they were permitted to skip church on Sundays; they were permitted to get dirty and charge wildly around the house; they were permitted to go to The Chocolaterie and eat as much chocolate as they were able; they were permitted to do their homework *after* they had played games, and to ask him to bring them back pretty clothes and toys as souvenirs from his business trips.

It was a light-hearted, free atmosphere that reigned in the chocolate-maker's home during those years, and the many little signs of neglect that began to appear in the once-immaculate house didn't seem to bother anyone, either; on the contrary, they added to its cosiness.

Stasia always remembered her early childhood, and the period of 'girl rule' in the house, with great fondness. But when her father came back from a business trip to Kiev one day in the company of a tall woman with a somewhat cool, but very impressive, Slavic appearance, who understood not a word of Georgian, and introduced her as his new wife, everything changed in an instant. A house without a wife was no house at all, their father said, and he was sad to be going through life alone. He had no intention of replacing their mother, he told them, but he implored them to accept Larissa (or Lara) Mikhailovna as a new member of the family with respect and open hearts.

But Lara Mikhailovna, who was a member of the Moscow aristocracy and had previously been married to a (now deceased) Ukrainian merchant with alcoholic tendencies, proved not so easy to accept. She was an imperious woman, used to people flattering and paying court to her. She liked luxury, and regarded her move to the Georgian provinces as unworthy of her. Unlike the girls, their father seemed untroubled by Lara's difficult character. Either she was delighting her new husband at night with her incredible talents, which made it worth his while to forget the hardship of spending the day at her side, or she possessed other intellectual qualities that were revealed only to the chocolate-maker. There was no other explanation for why he heaped expensive gifts on his new wife, subordinated everything else to her wishes and wants, and allowed her to treat him like a serf.

The cheerful, relaxed atmosphere of the preceding years gave way to an oppressive, hierarchical order, in which Lara set the tone.

She found the girls too wayward, and began to re-educate them at once. First, the two older children, Lida and Meri, were sent to a strict girls' school for children of the elite. Then she engaged a piano teacher, who practised tirelessly with them every two days, followed by a private tutor to work on their Russian — their accent was abominable, or so Lara said.

She herself, however, enjoyed the advantages that her spouse and his status brought her. Spa trips were undertaken, celebratory dinners given, balls attended, materials ordered from France, hats sewn, two new housemaids employed, and jewellery purchased, along with several Chinese porcelain vases that Lara particularly liked.

My great-great-grandfather also blossomed; Lara seemed to be the wife he had always wanted at his side. The fact that his children laughed less and less, became ever quieter, and were always sticking out their tongues at Lara as soon as she turned her back were things he was happy to overlook. Lara was more than fit for good society, adept at using the advantages of money; she loved the attention, the travel, the jewels, the gossip, went to church only at Easter and Christmas, and knew how to impress people, above all the male sex.

Two years after the wedding, Christine, the late arrival, came into the world. Seven years after Stasia.

The chocolate-maker still wanted a son, and didn't give up hope of an heir. But neither he nor Lara was as young as they once were, and there were no further pregnancies. And so — after several visits to health spas and a great deal of effort — Christine remained my great-great-grandfather's final attempt to produce a male successor.

Christine was to become the classic baby of the family: pampered, spoilt, and arrogant. She was declared by her mother — as if it were the most obvious thing in the world — to be the only princess in the house, and was idolised by her father. Admittedly, Christine was an almost supernaturally beautiful child. Nobody who visited the family could stop talking about the little girl's beauty, to the great pride of her parents. What a Madonna-like face, what grace, what perfect features, what fine limbs!

In fact, the girl embodied the ideal of Slavic-Caucasian collaboration. Particularly as, from a young age, Christine knew how to use her advantages, and was very good at getting what she wanted. For the older girls, life didn't exactly get easier.

Perhaps it was this change in the household that made Stasia develop a kind of spirit of protest. Unlike the quiet Lida, who was flirting with the idea of entering a convent, and the rather superficial and exuberant Meri, Stasia had realised very early on that she had to assert herself in this family. Otherwise, she would probably remain unnoticed, in the shadow of a toddler with whom she just happened to share a father.

She quickly learned to voice her own opinion, to concentrate on her dreams and desires, to do things that Lara, and therefore also Christine, would never do, like, for example, riding astride on Kabardin horses, taking an interest in women's rights, wearing no jewellery, caring little for luxury — and, above all, taking ballet lessons, dreaming of a ballet career, and planning her departure for Paris.

★

Time hurried by, and the political mood throughout the Russian Empire grew tenser by the day. The chocolate-maker had already started to worry about his own future and that of his children; the communists, who seemed to have been swarming all over the place for the past eight years, did not bode well for them. Like all members of the Georgian elite, my great-great-grandfather was afraid of the proletariat. He was happy to make charitable donations to them, but he still liked to keep them at arm's length whenever possible.

My great-great-grandfather didn't believe in socialism; he didn't believe in the revolution, or radical reforms; and, although he followed the news from Russia with some concern, he apparently always said that, in his country, the Bolsheviks would never prevail (the embryonic 'Third Group' was already hard at work in the Georgian capital and would declare Georgian independence barely a year after the October Revolution).

My great-great-grandfather viewed Simon Jashi's well-balanced mixture of *good old-fashioned values*, a longing for stability, and a commitment to moderate liberalism as a kind of guarantee for the future of his business. Simon was also a military man: should the going get tough, he could be useful to the Reds as well, and would thus be able to assure the family's future. With no male heir, the chocolate-maker wanted a man at his side: the future was already knocking at the door, and nobody knew what it would look like.

His first-born would never find a husband, monosyllabic, pious churchgoer that she was. And he started to come to terms with the idea of giving Lida over to God, whom she seemed to love above all other male beings — *Does God actually have a sex?* the chocolate-maker wondered on some evenings, as he sat in his study with a good glass of cognac, mulling over his thoughts.

The second eldest, who was by then already twenty-one — a good, marriageable age — proved to be no easier. At nineteen, she had become engaged to a hard-working banker's son, and nothing seemed to stand in the way of this promising new family alliance, until one day she announced that she didn't want to marry him after all: he was chasing after every skirt in the city, and that was hardly likely to change after the wedding.

'But darling, Meriko, my sunshine, you have to allow the poor boy a little pleasure in life. We men are weak creatures; we need more affection than you women. Let him look to the left and right a little — who's it going to hurt? There are many temptations along a man's path, and resisting them is difficult. He loves and respects you, and after all, that's the most important thing for a woman.'

This was how the chocolate-maker had reasoned with his second eldest daughter. But she had just snorted scornfully and said she wasn't that stupid.

She wasn't about to throw her life out of the window just so that he would finally have her out of the house. Of course, the banker's son was famed throughout the town as a Don Juan, and Meri was not domineering enough to take him in hand and turn his head firmly in her direction. And yes, my great-great-grandfather would have liked to marry her off: he was, after all, seeking allies for the chaotic times that lay ahead — was that so reprehensible? But at the same time he admired Meri's self-determination, and he let the matter lie.

Three years had passed since then, and nobody seemed good enough for Meri. One was too dull, another too old, a third had an awful mother, and so on.

Stasia, though, was the one who actually caused him the most trouble. Yet my great-great-grandfather couldn't help loving his second youngest with the most sincere, respectful love he was capable of giving his daughters. Stasia was the most quick-witted and nimble, the most contrary of his daughters, the one who vexed him most and most frequently provoked his rage. But he loved her mischievous ways, and he even loved her peculiar dreams and her addiction to dance. She knew what she wanted, and, unlike little Christine, things didn't just fall into her lap. She only did what seemed important to her. Perhaps her father recognised himself most in her; perhaps he had never overcome the guilt he felt about his late wife and Stasia's dead twin sister; or perhaps Stasia was simply more accessible, less outlandish and alien to him than his two elder daughters.

His deep love for her had a firm hold on his heart — so firm that it hurt at times — even though he and Stasia argued most often and loudest, and Stasia sometimes seemed impudent and lacking in respect. But he was adamant that she should be happy, and should lead a life that never completely excluded her dreams — although never for a second did he seriously consider sending his child to the Sodom and Gomorrah of the West, to Paris, to become a frivolous dancer.

And so the chocolate-maker was all the more pleased when Stasia responded to Simon Jashi's advances, and seemed to be far from averse to the young man.

Up to this point, Stasia had wanted nothing to do with men. She had refused to wear a Sunday dress to church, or to go out with her stepmother and sisters on a Friday and promenade along the main street — a kind of marriage market. She had also given the cold shoulder to the men who had flirted with her at several school and town balls.

It seemed that Simon could indeed become an anchor in the unfathomable waters of Stasia's nature.

But that was where my great-great-grandfather was wrong.

> Revolutions have always been characterised by rudeness;
> probably because the ruling classes had not troubled themselves
> earlier to accustom the people to good manners.
>
> LEON TROTSKY

My great-great-grandfather's concerns are understandable, Brilka: the times really were chaotic. Extremely chaotic.

At the point when our seventeen-year-old Stasia met her White Guardsman, the First World War had already been raging for three years. At the end of the nightmare that lasted a total of four years and raged across half the world, it had claimed more than seventeen million human lives and pulled almost forty countries with it into the abyss.

In our little country, and in our sleepy little town, people's awareness of the terrible repercussions came, for the most part, via our great northern neighbour and 'patron', where the economic, political, and social problems seemed to have reached their height. Thousands of disillusioned soldiers and peasants deserted the front, and returned to their homeland infected with a new ideology: socialism.

Those were the days when the White Lieutenant Simon Jashi would hold forth in his philosophy circle, smoking a contemplative pipe.

'Like all other totalitarian countries, Russia has spent centuries suffering from inferiority complexes — the most painful of all, and at the same time the most insidious, is probably its own imperialism, which is why sensibility to socialist texts and ways of thinking was, and is, particularly great in Russia. Even the beauty of St Petersburg is founded on serfs, and prisoners starved and beaten to death, who were forced to build a splendid city every bit the equal of Paris or Vienna.

'I know this country. I have served it. But the Russian ruling classes certainly have this complex. The Georgian ruling classes have it, too, believe me. Life for the ruling classes is too good for them to change anything, but the sight of the peasants, most of whom are illiterate and enslaved, is too ghastly. Personally, I do not believe that revolution is an outcry from the people; rather, I believe that it awakens in the guilty conscience of the privileged,' he added in a particularly contemplative tone.

'So you believe that when our Liberator, Tsar Alexander II, passed a law to abolish serfdom, he was also motivated by such a complex, but did not consider that this step might end in economic and, above all, ideological disaster?' asked a particularly keen high-school student.

'Yes, that is what I believe. Granting freedom to the peasants only made the discrepancies in society even more apparent. Nor should we forget that, in the last few years, thousands of young people have moved from the cities to the countryside to spread enlightenment among the peasants, only to meet with lack of interest, resignation, and incomprehension.'

'And you think that the assassination of Alexander the Liberator was the thanks he got for this very act?'

'I can't answer that definitively; that would be mere conjecture on my part,' Simon continued, distinctly enjoying his role as lecturer. He could feel the rapt gaze of his boys fixed upon him.

'And do you believe that this Lenin is acting for personal reasons?' asked a red-headed anarchist in the back row.

'How do you mean? And please stand up, I can't see you.'

'Well, after all, his brother was one of the five conspirators who were executed after the failed attempt on the life of Alexander III.'

A few young men in the front rows huffed demonstratively, apparently annoyed by the red-head's showing off.

'I can't say that for certain either, my friend, I can only conjecture.'

'And what about Nicholas II?' asked the keen student, growing agitated (and forgetting about the psychological motives behind Lenin's actions).

'Nicholas II has never been able to choose between his God-given autocracy and western liberality, and that has now sealed his fate. In particular, following our defeat against Japan he fell into an unworldly apathy, which increased the aggression of the peasant uprisings all over the country threefold. And here I do know what I'm talking about: he should not have allowed them to fire on unarmed demonstrators at those gatherings in St Petersburg in 1905. He's much too educated for that, and he should have known better: it was these hundred deaths that led to the formation of the first workers' "soviet". Really, that was their legitimation. It was he who gave them that trump card, if you ask me.'

The keen student nodded pointedly and wrote something down. This pleased Simon: already he was being quoted. And in order to impress them further, he added:

'And Nicholas made a second grave error when he started sending peasants to the front for lack of soldiers. He didn't consider that these peasants would come into contact with soldiers and their ideologies there, and would become infected with socialist ideas, spreading this anti-tsarist ideology around their home villages on their return.'

Simon blew out a slow, deliberate plume of smoke and let his gaze roam over the heads of his listeners.

★

In any case, Brilka, what we do know is that in the cold winter of the same year that Stasia believed she had found love, the unrelenting mass demonstrations, the ongoing violence, and the consequences of three years of war finally led to the tsar's abdication. Bunin recorded the words of a coachman at that time: 'The people are now like cattle without a herdsman: they keep shitting all over and destroying themselves.'

Thus, in the year of my great-grandmother's love, the Romanovs were replaced, after three hundred years of rule, by the workers' and soldiers' councils and a provisional government.

And all that, Brilka, happened exactly ten years after one of the most spectacular robberies of the tsarist era. A robbery that took place on a warm June day, in Tbilisi's pretty Yerevan Square (later Lenin, and even later Freedom, Square):

It's ten-thirty on a beautiful sunny morning scented with cardamom, coffee, dust, and cloves, the kind of morning you will only find in Tbilisi. One stagecoach and two Cossacks, the tsar's mounted soldiers, laden with more than a quarter of a million roubles, the tsar's private budget for the year, reach Yerevan Square.

The coach is about to turn right, towards the great classical building of the Central Bank, when some small round objects roll between the horses' legs. They are followed by a deafening noise, screams, spurts of blood. Peasant boys, appearing out of nowhere, start firing machine pistols at the guardsmen who come rushing over. In the midst of the smoke, uproar, and blood, a man gallops up on a horse, snatches the bags of money, and rides off.

And although the entire Russian Empire looks for the money, the whole city is turned upside down, and apartments are searched, it cannot be found.

Later, it arrives in Finland, sewn into a mattress. It is delivered into the hands of Comrade Lenin, who launders it there and sends it back to the Russian Empire, to the coffers of the Party.

The leader of this band of robbers is a Georgian cobbler's son, a clever child of the lower classes, a twenty-eight-year-old seminary dropout. Lenin thinks very highly of him, and that must mean something. He has a lot of aliases; he's been wanted by the tsarist secret police for some time now, for robbery, arson, and political agitation. The list of his offences against the authorities is long — but he does not yet bear the epithet with which he will go down in history; he is not yet called the *man of steel*.

★

Anyway, in the summer of 1917, the Bolsheviks, with around five thousand followers, represented a minority in the sea of political sympathies. But, by the end of October, when Stasia was still riding happily across the steppe, the Bolshevik military committee had occupied all the post offices, bridges, and stations in Petrograd. On 25 October, the transition government met in the Winter Palace. It was protected only by a few hundred junior officers, one hundred and thirty women from the women's battalion of the army, and several hundred cavalry veterans.

The Bolsheviks, including around two thousand Red Army soldiers, walked up and down in front of the Winter Palace all day. That evening, three thousand sailors arrived to support the Red Army soldiers. The square outside the Winter Palace filled up.

Celebratory shots were fired from the *Aurora* and the Peter and Paul Fortress. The officers inside the palace began firing on the sailors, but, in the meantime, some of the sailors had infiltrated through the unguarded side entrances and arrested the transition government. This took place at two o'clock in the morning on 26 October 1917.

And with that, the 'Storming of the Winter Palace', so often invoked and represented in Soviet propaganda films, was at an end.

It left a total of two people dead.

★

'People are losing faith in the transition government. Inflation in Russia is on the rise. The economy is stagnating. We hear that attacks, conflicts in the military, looting, confiscation of land, and criminality of every kind are the order of the day. Food supplies are dwindling, and the country may well be nearing bankruptcy. And this opportunist, Kerensky, who's supposed to be leading the transition government, is trying to use symbols to increase his strength, and is losing more decision-making power and trust each day. What more could the Reds wish for?'

Bent over his newspaper, my great-great-grandfather was working himself into a lather. He was drinking his morning coffee in the chocolate factory, where he had invited Simon to join him.

'In the elections, the Bolsheviks are sure to concentrate on the two big cities, Petrograd and Moscow, and will put almost all their finances into establishing and equipping an army. And, if they win, they'll lead the Petrograd Soviet; apparently they've earmarked this odd fellow, Trotsky, whom I wouldn't trust an inch, to do that. We're lagging behind here, as usual. While the Russians have carried out their damned revolution, we're still mulling over what the future of our country should look like, and that's not good, Simon, not good at all.'

Both men were drinking black coffee, eating chocolate-filled almond croissants, and, as they had done almost every day for the past few weeks, talking of nothing but politics.

> Georgian political life was sunk the moment Georgia allied itself to Russia. After this annexation, and after a very nebulous agreement had been made on the retention of our own national identity, the Georgians threw aside all political ideas and plunged wholly into the whirlpool of Russian life.
>
> THE CAUCASIAN HERALD

All these White Guardsmen, nationalists, liberals, even a few Mensheviks who met daily in their billets, the hordes who passed by Stasia's girls' school speaking in excited whispers, seemed united in a single aim: to seize the moment and declare Georgian independence. The balcony of Europe — an ironically poetic description of our homeland — should finally be released from bondage and given the freedom for which it had yearned for so long.

But Stasia took no notice of them. She just shrugged, and went on dreaming of her ballet career. She had little time for all these discussions — after all, there was so much beauty, so much delight in the world, especially when you were experiencing the first signs of love, and imagining your future in Paris with the *Ballets Russes*. No matter what her father, her husband-to-be, even the whole country wanted — all Stasia wanted was freedom and Paris, but above all: to dance, dance, dance. Let these sombre-looking gentlemen punch each others' lights out; she would dance on towards her dreams, and, like Ida Rubinstein, appear as Scheherazade at the *Théâtre du Châtelet*.

Every day, she waited for her White Lieutenant to pick her up from school in the afternoon, so that she could give free rein to her competitive spirit on the steppe. Then, all the political talk fell silent. Then, everything fell silent, and all that remained was her beating heart, the breeze, the echo, and the sound of horses' hooves on the red earth.

Our seventeen-year-old Stasia, in love for the first time — Stasia, who would rather learn Latin and astronomy at school than knitting and crochet — rode, was free and full of life, and neither socialism nor democracy could do anything to alter that. She was already plotting ways to convince her husband-to-be to go to Paris and start a new, quite different life there.

And when, one evening, as they sat on a fallen tree-trunk, Simon asked Stasia if she could imagine going with him, as his wife, to the cold, northern country where a career awaited him, Stasia was suddenly at a loss.

She wept inwardly for that other life — no matter which — that, with one decision — no matter which — she would have to give up. Didn't one have to be born twice — three, four, countless times, even — in order to do justice to one's desires? To the possibilities of this world? And, as always at such moments, she thought of her dead twin sister, whom she called Kitty, after Kitty in *Anna Karenina* — Tolstoy's Kitty who, following many romantic troubles, finds a home port in Levin after all — and felt even more despondent.

The White Lieutenant was mulling over quite different things, and was searching for a solution. For some time he had been feeling straitened both ideologically and financially, and his hope that the liberals would defend his country against the communists was dwindling with each day that passed. The situation in Georgia was too uncertain for him to remain there: he didn't trust all the local unions and coalitions.

He had to act; he had to pick a side. Under no circumstances did he want to remain trapped in his little hometown. Out there, people were shaping whole countries anew, and that was where he wanted to be — not sitting in smoke-filled rooms in this provincial town, talking to high-school students about what others were accomplishing, far away from him.

These were great days, when you could rise to the top or be declared an enemy with equal speed. Under no circumstances did he want the latter.

But, if democracy were to fail in his homeland, the Bolsheviks would achieve definitive victory, and then he would have no chance here.

On the other hand, the Reds needed helping hands — as many as they could find.

And so he sat there, beside this girl who so enchanted him, not daring to confess to her that he was about to join the RKKA, the peasant army, the expansion of which had just been ordered by Trotsky himself.

In any case, Stasia wept inwardly beneath an oak tree — I'm sure it was an oak, and I'm sure it was very old. Quite sure. Simon grasped Stasia's shaking shoulders, under the pretext of comforting her. Of course, the first kiss was wonderful — I'm sure it was, very sure, Brilka: the first kiss of our story *has* to be wonderful!

I don't know whether Stasia gave her consent immediately, that early evening, but what is certain is that three evenings later, Stasia entered her father's little study, which always smelled of chocolate and lavender, sat down in front of him in the heavy leather armchair, and informed him that she was going to marry Simon Jashi the following day.

The chocolate-maker looked up from his papers, took off his reading glasses, fixed his eyes on his daughter, and laughed.

But that wasn't all. Stasia went on: 'I don't want a wedding party. I want to take the money for that, and for my dowry, and use it to finance my dance training. As far as I know, this marriage is in accordance with your wishes, Father, and now I simply expect you to say yes.'

Her father was still laughing, but now he put on a stern voice, and said there was no way *that* was going to happen (or some phrase of the time to that effect) and that he wasn't going to make himself the laughing stock of the town just because his daughter had fanciful ideas in her head. Everything had to be done properly: the engagement, the period of waiting, and then a wedding befitting their status. She was, after all, the first of his daughters to marry — that called for a big celebration.

And then he would have to have a serious word with his future son-in-law: a respectable young man such as Simon couldn't go letting his wayward wife call the tune.

Stasia listened to all of this calmly, even declining the delicious-smelling Turkish coffee her father offered her. Finally, she stood up and said that she would either get married in this way or not at all, and in any case Simon would soon be leaving for Petrograd. She must have uttered this sentence with an air of such determination that, although her father did not agree, he did nothing further to prevent his daughter from walking up the aisle the following morning, in a simple white dress that had been made for her elder sister Lida's first ball.

The chocolate-maker must have wrestled with himself and his doubts for a long time before deciding to keep his promise and give Stasia his recipe in her dowry. Perhaps, in the years after his first wife's death, he had decided to trust his business sense more than his superstition. After all, it was this recipe that had enabled him and his family to live a good life all these years, even if he hadn't expanded into the big cities and still hadn't put the hot chocolate on sale. But, in small doses, this mixture of ingredients didn't seem to do any harm — on the contrary, it brought people joy and allowed them to forget their troubles for a while, without exacting a fatal price. He had surely done the right thing in keeping the hot chocolate under wraps, the chocolate-maker mused the night before Stasia's wedding, although he now no longer knew whether his reasons for that were the same as they had been when he came back from Europe with the recipe in his pocket.

The decision not to sell the hot chocolate gave him a good, secure feeling, as if he had thereby warded off further calamity, which would have struck had he disobeyed his instincts. Of this he was quite sure. Even if he would never say so openly, especially not in front of his employees or his wife, even if he sometimes found his own speculations ridiculous, this black premonition had remained at the back of his mind ever since the deaths of Ketevan and Stasia's twin sister. Against his expectations, it didn't wane over the years; on the contrary, it grew all the stronger with time and solidified into a conviction.

But Stasia was not one of his employees, and she certainly wasn't Lara Mikhailovna. Stasia was perhaps the only person to whom he could entrust his secret without fear of ridicule.

And so, the night before her wedding, he summoned all his courage and knocked on Stasia's bedroom door (she was awake; she couldn't sleep all night for excitement) and asked her to get dressed and follow him. Stasia put on her clothes, her father took her by the hand, and they walked over to the chocolate factory.

He unlocked the door, flicked on the electric light (still a rarity in the little town at that time), led her into the production room, and asked her to take a seat. Then he began to prepare the chocolate. She was to observe him very closely, he said, to take note of the ingredients in the spice mix and repeat them aloud as he mixed them. Stasia, astonished at her father's secretive behaviour and the reverence he was displaying, suddenly forgot all restraint as the most magical aroma she had ever smelled began to spread through the room.

As the daughter of a confectioner famed throughout the land, she was used to all kinds of delicacies, but she had never smelled such a bewitching scent, let alone tasted it. As if hypnotised, she listed all the ingredients one after another, repeating the quantities with rapt attention as she felt her mouth starting to water. After that, her father instructed her to write down, with great precision, everything she had heard: the ingredients, the preparation time, and — *very importantly* — the exact dosage. A pencil and a piece of paper were set out for her on the table, and she noted down her father's secret neatly, in her best handwriting. She had to concentrate hard because of the intoxicating aroma filling the room.

Then she was given a small, delicate cup, as light as a feather, filled with a heavy black liquid, which she began to devour with a silver spoon. Her gums: awakened to incredible joy; her head: intoxicated by the taste; her tongue: drugged. She savoured the chocolate, one spoonful at a time, and for a few minutes forgot the world around her.

'What in God's name was that?' she asked, once she had licked the cup clean like a hungry cat and set it down carefully. 'And why have you never shown it to us before?'

'Because it's a secret recipe. I mix a small dose of my secret into all our chocolate products, but the recipe was originally invented for this hot chocolate, which you have now been allowed to taste. But ...' He paused and gazed at his daughter steadily. 'But it is dangerous.' He hesitated again, as if searching for the words to describe something that could not be described in words.

'What do you mean, dangerous?' Stasia asked, still with the ecstatic feeling in her breast that the taste of the chocolate had left behind.

'You have to believe me, Stasia, my girl. What I am about to tell you may seem strange, but you have to believe my words — promise me!'

'But Father —'

'Promise me!'

'Yes, all right, I promise. Of course I promise.'

'Too much of a good thing can bring about too many bad things. And I have never seen a person taste this chocolate without demanding more, and, yes, craving more. But the combination of craving and enjoyment can lead to dependency. Please remember that!'

'Of course people want more — it's so sinfully delicious!'

'No, you don't understand. This chocolate can only be enjoyed in small amounts. A very small quantity of the ingredients can make any chocolate product a true delight, but in its pure form, in this form, Stasia, it can bring about calamity.'

Stasia, who was not used to hearing such words from her father, let alone the reverent tone in which he pronounced them, tried not to let her consternation show and assumed the most serious expression she could manage.

'You must promise me, by all that is holy to you, that you will keep this precious secret as the apple of your eye. This recipe must never be allowed to leave the family. Outsiders must never be allowed to use it. You must never use it lightly, or prepare it for some party or other. It should remain something rare and special. If I had sold this chocolate in the shop I could have made a considerable profit from it over the years, but I decided against it.'

'But why me? Why are you giving me the recipe?'

'Because when you were born I swore, in memory of your mother, that one day you would inherit the secret, and ...'

'And?'

'Because you had survived the calamity and, as it seemed to me ...' He didn't finish the sentence. Stasia didn't entirely understand, but nor did she dare ask any more questions. There were other things occupying her head besides some calamity that her father imagined this heavenly chocolate had provoked.

'But sometimes ...'

'Yes, sometimes. Just make sure that these times are rare and that the occasions are special.'

That night, Stasia took an oath, swearing to learn the recipe by heart and destroy the paper. And when she was lying in her bed again, recalling the taste with all her senses, she was sure that this secret recipe could heal wounds, avert catastrophes, and bring people happiness.

But she was wrong.

★

On the day of the wedding, the chocolate-maker's second eldest daughter, Meri, was in the countryside with a sick aunt, and their stepmother feigned a migraine. It was just timid Lida and ten-year-old Christine — carrying large bunches of flowers, the only one to approach the day with enthusiasm — who accompanied their sister to the altar. The monk Seraphim, Lida's confessor and a family friend, conducted the wedding in the little Church of St George.

Simon consoled his father-in-law with the prospect of a belated wedding party befitting their status. He promised to be there for his wife in good times and in bad, and to care for her. They spent the wedding night in a guesthouse not far from the cave city, and the next morning Stasia smiled the tenderest smile she was ready to show. She had not yet mastered the smile of a married lady, and the smile of the freedom-loving girl who rode astride had already faded.

Simon left the town barely two weeks after the wedding, taking first a carriage to the railway station and then the train north, and Stasia returned home a married woman.

All this happened at the start of the chaotic year of 1918, the same year that our countryman, who was then simply called Joseph, Koba, or, affectionately, Soso, was made commander of Trotsky's Red Army.

The same year in which the Bolsheviks issued a decree with the title *The Socialist Fatherland Is in Danger*, paragraph eight of which read: 'Enemy agents, profiteers, marauders, hooligans, counter-revolutionary agitators, and German spies are to be shot on the spot.' The first year of the Cheka. The Cheka, which was later renamed the NKVD, and would finally be called the KGB.

> The Russian masses have to be shown something very simple, very accessible. Communism — is simple.
>
> VLADIMIR LENIN

I WONDER WHAT MY AMAZON IS DOING NOW — WHEN WILL I BE ABLE TO PUT MY ARMS AROUND HER AGAIN or *LITTLE DOVE DO YOU MISS ME I HAVE FOUND US A VERY PRETTY PLACE TO STAY NOT FAR FROM THE NEVA YOU WILL LIKE IT — THEY KNOW OF A GOOD BALLET MASTER HERE TOO*, said Simon's telegrams from Petrograd. Frivolities of this kind vexed the town's postmen, and people cast outraged glances at Stasia — this sort of thing just wasn't done.

Later, the lines changed, growing more worried: *LITTLE DOVE THERE IS UNREST HERE WE DONT KNOW WHAT IS TO COME TAKE CARE OF YOURSELF* or *LITTLE DOVE BAD THINGS ARE HAPPENING IN THIS COUNTRY BUT I CANT HELP*... (the rest was missing).

Only after several requests did Stasia manage to discover exactly what her husband was doing: he had joined the RKKA, and was responsible for procuring bread.

Since January 1918, Russia had been in the grip of terrible hunger. The RKKA had the task of confiscating bread; farmers were unable to maintain the required rate of production, and were subject to looting and raids.

In May of that same year, the first Democratic Republic of Georgia was proclaimed. The chocolate-maker breathed a sigh of relief, and, in May, he met with the first minister for economic affairs in Tbilisi to talk about expansion plans for his business. A large patisserie in the capital — nothing now seemed to stand in the way of this proposal. Afterwards, the chocolate-maker held a celebratory dinner, and invited the provincial town's high society to celebrate the future that seemed to be looking so bright for him.

Stasia and her husband had agreed that she would follow him in February. After months of waiting, she could stand it no longer, and, when summer arrived, she informed her father that she wanted to go to her husband and stand by him, come what may; her dance training could be put on hold for the time being. Her father, irritated at seeing his independent daughter so willing to sacrifice herself, tried to console her. Under different circumstances, he would have wished his daughter to be at her husband's side, as befitted a wife. But, given the situation, my great-great-grandfather opposed her plans. The long battle over her departure that followed wore Stasia down so much that she would spend hours sitting in the garden on the old swing seat that had belonged to her mother, staring into space, in the hope that her tragic appearance would soften her father's heart.

'Men always want to be in charge of you. What kind of life is that? I may as well have been born a dog; even as a dog I would have more freedom,' she complained to Lida, who just shook her head in horror and accused her younger sister of blasphemy.

When, in July, the telegrams stopped, concern for her husband finally brought Stasia's free-thinking ideals crashing down, and she went to the Church of St George, sought out the priest, Seraphim, and asked him for help. Afterwards, she was said to have knelt in the little church and prayed aloud for two hours: 'Please, God, please, please: if it is Your will, then I won't dance, or only later, but bring Simon back to me, or make my stubborn father take pity on me and let me go to my husband. I believe I really do love him, really, and it's so unfair, God, You can't have made me, with all these thoughts and wishes, and then have willed that I must only ever obey; please make it so that I have the same free will that You do. Yes, I know I should say ten Our Fathers and bring red eggs to the dead every Easter Monday and pour wine on the graves. I have neglected my Christian duties. I will gladly make up for it all, but please be a little lenient with me. I mean, if You created everything, then You created dance, too, didn't You?'

At that moment, a strong gust of wind blew open the church door, and Stasia leapt up in fright (at least, this is how I imagine it: in my imagination Stasia's prayers were answered on the spot).

In the doorway stood Seraphim, in his black habit, with a slip of paper in his hand. He went to Stasia and whispered in her ear that a carpet-seller had agreed to take her as far as the station in his coach. He couldn't get her past Military Road, but if she dared make the long train journey alone in these troubled times, then he would get her to the train. And, as love was the most divine thing of all and the bringing together of lovers who had married in the sight of God was the most wonderful duty of all, Seraphim would support her with his prayers.

Stasia threw her arms around Seraphim's neck, forgetting that he was a priest, and then discussed the details of her escape plan with him in whispers.

Three days before her departure, everything was already prepared, and Stasia had packed her things. Most importantly, she had taken a few banknotes from Father's trouser pockets, and a little jewellery she could count as part of her dowry, and had sewn them into her dress.

At dawn, she fled her home in a carpet-seller's carriage. She left a letter for each of her sisters and for her father, begging their understanding for what she had done.

I know little about the long journey she made through the increasingly ravaged landscape. I only know that her father sent out some men to fetch Stasia back, and that Seraphim withdrew to the cave monastery, claiming to have taken a vow of silence during the fasting period. And I know that Stasia arrived in Russia. Three weeks later.

*

In the meantime, the Russian Empire, so recently so powerful, sank ever deeper into chaos: the expropriation and communisation of property, banks, and housing, and the downfall of the free-market economy, had catastrophic consequences. As did replacing the courts with so-called people's tribunals.

The whole country was in the grip of unrest, as there were not enough professional organisers to implement these radical reforms. The Soviet Constitution, established in July, denied entire social classes in the country their rights. Only eight months after the revolution, a leadership profile had established itself that would lead inevitably to civil war: the concentration of power in the hands of a few leaders, the pursuit of economic and information monopolies, and discrimination against certain sections of the population.

And, by the time Stasia reached Petrograd, Nicholas II and his blue-blooded family were no longer alive. Their story had ended anonymously, with shots fired in a cellar in Ekaterinburg.

But, as yet, Stasia knew nothing of this. Nor did she know where Simon Jashi was to be found. At his official address, which should have been their 'lovely place not far from the Neva', Stasia found only drunken Red Army soldiers. It was a headquarters, not an apartment, and Comrade Jashi was not among this rabble. She wandered the cold streets of Petrograd, asking for her husband in her accent-free Russian, which was spoken at the time by every sophisticated lady on her side of the endless Silk Road.

She was finally forced to send a telegram home asking her father for help, though having to do it made her die a thousand deaths.

Scarcely an hour later she received her father's reply:

WE NEARLY DIED WITH WORRY HOW COULD YOU BUT THANK GOD YOU ARE WELL — GO TO THEKLA SHE IS THE COUSIN OF MY COUSIN DAVID FROM KUTAISI — SHE LIVES BY THE FONTANKA — SAY YOU ARE MY DAUGHTER — I DONT KNOW THE HOUSE NUMBER — ITS A BIG HOUSE AND SHE IS KNOWN IN THE CITY — ASK AROUND — WRITE AS SOON AS YOU ARE SAFE.

Stasia had never heard of a Thekla-who-is-known-in-the-city. Which didn't mean much: Stasia didn't really know half her relatives, and was always discovering them at the birthday parties, weddings, and funerals her father made her attend.

For three hours, Stasia wandered, confused and frightened, through a city that had gone mad, until she found a drunk Cossack who said he was prepared to take her and her meagre luggage with him as far as the Fontanka.

Stasia, whose worry and fear made her unreceptive to the beauty of the city, stared open-mouthed from the cart as they thundered through the streets.

Uniformed men were patrolling the countless bridges. Peasants pushed wheelbarrows laden with furniture; there were endless queues outside the shops, and people were running about with worried faces. Even the river, murky, angry, and loud, seemed to be in tune with this strange atmosphere.

Outside the imposing St Isaac's Cathedral, a public assembly was taking place: a large crowd of people stood holding banners and constantly shouting noisy slogans.

On the Fontanka — the riverbank promenade with its light green and pale yellow villas and courtyards — people were clustering around fire pits where food was being prepared. The manicured city of the tsars seemed absurdly contradictory as a backdrop to these goings-on.

The Cossack had to stop three times to ask people about Thekla, and finally informed the speechless Stasia that he didn't have the time to go looking for a landowner. At that moment, one of the girls clustering around the bonfire shouted that it must be the pretty yellow house up ahead on the left. Stasia didn't know what she would have done if this girl hadn't come to her aid.

She paid the Cossack, unloaded her luggage, and knocked on the classical villa's monumental iron door — no, she positively hammered on it with the door knocker, as a column of shouting people was coming up the promenade towards her and if she didn't get to safety right away she would be swept along by the crowd. Eventually, a frightened girl wearing a traditional Russian headscarf opened the door and hastily bundled Stasia into the house without saying a word. Then she slid home the numerous bolts and barricaded the door with furniture.

Cautiously, Stasia looked around. She found herself in one of the most beautiful houses she had ever set foot in. A marble staircase led up from the wide, welcoming entrance hall. The floor was inlaid with beautiful black and white tiles. Stasia was shown into a light, spacious drawing room, in which, to her surprise, there was no furniture beyond a fantastically long oak table and two chairs. The girl left her alone, telling her to wait there and not go anywhere.

After a while, she heard footsteps, and a woman appeared at the top of the staircase. She might have been in her mid-fifties, but she could have been older or younger: her biological age was masked by a thick layer of make-up. She was wearing a pale-pink dressing gown decorated with a feather collar, like a dancer in one of the morally dubious dance halls her father had so often warned her about. The figure rushed towards Stasia and wrapped her arms around her.

'Oh God, such a big girl, the last time I saw my dear cousin was at the New Year's ball in Kutaisi, I don't believe it, what a beauty, you have his solemn eyes, so serious!'

She ordered the peasant girl, who was the only servant to have stayed on in the house, to prepare some strong tea and fetch some biscuits from the pantry.

'But the biscuits are for emergencies,' the girl muttered, before being silenced by a stern look from the lady of the house.

'And what does this look like to you? My own flesh and blood, arriving here from my homeland, in times like these … What do you think it is?' she called out after her.

Over hot tea and very dry biscuits (which to Stasia still seemed like the eighth wonder of the world), Thekla quickly told Stasia her whole life story. Stasia drew her own conclusions as to why she had never heard of Thekla-who-is-known-in-the-city.

Thekla was a member of the minor nobility from the valleys of central Georgia. She had realised very early on what she wanted from life, and also how to get it. Gossipy Kutaisi, her hometown, did not offer her enough breathing space, so she married young. Her husband was a rich merchant from Tbilisi, who managed a number of vineyards and sold Georgian wine to Russia. It couldn't have been particularly difficult for Thekla to find a willing candidate: if you looked closely — once you had grown accustomed to the layers of make-up — she had a very delicate, soft face, a gentle aspect inviting daydreams, along with a truly voluptuous and appetising body which featured a high, larger-than-life bosom. But the marriage had been without passion: her husband had been more in love with his vines than with her, Thekla said, and on one of their business trips to Petrograd, or St Petersburg, as it was then, she had fallen in love with Alexander: irrevocably, powerfully, tremendously. Alexander Olenin, a descendant of the rich Petersburg Olenin dynasty, which had brought forth patrons of the arts, art collectors, and the founder of the St Petersburg Library, was an educated, elegant, free-spirited man — 'outrageously beautiful, moreover' — and a member of the tsar's army.

Following her return to Tbilisi, Thekla informed her husband that she would forgo all privileges and leave his house without a gold ring, if he let her, because she had fallen irrevocably, powerfully, tremendously in love with another man.

Of course, there was a scandal. Her husband thoroughly destroyed her reputation and refused to divorce her for years. But, as the marriage was childless, Thekla was able to travel to Petersburg without a gold ring, although she was still officially married, and play at being Anna Karenina in the city of the tsars.

Olenin must have been an honourable man: unlike Count Vronsky, he stayed with his beloved and introduced her to St Petersburg society as his rightful wife. Although this society initially rejected her, Thekla managed to get a foot in the door, and even find friends. Eventually she managed to gather a real community around her, which must have been due to her truly unconventional and vivacious character. Her 'outrageously beautiful' Alexander bought his beloved this wonderful house, and began to enjoy the good things in life to the full with his Thekla, who was eager to experience them all. They lacked neither means nor opportunity, and invited artists and 'all kinds of crazy people' to the house, all of whom were 'illicitly interesting', thus continuing the Olenins' tradition of patronage and engaging in philanthropy. They travelled around Europe and enjoyed the piercing beauty that the world has to offer when one is so 'obliviously in love and beloved'.

'Alexander and I were married for only two years,' Thekla confessed sadly. It took a very long time for the Georgian to grant her a divorce, but when he did, Thekla and her Alexander were finally able to marry and seal their love.

'We were as happy as children. Life was good to us. I know I have had a great deal of happiness in my life.'

But, since then, she had not been back to her homeland.

In the accursed year of 1904, Alexander fell in battle in Japan, a war hero. Something in Thekla was forever broken by his death. It took years for her to get over it, she said — but then, to honour his name, she used her lavish inheritance to help out wherever she could. She went on hosting the salons, the literature and music circles, at their house. She took trips to health spas, made new friends, and, above all, put the money to good use.

'But Alexander and I had to pay a high price for our happiness: he went before God had blessed us with children.'

With that, Thekla brought her account to an end, and sipped from the expensive porcelain cup that the housemaid had produced from the kitchen.

In terse sentences, exhausted and shivering slightly, Stasia then told the story of her journey to Petrograd, of her new husband, his inexplicable disappearance, and her own desperate situation.

'If I could just stay here for a few days — you know, until I've found Simon. I won't be any trouble. And I can help with the housekeeping,' Stasia murmured shyly, before she was silenced by Thekla's mighty laugh.

'What housekeeping, my dear? Of course you can stay. The house is big enough. Those swine may have taken away everything they could find, but I'm permitted to remain in the house. There are two beds left. And I think this is a temporary state of affairs. Those imbeciles can't stay in power forever, the resistance is too great, and then ... Then everything will go back to how it was before. I'm glad you're here, Anastasia. Since those idiots started rampaging around, a lot of my friends have fled abroad or taken to hiding in their houses, and it's grown rather lonely here. But we two can have fun again — splendid!' Thekla cried triumphantly.

> The keen-sightedness of our days is the sort that befits the dead end
> whose concrete begs for spittle and not for a witty comment.
> Wake up a dinosaur, not a prince, to recite you the moral!
>
> JOSEPH BRODSKY

The house really was outrageously large. But the absence of furniture made it seem like a strange, purposeless palace. Like the warped memory of a place from *before*.

The old wallpaper, the few expensive curtains that remained at the tall windows, and the isolated pieces of furniture that had been spared hinted at its former glory. Thekla also kept a large, secret cellar of provisions, which the Bolsheviks had not been able to access. It was full of wonderful things: peppers pickled Venetian-style, artichokes from Greece, chocolates from Moscow, jams from the Crimea, Spanish ham, English butter biscuits, and several bottles of expensive wine, cognac, and even champagne.

Every day, Masha, the peasant girl, who had remained with her mistress more out of hopelessness than loyalty, conjured up a small portion of these delicacies to go with the daily bread rations and the two or three eggs she managed to obtain on her forays into the city. She was the only one who left the house.

Thekla spent most of the day in the half-empty bedroom on the second floor. From time to time, she could be heard singing, or playing one of her gramophone records — always French *chansons* or Russian love songs. Or she would sit wrapped in a blanket in the spacious reception room, reading a romantic novel, of which she owned a large number, and in which the Bolsheviks had apparently shown no interest.

There was enough tea in the house and, on special days — Thekla decided which days counted as special — there was coffee, too.

Stasia noticed that sometimes, before the peasant girl set out into the city, Thekla would slip her a necklace or a ring and whisper something to her. On those days Masha usually brought back more than just eggs and bread.

Stasia occupied Thekla's former dressing room, which was as large as the dining room of their house in Georgia. She was given clothes, scented soaps, and a pair of wonderful leather boots. It grew steadily colder, and Stasia was grateful for such a present.

The lady of the house had as little interest in knowing about the civil war raging around her as did the house itself. Thekla dressed and made herself up as if she was hosting a gala dinner in the house every night — as if, at any second, they would smell the aroma of delicious food, the great front door would open, the high society guests would stream in, an orchestra would immediately start playing, and stylish ladies and gentlemen would take to the floor for a foxtrot, just like *before*.

The house had been looted months ago, but Thekla had succeeded in bribing the Bolsheviks to let her stay: it must have cost her a great deal of money, or other goods, as they were in the middle of a brutal war over expropriation and living space.

Through Masha she maintained a little contact with the outside world. But when Masha so much as started to report some event or other from outside, Thekla would wave her white, manicured hand, signalling to her to be quiet.

Thekla harboured the illusion that one merely had to wait it out, to make it through the winter, and soon this idiotic *putsch* would be over, too, and everything would be the same as before. Thekla didn't want to move away from her beloved Petersburg (definitely not Petrograd!). Countless friends had already left the country, or had simply disappeared, but she refused even to entertain this possibility for herself. She lived in hope, and she needed this hope like she needed air to breathe.

Thekla missed her salon, the loud gatherings, the guitar and piano players, the gypsy songs, and the debauched nights with the rich and beautiful denizens of the city, so this young, doe-eyed relative came as a welcome diversion. They played cards together in the evenings, ignoring the noise outside, the screams, the footfalls, the slogans, the threats, the hammering, and, yes, also the occasional shot. During the long, silent evenings of sombre loneliness in the house, they gradually grew closer: the taciturn Stasia and the voluble Thekla. The girl with the endless plaits and simple clothes, and the glamorous lady in her feather boas. The waiting united them: it made them into silent accomplices in the creation of a spectacle, the outcome of which was still uncertain. Outside, hundreds of thousands of workers went on strike against the 'dictatorship of the communists', businesses were crippled, hunger brought more and more criminals into the city, pogroms took place as regularly as clockwork, and the bread ration fell to a hundred grams, while the Cheka, which was already operating successfully, went on arresting and shooting people. Meanwhile, the two of them sat there, drinking tea and playing patience, in the belief that the horror would not find its way into the house.

After a time, Stasia could stand it no longer, and started sneaking out of the house with increasing frequency, against Thekla's strict instructions. She searched the Reds' bases for Simon Jashi, but nobody seemed to know him; nobody seemed to have any information about him.

★

Autumn fell suddenly over the white city. It was not the mild and gentle autumn Stasia was familiar with from her homeland, and waiting for a message from Simon was hard. It paralysed everything, made her body lethargic and her mind fearful. Stasia hated this waiting. She spent hours sitting by her bedroom window, staring through the little hole she had made in the sheet that hung over it, and hoping, without knowing what she was hoping for. Stasia's only regular contact with the outside world was the telegrams to and from home.

Some days, she was overcome with an almost hysterical euphoria, and then she would run down the wide staircase into the kitchen, light candles or paraffin lamps, and clatter about, making noise just to reassure herself that she was still alive, that she had not already become a ghost. She ran out into the drawing room, through the guest room, into the guest bathroom, back up the stairs and down again, and then, cheered by her own energy and driven by a strange desire, she began to dance. She whirled, leapt, flew, and, for a few moments, forgot the world around her. The world outside the house, and the world inside it.

As the cold set in, it seemed to spur the people on to greater bitterness and cruelty. Here and there, government buildings and houses in the neighbourhood were burning. And the shots were now an everyday occurrence.

The ominous quiet of isolation reigned in the big house on the Fontanka, an ice-cold peace and a preserved past; but the present reigned outside, on the streets, on the grand promenades and riverbanks, and it was cruel, bloody, dangerous, full of hunger and want.

★

As October reached its end, Thekla was seized with a peculiar apathy. She locked herself in her bedroom and remained shut in there for days at a time. Masha and Stasia did everything they could to tempt her out, but she refused anything more than the little food that Masha left outside her door. Stasia thought long and hard about how she could cheer up and reinvigorate the lady of the house, and then it came to her: her father's life-changing, happiness-bringing chocolate, the recipe for which she had carefully committed to memory. And so, for the first time since she had come to live in the house, she asked Masha for the key to the cellar. Masha just gave one of her it's-all-the-same-to-me shrugs and handed her the key. She found everything there. Apart from sugar and butter, all the ingredients she needed to prepare the chocolate were to hand, and she asked Masha to procure the rest on the black market, promising her a silk scarf she had been eyeing up in return.

In the night, Thekla was woken by a heavenly scent, and she hurried into the kitchen, somewhere she hardly ever set foot.

She found Stasia at the stove, stirring a black substance, and, in that moment, Thekla was bewitched by the little girl with the long plaits. She was bewitched by this sight and this smell, by the promise of something that would make her forget everything else. Especially in that dying world the two of them found themselves in, the magic must have had an almost irresistible effect. And when at last she was served the chocolate, Thekla was utterly lost.

From then on she often begged like a dog, screamed and stamped her pointed boots on the marble floor of her house, and shed tears like a child, wanting Stasia to make the chocolate for her.

★

They celebrated the New Year with a little fir tree branch, a bottle of champagne, the rest of the butter biscuits, the strawberry jam, and three slices of ham, behind windows that had been barricaded with table-tops. The frost that was spreading through the house made the mood tense and irritable, and, to top it off, on the first day of the New Year, Masha gave her notice. She was going to join her fiancé in Volgograd. He was fighting there, and she was fed up with making this 'inhuman' effort, in this 'godless' city, and receiving no recognition for it whatsoever from the mistress of the house.

Stasia and Thekla knew neither what to do in the miserably long bread queues to make sure they actually got bread, nor even where the black market was located. Without Masha they would starve, they would perish, and they would quite certainly go mad — of this they were sure.

But then came temporary relief, albeit one that at the same time provoked great anger in Stasia. A letter reached her from Simon:

My little dove, how miserable I feel to have brought you this heartache, and how worried I have been since I heard that you were residing here. What an Amazon I have married, bravely taking this long road to reach me! I bow down before you, my sunshine. I want you to take care of yourself. Your father wrote to tell me that you are staying with a relative. We are making slow progress: the resistance has many sympathisers and therefore many helping hands, but we believe in the final, rightful victory! I would like you to seize the very first opportunity to go home. Travel via Odessa — it is still the least dangerous route. It is not safe for you in Petrograd and I will come and visit you just as soon as I can. I love you and am with you in my dreams. Your Simon.

The letter made Stasia want to scream. He should be with her in reality, not in his dreams. The very least he should have written was that he was going to drop everything and hurry to her side; that would have been an appropriate recompense. She wrote back to him with a trembling hand, telling him of the ordeal of the last few months and firmly requesting that he come for a few days, at least. She signed herself *Your wife*, which she had never done before.

At once, she felt a deep sense of relief that loosened her limbs, expanded her ribcage, and cleared her airways; and when she heard a beautiful, unfamiliar, and, for once, not hopelessly sentimental melody coming from Thekla's room, she started to dance.

Her limbs were stirred into new life, warmth rose in her breast, and she forgot her continual hunger and the accursed cold, which troubled her more than the hunger did. She spun around, leapt into the air, turned and stretched, growing soft and supple, and laughing out loud.

Thekla, who was just coming out of the kitchen, started applauding for all for she was worth. Stasia broke off her dance and sank down on the landing in a daze. Thekla may not have taken much interest in this life, but she knew beauty when she saw it.

'Forget that man: the only thing in his head is his sick politics. Leaving you sitting here, it's an outrage — you — look at you, what a sight! Beautiful things seldom come from waiting — you should dance, my darling!'

And she floated theatrically up the stairs in her lilac coat.

> The goal is nothing to me, the movement is everything.
>
> EDUARD BERNSTEIN

Three days later, Stasia received a visit from Peter Vasilyev, a master of the old school and former soloist with the Royal Ballet. He gave Stasia his hand and said, 'Only Thekla would think of engaging a dancing teacher in times like these, but she thought it might provide me with a little distraction, too.'

The house's large, empty rooms provided ideal practice space, and Peter Vasilyev brought new records with him for the gramophone.

Vasilyev had grey hair. He was tall, artificial, worldly, and authoritarian. Stasia worshipped him from the moment they met, and counted the hours until he arrived.

She had received basic training in classical ballet, but Vasilyev was quite different: imperious, demanding. He knew only the best exponents of his art, and had danced in a number of magnificent halls. If the revolution hadn't intervened, Peter Vasilyev would probably be the director of the best ballet school in the city, Stasia thought.

With his tireless discipline, his talent, his awe-inspiring manner, and Stasia's great determination to spend hours practising despite the bestial cold, her hopes for Paris had returned. Everything seemed possible again. With Simon, or without him.

Thus Stasia danced through the winter; through the snowstorms, the icy wind, the frosty days and nights; through the demonstrations and skirmishes, the uprisings, strikes, and — again and again — through the hunger. Simon did not come.

★

In March of the year 1919, workers began to strike in almost all the notable factories of Petrograd. And Masha finally left them. She had inducted Stasia into everything: she had twice taken her to buy bread, introduced her to a Siberian girl who knew people from the black market and would help her in emergencies, and explained the principles of shoving, shouting, and getting oneself noticed, which were needed in those times in order to survive. Then, with a small bag on her back, and showing hardly any emotion, she bade a cool farewell to the weeping Thekla and walked out of the door, which Stasia fastened behind her with numerous bolts.

In April, Simon's next letter to Stasia informed her that his visit to Petrograd would be delayed further. They still couldn't grant him leave, as they were currently anticipating an assault on Moscow, and he was being sent there. He put her off until the summer.

By this time, the chocolate-maker had somehow managed to send his daughter a large crate of groceries. God alone knew who he had had to bribe to get it to her. These groceries, together with the spring weather, which was finally starting to beat back the merciless winter cold, granted the two women a few weeks' peace, and released them from their daily worries about how they would survive the following day.

Dance always helped. The taxing, monotonous exercises and the small successes. After every practice, Stasia felt a little happier, freer, more light-hearted. There had been many times when, had it not been for Thekla, who refused to admit defeat despite her loneliness, and the hard-working Peter Vasilyev, who doggedly made his way to the house by the Fontanka three times a week, Stasia would have thrown in the towel and either taken the next train south or simply gone to bed and never got up again.

Standing in the endless queues for bread, Stasia eavesdropped on people angrily discussing the country's future. The front at the Don, the front at Kharkov, the front at Novgorod, the front near Minsk, the front near Irkutsk — the very word 'front' made her feel sick. The peasants just wanted to be left in peace. The Cossacks wanted to defend their independence and their worldly possessions; the monarchists didn't want to cooperate with the Mensheviks because they were collaborating with the Reds; the Mensheviks were drawing ever closer to the Bolsheviks, to escape the chaos of the monarchists and the liberals; while people with no affiliations, anarchists, and criminals were taking advantage of the situation: they were seeing to their own prosperity and earning money on the black market.

'Maybe we should go to Georgia together, Thekla. Unrest or no, we'd be safer there and we'd have no shortage of food,' Stasia said to Thekla one morning in the kitchen, over insipid tea. (Unlike Masha, she was never able to get hold of the good, strong tea; she always got ripped off.)

'Oh, my darling, I'm far too old to make a new start like that,' Thekla replied.

'Oh, come on. You're not that old, Thekla. And anyway, nobody's talking about a new start; this is more a case of getting through the winter, as you call it. Until all this is over.'

'Will it ever be over?' Thekla asked, with a harrowing sadness in her voice. And Stasia knew that Thekla would never leave this city and this house, and she also knew that it would be impossible for her to leave Thekla there alone.

And so Stasia and Thekla stayed together over the following months, in the shadowy, damp isolation of the big house, brought to life three times a week by Peter Vasilyev's visits and his dance lessons. But the constant fear, and continually having to fend off the people who hammered on their front door looking for somewhere to stay, or simply wanting to loot the place, sapped Stasia's strength. At these moments she would have liked to have boxed Thekla's ears for leaving her to defend the house alone, as if it weren't Thekla's own beloved home.

★

In the summer of 1920, Stasia reached the second anniversary of her Petrograd imprisonment. A few days had become two full years since she had left her home and her family to be with a man whose wife she had been for only a matter of days. Sometimes Stasia seemed already to have forgotten why she had come to this city.

On one hot July evening, swarming with mosquitos, Peter Vasilyev appeared at the front door unannounced. He had a bottle wrapped in newspaper under his shirt, and was beaming from ear to ear.

'Come, ladies. I would like to drink a toast with you and bid you farewell!' he cried, walking triumphantly into the kitchen. There he filled three glasses with Crimean sparkling wine, and informed Stasia and Thekla that in two days' time he would be leaving the country, and the lessons were therefore at an end.

'I have a cousin in Baden-Baden. She has a shrewd banker for a husband; she's offered to help me, and my two sisters are already there. I can't stand all this any longer. They've sent money for my passage and arranged the necessary papers for me. For once, I'm glad that I never quite escaped my Jewish relations.'

Years later, when Stasia heard about Auschwitz and Birkenau, she often thought of Peter Vasilyev, whose fine-sounding Russian name was a pseudonym, and she hoped fervently that Isaac Eibinder, as Peter Vasilyev was called, was not numbered among those millions.

After Peter Vasilyev's departure, everything suddenly seemed stale and futile. Thekla hardly left her bedroom, and Stasia wandered aimlessly about the house. To begin with, she practised and danced even without Peter Vasilyev's strict instructions, as he had told her to do, but she found it increasingly difficult; her dream seemed to be fading again, as if she were constantly in need of allies to keep it alive. She started buying strong sailors' tobacco on the black market, which she rolled into thin cigarettes and smoked (a vice that would stay with her all her life; even when she could have afforded to smoke better cigarettes, she never swore off the cheap, strong tobacco).

One morning, a few weeks after Peter Vasilyev's departure, after a sleepless night, Stasia went into Thekla's room and sat on the edge of her bed in the dawn light. Thekla lay with her back to her, asleep, or pretending to be. Stasia woke her.

'It can't go on like this. One way or another, they'll take the house from you, or people will just break in and stay here. Only yesterday I had to threaten two of them with the carving knife again, when they tried to climb in through the cellar. If only I had a gun — they're more afraid of those than of my knife … I don't have the strength any more to stand in these queues for hours, to always be afraid that somebody's going to break in and cut our throats. A silver ring and a chain are all that's left in your casket. The bonds you still own are worth nothing any more, and the tsar is dead. I know you don't want to believe it, but it's true. You've always said, Nicholas will come back, he won't hand over his country to these wretched drinkers, but that's not going to happen. They shot the tsar almost two years ago. In Ekaterinburg. His children, his wife — they're all dead. We're at war. Everywhere is at war. It will never again be like it was *before*. Never. I'm sorry. But we have to do something, Thekla. I'm going home.'

> Civil war has its laws, as is well known, and
> they have never been the laws of humanity.
>
> LEON TROTSKY

At the start of September 1920, Stasia began her travel preparations. She wrote to her husband at the Moscow headquarters of the Red Army, informing him in a cool tone of her plan to return home. She no longer ended her letters with the phrase 'with love'. The last piece of jewellery was sold, as was Thekla's lambskin coat. With money for bribes, and after weeks of waiting, she finally managed to buy tickets for a train to Odessa, leaving at the end of October. From there, they would take a boat to Georgia. After she had got hold of a heavy suitcase — Thekla's expensive, hand-made suitcases had been sold off long before — Stasia returned to the powdery-yellow house on the Fontanka, soaked and frozen from the rain, but pleased with her success.

'It's worked: we have the tickets, we can go next Monday!' she called out, and then suddenly fell silent, confronted with an unaccustomed icy stillness. Cautiously, she went into the kitchen. A seductive scent emanated from it. There was nothing there, but she was familiar, very familiar, with the smell.

Quietly, she went upstairs. The scent led her to Thekla's bedroom door. She knocked: there was no reply, so she turned the handle and peered into the room. Thekla, her back to the door, seemed to be asleep. A tin cup stood on the floor beside the bed, with the sticky remains of chocolate inside. How many weeks had it been? It seemed an eternity since the last time Stasia had made hot chocolate for Thekla. She recognised the cup she had brought her the chocolate in last time. Thekla must have saved the remains and reheated them. Stasia lifted the cup and smelled it; the scent was delicious, magical, intoxicating, but there was something else mixed with the sweetness, something metallic.

Stasia slowly put the cup back on the floor, her knees trembling. Thekla lay motionless on the bed. Something had been mixed into the chocolate; something final. A cold shudder ran down her back, and she saw her father's reverent face in the chocolate factory, the night before her wedding. She heard him speaking of calamity, something she had dismissed as a figment of her anxious, troubled father's imagination. This word — calamity — the meaning of which she had not been able to imagine now resounded inside her head. Was he talking about this horror, this pain, this fear that she now felt, looking at Thekla's back? Had she brought on this calamity, believing she was bringing Thekla a little joy, and had Thekla known the price this black happiness would exact from her? Or was it she who had used the chocolate for something as *calamitous* as her own end?

An eternity passed before Stasia dared to go round to the other side of the bed and look at Thekla's face. She had expected something terrible, but Thekla lay there as if sleeping peacefully. Beside her was a sheet of white paper:

Darling, I will be with you always. Your coming into my life at such an unspeakable time was a gift from God. This life, the life that awaits us, is not made for me — I no longer have a place there. I knew the tsar was dead. I knew from the start, but I thank you for keeping it secret from me for so long. I am so very tired. Don't be angry with me. I have left you a little money, in the sugar tin in the kitchen. That should suffice for the burial, and hopefully also for your journey back. Look after yourself, and remember: if there should be anything beyond this eternal sleep, I will be there watching over you. Forgive me, and accept this last gift from me.

Underneath the note was a watch. An incredibly beautiful, gold wristwatch. It was only after several minutes that Stasia realised the letter was written in their shared mother tongue, in the ornate script that looked to outsiders like a kind of secret code, the script that Stasia had almost forgotten, the script that had made her tear her hair out at her girls' school when she hadn't been able to write beautifully, in a manner befitting a lady. She and Thekla had almost always conversed in Russian, and this last letter was a painful reminder that she would never again be able to speak to Thekla in the language that went with the script.

Stasia herself didn't know how many hours she spent nestled against Thekla's dead body. At some point, she said, she shouted for help, and people came charging into the house. Strangers.

Three days later, Thekla was buried, without a funeral service, without a priest. The churches had shut their doors for fear of pogroms. Stasia remained standing by the grave for a long time, crying uncontrollably. She had not been able to cry before. Even lying beside Thekla's dead body. But now, standing at her graveside, with Thekla's farewell letter and the gold watch in her pocket, the tears came.

★

By the time Stasia came downstairs with her suitcase the next day, people had already forced their way into the house and were running around in a frenzy, stuffing whatever was left to steal into their pockets and arguing about the rooms.

At the station, she was told that she required an exit visa for Odessa. Stasia, at her wits' end, trembling, showed them all the papers she had, including a copy of Simon's RKKA certificate, which he had sent her a few months earlier for safety's sake. She begged with tears in her eyes, but it was no good. Eventually, the lady in the ticket office took pity on her. She couldn't go to Odessa, but, as the wife of a Red lieutenant, she could follow him to where he was posted; this she was permitted to do. Where was he stationed, she asked.

'In Moscow,' an exhausted Stasia replied, sitting down, dejected, on her suitcase.

'There's a train leaving for Moscow at six o'clock in the morning; I'll exchange your ticket, and your husband can get you an exit visa in Moscow. Give me your ticket.'

Stasia absentmindedly handed her both tickets.

'There are two here. Who's supposed to be travelling with you?' the uniformed lady asked.

'She's not coming now.'

On the train she sat in silence, listening to the monotonous sound of the wheels. She told me she kept thinking about Thekla's rigid body, and the simple shirt that was the last thing she wore, a simple white cotton nightshirt, a plain nightshirt, as if she had put it on to set out on a journey into a dream of *before*.

★

There were propaganda posters all over Moscow depicting a soldier in a white uniform, pointing his finger at you. Underneath, they said: 'Why aren't you in the army?' On the others, the Reds' posters, there was a soldier in a red uniform, pointing at the viewer. Underneath, they said: 'Have you joined the volunteers yet?'

Stasia was in luck. At the address she had been given, everyone knew Simon Jashi. It was a barracks, somewhere on the edge of town. Stasia, exhausted, frozen (her boots were stuffed with newspaper, as they were full of holes), sat in the corridor of this barracks, having finally arrived there in a hired *droshky*. Two young soldiers brought her a mug of tea and a little schnapps — that would do her good, they said. She drank the schnapps, holding her nose, and it did bring her some relief. Simon, they said, was at a union meeting in some factory or other, and would be back that evening. In the meantime, they showed her to his room, which he shared with two other soldiers, and covered her with all the bedcovers they could find.

She slept, long and deep.

A man woke her. He was sitting at her feet, his arms wrapped around her hips and his head on her stomach. He was sobbing. As exhausted and empty as she was, Stasia was unable to express any kind of emotion. She ran her hand absentmindedly through his hair. It was a strange state of affairs. All that time she had been waiting for this, playing out the details of the scene hundreds of times over, conducting daily conversations with Simon Jashi in her mind. She had such a long, cruel, cold, hungry journey behind her, and now she was able to feel so little. As if all her feelings and her words had been used up. As if the Petrograd years, Peter Vasilyev, and Thekla, above all, had taken from her everything that Stasia had been hoping to save for her husband. They held each other, without talking much. He warmed her feet and brought her hot *borscht* and a whole loaf of bread, a thing that Stasia had not held in her hands for two years. She ate greedily, and later fell into a deep sleep.

When she woke in the morning, they were alone in the room. He was lying beside her, fully clothed and sleeping. She sat up and looked at him for a long time. There was so much she wanted to tell him, so much she wanted to ask, to explain, but she didn't know where or how to start. He was sleeping peacefully, his grey wool coat with the red star sewn onto it hung neatly on a hook on the wall. His boots, which were old and worn, but clean, stood on the floor.

He was now well over thirty, but his face still seemed very boyish to Stasia. His thick brown hair, good-natured brown eyes, thick lashes, bushy eyebrows, his long, straight nose, well-shaped lips, and, in particular, the little moustache he had grown. She looked at him and sensed that it would be very difficult ever to forget these years, this separation, ever to overcome it — that it would be very difficult for her to become the old Stasia again, with a head full of fanciful nonsense and feverish dreams. She felt empty and dreamless, exhausted. His sleeping face did tease a smile from her, but at the same time she felt an immense sadness.

Outside, she could hear footsteps, the shouts of soldiers; it sounded as if they were mustering.

'Simon, wake up, I think you have to go,' she said to her husband. He sat up, looked at her in disbelief, and shook his head.

'They'll manage without me,' he said, and kissed Stasia on the lips. These words made Stasia furious. Suddenly, her sadness gave way to anger. Then why, why had he never come, not once? If they could spare him here, if he wasn't out there saving lives, then what and who excused him for leaving her alone for so long — and worse, for leaving her there in suspense?

Stasia felt tears welling up in her eyes, full of disappointment — but again she said nothing, she made no accusations, she didn't scream at him; she swallowed her rage and let him undress her. To begin with, Stasia found it difficult to let herself go: she was listening to the footsteps in the corridor, the shouts and the conversations in the yard. It seemed she couldn't remember what it was like to soften, to feel this special joy, to no longer be tense and filled with fear. It took a great deal of effort for her to make love to her husband. Only it was not as it had been on their wedding night, in the guesthouse, where she had felt this euphoria, this joyous excitement. She simply lay there, patient and quiet, her eyes closed. But even like this she could find no relief; she kept seeing Thekla's stiff back in a simple cotton nightshirt, the sheet of paper with her name at the top, and the watch, which she had sewn into her underskirt.

'I want to go home. I need an exit visa. I can take a boat from Odessa,' said Stasia finally, when they were lying naked, side by side, breathing in time with each other. For a brief moment, Stasia hoped he would say that he didn't want this: that he wanted her to stay, that he would do everything humanly possible to keep her by his side, but then he replied:

'Yes, it's time you went home.'

'How long will you have to stay here?'

'How do you mean?'

'How long is everything going to be like this? What was the point of our getting married?'

'Stasia, there's a war on, and things are no better for us here, believe me. I'm kept regularly informed, and ...'

He spoke for quite a while about the necessity of the Bolshevik victory, various fronts that still had to be defended or wrested from the Whites, a few adventures that he and his team would have to face in Moscow, and difficulties in the Party leadership. Stasia barely listened. She found it hard to follow him; she had no idea why he was telling her all this, and she doubted his socialist convictions. Everything he said sounded like a poem learned by heart. Something in his voice sounded very tired, empty, resigned — a state that felt familiar to Stasia. But he didn't admit it; he wanted her to go on thinking of him as the confident lieutenant, sure of himself and his work. And yet, thought Stasia, it would be so much easier if he, or she, were to tell the truth. Then, perhaps, it might be possible for them to come together. If they would only try.

★

Stasia finally saw her hometown again at the end of 1920, after an absence of almost three years. She was met by her eldest sister, Lida, who had spent most of that time in the Church of St George; her grey-haired, sad-looking father; her smartly dressed stepmother, who had put on weight; and an almost surreally beautiful Christine, who had just celebrated her thirteenth birthday. Meri, the second eldest, had finally found a suitable husband, a notary from Kutaisi, and had followed him there. When she arrived in her homeland, Stasia did not yet know that, in addition to all these people, there was somebody else at the family gathering — in her belly.

At this point, she was already pregnant with her first child, my grandfather.

The patisserie was still going, though they were constantly afraid for all the family property, which was threatened with expropriation. Democracy was on a shaky footing in Georgia. There were daily workers' and peasants' uprisings and factory strikes, and the socialists were boycotting the government. Nobody knew what the next day would bring, and the nation was disconcerted by the unclear political axis of the various parties and groups. Nobody knew who to vote for, or why; the laws, the demands, the promises changed every day.

Stasia's return to the bosom of her family was given the celebration it deserved. There was weeping, arms were constantly being thrown around her neck, and even Lara, who was usually so reserved, shed a few tears. Stasia told her family in detail and at length of her hardships and battles in Petrograd — everything she had not told her husband. It was only the end of the story that she kept to herself, until the evening when she confessed it to her father in his study, after allowing herself a sip of his cognac. Her father's gaze was fixed on the floor as Stasia gave him her account in a wavering voice, though she said nothing of the chocolate and the poison. She didn't want to disappoint her father, or give him the impression that she had acted recklessly, abusing her knowledge, and, most importantly, failing to keep the promise she had made him. But, above all, she didn't tell him because she had still found no answer to the question of whether, in this case, the chocolate and the poison were one and the same, and she was afraid of this answer.

She was back home. She had survived. Even if, once again, Paris seemed so far away, and Thekla had left her in the lurch — or was it the other way round? — even if at the end of it all she still wasn't with her husband: she was still alive, and that was good.

★

A week later, Stasia was to finally discover the reason for her sentimentality and hypersensitivity: the pregnancy.

The discovery made her feel a strange mixture of irritation and excitement. In view of the circumstances, she wasn't entirely sure whether to be glad about the news. The ministrations of her father and Lida, however, alleviated the pain, the longing, and the dark memories to some degree. Lida had grown to be a sort of dove of peace for the family. She strode about the house with her crooked gait, performed all kinds of services, helped out in The Chocolaterie, did Christine's homework with her, and was responsible for the whole family's wellbeing. In her mind, she had already become a bride of Christ, although her entry into a convent was perpetually delayed by her father's objections.

In the evenings, Stasia sat in her father's study, sometimes with a newspaper or a book, while he engrossed himself in his papers. His presence gave her a sense of safety.

'I always used to think you were too dreamy to love seriously, but now I suspect I was wrong. Still, no woman should travel so far for a man, and no man should leave his wife alone for so long,' he told his daughter one evening. He asked if she would like a hot chocolate — he would make one for her, just this once — and Stasia had to run out and vomit.

The Red front relocated to Azerbaijan. When the Bolsheviks were able to safely suppose that England would abandon the competition for access to the Orient, and therefore to oil, fighting officially commenced. The war finally ended in victory for the Reds, and the Sovietisation of the country, as Stasia's belly inexorably grew. The neighbouring country of Armenia, weakened by the war against the Turks, was also unable to put up any further resistance. The Crimea was now under occupation, and Kiev had been firmly in Soviet hands since the summer. The question was how long Georgia, which the Bolsheviks had so far recognised as sovereign territory, would be able to remain an independent country.

But in February 1921, the dam broke. The Georgian Bolshevik Filipp Makharadze and his followers proclaimed the Soviet Republic of Georgia, and called on the Russian Central Committee to provide military support against the 'Third Group' and the Mensheviks.

The 11th Army took just nine days to capture the capital, meaning that by 25 February the resistance had already been broken and the country belonged to the Reds. The 'Third Group' government had fled to Kutaisi, and left the country altogether a short while later.

During Stasia's pregnancy, the Reds had brought all supplies of wheat and weapons under their control, as well as the entire rail network. At the same time, the people in thirty-seven Russian governorates were starving, and the western press was already carrying reports of cannibalism and of many thousands of children with rickets. When somebody was facing the firing squad, their life could be bought for around four litres of sunflower oil and three litres of vodka.

Yes: all of this happened while my grandfather was growing in his mother's belly, and when he came into the world that hot August, his country already bore the name of the Georgian SSR. Two weeks later, in the Church of St George, one of the few intact churches left in the city, he was baptised Konstantin, but from then on everyone called him Kostya.

★

A little less than a year after Kostya's birth, just before his father met him for the first time, the chocolate-maker's property fell into the hands of the state, as they had feared, and the spacious house in the city centre was divided in two. The upper floor and the large attic room now accommodated two workers from the wood factory and their families.

The Chocolaterie continued to exist as a nationally renowned institution; now, though, it belonged to the state, and my great-great-grandfather was a state employee.

From this point on, as a silent protest, my great-great-grandfather stopped adding his secret ingredients to the chocolate mix, which quickly led to a loss of custom. He was forced to change the shop's decadent, capitalist décor in favour of the Party-approved style, which would not necessarily have delighted most of his customers, either: they went to the shop to enjoy the Parisian or Viennese atmosphere, not the dismal reality of an occupied Soviet town. The servants were dismissed, of course — there was no place for a nanny in this new proletarian life — and so Stasia and Lida spent their time child-minding. Only occasionally did Stasia manage to escape her day-to-day life and ride out into the steppe, on a Kabardin she borrowed from the stud farm.

The range of food on offer decreased with every day that passed; people's clothes lost their colour, and the town's only dance school — and Stasia's only hope — was closed down. Instead, they opened a branch of the Komsomol, the 'All-Union Leninist Young Communist League', a Party youth organisation, which continually struck up patriotic songs and glorified the October Revolution, and whose goal it was to raise young people as 'loyal communists'.

> Rally the ranks into a march!
> Now's no time to quibble or browse there.
> Silence, you orators!
> You
> have the floor,
> Comrade Mauser.
>
> VLADIMIR MAYAKOVSKY

By the time Simon Jashi met his son, Kostya could already say '*Deda*'. Simon had had a leave request signed off for the first time. Stationed somewhere on the Don, where the peasants kept calling for uprisings, his brigade was responsible for re-education. Stasia and Simon went for walks and ate her father's chocolate cake, which didn't taste the way it used to. They played with their son, visited the town's first cinema, and even rode out into the steppe together, but Stasia couldn't help feeling as if she was living a stranger's life: this husband simply didn't feel like hers, and, when he departed, she experienced a real sense of relief. Alone, she was at least able to carry on dreaming of the life she had once wanted to lead, which had nothing in common with the one she was leading now.

Kostya had just started attending the town's first state kindergarten when Simon Jashi suddenly turned up unannounced one March morning: a gaunt lieutenant with a full beard, standing outside the entrance to the house, calling for his wife. Three broken ribs that had never healed properly had given him a pulmonary embolism, which he had survived; he now limped, and his hands trembled. He had been *assaulted* by a peasant with a shovel, and given leave from the army for a few months as a result of his *physical impairment*.

Stasia, who was just tasting her son's porridge, hurried to the door with the spoon in her hand. She looked at her changed and dramatically aged husband up and down and tapped the spoon against her thigh, not knowing what else to do. This man, the father of her son, who she had always wished would love her more than he loved his duties, stood before her in his pitiful state, but neither she nor he uttered a word. They stood facing each other, with no idea where to begin.

My great-great-grandfather suggested to the newlyweds — for how else should one refer to a couple who had shared a bed for only a few nights in more than five years — that they go to the countryside, to one of the villages close by, and take some time there for each other and the child. He had a friend whose summer residence had not been expropriated: a simple, traditional Georgian lodge, just a few kilometres from the town, but far enough from the hustle and bustle of the world. They were to get to know each other again there, and Simon was to get well. The owner of the house wouldn't bother them; they would just have to look after a few hens, two cows, and a bit of greenery.

★

The simplicity of the house, the peace of the countryside, the remoteness from politics, their everyday occupations, the friendly local peasants — all of this suited the couple very well. At first, Stasia even enjoyed working on the land and with the animals: it was a change, after all, and she was determined to give her family a fresh start. They could begin a new life. Somewhere, the remnants of that first, foolish, crazy, provocative feeling of being in love must still exist. There were horses in the village, too, which could be rented and ridden. A good start, Stasia thought, since riding had been their shared passion. But Simon was so fragile, so tired, that he couldn't even manage to mount one of the horses. Most of the time he stayed silent, gazing listlessly into the distance, giving his son an occasional smile, only eating when Stasia reminded him to. Stasia still couldn't see — she refused to see — that something within him had been irrevocably extinguished.

Meanwhile, in Russia, coroner's reports were piling up:

Corpse no. 1: skull completely shattered, lower jaw broken.

Corpse no. 2: skull smashed by two bullets.

Corpse no. 3: skull and surrounding area shattered by a metal object.

Corpse no. 4: a soldier, judging by clothing, three bullet holes in the skull.

Corpse no. 5: certainly the bishop, cause of death difficult to determine, as he was apparently buried alive.

Simon Jashi had seen enough of that. More than enough. The handsome horses, his wife's energy, and the love of his son could not make him forget it all.

Stasia's effort to put on a cheerful, beaming face every day, whether she was doing the laundry or mucking out the cow shed (a task she took as seriously as saving her marriage), whether she was peeling potatoes or telling little Kostya a story, had no effect. Everything seemed to pass Simon by without leaving any impression on him. He rose late, spent an eternity sitting over the strong coffee that his father-in-law sent from town every three weeks, and read the paper, which always reached the village two days late. He ate what was put in front of him, as if he had no further desires or needs, and afterwards he went for a walk, returning home only late in the afternoon. After supper, he went out to play cards with the neighbouring farmers, and, when he came back at night, Stasia was usually lying in bed awake, but with her eyes closed, hoping he would want to wake her, tell her about his thoughts and worries, ask her about her own, plan the next day, *something* — but nothing of the sort happened. Deadened as he was, empty and resigned, he lay down silently beside his wife, turned his back to her, and fell asleep straight away.

During this time, the only one who seemed to be alive was Kostya. He grew, and was delighted by each new discovery; he learned to walk and talk, he laughed and cried. The little village constituted his whole world, and he wanted nothing more. And if his parents, who were so wrapped up in themselves, happened to laugh, it was mostly due to Kostya having done something funny or said something inappropriate for a toddler.

Although the couple's country life was only supposed to last a couple of months, and at the start they said that Simon would soon be redeployed, nothing happened. For some reason, Simon seemed to be in no rush to take up his promised post, and his superiors didn't seem to be missing him too much, either. And so his leave stretched out into an eternity, or so it seemed to Stasia. He received a small, regular pay packet, and, with her father's support and hardly any demands on their money, they managed quite well. The time the Jashis spent in the countryside passed slowly and languidly, and, above all, quietly.

On rare occasions, Stasia took Kostya into the town to visit her family, and, every time, she found herself on the verge of never going back to the village and the sleepy little wooden house. But the chocolate-maker's household was a far cry from what it once had been. They had nowhere near enough money. Inflation had reached Georgia. The Party was setting about the project of collectivisation and industrialisation, and living space was tight. The wood factory employees and their families did not get along with the chocolate-maker's family. They were living on top of each other, and Lara, who seemed to be gradually expanding out of sheer vexation, was always bickering with the workers' wives.

With the political situation and his social degradation, Stasia's father's health had suffered badly, and his character had changed. He had developed a fiery temper, and become more cantankerous and impatient. Lida was still trying to hold the family together, but was no longer having much success. Meri's husband had lost his job, and Meri kept fleeing home from Kutaisi to sleep in Lida and Stasia's former room.

Only the youngest, Christine, seemed really to blossom during these hopeless times. She had reached her sixteenth year, and her beauty seemed to grow more supernatural from one day to the next, such that she was hardly allowed out of the house without a chaperone. Whether grammar school boys or married men, old men or young working-class Komsomol members, she stopped them all in their tracks. Some whistled at her or wrote her anonymous letters, which came fluttering through the window of her classroom, and which Christine laughed over with the girls in her class.

★

After almost a year of country life, Stasia's gloom reached its zenith. Every plate she washed, each egg she had to fetch from the hen house seemed to her like an unjust punishment. She felt her resentment of Simon growing; his silence seemed to mock her, and his withdrawn manner was pure provocation. She often lay down in the hay in the cowshed and cried until she could cry no more. Some days, her aggression also spread to little Kostya, who refused to acknowledge the iciness between his parents and continued to demand unlimited love and attention from them both.

'I can't stand it any longer. I don't know who you are any more. I want to leave, I'm suffocating here, you do nothing to help me, and if we don't do something about it soon, I'm going to start hating you.'

Stasia had, yet again, been lying awake in bed, and when Simon came home tipsy from playing cards with the neighbouring farmers, lay down beside her, smelling of schnapps, and was just about to turn his back, she said this in a calm, quiet, measured voice.

'What exactly would you like to change?' was his response. His voice, too, was calm, quiet and measured.

'I'm not a peasant, I'm not built for this life. I never wanted to live like this.

Never!' she replied, speaking louder and more quickly this time.

'I've killed a man,' he said suddenly.

'But you were at war.'

'No, not in the war, it wasn't defence.'

'What exactly does that mean?' Stasia asked, slowly taking in what this stranger, her husband, had just told her.

'We were in Crimea. They'd sent us there, to a pretty little town not far from Taganrog. There was no end to the uprisings around there. So many, again and again. I mean, I understand it. They want to wipe out the *kulaks*, as a class. They want to completely nationalise agriculture. To them, the economic reform means that the farmers sell their wheat below the going rate, the Party buys it and sells it above that rate, and the profit flows into the arms industry and goes to build factories. But what they don't consider is that a farmer has no interest in selling his produce at a loss. He'd rather harvest nothing: either way, he's headed for poverty, and he'd prefer to be poor without having to toil for it. They'd sent plenty of army troops there before us, but the farmers wanted to keep their land for themselves and sell their wares at a decent price again. Why should they sell their produce to the state more cheaply just because it's the state? So it was always a case of oppressing them, expropriating their land, resettling them. We'd been there two days when we were sent into this village, in the interior. A village collective was occupying the administrative building and stopping the commissars from doing their work. Their leader was a farmer who used to own the largest maize and wheat fields. Two of us went, in civilian clothes — we were supposed to assess the situation, and then the army would follow. A brigadier and me. The whole thing was supposed to go off without a lot of fuss; there was enough unrest in the area already. We tried speaking amicably with the man — a bear of a man, a colossus, a life of working the land ingrained in every pore. But he proved inflexible. I tried to persuade him, telling him it was pointless to be so intransigent: all his land had already been confiscated, and he wouldn't be able to sell his produce elsewhere. He was just endangering the whole village with his resistance. But he just kept saying that he didn't give a damn about the accursed communists and had no intention of handing all his years of work over to these swine.

'The brigadier who'd accompanied me — he was one of the volunteers — quickly started to lose patience. We didn't have rifles with us, otherwise we wouldn't have got into the village; I'd introduced myself as a commissar, and there was no talk of the army, but the scoundrel whipped out a little pistol and suddenly we found ourselves in the middle of a battlefield. In no time at all people were picking up shovels and sickles, and blood would start to flow any second, I knew it; so I snatched the pistol from the brigadier's hand — God knows where he'd got it from — and aimed it at him, demanding that he calm down. I thought we were out of danger, and I started negotiating again. But the brigadier was cursing and screaming and calling me a traitor, and when he came at me, I pulled the trigger. I don't know why, I don't know what for, he wasn't armed; he came towards me and I pulled the trigger.

'That same night, I went to Taganrog and reported everything to my commander. I was prepared for anything, but not for what he decided. The news seemed almost to delight him; he shook my hand and congratulated me. Imagine that, Stasia. He congratulated me. I only understood the following day. They marched into the village and slaughtered the lot of them because it was said the farmers had shot a Red Army soldier. So now they had the right to do that. Anyone who defended themselves and their families they shot dead, and those who remained were resettled. That's why I was able to come back to you. That's why I've been able to stay here so long: because I killed a man, Stasia.'

She laid her arm around his waist and pressed her head against his shoulder, pressed herself tightly to him, and finally rolled onto his body. She felt pity for him, even if her store of pity had been substantially depleted over the last year. All this time she had been waiting for him to start speaking, as she had waited for her son's first words, for his first *Deda*, but now that he was speaking, the main thing she felt was anger.

No, no, I don't want to hear all that, why are you telling me all that? What am I supposed to do with this story, where should I put it? It's this goddamned war — you could have stayed here, with me, you could have avoided this war, you would have been able to find another position, you wouldn't have had to condemn me to go after you and end up in that hell and witness the suicide of a person I had started to love. You were the one who wanted it. You didn't have to put me in this position, coming here, and then not being able to speak to me all this time. I'm sorry for what happened to you, you and the farmers, and I'm sorry that the whole world has lost its mind, but what about me? I never thought it would be like this. I married a charming, quiet, self-assured young man, and now I have a silent, sad, empty, wounded old man, and I'm supposed to nurse him back to health, but I don't know what to do, I simply can't go on. You didn't summon me to Moscow, nor did you come to me in Petrograd. And when you came back, you didn't even ask me if it wasn't too late!

All this she wanted to say, but instead she kissed his temples, stroked his chest, and began to undress him. And he allowed her to comfort him. They hadn't touched each other for months, and he was relieved that his words had broken down the physical barrier, at least.

★

Simon's confession brought about a change in the couple's relationship, and another pregnancy for Stasia. It softened the fronts slightly, and made the silence a little more permeable. But unfortunately it wasn't able to turn the silent, sad, wounded soldier back into a witty, charming, quiet, and self-assured young man. And when their daughter, Kitty, came into the world in the year of Lenin's death, the couple still didn't know how to help each other with their respective wounds, their disappointments, and their loneliness.

In 1924, the year Kitty was born, there were twelve work camps and fifty-six other prisons in Moscow alone. Bukharin had proclaimed: 'Yes, we will remodel the intelligentsia, like in a factory.' And Leon Trotsky, the man seen as Lenin's successor, was still too preoccupied with the 'idea of permanent revolution' to notice that the former bank-robber from our homeland had started to gather power around himself. In May 1924, our countryman, Joseph, Soso, or Koba, who two years previously had been named General Secretary of the Party — in spite of the warnings issued by an already seriously ill Lenin — prevailed against the Party's internal opposition, led by Trotsky, and secured his supremacy at the 13th Party Conference.

But Kitty, who bore the name of her mother's dead twin sister, was granted life. She was greedy and loud, as if living for two people at once.

Simon's walks became shorter, and he started to throw his wife a few grateful glances in passing. And, just as Stasia started to believe recovery was in sight, first of all a couple of official letters arrived, and then, one winter's evening, a commissar, who wanted to talk about Simon Jashi's future. The gentleman in the brown wool suit, which was a little too tight for him, sat in the small living room drinking the wine that Stasia had offered him.

'It's almost a year since Comrade Lenin died. The father of us all and the brightest star in the Soviet sky. To Lenin!' He raised his glass. The lieutenant had to clink glasses with him.

'You have always done your duty. We have been informed about it. You can bank on a promotion, Comrade Jashi. You want to continue serving the Motherland, don't you? Of course you do. I see it in your eyes.'

The gentleman lit a cigarette.

'Though I have to tell you, you will only learn the exact location of your posting once you're in Moscow, where you are expected on the first of next month.'

Stasia shut her eyes. She felt dizzy. In the few seconds that passed before her husband replied, she hoped. And then she heard Simon saying:

'Yes, of course, yes.'

'And what about us?' Stasia couldn't stop herself.

'What do you mean?'

'I mean, he's going to be sent God knows where again, and I'll have to spend years waiting for him again, here, with two small children? In the hope that at some point my children will get to set eyes on their father again for a day or two?'

Simon looked angrily at her, but she didn't care.

'Comrade, as the wife of a man who is serving his Motherland and the development of our socialist country so honourably, you should support him, instead of making things more difficult for him.'

'It's not his Motherland,' Stasia let slip. She turned her face to the wall so she wouldn't have to bear Simon's gaze any longer.

'You still seem rather flustered, Comrade. Understandable, in view of the difficult birth on the rainy night of the …'

Stasia was winded. He knew everything; all this time they had supposed themselves alone, but they never had been. Simon would never escape, no matter where they went. Her husband had killed, and must continue to do so — Stasia suddenly realised this with ghastly clarity. Once — even if by unhappy chance — he had demonstrated his talent, and now this talent was what they were after. She glanced at Simon, who was sitting at the table, looking rather paler than usual. He didn't defend himself, didn't refuse, displayed no emotion.

She blinked. Her head hurt. She tried to think of a solution. For her. For the children. She tried to picture her future — a future that from now on would be an extension of this present, this dreary everyday life, with love and affection reduced to a minimum; of this silence, this marital taking-for-granted and banality.

She looked around and saw the shabby room with its old furniture. She saw the washing hanging outside in the yard, the white flags fluttering in the dark of the night, the darned tablecloth, her worn-out gloves, her son's sad, scattered toys, and saw herself in ten years' time, probably exactly where she was standing now, her slippers even more trodden down, a little more weight on her hips, and even more grey hairs in her chestnut-brown plait.

Repressions are educational measures

POSTER SLOGAN

Stasia packed Simon's things for him, with a kind of contrary satisfaction. She said, almost casually:

'I won't come to visit you in Moscow, or wherever else you'll be. This time, you'll have to visit us if you want to see me or the children. And I won't stay here, either. The children and I will live at my father's until they put me on the list for an apartment. I've heard that you can't rent living space privately any more, but since you're such an *honourable comrade* now, I may stand a better chance. I have to get out of here. I hate this farmyard, these cows, I hate my hands stinking of the cowshed, and this mud under my feet.'

'Stasia, I had no choice. I fear there's no other path for me now. The path others have taken leads to the Solovetsky Islands, from which no one has yet returned. I would have liked to have spared you all this, believe me — even if I'm no longer capable of proving it to you.'

Four days later, the White-Red Lieutenant took the night train to the capital, and from there to the capital of socialism. He was posted to a training camp, where he was to teach the young, dedicated, *honourable* men of the Cheka — an association that was on its way to becoming the most powerful and feared organisation in the whole Soviet region — to 'detect and combat counter-revolutionaries and saboteurs'.

★

Stasia and her two children moved into her father's halved house. Christine's room had become free. Just before Kitty's birth, she had married a man named Ramas Iosebidze: twenty years her senior, with exquisite taste, known in society as one of the best Georgian toastmasters, or *tamadas*, an art lover, gourmet, and one of the richest and most powerful bachelors in the capital.

Iosebidze was also a Chekist, and he was a subordinate and close confidant of a fellow Georgian with a striking *pince-nez*, who usually dressed in the typical Cheka uniform of jodhpurs and tunic coat. A short, bald man, who, over many years in the South Caucasus and in Russia, had done everything he could to make a name for himself in the Bolshevik Party, and who had now returned to Georgia; who, at that time, still occupied a modest flat in Griboyedov Street, only to have a splendid villa built shortly afterwards two streets away. Ramas, in stark contrast to his superior, was a majestic-looking man. He had a very imposing belly, a balding head, large, kind, dark brown eyes, huge hands, and he stood at the impressive height of one metre ninety-three. However, in addition to their political convictions and political ambitions, Ramas and his friend had another quality in common: they both appreciated beauty in women.

BOOK II

★

CHRISTINE

> We are, somewhere else, everything that we could have been down here.
>
> AUGUSTE BLANQUI

Ramas had been visiting their little town on official business. A reception was held in his honour, and he was introduced to the town's most presentable businesses. Finally, he and his delegation were invited to the chocolate factory for a piece of cake and a cup of Georgian tea (by this time, national production was taking priority). The chocolate-maker had been instructed to receive the delegation and entertain them personally, which he did, though with limited enthusiasm. The guests sang the praises of The Chocolaterie's products, then fell upon them. Bellies full, they were preparing to set off — their train to Tbilisi was leaving late that evening — and a great shaking of hands was underway, when seventeen-year-old Christine came into her father's shop.

She wanted to go to the races, and had come to ask her father's permission. She was wearing a yellow summer dress and a black beret, which she had placed on her head at an angle, in the French style. She always changed her clothes after school; the drab uniform was an insult to her beauty. Floating daintily across the floor, paying no attention to any of the guests, she headed straight for her father and gave him her most beguiling smile (she wasn't usually allowed to go to the races). The guests turned their heads in unison, some with open mouths, conversations interrupted, others unwittingly letting out a gasp of laughter. It was a reaction the chocolate-maker knew only too well: Christine's God-given beauty took people aback every time. Her father looked at his daughter and couldn't suppress a smile: she really was confoundedly pretty, he thought for the thousandth time.

She had delicate, flawless white skin, like porcelain (nobody in the family was that pale, the other girls were olive-skinned, like him), a bony, elegant figure, and supple limbs. Her features were almost perfectly symmetrical: a small, straight nose; high cheekbones; shapely, wine-red lips; a long swan neck; and, most notably, almond-shaped eyes, marsh-green and framed with thick lashes. Countless little devils seemed to have gathered in these eyes, and were kindling fires there.

But my great-great-grandfather noticed one reaction in particular: that of the big man, the head of the delegation, whom everyone had been so eager to please. He seemed to be devouring her with his eyes; his coarse face had even reddened a little, and he looked as if he was about to say something, then suddenly shut his mouth again.

Christine, who was accustomed to these reactions, ignored him, with her air of refined indifference, and linked arms with her father.

'My daughter, Christine,' said the chocolate-maker.

'You're not an actress, are you?' one of the men whispered. She laughed, and shook her head.

'She won't even finish school for a few months yet,' her father explained.

There followed a few comments regarding her beauty; she received them as if they were entirely self-evident and waited for the party to leave The Chocolaterie.

The last to leave was Ramas Iosebidze, who kissed Christine's hand in parting.

*

Three days later, she received a huge bunch of red roses, with a scented card tucked into them: *These flowers are not worthy of your beauty, Christine. But I think it is worth an attempt to pay tribute to you. Count me as one of your admirers, of which, I assume, there are a great many. I will try to find ways to express the depth of my admiration. Ramas Iosebidze of Tbilisi.*

Christine hadn't shown her parents the many cards and letters she had been sent over the previous few years. She laughed at the young men from the neighbourhood; she and her school friends would make fun of their clumsy declarations of love, and eventually she would tear all the letters up.

But the flowers, which had been sent to her father's address, could not be overlooked. And so Christine had to show her father the card. He merely smiled — which was the last thing she had expected. She had been prepared for him to curse and throw the card away in exasperation. But no. He even gave her a kiss on the forehead.

Flowers and other gifts arrived with increasing frequency over the months that followed. Christine, who was preparing for her school-leaving exams, was often interrupted during her studies by a courier bearing bouquets of lilacs or bottles of French champagne, exotic perfumes, an Italian feather boa, cashmere shawls, a necklace of black pearls, or silk for petticoats.

Christine barely recalled this man — all she could remember was that he was tall and old. Like her mother, she loved luxury; she didn't share her older sisters' modesty. She loved parties and high society, and she loved people paying her the right amount of attention. She loved everything that brought joy and levity; she was choosy, and didn't worry too much about her future. She had neither grand dreams nor a rebellious streak. She had been raised as the sun-kissed child, universally adored, admired, and idolised, and she wanted nothing more than to continue to receive this treatment. Her favourite pictures were watercolours; she hated apple cake and cinnamon rolls, took long baths in rose water or peach-blossom bubble bath, rubbed honey into her hands, and spent hours looking at herself in the mirror. She pored over fashion magazines — which were becoming ever rarer, and ever less fashionable — and thought about all the beautiful dresses she could wear.

And she had another passion: she loved children more than anything, and in particular her nephew, Kostya. And he seemed to return her love. Whenever he saw her, he fell silent and stared at her unblinkingly for a long time. They could spend hours playing, laughing, and messing about together. Christine hated the narrow confines of her house now that the rough, uncouth workers and their families had moved in upstairs; leafing through magazines like *The Fashionable Woman*, or at her beloved cinema, watching foreign films in which the women were so elegant, well-dressed, and grand, she became exasperated by Lida's piety and her requests that Christine dress less conspicuously, by her mother's exaggerated care and watchfulness, and, above all, by Lara's growing small-mindedness and parochialism. Yet, nonetheless, Christine was very happy at home.

In June 1923, once she had her school-leaving certificate in the bag, the decisive letter arrived: an invitation for the whole family to attend Ramas' birthday celebrations in Tbilisi. He was planning a grand party for his thirty-sixth birthday. After much discussion, Christine, her father, mother, and Lida travelled to Tbilisi. They stayed in a pretty guesthouse close to the 'holy mountain' of Mtatsminda, where they were treated like royalty.

The party took place the following evening at Ramas' house on the right bank of the river, in the old-town quarter of Vera. The majestic villa from the previous century, covered in ivy and surrounded by a lush flower garden, the illustrious guests, Ramas' generous hosting, his *élan*, his humour and apparent popularity, his wealth, and the impressive party left the required impression on the family. Ramas was now free to woo the youngest daughter.

A 'big cheese' like Ramas guaranteed his daughter an untroubled future, thought the chocolate-maker. After his disappointing experience with Simon and Stasia and their over-hasty wedding, and the failure of Meri's marriage, this was an excellent opportunity for Christine and the whole family. (Meri, who had for long enough felt humiliated and embittered by her unhappy marriage, kept writing her father despairing letters from Kutaisi, begging him to help her and give his consent to a divorce.) Such husbands were not what the chocolate-maker had wished for his daughters. He was particularly pained by Stasia's lustreless eyes, her hands, rough from farm work, and her taciturn manner.

Christine was his last hope, and this time he wouldn't, and couldn't, make a mistake.

Christine — I don't think she ever found time to consider what all this meant for her. She didn't even have time to fall in love, least of all with the much older Ramas Iosebidze. On the other hand, she was impressed by his splendid gifts, his generous invitations, his yearning gaze, his height, and the size of his properties. And in high summer, with the encouragement of her parents and the prospect of a move to the capital, she gave her consent when he asked for her hand.

The wedding the following spring was magnificent: at last, a celebration befitting the family's status, with an immense train and a thousand white roses, countless guests and friends from the north and the south, from cities and villages, a long table laden with all kinds of delicacies, including, of course, the world's best chocolate gateau. I'm told the likeness of the bridal pair was moulded in chocolate and placed on top of the cake — even if the real bridegroom didn't quite match the chocolate version, with his full beard, the impressive circumference of his belly, and his balding head. The guests ate, drank, and danced; there was laughter and embracing and congratulations. The band played jaunty music. The night wore on and became stifling.

Stasia left the ballroom and went out into the dark garden, wanting some fresh air and a chance to look back over the events of the day. She sat down contentedly on a bench in the darkness and laid her hands on her belly.

It was already cold, and multi-coloured leaves covered the ground. She felt a light touch on her back and saw Christine, shining white, standing beside her.

'I had to get out into the fresh air for a while as well. It's so exhausting, getting married!' she said in her precocious way, and sat down beside Stasia with a groan.

'You don't love him, do you?' Stasia suddenly blurted out, and regretted the question even as she asked it. Christine straightened up and frowned at her sister, who, by comparison, looked like a boy who had grown too tall. Her long plait hung down her back and, despite the occasion, she wore no make-up and had on a simple blue and white spotted cotton dress.

'But he loves me enough for two. And anyway, I already love the life I'm going to live,' Christine replied with disarming honesty.

'You're too young to talk like that.'

'Oh, Stasia — still the old romantic. And I want to have children soon: preferably a boy first, just as pretty as your Kostya.'

Christine laid a hand on Stasia's belly.

'I wish you a great deal of happiness, in any case, little sister,' said Stasia, with a smile.

'And what happiness did your great love bring you, sister dear?'

The question took Stasia by surprise, and she shifted a few centimetres away from Christine. But, at that moment, someone called Christine's name. As the band struck up the loudest chord of the evening, Stasia's sister, in her beautiful dress, hurried back into the ballroom and into her new life, and Stasia remained behind. She looked sadly up at the stars and wondered what Peter Vasilyev was doing just then, and which girls he was teaching, and what would have become of her if she hadn't allowed her head to be turned by Simon Jashi's sweet enticements. Even her little sister seemed to be cleverer and more calculating than she, who would soon be a mother of two.

And so Christine moved to her influential husband's house in the capital, and Stasia and her children moved into Christine's old, light-green room, while posters continued to appear all over their home town bearing slogans like 'The spy aspires to Party membership' and 'The enemy behind the director's mask'.

Stasia lived in the house where she was born for another four years, forever waiting for her husband to be granted leave. He was released at the beginning of June every year, and allowed to return home for four weeks. He was admittedly more lively and talkative than before, but the old Simon, whom Stasia still loved and looked for, never came back.

Her father went to the chocolate factory less and less since he had been demoted to second deputy director. Christine wrote rosewater-scented letters, in which she enthused about her splendid life and the wonderful trips she had taken, or complained about the housemaid. Now and then she would send a parcel full of rare and expensive items: an Armenian cognac for her father, good-quality wool for Lida, caramels and nice trouser material for Kostya, pretty earrings for her mother, and so on.

Stasia darned socks, and was often to be seen sitting on the tiny wooden balcony of the shrunken house, which looked out over the fabric shops and the fruit market now managed by the municipality, gazing into uncertainty. Occasionally, and mostly out of habit, she wrote letters to her Red Lieutenant, mainly concerning the children and money matters. Every six months she went to the photographer and had the children's pictures taken. She enclosed the brownish photographs, glued onto stiff cardboard, in the letters to her husband.

★

At this point, Brilka, I should give a more detailed introduction to the little man with the *pince-nez*, who was on his way to becoming *big*.

This little man, born in an Abkhazian-Georgian village called Merkheuli, came from a poor background. He didn't particularly excel at school, and, following his apprenticeship as a technical engineer in Baku on the Caspian Sea, he found a position in the oil business. These were early days for the industry, which, at that time, was still dominated by the Swedish Nobel family (yes, yes, *that* Nobel!).

Rumour had it that he owed his appointment to the Azerbaijani government's secret service, which reported to the British secret service and had its eye on Transcaucasia. He had joined the Party as a twenty-year-old, in 1919 — though he claimed to have been a first-wave communist who was already a Party member in 1917. But then, he had always had a rather idiosyncratic understanding of truth. Unlike his more famous countryman, he had no proven criminal past, and — this was the most surprising thing — hardly any political ambitions. Those who had known him as a young man said that, for him, it had always been about 'making it', compensating for his lack of education and his low social status, providing for his mother, who lived in poverty, and his deaf-mute sister, and being able to impress beautiful women from better social circles. Pretty banal ambitions, in retrospect.

But he developed an almost pathological urge to join the upper classes, initially failing because he never appeared educated, sensitive, and charming enough to get a foot in the door of high society. But, one day, this little man with the love of opera and feminine beauty finally did make it: in 1922, he came to Tbilisi at the head of a secret operations unit of the Georgian Cheka to conduct a highly effective campaign against counter-revolutionary scum. A year later, he had done such a thorough job that he was awarded the Red Banner. In the year that Kostya started school, this man had already become head of his organisation, and was working on securing a personal meeting with his countryman, who was no longer called Joseph, Soso, or Koba. After a dizzying rise to power, he had smashed the Party triumvirate and was on the way to placing himself alone at the apex of the vast empire: he was now the *man of steel*, soon to become the *Leader* and *Generalissimus*.

CPSU is the brain, the honour, and the conscience of our epoch

POSTER SLOGAN

One morning, Stasia received a telegram from the capital: an invitation from her sister Christine to a New Year's ball. Christine also informed her that Ramas had recently been promoted to become the little man's deputy, and that she looked forward to celebrating this important development with her sister. She requested that Stasia wear an imaginative costume. Everything else was taken care of.

Lida said she was prepared to look after the children, and Stasia decided to forget her day-to-day worries for a little while and travel to the capital city, which, so they said, was flourishing and prospering and receiving a record number of visitors, thanks to the Communist Party of Georgia.

By train, the journey took just one night. Stasia had always wanted to go to Paris, and now here she was arriving in the Paris of the Caucasus. Well, that was something. The city with the spice markets, the new cafés and old houses, the long, paved, dusty boulevards. With the kosher butchers and Catholic churches, the magnificent carriages and lacquered automobiles that, between them, dominated the streets; with the pet shops, the wine and carpet merchants; with the literature, dance, and theatre circles; with the theatres and opera house; with the half-built apartment blocks and Bolshevik architecture; with the centuries-old fortresses and myriad church towers; with the winding alleys of the city's Jewish and Armenian quarters; with the sulphur baths, the shabby rear courtyards, and the imposing villas in the east.

Outside the railway station, people were scurrying around like ants. Sales girls in white aprons extolled the virtues of the warm bread from the clay ovens, and gypsies with budgerigars offered to tell your fortune. There Stasia stood, with the black suitcase she had brought back from St Petersburg, waiting for her sister. She had visited the capital once as a child, but that was many years ago, and this city was a different one.

Instead of Christine, an old man appeared and asked her to get into one of the motorcars that the horse-loving Stasia could never get used to.

At the viceroy's former residence, the driver turned into a side road and drove up a steep incline. Taking a series of little, winding one-way streets, they came to the top of a hill that afforded a wonderful view of the old town.

There, outside one of the grandest villas, they stopped. A slender boy opened the gate, and Stasia entered a beautiful garden, at the centre of which stood a small fountain with a Cupid statue, water spouting from his little penis. Before Stasia had overcome her amazement, she heard a rustling sound, and her sister came hurrying towards her in an azure-blue dress that was only knee-length. And, as was presumably the norm in the capital, she pressed a little kiss onto each of Stasia's cheeks.

'Stasia, how wonderful that you've come! I'm so thrilled,' Christine cried. She led her sister into the pastel-coloured, ornamented, two-storey house.

There were sofas from Tehran, hand-knotted rugs, and a huge number of pictures on the walls. There were even bamboo rocking chairs and seventeenth-century sideboards. Dark green velvet drapes, a housemaid, a cook, two Persian cats, a wireless (Stasia had read about these in the newspaper), several gramophones, and gold-decorated vases.

Stasia was given a spacious room with a glorious view and an ornate bedstead, made up with white sheets. A Chinese folding screen stood in front of it, and the walls were hung with silver-framed mirrors.

★

Christine and her husband proved to be superb hosts. It was a quality that the rich and beautiful people of Tbilisi society also appreciated.

Ramas' family originally came from a little village in the southwest. In the time of the tsars, they had enjoyed an excellent reputation as silk exporters, with two silk mills in the south that had been in the family for generations. Ramas, the family's only son, was given a first-rate education and travelled all over Europe in his youth. He spoke four languages fluently. He came into contact with Marxist thought — much to his family's horror — during the few months he spent in Germany, of all places, and, on returning to his homeland, he became an early member of the Communist Party. Shortly afterwards he was detained for anti-tsarist agitation and sent into exile in Turukhansk, returning two years later with a pardon. His cellmate there, so people said, had been none other than his countryman Joseph, called Soso, or, affectionately,

Koba, though this fact has not been proven. (Perhaps people only said it to explain his meteoric career, and the protective hand that hovered over Ramas, so successful, so favoured by life — because to many people it must have looked as though Ramas had a protective hand over him.)

Ramas' father, a man of the old school, hated the communists and belonged to the Georgian nationalist movement. They say he gave financial support to the 'Third Group' in its early days, and was therefore not entirely uninvolved in founding the Democratic Republic of Georgia.

After the Bolsheviks took over the country and their factories were closed down, the family emigrated to Paris, following the example of many of the Democratic Republic of Georgia's founding fathers. Ramas stayed in Georgia.

As Ramas had put a large part of his inheritance into the Party, thereby enabling the Reds to carry out many of their plans in his homeland, they allowed him to keep the rest of what he had inherited, meaning he was able to continue his cultivated and hedonistic lifestyle — even as a dedicated Bolshevik and Chekist. He never spoke to anyone about his business, particularly not his wife, though she had no real interest in it, anyway. He was a fervent communist who believed that socialism was right and would soon be successful. Like Trotsky, he was a proponent of permanent revolution, believing that sooner or later the whole world must be revolutionised. The only thing Ramas retained from his imperialist upbringing was his passion for art. And not strictly Bolshevik or socialist art. No homages to the homeland, proletarian hero figures, or socialist realism, the art his Party called for artists to create.

He loved and collected art, in particular the work of Impressionists, Symbolists, and young, unconventional painters. He stored the imperilled paintings in a small, secret room, accessed through a cupboard door in his study. He could spend hours there, admiring them.

Ramas had previously been famed throughout the city as a Don Juan. He was said to have had numerous affairs with actresses, *salonistes*, widows, female patrons, and even servants. But he hadn't married any of them. When the news that he had wed an underage girl from the provinces spread throughout Tbilisi, it became the number one topic at salons and dinner tables all over the city. People gained access to his house on the most absurd pretexts to admire his young wife. And, although everyone had to admit that Ramas had excelled himself in his choice of bride, they were all still of the opinion that this marriage would not last long, and that, in a year at most, Ramas would be back to chasing every pretty skirt in the city.

But Ramas never left the house without his wife, except when he went to work. He took her on business trips, went to premieres and exhibition openings with her, and held great dinners and parties at his house in her honour.

They were an unusual couple. He: huge, powerful, a colossus with a balding head, a wide mouth, and sincere, permanently moist, eyes. And she: a delicate, dainty creature, a work of art, carved from ivory. She too was tall, though she barely reached his shoulder — and yet he seemed small, almost unremarkable, in her presence.

The expected scandal in the Iosebidzes' magnificent house did not materialise. On the contrary, the couple seemed happy. Of course, people thought the girl had only married Ramas for his position and his money, but whenever she appeared with him in public she seemed almost fixated on him; she was never seen gazing at other, young, good-looking men, or seeming bored at her husband's side, and finally, the city was left with no choice but to trust in their happiness.

During her visit, Stasia, who had also greeted her sister's family idyll with mistrust, was forced to acknowledge that Christine really had found her place in the world. While Stasia strolled through the streets (she had vehemently declined the offer of a chauffeur, despite Christine's repeated attempts to convince her of the advantages of the motorcar) and visited the various markets, parks, and cafés, the younger woman prepared for her New Year's ball, which was to be the event of the year.

On 31 December — it must have been the last day of the year 1927 — both sisters were to make acquaintances that would change their lives forever. The carpet of our story, Brilka, would continue to be knotted, and the patterns that emerged would be ostentatious, colourful, carnivalesque, but also dark and sinister.

Perhaps that was the night when Fate became aware of us all for the first time. Perhaps, without it, the carpet would have been kept beautifully simple, in pastel shades, with no more powerful colours knotted into it. Or perhaps it was pure chance that brought these people together in the same place, or a whim of nature — an unstoppable, swift, cruel whim.

But, as yet, none of the actors knew what play they were performing. It was still just a lovely, festive New Year's Eve.

Christine had mobilised a whole horde of cooks and servants, and a band, and had decorated the entire house with flowers. Stasia couldn't help admiring her: with what ease, what panache, she played the lady of the house, so naturally and at such a young age. She was like a *grande dame*, a *salonnière*, doing everything she could to give her guests a unique experience as soon as they entered her house.

Stasia wondered how it could be that, having grown up in the same house, with the same upbringing, the same father, they could be so different; as if Christine, in all her perfection, had been raised to enchant people and have them pay court to her. Stasia also had to admit that her sister looked wonderful amid all this hustle and bustle, remaining cheerful, relaxed, easy, charming, and attractive in her own distinctive way. Attractive in a languorous, offhand way, her manner bordering on arrogance.

Later, when Christine appeared after barricading herself in her bedroom to put on her costume, Stasia even let out a little gasp of astonishment, so nearly *perfect* did her sister look that evening.

Her original choice of costumes for herself and her husband had been the Sun King and Marie Antoinette, but Ramas had deemed them too decadent (they could be misinterpreted, seen as a provocation) and asked his wife to come up with something simpler. Christine had retorted: would ancient Rome be *simple* enough for him? Ramas liked that suggestion even less: he didn't want his wife's incredible body paraded half-naked before other men's eyes (and he couldn't imagine himself in a Spartacus costume, either). Finally, they agreed on a simple, sophisticated option: they would wear elegant Venetian masks. You couldn't go wrong with those, Ramas reasoned. They would give rise to no misunderstandings.

Christine was swathed in a dream of turquoise silk, truly simple, no doubt about that. The dress was fitted, but not too tight; it was modestly cut, and, although the choice of colour was perhaps a little unusual, it didn't even have a plunging neckline — quite the opposite, it was high-necked, and her only jewellery was a long chain of black pearls, a gift from her husband when he was courting her.

But, as Christine went by, Stasia had to suppress a burst of laughter. The dress was cut low at the back. A little collar around her neck held the material together, but nothing more. It was cut so low that it exposed the two little dimples above her buttocks.

'What?' said Christine, looking at her sister with a mischievous smile.

'And *what* are you supposed to be dressed as?'

'If anybody asks me, I can say I'm a courtesan who's been fortunate in her admirers. She has regular customers, all of them noblemen or from merchant families. And if nobody asks, then I'm just me, in a divine dress,' she replied, before sweeping into the next room to make herself up. 'Hurry up!' she called over her shoulder.

At around nine o'clock, the house began to fill with voices. Twice

Christine sent the housemaid up to her sister.

And then Stasia did a peculiar thing: she started covering up all the polished mirrors in Christine's dressing room. She draped them with sheets, coverlets, and robes. Perhaps to preserve her dream as a dream, and not experience it as a failed reality. But perhaps also to give her the courage to put on her costume.

She tied her hair back, took off her wedding ring, which didn't really go with the image of the dying swan, and, before leaving the room, closed her eyes once more. She imagined herself in the large, chilly hall in Thekla's villa, heard the music from the gramophone and Peter Vasilyev's remarks, saw herself floating over the parquet floor, and danced a few steps before gliding down the stairs to join the illustrious ball.

Witches and queens, pirates and musketeers, thieves and contortionists, and, above all, peasants and soldiers were laughing and drinking champagne. On this mild New Year's Eve at the start of 1928, the band played something light, something pretty — at least, that's how I imagine it. Perhaps even a little swing from the land of the capitalist enemy? Why not ...

And there she was, our Stasia, a swan woman, a white phantasm, floating down the stairs. She wasn't as elegant as Christine, to whom all eyes were drawn, but she was enchanting: because what she was wearing was a dream, a thought, an idea, a possibility perhaps ... Even if her legs were a little bowed from all the rides across the steppe, and a touch too thin; even if her face betrayed a little hesitance and uncertainty; even if her hands trembled slightly, and the end of her nose was a little red; Stasia was still happy. That evening, she was happy; happy that people were looking and smiling at her, that she was briefly able to believe it could be true, that the dream might, if only for a moment, be real.

Perhaps it was that night's happiness, surrounding her, that drove her into Sopio's arms. In a literal sense.

Whenever I asked Stasia about this encounter, dragging more and more details out of her against her will, she always replied, in her dry, terse manner: 'I came down the stairs, and she was standing at the foot of the staircase; she looked at me, I looked at her. At that moment I stumbled, and she had to support me. It was that simple.'

So, the swan came down the stairs — wobbly, hesitant, but proud — and stumbled, and there she was: a tall woman in a man's suit, wearing a bowler hat and carrying a walking stick (which may have been the most scandalous costume of the evening; this wasn't the Golden Twenties in Berlin, and Sopio wasn't Marlene Dietrich).

Green-eyed and proud, with an unforgettable nose — *à la géorgienne* — and an inner glow. A strand of blonde hair had broken free from the prison of the hat and made its way down her high forehead. Her tall stature and powerful build suited her costume. They met: Sopio Eristavi as a man, and Stasia Jashi as an unlived dream.

★

'And *then* — what happened then, tell me, tell me, Stasia, come on!' I would press her, and she would explain, as usual, in just a few words:

'Yes, it was how it is when two people find each other. We introduced ourselves; we liked each other. More than that, we were delighted with each other, and we knew we were going to be friends. We fetched our coats and went out into the garden, which was empty and cold. But we didn't care. We drank champagne, smoked, and told each other our life stories.'

In my imagination, I could smell the delicious food in the house, I could hear the swing music, see the coloured lights that decorated the house, and the gigantic Christmas tree topped with a red star (we had one like it, all through our childhood!). I could see two women, giggling, cackling, smiling beside one another in their basket chairs, the tips of their cigarettes aglow.

★

On the very first night of their acquaintance, Stasia learned that Sopio came from an aristocratic family; she was born an Eristavi, the *head of the people*. She had spent her childhood in Borjomi, the tsar's resort by the healing springs, and later at a girls' boarding school in Lausanne. There, she came into contact with some interesting women who organised regular meetings to promote women's rights, and held numerous demonstrations. Stasia also learned that, even more than campaigning for women's rights, Sopio loved to write poetry, and was a fervent devotee of symbolism. She named several poets who Stasia had never heard of, and recited a few verses that meant nothing to Stasia.

Stasia learned that the Eristavi family's property had been expropriated, and they now lived in exile in Switzerland. Sopio herself, however, had stayed with her husband, a cultured Georgian who had reminded her of her dead father, and who apparently sang no worse than Chaliapin himself.

They had a son, but, as her husband started being unfaithful to her while she was still pregnant, drinking away his inheritance, and swiftly forgetting his vows in other ways as well, she decided to file for divorce and give her son her own name, which at the time was as good as officially baptising the child *Bastard*.

'The whole of Tbilisi dragged my name through the mud over the divorce; I don't know anyone else who would have gone through with it. But I don't regret it. My Andro and I get by very well. We learned to survive early enough. It's character forming,' said Sopio, smiling at Stasia. And this smile made Stasia believe in her dreams again, all night long.

But, at that moment, alongside the happiness that pattered down on Stasia like golden confetti, a little door opened. It was a door beyond time and beyond fate, beyond all laws. The world of ghosts awoke for a moment, the moon took on a greenish pallor, the snow and the icicles in the garden glowed, and little particles exploded in the champagne. Confusion broke out; for a fraction of a second, the world hiccupped. Everything churned and groaned, though all were oblivious to it. It was just the wrong door, thrown open for a barely perceptible moment and slammed shut again — but that was time enough for something black to crawl out. Or perhaps it wasn't black at all; perhaps it was colourless and imperceptibly slight — but it was cruel and icy, and what it craved was ruin. This was the moment when betrayal was born.

And something nameless was begun, set free, released into the world to bring madness upon everyone, to afflict the brain and numb the soul: to snatch away life, huge and insatiable.

The door was thrown open, and somebody came in.

Shortly before midnight, shortly before the champagne corks started popping, shortly before the fireworks were lit, and while the two new friends were still sitting in their basket chairs by the fountain telling each other their life stories, a great murmur of amazement ran through the villa. There was a rustling as people whispered in each other's ears and stepped aside: the Little Big Man had been announced. Head of the Chekists, the most powerful man in the country, the host's superior and his personal friend. And he was joining the select gathering to celebrate the start of the year 1928 with them. What an honour!

Christine hurried into the kitchen and put all the servants on high alert: everything the household had to offer must be brought out. He came with his entourage, with his *pince-nez* and his polished, bald head, in his usual uniform — which in the midst of all the costumed guests looked almost like a costume itself — surrounded by similarly uniformed men, who walked silently beside him. He entered the drawing room with a smile, and immediately asked for a

Georgian wine. Since the Kremlin had started placing orders for Khvanchkara, the new leader's favourite wine, this was the wine the Little Big Man favoured as well. He was handed a glass, and drank to the Party and everyone there, in particular the host.

When they asked him what music he would like to hear, he requested a Rachmaninov prelude, a wish that was instantly fulfilled. He politely declined the food, saying he had already eaten, and, as he listened to the piano piece, he closed his eyes reverently. The only guests who missed this spectacle, who had not even noticed his arrival, were Sopio and Stasia.

At the start of the fireworks, which Ramas had ordered specially from Moscow, everyone hurried out into the garden and onto the street. People clinked glasses, embraced each other, and even the Little Big Man sent his guard off to one side and was unusually merry and open-hearted.

Every time I asked her to tell the story, Stasia stressed that the little man had immediately become fixated on Christine, whom he must have noticed straight away. Unlike her husband, Christine had kept her Venetian mask on, even when standing with the important guest and entertaining him in person. Nonetheless, after his first glass he had started heaping compliments on her, praising her costume, her qualities as a hostess, and her beauty, and he was not ashamed to keep telling her what an indispensable colleague and true friend Ramas had been to him. Soon after the last firework had gone out, he asked the lady of the house to show him around. It may even have been the mask that spurred him on to look at Christine more closely. Perhaps it sparked his curiosity.

Christine led him around the house, they chatted about the garden, and he asked her to advise him on plants, saying he wanted to plant a large garden at his villa in Machabeli Street: perhaps she could help him. Standing on the balcony of the upper floor, they raised their crystal glasses and drank to the Leader, to the Party, to her husband, to love. Ramas, who was unquestioningly loyal to his commander, kept his distance that evening and left his enchanting wife to his superior. He was familiar with the magic that Christine worked on men, but, more importantly, he was also familiar with Christine's indifference to her admirers, which sometimes bordered on rudeness. Even in the knowledge of his superior's cruel voraciousness, he trusted that Christine would be able to extract herself from the affair with ease and tact.

Perhaps that was the greatest mistake of his life.

For, after the toast to the great Socialist Revolution, the Little Big Man asked her almost in passing to take off her mask: it bothered him a little, he said, even if the mask itself was, without a doubt, a work of excellent craftsmanship.

But Christine refused, saying she had decided to maintain her mystery that evening, and not to show her face: she was sorry. At which the Little Big Man nodded, as if he accepted her reply, and then called her husband upstairs. In his presence, he repeated his request.

There was an icy, fractured pause.

Everyone involved, particularly husband and wife, was aware of how delicate the situation was. After a moment of hesitation, Ramas turned to his wife with a laugh and carefully removed her mask; the Little Big Man stared unwaveringly at Christine, smiling, self-assured, and satisfied. Apparently, he then cleared his throat and apologised for his curiosity. Christine was quivering with rage, but she didn't let it show, and cheerfully raised another glass to the leader in Moscow.

In the morning, when the couple got into bed, tipsy and overtired, with swollen feet and skin smelling of smoke, the wife turned to her husband, regarded him contemptuously, coldly, full of obstinate aggression, and said, 'You shouldn't have done that.'

> Brothers, unite your hands,
> Brothers, Death laughs!
> An end to slavery forever,
> Holy the final battle!
>
> SOCIALIST SONG

Stasia had dusted off her dream once again and given herself to love. She pumped Sopio for information about Paris; she talked constantly with her free and free-thinking friend; she never wanted to leave Sopio's little flat on the hunchbacked hills of Avlabari, with the colourful wooden balconies, the noisy taverns and the old fortress, the simple, jovial people, and the Armenian music. She accompanied Sopio to the women's meetings she organised on a regular basis, in weaving mills, laundries, and dye-works, to tell women about their rights — an initiative that was supported, oddly enough, by the Party.

Stasia fell in love with this city, which had so much freedom to offer. Above all, it was Sopio's city: she saw it now through Sopio's eyes, and it was a very different city from her sister's. A city full of street-sweepers, washerwomen, cobblers, fortune-tellers, seamstresses, fruit-sellers, and showmen. A friendly, roaring community that dwelt on the hills, sang songs with dubious lyrics far into the night, played accordion and cards. Little dilapidated apartment buildings, constructed in the previous century and never renovated, with communal showers and outdoor privies in the rear courtyards.

These people had always lived here, and they remembered the age of kings and tsars, and the rafts on the river with the *Karachokhelis*, whom you hired to win the heart of the woman you loved, drinking away. They were a people who learned long ago to live for today because no one knew for certain whether there would be a tomorrow. And when tomorrow did arrive, it was usually noisy, dusty, once again bringing too little money, only rough insults or loud laughter and obscene anecdotes.

Sopio had little money and couldn't make contact with her family, let alone accept any kind of support from them, without immediately being denounced as a spy, which was why she had come to live in this rather impoverished quarter — but she had quickly taken it to her heart, along with the cackling Kurdish woman who sat in the courtyard day in, day out, supposedly combing wool, but actually keeping an eye on the whole courtyard and what went on there. And Aunt Natasha, a sixty-year-old Russian who was crazy about children (and whom the Kurdish woman always described as a hussy), who offered to look after Sopio's son any time she was late getting home. And the Georgian couple who sold fruit on the street in order to feed their six children, and yet were able to invite all the neighbours to hearty feasts on Sundays.

Stasia fell in love with the feeling of being young and alive again.

The two of them strolled through the streets or climbed aboard the crowded trams, drank beer, ate kosher food (which Sopio swore by) in the Jewish quarter, and visited the sulphur baths, where they were scrubbed down by fat, strong women's arms as they giggled like schoolgirls. They visited the old town's increasingly empty churches, and in the evenings they spent hours sitting in the lantern-lit park, watching as Andro used his little teeth to extract sunflower seeds from their shells before eating them greedily.

The city that Sopio showed Stasia was a different city with different people, a labyrinth hidden behind the city wall of the old town, whose streets Sopio knew so well. Stasia felt a strong affection for little Andro, with his mother's straw-blond curls and his blue saucer eyes: the child moved her in a special way, and when she was with him she abandoned the strictness with which she treated her own children. Perhaps it was because of the boy's modesty, a kind of joy in simple things. Sopio could never afford enough clothes and toys for him, but so that little Andro would not feel the lack of material things, she cultivated a spellbinding imagination.

She mixed egg yolk and sugar and presented it to him as the most delicious thing in the world, and he accepted it gratefully, and believed it. Spent hours telling him stories about the ants and the butterflies, the little cats and the hedgehogs, in place of beautiful children's books. Invented bedtime fairy tales for him; knitted and sewed things for him out of material from her old clothes, which he wore proudly and showed to everyone. Stasia's children weren't exactly spoiled, but still she almost felt guilty when she looked at Sopio and Andro.

Sopio had to work hard for everything she had, and Stasia admired that. She herself was too rich for the proletariat and too poor for the elite: she found herself in a strange in-between class, which to me explains her guilty conscience.

★

Those two weeks, in which Stasia hardly spent any time with her sister and brother-in-law, went by in a flash. Inspired by all the little exhibitions, cellar performances, and poetry evenings that Sopio had taken her to, and above all by Sopio herself, Stasia felt reluctance at the thought of having to go home to her dreary little town; it almost made her feel faint.

'I need your help!' Stasia said at breakfast the day before her departure. Her younger sister was just pouring herself some milk.

'Why, what's wrong?' asked Christine in her usual bored tone.

'I'd like to move in with you. I don't want to go home. I'll bring the children with me, find a job, and stay here.'

'And what will Simon say about that?'

'I'll write him a letter. I've wasted so much time, always waiting for other people to give their blessing to what I wanted ...'

'You still don't want to grow up, do you, Stasia?'

'It's only temporary, mainly because of the children, until I've found somewhere of my own. Or you could just take the children — I can stay with Sopio.'

'You need to your get over your affinity with this person. She's not exactly ... well, socially acceptable. I have no idea how she got into our party: somebody must have smuggled her in. She may write lovely poems, but she's a dubious woman.'

'How can you be so young and so old at the same time, Christine?'

'So old? I'm not old; if anything, I'm more mature than you, Anastasia. And I'm just thinking of the future.'

'I never imagined that, by inviting me here, you would bring me so much happiness.'

'I'm glad to hear it. And you really want to work?'

'Yes.'

'Isn't Simon sending you money any more?'

'Yes, he is, but I want to earn my own money.'

'Did Sopio Eristavi put that idea in your head?'

'No, she just showed me that it was possible. She teaches foreign languages — she gives private lessons, and takes care of her son and herself.'

'I'm glad to hear it, but you're not like her.'

'I'll leave tomorrow, and as soon as I've got everything ready for our departure, I'll send you a telegram. In the meantime, maybe you can put us on the list for an apartment.'

'I'll be glad to have Kostya so close.'

'Why haven't you got any children yet, Christine? I didn't think you wanted to wait so long.'

'Some day we'll have a wonderful son, just as pretty as Kostya. I promise you that. Now please excuse me, I have to go to the kitchen and give instructions for lunch.' Christine gave a melodramatic groan.

It would be a month before Stasia convinced her father that this was the right move for her and the children; before she packed all her belongings into crates and chests, reached her husband in some military barracks or other and informed him that he would have to visit her in Tbilisi from now on. Before she had convinced the anxious Lida that there was no impropriety in living in the capital without a husband. Before at last she packed Thekla's gold watch, which she had been keeping in a glass box in her bedroom, and boarded the train with her children.

★

At the peak of compulsory agricultural collectivisation, Stasia arrived in Tbilisi with Kitty and Kostya.

Sopio and Andro were waiting for the family at Christine's house, and Christine ordered the cook to prepare a feast. Kostya, who reciprocated his aunt's boundless love, threw his arms round her neck, and refused to let go until it was time for bed. Andro and Kitty, who were about the same age, hit it off straight away and started racing around the fountain. Everything seemed to be going well. The garden was a little paradise for the children, and Kostya started school without a hitch — he was to attend the best school in the city, on the recommendation of Christine's husband. A Russian school, of course.

While Christine devoted herself to the little ones, Stasia began to blossom at the side of her new, golden-haired friend. She spent whole nights watching Sopio sitting at the round wooden table, writing poems by the light of the paraffin lamp (in this part of the city, the electricity supply left a lot to be desired), leaping up now and again to light a cigarette or, if something had turned out well, to wrap her arms around her sleepy friend.

'Sometimes I'm afraid. Really afraid,' said Sopio pensively one windy night. She lowered her head and sat very still. Stasia, confused by her friend's sudden change of mood, touched her hand gently. Outside, the wind whipped against the shutters.

'Of what?' she asked, and put water on the wood-burning stove to make herself and Sopio some of the strong tea that Sopio liked so much.

'I'm afraid they'll come for me.'

'Who are *they*, Sopio? And why — who would want to do that? You haven't done anything, have you? I know you're not in the Party, but ...'

'Where are you *living*, Stasia? Can't you see it, can't you feel it, can't you smell it? Today, at the gallery, I heard that soon you'll have to apply for an exit visa if you want to cross the border, no matter where you're going. And that you won't get a visa for a country that isn't one of the *brother states*.'

'You're seeing it all too gloomily.'

'I suspect I don't see it gloomily *enough*, Taso.' (Sopio refused to shorten Anastasia to Stasia in the Slavic manner; instead, she used the Georgian diminutive and called her Taso.) 'And then there's this dream. In the dream, I'm walking along a street. An empty, deserted street somewhere here in this city, only I've never seen it before. But it's here, somewhere just around the corner — in the dream, I know that. There's a house, a great villa, simple and light, with round archways and winding staircases. It's lovely there: I want to go there, though I don't know what I'm looking for. I reach the gate, tired out from endless walking. A man is standing there, a handsome, well-groomed man, who invites me in. I've never seen him before, never heard his deep, soothing voice. I trust him. I follow him because he knows the way ... The way — I don't know where to. We walk through a garden that looks like a biblical place, like paradise. With roses, so red, so red, Taso, and a wonderful waterfall, like the botanical gardens, and cats and dogs stretched out in the sun, and exotic plants and trees; and the garden seems to go on forever — I can't see the end of it. I walk and walk, and the man leads me around. And then he leads me to a well, on a hill so green it hurts. And then he says that we've arrived now and everything will be fine, that I'm home, and he asks me to climb into the well, and I obey him, I don't want to escape or run away, I swing my leg over the edge and ... There's a good smell coming from the well, and it's damp. I'm not afraid, even though the well is deep and I can't see the bottom. And he waits and stares at me as I climb down, he even smiles at me, and then finally, partly out of fear that he might push me down, I do it, I jump and fall and don't land anywhere. And as I'm falling and falling, I wake up.'

The water was boiling, and Sopio covered her face with her hands and started sobbing. Stasia had rarely seen anybody cry with such racking sobs, such devastation, such hopelessness. She took her in her arms, not knowing what to say.

Until little Andro appeared in the doorway in his white pyjamas, frightened, with tears in his eyes, asking what was wrong with mama. He said *Maman*, in French, something he did all his life. With the emphasis on the last syllable, the French pronunciation.

Sopio wiped away her tears, laughed her loud, hearty laugh again, and replied: 'I was just trying something out: I wondered what happens if someone cries for long enough — whether the tears dry up. Everything's all right, my sunshine.'

'And do they dry up?' asked Andro, wiping the snot from his nose with his shirt-sleeve.

'Yes, they dry up, my darling; tears run out, too, eventually.'

★

In the hot July of Stasia's first summer in Tbilisi — Christine had gone to the coast with her husband, and Stasia had the house all to herself — the Red Lieutenant came to visit his wife.

Stasia had given the housemaid, the cook, and the gardener time off, and was enjoying evenings with Sopio, immersing herself in playing all sorts of ball games with the children, and accompanying her friend to her women's meetings. She had got to know Sopio's friends, all of them penniless and fond of a drink, and was on the point of declaring herself almost happy.

She took the tram to collect her husband from the station. After a year's separation, they were distant and cool with each other. No kisses on the platform, just a brief hug. No accusations; to begin with, the head of the household was received, waited upon, and left alone with the children.

But the following evening — after Sopio had retired with Andro — the Red Lieutenant and his wife had their first heated argument. And it must have been so loud that a neighbouring professor considered calling the police. All the stored-up, unsaid words were spoken; everything Stasia had suppressed over ten years of marriage, as her dreams slowly withered away, was screamed out loud.

At dawn, when the argument finally fell silent, Simon Jashi said to his wife: 'Life is more than just dreams, Anastasia. Let's become a proper family. Because I'm tired. Really tired. I bend over backwards every day, and I still can't live up to your expectations. You're longing for something that's already in the past. I'm almost afraid to see you again because I can't bear these accusations, the disappointment in your face. It has to stop if we want to be good parents to our children. I miss them, and I miss you, too. You, before you started punishing me with every gesture. I need a family — *my* family, Stasia.'

But then — then Stasia knew that her love had already broken off, like a dry branch.

★

Christine and her husband returned, and the children were overjoyed with the wonderful pralines they had ordered specially from Eliseevsky in Moscow.

Shortly before Simon Jashi set off again, Stasia and her friend took a stroll in the park with the lanterns. It was a hot August night, and the city seemed jaded, thirsty, and worn out.

'Why do you lie? Doesn't it make you tired?' Sopio asked her friend unexpectedly.

'What are you talking about?'

Stasia could play fabulously obstinate and stupid, preferably both at once.

'You know what I'm talking about. You want to be free? Then be free. You want to dance? Then dance! You want to be a wife — then be one. It's no disgrace. But you can't do everything at once. Having everything is like having nothing, Taso. You need to see that. You wanted to dance, but at the same time you wanted to be a good wife to your husband; you want to be friends with poets, and at the same time you want to dine at Party receptions; you want to live independently and work, but you've been here almost six months now and you're still living with your sister. You want to have children, but they feel like a burden to you. What exactly do you want? Who are you pretending to?'

Stasia said nothing; she watched the stray dogs roaming pack-like through the park.

★

The lieutenant departed without the couple having reached a decision. Everything was left as it had been before, since they had no better alternative, and they pulled themselves together for the sake of the children. Stasia made half-hearted enquiries to the accommodation commissariat about available accommodation in the city. They acknowledged that she was the wife of a Red lieutenant, but at the same time they had to point out that she was the sister-in-law of Ramas Iosebidze, and his house was luxurious and more than spacious enough.

★

Those were the years when the Little Man rose above himself and finally became the Little Big Man. And people were already starting to fear the name of the Cheka. Political resistance had practically disappeared; all enemies had been cleared aside, banished abroad, or sent to the work camps. Industrialisation demanded a great deal of strength and a great many human lives; unlimited productivity was expected from the new factories and the forced *kolkhoz*. The transformation and, above all, the renaming of cities was in full swing. Across the Soviet Union, countless cities were renamed, and the new names wiped out the past, as if there had been no life before the Revolution. The age of the tsars was declared an age of murderers and thieves, and the Party's propaganda machine was working overtime.

Whenever Sopio complained to Stasia about the lack of certain goods and produce in the shops, Stasia would search the pantries and cellars in Christine's house and was pleased, even a little proud, that she was able to help her friend feel such deficiencies less acutely: at Christine's, she always found the things that Sopio couldn't get hold of in the city.

Even when Sopio told Stasia how indignant she and her friends had been at a recent cinema screening of *The White Eagle*, when there had been an introductory lecture on how the film should be understood, Stasia refused to see any serious propaganda behind it, and shrugged it off as an artistic quirk of the director's.

And, as all freedom in this joyful, happy country disintegrated like an inexpertly woven spider's web, the *Ballets Russes* in far-off, free Paris was also dissolved — and Sergei Diaghilev took a piece of Stasia's dream with him to the grave.

Stasia learned of this only by chance: someone had heard it from someone who knew someone in Paris, and this person told Sopio, and she — very quietly — told Stasia. Stasia went up to her room with the beautiful wallpaper in Christine's villa, got into bed, and stayed there for many hours. She thought about Peter Vasilyev, and the ghosts of unlived dreams that are doomed always to pursue you. She saw herself one last time floating across the stage in the *Théâtre du Châtelet*, sought-after, loved, applauded; smiled, and buried it deep inside herself, her lost other life, full of freedom, unbridled passions, provocations, one of the chosen, exceptional few ... until at last she forced herself out of bed because Kitty and Kostya were fighting and Christine couldn't make them see sense.

★

One afternoon, when Stasia was once again visiting the tiny flat in Avlabari and saw her friend staring glumly into her hot tea, and heard her complaining that three of her pupils had cancelled their lessons, she suddenly leapt up, asked Sopio to wait a little while for her, and ran out into the street.

She wanted to give Sopio a boost, wanted her to read out her poems to her again, or tell her about the miracle of psychoanalysis — this Viennese healer called Freud; wanted her to tell her about the Impressionists, and about the Symbolist plays of someone called Maeterlinck. She wanted her to recite Persian love poems and talk about the new movement in Georgian poetry that called itself 'The Blue Horns', whose poems Stasia thought so incredibly beautiful.

She knew what remedy could make Sopio forget her worries and make her herself again, but Stasia was afraid. The last time she had made the hot chocolate for someone, her father's prophecy had been fulfilled. Since then, she had been unable to banish the image of Thekla's stiff body from her memory. But how could she be sure that her father's chocolate was responsible for Thekla's death? Wasn't it the poison that had rocked Thekla into eternal sleep? Wasn't it the times they lived in, the war, the hopelessness that led to her end? Perhaps her father was wrong; perhaps the link he had made between misfortune and this mysterious drink was just a figment of his imagination. Perhaps it was the guilt he felt at having pressured his wife into having another child that had caused him to make this strange assumption — that the chocolate was to blame for Ketevan's death. And anyway, he himself had claimed that she, Stasia, had 'survived the calamity'. So what was she to make of it all? If this supposed calamity had not touched her, then it would be even less likely to harm her brave and fiery friend. No, it was clearly childish to accept this absurd conjecture so blindly; there was no logic to it.

The 'speculators' had cinnamon, the best cacao in the city could be found in the Jewish quarter, and there was brown sugar and cloves in Christine's pantry, as well as the other, secret ingredients.

Two hours later she returned, with a bag full to bursting, and made the hot chocolate for the first time since Thekla's death.

★

Stasia went to the little, blackened stove, and, after a few minutes, the aroma began to envelop the apartment, the staircase, the back courtyard.

'What are you making?' asked Sopio, puzzled.

'I'm making my hot chocolate.'

'You're making chocolate for me?'

'That's right.'

'I've never seen you make hot chocolate before.'

'It's a secret recipe; I can't give to anyone, not even you. It has to stay in the family. My father made me swear to it.'

'I feel like I'm part of a conspiracy. Come on, it's only chocolate.'

Sopio laughed. For the first time in days.

And, of course, Sopio, too, fell for Stasia's hot chocolate, and even when it became increasingly expensive and difficult to obtain the necessary ingredients, it seemed to be the only thing that could drive away her gloom and conjure a smile back onto her face — and so Stasia went on making her magic drink for her friend twice a week.

★

Christine was expecting an important visitor. The children were dressed in their Sunday best, the whole house was decorated with lilac blossom, the silver came out of the cupboards, and her most expensive dress was taken out of the wardrobe. Fresh food was bought from the market and wine ordered from Kakheti. For two days, there was a state of emergency in the house of the busy Party Secretary Ramas Iosebidze (who was overweight and now almost completely bald) and his wife Christine (as wonderfully pretty as she had always been).

Stasia arrived in the middle of the morning's preparations. 'What's going on? Is someone from Moscow coming?' she asked her sister.

Christine — with slices of cucumber on her face and olive oil in her hair — just gave an exasperated groan and shook her head. 'You really don't pick up on anything, do you?'

She seemed anxious, and Stasia resisted the temptation to respond to her sister in kind. Simon may have been sending money every month, but it certainly wasn't enough to finance the lifestyle to which Stasia had now become accustomed.

Later, the cook told her that they were expecting the head of the secret service himself, the *friend of the family*, along with a few of Ramas' other colleagues. His superior, she said, was a great connoisseur of good food and fine wine. A great lover of opera and fine art, like the man of the house himself. That may have been the first time Stasia considered what exactly it was her brother-in-law did, and who his friends were. A peculiar sensation made her shudder. She couldn't put it into words, she told me years later; it was as if something were cutting off her air supply.

She hurried over to Kostya and Kitty, who were quarrelling over some treat or other, and ordered them to come with her, intending to take the children and spend the night at Sopio's. Just then, Christine came into the hallway and stared at her, nonplussed.

'What are you doing?'

'I'll leave you to your preparations. We'll stay at Sopio's tonight.'

'Have you lost your mind?'

'What do you need me for? You know I don't particularly care for these dinners.'

'Do you have any idea who we're expecting? You can go, as far as I'm concerned, but the children are staying here. They're going to meet him because one day they'll be glad to have made his acquaintance. Kostya, Kitty, come to Auntie!'

And the pair of them, with their ribbons and patent-leather shoes, almost seemed relieved as they ran to their pretty aunt, who managed not to look ridiculous even with slices of cucumber on her face.

That must have made Stasia feel incredibly mean. She stayed, and bore witness to the Little Big Man eating the quails in coriander sauce, drinking the Georgian wine, giving grandiose speeches about their homeland and the jewels of its cuisine, telling anecdotes, while everyone round the table fawned and exclaimed, 'How enchanting', 'Oh, how fabulous', 'Incredible!' and smoothed the tablecloth with their trembling fingers. And the man with the *pince-nez* began eyeing her sister like an animal he was determined to bring down, his gaze growing ever more brazen and aggressive as he stared at her shapely lips, her small breasts, and her slim wrists, and embarked on a tipsy ten-minute toast to Georgian beauty without taking his eyes off Christine for a second. And her husband sat there nodding contentedly, smiling peaceably, and his chin quivered just a little.

By that time, if not before, Stasia knew that the skin of the world would tear. She knew that the earth would disgorge itself and the ruins would become visible, that a bottomless fissure would run through all the centuries, splitting the earth open to reveal a blood-soaked abyss.

Later, as the Little Big Man stood smoking his pipe in the garden with Christine and her husband, chatting to his hosts, and, his tongue now thoroughly loosened, saying something obscene at which they were forced to laugh, Stasia stood in the lavishly decorated dining room and observed them through the window. She observed his every gesture, the way he casually touched her sister's elbow; she saw his teeth flash in the dim light of the garden every time he let out a drunken bark of a laugh at one of his own jokes, and hated herself for not running out there and pulling her little sister away from them. Christine, demonstrating remarkable acting skills, was not letting her feelings show. Or could she actually be enjoying the attentions of this awful man? Stasia quickly banished the thought.

★

In 1931, Kitty was in her second year at the Russian girls' school, where she was already attracting attention with her strikingly full lips, her curly chestnut-brown hair, and her honey-brown, almond-shaped eyes. Kostya had grown into a tall, handsome boy with jug ears and the same chestnut hair, but straight. He was top of his class, and gave the appearance of being older and more serious than most of the other boys. That year, the Little Big Man finally became head of the Georgian Communist Party. He appointed Ramas Iosebidze as his private secretary.

Sopio now barely left her apartment, and was only able to make ends meet with help from her friends. She had no more pupils, and was banned from publishing after the writers' union told her that her work fell outside the social norms and morality of the great Socialist Republic.

One afternoon, the head of the Communist Party telephoned the Iosebidze residence. He was put through to the lady of the house. The phone call lasted a quarter of an hour. Afterwards, Christine was collected by a black Bugatti. She was wearing her red, sequinned chiffon dress, her long black velvet gloves, and the black hat with the peacock feather. At the opera, the head of the Party received her in person, in his box, and showed her to the seat next to his. The opera was Bellini's *Norma* — which, astonishingly, had not (or not yet) been banned for its religious content.

During the 'Casta Diva' aria, rustling and whispering could be heard from the box. Countless heads turned discreetly towards the royal seats: in the dim light from the stage, they could make out the figure of a woman who was definitely not the head of the Party's wife. Then there was nothing more to be seen. But at the line '*Ah! bello a me ritorna*', a woman's hand appeared in a black velvet glove, clinging to the red velvet balustrade. At '*Del fido amor primiero*' there was the sound of something heavy falling to the floor. At '*E contro il mondo intiero*', some may have heard a suppressed scream. And at '*Difesa a te sarò*', slowly and hesitantly, the hand withdrew.

The couple were the last to leave the auditorium. The audience had already departed by the various exits, and the rumour quickly spread that the head of the Party had not enjoyed the performance, as his applause had not been particularly enthusiastic. This occasioned weeping in the ensemble, but the rumour was false. Later, the head of the Party even made a public announcement to the effect that he had enjoyed the performance very much. The truth was that he had seen nothing of it, or only very little. The truth was that Christine's chiffon dress was crumpled and her make-up had run, and they had waited until the hall was empty to allow them to get back to the Bugatti without being seen.

Since Ramas was in Kiev, at a conference on how to solve the agricultural question, Christine went to sit in the reception room and asked for some cherry liqueur. Stasia, woken by loud noises and the slamming of doors, came downstairs and saw her dishevelled sister drinking, at alarming speed, straight from the bottle.

'What's happened? Is it Ramas?'

'Oh, no, he's all right. Everything's fine. Come and have a drink.'

'But where have you been?'

'It was just a little rendezvous, *without obligation*.'

After numerous attempts to get more information out of her sister, Stasia eventually gave up and started knocking back the sweet, sticky liqueur to try and keep pace with her.

Over the next few days there were more phone calls, and each time Christine would disappear for several hours afterwards.

> The workers of the Soviet Union will live
> ever better, ever more joyfully!
>
> POSTER SLOGAN

Over the next few months, the private secretary's mandatory official trips doubled in number, and Christine's outings trebled. Ramas was busy with issues of espionage, exit visas, the press, the administration of the gulags; the Little Big Man was busy trying to satisfy his insatiable hunger for feminine beauty.

I don't know what made Stasia do it, but one afternoon she followed the black Bugatti that came to collect her sister after these phone calls. I don't know whether Stasia followed on horseback, or took the tram, or an automobile; what I do know is that she arrived at the grandest villa in the city, reminiscent of a villa somewhere in South America, with a beautiful garden full of exotic plants and palm trees that screened the house from curious eyes. Everyone in the city knew whose house this was, and that it wasn't just the master who came and went there, but some of the city's most beautiful women, too. Stasia watched the black car pass through the gilded gates with her sister inside.

Back at Christine's house, she sat down at the long table in the kitchen and didn't move until her sister returned late that evening. Stasia had given the staff the evening off and sent the children up to their room early. Something in her voice had made the two of them realise that resistance would not be tolerated, and they obeyed.

Christine came into the kitchen, took off her shoes, picked up the liqueur bottle, and sat down with her sister. Stasia, rendered almost sexless by the years of hunger in Petrograd and the bitter aftertaste of her Red Lieutenant's love, and Christine, blooming in her femininity and elegance. Stasia, wearing a plain, calf-length cotton dress with tiny buttons, and Christine, in a claret-coloured jacket with a hand-embroidered collar and a floor-length black silk skirt. Stasia drew on her cigarette and stared, glassy-eyed, at the floor.

Christine was babbling about the weather and holiday plans and the stresses of city life when Stasia interrupted her.

'I followed you.'

For a long time, Christine didn't reply. She just went on drinking her liqueur. Then she whispered, 'Why?'

They sat facing each other like two moles, frightened and blinded by the light, staring as if recognising each other for the first time.

'I didn't want to believe it. I couldn't believe you were really doing this.'

'What? *What* am I doing?' Christine yelled. Stasia realised it was the first time she had ever heard her sister shout.

'You ...' said Stasia, but her voice failed her.

'I have to do it.'

'Why do you have to do it?'

'Well, someone has to lay themselves on the butcher's slab so the others can go on celebrating, don't they?'

Stasia suddenly heard so much contempt, so much spite, so much self-hatred in Christine's voice that it frightened her, and she instinctively shifted away from her a little on her chair.

'You disgust me.'

'But the good life, the wonderful food and the nice clothes, the day trips, the private lessons, the good schools for your children — they don't disgust you?'

'I never asked for those things. Why, why, Christine? Ramas has money enough.'

'You understand so little, so little, sometimes I could scream in disbelief! You still don't understand just *who* he is and *what* he's capable of, do you? Can you still not see *where* it is we live?'

Christine abruptly fell silent, took a generous swig from the bottle, and left the room.

The future had become the present.

Everything would arouse mistrust; words and hearts would become battlegrounds. They would slip into tunnels that offered no way out. Stasia would have to fight, but what was worth fighting for when everything had begun to taste of hopelessness? Where could you look and not see the teeth of the Little Big Men laughing in your face? How tightly would you have to shut your eyes from now on, to avoid seeing the ruins being unearthed? How much effort would it take to laugh, when you could feel all those bodies beneath your feet?

Stasia closed her eyes and saw Thekla before her, rosy, laughing, she was reaching out to her, calling her — Stasia quickly opened her eyes again to escape her ghosts, but it seemed reality was filled with ghosts as well.

★

In the first week of January 1932, the Little Big Man assumed the leadership of the Communist Party in the whole of the Transcaucasian Republic, and transferred his private secretary to the Party headquarters in Baku, meaning that Ramas Iosebidze only got to see his wife on the last weekend of every month. A new wave of peasant deportations and mass executions was in progress — it wasn't yet apparent in the cities, but it was getting closer, creeping slowly into the metropolises. There were stories of marauding gangs of children all over Russia, of miserably long queues outside grocers' shops, of female workers selling their bodies to feed their families. Stories of editors who had strayed from the 'happy and joyous life' and been arrested. Stories of millions of peasants who had been executed or deported from Ukraine to Kazakhstan over the previous two years. And people saw the state-sponsored posters that read: 'To eat your own children is an act of barbarism!'

The people of the sunny Southern Caucasus had not yet felt much of this; they might know someone who knew someone to whom something had happened, but they still hadn't felt it, they still didn't want to see it.

All the same, Stasia was worried, not just for Christine, but also for Sopio, who often stayed out all night and hardly spoke to her friend any more.

When Stasia confronted her about it, Sopio avoided the question and invented excuses. The first night Sopio disappeared, Stasia knew that this was the end of her self-imposed asceticism and seclusion in her dingy apartment; or rather, she knew that Sopio, following her natural inclination, had begun to rebel. Stasia was tormented by doubts and indecision, afraid of the dreams that had died and afraid of a life without dreams. She was tormented by Sopio's silence, and by her fractured love for her husband; she was tormented by the hardness that had taken root in her younger sister these last few months. And yet she capitulated, even now, paralysed by her inability to intervene.

Not even that bloody March night, the night she only told me about much later, could bring her to her senses. The night she returned from Sopio's apartment to Christine's villa, holding Andro by the hand (his mother had asked her, once again, to take the boy with her), and heard cries coming from Christine's bedroom.

She told Andro to go up to the nursery, and hurried into the room where her sister and her absent brother-in-law slept. There she found her sister, enveloped in the scent of lavender from the dried flowers that stood on the chest of drawers to guarantee the couple a good, peaceful night's sleep. She was lying on the starched white sheets of the four-poster bed, with the white mosquito net stretched above it, and beneath her was a lake of blood.

Christine was groaning and crying out through gritted teeth, clinging to the bedstead. Stasia ran to her and said she would fetch the doctor, but at that Christine screeched so loudly, like a wounded animal, that Stasia froze and, eventually, obeyed.

'No doctor, no doctor ... No one must know ... I've sent them all home. No one can —'

'You could bleed to death! What have you done?'

'In the black notebook on the table, on the last page, at the bottom, there's an address. Go there and bring the woman back here with you. She knows how to stop the bleeding.'

With cold sweat on her brow, Stasia fetched compresses, made towels into makeshift bandages, then hurried to a suburb of the city where she found a wrinkled old woman in a tin shack and took her back to her sister's house. A backstreet abortionist, who had given Christine a mixture of herbs to get rid of the unwanted child.

Stasia sat by Christine's bed for two days, and, at the end of the second day, she went to the kitchen, sent the cook away, and prepared the hot chocolate for her ailing sister. And when Christine drank it — after shooing away the children, who had come running at the aroma — she smiled again, and a little tear rolled from her left eye.

'I'll never have children with Ramas. We've been to see several doctors,' she said quietly, sipping the chocolate.

Stasia sat in silence on the edge of the bed and tried not to look at her sister, who seemed so fragile, so weak and sickly, with her colourless lips and the deep circles around her eyes.

'I thought it was me ... Isn't that a bad joke?'

'I thought you didn't want any. Not yet. You told me you were still enjoying life, and —'

'I lied to you. I hoped it would happen eventually. When you thought I was at the seaside, we were in Warsaw seeing a specialist. Why now, why like this, why?'

Stasia tried to hold back the tears, tried not to make the whole unhappy situation unhappier still.

'Finish with him, please. Even if you're frightened, finish it. Please,' she whispered at last, handing her sister a glass of water.

'You know I can't do that.'

'But you're even less able to do *this*, Christine, don't you understand?'

'I can't, Stasia!'

'Let's go away. Disappear somewhere.'

'Don't be silly! Anyway, he would find me, no matter where I was.'

'He's not God, Christine!'

'There is no God any more, no God can rescue anyone from this misery. That's just the way it is now. He's ... he's addicted.'

'Addicted?'

'To me.'

'What are you talking about? He's a —'

'He'll need it again and again, he'll do anything for it; he's in thrall to me. He'll need it again and again.'

'It? You mean you and —'

'Let me sleep now, Stasia. I'm so tired. And tell them downstairs that I'll need my green dress tomorrow. They should iron it and starch the collar, and — oh yes, polish my hair clip as well, the one with the butterfly on. It's silver, tell them to use salt.'

'Christine!'

'Tell them. I don't want to get up tomorrow and find that the dress is still in the laundry.'

'Tell Ramas.'

Christine laughed, a scornful laugh, and turned away.

Young people still do not feel deeply enough the poetry of work.

MAXIM GORKY

That summer, Stasia travelled back to her hometown with her husband and the children. She spent her time there with Lida, who had grown even more pious, her stepmother, who since her only daughter got married seemed to do nothing but eat, and her father, who appeared increasingly preoccupied and melancholy, ever thinner and more frail.

For the first time, Stasia wondered whether there might not be a rightness to all of this — life, as it *usually* turned out — and whether dreams might not just be obstacles that kept you from what was real.

While the lieutenant met with old friends every day to play backgammon, Stasia took her eight-year-old daughter to the stables, hired a Kabardin, and taught her to ride. Astride, naturally. She showed Kitty her childhood haunts. And Kitty, who was now much quicker, noisier, and more energetic than either of the boys, laughed and squealed with delight. This city child, used to being driven everywhere in her aunt's car, blossomed, and made Stasia think of something peach-coloured, beautiful, joyful. And this something moved her very deeply. Stasia showed her daughter the oak tree — let's agree it was an old oak tree — the cave monastery, the barren landscape. They looked up at the painfully bright stars, the yellow moon, and they smelled the old earth, which knew so much and gave away so little.

Meanwhile, Kostya was trying to keep his jealousy of Andro in check, and to reconnect with his father, whose constant absence had made him a stranger to his son. Caught between the adults' quarrels and frontlines, between his insatiable longing for his father and peculiar distance from his mother, Kostya lost himself in approaching adolescence. He lost himself in his rage against the restless, unpredictable women around him. He was desperate for consistency and order, and he missed Christine, the queen of his little world. She had changed. She didn't spend as much time with him as she used to. She seemed to have stopped putting him on a special pedestal — it seemed he wasn't her prince any more. She kept disappearing, and when she came back she would sit alone in the kitchen, never switching on the light, drinking that sweet, sticky stuff straight from the bottle, and staring into space. She retreated into her silence, for which he had no explanation.

He wanted recognition from his father, but he wanted love from Christine.

He wanted her to tell him how handsome and different he was, how clever, and how few worries he caused the adults. What good manners he had and how *like* her he was. It was what she had always told him, ever since he was born. It was Christine, not his mother, who seemed to need him most, who spoke to him as an equal. Who made him believe that one day he would make something of himself, that he would be a *king*.

Above all, he missed the sense of being her favourite. Because Christine had always made that quite clear, too — that she thought him better than all other children. More than anything, Kostya wanted not to be like everyone else. Least of all his younger sister. He was almost offended at having been brought down to the same pitiful level as his sister and Andro, having to compete to get himself noticed and distinguish himself from them.

That boy — that curly haired Andro. Who was weak and fragile, and seemed to have no ambition of any kind beyond reading books or being read to, who always sang when he thought no one was around, who could recite poetry in three or four languages, who loved carving those pointless wooden figures. And who earned so much admiration for it. And for supposedly being so nice, so considerate, so self-sufficient, so forgiving, as if that were the most important thing in life: to be nice, considerate, self-sufficient, and forgiving.

And his sister, who had nothing in common with him besides a surname and the shape of her fingernails. Who wound him up, worked him into a white-hot rage, with her insolent manner and lack of sensitivity. Who was clumsy, with a head full of nonsense; who was lazy at school, and whose greatest talent was clowning and silliness, with which, however, she always seemed able to amuse adults and win them over. Who was constantly giggling and smacking her lips and pulling faces. Who always had a ladder in her stockings, and who clung to Andro like a limpet.

And secretly he always blamed his mother for the fact that he was separated from his father, the man with the medals — which he too so desperately longed for, and which his later career would bring him in abundance. Konstantin Jashi would spend a few more years stuck in his own and his family's inner landscape, until he had clearly separated the fronts, fixed his truths, and chosen his means.

★

There must be a new man in Sopio's life, thought Stasia, on her return to the city in the autumn. This, at least, was how she explained Sopio's moods, her long absences and secretiveness.

A man had, in fact, entered Sopio's life. He was an architect. He had studied in Florence, created a few wonderful designs, and had begun to realise them, too, until he was declared too decadent and western, and the authorities removed his professional accreditation and stuck him in a communal apartment where he shared a bathroom and kitchen with some potato-sellers.

But this man had not awoken in Sopio the kind of love Stasia suspected. Rather, he had laid a thin, delicate band around Sopio's shoulders, the ends of which were tied firmly to his ideas. The architect was forced to work in a canning factory and had no choice but to sketch his designs — for houses, at first, and then for the world in general — at night, by candlelight, in a crumpled exercise book that he hid under the mattress in his communal apartment.

He had shown this book to Sopio; she had come to the factory one day to inform the female factory workers of their rights. Most of the women had stared at her without interest, nodded, and gone back to work, but the architect had stayed. He had been listening in the back row, and Sopio was pleased to see a man in the audience. Thus it was they fell into conversation.

★

This man looks like a drinker! was the first thing Stasia thought when she saw the architect. Bloated, sallow, hunched. Stasia felt a kind of anger towards him from the moment she laid eyes on him, when he arrived at the apartment and began sipping the black tea Sopio had made for him.

If at least he were an interesting man, if at least he were really special — if ... she thought.

When he finally left, she interrogated Sopio. Was she intending to expose herself to neighbourhood gossip, or to make the whole thing more official? And Sopio said how tremendously sad it was that Taso was yet again shutting her eyes to everything that was unfamiliar to her, and that, for the umpteenth time, that wasn't what this was about.

'For a start, there's nothing going on between us that would need to be made official. Secondly, he's being watched, and I can't put Andro in danger;

thirdly, you're really not making this easy for me; and fourthly, I can't let him down,' she said tersely, and hurried to the door, where Andro was knocking, having just got back from school. He went to a Georgian school that was rather less elite than the selective Russian schools Kitty and Kostya attended, and his journey home was shorter than theirs.

★

Not long after Stasia's first encounter with the architect, Christine summoned her sister to her husband's study (he was absent, as usual), and set a glass of her favourite cherry liqueur in front of her.

Christine's appearance revealed none of her troubles: she was beautifully attired, and held herself erect. Her hair was wound into an elegant, intricate knot, jewellery sparkled at her ears and wrists, and her lips were painted cherry red. Christine remained an impossible puzzle to Stasia.

They sat down. Both women had a glass of liqueur and exchanged a few banalities. Kitty had received a bad mark in maths the previous day, and the teacher had told her off; Kostya was doing wonderfully well, top of his class in calligraphy; the cook had over-salted the omelette — well, she was getting on a bit now; people said the price of wheat was going to go up; and so on.

Stasia watched her sister's dancing fingers, with their wickedly expensive rings, and tried and failed to work out what it felt like to be Christine.

'I wanted to talk to you about your friend,' Christine said, and her tone suddenly changed, becoming more abrupt and distant, as if she had just cast aside the role of sister and was now playing the politician's wife to perfection.

'What about her?'

'She's started moving in dissident circles, and her new boyfriend ... Well, he's being watched. She sympathises with the wrong people. It could get her into real trouble. That man has *mistaken* ideas, if you understand me. She needs to break with him as soon as possible.'

'That man is harmless. Any problems he has are psychological, or with alcohol, if you ask me. He's not capable of having any ideas at all,' replied Stasia snippily.

'I just wanted to tell you. I've already put in a good word for Sopio. But that's not going to help her in the long run if she doesn't watch out for herself. She needs to watch out, and so do you.'

'Why me?'

'You're her friend.'

'But I'm *your* sister.'

'Of course you are. All the same, I wouldn't like you to get into trouble. I'm not all-powerful, Stasia.'

'But you're his …'

'What? Courtesan? Lover? Whore? What do you want to call me?'

'Nothing.'

'Go on, say it!'

'What do you want from me?'

'Me? Me? I'd just like you to be able to go on living a life without cares. Please take what I've said seriously, that's all.'

Stasia left the room with her mind in turmoil and walked out into the garden, to the fountain, which had been dry for months and was full of leaves, to smoke one of her long cigarettes. Something about Christine's words had affected her deeply.

She just didn't know exactly what.

Maybe it was the whole situation, which to her felt bizarre and disgusting — her sister's situation, which she, Stasia, was doing nothing to change, from which she was even profiting.

Or maybe it was the comfortable state of dependency in which she had now been living for several years. Or the strange mood that had suddenly started to spread through her country like a virus, a mood that made her afraid, a mood she didn't want to think too much about. She felt miserable and powerless. She didn't admit to herself that she was haunted by the sense of having failed, on all possible fronts.

She marched into Kostya's room and made him get up. He had just gone to bed and was reading *Treasure Island*, a book he dearly loved. Puzzled and yawning, he followed her into the dining room and poured himself a cup of milk.

Stasia stared at her son, surprised at how much of a stranger he seemed. So serious, so un-childlike, so fierce, and yet somehow so lost in his grown-up manner. She was surprised at how little he played with other children, at his preference for being with the adults, at his constant quarrels with Andro and Kitty; the quarrels with his sister were sometimes so heated that they came to blows.

'Are you all right?' Stasia began.

Konstantin, now even more puzzled, nodded and took a large gulp of milk, while Stasia lit another cigarette.

'Is there something the matter, *Deda*?' he asked.

'I was wondering how you were. We don't talk very much, you know.'

'What should we talk about?'

'Oh, everything. Anything you like. About you, me, Kitty, your father, Christine.'

'Is something the matter with Aunt Christine?'

'Why do you ask that?'

'Well, she's been a bit irritable lately.'

'Yes, she has. Things aren't easy for her at the moment. She's probably missing Uncle Ramas.'

Even as she said it, she could have kicked herself for the lie.

'Or maybe she doesn't miss him at all any more, like you don't miss Papa,' retorted Kostya, staring into his cup, which he had quickly drained.

'What makes you think I don't?'

'Well, you just don't look like you do, *Deda*.'

'And do you miss him?'

'Yes, sometimes.'

'Do you write to him?'

'Sometimes.'

'And what do you say in your letters?'

'That I miss him and that I'd like to visit him.'

'And what does he say to that?'

'He says he wants to have me there, once I'm in senior school.'

'And is that what you want?'

'I just want to see what it's like where he is. And I want to try shooting, and see what that's like, too. Papa can teach me.'

'What for?'

'What do you mean, what for? Why does anyone shoot? So you can fight, and defend yourself, of course.'

Stasia sensed an ever-increasing distance between them; she sensed the almost total lack of compassion and empathy with which her son regarded the world around him. The bid to redeem her evening by attempting a rapprochement between them had failed entirely and left her feeling even more confused and powerless.

When she finally fell asleep, as dawn was breaking, she dreamed of Kostya shooting at everything around him; she woke that morning dripping with sweat.

★

I believe Stasia tried several times to speak to Sopio — whenever I asked her, she said she'd given her warning signals — but to this day I can't explain why she didn't do a better job of warning her friend or repeating Christine's words to her. I suspect that, once again, her immense capacity for repressing things was to blame.

The end began with suicide of the Leader's second wife, Nadezhda Alliluyeva. She was twenty-two years younger him, the mother of two of his children, and her husband had placed her under the same surveillance to which he would later subject the whole country. They say she once told her husband that he tormented his wife as he tormented the entire population. And yet she had made such an effort to be a good wife, a good mother, a good Party member. Almost all the socialist history books, right up to the late 1980s, gave her cause of death as appendicitis. On that cold November day she had appeared at a military parade to celebrate the fifteenth anniversary of the Revolution, waved, smiled, beamed, attended a reception afterwards for the Party elite, fallen out with her drunken husband, returned home, and shot herself with a pistol.

Not quite two months later, at the dawn of the year 1933, the architect was arrested. He was by now wholly confused and frightened, having endured two years of harassment, intimidation, and questioning. He was found guilty of treason and counter-revolutionary activities and sentenced to death.

Sopio, who until then had been cautious, quiet, and mild in her protests, could no longer contain her hatred.

They say she ran through the streets, yelling at people; they say she wrote a cycle of poems with the unambiguous title *The Festival of Blood*. Just four weeks after the architect was shot dead, two gentlemen in uniform came for Sopio in the middle of the night and took her to a psychiatric hospital. Apparently she was endangering her fellow citizens, and very probably suffering from hysteria and madness — at least, that was the reason they gave.

Andro had to watch his mother being dragged from the apartment, shrieking, struggling, cursing, spitting at the men, though all the while she kept shouting to him, telling him never to be afraid, not of these beasts, not of anything or anyone! But Andro *was* afraid. He ran up the steep streets of Vera and hammered on the iron gate of the villa until a sleepy Stasia flung open the door and the light went on in Christine's bedroom. He hadn't been able to stop sobbing all the way there, and it was a very long time before he could string a sentence together.

Stasia took him into her arms. She comforted him, told him Sopio would be back soon, lied to him, said his mother was getting better and sent her love.

Kitty seemed to be a support to him, a source of energy. She was a survival artist. She went on smiling and digging the boys in the ribs; she pinched Andro's arm in passing and threw sunflower seeds at her brother. Despite the dark mood in the house, she went on listening to music on the bakelite wireless, meeting up with school friends, and playing football in the playground, even though she had been told several times that it was indecorous. She went on pulling faces, and greeting each new day by cheerfully exercising to the early morning callisthenics broadcast. Though she did all of this more quietly, more cautiously than before.

The more her behaviour seemed to annoy her brother, the more Andro sought her out. Kitty intuitively did all she could to make Andro laugh again and overcome his fear. She drew pictures of her teachers as animals, or sitting on chamber pots; she spat sunflower seeds from the attic window onto the heads of passers-by; she stole sweets; she cut off her hair. She did everything she could to evade the speechlessness of the adults. Even though she had to spend hours standing in the corner, was told off repeatedly, and given punishments and detentions; even though Stasia read her the riot act and Christine called her a boy. Even though they threatened to pack her off to her father in Russia, where she would have to live in a military barracks, eat nothing but porridge and groats every day, and would at last be shown a firm hand.

Andro took comfort in books. They seemed to form a bridge between him and his mother. She had always read aloud to him, had told him that literature was the 'anchor in the black lake of life'. He wanted to feel close to her, wanted her to know he wouldn't disappoint her, and he began to read obsessively. He read everything he could get his hands on. Ramas must have possessed a first-rate library, which may even have included books you wouldn't necessarily expect to find in a model socialist household.

Andro and Kitty had been a good team from the very beginning; they'd always been able to occupy themselves and play together better than she and her brother could. But now this alliance seemed to be becoming a front. A front against Kostya.

★

The devout communist Ramas Iosebidze fell into a deep abyss — so immense, so dark, that the only way out he could see led to the final darkness.

He had given up everything, including his family, for an ideology — and had done nothing but serve this ideology for years. This portly, generous hedonist, whose greatest loves were communism, the Party, and his wonderful wife, lost all of them at once. The three seemed inseparably bound together; they had fused into a whole.

It started with a growing disillusionment with his work — the means to an end that was becoming ever harsher, harder, bloodier; supposedly in order to strengthen the Party, to serve the cause. But the cause was no longer the one he had once believed in, the one for which he had sacrificed so much. And the people with whom he could have banded together in another struggle against the apparatus of death were all either dead or in exile. The Party's allegations became increasingly absurd, and the general mistrust of everyone and everything grew to ludicrous proportions. Treason was being committed on an hourly basis. People pointed the finger at their friends, their neighbours.

Ramas had believed in Marxism. He had become a communist at a time when you paid for this conviction with your life. He had rebelled against his father, believing that what was due to him was also due to others. And he had believed in the Little Big Man.

On the night of the fateful New Year's Eve party, he had already seen it in his eyes: the lust, the unbridled lust for Christine's narrow hips, her porcelain wrists and ankles, her swan neck, her drowsy eyes, her stern lips, her small, girlish breasts, the magnificence of her hair, her dignity.

It wasn't the same lust, the same longing that other men were unable to suppress at the sight of Christine. Deep down, Ramas even took pride in the way other men looked at her — yes, pride, like a collector who is the envy of all because he owns a particular work of art. No, the Little Big Man's lust was different. It was the lust of a murderer.

Ramas couldn't have put this into words at the time. He hadn't dared to think such a thing, had not admitted it to himself. He had played it down; after all, he'd been loyal and faithful to this man, had stayed by his side on every path he had taken.

But this person sent other people to torture chambers and death cells without batting an eyelid. Ramas knew that; he had already begun to suspect it by the night of the party, and was now seeing it for himself. He also knew what that meant for him and Christine.

He had taken her for himself — but even now Ramas couldn't believe that his Helen, the most beautiful woman in the universe, had allowed herself to be taken.

He had suspected it for a long time, ever since his official trips had become more frequent — there wasn't all that much for him to do in Baku, Yerevan, or even in Tashkent, he was surplus to requirements. His doubts were confirmed when Christine began to offer herself up to him whenever he was at home. She had never shown any desire for physical intimacy. She had regarded her marital duties as a kind of burden, though he had always hoped she would gradually discover her own desire and give herself to him, let him in. It hadn't really troubled him; this inertia, this absence was part of her beauty, and, as a great connoisseur of this beauty, he knew it soon dissipated if too many demands were placed on it. He was a realist, and when he had married this fabulous woman twenty years his junior he had known that she would never desire him as he did her, that she wouldn't love him straight away, that he would have to win her love in some other way than with his body.

In the first years of their marriage, Christine quickly realised that she had found the right husband. Ramas was the man who would give her the life she'd always wanted to live, the life she felt she was made for. She had stopped giving him the brush-off when he thrust his hand under her long nightdress, stopped ignoring him when he whispered sweet nothings in her ear, stopped regarding him with irritation when, excited and flushed, he covered her in kisses, worshipping her. These days she even, occasionally, slid one of her feet from her side of the bed to his. She no longer found it embarrassing to see him naked, and some mornings she even flashed him a conspiratorial smile. And he had thought himself the luckiest man in the world.

Until that New Year's Eve, after which his official trips began to pile up; until the evening when he found a theatre ticket in the wastebasket, with a note on the back written in an all too familiar scrawl: *I'm crazy about you.*

Then Ramas Iosebidze's world collapsed, and his dream crumbled into ashes. The swansong began with pathos and grandeur, accompanied by a Greek chorus. Ramas lived large, in every sense. And so his unhappiness was created from the rib of life: bloody, painful, and ugly. The rib violently torn from Ramas Iosebidze's life, dreams, and hopes. Just as he knew he should never have left her alone with him, should never have underestimated him and overestimated her, should never have relied on her to be strong enough, he also knew he would never be able to forgive her. He had raised her up to such heights of admiration and adoration that the fall from that Olympus would be correspondingly extreme.

He couldn't change the fact that he still loved and desired her, and that made him detest her all the more. He convinced himself that he had hoped for salvation and searched for a solution. He wished she had at least given herself to a young king, someone equal to her presence, her radiance — but the reality was much crueller.

Life had given a free hand to death. To the many skilful executioners.

★

Stasia had long since stopped begging her sister not to get into the black Bugatti. She had come to terms with lying to her brother-in-law, participating in the whole masquerade, even warning the children not to say anything about Aunt Christine's outings. She had reconciled herself with arranging for the plump cook and the pale maid to be absent whenever Christine went out. She had tacitly signed this pact because she was afraid — yes, indeed she was. She was afraid for Andro, frightened that someone might take him from her. She was afraid for her husband, even if he seemed to be doing well and regularly sent money for his children. And most of all she was afraid for her little sister.

Christine always came back. She never stayed away longer than three hours. Stasia had never spoken to her about how she felt, or what it was like for her to get into that car wearing those elegant outfits. About how it could be that Christine actually seemed to be flourishing, becoming more beautiful, more spirited, more aloof. About how it could be that Stasia never saw her little sister shed a tear, never heard her complain. Because the thing she was most afraid of was a question, which she would have to ask loudly and bluntly: 'Did you enjoy it?'

'You have to stop it happening,' Stasia said once again, in a soft voice. She was sipping a glass of her cherry liqueur and looking out at the garden, which had been left to its own devices and was running riot.

'I'm doing my best, I hope you know that. I have been for months now. But I'm not all-powerful. I'm just one of many.'

'You're the favourite.'

'The favourite. Oh, nicely put, thank you.'

How do you feel in the arms of this man? Who is he and who are you? Who am I, if I can't save what I love? What kind of person am I, what kind of woman, what kind of mother? Why does this life feel as if we've all taken a vow of silence? What happened to our childhood? Why does the lilac only blossom for such a short while? Have you seen the cherry tree? I think we need to do something: it isn't really thriving any more. Where is Ramas, what does he think? What will happen if no one protests against all these prohibitions, these rules? What are these propaganda posters doing all over the streets? Why do I still feel, at the age of thirty-six, as if I still have to learn everything, as if nothing comes naturally to me? Why don't birds drop out of the sky when they die? Can you not die with outstretched wings? Do you believe in miracles? Where is Sopio? How is she surviving? What's she being forced to do? I left her all alone. I didn't understand her. I've never felt such a sense of belonging as I did with her. Nothing must happen to her — nothing more than has happened already. I'm longing for our hot chocolate, are you? Maybe I should visit Father. Lida wants to enter a convent, forever, did you hear? Father wrote. I hardly miss my husband at all, isn't that strange? I'm worried about Kitty. She's too quick-tempered for the times we live in. I've been feeling so unbearably tired lately. I wonder why; I do so little. I'm no good for anything. You truly are beautiful. I think it every time I see you. Even your eyebrows, your tongue, the hair on your arms, even your feet and the veins that shimmer through your skin are shapely and beautiful. My son idolises you. I believe things are easier when one is as beautiful as you are. You never have to do much to arouse others' curiosity. And your husband really loves you, I think it every time I see you together. I respect him, he's a clever man. We should change the tablecloth, it's stained.

All this Stasia would have liked to say to her sister; all this went through her mind. Instead, she just said, 'I'm going out for some fresh air.'

Islands of powerlessness formed. Clouds gathered, the sky lacked lustre and took on the colour of a chameleon. The willow on the riverbank bent lower and caressed the earth to comfort it: worse was to come, and Nature had to arm itself.

Little wrinkles formed in the city's potholes, in the rainwater, green and dull. Screams formed in people's throats, and had to be swallowed down like bitter medicine.

Grey shadows formed on the walls, the ghosts whispered hoarsely; no one heard anything. For years to come, the words would go on dissolving in people's mouths. For years to come, the streets would reek of ridiculous despair, undignified and treacherous.

Armies of restless insects formed in the gutters and the dusty corners of houses. They hissed and tore their wings to shreds in an effort to be heard, but no one noticed.

Blotches formed on people's faces from all the suppressed desires, from all the dreams that had been driven away.

★

At the dawn of the 'great purge' of 1935, the year that saw the grand opening of the legendary Moscow Metro, Sopio Eristavi was deported to a labour camp. They said she had been banished to Central Asia. Months would pass before, thanks to Christine's help, Stasia discovered that she had been taken to an

NKVD colony with the simple abbreviation SasLag, in the Uzbek SSR. The camp focused on agricultural labour, and Sopio Eristavi had been assigned to cotton processing.

It was only after several miserable trips to the *militsiya*, with much begging, queuing, and humiliation, that Stasia was able to send her friend a long letter and a parcel containing provisions, photos of the children, a skirt she herself had made — would Sopio even be able to wear it *there?* — postcards from Kitty and Kostya, and a heart-rending letter from Andro.

> We cannot expect mercy from nature;
> it is our task to take what we need.
>
> POSTER SLOGAN

It was the start of an exciting year! A year that saw the founding of the German Luftwaffe, the first performance of *Porgy and Bess* and 'Summertime', and a ban on jazz in the German Reich. It was the year in which jukebox culture started, in which Billie Holliday sang 'What A Little Moonlight Can Do' in a jam session, and a year in which the Soviet leader started work on a new constitution that would come into force the following year, costing millions of people their lives.

A year in which a certain Mr Mairanovsky (who was also born in our sunny homeland) was taken under the Little Big Man's wing, and went on to head what became known as Secret Laboratory 12. This laboratory, under the auspices of the NKVD, and therefore the Little Big Man, manufactured poisons and tested them on prisoners. The work done in the laboratory was intended to 'assist' Soviet spies in capitalist countries. Mairanovsky's main contribution was the invention of the poisoned chair.

An exciting year, yes. A year in which Elvis Aaron Presley was born, in Tupelo, Mississippi (in the company of a dead twin, just like our Stasia).

The year in which the Soviet judiciary upheld a law that any action intended to weaken the leadership was punishable as counter-revolutionary.

The exact meaning of 'weaken' remained vague, nebulous, and therefore applicable to any action that displeased the Party. The law also stipulated that, in cases in which the charge was terrorism, the accused lost all right to a defence and the only punishment was the death penalty. The law meant that anyone who had ever laughed at an anti-socialist joke or read an anti-socialist book, visited Europe or given his wife a western perfume could be picked up by NKVD officers without any warning or explanation — preferably at dawn.

Of the twenty-one men on the Central Committee in 1917, only one was left alive by 1938: the *man of steel* himself.

★

Then Christine said they urgently needed to change Andro's surname, and that Stasia and Simon should officially adopt him.

A single letter reached them in September 1936, a month that blanketed the city in a murderous heat. Sopio's handwriting was the same — generous and broad — but everything else had changed. Her train of thought was interrupted, every line spoke of fear, you could smell it; you could smell the censorship through which the letter had passed.

Dear Taso, my dearest darling Andro, my wonderful Kitty, my clever Kostya, the package and the letters gave me such joy. I am well. We work a lot. I miss you to distraction, but my confidence has not left me, I hold on tightly to it. A lot has changed and I am sure a lot more will change, but one thing I know with absolute certainty: I love you all with all my heart. Be together, be a little brigade, because then we will pull through, whatever happens. Forever yours, Sopio.

I don't know if Stasia wept, felt ashamed, or chewed her fingernails to the quick with rage. But I am sure that this letter, and what happened afterwards, were a powerful injection to Stasia's heart that anaesthetised it for a very long time.

The news of Sopio's death reached Tbilisi two months after the fact. The exact circumstances of her death, and the place of her burial, were unknown. The letter was clinical, clear, and businesslike. As if Sopio's death were simply unavoidable — as if she had been suffering from a terminal illness and her sad end had been predicted long ago.

The only visible sign of Stasia's grief was when she wandered out into the garden one morning — the children were at school, and Christine was at her dressing table, putting on her make-up — and trampled all the flowers. She stamped on the snapdragons, the begonias, tore up the radiant yellow sunflowers and the pale yellow marigolds. She ripped them out by the roots and crushed them. It was a massacre of beauty.

They kept the news from Andro. At school, he was learning to sing hymns in praise of his homeland, not knowing that his mother had been executed in the name of this very homeland, with a three-rouble bullet to the head in a dirty backyard. They wanted to spare him, but the main reason was really that they didn't know how to explain the grim, senseless event to him, and were afraid of what they might read in the child's eyes.

> The people's flag is deepest red,
> It shrouded oft our martyred dead,
> And ere their limbs grew stiff and cold,
> Their hearts' blood dyed its every fold.
>
> SOCIALIST SONG

The Frunze Higher Naval School offered four courses in different areas of naval training and sciences. Kostya was most interested in navigation.

For Kostya, who was top of his class, getting accepted by the academy — with additional help from some excellent references and Simon's contacts — was child's play. Over the past two years, he had worked on himself and his body with something bordering on obsession, swimming several hundred-metre lengths three times a week, lifting weights, and joining the athletics programme at the Youth Sports Palace.

Stasia, who had guessed his intentions, stopped bemoaning her failure and came to terms with the fact that Kostya wanted to be placed in the care of the father he idolised. She wrote letters to her husband, and even had long-distance telephone conversations with him from the post office, asking him to take good care of Kostya. She added that the boy was more sensitive than he looked; the lieutenant should not be deceived by his physical strength. Simon was proud of his son and promised to do everything in his power to see that his development continued just as splendidly.

There was little difficulty in arranging Kostya's departure, and the farewells at Tbilisi's Central Station also took place quickly and without tears.

'Do try and learn how to have some fun!' Kitty called after him as he was getting on the train, and he muttered that she should learn how to behave like a girl. Stasia kissed him on the forehead, pressed a bag stuffed full of treats into his hands, and turned her face away as the train began to move.

★

And just as Sopio's death and the destruction of the flowers could not have been averted, the year 1937, which was to be the bloodiest and most rabid in Soviet history, brought with it an unavoidable catastrophe — like a storm, but without thunder; silent, but extreme.

It was inevitable that one mild October day, just a few weeks after Kostya's departure, Ramas Iosebidze would return home earlier than planned. It was a glorious, golden evening. There were still melons to be had for dessert; it was still warm enough to sit outside. The children happened to be spending a week with Stasia's family in their sleepy border town. Christine had gone to bed early with a headache, and Stasia was still sitting in the garden doing a crossword puzzle. The cook and the maid had already gone home.

'Ramas?'

Surprised, Stasia went to meet her brother-in-law. He smiled. He seemed to be in a sentimental mood, for he embraced her, which he seldom did, and sat with her in the garden for a while. He had his briefcase with him; he told Stasia about the stresses and strains of his trip, and asked after the children.

For years, Stasia believed that the children's absence must have been the final incentive Ramas needed to go through with his deed. But I think he had been planning it for months, and would have carried it out one way or another — perhaps not on that October evening, but there would certainly have been another opportunity. It would have been enough for the children simply to have been at school.

Ramas said he was tired and was looking forward to waking Christine and seeing her, and went up to their bedroom. Stasia went to bed as well.

Ramas lay down beside his wife and hugged her tightly.

'What are you doing here, when did you arrive?'

'Just now. I had to see you. I couldn't stand it any longer.'

'Did you leave without permission? Isn't that against the rules? I don't want you to get into trouble.'

'I want you so much ...'

He started to tug at Christine's nightdress. Finally, Christine gave in; she felt guilty, of course she did, she felt miserable. But she took off her nightdress, because in the last few months she had learned that her nakedness rendered men more helpless than when she kept her clothes on.

He stretched out on his back and made her straddle him. They had never made love like that before. She looked at him, his face contorted with pain or pleasure — she couldn't tell which, but she had to look at him because he was staring unwaveringly at her. He didn't look at her pert white breasts, he didn't admire her flawless body, he didn't touch her most secret places; he stared into her eyes throughout.

She moved slowly at first, disconcerted and hesitant, surprised by her own desire. Willingly she took the hands he offered as support. She was confused by the fact she was starting to enjoy what she was doing. Her breath came more quickly; he saw little beads of sweat appear on her forehead, he smiled, he was entirely with her, as if what she was doing was not happening to his body. As if they were two different bodies, beings, not joined together, but isolated in their pleasure.

Christine wanted to cover her face, she wanted him to stop staring at her like that — she groaned, though she was usually so quiet when they made love. Until now, the worldliness of Tbilisi had been no match for her provincial Christian upbringing. He held her hands tightly, steadying her.

She wanted to stop, to lie down beside him and stroke his forehead, because what she was feeling made her heart hurt — painful little jolts — she felt something move inside her, she wanted to weep out loud, beg him for forgiveness, undo everything that had happened, she wanted to move out of the city, to the countryside, to make a new start — even without money, without power, she was prepared to take him as her husband.

This she understood as she began to sense something she would never have thought possible; as her moans grew louder and louder, as she forgot her inhibitions, her manners and the Bible. She understood that she would follow him, no matter where, this gentle man with the deep sadness in his eyes, as if he knew about everything — yes, he knows, she thought. And he started to laugh loudly, though there was no scorn in his voice — his laughter was understanding, indescribably beautiful, very gentle, very loving, as if he couldn't believe his luck, and he whispered: 'Yes, yes, you're so very beautiful, yes, my sunshine, please, yes, please.' She couldn't entirely overcome her embarrassment; the way he was looking at her and talking to her made her uncomfortable, but the enjoyment was so great, it felt so good to let herself go.

This time, she was taking someone else's body; she was not the one who had to give herself. As she had always thought you had to when you were someone's wife, courtesan, mistress, yes, whore — yes, at that moment, those were her exact thoughts. Engulfed in this feeling, she wanted to scream everything out of herself — why had she never been able to feel it before, she wondered — and she closed her eyes. She was filled with an immense warmth; a gentle and very delicate feeling spread through her ribcage, something contracted, again that painful jolt, and her lips formed words she had never wanted to say before: 'I love you.'

She was amazed: when he had said those words to her, she had always just said 'Me too', never thinking what they meant, those words everyone else was so desperate to hear. They had never been all that important to her. The jewels, the receptions, the admiration, the appreciation always seemed more important. That was what she wanted from him: this life, yes, this one exactly. Love just seemed to come to her, without her having to do anything for it; it was enough that she existed and delighted people with her presence, nothing more. He had never asked: 'Do you love me?' He had always seemed satisfied with her 'Me too', never demanding more from her.

She hated him. And she loved him. And this contradiction was tearing her chest apart — it had to be released in a yell. He heard the words and gave his tears free rein; there was no doubt now that these were tears, and he was crying. But she didn't know why. She hoped they were tears of joy, but she couldn't be sure. Her pelvis moved faster, he moved in time with her, offered up to her his sluggish body, which she now found so desirable. He was there only to give her pleasure, to give her this sense of boundless freedom.

In her room, Stasia woke, sat up in bed, and listened. She heard her sister and her mouth fell open in the dark. Christine was making love to her husband, Christine was doing something other people did, Christine was becoming human, flesh and blood. Stasia couldn't believe her ears. It made her giggle, and she resolved to tease her sister about it at the next opportunity. She sounded excited; it seemed to be doing her good. These were sounds of joy, and it had been a long time since anything so beautiful had been heard in this house.

★

And then came the scream, so loud its reverberations seemed to wander down all the hallways of the house and creep into all the corners and alcoves. The scream was like a birth cry, it was like an anthem, a celebration of desire and intimacy, it rose up like the start of an aria, a pure, ringing voice.

Stasia shook her head and sat up once more. *What the devil are they doing in there?* she wondered, and suppressed a grin. Christine screamed and her husband laughed, laughed with happiness and gratitude. She had closed her eyes and was writhing like a snake at the sound of a charmer's flute in the bazaar. Something exploded inside her, and tiny stars danced before her eyes.

She didn't see her husband's hand reach for a little bottle beside the bed.

'I'm doing it for us. Only for us. For you and me. Because there's no other escape for us,' he said, gripping her by the wrist.

Still dazed, Christine opened her eyes. She noticed the small, elegant bottle, which looked like a perfume bottle, and smiled.

'What's that, my darling?' she asked, stretching her back.

'I'm sorry I let you down. No one has ever given me as much joy as you have. It's not your fault.'

Christine, now a little more alert, and frightened by her husband's calm tone, tried to free herself; it was only then that she realised how firm his grip was, how steely.

'What are you doing?' she asked, and fear crept into her voice.

'Otherwise it will never stop. As soon as you say no, you'll pay for it with your life. There's no other way.'

A shudder ran down her spine; she stared uncomprehendingly at the bottle. But there was no doubt now: he knew everything. She prepared to defend herself, struggling against the remnants of desire in her body; she drew herself upright. She felt nothing but immense gratitude, humility, and something like affection.

'Ramas, what's wrong?' she stammered.

At that moment he threw the contents of the bottle in her face. It was just a few drops, and at first she thought it was water, but then the hellish burning started. She could smell its stench, not realising that it was she who was burning, until the pain spread across the left half of her face and paralysed all other sensations, making her mind reel, her body cramp. Christine screamed, even more loudly — so loudly it made all the glass in the house ring. This time, the scream was inhuman. Ramas, who had spilled a few drops of the acid solution on his hand, gave a similarly bestial cry. Trying not to look at his wife, he leapt up, grabbed his trousers, and strode out.

Stasia rushed out of her room and, to her astonishment, saw that the door of her sister's bedroom had been flung open. In the dark, all she could see was her sister lying on the bed, naked as God had made her, thrashing about as though she had lost her mind. She thought it must have something to do with Ramas: he must have done something terrible to himself in his despair; she thought the blood was his. But then Christine turned towards her and Stasia saw that the left half of her face was a single blood-drenched wound that smelled of burnt flesh.

★

The next morning, Ramas Iosebidze's body, wearing only shoes and trousers, was found in the Kojori woods. He had shot himself in the head with a Walther PPK. The gun had been a birthday present from his friend, mentor, and commander.

By some miracle, Christine's eye was spared; but the left half of her face was disfigured beyond recognition.

The hot chocolate was the only thing that could bring a hint of a smile to Christine's lips. Over the long weeks of bed rest and closed curtains, of hiding her face, of pain and half-suppressed screams, it was the only thing that brought any kind of relief.

BOOK III

★

KOSTYA

> We thank our leader for our happy childhood!
>
> POSTER SLOGAN

Kostya came to Leningrad (previously Petrograd, the former St Petersburg) to train as a sailor at the Frunze Higher Naval School.

It was in an old building on beautiful Vasilievsky Island, right on the Neva. The training centre had recently been awarded the Order of the Red Banner on account of its discipline and exemplary character. Kostya had come to what was possibly the most European city in the East, built, in the competition for western appreciation, by forced labourers and prisoners, who all too frequently paid for this beauty with their lives (the gilding of the twenty-six-metre-high dome of St. Isaac's Cathedral alone resulted in eighty dead). The white city. With its proud Neva, the islands and bridges, and the beautiful black cats and undaunted ravens that — majestic, complacent — permitted anyone to feed them. The dark, interconnected interior courtyards; the secret passages. A city with the *raffinesse* of a French bride and the *grandezza* of an Italian widow.

But Leningrad was, above all, the epicentre of communist ideology. This was where the *Aurora* had fired the first shot and the imperial palace had been stormed; this was where Lenin had arrived, as if by a miracle, at the Finland Station, to save the country. This was where the Party bigwigs had started out. This was where a new calendar had begun!

Already, as his train pulled in to Moscow Station, Kostya's breast was filled with pride and awe. For him, it was an honour to be here, at the heart of Communism, following in his father's footsteps.

He thought it very laudable that his father lived in such a modest abode, a tiny apartment on Petrogradsky Island, in a classical, nineteenth-century house that had been converted into *kommunalkas* and allocated to soldiers and their families. None of the splendour and luxury he was familiar with from his aunt's house; no superfluous items, no wasted labour.

He could have burst with pride when his father took him out and showed him the city, even allowing him a glass of vodka with some of his colleagues. Kostya was sure he would soon give his father plenty of reasons to be proud of him. He would demonstrate to him how upright he was, how hardworking, how disciplined, and how faithfully he served his country.

And then his happiness on seeing all the ships. At last, he had escaped the fetid, oriental seclusion of the Caucasus and was here at the heart of world affairs. Even his tiny room at the boarding house filled him with childish delight. The plain wooden bed, the old woollen blanket, the little table, the musty wardrobe — this was all he would need in the coming years. And he would make friends, kindred spirits who shared his passion for the Navy.

★

His first minor disappointment came on the very first day of training, when he discovered that his roommate was by no means a genteel Leningrad native, but a small, slight, rather unprepossessing Georgian with thin hair and overly narrow shoulders. He spoke with a southern Georgian accent, which softened all his words and which Kostya thought sounded smarmy. Giorgi Alania, as the boy was called, seemed insecure and overawed, and didn't correspond in the slightest to Kostya's image of the ideal roommate.

Kostya complained to his father, asking him whether it was customary in Russia to allocate roommates according to nationality. His father laughed and said no, it was just a coincidence: he should be pleased that he still had an opportunity to speak his mother tongue. However, what with the strict drill at the traditional academy, the onset of the northern winter, and Kostya's pathological desire to be the best and to prove it to the world, he quickly forgot this initial disappointment.

He rose at six in the morning, did callisthenic exercises in his room, had breakfast in the canteen, attended his courses, then went to the academy library and read up on engineering so that he could show off his knowledge in class and gain favour with the teachers. He was eagerly looking forward to the first training exercises in the Gulf of Finland because he was a practical sort of man and knew he would come out of them looking good.

Soon, most people were calling him '*Krasavchik*' — 'Mr Handsome' — and even the older students started seeking his company. He was said to be a 'real man', as good at drinking as he was at studying.

Yet the harder Kostya tried to win his father's affection, the busier and more dismissive the latter seemed. Simon Jashi's slack posture, constant tiredness, pallid skin, and his restless, wandering eyes spurred Kostya on to ever greater boldness, daring, and accomplishments. For so many years, he had preserved the statue of his heroic father in his imagination; he wasn't prepared to drag it down from its pedestal so soon. The more assignments he was given, the more energetic he became. The more strenuous the training manoeuvres and sporting activities, the more enthusiastic he was. He never complained about the teachers' severity, never longed for the weekend or the holidays. And at the same time, he never missed any of the gatherings in the various rooms of the boarding house or the *kommunalkas*. He drank, he sang, he was always the first to raise his glass. This soon earned him a reputation for indestructibility, and the respect of his fellow students.

Giorgi Alania was the exact opposite. A loner, he was always buried in his books. His comrades didn't invite him to the gatherings; they never saw him drink or swear, never heard him make lewd jokes. He clearly struggled to meet the Academy's high standards in the physical disciplines, but in the theoretical subjects — mathematics above all — his performance was remarkable. Soon, people were casting envious glances in his direction and calling him a swot behind his back.

Alania's fellow students only approached him when they needed his assistance with their exams. He was happy to help, and did so without protest, but it never occurred to anyone to invite him to the weekly drinking sessions in return. Kostya, too, steadfastly ignored him at first. Their conversation never went further than an exchange of banalities. Sometimes they lent each other books or read *Pravda* together, but that was all. The only classes they both attended were the mandatory ones; Alania had decided early on to study shipbuilding, and that suited Kostya just fine.

On this particular evening, though, when Kostya put down the book he was reading, he observed Alania more closely; he was finding it hard to concentrate, and was looking for some distraction. Alania was in the middle of peeling a cucumber, so meticulously that Kostya was impressed. As if the cucumber were a bomb that required defusing.

'What are you doing?' asked Kostya, curious. He generally addressed Alania in Russian.

'My mother sent me a parcel with all kinds of treats in it. I bought cucumbers too, to complete the meal. And you're most welcome to share it with me, if you like,' he answered in his soft Georgian.

Indeed, Kostya's mouth began to water when he saw Alania laying the little table. A constant diet of black bread, groats, and fat-free *borscht* was too meagre for his stomach, and although he might not have wanted to admit it, he missed the sumptuous meals he had enjoyed at home.

Alania prepared the food with great care and attention: he sliced the bread, put the spicy *adjika* in little bowls — God knows where he'd found them — cut the smoked cheese into thin slices, patiently stirred the cucumber salad in the bowl, arranged pickled garlic on a plate, and uncorked a bottle of Saperavi.

At the sight of this lavish meal, Kostya's reserve evaporated. Quickly recalling Georgian dining tradition, he proposed a hearty toast to the dinner. The wine loosened their tongues, and Alania told him about his childhood in a small village, Machara, on the Black Sea. He was an only child, which was most unusual in that region. He spoke very highly and with the greatest respect of his mother, a teacher in the local village school. He did not, however, mention a father.

Kostya wondered how, as an ordinary village boy, Alania had managed to get into the Frunze Academy in Leningrad. He soon decided that Alania must be one of the token students from the *kolkhoz* that almost all the educational institutions were required to take. Alania's knowledge of natural sciences and mathematics was very impressive, so it wasn't hard to imagine that a headmaster or a *kolkhoz* representative had recommended him. By the early hours of the morning, they were already singing the Georgian song 'Suliko' together and slapping each other on the back.

Kostya became Giorgi Alania's only friend, and, although he couldn't have known it at the time, Alania was to become Kostya's best friend, and the most loyal.

Because, Brilka, the friendship sealed that evening traces what is perhaps the most interesting and improbable pattern in our carpet. By the end you'll agree with me that, without Alania, parts of our story would never have come together; that, without him, I might not be able to tell this story this way.

★

In 1922, before Alania came into this world, the first official constitution of Soviet Georgia was accepted. That year saw the start of the agricultural reforms, collectivisation, and *kolkhozation*. But it seemed that none of this could prevent a schoolgirl of barely seventeen from graduating from her village school with a gold medal and looking forward to her future. In her case, this future showed tantalising promise: as the best student in her class, she had a good chance of gaining a university place — and that was a very big deal for a girl from one of the remotest villages on the Black Sea coast.

Her family were less than delighted by this prospect. A girl was supposed to get married — she was quite good-looking, there would have been a number of interested parties — and for that, in this rural region, a woman didn't need to be able to do more than read and write and add a few roubles together. And be good to her husband and not work-shy, because there was work aplenty in the tea plantations round about.

But Gulo, their 'little sweetheart', wanted nothing to do with all that. She explained to her parents, who had had only three and five years of schooling respectively, that the tea plantations were not for her; she was interested in higher mathematics, and there were far more exciting challenges in the world than mucking out cowsheds or picking tea. Besides, she had two older sisters, both of whom had been married for some time and shared the responsibility for the farm and the next generation; and there was her brother, who would inherit everything anyway and was already following in her father's footsteps. So they needn't have any concerns about releasing her from the clutches of the family.

Her mother complained about her ungrateful child; her father painted grisly pictures for her of what he believed went on in the cities: murder, rape, exploitation. But Gulo, or Guliko, as she was usually called, just kept shaking her head and repeating over and over again that she would take her father's hunting rifle and put a bullet through her brain that instant rather than marry some village idiot and die a lingering death out here in the back of beyond.

It was only when Gulo's teachers, convinced of her academic promise, went so far as to pay her father a visit to urge him to allow Gulo to go to university that her parents finally admitted defeat.

The very next month, Gulo became the first woman in the history of the university to be offered a place at the Faculty of Mathematics in Kutaisi. If she successfully completed the four years in Kutaisi, she could then, with top marks and a diploma, apply to the Institute of Astrophysics in Moscow. Astrophysics was her ultimate goal: she dreamed of a career in research. She had no doubts — nothing else stood in the way of her dreams, and she would give everything she had to achieve her aim; of this she was firmly convinced.

The only thing that, to everyone's astonishment, Gulo considered a disadvantage was her outward appearance. Her unusually pretty face, her flawless skin, her large eyes the colour of an autumn lake, her marvellous head of hair, and her strong, tall, curvaceous figure didn't really seem appropriate for a girl with a passionate interest in physics and mathematics.

And indeed, had her striking appearance not got in the way, her life after that summer would have been a very different one. Perhaps it really would have gone according to her plan.

A month after the final school examinations, Gulo's class teacher invited her on a trip. As the top graduate in her year, she had the honour of spending a week in the oil town of Baku, along with other girls from the region who had similarly distinguished themselves. The trip was financed by the Transcaucasian Federation and was intended to promote understanding between the peoples of the Caucasus.

For Gulo, who had only ever left her village once, on a school trip to Sokhumi, it was a very welcome opportunity. Baku was an expanding metropolis; the financial aristocracy, the Rothschilds and the Nobels, had changed the face of the city, and Gulo was happy to have the chance to absorb some of its big-city atmosphere before beginning her studies. She wanted to be able to hold her own with her future fellow students; she didn't want to look like a country girl.

The first few days were marvellous. Gulo was impressed by Baku — the colourful oriental markets and the friendliness of the people — and it didn't even seem to bother her when men ogled her on the street. She enjoyed the strong tea, the honey-drenched baklava, and the bustle of city life with its trams and horse-drawn carriages.

She felt like an adult: it was her first taste of the sort of freedom that awaited her in Kutaisi, and it filled her with euphoric happiness.

The girls stayed in a communist youth hostel, where they all shared one big dormitory. It was hot and dusty, and the nights were long. Full of new impressions, they chatted in whispers throughout the night, talking about their new lives that would begin at the end of the summer.

On the fourth day of their visit, they attended a public event organised by the local Communist Party. Their teacher, a staunch communist, believed it would do the girls no harm to think about ways to improve living conditions for the working classes — the subject of the event — and urged her protégées to go with her to the National Library. The room was packed; the audience listened with great reverence to three men who spoke one after the other, tediously and at length, in heavily Caucasian-accented Russian, about the measures that must now be taken to improve working conditions in the *kolkhoz*.

The teacher went on clapping enthusiastically long after the obligatory applause had subsided, then dashed over to one of the men as he was heading for the exit, practically dragging Gulo along behind her. The man with the glasses was Georgian, the teacher explained, and he must be important if he was permitted to give a speech here. They had to seize the opportunity and make his acquaintance.

The teacher introduced herself and her group of girls, and enthused about what the man had said and the suggestions he had made. He listened to her patiently, nodding thoughtfully a few times, and as he was about to shake her hand and excuse himself his eyes fell on Gulo, who was standing mutely at her side. Suddenly, he switched from Russian to Georgian and asked which village they had come from. The teacher, delighted by his unexpected interest, started gushing like a waterfall. They were from a small village, not worth mentioning, she said, Machara; their trip was to promote understanding between peoples, and she and the girls were extremely pleased to have had the honour of hearing his lecture.

He himself came from Merkheuli, a nearby village — what a funny coincidence! — the man cried, and added that this absolutely must be celebrated. The ladies had undertaken such a long journey and should therefore be entertained appropriately, to seal this friendship between peoples. There were a few restaurants here, he said, that served excellent lamb cooked in all manner of ways, and delicious desserts — the girls liked sweet things, didn't they? All girls like sweet things!

Barely able to contain her enthusiasm, the teacher summoned the girls, and after the little man had consulted his colleagues, they made their way to the exit, accompanied by two Red Army soldiers. The group was split up into three carriages and driven to a restaurant on the promenade, overlooking the sea.

The girls were overwhelmed to find themselves the object of so much male attention. They didn't know how they were supposed to behave, and kept glancing across at their teacher, whose rapture now knew no bounds; she seemed just as overwhelmed as her wards.

Sweet wine was brought to the table, and although for a while the teacher protested and forbade the girls to taste it, their glasses were eventually all filled to the brim. A brass band was soon summoned and the mood grew increasingly jolly and relaxed. Bit by bit, the girls lost their inhibitions, and soon some of them were dancing with the inebriated Red Army soldiers.

Gulo remained sceptical. The leader of the group was paying her far too much attention. He had sat down beside her and kept pouring her more wine; he entertained her with anecdotes and paid her compliments. The teacher didn't see the man put his arm around Gulo and brush his knee against hers.

It got late, and although the teacher kept saying that they had to leave, the bespectacled man ignored her protests and ordered more bottles of wine. One of the girls threw up in the toilet. Another fell asleep with her head on the table.

Eventually the carriages were brought round and they split into three groups again. The gentlemen insisted on driving the ladies back to the youth hostel. Gulo had no choice. Relieved, she climbed into one of the carriages in the hope that the evening was now over, but the man got in and sat down beside her. One of the girls didn't have a seat, and Gulo called out to her: on no account did she want to be alone with this man. Nelly, as the other girl was called, was of a cheerful disposition; she had been dancing a lot and laughing very loudly. Gulo knew her from the village; she was the daughter of the village commissar, and always wore strikingly beautiful clothes that emphasised her generous bosom.

Nelly wasn't nearly as stupid as Gulo had originally thought, but that evening she had clearly drunk much more wine than was good for her, and had to be lifted into the carriage by one of the Red Army soldiers as she could hardly stand. The soldier went to sit up front with the coachman and they set off.

Initially, they drove along behind the other carriages, and after a few minutes Gulo's unease lessened. Soon they would be at the youth hostel; soon it would be over. But when their carriage suddenly turned right while the other two carried straight on, Gulo felt herself starting to panic.

The bespectacled man assured her that there was no need to worry, they were just making a small detour, he had something to attend to *en route*. Nelly laughed stupidly again and laid her heavy head on Gulo's shoulder.

Eventually the carriage stopped in a dark alleyway and the girls were asked to get out. Gulo could hear her heart hammering. Nelly began to whimper; Gulo took her by the hand, trying not to betray her fear. They were invited into an interior courtyard. The man was talking at her non-stop: everything was absolutely fine, no need to be afraid, they were just taking a little break, and Nelly could go to the bathroom and freshen up.

Gulo helped Nelly up the spiral staircase to a wooden gallery. From there, they passed into a small apartment with low ceilings and lots of tapestries. As if by magic, the Red Army soldier produced a basket of fruit, and the bespectacled man offered Gulo lemonade, which she politely declined. The apartment was dark; the men had lit two candles, but the silence all around only served to heighten Gulo's fear. The gentlemen laughed and tried to revive the jolly atmosphere from the restaurant, telling jokes and paying the two girls more compliments.

Gulo excused herself, took Nelly's arm, and dragged her into the little bathroom, which had a bidet and a washbowl. Nelly didn't really understand where she was, and was slurring incoherently. Gulo took some water from the bowl and threw it in Nelly's face. Nelly screamed and pushed her away with both hands, but Gulo grabbed her wrists, brought her face up close to Nelly's, and compelled her to look her in the eyes.

'Listen to me. We've got to get out of here. You have to wash your face and try to sober up. Do you hear me? We've got to get out of here. The door's right here, at the end of the corridor, and it's not locked. There's only a chain. You just have to pull yourself together and be absolutely quiet. Do you understand?'

'I feel sick!'

Gulo threw more water in her face. Nelly stopped resisting.

'Do you understand?' Gulo repeated. This time Nelly nodded hard and wiped her mouth with the sleeve of her dress.

A few steps and they would be outside. Gulo held her breath. She pushed the chain aside and opened the door, slowly, carefully, as soundlessly as possible. She turned to Nelly and placed her forefinger on her lips, then let her go on ahead.

And that was when it happened. Nelly stumbled and fell, crashing flat onto the floor. For a split second Gulo considered stepping over Nelly and running down the spiral staircase; not looking back, running out, away from these men, away from their mocking laughter. But she couldn't do it. She saw the girl lying on the floor, pathetic, feeble, drunk, stupefied. And although she didn't know exactly what staying would mean, she did know that if she ran away she still would not escape. And she stopped, and closed the door, even as she heard the men coming down the corridor.

He bore down hard on her on the old sofa, which kept sagging more and more beneath the weight of their bodies. She focused on the whimpering coming from Nelly in the corridor. She heard the panting above her, and the same words, over and over again: 'You're so beautiful — so beautiful!'

With one hand gripping the arm of the sofa, she struggled not to turn her head so she wouldn't have to look at him. She closed her eyes and tried to erase the image from her mind: the image of Nelly in the corridor, lying on the floor like a lifeless doll, legs spread, and the Red Army soldier kneeling in front of her, pulling her thighs towards him with increasing force, lifting her pelvis, driving himself into her.

She tried to think about Kutaisi, about the day she would pack her bags;

she tried to think about her home, the farm, her sisters, the school; she even tried to think about the cattle, the cows and the pigs, the oilrigs off Baku, the green countryside she had seen from the train; she tried not to think about the pain in her abdomen, not to breathe in the smell of the bespectacled man above her, not to scream out her despair and disgust; she wanted not to hear Nelly's terrible whimpering and her heartbreaking cries for help.

When the two of them were dropped off outside the youth hostel at dawn, nothing was the same as before. Yet their bodies betrayed nothing of what had happened to them. No traces of blood, no ripped clothes, no bruises.

When they got into bed, everyone was still asleep.

Why hadn't they looked for them? Why hadn't they fetched help? Why?

At breakfast, the teacher gave a speech about the importance of yesterday's meeting. No one asked what time the two girls had been brought back to the hostel. The teacher avoided Gulo's and Nelly's eyes, patted them absent-mindedly on the cheek, and didn't even question them when they both said they were sick and asked to stay at the hostel and be excused from the day's events.

'Had a few too many last night, did you?' one of the girls joked half-heartedly as the rest of the group headed off and Nelly and Gulo remained behind in the canteen.

Afterwards, they returned to the dormitory and lay down on their beds.

'We should go to the *militsiya*,' said Gulo, after staring interminably at the ceiling and listening to the regular breathing of her companion in misfortune.

Nelly just laughed. Her laugh had a scornful edge and made Gulo feel even more wretched and helpless than she did already.

'Why not?' asked Gulo.

'You don't seriously think they'll hold them accountable? Them?'

'Why not?'

'They'll stick us in a mental hospital and pump us full of drugs until we believe we invented the whole thing.'

Sober now, no longer whimpering and slurring her words, Nelly seemed almost too grown-up. Her tone was practically vicious.

'So what do you suggest?'

'What do I suggest? We say nothing, go on living our lives, and remain spinsters forever.'

'But why?'

'What, you think men are going to be queuing up for us, now that we're …'

'But —'

'Forget it, Gulo. And not a word to anyone — not a word, you swear!'
'Nelly ...'
'Swear!'
'I swear.'
Two days later they returned home.

Gulo went to Kutaisi and embarked on her studies. She was staying with an old lady who gave piano lessons and served as a kind of chaperone. One month later, she discovered the reason for her unusual irritability and sentimentality: pregnancy. She knew that this was the end.

As she didn't have enough money to go to an abortionist, she tried all kinds of herbal concoctions that were said to cause women to miscarry, and when none of them had any effect she climbed up a ladder and jumped off, hoping that this would rid her of her unwanted burden. When nothing happened, she began to have terrible pangs of conscience.

Every night she cried into her pillow, her hands clamped over her mouth so her landlady wouldn't discover her problem and turn her straight out on the street.

Her work started to suffer. From the very first day, the male students had seen her presence as a kind of insult; now, in light of her shortcomings, they took every opportunity to make this clear.

Gulo cursed the man who was the author of her misfortune; she cursed her gender, her powerlessness; she cursed the heartless people around her from whom she could expect no sympathy.

After three months, she went to her professor and explained the situation. He tugged his goatee, cleared his throat, shook his head, and told her he could see no way of keeping her coveted place at the university open.

'You see, Comrade Alania, why we are so reluctant to allow women to study here? When it comes down to it, they always have something better to do than apply themselves to mathematics. I thought you were an exception,' he concluded, affecting an expression of commiseration, 'but now all this exception does is to prove the rule.'

When she was six months pregnant, Gulo packed her bags and left Kutaisi. She swore to herself that as soon as the child was old enough she would try a second time, that she would apply to every university in the country.

She went back to her hated village.

Endless interrogation followed. Who was the father of the child, Gulo's father demanded in fury. Was he a fellow countryman, or just some nobody? Was he even a Christian? He must be tracked down and called to account; and so on.

Gulo endured it all with stoicism. After interminable weeks of contempt, tirades of abuse, ostracism, violence, her family abandoned their attempts to discover the identity of the child's father. Gulo was packed off to her elder sister, who was married to a forestry worker and living an isolated life at the edge of the woods. Gulo was to keep house there while her sister worked on the tea plantation. Away from the village, the villagers were less likely to spread malicious gossip about her.

When her time came, no midwife was called because the family were ashamed of her, and she had to give birth with no outside help, alone in her attic room, reluctantly assisted by her childless sister. This was how Giorgi came into the world.

When Giorgi reached his second birthday, Gulo applied again to every university in the country, but received only letters of rejection. After this, she accepted a post as a maths teacher in the village school. Because there was no one to look after her child, she always took him with her to class. Giorgi could already read, write, and do arithmetic before he formally started school.

She would never have thought it possible, but her love for her son was unburdened by his history, as if he had come into being through immaculate conception and not through rape. She passed on to him all her knowledge and skills; she told him about the things she wished for, and the things she had wanted to discover and explore; she garlanded him with her dreams like a necklace handed down from generation to generation.

When Giorgi was in his seventh year at school, the principal commended him to the science college in Sokhumi. It was during his time there that he fell in love with the sea — the only love he did not share with his mother. He graduated from school at the age of just fifteen, and his teachers and the chairman of the *Komsomol*, the Communist Union of Youth, made an application for him to attend the Frunze Higher Naval School in Leningrad.

Giorgi first asked who his father was at the age of five. At the age of seven he even threw a temper tantrum about it in front of his mother. At the age of twelve he cried and begged her to tell him. But Gulo always gave him the same answer: 'I'll tell you when you're old enough.'

And so he had no choice but to wait until he reached this eagerly anticipated age. But life had other plans for him, and the wait was to be a very long one.

Many years later, Nelly, the girl Gulo had been unable to walk away from that terrible night, came back to visit her home village, and called on Gulo. After that summer, Nelly had moved to Batumi, the white seaport, and Gulo had heard nothing from her since. She had often thought of her companion in misfortune and hoped that that night had not had the same consequences for Nelly as for her.

Now, all of a sudden, this heavily made-up woman was standing there before her. Gulo focused on her features and tried in vain to find some trace there of the girl from years ago. This was a voluptuous lady in rather vulgar clothes, who had an artificial laugh, smacked her lips, feigned an insincere cheerfulness, and spoke in a voice that was excessively loud and over-articulated.

She had brought Gulo a gold box of chocolates, and sat down in her sparsely furnished living room. She had a 'marvellous' life, Nelly proclaimed at the top of her voice. Batumi was a great city, and she lived in a house right on the promenade.

They sat drinking lemonade in Gulo's cramped, shabby apartment, and Gulo kept trying not to look at her guest. She found it hard to look Nelly — the person she had become — in the eyes. She had so hoped that Nelly at least had made a life for herself; that she had had better luck than Gulo herself had done.

'Tell me, have you got a drop of wine, or something stronger? I can't endure this place without alcohol. Really I can't,' said Nelly suddenly, and gave that false laugh again.

'No, I'm afraid not. I don't drink. I lost the desire to drink a long time ago,' answered Gulo; and for a fraction of a second the women were silent. Then Nelly spoke again, too loudly.

'I'm very sorry about what happened to you. It's a boy, isn't it?'

'Excuse me?'

'You know — the child.'

'Yes, he's a wonderful boy. Do you have children?'

At that moment Gulo realised that this strange woman was the only person other than herself who knew the identity of Giorgi's father. It dawned on her that this accursed secret bound them together forever, like invisible handcuffs, and the realisation made her deeply uneasy.

'No, no. That's not for me. Hahaha. I enjoy life far too much, you see. And men — men are very egotistical creatures, too. They demand your full attention.'

There was something in the way she said 'men' that made Gulo feel nauseous.

'Maybe you'll come and visit me and the two of us can have fun! I have lots of influential friends, believe me!' said Nelly, rising, as their awkward conversation drew to a close.

A car was waiting outside. Gulo watched as Nelly ran out into the street and a Red Army soldier opened the door for her. For a moment Gulo thought she was having a moment of déjà vu, and screwed her eyes shut. The man slapped Nelly's bottom lightly, and she feigned an outrage as artificial as her laugh, before getting into the front seat. How young and beautiful and light-hearted she had been back then, thought Gulo; and she closed her eyes again to escape the image that had haunted her for years.

The image of Nelly being put into the carriage by a Red Army soldier. Of how she had lain her heavy head on Gulo's shoulder, so trusting, so relieved, with absolutely no premonition of what was to follow.

Gulo kept her eyes tight shut to drive away the thought that usually followed this image: the thought of what it felt like to close, with your own hand, a door that would never open again.

Dictators have always had time for illusions.

ANTON CHEKHOV

The first year Kostya spent in the white city can be said to have been a happy one. He applied himself assiduously, both at the Naval School and during manoeuvres in the Gulf of Finland; he spent many nights with Alania, immersed in discussions about life and the world; he walked over the Anichkov Bridge with his comrades, drunk and singing lewd songs, and wolf-whistled at Pioneer girls. He did everything in his power to try to impress his father, and ignored the rest of the world with the indifference and self-confidence of youth. At a time of shootings, at a time of arrests and forced resettlement, at a time of suicides, Kostya blossomed, and believed he had found his place in the world. He rejoiced in himself and in life, at the height of his youth.

He wasn't yet interested in knowing how very alike the score of life and the score of death can be.

★

Sometimes, Brilka, stories repeat themselves, and overlap. Even life lacks imagination occasionally, and you can't blame it for that, don't you agree? And so I need to tell you about two more knots that were being tied simultaneously in our carpet.

On the same January night that Kostya attended the Academy's annual Naval Ball, his fifteen-year-old sister, who had cut her hair into a pert bob, was waiting for someone in the park, in the little town once destined to become the Nice of the Caucasus. Kitty and Andro always spent the winter holidays with Kitty's grandfather, the chocolate-maker. Christine still didn't believe she was strong enough to go out in public; she relied on Stasia's full and unqualified attention. And so, late that evening, Kitty was sitting in the park, chewing her fingernails, freezing, waiting.

It was a game. She was putting Andro's love to the test. She hid, and he had to find her. Sometimes she would send him on a wild goose chase all over town, leaving him little clues on scraps of paper that she slipped into the pockets of his trousers.

She hid everywhere — in the old school building, behind the bakery, sometimes in the empty chocolate factory, sometimes in the garden of the cloistered Church of St George, even under her own bed. But she knew that he would find her because he had never let her down; he had always been able to follow her trail. And so it would be again today, although she was already a little annoyed; she should have sat somewhere warm, not out in this damned cold, because Andro was taking his time.

Since his mother's disappearance, it was more difficult to persuade Andro to join in with all the games they used to play together, but he always did with this one. He refused to play tag with her, didn't want to touch the cards any more, didn't want to sing, either; but when she challenged him to seek her, he would seek, and find.

For some time now, the only woodcarvings he had made were of angels, which worried Kitty. This passion had developed into a downright obsession. Whereas before he would carve figures of animals and little houses, now it was only angels: old and young, with outspread or folded wings. The chocolate-maker's house was populated by an army of angels, and in Christine's house too they stood in rows, on the mantelpiece, on window ledges, on chests of drawers.

She saw him coming. He was running. He was out of breath. It was going to snow, her grandfather had said; the whole town was blanketed in thick fog. And this fog made people silent and careful, more fearful than they already were. He sat down beside her, smiled at her in affirmation, and she gave him two smacking kisses, one on each cheek, as a reward for finding her. Neither of them was in any hurry to return to the gloomy atmosphere in the chocolate-maker's house: since his retirement, all he did was indulge in reminiscences, look at old photographs, or jot down secret recipes in an old notebook.

Lida's demonstrative piety didn't make their home more inviting, either, and nor did Lara's strangeness. She couldn't understand why her only daughter hadn't been to visit her for two years. She spent most of her time making jam, and hid banknotes between books which she then couldn't find again.

'I want to leave. But I don't want to go without you,' said Andro suddenly. He started to scrape at the frosty earth with the toe of his boot. 'Would you come with me?'

'Where do you want to go, you lunatic? You don't have any money; and anyway, you have to wait for your mother.'

'My mother may not be coming back any time soon.'

'How can you know that?'

'I just know.'

'And where do you want to go?'

'I want to go to Europe. Remember when I showed you the map of the world the other day? I've marked it up. All the places I want to go. I want to go to Rome and Paris, Madrid, and Vienna — especially Vienna, they say it's very beautiful there. You'd like it there, Kitty.'

'But we can't, not on our own ...'

'Would you come with me?'

'I don't know.'

'Are you scared of going away?'

'What do you want to do in Vienna? There are only poor people and rich people there, and the rich people don't give the poor people anything, and the poor people starve and freeze to death on the streets. And anyone there who isn't blond gets kicked up the arse,' she said, and giggled.

'Don't be ridiculous.'

'Fine. All right, then, of course I'll come with you. You know I will!'

And Andro bent over his Kitty, the girl with the most beautiful almond eyes in all the world, and kissed her on the lips. The fog-filled town, the green-painted park benches; tall, gangly, quiet Andro, and restless, frenetic Kitty, both numb with cold and excitement in equal measure.

And as Kostya's sister pressed her fingers to her mouth, holding on to the first real kiss of her life and the taste of Andro's lips, her brother, three years older, was losing his virginity. I don't know whether these two events really did take place at precisely the same moment, but I like the idea that it might have been that way.

★

After the Naval Ball, Kostya's friends dragged him up an old staircase on Vasilievsky Island and left him in a dark, narrow corridor in front of a wooden door. They hammered on the door for all they were worth before sprinting off, laughing, down the stairs. At first, Kostya, who had already drunk a good deal of vodka, didn't really understand what was going on. He could only move slowly, and because he knew he wouldn't succeed in running away so easily he decided to stay there, come what may, even though his heart was beating so loudly he felt the whole house must be able to hear it.

The door was flung open and a tall, dark-haired woman in a long dressing gown, with rings on every finger, stared out at Kostya in his blue uniform, standing there like a kicked dog, red-faced, not knowing where to put himself.

'What's all this about?' asked the stranger indignantly, stepping towards him.

'Oh, excuse me — I don't know, either — they …' stammered Kostya, in accent-free Russian.

'If you're looking for that … hmm … *lady*, she doesn't live here any more. I live in this apartment now.'

The woman was about forty. She had olive skin and her eyes were jet-black, like her hair, which was loosely held up with a clip.

They'd played a trick on him. Kostya needed to think fast — how could he extricate himself from this awkward situation and pay them back? You were only a real sailor when you were as good at sea as in a woman's arms, that was what they'd said, and Kostya had allowed himself to be swept along, had walked here with them through the snow-covered streets, because this was the home of that lady who, for a few roubles and without any fuss, would initiate him in the art of love.

He was already on the point of turning round and walking briskly away, but she stopped him and asked, 'What's your name?'

'Konstantin. Kostya.'

'Hello, Konstantin. And how old are you?'

'I'm seventeen.'

'Aha. And where are you from, Konstantin?'

'From … from … Georgia.'

'From Georgia. Oh, that is nice. I spent a summer there once as a child, beside the sea. I ate a lot of pomegranates. I love pomegranates. Do you like them, too?'

'They're all right.'

'Would you like a tea, Konstantin? You look frozen to death.'

There was something about this unknown woman that Kostya found attractive. He couldn't have said himself what it was: her slightly sarcastic tone, her mischievous smile, or the sparkling rings on her hands.

The apartment must once have consisted of several rooms, now partitioned off by thin walls. The space he entered was only one room, with the kitchen in an alcove. The bathroom was in the corridor and was probably used by the neighbours as well. An entire corner had been taken over by indoor plants; on the dining table were piles of books, all of them open. The room was illuminated by a single lamp. It smelled good here. Kostya immediately felt at home.

He did indeed get a strong cup of tea, and his coat was hung over a coal-fired stove. He took a closer look at her in the light: she was almost as tall as he was, with a narrow frame, bony joints, and hips that were a little too wide. Her wrists were as slender and delicate as those of a young girl. Her face appeared to be hiding something, which Kostya found slightly arousing. A long, pointed nose, thin lips, slightly hollow cheeks. But it was her dark eyes, above all, that gleamed seductively in the dim light, as if coated with a film of oil. Hers was a sickly beauty, already starting to fade.

When the unknown woman asked him if he wanted to have a glass of wine with her, Kostya realised what it was about her that he found most attractive. It was her voice. She had a deep, rich voice that was also somehow very brittle, as if liable to crack on the very next word. She fetched a bottle of wine, handed him a corkscrew, and asked him to open it. Then she brought two glasses, snatched the bottle from his hand, held it up to the light for a moment, and poured. She sniffed at the red liquid before taking the first sip.

'This is a Bordeaux. It's very old. And very good. Very good. Wines are a special business — as I expect you know, Georgian. I've kept this bottle long enough. I was always saving it for that special occasion. But we'll drink it now.'

Kostya, even more confused, and preoccupied with trying not to let his confusion show, obeyed without protest. Beside the bed he could see an old piano draped in white cloth. After they had raised their glasses to each other, and the unknown woman had emptied hers in one go, she stood up, went over to the gramophone on the floor beside the piano, and put on a record. A *chanson* by Vertinsky began to play. She approached Kostya, stopped in front of him, and extended her hand.

'Would you dance with me, Konstantin?' she asked him, with an ambiguous smile. Kostya leaped up, excited and clumsy, and seized her hand in one of his, encircling her waist with the other.

She felt good: somehow, in a strange way, very familiar. In the middle of the dance she stopped, removed his hand from her waist, disengaged herself, and threw herself onto the little metal bed, which was covered with an old plaid blanket. A few moments later she had buried her face in both hands and was sobbing desperately.

Kostya stood in the middle of the room, rooted to the spot, not daring to look at the weeping woman. At last, he went over to her and, moved by her despair, knelt before her and placed his hand cautiously on her leg. The woman immediately flung her arms around his neck and dragged him onto the bed. He fell, and she pressed herself against him, started unbuttoning his jacket. Not thinking about what was happening to him, Kostya allowed himself to be led by instinct: with a sweep of his hand he opened her dressing gown and started kissing her, and she gripped his hair with her beringed fingers, guiding his head to where she wanted it. He didn't mind her leading him. Before he knew it, she had undressed him, and with hurried movements and trembling hands he helped her, undid her suspender belt, slipped off her petticoat. The open dressing gown exposed her small breasts, her smooth, soft skin, and the dark triangle between her legs.

Although she was brusque and possessive, very domineering, and expressed her lust with abandon, Kostya found her behaviour touching. There was something lost about her urge to possess him; her passion was fragile, as if at any second it might be extinguished as unexpectedly as it had been kindled.

For a moment, Kostya felt as if he were losing consciousness, while the unknown woman kept her eyes firmly closed, kissing every inch of his face and smiling through her tears.

Hold sacred all the riches of our homeland.

POSTER SLOGAN

For days after this encounter, my grandfather was stupefied. He walked around as if in a dream, astonished at the peculiar turn of events that had catapulted him not into the arms of a prostitute, but straight into his first love affair. He was torn between his days at the Naval School with its strict discipline and the nights of abandonment in the dimly lit apartment on Vasilievsky Island.

To his father, he pretended to be a model son; in the drinking sessions with his comrades, he played the ringleader with tremendous panache. But in his thoughts, Kostya was constantly in the dizzying proximity of the unknown woman, whose depths he began devotedly to explore.

'Ida.' This was the name his lips would form during class, or on board ship in the Gulf of Finland; he would repeat this name in his thoughts like an incantation as he lay in bed, sleepless, at night. He would cling to these three letters when the longing for her skin, for her deep, smoky voice, for her ambiguous smile, became too much and he didn't know how to quench his painful desire for her.

Some nights he could stand it no longer. He would jump out of bed, grab his coat, and run down the street like a man possessed to hammer breathlessly at her door, hoping she would open it and take him in like a hungry, homeless animal, feed him and care for him, give him warmth and protection.

And she did. Always. She never left him standing outside.

With a mischievous smile, she would open the door a crack, look at him, sometimes with curlers in her hair or an open book in her hand, then shake her head and say, 'Konstantin, what is it now? I wasn't expecting you until tomorrow evening.' She would say it in a tone of mild reproach, and at the same time he could sense how pleased she was that he didn't stick to their arrangements, that he was paying her a surprise visit. He could speak to Ida with his body; he didn't need words. From the taste of her skin, he could guess the measure of her sorrow; from the way she touched him, he could guess her fears; from her kisses, he could tell whether that night she would behave with particular abandon.

During the daily shooting practice, he had to screw his eyes tight shut so as not to blink, then open them again, close them, open them, until the images from the previous night had gone from his head and he could concentrate on the target again.

All his life, Kostya would remain in thrall to this incurable beauty — incurable because, to him, she radiated a sense of something endangered, something utterly unprotected, a beauty with the capacity to destroy you.

For the rest of his life, he would never stop seeking this beauty, and his ability to love would depend on the extent to which he found it again in his subsequent love interests. As if he could only experience desire when he felt this desire would destroy him. As if he needed to dive for hidden pearls, concealed in the deepest depths of the sea, and in doing so run the risk of drowning.

★

In her previous life, Ida was meant to become a pianist. She had studied with one of Rubinstein's star pupils. She came from a well-to-do St Petersburg family of Jewish intellectuals; her father was a doctor, and her mother had also aspired to a career as a concert pianist until severe depression rendered this impossible. Ida had spent half of her life in Paris, where her family had settled after the Revolution and the subsequent wave of anti-Semitism in Russia. In her early years, she was said to have had a nervous disposition, anaemia, a marked tendency towards excessive passion, and inspired fingers, destined for a world-class career. But she cut the umbilical cord of predestination with her own hands when she announced to her family that she had fallen hopelessly in love with an exiled violinist, who had a wife and two children in a little attic apartment in Paris, earned his money in dubious locales, and could scarcely keep his head above water. Despite pleas and threats from members of her family, Ida appointed herself the saviour of the violinist's battered soul; she, of course, considered him brilliant, and even converted to Christianity in the hope the violinist would want to marry her once he was legally divorced from his wife.

That, however, didn't happen.

Instead, he lived with her in a seedy room in a hotel that charged by the hour; he allowed her to cook for and spoil him, was also very happy to take the extra money Ida earned giving piano lessons, and never even dreamed of asking his wife for a divorce. One day, he announced to Ida that he was in trouble: he had run up a mountain of debts, and his only hope of escaping the debt-collectors was to flee to Russia. All attempts by Ida's family to stop their daughter failed; Ida returned with her martyr to St Petersburg, which was not even called St Petersburg any longer, and where nothing was as it had been before.

They moved into a communal apartment on the outskirts of the city. Ida taught piano and worked at surviving the post-war years. She provided her violinist with food, began to hate him, berated him, lamented her suffering, missed Paris and her family's affluence, reproached herself, and was ashamed of her miserable existence. The violinist would disappear for days at a time while Ida, caught up in her masochistic feelings of love and loathing, was being driven up the wall by worry, disgust, and socialism, which was profoundly abhorrent to her. She started punishing the most precious thing she owned for her unhappiness: she draped a cloth over her piano, the only valuable thing she had sent for from Paris. The violinist doubled his alcohol consumption and ran up more debts, with, among others, a Siberian butcher who controlled the black market. There was a fight. The violinist was given a kicking; he cracked his head against a wall, and crawled through the streets on all fours until he reached the hallway of the communal apartment, where he collapsed. He died of internal bleeding before a doctor could get there. Ida managed to procure this single room on Vasilievsky Island, formerly inhabited by a lady from Dnipropetrovsk who, as previously mentioned, earned her living with her sturdy body until one day someone reported her to the authorities and she was sent packing.

The only thing Ida took with her from her old life was the piano. She found herself a job as a ticket attendant at the theatre, applied twice more to leave the country and was rejected both times, upon which she cut all contact with the people from her old life, but did not try to make any new acquaintances, lived with her records and books, and drank her strong black tea.

She lived like that until one day Konstantin Jashi appeared at her door.

When Kostya's youth and willing body fell into her hands, Ida pounced on him as if famished: she lost herself, let herself go, forgot, and began to hope.

Even if Ida was now a woman who no longer had any romantic illusions, there was nothing she could do about the fact that, with Kostya at her side, she had started to hope again — unintentionally, against her will, entirely without wanting to. Because until then hopelessness had been the only constant in her life, and the gradual erosion of this constant frightened her; she believed that, for her, the renewed hope of a different life could be life threatening.

With each day that passed, Ida let another little piece of hopelessness drop away. With every word Kostya addressed to her, with every touch, she scratched the thick layer of desolation from her skin and allowed herself to be infected by his youth, his greed for her, his joy in her body, and in an unspoken future.

And Kostya, fearful and insecure, because he craved her nearness, her nocturnal enchantment, her secrets, stumbled after his desires at night only to punish himself for it the next day. He didn't tell his fellow students about his new love; he was embarrassed about it because he assumed Ida would not be seen as a suitable match for him. He reproached himself for the fact that he could never take her out for a meal, never go for a walk with her; that she existed for him only at night, and by day he tried to banish her from his thoughts, from his daily life, acting as if she didn't exist.

But Ida was good at hiding her feelings: it was something she had learned well in her years of struggling with life, or with what life had denied her. She had learned that words are not always promises, that music cannot save you, that your own abilities do not always lead to their predestined objective, that love is sometimes just camouflage for something much worse; she had learned to tame her dreams, had learned to paint over her disappointments with a dash of lipstick; and so Kostya knew nothing of how painful she found the waiting for those nights, the effort it cost her to keep pace with his pent-up longing; all the words she left unsaid, all the reproaches she spared him, the understanding his divided life required of her, how impossible it sometimes seemed to her to be part of his parallel world. And how moved she was by his desire to experience love through her; and how much, at the same time, it frightened her.

But Ida had always been a good teacher, and all the things that, years earlier, she had tried to show her students, on the black and white keys, she now taught Kostya, devoting her entire body and soul to the task. She taught him to prepare a nourishing winter soup from leftovers, taught him to iron his uniform immaculately, taught him to keep secrets, and to speak without words.

Holding each other close, they danced to every Vertinsky song in Ida's record collection: for every song, a different dance. Their dances were slow and fast, restrained and unbridled, risqué and accompanied by full-throated laughter, sad and oblivious to the world around them; they danced together and alone; they danced and danced.

She told him the stories behind each of her many rings, kissing the tips of his fingers as she did so; she laughed at him when he bored her with lectures about ships; she tickled him as he slept and woke him to show him the full moon, which was particularly yellow and sickly that night. She showed him photographs of her old life while he massaged her feet; she told him that her house plants were her true friends, and introduced them all to Kostya by name. She giggled like a schoolgirl when he took off her clothes, and ordered him to undress with the stern face of a headmistress.

They lent each other happiness. They lent each other the present, and gave each other memories for the future.

★

She stretched luxuriously, like a Persian cat, on the squeaky metal bed. Kostya was ironing his shirt; he had to be at the academy in less than an hour. Suddenly, as if stricken, Ida jumped up, rushed over to Kostya, flung her arms around him, and clung on.

'What's the matter?' he asked, laughing, already calculating in his head whether he had enough time to comfort her with another, brief bout of lovemaking. But Ida pulled away and gazed at him, wide-eyed.

'There's going to be a war,' she said quietly, backing off.

'You're not really afraid of the stupid fascists, are you, Ida? Come here, come here, you silly thing.'

'You should turn on the radio.'

'Just because the Germans are marching into Poland, you're afraid they'll come all the way here?' He laughed and hurried over to give her a kiss on the tip of her nose. 'They gave us a long talk at the Academy. When I come back tonight I'll tell you a bit about how cleverly the Generalissimus is dealing with the Germans. Apparently he held a secret meeting at the Politburo on the nineteenth of August. At the Academy they're saying he told them the Soviet Union would definitely reject the Franco-British alliance against Germany, and would extend its hand to the Germans. Because, they said, it's impossible to promote communism in Europe in peacetime, but if the Anglo-French declare war on the Germans both sides will quickly overextend themselves, and the Soviet Union can advance the cause of socialism in Europe undisturbed. I think that's an incredibly far-sighted attitude, don't you? ... Ida, are you even listening to me?'

'Even if they do start fraternising with the Germans, it doesn't mean the Germans will be happy to give up territories to the USSR, Kostya. And that's the whole point. Without this alliance with the Nazis, the Generalissimus doesn't stand a chance of getting his hands on those areas. Think about it: the Germans are constantly talking about the need for *lebensraum*.'

Ida fell silent and began to stare at a spot on the wall as if she could already see the future there in front of her.

'All right, listen. I'll tell you a secret. You've heard about this trade agreement, haven't you — this Molotov-Ribbentrop thing? The one that was all over the newspapers? Do you know what they told us at the Academy? Behind the trade agreement there's a secret protocol that's far more important than the actual agreement itself.' Kostya lowered his voice. 'Apparently, it talks about neutrality for the USSR in the event of a European war. There — is my Ida reassured now? The Generalissimus knows how to deal with the fascists. You mustn't doubt that!'

Suddenly, Ida began to laugh at the top of her voice. She doubled over and slapped her hands on her knees. Kostya stared at her in bewilderment.

She took a copy of *Pravda* out of her bag and held it under Kostya's nose.

'Isn't it hilarious, my angel, the world we live in? The biggest newspaper in the country calls this agreement, and I quote, "an instrument of peace". Yet what it really is is two madmen squaring up to each other and misusing the world to benefit themselves and their ideologies; two madmen who will stop at nothing. Isn't that hysterical, Kostya? Two madmen are never going to allow one to become greater than the other.'

'What madmen? Ida, calm down! Ida, look at me. I'm here, I'm with you, nothing's going to happen to you. I won't let anything happen to you.'

'The only question is, for how long,' murmured Ida, going back to the bed.

'How long what? What do you mean?'

'Go on, get dressed. I don't want you to be late.'

★

The news of Christine's disfigurement, which Stasia had kept from Kostya for almost two years, reached him along with the news that war had indeed broken out in Europe. On the same day that the whole of Leningrad started talking about the German invasion of Poland, Kostya finally learned the real reason Stasia had asked him not to come to Tbilisi these past two summers, but to spend his holidays in Russia. In her letter, Stasia recounted Christine's tragedy in detail — without naming names, of course, as post office workers might read the letter.

She described the terrible deed, Christine's time in intensive care, her deep depression, her silence. She told him about Ramas' funeral, which had taken place anonymously in order to avoid a scandal, and about the sale of his paintings. She ended with news of the death of her stepmother, Lara; Christine's tragedy had caused her to have a stroke.

Kostya came to Ida's apartment in the middle of the night, lay down on the bed, and wept for more than three hours without stopping.

Ida asked no questions: she let him grieve, because she knew about grief; for many years it had been her most dependable companion. Ida knew that the world — both her own and, above all, the fragile world of all-encompassing intimacy she shared with Kostya — was doomed, but she faced this doom with her eyes wide open, awaited it, stoic, erect, standing to attention, like a steadfast tin soldier.

War came to Kostya long before the German invasion of the Soviet Union. The horrendous news of his aunt's misfortune unleashed a struggle within him and presented him with the almost impossible task of reconciling his feelings, his duty, and his future.

He tried to imagine Christine's corroded face, and saw before him Ida's olive skin, the blackness of her eyes. He felt anger towards his mother, who had kept him in the dark, had kept him far away from Christine and her sorrow, and he tried to fill in for himself the gaps that Stasia's truth had ripped open. Because in her letter Stasia had not told him who, other than Ramas and Christine, was involved in this jealous drama. In his mind, Kostya laboriously went through all the renowned communists in his homeland who had been guests at Christine's house. He tried to imagine what man had possessed such power that Ramas hadn't dared to rebel against him; someone from whom Ramas had believed he could only protect his wife by inflicting this cruel disfigurement upon her.

Kostya's deliberations left him in no doubt, but even in his thoughts he didn't dare say the name of the Little Big Man, who the previous year had become the head of the entire Soviet NKVD.

There were many things Stasia had not told him.

She had not told her son that, after the tragic event, his adored aunt was paid a generous pension as the widow of a hero of the Soviet Union, which Ramas was posthumously declared to have been. She had also not written about the scented roses Christine's lover had sent her every week in hospital, and then later at home, all of which she had thrown away. She had not written that the Little Big Man never again visited the first lady of his harem after her face was burned away, for fear he would be too revolted by her devastated beauty.

★

When Kitty called her brother from the post office in the little town, she noticed that he seemed irritable and distracted, inattentive and demanding.

'Giorgi, my good friend and roommate, has been granted leave and he's heading for Georgia. I've given him a small parcel for Christine. There are all sorts of things in it that she really likes. I want the parcel to get there quickly, and he's offered to make a little detour and change trains near you. He's not going as far as Tbilisi, but you can meet him tomorrow and send the parcel on to Tbilisi. It won't take as long then.'

Kitty was annoyed that he had paid so little attention to what she had been saying, and hadn't asked after either herself or Andro. He didn't even seem surprised that she and Andro had been living in the countryside for months, banished to her grandfather's house. That they had had to change schools, and now lived far away from Stasia and Christine.

'Incidentally, I'm sorry Lara died so suddenly. Is Grandfather bearing up?' was the only thing he wanted to know.

'He's trying,' she answered, reluctantly. She promised to take receipt of the parcel and send it on, although she secretly wished it were a parcel for her, and that she didn't have to live with the feeling that her big brother had forgotten her.

★

That evening, she walked to the station on her own. An unprepossessing lad in glasses and a sailor's uniform stood waiting in the little station hall, which was almost completely empty. He introduced himself as Giorgi Alania; he was passing through on his way to Abkhazia to visit his mother; she wasn't well, which was why he'd asked to go on leave. He had travelled via Vladikavkaz, had got off here to hand over the parcel, and would take the night train for the Black Sea coast later on.

'Isn't it very inconvenient for you to make such a detour on account of this silly parcel?' asked Kitty, still annoyed with her cold, domineering brother.

'Oh, I don't mind. Your brother's really very important to me. Believe me, I would do a great deal for him.'

Kitty marvelled as to how her narcissistic brother had managed this.

The lad asked her whether she would like to have a coffee or tea with him; he still had a while to wait for his train, and he'd be very glad of the company. But Kitty politely declined; she had homework to do.

He seemed disappointed by her refusal, but he remained courteous and immediately handed over the parcel. She wished him all the best for his onward journey, and turned to go. Outside on the street, though, with his disappointed face still before her eyes, she stopped, turned round, and went back into the station.

He was standing in the middle of the empty hall with his little suitcase, waiting for something: it had to be more than just a train. When he saw her coming, he smiled gratefully at her, and she suggested they go for a little walk, perhaps sit in a park; the station café had already closed, and in any case the station concourse wasn't very inviting. He agreed thankfully, and beamed at her as if she had just accepted his proposal of marriage.

They went out onto the street, and Kitty led him to the little park nearby where she so often met Andro. Giorgi didn't seem to be all that used to feminine company, and kept thanking Kitty for her time.

They exchanged some small talk. When he started speaking about Kostya she hedged and changed the subject. They chatted about politics, in which Kitty had no interest, about mothers, and about school, where he had apparently done well; they even laughed about this and that, and later Kitty accompanied the lad to his platform and waited until he had boarded his train. She gave him a hug, feeling as she did so that he was trembling slightly. It couldn't possibly have been from the cold. She waved to him from the platform, and he stuck his head out of the window and waved to her for a long time as darkness settled over them, until it swallowed him completely.

★

In the first week of September, the Wehrmacht advanced eastwards as far as Warsaw. On 17 September, the Red Army entered Poland with 620,000 men. On 22 September, the Germans and the Russians organised a joint military parade in Brest-Litovsk, and on 28 September, Ribbentrop and Molotov signed a further treaty on 'friendship, cooperation and demarcation'. In November, the USSR then expanded to include regions in western Ukraine and Belarus — Polish territory since 1920.

The Kremlin knew it couldn't turn its new subjects into model Soviet citizens overnight with laws and dictates alone. Nonetheless, in the new territories they had to fast-forward through the years of 're-education'. Here, too, ethnic conflicts were to be intensified — the strategy of playing different ethnicities off against each other had, after all, proved effective in so many other regions. The invasion of Poland was presented as the liberation of the Belarusian and Ukrainian populations. The Soviet press praised the 'reunification' of these peoples with the Soviet Union, great friend to and helper of all oppressed nations. The tactics soon had the desired effect. In Novgorod and Łuck, Ukrainian farmers attacked Polish officers; in Pruzhany, Belarusian farmers stoned another officer; the NKVD looked on approvingly. However, when the resistance went too far, they resorted to more direct methods: both commanders and partisans who defied orders were summarily shot without trial.

By the end of September, more than 250,000 Polish soldiers had been imprisoned. Transit camps were set up for them because some of the prisoners were to be packed off to the Germans. Almost 43,000, all of them Jews, were handed over to the Germans in November.

Estonia, Lithuania, and Latvia were coerced into providing the USSR with military assistance. With around 60,000 Red Army soldiers stationed in the Baltics, the countries had no choice but to prepare for annexation, which took place in the summer of 1940. That same year, the USSR expanded to include the Socialist Republic of Moldova. Northeastern Romania was occupied, Ukraine extended. The Latvian and Estonian presidents were arrested; one died in prison, the other in a psychiatric institution. Only the Lithuanian president managed to escape. Border fortifications were hastily erected between German and Soviet territories, and all private radios were confiscated: only Party-approved information was to reach the population in the border areas.

★

In March 1940, the Generalissimus received a letter from the Little Big Man in which the latter proposed that the 25,000 Polish officers, officials, landowners, police, spies, constables, and prison guards currently under arrest should be shot then and there. This request was justified as follows: they were 'all sworn enemies of Soviet authority full of hatred for the Soviet system'. The people in question were 14,700 state officials from the camps and 11,000 spies and counter-revolutionaries from the prisons.

The Generalissimus gave his approval the very same day, and forced another five Politburo members to put their signatures to the document. A *troika*, made up of close allies of the Little Big Man, was tasked with implementing it, and set to work at the beginning of April. First, rumours were disseminated in the camps and prisons that the prisoners would soon be released; their food rations were increased, they were vaccinated against typhus, and then they were fetched. They were taken by train to Kalinin, to Kharkov, and to the forest of Katyn near Smolensk. A number of NKVD men arrived from the capital especially for the operation with pistols in their suitcases. In the basement of the prison in Kalinin, two men held each prisoner still while a third shot him in the head. A maximum of two minutes was allocated for each execution. In Kharkov prison, they burned all the inmates alive. Afterwards, the bodies were taken away in trucks and buried in mass graves in the surrounding forests.

Regional prison directors and public prosecutors were present during the operation, as was Vasili Blokhin, the Lubyanka commandant who had already proved his loyalty on numerous occasions and was one of the people the Generalissimus trusted with special tasks. A man who liked to wear an apron, gloves, and rubber boots at executions, and who is said personally to have sent more than 15,000 people to their deaths in the course of his 'career'. It was also Blokhin who got his employees and subordinates to sign a document stating that 'educational measures' should be used against those condemned to death to prevent the name of the Generalissimus from passing their lips. 'Educational measures' signified blows to the head.

At the Little Big Man's suggestion, once the operation had successfully been completed, Blokhin's men were given an extra month's pay. Just six years later, Roman Rudenko, the deputy public prosecutor from Ukraine who had been summoned to Kharkov to observe the execution of the operation and ensure everything went according to plan, was one of the Soviet Union's chief prosecutors at the Nuremberg trials. Throughout those trials he accused the fascists of being responsible for this indiscriminate orgy of killing.

Blokhin himself was showered with medals and later made a general. He served the machinery of killing with loyalty and devotion for almost thirty-six years before being forced into retirement in 1953. He was buried in Moscow's Donskoi Cemetery, where many of his victims had been burned and bucketfuls of their ashes poured into anonymous graves.

> I prayed that my son would be a good student
> and would grow up to be an independent man!
>
> EKATERINE DZHUGASHVILI, THE GENERALISSIMUS' MOTHER

Andro had graduated from the local school with average grades. With the future of the country so uncertain, he was advised to learn a proper trade, and was apprenticed to an Armenian carpenter. His carvings were already laying siege to every room in the house. The young journeyman carpenter pursued his apprenticeship with the same disciplined indifference as his schoolwork, and, slowly, began to understand that his mother wasn't coming back.

Andro hadn't wanted to see the truth; he had been too afraid. He dreamed of his mother incessantly. He searched for her in his sleep; in his dreams, she seemed relaxed and free, but when he enquired as to her whereabouts, she only gave him a loving smile. When he woke, he was always overwhelmed with hysterical excitement and would spend long minutes in the bathroom trying to calm down. Yes: he was afraid of the moment when any further hope would prove futile. Sometimes, without warning, a fit of fury would seize him and he would start smashing his wooden figures, because something about their naivety, their sweetness, made him incandescent with rage. He would take his tools and batter their heads and limbs to pieces, gouge out their eyes. The only things that remained unchanged were Kitty and his absolute trust in her. He knew that however angry, however sad, however desperate he might feel, she would make him laugh, play her games with him, clasp him in her strong arms so tightly he couldn't breathe. Kitty gave him the confidence that better times were coming soon, that they would leave this place and start a new, different life. She was so full of life, so full of energy, and he relied on her sharing this energy with him. Above all, she was so fearless. Things she was forbidden to do, she did anyway. Things she was scolded for, she practised with even greater conviction, and this obstinacy fascinated him. Kitty gave him the impetus he needed to outwit his dismal reality.

They were ridiculous games, utterly pointless and childish, but he went along with them all: if she decided to hide from him all day long until he found her, or they had to rescue three homeless kittens from a ditch, or the game was a race, or to see who could gobble their bread and jam the fastest — Andro went along with it because they were the only moments of fun and freedom in their daily life, between Christine's recuperation and the chocolate-maker's slow decline. Between the hot Tbilisi summers and the cold winters in the little town.

Sadness lay over them both, and the moody petulance of puberty was already apparent. Their love became more than platonic. Despite this, they remained bound to each other: to each other, and their childhood.

And while the German army was marching into the Netherlands and on to Belgium and Luxembourg, and my grandfather was graduating from the Naval Academy with a gold medal, and Giorgi Alania was preparing for his shipbuilding exams, Andro was staring at his future with empty eyes. It held so little that he could look forward to.

★

On that mild June day when Italy joined the war on the German side, four days before the 18th Army of the Wehrmacht took Paris, Christine started to speak again, and Ida came to look for my grandfather in his room at the boarding house for the first time — the first and last time she saw him outside her little plant-filled apartment.

She pretended to be a relative of Comrade Jashi, ascended to the second floor of the boarding house, and knocked on Kostya and Giorgi's door. My grandfather was just getting ready for the graduation parade in honour of the Soviet Navy, and when he flung open the door and found himself face to face with his lover, he froze.

'What are you doing here?' stammered Kostya, quickly pulling her into his room.

'I had to see you. I had to see you just once by daylight. Your skin, your eyes, your lips, without that wretched bedside light, the gloom. Because I want to remember you the way you are now: bright.'

'What are you talking about?'

'I'm leaving. And I want to leave before you. I don't want to be left. Let me have that pleasure. Let me leave you, Konstantin.'

'I don't understand you.'

'We have to stop this. You'll soon be going to join the fleet, and I won't be able to manage without you. I'm already far too dependent on the hours you find for me, and they're getting fewer and farther between, shorter and shorter. I won't manage, Konstantin.'

'Yes, they've given me a special award, I'll probably even —' Kostya broke off, only now understanding what Ida had said.

'You're too good for war.'

'But we're not at war — and if it comes to that, I'm more than ready, believe me. I'll be able to sink ships like little stones! *Pow, pow, pow!*'

'You're happy because your ignorance protects you from yourself and from what lies ahead of you, and from missing me, but it will come, this realisation; it usually comes at a very inopportune time, my dear Konstantin, and I don't want it to tear you apart, I don't want it to change you; you have to promise me that, all right? All right? Will you do that?'

'Ida, what are you talking about? I'm not going anywhere; I'm here, and even if I do go to sea, I'll come back again. Listen, my parents —'

'I can't — forgive me, and grant me this prerogative. Please.'

'The prerogative to do what? You're not going anywhere. You've fallen prey to gloomy thoughts again. You should distract yourself more, get out of the apartment more often.'

'And now I want you to sleep with me.'

'What?'

'Let's go to bed.'

'But it's not night-time, and besides —'

Ida started to laugh. She seldom laughed, but when she did her whole body shook. She wiped tears from her eyes, bent double, slapped her knees and thighs with her hands. Kostya watched her; he couldn't help admitting to himself how much he admired her, how desirable she was. He felt both fear and excitement rise up in his body. He went to her, put his hand over her mouth; she bit it gently, which aroused him even more; he pressed harder, still hesitant because of her presence in this, his world, where she did not belong. He put his arms around her, lifted her slightly off the ground; she defended herself, still laughing; he pushed her against the wall, grew bolder, more impatient, she should stop laughing, he didn't like the thought that she might even be laughing at him. He narrowed his eyes and looked at her; her eyes were so dark that he assumed she must see everything around her through a kind of black filter. He thrust his forefinger between her teeth. She bit down again. Suddenly she fell abruptly silent, as if a terrible thought had cut off her laughter for ever; she grabbed his thick hair, pulled his head towards her, and, for a moment, breathed calmly and evenly, as if inhaling his scent. He kissed her.

It was so easy, as soon as she was near him, to forget that anything else existed. It was so easy, as soon as she touched him, to shake off all thoughts of the outside world. In moments like these, he was sure he had absolutely no need of it. The whole Soviet fleet, the parades, his roaring fellow students, his impressive achievements, his plans for the future, were so effortlessly swept aside by her mere presence, so effortlessly replaced. As if the world without Ida were just an illusion.

He pushed up her calf-length skirt. Pressed even harder against her warm, sinewy body. They were almost the same height; he looked her right in the eyes, which alarmed him a little because they seemed so feverish, even darker than usual. He tried to open the buttons on her grey blouse with his teeth, and, when he didn't succeed, he bit two of them off. The familiar smile spread across her face. As if she understood both his weaknesses and her strength; as if they were mutually dependent. She whispered something, her lips formed words, but he couldn't hear them any more; he was intoxicated by her smell, by her dangerous proximity, by the possibility that someone might catch them. Perhaps he even longed for it; perhaps he wanted someone to come across the two of them here, frozen in a tableau that left no room for interpretation, frozen in their clandestine love. So that he would finally be able to take a deep breath and shout at the top of his voice: *Yes, this is her, the woman I carry with me in every thought, every fibre of my body, who is so beautiful it pains me, because she is unsaveable, because I know I can't save her, not from herself and not from the world, either. The woman who taught me to forget, and to feel, with hands and eyes and the hollows of the knees and the ankles and the tip of the nose and the earlobes. This is how I want it — this is exactly how I want it!*

Perhaps that's exactly what Kostya wanted. Perhaps.

She kissed his neck and held his head firmly; the pressure grew firmer and firmer, his ears were closed, he could hear nothing, she was sealing him off from something, from what was to come, perhaps, as if she were his oracle, his portent, his Cassandra, condemned to know the future without a single person to believe her.

Kostya crooked her leg and she adjusted to him, made herself small and round, made it easy for him to love her, even here, even now, pressed up against this cold wall. She could not do otherwise; perhaps there was nothing she could do but follow her destiny, and her destiny was simply to be a fateful, unique, unrepeatable experience for him. But perhaps, too, she knew very well that this man, this moment, this sad, almost furious proximity was the last happiness to which she was entitled, and she seized it with animal strength.

I don't know, Brilka, and I'll never know for sure. But what does that matter?

*

Gasping, he buried his face in her neck. He felt her hand gripping his head, felt something brutal, terrible in her grasp; it frightened him, but his lust enabled him to contain his fear, to not think about it. Suddenly his heart leapt: there was a knock at the door. Kostya froze, forgetting even to breathe. Ida did not let go.

'Yes?' he called, carefully clearing his throat in an effort to conceal the excitement in his voice.

'Hey, Krasavchik, hurry up, we have to go — the boys are already waiting downstairs!'

'I'm coming!' Kostya answered, with considerable effort.

'No, stay here, please stay with me!' Ida begged him.

'I can't — I have to go. It's our graduation parade and we've been practising for it for weeks. I ... I'll come to you tonight. I'll come as soon as the parade is over, and we'll talk about everything.'

'Don't leave me behind like this, please don't — no, don't stop!' Ida clung to his shoulders, pressed her head against his chin, caressed him with her skin. But he pulled away from her, intoxicated, swaying, his desire still unsatisfied. He staggered to the bed and started hastily putting on his shirt.

Slowly Ida pushed down her petticoat, then her skirt, and turned her back to him. She laid her face against the wall, pressing her forehead into it as if trying to break through it, as if she knew of a way out, a secret way through the wall into another world.

'I really do have to go. My father will be there, too, and ... I'll come tonight, Ida. I'll come, and I'll stay as long as you want, all right? And we'll talk about everything you want to talk about. You can tell me everything that's troubling you.'

For a while she didn't move, and he didn't know what was going on; whether she was crying, or cursing him, if she were wishing herself invisible, if she regretted coming. Then she turned and looked at him. She was smiling. Her hair was dishevelled; her bun had come loose and a few long, dark strands hung in her face, and once again Kostya was on the point of tearing off his uniform and rushing to her, taking her in his arms, and locking the door — but her smile reassured him: things weren't so bad, and, after all, he would come to her soon.

'It's all right, Konstantin, my beautiful, beautiful boy. Look after yourself.'

'Hey, I'm not a boy any more, remember that!' He gave her a hasty kiss on the lips and dashed from the room.

★

During the military parade, Kostya was overcome by excruciating fear. He saw his father standing on the pavement, waving to him, but all of a sudden this sight no longer meant anything to him. He walked in step with the other sailors, shouting the slogans they had learned by heart, and tried to adopt a reverent expression as the cannons were fired into the Gulf of Finland. But in his breast all he felt was a fear that seemed to clench all his internal organs.

As soon as the parade was over, he ran. He ran until he could run no more, he stopped and sat down in the middle of the street, caught his breath, ran on, flew up the steps, stopped outside her apartment, gasped for air, and hammered on the door — but no one opened.

He went back downstairs, out onto the street, and looked up at the third floor, but no lights were on.

He went up again, knocked and knocked, screamed, shouted for her.

For three days and nights he returned again and again, until finally a neighbour told him that the lady had gone away, he had seen her leave the house with two suitcases but didn't know where she had gone; she hadn't been a very talkative neighbour.

Later, Brilka, I learned that Ida hadn't gone anywhere; that she had slipped her neighbour a few roubles, asked him to tell a white lie, and that all those days and nights she was standing behind her locked door, holding her mouth shut to prevent her voice and her longing from betraying her, while my grandfather hammered on the door and called her name, no longer able to make sense of the world around him.

★

The National Socialists owed their swift and stupendous success at the start of the Second World War in part to the friendly neutrality of the USSR. The Generalissimus supported Hitler not only with the Molotov–Ribbentrop Pact; he also facilitated German import and export shipments across Soviet territory.

So the occupation of Bessarabia and Bukovina in northeastern Romania by the Reds in 1940 came as a surprise to the National Socialists. To stop the Generalissimus getting the idea that he could advance any further, Hitler stationed Wehrmacht troops in Romania as well. In July, at a meeting of the High Command at the Berghof — Hitler's little piece of paradise — a certain unease was apparent as soon as the discussion turned to the Soviet Union. According to General Halder's notes, Hitler spoke in favour of launching 'Operation Draft East' earlier than planned. In November, Molotov travelled to Berlin again, but this time the negotiations were unsuccessful: no further agreement was possible on territorial division. Hitler began to find the Generalissimus' demands too outrageous: he had laid claim to Finland, Bulgaria, Turkey, and numerous other territories from the southern Caucasus to the Persian Gulf. On 18 December 1940, Hitler authorised the plan for 'Operation Barbarossa', and set 15 May 1941 as the date for its commencement. By the spring of 1941, there were only five neutral countries left in Europe: Sweden, Switzerland, Portugal, Spain, and Turkey.

The war in the Balkans forced Hitler to postpone Barbarossa by a few weeks. The Soviet foreign intelligence service informed the Generalissimus of Hitler's plans, but our Great Leader deemed them an intrigue, an invention of the British secret service. He laughed at the warnings, saying that the people making such claims had 'brains as small as my thumb'.

The Generalissimus could not conceive of the possibility of a war with Hitler's Germany. The Soviet Union had adhered strictly to the trade agreement: in the first two years of the war, it had supplied Germany with tons of wheat, oil, and steel. At this point in time, there were almost five million people in the Red Army. Its equipment was inferior to the Germans', not to mention its organisation: the Generalissimus had had almost all the renowned army generals and officers arrested or shot some years earlier. But Hitler and his entourage, emboldened by the recent successes of the Blitzkrieg, were planning the swift subjugation of the Soviet Union. What Hitler didn't know was that the terror and misery the Wehrmacht planned to bring with its invasion were already part of everyday life in the USSR. That the Soviet horror of recent years had prepared the people all too well for the horror Hitler planned to inflict on their country.

> The right to sorrow is a privilege.
>
> DMITRI SHOSTAKOVICH

Kostya Jashi was now a junior lieutenant in the Soviet Navy. After staring in despair at the locked door of Ida's apartment for the last time, he had requested an urgent transfer out of the city. His application was approved, and in April he was transferred to Crimea, to a training ship in Sevastopol.

On 22 June 1941, three Wehrmacht army groups crossed the Soviet border: Army Group North, heading for the Baltic states and Leningrad; Army Group Centre, heading for Smolensk and Moscow; and Army Group South, heading for Kiev. One of the biggest invasions in military history had begun. From the Baltic Sea to the Carpathians, the Generalissimus' huge empire was being attacked from all points of the compass by more than three million German soldiers. Hitler 'thawed' after the order was given, 'all tiredness gone', noted Goebbels, in a diary entry following the invasion of the Soviet Union. The attack rendered all prior military agreements, laws, and rules invalid.

The earth began to turn faster.

Despite the warnings, the Generalissimus continued to cling to his belief that the mobilisation of German troops at the borders was an exaggeration by the secret services. He retreated to his dacha in Kuntsevo, and addressed the people only eleven days later in a calamitous radio broadcast in which he declared the 'Great Patriotic War'.

Kostya could not have foreseen when he was transferred that the German invasion would come as a complete surprise to the western parts of the Russian fleet stationed in Sevastopol, and that he would be catapulted into the epicentre of the war much faster than he would have liked. The sailors' training manoeuvres were replaced alarmingly quickly by actual warfare, and Kostya Jashi was caught up in the three-day raid on Constanța.

In early July, Army Group North began to advance on the Baltic States, and the Soviet Baltic Fleet was forced to fall back to Kronstadt. Army Group

Centre took Smolensk on 16 July. Minsk fell into German hands in the first few weeks of the invasion. Novgorod succumbed on 16 August, and on 8 September the Germans reached Lake Ladoga, encircling Leningrad.

One week after war broke out, the Red Lieutenant Simon Jashi was sent to the front in Minsk.

The Wehrmacht's success was colossal. The Red Army's general staff — hesitant, caught between fear of the Kremlin, still crippled by indecision, and the necessity of taking swift action — remained passive. The paralysis in the Kremlin affected the whole country. It resulted in the loss of countless lives during the first months of the war. In July 1941, Goebbels wrote triumphantly in his diary: 'There can no longer be any doubt that sooner or later the Kremlin will fall.'

Having obtained excellent marks in his shipbuilding diploma, Giorgi Alania was posted to the Amur shipyard on the Sea of Japan. Alania hesitated; he didn't want to go to the other side of the world, to be separated from his best friend. He hoped he wouldn't have to stay there more than one or two years. In hindsight, the Sea of Japan proved to be his salvation, as the posting to Amur meant he escaped the war; because he worked in heavy industry, he was spared the front.

When the Germans invaded the Baltic States and Ukraine, no one thought the Bolsheviks would come back. The Germans were celebrated as liberators. When Wehrmacht soldiers entered Ukrainian villages with tanks and trucks, farmers stood in the streets holding out bread and salt as a sign of hospitality.

The Soviet NKVD, by contrast, had done a thorough job in a very short time. Prisoners had been executed in the jails; inmates in psychiatric hospitals had been killed. Later, villages and towns would be burned — nothing was to fall into German hands.

Reports in the Soviet press about Nazi crimes, about Jews being rounded up and taken off to some place from which no one had ever returned, were dismissed as lies and Soviet propaganda. Consequently, many Jews decided not to flee. For years, they had been fed lies and invented realities, but this one, out of the mouth of the oppressor, was more blatant than any lie so far: that in the Caucasus and Ukraine ethnic minorities were being recruited by the Wehrmacht to serve as 'volunteers'.

In the panic that prevailed in the first months of the war, many Party functionaries, directors, and commissars fled their posts. People believed they had been abandoned, and took liberties they would never otherwise have dared to claim: they refused to work, looted, even threatened their superiors. The

Bolsheviks' unassailable status was called into question.

In August of that year, the Generalissimus issued order number 270, according to which any soldier who allowed himself to be taken as a prisoner of war was to be considered a traitor. Red Army soldiers had only two options: to let themselves be shot by the Germans, or be shot later by their own people.

★

The day Kostya Jashi took up his rifle to shoot at people for the first time, his little sister graduated from her all-girls' school and ran into the arms of Andro, who still spent his time compulsively carving wooden angels and had shaved off all his curls.

That same night, my great-great-grandfather died peacefully in his bed after going through the secret recipes in his black notebook, thinking himself back in the chocolate factory, which had ceased to exist three years earlier, and was now a government canteen serving mashed potatoes and cheap meatballs. He died believing himself back in the sweetness of his past life, surrounded by the most tempting aromas in the world, full of plans for the future of his hometown, the putative Nice of the Caucasus, in the company of his four daughters, each one lovely and full of the brightest hopes, undimmed by the cheerlessness of socialism. He had taken his leave of the present gradually, over time, until it grew thin and transparent and finally tore. Old, feeble, frail, with weak kidneys, no social standing, and no longer surrounded by the dark fragrance of grandeur, heavy sorrow had formed a crust around the chocolate-maker — impenetrable, impossible to soften. His decline was hard for his family to bear. And although Lida and Kitty did their best to keep from the old man the terrible news of what was happening in the world, they could not rid him of his sorrow. Again and again he asked after Christine, who hadn't dared to return to the house of her birth since her disfigurement. He never spoke of what had happened, nor of Ramas: as if Christine had never married, as if no one had done to Christine the things that had been done to her. To him, she remained the young girl for whom the gates of life were open, with everything before her; and Lida and the others had to play along, had to declare the past the present and learn to hide their own sorrow, their own worries, from him.

Beeswax candles, which Lida kept hidden in her room, were lit. Lida sat at her dying father's bedside and prayed for hours on end. At daybreak, Andro was dispatched to the post office to send a telegram to Tbilisi.

Later, as they sat by the window looking down on the sleeping street,

Andro asked Kitty if she wanted to be his wife and go with him to Vienna. 'To our very own, private Vienna,' he added.

★

Dressed all in black, supported by Stasia, her face hidden by a veil she had cleverly woven into her hair, Christine took a seat at the window of the compartment and leaned her head against the glass. The station was crowded; people were running around like industrious ants. The little boy selling newspapers was shouting at the top of his voice: 'War! We're at war! Fascists attack Soviet Union! Generalissimus declares Great Patriotic War!'

Christine tried not to listen to his words. But Stasia, who was putting her suitcase on the rack, turned sharply and stuck her head out through the narrow gap in the window, waved the boy over, tossed a few kopeks into his hand, and took the paper. Absorbed by the news, she gasped as if she were having an asthma attack and sank weakly into her seat.

'Kostya!' was all she said, as if she had seen him standing in front of her. She gripped her veiled sister's wrist. 'Simon has taken my only son and he won't stop him going to war. He'll even be proud of him. Oh my God, Kostya, my only Kostya!'

'We don't know anything yet. We'll contact Simon and Kostya first thing tomorrow morning. Try to calm yourself.'

Christine looked out of the window and watched the green, hilly countryside roll by. At daybreak, the sisters reached the town where they were born, which had become anything but the Nice of the Caucasus. By now, news of the war had reached here, too; people were wandering the streets, older men were standing on street corners with their pipes, recalling the horrors of the last war, and the women, who had set out little tables in front of their houses, were gathered around big wireless sets with pots of coffee, drinking and shaking their heads. Only the children still carried on as normal, playing ball and hide-and-seek, running races, and making a deafening racket.

Lida was sitting silently beside her father's coffin, a sexless creature in a black cotton dress and black headscarf. Kitty and Andro were hovering at the bottom of the stairs. When they spotted Christine with her masked face they both started crying in unison, and pretended they were crying for their grandfather, who in his last few years had taken hardly any interest in their lives, or indeed in anybody's, including his own.

The mirrors were taken down and all available icons positioned around the coffin. Lida had even summoned a priest to the house, in civilian clothes, of course. Meri arrived from Kutaisi, with a discontented expression that seemed to be stuck on her face, as if she held her sisters personally responsible for her unhappiness. Chairs were set up around the coffin; the women sat, while the men stood in the corridor, elbowing one another, to receive the mourners. The lights remained on for three days and nights; all the doors were opened; food from the funeral feast was given to the poor, the deceased's belongings given away.

Kitty and Andro were constantly being sent off somewhere, to fetch bread or wine; no one had time to notice Kitty's sparkling eyes, the restlessness in Andro's knees, or how they seemed always to be casually touching.

'Yes, all right. We'll get married, then,' Kitty had said to Andro, the day her brother aimed his gun at another man for the first time, the day her grandfather died. And as they kept vigil beside the body they whispered constantly about their future, because their love, unlike Kostya's, couldn't do without words.

Christine, in her veil, kept calling the two of them over to her and patting them like little children.

'Don't be afraid, it'll all be all right again,' she kept saying. Yet it was she who was afraid. Afraid of the infinite loneliness that imprisoned her; of the darkness she had not yet found her way out of; of the moment when Stasia would return to her old life and would have to leave her behind, alone with her ghosts. Afraid of the war, but above all of not knowing how she was to go on living, with half a face and a heart that belonged to a suicide.

★

On 5 July, the chocolate-maker was buried between his Russian and Georgian wives, and the mourners sat down around the big wooden table to drink coffee and discuss the future of the Jashi family.

'I have to go and get Kostya back,' said Stasia suddenly, lighting a cigarette.

'Calm down, Anastasia. God will look after him, he's a brave boy,' whispered Lida.

'Shut up!' cried Christine, helping herself to the schnapps that someone had left on the kitchen table.

And before Lida could cross herself and ask God to forgive her sister's insolence, Kitty said, 'We're getting married.'

She looked proudly at Andro, who sat silently with his head bowed, staring at the floor.

'Excuse me?' laughed Christine.

'We want to get married and then go away,' Kitty repeated.

Lida finally crossed herself, and Meri snorted contemptuously, as if this announcement were a personal affront.

'Have you taken leave of your senses?' asked Stasia eventually, still quite composed.

'I know I should have spoken to you, but when you were here there was never any time ...' Andro began slowly.

'Holy Mary ...' whispered Lida.

'My mother's dead, isn't she?' asked Andro suddenly. He received no reply, only evasive looks. Lida crossed herself again.

'There's a war on. You don't get married in wartime,' said Stasia.

'Or that's exactly when you do,' answered Andro.

'I don't know what to say to you both. It's your life. Either way, this is the worst possible moment for such childish nonsense,' said Stasia, and left the room.

She didn't come back until the following evening. Lida was all for sending out a search party, but Christine stopped her. She guessed that Stasia had borrowed a Kabardin and ridden out to the cave city. Probably astride.

★

As the Wehrmacht was crossing the Don, Lida left for a convent in Racha, where she was to stay for the rest of the war. The apartment was locked up, and Christine, Stasia, Kitty, and Andro took the train back to the capital together.

After arriving in Tbilisi they all went to live at Christine's villa, which felt shabby and empty behind its ostentatious façade, as everything rare and valuable had disappeared over the last few years or been sold on the black market. Telegrams were sent to Leningrad; no answer came. In Tbilisi there was panic; rumours were circulating that the fascists were planning a secret operation in the Caucasus. People said Hitler had declared the Caucasus, and Caspian oil in particular, his top priority.

Daily life in the city became quieter, more cautious, more hesitant, more gloomy — but at least it went on. Food production companies and factories were working flat out. The *kolkhozes* had to double their production. September brought the first news of the Leningrad blockade. Shortly afterwards, Stasia received a letter from her husband (oh yes, Brilka, marriages can last much longer than love) in which he informed her that Kostya was well, had fought heroically in the raid on Constanta, and was now serving in the Baltic Fleet: the defence of Leningrad was at stake. She wasn't to worry; they had corresponded, and Kostya had everything he needed. Simon himself was currently in Moscow, leading a division of the 2nd Rifle Corps and awaiting redeployment.

*

As Stasia paced about her room, appalled, puffing on her cigarettes, cursing, and trying to fight back tears of outrage, Andro walked with Kitty in the Botanical Garden. With her, he sought out secret, empty paths, and climbed up the steep crags. When it grew dark, they sat down right beside the waterfall, and when Kitty asked him if it weren't time to go — the garden would be closing soon — he replied that they could stay there overnight. He had taken care of everything, and had told everyone at home something about a public meeting, so no one would expect them back. He spread out a blanket, took some bread and cheese from his bag, then a bottle of wine, and looked at her, eyes twinkling.

I'm sure they listened to the little waterfall I used to love jumping under as a child, and I'm sure they marvelled at the size of the pale September moon. I'm sure they were intoxicated by their return to the big city, but intoxicated above all by each other and their physical attraction, which they now permitted themselves to acknowledge openly and experience for the first time. And I'm sure Kitty's back must have hurt on the rocky ground beside the waterfall, but I'm sure she didn't care because she was kissing her Andro as she had never kissed him before, and allowing herself to be undressed, touched, tasted, and smelled, allowing her body to be explored, forgetting her embarrassment, forgetting the war. Forgetting the army of wooden angels that was supposed to protect them both from something that was advancing upon them. And I'm sure that afterwards, exhausted and overwhelmed, they will have jumped under the waterfall. That's what I would have done, Brilka, if that had been where I spent my first night of love.

*

Three days later, Stasia gathered the members of the Jashi family in the spacious reception room, which hadn't been used since Ramas' death and was impossible to heat in winter because it was too big. Puffing on her cigarette, she spoke: 'I can't stand it any longer. I can't let my life be destroyed all over again by a bloody war. I have to find him. Kostya. I'm going to speak to Simon, make him pull some strings; maybe then he can get him a transfer. What's a Georgian doing in the Baltic, anyway? They should send him back to us; it's still calm here, and the Black Sea Fleet isn't a war fleet. Kostya has to get away from there. I'll tie him up and bring him back myself if I have to. I am not going to sacrifice my son as well. I've had enough. And you —' she looked at Andro and Kitty, sitting subdued in the corner '— you are not getting married. This is the wrong time to marry. Andro, see that you make something of your life: these are hard times. And you, Kitty, what's to become of you? All this dancing and singing and prancing about? Do you suppose anyone can live from that? Be sure to listen to Christine. You're old enough. I have no desire to treat you like little children just because that's how you behave.'

Then she gave each of them a tentative kiss on the cheek, took the old suitcase she had brought back from Petrograd, and drove to the station. All Christine's pleas, all her threats, all her attempts to stop Stasia making the dangerous trip across Russia failed utterly. She didn't want to hear a word about the futility of her plan.

She travelled for days on end — by train, in freight cars, by bus, even in a donkey cart, so she told me — and finally reached Moscow at the end of September. It had been raining heavily and the city was drowning in mud. The mud washed Stasia into the city, and into the war. Just like the last time, almost seventeen years earlier, when she had taken the Military Road in the hope of finding her newly wedded husband, and had found herself in the midst of a civil war. Only this time it wasn't a civil war, but a world war. This time she was looking not for her husband, but for her son. This time she intended to find him without having to wait two years; this time, even if the whole world came to an end, the outcome of her journey would be a good one.

Stasia couldn't know — the Sovinformburo had not divulged the information — that by this time there were already more than one million dead to be mourned on Soviet soil.

The Soviet rocket was created to promote peace.

POSTER SLOGAN

Simon Jashi couldn't believe his eyes when he saw his wife standing before him in the old barracks. He blinked, as if he needed to make sure it wasn't Stasia's ghost. She had changed. Her shoulders were stooped; she seemed smaller than before, as if her sister's misfortune, the separation from her children, the absence of a married life had caused her to shrink. Her calves, once hard as steel, were less muscular; her back was no longer as strong and straight as before; there was no colour in her lips, and the lines around her mouth were very marked. He tried to hug her, but the embrace proved more difficult, more artificial, than anticipated. He had forgotten what it felt like to feel.

'This is absolutely ridiculous!' Simon told his wife, once she had apprised him of her scheme. 'In case it hasn't got through to you yet: we're in the middle of a world war, Stasia! What, you think I'm going to get him some sort of fake authorisation? Like hell I will! We're the Red Army, not a bunch of amateurs. If we lose, we're all done for, don't you understand? We'll all become slaves; we'll lose everything we have, not just our freedom — the future, our country, our home.'

'I'd rather be a slave and know that my son is alive than a free woman with a dead son,' she cried, somewhat theatrically.

'Stasia, listen to me! Kostya is in the Navy. He's a sailor through and through. It's what he wanted. He's a grown man. He's serving his country. Even if that were not the case, nobody posts a capable sailor somewhere strategically unimportant like the Black Sea. It won't be long before all young men are conscripted. It'll happen in Georgia, too. Don't kid yourself: this isn't going to be over any time soon. We have to do everything we can to make sure we win this war.'

'He's not a grown man, he's not ...' Stasia kept shaking her head, as if the only thing her husband had said that she had understood was the bit about Kostya's age.

'He'll get through. He'll fight. He won't allow himself to be enslaved; he's a model of courage and loyalty. You should have seen him, at his graduation parade, when he —'

'You don't understand. You're the one who doesn't understand all this, Simon, not me.'

Stasia drew on her filterless cigarette and flapped away the smoke.

'You have to leave the city right away, Stasia. We're doing our best, but Moscow may have to be evacuated. You must go back to Tbilisi while you still can.'

Simon made another attempt to take Stasia in his arms. This time it was slightly more successful. As she allowed herself to be embraced by her husband, Stasia wondered why she didn't worry about him as much as she did about her son. The thought made her feel ashamed, and she wriggled away.

The Red Lieutenant kept talking to her; he tried to change her mind, tried to encourage her to return home, but Stasia kept repeating that she had to see Kostya at least once before she would leave. She had to try, at least once, to speak to him. But Kostya was already at Lake Ladoga; he and his fellow marines had been assigned to safeguard supplies coming in via military road number 101 — the road that would later go down in history as the Road of Life.

Stasia stayed in Moscow.

Stasia stayed in the barracks and cooked potato soup for the soldiers in the barracks kitchen.

★

The Germans' triumphal progress that summer seemed almost unreal. The success of Operation Barbarossa confirmed Hitler in his belief that he would soon defeat the Kremlin. Army Group Centre began to advance on Moscow. In the autumn of 1941, the Red Army regrouped and planned counter-attacks. Under General Zhukov, seventy new divisions were set up. All deserters and mutineers were to be shot on the spot. The autumn mud that made the roads impassable did Moscow and the entire Red Army a great favour. The Wehrmacht's advance was delayed by weeks, and fuel, munitions, supplies of every kind, in particular winter clothing for the German soldiers, got stuck *en route*.

Workers' regiments were already on standby in the various municipal districts. And as Stasia continued to hope for a meeting with her son, Andro Eristavi received his call-up papers for military service. The majority of Georgian soldiers called up in the winter of 1941 were sent to defend the Western Front, and ended up in Kerch in Crimea.

*

Since her sister's departure, Christine had shown impressive discipline. As if she had been waiting all along to be left on her own with two adolescents, she came back from her shadow world of cherry liqueurs and opera arias to grubby, careworn reality. She drew up daily plans for their family of three, assigning the chores: there was housework to be done, food coupons to be redeemed, donations to be collected.

While Andro worked as a volunteer at the post office, Kitty helped Christine collect lint and bandages for the front, and together they planted vegetables in the garden; the food rations didn't stretch nearly far enough. The war seemed to have given Christine a new purpose in life. Andro and Kitty went about inseparably entwined, like Siamese twins; they winked at and pinched each other, and were constantly challenging each other, as they so loved to do: whoever gets to the next crossroads first, whoever gets to the front door first, whoever plants more vegetables, whoever collects the most donations.

'For our soldiers! Donations for our soldiers! They need warm winter clothing, socks, underwear, shirts. Everything welcome!'

Kitty had caught the flu, so Andro was standing alone beside his big box outside the teahouse, calling on people, with a friendly smile and a loud voice, to donate for the front. All of a sudden a fine gentleman was standing before him, extending his hand.

'You have my respect, young man! Such enthusiasm! That's what I call true loyalty to your homeland. Many young people your age just laze about and think of nothing but fun. They don't know what it means to be at war, but you — I take my hat off to you!' He made an affected little bow, then took a donation, wrapped in newspaper, from his briefcase and laid it carefully in Andro's box.

The gentleman had the air of a foreigner, although he spoke flawless Georgian; he wore a perfectly tailored pinstriped suit and a strangely shaped hat with dark green trim. He introduced himself as David.

'That should be enough for the time being,' he said. He took an interest in the carvings Andro had with him, and held forth at length about trends in modern art. But the art he talked about was European, and he named names Andro didn't know, impressing him all the more. The fine gentleman must have seemed to Andro like a being from another planet.

'Yes, there are many interesting things in this world; unfortunately, we don't hear much about them here, do we, Andro?' said the gentleman, concluding his monologue; and Andro was flabbergasted, because he had not yet told the fine gentleman his name.

Before Andro could ask how he knew it, the stranger placed a matchbox on top of Andro's carton and went on his way without saying goodbye. Andro picked up the matchbox and examined it. Finally, on the back, he found what he was looking for: an address, scrawled in tiny letters.

Andro felt like a real man of mystery. For three days he walked around with the matchbox in his pocket and didn't even tell Kitty about this remarkable encounter. He imagined all kinds of adventures the fine gentleman might be caught up in. He wondered what such an urbane, sophisticated man could want from him, and how on earth he knew him. After three days he could no longer suppress his curiosity and set off to the address he had been given.

A winding staircase led up to the little attic apartment. There he was received by the gentleman, now wearing a dark blue suit and holding a glass of brandy, a drink Andro had only ever encountered in books.

'You're a fine young man. You combine many useful qualities: you have tact, curiosity, and good manners, too; you strive for something greater, and you're loyal. But, alas, we are not living in a time in which such qualities are valued. Coarseness, betrayal, and greed are the order of the day.'

The man quickly came to the point — a little too quickly for Andro's liking. They had sat down in front of an old tiled stove and Andro had just taken his first sip of brandy when the man started to speak very insistently.

'Socialist ideology has been betrayed. We have been betrayed. And now we find ourselves at war, although we wanted peace. Now we find ourselves in the state of slavery we wanted to fight; we find ourselves in a dictatorship, my boy, although we longed for freedom. Our ideals have been violated.'

The man nodded meaningfully, as if to lend his words greater significance. Andro said nothing and looked at the floor: he felt pathetic and stupid, and didn't wish to appear inexperienced and clueless. By remaining silent, he could at least convey the impression that he was thinking very carefully about what the gentleman was telling him.

'But there is still hope,' the man continued, and this time he sounded like someone giving a lecture before a large crowd. He rose to his feet and came to stand at Andro's side. 'There is a way to overcome these forces and establish a free Georgia, from which it would be no problem for people to travel to Paris or Vienna, as they used to do. For that, though, we need good men. You want to go to Europe, don't you?' The warming brandy was generously topped up. 'We need men who know what's important, and it seems to me, my boy, that you're one of them. If we *win* this war, all our hopes are buried, all ideals are dead, all borders closed. You understand what I'm saying?'

Andro, befuddled by alcohol, nodded seriously. He looked up again and returned his host's wide smile.

The apartment was spartan, not at all in keeping with this David person's suave charisma. Perhaps that was a sort of disguise, Andro thought to himself. He felt he was being called upon to do something important, and even if he didn't know exactly what his assignment was, it was certainly exciting. Something inside him told him he should not disappoint this man.

The man himself held forth about freedom and values, about borders and oppression. He spoke of Europe; again and again he mentioned names and places that were sheer magic to Andro's ears, so unattainably remote, and so romantic. Places he had always wanted to visit; places he had so often rhapsodised about to Kitty; but in this man's mouth they sounded familiar, not at all remote, no longer unattainable. As if he had just that moment returned from a stroll around Montmartre and was asking Andro if, next time, he would care to accompany him.

With this man it was so easy to imagine the casino tables in Baden-Baden, the dance clubs in Paris, the Viennese coffee houses. This man, in his fine clothes, kept talking to Andro, feeding his imagination with marvellous images that promised him the world and guaranteed him Vienna, freedom, wonderful prospects. He could develop his talent and aspire to a career as a sculptor. He could study in Europe.

'The Germans are striving for freedom for Georgia. They know very well that the cradle of our race and our civilisation lies in the Caucasus.' The man was whispering now. He had sat down opposite Andro again and was looking him straight in the eye. 'Have you heard of the Georgian Legion, my boy?' Andro shook his head. 'These are men who are fighting from abroad, mainly from Berlin, for a free Georgia. In the past few years there've been secret discussions with the Germans; they've assured us that as soon as the Soviet Union is defeated we will be free again. That we will form an autonomous state as part of the Greater German Reich, and that we will be given our due, if you understand me.'

Andro nodded cautiously, although actually he wasn't sure he really had understood what the man was saying.

'You can help us, Andro. You can help us win this war. You can help us shape the future of our country. You can be free, my boy. You've been called up, haven't you?

Again Andro wondered how it was that the man knew so much about him. This time he nodded firmly.

'You'll soon be sent to Crimea by the Soviets. Someone will contact you there and give you the details of your assignment. You have no military experience, so you'll probably be trained in radio communications. A very important job, my boy. In a few months' time we'll fetch you and take you to Europe. You'll be able to operate with us from there. We have cells everywhere. All over western Europe, and soon all over the world. And when all of this is over you'll be able to go anywhere — wherever you like.'

Andro, now flushed and slightly drunk, leaned further forward and downed the last of his brandy.

'Uff, that's strong,' he said with a smile. 'And what about my wife?'

'You have a wife?' asked the gentleman in surprise.

'Yes, soon she'll be my wife.'

'Oh — I see. Nothing should ever stand in the way of love. I can assure you that as soon as you've arrived in Europe and assumed your duties, we will send her to you. But all that takes time. We're right in the thick of things. There's still a great deal to do, and helping hands are important, Andro. We'll arrange false papers for your wife and get her out of the country — with the highest level of protection, of course, that goes without saying.'

'Are you spies or something?' asked Andro, and laughed uncertainly. His head ached. He tried to interpret the man's words. He tried to weigh up the offer. The gentleman slapped Andro on the back.

'We're just doing our work — working for a free Georgia.'

'But ... doesn't that mean you're working with the fascists? Why would the fascists particularly want Georgia to be a free country?'

'Listen to me, Andro, listen to me very carefully.' The man sat on the arm of Andro's chair again, and this time his voice was rather sterner. 'Perhaps you'll have heard the name Shalva Maglakelidze. One of the original Georgian democrats, and a first-rate commander. Before the revolution he was governor general of Tbilisi. After the occupation of Georgia he left the country and emigrated to Europe, where he founded the Tetri Giorgi resistance organisation in 1924. The purpose of this organisation was to liberate Georgia from the hands of the Soviet occupiers. When war broke out, he founded the Georgian Legion in Berlin and made an agreement with the Germans, according to which Georgia was to become a free state within the Greater German Reich.

Maglakelidze has gathered together the best Georgian soldiers in exile, and has allied himself with the Wehrmacht. The Georgian Legion will soon number thirteen thousand soldiers, Andro, divided into twelve different battalions. Every day, more and more Red Army deserters and prisoners of war are joining the Legion. And Maglakelidze has already been promoted to major general.'

'I think I should probably be going now ...'

Andro stood up and started looking for his hat. The man remained seated, motionless, his eyes fixed on Andro.

'Your mother is dead, Andro. Shot, like a cheap whore. I can put the details in writing for you, if you're interested. Even the exact price of the bullets they used to kill her. Shot because she wanted to remain free, in a free country.'

Andro, already at the door, slowly turned and looked the man in the eye. The transformation of conjecture into certainty changed him, and his future, forever.

★

A few days before the year's end, Andro, along with other soldiers, left Tbilisi for Crimea. Kharkov was in German hands, and rumours were spreading that it was only a question of time before the Wehrmacht reached the Caucasus as well.

The night before his departure, Andro crept into Kitty's room, woke her, and confided his plans. Kitty became virtually hysterical; she insisted that he shouldn't take this risk, it was too dangerous and he was too inexperienced, the Reds could find out at any time and arrest him, and then nobody would be able to save him. There was no way Kitty wanted the fascists to win the war; she didn't want an autonomous state within the Greater German Reich. The idea that a fascist victory would mean freedom for Georgia was an illusion. He shouldn't be so naive, he should come to his senses. He was putting himself and the whole family in grave danger.

It would all be all right, Andro insisted. After all, it was in the gentleman's interest that his cover should not be blown. But when Kitty still refused to agree he shouted at her, grabbed her by the elbows, shook her violently, and insisted that she had to believe him, she had to trust him. He had no future in a country where they had shot his mother like a sick animal, a country with a system like this. He preferred to stake his life on a hope than perish in this cesspit.

Kitty stared at him, wide-eyed. She had never seen him so beside himself. Finally she pressed his head against her breast as if he were a little child. Her attempts to comfort him turned into passionate kisses and they ended up in her bed.

'As soon as it's possible they'll make contact with you, and then you'll follow me,' said Andro quietly — naked, curled up in a ball, lying like an embryo at Kitty's side. 'You will come, won't you? Won't you? Promise me!'

He gazed at her expectantly.

'Yes. Yes, I'll follow you,' she said, placing her forefinger on his lips. For the first time in their life, his dreams frightened her.

★

The world was dancing in circles. The skeletons beneath the earth beat time. Roses no longer bloomed in any colour but black. All paths felt like rope bridges, swaying, ready to collapse at any moment. Even the snow acquired a bluish tinge. The sky was peppered with holes; you could see bullet holes on the horizon, too, and although the sun shone wearily down it could no longer impart any warmth.

The trees came to a whispered agreement, and hanged themselves on one another's branches. Birds fell from the sky, because at the sight of the dance they forgot how to fly; children became adults overnight and polished grenades. Tears became rare, expensive things. Only grimaces were free.

Chocolate was now just a memory of another age, and without chocolate people forgot sweetness, and without sweetness they forgot childhood, and without childhood they forgot the beginning, and without the beginning they couldn't see the end.

And the voice of the Soviet Union, the voice of the Sovinformburo, Yuri Borisovich Levitan, echoed through the ether, inimitable, omnipresent, reporting tirelessly on horrors that, from his mouth, always sounded a little less horrible. His voice — even the Generalissimus believed it — gave the nation confidence. Levitan talked and talked:

'... The Germans have been pushed back from Rostov. Successes at Lake Ladoga; the Road of Life is passable again. Frost has brought the front to a standstill. The Germans are attacking from the south; they are crossing the Volga. The Germans are approaching Stalingrad. Orders are: do not give an inch. 240,000 German soldiers encircled ...'

And the snow fell and splintered into shards, and the ghosts roamed the hills telling rosaries for those who had frozen to death.

> In Germany you cannot have a revolution
> because you would have to step on the lawns.
>
> VLADIMIR LENIN

Meanwhile, at the end of September, the Red Lieutenant was posted to Kamyshin on the Volga, and Stasia telegraphed her sister in Tbilisi to say that she couldn't get away from Moscow, the roads were impassable, and besides, Kostya was stationed near Leningrad. She stayed on alone in the Moscow barracks, and gradually began to realise the absurdity of her plan. In retrospect, the desire to make her way to Kostya in Leningrad seemed like utter foolishness. She asked herself how she could have acted so impetuously, leaving her daughter and Andro behind.

Before his departure, Simon had promised that as soon as an opportunity presented itself he would get her out of the city so she could make her way home. However, given the situation, this too seemed to her an impossible undertaking. No one could guarantee her safe passage any more. Once again, she was trapped in a theatre of war, fearing for her family, enduring cold and hunger, and wondering how she could have been so stupid. She asked herself why every attempt she made to unite her family ended in war.

This time, though — unlike before, in Petrograd — Stasia was better prepared. She knew to whom she could turn to get black-market goods; she knew how to deal with the soldiers who had remained, which of the superior officers looked favourably on her husband, and which were in Simon's debt. She actually succeeded in requisitioning the room at the barracks for herself alone. She made herself useful in the barracks kitchen. She darned and sewed coats, shirts, uniforms. But her main thought was of escaping this dangerous, child-devouring place.

Christine hadn't told her that Andro had been called up. But Stasia guessed it wouldn't be long before he was sent to the front — and, unlike Kostya, Andro was no fighter. Stasia thought of Sopio, focused her mind on her friend, and begged her forgiveness for not staying in Tbilisi and taking better care of Andro.

When the first bombs fell, making Stasia's ears ring; when, for the first time in her life, she found herself in one of the air raid bunkers that had been set up in the metro stations, she finally realised that not only had she failed to save her son and protect her adoptive son, she had also put her own life at risk. And then she really was mortally afraid.

Suddenly, she was no longer an observer: she had become part of this terrible spectacle, and many years lay between her and the ordeals she had survived in Petrograd.

Some half a million citizens, the majority of them women, erected fortifications outside Moscow. Façades were painted over in painstaking detail to camouflage them during German air raids.

And Stasia laughed at herself, a cynical, violent laugh, at how naive she had been to think you could drive war out of a person, when you inevitably ended up becoming part of the war yourself.

The mass mobilisation began. Stasia hauled sandbags with the other women, and lent a hand when another barricade needed building, or windows needed covering, as a total blackout had been imposed during the air raids. Some of the Red Army officers' wives moved into the barracks with their children. The men had been pulled out. On these dark nights, Stasia sat over cabbage or potato stew in the barracks kitchen and couldn't believe how real the prospect seemed that she might never get out of here again; that she might never see her children, her sister, her husband again.

The great rain stopped, the mud dried out, and the Germans marched on Moscow. Mass panic erupted when the evacuation of the city began. Frantic people burned files in the street. Men ineligible for military service were deployed to lay mines in important buildings. Careful as jugglers, they could be seen walking along the pavements with the explosive in their hands, as if part of a choreography both elegiac and macabre.

Lenin's body was removed from the mausoleum, the Kremlin painted green. Captive balloons floated up from the arterial roads to deter low-flying aircraft. Documents were burned in the archives. All factories, schools, and institutions were closed, and finally public transport was suspended, too.

The train stations were overcrowded. The trains were heading to Kyrgyzstan, Tatarstan, Kazakhstan, to places one had never heard of before; far, very far away, train journeys of several days, weeks by boat. Lists were compiled of professional groups, and a destination for evacuation was assigned to each. Communist Party members, the Authors' Association, the Academy of Sciences, doctors, botanists, engineers, chemists, physicists, train drivers, even brass bands were all assigned to specific trains. The privileged were able to jump the queue; those who had little to boast of had to wait, keep pushing; occasionally someone without a seat reservation managed to secure themselves standing room in one of the carriages.

Swept along by other women from the barracks, Stasia vanished in the crowd, got lost, resurfaced; someone pulled her by the hand, let go of her again. The certificate of evacuation to Tatarstan was in her passport in the inside pocket of her coat. At Kazan Station the crowd of people blurred into a single, enormous body with two huge arms and two legs, a formless trunk and a monstrous head. Stasia stood still, fell back from the other women hurrying to the platforms with children and suitcases. A small group of people, unlike all the others, had caught her attention, and she stood there, unable to look away.

These people were boarding the train with almost unnatural slowness and elegance; they were helping each other with their luggage, and kept looking around, as if it was hard for them to leave the city. Stasia asked a man which professional group these people belonged to, and the man replied irritably that they were dancers from the Bolshoi Theatre.

Stasia couldn't tear her eyes away from the dancers. One dainty young woman spotted her and waved. Stasia stepped closer.

'Which theatre are you from?' the young woman asked, giving Stasia an empathetic smile. Hearing this question from a Bolshoi ballerina gave Stasia a childish rush of joy, and for a moment her breast was filled with pride. She'd thought she was a dancer, too! Stasia bowed her head, embarrassed, and murmured something about a provincial town.

'That doesn't matter. We artists must stick together more than ever in these terrible times, mustn't we?' the young ballerina said encouragingly. She beckoned to Stasia. 'You've got your evacuation certificate with you, haven't you? We're sure to find you a seat, don't worry.'

Stasia came within a whisker of accepting the invitation and boarding the train for which she had no authorisation. For a moment, she succumbed so effortlessly to her illusion, picked up so easily where she'd left off years ago, imagining herself seventeen again, with Paris and the *Ballets Russes* waiting for her, and if she just worked hard enough and took enough ballet classes she was sure to be able to dance Scheherezade at the *Théâtre du Châtelet*.

Her hand wandered across her breast, and there, inside her vest, she felt something heavy that she carried with her always, that gave her a peculiar sense of calm: Thekla's gold watch. She stepped back, caught the dancer's puzzled expression, shook her head with a grateful smile, and disappeared again into the crowd.

An officer's wife from the barracks had seen her and was waving at her.

'Hurry, Stasia! The train's already so full — come on!'

But suddenly Stasia felt a terrible emptiness. An all-encompassing indifference. She kept looking back, trying to catch a glimpse of the dancer, but there were too many people thronging between them.

Why in the world would she go to Tatarstan?

The only sensible destination was home. She didn't want to get on this train, she didn't want to chase after the wrong life. She should have lived a life that would have led her to the train with the dancers, not the one to Kama, Tatarstan. Not there. She didn't belong there. And she didn't belong here, either.

The officer's wife waved and waved, called her again and again, but Stasia turned her back on her and pushed through the crowd in the station concourse, emerging into the cool air, the grey daylight; she ran blindly through the streets, simply following her feet, further and further away from this station with its overcrowded trains. She lugged her old suitcase along with her, like an abdicated king dragging his sceptre. As she reached a wide, alarmingly empty boulevard the sirens began to wail: even then she still felt nothing.

She turned into a side street and sat down in the empty entrance to a house. She took a cigarette out of the bag and lit it. She looked up at the sky. No bombers to be seen. Good. That was something, at least.

*

In another city, at this moment, another woman also sat down and looked up at the sky. This city, though, had been cut off from the world for months; survival there was akin to a miracle. The woman was gaunt, taller than Stasia, with olive skin; she was bony, like Stasia, but she looked older, sickly, and there were grey streaks in her jet-black hair. She was wearing a patched autumn coat and her hands were covered in earth. Her cheeks were sunken, her lips dry and cracked, and her fingers bare, not a single ring left on them. She had just been harvesting vegetables alongside other women in one of the public parks, and had sat down, exhausted, on the damp ground. This last winter she had lost more than eleven kilos, and had sold the most precious thing she owned: her piano, which was used not to make music, but for firewood. Almost all her records had gone, too, as she could no longer bear to hear music, since the blockade; music made her vulnerable, and she couldn't allow that. Not any more.

She had survived the mass deaths. She had survived the famine. She had survived the reduction of the bread ration to two hundred grams. She had survived the sight of starved, frozen bodies on the streets. She had seen people eating their shoes, or dogs, or cats, starch paste, and crows. She had survived thousands of bombs that had been dropped on her since the city came under siege. But she would not survive music. Music, she believed, would cause her heart, still beating dully in her breast, to contract so unbearably that she would die on the spot.

Because she was unmarried and had no children, because she was neither disabled nor wounded, she was very low on the list for urgent evacuation. Along with the other seven hundred thousand people left in the city, she had braced herself for the coming winter. The last one had seared itself into the minds of the city's populace with such cruelty that they were now going about preparing for the next coming horror as best they could, mechanically, without feeling. Because no one doubted that the horror would return, in all its shattering glory. She looked down at her cracked and reddened hands, covered in dirt. She was living in the present. In this moment. She asked herself, as she had so often before, whether she actually knew why she was trying so hard, so doggedly, so desperately to stay alive.

★

The thermometer read minus 34 degrees. The Generalissimus issued the order to begin the counter-offensive, led by Zhukov. On 6 November, he gave a ceremonial speech in the Moscow metro, praising the tenacity of the Soviet people and the Red Army's powers of resistance. The following day, there was even a parade on Red Square to commemorate the October Revolution. The Russian army was marching — with or without winter clothing, with or without helmets. (After the war, General Eisenhower is said to have expressed his outrage to Marshall Zhukov over the way the wartime leadership in the Soviet Union had recklessly thrown away human lives. Zhukov is said merely to have smiled and replied, 'It doesn't matter; Russian women will bear more.')

At the end of November, the Germans were just twenty kilometres from Moscow. On 2 December, a tank battalion penetrated a Moscow suburb; they could see the Kremlin through their binoculars. The symbolic power of this development generated downright euphoria among the German soldiers; the dangers of the Russian winter seemed to have been superseded by joy over the imminent capture of Moscow. In Moscow itself there was talk of a march Hitler had personally commissioned to be played during the capitulation of the city.

As the NKVD was able to confirm that Japan was not planning an attack on the Soviet Union, various divisions were pulled out of the north and sent towards the capital. The infantry marched on Moscow in skis and snowshoes. On the night of 5 December, Soviet parachutists landed near Yukhnov; railway lines and important roads were secured and occupied. At the same time, the counteroffensive was launched in the west.

The Wehrmacht had no longer reckoned with such a fierce counter-attack. Its reaction was belated and uncoordinated. There was no time: the army group only received the order to take evasive action on the evening of 6 December.

On 7 December, the Sovinformburo announced another sensation, this time on the other side of the world: the Japanese had attacked the Pearl Harbor naval base near Honolulu. As a result, the United States declared war on Japan, thereby officially becoming part of the universal apocalypse. And Hitler, for fear of losing Japan as an ally, declared war on America.

It wasn't until mid-January that Hitler ordered the retreat from Moscow, but by then the German troops had already suffered massive losses, not just from Russian bullets and grenades, but above all as a consequence of the freezing temperatures that winter. During the retreat, the German soldiers had to leave almost all their munitions behind, as they had neither horses nor the machines and fuel at their disposal to transport them back in an orderly manner. Frozen and dejected, the soldiers left the city, singing quietly to themselves:

> Before the gates of Moscow stood a battalion,
> The proud remains of Wehrmacht 34th Division.
> The Kremlin was just in sight
> But they were forced to leave the fight
> Just like Napoleon.

> The Soviet power does not punish, it improves.
>
> POSTER SLOGAN

Kitty walked up the little hill to Christine's house. She went into the neglected garden and lay down on the damp earth. She screwed up her eyes, counting the glow-worms above her as they turned into stars. Christine had just got back from the hospital, where she had taken a full-time job as a nurse, and where, in recent weeks, German prisoners-of-war had kept arriving, as well as the numerous Soviet casualties. She stopped by the glass door and watched her niece, who was stretching her limbs and staring into space with a glazed expression. Christine picked up a little stool and went and sat next to Kitty.

'What's Andro planning? You have to tell me. I can see you're not happy about it, that you're suffering. Tell me.'

'It's nothing; you're exaggerating, Christine. It's really nothing. I just miss him so terribly, and I'm worried about *Deda* too …'

'Don't lie to me.'

'Really, I don't know anything.'

'It's important that you tell me what you know. We might get into trouble, Kitty. Big trouble. You must talk to me. Where is he? And why can't I find him through the commissariat?'

'I don't know where he is. I wish I did!' Not a scrap of truth escaped from under Kitty's thick eyelashes. Christine fixed her one good eye on her niece. How many times Kitty had feigned ignorance … What was she trying to protect Andro from? What was she afraid of? The obvious suspicion was that Andro had joined a partisan movement. But as long as it remained no more than a suspicion, Christine could protect neither Kitty nor herself. Perhaps he had already been killed in action, and Kitty was scared of this finality. But something told Christine this wasn't the case.

Suddenly she thought of her nephew, Kostya, about whom she had forbidden herself to think these past few months. She saw his well-manicured fingernails, his dark eyes, his upright gait, heard his gallant way of speaking. She would so like to hold him in her arms, gently kiss his cheeks, as she had always done when he was small and they all lived in one house. She would ruffle his hair, slip him a sweet, and everything would be as before; Ramas would walk through the door, would call out for her ...

Christine began to take out the hairpins that kept her face-covering in place. No one but Stasia was allowed to see her divided face.

How little we know, she thought. We, the left behind, the silenced, how we fear what awaits us in the end. How we hate to be the ones left behind, and yet how little we can do about it. She touched Kitty's shoulder. Kitty was still lying motionless, her face turned away.

'Turn round. Look at me.'

'Please, Christine ...'

'Look at me!'

Slowly, listlessly, Kitty obeyed, sat up, and involuntarily put her hand over her mouth to stop herself crying out. Her wide eyes betrayed her horror. Her head wobbled like a *nevalyashka* doll's.

'That's right — look at me. I survived even this. I'm not afraid of anything any more. We can get through this together,' said Christine, trying to stretch her lips into a smile.

Kitty's hand was still clamped over her mouth.

'Where is Andro?'

'Please.'

'Tell me where he is. Perhaps it's still not too late. Stasia doesn't know he's disappeared. She thinks he's in Crimea.'

'I'm sure he is! That's where he was posted.'

'But he wasn't planning on staying there, was he? Is it the partisans, the anarchists, the liberals — which bunch of lunatics has he joined?'

'I don't know.'

'Tell me!'

'I can't do this any more ...'

Kitty started to sob. She wept uncontrollably. She wept and wept and would not be comforted. Christine watched her without a word; she sat on the stool and waited until the spasm had passed.

'What can't you do any more?' she asked.

Suddenly, Kitty sat up and lifted her clothes to reveal the sharply protruding dome of her belly. Christine rose from her stool. For a brief moment Kitty thought she saw anger and disgust in Christine's eyes, thought she had been betrayed, and waited for the words that would confirm this suspicion, but Christine just gave an expressionless nod and went back inside. Kitty followed her a moment later. When they reached the kitchen, Christine said, 'I have ingredients for precisely one portion. I kept them in case the worst should happen. Or perhaps the best. I think this is both. So I'm going to prepare it for you now. I took Papa's notebook after the funeral — Stasia didn't want to give me the recipe! And the ridiculous reasons she gave me! It's dangerous, it brings bad luck, there was a reason why Papa guarded the recipe with his life — I mean, really!'

'What are you talking about?'

'Sit down.'

And so Christine made Kitty her first hot chocolate, little suspecting that the misfortune her father had feared was inherent in his creation, the misfortune Stasia came to believe in when she returned to Thekla's abandoned villa on the Fontanka with two tickets and such high hopes, would not pass Kitty by, either.

★

That same evening, Stasia had a waking dream. Thekla visited her and took her by the hand, leading her through the empty rooms of her St Petersburg villa, where there was no furniture apart from mirrors that had been taken off the walls. Stasia followed her, but whenever she thought Thekla was close enough for her to catch the sleeve of her robe, she slipped away and called to her from another room. At last Thekla stopped, in front of one of the big mirrors that now stood propped against the wall, and carefully removed the dustsheet. Stasia saw herself in the mirror, Thekla's benevolent face beside her; she gazed at their reflections, but when she turned round to look at Thekla directly, Thekla was no longer there.

Stasia stayed in Moscow. There was still no way to leave the city. She stuck it out, waiting for a sign of life from her husband, her son, her sister. But, at Kitty's request, her sister kept the most important news a secret from her: that in the midst of all that dying a new life had been created, and a new addition to the human race was on its way.

★

Every morning, at 05:14 precisely, Konstantin Jashi awoke with a start and a loud cry that made the other three sailors who shared his berth flinch. They would look at him, smile reassuringly, persuade him that everything was fine, make clear to him that he wasn't in mortal danger, that they were all still alive — luckily, or unfortunately? Kostya couldn't tell from their expressions.

He had been in action on Lake Ladoga since September and thus, without knowing it, perilously close to his beloved. In Leningrad, which had been divided into six sectors, Ida, alongside many other women and men, was erecting metre-high barricades. She helped patrol the streets, and was put to work building obstacles to stop the German tanks. She had to keep busy; she was clinging to the last remaining scraps of her sanity.

Each knew nothing of what the other was doing, had no idea that there were only thirty-two kilometres between them. Kostya didn't know that in the first year of the blockade the woman he could not forget, whose scent, like the memory of some terrible deed, refused to leave him, had already, along with all the inhabitants of her beloved city, survived bombardments of up to eighteen hours, 70,000 bombs, hunger, sickness, and cold. And Ida didn't know that as a sailor in the marines, tasked with securing the 'Road of Life', Kostya had helped get more than 44,000 tons of food and more than 60,000 tons of kerosene into Leningrad by tug and motorboat. That he had evacuated more than 50,000 people, and that he, too, had survived eighteen-hour bombardments, hunger, sickness, and cold. Kostya didn't know, either, that Ida thought just as often as he did about their wordless intimacy, so ridiculously impossible and yet, in retrospect, so fundamentally essential. And Ida didn't know that the marines and the soldiers of the 54th Army had voluntarily reduced their rations in favour of the besieged population, to mitigate the hell of that savage winter. Ida didn't know that she was eating a piece of Kostya's bread.

The winter was merciless. The lake was frozen. The transport of supplies was laborious and subject to long interruptions. People drew water from the Neva. Fires broke out all over the city; furniture and apartments burned. Both Ida and Kostya heard the same warnings on the radio. Both drank a glass of schnapps on the last day of 1941. They were separated by thirty-two kilometres of the Road of Life — or Death, depending. Neither knew what awaited them.

Kostya's unit was on the southern shore of the lake, the Schlüsselburg side. He himself never got as far as the city. He hardly wrote any letters any more. The previous year he had still received imploring letters from his mother, postcards from his sister covered in cherry lips, and encouraging telegrams from his father. But he had not had any such news for some time now, and he no longer bothered to make contact with his homeland, either. The war had robbed him of speech and of the capacity to feel. All the dead pursued him, and he had already seen far too many die. He renounced his memories.

There was only one memory he could not shake off: the memory of the woman with the ringed fingers on Vasilievsky Island. He was haunted by her scent, stronger than the stench of death. Her memory clung to him, to his hair, to his skin; it was unmistakable, indestructible, and threatening: it weakened him, made him vulnerable.

In the spring, Hitler himself gave the order to Army Group South to advance on Stalingrad. Stalingrad was Hitler's top priority in the summer of 1942, because of its geographical, strategic, and above all symbolic significance. The great Volga river ran through Stalingrad — one of the most important supply lines for the Soviets' war materials. As for symbolic significance: it was in 1918, in this city that now bore his name, that the Generalissimus had been appointed commissioner for the mass shooting of saboteurs and partisans. This was where his ascendancy had begun.

O God, now I have but a single request of Thee:
destroy me, shatter me utterly,
cast me into hell, do not stop me before my course is run,
but deprive me of all hope and swiftly destroy me forever and ever.

DANIIL KHARMS

In August 1942, the Wehrmacht occupied Krasnodar and crossed the Kuban. Not long afterwards, the Georgian Military Road fell into German hands. The Nazi flag fluttered at the top of Mount Elbrus.

Kitty's child was due in September — by which time people were dying in their thousands in Leningrad while her brother worked tirelessly to try and prevent it; a few months before her lover would be transferred to the Georgian Legion, to the French front. But in August, when the eighteen-year-old Kitty had to give up her voluntary work at the hospital on account of her girth, three Red Army soldiers came one warm, late summer's afternoon to collect her from the villa in the Old Town.

She offered no resistance and got in the car. Perhaps she hoped it was a secret sign from Andro — the news she had been waiting for for so long. A glimmer of hope. A little piece of future.

After a two-hour drive, they stopped in a village south of Tbilisi — I'm afraid I don't know the precise location — got out, and entered an abandoned school building. Kitty's companions had been silent throughout the journey; her enquiries about their destination had gone unanswered. They entered a bare room with an outsized, badly painted portrait of the Generalissimus on the wall. Two empty school benches, a broken chair, a carafe of water.

Kitty was left alone in this room for almost an hour, tired, her legs swollen. She kept peering round the door; she called out that she didn't want to be left here so long, someone should come and talk to her, but no one answered. Finally, a woman in a Red Army uniform entered the room, followed by a man in civilian clothes. They sat down opposite her and offered her a glass of water.

The woman gave her a friendly smile; the man tried to avoid Kitty's eyes.

'Comrade Jashi. We're sorry we've kept you waiting so long. We know it's not easy for you in this heat, in your condition. So we'll quickly explain to you our concern. As you know, our Motherland is in the midst of a devastating war. The Generalissimus is attempting the impossible in order to safeguard freedom for our country and independence for our people. Our country's best men are fighting in this murderous war, and you'll understand, won't you, how important loyalty, allegiance to the homeland, and belief in socialism are in times like these? And you'll also know what a grave matter treachery is at such a time? Do you agree with us, Comrade Jashi?'

The woman spoke Russian with a Moscow accent. She had delicate features and was wearing red lipstick. The lipstick had smudged a little in the heat, giving her mouth a clownish aspect. Kitty couldn't stop staring at this mouth. The nondescript man started walking up and down in the gathering dusk. No one turned on the light.

'What do you want from me?'

Perhaps it was only then that Kitty understood this journey would not lead to the hoped-for message from Andro. But she still didn't realise where it was all heading. Because she had nothing to hide. And she was heavily pregnant. She remained calm. She still didn't know then the price she would pay for her dreams.

'The child's father has betrayed his Motherland. He was recruited by the fascists and is fighting against us. Against his homeland. Against his friends. I'm asking you outright, woman to woman, comrade to comrade: where exactly is your fiancé at present? You are engaged, aren't you? Tell us his current whereabouts and we'll drive you straight home.'

Kitty continued to stare at the woman's lips. She had a pleasant voice, very soft, with a velvety timbre. Although her words were clear and almost brusque, her manner peremptory, her voice made it sound as if she were flattering you and giving you compliments. The words she spoke did not fit the voice.

'I haven't had any news from him at all since he was called up. I'm afraid I don't know where he is at present, and also I very much doubt that Andro would betray his country,' squeaked Kitty, clasping her belly. 'Please could you turn the light on? I can hardly see you.'

'Believe me, Comrade Jashi, we'd also like to go home soon, but you must cooperate with us. Otherwise we'll be stuck here for a long time yet.'

All Kitty could see of the woman now was her silhouette. She sounded genuinely concerned, as if she found it unpleasant to have to ask these questions. Her mild tone gave Kitty hope that she might indeed soon be going home. For some reason it seemed comforting that the person interrogating her was a woman.

'I really don't know anything. But Andro isn't a traitor, I can assure you of that; he would never ...' Kitty felt helpless; she didn't know what more she could say.

'We're not going to leave this room until you talk.' The woman propped her face on her right hand and leaned forward a little.

'But I really don't know anything.'

And so it went on: hours that felt to Kitty like days. The blonde woman's calm, compassionate tone; always the same answers from Kitty. The silent man in the background. The darkness. The pale moonlight that crept in through the uncurtained window. Kitty's nervous movements, teetering on the chair, shaking her head, chewing her fingernails. Sighing. The groans, and the woman's calm, mild tone that suddenly no longer seemed reassuring, but almost eerie. Her voice had deceived Kitty. It had given her false hope. Gradually, her sense of time began to recede, and eventually dissolved altogether. When the sky began to pale, Kitty wept. A weeping that became hysterical sobbing. She was hungry, she was afraid; she felt the baby kicking in her belly, she felt its fear.

She begged and pleaded with them to let her go, to take her home, she didn't know anything, she didn't know anything, she didn't know anything. When the woman ignored her pleas and just went on mechanically repeating her questions, Kitty started calling for help. At this, the woman, who had been sitting so still all this time, as if made of marble, jumped up and ran out. Two Red Army soldiers entered the classroom, grabbed Kitty by the elbows, and dragged her out into the corridor. She was taken down to the basement of the school building and locked in, in total darkness. She rattled and hammered on the door, shouted furious insults, threatened, cursed, finally begged them to let her out, appealed to their consciences, the baby was hungry, it was permanently agitated; but no one responded, and so she sank into a state of profound exhaustion, lay down on the cold floor, and fell asleep.

When she woke, she was lying on a stretcher, strapped down by two leather belts across her thighs and upper body. She was in the same classroom in which she had been interrogated the previous evening, only now the benches had been removed and the portrait of the Generalissimus taken down: it stood on the floor, turned towards the wall, leaning against it. A pale rectangle marked the spot where it had hung, wonderfully symmetrical and impressively clean.

She didn't have the strength to scream. Nor did she make any attempt to free herself from the straps; she knew it was useless. She wriggled a little to the left, trying to find a more comfortable position, a position in which they didn't cut into her flesh so deeply. A naked light bulb hung from the ceiling, blinding her with cold, almost white, light. Kitty blinked and tried to turn her head away from its glaring beams.

The uniformed woman was sitting in a corner. Kitty looked over at her and once again was unable to tear her eyes from those red lips. They were perfectly made up today. The woman had beautiful, harmonious features, a dainty nose that almost looked painted, and she wore her hair in a sophisticated, pinned-up style that seemed strangely incongruous here, in such a place. As if she had hurried over from an elegant party to get this bothersome and disagreeable work over with and return to the party as quickly as possible. Who was she? Where did she come from? From what sort of world? What did her world smell like? Was she loved there? Did she love? Was she sad sometimes, as well? Did she like tomatoes, or did she prefer cucumber? Was she a mountain person, or did she love the sea? Did she go to bed late, did she have children? Did she have a mother who had sung her nursery rhymes? Did her skin smell slightly sweet, as Kitty imagined?

Kitty looked at her for a moment, even though it was difficult for her to turn her head in that direction, as the strap cut into the flesh of her thighs. She was morbidly pleased to see the woman again. She was still there. She still wanted something from her. She still looked composed and compassionate, as if she wouldn't hand Kitty over to these coarse, silent men, as if she wouldn't push things to the limit. But what exactly was the limit? A black, dark hole, bottomless and noiseless? Would it be a cell with dripping pipes? More straps? Or just her endless repeated questions about Andro's whereabouts? The blonde woman's skin shimmered like porcelain in the bluish light. She didn't belong in this deserted, dysfunctional place. No, this woman wouldn't take things to the limit, Kitty was sure of it. She was too beautiful, too smartly dressed for the limit. And besides, she was a woman. A woman, like herself.

★

Beads of sweat stood out on Kitty's forehead, she was ravenously hungry, and her lips were cracked. The woman stood, walked slowly towards her, and put a carafe to her mouth, and Kitty drank the water from it greedily. Half the liquid ran over her face, but its coolness felt good on her skin.

'I appreciate that it's very upsetting for you to have to endure all this, but you must cooperate with us.'

The blonde woman wiped the sweat from Kitty's forehead with a delicate handkerchief plucked from the inside pocket of her uniform jacket. The handkerchief smelled sweetish, as Kitty had presumed the woman's skin would smell. Sweetish, seductive; even, Kitty was shocked to discover, slightly familiar.

'I'm hungry ... I want to go home. Please. I don't know anything.' Kitty mumbled her words mechanically, almost apathetically, without much emphasis. Her eyes were fixed on the white rectangle on the wall. Was it midday, or was it afternoon? Was Christine already looking for her? If so, what were the prospects of her aunt finding her?

'Tell me where he is, give me the recruiter's name, give me an address, give me some information I can use, and I will drive you home myself. But you have to give me something, Ketevan!'

'Do you think I would do this to my child if I knew anything? I've waited so long for a message from him; I don't even know if he's still alive, and he doesn't know we're expecting a baby, and in a month it'll be born. Andro isn't a traitor, he just wanted to go to Vienna ...'

'To Vienna — good, good, that's a start. Who did he know in Vienna? What did he want to do there?'

'He didn't know anyone, he just wanted to go to Vienna because there are such beautiful coffee houses there and they do psychoanalysis there and sculpture is something you can ... Andro wants to be a sculptor. Please. I don't know anything. The baby's frightened, I can feel it.'

'My dear girl, you're little more than a baby yourself. Your parents should have done a better job of protecting you.'

'My father is with the Red Army, my brother's serving in the Baltic Fleet. They're serving the Motherland, they're serving the Generalissimus, they—'

'That is why we find it all the more regrettable that you, of all people, have chosen a traitor to be the father of your child.'

The sentence echoed in Kitty's head. There was something sickening about the way the blonde woman said it.

She was taken back to the basement, then brought out again and strapped back onto the stretcher. Hours passed. She no longer knew what day, what time it was. Her body ached; her baby was frightened. Twice she was given a little unsalted porridge. Three times a chamber pot was shoved under her backside. She got cramps in her arms and legs. Her strength diminished; she started to hallucinate; the bright light made sleep impossible, and she squeezed her eyes shut the whole time. Whenever the baby stopped kicking against the wall of her belly she had a panic attack and started screaming for help; only when it made its presence felt again did she sink back into exhaustion.

Suddenly, the blonde woman was standing very close to the stretcher. She was holding a syringe in her hand and scrutinising its contents in the white glare of the light bulb.

'If I don't get any useful information from you in the next few minutes, Kitty —' the way the woman said her nickname felt like more of a threat to Kitty than the syringe in her hand '— we will induce labour and you will suffer a stillbirth.'

The woman spoke deliberately, dragging out every word with artificial emphasis. But her tone remained soft, almost flattering, as if she were informing Kitty of a pleasant surprise, not putting the unthinkable into words.

Kitty started pushing against the straps with all her might, with her whole upper body; she tried to leap up, was astonished, wondered where she had suddenly found the strength to try and free herself. As she did so, she let out a scream, deafening even herself for a moment; a terrible, inhuman sound. The woman stayed at her side, impassive; she kept shaking her head regretfully. Kitty reached a hand down through the strap and grabbed at the corner of the uniform jacket. The blonde woman continued standing there; she didn't try to remove Kitty's hand, and went on holding the syringe upright in hers.

'You don't really mean it, do you? You just want to frighten me, I know it, I can see it in your eyes. You're nice, you like me, you care what happens to me, don't you? Isn't that right? You don't want to hurt me, you just want to frighten me, and the syringe is just full of water, no, you don't mean it.'

Kitty spoke quickly, the words tumbling out breathlessly one after another. For a moment the woman seemed caught between Kitty's hand on her jacket and her own eyes on the syringe. Between the decision to keep playing this wicked game, or to free Kitty. At least that's what Kitty thought. Yes — she too was a woman, she was ten, perhaps fifteen years older than Kitty, she was sure to have children. Surely she would never be able to go through with what she was threatening — she just wanted to prove to her superiors that she was second to none of her male colleagues. Just then, though, the woman called someone into the room.

A young girl in a white tunic entered. She was about Kitty's age, and she was afraid — very afraid. You could see it: her hands were trembling, although she kept them hidden in the pockets of her tunic. She didn't dare look the blonde woman in the eye; she didn't look directly at Kitty, either, kept her eyes on the ground, wishing that this place, this classroom, these people didn't exist.

She was definitely a country girl. She had red cheeks and sunburned skin. Perhaps her parents or husband had a farm to run. When she stopped in front of the woman it was impossible for her not to look at Kitty, and she began quietly reciting the Lord's Prayer, earning herself a contemptuous look from the blonde.

'Comrade Jashi doesn't want to help us, Mariam. Comrade Jashi is betraying her country. Comrade Jashi is shielding a traitor to his country; she even means to bring another traitor into the world. Do you think that's right? Do you think that's a good thing, Mariam?'

At these words, Kitty felt the urge to be sick. She started retching, but brought nothing up: the porridge was long since digested and her stomach was empty. She tried to concentrate on Mariam, the frightened girl, who had been roped into something that was beyond her imagination, that turned her knees to jelly, that made her go pale. Mariam, Mariam, Mother of God, thought Kitty to herself; and if she could, she would have laughed out loud. She had always mistrusted the saints that were still revered with such fervour in her country, even at the height of socialism. She had never understood why people allowed themselves to be tortured and tormented in the name of God — in the name of a God who had not redeemed them by his suffering, had not saved them. Mariam could have passed for a saint with her white tunic and her trembling hands, with her innocent calf's eyes; but she couldn't save Kitty, and she couldn't be saved, either.

The blonde pressed the syringe into the saint's hand, and with her other hand she grabbed Mariam's wrist and looked her in the eye. Mariam whimpered, tried to say something, fell silent, shrank back, but the woman went on staring at her intently. Mariam's fingers closed around the syringe. The woman took a few steps back and nodded at her. Mariam gasped for breath; her lips opened and closed like the mouth of a fish taken from the water.

'Do it!' Kitty heard the blonde say to Mariam, and she felt Mariam brush her elbow. Kitty narrowed her eyes. Any second now her heart would explode, she was sure of it. She tried to speak to the baby in her mind, tried to calm it. She didn't want it to be afraid. She held on tight to the stretcher with her fingers. She felt something salty fall on her face and saw Mariam's face bent over her, saw Mariam's tears dropping on her face, looked directly into Mariam's eyes for the first time: with the bright light of the bulb above her it was as if a halo had formed around Mariam's head. Kitty licked her lips and tasted Mariam's salty tears on her tongue.

'God have mercy upon me, God have mercy upon her, God have mercy upon us, God have mercy!' whispered Mariam, bending low over Kitty's head. In the background, the blonde stepped over to Mariam and said something in her ear; Mariam's face contorted horribly; then Kitty felt her hand on her forearm, felt it search for a vein, felt something cold and irrevocable being injected into her.

The blonde went out of the room and left Mariam alone with Kitty. Mariam undid the straps. Bruises had come up on Kitty's arms and thighs. Mariam sniffed, allowed the tears to flow; she didn't even attempt to wipe her face. Praying non-stop, she helped Kitty sit up. Everything hurt, every single part of her body; with every movement, Kitty groaned and stroked her belly.

'What was in the syringe?' She could hardly speak; she allowed her legs to dangle off the stretcher. Instead of answering, Mariam just shook her head.

'What was in it? What?' This time, Kitty raised her voice, reached out for Mariam, but before she could grab Mariam's tunic and pull her towards her, she was flung back onto the stretcher by inconceivable pain in her abdomen.

'Oh God, no, no, it can't be, it can't be, oh God!' Kitty began to scream. The contractions set in with fearful violence, ripping Kitty's body apart. She no longer believed she would survive this. In the few moments when the mind-numbing pain subsided, she tried to come to terms with death, tried to recall the face of her dead grandfather: how peaceful he had looked, his lips bluish, discoloured; perhaps she would manage that as well, slipping away peacefully and without fear, and it would feel like a deep, healthy sleep. Anything was better than this. Anything was better than this pain. Anything was better than this classroom and the white rectangle on the wall.

Again and again, Mariam squeezed her hand, encouraged Kitty to push. Again and again, she urged her to breathe. And when Kitty was no longer in any doubt that she would die that very second, she felt something large, round, slide out between her legs, felt Mariam's hands pull the little body out, and she fell back onto the stretcher. The pain abruptly subsided. She kept her eyes closed.

'Keep praying. I want to … with you …' Kitty didn't dare open her eyes. Mariam started saying the prayer, and Kitty repeated every word after her.

'Our Father, who art in Heaven, hallowed be Thy name.' There was no cry. No cry. Not a sound. 'Thy kingdom come. Thy will be done.' The child was mute. Perhaps it was just mute, it must be mute. 'On Earth as it is in Heaven.' A kind of rustle. Mariam was moving. Perhaps the baby had stirred.

Perhaps it had taken a breath. 'Give us this day.' Kitty couldn't bear it any longer: she opened her eyes, saw Mariam's back, the splashes of blood on her apron. She saw Mariam holding her baby in her arms. 'Our daily bread. And forgive —' Kitty put a fist under the small of her back and propped herself up so she could see better '— us our trespasses, as we forgive those who —' Mariam turned around. She didn't finish the prayer. There was nothing left to be asked of God.

'Go on, go on!' Kitty yelled at her, but Mariam just shook her head, holding the tiny, bloody body pressed tight against her.

'Strap her back down!' they heard the blonde say through the door. But Kitty crawled off the stretcher and stumbled to the door, without taking her dead child in her arms. Before she could fling it open it was opened from outside, and a Red Army soldier, one of the three from the car, stopped in front of her, lifted her off the ground, brought her back to the stretcher, put her on it, and strapped her down.

'The placenta hasn't come yet, you have to let her —' cried Mariam, horrified. 'What kind of people are you, what are you!' Her Russian was clumsy and broken, her voice hoarse and rasping.

Kitty heard nothing more. Total darkness filled her head.

She didn't watch as Mariam wrapped the dead body in her tunic and carried it out of the room.

★

When Mariam returned and found Kitty unconscious, she started shouting for help, and the blonde returned.

'She won't stop bleeding, she's going to bleed to death. So much blood — Mother of God, Jesus, Holy Child, we have to stop the bleeding, or she'll die ...'

The blonde gazed for a while at Kitty's blood-drenched lower abdomen with an expression of resignation, then turned to Mariam.

'You will stop the bleeding. You'll find everything you need in the basement, in the metal cupboards. You have to operate on her. You have to remove her womb. Otherwise she'll die a miserable death, and you don't want that. Otherwise she may get it into her head to bring more traitors into the world. You can operate, can't you?'

'What? No, no, no — I can't do that. I've never operated myself, I'm not a doctor, I just helped out in the outpatient department; I only watched, I can do sutures and take them out again, but I can't do this.'

'But I was told you were good. That's why you're here. So see that you complete the task. I'll have them bring you morphine. The disinfecting agents are in the basement as well. You can start right away!'

'I can't. I can't!'

Mariam was getting increasingly hysterical.

'Well, then she'll just have to bleed to death.'

'Please, no, no ... You can't do this to me. Call a doctor. Please!'

'One of my men will assist you. Don't worry, he won't pass out. And you know what will happen if you get any ideas.'

'All right, all right. I'll do it. I'll try.'

'If she survives, you'll take her with you to the village afterwards, and when she can walk again you'll send her home. And you'll be good and keep your mouth shut, won't you. And tell her: as soon as he makes contact with her, she should go to the nearest commissariat of her own accord, if she doesn't want ... Well, I think now she'll understand.'

★

Mariam called the Red Army soldier, instructed him to clean his hands with spirit and pass her the necessary tools when she asked for them. She kept talking to Kitty all through the operation.

'You mustn't give up. You're strong. We can do this, but you mustn't stop fighting. I know it's hard for you to trust me; it's hard for you because I'm not a doctor. But I always wanted to be one. I assisted in the outpatient department, they had a very good doctor there, and because we don't have a proper hospital in the village he would perform operations as well, and he was good. Everyone got well again. And of course there were births, as well; jaundice, gout, TB, I've treated everything. We had a miscarriage once, and that woman's alive and healthy. I can do this. I'm good. Do you believe me? You do believe me, don't you?'

Mariam was speaking only to Kitty now. Not to God any more. Mariam removed Kitty's womb, in a classroom that had served as a torture chamber and was now an operating theatre. In a classroom where they had taken down the portrait of the Leader so as not to insult his eyes with the degrading sight of a stillbirth and a blood-drenched woman. Mariam kept her word. She saved Kitty's life, and her own. She could not save Kitty's child.

★

After the blonde woman and her entourage had left the village, Mariam took Kitty to an isolated barn and nursed her. She had taken the necessary medicines from the school basement; she found Kitty a clean mattress and fresh bed linen, fetched her milk and warm bread, slaughtered a chicken with her own hands and roasted it over an open fire. She treated Kitty's inflamed stitches and stroked her head. The fever had to be brought down, Kitty had to be fed; she gave her herbal mixtures to relieve the pain, lay down beside her on the mattress, and stared with her into the nothingness on which Kitty's eyes were fixed. It was days before Kitty turned and spoke to her for the first time.

'Where am I?'

'In my brother's barn. He's at the front, somewhere in the northern Caucasus. I didn't want to take you home with me, to my parents. There would have been unnecessary questions. People in the village are afraid. The NKVD have been here a few times already. They use the old school building for … Well, people are suspicious, anyway; no one wants trouble. We're safe here.'

'Why did you take me with you?'

'What sort of question is that? What else could I have done? You would have died. Rest now. Drink the milk. We have cows, we always have fresh milk. You had a high fever, but that's normal.'

'I have to go home. I have to telephone Christine. How long have I been here?'

'Exactly a week. You can't get up yet, and you're not allowed to go, either.'

'What did you do?'

'They would have shot us. They took a girl from a neighbouring village, a nurse; she never came back, just because she refused to operate. I had to do it, otherwise they would have shot me — both of us. Last week they brought three men here, shot them, and buried them in the woods.'

Mariam covered her face with her hands. Her body was trembling. Kitty sat up and looked at her, her expression blank. She made no attempt to comfort her. Finally Mariam clasped Kitty in her arms. Kitty didn't move.

'I know it can't ever be put right.' Mariam groaned and pressed herself against Kitty's shoulders, buried her face in her neck.

'What exactly do you mean?' Kitty insisted.

Mariam stuttered. 'You … can never have … I … I … your womb …'

In the nights that followed, Mariam stayed with Kitty, lying on a simple blanket beside her mattress and falling into a deep, dreamless sleep only as dawn approached. Eventually, one day, Kitty got up and went out into the warm sunlight with Mariam supporting her. It was quiet; you could hear the crickets. The barn was next to a cornfield, at the end of a narrow path lined with tall cypresses. Green, hunchbacked hills stretched away into the distance. Kitty's eyes were burning. Her mouth was dry; the sunlight hurt her skin. Nevertheless, she allowed the sun to warm her cold limbs. She stood there, moving her head gently from side to side, slowly raising her arms above her head, wriggling each finger cautiously, one at a time. She moved as if for the first time, as if she first had to learn how to do it: how to walk, to move, to think, to live.

That night, Mariam lit a small campfire and the two of them sat beside it. The night was clear, the sky full of stars, and the moon, white as marble, radiated a greenish light.

'What exactly did you do?' asked Mariam, almost inaudibly. She poked the ashes with a stick. 'You're so young; what can you possibly have done for them to do something like that to you?'

'Nothing.'

'What did your husband do?'

'He just wanted to go to Vienna … It was a boy, wasn't it?' Kitty asked suddenly, concentrating on the glowing coals.

'Yes.'

'What was he like? Was he big, small? Did he have lovely little fists? Did he have hair on his head?'

'He was wonderful. He didn't suffer. He didn't even feel it. It happened very quickly.'

'Where did he go?'

'He's with the angels now.'

'Stop that nonsense. Where did you take him?'

'I buried him. In the garden behind the school.'

'Please don't start bawling again. Pull yourself together.'

'Oh God, Kitty … It would have been better if they'd shot us.'

'That's enough. Stop it. Don't cry. Not again. You had no choice. You saved my life.'

'No, I didn't. I destroyed everything.'

Kitty got up and started turning slowly round in circles. Head tilted back, looking up at the stars, her lips widening in something like a smile.

'Careful, you mustn't move around yet. Please take care — the stitches!'

Kitty took a deep breath and released it again.

'When all this is over, it doesn't matter how or when, I will find out who she is, and I will kill her.'

She spoke with great composure. Mariam did not reply, and they went back inside the barn.

*

Once Kitty had recovered her strength and could get about without help, she walked to the abandoned school building with the broken windows that looked so normal, anything but menacing, and wandered through the cold corridors and empty rooms. She looked for the room where they had cut her child out of her belly. The portrait of the Generalissimus was back on the wall. She stared for a long while at the man's moustachioed face; for a very long while, as if seeing him for the first time. Outside again, in the open air, she sat down on the dry earth in the courtyard. A few pigeons were cooing and scratching at the ground in search of something edible. The earth was warm, the sun shining impassively. She heard a tractor drive past in the distance. Her gaze moved across the yard. Somewhere here must be the spot where Mariam had buried her boy. Somewhere here his body must lie. Beneath an oak, almost at the very end of the school grounds, she spotted a little pile of earth: small, so incredibly small. She went over, sank to her knees in front of it, and started digging up the mound with her bare hands. The earth was stubborn and rough, as if trying to thwart Kitty's intentions. She touched something. Felt it. Felt the nausea well up inside her. Closed her eyes, kept digging. There was a smell of something definitive; she vomited, then screamed, just once, just briefly. The scream sliced the air. Then there was silence again, and the silence felt holy; it was a good day for life to begin, a day of delicate ladybirds and lazy bumblebees flying on the breeze, a day for lying in the shade eating ripe figs and soft persimmons. A day that belonged entirely to life.

She saw with her hands: the nose and the oval of the face, the tiny eyebrows, the lips. She gazed at his face as it arose in her mind's eye. She recognised him. She would keep him in her memory all her life. His face that she had never seen, never stroked, not even once. That she would never see either crying or laughing, sleeping or awake. She would keep him forever in her dreams, in a parallel universe that existed only behind closed eyelids. She would live there with him, go to sleep and wake with him. She gave him a name. She threw the earth back over him.

Again she retched, but this time didn't vomit. A flock of birds flew past above her head. The stitches pinched. Gently she stroked the mound of earth with her palm. 'You can visit me in my dreams; you will, won't you? I'll sing you songs, I'll sing you all the songs in the world, and that will be our sign; you'll know then that I'm calling you. I'll take you with me everywhere, no matter where I go. You'll know I'm there, and I'll know you're there. That'll be enough: it'll have to be enough for a lifetime.'

She stretched out on the ground, laid her face on the earth, tasted it on her tongue. If she could swallow the bitterness, she would taste the essential thing: this love for her son, fragile, almost painful, physically present yet at the same time soft as butter — this love that eclipsed all other feelings. A love they would never have been able to cut out of her. A love that ripped her apart from inside, that pinched her with every move she made, a thousand times worse than the stitches.

Broken rays of sunlight wandered across the hills, down into the valley, to the village, to the school playground, to stroke Kitty's ankles, light the colour of a weathered brick. Somewhere a crow was crying. Kitty forced herself to stand. A last, overripe fig fell from the tree beside her. Summer flies buzzed around.

★

At this moment, Kostya was carrying a heavy sack of flour and passing it on to a sailor who hoisted it onto the bed of the truck. Suddenly it was as if there were a heavy scent in his nostrils, a seductive, familiar smell. He wondered where he recognised it from. It was the smell of his grandfather's chocolate factory. He wiped the sweat from his face, and without knowing why he suddenly thought of his younger sister, from whom he had heard nothing for such a long time. *Don't you miss your brother? Or are you always thinking of your Andro? Where is he now? Was he sent to the northern Caucasus?* These thoughts passed through Kostya's mind, but he preferred not to dwell on them, and seized the next sack of flour. Shots could be heard in the north, but he had learned to ignore them; they were far enough away.

★

Kitty prepared for her departure. The trains were running irregularly; there were reports of bands of robbers in the stations. It would be safer, Mariam suggested, for her to ask a farmer to take her to the city. The post office in the village had closed some time ago. There was no way of sending a telegram to Christine. Kitty was uncomfortable about taking the roubles she needed for the journey from Mariam, but she had no choice.

'What will you do?' Kitty asked her friend — her friend, despite everything — as they said goodbye.

'I'll go home, to my parents, and see whether I can be of any assistance to the doctor in the next village. They closed our outpatient clinic a few months ago.'

'Come to Tbilisi.'

'Is that a joke? What would I do in the city?'

'There's a shortage of doctors everywhere. I worked in a hospital, too.'

'But I'm not a doctor, Kitty.'

'You're the best doctor I know.'

Kitty hugged her saint tightly. Mariam brushed back a lock of hair from her forehead.

'Please forgive me, if you can,' she whispered in her ear as they parted.

★

Christine's hand flew to her mouth when she opened the door and saw Kitty standing before her at last. Kitty — without her belly. The farmer had set her down at the main market and she had walked the steep streets all the way up the hill to Vera. Christine knelt down in front of her and started kissing her hands. Kitty had never seen her aunt so beside herself. Christine stroked her face, hands, shoulders, kept running her hands through her hair; she kissed her forehead, her cheeks, her neck. She had spent days on the phone to the administrative authorities, had been to every commissariat in the city, had interrogated all her old acquaintances, to no avail. No one had been able to tell her where Kitty was.

'What did they do, what did they do to you …?' asked Christine, again and again.

Kitty allowed herself to be kissed and stroked, but her eyes remained glazed, and she didn't want to talk, either.

'I'm hungry, I'm so hungry, I'm so tired, I have to eat something and then sleep, just sleep.'

Christine quickly started opening the kitchen cupboards and putting everything she found on the table. She put a saucepan on the gas and heated the frying pan.

'I nearly died of worry, I didn't know what to do … What on earth happened, Kitty?'

As she sliced the bread, Christine cut her forefinger and froze at the sight of the blood running from it. She continued to stare at the red liquid in fascination. Kitty got to her feet, led Christine to the sink, and ran water over the fingertip.

'It's all right, it's not that bad,' she said, looking at her aunt. Christine's expression was one of horror.

That night, Christine sat beside Kitty with the beautiful half of her face turned towards her, and clung to her hand. Kitty wanted to be left alone, but Christine seemed so frightened that she didn't dare send her aunt away.

'Where's the baby?'

The room lay in darkness. Kitty could see Christine's silhouette, her flawless profile, and felt an inexplicable urge to touch her face. But it wasn't the flawless side she wanted to touch; it was the side with the scars, the burned left side she had revealed to her not all that long ago, to tell her that together they would make it, that they would get through this, whatever happened. But they hadn't made it.

'What are you doing?' Christine shrank away slightly as Kitty's hand moved across her cheek, across her nose, towards the left side, which was hidden beneath a blue veil.

'Let me, please,' said Kitty, gently touching the shrivelled skin that felt so hard compared to the intact half of Christine's face. As if she were stroking a prehistoric animal, the last survivor of an extinct species. Her instinct was to withdraw her hand, but she overcame it and went on exploring Christine's face with her fingers. Kitty began to speak. Calmly and in detail she told Christine about the hours in the school building, about the blonde woman, about the straps that had bound her, about the syringe, about Mariam, about the questions, those questions they kept asking her again and again, to which she had had no answers. She told her about the contractions, about the stillbirth, about the operation, about the days in the barn where Mariam had nursed her. And all the while she ran her hand over Christine's scars, felt her way across the bumps and hollows in the hope that by studying Christine's map she would be able to create her own. A map of her own that would show her how to go on living. A survival map. One that would help her to get out of the classroom with the white rectangle on the wall and cross her own desert, where there was nothing but burning sun and a little mound beneath a tree.

Her hand touched the eye socket. She touched the place where once there had been an eyebrow. The spot where Christine's husband, perhaps, had kissed her every morning when they awoke; or where perhaps, as a child, she had contrived to cut herself and received a kiss from her mother, right there. Or perhaps from her father. A spot that had had stories to tell and that now no longer existed, that could no longer write stories on this face. A spot obliterated by the dark wing of a poisonous bird that had flapped over Christine's head and brushed her as it passed.

'Where is Andro?' asked Christine, once Kitty had fallen silent and taken her hand away from her aunt's face.

'Please, don't ever ask me that again. Never, never, never again, you hear?' Kitty suddenly let out a scream, turned to face the other side of the bed and drew up her knees. 'I don't know where he is, and I don't want to know any more.'

The USSR guards the peace of all peoples!

POSTER SLOGAN

General Paulus was appointed commander of the entire German 6th Army, which had more than a quarter of a million soldiers and several tank battalions at its disposal. On 23 August 1942, the first German tanks reached the Volga north of Stalingrad. That same day, the Luftwaffe attacked the city. The Generalissimus had absolutely no intention of allowing an evacuation; the city that bore his name was too important to him for that.

In early August, Lieutenant Simon Jashi was appointed commander of a company in the 38th Rifle Division under the leadership of Lieutenant-General Zhukov, who led the overall defence in the battle for Stalingrad. Of the almost 600,000 inhabitants who were still in the city in the summer of 1942, 40,000 were killed in the first days of the offensive. For the Kremlin, not even the massive death toll, the starvation, and the bombardments constituted an argument for evacuation. On the contrary: on 25 August, the Generalissimus announced that he was going to 'turn the city into an invincible fortress'.

The ghosts started giggling hysterically from the late-summer treetops and the great branches of the oaks.

On 12 September, parts of the 6th Army penetrated the city — the flag at the main station changed three times in as many hours. The city was transformed into a lunar landscape, its architecture designed by the Luftwaffe. Fuel from wrecked cars and broken pipes ran straight into the Volga, lending an additional morbid drama to the inferno. Ten days later, the Germans had taken the station, which by then had changed sides fifteen times. A grotesque battle began for every house, every street. Every centimetre counted. After forty days, the city had been transformed into a deadly labyrinth with no way out. People called it the 'War of the Rats', because the majority of the population was forced to live in the sewers. As many as two thousand Luftwaffe Stuka bombers were sent out over the city. In November, practically the whole of the city was in German hands. When the final German offensive began on the eighty-first day of the battle, there were only a few Russian bases in the city still holding out against attack. And it was here that, once again, the relentless cold came to the Red Army's aid. The Luftwaffe was unable to carry out aerial attacks because of bad weather, and supply routes on the ground were blocked, giving Marshal Zhukov time to launch a military counterattack codenamed Operation Uranus. Zhukov mustered almost one million soldiers on the southern and northern fronts, and began to draw the noose tight around the city. The northern and southern forces joined up on 23 November: they began to encircle Stalingrad, and with it the entire 6th Army.

Even when the German general staff sent desperate warnings to Berlin requesting permission to retreat, or risk the deaths of many thousands of German soldiers, Hitler bellowed into the receiver: 'I'm not leaving the Volga!' Göring assured them that the Luftwaffe would guarantee food supplies from the air. Field Marshal von Manstein was to make an immediate plan for the German counteroffensive.

The Germans spent Christmas 1942 in foxholes, freezing and starving, hallucinating Christmas trees and fragrant Christmas biscuits. Softly whistling 'Silent Night', the ghosts of war climbed over the barricades and crawled into the soldiers' dreams. There they metamorphosed into the faces of their mothers, fathers, sisters, brothers, their wives and sweethearts, warmed their hands and whispered lovers' vows in their ears. The ghosts knew nothing of time, and created bright illusions in the soldiers' heads. The dreams tasted delicious, and waking was unbearably hard.

In desperation, wounded, starving soldiers clung to planes taking off for home just to escape this hell, only to fall a few moments later, frozen, to their deaths. In Stalingrad, Death was dancing his wildest dance. The Soviet command had death songs specially composed and played all over the city via loudspeaker: 'Every Seven Seconds A German Soldier Dies', 'Stalingrad: A Mass Grave'.

The Red Lieutenant, his hair now totally grey, sat in a headquarters near the Red Barricades ordnance factory and wrote to his wife with a shaking hand, unsure whether he would ever be able to send the letter: *My Anastasia, how I wish now that I could turn back the clock* ...

On 10 January, the 6th Army launched its final, decisive counteroffensive against the Reds, which led to the division of the army and its encirclement in two pockets. The Germans' supply lines were cut off completely.

After this day, the White-Red Lieutenant disappears without a trace. It is said that he was seen again on 31 January in the Univermag department store, the headquarters of the 6th Army, which was stormed by his division and blown up in the general orgy of destruction. It's very likely that Simon Jashi was in the building. But perhaps it wasn't like that at all; perhaps he died some other death, in some other place.

I've always had a picture in my head of the ruined department store: the skeleton of the building before my eyes, its shell, its bones. And the haggard shadows inside that have forgotten what it feels like to be human. I picture Simon Jashi yelling something, I picture soldiers stumbling past him like an emaciated herd, aimless, uncomprehending, following a brute survival instinct. Dust falling from the ceiling, and the biting wind creeping through the smashed windows, the broken-down doors, the façades, now shot to pieces, and spreading out, encompassing everything, blowing everything away, all of time, except for this one moment in which Simon Jashi stops. Perhaps he hears someone, a young soldier, shouting: 'Get out, get out, quick, get out of here!' But he is unable to move. He stands staring out through the shattered glass, out through a hole in the wall at this great graveyard of humanity, the apocalyptic landscape, this terrifying beauty of the end of days. He sees the gardens of rubble and stones, the skeleton architecture, sees the patterns of blood, sees the sculptures of mangled reinforced concrete, and is amazed that everyone but himself is oblivious to this doomed symphony of death and destruction. Simon Jashi stands silently and doesn't understand why he cannot move. It lasts only seconds, or perhaps minutes, but to Simon it feels different: as if time has been slowed down, as if everything were happening in slow motion. Always, in my imagination, Simon has forgotten the war and the thoughts of his terminal future, the hopeless days, the sense of failure, the disappointed eyes of the wife he was unable to make happy, the tsar, Lenin, the Motherland, and the Generalissimus; yes, even the steppe, which could have been the start of a better future. And suddenly the noise is very loud, a deafening thunderclap, and blood starts to flow from his ear. He knows that more detonations will follow, that time has run out, but he's not thinking about that any more, he can't move any more and he doesn't want to.

Beat the fascists to death!

POSTER SLOGAN

As if by an irony of fate, Simon Jashi's son had celebrated his greatest victory a few days before that final decisive battle for Stalingrad in which his father most probably lost his life. On 18 January, the Reds captured the shore all the way around Lake Ladoga. An eleven-metre-wide corridor was created, and with it a link to the mainland. Konstantin had distinguished himself through outstanding service in the battle to liberate Leningrad. When radio communications broke down completely one night during Operation Iskra and the commander-in-chief was unable to issue any further orders, Konstantin Jashi had assumed command of one of the ships in the Gulf of Finland.

Kostya celebrated the victory with his comrades. The schnapps he hadn't tasted for months warmed his stomach, went to his head, and made him so euphoric that he climbed the mast of the ship, yelling that the fascists were finished.

★

Less than forty kilometres away, a gaunt, dark-haired woman crept out onto the street. Her hands were purple and her eyes sunk deep in their sockets; her hair was thin, her boots full of holes, her back bent. She dragged herself out of the dark entrance of one of the houses and onto a cobbled street, staggered in the direction of Nevsky Prospekt, stopped, took several deep breaths. She was heading for the post office on Karavannaya Street, where a registration office had recently been set up to compile an evacuation list.

The past month had robbed her of her remaining strength. She barely managed to leave the apartment, negotiate the stairs, or survive the interminable queues for food rations. However, the news that the siege had been broken had conjured a smile to her lips, and she had decided to go to the registration office again. Surely just one look at her would be enough to put her at the top of the list.

She had been coughing blood for some time now, but she didn't want to think about that. She had to make it there; she had to get to the post office.

Perhaps she really had lost her mind, like the street-sweeper last month, who had stood naked in the street shouting obscenities. She didn't know what day it was, or what else was going on in the world. In some of her daydreams she hallucinated that the rest of the world had long since ceased to exist, that Leningrad was the last island of survivors. Today, though, Ida was struggling to banish all her destructive thoughts and concentrate on getting to Karavannaya Street.

The sky was not as dusty, powdery, and overcast as it usually was at this time of year. A few rays of sun were even shimmering through, and beneath the hard ice the Neva had begun to flow again. A couple of ragged children ran past. A woman walking in front of her was pushing a pram, as if it were a perfectly ordinary day in a perfectly ordinary town, but when she drew closer, Ida saw that the pram was full of stones. She heard a car in the distance: a good sign — there must be petrol again.

The little junk shop on her street had reopened its doors; another good sign, she thought. Even if there was nothing to buy there.

You really could have supposed that this was a perfectly ordinary day in a perfectly ordinary town. Perhaps she ought to persuade herself that this was actually the case. Perhaps that was her best chance of holding on to what remained of her wits; but the ghostly silence that hung over the city made her doubt this possibility. She stopped, breathed deeply, swallowed; her mouth was dry, her eyes burned, she was barely accustomed to daylight any more. In her apartment she kept the curtains closed, initially on account of the air raids, then out of habit; now she could no longer imagine it any other way.

The last three times she hadn't even gone down to the bunker when the air raid siren went off; she'd been unable to summon either the necessary strength or the necessary hope. Back in the first year of the blockade there had been old people who had stayed in their apartments despite the alarm. Ida used to get upset about these people; back then, she had still possessed the optimism and the memories necessary to want to survive. Now she herself was one of these people. Now she too was one of these mummies whom both life and the war passed by.

On Nevsky Prospekt she stopped. She had caught sight of her reflection in the window of an old shop, long since closed. She had known this street so well, before, in her old life; now she couldn't even begin to remember what shop had been here. Perhaps the upmarket fabric shop, or the bookshop ... What was the point, anyway, in reconstructing something that would never be that way again?

The question was banished by a vague memory: the memory of his face. Or what her memory had turned it into. Did he still look so touchingly young, in his dark-blue uniform with the white-gold braid on collar and sleeve? Did he still have that thick, wavy hair? Could he still laugh with such abandon? Utterly childlike, utterly free, utterly unforced, forgetting his habitual seriousness? Was he still so eager to please, to be acknowledged and accepted by those in power? What was he afraid of? Had she become the same indelible memory for him that he was for her?

On her darkest days, Ida pictured Kostya's death. Believed he was already dead. Wallowed in this fateful, ghastly certainty. She pictured terrible scenarios: Kostya, hit by a grenade, falling into the sea; Kostya drowning, or shot, wounded, bleeding to death on some distant shore.

On better days she put him at the side of a young girl with big doe eyes and pigtails that hung halfway down her thighs. Pictured him teaching the girl, with the same devotion, all that she had once taught him.

She turned into a side road. The street sign had disappeared long ago. She knew the street, but couldn't remember its name. Suddenly she had to stop again, because she had heard something; a noise, a sound, something very familiar. It was music — a piano, definitely. A well-known melody that, like the street, Ida was unable to place. But she followed it: without thinking what she was doing, she hurried after the notes. The melody grew clearer and louder with every step.

Where did she know this melody from? What was it? Ah, yes: in another life — or was it a dream — she had played the piano. She could feel the keys under her bare, transparent fingers, which had long since lost their rings: the ivory, the cool, beautiful material of her childhood grand piano.

Once there had been all this, and much more. Now there was shattered debris, shards of glass, hunger, and the siren that announced the air raids.

It was Grieg. Yes, Ida remembered now. Grieg. The Romantic. The romance of ruin, she thought. She kept following the music and came to an inner courtyard where an old house with broken windows had managed to withstand the bombs. A first-floor window was open; the piano music was coming from this apartment.

Ida entered the dark stairwell and climbed the few steps to a wooden door that stood ajar. All this time her brain was trying without success to reconstruct the title of the piece. She knocked, but heard no footsteps; the piece continued uninterrupted. She peeped through the gap and stepped over the threshold.

She found herself in a spacious hall, empty and damp, with grey, wet patches on the walls. She followed the Grieg and came to a room with a fox-coloured parquet floor and a bare mattress in one corner. At the window stood the piano: undamaged, beautiful, well tuned. A young girl was sitting at it, lost in the melody, playing the 'Ballade for Piano in G Minor' — yes, that was the name of the piece, she remembered now.

The girl didn't turn, didn't look round. From behind, Ida guessed that she couldn't be older than fifteen.

'Excuse me — I heard you playing and I followed the music. You play beautifully.'

Cautiously, Ida approached the pianist. The girl continued to play. She nodded her head almost imperceptibly.

'An audience of one, at least. Come in, do come in. I'm afraid I don't have a chair; you'll have to stand. We burned all the furniture when it was so cold.' The girl didn't turn round; her fingers continued to dance across the keys without a single mistake. Ida sensed goose pimples creeping up her arms; it was disconcerting, as if her skin had forgotten how to feel. Carefully, Ida positioned herself at the piano, glanced at the girl's face for the first time — and shrank back, holding her breath so as not to betray her shock. The girl's eyes were missing. There were two dark hollows where her eyes should have been. But she was smiling.

She was wearing a grey worker's dress full of holes, and warm felt boots on her feet. Her thick, light-brown plait hung down her back.

'I'm practising for my third young musicians' competition. I was supposed to travel to London, before ...' said the girl, her body swaying slightly to the music.

'You're going to be a pianist?' asked Ida, still not quite over the shock.

'I was supposed to become one, yes.'

The girl stopped abruptly. Her fingers rested on the keys, suddenly quite stiff and without purpose.

'You still will, I'm sure. If you're practising in these conditions.'

'I wasn't able to practise for a long time. My mother wouldn't let me, after ...'

'After ...?'

'It was because I was practising that I didn't make it to the bunker in time. I was hit by a piece of shrapnel — here, you see ...' The girl turned her blind face towards Ida, as if she wouldn't notice otherwise that her eyes were missing. 'Now Mama is dead, and I can play again.' The girl spoke with as little emphasis as if she were talking about the death of a pet.

'And your father?'

'He was killed. At Minsk. My brother's at the front, too, but he's alive. I know he is. Sergei's still alive and he'll come back, I'm sure of it.'

'Definitely. Definitely.' Ida noticed that her voice sounded tender, almost loving. 'I like music. I used to think that I'd become a pianist, too.'

'What stopped you? The war?'

'Not quite. But something similar,' said Ida, and laughed. Suddenly the girl got up from the stool and stood in front of her. She was tall and bony, but not undernourished. That was a good sign — a very good sign, in fact. The girl raised her hand.

'May I?'

Ida consented, and the girl touched her face. She ran her fingers gently over Ida's features. She touched her mouth, her nose, her eyes, her lips. Ida shuddered. How long ago was it that someone had last touched her. How worn-out and terrible, how cold, how rigid, how ancient she must feel. But the girl didn't seem to mind.

'I have to do this so I can imagine a face, and I can often guess a person's age as well. Shall I tell you how old you are?'

'Go on, then.'

'Mid-forties?'

'I don't know myself any more. I've stopped counting.'

'I'm fourteen.'

The girl said it with pride, as if being fourteen were a great achievement. And perhaps it was. Perhaps, in this city, it was a great achievement to have reached your fourteenth year.

'Do you live here alone?'

'My cousin is here sometimes. But she has to look after my grandfather; he's not well. And she works at the school. But I manage. I'm allowed to play again. Fortunately we didn't chop up the piano for firewood. Mother was planning to, but I wouldn't let her.'

'Please, could you go on playing? I haven't heard music for so long.'

'You could play with me. Something for four hands.'

'No, no, I couldn't; my hands are like claws. It would be horrible. I'd like it to be beautiful.'

'As you wish. My teacher once told me that I had a flair for the French composers. Shall I play something by Debussy? I'm so fond of him. Something from the Preludes, perhaps?'

'Whatever you like.'

The girl concentrated, rubbed her hands together, blew into her fists, and began to play. Ida leaned against the wall and listened, enchanted. She followed the girl's playing, and with every note the war was driven from her arms, her body, her head; she was transported her to another world. A world of brightly lit cafés and shining boulevards where well-fed people strolled up and down. A place with purple Chinese lanterns, neat entrances to buildings with furnished apartments; a place where you could order apple cake with your tea, a place that smelled of French perfume. Where people wore warm coats and leather gloves. Where you could go to the cinema or listen to concerts. A place where the girl playing the piano had a mother, and sparkling green eyes.

'Sacred Dance. That's what he called that piece.'

The girl's voice broke into Ida's thoughts, brought them abruptly tumbling down. Ida looked out of the window at the empty courtyard. She remembered that she had to go to the post office and shook her head, as if trying to rouse herself from her dream.

'Why are you still here? Why weren't you evacuated long ago?'

'I wasn't an invalid back then,' the girl said. Her directness was both disarming and somehow brutal.

'But ...'

'My mother worked for the Road. We got by.'

'You have to come with me.'

'Where?'

'To Karavannaya, to the post office. They're compiling new evacuation lists. The siege has been broken, haven't you heard?'

'I haven't been out for days, and my cousin hasn't been able to come.'

'When was the last time you ate?'

'My neighbour, Comrade Tashkova, gives me some of her food, because I play for her son. He's mentally handicapped, and it soothes him.'

'Stand up.'

'I don't have a coat. I can't go outside.'

'I'll give you mine. You have to come with me, now.'

'But ...'

Ida was already pulling the girl to her feet and putting a coat around her shoulders. She wrapped her in the scarf that she had knitted herself, and they went outside. The girl sniffed the air like a dog. Ida took her hand; she pulled it back and answered proudly, 'I can manage on my own. I've been blind for two hundred and thirty-four days now. I'm learning.'

The queue was visible from a long way off. They had to wait in line, and by the time they finally entered the building the light had gone.

Behind a little table — more like a school desk — sat an older woman and a young Red Army soldier. Ida gave her name.

'I'll have to look.'

The woman started leafing through an enormous file. People are happy to burn pianos, but files are sacrosanct, thought Ida.

'I was assured in October that I'd be put on the priority list,' she pointed out.

After a few minutes the woman did indeed find her name on the list. Ida had to present her passport and her tattered, crumpled health certificate, which had been issued to her by a malnourished doctor after a cursory examination: it did not look good. The woman rummaged again in her mountain of files.

'February the twelfth. Mikhailovsky Garden. It'll be a transporter. You may take no more than one suitcase, and don't forget your passport. And this document I'm issuing you with — don't let it out of your sight.'

When the woman said this, Ida thought she would be sick. The girl just stood beside her, motionless, as if she hadn't heard.

'This girl has to come with me,' began Ida timidly. 'She lost her eyesight in an air raid and her mother's dead. She has no other relatives, which means she's a first-degree invalid.' Ida tried to speak as neutrally as possible so the girl didn't get the impression she pitied her.

The woman slowly raised her head and stared long and hard at the girl. 'I really am very sorry, but I'm afraid there's nothing I can do. She has to get on the list first, like everyone else. They've all been waiting for months already, if not years.'

'It's all right,' said the girl. Her face betrayed no disappointment.

'No, it's not all right!' Ida shouted suddenly. She was surprised by how loud her voice was. 'Nothing is all right. Look at her! This damned war has taken everything she has, and yet she's still sitting there, forgotten even by God, in a cold, empty apartment, playing the piano. She could be an extraordinary pianist. She has to stay alive, she has to get something to eat, she has to play! She's only fourteen!'

The older woman looked at Ida with indifference, as if she was used to outbursts, breakdowns like these. No one in the queue dared say anything; everyone was entirely focused on their own survival. The girl was clearly embarrassed by it all; her head was bowed in shame.

'Come on, please, let's go ...'

'No!' Ida shouted again. 'You have to get out of here!'

'Then give her your place, for heaven's sake, and put yourself on the list again!' a one-legged man behind her shouted, visibly annoyed at the delay. For a moment the room went quiet. Ida said nothing. She looked at the girl.

'No, for God's sake — don't do that!' the girl blurted out, turning her eyeless face to Ida.

But Ida was already bending over the desk, and saying to the woman, 'Please make out the document in her name. And put me on the next list.'

The girl seized Ida's hand and tried to drag her away.

'No, absolutely not, you mustn't do it. Your hands are alarmingly cold, I can feel it. You're not well. You have to leave. My cousin —'

'Stop it and do as you're told!' The customary hardness returned to Ida's voice.

'Name!' said the woman at the table.

'What's your name?' Ida realised she hadn't asked the girl before now.

'Ida,' she said.

'Your name — I mean yours,' Ida insisted.

'Yes: my name is Ida. Ida Efremova.'

'Well, that's convenient. So I only have to change the surname and date of birth,' said the woman behind the desk.

Ida's knees buckled.

★

They spent the days before her departure together, in Ida's darkened apartment on Vasilievsky, and in Ida Efremova's empty apartment; I don't know its exact location.

Ida heard music again for the first time since the start of the blockade. The younger Ida was always ready to play something for the elder, who would first warm her hands for her by placing them in her armpits: the two of them would stand like that for a while, until the younger disengaged herself and ran, with a laugh, to the piano. Then she would play, lost in the music, while Ida stood beside her with her eyes closed and followed the melody back to her past.

Ida E. spoke incessantly about the future. About sharing an apartment, somewhere where it was warm; about piano lessons, because Ida E. was sure that, once the war and the cold were over, the elder Ida would want to play again. She talked about the hens they could have that would lay eggs every morning, about the competitions she would take part in, and envisaged herself travelling the world with Ida as her companion.

One afternoon, as they were standing in the courtyard warming themselves around a fire the neighbours had lit, Ida E. touched Ida's shoulder and suggested she adopt her.

'I mean, you don't have any children of your own, and I'm sure you want some. It would be ideal. Besides, I'm almost grown-up already; you don't have to change my nappies or spend sleepless nights with me. You'd have a ready-made child who can play you beautiful music. What more could you want?'

Ida had to smile at Ida E.'s direct, precocious way of explaining her vision of their future together. She gave her a tender kiss on the cheek.

Before the girl took Ida's place on the back of the truck, and seized the tentative, trembling hand of life, she asked Ida if there were anyone on the outside she could send a message to: a family member, a friend.

'Before you join me,' Ida E. added.

'I don't know ... Perhaps you might be able to find an officer in the marines — Jashi is his name, Konstantin, also known as Kostya. If he's still alive. He trained here in Leningrad at the Frunze Higher Naval School, and as far as I know he's serving in the Baltic Fleet.'

'And what should I tell him?'

'If ...'

'I'll find him.'

'That I wish him happiness.'

'That's all?'

'That I haven't forgotten him.'

'And?'

'That I ... You think of the rest. You have a vivid imagination — embellish it for me. Tell him something nice. Tell him whatever nice things come into your head.'

'Right. I will.' Ida E. nodded firmly.

They put their arms around each other and stood there, motionless, as people pushed impatiently past them and threw their suitcases into the truck.

'We'll see each other again, in May at the latest, in some Kazakh village. And by then I'll have tracked down a piano, and found my brother and your sailor. And until then you must take care of yourself. All right?' The girl pressed the tip of her nose against Ida's and breathed in Ida's scent. She felt her face with her fingertips and Ida sensed that at that moment the girl saw her — really looked at her — that she knew her, for all that she was, all that she had dreamed and missed out on, all that she had loved and lost, sought and found, aspired to and failed to achieve, wished for herself and never had, all that she still hoped for, and feared.

Suddenly she felt something warm, damp, running down her cheek. Ida E. was crying. Ida wouldn't have thought it possible, but those dark hollows had come to life, and tears were running from them.

★

Ida died just two months later. A neighbour found her dead outside the door of her apartment. The door she had once flung open to Kostya. That he had hammered on so bitterly at the end. She had collapsed after climbing the stairs to the apartment. She hadn't made it inside, to her bed, where she and Kostya had once celebrated their love and all obstacles had seemed so effortlessly overcome.

Ida E. became a renowned concert pianist. Her career reached its peak in the late fifties and sixties. Whilst on tour she played a date in West Germany, and stayed there; three years later she enabled her husband, a viola player she had met during her studies at the Moscow Conservatory, to leave the USSR. She became known above all for her daring interpretations of French composers. The dark, oval glasses she wore during her concerts became her trademark. Her autobiography, published in Germany in 1982, was a great help to me in researching Ida's story. The book was dedicated to her.

It was many years before Ida E. found my grandfather, but she found him.

More metal, more guns!

POSTER SLOGAN

Because of the Germans' heavy losses at Stalingrad and the devastating outcome of Operation Edelweiss, Army Group A was ordered to withdraw from Vladikavkaz, which at the time was still Ordzhonikidze, and by the end of the year, the Military Road was open and passable again. Stasia was able to make her way home. In March 1943, she reached Tbilisi. Simon's last letter, unusually sentimental for him, had frightened her, but she would not allow herself to think the worst. She knew from Christine that Kostya was alive and had served with distinction on the Leningrad front. She reached the grand house on the hill whose garden had long since run wild, its fountains dried up, its treasures sold on the black market. She fell into her daughter's arms and tried to weep, to experience some sort of relief, but she couldn't. It was only bit by bit that she learned from Kitty and Christine what had happened in her absence: Andro's disappearance, and the sad, anxious months in Tbilisi, where at least no shots had been fired. It was only much later that Kitty mentioned a miscarriage, as if in passing, without wishing to discuss the subject in more detail.

They sat in the kitchen, baked corn bread, and gazed at each other in rapture. Christine kept massaging her older sister's shoulders; she made her a face mask of cucumber peel, prepared hot hibiscus tea to renew her strength, heated buckets of water for her so she could take a bath, gave her new stockings and boots, and cut her hair.

For the first few weeks, Stasia was in a sort of daze. She couldn't bring herself to go out, couldn't concentrate during their conversations. Her eyes would close of their own accord, and she would yawn constantly. Kitty and Christine went about their daily business: they took the food vouchers and went shopping, went to the hospital, cleaned, cooked, darned jackets and coats for soldiers at the front, fetched wood, cooked meals, and listened, spellbound, to the old Blaupunkt radio.

Some nights, Stasia heard loud screams in the house; heard Christine's bedroom door open as she hurried down the corridor to the former playroom where Kitty slept. Heard her daughter whimpering, moaning, raising her voice, then Christine's soothing words. Sitting up in her bed, she heard Christine talking to Kitty for some time, until their voices fell silent again and Christine returned to her room.

On those nights Stasia wished she could find the strength to go down and take her daughter in her arms. To whisper just such soothing words in her ears; to ask her where this despair came from, what had made her so afraid. But she feared the secret Kitty shared with her aunt; she feared Kitty's nightmares, which might be contagious.

★

Spring brought people out onto the streets, into the parks, into the wide boulevards and the narrow alleys. The ice-cream sellers were heard again, touting their wares; the neighbourhood women, sitting on benches, exchanging the latest gossip; the dice rolling across the backgammon boards. Fresh laundry hung again in inner courtyards, transforming them into white, war-free zones.

The old man who used to have the big fruit stall on the corner now sold his few apples and plums out of zinc buckets. The academic's fat wife wore feathers in her hat again; crowds of gypsies wandered the streets telling people's fortunes — only the happy, bright, promising ones, of course. Bad tidings in wartime could lead to a sound thrashing.

On sunny days like these, Kitty, Christine, and Stasia went for walks around the hilly streets of Vera, ate sunflower seeds, drank malt beer. By May there was still no news from Simon, so Stasia went to the military People's Commissariat and submitted an application in the hope of learning something of her husband's whereabouts. Stasia had already given up hope when a letter arrived for her with a Moscow postmark. The message was brief: the Red Lieutenant had most probably lost his life in the glorious victory of the Battle of Stalingrad. She should take this letter to the relevant commissariat in Tbilisi. They could be of more assistance to her there, particularly with regard to her widow's pension.

At the commissariat a young woman in uniform explained to her that, although her husband was not to be found on any of the casualty lists, she should be aware that they had suffered very high losses in Stalingrad.

'You mean there's no body?' asked Stasia, sounding composed.

'We've contacted his division. Your husband is still registered as missing. But it's assumed he was killed in the final days of the battle.'

He had fought heroically, would probably be awarded a posthumous medal for bravery. Stasia interrupted her. 'As long as there's no body, he can't be dead,' she declared. Then she turned and walked out of the building.

Christine and Kitty were stunned when Stasia repeated to them, calmly and collectedly, what they had told her at the commissariat. Kitty chewed her lower lip nervously, and Christine's eyes filled with tears. It was clear from her expression that she accepted the news of Simon's death as fact. She wondered whether the certainty that Simon would not return also gave her the dreadful certainty that Andro could never return, either.

And Kitty wondered whether Christine was weeping for the loss of her own husband, and of her face; and she wondered whether Kostya would share Simon's fate.

Suddenly Kitty too began to sob.

'Why are you crying?' asked Stasia. 'He's not dead. He's just missing. This man has been missing for half his life; it'll be no different this time. He'll turn up again, don't you worry.'

'He's dead!' gasped Kitty.

'Where there's no body, where there's no grave, there are no dead, either!' Stasia's tone left no room for doubt. She seemed absolutely certain.

'But of course there are dead with no graves!'

There was something leaden, something lifeless, in Kitty's voice that made Stasia sit up and take notice. Timidly, she rose to her feet and went to her daughter. The abyss in Kitty frightened her; she didn't trust herself to peer into it, she was afraid of losing her balance. She tried to take Kitty in her arms, but Kitty recoiled.

★

Konstantin Jashi survived. In the last days of fighting, he sustained a serious leg injury and had to have an operation. The clinics in Leningrad were full to overflowing, so he was flown out on an NKVD plane to a military hospital in Moscow. Far away from the shooting and grenades, well fed, and under a warm blanket, the stay in hospital must have seemed to him like a sort of paradise. He was given two weeks' home leave, which he took, with some hesitation: it was akin to a medal of honour, as it was not generally permitted to Red Army soldiers. Someone must have put in a good word for him. Who could it be, Kostya wondered; but his deliberations did not supply an answer.

It was years since he had last been in his homeland. During the first two years of the war he had corresponded regularly and at length with his father and Giorgi Alania, his former roommate, but he only ever sent short telegrams to Tbilisi. He didn't know how to put the things he had experienced into words that would be comprehensible to his aunt, his sister, his mother.

He had preferred to remain in a state in which he asked no questions and hoped for no answers, no meaning. He wanted to forget that anything else existed beyond the daily certainty of death. Things like grief, happiness, disappointment, hope, and, above all, intimacy. Happiness had been a sip of schnapps and a piece of black bread smeared with fat; happiness was the sacks of flour and tins of food they smuggled into Leningrad for months on end; happiness was ships unscathed; happiness was mere survival. And everything that had existed beyond this no longer mattered. It didn't exist any more, and Kostya felt the hope of its return as a hindrance — dangerous, even, in certain circumstances.

Memories make the heart soft and transparent. You can't shoot well with a transparent heart, Brilka: you miss your target, and soon become a target yourself.

★

It seemed an age before Stasia, who opened the door to her son when he arrived, finally took him in her arms. Her whole body was trembling, and she pressed his head to her neck so hard he almost suffocated. Stasia yelled for Christine, and her voice filled the house. Kostya staggered, but quickly regained his balance by leaning on the walking stick he was to rely on for three weeks after his operation. Christine appeared at the end of the long corridor. It was where she used to stand when he was little, waiting for him to dash up to her after school and fling his arms around her neck. He stared at the unveiled right half of her face. How beautiful she was, he thought; and at the same time her halved beauty made him infinitely sad: his heart contracted, and he felt his palms grow damp. Looking at her, he couldn't help thinking of Ida.

Christine stopped in front of him and gazed at him, as if they had been writing love letters to one another all their lives and were meeting now for the first time.

'Kostya, Konstantin, my beautiful Konstantin, you're back, you're here, with me!' Stasia stepped back, allowed her younger sister to celebrate her symbiotic intimacy with her nephew, allowed her son to accept this intimacy, to garland himself with it, for everything about his body and his face suggested terrible hardship.

Later, when Kitty came home from the hospital and heard her brother's voice in the kitchen, she stopped for a while in the corridor, pressing herself against the wall, taking deep breaths, trying to get her body under control; and before she burst into the kitchen she spent a few seconds practising her old, unbridled laugh, trying to remember what her voice had sounded like when she had been happy.

★

Unlike Stasia, Kostya had a lot to say. He described in unremitting detail his time in Sevastopol, the raid on Constanța, and, above all, what had happened at Lake Ladoga. He wolfed down everything that was put in front of him; his hunger seemed insatiable, and he drank the bitter *chacha* that loosened his tongue still more.

But Kitty noticed that the way he talked about all these things — the battles, the attacks, the bombs, the hunger, the harsh fight for survival — sounded artificial, almost dispassionate.

Christine and Stasia told him many things, too, but their stories were less tidy: they interrupted one another, argued about details that each remembered differently. When the conversation turned to Andro, Christine lowered her voice and told him what she knew, or rather, what she didn't know: that it was assumed he had joined a partisan movement and was fighting on the side of the Wehrmacht. Kitty felt betrayed by Christine's words, even though Christine was just reporting facts; she was also annoyed that Kostya had managed to draw Christine entirely into his orbit in the space of just a few hours. Andro's story provoked a tirade of abuse from Kostya. He grew heated talking about this betrayal of the Motherland, and launched into a monologue about the importance of the correct ideology, about loyalty and fidelity, about the duties of every Soviet citizen, and repeated that he had always suspected Andro would go astray, that he would bring shame on the family.

Kitty didn't dare intervene; she didn't want to get into a fight with Kostya on his very first evening with them, disappointing her mother and aunt. She also knew that her arguments in support of Andro were too weak. Nonetheless, it was hard for her to see him portrayed so simply as a traitor to the Motherland. It wasn't the truth. For the others, the easiest thing to do was to sacrifice him to his own mistakes.

'Father's dead, isn't he?'

Kostya's question came very suddenly, as unannounced as a summer storm. He had just been speaking of his experiences in Moscow. Christine bowed her head. Stasia cleared her throat briefly and scratched her forearm.

'You should know ... he's missing, he's just disappeared.' Stasia tried to answer as casually as if she were talking about the weather.

'Will you stop this!' shouted Kitty.

'He's disappeared, we have no proof that he's dead!' Stasia sounded indignant, as if offended that her truth was being called into question.

'He was last seen in the final days of Stalingrad, outside the German headquarters, just before it was blown up.' Kitty was breathing fast.

'And they haven't found his body!' Stasia remained stubborn, repeating it like a magic spell that would protect her from reality.

'Tell her, Kostya — we have to have him declared dead, we can't go on living like this,' Kitty implored her brother.

'I'll go the commissariat myself tomorrow. They'll give me more precise information,' he answered calmly.

★

With the arrival of the summer heat the whole family set off for the town where Stasia and Christine were born. They stayed in the chocolate-maker's old house, where Lida now lived alone in the half that was still hers. They visited their parents' graves. They gazed at the gravestones, sat on the grass. They all repeated 'Amen' after Lida said a prayer for the dead. The very next day, Kostya commissioned a new gravestone engraved with the name 'Simon Jashi' and had it erected beside the graves of his grandparents and his mother's twin sister. Stasia refused to accompany them to the graveyard to mourn her husband. She announced that she would only acknowledge her husband's death when his bones lay beneath the gravestone.

In the little town that was once destined to become the Nice of the Caucasus, it seemed unimaginable that somewhere out there a cataclysmic war was raging. Everything appeared so peaceful, almost provocatively quiet.

Kitty and Kostya were bewildered when their mother borrowed a Kabardin and disappeared into the steppe. Christine, too, was bewildered, wandering the little streets and alleyways of the town where once she had walked so proud and aloof. She stood for a long time in front of the barred doors and boarded-up windows where the chocolate factory used to be; where — it seemed like centuries ago — she had first met her husband. On her walks through the town, Kitty avoided the park with the green-painted benches. She avoided all the streets where she had walked with Andro, and the places where she had hidden from him in the hope that he would find her.

The evening before their departure, Kostya and Kitty walked again side by side through the crooked streets of the old town, stopped in front of the closed shops, argued over what used to be in this or that building. They bought candyfloss from an old woman on a street corner, and both nibbled on the sticky cloud. Kitty took Kostya's arm; he kept stopping because of the pain in his leg.

'Aren't you afraid?' she asked her brother suddenly.

'What would I be afraid of?'

'When you're out there: that this could be the end? I mean really every second.'

'Yes, sometimes.'

'How can you stand it?'

'I don't think about it. I just try and do my duty.'

'Which is to kill or be killed?'

'Which is to make sure that as few of us as possible are killed. And as far as the enemy's concerned: if you don't kill them, they kill you. There's no mercy. You don't think about it.'

'Aren't they human beings?'

'They're sick fascists.'

'And what are we? Sick communists?'

'Only you could say a thing like that! Is that your boyfriend's sick ideology?'

'We grew up together, Kostya, all three of us. He was like a brother to you.'

'No. A traitor cannot be my brother. He shouldn't have done it.'

'He just wanted to be free.'

'Free? With the fascists? Are you serious? And you shouldn't have got involved with him.'

'We were engaged.'

'You were engaged?'

'Yes. And now I don't even know if he's alive.'

'Grow up, Kitty. It's high time. Engaged!' Kostya shook his head vigorously.

'The fact that I refuse to see this world with your eyes doesn't mean that I don't see it at all.'

'Don't cry over him, he's not worth it. He's deceived our family — the family that saved him.'

'Saved? His mother was shot. What was her crime? Are you surprised he refused to accept this system as just? Wouldn't you feel the same way if *Deda* or Christine or I —'

'They'll have had their reasons.'

'How can you say such a thing? You know it's not true. You know it's not right.'

Kitty had stopped walking and was looking at her brother in total incomprehension.

'The war won't last forever. The Germans are finished. The whole world is against them. Afterwards, everything will get on the right track.'

'People are waiting, you're waiting, and nobody knows what's coming.'

'Even the USA is supporting us now. They're supplying us with new tanks,' Kostya continued, as if he hadn't heard his sister's objection. 'We're all fighting together now against the Germans.'

'And you?' They had stopped at a junction. The silence on the streets was almost ghostly. 'What do you plan to do, afterwards?'

'If I survive this, you mean? I'll do what my duty requires of me.'

'And what is your duty?'

'To carry on working for the good of my country. It's that simple, Kitty.'

'But ...'

'But what? What do you think Papa gave his life for? Why do you think countless heroes have lost their lives?'

'Papa lived for the military. You're not him. He was never there; we missed him all the time. You, me, *Deda*. Do you want to live like that, too?'

'What's that supposed to mean? We missed him? How can you dare to question the path he took?'

'What I'm questioning is the paths you and I are taking.'

'You'd do better to see to it that you forget all this rotten ideology your boyfriend has filled your head with, as fast as possible. You should find yourself a real man!'

'He has a name — his name is Andro! You won't infect yourself by saying his name!'

Kitty flung the stick of candyfloss aside in fury and strode on ahead.

How did you serve the front?

POSTER SLOGAN

Some time after his deployment to Crimea, Andro Eristavi fetched up in a Georgian Legion combat battalion in Poland. As a radio operator in Lvov he was responsible for safeguarding rail services. Later, he was transferred to the division with the patriotic name 'Queen Tamar' and sent to France. During this time he learned German and French. In the Pyrenees, he was charged with decoding enemy communications. In the last year of the war, he was posted to Haarlem in the Netherlands, where he again worked as a radio operator in charge of railway security.

Unfortunately, I have little information about Andro's state of mind at the time. I don't know whether he realised while he was still in Crimea what it was he had got caught up in, or whether he regretted his decision; bit by bit his hopeless situation must gradually have become clear to him. He must have understood that Vienna was slipping further and further away as, at the same time, the possibility of returning to his homeland also faded. From 1944 onwards many Georgian Legion battalions began to desert, and the Wehrmacht disbanded the unit. The dream of a free Georgia had died long ago, and from this point on it was down to each individual to try to secure his own survival.

Andro didn't desert: he stayed with the Queen Tamar. Quite simply, he could see no way out for himself — he knew of no alternative. Looking back, I think in the end it was this paralysis that saved his life. The staunch pacifist Andro Eristavi found himself on Europe's last battlefield: he became one of the insurgents on the island of Texel.

★

Following the Nazi occupation of the Netherlands in early 1940, this Dutch island in the North Sea became a German military base. The Queen Tamar

Battalion was responsible for, among other things, protecting the Haarlem–Amsterdam railway. In early 1945, Andro received orders to go to Texel. There was a camp on the island where many Georgians who had been taken prisoner on the Eastern Front were being held; the Wehrmacht was now using them as auxiliaries. In the night of 5 April, an uprising was organised in the camp after news spread of a Wehrmacht order to send them back to the front. The Georgians managed to gain control of the whole island, with the exception of the naval batteries. Even after the German capitulation in Denmark and the Netherlands, the bitter fight for the island continued.

I don't know when exactly Andro reached the decision to join the uprising, but I presume he saw this rebellion as his only chance of making amends for his disastrous past and ensuring his own survival.

Andro hid in the fields for days. He saw the farms go up in flames. Heard screams, a lot of gunfire. Heard the battleships' horns. Heard sentences in Georgian and German; his brain could no longer keep the two languages apart. It no longer made any difference who was killed and who survived. More shots. Which side were they coming from? Where should he run? And what should he shoot at? His rifle felt so heavy; it would take such effort to pull the trigger. He saw something lying in the field, not far away. Andro crawled in its direction, then ducked down: more gunfire, very close this time. He crawled on, belly to the ground. He could smell the spring.

It was a man. A soldier in a Wehrmacht uniform. He had lost his helmet somewhere. Was he still breathing? No. His face was already discoloured. How old might he be? The German rifle lay beside him like a faithful friend. His leg was twisted; he was lying in an unnatural position. Andro lay down beside the dead soldier and stared up at the sky. Soft white clouds were dancing around each other, dispersed by a gentle wind.

Shots.

One, two, three.

Andro whispered to himself: *Maman*. But his mother didn't answer. Nor did the sky, and nor did the dead soldier.

Four, five, six.

He heard shots, again and again.

Seven, eight, nine.

He watched a cloud fly away. He smiled. He counted and waited for a reply. Or for death. Perhaps he should envy the German soldier: he couldn't hear the shooting now, it was all behind him. He had nothing more to do with any of it.

Ten. And another shot. Then a deep, spreading silence that was far from reassuring.

Two weeks after the end of the Second World War, Canadian troops put a stop to the bloodshed on the island, which came to be referred to as Europe's last battlefield.

Andro Eristavi survived, along with two hundred and thirty other Georgians.

Andro remained on the island until the summer, living with five other Georgian survivors on one of the burnt-out farmsteads.

He never made it to Vienna.

If one man dies, that is a tragedy. If millions die, that's only statistics.

THE GENERALISSIMUS

Kostya spent the last months of the war in the Baltic Sea, where he and his fleet division safeguarded transatlantic convoys bringing in weapons. He lost more than half the men with whom he had joined the Navy, and it was only by a miracle that he himself survived a bomb blast in the Curonian Lagoon in the autumn of 1944.

Stasia went back and forth between Christine and her daughter in the orphaned house on Vera Hill, and Lida in the divided house of her childhood, where they planted vegetables and kept chickens: food rations in the city were getting ever smaller and there was less and less to be had, even on the black market. In May 1944, Kitty Jashi registered with the Rustaveli Theatre Institute in Tbilisi, which had just started teaching again, to take the entrance examination for the acting course. In September of that year, she started training to be an actress. Neither Stasia nor Christine was keen on Kitty's new choice of career, but they did not oppose her decision.

★

'The events of the past twelve months ... have compelled me to dedicate my full attention and capacity for work to the single task for which I have lived for many years: the struggle for the fate of my people ... In this hour, as the spokesman of Greater Germany, I therefore wish to make the solemn avowal before the Almighty that we will loyally and unshakably fulfil our duty also in the new year, in the firm belief that the hour will come when victory will definitively favour the one who is most worthy of it: the Greater German Reich.'

So said Hitler in his 1945 New Year address, which was to be his last. The year did not begin well for him: on 1 January he was informed of the German forces' retreat before American and British troops near Koblenz.

The Generalissimus was now vigorously urging his armies to storm Berlin. Like Stalingrad for Hitler, Berlin was of huge symbolic significance for Stalin. Besides, he didn't want to be left empty-handed when Germany lost its sovereignty and the world was re-divided; rather, he was creating facts on the ground. First, though, Auschwitz was liberated by Soviet troops. Ukrainian units found six hundred and forty-eight unburied corpses there, and around 7,600 living dead; they smelled the sharp stench of the poison gas Zyklon B. On 3 February Berlin experienced its heaviest bombing by US forces, resulting in 22,000 deaths.

On 13 February, Dresden was annihilated — the joint work, this time, of the British and American air forces. The countless victims of the bombing were so badly burned they could not be identified. The piles of rubble weighed eighteen million tons. At the end of February, the Western Allies reached the Rhine.

German radio continued to play 'Das Wunschkonzert', a programme of popular songs and operettas decreed by Goebbels, interrupted by news of the war.

On 16 February, the Swiss government froze all Nazi assets in Switzerland. In March, the Americans occupied Frankfurt. Air raids continued all over Germany; the deafening noise was the lullaby of that winter. In the same month, trials of collaborators began in France; thousands were condemned and executed in dubious judicial proceedings, while others had their heads shaved and were paraded and taunted on public squares.

A girl so thin you could see right through her died of typhus in Bergen-Belsen. She had been brought there from Auschwitz just a couple of months earlier, along with her sister, and certified as a person who was sick but could potentially be restored to health. She died not knowing that her diary would survive her and be read by millions.

On 16 April, the 1st Belorussian and the 1st Ukrainian Fronts under the leadership of Zhukov and Konev launched the attack on the German capital. The 9th Army was crushed in no time. On 22 April, they advanced on the city centre.

Meanwhile, in the bunker — it was the night of 28 April — the Führer's last will and testament was being drawn up. Grand Admiral Dönitz was to become president of the Reich. Goebbels was to be chancellor. Then the world's most macabre wedding took place: Adolf and Eva were man and wife at the end. Two days later the *Hamburger Zeitung* reported: 'This afternoon, fighting Bolshevism to his last breath at his command post in the Reich Chancellery, our Führer, Adolf Hitler, died for Germany.' No mention anywhere of a bullet or of the potassium cyanide taken by the newlyweds. Just eight hundred metres away, on 2 May, the Soviet flag was raised above the Reichstag. 150,000 Wehrmacht soldiers were taken from Berlin into captivity. On 7 May, the unconditional German surrender was signed in the French city of Reims. It came into effect on 8 May at 23:01.

The war was over.

There were no more words. But there was shouting. And the drinking of strong schnapps.

The Red Army soldiers looted, taking everything that wasn't nailed down — and everything that was.

Duke Ellington played 'I'm Beginning To See The Light'. And couples danced in Times Square, and there was a lot of passionate kissing.

In Europe, the air smelled of ashes.

The ghosts choked on their own threnody. The butterflies refused to emerge from their cocoons. And Sinatra sang 'Dream When You're Feeling Blue', and people fainted.

The war is over. Those words, again and again. It sounded so simple, proclaimed on every wireless programme and on every cinema screen, so surreally simple: The war is over. Followed by marching bands.

On Red Square, Lenin's legacy was invoked, and neither Ellington nor Sinatra were played, but there was kissing all the same and people probably fainted there, too. And the Generalissimus bragged, 'Three years ago Germany aimed to dismember the Soviet Union by wresting from it the Caucasus, the Ukraine, Belorussia, and the Baltic lands. However, this was not fated to come true. Germany is utterly defeated. The German troops are surrendering. Comrades! The Great Patriotic War has ended in our complete victory! Glory to our heroic Red Army, our great people, the people victorious! Eternal glory to the heroes who fell in the struggle and gave their lives for the freedom and happiness of our people!'

Although he didn't know it, the end of the war also marked the beginning of his personal end. A few months earlier he had survived his first stroke, but soon his doctors would diagnose him with hypertension, arteriosclerosis, myocardial insufficiency, and chronic hepatitis. But the Generalissimus was content: the Soviet Union had emerged from the Great Patriotic War a global superpower.

★

Andro was transferred via an assembly centre for displaced persons to the Plattling concentration camp near Regensburg. He hoped that there he would be given permission to leave the country.

At the Yalta Conference, however, it was decided that all Soviet citizens would be unconditionally handed over to the USSR. Neither the International Committee of the Red Cross nor the United Nations Relief and Rehabilitation Administration could do anything about it. Even before this decision, the British had already started to extradite thousands of Soviet prisoners of war to the USSR. A similar fate awaited all returnees: some were shot immediately on arrival in the ports of Murmansk and Odessa; others were transported to the gulag, or sent to the Manchurian front shortly before the end of the war. The most tragic extradition took place in Dachau in 1946: out of one hundred and forty people who were due to be sent back to the Soviet Union against their will, fourteen cut their throats with shards of glass. The Americans described the act as an 'inhuman orgy of suicide by the Red Army traitors'.

Andro Eristavi was handed over to the Soviet authorities along with one and a half thousand other Soviet prisoners of war in Plattling and taken to a Siberian gulag near Nazino, infamous for the 'Nazino tragedy' of 1933, when six thousand Soviet internal deportees were simply left on an uninhabited river island with no shelter, no provisions, and no tools. After two weeks, only two thousand were left alive. Four thousand had starved or frozen to death, or disappeared, or, notoriously, fallen victim to cannibalism.

And so the dream of Vienna was hung, drawn, and quartered.

★

A few days before the official end of the war — the day Benito Mussolini and his lover, Clara Petacci, were captured on the run, shot by partisans, and their corpses hung upside down on the Piazzale Loreto in Milan — the war also ended for Kostya Jashi, when he was recalled from the Baltic and sent by train to Moscow.

He was received at the naval commissariat by an elegant, soft-spoken man in a smart dark coat with a fur collar. It was only on closer inspection that Kostya recognised his best friend, Giorgi Alania.

Giorgi took him to his light and spacious apartment right on Tverskoy Boulevard and entertained him like a king. Exclusive apartments like this were the sole preserve of ministerial employees, but initially Kostya wasn't interested in such tedious details; he just wanted to enjoy the luxury and eat the good food in peace. Giorgi mentioned in passing that he had been promoted and was now working for the NKVD, the People's Commissariat for Internal Affairs. He didn't go into how he had got there or what exactly he did there; only later did he indicate to Kostya that he was not yet authorised to discuss his precise activities. Kostya, however, was more than happy that his friend was still devoted to him, admired him, and could clearly anticipate his every wish. Giorgi took him out, invited him to opulent dinners in restaurants to which Kostya couldn't have dreamed of gaining entry, and never tired of praising Kostya's courage and heroism. He confided in his friend that he too was soon to be promoted to captain.

How Giorgi Alania had managed to get from the humble shipyard at the end of the world to the ministry remained a mystery. Kostya was forced to admit to himself that he had underestimated his friend.

On certain days, though, between the popping of champagne corks and the lavish visits to exclusive restaurants and the long conversations that went on into the night, he was seized by a sudden fear — the fear that he could no longer hold back the memories. He had survived the war; bombs were no longer falling. There was no shooting. Yet Kostya found it hard to get used to. As paradoxical as it seemed, even to him, it was only now that he felt unprotected. He didn't know how to handle daily life. He knew, though, that the memories would come: a terrible army of them. They would not spare him. And somewhere in the deepest recesses of his mind there dwelt a woman with a ring on every finger who refused to be banished, no matter how hard he tried. The fear that she might no longer be alive was driving him mad; he was losing himself in search of a shadow.

Giorgi Alania invited beautiful women to his home, swathed in furs and laden with jewellery. They wore blood-red lipstick and fluttered their eyelashes, flirted with Kostya the war hero, took him into their midst, touched him, admired him, asked him to fill their wine glasses, vied for his attention; but when one of them put on a record and invited him to dance, he left the room and asked his friend to send the women home. Alania obeyed, but visits of this kind became a regular occurrence: Alania no longer came home without female company. Until one evening, emerging from the kitchen, he spied Kostya on the sofa with a blonde, and saw that Kostya was allowing her soft, velvety lips to heal his wounds and dispel his gloomy thoughts. Alania gave a sigh of relief, visibly pleased that love could, after all, still be bought.

'And what do you plan to do now?'

Alania was sitting with Kostya on the balcony the following evening, watching the people on the street below.

'Wait for my next posting,' Kostya replied, cracking his knuckles. 'You deserve something better. I could help you.'

'Help me what?'

'Ensure you're treated according to your merits.'

'What exactly is it that you do, Giorgi?'

'I already told you: I'm at the NKVD.'

'And what's your line of work?'

'I can't discuss it.'

'Come on, Giorgi, we know each other. Stop being so secretive.'

'A lot of departments have been established there, and —'

'Departments? What are these departments for?'

'Our group is responsible for the repatriation of Soviet citizens abroad. Right now they're preparing us for foreign assignments. I'm afraid I can't tell you any more than that.'

'Repatriation? What's so mysterious about that?'

'I'm afraid I can't tell you any more, Kostya. I hope you don't think it's because I don't trust you.'

'No, it's all right. But how can you help me?'

'I'll put in a good word for you at the ministry.'

'Was it you who had me brought to Moscow that time? And was it you who arranged for me to be granted home leave?'

Alania didn't answer.

'So it was you! I can't believe that didn't occur to me. But — many thanks. What else can I tell you? I'm not cut out for a desk job, you know that.'

'Yes, I know that. Your skills and preferences will be taken into account, don't worry.' Alania had stood up and was leaning over the balcony railing. Kostya came and stood beside his friend and put his arm around his shoulders. 'You know you mean a great deal to me, don't you? I'd do anything to make things all right for you again.'

'There is something you could do for me,' Kostya murmured.

'What? Tell me — it doesn't matter what it is.'

'I'd like to ascertain the whereabouts of a certain woman.'

★

That autumn, people started to clean up the mess in the world and enlarge the cemeteries in the cities. Kostya returned to Tbilisi. He spent his first weeks at home sleeping or listening to the Blaupunkt radio. It was during these weeks that Kitty played her first lead in a student production; in my imagination it was Antigone. But that play was probably banned at the time, so you can decide for yourself, Brilka, what role it was that Kitty played. Two days after her premiere she received a letter, and immediately recognised Andro Eristavi's handwriting. She ran to the bathroom and threw up. She sat on the edge of the bathtub for what seemed like an age before she found the courage to open the letter. Then she went into Kostya's room, woke him, and sat down beside him on the bed.

'You have to help me.'

'What's wrong?' Kostya, half asleep, rubbed his eyes and sat up.

'Andro's alive. He's in a gulag. I have an address. We've got to get him out of there. You have to find out what he's done and —'

'What he's done? Are you out of your mind? He betrayed his country! He's a deserter, a coward. I'm surprised they've even let him live.'

At this, for the first time in her life, Kitty slapped her brother's face. Shocked and angry, Kostya leapt up, quickly pulling on his clothes.

'Please, please, forgive me — you must help me! Kostya, please.'

'You're crazy! You're putting us all in terrible danger!'

'Perhaps we can apply for a transfer, to somewhere nearby, where I can visit him ... He'll die there, Kostya.'

Kitty had fallen to her knees in front of her brother, clinging to the jersey Kostya had just pulled over his head. Kostya stepped back in disgust and tried to pull his sister to her feet.

'Stop humiliating yourself! Get up!' he said loudly, turning his face away from her and her piteous gestures. He pushed her away and fled the room.

Learning from the Soviets means learning to be a victor.

POSTER SLOGAN

The post-war world fell into a frenzy. People wanted to celebrate life and clear away the rubble; they wanted to dance heathen dances of survival, they wanted to drink, they wanted to celebrate, they wanted to gorge themselves on all the things they had lacked in recent years. People wanted shallow operettas, they wanted risqué songs, they wanted nice, sentimental films with rural settings. They wanted to forget; they wanted to live as if there were no tomorrow — and no yesterday. The euphoria was infectious, dangerous, charged.

In our little homeland, too, people sang and celebrated until they felt dizzy. And of course the regime celebrated itself; people organised insane orgies of gratitude in its honour and extolled its cleverness and might. They celebrated the Generalissimus, the great Father of the People, who had led his country victoriously out of the apocalypse and back into the light of socialism. New legends and myths sprang up around him, praising his bravery and self-sacrifice on behalf of his country. Perhaps the most powerful myth was about him and his son. In 1941 his oldest son Yakov had been taken prisoner by the Germans. When the fascists found out who this prisoner was, they suggested exchanging Yakov for General Paulus, who had been captured by the Russians at Stalingrad. But the Generalissimus — so the legend went — replied: 'I do not trade field marshals for lieutenants.' And so Yakov met his miserable end, shot in the back of the head with a German gun.

This legend testified once again to the selflessness of the Great Father and his loyalty to his homeland. The act was not seen as inhuman; on the contrary, the story showed the extent to which the leader suffered with his people and the — yes — superhuman strength he demonstrated in taking this almost biblical step and sacrificing his son. The Soviet Union shone. The Generalissimus was a victor. And victors are forgiven everything.

★

After the war, Stasia returned to Tbilisi permanently and registered for the first time with the People's Commissariat as a person in search of work. Christine continued to work at the hospital. And Kostya seemed in no hurry to be redeployed; he enjoyed the ministrations of his mother and aunt, slept for days on end, went to the sulphur baths almost daily, as if he wanted the hot steam to scald the war from his skin, and flirted with students in teahouses. Kitty reeled from one emotional extreme to another, and it sometimes seemed to her that there were two people living in her chest, two completely different entities who were compelled to fight each other. The happy, light-hearted Kitty had not reappeared since the day they drove her out to the village school; but vestiges, hints of this happiness, still flared up in her occasionally, like charred branches in a dead campfire. On days like these she enjoyed her studies, the different parts that she tried on like new clothes. She enjoyed her fellow students, who were all able to party with such glorious abandon; she enjoyed survival, and new beginnings.

She wrote regular letters to Andro, described her daily life, gave him hope, continued to play her old, cheerful self, told him about the new books she was reading and the theatre premieres she went to. But she never wrote about anything real. She never mentioned her worries, not with so much as a line. She was afraid that he wasn't strong enough to withstand the endless tortures of the gulag, and wished with all her heart that he would return, but didn't know how it was possible. Even if there would be no Vienna for them now, even if their illusions and hopes were irrevocably shattered, even if they would never kiss one another on green-painted benches ever again, she would never give up hoping for his return. His replies were never longer than half a page. The letters were read, of course. He only ever wrote, in his small, spiky hand, about daily life in the quarry, his delight in a sunny day, or a soup that was more substantial than usual. Only once, in his first letter, had he written the word 'Forgive' at the end. But she hadn't commented on that.

So far, Kitty had kept this correspondence secret. She intercepted the postman, and took her letters to the post office after lectures. She had hoped that Kostya would help her, but she had to accept that this was not going to happen, and one day she approached Christine — who still had good contacts among the *nomenklatura* — with her request. They were sitting in a newly opened ice-cream parlour on Rustaveli Boulevard. Kitty stared at a big poster announcing the new opera season.

'How long have you known?' Christine stirred sugar into her cup of tea.

'A few weeks. I got a letter from him. But Kostya —'

'You should keep him out of it!'
'Stop leaping to his defence all the time!'
'What are you hoping Kostya could do?'
'I thought he might make it possible for Andro to be transferred. There are plenty of labour camps around here, too.'
'So you still think you have to love him?'
'What do you mean by that? I'll always love him — he's our Andro.'
'What you love is the memory. You're not the same person, and I'm sure he's even less the person he once was — the one you know. You can want to help him, but do it for his sake, not your own.'

Christine finished her tea. Kitty fell silent, chewed her thumb, and gazed out at the street, where young lovers and parents with children were strolling up and down. Although Christine didn't promise her anything then and there, in the days that followed she considered what she could do. If Andro really had been accused of treason, it was highly unlikely that he would still be alive. It was possible, then, that in the last years of the war he had actually had second thoughts, that he had perhaps been of service to the Reds in some way, and they were thanking him for it now by letting him live. She asked some of her husband Ramas' old friends for advice, enquired as to whether there was any chance of seeing Andro's file, and informed Stasia that Andro had made contact with her daughter.

Stasia was racked with guilt. She refused to think that Andro might suffer the same fate as his mother. She could never have forgiven herself for that. She had followed her son to Russia, naively assuming that she could save him, and had left the gullible, inexperienced Andro, to whom nothing was more alien than warfare, to his own devices. If she thought about it long enough, she couldn't even reproach him for taking this disastrous path and, in doing so, infecting her daughter with misfortune, too.

Stasia made up parcels of food and clothes, and slipped rouble notes into the pockets of post office and customs officials to ensure the parcels reached Nazino; and she took her son to task. He should contact someone in the central administration, she told him, to find out why Andro Eristavi had been sent to Siberia.

Eventually, Kostya could no longer withstand the constant pressure in the house — his sister's expectant, beseeching looks, Christine's intercession, Stasia's insistent demands — and called Giorgi Alania in Moscow. Unlike the search for Ida, which was proving extremely difficult, where Andro was concerned Alania quickly found what he was looking for. In a late-night telephone call he described to Kostya in detail the path Andro had taken. The only reason he was still alive, Alania explained, was his involvement in the Texel uprising.

★

A magical scent wafted through the house. Kostya had gone out, and Kitty was still at rehearsal. Christine, in her nightgown and already on her way to bed, came downstairs and into the kitchen. Since that terrible night, Stasia had never made the hot chocolate for her again; she didn't know that Christine had been in possession of the recipe for quite some time. Christine sat down at the table with her sister.

'You haven't made it for ages.'

'True. But I thought we two had earned it.'

Stasia poured the thick liquid into two porcelain cups. They began to spoon it up slowly, relishing it.

'You have to contact *him*,' Stasia blurted out suddenly.

'Whom should I contact?'

'You know who.'

'Excuse me?' Christine's voice grew icy.

'We have to get Andro out of there. He won't survive otherwise.'

'And how are we supposed to do it?'

'We're responsible for this boy. Yes, perhaps he made a mistake, perhaps he made the wrong decisions. But he was so young, Christine. What happened to Sopio cannot be allowed to happen again. We'd never forgive ourselves.'

'And would I forgive myself for seeking *him* out again, looking him in the eyes, after all that's happened?' Christine's tone remained icy, and her expression was filled with disgust.

'It would be to save a life, Christine. To save Andro. We raised him like our own child; imagine if it were Kostya ...'

'I can't, Stasia. I simply can't.'

'I hate myself for having to ask you for this favour, but there's no other way. With his history he won't stand a chance, unless ... He's the only one who can help him.'

'I don't even know if he would be prepared to receive me, to listen to me, or where I could even reach him. He's in Moscow most of the time.'

'He'll listen to you. I'm sure he will always want to see you.'

'But he hasn't. Not in all the years since.'

'I saw his look.'

'What look?'

'The way he used to look at you.'

For a while, Christine said nothing. She licked the last remnants of the chocolate from the cup with her finger. Suddenly she looked up and said, 'All right. But in that case ...'

'In that case what? I'll do anything.'

'In that case, you have to accept that Simon is dead.'

Stasia gulped. She stood up. Sat down again. Lit a filterless cigarette.

'Say it,' repeated Christine sternly, fixing her sister with a look of *schadenfreude*.

'I don't know. I don't know. Why do you want me to —'

'Say it!'

'He ... he ...'

'Say it, and yes — I'll seek him out and petition him for Andro to be pardoned.'

'He's ...'

'Stasia!'

'... dead.'

BOOK IV

★

KITTY

> Got a moon above me
> But no one to love me
> Lover man, oh, where can you be?
>
> BILLIE HOLIDAY

After one of the student performances, there was a knock at Kitty's dressing room door. She threw it open in irritation — and froze, speechless. Before her stood Mariam. In a pleated skirt, her hair tied back in a loose ponytail. She held a little bunch of violets clutched tightly in her fist. Kitty hesitated for a moment, then flung her arms around the neck of this girl who should never, by rights, have been her friend. Neither of them knew what to say, or how to describe their feelings. Kitty offered Mariam her chair in front of the make-up table, and sat down on a low stool at her feet.

Although she had never believed it possible, Mariam had been admitted to the Institute of Medicine. It was very unusual for a simple village girl to be allowed to study medicine in the capital, but there was a shortage of doctors. She told Kitty how happy and excited she was, how much she was looking forward to moving to Tbilisi. She had seen Kitty's name on the poster at the Theatre Institute and had come to watch the performance. For a long time she had been in two minds about seeking Kitty out; she hadn't been sure whether Kitty would even want to see her, but then she couldn't stand it any longer, and so here she was.

'What are you talking about! Of course I want to see you. I'm so pleased.'

★

Soon afterwards, Mariam moved to the capital, and they began to see each other frequently, meeting up and going out together. Kitty showed Mariam the city, took her along to see friends, and later took her home as well, where she introduced her simply as a friend. No more than that. They never said a word about the events that had brought them together, although the unsayable was always there between them. In the face of what they had been through, words were powerless. Yet their mutual knowledge of one another, of their shared tragedy, was constantly present in their minds.

Unlike with other, ordinary friendships, it wasn't important to either of them whether they had interests in common, or shared the same sense of humour; whether they could really talk to each other at length; whether they giggled easily and uncontrollably. None of this carried any weight compared to what had created this involuntary friendship. Yet nothing was forcing them to be together. There was mutual empathy, an awareness of their visible and invisible scars, and this prompted a very special kind of love that suppressed their own self-hatred for a while and numbed the worst feelings of guilt. Both of them immediately felt this love to be absolutely essential; they needed it in order to cope with their daily lives, in order to keep doubt at bay — the doubt that they had the right to be alive.

Strangely, since Mariam had come back into her life, Kitty had recovered a little of that former self she'd thought had gone forever: the lightness, the playfulness, the silliness returned, and she blossomed, laughed, and sang along at student parties at the top of her voice. Christine appreciated Mariam's modesty and reserve; Stasia, too, was surprised that her wild daughter had become best friends with such a simple, reticent girl, and saw it as a good sign.

Mariam was almost excessively polite, and pleasantly shy; not at all noisy, let alone coquettish. She was curious but not intrusive, helpful, and anything but selfish: other people's wellbeing was always more important to her than her own. Above all, though, she charmed people with her talent for showing gratitude. As if she never expected anyone to praise her for anything, to give her a present, or to recognise her merits, and when this was in fact the case, she seemed so happy, so grateful, that it was worth giving her compliments and presents just to see the look on her face.

Right from the start, Kostya found Mariam completely different from cheeky, insolent Kitty. Although he would never have admitted it to himself, I suspect, Brilka, that, in some way that's hard to understand, that isn't even logical, Kostya feared his little sister. Perhaps it was her unpredictability, or the way she had distanced herself from him since Andro had driven a wedge between them; or perhaps it was her impetuous, volatile nature, which was too much for him and made him angry.

I'm not sure whether he was trying to connect with his sister through Mariam; what is certain is that, very soon after meeting Mariam, he started picking the two girls up after lectures and taking them out, inviting them for meals, going with them to the cinema and to dances; occasionally he would give Mariam flowers. At first, Kitty interpreted these gestures as her brother's attempts to make amends for his refusal to help Andro. The longer she lived with him under one roof, the harder it was for her to accept his rigid world view, his iron discipline, his excessive demands on those around him, his peremptory military tone, and his taciturnity. After his return, she had tried many times to speak openly with him, but in vain. So when his behaviour suddenly changed and he started making an effort with her and her friend, asking them questions, taking an interest, even coming to the student performances and praising Kitty's talent, his sister decided not to spoil this chance of a rapprochement. But she was still annoyed by his officious, domineering manner. And it bothered her that Mariam was impressed. She started to keep her meetings with Mariam secret from him; she invented excuses and lied to him when she was going to the cinema with her friend, or planned to go to a concert. She tried to keep him away. Kostya, however, had always exerted an extraordinary power of attraction over the opposite sex, and Mariam was no exception.

Whenever Mariam was alone with Kitty, the conversation would constantly return to Kostya. She raved about what an elegant figure he cut, how gallantly he treated her; she spoke of his solicitude, his excellent conversation, his attentiveness. Kitty didn't respond and tried to change the subject. Now, though, it was Mariam who insisted on going out with Kostya, inviting Kostya, going dancing with Kostya. And even when Kitty didn't have time to accompany them, Mariam did not forgo the opportunity of meeting Kostya. Kitty was secretly puzzled by her brother's interest in Mariam. Kostya couldn't and shouldn't like a woman as simple as Mariam; all the other young women he knew and had flirted with were striking, unapproachable creatures from good families. Mariam was neither experienced in the arts of love nor liberal enough to allow Kostya to initiate her in them. He wouldn't be fobbed off for long with stolen kisses and the surreptitious holding of hands, his sister was sure of that. Which meant that soon he would drop Mariam; not to mention the fact that he might leave the city for the north at any moment.

But the longer Kitty observed her friend and her brother, the clearer it became to her that the two had moved on from Mariam's initial interest and Kostya's posturing to impress her; they had really fallen in love. A light-hearted flirtation had set off an emotional chain reaction. Initially feather-light, joyous, and full of yearning, Mariam's feelings grew leaden, heavy, and mistrustful. Her paeans to Kostya practically became interrogations, to which she subjected her friend on the pretext of trying to understand Kostya's mind: she wanted to know his preferences, to work out how he thought — every word he said to her was carefully analysed, every look assessed, significance ascribed to every touch. Kitty hadn't thought anything could surprise her, but she had not thought her friend would lose her head so completely, and in such a short space of time; that she would fall for Kostya so entirely, become so desperate for his attention.

★

One mild April evening, Kitty came home from rehearsals and saw Kostya sitting with Christine in the garden, which the two sisters had recently replanted and begun to tend. She stopped abruptly, because something about the picture didn't feel right. For some inexplicable reason, as she observed them, Kitty felt like a voyeur witnessing something not intended for her eyes. Yet it was just her aunt sitting with her nephew in easy intimacy. A familiar picture; nothing unusual. The two of them were sitting at the old garden table, Kostya leaning forward slightly, holding Christine's hand in his. The beautiful half of Christine's face was turned towards her nephew, and she was listening, captivated, to what he was saying. Suddenly she burst out laughing and threw back her head. Their intimate conversation, their uninhibited laughter, their togetherness were so self-contained, so self-absorbed, that Kitty pressed herself against the wall and lowered her eyes in embarrassment. This sight, so seemingly ordinary, concealed a truth the participants themselves were probably unaware of. They're the perfect lovers, thought Kitty suddenly — and dismissed the absurd idea as swiftly as it had come. But she couldn't tear herself away from this sight, this image, which made such coherent sense.

Perhaps it was not his aunt's physical beauty Kostya had fallen for, Kitty considered; rather, that there was something concealed behind that beauty, something vulnerable, mournful, unhappy. And perhaps he needed the aloofness that Christine radiated in abundance; needed to immerse himself in it, to lose himself, so as not to have to face reality. Perhaps, Kitty speculated, it was fear that governed him: the fear that he could not stand the test of the world.

Perhaps his discipline, his longing for power, was nothing more than a constant effort to annihilate this fear. The fear of mistakes, the fear that everything around him might one day turn out to be meaningless. One day — when he might lose something, something he could not hold on to.

Or had it already happened? Had he lost something? And if so, what — or perhaps she should ask herself: who?

He would never be able to look at Mariam like that. The thought flashed through Kitty's mind like a bolt of lightning. For Mariam had survived the darkest of all worlds. Like Kitty, Mariam had stood the test of Hell and could no longer have any fear of the world. Mariam would never awaken this longing in Kostya; and Kostya would always avoid his sister because, however paradoxical, however incredible the observation seemed, in this moment Kitty was quite convinced that her brother was governed by this fear just as much as Christine.

Kitty went to her room, closed the door behind her, lay down on the bed, and thought. She would have to amputate her own past, she thought, in order to recover the life she had been observing from the sidelines for so long. She reflected on how wrong it had been to take in Andro's dream, that it had made her ill, but she was equally aware that for her, unlike the other members of her family, her unfulfilled dreams could actually put her life in danger. Because it was imperative that she be herself, even if enduring that self, living with it, caused her pain.

When she thought about amputating the past, she was certainly not thinking only about the classroom and what had been done to her there. It was beyond her power to forget that, to suppress it, because to do so would also mean erasing her lost child from her memory. Unlike Kostya, who hid his loss — whatever and whoever it may have been — so well, vanishing ever further behind a mask of ignorance, indifference, and strength, she would remember what had happened to her every single day. But everything before that day — before the classroom, before the straps — all that had to disappear. She would have to bid it all farewell.

★

In May, Kostya and Mariam announced their engagement. Kitty refrained from making any comment; she kept her doubts to herself and congratulated her radiant, happy friend. She didn't question why Kostya had let himself get so carried away as to take this decision; it made no difference to her now, anyway. The most likely explanation was that Kostya wanted to see himself through Mariam's eyes: as the honourable, courageous, determined, cultivated man who kept his word, never violated a woman's honour, and had a brilliant future ahead of him. When Kitty came to think about it, all her brother had wanted all his life was to be just such a man. But he wasn't, and he never would be. And Kitty would have to keep this secret from her friend, his future wife, forever.

Mariam's family, who had come to Tbilisi for the engagement, glowed with pride all day long. It was already a miracle that their daughter had been granted a place to study medicine, and now she was getting engaged to a naval officer. Nothing now seemed to stand in the way of her extraordinary happiness.

Stasia and Christine had also seemed bemused when Kostya broke the news to them. Stasia, with her characteristic passivity, kept out of her son's private life; she gave him a little kiss on the cheek, which Kostya interpreted as her approval of his intentions. And Christine was sufficiently tactful not to express her doubts openly. The wedding was to take place the following summer.

After the engagement party, Kostya left Tbilisi. He was going to spend two months in Moscow, where, he said, he wanted to sort out his future. Telegrams had started arriving for him; he'd sat hunched over them in the garden, deep in thought. If anyone asked about them he would get irritated and evade the question, saying that these were his private affairs.

★

Christine, meanwhile, received the letter she had secretly, fearfully, been waiting for, and opened it with trembling hands. There was no official stamp on the envelope. Would he want to see her? What price would he demand of her in return? Or did he still not have the courage to behold the work of art that Ramas, because of him, had drawn on the living canvas of her face? She extracted the single sheet of paper, smelled it. Did the paper smell of him? Would she recognise the smell? If so, how would it make her feel?

But she felt nothing. There was just an infinite emptiness inside her. Not even anger, her one constant emotion in recent years. He wrote that, after much consideration, he had decided to help her, even though the boy's file contained nothing concrete that suggested a satisfactory solution; still, he would see what could be done. And he was pleased to have received a message from her, even though it had only reached him months later. As she was aware, he was very busy, but he would always make time for her. The letter, which was unsigned, ended by conceding that he had not forgotten her.

Of course he wasn't prepared to see her. Of course that would have been asking too much of him — too much for his eyes, which he hid so well behind the round lenses of his glasses. All day long, Christine sat in her room, the letter on her knees, trying to imagine what it would be like if she were to meet him again somewhere, some day. Would she feel the same sense of shame, and, at the same time, this bitterness? Would she be able to face his passion with the same indifference as she had years ago, in another life?

Christine sat down on the window seat and drank her cherry liqueur. Darkness had fallen; the streetlamps were being lit outside. She thought of his wife, the angelic Nina, whom she had seen only once, at the opera. Christine was still happily married to Ramas back then; back then, there was still no fear, no trembling at the unexpected calls, the Bugatti on the street corner, come to pick her up. Nina had been wearing an apricot-coloured dress and the melancholy expression of a lamb about to be slaughtered for gods it had no knowledge of and didn't believe in. Nina had given her a slight, almost imperceptible nod, and Christine, smiling, had passed her by and walked on, past all the busybodies bad-mouthing the Little Big Man's beautiful wife. How safe she had felt, arm-in-arm with Ramas — Ramas, who had escorted her safely to her box. Back then, she had felt pity for beautiful Nina, always surrounded by security men, and had questioned Ramas about her. Back then, she didn't yet know that she would soon be the one deserving of pity. Had this shy and retiring woman, the most mysterious of all the Kremlin wives, already been suspicious that evening? Had she sensed that one day, on that very spot, during another performance, in the box where they were sitting, her husband would take Christine, with such brazen, brutal nonchalance; would make her his own, like a wild animal he had to tame? With the same neutral nonchalance as the many women who came before and after her?

In the first years after Ramas' death, she had often found herself thinking of the silent Nina. She couldn't have said why, but Nina's face often materialised before her during her stay in hospital. Again and again, she had asked herself why, of all the many beauties, the gentle, dreamy beauty of his wife was the one he seemed to need and desire the least. Unlike all the other Kremlin wives, Nina led a shadowy existence. She was never seen with her husband at an official reception, or accompanying him at a military parade. Very occasionally she would go with him to theatre or opera premieres, but for a long time she had not even done that.

After her husband had consolidated his power and was finally summoned to Moscow, she followed him, spending most of her time living in her dacha while he resided alone in the magnificent villa on Triumfalnaya. People said she worked in a little chemistry laboratory; she had studied agricultural sciences. However, very few fellow workers had actually seen her. They said she was driven to work every day in a car with tinted windows, and after work it picked her up again. Patient Nina. Why was it that she couldn't help thinking of her, even now, Christine wondered — and was unable to answer. Nina had borne her Little Big Man a son, had tolerated an army of other women in his rooms, never asked anything of him, never got involved, never put him in an unpleasant situation. How does it feel to be someone like that, Christine wondered. How does it feel to decide, yourself, not to want to know anything that could pull the ground from under your feet? Or did she really believe in the rightness of what her husband was doing? Did she believe in his magnificent work, his extraordinary sacrifices for the Soviet people?

At the end of a long life, Brilka, when she gave her first and only interview at the age of eighty-six and was asked about her husband's predatory infidelity, Nina was indignant. She replied, 'He worked day and night; when would he have had the time to satisfy a whole legion of women?'

> Submissive to you? You're out of your mind!
> I submit only to the will of the Lord.
> I want neither thrills nor pain,
> My husband — is a hangman, and his home — prison.
>
> ANNA AKHMATOVA

Andro Eristavi returned to Tbilisi in the autumn of 1946. He was released without further explanation and put on a goods train to Moscow. There he was met by a couple of men from the NKVD — now the MVD — and taken to a police station, where it was made clear to him in no uncertain terms that he could hope for neither proper employment nor any kind of social integration. He was a parasite, and in future would be treated as such. He was to keep his mouth shut, live inconspicuously, think inconspicuously, never draw attention to himself, and content himself with employment in a *kolchoz* somewhere in the mountains. There was no chance of him obtaining the necessary registration certificate to live in Tbilisi. He should consider himself lucky to be alive; if he hadn't had influential friends, he would have been hanged in a few months' time — even a bullet was too good for scum like him.

Right up to the last minute, Christine didn't say a word about Andro's release and return. She was also the one who picked him up from the bus station and took him to a little apartment in the new town. The house it was in was still under construction, meaning that it was completely empty; it belonged to one of Christine's doctor friends, who had said she could use it for a few weeks.

Andro looked worse than she had expected. Like a haggard old man, with cheekbones that stood out so sharply you could cut yourself on them.

She disinfected his clothes, brought him new ones, washed him, shaved his lice-infested head and his beard, cooked him light, non-fatty meals. He didn't speak much, but thanked her for every little thing, which drove Christine crazy. She asked him what he would like. He requested a few books, which she brought from home, and a little schnapps, which she also obtained for him. He spent his time reading or listening to the little radio she had bought him, waiting for her to come back and bring him something to eat.

It was only when she judged that Andro was stable enough to cope with the impending meeting that she picked Kitty up from university and took her to the new town. Buildings were being constructed on every street corner now, mostly by prisoners-of-war.

'Where are you taking me?' asked Kitty suspiciously when they were in the tram.

'I have a little surprise for you. But I must ask you to control yourself as best you can,' came the unexpected reply.

After they had battled through the jungle of apartment blocks, all of which looked the same, Christine knocked at a rough wooden door on a half-finished staircase. There were no tears, no screaming: in fact, there was *nothing*, at all. There were two people — a young woman with dark, bobbed hair, in a green raincoat and knee-length boots, and a haggard, prematurely aged young man, stooped and short-sighted, staring into space, whose hands shook as if he had Parkinson's disease. They stood there in front of one another. They didn't touch. Eventually Christine's voice wrenched them out of their daze and called them to the table she had just laid.

'I've made chicken stew. I took a lot of trouble over it. So come, eat something. And there's cherry liqueur.'

Christine tried all evening to cheer them up a little. She chatted about the weather, about her work at the hospital and her unruly patients, but neither of them laughed, not even once, or said a word. Late that evening she picked up her handbag and left them alone together.

★

Kitty stayed in this apartment for the next fourteen days. What exactly she did during those days, I don't know. Perhaps she nursed him, as Christine had before her, cooked for and washed him. Perhaps they just drank cherry liqueur in silence, or read each other the poems of Lord Byron, of which Andro is said to have been particularly fond. Perhaps Kitty tried to cheer him up, telling him all sorts of anecdotes, or perhaps she just lay beside him and held his trembling hand in hers. She brought him his old things, which she had kept safe: a whole tool-bag full, so that he could start woodcarving again.

After these two weeks, Kitty went back home and took out her old guitar, which she had scarcely used before then and could only play badly. At first there was no music, no harmony, in the chords. She kept on trying until a simple but clear melody emerged from beneath her fingers. The next day she got herself a couple of music books and started to practise every day.

★

During that first meeting with Andro, it was immediately, searingly clear to Kitty that the days when wishes were flexible, pliable, were gone for good — buried on all the countless battlefields in the west and the east, the south and the north. She looked at Andro and saw a shadow who was unable to speak of the horror. In the first few days she had so hoped, had so wished, that he would ask her; that he would feel his way towards the unspeakable, towards her burning wound; but he didn't, and she didn't succeed in putting everything she had saved up, accumulated, into words. Like the rest of the family, the two of them were swallowed up by silence: silence consumed them, like a great whale in whose belly all of them, one after the other, had landed.

She soon felt more miserable around him than without him. She could bear his forlornness, but not his absence, the fact that he no longer had anything to communicate to the world. Even his eyes seemed to have lost their radiance; their blue seemed dull and watery now, and his dreamy gaze was gone for good. The war had beaten, shot, obliterated the dreams from his body, from his head.

She sensed the way he avoided the sight of her firm, well-rounded body, how he looked away whenever she drew near, how he resisted being touched by her, as if she contained explosives and he feared that her very first caress would blow him to pieces.

Only once, in the depths of her despair, did she touch his forehead with her hand and press her lips firmly to his, leaving him no chance to evade her — but he did not return her kiss. He remained cold; his body betrayed no sign of desire. Ashamed, he rose and went into the kitchen, and Kitty tried to force herself to smile through her tears so he wouldn't feel she thought him weak and incapable. Incapable of loving.

Lying awake at night on the mattress, with him on the sofa just a few feet away, she sometimes felt an insatiable desire to leap up, throw water in his face, scream at him to wake up and help her; to tell him of the price she had paid for his dreams. But she knew that if she did she would pull the ground from under his feet once and for all.

★

When Kitty returned home, Stasia happily took over Andro's care, and from then on Kitty stopped visiting him. Neither Stasia nor Christine questioned her about it. It was only weeks later, as she was returning home from a play, that she decided to pay him a spontaneous visit. She was wearing an elegant dark-blue dress with a plunging neckline.

She regretted her decision the minute she entered the apartment. Andro greeted her more sullenly than usual, and when she took off her coat he abruptly turned his back, muttering to himself. She followed him into the cramped kitchenette, where he put some water on to boil.

'I've brought you some of those sour barberry sweets you like so much,' she said, trying too hard to sound friendly.

'Will you stop it!' he shouted suddenly, banging his fist on the edge of the table. 'You can see that ...'

'What have I done? Why are you yelling at me?'

'You come here, you pretend everything's all fine and dandy, and every time you come your clothes get more outlandish, and the sweets get sweeter, and you expect me to —'

'What, what do I expect? I don't expect anything, I just want you to be all right.'

'I can't do it. Stop deceiving yourself. You're so beautiful; I look at you, and it makes me want to weep. But I can't bear this any more. Your being here makes it so blindingly obvious to me that I've fallen apart; I can't stand it. I don't have any strength left, I don't even know how I'm supposed to get through the next day, let alone —'

'But I don't expect anything of you.'

'Yes, you do. You expect me to give you hope. Sometimes I even ask myself whether it was the right thing to get me released.'

'You are so ungrateful. That is so bloody unfair — I could kill you right now.'

'So do it! Maybe then we'll both be free.'

Kitty froze. She staggered backwards. The bag of sweets slipped from her hand, and the contents rolled across the floor. They both looked down at the little sweets in their colourful wrappers, and the sight made them even more dejected. Everything about this felt wrong.

'I'm sorry,' she whispered.

'Me too.'

'Don't you love me any more?'

'How am I supposed to still love you, how am I supposed to feel anything at all, when I'm not even a man any more?'

'It was terrible for everyone. You should be happy that you're alive.'

'To be happy you must first be able to feel something.'

'We all want you to —'

'I don't care what you all want. I've lost everything I had, can't you understand that!'

'So have I, you ungrateful man! Guess what — I've lost everything, too!'

And just as Kitty was ready to shout out the unspeakable, Andro brushed past her and left the kitchen, saying, 'I'm not a man any more. I'm not man enough to love you any more, Kitty. I don't feel anything any more.'

Kitty stood there, still staring at the brightly wrapped sweets, and suddenly felt the urge to laugh. She didn't know why, but she had to keep her mouth pressed firmly shut so as not to burst out laughing. *Well, don't we just make a perfect couple*, she thought. *It seems he can no longer father children — and I can no longer have any. What a perfect, perfect couple, in a perfect, perfect world!*

But she had misunderstood him.

And that night, as she sat alone on her bed and lit herself a cigarette cadged from her mother, words started running through her head, followed — accompanied — by a melody: *What a perfect, perfect couple, in a perfect, perfect world, look at us, wouldn't you say we're perfect?*

By daybreak Kitty had composed her first song.

She was humming it during one of her theatre company's rehearsals when the director asked her to sing him her 'little ditty', as he called it. He found it enchanting, and immediately worked it into the play, in a kitsch love scene where Kitty, with her guitar around her neck and a sorrowful expression on her face, sang it with feeling while gazing adoringly at her leading man.

And it's true, Brilka: soon every happy, lovestruck couple in the city was singing her song; then all the unhappy ones, and the forsaken lovers. And when Kostya returned to wed Mariam after months away from home, he heard his sister's voice on the radio.

★

Kostya had stayed in Moscow longer than planned. He appeared to be waiting for something big, something important, but he kept his worries and his hopes to himself. Not even Christine had any idea about the scheme her nephew was hatching.

★

Kitty's song, so captivating in its artlessness, so memorable in its clarity, gained her national popularity overnight. People stopped to talk to her on the street; one of the theatres offered to schedule an evening of her songs. Kitty was overwhelmed by her unexpected success. She used the holidays to practise the guitar and write more songs, because it was embarrassing to admit in public that 'A Perfect, Perfect World' was her *only* song, born of her inability to say what she wanted to say. Now, though, she found the words she had spent so long searching for. They only came to her through the music. As if her language needed crutches to lean on. And again I find myself thinking of you, Brilka; you played me those songs on our car journey, and sang along. How your eyes sparkled when you sang for me! It was a real struggle for me not to show how moved I was, how deeply moved, not to let you see the emotion those lines of yours, sung with such enthusiasm, evoked in me. But there were so many other little marvels you revealed to me on our journey, Brilka, so many that if I were to start talking about them I would never stop, and our story would probably never end. But I have to share you with all the other people, because our story is also theirs, and theirs is also ours. And we haven't got as far as us yet ...

★

With Kostya's return late that autumn, happiness came back to Christine's house. Mariam, who had tended to avoid Kitty these past few months, also appeared unannounced every evening. The whole family gathered in the kitchen or the garden for extended dinners, although Kitty never stayed at the table any longer than necessary. This relaxed mood didn't last long, though. After the time he had spent in Moscow, Kostya's hometown seemed to him too small, too constrained, too provincial. And when his mother and Christine spoke to him late one evening and confessed that Andro had come back, he openly expressed his displeasure and incomprehension at their support for a man who had betrayed his country. He grew bad-tempered, accused his mother and aunt of trampling Soviet values underfoot and abandoning all sense of morality and responsibility. Christine denied it, but of course Kostya knew that Andro's unexpected release would never have been possible without intervention from above. He shouted at the two women and forbade them ever to let that traitor into the house.

His bad mood didn't lift, and soon not even Mariam was spared. Kostya kept leaving her at home on her own. He no longer took her out, no longer went with her to the cinema, was uncouth and hurtful, responded to her excessive care and kind, affectionate nature with irritation. He virtually fled the house, stayed away for nights on end, looked up old school friends, made fleeting acquaintances, went to parties, sought diversion. As if he were trying to wring a new taste from life, to reinvent himself, but was constantly being thwarted by what had gone before.

He needed the body of one particular woman; he needed to lose control at night in order to stay in control during the day.

He needed to see admiration in a woman's eyes; he needed game playing, flirtation. Not this orderliness. The security, the clear prospects Mariam offered weren't enough for him. He was too sure of her, and it began to bore him. Security was not enough of a challenge. At the same time, he was aware that if he broke off the engagement, Mariam would never recover from the shame; for her, it would be the end of the world. Her honour would be violated, her faith shattered.

Kostya was about to head out on another of his nocturnal excursions when Kitty, all dressed up and perfumed, planted herself in his way.

'What are you doing?' asked Kostya irritably. He had changed out of his uniform and was wearing an elegant suit.

'I'm coming with you. I feel like going out. We haven't done that for ages.'

'I thought you had to work on your successful musical career?'

'I'm going to pretend I didn't hear that outrageous remark. I'm going to carry on being nice. I'm going to link arms with you now, and I expect you to take me out.'

'Alright, but behave yourself and please keep your judgements to yourself. It's a high-class place we're going to; I don't want you embarrassing me there.'

Kitty, surprised that he had agreed so readily to her request, nodded obligingly. She was also surprised that her brother would be in high-class company on his dissolute nocturnal outings. She had assumed that he went to one of the bars by the river, ate smoked fish, drank beer and schnapps, and then disappeared into a guesthouse in Avlabari with some buxom lady, between the Tatar tea houses and the Armenian laundries.

Kostya hailed a taxi and they drove up the Mtatsminda, the 'Holy Mountain', along cobbled streets that led ever more steeply upwards, before finally turning into a cul-de-sac at the end of which a large new house was proudly enthroned on a little hill. There were cars parked in front of the high black gates; loud music emanated from the house, along with a hubbub of voices from the large crowd drinking and talking inside. The people who lived here clearly had money, which meant they were either of significance in the Party or the children of people who were. Kitty could already sense her reluctance as she crossed the threshold, and even considered turning round; she had seen enough, she knew Kostya wasn't slipping into debauchery on his nights out, as they had all feared. But just then a small, rather plump, young man appeared and walked towards them, laughing.

He introduced Kitty to the assembled company, who greeted her effusively. She learned that the owner of the house, the plump boy's father, was the director of the silk factory and currently on holiday in Karlovy Vary. The son and his sister were looking after the house, which was full of would-be sophisticates and the *nouveau riche*, spoiled daddy's boys and girls whom Kostya, by his own standards, ought really to despise. Instead, he seemed to find them entertaining; he was playing the wit, the charmer, the dancer, the intellectual, and above all the ladies' man. Kitty found herself surrounded by women with elaborate hairstyles and interesting skirts, all of whom found it incredibly exciting that she of all people, Kitty Jashi, whom they knew from the radio, was the sister of the best-looking bachelor in the city. Now Kitty understood what was going on. Of course he had had to distance himself from Mariam in these circles, to deny her existence, so that he could play this game. The short, dark-haired girl who laughed loudest, waving her hands with their scarlet fingernails in the air, was the host's sister; she seemed exceedingly interested in Kostya.

Kitty found herself monopolised by some self-satisfied boys whom she found intensely irritating. They all wanted to know who the lucky man was who'd inspired her to write that fantastic song and whether she was still having an affair with him. The very word 'affair' made Kitty feel so out of place that she would have liked to have run straight back home again. She thought of Mariam and what she would have to say about all this; what then could she still find to love about Kostya?

'Come on, I'll show you something.' Visibly intoxicated by the heavy red wine, Kostya smiled his captivating smile, dragged her away from the crowd, and led her out onto the terrace. From here they had a superb view of the glimmering city and the lush green hills with the lizard-coloured river winding among them. Sunk in the night, the city looked content. Seen from up here, everything shone so beautifully; and Kostya was such a natural part of this shining, standing here beside her, so broad-shouldered and proud, looking up at the sky, breathing in the fresh air.

'Why are we here, Kostya?'

'I thought you wanted to get drunk with me tonight.'

'I mean, what are you doing here? With these people?'

Before he could answer, another group of clucking girls appeared, with the hostess at their head, and gathered around Kostya and his sister.

'Please, please, sing the song! We've brought you a guitar specially; please, please sing "A Perfect, Perfect World",' they beseeched Kitty, champagne glasses in their hands.

Kitty stared at their faces and saw Andro before her, his little room, his slumped posture, his sunken cheeks and bald head. She thought of how much she missed his golden curls that would never grow back as luxuriantly as before. 'What a perfect, perfect couple, in a perfect, perfect world, look at us, wouldn't you say we're perfect?' And they all sang along; they all sang the same words, they all raised their voices when they got to the 'perfect world', and they all lowered their voices when she breathed, '... so how can it be, that, without you and me, the world is still so perfect?'

With her audience applauding rapturously, Kitty knocked back two glasses of champagne in quick succession, excused herself, and looked around for her brother, but he was no longer with the group outside on the terrace. She hurried back into the house; she wanted to let him know that she had to leave, that she couldn't stand these people any longer. But Kostya was nowhere to be found. She crossed the big room with the dancing couples, ran up and down the brightly lit corridors, peeped into various rooms, asked after him again and again, but no one had seen him; no one knew where he was.

At last she gave up: she feared that he must have retired with the hostess to some quiet corner where no one would find them, and she ran to the door without taking her leave.

Outside, she breathed a sigh of relief. The cul-de-sac was dark; the only light came from inside the house. She sat down on a ledge a few metres from the front door. Suddenly, she heard a noise. At first, she paid it no attention, but then she recognised her brother's voice, low and persuasive. Hadn't they managed to find a secluded part of the house in which to indulge their flirtation? Kitty felt uncomfortable about spying on her brother, but curiosity prevailed, and she followed his voice down the left-hand side of the house. She saw two shadows beneath a balcony, and recognised Kostya; he was propping himself against the wall with one hand and leaning over someone, dangerously close to this woman's face, as if they had just kissed, or were about to. He was speaking to her insistently. But it wasn't the little dark-haired girl, the hostess; this woman was tall and blonde.

Kitty squinted and craned her neck as far as it would go. Which of the squeaking, childishly over-made-up women was it? One of the ones who had been standing upstairs listening to her sing? The woman was pressing her breasts up against Kostya and looking attentively into his eyes. Then she ran a hand carefully down his cheek, and he glanced around warily; it seemed he didn't want to be seen with her. Once Kitty's eyes had grown accustomed to the dark, she focused on the woman's profile. She was tall and elegant; her hair was pinned up and elaborately styled, and she wore a tight beige skirt that emphasised her waist, with a flattering slit up the side exposing a long, muscular leg. Above all, though, she was older; older than Kostya, and older than all the other guests in the house.

'I want it, too ... Of course, how can you doubt that?' Kostya was whispering things Kitty could hardly hear, and the woman pulled him close and pressed her nose against his. Soon she would touch his lips, thought Kitty; Kostya's body grew tense, he leaned in towards her, but she didn't let him, she didn't kiss him.

Then Kitty heard the blonde woman say, loud and clear, 'You know I hate it when people keep me waiting, Kostya' — and suddenly she was overcome by dizziness. She felt her legs turn to jelly and, leaning against the wall of the house, she slid to the ground.

The voice. She knew that voice! She would never forget that voice. She would never fail to recognise that soft, cajoling tone.

It was her. The woman from Hell.

Kitty got to her feet again, clinging to the wall of the house, and walked backwards until the two of them disappeared from view and she was at the front of the house again. From there she ran back inside, locked herself in the nearest bathroom, ran some water, and held her head under the tap until she was able to control her breathing. But her body refused to obey her: her knees were shaking, and she could hardly stand. She forced herself down onto the cold, tiled floor and counted to one hundred until she felt able to get up again.

Then she went back to the main salon, grabbed a glass of wine, and knocked it back in one draught. By the time Kostya reappeared, she was standing alone on the terrace and had downed about three more glasses.

'I've been looking for you,' said Kostya. 'Where the hell have you been hiding? You look sort of ... Have you drunk too much?' He was cheerful; his voice was bright. 'I heard you sing. You seem to go down really well, with your funny song — really, I'm impressed.'

'Who is she?'

'Sorry, who do you mean?'

'Who is that woman?'

'Have you been spying on me?'

'*Who?*' She turned and looked at him. Her face was contorted; the expression in her eyes was somewhere between revulsion and physical pain. Kostya's relaxed manner instantly switched to aggression.

'That? It's nothing serious. You needn't be concerned on Mariam's account.'

'Does she know you're getting married? Does she know her name? Does she know your real name? How well do you know her?'

As Kitty uttered these questions, she suddenly realised the full, irreversible, dark implications of the ancient sport the gods were playing with them.

'Is this an interrogation? I'm a big boy, Kitty; pull yourself together. I don't need a chaperone. Are you, of all people, going to talk to me about morals?'

'I don't give a shit where you choose to put your dick. I just want to know her name.'

'Don't you dare —'

Kitty was sure the blonde woman would not set foot inside the house. She had vanished into the night just as she had appeared, without a trace. Where had she come from? Where had he met her? Did he only come to this house in order to meet with her in secret? It made no sense. Kitty's head ached. She narrowed her eyes, frowning ferociously.

'Tell me who she is and I'll leave you alone!'

The volume at which she made her demand surprised even Kitty herself. She seized her brother by the shoulders and began shaking him as hard as she could. Kostya was startled by the violence of her reaction; he staggered back, but didn't defend himself.

'Kitty, Kitty, please, calm down — come on, I'll drive you home, it's all right, calm down. I promise you I won't hurt Mariam; what you saw is something else, come on now.'

'Who —?' she screamed.

A few guests had started to come out onto the terrace, and Kostya was clearly finding the scene uncomfortable. He seized her wrists and dragged her into the house, and when she grabbed hold of the banisters and refused to go any further he picked her up, threw her over his shoulder like a sack of potatoes, and carried her downstairs. He only put her down again on the wide road once they had left the Holy Mountain behind them. She slumped onto the pavement and started to weep.

She wept almost soundlessly, but it was a terrible weeping; a weeping like Christine's, the silent weeping of the women of the chocolate house. Kostya stood beside his sister in bewilderment, looking down at her, incapable of comforting her and incapable of leaving her alone. Eventually he sat beside her and tried to put his arm around her, but she pushed him away.

'I expect some sort of explanation from you, right now!' he said, loudly, once she had calmed down a little and wiped away the tears with her sleeve.

'I just want her name. I don't want anything else from you. I won't say anything to Mariam, I just want the name.'

'But why, what for?'

'I know her.'

'Where do *you* know her from?'

'Who is she?'

'She's just a beautiful woman I met at a banquet, and she's married, which is why it wouldn't be very advisable —'

'Just a beautiful woman … just a beautiful woman.' Kitty repeated her brother's words in disbelief.

Just a beautiful woman, you say. It didn't hurt, didn't hurt, because she was a beautiful woman. Such beautiful lips, I thought, as she sang me the song of death. Just a beautiful woman. But look at me, look at me — I'm a woman too, not beautiful like her, dead and risen again, but a woman, like her.

I doubt, Brilka, that the people who were to sing this song in the years to come, and still sing it, know that it's not a song about jealousy.

★

He didn't relent. He didn't reveal her name. Kitty wasn't sure who exactly he was trying to protect, but she knew that she would not yield, that she would do everything in her power to find out the blonde woman's name.

She tried using tenderness, deploying her acting talents to play the concerned and loving sister; she intimated that if he didn't relent she would tell Mariam. But apparently there was much more at stake for him than just Mariam. She made his life difficult, persecuted him, gave him no peace. He was losing patience; eventually he would give in. He couldn't stand this persecution, this curtailment of his freedom for long, thought Kitty. And she would dog his heels, would allow him no rest. She was tough, tougher than he could ever have dreamed.

At the end of the month, when the rain had been beating down on the roofs non-stop for days, stretching the nerves of everyone in the house to breaking point, Kitty made yet another nasty comment about Kostya's nocturnal escapades, and he lost patience. He grabbed at her dress, dragged her into the mud-soaked garden, and flung her to the ground. The rain kept sluicing down. Within seconds, brother and sister were soaked to the skin.

'Stop it — stop it! Do you hear me?' he bellowed through the rain.

Full of hatred, he glared at his sister, who leaped back onto her feet and started circling him like a wildcat.

'Tell me her name!'

'You're completely mad, insane, you should be locked up, you should be ashamed of yourself!'

'Tell me her name and I'll leave you in peace!'

'She's done nothing to you — leave her alone. I just had an affair with her, my God! Just a little affair. Her husband is very powerful. And if anything goes wrong, if you do something foolish, you'll be in trouble and I don't want to carry the can for you yet again — just let things lie!'

'Fuck her senseless if you want — you think I'm interested in that? I just want her name!'

'You're talking like a cheap whore! Father would turn in his grave.'

'He doesn't have a grave! He doesn't even have a grave!'

At that Kostya caught hold of his sister again and hit her hard in the face. She fell, and rolled in the mud; when she raised her head, blood was running down her chin. Her bottom lip had split. She didn't cry; she didn't even touch the wound, as if she were immune to the pain.

Just then Christine ran outside and stood between them, screaming at the top of her voice for them to stop. Dazed, Kostya paused, his hair stuck to his scalp, clothes dripping; he couldn't quite believe what he had done. But Kitty's face showed no remorse, no fear: she looked him dead in the eye, haughty and self-assured. The blood on her face mixed with the rainwater, creating the illusion of war paint.

Stasia, too, came out into the garden, stood in Kostya's path, and grabbed him by the collar. 'What have you done?' she snarled at her son.

He looked her in the eyes, and said, 'I hate you both!'

And those words tore us all apart.

★

A few weeks later, Kitty called Mariam and asked to meet her in a café. Mariam, who found both the strained atmosphere between the siblings and her fiancé's aloofness and irritability upsetting, was happy to receive the invitation and accepted with relief.

They met in a fashionable café that had just opened near the Technical University. Mariam had taken great pains not to seem in any way inferior to the rest of its clientele. She arrived wearing a chocolate-brown suit that didn't really do her figure any favours, hugged Kitty, and ordered a Turkish coffee, although normally she only drank tea: one *had* to drink coffee in a place like this.

'I simply have to tell you how happy I am you called. The last month hasn't been that easy for any of us, has it? All this time I've been hoping we'd be able to find a way, be able to talk about everything again. I don't want you to be cross with me.' Mariam gushed at her friend like a waterfall.

'I have to speak to you.'

'No, listen to me. Please. I've hardly been able to sleep these last few weeks. I don't want anything to come between us. It'll all sort itself out. I'm sure of it. We'll sort this out, the two of us. We've come through so much together, we just have to want it.'

Mariam was agitated; her cheeks were burning. She grabbed Kitty's hand across the table and held on to it.

'Mariam ...'

'We'll make up for everything, won't we? We can't give up on our friendship just like that, that's just not possible. I miss you, I miss you so much, and I don't want to be without you. Yes, I love your brother. But that doesn't mean you're any less important to me.'

Tears welled up in Mariam's eyes.

'I don't want to drive a wedge between the two of you, I don't want you to quarrel, especially not because of me. I would never forgive myself. You're such a wonderful brother and sister. Fascinating, talented, clever, beautiful. No — that can't happen, Kitty. I'd never forgive myself.'

Mariam had turned away and was staring at the pigeons strutting up and down the pavement.

'Mari, I have to tell you something important.'

'I love you. But I love him, too. You're two halves of a whole. That may sound strange, but I've thought about it a lot, and I know what I'm talking about. I —'

'He's cheating on you.'

'Kitty!'

'He's having an affair. I've seen her, but I don't know her name, and I will gladly help you if you find out who she is.'

'Kitty.'

'If you don't want to believe me, that's your decision. The quarrel wasn't because of you, it was because of her. Check what I've told you, and if I'm wrong, just forget all this. If not …'

'Yes — if not, what?'

'Then think about whether you want to spend your life with a man who will never love you.'

'Why are you trying to ruin everything?'

Tears were rolling down Mariam's red cheeks.

'I can't ruin something that was ruined long ago.'

Kitty hated herself. But she hated that woman far more.

★

That night, Kitty persuaded her aunt to make her the hot chocolate. Kostya came home late, and when the smell of the chocolate reached his nose he hurried to the kitchen and demanded some of the magical drink. Kitty reluctantly divided her portion, shared it with her brother, and they fell on their cups like starving dogs. Wakened by the smell, Stasia too stumbled into the kitchen to see her children licking the last drops of chocolate from their cups. She screamed at her sister — how dare she, where had she got hold of the recipe — sank helplessly onto a chair, and howled. Even if Stasia still wasn't sure what price her father's hot chocolate exacted from those who tasted it, she was no longer in any doubt that there was certainly a price to be paid. She had wanted to protect her children from temptation, from becoming greedy for more, because she was sure that this was the danger her father had spoken of back then, the danger inherent in the chocolate: the fact that no one who had so far succumbed to the temptation of sampling it was able to do so just once.

Christine, still holding the tin bowl she had made the chocolate in, snarled back that he was her father, too, and she also had a right to the recipe, whereupon Stasia seized the bowl and threw it on the floor. For a moment they all glanced back and forth between the furious Stasia and the few drops of black liquid that had trickled out of the bowl.

Suddenly Kostya bent down, sank onto all fours as if hypnotised, and started wiping the residue off the floor with his fingers, sticking them eagerly into his mouth.

The women stared down at him, speechless. When he had wiped the last drops off the floor, he got up and calmly left the kitchen.

'What was *that*?' asked Christine. She looked at her sister, bemused.

'His first chocolate, I imagine,' Stasia answered reproachfully.

> I was there, too. I drank mead and beer;
> they flowed down my beard but did not go in my mouth.
>
> RUSSIAN FORMULA FOR THE HAPPY ENDING TO A FAIRYTALE

The tall blonde woman with the cherry-red lips was called Alla. She was forty years old and the neighbour of the silk merchant who let his children throw parties in the big house. It was at one of these parties that Kostya had met her. She had studied medicine in Moscow, where she was regarded as an up-and-coming star in the field of psychiatry. As a result, she was approached by the NKVD and joined the organisation. On one of her business trips she met her future husband; he, too, worked for the NKVD, but with the Georgian branch. She moved with him to Tbilisi and continued her work in the Caucasus. Her husband was about twenty years older, and she soon grew tired of him; for Alla displayed a healthy appetite, not only for tracking down 'spies and counterrevolutionaries, saboteurs and other vermin': her body also had a great hunger that her husband, a very busy man, was soon no longer able to satisfy.

In the twelve years she had so far spent in the service of the most powerful organisation in the country, she had had nine abortions — all children of different men — the last of which had gone wrong, and since then she had been barren. Infertility, then, became her punishment for the toughest women who fell into her clutches — her small, personal revenge — and it bore impressive fruit. She was known as one of the NKVD's most loyal employees, and also one of the most feared. It's even said that the Little Big Man had pinned a medal to her breast with his own hand. But I don't know that for sure.

When she met my grandfather, her appetite was piqued. That very night, she dragged him into the house next door and unbuttoned his trousers. Her alacrity and decisiveness reminded Kostya of Ida, and he willingly surrendered to Alla. From then on they met regularly.

I don't know how she did it, but Mariam found her. The humiliation of a woman scorned can work miracles. She must have lain in wait for Kostya night after night, standing outside the glittering house. The laughter and loud music coming from within must have felt like being slapped, until she found what she was looking for.

Mariam followed the blonde woman, who kissed her fiancé goodbye behind the house before hurrying down the cul-de-sac, where she stopped in front of the first house. Before, in the dark, all Mariam had been able to make out was her tall figure and elegant clothes, but now, as she stood directly in the light from the streetlamp, looking for her front door key, Mariam too recognised the woman from Hell.

The soft, blonde hair, the red lips, the slow movements, the litheness of her body.

Mariam's horror at the thought of this woman making love to the man she planned to marry was inconceivable. And it was easy for her, so appallingly easy, to picture those manicured fingernails digging into Kostya's back: the coquettishness with which she would throw back her head, snarling at him, lips and eyelids moist with lust. It was so easy for her to imagine the woman urging Kostya on, using the same soft words with which she had once ordered Mariam to pick up the syringe of poison.

★

That night, Mariam threw gravel at Kitty's window. Kitty slipped on a coat and hurried out into the street. When they were far enough away from Christine's house, they sat down on the pavement, and Kitty knew that Mariam had found what she herself had sought so long and so bitterly.

'You wanted me to see her, didn't you? You knew who it was, and you didn't tell me.' Mariam spoke quietly. Her face was empty. It didn't even express anger. 'Why didn't you tell me then and there?'

'You wouldn't have believed me,' murmured Kitty, not sure whether she had done the right thing, whether she'd had the right to let Mariam walk into this trap.

'How long has it been going on?'

Mariam crumpled like a pricked balloon.

'How should I know?'

'How could he … It's too ridiculous to be true. Why did you let me …?'

Mariam stood, walked a few steps along the dark, empty street, turned back, and sat down again. Her whole body seemed to baulk at this outrageous fact, as if refusing to acknowledge the truth.

'I can't even blame you. What sort of degenerate is he, arranging to go to someone else's house for a rendezvous with a woman who isn't even invited to the party?'

She laughed. Her laugh sounded shrill, forced. Kitty's thumbnail was bitten down to the quick.

'I don't know why I sent you there. Perhaps I wanted you to confirm that it couldn't possibly be her. But it is. It's her, and none other!'

Kitty wondered what reaction she had anticipated from her friend. Certainly not this. Fits of weeping, perhaps; hysteria, panic, but not this emptiness in her face, this irrevocable determination in her voice.

'I'll go and find her and talk to her. It's nothing to do with you any more.' Kitty got up off the pavement and looked down at her friend. She hoped this position would lend weight to her words, but Mariam was laughing again. She was laughing in her face.

'Talk — to her? Are you pretending to be more stupid than you really are, Kitty, or what are you actually saying? And don't tell me it's nothing to do with me. If that were true, you wouldn't have set me on your brother like a bloodhound. Be honest enough at least to admit that to yourself.'

Kitty couldn't think of anything to say. Of course she should never have sent Mariam to the house, but it was too late. Kitty refused to think about that; she couldn't hesitate now. It would only make Mariam more determined, whatever that might mean.

'Yes, perhaps you're right, but please — let me put an end to this by myself.'

'Put an end to it? What, are you going to report her to the police?' Another derisive laugh.

Kitty was gradually losing control of the situation. Mariam was steering this conversation, this whole situation, in a direction that made Kitty very uneasy, one she couldn't fathom. She cursed her own rashness, her impetuosity.

Perhaps for both of them the blonde woman had once been an angel of death, but to Mariam now she was, above all, her rival for Kostya's affections; the classroom, the village school, were just an inevitable black mark on her immaculate white skin.

Kitty began to shiver. She rubbed her hands.

'You want to put an end to it, but you've already made me your accomplice. Here I am again, and we'll put an end to it together. Because that was how you wanted it, and apparently God did, too,' said Mariam, before turning her back on her friend and walking swiftly away down the road.

★

When she got home, Kitty sat on the window sill and asked herself, for the first time since that mild evening on the Holy Mountain when she had seen with her own eyes something she would never have thought possible, what exactly it was she really wanted. Whole armies, political organisations, countless people in uniform and Little Big Men stood between Kitty and her angel of death. Between them lay mountains of weapons, files, and bones, over which she would never be able to climb. Feverishly, Kitty ran through her options. The easiest thing, of course, would be to confide in the woman's husband — obviously a very powerful man — and reveal to him that he was a cuckold. But a man married to a woman capable of brutally robbing another of her unborn child would surely be her equal in this respect. His fury would be directed not against his wife but against the man she had chosen. And his revenge would be no less terrible than his wife's. Kitty couldn't risk putting her brother in such danger.

By the time she fell asleep, exhausted, she had come to the conclusion that taking revenge was no less a burden than renouncing it.

★

Mariam withdrew. She didn't show up at the Institute, didn't leave the boarding house, didn't meet Kostya any more, and didn't respond, either, to the notes Kitty shoved under her door. Kostya tried to confront Kitty, but she denied having anything to do with Mariam's behaviour.

Kitty focused on her studies, the theatre, and above all her guitar. But at night, when she was alone, an ice-cold fear that made beads of sweat stand out on her brow would overwhelm her, and she would toss and turn, trying to find a solution. She sensed, however, that after all the weeks Mariam had spent obsessively searching for the blonde woman, she was not just going to walk away from this, would not just let it go.

When she thought of what Mariam might be going through, she pictured all kinds of dreadful scenarios. Memories of the days in the classroom, the days in the barn, began to plague her, and when her nightmares started to pursue her in the daytime, too, she went to the student boarding house where Mariam lived and sat down in the corridor outside her door. She decided she would wait for her friend for as long as it took. Sooner or later Mariam would have to go out — sooner or later she would at least have to eat something.

For the first two days, Kitty's efforts were fruitless: the door remained closed. She hammered on it again and again, slipped many more notes under it, begged, pleaded with her friend, tried all her powers of persuasion, but nothing happened.

On the third morning, after most of the students had gone to their lectures, leaving the boarding house empty, Mariam appeared at the door. She was wearing a long raincoat and had done her hair.

'Let's go for a walk,' she said, as if nothing had happened, as if everything were as before, when the two of them had had an — almost — normal friendship and would stroll through the alleyways chatting and eating sunflower seeds. Mariam strode out purposefully into the street and marched over to the bus stop. Everything about her seemed cheerful, smart, the same as always. Only the dark rings around her eyes betrayed something of the grim labyrinth she was trapped in.

'We're going to the Old Town,' said Mariam, as they boarded the first bus that came along. Kitty sat beside her friend. It was foggy and damp in the city. The sky was overcast. The autumn still hadn't really arrived; it wasn't chilly yet. They stared out of the bus window at the streets, the passers-by, the people fleeing the grey day. Kitty laid her head on Mariam's shoulder and breathed a sigh of relief.

They got out at Lenin Square and walked up Kirov Street. Mariam set the pace and the direction. In a cheerless, empty grocery shop displaying half a sausage and two types of cheese, they bought some malt beer, which they drank quickly. Mariam didn't stop anywhere for long, but continued unerringly on her way, which led up and up into the green hills. Kitty asked no questions; she was happy just to be walking here with Mariam, and tried to keep pace with her friend.

They left the big, screened garden of the Central Committee building behind them, turned left, cut through some side streets, sat on a lonely bench for a moment, passed the cable car stop, and watched the people getting into the little cabins.

All at once, Mariam turned to Kitty, reached out, and lifted her jacket and jersey. She stared at Kitty's bare belly. With her other hand she pushed down Kitty's skirt and tights and studied her abdomen.

'What are you doing?' Confused and unnerved, Kitty permitted herself to be examined.

'I wanted to see your scars again. The ones I left you with. Whether they've healed well. I haven't seen them since *then*.'

They left cobbled Chitadze Street behind them, and were already looking up at the artists' cemetery when Kitty realised where Mariam was heading. The silk merchant's house was just a few metres away. She stopped, demanding that her friend explain what this was all about, where she was going. But Mariam didn't stop. She called for Kitty to follow her: it was all right, *her* husband was away.

Kitty tried to protest, but Mariam was already pausing at the corner of the street and climbing the three steps that led up to a red-brick house. Kitty screamed at her not to do it, but before she could reach the house her friend was banging on the front door with a metal lion's head knocker.

Kitty had just set foot on the bottom step when the door was thrown open and Alla stood before them, a cigarette between her painted red lips, curlers in her hair, in a full-length white silk slip.

'Yes?' she asked in Russian, looking at them both crossly. Kitty wanted to grab Mariam's sleeve, to drag her away, but she stood there, firm as a rock, staring spellbound at those scarlet lips.

'Yes?' the blonde woman repeated, and her tone was unfriendly, as if she had just been disturbed in the middle of something important.

'My friend's hurt herself, she fell over and grazed her knees, we'd like to use your bathroom for a moment, if ...'

Mariam's voice was frighteningly calm. She asked the question in Georgian. Kitty's legs were clad in dark woollen tights; the woman, who glanced only briefly at Kitty's knees, couldn't see anything. She seemed to consider for a moment. Her face tightened a little. Perhaps she had recognised one of them, or both. She must have done, Kitty thought. It was madness, really, to assume that someone like her, at the top of her game, would simply let them into her house, right into the mouth of the dragon.

But she did. She gave a brief nod, and just added curtly, in Russian, before opening the door wider and letting them both slip inside, 'Hurry up, though, please, I don't have much time!'

Kitty could feel her whole body trembling. Mechanically, she followed Mariam, who was following the blonde woman, who was showing them to the bathroom. She couldn't believe it, she couldn't take it in. This couldn't be happening. Not like this, not now. Surely it couldn't be this *easy.*

It was a high-ceilinged, airy house, cool and shady. It smelled of fresh coffee beans. She led them through the dark hallway into a tiled bathroom with a bidet and a porcelain washbasin. Kitty closed the door behind her and started hyperventilating.

'What are you doing?' she whispered, suppressing a scream.

Mariam smiled, which disturbed Kitty even more; she was just looking at the door and smiling. Kitty turned on the tap.

'This is what you wanted, isn't it? We're here. At last we're here.'

'I'm sure she doesn't live alone. And anyway, what are you intending to do? If she takes a closer look at us, we're done for. Let's get out of here, fast.' Kitty was stuttering with anxiety.

'No. Everything is as it should be. She didn't recognise us, she didn't even look at you — not even *you*, Kitty. But she will remember us, I promise you that!'

And before Kitty could say anything else, Mariam stormed out of the bathroom.

Kitty felt nothing but horror: overwhelming, paralysing, all-consuming. She stood there, petrified, listened to the running water, tried to calm her breathing.

Suddenly, she heard something fall to the ground, followed by screams, but she couldn't work out whose. She tugged at the door handle and peered cautiously into the corridor, which was still in darkness.

Slowly, she left the bathroom and followed the sounds, which had come from the depths of the house. She reached the end of the corridor and entered the kitchen. Heavy, dark cupboards on the walls, a wide dining table, a fruit basket filled with oranges. Two unwashed plates beside the sink. A faded landscape painting on the wall. Then a small portrait of the Generalissimus, then another photo, of the blonde woman with an older man, his arm around her shoulders.

'Mariam?'

Kitty's voice seemed to be swallowed up. It was eerily quiet in the house, as if she were completely alone. Suddenly, there was a laugh; it came from her right, where a door led out of the kitchen. Kitty opened it and stepped into the living room. In the middle of the room stood a tapestry sofa; in front of the sofa was a glass table with fashion magazines on it. *She* was sitting on the sofa in her slip, chest heaving, eyes wide and clear as glass. She was laughing in Mariam's face, laughing so grotesquely that one might have thought she found the situation hysterically funny. A rough, almost vulgar laugh that didn't seem to fit her sophisticated manner at all.

Mariam stood in front of her, and it was only now that Kitty realised she was holding a large kitchen knife; she must have had it in her bag all along. Her hand wasn't shaking; her grip was firm, as if she'd been practising this for a long time. But her face was contorted; she clearly didn't know how to deal with this laughter. When she turned to Kitty, her eyes were clouded, swamp-like.

'Mariam ... what are you doing?'

Kitty took a tentative step towards her friend.

'I want you to look at her. Well? Do you remember now?' Mariam turned to the blonde woman. On the ground beside the sofa lay a shattered vase; it must have got knocked over when Mariam forced her to sit down.

'Stop laughing, stop laughing!' screamed Mariam suddenly. Kitty felt as if she were about to faint.

'Mariam, please, don't make a mistake here!' Kitty reached out her hand to her friend.

'What? Isn't this what you've wanted all these years? Didn't you want it? Huh? Now you've got it. Here, go ahead, enjoy it!'

The blonde woman suddenly sat up, picked up a cigarette case from the glass table, took out a pink cigarette, and lit it. A couple of rollers had fallen out of her hair, and thick, wavy strands were dangling in front of her face. Not even now, not even in this dreadful situation, could she manage to look ugly.

'You're creating some really big problems for yourselves right now, my darlings. Really big. So I suggest you put that silly knife down right away, say what you have to say to me, and then get out. I'm not angry yet, which means you've been lucky so far, but you won't be for very much longer.'

'She doesn't understand — what a shame! We'll just have to make it clearer for her. Come here, Kitty, come here!'

Mariam waved Kitty over.

Hesitantly, Kitty put one foot in front of another, as if fear had made her forget how to walk. Mariam grabbed her wrist, pulled her towards her, tugged at her skirt, and lifted it to reveal her belly. Rigid with shock, Kitty resisted, reeling backwards, but Mariam held on tightly to the hem of her skirt and lifted it up again. Alla shrugged, and watched with complete indifference as Kitty was exposed.

Kitty felt nausea rising in her chest again.

She was faking — of course she had recognised them both by now, it was impossible that she hadn't — she's just faking, thought Kitty. That ostentatious body, on display, that supercilious smirk around her garish red lips, that cold face: this was all part of her game. Perhaps it even amused her; perhaps it even gave her a bizarre pleasure.

Kitty felt herself seized by unexpected revulsion. A revulsion that tipped over into hatred. A hatred that deadened all other feelings, even puncturing her fear: suddenly, all that was left was this one, single emotion.

'Do you remember now? Is it starting to come back to you?' shouted Mariam. But the woman didn't stir. Her expression remained unchanged.

'You're very confused about something here, darling!' she said, in Russian, and tapped her cigarette ash onto the floor.

'But *we* remember — we remember you! Bloody well, in fact, don't we? And if you hadn't got your harlot's hands on Kostya, too, perhaps we wouldn't even be here.'

Mariam was raving.

At the mention of Kostya's name, the thin, painted eyebrows shot up. The woman opened her mouth and blew a perfect smoke ring. The smirk vanished; she appeared to be thinking. Apparently Kostya's name didn't fit into her game.

Kitty looked at her red-faced, sweating friend, who looked so lost, so weak, compared to this angel of death; she looked at the stockings that had fallen down and were sagging around her ankles, at her shaking hands; she felt the sweat on her forehead, felt how powerless she was, how ridiculous and hopeless, and knew that she had made a mistake. *And if you hadn't got your harlot's hands on Kostya, too, perhaps we wouldn't even be here.*

She should never have told Mariam about this woman. Mariam, who apparently still believed that the woman sitting smoking in front of them had stolen her man — the man who had promised her a happiness that tasted of the great wide world. She didn't realise her mistake. She didn't realise that this woman was just a proxy, one of the many Kostya lusted after. And Kitty herself, standing here with her scars exposed, in this surreal tableau of intimidation, this ludicrous attempt to achieve justice, had been no less mistaken. It had been a disastrous mistake to believe that anything would change, that the acknowledgement of an unspeakable guilt could provide any kind of reparation.

This woman's crystalline blue eyes told Kitty that she would never receive any kind of reparation from her; that no matter how many knives she was threatened with, she did not and would not acknowledge her guilt. She believed in her life, in the man she served; she believed in the state she was helping to shape, and neither Mariam nor Kitty, nor the scars on display, nor the knife were going to change that in any way. Someone who was capable of feeling remorse, someone with compassion, someone who was able to put the truth of a human being above the truth of a state would not have driven to the village school, would not have converted a classroom into an operating theatre, would not have made a nurse into a murderer and a heavily pregnant girl into a childless mother.

Kitty realised that no matter what the outcome of this afternoon would be, she would always feel her dead child's body under the earth, all the time, every day. She realised that her scars would always reveal traces of Hell whenever she ran her hand over them. She realised that whatever happened she would remain powerless, a victim. This was how it had been, and how it would always remain, because the days she had spent in the village school had branded themselves onto her. This realisation was so abhorrent to her, so sickening, so repulsive, that she turned her face away, shrank back, and vomited in the corner.

'What the hell are you doing?' said the blonde woman angrily, jumping to her feet. Mariam thrust the knife towards her; the tip was just a hair's breadth away from touching the fine silk slip. The woman sat down again.

'So what's it like, then? What's it like with him? Do you run after him like a bitch on heat? Do you enjoy it?'

Mariam was still chasing her desire for personal retribution.

'What do you mean?' Alla's face darkened. 'I don't know you; I don't know either of you. This has gone too far. I'm starting to lose my patience, and believe me, darling, once that happens you will know about it.'

'We mean nothing to you, the classroom means nothing to you, the syringe means nothing to you, all that blood means nothing to you, the dead baby means nothing to you ...? Look at these hands: they cut out this woman's womb. Does that mean nothing to you either? But Kostya's dick means something to you — how wonderful!'

Kitty was astonished at Mariam's choice of words, at the way she was reviving the memories.

'Please, Mariam, stop, there's no point ... Please. Let's go. I feel sick.'

Kitty wiped her mouth on the sleeve of her jersey.

'You feel sick now, do you, Kitty? And how did you feel then, when she asked me to kill your son? Didn't you feel sick then? So sick that you wanted to die? We're not going anywhere until this whore —'

'That's enough. Get out of my house!'

How composed she is, despite everything, thought Kitty. How well she has mastered her game.

★

Outside, night was drawing in. The room was dissolving in the twilight. Features grew increasingly blurred. Memories, like first snow, slowly settled on this woman's beautiful, half-painted eyelids; they settled there so softly, they were almost transparent, and Kitty would have liked to gather her hatred into a single lump, to take that lump of hatred in her hand and hurl it with all her might at the woman's face. The hatred would hit her and smash her beautiful face to pieces, disfigure her forever; it would rain down onto her shoulders, force her to her knees, she would have to cut open her ribcage, maybe Mariam would help her, a clean, thin cut, and it would disappear inside, that heavy, bloody lump, then Kitty's blood would run through her veins, would mingle there with her blood and turn to poison, in seconds her blonde hair would turn white —

'Kitty!'

Mariam's voice shook her out of her reverie. The woman had stood up and was approaching Mariam.

'Put that damned knife down, you don't know what you're doing or who you're dealing with; put it down and then get out of my house. I'm giving you one last chance. I've had enough, you crazy, feeble-minded little monsters!'

She kept moving slowly towards Mariam, who took a step back, still gripping the knife.

Despite the quickly gathering darkness, Kitty could make out the tears on her friend's face. Would they always have to keep losing, again and again, in this senseless battle?

'Kitty, do something. Why don't you help me, damn it?' Mariam began to moan.

'You're finished — this is the end for both of you! I should never have let you live, I should have finished you both off back then, you ungrateful little monsters, you scum!' Alla's voice was clear and piercingly high.

At these words, Kitty froze, and, for a fraction of a second, Mariam loosened her hold on the knife. For a moment, time seemed to stand still, the earth stopped turning, thoughts tumbled thick and fast. The woman from Hell was acknowledging that this hell had really existed. She admitted to being its ruler. But, at the same time, her brutal admission made Kitty feel more helpless than ever.

Naked fury was now written on Alla's face. She was glaring at them both, full of hatred. Kitty took a step over to Mariam, who was backing towards her.

'What do you think is going to happen here, you little monsters? You come into my house just like that, threaten me with this ridiculous thing, and expect me to be moved, to burst into tears? Do you have any idea what punishment is? Do you have any idea what pain means? Not enough, apparently; it looks like it's time you learned.' Her eyes glittered unhealthily in the dim evening light. For the first time, her beautiful face was twisted and ugly. She was very close to Mariam now.

'Don't come any closer, don't you dare — stop there!' Mariam screamed, and Kitty sensed her friend's fear.

They had gone too far. They could no longer just walk out of this room; however often and however much she had to vomit, they would have to stick it out.

The blonde was standing right in front of them now; they could smell her cloying scent, her lipstick.

It was as if they had switched roles, and Mariam was now the observer. She stepped to one side and switched on a little table lamp. Just at that moment, Kitty's ribcage expanded and a scream came out. It came from the very centre of her body; she let herself be carried along by it, followed the sound, and threw herself at the woman. The blonde seemed startled; she didn't defend herself, fell — and suddenly there was blood. Her bare body had fallen on the shards of the vase and she had cut herself. She groaned, but even in her pain she kept her composure.

Kitty was breathing heavily. Alla sat up and examined the cuts on her knee, her wrists, her elbows.

There was a moment's silence. Then she stood, put her hands around Kitty's neck, and her manicured, white, bloodstained fingers began to squeeze.

'You pieces of shit, you're finished, you're —'

Kitty clutched at the hands and tried to pull them away from her neck. She couldn't breathe.

Mariam threw herself between them, knocking over the lamp as she did so, and they were plunged back into darkness. She yanked at Alla's blonde hair, dragging her off Kitty, who crawled aside, coughing.

'I shouldn't have taken pity on you. People like you must be exterminated, you never learn anything, you're not worthy of our society,' the woman yelped, hugging her knees, which were now bleeding heavily. 'I need a bandage, I have to ... I have to go to the bathroom,' she added, almost pleading.

'You're not going anywhere. She bled for long enough, too, back then.'

The knife was clearly visible in Mariam's hand.

'What do you want from me? What do you wretched bastards want?'

For the first time, there was something like desperation in her voice.

'She still doesn't understand. Well, Kitty, what do you think, shall we clarify it for her? Shall we do her that favour? Yes, come on, we don't want to keep such a nice surprise from her!' Mariam seemed to feel secure again, back in control of the situation. 'This is his sister. She's Kostya's sister. Do you get it now? Whose baby and womb you ordered me to remove. The sister of the man you're running after like a bitch on heat, the man you put these curlers in your hair for, who you can't wait to have mount you!'

'Stop, stop, stop, please, please, stop!' begged Kitty, her hands over her ears. The blonde woman's face slowly twisted into a grimace; in the darkness, it was hard to tell if it was of disgust or fear.

★

Just as Alla was slowly beginning to understand how all the elements of this macabre spectacle fitted together, Stasia was sitting down on an old rocking chair in a corner of her sister's garden and lighting herself an unfiltered cigarette. What she saw before her made her mouth fall open in astonishment; the glowing cigarette dropped out and she leaned against the back of the chair so hard that she tipped over backwards.

At the little wooden table where Christine and Kostya liked to sit, where she herself had so often sat drinking cherry liqueur with her sister as the daylight faded — there, now, sat Thekla and Sopio, playing cards. Thekla wrapped in a pink peignoir adorned with a feather boa; Sopio in a dinner jacket. There they sat, absolutely tangible, absolutely real, absolutely *alive*, playing cards! Stasia blinked several times and looked again, in the hope that it might just be a silly daydream, but the two of them had by no means disappeared: they were still sitting at the table, playing placidly and with total concentration. Stasia's throat tightened.

★

Alla had lost control. Her fear was palpable now. In a single movement she had reached out to grab Mariam's sleeve and struck her in the face. It was pitch dark in the room; Kitty heard noises, a piece of furniture falling over, cries. She couldn't see clearly who was hitting whom, but Alla now had hold of Mariam. Kitty flung herself on the blonde woman, clasped her body with both arms, clenched her fist, and punched her in the back with all her strength.

Kitty saw the knife slip from Mariam's hand; she saw the glint of the blade, and heard it hit the floor.

Alla whipped round in a flash, letting go of Mariam; the curlers flew through the air and her magnificent blonde hair slapped Kitty's face, then Kitty felt her long fingernails on her face, felt the talons pushing her away; the sweetish smell of her skin reached Kitty's nose and made her feel dizzy. The woman twisted her whole body round to face her and punched Kitty in the stomach. In the very place where her son had struggled with his fear, as if he'd already known that being born always means that you must also die.

Kitty was winded; she hung on to the arm of the sofa to stop herself falling over backwards. She felt another heavy blow, a little higher, to her diaphragm: this time, the woman had kicked her. Kitty gasped for breath.

Mariam leaped on Alla from behind and clung on, and for a moment the scene was like a children's game that had got out of hand, one child whirling another around the room for fun, an improvised carousel. Until finally one of the children sank to her knees, because the other was holding a knife to her throat. And the third child saw the sharp blade against that delicate throat, pressing more and more firmly. Then Alla turned her head sharply, stretched out her arm — she looked like an acrobat, her arm so unnaturally flexible — and stuck her middle and index fingers into Mariam's eye-sockets, and the blood spurted, pattering like summer rain, it smelled of iron, it spurted lukewarm and heavy onto Kitty's face, her neck, her breast.

And Alla fell backwards as if in slow motion, with a rattling breath, and the bloody knife slipped from Mariam's hand and hit the floor with a loud, metallic clack, followed by a horrified scream, although Kitty wasn't sure whether it came from Mariam or the angel of death. Then silence. Nothing moved. Kitty tasted the iron on her tongue, and once more suppressed an urge to retch. And then she heard Mariam say quietly:

'*Arteria carotis communis* ... We had it in a lecture recently.'

Her voice seemed to come from a distant planet.

> Like a beast in a pen, I'm cut off
> From my friends, freedom, the sun,
> But the hunters are gaining ground.
> I've nowhere else to run.
>
> BORIS PASTERNAK

Alla's time of death was later established as between ten o'clock and midnight. The cause of death was given as the severing of the carotid artery, the *arteria carotis communis*. The death certificate did not, however, state that she had died at the hands of a virgin raised in the Orthodox faith. One who wanted to marry a naval officer, complete her medical training, and work in an outpatient clinic or, if all went well, in a city hospital; who wanted to bear children, bring them up, love them, spoil them, and raise a glass of sparkling Crimean wine in a toast with her husband.

★

Mariam had initially refused to leave the house, to wash the blood off her hands; she refused to flee at once, refused to contemplate the possibility that perhaps it had, after all, been an accident, or at least self-defence, and that perhaps she wouldn't have used the knife if Alla hadn't stuck her fingers in Mariam's eyes. Dazed and covered in blood, Kitty went to the dead woman's bedroom, picked out some clean clothes, stuffed her own things into her handbag, and left the house.

'You go to Kostya and tell him what's happened, tell him everything, everything he needs to know — tell him our story, yours and mine. I'll stay here. Then tell him to fetch the *militsiya*. I'm going to stay here and wait,' Mariam had said to her.

★

Kostya didn't look at his sister. He kept repeating the same questions in a monotone, sitting on his bed, still half asleep, in the growing light of dawn. Kitty reeled off the words once more, like a poem she had memorised that didn't rhyme. The house on the Holy Mountain. The woman. Mariam. The lion's head knocking on the door. The screams. The struggle. The knife. Mariam. Blood.

'You have to tell the *militsiya*, Kostya. Mariam's still there. I'll make a statement, I'll tell them everything they want to know. Right now I just want to sleep.'

Kitty couldn't stay on her feet any longer. She slid to the floor; her head smacked against the side of the bed, and the skin on her forehead split. She didn't move, just hung her head, clinging to the mattress with one hand.

'I will do everything I can to make you sorry you're alive!' he said suddenly, and forced his sister to her feet. Her knees kept buckling, but he held her up and looked her in the eye. 'You will now do exactly what I tell you! To the letter. Do you understand?'

Kitty nodded mechanically.

Kostya started punching the wall with his fists, pacing up and down; he was talking to himself, searching for a way out. He was desperate, and scared.

Her face buried in the blanket, Kitty began to speak. She felt nothing. Her eyes blind and her limbs like rubber, she told him about a baby in her belly, about a classroom with bare walls, about endless interrogations, about her fears, about the cold words and gentle looks of a beautiful blonde woman, told him about the straps and the torture, about Mariam and her soft hands, about the syringe and the stillbirth, about her womb, which Mariam had removed, about the half-dead days in the barn, the buzzing of flies, about touching the child's little corpse beneath the earth. She told him all this, and yet they were only words, which seemed so cruel it was impossible to imagine what they meant.

Kostya stood rigid, leaning wide-eyed against the wall. It was clear that he couldn't deal with this and didn't want to, didn't know how he was supposed to live with this from now on. And if Kitty hadn't told him, he certainly wouldn't have taken the decision he took, and, as so often in our story, Brilka, everything would have been quite different — and you wouldn't have taken the train to Vienna. (Yes, yes, Brilka, everything leads to that day and to its outcome!)

★

'She wasn't there. She wasn't there. Mariam said it herself, her statement will confirm it.' Kostya's voice was hard.

'But —'

'You will let me deal with it. None of you will be summoned as a witness. I will not allow any more damage to be done than has been done already, I will not allow us to be sucked into this disaster — and all because she loved that traitor — I'll kill him.'

'But how is it Andro's fault?'

'How is it Andro's fault, *Deda*! Just shut up. Just be quiet. Both of you. I don't want to hear another word.'

'But she keeps on saying that she wants to make a statement. When I brought her tea this morning —'

'Who cares what she wants? She'll keep her mouth shut, and you'll make sure of it. It's over. Mariam took her there, and the knife was from her institute canteen.'

'But Kostya ... There must be proof that Kitty was in the house, there must be proof that Mariam wasn't alone at the — er — scene of the crime?'

'There won't be now — there already isn't. I will not allow us all to perish because of her. No proof. That's it: the end.'

Kitty didn't understand the meaning of the things Kostya was drumming into his mother and aunt — loudly, furiously, even threatening them on occasion. They were talking about her, but she couldn't make the connection; she didn't feel like herself, didn't feel any of this had anything to do with her. Only sometimes, in the days that followed, when Christine or Stasia came to her room and brought her something to eat, did she try to ask when she would be picked up and interrogated. But they never replied. They told her she should calm down, she should sleep, she shouldn't ask any more questions.

Kitty was convinced that punishment awaited her: soon, very soon. Perhaps Kostya had been able to postpone it for his sister, but Kitty had no doubt that it would come. They would come and knock on her door no matter what Mariam said or claimed had happened, and she relied on that, she hoped for it. She heard Kostya coming and going several times a day; she heard Stasia and Christine hurry to meet him and speak to him urgently, in whispers. But nobody else came. No strangers, no *militsiya*. Every morning Kitty thought: *This is it, it'll be today for sure.* And every time she was wrong.

★

'I went to see her today. They let me speak to her. She's being treated well. They'll have to transfer her, though; they can't keep her in the city forever, waiting to be sentenced, it might take a while. She agreed with me. She said that was how she wanted it, too. And if we are summoned, that's the testimony we'll stick to.'

Kitty heard her brother in the kitchen. For the first time since she had confessed to him in the early hours of the morning, she got up, put her feet on the ground, and tottered out of the room. She went down the stairs. The hallway seemed never-ending, but she managed to make it to the kitchen, where the whole family was gathered around the table. They all turned their heads towards her simultaneously in alarm, as if they had seen a ghost.

'Go back upstairs!' Kostya ordered.

'Do you need something?' asked Christine. Stasia said nothing; her eyes were swollen.

'You have no right. I was there. I'm just as guilty. I know what you're asking of Mariam, and it's inhuman. I want to be held accountable, too. And stop calling Moscow all the time, stop protecting me. They have proof that I was there. They all know Mariam couldn't have done it alone.'

Kitty spoke quietly but resolutely, summoning all of her strength.

'I told you to just keep your mouth shut and let me deal with it. I don't want to hear any more of these silly arguments. This isn't just about your future; it's about the whole family. You dragged us all into this disaster. Now you have to live with the consequences.' Kostya looked at her with contempt.

'But those are the wrong consequences. That's what I'm talking about. I want the consequences; they're all I do want.'

'Well, we don't always get what we want, do we?'

'Stop being such a monster. Have pity. She should have been your wife. How can you hand her over without a scruple? It's all lies. What good does it do you if I go unpunished? And why don't you two say anything, why are you just sitting there silently, why don't you say what you think?'

Kitty tried to look her mother and aunt in the eye, but they avoided her gaze.

'Kitty, just go back upstairs. My patience is exhausted. I'm trying my best. I'm trying to salvage the remains of our family honour.'

'And for that you're sending the woman who loves you to prison?'

'The women who love me aren't *murderers*. I didn't pressure Mariam into doing anything. She said from the start that she alone committed the crime, and why.'

'She's saying it because she believes she's doing you a favour. She's doing it for you, you monster —'

Kitty's voice failed her and she leaned against the kitchen wall, pressing her face against the cold tiles.

'She killed her. That's what counts. And you told her about it. You sent her there. Now you have to live with it, sister, like it or not!'

'Kostya, please.' Christine tried to put her arm around his shoulder, but he shrugged her off.

'Then let me, let me live with it! I want to go there. *Deda*, say something, it's not right, we can't do this. I can't sit here while Mariam … *Deda*, please.'

She was sobbing. Her whole body heaved. She scratched at the tiles with her fingernails.

'You dragged us all into this with you, and believe me, that's punishment enough, having to live with this!' bellowed Kostya, slamming his palm down onto the table.

'It wouldn't change anything if you were arrested. It wouldn't change anything now. It would just make it worse. For all of us,' murmured Stasia.

'You haven't the faintest idea! You don't know what it was like then, or now. You simply *had* to go away and rescue your precious son!' Kitty screamed, wiping the tears from her eyes. 'How can you condemn me to live with this?' she asked her brother as she left the kitchen.

'Go on then, do it — go to the nearest *militsiya* and make your confession. Confess what you've done! Confess how many people's lives you've ruined! Confess, off you go!' he shouted after her before he, too, left the room.

Christine laid her head on the table and sighed. Stasia was standing in the middle of the room with her palms turned up, as if waiting for the ceiling to burst open and an angel to appear: an avenging angel, or a redeemer.

'He's been offered some sort of important position, Stasia. I've seen the letters on the chest of drawers in his room. They're all stamped by the MVD. The last time he received a letter he jumped up and down for joy, so I assume that he …' Christine spoke without lifting her head from the edge of the table.

'That he what?'

'Think about it.'

'What are you getting at? I don't understand …'

Stasia emerged from her stupor and sat down at the table with her sister.

'Which organisation would have the power to let a guilty party go unpunished, someone who was involved in the murder of an MVD officer?'

Christine slowly lifted her head and looked her sister straight in the eye.

Stasia's eyebrows lowered as though a storm were gathering in her face.

'That's not possible. Kostya's in the Navy. He's a sailor through and through, he loves the sea. He wouldn't ...'

'You can work for *them* in various capacities.'

'That can't be right, no, that can't be right.'

'If it weren't, Kitty would long since have been where Mariam is. When you look at it that way, perhaps it's a blessing in disguise.'

'A blessing in disguise?' Stasia would have liked to slap her sister's face.

'Yes. That's exactly what I mean. Which would you rather: your daughter in prison for the rest of her life, or being sent to a work camp somewhere at the end of the world, or a son who works for the MVD?'

★

Exactly three weeks before Alla's death, thanks to Giorgi Alania's enthusiastic recommendation, Kostya Jashi had indeed joined the all-powerful Ministry of Internal Affairs, or MVD, formerly known as the NKVD. Alla's death and the associated scandal, which went down in Tbilisi legal and salon history as a 'dreadful *crime passionel*', obsessed people in the city for months, giving them plenty to talk about and prompting a great deal of speculation. All the files that could have attested to Kitty Jashi's involvement were destroyed in the first few days of the investigation. True, there were a lot of rumours and gossip, but her name was not publicly associated with the trial.

Would anything really have changed if Kitty had made a statement and confessed her involvement in the murder? Who could she have saved? Who would people have believed? Her, or her brother's powerful friends? Eventually, she let herself believe that her truth really could differ from Mariam's. She let herself believe that she would not have used the knife, that she would not have left the house, that she could never have mustered the strength to do it; she let herself believe that she was not a murderer.

A few weeks later, Mariam was deported to a women's camp in Sverdlovsk.

★

Kostya was posted to Baltiysk near Kaliningrad, soon to become the home port of the Soviet Baltic Fleet, which would be responsible for the shipment of goods, primarily for military use. Many of the Soviet Union's battleships were stationed there, as were some of its cargo ships. Kostya, now a captain, was to supervise and support the expansion of the submarine network in the North Sea. The goal was to create a fleet of nuclear-powered submarines.

When he took up his post, Kostya Jashi, heart thumping, put his signature to the document in which he pledged to keep secret both his field of responsibility and all research results associated with it. When he came home to visit, he seemed different: happy, relaxed, jocular. He spent a lot of time at home again, let the women cook for him, and talked a lot with Christine. The steely body, thrust-out chest, straight shoulders, upright walk — everything about him exuded a profound satisfaction, as well as his restored confidence and pride.

Next to her brother, Kitty seemed all the more miserable and depressed. When she laughed, deep lines appeared at the corners of her mouth, as if laughing were a huge effort for her. She had resumed her studies, but her eyes were still dead, and her guitar stayed in the corner. Her voice was thin and uncertain. Her brisk walk, her effortless, floating movements, had been replaced by a vague leadenness, a lethargy ill-befitting her age.

Brother and sister scarcely spoke any more. At breakfast and dinner, they chewed their food, didn't talk to each other, didn't look at each other; neither of them even asked the other to pass anything. They seemed to have sworn an oath to which they were blindly faithful.

It was only on the evening before his departure that Kostya turned to his sister and asked her to come to his room after dinner. When she entered, she saw him bent over the ironing board, ironing his uniform — something he would entrust to neither Stasia nor Christine. Kitty smoothed the curtains nervously, as if she were unable to speak and this action her only reason for being there.

'It has been brought to my attention that it may be dangerous for you to remain in Georgia,' Kostya began, concentrating on the iron as he ran it over his trousers.

'What's that supposed to mean?'

'People don't stay in the same posts forever. Sometimes they leave, new people come; it could happen at any time that a young, ambitious employee might suddenly look into Mariam's file again, and because he wants to further his career, he … well, he might come to quite a different conclusion. And the case can be reopened at any time.'

'So what are you trying to tell me?'

'That I can't cover for you forever. That I'll be putting myself in danger if I go on doing it, and others with me. I have a position of some responsibility now.'

'Yes, we've all gathered that. Congratulations!'

'Spare me your sarcasm. I'm trying to help you.'

'You've already helped me, thanks.'

'You used to be less ungrateful.'

'Ah well, times change. So do people, by the way. I've written to Mariam, many times, but I haven't received a single reply. Apparently she's banned from corresponding.'

'I didn't summon you here to talk to you about Mariam. We're talking about you and your future, Kitty.'

'Do I still have one? I didn't realise.'

'This is serious, damn it.'

For the first time, he looked up from his trousers and turned his head towards Kitty.

'I look at you and I don't know who's standing in front of me any more. I don't know you. I don't know who you are,' said Kitty, lost in thought, as if she hadn't heard him.

'Don't change the subject. It's important that we work together to find a solution.'

'Together? When did we ever do anything together?'

'You're being impossible, as always.'

'Really? And what should I do, in your opinion? Run away? Hide? In the forest?'

'Well, this is what happens when you get mixed up with deserters and traitors.'

'I despise you.'

'Fine. I'll just have to live with that. Listen: I will help you one more time, one last time, and then I want you to stay out of my life.'

'I'll be very happy to do that, Kostya, even without your help.'

Carefully, he set the iron aside, smoothed the trouser-legs with his hand, and stepped towards his sister. Then, lowering his voice, he said: 'As far as I recall, you had an offer to perform a song recital. You're sure to get another of these, and you will accept. Later there'll be an invitation to go on a tour, of the Soviet Union, perhaps; perhaps even to one of our sister states. Let's say Eastern Europe. Let's say Prague. You will stay there. You'll be provided with papers. You'll be looked after. There you'll receive further instructions, and as soon as it's possible you will leave Prague for the West. I don't have the precise destination yet. You will not contact us. If necessary, I will find you. But a friend of mine will look after you.'

Kitty slid off the window seat and walked up to her brother. She smelled the sharp scent of his eau de Cologne, she breathed it in, she put out a hand to touch his face.

'What are you talking about?' she whispered.

'There's no other way. Believe me.'

'And what if I say no?'

'You don't want to put your friend Andro in danger, do you?'

'What's he got to do with it? Why Andro?'

'He may have been reprieved, but he's still a traitor.'

'Kostya …!'

'You have no choice. You wanted your punishment. Now you've got it.'

For a moment they were silent. Tentatively, she laid her hand on his cheek. She wanted to touch him; she wanted to know what he felt like. It clearly made him uncomfortable, but he kept still and didn't resist her caress.

'Kostya, where am I supposed to go? What am I supposed to do there?' she asked, in a voice of abject despair.

'Didn't the two of you rave about the West all the time, about Vienna and Paris?'

'But there is no *two of us* any more.'

'But there is you.'

'I don't believe you, I don't believe you really mean it.' Shocked, she withdrew her hand, as if she had just felt his innermost self in his face.

'You drove my fiancée to commit murder. You. Not me, Kitty.'

'The fiancée you betrayed with a child killer.'

'Having an affair is a lesser crime than murder, though, don't you think?'

Kitty stared and stared at him in the hope of seeing something familiar: she stared at him until she couldn't see anything any more.

★

The death sentence was abolished in the Soviet Union in 1947. It was reintroduced in 1950, as if those in power had been frightened by their rash decision and had quickly reversed it. Mariam was one of the first to fall victim to the law when it was reintroduced. As was customary with traitors, deserters, and dangerous criminals, her family was sent the bill for the bullet they used to shoot her in the back of the head.

The illusion was broken and the people disintegrated into atoms.

ANDREI SAKHAROV

Andro Eristavi was working in the metal factory in Rustavi, a nearby industrial town. Because he couldn't get a registration certificate, he had to move on every month, staying in various different barracks and rooms before finally ending up at Christine's house again, even though he had firmly resolved not to go back there. He had no choice.

He left the house early in the morning, came home late at night, and no one noticed when he stayed in his attic room all day on Sundays. His presence was without sound and without smell. He ate little, but thanked them politely, like a well-behaved child, after every meal they put in front of him. The only things he consumed in abundance were Christine's liqueurs and the homemade schnapps he bought from the factory workers. He never participated in family conversation, and when he sat with Christine or Stasia in the garden he would carve little figures out of wood. They weren't angels any more, though, but strange creatures with outsized heads and bellies that no one really wanted to put on their shelf or mantlepiece.

At first, Kitty had fiercely opposed his presence in the house. Eventually she had had to relent, with a sour face, when she realised he had no option but to move into Christine's attic room. His silent, passive manner aggravated her, goaded her into making barbed and cynical remarks. When she secretly observed this man who was now no more than a shadow, something inside her contracted, causing her almost physical pain.

One morning, she came across him sitting on his own in the garden. Christine and Stasia had gone out, and he shouldn't really have been home from the factory yet. But there he sat, wrapping a bandage round his wrist, a bottle of schnapps placed squarely on the table in front of him. Blood-soaked cotton wool lay on his knees. Apparently he had cut himself carving.

'Hello, Andro,' she said, sitting down opposite him. 'Shall I help you?'

'I don't know ... Yes, maybe.'

She fetched fresh cotton wool and some lint from the house, moistened the cotton wool with schnapps, and dabbed carefully at his wound. His expression didn't change; if it hurt, he wasn't letting it show.

'What happened?'

'Cut myself.'

'But how?'

'My hands tremble sometimes.'

'Nearly done. I'll tie the bandage a bit tighter. Why are you home already?'

'They informed me today that I can't work there any longer. A letter came from the commissariat. I'm being sent to the mountains. To some *kolchoz* or other.'

'I don't believe it! Those bastards.'

'I don't care. Things can't get any worse. At least up there I'll have my own four walls. And the mountains ...'

'You were never a big nature lover.'

'Will you have a drink with me?'

'Yes, why not. I'll fetch a glass.'

'No, stay there. I'll fetch you one.'

He quickly returned and poured her some of the clear liquid. Kitty shuddered at the thought of the bitter taste, but she didn't want to disappoint him by rejecting one of his rare invitations. She noticed his smell, the smell of tiredness and drunkenness mixed with the sharp tang of blood: this smell no longer had anything in common with the scent she had breathed in from his skin that night in the Botanical Garden and had held in her memory throughout all the years of the war.

'You're unhappy,' he stated matter-of-factly, raising his glass.

'You've never asked me about it.'

'What good would it do? I can't change anything anyway. It's like I'm an invalid. I can't do anything, I'm not allowed to do anything. The way they look at me in the factory sometimes ... In their eyes, I'm scum.'

'Yet again, you're feeling sorry for yourself.'

'So what? Don't I have a right to? Cheers!'

'Oh, Andro ...'

'Stop giving me those meaningful sighs. Is it something to do with Mariam?'

'I'm not allowed to tell you. He'd ... Forget it.'

She downed the bitter drink in one gulp. Her whole throat burned, but she didn't let it show.

'I wish you'd stayed with me,' she said, holding her glass out for him to refill. Two doves settled on the fig tree. She wanted to touch Andro, to anaesthetise her pain by being near him, but she couldn't. She didn't move. There they sat again, side by side, mute, trapped by their own impotence, just as they had back then, after his return, in the half-finished apartment in the New Town.

'Do you know why we're a threat, in their eyes?' Andro began. 'Why they banish us, forbid us to have contact with other people, why they want to get rid of us? Because we understand — because we've seen it all with our own eyes! We're the ones who've survived; we've come back, and *they* know we can't go on living inside the lie, and they don't know what to do with us. We're too much for them. They want us to forget everything, they want us not to remember all the things we've seen, but they know it won't be possible. Things they've kept from us all these years, and will go on keeping from us. Things that are beautiful. Those of us who've crossed the border understand what a shithole we all come from, how we've been lied to and abused. Now lots of these men are back again, in this emptiness, this darkness, and they have to start singing the praises of our state again. How do you bear that? How do you live with it? And the worst thing about it is not that this bloody war has turned us into cripples, taken away our friends, destroyed our lives, but that the war has actually legitimised the whole thing. Now they say: "Look, our great Leader led us to victory, we did it, we defeated the fascists, we survived. It was right, all of it, the path that brought us here." They say it was necessary, the sacrifices we had to make — yes: that it was necessary. And it's so horrifically stupid, so unfair.'

For the first time, Andro talked about the war and the images that refused to let him go. He talked about his time in Crimea, about his hopes, about the Georgian Legion, about the letters he wrote to her and then destroyed. He talked about Texel.

Kitty listened, spellbound. It was too late to cry, and there was nothing left to laugh about. She listened attentively, grateful that he was letting her share his memories; and she struggled with herself, suppressing her desire to unlock her own chamber of memories and release her nightmares.

'What exactly did you do?' he asked her suddenly, out of nowhere. He looked her in the eye. Normally, he couldn't bear to hold her gaze, couldn't bear her eyes demanding something of him, but this time he looked straight at her.

'I tried to put something right.'

'Is it something you'll be able to live with, Kitty?'

'I think her death doesn't even begin to match the death she made me die.

Perhaps I'll be able to tell you one day. Perhaps. But not now. Not yet.'

That night, Kitty crept into Andro's room and lay down beside him. He woke with a start and hastily tried to get up, but she clung to his body with all her might, pressed herself against him, held him tight, waited until his muscles relaxed, until the fear left his skin, until he no longer had the strength to push her away. Then she laid her head on his chest and ran her hand over his body, feeling the unfamiliar bumps, the scars, the strangeness of him.

He felt so hard, so impenetrable, but she didn't want to give up so easily this time. She wanted to rediscover the familiar within this strangeness. She wanted to find the traces of Andro, her lover, the father of her son. Because he must still be there; that afternoon in the garden, listening to him speak so openly, she had believed it, had seen in those dull, clouded eyes the clear blue of long ago. She gently stroked his skin, kissed him hesitantly on the lips. She ran a tentative hand over his bald skull; this was the hardest thing for her to do, because she so longed for his curls, for the old days.

His body remained tense, but he didn't push her away, didn't look at her scornfully, didn't laugh at her hope, allowed her to search for the old days. She stroked his body until it softened, and he placed his hand uncertainly on her scars. The second person after Mariam to touch her there.

With her body, she gave him the gift of forgetfulness and herself the gift of remembrance. But they would never make it anywhere, never feel they had arrived. They would sense each other, but would never get past the barriers; they would find no relief. They knew this. And they didn't hope for it from each other. It was enough to be able to succumb to an illusion for just one night.

'I may be going away soon,' Kitty murmured into the dark.

'Where? What do you mean, going away?'

'I may have to.'

'I don't understand.'

'That's how Kostya wants it.'

'Tell me. Tell me everything.'

'No.'

'Why not?'

'Because your hands tremble and your heart is full of holes.'

Two weeks later, Andro Eristavi left Tbilisi. He was sent to a mountain village in Racha, where he was assigned to the local *kolchoz*.

★

Kitty Jashi finished her studies, and, as her brother had predicted, she toured various Caucasian cities, performing her songs in youth clubs and arts centres. The idea that she might have to leave her homeland one day still seemed unreal to her. She comforted herself with the belief that Kostya had been making empty threats, hoped she had avoided the banishment he had warned her of, hoped that other ways had been found to ensure that her file remained under lock and key. Soon she would get a permanent contract from a provincial theatre, and would play all the Desdemonas, Julias, Mashas, who would distract her from herself until she disappeared completely behind the characters.

But it was not to be. In the spring of 1950, she received a telegram from Kostya informing her of Mariam's death. Kitty became so hysterical at the news that Stasia had to slap her several times to put a stop to her ear-splitting screams. Kitty kept repeating the same question: *But how can it be? How can it be? How can it be? How can it be ...*

After that, Kitty knew she would not be able to stay.

★

The same day — at least, in my imagination it was the same day he sent his telegram to Kitty — her brother opened a letter from Giorgi Alania. He knew that his best friend was due to leave the country in the coming weeks, and would finally be taking up the post in London for which he had been groomed for years. Kostya was hoping for a sentimental but cheerful letter of goodbye. But the letter he held in his hands was a different one. In the cold light of the room, between the portraits of Marx and Engels, the busts of Lenin and the Generalissimus, he decided that he would never allow himself to read lines like these again. Never again would he put himself in a situation where he might have to bear such pain.

Ida was dead. This, no more and no less, was what this brief letter said. He had lost the woman for whom, if there had still been any hope for her at all, he would have endured the hunger, the cold, the shooting, the bombs, all of it, all over again. If he hadn't had to read that this woman, whose loss now killed him more definitively than death could ever have done, had not boarded any of the trucks that he, with such effort, such labour, such anxiety, had sent into the city. No: she was dead, and he had lost her. Because of a parade. He had gone to the parade, had not taken her premonition seriously. He had not finished loving her. His naive desire to be a hero. A hero for whom a forty-year-old Jew with rings on her fingers and melancholy eyes would not have been a suitable partner.

He should not have gone to see Mariam in that cell, and he should never have lied to her, should never have told her that Alla had been only a little, insignificant affair, that Alla had meant nothing to him. But he had said it, so that she would cover for his sister, a woman who viewed the world with radical indifference. He had sent her to her death, promising her that by forfeiting her own life she could attain divine power and save another person's life. But this power did not exist. He did not have this power. Just as Mariam didn't. He hadn't known who Alla was and what she had done. He hadn't known about the path Mariam and Kitty had walked together. But he could have done. He could have known so much more.

With Ida, Mariam also died. And with Mariam, his sister also died. At least, she was dead to him. And Alla, with her blood-red lips, died, too, as did the possibility of making amends. Hunched over the lines his friend had written, Kostya Jashi understood what it was to lose. He had lost. He was fatally wounded, but his death throes would last a lifetime. For this war was not a war against enemies; it was a war he had waged against the people he loved.

★

Kostya ran out of the building. The sky was overcast and sulphurous. The sea reflected the ships anchored in the distance. It was cold; the air was piercing, icy. He ran down to the quay, down the long jetty. He had come out without his coat, but he didn't feel the cold any more. He was still holding the letter in his hand; it burned his skin. Somewhere a freighter sounded its horn.

He ran alongside the sea. The sea, which carried the winter within it, and somewhere, in the distance, a door, a door to the sky. Perhaps he could swim out to this door; perhaps he would manage to reach it. Perhaps there was a way to get back to that shadowy room on Vasilievsky Island and find Ida there.

He threw off all his clothes. In seconds, he was standing on the beach in his underpants, plunging into the water as if rushing to the aid of a drowning man; but he was the one who was drowning.

Not even the heavy sea could revive him. Not even the shock of the cold. To dive in and never come up again — what peace that would be, he must have thought. How was it possible to want someone so much, to need someone so much, to love someone so much, and for death to make no allowances for that?

Ida! My grandfather roared into the cold and the waves, swimming further and further out to sea.

A crowd had gathered on the shore; somebody shouted his name; he didn't care. He didn't want to go back. His trousers were on the beach and in the pocket that letter, the finality of it. He couldn't go back there. The only thing he could do now was swim, swim, swim until he couldn't go on, until he found the door. If he had held her, if she had survived, he would never have gone to Tbilisi, would never have met Mariam, would never have been at a party with insincere toasts, and would never have seen a beautiful blonde woman there who killed babies and yet was so hungry for his love; he would never have allowed her to unbutton his trousers in the bathroom, and her pent-up, uninhibited lust would never have broken over him. Then Mariam would still be alive. And his sister would never have met her son's murderer.

If Ida weren't dead, he would still be alive.

Infinity blurred before his eyes, and, even in the depths, Ida was nowhere to be found. Just like the door in the sky.

Kostya swallowed water; his strength began to ebb.

Then he heard shouts and saw a dinghy approaching. The next day, he gave a statement saying he had jumped into the water because he'd thought he had seen someone drowning.

★

Over the next three weeks, which Kostya spent in a clinic, seriously ill with pneumonia, he sloughed off everything that could ever put him in such a situation again, and anaesthetised his conscience.

He read the letter one last time before burning it over a candle flame.

My dear friend,

I hate myself already because I know that with these lines I am going to cause you great pain, but I made you a promise and unfortunately it is not in my power to spare you this pain. And so I am writing to tell you what you wanted to know, what you've been waiting for for a long time, and yes, I think you've already guessed it. She is dead.

She was in Leningrad throughout the blockade. She did not leave the city. In the final year of the blockade she was given an evacuation certificate, but for some inexplicable reason she swapped it with someone else, whom we cannot trace. She died in her apartment on Vasilievksy. Her grave, unfortunately, is unmarked.

By the time you receive this letter I will no longer be in Moscow. I will write to you again as soon as possible, and will look forward to your replies. You know how much you mean to me, Kostya. I am so very, very sorry, my friend. I know you have not forgotten her, I know that you loved her, that you still do even now. I will take care of your other 'problem child'.

I embrace you and send my deepest sympathy,
Giorgi

★

Giorgi Alania officially assumed the position of cultural attaché at the Soviet Embassy in London. Unofficially, he was to locate renegade Soviet citizens and 'repatriate' them, as it was called. With lies, with false promises, and, if necessary, by force.

That summer, Kitty received the message she had been waiting for from her brother. Everything happened as he had foretold: it was as if all his words were coming true. She received an invitation to take her *chanson* evening to Prague, and she accepted, having realised now that she had no choice. She travelled in the company of a security serviceman, who was to keep an eye on her. After her performance in Prague, he handed her false papers, took her to a rented apartment on the outskirts of town, and ordered her to stay there and await further instructions. In Moscow, Kitty Jashi was declared a traitor; the authorities' assumption was that she had been a western spy and had now fled to the West.

Stasia knew why Kitty had left, and who had helped her do it. She knew that she would bear this burden with the same silent grandeur as she bore all the other unavoidable events in her life. That day, when the MVD men came calling and took her to be interrogated about her daughter's disappearance, she finally realised that the ghosts were back: the road was open again, the road between times, between all possible, conceivable worlds.

Combat rootless cosmopolitanism!

POSTER SLOGAN

Kostya became what he would never have become at Ida's side: my grandfather and your great-grandfather, Brilka.

That summer, he returned to his homeland, and travelled on from there to Abkhazia for his paid, state-prescribed holiday on the Black Sea. This was where he met my grandmother, Nana. Sensible, gentle, bright Nana. Nana, whose grandparents — both linguists at the University of Tbilisi — had been victims of the purges. Her father, an archaeologist, was imprisoned in Ortachala city prison, the son of supposed spies and counter-revolutionaries; he died there at the age of just forty-two, of untreated pneumonia. Nana was raised — and pampered — by her mother, and her father's two unmarried sisters. The women tried to compensate for the misfortune that had befallen the family by taking excessive care of little Nana and showering her with love.

Nana — straightforward, open, not remotely mysterious, not even elegant — should never have appealed to Kostya. Nana was healthy. In every sense of the word. Too healthy for Kostya. She wouldn't infect him; she wouldn't ruin him. And that was precisely the reason for his sudden interest in her. As if his hopeless, indifferent eyes had spotted the healthiest woman on the whole Black Sea coast, and he had taken her by the hand, wanting her to heal his sickness.

Perhaps he also hoped he could break the old patterns, step out of the shadow of the dead and make a completely new, completely different, start.

When I look at Nana in old family photos, she looks to me like someone who has never doubted herself or the world. Someone who has never encountered failure. A tall young woman, not as youthful and reckless as she should have been at that age, but clearer and more confident as a result, as if she knew precisely how her life, which still lay before her, was going to unfold. Blonde and strapping, with a thick plait that she wound round her head, and smart, well-tailored, but modest clothes. Not conspicuous, but not unremarkable, either. As if everything about her aspired towards solid normality and clear structures. There was something attractive, but never vulgar, about the way she pouted, or gesticulated wildly with her hands; the way she wrinkled her forehead as she pondered a question, or demonstratively crossed her legs when she was excited about something. She was conservative, believed in clear value systems, and until she met Kostya she dreamed of the things most girls dreamed of in her day: social recognition, a conventional path — in her case, a respected university career — a family, children; all of which should be romantic, if possible, but not too dramatic; a little exciting, but not too wild. That summer, Nana had just completed her degree in Georgian language and literature and, following in her grandparents' footsteps, had developed a passion for linguistics. She wanted to do a doctorate, and that summer on the Black Sea, where she was holidaying with friends to celebrate her graduation, she was trying to decide the subject of her thesis.

Until then, she had never really been in love. She had had a few flirtations with fellow students, but had ended each one after just a few weeks. She focused on her studies, enjoyed spending time with her female friends, cooked with her mother and aunts, and made plans for the future. She had never wanted for anything, and she'd never really missed the much-vaunted ideal of love, either. She wasn't a dreamer, and if a book she was reading got too dramatic and passionate for her liking, she would set it aside without compunction. She didn't want to dream of something she would never experience the way it was described; nor did she want to experience it.

Naturally, it was coincidence that brought these two utterly different people, Nana and Kostya, together. In the cafeteria of the spa hotel where they were both staying, Nana and her friends were having breakfast at the table with the best view when Kostya asked, with a polite smile, whether he might join them, as there didn't seem to be any tables free. He quickly fell into conversation with Nana's friends, who were just as quickly impressed by his charm and his skill as a raconteur. Nana stayed in the background; she said little, and concentrated on eating her breakfast. She was therefore astonished when, on leaving the cafeteria, he kissed her friends' hands in farewell, but asked her, of all people, whether he might take her out to dinner.

She agreed, more out of curiosity than interest.

That same evening, they went to a fish restaurant right on the promenade that Nana would never have been able to afford. There, they were served chilled white wine and fine sea bream. Kostya treated her to a long lecture about the sea in general and fish in particular, and afterwards there was Armenian cognac.

Nana, who didn't want to appear in any way inferior to Kostya, demonstrated her expertise on the subject of regional cultures and their customs. On their first rendezvous, they both showed off their knowledge and didn't get close at all. They didn't even really get to know each other. But at the end of the evening, they both decided that they wanted to rectify this at a second meeting.

In the days that followed, Kostya accompanied the girls to the beach, played cards with them, entertained them with all sorts of anecdotes, bought them coffee and ice cream, and never left their side. Three days later, he took Nana to a dance club on her own and proved to be a good dance partner. After several dances and a few glasses of Crimean champagne, Nana found herself willing to believe in something as irrational as being in love. On the way back to the hotel, she indicated that she would not be averse to his continuing to court her.

★

They met again in Tbilisi. He invited her for meals, took her dancing, went with her to the cinema and for walks in the park. Nothing out of the ordinary; nothing demanding. Gallant and patient, Kostya wooed her as he thought she wanted to be wooed. They didn't touch each other, they made no plans, and they didn't talk about the future. A few days before Kostya's summer holiday came to an end and he had to leave for Baltiysk, he asked soft, blonde Nana if she would be his wife. They had just come out of the cinema, where they had been to see an upbeat rural film — or that's what I imagine, anyway — and were strolling up the cobbled street of Varazi Hill. As if he had asked some trivial question about the film they had just seen, Nana's expression didn't change; she went on slowly walking, without saying a word.

'I won't expect anything from you. If you want to stay in Tbilisi, that would be fine, too,' Kostya added to his proposal.

'I hardly know you.'

'You know me well enough.'

'We haven't even kissed.'

'Would you like us to?'

Kostya took her head in his hands and gave her a tentative kiss on the lips.

'Now we've kissed each other,' he said, satisfied, and gave her another kiss, more daring this time, and a lot more moist.

But this kiss didn't taste of St Petersburg, it didn't taste of white nights, of the hours of abandonment there, didn't taste of a woman with rings on all ten fingers; it didn't taste of death.

'Just say *yes*,' Kostya insisted, still holding her chin in his hand; and Nana, who felt very uncomfortable about allowing herself to be kissed by a man in the middle of the street, and wanted to put an end to the awkward situation as quickly as possible, said yes.

★

Kostya wrote to Baltiysk and asked for another two weeks' leave to prepare for his wedding, which he was granted. And so they had a modest wedding in Christine's house. There was spinach with pomegranate seeds, suckling pig marinated on wood, lamb in mint, and fresh Kakhetian wine. Stasia made a big wedding cake laden with condensed-milk *crème pâtissière*, and the table was decorated with mountains of grapes, pears, persimmons, figs, melons, and pomegranates. The newlyweds spent their wedding night, which Nana of course came to as a virgin, in Nana's mother's apartment, which she generously surrendered to the couple.

After Kostya's departure, Nana moved into the big house on Vera Hill. She was accustomed to the company of older women. She had made it clear that she did not want to move to the cold north to live with her husband, and reminded him that he had told her she could stay in Tbilisi. She wanted to apply for a university place and start work on her PhD thesis.

★

Kitty was living on the outskirts of Prague in a small room barely three metres square. She received no letters, no instructions. All she had was one suitcase and her guitar. And a new passport, with a different name. At the start of each week, an envelope was pushed under her door; so far, all her attempts to catch the person delivering it had failed. The envelope contained a few banknotes — always the same amount. The money was sufficient for her to buy food. She never went into the city centre, she never left the area where she was living, she spoke to no one. She greeted the old lady who lived next door with a nod of her head.

Her new passport identified her as a Luxembourger with the name Adrienne Hinrichs.

She felt as if her real self had been amputated.

Three times, she had contemplated handing herself in by going to the station or the airport and approaching the nearest security or border guard.

The isolation she was living in sometimes made her doubt her own sanity. She listened to the Voice of America, turned down low, on the old radio she found in the room. Including the programmes in English. She didn't understand the language, but its melody seemed reassuringly foreign to her, reassuringly benign. It was only after she had been living in the city for three months that she received, in her weekly envelope, an unsigned note. It told her to go to her local post office the following day at precisely three o'clock to receive a long-distance call.

On the other end of the line was an unfamiliar male voice. Kitty had squeezed herself into the small, stuffy telephone box.

'I will get you out of the city. You've been keeping a low profile. That's good, very good. I understand your situation, but you have to trust me and be patient for a while. As soon as it becomes possible, we will get you out of the city. As soon as the danger has passed. I promise you.' The man spoke with a soft voice that inspired confidence.

'Who are you?'

'I'm your friend. Your closest friend.'

'But —'

'I can't tell you any more at the moment.'

'How can I trust you? How do I know that you —'

'You don't have a choice. You'll just have to. From now on, I'll call you on this number at the same time every week. We'll stay in regular contact. Can you get by on the money?'

'Yes, of course, I don't need much, but —'

'Just trust me.'

He kept his promise. He called every week. Assured her that she would soon be leaving the city for the West. That everything was all right, she was safe, no one was going to hurt her, he was watching over her, he was thinking of her, he was her friend. Because she had no choice, she accepted him as her friend. Her only friend. But as soon as she tried to find out his name, or where he was, he would fall silent, always repeating that he wasn't allowed to tell her. She cursed her brother, her life, her country, the past, the present, the future, but her interlocutor remained unruffled. He listened to her, and went on talking in his soothing tone.

He told her about Georgia. Banal, unimportant news that Kitty, nonetheless, absorbed with the greatest attention. He also told her that her mother and aunt had bravely withstood questioning by the secret police, and that her brother was happily married.

But Kitty no longer knew what day it was, or what she was doing in the city.

'I don't know a single person here. I don't speak the language. I never go out. I'm dying,' she confided to the telephone receiver after six months. She was distraught.

'You're strong. You can do this. We can do this together. I need you. I'm not just saying that to comfort you. I really do need you. You'll leave the city soon. You'll be able to live a free life. I promise you that. But you have to believe in it, too. I can't do this on my own. You have to help me. I've promised your brother that nothing will happen to you. And I keep my promises. I believe you'll get through this because you're strong, because you've already got through *worse*.'

'What do you know about me?'

'Enough.'

'Say my name.'

'I beg your pardon?'

'You never call me by my name. You never say it. We're two nameless people. Faceless people. Say it!'

There was a short pause, and she thought he would deny her request, but then he said what she wanted to hear.

'Yes, Kitty. I'll say it. Kitty. Kitty. Kitty.'

The name felt foreign, as if she were hearing it for the first time, as if she had left behind all the stories attached to this name. But she clung to those five letters; she wanted to remember again, she wanted her past back, regardless of how much she hated it, because her past was the only thing that gave her the right to her real name. And she wanted it back. More than anything, she wanted it back.

He went on talking, and his quiet, velvety voice calmed her, cradled her in its arms. She wiped away the tears with her sleeve and pressed her face to the wall, clutching the receiver with all her might.

★

Her isolation was to last many more months. Kitty stayed in Prague for almost two years. But from that day onward, after he spoke her name, she was able to deal with it better. She learned a few words of Czech, and sometimes talked to the neighbours' children or the elderly lady next door. The lady spoke hardly any Russian, so she couldn't ask her any unwelcome questions.

She cooked for herself regularly, went for a walk three times a week in nearby Malešický Park, listened to her radio, bought herself an English dictionary to help her understand the programmes on Voice of America, and practised the guitar. Although she was not in the right frame of mind for composition, she tried to perfect her technique. She didn't think of home any more, of the people she was close to; above all, she banished all thoughts of the blonde woman with the red lips, of Mariam's blazing eyes, of her friend's death.

Each time Tuesday came around and she hurried to the post office, she felt quite euphoric. The thought of hearing his voice filled her with a childlike glee.

Sometimes she looked at her passport and imaged what Luxembourg was like, what she had done there, whom she might have loved there. Imagined a different life for herself, a different biography. In the beginning, she would jump out of her skin if someone knocked on her door or spoke to her on the street, if someone asked her for the time, but she grew accustomed to it and would give the required information in her still halting Czech. She met a Polish student in the park who wanted to take her for a beer, but she rebuffed him, saying that she was married and her husband wouldn't approve.

She stuck to his rules. She avoided places where there were a lot of people, avoided trams and buses. She lived as inconspicuously as possible. Sometimes there were days when her life even started to seem normal to her. As if she had never led any other; as if it had always been like this, and even the fact that she was otherwise silent for months on end, scarcely speaking to another human being, no longer seemed so terrible to her.

The envelopes still arrived regularly. Her only friend must have plenty of helpers in the city, and apparently he was taking steps to ensure that none of the property managers and no one from the foreign nationals' office knocked on her door.

It was a time of social, emotional, and artistic abstinence; a sort of righteous punishment for what lay behind her. But when she said this to her anonymous friend in one of their phone calls, he got quite worked up. This period was tragically unavoidable, he told her; it was not a punishment.

Exile grew to be part of her very skin. And the perpetual fight against memory became the defining trait of Kitty's character; the fear of dreams in which Mariam might haunt her became her constant companion.

At least Kitty was spared the paranoia of the Generalissimus' final years, which afflicted the whole empire with undreamed-of ferocity. She didn't have to see Party men disowning their wives because their smiles had aroused the Generalissimus' mistrust. She didn't have to see memories of the bloody thirties revived in the collective consciousness, the number of state security ministers increased from four to seven, the orchestration of hate campaigns. Didn't see the Generalissimus reduce his entourage to clowns, pillory them, force them into public displays of remorse, like mangy dogs. She didn't know that the man from the weather bureau who was responsible for reading the weather forecast on the radio had been summoned to the Kremlin and cautioned, because the Generalissimus had complained about a particular weather forecast and his entourage were afraid that they would have to pay for it with their lives. She didn't hear that the Leader now ruled the empire entirely from his dacha, where he made his men dance and drink themselves into a stupor. Didn't know what Khrushchev had said of these binges: 'When the Leader says dance, a wise man dances.'

One morning, when she opened the usual white envelope containing the banknotes, she found a typed letter inside, again unsigned:

Read the following very carefully. Memorise it well, then destroy the message you are reading!

You will travel to London. In London you will be safe. Go to the telephone box next Tuesday at precisely the usual time. You will find an envelope with the necessary visas and papers. Take good care of your passport. The next day, Wednesday, take the 14:20 train to Dresden from the main station. A man will meet you directly on the platform; he will give you a bunch of roses and kiss you, and you must return the kiss. Officially he is your fiancé; his name is Jan and he works as an engineer in the Dresden printing press factory. He will talk to you in sign language; nod agreement or shake your head from time to time. If you want to improvise — which is something you are surely capable of — you too should improvise a conversation in sign language. As soon as you are in a safe place he will explain to you in detail what will happen next. He will accompany you over the border. You will be driven to Hamburg in a British military car, and from there you will take a flight to London. Until you arrive in London you are Adrienne Hinrichs, a deaf-mute from Luxembourg ...

So many times Kitty had dreamed up a love life, a life story, for her other self, for Adrienne; but it had never occurred to her that she might be a deaf-mute, although the idea was such an obvious one. She read the letter again and again, and heard her faceless friend's soft, confident voice in her head as she did so.

*

London. Kitty's arrival. We'll skip the obligatory rain, shall we, Brilka?

Trafalgar Square, and Kitty's peach-coloured arms outstretched to greet the British air: air that was different here, that smelled different, tasted different.

Piccadilly, and the sudden thought of the knife, the blood flowing from the severed artery. Hyde Park, and the classroom. Tower Bridge, and the dim light of the room on the Holy Mountain. Whitehall, and Andro's head on her breast. The green-painted benches of the little town that once held a promise of the future. Downing Street, and a hand exploring the scars on her abdomen. Past County Hall, and the images from the Botanical Garden; and Andro, always Andro.

The Thames. Kitty stopped, and gazed down at the stately river. Was this what freedom tasted like? Was this how it smelled? Ought she to be happy now? Had she survived? And what about all the days, weeks, years that lay before her? Back then, she had wanted to go to Vienna, to accompany her Andro with the introspective eyes, so that he wouldn't get lost, so he would go on carving wooden angels, so he could excitedly explain the world to her, a world she had seen through long ago. But when *her* Vienna was beheaded, along with Andro's dreams, she had decided she would seek no new worlds, no new continents, no cities of dreams, because castles in the air cannot withstand the storm.

On arrival, she had put a match to her passport and burned it to ashes. Adrienne Hinrichs was gone, incinerated, turned to dust; the way was now clear for Kitty Jashi. But as she walked around central London, Kitty Jashi couldn't find herself anywhere; and now she felt as if, with Adrienne, she had turned the remnants of her self into ashes, too. Somewhere near Buckingham Palace, her tears began to fall. Silently: the weeping of the women in the tearless palace on Tbilisi's Vera Hill. As if they wept not to shake off the sadness that oppressed them, but to grieve the loss of grief. Grief: the normal condition for the chocolate-maker's heirs.

At St James's Palace, she felt, for the first time, something like relief. Like the thought of something terrible coming to an end. She looked down at her patched autumn coat, her dirty, worn-out shoes, the shapeless, pleated skirt. Ran her hands through her dishevelled hair, which should have been cut long ago. Felt her own ugliness all the more painfully, surrounded by so much beauty. She wanted to hide: for a moment she wished herself back in Prague, back in her little room. Then she quickly dismissed her doubts and walked on, went on exploring the city. She was free.

> Blood runs, spilling over the floors.
> The barroom rabble-rousers
> give off a stench of vodka and onion.
>
> YEVGENY YEVTUSHENKO

She took the Underground to the East End and went to the address her Dresden fiancé had given her. It was a Red Cross shelter. Once she had filled out the forms and registered as a stateless person, she was assigned a room with a plank bed, a washbasin, a clothes rail, and a radio. She took a long shower in the communal bathroom, threw herself onto the bed, and fell into a comatose sleep that lasted more than twelve hours.

Hunger woke her. She went outside, bought herself fish and chips at the first shop she came across, and ate them as if it were a meal fit for a king, sitting on the pavement and watching the passers-by, trying to work out what she was feeling. He had not deceived her. He had kept his promise, and Kitty knew that whoever he was she would keep him in her life, that she wasn't willing to let him go, that she wanted him always, always to speak to her and call her by her name. And one day, perhaps, she would find him — would set eyes on him, put a face to the voice, and thank him.

She was given temporary papers. She was sent to the Red Cross offices, given warm clothes, and enrolled in an English-language course. She wasn't asked any questions she couldn't answer. The friendly lady from Social Services sent her to a soup kitchen, where she was given regular meals. Two weeks after she registered, a Jamaican woman who worked at the shelter stopped Kitty on the stairs and told her that a cousin of hers ran a pub in the East End and was looking for someone to do occasional shifts. He wasn't bothered about a work permit, she said; Kitty should get in touch, that way she could earn a bit of pocket money until everything else was settled. Overwhelmed by such kindness, yet suspicious, wondering whether she could really trust the woman with the brightly coloured headscarf and benevolent eyes, Kitty had stood uncertainly on the stairs, chewing her thumb. But the woman was accustomed to such reticence; she put her arm around her and offered to go with her.

The following day, Kitty had a job at the pub.

★

She was frightened of words. And of the friendly smile she had to conjure onto her face. Over the past two years, she had grown accustomed to being alone. Crowds of people made her panic. During her first few days at work, she had to keep disappearing into the toilet in order to catch her breath, wipe the sweat off her forehead, look in the mirror, and remind herself to stay calm. But most of the customers who came to the pub paid her no attention; they didn't want words, they wanted alcohol. The people who strayed in here hardly ever smiled themselves. Construction workers, taxi drivers, drug dealers, cooks, prostitutes; all just looking for diversion, a moment's distraction, glad to escape their daily routine for a few hours. Many of them were immigrants, too. They came from India, from Pakistan, from Nigeria, Ghana, Jamaica, Guyana.

Kitty quickly felt at home among them. She liked their rough voices, their jokes, their different languages and accents, even their vulgarity. They didn't look at her with pity: they were just as inconsiderate, crude, and indifferent towards her as they were with their friends, their companions, and themselves. Nonetheless, the hours Kitty liked best were always when she stayed on in the pub on her own after everyone else had gone, putting stools on tables and scrubbing the floor, washing glasses and sorting crates. When the customers had gone, when the pub had closed and the owner had gone back to his family — that was when she felt good, felt safe. She would put a coin in the jukebox and listen to the loud music, and her body would move to the different rhythms of its own accord.

The hard work exhausted her, but she was grateful for it, because afterwards the night would be dreamless and her mind too tired to think. When she wasn't working she would stay in her room and play her guitar — listlessly, aimlessly, and without much passion, but at least she played. Apart from her physical work, the guitar was the best way for her to take her mind off things.

I've come this far / searching for ghosts / you promised they'd wait for us. / But they're gone, just like you / gone so far away. / So I'm walking through the city of ghosts / just walking ahead, asking myself / Should I go on, should I begin? / Should I wish or should I die? / 'Cause you've not come as far as I…

If I'm not mistaken, this was the first song Kitty wrote in London. Initially, she wrote it in her mother tongue; the song was translated only later, and she would sing it in English with her strong but unidentifiable foreign accent. I remember, Brilka, how we listened to this song together in the car, how you explained to me then that it marked a new direction in Kitty's music. I love this song, but I love it mainly because of you, Brilka; because you sang it to me, and you sang it so passionately, with such abandon. And I love it because it doesn't make me feel sad, like most of Kitty's songs, because at that moment I was driving along the endless, dusty coastal roads with you by my side, and I was happy, even if I didn't know at the time that it was happiness I was feeling.

★

The city had been wearing its Christmas costume for weeks now. On Christmas Eve, the customers left the pub early. Even the poorest among them seemed to be preparing for the holiday, readying themselves to enjoy the time with their families. The owner left the pub earlier than usual, too, as there were hardly any customers; he told her to treat herself to a couple of drinks on him, and put a few extra coins on the counter for her. She'd earned it, he said. Then he wished her a happy Christmas and left her on her own. Kitty was in no hurry. Christmas was something they used to celebrate in her country before she was born. After that, those festivals stopped; after that, God was replaced by the Generalissimus, and people celebrated the anniversary of the Revolution, or the Leader's birthday. It was only her deeply religious Aunt Lida who used to light candles on this day, in silent devotion, and retire to pray.

One after the other, all the customers left. She had soon finished tidying up, but she didn't want to head back to the shelter just yet. She wasn't tired enough, and the city was so alarmingly quiet: her memories would return and take her hostage. She sat at the bar and, after some initial hesitation, poured herself her first whisky. She had never drunk whisky before; the strong drink warmed and burned her throat pleasantly. She allowed herself another. The alcohol, which she had forbidden herself in her former exile, soon took effect. In Prague, she could not have afforded to be sentimental. It might have had unpleasant consequences. Here, that no longer applied; here, she could let herself go, especially when she was alone. No one cared.

She felt relaxed, and the dreaded melancholy did not materialise. On the contrary, she was cheerful; she could have danced all night. She started to hum one of her songs; her voice grew stronger, louder, until she was singing as loud as she could. She let herself be carried away by her own voice, grabbed the whisky bottle and held it to her mouth like a microphone. She whirled around the pub with all the showmanship she could muster, then closed her eyes and bowed to her imaginary audience.

Suddenly she heard clapping coming from the street. A tall, sturdy woman in a strikingly fashionable red coat was standing at one of the windows, applauding enthusiastically. Kitty came down to earth with a bump; mortified, she put the bottle down on the table and staggered backwards. She hoped the woman would disappear, but she stayed where she was and went on clapping, then knocked on the window. Kitty felt obliged to go to the door.

'We're closed,' she said, opening the glass door a crack.

'Your singing is fantastic. Fan-tas-tic! Incredible! What language was that?'

'I only speak a little English.'

'Was that your language you were singing in just now?'

'That was Georgian.'

'Oh ... Isn't that somewhere in Russia?'

'No, it's in Georgia.'

The woman laughed, and indicated to Kitty that she wanted to come in.

'But we're closed, and I've already —'

'I'm not a demanding customer.'

Kitty turned the light on again above the bar and put a glass down on a coaster in front of the woman. She had asked for a whisky, too. Her soft blonde hair was pinned back on one side with a hair slide, and she had clear, friendly features, harmonious and symmetrical. Everything about her was inviting, but although Kitty sensed that she could trust her, she felt uncomfortable: she was ashamed of her own inability to speak, and annoyed that she had let herself go like that in front of her. Initially, their conversation was stilted, but the woman persevered. She introduced herself as Amy — just Amy. No Miss, no Mrs. She questioned Kitty about where she came from, and about her songs. How had she learned to sing so well? What songs were they? What was she doing in London?

Although one wouldn't have thought it, judging by her elegant outfit and genteel way of speaking (ladies like her were an unusual sight in this part of town), she drank every bit as much as the regulars at this pub, and let Kitty keep refilling her glass. Kitty's tension had dissipated, and she too carried on drinking steadily. When the woman asked her for the third time if she would sing something, she relented, and began, quietly at first, hesitantly, then louder and more confidently, to sing her songs. Songs she hadn't sung for two years.

Songs that were there in her head, that accompanied her everywhere, that went on writing themselves in her mind, that wanted to be sung.

The woman didn't take her eyes off her. Her expression was tense, attentive, and at the same time blissfully content. From time to time, she raised her eyebrows or closed her eyes when she wanted to concentrate especially hard.

'I may not know much, but I know what good music is. Music is my passion, and I can tell you that your music is good — very good, even. You should do something with it.'

Before she left, she gave Kitty an extravagant tip, and wrote her address and telephone number on a beermat.

'If you want to take your music further, give me a call. I'd be happy to help you,' she said, shaking Kitty's hand.

'I have one more question,' said Kitty. She couldn't contain her curiosity. 'Aren't you celebrating Christmas? Why are you here on your own at this time of night?'

'I'm a staunch atheist, darling.'

★

Kitty was driven by mistrust: a profound, inherent mistrust of other people. As if all she wanted was to assure herself that other people never meant well by her, that they never kept their promises. It was with this mistrust that she called Amy's number in early January, and when Amy sounded genuinely excited that she had called and immediately suggested that she come and visit, her mistrust only increased.

Kitty took the Underground to King's Cross, a part of town she had never been to before. Amy's was a modest but respectable brick house in a tranquil street, concealed by a black iron gate.

Kitty stopped outside the gate. For a moment she hesitated, wondering whether it wouldn't be better for her to turn round. She had become used to the East End. It was full of people like her. There, she wasn't conspicuous. Here, even the shadow she cast on the street seemed conspicuous in its poverty: too big, too coarse, too proletarian for this pavement, these walls, these windowpanes. Then she summoned her courage and rang the bell. The glossy black door with the gold knob flew open, and there was Amy in a navy-blue dress, stepping towards her guest and beaming from ear to ear.

Kitty's sense of being out of place here was reinforced on entering the house. She had assumed that Amy lived in a flat, not that she was the mistress of this three-storey abode. She was led into the drawing room and offered Earl Grey tea and apple cake. Sitting there on the floral sofa, she felt like a Siberian bird that had strayed into the tropics. Embarrassed by her plain Red Cross smock, she kept her arms crossed over her chest at first, as if she could conceal the ugliness of her clothes. And when an immaculately dressed maid entered the room and asked her mistress if she could bring them anything else, Kitty felt a powerful urge to flee.

But the lady of the house didn't really comport herself in a manner suited to the genteel atmosphere. Her laughter was too loud and too immodest, revealing her big white teeth and pink gums; her gestures were too uncontrolled; and the way her eyebrows shot up when something surprised her, the way she pursed her lips when she was particularly delighted by something, or the way she left her mouth open when she wanted to emphasise something she had said — none of this seemed at all fitting for a sophisticated lady with a parlour maid and a floral sofa. In spite of her expensive clothes and the patchouli scent she wore, she was simply too unpolished for this environment, too lacking in self-possession.

This time, too, their conversation was very stilted. However, once Kitty had stifled her discomfort, she proved more talkative than during their previous meeting in the pub. If she got stuck she would reach into her pocket for the tattered English dictionary she had bought in Prague — the only souvenir of her banishment — and point to the word she was looking for. Each time, Amy nodded to show that she understood, and was delighted, as if it were a miracle that the same word appeared in both their languages.

Amy had been born in India, and had lived there until the age of fifteen. She was the youngest child and only daughter of a British officer who had married the daughter of a wealthy industrialist. Her father had served in the British Army almost all his life, and had spent two decades in Calcutta. For many years, Amy and her three older brothers, whom she idolised, knew no other home. In India, Amy could run and climb, play cricket and roll in the mud, skip and run races, tell dirty jokes and stick her tongue out at people — as long as she was with her brothers, as long as they kept her with them. For it was only with them that she could escape all the awful doll-filled prisons and the tedious poetry evenings, the pale English girls with their bloodless dreams who all suffered so in the tropical climate, the violin and singing lessons — all the things her mother intended for her. Later, though, all three of her brothers joined the Army, one after the other, in great despair at having to leave behind their Indian life, their carefree games and adventures. At the age of fifteen,

Amy was put on a steamer and sent to an English boarding school. She arrived at a school for upper-class girls in Devon, and everything changed. Her childhood remained her secret garden, which gave her so much that was good and wonderful that she was able to nourish an entire unhappy life on the memory of it. Two of her brothers lost their lives in the war; Amy herself escaped an arranged marriage when war broke out, and so, after finishing school, she found herself alone in London, though she was now financially independent, thanks to a sizeable inheritance from her parents.

She and her brother John had always shared a passion for music. Music was a secret language of symbols that, in their family, only the two of them had mastered. They had always loved Chopin and Schubert, but they had also listened to the disreputable music called jazz, had danced wildly to be-bop — still an insider tip at the time — had vied with each other as to who was the better musician, who knew more pieces, who had the better ear, who was more knowledgeable about music history. However, they were both sufficiently realistic to know that neither of them would ever be more than mediocre as a musician, and so they decided to become the best listeners in the world. Amy went dancing in Blitz-ravaged London, a city hungry for resurrection; she went to the East End in search of the newest clubs where the wildest, most exciting, most offbeat musicians played. She developed an infallible intuition for good music. She befriended dubious club owners, frequented pubs and basements that lived in fear of the vice squad; she didn't shy away from even the most out-of-the-way venues and the shabbiest houseboats in the harbour if she thought that was where she might discover an unknown talent.

It was around this time that she spent her first night with a woman. Her brother John, the only one she spoke to openly about her inclination, introduced her to a friend of his, Magnus, whose reticence and sensitivity reminded Amy of her second-eldest brother. Magnus' father had made his money — and there was a lot of it — in the diamond trade, and it meant a great deal to him that his homosexual son and only male heir should at least appear to live in a socially acceptable manner. The wedding was hastily organised, and Magnus and Amy were finally at liberty to do whatever they felt like doing with their lives. Amy bought the red-brick house in King's Cross, which she decorated according to her parents' taste as a way of maintaining the appearance of normality. Magnus spent most of his time in his country house in Wales, which served as his retreat and love-nest, and which Amy, out of consideration for his privacy, never visited. Instead, she stayed in London. Magnus treated her with equal discretion and never came to town unexpectedly. He was sufficiently tactful not to want to put his wife in an awkward situation. Without having to lift a finger, through mere fact of their existence, and this absurd state of being man and wife, they gave each other what they most needed in order to be happy: freedom.

★

In one of Magnus' regular haunts in Soho, between hidden erotic cinemas and houses of ill repute, Amy met Fred, the red-haired sorceress.

A little-known Austrian-Jewish painter, her full name was Friederike Lieblich, and she compensated for her lack of success in the artistic arena with a legendary love life. Rumour had it that the number of her conquests would have made Sappho pale with envy.

By day, restless, cold as a stone, insolent, hurtful, egocentric, and offensively unconventional, by night, she was, in equal measure, permissive and uninhibited, morbidly passionate, a real nymphomaniac. People said that any good-looking woman, regardless of sexual orientation, would do better to steer well clear of her: she always got them in the end. People also said she was nothing but trouble: she had no money, and no permanent abode; she would crash in like a November wind, flay you, take everything you owned, and vanish again as quickly as she had appeared. The consensus was that it was best to beware of the sorceress.

To Amy's ears, however, all the less-than-flattering rumours about Fred Lieblich sounded like compliments and enchanting promises. And when she saw the strange, slender woman sitting at the bar, and all the other customers whispering about her, she was determined to get the redhead to approach her, and sent over a glass of the most expensive whisky the bar had to offer.

Fred didn't have to be asked twice, and came to sit at Amy's table. She had a dreadful German accent and narrow cat's eyes; she was wearing a man's white shirt and working-men's trousers turned up at the bottom. In the dim light of the bar, her hair glowed fiery red, like a warning.

Although Amy left the bar that first evening without returning Fred's advances, and didn't show her face there for weeks afterwards, her curiosity had been roused. She wanted to know whether the sorceress really could cast a love spell. Despite the various experiences she had accumulated in this field over time, in bars, on houseboats, in clubs, and at private parties, Amy still felt gauche: she was ashamed of her lust, ashamed of her preferences, and never knew to what extent it was acceptable to express her desires. So Amy went back to Soho, and after three nights during which she spent several hours sitting at the bar, drinking a lot of gin and tonics and trying to look as indifferent as possible, Fred finally appeared. This time, she didn't have to buy her a whisky; Fred marched straight up to Amy and shook her hand. She told her she had sold a painting and was feeling flush. It was her turn to buy the drinks, and show her a few places that were more interesting than this dive.

They meandered around town, having fun, drinking, kissing uninhibitedly on the street, and finally ending up at Amy's house. The sorceress stayed on for several days, being waited on by Amy's maid and cook, and beguiled by her hostess, who gazed at her wide-eyed with lust and delight. Then the redhead disappeared again for many long weeks. Although Amy knew she had no right to expect Fred to be anything other than what she was, she still felt cheated. She wandered around, asking the creatures of the night whether they had seen her lover, slipping barmen some coins to try to glean information about Fred's whereabouts, but in vain.

Fred was nowhere to be found. She could only ever be tracked down when she wanted to be: that was a lesson Amy learned in the course of those weeks. And when she turned up again and rang her doorbell as if nothing had happened, Amy made a scene of which she was subsequently ashamed. But there was nothing for it; she had to admit to herself that she had never craved any other person on this planet as she did this small, almost plain woman, a woman one noticed (if at all) only for the colour of her hair, who had absolutely no manners, let alone good taste, or anything approaching consideration.

Of course, like every woman before and after her, Amy wanted to be the first great exception in Fred Lieblich's love life. With patience and great forbearance, with many enticing suggestions, with her unconditional acceptance, her soft, compliant character, her cheerful disposition (because her Austrian friend was distinctly inclined to melancholy), and with her impressive audacity in lovemaking, she would tame the sorceress, teach her reliability. Besides, Amy had something the sorceress did not; something on which she, like every other person, was dependent — money.

Although Amy's affluence didn't mean as much to her as one might have thought, she did know exactly the sort of power one could wield as a patron.

Over the next few weeks, she rented an old storeroom in Soho and had it converted into a studio for her lover. She called some of Magnus' art-loving friends, commissioned paintings from Fred Lieblich under false names, and equipped her with everything she had so painfully lacked in the past. But Amy didn't know her lover well enough yet. She couldn't know that, ever since she was a child, Fred had suffered nothing but deprivation; that, for her, lack and self-denial were normal.

What she didn't have, she took: cruising Soho and the East End, sneaking out of the cheap bed-and-breakfasts, rented flats, and basement lodgings the next morning, each time leaving a naked, sleeping woman behind her. Then, for a short while, she felt as if she had everything, as if she owned the whole world, until longing drove her back out onto the streets. If she ran out of paint, she drew on a napkin with a pencil. If she had no winter coat, she just took a blanket and wrapped herself in it. If she had no money to pay for her drinks in the bar, she fixed her cat's eyes on one of the female customers and stared at her until she asked if she was all right. After that, getting her to pay the bill was child's play.

Amy had no option but to accept Fred as she was — in between fits of rage, heartrending declarations of love, and curses. But this acceptance was only possible because she still hoped that one day she would be allowed to call Fred Lieblich her own. She had India in her blood, after all; she too was familiar with self-denial and deprivation; she always got what she wanted; and she wanted Fred, of that she was quite certain. Even if Magnus, John, and their friends were constantly trying to convince her otherwise, she would learn to make herself indispensable to her lover. One day Fred would need something — more than anything else, more than these wanton, escapist affairs, more than life itself — and Amy would be able to give it to her. Whatever it might be.

★

Perhaps weary, heartsick Amy would not have leaped so precipitously into the Kitty adventure had two events not preceded their meeting: Fred's renewed disappearance, and John's return to India. With his departure, Amy felt as if the connection to her childhood had been severed, and she was scared of loneliness. Magnus was either travelling or in Wales. He was living his life. But some days Amy didn't seem to know where she belonged any more. Who or what would remind her of her origins, which she seemed to need so badly, in order to reassure herself that her life remained true to these origins, to this childhood? Should she travel abroad? Follow her brother? And so Kitty's appearance in her life was the straw to which Amy clung. Someone needed her.

A refugee from the Soviet Union; a talented one, a brilliant singer. A minor sensation. Escaped from the dark clutches of communism, catapulted into the capitalist utopia. And before her new trophy realised that this country and this city were no place for utopias, no place where newcomers' dreams came true, Amy had to act: she had to imbue this melancholy and mistrustful creature with her very own personal utopia. She had to corral her with a fence woven from dreams, so that she would stay, so that she wouldn't waste her talent, so that she didn't long to return to her homeland, so that she went on singing. Just as she had once created a garden with her brothers, a garden of mud and happiness, of sand and wood and promises each made to each other.

*

At their very first meeting, Amy suggested that Kitty Jashi move in with her, to a flat on the top floor of her house. Her husband, she said, was never there, and she was usually alone. She had enough money. She was happy to help. She emphasised this again and again, and when she realised that Kitty was too proud to accept charity, she suggested a different form of payment in lieu of rent: her music. 'I'd like to introduce you to some friends of mine; they're all in the music business. One of them owns a jazz club. I can take you there. I just want them to listen to you, and perhaps you'll get some work out of it. Then, and only then, you can pay me rent.'

It took some time and all Amy's powers of persuasion for Kitty to agree to the plan, but when she arrived at the house in King's Cross, carrying her one suitcase and her guitar, and saw the little attic flat, she was deeply touched.

The new bed standing there, the empty bookshelves smelling of fresh paint, the new crockery in the little kitchenette, the unused handtowels — all this made her feel welcome. Amy had gone to great pains in decorating the flat. Kitty sat down on the edge of the bed. She stayed there for more than an hour without moving, feeling something between grateful amazement at such generosity and a certain unease that came over her at the thought of moving in with this woman she didn't know.

Amy's house began to fill up. Friends came to marvel at the Soviet *wunderkind*. They all wanted to know how she had managed to flee, why she had come to London, and what she had done in her previous life. Atlases were brought out to look for the Black Sea and Georgia. Even Magnus made a special trip to London from Wales to inspect his wife's new discovery. Everyone admired Amy for wresting Kitty away from the refugee shelter and introducing her to London's free spirits. As all the visitors, and especially Amy, kept repeating, she was a rare talent who should be encouraged and admired. Kitty, who was still working in the East End and waiting for calls from her faceless friend, accepted Amy's praise and her friends' interest in her music with indifference, as a matter of course. Her acting talent stood her in good stead: she invented stories about her escape, mixing fact with invention, and gave the visitors, who marvelled at her as if she were an exhibit in a museum, what they wanted to see and hear.

And at precisely the moment when Kitty had acquired a degree of renown in Amy's circles, Fred reappeared.

> *Wunderbar, wunderbar*! What a perfect night for love.
> Here am I, here you are — why, it's truly *wunderbar*!
>
> COLE PORTER

Fred materialised out of nowhere one foggy evening. She arrived in King's Cross, sat down at the table in the drawing room, and asked if she could get something to eat. Simultaneously overwhelmed with joy that her beloved had returned and outraged at her chutzpah in simply bursting in and demanding a hot meal, Amy hurried to the kitchen herself, as both the cook and the maid had the day off, and prepared Fred a lavish supper. Then she sat at the other end of the table and watched her eat, as if she were a child with a poor appetite who had finally announced that she was hungry.

Guitar chords drifted down to them from upstairs, and Fred, her mouth full, cast her eyes to the ceiling.

'I bet you haven't heard about my new girlfriend yet,' Amy began cautiously. She chose the word 'girlfriend' very deliberately. Fred shook her head and replenished her plate.

Amy spoke of Kitty with enthusiasm, watching closely to observe her lover's reactions. She was hoping for jealousy, but all she saw was curiosity. Nonetheless, she instantly relented when the flame-haired Fred came over and began to caress her, whispering words in her ear that testified to her desire and concomitant suffering.

It wasn't long before they ended up in Amy's bedroom.

A melody had been playing in Kitty's head the previous night, and all day she had been torturing herself with the new song, which wasn't coming to her as effortlessly as usual. She set aside the guitar in irritation and went down to ask Amy's advice. Amy really did have a remarkable feel for the right melody, and even if Kitty didn't for one second hope that she could actually help her establish a music career, as she was always claiming, she had at least convinced her to believe in her own music.

But there was no one in the drawing room: the remains of a meal were the only indication that Amy was in the house. Kitty felt uncomfortable sitting there in her absence, and had just retreated to her attic again when she heard furious shouting on the ground floor. And an unfamiliar woman's voice. Then she heard Amy swear, and the front door opening.

'Do what you want, and see how you get by. I'm not your bloody cook; that's not my mission in life, thank you very much!' And Kitty heard the front door slam.

Cautiously, she opened her bedroom door and peered down into the hall. She quietly crept down a few steps and saw the figure of a woman going into the drawing room. The woman stopped when she noticed Kitty, then walked up to her and held out her hand. Kitty couldn't move, didn't know where to look, because the stranger was stark naked.

'I'm still hungry. Would you like to keep me company?' the red-haired woman asked casually. She went on into the drawing room, where she got stuck in to the remains of the food. 'I'm Fred, by the way,' she added.

Kitty didn't want to appear rude. In her homeland, it would be outrageous to leave a guest to eat alone. But she was no longer in her homeland, and besides, in her homeland the guests weren't naked. She followed her into the drawing room, silently, head bowed, like a faithful servant, positioned herself at the window, and looked out at the little front garden in order to escape the strange woman's nakedness.

Fred smacked her lips noisily, wiped her mouth, and fetched herself a whisky from the drinks cabinet — clearly well acquainted with its precise location. She came up behind Kitty and offered her a glass.

'Come on, what's wrong with you? Haven't you ever seen a naked woman before? I was in a hurry and couldn't find my clothes. If you lend me your cardigan, darling, you won't have to endure the sight of my divine body any longer.'

Kitty immediately removed her cardigan and handed it to her without looking round.

'Thank you, darling.' The red-haired stranger laughed and set Kitty's whisky down on the window sill. 'Cheers!'

Only now did Kitty dare to turn round and look at the guest. The woman was standing close to her; too close. She smelled Amy on her; she smelled Amy's fury on her. The red-head smiled. But her smile was different from the friendly smile of the West that Kitty had come to know. It was cheerful, but cheerful *despite*, not *because*. The woman's green eyes glowed unhealthily. Her thin lips were an artificial red, although she wasn't wearing make up. She gave the impression of someone who wants too much and gets too little.

These red lips reminded Kitty so forcefully of the dark apartment on the Holy Mountain, the blood flowing from the cut throat, that she knocked back the burning liquid in one gulp and squeezed her eyes tight shut because she didn't want to lose her equilibrium in front of this peculiar creature.

The proximity, the smell, the hand with which she propped herself up on the windowsill, the other hand holding the whisky glass: it was all too close, too disturbing. Perhaps it wasn't even her nakedness that had so unsettled Kitty; perhaps it was this alarming intimacy. The moment was too much for her; it was dangerous, because here, standing in front of her, for the first time since she had left her country and her life behind, was a person who confronted her as an equal. Demanded that she look her in the eye, instead of up at her from below. It was not a look that wanted to change her.

The red lips and the dead baby. The birth that should have been a celebration of life, pledged instead to death. The hair curlers on the floor and the urge to vomit. Mariam, Mariam, Mariam, Mariam.

Kitty wanted this woman to leave right away. She hated her for her penetrating gaze. Hated her nakedness. Hated her presence in this peaceful house, which was like a declaration of war. She hated the role of museum exhibit that she, Kitty, had to play in this house, because this woman saw it for what it was. They were silent, and the red-haired woman's face changed. It grew serious: the corners of her mouth turned down, her cat's eyes narrowed to slits.

Kitty wanted her to leave, and at the same time she wanted her to stay. Wanted to claim this sincerity for herself. Wanted this woman to hold up a mirror to her, a mirror in which she could see herself in the woman's pitiless light. Without false hopes. Without false aspirations and expectations.

Life had betrayed her; or she had betrayed life, it was more or less the same thing. In the mornings, in her attic room, listening to the city as it woke, Kitty would ask herself whether she was still human. Whether it still made sense to going on living. And whether all her songs were nothing more than failed, pathetic attempts to justify her existence.

Now she was even starting to wonder whether these months, these people, these streets, these places and hopes were perhaps all just a daydream. Perhaps she didn't even exist any more. Perhaps she was just a body, forcing itself to go to the Underground station each day, and everything that she had ever been, that had ever made her who she was, had died: on the stretcher in the classroom, in the dark apartment on the Holy Mountain, or at the moment she received the news of Mariam's death.

Perhaps the most tragic thing about exile, both mental and geographical, was that you began to see through everything, you could no longer beautify anything; you had to accept yourself for who you were. Neither who you had been in the past, nor the idea of who you might be in the future, mattered.

Fred had sat down on the window seat, her bare legs dangling. There was something profoundly childish about her as she sat there, looking at Kitty. She reached for the bottle and refilled Kitty's glass. Kitty found this physical proximity uncomfortable, but didn't dare break the moment. Because like this she could simply breathe, drink, be silent, look out at the foggy day. Not have to do anything else. The woman radiated a playful nonchalance that Kitty found reassuring. She could have gone on sitting there even if there had been an earthquake and the whole house had collapsed. She was just opening her mouth to say something when they heard the door open downstairs and Amy's footsteps in the corridor.

Kitty turned abruptly and hurried out of the drawing room, shamefaced, as if she were afraid of being caught doing something forbidden. As she left, the red-haired woman threw the cardigan after her; it was as if she had guessed what Kitty was thinking, and was playing along.

*

Fred stayed in the house for the next few weeks. They all ate together and listened to music. Fred and Amy went out in the evenings, and only came back in the early hours of the morning. Amy seemed happy; she was making an effort to look more attractive than usual. She seemed rejuvenated, playful, joking, ready and willing to anticipate her beloved's every desire.

At first, Kitty could barely overcome her embarrassment when she was asked to join the two of them for meals: in part because it was a scandalous thing for her, this openly expressed passion between two women, but also because she could not forget that first, wordless encounter in the drawing room. Fred played the charming, gallant, interested lover. Whenever Kitty entered the drawing room to borrow one of Amy's many records, she would find Amy sitting on Fred's lap, lost in a deep, warm ecstasy, running her hands through her lover's hair or kissing the tip of her nose. Kitty would lower her eyes, excuse herself repeatedly, dash to the large cabinet where Amy kept her record collection, and vanish from the room again as quickly as possible. Amy seemed unconcerned; she asked her if she wouldn't like to stay, play a game of cards, or go with them to the cinema. Each time, Kitty thanked her and declined. After work, she preferred to wander the streets of the East End in the dark rather than head home, just so she wouldn't cross paths with the strange couple.

*

It was Kitty's day off. She had decided to stay in bed and learn vocabulary for her first English exam. She was excited because she knew that her nameless friend would be calling the following day: he would call her here for the first time, on her own private number. Amy had had a separate telephone line installed for her protégée. From now on, Kitty would no longer have to run to the telephone box; she would lie on her bed with the receiver pressed firmly to her ear, forming words in her mother tongue. She would be quiet, intimate; she wouldn't have to keep turning round to make sure no one was watching them, that their words were safe.

The house was silent. Amy and Fred must have gone out for a late breakfast. Kitty sat up, picked up her guitar, and began to play, wildly, chaotically, plunging from one song into another without a break, singing along, stopping, starting again.

Suddenly, she heard a knock at the door. Amy never came up to her room. If she wanted her for something she would ring a bell downstairs; lately, she had even started calling her on the phone. So it must be the red-head who was at her door. She glanced cautiously in the mirror, pushed her hair out of her face, and threw on a dressing gown over her nightshirt.

'May I come in? I've never been up here.'

She walked in without waiting for Kitty's answer. She was wearing white linen trousers and a white vest. White suited her. Her red hair, which hung in waves across her forehead, contrasted beautifully with her white clothes.

She looked around, taking in the furnishings and the personal items. The rail with just a few items of clothing (Kitty refused to accept the clothes Amy tried to give her), the two pairs of polished shoes lined up neatly. The guitar case. The plates spread out to dry on a kitchen towel.

'You don't have to stop. I was standing on the landing the whole time, listening to you. You really do sing very well.'

Kitty said nothing. She hesitated a moment, then went back over to the bed, sat on it cross-legged, picked up the guitar, and began to play. Although she never refused when Amy made this request, because it was her rent, she never played as uninhibitedly as she did now.

Eyes closed, lost in her own world, she sang in Georgian. It was a long time since she had sung with such relish, had been so completely at one with her music. When she opened her eyes, Fred was kneeling in front of her. Her face was serious and concentrated, as if she had been studying Kitty's features the whole time. It was an expression she never wore in Amy's presence.

Kitty put the guitar aside, stretched out her legs, and turned her face away. She didn't want to be looked at in such a penetrating way.

'Is everything all right?' she stammered, when the tension became too much for her. She started to get up. Suddenly the red-haired woman seized her wrist, forcing her to remain seated. Then she pressed her nose against Kitty's, and stayed like that. Kitty didn't trust herself to move her head. This closeness was not soothing; it was like the look they had shared when they had first met. Binding. It was a closeness born of knowledge, not of lust. And it was serious. They were so close, she couldn't focus. The contours of the other woman's face dissolved. Kitty didn't know what she should say or, above all, how to say it. And it would have been the same even if she had been able to say it in her mother tongue. For the first time since her arrival in London, she didn't feel that the foreign language was the crucial barrier.

But before she could formulate a sentence, Fred had pressed her lips to Kitty's. She didn't move; her tongue stayed in her mouth, and the kiss was dry and circumspect. As if they were two young girls, practising kissing for their boyfriends. Kitty reached out an arm and pushed Fred away, then shuffled back up the bed towards the wall.

'I don't think ...'

Kitty interrupted herself. What was it she didn't think? That it wasn't right for Fred to kiss her because she was with the woman who provided Kitty with a roof over her head, or because she herself was a woman, and this fact was an insurmountable hurdle? Or simply because she thought that this woman would not be good for her; not because she was so brazen and uninhibited, so egocentric and inconsiderate, but because with all her splinters and scratches, her wounds and hopeful forlornness, the two of them were too alike? Kitty knew nothing of the path this woman had travelled, and she didn't think she wanted to know, but there had certainly been a landslide in her life, a colossal, brutal landslide that had torn the ground from beneath her feet and taught her to fly. Of this, Kitty was convinced.

'You're close to me; that frightens me. I've been asking myself why that is. I've been asking myself that all this time and I can't find an answer.' Suddenly Fred was speaking German. The language took Kitty by surprise. It felt familiar to her, more familiar than English. It was a language she had studied in school; she had wanted to learn it with Andro. For Vienna. She didn't know what to say.

'You understood me, didn't you? You understand German?'

'No.'

'Yes, you do. You know exactly what I just said.'

'No.'

Kitty drew up her legs and wrapped her arms around them. She wanted the woman to go. She wanted the woman to stay. Perhaps right there, in this gap, in this intermediate state, she could escape herself. Not think of the house on the Holy Mountain. Not sing about death. Not miss the curls on Andro's head. Not regret anything. Not hate her brother. Not hate herself for sacrificing Mariam. For surviving — for this survival, this miserable existence. Not think about her mother, her aunt; not have to worry about them, about those she had left behind. Not have only one nameless and faceless friend. Not be here. Not be there. Not be herself.

Fred came and sat with her on the bed. She wasn't looking at her any more. She reached out her hand, took Kitty's, and Kitty let her, didn't pull her hand away. Fred's hand travelled up her arm to her collarbone, then to her face, up into her thick hair, down to her neck. She was sitting beside her now, but not looking at her. It was better that way.

These caresses made Kitty feel melancholy. Fred's caresses were easier to bear than her gaze. She stroked Kitty's torso, her face, without stopping; as if summoning up heathen gods, as if driving the fear out of her body. It was as if her thoughts had been blown away. Kitty felt an inner emptiness that came as a relief; an emptiness that was completely calm. Her body merely sensed the gentle caresses without her head contriving to categorise, to judge them.

What happened next happened quickly and was shockingly easy. This red-haired woman seemed to be so shamelessly accomplished at what she was doing. There was something about the feeling of these hands all over her body that was like healing. Kitty asked herself how that was possible. Why her body wasn't outraged at being touched in this way by a woman. Why nothing in her rebelled. Why she surrendered without a struggle, without a word. Perhaps her body believed that what this woman was doing was a healing ritual.

When Fred's hand reached her crotch, she pressed her legs firmly together, as if protecting a secret, and turned her head aside. There was something unfamiliar to be celebrated, but Kitty had been unable to celebrate anything for a very long time. Certainly not anything unfamiliar.

'It's all right,' said Fred, leaning over Kitty. It was a muggy morning, and the room was airless. They could hear cars driving past outside, pedestrians walking by. 'My father was from Vienna. My mother from Stockholm. They met in Vienna. He was still a medical student at the time. Later, he became a psychiatrist. She was interested in psychoanalysis, which was why she'd come to Vienna, but then she fell in love, married, and got pregnant. I was born and grew up in Vienna.' She spoke quietly, in German, leaning on one hand next to Kitty's head while the other ran over Kitty's skin. 'I had a younger brother. A late arrival. Eight years after me. I think my parents were happy. Yes, they were, in their way. They weren't religious. I mean, yes, we celebrated Hanukkah and Passover; my brother was circumcised; but that was all. The only thing they fought about was Vienna. She hated the city; he loved it. I loved it, too, but only because I didn't know anything else; and Stockholm, where we sometimes went to visit my grandparents, frightened me, so northern and aloof.'

Kitty's breathing grew calmer. She closed her eyes and tried to imagine Vienna; not her and Andro's Vienna, but this woman's city, this woman who was, at this very moment, embracing her. Kitty didn't understand all the words, but she could follow the context; she could sense, feel the words she didn't know, taste them on her tongue and draw out their meaning. As if a foreign language were no barrier between herself and this woman. As if it could not be a barrier.

'At the same time, they must both have been unhappy in their own way, but on the whole they were more happy than they were unhappy; at least, I think so. Perhaps just because I want to think that. And they were good parents to us, they loved us in the way they thought we wanted them to. And perhaps they were right: this kind of balanced, composed, chastising yet gentle love. Perhaps it was the best love for us.'

Fred's hand explored Kitty's waist and slowly wandered lower. Kitty felt her stroking her scars. She didn't want Fred to stop talking, to stop touching the hardened skin where once the stitches had been. Mariam's stitches. Mariam, seared into Kitty's body for ever and ever. The hand paused.

'I still remember exactly how it began. How it started, with that nauseating Jewish star. With my father being barred from his job. With my mother's panic attacks. She wanted to go to Stockholm, all along she wanted to get away, but he told her that was no escape. If *they* came to Vienna, they would come to Stockholm, too. He had no illusions about what awaited us, but neither did he make any attempt to leave the country, to flee. Many of his friends had already left. If he hadn't waited so long, perhaps we too could have ... But he simply didn't believe there was any point in running away. My mother couldn't understand it. I still remember very clearly what it was like when they came. Dressed all in black. Posturing with their guns. The sharp tone of voice. As if they were speaking a different language, not my mother tongue. The papers, the stamps, the train journey. First it was to the ghetto in Theresienstadt. Then we were split up — men there, women here.

'My mother wouldn't stop screaming. My brother wet himself as my father took his hand and pulled him away from Mother through the crowd. My mother had implored this SS man, hugged his knees and tried to kiss his hand, I still remember how ashamed I was of her, yes, even in those circumstances: I knew that my brother's wellbeing was at stake, and I was ashamed of her for humiliating herself. She implored him, kept repeating that he was so little — so little, sir, she said, so little, he needs his mother.

'I didn't understand any of it. I couldn't grasp any of it. I wasn't that young any more, I should have understood, but I couldn't. I couldn't conceive of what it meant: labour camp, concentration camp. Camp, camp, camp. It was only hunger that brought me closer to these terms. Hunger was the road to understanding. Yes, I believe that without the constant hunger I would have gone on refusing to understand what was happening.' She paused for a moment, looked up at the window as if she needed to draw breath, to prepare herself for what she still had to say.

'It's so ironic that my father and my brother stayed in Theresienstadt, and my mother and I were sent back to Austria. She never wanted to go back there. We arrived in Mauthausen. Do you know this place? No, you don't; better that way. Mauthausen had a lot of satellite camps. The earthworks, the stone quarries, the granite quarries, work for heavy industry. And it had a lot of brothels. It was a Category III camp, meaning *extermination through labour*. The only camp in this category within the territory of the German Reich, incidentally. People categorised as anti-social — criminals, ex-convicts, people with behavioural problems — were concentrated there and were supposed to work themselves to death. Why my mother and I were considered anti-social, I can't tell you. Mother was assigned to work in the quarry. At first I was assigned to the maintenance and disinfection of the brothel barracks, as I couldn't do the very heavy work on account of my weight. These were the only barracks that weren't ridden with lice and disease. The brothels were actually intended as an incentive for prisoners to work harder, but pure-bred German dicks often saw action there, too, even though it was forbidden. I saw everything. From the back and the front. From above and below. Most of the women who *worked* there came from Ravensbrück, and after a few weeks in Mauthausen most of them wanted to go back. At least there they could wait for death without having to sell their bodies at the same time.

'They didn't even send me out when they started going at the women. It didn't bother them that I was there, that I was watching them. Some of them even liked it, and every day I waited for it, every day I expected it — expected them to call me over, say lie down, pull up your shirt, spread your legs, suck my dick. I think it was the women's glances that protected me. I know it sounds stupid, but it's what I believe. I'm certain — absolutely certain. As the men were mounting them they would turn their heads towards me and look at me, as if to say: I'm doing this so you don't have to.

'Then along came Martin. Pure-bred Martin was a popular man in the brothel because he didn't want anything unusual; he didn't want them to stand on their heads and spread their legs, or crawl around the barracks on all fours, he didn't want them to hold their arse cheeks apart or grunt. He didn't want anything like that. He wanted to lie down, sleep with them, get up, and leave. Sometimes he would even hug one of them, if he felt inclined and let himself go. I even saw a tear roll down his cheek once when he came. Yes — good old Martin had a sentimental streak. And Martin stared at me. The whole time. From the moment he first saw me, he stared at me. Hesitantly at first, only when he thought I wasn't looking at him, then more and more blatantly. Until he only ever looked at me, just at me, while he mounted the other women. I was scared. I didn't know what it meant. I hadn't yet learned to interpret his look. The other men looked at me in order to affirm themselves. To see, in my eyes, what unparalleled lechery or perversity they were capable of. They wanted affirmation. And I learned to give it to them. I learned to look at them in such a way that they thought I was impressed. I learned to suppress my sympathy with the women and ally myself with them. With the murderers, rapists, sadists, masochists, with the sick and the impotent. I looked, and my eyes told them I admired them for their sick, uninhibited lust. I learned to do this. Over time, it came more and more easily to me. But Martin was different. His looks were different. I didn't know what they signified.

'Sometimes he looked at me fearfully, as if he were afraid of me and my presence; sometimes he looked at me just as lecherously as the others, with the same demented, glazed expression; sometimes I even thought I saw in his eyes a cry for help, as if he wished I would go to him, grab his gun, and release him from himself.

'We had been in the camp for four months and twelve days when he spoke to me for the first time. He arrived at daybreak, as I was starting work, on my own. Suddenly, there he was, as if from nowhere, standing in front of me. He asked me if I was a virgin. I nodded. I didn't know whether that was my death sentence or a free pass. He smiled at me and asked if I would be prepared to go with him. I asked him where to. He grinned from ear to ear and brought his neck close to me. There was the skull, emblazoned on his collar patch. I'd never have thought that Martin — such a normal man — was one of them. He told me he had been assigned to supervise the Wiener Neustadt SS labour camp. The Raxwerke plants were manufacturing goods for the armaments industry; I think by then they were already working on the V2 rockets. He told me he could take me with him, that I wouldn't have to work as hard there. That I was his personal protégée. That I would have my own room and enough to eat. And he would visit me at night. But only him. There wouldn't be anyone else I would have to … A fellow soldier had caught a nasty venereal disease; he couldn't risk that, the hygiene in the camp was a disaster, he would like to have a 'normal' love life. Yes, that's what he said, a normal love life — and I was so beautiful, and my red hair, and …'

Now Kitty seized the back of Fred's neck with both hands, pulled her head down and kissed her. She wrapped her legs around Fred's body and clung to her tightly, like a little monkey. But Fred could no longer stop; she kept on talking, the words seeming to pour from her mouth despite herself.

'I said yes. But I said I couldn't go alone. I could see my mother wasting away; every day I saw a little piece of her disappear, saw her being broken down. I knew she wouldn't last much longer. For a moment he was angry, and I thought it was all over. First he cursed me, called me an ungrateful whore, a Jewish pig, but then he calmed down, as if nothing had happened, and he said he'd see what could be done. And before he left he asked me again whether I was sure about my hymen. Whether I really hadn't let anyone near me. I swore to it.

'He kept his promise. We were housed in an external barracks. My mother and I. She knew exactly what price I had to pay for it, but we never spoke about it. Only that in the nights when my SS man stayed away, she would come to me, stroke my hands, and kiss my temples.

'Every night, as he lay on top of me — that was how he liked it, how he liked it best — he declared that he loved me. And sometimes he even wept when he came. He told me we had to stay together, no matter what happened. That he couldn't let me go. That he had to stay with me.

'When the air raids started, he put us in his car, at daybreak, in a cloak-and-dagger operation. We drove to Vienna; I remember clearly how my mother threw up when we reached the sixth district. The area where our apartment was, where we had lived. My father, my brother, she, and I. And Martin scolded and cursed her. Looking back, I think he was always a little afraid of her; perhaps he sometimes imagined that one day she would plunge a knife into his back as he lay on top of me.

'We had to stay in the car. He had found us some civilian clothes specially for the journey. Everyday clothes. Perfectly *normal*. Yes — we could have passed for a perfectly normal family. My blonde mother, her red-haired daughter, and blond Martin. The three of us could have passed for a perfect family. To some, we might even have looked like a loving brother and sister out with their mother.

'Mother and I spent two days hidden in an insurance-company building that had been evacuated. Then he took us to Mödling, a tiny backwater outside Vienna, to a deserted farmhouse. We had nothing to eat, but suddenly we had hope again.

'He drove back to Vienna. The city was being carpet-bombed, and they needed all their forces to secure the fuel depot. Even when people were saying that the Reds had taken Wiener Neustadt, that it was only a matter of time before Vienna fell to the Allies, he still came to me and lay on top of me. Still talked about a future together in Germany. Said he loved me. Deep down, I was still afraid he might shoot us both like a couple of animals. To cover his tracks.

'And then I said it to him. I told him that I loved him, and that I was looking forward to our German future. Yes: I said it to him. I said it in my mother's presence. I still remember how she froze, but I was afraid we wouldn't survive those final days. He kissed me before he drove off, promising he would be back within the week to take us to Germany. I'd gained us a couple of days to prepare our escape and try to reach the Reds or the Allies. I don't know whether he returned to the farm. I ran away.

'My father and my brother did not return. They both died in that first year in the concentration camp. My father of typhus, and my brother of starvation. My mother ...'

Fred abruptly fell silent, as if she had run out of words. She buried her face in Kitty's neck and took off her trousers. Kitty now wanted her to go on talking; she asked her, pleaded with her, but Fred said not another word.

Love was a slow, creeping poison, love was treacherous and insincere, love was a veil thrown over the misery of the world, love was sticky and indigestible, it was a mirror in which one could be what one was not, it was a spectre that spread hope where hope had long since died, it was a hiding place where people thought they found refuge and ultimately found only themselves, it was a vague memory of another love, it was the possibility of a salvation that was ultimately equivalent to a *coup de grâce*, it was a war without victors, it was a precious jewel amid the broken fragments you cut yourself on: yes, Brilka, in those days, that was love.

Kitty felt Fred kiss her out of her poisoned sleep with her words; felt that someone was holding her, with black tears and trembling eyelids, someone who had the urgency of a *survivor*.

★

The grey light of the last day of February shone through the flimsy curtains into the room. Fred had risen and was doing stretches, pulling in her legs and extending her arms. Her skin was a translucent white. Blue veins shimmered through in places. The triangle between her legs glowed provocatively red. Eyes squeezed shut in contentment, she stretched in the light.

Naked and exposed like this, her body suddenly seemed so fragile. Kitty studied it closely, yet it seemed to reveal nothing to her, to tell her nothing, as if this body kept everything that mattered to itself, as if it wanted to be just a body, autonomous, without any visible history, just the pale, white body of a woman. Wearied by the morning's lovemaking, nothing about it appeared vulgar or even seductive. It seemed to Kitty inconceivable that she had desired this body only a few minutes earlier. She buried her face in the pillow.

★

A secret conference took place in the commissariat of the Soviet Navy in Moscow to discuss the construction of the first nuclear-powered submarine, which bore the heroic name Leninsky Komsomol. Afterwards, the naval captain Konstantin Jashi was selected as the project's deputy manager. He signed the document with pride, pledged to keep these official secrets, and went for a gourmet dinner with scientists and other representatives of the Navy.

That evening, the Generalissimus was sitting with his entourage in the Kremlin's lavishly appointed cinema, forcing his men to watch (as usual) one of his beloved American cowboy films, or else a comedy.

His paranoia had reached unprecedented levels. The randomness with which he would lash out, like a dragon incapable of controlling its fire, was terrifying, and reminiscent of the despotism of the thirties. As if this despotism had been briefly interrupted by the war only to return again now in all its former cruelty. Overnight, he would change his mind; overnight, his generals would fall out of favour. At his dacha in Kuntsevo, a village on the western fringes of Moscow, he humiliated his ministers, made his men dance and sing, made them stuff themselves until they could eat no more and drink until they vomited. The atmosphere throughout the Kremlin, and thus in the entire realm, was wholly dependent on the way he smoked his pipe. If he smoked it cold, it meant arrests and firing squads; if he just held it in his hand without smoking it, he was about to fall into one of his dreaded rages, and one of the members of his court would lose his head. If he scratched his moustache with the pipe — then, and only then, would it be a good day. Turning down an invitation to a drinking orgy at the Leader's dacha, or even failing to receive the invitation, meant you could be deported, arrested, or shot.

For some time now, even the Little Big Man had not been able to count on his favour. The Georgian party chairman had recently been deposed; his followers had been arrested; the Generalissimus had even decreed that the Little Big Man must investigate himself. Everything indicated that he wanted to weaken the Little Big Man's undisputed supremacy in their homeland.

After the film screening, the Leader ordered cars for himself, the Little Big Man, and three other party functionaries, and they were driven to Kuntsevo. A lavish Georgian buffet was already laid out in his dacha, with copious quantities of Georgian wine on hand. During dinner they discussed the so-called 'doctors' plot'. The Generalissimus had just had the country's leading doctors arrested, including the Kremlin's own. The majority were Jews, whom he accused of being American agents conspiring to overthrow him.

It was four in the morning when at last he dismissed his entourage. He even permitted them the luxury of a little sleep. When the Generalissimus had still not appeared by midday, the guards became uneasy. But no one dared wake the Leader, for fear of paying for the disturbance with their lives. It was only towards evening that the senior lieutenant of the guard entered the room where the Leader normally slept on a pink sofa. He breathed a sigh of relief: the Generalissimus was in a normal state of mind; he gave him instructions and ordered him to fetch the post from the Kremlin. However, when the lieutenant brought him the post at around ten o'clock, he found the Generalissimus lying on the floor in his pyjamas, conscious, but unable to speak. He had wet himself.

His bodyguards carried him into the big dining room, hoping he would find it easier to breathe in there. Calls were made. No one knew who was responsible in such a situation: the Generalissimus had made no provision for it. The Little Big Man, Khrushchev, and Malenkov — the illustrious trio — were informed. However, the Little Big Man could not be reached at first, and no one knew which lady he was currently with. When at last he telephoned Kuntsevo, he ordered the guards not to inform anyone, not to make any more phone calls. Khrushchev, Bulganin, and Malenkov reached Kuntsevo around midnight. Without looking in on the Leader, they informed the household staff that he was merely drunk, and told them not to bother him in his sensitive condition. They then left the dacha.

It was only much later, in the early hours of the morning, that the Little Big Man also appeared and berated the guards. It was an outrage, he said, for them to be spreading panic. The Leader was snoring; everything was fine. But the household staff would not be reassured. They begged him to call a doctor. They protested that the state their master was in was not normal.

Deliberations began as to which doctor they should bring in. The country's leading doctors had been arrested; a Jewish doctor was definitely out of the question, but he had to be a professor at the very least. At seven o'clock in the morning, the team of doctors finally arrived. It is said that their hands trembled so badly during the examination that they had difficulty even taking his pulse. None of them knew whether they would leave the room alive. That morning, the doctors announced their diagnosis to the assembled Politburo: arterial haemorrhage in the left hemisphere of the brain. His condition was extremely serious.

Was it relief, fear, or consternation that spread among those gathered there? It was too long since each had discarded his own will, his own opinion, even his own feelings; now they sat like marionettes abandoned by their puppeteer.

The Little Big Man put himself in charge. His priority now was gaining time for the coming power struggle, although publicly he had to ask the doctors to do all they possibly could to try and save the Leader. Two men from his personal bodyguard were to keep watch at the sickbed; that would make it easier to monitor the situation, the Little Big Man said. To everyone else it was perfectly clear that, after all the years of torment, fears, threats, and humiliation the Generalissimus had inflicted, he believed his turn to wield the sceptre had finally come.

On the fifth day of his death throes, the millionfold murderer finally succumbed, surrounded by his weeping entourage — including the still-triumphant Little Big Man.

The Generalissimus would have approved of his funeral. Even dead, he still had the power to kill people. During the service on Red Square on 9 March 1953, hundreds were trampled to death or suffocated in the crowd.

Yet even inmates of the camps — whose lives the dead man had destroyed, who had been robbed of their futures, declared slaves, subhuman, whose families he had annihilated — hit their heads on bars and barbed wire in utter despair when they heard of the Leader's death.

★

Somewhere between Camden High Street and Arlington Road, Kitty laughed out loud. A little earlier, she had spoken to her nameless friend on the phone and discussed with him Amy's plans for her future.

'If there's any interest from the public you're welcome to tell the press whatever you like, but not, under any circumstances, anything about how you came to this country, or which city you were in beforehand. That goes without saying,' the nameless man had calmly replied.

'I won't,' Kitty promised. 'I don't want to make any trouble for you, which is why I wanted to make sure ... You've done so much for me.'

'You won't be able to put me in danger. Just look out for yourself. And if anyone from your homeland tries to contact you —'

'I won't respond; yes, yes, I understand.'

'You sound very cheerful, incidentally, on this fateful day.'

'What fateful day?'

'Haven't you heard? There's been nothing else on the radio in London all day, and the newspapers are full of it.'

'What's happened?'

'Well ... Our homeland is stricken with shock and grief.'

'Just tell me what's happened!'

'The Generalissimus is dead.'

Kitty paused. Her mouth silently repeated the sentence. She let the words dissolve on her tongue. *The Generalissimus is dead!*

'You must really be my guardian angel,' she said suddenly, and sensed a slight confusion at the other end of the line. The person the voice belonged to cleared his throat; it sounded as if he were smiling, or trying to suppress a smile. 'You always have fantastic news for me!' she almost screamed.

'I am definitely not allowed to hear such things. I'm going to hang up now, and we'll speak again in two weeks. At the same time?'

'Yes, yes, wonderful, let's do that — thank you!'

Kitty ran out onto the street and started singing at the top of her voice. She skipped along the pavement, danced, pirouetted, applauded, laughed joyously at passers-by.

She started to recite the names of all the victims she could think of. First, prominent victims from the fields of art and science, from the intelligentsia. Then she remembered the parents of classmates who were no longer allowed to mention them; the grandparents of fellow students; she remembered doctors who had suddenly stopped coming to work; she remembered the lecturers and teachers who had abruptly disappeared; she remembered friends of her mother and aunt, all of whom were missing a husband, son, wife, mother, father. The list of names was endless. The whole of Arlington Road was not enough; she had to walk down side streets as well in order to say out loud, at least once, all the names that occurred to her.

Not until she reached the station did she say: *Ramas, Sopio, Andro*. She paused for a long time; then she said to herself, in a mere whisper: *Mariam. My son.*

The same day, Kitty Jashi gave a radio interview, accompanied by her patroness, Amy, who now also acted as her interpreter. There, Kitty had the chance to perform one of her most recent songs — in her mother tongue — and talk about the hardships of life as a Soviet artist in exile. Shortly afterwards, she received an offer to perform twice a week in a jazz club in Soho, which she accepted with delight.

After the interview had been broadcast, and recorded in the Lubyanka, Kostya Jashi was summoned by the Russian secret service. Following a lengthy interrogation, he was made to confirm in writing that he had no intention of contacting his sister, and to publicly distance himself from her — more: to denounce her as an informer against the Soviet state.

> They wiped your slate
> With snow, you're not alive.
> Bayonets twenty-eight
> And bullet-holes five.
>
> ANNA AKHMATOVA

The despondent, fearful atmosphere of mourning that reigned across the country had infected Nana, too. As she walked up the hill towards Christine's house, her steps were hesitant, for she had at last decided to tell the world about her pregnancy, the news of which had been broken to her shortly after Kostya's departure; in any case, she couldn't conceal it any longer. And the more her belly swelled, the more an indefinable anxiety also swelled within her about her imminent motherhood. The news of her pregnancy had thrown her completely off balance: she had just been offered a place as a doctoral candidate at the Faculty of Linguistics, and had been preparing for this new phase in her life.

Once Kostya had left, everyone around her seemed far more enthusiastic about her status as a wife than she was herself. She felt nothing; she would have liked to have been more euphoric, more excited, less sensible, too, perhaps. But she could not identify any major changes in herself. She was still the same person; she had just moved into a different house. They all looked after her, had plenty of advice about how to be the best wife in the world. But she looked around with her big blue eyes and simply couldn't understand what was so special about marriage. The little time she had been able to spend with Kostya had not been enough for her to be sure of him, to know whether she was really in love.

The news of her pregnancy had just exacerbated her doubts about the whole enterprise of marriage, love, and so on. She had not said anything to anyone, not to her girlfriends, not to the family, and not to Kostya, either. As she sat poring over linguistics books in Kitty's old room, she often asked herself whether she knew her husband well enough, whether she even knew where he was heading. Whether she would ever be able to accompany him on his journey.

Stasia opened the door to her. 'Did you forget your key?' she asked in surprise, following her into the house.

'No, but I have to tell you something. Is Christine back yet?'

They went into the kitchen. Christine was preparing dinner. Nana, who so far had still not really become part of the family despite all the weeks they had lived together, stuck out her belly and said, 'So — does anything look different?'

'You didn't seriously think we hadn't noticed, did you?' Christine answered, with a mischievous smile. She shook her head in disbelief. Nana gave a coy laugh, a little disappointed that she had failed to surprise.

'How long have you known?'

'I think we knew you were expecting a baby even before you did. You must be in the fifth month now, at least?'

'Why didn't you say something to me? If my mother had suspected anything, she would have interrogated me.'

'She knows as well, my dear. It's very difficult to hide a thing like that.'

'May I ask you something?' said Stasia. She watched Christine's slow, considered movements, the careful slicing of the bread, the way she gently buttered it. 'What are you afraid of?'

'Afraid? What makes you say that?'

'You're afraid, and I'd like to know what of. Why are you hiding yourself away from the world? And your child along with you?'

'I'm not hiding from …'

Nana didn't finish her sentence.

That night, when Stasia had gone to bed, Christine made her nephew's wife her first hot chocolate, and comforted her. The chocolate would exorcise her fear, she thought to herself. Stasia had tried so many times to convince her sister that the chocolate exacted a high price from those who tasted it, but Christine had laughed at her and accused her of being superstitious and naive.

And so, that night, Nana tasted her first hot chocolate, made according to my great-great-grandfather's secret recipe, and experienced a powerful, stupefying, incomparable sense of bliss, the pure, vibrant joy of being at one with the world. A world in which a loving husband awaited her somewhere beside the cold sea; in which it would be possible to offer their child a beautiful, sheltered, happy life.

The next day, Kostya was called and informed that he was soon to be a father. His irritation that his wife had kept this news a secret for so long was quickly forgotten amid the great joy over the impending birth. Once the news was officially announced, whole armies of women flocked around Nana and didn't let her out of their sight until my mother was born, on 26 June 1953. They plagued her with fresh apples and cornmeal porridge, yoghurt, soups, and chicken broth, overripe plums, and many, many words of advice.

★

One morning, a month or so before the birth, Christine was sitting in the garden reading the newspaper, when she suddenly recoiled at the sight of *his* face splashed across a whole page. She lowered the paper, but her eyes were still glued to the photograph, as if in an instant it had turned back time. As if this were one of the days when the black Bugatti would drive up Vera Hill and pick her up on the street corner. As if she were still living in constant fear of Ramas coming home unannounced.

Trying to shake off the uninvited memories, she finished her coffee and inhaled the scent of lilac that enveloped the city at this time of year. She relished the abundance of nature that bloomed so marvellously in Tbilisi every May, but there was now no way she could make this day go according to plan. She picked up the paper again and read the text beneath his portrait: it was about the party the Little Big Man was to give the following Sunday in his majestic villa on Machabeli Street.

It was a celebration of his return, a tribute to his future. He was thought to be on course to achieve ultimate power. And at that point in time, all the signs, all the stars, did seem to indicate that he would soon be appointed the next ruler of the Red empire. First Deputy Premier, then Minister of Internal Affairs of the Soviet Union, the man who had succeeded in merging the Interior Ministry and the secret service in such a remarkably short time, the man who had even been given the title of Marshal, the man behind the Soviet nuclear bomb — admitted at last to the Central Committee's illustrious inner circle. Yes, everything indicated that the Great Georgian had finally made way for the Little Georgian, and left his vast territory in his hands.

Christine stared at the picture again. His features, his eyes, his expression, his gaze — all were so appallingly familiar. She wondered how many women like her he had, in the interim, sampled, chewed up, and spat out again. She tried to imagine the new, younger, beautiful women at his side.

She remembered his last, unsigned letter, in which he had given her hope that Andro would be saved. She remembered her fear of this letter, how long it had taken her to open it. She remembered the roses he had sent her every day for a year, all those painful months when she was bed-ridden, unable to look at herself in the mirror, when her sister had made her the chocolate ... The hot chocolate! Suddenly, a malicious grin spread across her face.

She lifted the newspaper and pressed the page with his face on it to her chest. Like a small child in a moment of great indecision, standing with a new doll in her hand, not knowing whether to accept it or smash it against the wall.

As if struck by lightning, she let the newspaper fall and rushed into the house. She went down to the cellar that had once housed Ramas' collection of rare and expensive wines, and where now old clothes, banished memories, and things that were no longer of use mouldered away in cardboard boxes. She started ripping boxes open, rummaging in them, working her way through the dusty mountain of old possessions — until at last she found what she was looking for.

She may have been past her prime — approaching forty-six — but she still knew exactly how to deploy make up to conceal the passage of time and present her halved beauty in the best possible light. She ran up to her room with the turquoise silk dress in her hand, held the fine material up to the light, searched for and found every blemish, and set to work. The tiny moth holes could be filled with pretty embroidery; with proper laundering and a little dye, the radiant colour could be restored. The most important thing was that she must still be able to fit into the dress.

She took off her clothes and slipped the dress over her head. After Ramas' funeral, she had wanted to cut it to pieces, but she couldn't bring herself to sacrifice the expensive material, with its artful cut and breathtakingly elegant shape. She had, however, banished it to the cellar so she wouldn't have to look at it every day, and until this morning had never even contemplated getting it out again.

Now, as she put it on and sensed the flattering material on her hips, her legs, her breasts, for a moment she felt regal again, sublime. The feeling she had always had at Ramas' side. The feeling that had seemed so essential to her in her old life, and which had abandoned her so utterly since Ramas' death.

That evening, she had worn a necklace of black pearls. That evening, the last of the year 1927. The pearl necklace had been sold a long time ago. A simple silver chain would have to do.

The dress fitted perfectly. The silken, turquoise dream. The dress with the dizzying back view that revealed the dimples above her buttocks. The dress her husband had approved, with an awed, surprised, ostensibly reproachful shake of the head. Her husband, who had been rendered momentarily speechless by the sight of his wife. Who had been bowled over by her ingenuity; who had presented her so boastfully to his boss, his *friend*. His choicest work of art. His goddess.

And if she had still possessed the Venetian mask, and had put it on again, she would have closed her eyes and heard the sounds all around her, the laughter, the clinking of champagne glasses; she would have smelled the delicious food. She would have been able to see the tinsel, glimpse Stasia in her swan costume, Sopio Eristavi dressed as a man, Ramas in his expensive dinner jacket. And in her imagination, at least, she would have refused to admit the illustrious guest whose arrival was awaited with such excitement. Would not have shown him around the house, would not have chatted to him, and would have prevented her husband from revealing her to his guest like a unique and precious jewel, when he knew full well how much this guest coveted such jewels, how he seized them for himself.

All that night, Christine worked on her transformation. Dipped the dress in dye, washed and ironed it. The following evening, when she looked at herself in the mirror, she could almost have been the old Christine, the Christine from before the New Year's ball — had she not been wearing a little black lace mask over the left half of her face. But she was content.

Then she went to the kitchen, packed the necessary ingredients — which she kept in a secret hiding place, concealed from Stasia — into her handbag, and lay down on her bed with a racing heart.

★

Black-clad security guards asked again and again to see her invitation, but she stubbornly insisted that they go and fetch the host. She felt their astonished eyes on her back, on her hips, and knew she would get in. She knew, too, that she would succeed in turning back time. They conferred among themselves; one of their number was dispatched into the illuminated villa. There was an embarrassed clearing of throats; they were visibly uncomfortable at the thought of having to turn this beauty away just because she wasn't on the guest list.

Limousines drew up outside the villa; ladies in elegant dresses and men in dark suits got out. And in their midst, Christine, uninvited, yet attracting everyone's attention. Standing there in this dress in front of these high gates, it was so easy to be the old Christine, the woman everyone turned to look at, whom everyone marvelled at, who was loved, and who loved, without even knowing it, with such excruciating completeness. Loved her big, sad, disillusioned husband. It seemed so easy to believe that he was still alive ...

Then she saw *him* striding down the wide avenue of palms, through the beautiful garden he had created over the years and which surrounded his villa like a protective wall. With its stately cypresses and the lush greenery. Its exotic plants and little stone-paved paths. A real Shangri-La — if you didn't know who lived in this villa, who was lord of this magical garden.

He greeted some of his approaching guests, shook their hands, smiled. Suddenly, he stopped, his eyes fixed upon her. His expression changed, but at this distance she couldn't tell, couldn't decipher, what it was he was feeling. For a moment, she thought he would go back into the house and leave her standing at the entrance, but then he took a purposeful step towards her, ignored the other guests arriving, and like an emperor striding through his subjects — who fall back before him out of admiration, out of fear — he came to her. The guards stepped aside, allowing him to make a dramatic entrance, as if it were a carefully rehearsed piece of choreography. She smiled the most enchanting smile she could muster and held out her hand. He clasped it in his warm, moist fingers, and his face assumed an expression of the most profound humility.

'I thought you wouldn't want to accept my invitation; I didn't want to put you in an awkward situation.'

'And now I've put *you* in an awkward situation.' She said it quietly, scarcely moving her lips. She said it not apologetically but proudly, in a tone of mild reproach.

'No, no, don't be silly. Please — you are my most welcome guest!' he replied, and offered her his arm. It happened so quickly; she was assigned the role of empress so quickly. And she accepted the offer: tonight she would play this part with the greatest of pleasure. And this time she would need no rehearsal. For she had had time to prepare herself for the role, ever since the night her face was split in two.

★

Intoxicatingly beautiful, provocatively flaunting her beauty. Confident, unapproachable, she stepped through the great gates. At his side, on his arm.

Beneath the burning, envious gaze of the illustrious assembled company.

She entered the packed ballroom: floors of finest marble, gold ornamentation on the hand-crafted stucco that adorned the incredibly high ceilings. Already the chamber orchestra was playing, champagne corks popping, alcohol flowing.

Only the powerful and the beautiful were here. The most powerful and the most beautiful. Men who for years had done nothing but play at being gods, and women who spent their lives in a state of constant, self-absorbed exhilaration. The best singers from the National Opera House performed arias, because the host loved grandeur and opulence, he loved the monumental — yes, he loved beauty.

Christine didn't let him out of her sight all evening. The Little Big Man, at the heart of his marble palace, drinking champagne, talking animatedly to his guests, listening, entranced, to the singers and to the chamber orchestra which, terrified of making a mistake, gave a truly first-rate performance. She watched him dispense compliments, carelessly brushing countless bare shoulders and arms as he passed, hips and breasts draped in light, floating material; making witty jokes, sparkling amid this spectacle of horror.

Decades later, Brilka, when digging up part of the garden, the human rights organisation then resident in the building — let's call that an irony of fate! — would come across human remains, and this discovery would lead to a lengthy debate in Georgian society over what should be done with the house. Some people demanded that the municipal government demolish it, raze it, erase from the collective memory all the horrors — whatever they may have been — that had taken place within these walls. Others wanted to preserve this architectural marvel; some just shrugged their shoulders, unable to come up with a solution. Nobody inquired about the dead; nobody tried to trace them.

> Sing not, my love, sad Georgia's songs,
> For they recall to me once more
> A place for which the heart still longs,
> Another life, a distant shore.
>
> ALEXANDER PUSHKIN

Christine joined the ranks of the elegant ladies, who were all listening to the sounds of the orchestra and looking very moved by them, and who pinched each other's elbows as soon as Christine arrived.

The Little Big Man raised his hairless head, pressed his round glasses more firmly onto his mole-like eyes, and stood motionless, as a pale woman and a short, fat man in a green suit launched into 'O soave fanciulla' from *La Bohème*. His eyes kept meeting Christine's across the room, across the many shoulders, necks, heads, arms, mouths, and glances. As the soprano responded to the tenor's declaration of love with '*Ah, tu sol comandi, amor*!', he walked up to her and stood by her side, and that was when she knew she would win. Tonight, she would win. She towered over him by almost a head — she and her body that she flaunted so openly, a body that was not disfigured, that the acid had spared. As if by accident, he touched her shoulder with his.

The singers' voices united in harmony, soft as butter, and he whispered in her ear in his sticky, soft, West Georgian dialect, 'Stay here, stay until they've all gone. You are so stunningly beautiful.' And she nodded, turning her head slightly away from him.

The exhilarating atmosphere was tremendously seductive; everyone loved to lose themselves in it. And at this exclusive ball, Christine sat in majesty on the high throne of fearlessness. She had already lost everything; there was nothing left for her to lose. She didn't need to contort herself, didn't need to hide anything, as the other guests did; didn't need to be loved and accepted by them. She triumphed over those who envied her, over their fearful dependency, over their burning desire to be counted among the vassals of their host.

Again and again, she slipped her hand into her handbag and felt for the slabs of dark chocolate, the little bottles of spices.

She had never believed her sister; she didn't believe in curses, or gods, not any more: the red star had supplanted all gods long ago. But for this one night, she wanted to believe in them again. She was hoping for their support. For this one night, she would borrow her sister's belief. She would believe that the black temptation her father had created possessed the power ascribed to it by Stasia. That these ingredients in her handbag could be the source of the sweetest revenge. She would believe in it, just for tonight.

Long after midnight, the room began to empty. He commanded the exhausted musicians to play a waltz just for the two of them, and with impeccable manners he asked Christine to dance. He danced with her slowly, out of time, wearied by all the golden champagne, but with great devotion. It occurred to her that she had never danced with him before. Yet how often she had danced with Ramas. Perhaps this time she would manage to close her eyes and imagine her husband leading her across this room, so proud to be holding his Christine in his arms. So happy.

She put her arm around his narrow shoulders. She accepted that for one night she was mistress of this cruel world. One of those countless women who liked to let themselves be dazzled and exhilarated by the sheen of ignorance, of repression, of obliviousness, rejecting all responsibility for tomorrow because their purpose in this world was pleasure and delight, to arouse male passions, to love and be loved.

★

I always imagine them, after this, going up the wide marble staircase to his private chambers, entering the enormous bedroom that Christine had had to enter so often before, in her previous life. I imagine that she was the one who stopped in front of him and began to take off her clothes; imagine her undoing the button at the back of her neck with a single flick of her hand, the soft fabric falling to the ground; imagine her making herself indispensable to him.

Satisfaction was what she felt at that moment: the satisfaction of suspending time for a few hours, the time between the present and the past. Of disrupting it, letting it slip completely out of joint. Not so that she could be young again, and beautiful, with a whole face instead of half of one, but because for a fraction of a second it felt as if Ramas were still alive. If she was sleeping with *him*, if she had to sleep with *him*, if she was here, in this room, on this bed, she could imagine that afterwards she would drive home and wait there for her husband. Her husband, who knew everything, who had understood everything long ago, even the future.

I always imagine, Brilka, that she was prepared to take this man in her arms over and over again in order to give herself the gift of this one lie. Anything was better than Ramas' death. Perhaps tonight she would manage not to think of her husband's body beneath the sheet, the husband for whom she had not been able to weep because she had had no face with which to do so.

He leaned over and kissed her neck. Her unblemished neck.

She sensed in herself a strange, alarming lack of inhibition, as if she had taken off a corset for the first time in many, many years. A corset of nightmares. She lay down on the bed. Her body naked, her face half veiled. He bent over her; she removed his pince-nez, stared into his eyes, and pressed her lips to his. Hard, harder, she would give him everything, everything, so that in her thoughts she could, just once, bring Ramas back to life; so that in her imagination she could, just once, have a whole face again, not a monstrous cratered landscape. Beside the bed was a framed photograph of his wife: soft, silent Nina. Christine banished the question of how much self-hatred one person could take, and clasped her arms around him.

Yes, I imagine how effortlessly she faked passion for him in order to reclaim her past. How she remembered Ramas; how she believed — yes, Brilka, it is that macabre — that she could be close to her husband again by being with his murderer. How she took control, took the lead in this game he had mastered so well. I imagine *him* gazing on her sundered beauty, growing intoxicated on it again and again. Imagine the barbed wire around her heart slowly loosening until she believed she had cut through reality and entered the realm of ghosts.

And then I see her rise up above him, like an ancient goddess appearing in order to dispense mercy or to condemn. In my mind's eye, I see her look at him, euphoric at the thought of what is to come, making him uncertain as to what that look might mean. See her sit up and slowly, with deliberate, controlled, very precise movements, remove her mask. Unveil her face. Her moonstruck beauty and her unbearable ugliness. Possibly feeling pleasure at being able to reveal to the man who had caused it the damage from which he had fled so many years ago.

He had wanted to look at her back then, that New Year's Eve; he couldn't abide her mask. Now he had no choice: the damage had become part of her face, he couldn't now remove the rough, maltreated visage, and for the first time in her life she felt a cruel gratitude that the nightmare was recorded in her face.

She let him look.

'I have a request,' she said.

'Anything you want,' he said, and looked away.

'I've brought something for you. I just have to prepare it. I'd like to thank you. For Andro. I'll go down to the kitchen, then I'll bring you my surprise. And I want you to taste it. I'll taste it, too,' she added, so as not to arouse his suspicion.

He nodded, relieved that she was going to leave the room, that he would no longer be forced to endure the sight of her corroded features.

She went downstairs, naked as she was, as God and the Little Big Man had made her, and prepared the hot chocolate.

She served the black, sinful concoction with the magical fragrance on a silver tray. She sat beside him on the bed, her right side turned towards him so as not to spoil his appetite, and thrust her finger into the thick, sticky mass. Then she licked off the chocolate. Fascinated, he brought his open mouth towards her and waited for her to feed him from her finger. Patiently, with great satisfaction, she initiated him in her father's secret. He devoured the chocolate; he wolfed it down.

★

At the Central Committee meeting on 26 June 1953, the day my mother came into the world, the Little Big Man was arrested. This was the culmination of a conspiracy by the other nine members of the Politburo, headed by Nikita Khrushchev.

The Little Big Man had come back from summer manoeuvres in Smolensk, where they had sent him to gain time while they meticulously planned his disempowerment. The meeting began in the conference room, in the Little Big Man's presence. One hour later, five armed men from a special division entered the room. Meanwhile, seventeen members of the MVD, the Little Big Man's vassals, were sitting in an antechamber with not the slightest inkling of what was happening behind closed doors.

'He is to be arrested in the name of the law,' declared Malenkov, and weapons were drawn. The same Malenkov who, like the Little Big Man, had been one of the Generalissimus' closest confidants; who had an estimated 150,000 people killed over the thirty years of his activities in Armenia and Belarus;

the Chairman of the Council of Ministers, nicknamed 'Malania' on account of his wide hips and squeaky voice; a man of whom the Little Big Man was supposed to have said, 'If the Leader gives an order for one person to be killed, Malenkov kills a thousand.'

This Malania, this caricature of a ringleader, now stood alongside Khrushchev, in front of *him* — the most feared man in the whole Soviet Union, the man the Leader himself had called 'our Himmler' — ordering guns to be levelled at him! In the Little Big Man's inside pocket was a crumpled piece of paper with the word 'Alarm' written on it, over and over again. It seems that he'd suspected something was up before the meeting, but had had no opportunity to pass the paper to his guards.

On the night of 26 June, the Little Big Man was secretly smuggled out of the Kremlin in the back of an SIS-110 and taken to an interrogation facility. The interrogation continued for six months; he confessed to little, but wrote numerous letters of pardon or accusation to various Central Committee members, such that in the end he was even banned from writing and corresponding from prison.

For the first time, his melancholy wife, Nina, grew active. She appealed to one of her husband's colleagues and wrote a letter to Malania. She was sure, she wrote, that this must be a misunderstanding; she believed in her husband, believed that he was a true communist who had always acted in the interests of the Motherland, Lenin's legacy, and the great Generalissimus; finally she requested that, if he had indeed committed some crime of which he had been unaware, she, too, should be held fully responsible. The Central Committee members were impressed by such loyalty; particularly those among them who had denied their own wives, brothers, parents, and friends at their Leader's behest and had them arrested. In December 1953, a secret trial was held: the death sentence was pronounced, and apparently carried out the same day. He was shot. The body was burned. Nina's wish was disregarded; she was left alive. She was to be granted many more years in which to preserve her husband's memory and maintain her blind fidelity.

The trial records are preserved in forty volumes. The indictment includes accusations ranging from unlawful persecution, arrests, and torture, to rapes, misuse of office, poisoning, and shootings. Yet the Little Big Man pleaded 'Not guilty' right up to the day of his execution.

★

Once the great power struggle had been won, and Malania too was swept aside, the Generalissimus' great empire passed into the hands of a peasant boy from Kalinovka named Khrushchev, who had been to school for all of two years before his father declared that all the boy needed to be able to do was count to thirty, as he'd never earn more than thirty roubles anyway. So far, Khruschev's socialist career had been an enviable one. As early as 1937, he had written to the Generalissimus to say that he had personally identified 8,500 enemies of the system who, in his eyes, deserved to die; which was why 'our hand must not tremble, we must march across the corpses of the enemy for the good of the people'. For this, he was rewarded. Very generously. And now here he was, where his father would never have dreamed it possible for him to be. The peasant boy from Kalinovka who was to admit, shortly before the end of his life, 'My arms are up to the elbows in blood.'

> he left many heirs
> behind on this globe.
> I fancy
> there's a telephone in that coffin:
> the Generalissimus
> sends his instructions.
> From that coffin where else does the cable go!
> No, he has not given up.
> He thinks he can
> cheat death.
>
> YEVGENY YEVTUSHENKO

Kitty sat in Amy's kitchen hunched over the *Evening Standard,* which had a photograph of the Little Big Man splashed across the front page. Her body was racked by violent sobs. It was the third year in which she had heard nothing from her family, and her fearful longing had by now already assumed monstrous proportions. However, this was also the day when she admitted to herself that she loved a woman. Following her morning argument with Amy, Fred Lieblich had once again moved out of the house and retired to her studio on the pretext that she was in a productive phase.

Kitty had been avoiding Fred ever since their fateful encounter. Overcome with remorse and horror that she had let herself be seduced by a woman, she started spending more time at the jazz club. She would stay later than usual, sitting at people's tables after her performance and drinking a lot of whisky. She allowed customers to engage her in conversation, and played the part of the Soviet sensation to the hilt. She played up to people's fears and projections, and accentuated them with more horrific details. Little by little, she even began to enjoy it. Her imagination spat out ever wilder and more colourful tales of her communist past; scenarios became increasingly exciting and dangerous.

But although she let a few men buy her drinks, give her presents, and persuade her to accompany them to the cinema, and although she even permitted a few kisses on Amy's doorstep, none of it helped. She had now mastered the English language, but that didn't make any difference, either: the fact was that she had nothing to say to the people she met, nor did she wish to say anything to them. The only person she longed to hear speak was her anonymous friend. The only woman she wanted to speak to was Fred.

And whenever she couldn't help overhearing the two women giggling and teasing each other in the dining room, she was overcome by piercing jealousy; she wanted to run down and seize Fred, drag her up to her room, and tell her everything that was going through her mind. But she was too ashamed of her yearning, and instead would bury her face in the pillow, deep enough for their voices and laughter not to reach her.

One day, she plucked up all her courage, took the Underground to Soho, and looked for the address she had surreptitiously copied from Amy's address book. She secretly hoped that she wouldn't be in, that she wouldn't open the door to her, that she would have a visitor. But she was in, opened the door on the very first ring, and immediately invited Kitty in. She was alone. Kitty went on standing outside, as if she feared she would never find her way out again.

Fred stood in the doorway, observing her unexpected guest, tilting her head slightly. Then a smile spread across her lips.

'Please stop doing that.'

'What?'

'You always look at me like that, so ... Especially when Amy's there.'

'And when she isn't there?'

Fred seemed to find her embarrassment amusing. She lit a cigarette and leaned against the wall.

'So you absolutely don't want to come in? Or take off your coat? Or have tea with me? Or see my paintings?'

Kitty shook her head. Over and over again, as if reaffirming to herself what it was she wanted. Fred held out her hand. Not a single ring; short, clipped fingernails, very clean for a painter. She didn't move. Waited. She was, in fact, certain that Kitty would follow her. When she continued to hesitate, Fred dropped her hand and ran off as if someone were chasing her, disappearing into the big studio space Kitty didn't dare peep into. Music started up. Then the hostess reappeared with two wine glasses in her hand. They were sure to have come from Amy's drinks cabinet.

'This is beautiful. What is it?' asked Kitty. She couldn't help smiling at the sight of Fred making herself comfortable on the hall floor. She patted the ground beside her, inviting Kitty to sit down.

'You don't know Billie Holiday? — Okay, fine; if you don't want to come in, I'll come out. But I wouldn't have expected you not to know Billie Holiday. *You* of all people should know her.'

Hesitantly, Kitty sat on the floor, utterly mesmerised by the voice and its infinite sadness.

'You need to breathe, my beauty! More air, more freedom. You must be yourself again,' said Fred suddenly, and her tone was serious, thoughtful, the mischievousness gone from her voice.

'What do you want from me?' asked Kitty guardedly. She raised the wine glass to her lips.

'You,' said Fred, laughing again. 'Just you.'

'You're a woman.'

'Correct: I think you're familiar with my sex?'

'And Amy?'

'Amy doesn't need me.'

'She does need you, very much!'

'We're a good team. Believe me.'

Before Kitty could reply, Fred was already leaning over her, closing in on her mouth. Her kiss was no longer cautious. It was what it was: a kiss that would lead to many more.

'How do you think this is going to work?' asked Kitty, turning her head away. 'You know nothing about me.'

'I know everything I need to know. I see you.'

'I can't betray another person, not again. I can't do it.'

'Just close your eyes. Nothing's going to happen to you. I'll take care of you.'

★

Three months after the birth of my mother, a woman in a village in the Caucasus had a baby boy who was given the name Miqail. His family name was Eristavi.

That night, Stasia dreamed of her dead friend Sopio. She appeared to her — bright, affectionate, with a conciliatory smile on her lips — sitting in an armchair in an unfamiliar room, gazing out of the window at a sunny garden. Overwhelmed by the sight of her beautiful friend, who seemed not to have aged a single day despite the passage of almost twenty years, Stasia stopped in the doorway and stared at Sopio stretching in the sunlight.

'Come on in, Taso, it's warmer over here,' called Sopio. She beckoned to her. 'Don't be afraid.'

Stasia went to her dead friend and perched cautiously on the arm of the chair. The sunlight poured through the window, dazzling her and warming her cheeks.

'I've missed you,' Stasia whispered through the warm sunbeams. She stroked Sopio's shoulder tentatively.

'Yes, it's been a long time, hasn't it?'

'A very long time. Are you angry with me?'

'You couldn't have changed anything. It's so warm, so warm here, isn't it?'

'Sopio. How I miss you. My Sopio!'

Suddenly, Sopio clasped Stasia's hand. Her hand felt velvety and delicate, young and full of strength. Stasia was speechless. There was so much she wanted to say, so much to explain, confess, but she couldn't seem to do it; it was as if, all of a sudden, she had no words.

'Tell my boy stories of a good world. Do that. Do that!'

No sooner had Sopio said this, and stroked Stasia's head once again, than Stasia woke with a start.

★

The father of the boy who came into the world that stormy September evening was a taciturn *kolkhoz* worker who carved wooden figures in his room in secret by the light of a kerosene lamp (electricity was a scarce commodity in the mountains), and hid them under his bed, in case the figures were seen as immoral or destructive.

He had married a devout peasant girl who worked on the same shift as him at the grain factory; who sometimes brought him pickled tomatoes and plums, was one of the few who asked him how he was, and didn't watch him with stern, suspicious eyes, unlike most of the villagers, who saw the stranger with the full beard and bald head as a thorn in their side. Because he didn't know how to distil schnapps, because he wasn't one for making noisy drinking toasts, because he didn't ogle the girls, because he took no part in celebrations, be they heathen, Christian, or public holidays, because he refused to sacrifice sheep for the sake of a good harvest, and because from time to time he travelled to the provincial capital, went to the library there, and returned with books under his arm.

He felt profound humility before the rites of these people, who lived so free of doubt, so far removed from any kind of modernity, as if operating by a different calendar; but at the same time he loathed their tradition-steeped intransigence, their superstition, their unwillingness to place anything above the laws of their ancestors.

Every day he would try afresh not to look back. And every day the image of almond-eyed Kitty, the woman with whom he had wanted to share his vision of the world, faded a little more. Gradually, he learned that life consisted of breathing, eating, digesting, hard physical work, drinking schnapps, and sleeping, and that he had no right to expect anything else of it.

A human warmth he thought he had lost returned to him with the birth of his son: it commandeered the whole of his chest and made his heart swell. He was truly moved, for the first time in years, by the tiny bundle he held in his arms. Perhaps, he thought, through the child he would learn to love again, too.

One afternoon, when it had already started to turn cold, he went out into the street with the peacefully sleeping baby wrapped up snugly in a hand-knitted shawl. He walked past the farm and the stony path that led down to the valley; he passed the neighbouring houses, the factory, the shops, the school, met the shepherds driving their sheep back from the meadow, greeted the black-clad war widows sitting together as they did every evening around the village fountain, and the village elders in the square in front of the church, came to the village library, which housed nothing that had been written in the past forty years, and passed children playing, racing down the slope, noisy and sweaty, with a sheepdog at their heels; on he walked, into the evening, and came to the quarry in the southern part of the forest surrounding the valley. There he sat down on a large stone, not far from a waterfall that cascaded with immense force into the depths — heedless, imperious — and looked around. Miqa (as the boy would come to be known) went on sleeping peacefully in his arms; not even the ferocious sound of the water seemed to bother him. And Andro closed his eyes, hugged his son close, took a deep breath, and smiled. He had come here in order to be able to smile again. And when he smiled, he saw her face before him: the face of the young Kitty with whom he had shared first kisses on a green bench in a sleepy little town, and to whom he had dedicated all his ideas. And he remembered the war. He remembered the gulag. He remembered the dehumanisation he had experienced, which was apparently so easy to accept, as if the true nature of mankind were to be inhuman.

★

Telling this story, Brilka, I sometimes feel as if I can't breathe. Then I have to stop, go over to the window, and take a deep breath. It's not because I just can't find the right words, not because of the punishing gods, judges, and omnipresent choirs. Nor is it because of all the stories clamouring to be told. It's because of the blanks.

The stories overlap, intertwine, merge into one — I'm trying to untangle this skein of wool because you have to tell things one after another, because you can't put the simultaneity of the world into words.

When I was about the same age as you, Brilka, I often used to wonder what would happen if the world's collective memory had retained different things and lost others. If we had forgotten all the wars and all those countless kings, rulers, leaders, and mercenaries, and the only people to be read about in books were those who had built a house with their own hands, planted a garden, discovered a giraffe, described a cloud, praised the nape of a woman's neck. I wondered how we know that the people whose names have endured were better, cleverer, or more interesting just because they've stood the test of time. What of those who are forgotten?

We decide what we want to remember and what we don't. Time has nothing to do with it. Time doesn't care. But the injustice of our story, Brilka, is that neither you nor I have been granted the possibility of recalling everything, including all those who have been forgotten — the injustice is that I too must choose, for you; I must decide what's worth telling and what isn't, which seems to me at times an impossible task. I am fighting against my own personal, entirely subjective memory. Since I started to write our story down for you — this Where, How, and Why — I've been alone. But I'll tell you more about that later, when it's time to tell the story of my life, when at last I have been born and come alive within this realm of words.

For this, I have set aside all my own needs, if indeed I had any. I've even forbidden myself my daily dose of melancholy and devoted myself entirely to my task. After the last few years, in which I got so lost, went so far astray, this almost monastic asceticism and iron discipline did and does me good. It's my journey. It's a sort of cleansing process, in the course of which I myself am changing — and I don't even know what my final shape will be.

Tonight — it's Friday, and the warm evening has driven even more people out of doors — I could already tell that I needed to pause again for a moment. The noise, the clinking of glasses and bottles, the music — all this was mingling beneath my windows, creating that enticing, inescapable symphony of summer and making it impossible for me to concentrate on the task in hand. The present is too alive, too intrusive, and I can't listen to the past.

So I got up, went over to the window, opened it, let the hot, summery, dusty air into my room, and looked down on the heads of passers-by. And then something strange happened. In the distance, over by the crossroads, where the homeless man greets me every day and tries to sell me his newspaper — I saw Stasia standing there. No, I haven't gone mad; I don't believe in madness, in any case — but all the same ...

That was when I knew that the ghosts have come to me now; and I also knew that it really is the right thing to do, to record their stories for you. Ours. Yours. Mine, and those of all the others who have written their lives into ours. I suddenly knew why I was doing this, and that it was right to do it. I knew that I was carrying out a duty, the duty of an axe that shatters time: for you. Suddenly, all my doubts were gone.

I understood that one day all of them will come, all the ghosts with a story they have yet to finish telling, and they will pore over my words. And I laughed aloud. Yes, I laughed. I thought of you. I missed you terribly, with an unbearable longing, but I also felt a sense of relief — yes, I did.

I have finally arrived in that timeless time beyond the bounds of law, and even if I am losing my connection to the reality of the present a little more each day, even if I am less and less sure of what moves the people out there and what awaits me after all this, I do know what question I will put to you at the end of this journey, this story. Even if you're still far away, not here, even if you're still unaware of any of this, even if you feel justified anger towards me — I will come back. To you. And I will ask you my question, and you will give me your answer.

> How can we act as if we didn't know what went on?
>
> KHRUSHCHEV

They say she laughed all the time, as a baby and then as a child. My mother: Elene Jashi, Stasia's granddaughter, Christine's great-niece, Kitty's niece, and the daughter of Kostya and Nana. Mother to Daria and me. The woman who resembled no one, not even herself. The woman who for no apparent reason would decide to atone for her greatest mistake through her children.

They say she was very quick, as a child, quick to think, to want, to demand. She came into the world in the year of bewilderment, in the year of newly revived hopes, in this vast empire that now no longer exists. Her father took a leave of absence from his top-secret mission and spent a few weeks, enraptured and euphoric, at the side of his exhausted wife and laughing daughter. The casual calmness with which Christine and Stasia greeted Elene's birth seemed to Nana much healthier and more desirable than the excessive solicitude of her own family: she would retreat to her darkened room when the visits from her aunts and mother, with their top child-rearing tips, became too much for her. She felt she was in good hands here, and against all the advice of her relatives and girlfriends, Nana decided not to go and join Kostya for the time being.

★

When Christine heard of the Little Big Man's death, she fetched her old gramophone from the attic and played *Norma* so loudly it could be heard all over the house. She stood at the window looking out at the garden and listening to the music. Her expression remained a mystery: it betrayed nothing, neither pain nor alarm that the curse of the chocolate had proved true. Her sister had been right all along!

From that day on, she started buying opera recordings, obsessively, as if she had decided to amass a rare and valuable record collection. No sum was too high for her. Less than a year later, by which time my mother was refusing to start walking, Christine owned an impressive collection ranging from Purcell to Puccini. In the evenings, the whole house succumbed to the soprano and bass voices from the gramophone: the warmer it was outside, the faster the voices would swallow up the area around the house and its unruly garden, reaching the narrow cobbled streets of this part of town and touching the tops of the towers of the old, empty church.

Christine listened, spellbound, and refused to turn the music down, until in the end all those living in the house found themselves forced to tolerate her operas as the constant background music to their daily lives.

★

The unruliness began with the advent of freedom in the family house in Tbilisi. With Elene's birth. With her first sounds.

The plants sensed it, and sprouted like mad in the garden. Bit by bit, they also invaded the house. Even items of furniture started to emit curious noises, and all kinds of birds held their parliaments in the attic. Butterflies and crickets sought out the house, stray cats strolled around it, squirrels and martens were found.

The house sighed. It was bursting at the seams, taking off the tight corset that had held it in for years. It began to live. Noisily, expansively, palpably, and visibly.

The older inhabitants of the house didn't seem bothered by this degeneration; quite the opposite, in fact. The spiders and butterflies were welcomed; the plaster that occasionally came off the ceiling remained where it fell; the plants were no longer pruned; even the frogs that had set up home in the fountain were left in peace. The dust that gathered everywhere was not wiped away. Stasia even bought herself a hand-reared grey parrot, and christened him Goya. No one cleared up the crockery and lampshades, either, as they fell victim to Goya's aerobatics.

The only person annoyed by the rapidly progressing dilapidation was Nana, who tackled it with every means at her disposal. She ran around after the noisy bird, cleaned and scrubbed every day, and secretly hid any records she found lying about in order to avoid constant exposure to Christine's music. All her energy went into making the house look well-cared-for; she chased after vermin, shooed away cats, and put poison in the fountain for the frogs. She cried down the phone to Kostya, complaining about his mother's eccentricity and Christine's provocative passivity. He ought to speak to them; they wouldn't be a good example to the child. Elene would grow up amid chaos, and nothing good could come of it. Given the disorder in the house and the two sisters' neglect, Nana decided not to go back to university; she would put her doctorate on hold for the time being and devote herself entirely to being a mother.

My grandfather accepted these developments from afar, since they could not be influenced, but it was a burden Nana struggled with her entire life. Although Kostya was always quick to send money whenever Nana complained, so that rooms could be freshly wallpapered, pipes repaired, and a swing seat acquired for the garden, and although she even employed a gardener to come once a week to curtail the wild proliferation of the plants, the house contrived nonetheless to gradually transform itself into a fairy-tale dwelling, as if it had only just realised its true destiny and now intended to enjoy it to the full.

It meant that my mother was able to spend her childhood in an enchanted realm. As soon as her mother handed her over to her grandmother and great-aunt — which she did most reluctantly, as their educational methods were far from reliable — Elene's world was transformed into a place without constraints, where she was allowed to play with the parrot, wallow in dirt, smash the crockery, climb and romp about, eat sweet things, pull Christine's hair, and make faces with Stasia. In this enchanted world, with these two old women, it seemed to her that anything was possible, anything was conceivable, anything was doable. Here, nothing stood in her way; and there was no one who could have been made happier by this state of affairs than a growing girl to whom all doors were open.

★

At the Party Congress in the year 1956, in a secret speech that nonetheless became famous, the First Secretary of the Central Committee, Nikita Khrushchev, sharply criticised the Generalissimus and publicly used the word 'crimes' in reference to his predecessor's brutal purges. He spoke of 'mass extermination' and 'execution without trial'; he also spoke of his own responsibility, and asked, 'How can we act as if we didn't know what went on?' We are told there was an eerie silence; almost all those present, including the First Secretary, had participated in these arrests and executions with impressive dedication. Yet it was so unheard-of for someone even to name what had really gone on that doing so called into question all the rules, structures, and internal agreements that had applied until that moment. Until then, the silence and taboos surrounding certain political practices in the USSR had signified stability for the country. Now, after these words, no one knew what was to come.

When the speech found its way into the public domain, students began to demonstrate on the streets of Tbilisi. People were shocked; they felt aggrieved. Their national identity was being called into question; their great countryman, who over the course of decades had pacified the boundless Russian Empire, was being declared a criminal. Even people whose parents and grandparents had fallen victim to this countryman of theirs could not endure the truth, though they must have been aware of it for years. It was absolutely outrageous, the things that Ukrainian lout was coming out with. People stormed onto the streets and boulevards, surrounded the university, blocked crossroads, rebelled against the truth. Because the victims had long since become perpetrators; the perpetrators, victims.

The system continued to exact its toll. People were afraid of memories, of insights, knowing these might drag them into a bottomless pit, twist their own lives out of all recognition, and all of this could cause self-loathing to swell to immeasurable proportions. Besides, where was all this wretched truth-telling heading?

When the security forces rallied to oppose the students — the same security forces who a few years earlier had fought to oppose this truth — it became clear that the truth would be a hollow one, without serious consequences. Perhaps a few restrictions would be eased, a few bullet holes revealed through which it might be possible to see one's life from a different perspective: but who actually wanted to do that? What could you do with this view of things, other than subordinate yourself to this truth until it buried you beneath it?

The indescribable always builds a defensive wall around the describable, Brilka.

The Central Committee had started to announce an audacious turnaround, which was to go down in history as the 'Khrushchev Thaw'. I believe that this point in the history of the Soviet Union was a singular moment, one that would never come again — and, just as singularly, nobody took advantage of it. People opted for the old way of doing things. They could have bolstered Khrushchev's ego, let him play the hero and liberator a while longer; they should have expected those in power to show remorse and penitence for longer, and perhaps it really would have brought about viable reform. Reform that would have actually taken root, not the ridiculous prohibitions that masqueraded as reform.

Press censorship was eased, previously banned books were printed, the powers of security officials were curtailed, torture was outlawed, music that prior to this had not been heard anywhere was played, the silent were granted a voice. Gulags were closed, political prisoners released, hundreds of thousands of people acquitted. New residential zones were built; many people moved out of the seedy *kommunalkas* and got their own bathrooms, toilets, kitchens, things that had been an inconceivable luxury until then. People acquired a little privacy. And they showed gratitude for the little morsels of freedom they were thrown.

But the steps towards freedom were strictly numbered. For power always proves sweeter than revenge. And the further the 20th Party Congress retreated into the mists of the past, the sweeter the temptation became to demonstrate that power again, to let it shine once more.

When the wave of uprisings reached Eastern Europe and Hungarian students took to the streets in collective rebellion and a public expression of anger, the authorities reverted to the old ways, and blood began to flow all over again.

The Party feared a loss of control. The priority now was to take things firmly in hand. Threats were made, the army sent in, and all those who had believed in reform and run out onto the street were swiftly brought to heel. And 'peace' returned to this vast empire once more.

★

Nana and Elene travelled to the 'cold sea' in the north — this was how Nana would always describe any sea that wasn't the Black one. She had never been here before; it was the first time she had visited Kostya's world. She arrived at her husband's apartment, which, she discovered, was in an attractive old building and sparsely but tastefully furnished. She enjoyed the long walks along the promenade, the view of the harbour late in the evening. She marvelled at the raspberry and blueberry bushes that lined the country roads when they took Kostya's Volga and drove out of the city to spend the weekend at one of his friends' dachas or enjoy the heat of a Russian sauna. She enjoyed the classical concerts in Kislovodsk, where they spent a long weekend taking the health-giving waters.

She enjoyed the opportunities and prestige that came with her husband's high rank, as well as his undivided attention, his presents, the quiet evenings — rare, but all the more precious for it — spent together in the apartment, the breakfasts and dinners they ate together. She enjoyed the care he bestowed on Elene, his delight in her, for Kostya proved a besotted father, bursting with pride in his lively, chubby-cheeked daughter, and full of loving feelings for her. Nana kept asking herself whether these evenings with just the three of them, these long walks beside the sea, constituted happiness; whether this was what love felt like.

She took great pains to be a good wife, and to rein in her secret resentment of Stasia's and Christine's unworldliness. She did this out of respect for her husband; and she wanted to be a good mother to Elene, one who set clearly defined boundaries and rules, and paid her enough attention. Although she found it difficult, she even tried to show an interest in her husband's work.

But something had come over her since Elene's birth, something melancholy and leaden that seemed entirely out of character for her. Since becoming a member of this family and living with her idiosyncratic mother-in-law and her sister, she had been afflicted by this strange heaviness, and she didn't like it. She barely recognised herself.

Kostya was certainly a good husband; at least, that was what everyone around her said. He never insisted on things, had even bowed to her will and let her stay in their homeland, had not summoned her to join him in this foreign place, although he would have been well within his rights to do so. He enabled her to have a good life, he was attentive, gallant, he was a wonderful father — and yet there were days, when Kostya was at work at the port authority or busy on one of the freighters, when she felt as if she were paralysed, oddly apathetic, as if this family had drained all her resistance, as if between the two peculiar, unworldly sisters she had voluntarily surrendered responsibility for her own life. Sometimes her endeavours seemed to her to be futile: her pursuit of order, clarity, her yearning for clear structures.

★

'You never talk about the past, Kostya. Why not? Nor do your mother and your aunt. I know so little about you all. I found a box of old photos in the attic recently. You don't even have a proper family album. It's strange.'

They were walking along the beach on a quiet afternoon. Kostya smiled at Elene, who was drawing shapes in the wet sand and so totally engrossed in what she was doing that their conversation passed her by.

'She is very pretty. A colleague we met at lunch yesterday kept saying so. Don't you think so, too? That Elene is a remarkably pretty child?' he asked, instead of responding to her question.

'You see, you always change the subject, all of you. It's like a family tradition.'

'What is it you want to know? Just ask me.' Kostya was irritated.

'Are you actually happy? I don't even know if you're happy, for example. With me.'

'You don't ask something like that, Nana. You can just tell.'

'But you're always so ... hmm ... self-controlled.'

'Aren't you?'

'I don't know.'

'You don't know?'

'No.'

'That sounds rather naive. You do know that, don't you?'

'Well, then it's naive; my God, I don't know that. I don't know what *that* is.'

'You see? The problem you accuse others of having is the problem you have with yourself. You're the discontented one. I don't stop you from doing anything, I don't restrict you, do I? Do I?'

'No.'

'So ask yourself why that is. We have an adorable daughter, we have a good life, we —'

'Yes, I know. You're right. I'm sorry.'

Just at that moment, Elene, who had drawn a round face with a wide mouth and two dots for eyes and had added a mass of curls, cried out ecstatically: 'Kitty!'

Both Kostya and Nana abruptly fell silent. They went over to their daughter, who was pointing at her artwork, full of excitement and pride, looking up at her parents expectantly, waiting for their approval.

'Where has she got that from?' Kostya looked at his wife, who shook her head in bewilderment. 'She must have got it from someone. Did you talk about her — at home, I mean? You know that's not good. And my mother should know it best of all. In any case, I've asked you all repeatedly to make sure that this subject —'

'*I* have never talked to her about your sister.'

'She can't just have made it up, can she?'

'Elene, my darling ...' Nana bent down to her daughter. 'Who is that? Tell Mama again. Who is that in your picture?'

And Elene, very pleased with herself, repeated the same name over and over again: 'Kitty. Kitty. Kitty.'

★

That night, the couple lay in their heavy oak bed without speaking. Kostya had turned to face the wall, and Nana kept her eyes closed in the hope that she would be able to shake off all her questions and confusion. Finally, she couldn't stand it any more; she sat up in bed and turned on a little bedside lamp.

'Where is she? You know where she is.'

'I don't know.'

'Yes, you do. You got her out of the country. Tell me.'

'I don't know, and now please stop asking, I don't want you to talk about this subject in front of my daughter. Do you understand me?' There was an iciness in his voice, something Nana had never heard from him before, that brooked no contradiction.

'What did she do? What did she do to you?'

'Stop it, I said!'

He shouted so loudly that Nana flinched and put her hands over her ears. Her husband had never shouted at her like that. Nana started to feel frightened. She was frightened of the man who shared her bed, who had fathered a child with her in the dark one night, and who, in all the nights of love that followed, had never made a single sound. She was afraid of the silence that surrounded her, and of her own ever-increasing sense of powerlessness.

'What on earth's the matter?' Nana asked quietly, after a pause. She got up, went round, and perched on his side of the bed.

'I don't like to look back.'

'But Kostya, you can't live like that.'

'You have to. There's no point in doing anything else.'

Nana, confused and out of her depth, flung her arms around her husband's neck, hoping to soften him with her tenderness. He relented, let her kiss him and hold him tight, then finally lay on top of his soft wife, who had become a little plumper, rounder, more yielding, since the birth of her daughter; who smelled of raisins and fresh bread; whose hair hung down to her waist. His wife, lying beneath him, still young, radiant, full of life, and now full of questions, too. He pulled up her nightdress; his other hand reached out to the chest beside the bed, and he turned off the bedside lamp, as he always did when he was about to make love to her.

'Leave the light on,' whispered Nana — and received a very clear, loud 'No' in reply. She did not object. He moved his hand up her body, caressing her belly, her breasts, her neck; as always when they slept together, he seemed rather distant, rather brisk, rather absent. Before, she had accepted this sort of intimacy as something normal, natural; she had believed that this was how it was supposed to be. After all, she had nothing to compare it with. But Nana was intuitive enough to realise, as time went by, that making love had to be about more than just her husband's quick movements, which were almost like an assault; more than this act that always followed the same pattern; more than just wordlessness.

She pushed him off and climbed on top of him, gently removed his hand from her back and began to kiss his taut, strong body from head to foot. She felt her way, exploring every inch of his skin, every tiny mark, every slight curve, every little imperfection, every mole and every hollow. She hoped that lust would draw out his secrets; that this sensation, which suddenly overcame her more strongly than ever before, would soften him, too. She so wanted these answers from him; she so wanted, this night, truly to get to know him, truly to see him, to be able to see deeper and deeper inside him. She wanted this so much, for him at last to forget his iron discipline, his reticence and self-control, and for them to embark together in search of the unknown, to forge new paths. He must be able to break free of himself for once, to reveal what he was hiding; he must be able, at least once, to forget himself in her arms!

She struggled on, searching for the spots that would make him more accessible to her. And for a while she seemed to be on the right track: he did not resist her. He let himself be explored, breathed heavily; he closed his eyes, grabbed at her, unthinking. She conquered her shame — an unspoken thing, but one that set such firm boundaries — and raised herself up over his body. Something inside was telling her that he was familiar with this kind of passion, this lack of restraint. And at the same time the realisation frightened her, because she sensed how little this lack of inhibition had to do with her. Kostya, his eyes squeezed tightly shut, was revealing his lust to his wife; but she was just the proxy for another, and Nana wished she had never gone down this path, because now there was no going back, now there was nowhere to hide from the realisation of this night — the thing she had so cruelly and unerringly revealed to herself, which was that her husband's love did not belong to her.

Nana understood then that, deep within himself, he was incapable of forgetting, that he clung desperately to every single memory of his past, and this was precisely the reason he was constantly demanding that it be forgotten. It would take a while longer for her to discover that he was restless, restlessly seeking a point between the sea and the horizon where a meeting of past and present might be possible; and that the impossibility of ever reaching it drove him into the soft arms of countless beautiful, perfumed women.

After that night in the port city, it would no longer matter to her very much.

She would feel a sense of regret, a slight, stabbing pain, but she would no longer be capable of getting seriously upset about it, or doing anything to stop it. By then she would already have accepted indifference towards certain things as a permanent part of her life. And soon she would construct a carapace around herself, in the literal, physical sense: because on her return to her homeland from the 'cold sea', Nana began to put on weight — little by little, almost unnoticeably — until her circumference was such that it could wall in all her feelings.

★

Thanks to Amy's influential friends, Kitty succeeded in obtaining a residence permit, and then a valid work permit, more quickly than expected. Her audience at the jazz club was steadily growing, and Amy ran a tireless propaganda campaign on her protégée's behalf. Other clubs put in requests for this socialist insider tip. Soon Kitty was earning enough money to pay Amy some rent — well below what she could have asked for the flat, but it salved Kitty's wounded pride. After the arid Prague years, these were the years when Kitty's music blossomed. She composed and sang, let Amy put her lyrics into English, and eventually she even signed a contract with her benefactor. From then on, Amy was Kitty's manager, and keen to ensure that she would soon have her own record deal. Amy never tired of telling her fellow countrymen how great it was to help a talented, freedom-loving refugee from the enemy camp and provide her with the right opportunities. She put her organisational talent to work, and planned Kitty's career meticulously.

Kitty herself was simply happy to have such good fortune, and so many well-disposed people around her, to be able to make music and even earn money doing it. She expected no more of her future, and viewed Amy's ambitious efforts to make her a star with scepticism. However, she realised with regret that she missed *the voice* terribly, for their phone calls had become less frequent: she was no longer dependent on him to help her. They spoke only about essentials; he assured her that her family was well, told her about the general political situation in her homeland, and — as usual — nothing about himself.

Amy had grown accustomed to these phone calls; she asked no questions when Kitty retired to her room to hold a conversation in her mother tongue. At first it had bothered her, partly because Kitty wouldn't give her any explanation for these calls, but she had now come to accept these conversations as an integral part of Kitty's past, which was in any case off limits. In the meantime, Amy had often heard Kitty tell varying and contradictory anecdotes, and had realised how Kitty protected herself. She never spoke of the real reasons for her flight, and, if she talked about her family, it was only very sporadically. Besides, after these phone calls, Kitty was usually in a good mood and immediately started composing, which, after all, also benefited Amy.

On this particular evening, Kitty was sitting expectantly beside the phone. He never missed an appointment, and she loved that about him — his reliability. She had made herself a gin and tonic, and was waiting for the soft, soothing, so familiar voice. Sometimes she would picture his face; she imagined a tall, confident man with delicate features and thick, wavy hair. This voice deserved to have a body that matched.

'I'm so pleased you've called!' She wished she could address him informally, by name. 'Seven o'clock on the dot. I love your punctuality.'

'I'm pleased to hear your voice, too.'

She sensed slight embarrassment at the other end of the line.

'Will you go on calling me?'

'But I am calling you.'

'Even if you don't have to any more?'

'If you like.'

'I do like. I worry that you'll stop.'

'I will always call you, for as long as you need me.'

'It's not just that.'

'What is it, then?'

'I don't know. You're ... important to me.'

'Thank you very much. I thought I should give you a few tips concerning your new work permit ...'

'I don't want to talk about that now. May I ask you something?'

'Certainly.'

'Are you here? In the same city?'

'What gives you that idea?'

'You're here.'

'You know that, unfortunately, I can't —'

'It's all right. Do you like conkers? I saw some today. I love them. They remind me of home, of my childhood. Andro and I ... We always used to collect them, when we were children.'

'Yes, I like them.'

'What else do you like?'

'I like music. I like your music, too.'

'You haven't heard my music.'

'Yes, I have.'

Kitty thought for a while. Of course he was here, in London. They shared the same sky, the same streets, the same stations and faces. They shared the same rain and the same sun. It was a comforting thought. Perhaps he sat in her audience at the club, although she couldn't really imagine this genteel man in those surroundings.

'I would so like to know why you're doing all this. And what you're called.'

'You can call me whatever you like, I've already told you that. I'll gladly accept whatever name you give me.'

'I can't do it. There's no name that seems to fit ... to be good enough.' She heard him laugh: he seldom laughed.

'Is everything all right, Kitty?' he asked, his voice composed once more.

'I don't know. I'm confused.'

'What is it that's causing you confusion?'

'I love that about you, too. Your way of expressing yourself — like that: *What is it that's causing you confusion*. It's charming. You seem to me to be a daydreamer, and I've always had a great affinity for them.'

'I'm honoured.'

'I think I'm in love.'

'Well, that's wonderful.' There was no pleasure in his voice. He sounded very serious.

'No, it's not. I feel so foolish, so stupid. And I mustn't allow it.'

'Why not? Are there adverse circumstances?'

He's sure to be smiling to himself now, thought Kitty. She didn't want to pursue the subject, although she felt a deep longing to talk to him about it.

'I'd give so much to see your face right now,' she said.

Again the disconcerted silence at the other end of the line.

'Do what you think is right, and don't think about the adverse circumstances. Almost all adverse circumstances, or what we think of as such, seem but a trifle in retrospect, don't you agree?'

★

That somnambulant afternoon, with Billie Holiday in the background, Kitty had left Fred's studio with a clear *No*. As soon as she started thinking about copper-haired Fred, she came up against her own frontiers. She was trapped inside herself. That afternoon, she had run out because she didn't want to cross any more frontiers. Having crossed national frontiers, she capitulated before all others. She feared the consequences of her *No*, and feared the consequences of a conceivable *Yes* even more. She feared leaving the world that had been presented to her as the only right one, which was divided into men and women. She feared losing Amy's patronage.

That afternoon, Kitty had decided to settle and not keep moving on, knowing full well that the woman on whom she had just turned her back was not a person who planned to settle anywhere. Knowing full well that this woman was a libertine, an entertainer, a tightrope walker.

She had returned to the care of her perfect patron, for whom Kitty's career had become a *raison d'être*. And Kitty was not prepared to deprive her of that.

★

Two weeks after her visit to Fred's studio, she found her benefactor slumped over the back of the sofa in her spacious, cluttered reception room, chest heaving, sobbing dramatically. When she cautiously enquired as to the reason for Amy's tears, Amy told her Fred was going to America and didn't know when she would be coming back. She had accepted an invitation from a Boston textile manufacturer to help him buy artworks and design a new gallery, where she would also be able to exhibit her paintings. She had given up her studio, and had left Amy one of her scrawls on a napkin promising to be in touch soon; perhaps by then, thanks to her new source of income, she would be in a position to invite her to the Hamptons for a weekend in the summer. She had added a postscript in which she sent greetings to 'your timid little protégée, who unfortunately thinks so little of herself'. Amy flung the napkin melodramatically at Kitty's feet.

Fred's absence was to last two years, and despite the grief it caused — openly expressed by Amy, borne in secret by Kitty — it allowed the two women she left behind to come into their own. As if Fred Lieblich had sensed this, or even desired it; as if she had left the arena to the women she loved.

Kitty had left failure behind her in the East, Amy proclaimed, and now the West would start to make amends. She got her to record her first album in English, *You And I*. Her accent was her trademark, Amy said; under no circumstances should she try to lose it. The single was played on the English airwaves. And Kitty was invited to give radio interviews, always accompanied by Amy, her manager. She received offers from clubs that were far more upmarket than her jazz club. Amy began to think about a first public concert. Kitty diligently recounted her tragic past to journalists, different versions cobbled together for her by Amy; the more tragic the story, Amy said, the better the prospect that she would soon become a naturalised citizen.

The age of rockabilly was in full swing, Elvis and fiery rock'n'roll were on the horizon, and Kitty, who was never associated with any musical style or genre, gradually became — thanks to Amy — a face that people registered, with her eastern 'purity', the polyphony of her homeland, her music that always emphasised the power of melody.

Kitty: whose trail you set out to follow, Brilka, searching for yourself and at the same time refusing to become yourself, for fear that you wouldn't be able to shake off all the ghosts that pursue us as we seek a new beginning for your story, which would also become part of mine.

BOOK V

★

ELENE

> Spilling tears from blind white eyes
> A jet of water hits the skies.
>
> JOSEPH BRODSKY

As the Cold War set in, Khrushchev tripled funding for the expansion of the Soviet Union's nuclear arsenal and its submarine fleet.

The space race between the United States and the Soviet Union was in full swing, and the certainty of holding a nuclear bomb in their hands gave the superpowers a sense of omnipotence. The Soviet Union had detonated its first atomic bomb in 1949, an exact replica of the American bomb that had laid waste to Nagasaki. The Generalissimus had ordered his scientists to copy it, allegedly telling them that *experiments* were not permitted.

Now scientists were working around the clock, on Khrushchev's orders, to keep pace with their American competitors' advances in the field. Since Khrushchev's inauguration there had been an alarming increase in the number of nuclear tests. Soon there were to be as many as eighty detonations per year; seven hundred and fifteen confirmed nuclear tests were carried out between 1949 and 1990 in the Soviet Union alone. The consequences of this — specifically: radioactive contamination — were of no interest to the Party. Under Khrushchev, it began to pour money into the armaments industry. Forty thousand men worked at the shipyard where the first titanium submarine was built. The rest of the world, including the US, had a total of one-hundred and fifty-nine nuclear submarines during the Cold War. The Soviet fleet numbered two-hundred and twenty-eight.

Kostya Jashi travelled to Nizhny Novgorod to proudly examine the first example of a nuclear-powered submarine.

★

While the parrot Goya, Elene, Elene's eccentric grandmother, and her equally eccentric sister had formed an invincible fellowship, Nana had turned her attention back to her doctoral thesis.

Nana strove to provide a strong counterpoint to the sisters. They only obeyed their own rules, but Nana required greater discipline of her daughter. She wasn't always successful in this, however, as Elene had developed a very strong will of her own, for which Nana held her mother- and aunt-in-law responsible.

The rampantly overgrown garden, the screaming parrot, the loud opera arias, the old necklaces and ribbons from Christine's room fortified Elene's free spirit. She defied her mother whenever she had the chance, and refused to comply with her disciplinary measures. In the battle for Elene's favour, the two older women effortlessly, almost accidentally, conjured up one trump card after another. Their suggestions, their offers, their worlds were more exciting, more magical to Elene than Nana's unimaginative regime.

In the summer, when Kostya came home to spend a few weeks with his wife and daughter, under palm trees on the Black Sea coast or in the health spas and sanatoriums of Borjomi and Sairme, the image of a close, intact family was maintained only with difficulty. The sullen look in his daughter's eyes was not lost on Kostya, and Nana saw the question marks in them, too, when her child had the all-too-rare opportunity to be with both parents together. During those weeks, though, Nana really tried her hardest; she didn't want to disappoint Elene, not for anything in the world. In this time away from Stasia and Christine, when she had her daughter all to herself, she wanted to do everything better, to prove to herself and her husband that *her* childrearing methods were the most effective. Kostya seemed slightly exasperated with her embodiment of the role of strict Georgian mother. He didn't want the little time he was able to spend with his daughter to be taken up with pedagogical measures. He wanted to enjoy his daughter's company, to fulfil her every whim, to indulge her; he didn't want to have to ration his affection. And so these summer weeks became one long ordeal for the patient and otherwise peaceable Nana. Inwardly, she cursed the thankless role she had been assigned. She felt out of her depth, at others' mercy, misunderstood, unsupported.

One hot August evening, after the two of them had drunk the iodine-rich healing waters in Borjomi and dined with other well-to-do guests at the sanatorium, Kostja paused at his wife's bedside on his way to the bathroom, razor in hand, and informed her: 'When the time comes, Elene should go to a suitable school, and that won't be in this country. I want my daughter to have the best possible education, and thanks to my position I have certain opportunities it would be incredibly stupid for us not to take advantage of.'

'You surely don't imagine I'm going to leave my six-year-old daughter behind in a strange city thousands of kilometres away, do you?'

'I'm not discussing this with you, Nana. I'm just informing you well in advance, so you can —'

'Forget it, Kostya. Not on your life!'

'My God, Nana, when are you going to wake up from your patriotic slumber?'

'And when will you ever think of anyone other than yourself?'

That was the end of the discussion because Kostya didn't answer his wife; he went into the bathroom instead, to shave in peace. That night the couple slept in separate beds.

*

When the time came for Elene to start school, Nana had long since lost her battle for influence over her daughter to Stasia and Christine. Confronted with two evils, she chose what she thought was the lesser: she decided it would be better to have a russophile daughter who was, nevertheless, disciplined, independent, and educated, rather than one who was feral, unworldly, and, at worst, mad.

Stasia and Christine sounded the alarm when they found out about the plan to send Elene to Moscow. They protested, argued, and made threats, but Nana stood her ground, citing her husband's wishes. Elene cried, hid herself away, shouted obscenities, and stuck her tongue out at her mother, but this, of course, achieved little. Nana was adamant: her child was not going to grow up in this house in the company of two madwomen. Elene would finally get a decent education; she would learn to behave as a young girl should, not run around screaming like a Fury; she would dress properly, eat properly, speak properly.

*

Two nights before Nana — with a heavy heart, but a clear objective — was due to take her daughter to the airport, Stasia decided to employ her father's magic in the hope of changing her daughter-in-law's mind. For the first time in years she made the hot chocolate. As she had anticipated, the smell drew Nana to the kitchen and, not suspecting herself to be at Stasia's mercy, she sat down at the table and gazed at her mother-in-law with grateful eyes. She spooned up the thick chocolate ecstatically, and Stasia spoke insistently to her as she did so, trying to convince her not to part with Elene; the magical drink made her daughter-in-law so soft and tractable that she came within a whisker of agreeing. Just at that moment, though, a sleepy Elene in yellow pyjamas slipped into the kitchen unnoticed, presumably woken by the most enchanting smell in the world, and before Stasia could stop her she had stuck her finger first into her mother's cup, then into her mouth. Stasia froze, closed her eyes, and hoped for a miracle. A miracle that would undo this moment. But there are no such miracles, Brilka.

That night, Stasia lay in bed, unable to sleep, imploring all the gods, real and imaginary, to spare this wonderful child she loved so much from the chocolate's curse.

The following evening, as Elene — accompanied by Stasia's lamentations — was packing her socks and knickers into her suitcase, the doorbell rang. Still deeply despondent about the incident the night before, Stasia answered the door — and froze. Before her stood Andro Eristavi, bald, with a full beard. Holding his hand was a younger copy of himself. The same curls, but dark; the same eyes, but lighter; the same build, but stockier. Only the boy's nose was a little coarser, his lips a little more full.

A visit like a bad omen. For a moment, Stasia's conscience battled with her reason. Andro's mother appeared in her mind's eye, asking her to tell her boy stories of a good world. She fell on Andro's neck, kissing him all over his face, as if he were the same age as the child whose hand he held. Elene, happy that the unexpected visit had relieved her of the sad duty of packing her suitcase, rushed over to Miqa and examined him in her bold and endearing manner.

The table was quickly laid, and Andro and Miqa took their places between Stasia and Christine. They sat silently, heads bowed, as if they had no right to be there. Unlike Elene, who couldn't keep quiet during the meal and chattered away about whatever sprang to mind, the boy ate his cut-up meatballs like an adult and said thank you every time anyone handed him anything.

After the meal, Elene jumped up and dragged Miqa away from the table by his sleeve; she wanted to show him round the garden and introduce him to Goya. As they were drinking their Turkish coffee, Nana excused herself, too, saying she still had preparations to make for the trip. Alone with Christine and Stasia, Andro could finally broach the reason for his visit.

'I'd like to send him to school in the city. There's a programme for gifted *kolchoz* children, and Miqa's smart. You know I can't get a residence permit. But with you ... If Miqa could ...'

There was a long pause. Then Stasia put her hand on his and nodded.

'Of course,' she said. She could still see Sopio's face before her. This, she realised, was her chance to fulfil her duty to Sopio, to make good with Miqa what she had failed to do for Andro.

Christine cleared her throat, seemingly astonished by her sister's swift decision to take a strange child into the house, just like that. They had, after all, failed miserably at this undertaking once before. Andro put a tentative arm around Stasia and kissed her shoulder. It was a sad gesture and, at the same time, expressive of great humility. Stasia was filled with a sense of relief. Suddenly Andro rose, as if he wanted to leave already; then he sat down again, plucking nervously at the tablecloth.

'How's Kitty? Where is she?'

Stasia and Christine were startled. They wanted to object; to say that it was better not to broach this subject, that they didn't know anything either, and were weighed down by the burden of this not-knowing; that they were doing all they could not to go mad with worry about her, since Kostya refused to give them any information; all they knew was that she was in England, and safe. Instead, Stasia's eyes filled and she wept silently, tears rolling down her sunken cheeks. And neither Andro nor Christine attempted to comfort her, because there is no comfort for a mother who has lost her daughter. From the garden they could hear Elene's happy, bell-like laughter, and Miqa, panting.

Nana left for Moscow with Elene the following morning. Her husband's aged housekeeper, Lyuda, had prepared his apartment on Nikitsky Boulevard for the little princess' arrival. Starting on the first of September, Elene would travel from there to one of the exclusive schools, where she would share a classroom with the children of Party functionaries, directors, and high-ranking officers. And on the same day, the first of September, Miqa would step out of the house on Vera Hill to start first grade at an ordinary school in Tbilisi.

★

Elene hated Moscow right from the beginning, but she hated the school most of all. Elene hated her school uniform of heavy brown wool, the scratchy, starched white pinafore, the white bow in her hair; she hated the strict teachers, and her fellow pupils, none of whom she had anything in common with. She hated her parents for bringing her here, and she hated the cold, grey climate of this vast grey city.

She hated the gloomy, marble-floored corridors in the tall school building near Gorky Park. Hated her father's driver, who drove her to school and picked her up again each day. She hated the parades at the end of every month in honour of socialism and the Party; she even hated the Sundays when her father took the day off for her, and tried to talk to her as if she were a grown-up — as if he could expect that of her, as if she were old and clever enough. She didn't want to have to play the grown-up, to be old and clever enough for her father. Even though she liked Lyuda, who took care of her and made her blinis, her favourite, she hated the fact that she liked her.

But above all she hated the voice of the boy her own age who, uninvited, and, to her mind, inexplicably, had moved into her house the day she left and taken her place; that contented voice she could hear in the background whenever she spoke to her mother or grandmother or great-aunt on the phone. She should be where he was now. She should be him; she should be leading the life he led.

Miqa, on the other hand, loved everything that life in Tbilisi had to offer. The school, the city, the peculiar sisters; reticent, principled Nana; he loved the guilt-ridden attention that was bestowed on him; he loved having the right to be a child at last — because he didn't have to do chores in the house, he didn't have to keep the courtyard clean, he wasn't constantly told he should act like a man and not like a crybaby, nor did he have to take part in his home village's frightening pagan rituals.

Nana had to admit that Miqa was quite different to Elene: an absolute model of courtesy, good manners, politeness, and restraint. He was malleable, like soft clay; he was grateful for every gesture; compliant, shy, not the type to do anything silly. He was no trouble at all. He wasn't especially popular at school, but he got tolerably good marks, and he never had to be reminded to do his homework. His presence in the house was almost imperceptible. He never interrupted the grown-ups when they were talking, he didn't smack his lips while eating, he washed, he crept past the ladies' bedrooms on tiptoe, and he never gave any of the house's occupants any cause for complaint or rebuke. How had this country boy acquired such good manners, Nana wondered. Sometimes she would reproach herself and wonder whether she was a good mother, whether she had done the wrong thing by her daughter, whether it had been a mistake to expose her child to the influence of these unworldly women; whether it wouldn't have been better if she had gone with Elene to join her husband in Moscow while his offer to live what he called a 'normal family life' still stood. It was almost embarrassing to be forced to admit to herself that she would view the future with much less anxiety if her daughter were equipped with the same character traits as Miqa.

Miqa fell under Christine's spell right from the very first day. No matter how much Stasia made a fuss of him and always made him feel part of the family, Christine's attention mattered more. He would try to guess her wishes and gauge her moods. If *Norma* was playing, he knew she was in a good mood, and that he would be allowed to sit in the room with her, listening to the music at full volume. Initially it had bemused him, but, as time went by, he found it more and more beautiful and impressive. If she was listening to *Tosca*, she was in a melancholy humour, and he would pick her flowers from the garden. If she didn't want to listen to any records at all, she was tired or had a headache, and off he would go to boil water for her tea.

On the days when she picked him up from school, he could barely contain his pride at walking beside this elegant beauty. Though at first she was amused by his attentiveness towards her, ruffled his curls, laughed at and shook her head over him, which hurt his feelings, she gradually became increasingly tender. She didn't return his tremulous, dreamy love with the same fervour as she once had her nephew's; but she did return it, in that she made him her ally. Miqa was practically euphoric; he felt as if he were one of the chosen ones in Christine's secret realm.

At first, Christine saw the boy as a welcome distraction in her daily life, which had become sadder and more sentimental since Elene's departure. She also liked the fact that he was so well behaved, and she enjoyed his attentions. The way he would sometimes stare at her in amazement reminded her of Kostya; of before, of her heyday. Increasingly, she began to seek his company, as if he gave her something she had been missing for a long time, or was no longer able to accept from anyone else: he gave her a sense of *completeness*, as if he didn't see her veil, her disguise. As if he saw her whole.

★

A playful, somnambulistic peace descended upon the house. For a while it even seemed to Nana that it was tidier, more homely. As if the wildness and neglect had been halted in their tracks. She also managed to finish her doctorate at last. It had cost her two years of her life and put an extra six kilos on her ribs.

The peace was interrupted only by the evening telephone calls from Moscow. That was when the three women would gather round the phone to listen to Elene's somewhat distracted voice and to hear from Kostya how she was doing, what she was having for breakfast, whether she had a cold, whether they were wrapping her up warm enough, whether she was doing well at school, whether she had already made friends, and so on.

At times like these, Miqa would usually sit in the library in Ramas' old study; picking up a book he would try to concentrate on it, but still he couldn't help listening. He would hear the pride in Stasia's voice when she spoke to her granddaughter, the concern in Nana's, Christine's subdued delight, and they would put him in an odd frame of mind.

He would think then of the mountains, of the house where he was born, of his mother's suntanned skin, his melancholic father's cracked hands and alcohol breath, the village boys who considered him unmanly, and he would feel afraid. Because he didn't want to leave: he wanted to stay here, to go on enjoying the unconditional care he received in this house. But there was this girl, out there, far away, the girl with the thick hair and grazed knees, and her voice alone was enough to tear all three women away from him and focus their entire attention on her, for hours: this girl who was hundreds, thousands of kilometres away, whereas he, sitting in the room just upstairs, was forgotten.

★

Since Elene had been living in Moscow under her father's and Lyuda's supervision, she had become much more tractable than she had been in the realm of the women. She ate her meals without objection, did her homework, accompanied her father to various events, went with him to the cinema, theatre, museums; her behaviour was more grown-up, more ladylike, all of which gave her father the feeling of being in the right when he maintained to Nana that Elene was not a difficult girl at all, quite the opposite, she was the most obedient child in the world, you just had to know how to win her heart.

She saw the sparkle in Kostya's eye when she recited a poem for him or brought a good grade home from school. She liked the way he was so solicitous then. Even though she sometimes cursed him in her head for transplanting her to this cold and alien country, he was her only source of stability and a substitute for all those she missed. He was the great man people greeted on the street with their heads bowed low; a man who made important decisions, and sat up late into the night bent over plans that seemed to Elene like secret code.

Lyuda catered to her every whim and never raised her voice. Yet Elene longed for Nana's hysterical outbursts, her warnings, her constant discipline; wished she could be returned to Stasia's and Christine's negligent guardianship. Here, in these high-ceilinged rooms with the heavy, dark furniture, on these wide streets and marble staircases, there was no place for silliness; here, everything went according to plan. Kostya's plan.

Under his command, her duty was to be his best soldier. It was a role from which she recoiled. At the same time, she was afraid of disappointing him. In her eyes, he stood on such a high pedestal, was so unassailable, his opinion had always seemed so definitive, that she didn't dare to doubt him.

She wanted to walk, run, explore, seek, and find; instead she walked decorously, holding Lyuda's hand; sat in her father's big car like a fine lady; politely answered questions the grown-ups asked her; looked after her toys as she was instructed; and let her father read to her (mostly books he had selected) — only to press her face into her pillow late at night and cry until she fell asleep, exhausted. Only the prospect of the winter and summer holidays enabled her to get through it all, waiting for the day when she and her father would drive to the airport, board the plane, and fly to Tbilisi.

When they arrived, she flung her arms around everyone's necks, gave them all sloppy kisses, ran, jumped, skipped, and sang. Because here she felt at home. She wasn't afraid, not even of her father's anger, because in Tbilisi his rules did not apply. Here, there was a mother; here, there was Stasia, Christine, Goya — and they would protect her. She was deliberately obstinate so as to put her mother's and grandmother's love to the test. She gladly accepted being sent to her room for being naughty because anything was better than having to play the grown-up in Moscow.

Miqa wasn't at the house during the school holidays. His father came to pick him up and took him to the mountains. Nonetheless, he was omnipresent: his toys and clothes, and his books, carefully piled up on the old writing desk, were constant reminders of him. And when any of the women compared her with Miqa — *Miqa's so good, Miqa really loves that cake* — Elene's anger would bubble up, making her even more rebellious and uncontrollable. Kostya's aversion towards the 'parasite's son', as he tended to describe Miqa, was very apparent, and he would side with his daughter against him.

'Will you stop winding her up by going on about this stupid boy!' he said indignantly one evening in the kitchen after dinner. Elene had jumped up from the table and run out because Stasia and Christine couldn't agree on how Miqa liked his potato pancakes: with or without butter?

'If you want to bring the bastard up here and pay for him, that's your affair, but I don't want my child to suffer as a result.'

'What are you saying?' Christine's fir-green right eye widened.

'What am I saying? You took him in here behind my back — at my expense, mind — and not even my own dear wife felt it necessary to inform me.'

'Kostya, please!' Stasia admonished him.

'What? I'm not the one who fought for the fascists; I didn't plant the idiotic notion of capitalist freedom in my sister's head; I didn't bring a child into the world that other people have to pay for.' Kostya's tone was haughty and cold.

'Andro is like a son to me — he was like a brother to you!' Stasia had abandoned her meal and was looking her son straight in the eye, appalled. Nana stared fixedly at the floor, as if there were a secret door in it that could lead her out and away from this unpleasant situation.

'How can you say such a thing?' Stasia's voice was trembling. 'All of us — yes, all of us — are constantly striving to please you; I've accepted the worst thing, the worst thing anyone can do to a mother, and you're asking the same of your wife.'

Christine stared at her sister in astonishment.

'What's that supposed to mean? What exactly am I doing to my wife?' Kostya's voice cracked.

'You took Elene away from her, just because the child simply had to go to an exclusive Russian school; of course she had to live in Moscow, this is a veritable backwater, isn't it? You're taking her child away from her, like you took mine away from me.'

Stasia had jumped up from the table and fetched herself a cigarette. Her chin was quivering with emotion.

'I took your child away from you? *I* did? You're out of your mind, Stasia!' He had stopped calling her *Deda* long ago. 'I vouched for her, I staked everything — I risked my life, goddamn it, but it seems none of that's good enough for you. I'm sure it's easier to love a traitor and a murderess!'

The room fell silent. Christine slowly rose from the table and hovered uncertainly for a while, as if she didn't know whether to go or stay. Stasia stood frozen by the tap, filterless cigarette in hand, while Nana glanced anxiously back and forth between Stasia and Kostya.

'Don't you dare call her that again! I swear to you by all that's sacred to me —'

'I didn't think anything was still sacred to you!' said Kostya coldly. He rose from the table.

'Stay here, damn it, stay here! I want to know where she is, after all this time — I want to speak to my daughter. I can't go on living like this!'

Kostya, already in the doorway, turned round again and looked at his mother.

'I saved her from death. We have no information as to her whereabouts, do you understand me? You don't, and I don't. We know nothing.'

Stasia moaned. Kostya stormed out of the room and Christine followed him. Nana slowly got to her feet and began clearing the table. Stasia didn't move; for a long time she stood there in silence. When she looked up again, little Elene was standing in the doorway with a grazed elbow.

'I hurt myself. Because of stupid Goya.' Elene gave her grandmother an imploring look.

'It's all right; come here, I'll clean the cut and then we'll patch it up, all right?'

And Elene hurried over to Stasia, holding her elbow out in front of her as if it were a trophy.

> What is this moment
> What was yesterday
> What whirlwind runs
> Like a beast through the field?
>
> KONSTANTIN BALMONT

'Billie Holiday, the greatest female singer in the world, died five days ago. Perhaps she's making way for you. You're looking good!'

These were the words with which Fred greeted Kitty after a long absence. She had turned up outside Kitty's flat on Old Compton Street, in a white shirt and an expensive-looking leather jacket, and rung the bell. Kitty had moved in only a few weeks earlier. Now that she was earning her own money, she had, with Amy's approval, finally taken a flat of her own, since, according to Amy, she would soon earn even more now that she had British citizenship. Almost nine years had passed since Kitty had left her homeland and, apart from the scant information from her anonymous friend, she'd had no other news of her family.

Fred Lieblich strode, uninvited, past the dumbfounded Kitty and into the brightly lit flat.

'It's the end of an era. The bastards didn't want to admit her to hospital because she was black. I don't want to live in a country like that.'

Kitty, caught completely unawares in the midst of preparing for her first television appearance, stood in the hallway staring after Fred, who marched straight into the kitchen.

'How do you know where I live?'

'Oh, come on, don't be silly. I need a drink, I've come straight from the airport, I just dropped off my things with some friends.' Fred lit herself a cigarette.

'Amy will be picking me up any minute. I've got a show this evening.'

'Excellent, then I can see her too. Good old Amy. I'd never have believed she'd go all out for you like that. And your English is exemplary. Excellent! That song of yours — sorry, I can't remember the title — I liked that song very much. So I say let's all have a nice evening together, the three of us.'

'And how am I to explain your turning up at my flat?'

'I don't owe anyone any explanations. I wanted to see you, so here I am.'

'You don't, but I do. Because unlike you I have some principles, which I'm not prepared to throw overboard just because you suddenly reappear and think you can turn everything on its head again.'

Fred had found what she was looking for and was mixing two gin and tonics with practised ease.

'I can't drink anything. I've got a live performance!'

'Nice place you've got here! Cheers!' Fred took a large swig of the sparkling liquid with great relish and sat down at the kitchen table.

Outside, it had started to darken. The noises of the street grew quiet; an almost audible silence fell. A slight, rather tired scent tickled Kitty's nose: *her* scent, the scent of this emotional tightrope-walker. Kitty reached for her glass. She had to get through this, it would be over soon, she wouldn't give in, she would be strong.

She had been working non-stop. She and Amy had been shaping her new life; the foundations were still shaky, she had to keep going, battle on undeterred, she was on the right path. This person sitting in front of her, this brazen, egotistical person, was an obstacle, a threat, a catastrophe. She had to do something to stop her.

'Please leave now.'

'So Madame has changed, has she?'

That accent, that soft, cocky intonation — how intimately familiar it was to Kitty's ears!

'Please!' Kitty rose and gestured towards the door. Fred stood, leaving her half-full glass of gin and tonic on the table. Kitty felt churlish. But that which had been forgotten should not be remembered, no, not under any circumstances. The main thing was not to look at her, then soon it would be over.

In the hallway, Kitty was aware again of that almost imperceptible scent in her nostrils. She tugged at the door handle, kept her face turned away: don't look, don't. Suddenly she felt a cool hand on her cheek. Fred was stroking her face. Kitty spun round and slapped her, so hard that Fred staggered back and slammed against the wall. Kitty's palm was burning.

It wasn't possible to forget.

She couldn't see Fred's face; she had one hand pressed to it as if trying to smother the pain. Then Fred seized Kitty's wrist, gripping it so hard it hurt. Kitty cried out and tried to free herself from her grasp. Where did this diminutive person get such strength? The woman before her was quite a bit smaller than her, she'd never really been aware of it before. Fred's other hand slipped under Kitty's skirt, undid the suspender belt; one nylon stocking slid down to her ankle. Kitty felt shame. She watched her clothes fall to the floor.

The flame-haired woman pressed her against the wall so hard that she gasped for breath. Fred was still holding one of her wrists twisted behind her back, and it hurt. This time she wasn't numb; this time she was conscious of this woman's every movement, every impulse. It was a feeling somewhere between disgust and pleasure.

Suddenly, she felt the burning sun of the empty schoolyard on her face. She saw again the house on the Holy Mountain. The meticulously framed photos on the walls. The perfect couple. The ticking of the clock — had there really been a clock, or was it her imagination? And the knife: what had the knife been like, how big? She didn't know any more. And Mariam, had she screamed at the end; or was that her own voice? And the curlers in the blonde woman's hair, did they all fall out? Had she been smirking right at the end, too, as the knife cut into her throat? Did she in fact die instantly, or had there been a death rattle? And how could she have left Mariam there, with the dead woman in the empty apartment, without batting an eyelid? How had she got home, in someone else's clothes — in *her* clothes? How could she have done that?

What had been Mariam's last thought?

As the warm, intense, overpowering feeling took possession of her and she forgot the world around her — her flat and the night outside, the pot plants, her little room in Tbilisi with the old, narrow bed, which she had loved so much, Andro's eyes when she saw him again for the first time after the war, the green hills of her hometown, the little blue veins on her mother's arms, her brother's uniform — as she forgot the classroom, in that hot summer of sutured wounds, as she forgot Amy and the voice on the telephone to which she was still unable to put a name, she screamed so loudly she thought her eardrums would burst.

Fred stroked the hair out of her face. Kitty was sweating. Her body was trembling. She sank to the floor. Fred sat down beside her and pushed down her skirt, so innocent, so abashed, as if she hadn't ripped off Kitty's clothes just moments earlier.

'Why are you doing this to me?' whispered Kitty. She lay in the hallway on the cold, hard floor.

'May I ask you something?' Fred responded.
'What do you want to know?'
'Where did you get this scar?'
Fred went to put her hand on Kitty's belly, but Kitty shrank away.
'From an operation.'
'What operation?'
'They removed my womb.'
Kitty didn't know why she hadn't lied.
'Why?'
For the first time Kitty heard something akin to fear in Fred's voice.
'Before they did that, they aborted my child.'
Kitty heard her voice coming from far, far away. It felt strange, after so many years, simply to speak the truth.
'What happened?'
Fred's voice remained quiet, tentative, but it wasn't pitying. That made it more bearable. And Kitty told her, in an almost matter-of-fact tone, about her old life, the life that had led to the classroom and the blonde woman and Mariam.

★

'Where's *your* mother now?' Kitty eventually asked, when she had finished her confession.
'In the Jewish cemetery in Vienna. At least, there's a plaque there with her name on. As to whether her remains are there as well: I wouldn't swear to it. In all the chaos back then they weren't keeping too close an eye on who went where, with so many Jewish corpses …'
'But why? You'd —'
'She hanged herself the night we were supposed to flee Mödling. With Martin's belt. A good, strong leather belt. German workmanship, you know; it does what it says it'll do.'

★

The nights that followed were sticky and clung to the skin, even during the day. They couldn't be washed off; their languorous, salty taste could not be discarded. They were wordless and gentle, then urgent again, full of words that refused to run dry.

And during the day they had to be painted over with falsehoods; Kitty had to be ready with excuses to evade Amy's watchful eyes. Until one day Amy informed her that her lover had returned, and she had no intention of ever leaving her side again, and Kitty was filled with bilious anger towards Amy, a vicious jealousy, and became painfully aware of her own unfortunate situation. She congratulated her manager, then retreated, and refrained from making any comment at all in the days and weeks that followed, as she sat with Amy in her house in King's Cross, or in one of the many Soho cafés, discussing their work plans.

But then Fred started turning up at her flat in the night; she would throw a little pebble up at her window, as if to emphasise her role as secret concubine, and would stumble up the stairs in the dark. It was rare for all three women to meet: at Amy's welcoming party for her returned friend, or a picnic together in Hyde Park. Then Kitty and Fred would exchange stolen glances, secret messages; their shoulders would brush accidentally, there would be almost imperceptible touches, words whispered furtively in passing.

Kitty was surprised by how easy it was for her to lie. She was surprised by how quickly she had become a part of Fred's world, despite her constant resistance, her pride in refusing to allow that to happen. How carelessly she deceived her friend and patroness; how effortlessly she forgot Amy the minute Fred appeared beneath her window. What had happened to her resolutions and principles? Why was she jeopardising her relationship with Amy?

Kitty knew that the coming months would be full of splinters, that she would have to learn to walk on them so that they didn't leave scars. Secretly she longed for the moment when this edifice of lies, these false promises, this wordless, deceitful arrangement would collapse and implode. Because Fred never mentioned Amy; she didn't feel the need, as if this divided life were normal, as if this dreadful situation were a logical consequence of her character, her thoughtlessness, the egocentric blindness that sometimes drove Kitty mad. But they talked a lot, and for Kitty these conversations with Fred became a necessity; she needed them as she needed air to breathe, needed them even more than she needed the sense of abandonment as they overstepped the boundaries together. For so many years she had been mute, and now, at last, she could speak again. Without false pity, without false expectations. She could exhale: for a few hours she could break free of the shadow world inside her head and return to life, to the here and now. Completely.

Let the ruling classes tremble at a Communistic revolution.
The proletarians have nothing to lose but their chains.
They have a world to win.

KARL MARX

Elene and her father sat in front of their Rekord television set in the eastern half of the world, while Kitty and Amy sat in front of their Ferguson television set in the western half, all staring, spellbound, at a friendly man in the impressive outfit of a cosmonaut boarding a spaceship in Tyuratam, waving and calling out, 'Let's go! Goodbye to you, dear friends, and see you soon.' The spaceship was called *Vostok 1*, the calm, friendly man Yuri Gagarin. When the engines were fired up shortly after nine o'clock that April morning and the retention arms released, the Americans sighed and the Russians cheered. But all over the world people held their breath at the start of the first orbit of the Earth in history, and heard Gagarin cry, 'I see Earth! It is so beautiful.'

*

Her time in Moscow had shaken Elene's deepest principles and convictions. She became acquainted with doubt, and through doubt she realised something fundamental, something that cut her to the quick and profoundly changed her. She realised that the world was not a protective place, that people didn't always keep their promises, that love was replaceable, that intimacy was a silken thread that could break at any time, that feelings changed from day to day and affection could breed contempt. She understood that she had been wronged. This thought was liberating for her: ever since she had formulated it and written it on the back of her maths book, she felt surer of herself. Because it meant that it was not she who had failed, but the others: she had not deserved to grow up far from home and be replaced by a curly-haired boy; she had not brought this strict life in Moscow, these cold foreign climes, this loneliness upon herself. It also meant that this wrong that had been done to her could one day be redressed. This thought was sweet as honey; it gave her strength and coaxed a smile to her lips. The child who in Moscow was so reserved, so painstakingly polite, almost deferential, soon became a cheeky, lively, noisy, domineering girl again. Encouraged by thoughts of some time in the future, she returned to her roots.

Whereas in the past she hadn't wanted to be a Young Pioneer, had never wanted to go to summer or winter camp, now she was first in line at Pioneer parades and managed to become leader of the girls' group at camp. She was the first to put up her hand in class, and if one of the boys looked askance at her, played a joke on her, teased her, or gave her a condescending smile, he would receive a reply that made him lose any desire to do it again. Elene also became more assertive in dealing with her father — although there were certain boundaries that she would never cross. Kostya was surprised and pleased by his daughter's sudden transformation. It would serve her better in life to be like this, he thought. He failed, however, to see Elene's anger, bubbling deep below the surface.

But Nana — who only saw Elene in Moscow in the autumn, when she took time off from university, or in the summer holidays, which Elene spent with her — couldn't shake a feeling of unease. There was something exaggerated about Elene's constant cheerfulness and feverish energy. She sensed the strange artificiality in her child's behaviour, the slightly forced aspect of her carefree manner. Nana, who struggled with her guilt over allowing Elene to go to Moscow, knew that the battle for their daughter had never been about her wellbeing: it had always been more about her and Kostya, even though Kostya never tired of repeating how good Russian discipline was for Elene.

But behind her child's smile Nana sensed the black tangle of thoughts woven together from unspoken reproaches and injuries. She just couldn't put this insight into words. How could she explain to her husband that their marriage was now no more than a perpetual conflict of interest over their daughter? He would never believe it if she told him that the child lacked for anything, that she wasn't happy, that she was nurturing something dark inside.

And during one of those visits, as she watched her daughter sitting alone in the garden one evening, lost in thought, staring icily into space and apparently not even noticing the rain pelting down on her, Nana realised she had to do something or she would lose Elene completely.

She ran through all the options, held conversations with her husband in her head, tried to pit her arguments against his. She needed a strategy in order to formulate her plan in Kostya's language; she had to be unyielding, she had to be stubborn, at least as steely as Kostya himself. Just as spring turned to summer, she flew to visit her husband in Moscow.

As was to be expected, Nana's concerns met with little understanding from her husband. Kostya ridiculed her worries as the misguided fears of an egotistical mother who was prioritising her own wishes over her daughter's future. But Nana kept insisting that this was about their daughter, who was just as much hers as she was his; that this child had lived apart from her — against her will — for long enough. Elene needed her mother: Kostya may have refused to discuss it back then, but now it was her turn. Tbilisi wasn't just some village, after all; there were good schools there, too. Besides, she should be speaking her mother tongue again, and she should be among women. A single Lyuda was no substitute for all her female role-models.

Although it was hard for her, Nana refused to give in. Worn down by the long discussions with her husband and his egregious insults, she was repeatedly assailed by doubt as to whether bringing Elene back to Georgia was the right thing to do; but then she would remember the black look in her daughter's eyes and cast her doubts aside.

One night, she was sitting at the kitchen table, still awake, frustration having driven her to eat the blinis Lyuda had made for Elene's breakfast, when Elene appeared in the doorway in her flannel pyjamas and laughed at her mother in surprise. She fetched a plate and took a blini for herself as well.

'Everything all right, *Deda*?' she asked solicitously. Her Georgian had long since acquired a Russian tinge that made Nana livid.

'I just can't get to sleep, my sunshine.'

'Have you and Papa been fighting again?'

'We're not fighting, Eleniko, we're just having some discussions.'

'What about?'

'This and that. Mostly about the fact that I miss you so terribly.'

'And what does Papa say?'

'That he would miss you terribly, too, if you were to come home with me.'

Elene appeared to consider this. Her feet were dangling from the high chair; she skilfully rolled the blini and dunked it in the little *varenye* bowl with its dark red liquid. At that moment she looked so peaceful and happy that Nana's heart clenched: her thick, uncombed hair, her long eyelashes, the pyjama trousers that were slightly too big. Nana would have liked to bundle her into her coat that instant, run outside with her, and drive her straight to the airport.

'You want me to come with you to Tbilisi, right? For ever, right?'
'I just want you to be happy, my pet.'
'I am happy.'
'Really? Do you like it here?'
'Of course.'
'I mean: don't you miss us? Me, Stasia, Christine, Goya?'
'Sometimes. Yes.'
'I don't want you to feel you're lacking anything.'
'Why don't you all come here? There's plenty of space here. There's plenty of space for all of you, it's just ...'
'It's just what? What do you mean, Eleniko?'
'Well, the boy — Miqa, I mean — he couldn't live here. And he can't speak Russian very well, can he? So he can't go to school here either, and anyway Papa said that his papa is a nasty man, and they don't take children like that here.'
'Papa told you that?'
'Yes.'
'But that's not true. Miqa's papa is just poor, my pet. Miqa doesn't have as many opportunities as we do, that's why we're looking after him. He's going to school in Tbilisi so he can get a better education than he would in his village. You hardly even know him, Elene.'
'You all do, though.'
Nana froze. That aggrieved tone. She wished she could have recorded that sentence and played it back to Kostya. The deep-seated anger in Elene's voice!
'I'd rather stay here, in any case, with Papa. Why don't you and Stasia and Christine and Goya come? Why don't you come here?'
Elene ate the rest of her blini and put the plate in the sink like a good girl. She gave her mother a tentative kiss on the cheek, wished her good night, and went off to bed. Nana stayed sitting at the table for a while, thinking. How alarmingly deliberate and confident Elene's every word, every gesture seemed to be. She felt impotent, helpless. Had she ever considered that Elene might reject her suggestion that she go back? If she insisted, would it just increase Elene's rancour? Would she then switch to Kostya's side, against her, out of protest? She mustn't let it come to that: open division in two opposing camps would just make the whole thing even more unbearable for Elene.

To avoid Elene's curious questions, and looks from Lyuda, the couple had decided to share a marriage bed again in Moscow. Seldom had Nana found anything more difficult than lying down that night in the bed where Kostya was peacefully sleeping. A week later, she returned home, humiliated and exhausted. Elene remained in Moscow.

★

When I asked him about it, in the last years of his life, after the story had long since caught up with him, my grandfather admitted to having been in Severodvinsk in late 1958 when the keel of the K-19 was first laid. But a certain Captain Zateyev had been responsible for the K-19, he said; he himself had never had anything to do with this model.

The K-19 submarine, which acquired the less-than-flattering nickname 'Hiroshima' following a nuclear accident, and whose faulty construction cost many sailors their lives, was strategically important in the Cold War, since it carried nuclear weapons and was capable of transporting them over long distances, as far as the coast of America. K-19 was the first nuclear-powered submarine, meaning that it had to undergo special security tests. However, because of growing pressure from the Kremlin in the arms race with the American Navy, these were not always carried out.

In 1960, the naval authorities said the K-19 had already passed all the security tests, and the submarine was launched in July 1961. My grandfather, Kostya Jashi, was charged with recording the first training manoeuvres, so he went aboard. The manoeuvres were to take place in the Greenland Sea. Just off Jan Mayen Island, the commander reported an incident in the submarine's reactor. The cooling system had failed, and the reactor had to be switched off. They were facing a nuclear meltdown. Within the Soviet Union these manoeuvres were kept absolutely secret, and the crews of such submarines were under strict instructions not to transmit the international SOS signal, even in life-threatening situations. In any case, the ship's wireless antenna was broken; it was impossible to transmit a long-range radio signal, so they couldn't even call on the Soviet Navy for help.

The only way of saving the submarine was to send some of the crew into the reactor well to jury-rig an emergency cooling system. Until this provisional arrangement was in place, and because the temperature inside the reactor had now risen to a perilous 800 degrees, technicians used ordinary hoses to spray water onto the reactor. This hapless attempt caused a violent reaction when the cold water from the hoses came into contact with the reactor: the water evaporated instantly, releasing a massive dose of radiation.

Kostya never talked about the disaster. Never reminisced. Never said a word about this voyage from hell. But his memories of that day had buried themselves in his eyes, which, as a child, I learned to read. I wondered how close Kostya had been to the reactor well. Wondered what it must have smelled of there — burnt flesh, or something neutral preceding something appalling, or perhaps just ordinary chemicals? I imagined the ruined faces of the men in the reactor well, their cold sweat, their shaking hands, the careful steps, the muffled voices, the nearness of death, the radio silence, the icy quiet of the Arctic Sea, and the dignity of the icebergs, among which the submarine resurfaced, rescued from the loving embrace of the deep. I believe that on that day — for it was daytime — the stars were shining despite the sun, making the icebergs glow like Christmas trees. That the islands off Spitzbergen on the Norwegian side of the sea looked as peaceful and perfect as a film set.

I thought I saw these images in Kostya's eyes; I searched for them there, followed them, late, very late in his life, too late perhaps, but then I understood. There may have been nothing more to forgive; it was far too late for that, for him and for me, but this helped me understand a lot of things — this experience, this anteroom of the Inferno where he sat for so long, awaiting death. Differently, and with a different finality from that at Lake Ladoga; at the mercy of a different fate, of which he was differently, much more explicitly aware.

But perhaps Ida was in his thoughts, too; not as clear and personified as the dead who appeared to his mother, but clear enough. In his head. Holding on to her image, clinging to it, to a dead woman who promised him life, until he heard the men roar, their joyful shouts that the reactor had finally cooled and the worst was over — they had survived. Yes, that's what they were thinking at that moment: the immediate joy of having cheated death by a whisker, little suspecting that death, once it was aware of them, once it had got so close to them, would not release them from its clutches so easily, that *the worst*, for them, was still to come. I also believe that disaster wasn't averted back then, that it was only delayed. Perhaps just because Ida wanted to give her beloved another chance to lose his heart.

I don't know. Perhaps that was how it happened, perhaps it wasn't; all I can say with certainty, Brilka, is that the horror that branded itself in Kostya's eyes that day remained there for the rest of his life. You just had to look deep enough. Very deep.

A distress signal was eventually picked up by a nearby submarine, and the crew were evacuated, after twenty-four hours.

When they arrived in Moscow, all the crew had to sign a statement that said they were not permitted to speak of their own experiences in any form whatsoever from that day forward. The eight men who had cooled the reactor all died within six weeks of being rescued.

My grandfather, Kostya Jashi, was lucky. Along with other survivors, he was subsequently flown to Vienna and treated in a specialist private clinic. He lost all the hair on his head and body. Before the signs of his sickness became apparent to little Elene, too, he telephoned his wife and informed her that he had been posted on a six-month training manoeuvre in the Baltic Sea and she had to come to Moscow to take care of her daughter. Elene liked her blinis best with raspberry *varenye*, he added.

Unbreakable Union of freeborn Republics
Great Russia has welded forever to stand.
Created in struggle by will of the people,
United and mighty, our Soviet land!

SOVIET NATIONAL ANTHEM

While the German Democratic Republic went on claiming that it knew nothing about the building of a wall, on one side of which people would celebrate socialist happiness and Marxist brotherhood; and while the United States was stationing medium-range ballistic missiles in Italy and Turkey, armed with nuclear warheads pointing at the Soviet Union, the Kremlin launched Operation Anadyr. More than 200,000 tonnes of military equipment was shipped to Cuba. Half of the entire Soviet Navy was needed for the mission. The freighter *Omsk*, with medium-range missiles on board, docked in Havana on 8 September 1962. American spy planes took aerial photographs of the armaments the Soviets were installing on Cuba, which indicated the presence of missile sites: more than twenty rockets, all of which, if fired from Cuba, were capable of hitting large industrial cities in America. On 22 October, America declared a naval blockade of Cuba. Kennedy addressed the nation and put the US military on Defense Condition 2, the second-highest level of alert, threatening to launch a nuclear attack if Khrushchev didn't withdraw the missiles immediately. The world held its breath. Thekla and Sopio went on calmly playing Patience in Christine and Stasia's garden. Stasia watched the ghosts silently laying their cards and no longer knew whether she was losing her mind or whether reality wasn't, in the end, more flexible than she had previously assumed.

 She smoked one of her filterless cigarettes and felt for the gold watch she always carried with her. No missiles in the world would stop her looking for her daughter, no matter where, no matter how, she thought, trying to catch a glimpse of the ghosts' cards. As far as the CIA was concerned, there was every indication that Khrushchev and Castro had agreed to attack the US base at Guantánamo (yes, the same one that, decades later, did such damage to America's image).

Christine had picked Miqa up from school, and they were strolling through the narrow alleyways of Sololaki. He was eating a little tub of ice cream, which he loved, and excitedly telling her about his day. They walked down the wide road of Kirov Street and continued along Rustaveli Avenue. When they reached the Hotel Tbilisi, Christine stopped and stared at the imposing building.

'What is it?' asked Miqa.

'My husband used to dine here a lot. Back then, the hotel was called the Majestic, and only rich and beautiful people from all over the world used to stay here. It was a beautiful place in those days.'

'Do you miss him very much?' asked Miqa. He took Christine's hand.

'Let's walk on. We don't want to linger over sad things, do we?' She didn't answer the question.

In his bed in a private clinic in Vienna, Kostya turned over onto his left side, seeing his daughter's cheerful, beaming face in his mind's eye. He wanted to go back to Moscow, he didn't want her to grow up without a father, she didn't deserve that, he wanted to live, he wanted to survive, for her, for Elene. He couldn't die without seeing her again.

Little Big Men continued to toy with the globe, laughing gleefully all the while. The world escaped nuclear war by the skin of its teeth when the American Navy dropped depth charges on a Soviet submarine armed with nuclear missiles. The seconds that followed took the planet to the brink. A secret meeting took place in Washington. Bobby Kennedy agreed to Khrushchev's demand about removing US missiles from Turkey and Italy, and that night Khrushchev ordered that missiles be withdrawn from Cuba.

Elene dreamed about her father, and cried out for him. Nana slept in her daughter's room to dispel her fears, but it didn't help. When Kostya reached Giorgi Alania on the phone — their phone calls had become increasingly infrequent — his friend thought he sounded optimistic.

'I've survived. I'm out of danger for now. I'll be going home. To Elene. I've survived — no leukaemia, the doctors told me today.'

Alania didn't understand what this was about, but something told him it was serious, and the fact that the call came from a clinic in Vienna confirmed his assumption. These were not, however, subjects that could be discussed on the phone.

'I had to tell someone. I just had to tell someone,' repeated Kostya, euphoric.

Alania couldn't help thinking of Kostya's sister, the woman whose voice had become the most reliable reference point of his life in recent years; the now-famous singer who had just put out her second album, entitled *Summer of Broken Tears* (her single was currently competing with another new song with the rather more profane title *Love Me Do*, by that new band — you know, Brilka, the ones with the silly haircuts).

Sitting at the desk in his office at the embassy, Alania stretched. Kostya had his private number. Back then he'd told him: only in an emergency. Now he wished he hadn't said it, and that his friend had called him more often. Back then, after Kitty's escape, they had spoken more regularly — although it was usually he who had called his friend, always from different phone boxes. They were both all too familiar with the rules; they stuck to the regulations and to what they had agreed. Even if it was sometimes hard to reconcile these rules with their own needs.

'Are you still there?' Kostya's voice roused him from his reverie.

'Yes, sorry, I was just thinking about what you said. Whatever the reason for your stay there, I'm as happy as you are that you've made it. You were always a fighter, and you always will be.'

★

Kitty sat, naked, in the little wicker chair in her bedroom. She could hear the bathwater running in the bathroom: she would climb into the bath, lie there, and chase away the thoughts, the doubts, that haunted her. For four nights now, Fred hadn't come round; presumably she was at this moment asleep in Amy's lavender-scented bed. Or getting drunk with shifty characters in her new studio in Hackney, for which Amy was footing the bill. Kitty wondered whether she should ask Fred to go with her to Vienna. She was afraid of the look in Fred's eyes as she flung a cold 'no' back in her face. After fleeing Mödling she had never returned to Austria, not since the night her mother had taken the belt in her hands. But Kitty hoped that, if they went there, Fred would finally be able to shake off the curse of that city. And perhaps the city would also stop being her own unlived dream with Andro.

She dragged herself to the bathroom. Her steps were heavy. She tried to recall her mother's face. She tried to imagine what time had done to her. The time that lay between them. What was this time like? Leaden, icy, metallic?

She slipped into the foaming water; it was too hot, but she wanted to feel it scald her. It was always like this whenever Fred was absent, or her nameless friend didn't call for a long time: nothing reminded her of life. Not her performances, not Amy's euphoria, least of all the small, diligent success of her songs. Whenever she closed her eyes, the East came flooding back. How quickly the West deserts you as soon as you stop focusing on it, thought Kitty, silently enduring the hot water on her skin. Just as Fred was unable to scrub Mödling off her body, Kitty was unable to scrub away the East. The marks it had left on her were indelible. She looked down at her scars. Mariam was there, too. She would always be there. Mariam, and her son. Yes — once the East had embraced you and held you tight, once you had choked on the East, it never went away.

And I stubbornly repeat
Your name again and yet again
Softly and with angry lips,
Trying to wake my love again.

SOPHIA PARNOK

Kostya had been home less than a week when Nana stood listening at the door of his study, where her husband and some of his uniformed colleagues had gathered, and heard, again and again, the words 'nuclear, dead, sanatorium' and 'medal for bravery'.

Elene wasn't home from school yet. Nana went into the kitchen and swallowed her cold fury with a very large glass of water. Nana, whose daughter had celebrated her father's return with such squealing and cries of joy that she woke the entire household — Nana, who was dying of homesickness for Tbilisi, her university, her friends, even Stasia and Christine, quietly admitted defeat.

Unlike the reunion of father and daughter, their greeting had been almost formal. A tentative kiss on the lips, a quick hug; no direct questions, of course. But naturally she had suspected — no, she knew — that this had had nothing to do with the Baltic Sea, that he had not handed over his beloved child to her all this time just because of a training manoeuvre.

Nana heard Elene open the front door, drop her satchel on the floor, put on her slippers, and enter the kitchen. Usually the first thing she did was burst into her father's study; she must have heard the unfamiliar voices, which had discouraged her from going in.

She was tall for her age; her cocoa-coloured eyes were very like her aunt's, the aunt who'd been branded a traitor to her country. About whom they were all forbidden to ask. Elene's legs in their white socks were long and strong, her posture erect, her gaze reflective, mistrustful. Her hair was cut in a pageboy bob that sat against her round head like a perfectly knitted cap. She washed her hands and peered into the saucepans to see what Lyuda had prepared for her today. Satisfied, she turned on the gas oven without asking her mother if she would like to eat with her.

Observing her independent daughter, Nana couldn't help finding her behaviour almost repellent. However hard she had tried with Elene these last few months, she could not penetrate the iron wall Elene had put up around herself, this personification of her father's perfect daughter.

Now that Kostya was back, Nana had become superfluous. It was the deciding factor in Nana's final capitulation: the thorny truth that the long months she had spent on her own with Elene had all been wasted. Elene had not forgiven her. Had not taken her back into her heart. Would not leave the country with her mother and travel south now that her stay in Moscow was drawing to a close.

She looked at her daughter and understood that this had not been an easy decision for Elene; that she had had to choose a side, choose one of her parents, and unfortunately she had chosen Kostya. But wasn't it the case — though it was immeasurably hard for Nana to admit this — that the girl was more like her husband than her? Perhaps that was why Elene found it more desirable to emulate her father than the eccentric women in her family.

And despite the tentative suspicions Nana had had during the years of her marriage, in the bitter battle for their daughter's love and favour; despite her intuitions about Kostya's secrets; despite her hurtful realisations in the time she spent alone with her daughter in her powerful husband's realm — despite all this, the fact that she would have to return home alone again was surprisingly painful for her.

Had Kostya come back two weeks earlier, perhaps she would have been spared the insight into the miserable state of her marriage. Now, though, as Nana sat passively, helplessly, in the kitchen, fighting back tears, she was still trying to persuade herself that it wasn't Elene's fault, that she hadn't been taking revenge; that it was because of her childishness, her naivety, her innocence that she had inflicted such pain on her mother.

Two weeks earlier, Elene had been talking incessantly about Kostya again. Nana had felt the anger welling up inside her; she had felt she was being treated unjustly, being manipulated by her own child. She had wanted to scream in her face that she should stop punishing her for something that wasn't her fault; that Elene should show her mother more of the respect and love she deserved. That she should show her true face — candid, obstinate, quick-tempered, but so much more alive. Should go back to being unruly and loud, stubborn and emotionally needy. Should, should, should. Nana had held her tongue. One after another she stuffed chocolates into her mouth and stared at the bluish light of the television, which was showing the bedtime programme Elene loved to watch every evening.

'Don't eat so many sweets,' Elene had said suddenly, without taking her eyes off the screen.

Nana had just popped another sweet into her mouth; she froze, not daring to chew it. She felt ashamed, humiliated by her own daughter. As if that weren't enough, Elene added, 'Papa prefers women who are slimmer and wear lipstick, and perfume, too.'

A cartoon dog with unusually long ears was racing across the screen singing a cheerful song.

'And how do you know that?' Nana asked icily.

'I just know.'

'How?' Nana's voice grew louder. She finally swallowed the chocolate.

'He sometimes has visitors,' Elene said calmly, as if telling her about her day at school. Her eyes were still fixed on the dog, which was waving its ears and emitting a contentedly melodious *woof, woof*.

'Here? He has visitors here?'

'Yes, where else? This is where he lives.'

Elene reached for the bowl of sweets on the narrow coffee table.

'And who are these slim women with red lipstick?' Nana tried to control her tone. She felt like howling.

'Well, like I said: slim women with red lips in fluffy coats. They smell so nice. And sometimes they bring me presents.'

'Aha. They bring you presents, do they?'

'Yes.'

Elene unwrapped a chocolate and stuffed it greedily into her mouth. The long-eared dog had now been joined by a waddling duck who also joined in the singing, adding its *quack, quack* to the *woof, woof*.

'What sort of presents?'

'Mama, I'm watching television.'

'What sort of presents?' Nana was struggling to control her voice.

'Toys. Or a scarf. I've had gloves, as well.'

'And how long do they stay here?'

'No idea. Not long. Some of them come again, some don't. Look, that's Gaston, the duck. He's my favourite.'

Elene squeaked with delight, her mouth full of chocolate.

*

The dignitaries finally left. Kostya shook them all by the hand as he said goodbye. The gentlemen looked very serious and important. Just the way Kostya liked to see himself. Nana put Elene to bed as usual. It was Lyuda's day off. Kostya holed himself up in his study.

He had changed. He seemed thinner, weaker. She could hardly look at him; since his return all she could think of was what Elene had said: *Papa prefers women who are slimmer and wear lipstick, and perfume, too.*

Nana went into the bathroom. Took a long look at herself in the mirror. Her face betrayed none of her worries. The many pounds she'd put on in recent years hadn't touched that open, friendly countenance. Her cheekbones were still sharp and high, her forehead smooth, her eyes clear. She didn't look like a deeply unhappy woman. Over the course of her marriage her face had learned to lie.

She took her washbag from the cupboard, took out a red lipstick she hardly ever used, and dabbed the colour onto her mouth. She combed her thick, dark-blonde hair and pinned it up in an artful knot. Then she went into the bedroom and selected her best dress: it had a daring neckline, and was navy blue, which brought out the colour of her eyes. It was a little tight around the hips now, but it would do for tonight. She put on the only high heels she possessed; they were languishing untouched in a shoebox in the cupboard. She had bought them with Kostya beside the 'Cold Sea', all those years ago, when she had first realised that her husband did not desire her.

Then she bundled up her clothes and stuffed them into a suitcase.

She knocked on his door and entered without waiting for an answer. He was sitting poring over files by the weak light of a lamp. On his desk stood a bust of the Generalissimus; beside it, a few framed photographs of Elene.

When he saw her like that, it gave him a start. She had stopped dressing up for him long ago. Normally he would have told her that he still had things to do, thereby indirectly sending her out again, but something in her manner must have made it clear that he couldn't show her the door so easily this time. He offered her a chair. Some glasses and a half-empty vodka bottle were still sitting on the little sideboard by his desk. Apparently he and his colleagues had drunk a toast to something.

She reached for the bottle without asking and filled one of the used glasses to the brim. He opened his mouth to speak, but closed it again as she brought the glass to her lips and knocked back the contents in a single gulp.

'It seems I'm not the woman you need. What a pity I was so deceived in you, Kostya. It's not even your fault. You were right, I didn't want to wake up. But now I have, as you can see. I'm so awake, so terrifyingly awake, that sometimes I fear I'll never be able to fall asleep again. If you want to, we can get divorced. It's all the same to me. But if you want to stay married to me, we have to settle a few things. And you will have to take my wishes into account.'

Nana had refilled her glass, and, as her husband didn't speak, she continued.

'First of all, from now on I don't want you to question my authority ever again in front of Elene. I want you to stop belittling me and sneering at my "university nonsense", to stop criticising my parenting methods. Stop trying to make her believe that I'm not good enough for the two of you. Yes — the two of you, because you're a proper little team now, and all I'm allowed to do is sit on the reserve bench and watch you. This has to stop! Right now.

'Secondly, I insist that you never again bring any of your tarts — pardon my coarseness — to the apartment where my daughter is living. You can do whatever you like, but you will make sure Elene knows nothing about it. I'm going to tell you a little secret, Kostya, as a friend, not as your wife. All these women who seem so desirable to you, all these blonde and brunette angels for whom you get to play the Don Juan: they're nothing more than actresses who are very good at playing their part. Because that's all they've learned: the only thing they know how to do is provide you with exactly the feeling you think you need. They've learned to let you believe that they're magical, that their only purpose is to enchant you, and when they moan in bed — pardon my directness, but I don't have to please you any more — they do it because they think that's what you want to hear. And they're right: that is what you want to hear and see. Precisely that. And the more I think about it, the less I understand you, Kostya, the less I'm able to grasp how someone who grew up surrounded by so many women can understand so little about them. And it's sad that no matter how many heroic deeds you perform for your country, or how many medals they give you for it, you will always be weak — weak around women, because it seems you haven't learned to make them your friends.

'You know, you should have understood that you weren't doing yourself any favours by excluding me from your relationship with Elene, because I could have protected you. You know why? Because I saw you as a friend. And because I loved you. Yes, I did, even if for a long time I didn't know or understand what exactly this wretched thing called love actually is. And I hoped we could be friends to each other, that at least, even if we couldn't be partners. But you lied to me; for you, it was always about breaking my will, making me small and docile, because you didn't know anything else, because you didn't want anything else; because it seems your pretty, empty little dolls are just like that, aren't they? Submissive, docile, and uncomplicated, their only purpose to lift your spirits. And when I began to resist you, when I didn't submit, you started to take the most precious thing of all away from me; you declared a silent war on me. Over her, over our own child! You didn't understand that in doing so you've set yourself the biggest trap of your life. And it's partly because I've failed so dismally with her during my time here, because even in your absence I was always in your shadow, that I know she'll turn against us one day, and do you want to know why? Because she'll be a woman, a real woman of flesh and blood, not an empty doll, the way she's learned to be from you, in all those years of living by your side. One day she won't be able to stand it any more; she'll smash open this shell and start punishing you for the burden you placed on her when she was so very young. And it makes me want to throw up to hear her speak her mother tongue with that bloody Russian accent —'

'What's that got to do with anything?' stuttered Kostya, who throughout her monologue had been staring at his wife in utter disbelief.

'Thirdly: don't interrupt me! Just don't do it any more! And fourthly: when she finishes this school year, I'm taking Elene back with me to Tbilisi. And no, I don't want to discuss it. I'm just saying it so you'll have plenty of time to prepare yourself.'

All at once Kostya sat up. He too reached for the vodka bottle.

'I will not agree to a divorce.'

'Fine — as I thought. If you agree to my demands, I promise you in return that I will continue to be a faithful wife to you, and won't do anything that might endanger your reputation or your position. And you needn't worry about your daughter's admiration for you, either: I won't come between you. And yes, I'm flying home tomorrow. I don't think my presence is required here any longer.'

If only I could stand in line for a different fate ...

ALLA PUGACHEVA

'You're spoiling the boy!' Stasia told her sister one mild October afternoon in 1967. Once again, Miqa had refused to play football with the neighbours' son, and had instead taken refuge in Christine's bed, supposedly with a sore throat. Christine was sitting in the kitchen crocheting a tablecloth. Stasia stood in the doorway, in dirty gardening boots and old, rolled-up trousers at least two sizes too big, eyeing her sister crossly. Since turning sixty, Stasia had begun to shrink; her bones seemed to become more slender, she herself ever smaller and more delicate. By her eightieth birthday, she would have the figure of a little girl.

'What's the matter now?' Christine was irritated, but didn't look up from her crocheting.

'Can't you see what you're turning him into? The boy's behaving like an old man already. He never goes off to play with other children; he's always so serious, always with you. It's not healthy. Even his father's complained that he —'

'What are you getting at?'

'I'm trying to tell you that you're not a little girl any more, and the boy needs to be with children his own age.'

'I have no intention of being declared a fossil just because I'm not twenty any more.'

'He's a little boy, Christine, my God!'

'I try to give him everything he needs. He's happy. For me, that's the most important thing.'

'You're giving him what you think he needs. But he needs other things. He's not a toy. Besides, he's *not a girl*, and the way you are with him certainly isn't good for him.'

'You're jealous, you're just jealous, because I'm finally able to raise a child, and do it so that he's happy, whereas you ...'

Christine was shouting. The tablecloth slipped from her hand and she stared at her sister, enraged.

'You're still a spoiled brat! A blind, pampered, stupid creature, Christine!' Stasia returned her younger sister's furious glare. 'You're getting old — accept it! And get your satisfaction elsewhere!' Stasia stamped out into the garden, leaving damp earth on the kitchen floor.

Christine was annoyed. Why did her sister always have to be so frightfully humourless, so entirely lacking in charm, so serious and bitter? Yes, it was true, Miqa was a dreamer through and through, and perhaps her excessive pampering of the poor, frightened little creature who had felt so alone when first he came to them was not a good strategy for his future survival.

His features were coarser than his father's, but they suggested he would be a very attractive man one of these days, at least for the part of the female population that is drawn to brute strength. He radiated physical power and a healthy groundedness. Only his large eyes, clear and blue as the sky, betrayed the childish vulnerability within. His outward appearance belied his extreme shyness, his nervousness of strangers, his love of literature and loathing of physical activity. Certainly, the way he could sit for hours in the garden with little beetles on his palm, listening to the birds, did not really endear him to children his own age. But he managed to keep trouble at bay; his external appearance inevitably commanded respect.

How happy he always was, thought Christine, when he was able to come home to her after the summer holidays. How relieved not to have to act tough in front of his unsympathetic mother and drunkard father. How delighted he was then to be allowed to listen to the old gramophone with her as she told him something about each of the arias, or when she put one of her favourite novels on his pillow; when she took him out for an ice cream and told him tales about every street and corner.

And what was wrong with that? Why shouldn't she do all these things? Nana's critical looks had not escaped Christine's notice, either, whenever she and Miqa sat poring over a book or bent over a plant in the garden. Ever since she had come back from Moscow, Nana had regarded the world around her with alarming pragmatism. At first, Christine had assumed Nana was despondent because she was missing her daughter, but by now all she felt for her was irritation. She should have gone to Russia to be with her husband, then her relationship with Kostya wouldn't be so cold and distant! Then she wouldn't have had to share him with Russia and the Cold Sea, with state secrets, and, above all, with other women! But Nana and Kostya simply weren't suited. She knew her nephew far too well not to know this. Right from the start, Nana had maintained a certain distance; from Christine, but, above all, from the boy, as if she were afraid of loving him too much.

★

Over the past few years the thought of Kitty had become an obsession for Stasia, an inescapable prison that made her more bad-tempered, irritable, and abstracted than she already was; that robbed her of sleep, and made her inattentive at work at the library.

She had to see her. Otherwise one day — she was quite sure of it — she would simply not get up, would wait until Sopio or Thekla came to take her hand and lead her over the Jordan. If that was even how it happened. She sensed it: she had no doubt whatsoever that she would die very soon if she was not able to put her arms around her daughter at least once more.

The thought led her to start having conversations with her daughter, her lips silently forming the words she addressed to her. Was she eating properly? Could she bear living abroad? Or she would ask about the country Kitty was living in, tell her tales of daily life at the library, complain about Christine's infantile stubbornness, explain that Elene was growing up far away from her mother.

Lying in bed at night, her glassy stare fixed on the ceiling, she would dream of how she might contrive to see Kitty again. But in none of these scenarios could she find a way to bypass Kostya. He was the intermediary. The black angel who presided over the fates of both mother and sister. She knew her request could put him in danger. But how else could she find Kitty? Where in the West, where in England — if it was true, if that really was where she was living — should she look for her, and how would she get there? The mother of a traitor would never be allowed out of the country. Never!

Christine was no support: as was typical of her, she approved of Kostya's behaviour. He had a responsible position now, she said; they were all protected because of him; he couldn't take such a risk. Just think of all the interrogations the two of them had been subjected to after Kitty's disappearance; if Kostya hadn't had his position, those interrogations would have ended badly. They would both have been banned from working in public institutions like the hospital and the library — or possibly worse.

Back then, years ago, in another life — in another world, or so it seemed to her — she had travelled hundreds of kilometres across war-ravaged countries, first for her husband and then for her son; had had the courage to defy the Mensheviks and the Bolsheviks, and the fascists, too; and she had had no fear, because she'd been convinced that she was doing the right thing. And why shouldn't she do the same for her daughter? Neither of her journeys to Russia had had the desired outcome, of course; but she had made them, she had tried, she had done something, albeit in her own way, which was twisted, hard to comprehend, not always logical. Perhaps she had had less to lose back then — yes, perhaps, perhaps her behaviour had been thoroughly egotistical, but what did it matter? Wasn't this terrible inaction just as dangerous?

Even the card games played in her garden by the two dead women whom no one but she could see were no longer able to distract Stasia from her oppressive thoughts. Whenever the ghosts appeared, she turned her back on them and buried herself in a book or newspaper. What use were they to her if they didn't help her, if they didn't show her the way, if they showed no interest in anything apart from their cards?

But when Kostya returned to Tbilisi with Elene for the winter holidays and started to prepare for a big New Year's party, she said the unsayable. She set aside her fear of his anger and began to urge him, beg him, to tell her where her daughter was, to arrange some kind of contact between them, a meeting — it didn't matter where or how.

'That's absolutely out of the question!'

There was no mistaking Kostya's horror: his hand flew to his mouth as he spoke, as if he were suddenly afraid of his own voice.

Just then they were alone in the kitchen; she was helping her son to unpack and put away the lavish quantities of food he had bought at the central market.

'If I don't see her, I'll go mad. I dream of her all the time, when I do actually manage to fall asleep, and they keep giving me warnings at work because I —'

Kostya put a finger to his lips and glanced around in alarm. There was something pitiful about her, the way she was pleading with him, permitting him to glimpse her needs and fears, something she never usually did. He wanted to contradict her, to put an end to the subject as quickly as possible, but he couldn't help feeling profoundly moved. She was like a little child, frail and shrunken, sexless, so utterly lost, standing there waving her hands to emphasise her words.

But she didn't stop; she kept going on at him, and since it had already become clear to him that this was not something he could resolve quickly, he took her by the hand and led her over to the table. He suddenly felt like a giant beside her: her shoulders were hunched, her face so pale. The lines around her mouth were deep and depressing. Despite her grey hair, which, unlike her sister, she didn't dye, she didn't really seem old. She had the air of a person who, in some peculiar and obstinate way, was defying time, sticking her tongue out at it.

Her speech was confused. She jumped from one point to the next, from one memory to another. Craning her head towards him, desperately searching for something she could cling to, a shred of hope in his eyes. She touched his hands — she hadn't done that for a long time. She didn't reproach him. She flattered him. She called him 'my boy'; she really begged. It was all too much for Kostya. Fortunately, they were alone. The small, naked piglet lay on the draw leaf of the kitchen dresser, staring at them with sad, dead eyes. Mountains of oranges and mandarins, persimmons and dried fruit lay in several bowls on the table and refrigerator. Bottles of sparkling wine stood around in shopping bags on the floor.

He loved the New Year's party. The sumptuous meals, the excess, the ringing in of the new year, the grandiose addresses on television, the counting down from ten, the fireworks; he loved giving presents to his family, and he thought about the fact that she, his mother, who was now sitting before him and would soon prepare many of the delicacies he loved so much, had no idea that, not so long ago, he had had to come to terms with the thought that he might never enjoy such celebrations ever again; that, in a sickbed in a western clinic, he had stared death in the face for months on end.

This thought was hard to bear. He would have liked to have told her, when he didn't know if he would ever get well again, that despite everything he was grateful to her for having borne him. Despite everything from which she had not been able to shield him; despite everything she had withheld from him, had not given him; despite all the times she had eluded him. He had wanted to write her a letter, back then; in this letter he would have addressed her as *'Deda'* again, not by her first name, as he usually did, to maintain distance between mother and son.

He looked at her, and felt as if they had swapped roles. As if he were the father and she the child. As if it were unthinkable that another human being could have sprung from this ageless, childlike person. Himself. And his sister, for whom she now wept with such abandon.

But in the same breath he also felt anger welling up inside him; anger at this fragile person with the drab bun and the shining, colourless eyes. How often, as a child, had he stood before her, completely at a loss — and not just him, *her* as well, her beloved daughter, her ray of sunshine — how often had they both failed to reach her, frustrated by her unworldliness, her habit of retreating into an inner world to which they were denied access? How often had they wished they had a normal mother who didn't say and do such confusing things, but whose actions were straightforward and easy to understand, a simple woman with simple desires and maternal instincts? Would their lives have taken different paths, Kostya wondered, as he shrank from an unfamiliar fervour in Stasia's eyes, if she had been a better mother to them? If they hadn't had to vie for her love, her attention, to wear themselves out in this all-consuming rivalry? Were there even any answers to such questions? Or was it perhaps too simple to believe there was a single answer to their question, one that made all others redundant? Rather, didn't each answer conceal another answer, and behind that another, on and on, until it drove you mad?

Stasia told him about her journey to Russia, all those years ago, and her attempt to trace him. *Why is she telling me this now?* he asked himself, not knowing whether to be pleased or angry.

Was Kostya sorry? Did he feel any pangs of conscience? Did he question what had happened? Did he waste even a single thought on how Kitty was faring? I don't believe he did: he forbade himself to think about such things. Because here, too, he didn't believe in answers. The only possible definitive answer was the life that they were living.

His mother, this shadow trapped in a world of her own — no fairy, as Christine had once been — stood before him, weeping, her hand clamped round his wrist. He couldn't cope with her tears. He didn't want to have power over her: for what was perhaps the first time since the pursuit of power had become his main aim in life, Kostya felt it as a burden. He didn't want to sit in judgement over her tears. He wanted nothing to do with her suffering. But it was impossible: they were all far too tightly bound to one another, whether they liked it or not. They would never be able to disentangle themselves; nothing in their story was ever truly over, not as long as they lived. There were always other outcomes, twists and possibilities that revealed themselves after every supposed end.

He lowered his head; he raised her hand to his lips; he touched her cool, soft skin; it felt good to sense the possibility of forgiveness, the possibility of considering a different possibility, for himself and for their story together. Even if they wouldn't rewrite it, not now, even if it was impossible to preserve this peace, to believe in a new beginning, the illusion was nonetheless soothing, calming, reconciling.

When her speech got as far as his birth and its associated torments, he was cursing himself for letting himself get caught up in this mawkishness, this emotional indulgence, for not stemming this flood of words at the outset and setting about the profane activity of sorting out the food. But it was too late: for a moment he had been weak, for a moment he had allowed himself to be carried away by his feelings, and now he had to bear the consequences and listen to this sentimental mother-son claptrap.

'Yes — nine hours, nine whole hours the contractions lasted. You were big, even then; you weighed more than four kilos, I didn't have much strength left to push —'

'Stasia, please.' He didn't want to hear any more, didn't want to have to listen to the bloody details.

'And the midwife shouted —'

'Stasia!'

'— push, push, and I thought: I'm going to faint!'

'All right, that's enough! I'll think about it. I can't promise you anything, but I'll think about it.'

★

When the telephone rang, Kitty was standing in the middle of her living room, locked in a tight embrace with Fred, feeling for a moment as if she had overcome everything that separated her from happiness. She had been dancing with Fred, laughing as her red-haired friend floated dreamily across the dark wooden floor, twisting her body into peculiar shapes, while Kitty's own voice sang out of the big speakers.

They had fought the previous night. Perhaps for the first time it had been as fierce as the fights Amy had with this woman who was lover to them both. Kitty had never intended to let that tone creep into her voice, that contempt, which was really only an admission of her own dependency and powerlessness. She had been ashamed of her loss of control, the pointless reproaches, all aimed at Fred's ideas about life and morality. Kitty felt she had behaved shabbily in her desperation. The cross-examination she had inflicted on her beloved, the cheap, repulsive, almost vulgar insults and threats. Unlike Amy, she had never hoped she would be able to change Fred. Perhaps she had never wanted to, either, but equally she did not want to make her happiness, her contentment dependent on this woman. On the tiny morsel of clandestine love she threw her way. And Fred, as if she didn't take herself seriously in the role of cruel heartbreaker and thoughtless egomaniac, had waited for Kitty's anger to subside, only to sweet-talk and bewitch her again, to soften her up and explain to her once more that this lack of commitment, this unreliability, this freedom actually constituted the greatest fidelity of which she was capable.

Kitty hated it, and it seemed she would never get used to the idea that Fred didn't have a romantic bone in her body and had to reduce everything to sex. But perhaps it was easier to describe their relationship as a liaison with no commitment; perhaps it was easier to persuade herself that they shared nothing more than a bed and the traumas of their pasts.

As dawn was breaking, Kitty, hoarse and exhausted, had admitted defeat, after which Fred had coaxed her into going for a long walk, then had bought fresh fish with her at the weekly market and made her a delicious meal. Kitty would never have believed Fred's hands were capable of such a thing had she not been present and seen it with her own eyes: Fred, over-excited and giggling like a little girl, preparing the food in Kitty's kitchen with such patience, such attention to detail; the time she took over the cooking, the many spices weighed and tasted like a medicinal remedy.

After the meal, Fred put on *Summer of Broken Tears* and held forth about every song on the album. And once they had finished a bottle of wine, and Fred had rolled a joint, they were sufficiently uninhibited to dance to *Star Collector*, too, whirling around the room, singing over and over again: 'Let's pretend we are lovers and start to collect the stars.'

How many people there are in this one person, thought Kitty. She was constantly amazed by how deceptive and changeable Fred's body was. How transparent, defenceless, insubstantial as breath, weak, and devoid of all eroticism; how possessive. She could have danced with this woman for ever and a day.

The sound of the telephone roused Kitty from her stupor. She reeled back to the sofa, flopped onto it, and picked up the receiver. Even before he had said hello she recognised his even breathing. He had never called outside their prearranged times. What had happened? Her body tensed. No, please no, not bad news, not now, she thought.

'I've been asked to make you an offer.' He sounded particularly matter-of-fact.

Kitty took a deep breath and signalled to Fred to turn the music down.

'I thought something awful must have happened.'

'No, no. It's a good offer, in my opinion.'

'I'm happy to hear your voice.'

Fred eyed her with curiosity. It was the first time she had heard Kitty speak in her mother tongue. She watched her, fascinated, as if she were performing a work of art.

There was a crackle at the other end of the line.

'The Komsomol Club in Prague is interested in a performance.'

'Prague? Did I hear that correctly?'

'Yes, precisely.'

'That can't be right, that's —'

'Yes, yes, it is. In a few days' time your manager will receive an official request. And if I were you, I would accept the offer, because there, you might …'

He fell silent. Kitty's heart was racing. Prague. The city was full of scars; the memory of that city was full of bruises. She felt all her courage draining away. What she really wanted to do was ask him to go with her. Only now did she realise that he hadn't finished his sentence.

'I might — what?'

'You might meet someone; someone who …'

Kitty put her hand over her mouth to hold back the scream. Did he mean Kostya, her mother, Christine? Andro, perhaps? No, that wasn't possible, they would never give him permission to travel abroad. Most likely her brother. Never mind who, the main thing was that it would be someone from her family, someone from home, someone from her old life.

'Who?' she cried, overwhelmed by the joy filling her heart.

'You know the rules.'

'Yes, yes, I know the rules. Yes, I'll accept the offer, of course I will.'

'That's what I thought.'

'Do you know that I really like you?' Kitty could no longer suppress her laughter.

'I'm very glad. Because the feeling is mutual.'

After she hung up, she threw open both windows in her room and let the cool air flow into her lungs. Fred, who had gone into the kitchen, returned with a glass of whisky in her hand. Normally Kitty would have been cross and warned her that she drank too much, that she constantly needed some kind of stimulant to act as a crutch for her life, but this time she didn't care, she wanted to get drunk, too, wanted to celebrate this incredible news. She turned and flung her arms around Fred's neck.

What is needed is work; everything else can go to the devil.

ANTON CHEKHOV

Kostya knew he should not have made Elene his accomplice: firstly, because she was still far too young to be able to interpret the subtle signs of a broken marriage correctly; and secondly, because she was herself a woman. He should not have let her in on his secrets. He blamed himself for the fact that he now had to let her go, walking on the sad, broken shards of his marriage, even though the return of his cautious, disciplined girl to the emotionally unbalanced, chaotic, unstructured regime of the women, dictated by moods and whims, was not without danger. What Kostya did not foresee was that Elene's anger would blossom into a beautiful and poisonous flower.

He promised Elene that he would call at every opportunity, promised her the same pocket money she got in Moscow, promised her he would take advantage of every holiday and every opportunity to go on spending time with his 'best friend', as he sometimes called her. He even promised that he would make her the blinis she loved so much, according to Lyuda's recipe. And although Elene didn't protest, didn't make any hysterical scenes, didn't even cry in front of him, he knew that her heart was broken, that he had not protected her from a sense of being superfluous and unloved.

He had no say in the decision as to whether Elene should attend tenth grade in a Russian or a Georgian school. Nana had had enough of Elene's affected upper-class accent, she told him on the phone; those elitist mannerisms had to stop once and for all. She would go to a perfectly ordinary Georgian school in Vera, and she could walk there; a chauffeur was completely over the top for a fourteen-year-old girl.

Elene maintained a mild, polite demeanour, kissed all of her female relatives cheerfully upon her return, accepted, for her mother's sake, her demotion from an elite school to a normal one, even though it seemed impossible to her at first to change the language in which she was educated, and swore to herself that the minute she turned eighteen she would never do anything the adults expected of her ever again.

Her unknown aunt's old room was repainted in a hurry; a new writing desk was installed, rails were bought specially for Elene's many clothes, and the soft toys Elene had brought with her from Moscow were arranged on the freshly made bed.

In the first weeks after her return, everyone in the house seemed to vie for her favour. They only prepared meals she liked; whichever programme she expressed an interest in was the one they would watch; they made a fuss about ensuring Christine's arias didn't disturb her when she was doing her homework; and Miqa was warned not to keep her from her work and her daily routine any more than necessary. Elene sensed all this and cynically took it for granted. For her, their behaviour was confirmation — proof — that her family felt guilty about replacing their daughter, granddaughter, with an overly sensitive country bumpkin.

Miqa had been in torment since her return. Things he had previously taken for granted were now forbidden him. Nobody had given him an instruction manual for Elene. He tiptoed past her room, where she was often playing western music, and blushed when she sat next to him at meals.

She seemed so sure of herself, so sophisticated, so chic, with her white mother-of-pearl nail varnish, her absolutely symmetrical shoulder-length hair, and her constant cries of, 'Of course I know that. Why? Don't you have it here yet? In Moscow ...' He felt small and stupid around her, as if unworthy of her presence. Never the most popular pupil in his class, he envied the way friends started flocking to her soon after she arrived at the school. Everyone seemed to court the favour of this precocious, fashionable girl: from the teacher's pet to the cool kids, class clown to school heartthrob, everyone wanted to be around her. She radiated an aura of grandeur and self-sufficiency; she'd come straight from Moscow, had seen the world, her father was an important man, she possessed the rarest records, she knew about pop music, she had a sharp tongue, she didn't let anyone push her around, and above all she was very aware of the effect she had on people.

Life in the house on Vera Hill gradually normalised. Stasia and Christine went about their work; the previous year, Nana had finally secured a long-coveted full-time job as a professor of linguistics and was immersing herself in the day-to-day life of the university. Elene's return appeared to have been a success: she was integrating well into school life in Tbilisi, overcoming the language barrier thanks to the tutoring Kostya paid for, and seemed not to miss

Moscow and her father at all, as Nana had initially feared.

Elene and Miqa had agreed on a few unspoken rules so as to keep out of each other's way as best they could. Although they both had the same walk to school, they never walked together. At breakfast and dinner, when the whole family gathered around the kitchen table, they sat as far away from each other as possible so they wouldn't be tempted to chat or have to ask the other to pass something. When the weather was fine, Elene monopolised the garden; but she scarcely set foot on the first floor of the house, where Miqa's bedroom was, along with Ramas' study and library, where he loved to spend his time. That winter, when Andro collected his son as usual at the start of the school holidays, he sensed that, for the first time since he had gone to live in Tbilisi, Miqa was glad to leave the city and the house behind.

★

But after the winter holidays, which Kostya spent with his daughter as promised, even taking her to Bakuriani for a week-long skiing holiday, things changed. Nana was summoned to the school, where the class teacher informed her that her daughter was inciting other girls to play truant and engage in 'lewd behaviour'. She was shown rude words that Elene — so the teacher had been told — had pencilled on the walls of the girls' toilets for all to see. Nana defended her daughter: Elene was a model pupil, popular and hardworking, and so disciplined — this wasn't the kind of thing her girl would do.

However, the following week, when she found cigarette butts on Elene's windowsill, she started to suspect that Elene's rebellion might indeed have begun, and so she attempted to have an open conversation with her daughter. Elene denied everything, became very angry, and slammed her bedroom door in her mother's face.

Elene was grounded. Nana came home punctually from work and made sure that she did her homework. Her daughter's favourite meals were off the menu for the next few weeks, and Stasia and Christine were also asked not to pay her any attention. Nana believed she was doing the right thing; true, Elene went around looking sulky, but she did as she was told.

Until one day she didn't come home from school. They called her girlfriends, but no one could say where she might be. The alarm was raised. Nana grabbed Miqa and spent all afternoon with him combing the streets, but Elene was nowhere to be found. One of her classmates mentioned that she got on well with the older boys; perhaps she was at a party somewhere with one of them. Sure enough, long after midnight, a drunken Elene staggered into the kitchen as if nothing had happened and calmly started frying an egg: she was hungry, she said.

Nana exploded. Kostya was called in Moscow, and, after he had spoken to his daughter for an hour, Elene mumbled a half-hearted apology to her mother. Nana threatened not to let her out of the house for a month if she didn't stop this unacceptable behaviour immediately; but Elene just climbed out of her window and stayed out all night. There was another long phone call to Moscow that culminated in a fight between Nana and her husband, who accused her of ruining their daughter's future.

Elene was impossible to control. Sneaking out after dark became a habit. She would hang out all night with the rowdy boys from school on the field beneath the television tower, where they would drink wine or beer, play each other songs on the guitar, sing, dance, and — if they were especially daring — kiss.

Nana had bars put on her daughter's window, but the following night Elene escaped via the apple tree, which she reached from the window of the bathroom on the first floor, where Christine, Stasia, and Miqa's bedrooms were. Nimble and athletic as a result of her Pioneer training in Moscow, she climbed through the branches until she reached a strong one — where she sat, holding her breath.

A little bedside lamp was still on in Christine's bedroom, and Elene could make out two figures on the bed. She saw Christine, with the white veil covering the left half of her face, wearing a white nightdress, her shoulders bared. And beside her great-aunt she recognised the broad shoulders and heavy features of Miqa.

He was sitting on the edge of Christine's bed in silly pyjamas, listening while she told him some story. From time to time she paused, and they looked at each other as if there were nobody else in the world. Later, Christine allowed him to comb her long hair. Elene felt a peculiar mixture of disgust and attraction at the sight, which so overwhelmed her that tears unexpectedly sprang to her eyes.

At breakfast the following day, throughout which Elene stared at the floor as if she had something to hide, Stasia, beaming with joy, announced that she had had the extraordinary good fortune — so close to retirement! — of being invited to a librarians' conference in Prague.

As soon as Stasia left the house, Christine prepared herself a cup of hot chocolate. She hadn't dared make the dangerous drink since the Little Big

Man's death. The temptation to sample its delights at least occasionally was great, but since then she had grown more cautious. Still, her doubts were not strong enough, because after savouring her portion she left vestiges of the chocolate in the little zinc pan she had used to prepare it. And so it was that Elene, coming into the kitchen late that night to fetch herself a drink, was able to walk to the stove unchecked and devour the chocolate. I don't know if she recognised the scent, if she remembered the time when, as a little girl, before the move to Moscow, she had pounced greedily on the chocolate meant for her mother; but that didn't matter any more, because Elene tasted it — and not only Elene. For before she had scraped the saucepan clean, Miqa also appeared in the kitchen. He risked putting himself at the mercy of Elene's superciliousness, but the temptation was too great: the smell drew him towards the stove as if hypnotised. He even came and stood right next to her, and Elene, dreamily scraping the night-black mixture from the pan, did not complain, but closed her eyes in pleasure as Miqa tasted the chocolate by her side.

*

It had been a good day for Elene. A beautiful spring day. She had left the house without fighting with her mother and then — much more importantly — she had finally managed to get hold of her first record by her exiled aunt, in exchange for a brief, stolen kiss behind the school. She had always been intrigued by her father's absent, taboo sister, but had never been given a straight answer to her questions, so she had begun to do some research of her own. She collected everything she could lay her hands on that had anything to do with Kitty Jashi, secretly pilfering photos from old family albums and hunting down defamatory articles about her in the Soviet press after she fled to the West; and also, later, cuttings from foreign music magazines that mentioned her songs. Even these were rare, and worth their weight in gold. But they were nothing compared to an actual record — and it wasn't even a cheap, X-ray album, but the foreign original, with the original record sleeve!

Nothing seemed to stand between her and happiness when she returned home to find a note from her mother on the kitchen table. Nana had been invited to a colleague's birthday party and wouldn't be back before midnight. Christine was on a night shift; Elene's dinner was in the refrigerator for her to heat up whenever she liked; she should be very grown-up this evening, not do anything silly, and, above all, stay at home.

Elene had no problem with that. She immediately retired to her room and placed the album reverentially on the record player. She sat on the bed, listening with rapt attention to the foreign language with the familiar melodies, and getting up twice to smoke a cigarette out of the window. When the record had finished, she played it again, turned up the volume, and tried to guess at least a few of the English words. Her English was terrible, but she promised herself firmly that she would work on it, for this record, for her dissident aunt, for her revered anti-hero. She was sitting on her bed, utterly lost in the music, eyes closed, mouthing the beautiful-sounding foreign words, when there was a knock on her door. She had completely forgotten that Miqa was still in the house, and threw open the door in annoyance.

He stood before her, with that fearful, hangdog expression Elene found so irritating, and asked her what the music was; it was very loud, you see, he'd been listening to it and found it very beautiful. For a moment, she considered pulling his leg and telling him it was The Doors or Jimi Hendrix, because he didn't have the first idea about the new music; he was always listening to Christine's bombastic arias. But she dismissed the idea — he looked too pitiful, standing there in the doorway — and instead she did something she had never done before: she invited him into her room.

'That's my aunt singing. She's a star in the West. She's in all the big magazines and everybody knows her.'

'I know who she is,' said Miqa, in his unusually deep voice, listening again, attentively, to the chords of Kitty's guitar.

'And where would you know her from?' she asked, in a demonstratively bored tone.

'She used to go out with my father.'

Elena lost her composure. She jumped down abruptly from the window ledge where she had seated herself to smoke.

'What are you saying? That's rubbish!'

'He doesn't talk about it. But he still keeps a photo of her. And all the letters she wrote to him in Siberia, too.'

For a long moment Elene froze. She tried to calm the chaos in her head. How come she knew nothing about this? She suddenly felt so stupid, with her violent need to be different, her burning desire for protest and attention, her quest for points of reference. She had thought she knew something, that she had discovered it all by herself, that it was entirely hers, and yet again it turned out to be a half-truth, a coin of which she apparently knew only one side. It was enough to drive a person to despair!

This primitive loner was claiming to have better, more intimate knowledge of her idol; not only that, he was even telling her his father had been close to this woman, that they had been a couple!

What else was being kept secret from her? Was that why Miqa's family was bound so tightly to her own that everyone felt responsible for this peculiar boy? It was all too much for her, and in an attempt to show him that she still had the upper hand, she flung herself down beside him on the bed, sprawled out, pulled in her knees, stretching and writhing like a cat in the sun. To her disappointment, he ignored her contortions and concentrated instead on listening to the music, so in sheer indignation at his obtuseness she grabbed his elbow. He jumped, and stared at her in bewilderment. They were strangers to each other, and that was clearer to them than ever before in this moment of sudden physical proximity.

'You're hurting me,' he protested.

'Don't be a baby.' She laughed, and increased the pressure on his arm.

'Hey, Elene, what are you doing?'

Suddenly he was shouting. It amused her. Was he finally leaving his ivory tower of poetry and melancholy and deigning to come down to her unromantic level?

'What, are you afraid of me?'

'Elene!'

In that moment she jumped at him, like a monkey that has just discovered climbing, and threw him backwards onto the bed. Before he could say or do anything she had scrambled on top of him and was sitting on his groin. She started tickling him and pinching his belly. Feeling a mixture of arousal and pain, he tried to wriggle free of her arms and push her away, but she seemed to be enjoying herself too much to let him. She clung to him with all her might, even biting his neck. He could have pushed her back and off the bed with a single sweep of his hand, but something prevented him. He was trying to grasp what exactly he was experiencing, but it was all happening so quickly his thoughts couldn't catch up.

Was he allowing this game to continue because, although she made a point of flaunting her vulgarity and lack of restraint, she was still a girl with slim ankles and sharp cheekbones, small ears and delicate wrists? Or was it because it gave him some kind of satisfaction?

'Please, stop it!' Miqa repeated, not believing his own voice. She went on squealing with delight, squeaking with amusement. Beads of sweat stood out on her forehead; her cheeks were red, and saliva had collected in the corners of her mouth.

This girl, upon whose birth the stars had smiled, who only needed to stretch out her coquettish little hand to have whatever she desired, couldn't seem to leave him alone. The thought both scared and fascinated him. She was a stranger; she was ungrateful, she was spoilt, she was disrespectful, she was egocentric and moody, and she was the legitimate successor in this family. She, not him.

'You don't like girls, do you? Only old women …'

Elene was provoking him. He froze, stopped defending himself; she continued, undeterred: 'You think you're so superior, don't you? With your French and your secretiveness and your poetry?'

'Elene, stop it!'

He was livid. Perhaps it would do him good to have this fight with her at last, to wage war with her openly instead of hiding away so that they would tolerate him in this house, like a sick puppy. Perhaps he should tell her to her face for once what he thought of her; perhaps he should run the risk of her hurling her anger in his face? Or was it better to wait until she made a mistake, until she showed some weakness, then expose her? What should he do to put himself out of danger, so that he wouldn't have to relinquish his place in this family?

But his body refused to cooperate, would not respond to his thoughts. His body was trapped by his fear. He pinched her thigh and made her cry out in pain; then he grabbed her shoulder and threw her onto the other side of the bed by the wall, taking care that her head didn't hit the hard surface. She resisted, wrapping her slender legs in their white knee-socks sideways around his pelvis. Her brown school dress slid up, revealing her white cotton knickers.

'Stop it … Elene, stop it, please!'

He was imploring her. His voice was suddenly so submissive again that her desire to provoke him was immeasurably increased. She propped herself up, leaned down towards him, alarmingly close, and looked him in the eyes. He could smell her, smell her light perspiration, the scent of her skin perfumed with lavender soap; her hair hung down in his face, tickling him. He tried to look away. She suddenly looked so grown-up, so determined. Why was she doing this? What was she trying to achieve? What was she feeling? Why did she always seem to be a few steps ahead of him?

When would it end — this sense of inferiority brought on by her full-throated laugh, her ostentatiously flaunted popularity, the way she giggled whenever he passed her in the school playground? When were the insults and the provocation going to end?

'You're ruining everything! You idiot!'

Now her euphoria was mixed with aggression. Her voice trembled, and he saw tears glittering in her eyes. This was a battle she was fighting with herself. He was ashamed to have witnessed it, and he realised that she would never forgive him for having seen her in her moment of weakness. But he didn't want her to forgive him. The memory was sure to taste sweet. It would always be a trump card in his hand. Perhaps the best thing to do was to hold out, to wait until she disgraced herself in her family's eyes? Perhaps it wasn't really even a question of winning but of *allowing her to win?* Perhaps, in order to survive, it was more important to be able, at the right moment, to lose?

'We're just playing around, it's fun, don't you think it's fun?'

She was screaming now, like a madwoman. He couldn't tell from her voice whether she was about to roar with laughter or burst into tears.

And when — exhausted, sweaty, her hair tangled — she sat up over him and slowly started to lift the rumpled skirt of her dress, he knew that he had lost. But he didn't know whether it was the *right* kind of losing.

She pulled her dress over her head and sat there, like a little child, in a vest with a pattern of yellow ducks and a pair of white cotton knickers. Miqa was overwhelmed: so many feelings washing over him, shifting from one moment to the next.

No girl had ever been this close to him. But he hadn't wanted it like this; he had never dreamed of this. Not this arbitrariness, not this animality: it repelled him.

There was nothing tender or gentle about her movements, her expression. Nothing *happy*. It had nothing to do with him. And yet he couldn't prevent himself from being disconcertingly aroused.

She took off her vest as well, squatting before him in a polka-dot bra that encompassed her small breasts. She began to unzip the trousers of his school uniform. He wondered where she got this self-assurance, how she could deal with this situation so clearly and decisively; he was shivering all over, incapable of moving, of making any kind of decision. *If this is her revenge on me,* thought Miqa, *why is she hurting herself as well? Why is she humiliating herself?*

In one swift movement she pulled down his trousers and stared at his bulging underpants.

'Take them off!' she ordered, not taking her eyes off his crotch. When he didn't move, she tugged at the elasticated waistband of his underpants and reached inside. She touched him, tentatively, with mingled disgust and desire.

She lay down on top of him, clumsy, hesitant, her knickers the only barrier between them. He caught himself counting to ten: one, two, three ... She wrapped her right hand around his penis, holding it like a candy-floss stick, something wooden and lifeless. He tried to wriggle onto his side, to get away from her, but felt unable to throw her off. He loathed himself, and he loathed her even more.

And suddenly, with imperceptible speed, a kind of darkness descended on him. He sat up, threw her on her back, and buried her beneath him, beneath his broad chest, pulled her knickers down with one hand — as if it were the most natural thing in the world, as if he had done it a thousand times before — and pushed her legs apart.

He felt a numbing warmth spread through his body; he was somehow slipping below the surface.

He thought he had lost consciousness. Her faint cry reached him from afar, as if she weren't close, so close he could smell her breath, taste her skin, bury his head in her hair.

Her face contorted in pain; she bit his shoulder. He was hurting her, but what a wonderful feeling it was. How quickly his fear had abated. How good it felt not to have to think about whether or not he was loved, whether or not he was *good enough* for this family. How liberating! How wonderful not to have to be *good enough*, not even to have to be good!

After he had spilled himself inside her, as if in an epileptic fit, she moaned quietly and looked him straight in the eye. He recognised something like fear in her gaze. And it gave him satisfaction. For a moment he considered reassuring her, perhaps even cautiously taking her in his arms, but she sat up, leaned against the wall, and stared blankly at the thin trickle of blood running down her thigh.

★

There was something wrong with Fred. But Kitty didn't have time to deal with it now. She couldn't think about Prague and Fred at the same time. The two worlds were irreconcilable. She had to pack her suitcase, her guitar — no, actually, the first thing she had to do was phone the cultural attaché of the Czechoslovak embassy — or, no, she had to make it clear to Amy that she absolutely did not want a chaperone for Prague — or ...

Fred had not turned up the previous night, again. She had come round — most inconveniently — at midday, and had now been sitting in Kitty's flat for over three hours with empty eyes and an inane expression, lolling on her sofa in nothing but her knickers and staring off into space. Too much drink, too much smoking, too much … She must have pumped herself full of some infernal mixture; there was something abhorrent about this half-dead stare. It frightened Kitty. She had seen that look before. Not often, but often enough. Kitty had seen traces of this lethargy in Fred when she came to stay at her flat after partying through the night. It was the way she'd looked when she returned from America: when was that, exactly? Kitty had to think about it — no, no, there was no time for that now, she would have to talk to Fred when she got back from Prague, not now, she absolutely mustn't get on the plane without having had enough sleep.

And when the doorbell rang, Kitty was so lost in thought, so preoccupied with all the things she still had to sort out before she left, that she didn't even press the buzzer on the intercom but simply flung open the door. Amy was holding a paper bag with fresh fruit in one hand and beautiful long-stemmed amaryllises in the other. Her blonde hair was damp from the light summer rain. She marched straight into the kitchen and set down her purchases, then started looking for a vase. Kitty was speechless. How often had she feared this very moment? She felt suddenly wretched in anticipation of the storm about to break over them all.

'What's the matter, aren't you going to say hello? I need a vase. A pretty vase. I have some good news for you when you get back, but you know what I think about the socialist nonsense you're inflicting on yourself by going on this trip. And Madame doesn't want my company, either, although actually I wouldn't mind taking a peep behind the Iron Curtain — I mean, how often does one get an opportunity like that? — but fine, never mind … So what I wanted to say was: when you're back, there's a chance we might even leave Britain and go on tour to —'

She broke off in mid-sentence. She was standing in the living room, holding her flowers, staring at Fred dozing half-naked on the sofa.

Kitty, leaning against the cool kitchen wall, could hear her heart pounding. And she heard something fall to the floor. The beautiful amaryllises, presumably. Then footsteps again. Fred must be so out of it she hadn't even registered Amy's presence.

Amy walked past her, went to the sink, and ran some tap water into a glass. Without looking at Kitty, she asked, 'How long? How long has it been going on?'

Anything would be better than this composed voice, this control, this bitter chill.

'I don't know any more.'

Amy turned and looked at her. Kitty lowered her eyes. Suddenly, Amy burst into piercing laughter — the last thing Kitty had expected. She laughed and laughed, although Kitty didn't know whether this hysterical laughter was born of hopelessness or self-protection.

'I hope she behaves with you just as she did with me. So you'll know what you're doing to me. But — no, you know what, maybe you've actually done me a favour, maybe you've just rid me of this disease, maybe you've finally shown me what scum I've been wasting my energy on all these years. But you — to be honest, I wouldn't have expected this of *you*, Kitty. Why don't you say something? Can you not think of anything, or are you going to turn this into one of your album tracks as well? Will you put us all into an amusing little song?'

She shook her head in incomprehension, as if trying to rouse herself to fathom the unfathomable. 'This really is the limit,' she added.

'I didn't want this. I tried for so long ...'

'Sure, of course you didn't want it. As far as I'm aware, though, human beings don't just have sexual organs, they also have brains. I thought you did, anyway! But it looks as if I was very wrong about that.'

'Let me explain: I —'

'Ha! I doubt I really want to know the details. I need to think. And you can tell this cowardly, lying bitch that she's dead to me, and she'd better not dare to ask me for money or anything else ever again.'

'There's something wrong with her, Amy; there's something really wrong with her lately ...'

'Well, darling, from now on that's your problem. I've wasted my best years on this slut. And now I see working with you was a waste of time as well.'

'She's got problems; I think she's —'

'What a discovery! You should have thought about that before you jumped into bed with her.'

'Amy, please, I'm asking you ... I'm talking about a different kind of problem!'

'You're in no position to ask anything of me right now. And neither is she.'

> Communists should set an example in study;
> at all times they should be pupils of the masses as well as their teachers.
>
> CHAIRMAN MAO

Wild times were coming, Brilka. The East envied the West its blue jeans, and young girls in the West fainted at Beatles concerts. In the West, people were demonstrating against the Vietnam War, which was taking on ever more absurd and bloody dimensions, and had become, like the Berlin Wall, a symbol of the Cold War power struggle.

In Paris, students occupied the Sorbonne and erected barricades. Parents no longer understood their children. They didn't understand why these children, who had never lacked for anything, were suddenly taking a stand on behalf of unions and workers. Why they didn't take their own national identity seriously, why they were dragging its values through the mud; why they were taking to the streets to demonstrate for women's rights and against the military. Surely they didn't seriously believe they were bringing peace to the world with a joint and a few flowers plaited in their hair, or by wearing ridiculous batik sarongs!

In our glorious and powerful land we were still a long way from shameless demands like these, but there had, at least, been a change of leadership in the Soviet Communist Party. The Ukrainian peasant had been replaced by a more gallant, pleasure-loving man, who dripped with medals and awards for heroism, and had the bushiest eyebrows in the world.

The Communist Party of Czechoslovakia also had a new leader and, encouraged by this change, the people were calling for liberalisation of the system. Some straightforward reforms had been pushed through, and the populace — asked for the first time to help shape the future of their country — demanded further relaxation of laws, such as the abolition of press censorship and the democratisation of the Communist Party. A Kafka congress was held to rehabilitate the writer; more rehabilitations were set to follow.

The western protest movement seemed to have arrived in the East at last. The Kremlin quickly felt that things were getting too complicated. Party functionaries grew uneasy. Comrade Brezhnev insisted that the reforms already passed be reversed, but his decree did nothing to check the wave rolling across the country, and there was a fear that the Czechoslovakian situation, as they called it, might find imitators in other sister states.

In August 1968, things came to a head. People stormed onto the streets, called for the restitution of human dignity, demanded the release of all political prisoners and the complete abolition of the totalitarian regime. Dubček, the head of the Czechoslovak Communist Party — removed from power by Moscow shortly afterwards — said later in an interview that he had not believed in August 1968 that his people wanted the complete abolition of the communist system; for him it had just been a question of 'moderating the system'.

★

Stasia arrived in Prague on 20 August. She was picked up at the airport by Intourist staff and taken to a hotel, along with a few other Soviet fellow travellers. Kitty had arrived the previous day, and after a long and exhausting process at the airport, had been welcomed by two employees of the Komsomol Club and someone from the Ministry of Culture. She, too, was taken to a hotel — a much better one than her mother's. There, Kitty got a telegram informing her that she would receive a call on the telephone in the hotel lobby in half an hour. She instantly felt as though she had been transported back in time and, as if under a spell, sought out the telephone booth.

'Your concert on Wednesday has to be cancelled.'

He spoke more quietly and was more subdued than usual. He sounded nervous.

'What's going on? I've only just arrived.'

'I know. The circumstances ... It's all got a bit out of hand.'

'Are you all right?'

'Yes, yes, I'm fine. I just have to make sure that I get you out of there right away.'

'What's happened?'

'There's just been a crisis meeting in Bratislava to resolve the Czechoslovakian question. The Communist Party chairmen of the sister republics concluded that developments in Prague must be stopped by force.'

'Stopped by force?'

'That's the situation.'

'Who was I supposed to meet here? Tell me, who was supposed to come?'

'You needn't worry about *her*. She has a Soviet passport; you don't. And in times of crisis like this, they don't really like having western observers in the city, if you get my meaning.'

'She?'

Kitty's knees had turned to butter. Her mother. Her mother was here.

'Don't listen to the Komsomol people, wait for further instructions from me. Do you understand?'

Kitty hung up. She wouldn't take a single step out of this city until she had seen her mother again.

That same evening, Kostya too received a phone call from his friend, explaining the situation and asking him to contact his mother and prepare her; she had to take a flight to Moscow within the next three days. Kostya, who had spent the previous night in the arms of a twenty-seven-year-old blonde and had drunk a little too much Crimean champagne, was immediately fully alert and promised to take care of it.

'We shouldn't have taken the risk in the first place,' Alania sighed.

Kitty contrived to shake off the officious woman from the Ministry of Culture and slip out of the hotel. She wandered the streets of this city that had been the bridge to her new life, thinking back on the lonely months she had spent here. How long ago had it been? How many years was it since she had seen her mother? How many words, songs, meals, kisses, memories, how many disappointments, how many people, places, thoughts, encounters, borders, nights, and days separated the Kitty of today from the Kitty of then?

She walked along the cobbled streets of the Old Town, looking neither right nor left; she felt a tightness in her chest, and avoided people's eyes; after London, they seemed to her so serious and downcast, so lost in thought. She had no destination, no idea where her feet were taking her. She just kept walking straight on, and realised that she didn't know the city at all; that she had managed, back then, to remain invisible here. Her thoughts ran into each other, creating a colourful mosaic in her head. The city was restless. Her nameless friend had been right, as always. Hundreds of thousands of soldiers were marching against the desire for a different life. Battalions against a people. A whole army against her reunion with her mother.

She found herself thinking of Fred. Fred's eyes. Glassy eyes. Eyes that flirted with death. Yes — that was exactly what it was: the way she stared into space, this mental absence. Had she ever truly recovered from Mödling? What was she taking? What kind of drug?

At seven o'clock, the delegation met in the lobby. Kitty acted as if she had just come down from her room. They were taken to a restaurant with a pseudo-folkloric atmosphere and state-approved background music. There was plenty to eat, lots of beer, and exhausting conversation about nothing whatsoever from the curious, excited Komsomol employees and the tedious woman from the ministry. Kitty did her best not to let her panic show. Panic at the thought of having to leave the city without seeing her mother's face again. She smiled absently and asked no questions, but readily answered theirs about her songs. Everyone spoke Russian. Asked whether this was her first time in the city, she responded with a friendly 'yes'.

At one point she went to the toilet and splashed her face with cold water. She had to maintain it, this face; it could not be allowed to slip. Upon her return to the hotel she would probably find a message from her personal guardian angel. And just this once she would defy him. For her, there was no going back without meeting Stasia.

As she cut the *knedliky* into little pieces and dunked them in the wild mushroom sauce, Amy's shrill laughter echoed in her mind, the terribly artificial way she had laughed so as not to forfeit the last vestiges of her dignity when she found Fred half-naked in Kitty's living room.

The call came long after midnight.

'You must pretend you've got flu. You must leave the city as soon as possible. Cancel your performance before they come to you. You must do it, because I can't guarantee anything in the current situation.'

Kitty feigned acquiescence, and agreed. Yes, she would cancel her performance, pretend to have a bad case of flu, and would fly straight back to London the day after tomorrow. But there was no way she was going to sleep now. She couldn't leave. Her mother was here, all her old life was here. It was like a treasure chest, and all she had to do was open it. She couldn't just leave again. She had to open this chest. She had to find Stasia. Hundreds of thousands of soldiers notwithstanding.

★

The invasion began that night. Half a million foreign soldiers occupied the country. These fateful events took the decision out of Kitty's hands. Around nine o'clock in the morning, there was a knock at the door of her hotel room and, gesticulating wildly and bowing his head ever lower, the young *komsomolets* who had stared at her the previous evening with hostile admiration babbled something about politics, about Czechoslovakians and Russians, about the shadow now being cast over that great friendship between peoples, about her security, which, in the circumstances, the Komosomol Club could no longer guarantee, about her performance which now, unfortunately, had to be cancelled. All the leading party functionaries, including Dubček, had been arrested and sent to Moscow; all reforms were to be reversed immediately.

She stared at him, bleary-eyed, through the crack in the door. He told her he had been charged with taking her to the airport at once. The next flight left that evening, at nine o'clock.

'You mean, they're here already? Here, downstairs, on the street?'

Kitty was suddenly wide awake. She opened the door a little further and beckoned him inside, so he would have a chance to give her his own assessment of the situation instead of the stuff he had learned by rote.

'Yes, Comrade Jashi,' he continued in his faltering Russian, and entered her room with an awestruck expression. It was probably the most luxurious room he had ever set foot in. This huge, soft bed, the thick carpet, and the ornate, gilded mirror on the wall. She could already see his very own personal West light up in his eyes. This was how he imagined the West to be: beds like these, carpets and mirrors like these — for everyone.

'The streets are full of people. The president has called on the populace to show prudence and obedience. But ...'

He was clearly hesitating: he didn't know how freely he could speak with her.

'Tell me — it's all right, go on!' Kitty offered him a chair.

'The students have set up a pirate radio station. Almost everyone from the university and the institutes is out on the street. I had to fight my way through to get here. People are marching between lines of soldiers, carrying home-made banners. Street signs have been reversed so that the ...' He faltered again. Which word did he want to use? The Russians, the enemy, the invaders?

'The occupiers?' she suggested. He seemed relieved.

'Yes — so that it's harder for them to find their way around the city. My brother told me people are being arrested every minute. And the Soviet news agency claims that the Czechoslovakian Republic turned to the Soviet Union with an urgent appeal for help. A complete lie! They're actually claiming that we asked them *to provide help through military force*. Can you imagine?'

He had forgotten the Komsomol oath more quickly than expected; bit by bit, he revealed to her his anger and disappointment. Finally, he even confessed that he desperately wanted to stand by his friends and fellow students outside, but had promised his father that he would stay well away from the streets; one saboteur in the family was enough, his brother was very active in the protest movement and it looked as if he was about to be thrown out of university; besides, he had to get her safely to the airport, because he still hoped she would be able to give her concert one day after all; he was such a big fan of hers, such a big fan.

She fetched one of the ten copies of *Summer of Broken Tears* from her suitcase — she hadn't been allowed to bring any more into the country — and signed it for him. She promised she would be in the hotel lobby at seven o'clock precisely.

The boy would keep his mouth shut, regardless of how this worked out. He wouldn't denounce her. He would only give people the part of the truth they expected from him: I was there, she didn't come, I looked for her, I didn't find her, I did my duty, I couldn't do more than that. He wouldn't say: she seemed excited, curious, cross-examined me, asked me to report on the situation, gave me the feeling that she had anti-Soviet sympathies. *Et cetera*.

Yes, she had made him her accomplice, and the bed, the carpet, the mirror, and the album had been a great help to her in this.

In the collective memory of the West, Brilka, the 'Prague Spring' is celebrated as one of the biggest and most courageous revolts against Soviet tyranny. For the East, it was a threnody, a moment of sadness, because the curtain that had just been pushed ever so slightly aside would soon be drawn even more firmly closed.

★

Much has been said and written about the legendary tale of how Kitty, surrounded by tanks, took out her guitar amid the tumultuous crowd in Wenceslas Square and started singing an old folk song from her homeland. Some have claimed it was one of the Russian romances and not a Georgian folk song at all. Oh yes, there's a great deal of speculation and discussion over what that song might have been.

Later, of course, in the West, people idealised her actions, glorifying them as a great advertisement for peace and freedom. The West, with its prejudiced viewpoint, was always misinterpreting the East; in this case, it saw a deliberate protest by a courageous artist, oblivious to what was going on around her, who sympathised with the people and was trying to soften the hearts of the brutal mercenaries. In reality, when she walked into the square and started singing, it was an act of desperation, and her motivation was purely selfish, not remotely intellectual or political. Her behaviour had nothing to do with courage or political convictions.

She went to the square as a woman uprooted, filled with rage, driven by the thought that her journey here, to this city, the journey into her past, might turn out to have been in vain. That she would have to leave the city without having had the chance to reconcile with the part of herself she had left behind. There was the profound pain of having to leave without seeing her mother and asking her why she hadn't fought for her back then as, years earlier, she had fought for her son.

After the *komsomolets* left her room, Kitty started throwing her things into her suitcase, but stopped again a few moments later because she didn't know what to do with it. Instead, she took her guitar, slung it over her shoulder, and hurried out into the street. For more than an hour, she wandered aimlessly, until she got close enough to the epicentre of events and was swept along by the crowd. Of course, she was afraid; of course, the guns, the tanks, the uniforms awakened her ghosts; of course, she would have liked nothing better than to flee, to return to the safety of London; for a moment, she cursed herself for having come here — and, of course, the West was deaf, later on, to her real motivation.

But that's just the way it is, Brilka — we do things with a specific aim in mind and sometimes we achieve something completely different, just as you could never have dreamed, when you boarded the train to Vienna, that you would have to travel *backwards*, backwards to me, into the story you were so eager to leave behind.

And when an exhausted Kitty Jashi was swept into Wenceslas Square, took her guitar out of its case, and began to sing in an attempt to counter her own impotence, she too could not have imagined that a Magnum photographer would be standing nearby, would take a photo of her, would turn a woman who had seldom felt so discouraged, frightened, and lost into a figurehead of the resistance.

But Stasia didn't come to Wenceslas Square. Stasia didn't see her daughter singing. Stasia's son had called the previous evening and ordered her to keep quiet, to stay in her hotel, and to set off for home with the Intourist agent as soon as she was able. Stasia began to fear for both her daughter and her son.

Three women from Leningrad who had come for the congress were sitting in the hotel lobby, distressed and worried about the journey home. The men from Kharkov were talking to their 'tour guide' — who was really a KGB man — about the possibility of catching a train to Ukraine.

By evening, as the situation continued to escalate and became increasingly ugly, the tour guide managed to find a bus that would take the congress guests to the airport. He ordered them to quickly grab their suitcases and board the bus.

Stasia stood in the lobby, her hands shaking, her lips pressed together, her little suitcase at her feet. She was the first to see the uniformed man enter the hotel and walk up to the tour guide. He showed him a document, which the tour guide studied intently for a long time before nodding, impressed, and shaking the uniformed man's hand. Then he pointed his finger at Stasia and gave her a surly look. Stasia stared at the tour guide in amazement: she could hardly believe that anyone might want anything of her, and as the uniformed man approached her, she instinctively looked round, as if she expected there to be someone behind her who was the real object of the tour guide's finger. Then sheer panic overwhelmed her, and she felt paralysed. If she took a step to the right, towards the centre of town, she was endangering her son; if she stepped to the left, towards the airport, she was abandoning her daughter.

For hours she had been in a state of fear, incapable of doing anything, of making a decision. Where could she even look for Kitty? Who could she ask? Had they already got her daughter out of the city? Had her hopes been in vain? And who was responsible for creating this brutal, macabre scenario? Surely it couldn't be that every time she went anywhere, her journey culminated in a war! Was this her curse?

'I must ask you to follow me, Comrade.'

The uniformed man spoke Russian with a Caucasian accent. A whole map of medals adorned his chest.

'What's happened?'

'We have a few questions about your documents, and unfortunately we have to take you to the commissariat. Nothing serious — I'm sure we'll soon be able to resolve these problems, and then naturally we'll drive you to the airport as well.'

'But — what problems?'

'Follow me, Comrade, and we'll explain everything on the way.'

Strangely, Stasia's panic dissipated. She didn't feel afraid of this man. Something in the way he spoke to her, the way he bent down towards her; something in his posture, which had a youthful, relaxed aspect in spite of all the medals, made Stasia trust him.

He took her bag and headed for the exit; she followed him, accompanied by the patronising looks of the other congress participants. Typical Soviet citizens: suspecting everyone they met of being spies and enemies, capable of switching in seconds from kind, friendly librarians to informers. Already she could hear them talking on the bus: *I could tell from the start that something wasn't right about her, she was so quiet and withdrawn; she didn't want to go to the department store with us, either, and gave me and Martha such a snide look when we asked about the knickers and bras. I'd have so liked to buy those knickers, you know, you won't find a pair like that in ten years back home, and even if you do they've all already been sold under the counter, with a horrendous mark-up, you know what they're like* ... And so on. *Ah well, what can you expect of the population of a country where you can't buy proper underwear,* thought Stasia, and got in the back of the car.

They started weaving their way through the crowd. Screaming, running, aggressive, desperate, hopeful people. How awful, thought Stasia, that this scenario seems so familiar to me. How much older do I have to get before images like these vanish from my head?

The uniformed man was driving the car himself, although a man like him would normally have a driver. All of a sudden, she was suffused with relief. Her limbs relaxed, the back of her neck stopped hurting, her hands warmed up. She leaned her head against the window. As if the congress guests and the Intourist moles and the cut-throat tour guide had been the real threat; not this man, who was taking her with him into the unknown.

*

The photo was taken, and the film — miraculously — was slipped past the soldiers who arrested and searched the photographer on the spot, along with hundreds of others in Wenceslas Square. Kitty escaped before they could handcuff her, too; swept up by a mob of students, she ended up in a side street where she was carried along by the next wave of people, like a paper boat in the gutter, floating aimlessly, helplessly, from one street to the next, from one danger to the next; a throng of students swept her onto a bridge, where she walked straight into the arms of a Kyrgyz soldier who ordered her to show her papers. When she produced her British passport — exhausted, hungry, with an expression of dazed indifference — the Kyrgyz called on his colleagues for help. After some deliberation they decided to take her along to the nearest police station where there would be a more senior official who could deal with her case.

In the military vehicle, she explained to the soldiers — in accent-free Russian that nonetheless sat like lead on her tongue and would no longer flow light and sparkling from her lips — her reason for being in the city. She feigned ignorance about the events on the streets, claimed she had only got mixed up in this chaos out of curiosity, and kept repeating that she had to be back at the hotel on time because the *komsomolets* was supposed to take her to the airport.

This conversation took place at five forty-five. At five fifty-five, the Kyrgyz radioed the local *militsiya* with the news that a foreign woman had been arrested. At six fifteen, Stasia was fetched from her hotel. Almost simultaneously, Kitty arrived at the police station near the Charles Bridge, where Stasia, too, was brought shortly afterwards.

The Kyrgyz soldier's confusion upon picking up a British citizen in the tumult — even though she was clearly from the Soviet zone — had enabled Kitty's dream to come true.

Giorgi Alania had been on the phone all day; he had even taken the risk of using the telephone box right outside his London flat for the phone calls to his middlemen in Prague. When he had hung up the previous night, he had already suspected that Kitty would not stick to the arrangement, that the temptation would be too great, that with her British passport she would feel too safe not to give in to her hope of finding her mother in that sea of people. It was, of course, a daredevil recklessness that flared up in her so quickly, a recklessness bordering on naivety. He knew her well enough to know that she wouldn't be able to resist this temptation. He should have refused Kostya's request. This was a more than hazardous undertaking; he had allowed himself to be persuaded into something that was far too risky, and he had done it because, for the first time since he had been recruited by the NKVD, his emotions had clouded his judgement. He had put her, his best friend, and, above all, himself in tremendous danger.

From London, he placed calls to his accomplices and alerted them. No one could tell him where she was. But Fate proved merciful, and he was given a chance to rectify the only mistake he had ever made in all the long years he had spent on the Kitty Jashi file; for he was never wrong in his choice of accomplices. He received a call from the *militsiya* officer, whom for years he had secretly been supplying with little envelopes of banknotes (real British pounds, to be precise), informing him that Kitty Jashi had been arrested. And although he knew he was acting rashly and was taking an even greater risk, he told his confidant to bring Stasia to her daughter.

★

I often asked Stasia about this moment. Back then, though, the words she used to describe their meeting seemed to me disappointing, small, almost insulting. They weren't worthy of this moment, which could have been a scene from a classical drama, except that it wasn't the gods sitting in judgement over the destiny of mankind but the KGB. Back then, as a young girl nosing around my family's secrets, I wanted something truly dramatic, something that had the scent of Destiny; instead, Stasia talked about a small, dirty, foul-smelling interrogation room where she was brought by her Caucasian protector, and which her daughter walked into shortly afterwards. (At this point she always stressed that, at first, she had thought she was hallucinating.) She told me that the uniformed man with all the medals quietly informed them that they had exactly one hour before Stasia had to be driven to the airport and Kitty, who would now miss the flight she was booked on, was expected back at her hotel.

Stasia described the reunion with the usual unsentimental, almost banal words that were so typical of her, and that seemed even simpler and more commonplace the greater or more painful the event they described.

No tears. ('No, no, we didn't cry! What good would tears have done us then? Brought relief? Tears just fill gaps, act as substitutes. If the person you want to shed tears for is standing in front of you, you don't cry, you make use of the time you have. Tears can wait, after all; they can be wept later, at any time.')

I imagine the scene. The stark ceiling light in the empty room. At first, silence. Tentatively, they move closer. A few steps on either side; the echo of those steps. Kitty, walking up to Stasia and feeling her face like a blind woman. As if trying to trace the marks of the time that lay between them, the new wrinkles, the grey hairs: to identify the past.

'I've never yet made a journey that didn't end in a war.' Stasia was the first to speak.

'Oh, that's not true, *Deda*.' They both had to reaccustom themselves to the word; it was like a lump in Kitty's throat. 'You just have a knack for bad timing.'

'*Timing*; what's that?'

'Oh — never mind.'

'You've got an accent.'

'I don't get much chance to speak Georgian.'

'You've grown.'

'Grown-ups don't grow any more.'

'Yes they do; you've got taller. Do you really live in Great Britain? And ... you make music?'

'Yes. I sing. And I write songs. *Deda*, oh God, *Deda* ...'

Kitty covered her face with her hands. And Stasia put her arms around her daughter. Her body must have felt as light as a bird to Kitty; so delicate, after all those years, as if it were made of sand running through her fingers. At least, that's how it always felt to me when I hugged Stasia as a child.

Stasia told her about Tbilisi, and Kitty told her about London. Then Stasia told her about Christine and Elene and Nana and Miqa, and about Andro, too. Only the good things, the cheering things, the most optimistic things. And Kitty spoke about Amy, and kept quiet about Fred. Stasia told her about Kostya, about the library and her imminent retirement, and Kitty told her about her music.

They talked about many things — but not their fears and their hate and their impotence, and certainly not about the ghosts. But one question, the question that had pulsated under her skin like a deep wound for all the years since her flight, the question that had seared itself onto her retinas and through which she saw everything in the world — this question Kitty did ask.

'Why didn't you stop him? You knew it wasn't right, putting everything in a false light, deporting me like that, condemning me to blame myself all my life for sending someone to their death. Why?'

Kitty was clinging to her mother like a little child now: she wouldn't let her go, hugging her shoulders, burying her head in her neck, inhaling her smell, because these impressions would have to last, to endure in her memory for God only knew how long.

'I'm your mother. I gave birth to you. It's not in my power to send you to your death. I'm responsible for your life. Yes — I'm there to make sure you live. I stake my own life for that. No matter what the reason, no one can demand of a mother that she be responsible for the death of her child. It would be inhuman of you to expect such a thing of me. I kept you alive. I had no choice.'

As if he had been waiting outside the door with an hourglass, the uniformed man returned. Their time was up. Kitty didn't want to let Stasia go; she cursed and screamed, begged that they be granted a little more time. But Stasia kept stroking her face, and whispered in her ear:

'I will not die without having seen you again. No matter how long it takes, I will not die until you come home. So pull yourself together now, Kitty, do it for me; go, go, because you will come back to me again; the times are changing, Thekla says so, Sopio says so, yes, that's what they tell me, they're changing and you will come home and I will stay alive until then. Until you come.'

★

It took the armies of the Warsaw Pact just three days to put an end to the Prague Spring. The Czechoslovakian reformers, including the imprisoned Dubček, were summoned to Moscow and made to stand in the corner like schoolboy truants. Upon his return to Prague, Dubček, humiliated, had to tell his people that Moscow had rescinded all the reforms. In the course of the Prague Spring, tens of thousands of people fled the country. At Moscow's behest, the Czechoslovakian Communist Party was restructured and some members were expelled. In protest against the state's capitulation, two students immolated themselves on Wenceslas Square, near the spot where Kitty had stood and sung her songs.

I drink the grief of sunset
— The deep red wine.
No shame — what I knew, I forget
what's forgotten is buried in time.

ANDREI BELY

No, it couldn't go on like this, not one more day! For days on end, or was it weeks, the same record had been playing on repeat — and who was that singer, anyway? For days on end, the same refusal to go to school; for days on end, no eating breakfast or dinner together; for days on end, she had just lain in bed snapping at anyone who came to bring her something to eat. No, it couldn't go on like this. Either her daughter was in love or she had some other problem, which must have something to do with those boys at school and her bad marks, because Elene didn't have a fever, she didn't look ill, she even had a good appetite.

Nana considered how she might persuade her daughter to talk. At least she had succeeded in sending her to school that morning, despite her abject protests. Hopefully she really had gone. Nana couldn't go on lying to her teachers forever, telling them Elene had the flu. Her head already hurt from all the thinking and making of plans, and she absolutely did not want to call Kostya again and admit that she couldn't cope. The power struggle between them was enough of a strain on Nana's nerves, as was the fact that Elene discussed all her secrets with her father on the telephone, falling silent and looking irritated whenever her mother entered the room. Under no circumstances could Kostya be called upon for advice this time.

There was no counting on Stasia, who ever since she had got back from Prague a few days ago had been wandering around like a deer in the headlights, preoccupied with vague thoughts, which of course she didn't share with anyone. So Nana asked Christine for help, relying on her neutrality; perhaps she would manage to squeeze out of Elene whatever was causing her bad mood.

Christine agreed, and asked Elene, who had just got back from school, to sit with her at the garden table. It was a beautiful day, full of glorious, shimmering colours, as if dressed for a carnival. Christine was intoxicated by the sight of her wild garden. Wearing a black dress embroidered with red carnations, in which she looked like an old angel cautiously hiding its wings, she cut an overripe watermelon into little pieces for her great-niece, and Elene began stuffing them greedily into her mouth.

'Your mother says you're worried about something.'

Elene shook her head and wolfed down another piece of watermelon.

'Is something upsetting you?' Christine asked insistently. She lowered her face to Elene's.

'Miqa's a pig!' blurted Elene suddenly, and gulped down the fleshy red fruit.

'Excuse me?'

'Miqa's a pig.'

'Now what's the matter?' Christine groaned softly, and pushed the plate of watermelon aside. 'Look at me, please. You can go on eating later. Have you two had a fight?'

'No. He did bad things to me, and I want him to move out.'

'Bad things?'

Christine didn't buy her great-niece's feigned naivety.

'Yes.'

'Such as?'

'Ask him yourself. You two have a good relationship.'

There was something Christine didn't like about the way she had said 'a good relationship', but she didn't object, focusing instead on Elene's words.

'Well, you've got a sharp tongue; I'm sure you didn't let him get away unscathed,' said Christine tartly, surprised by how affronted she was. Elene's words were full of malice, and disproportionately hostile for her age.

'I want some more watermelon now.'

Truculently, Elene pulled the plate back towards her.

'Elene,' Christine began, aiming for a more pedagogical tone of voice this time, 'you're not little children any more. He may be very different from you, but you still have to respect him and be polite to him; he's part of our family.'

'Family don't do *things like that*.'

'Excuse me?'

Christine's blood ran cold. How could the little girl she had watched grow up, that lively, loving child, suddenly have such a mean look in her eyes, such a cruel tone of voice? What was she getting at?

'Yes — ask him, ask him, why don't you!' Suddenly Elene was screaming. Bright red watermelon juice spurted from her lips; her eyes burned as if they were on fire; she was completely beside herself. Christine shrank away. 'He shouldn't have done it, I told him not to, I asked him to stop but he didn't listen to me — he hurt me.'

She had reverted to a childish vocabulary that jarred with the winged Fury she was currently impersonating. Christine couldn't believe her ears. You could have accused Miqa of anything in the world, but the idea that he had hurt someone, that he had used violence against someone ... It was something Christine didn't want to voice even in her thoughts. It was a barefaced lie! It was impossible! Never!

'What are you talking about, Elene?'

Christine's voice was quiet, careful, as if she were still trying to find the right tone.

'What, don't you believe me? Of course not — you think I'm the guilty one, that I ...'

Oh God! She plays the part well, thought Christine. Elene was certainly a good actress, and indignation and outrage were what she did best.

'Stop this immediately!' Christine could no longer contain herself.

'You're telling *me* to stop? Me? I haven't done anything. He — he's the one who hurt me, he ...'

Elene started crying. Crocodile tears, thought Christine with revulsion: she was bewailing her lack of love, while claiming to shed tears over the injustice, the violence that she alleged had been done to her. Faced with Elene's audacity, her willingness to go this far, Christine was lost for words.

Quaking, she rose from her chair and hurried upstairs to Miqa's room. She had been completely focused on her sister, who had had some kind of experience in Prague that she didn't want to discuss. That made Christine insanely curious, so she hadn't given much thought as to why Miqa had recently taken to spending so much time in Ramas' room, why he came back so late from school, why he didn't come to her bedroom any more and ask whether he should brush her hair. Perhaps now, though, it all made sense.

He opened the door just a tiny crack. She saw his pale face, the dark rings under his eyes. Of course his extreme mood swings, his hollow gaze, couldn't simply be ascribed to puberty; she should have realised, because humiliation was written all over his face.

'Shall we go for a walk? I thought a little stroll might do us both good.'

'I have to go to bed, Christine.'

'Come on, like we used to before — we'd walk all over the place. We can stroll along the river. Come on, don't be a spoilsport, *Kotik*.'

Christine would often tease him with this Russian pet name: Kitten. He looked at her hesitantly.

'Get dressed and come with me, Miqa!' she requested, more firmly now. For a moment he seemed to be about to shut the door in her face; then he nodded, closed the door, and quickly started to get dressed. Before, he would have let her wait in his room, not outside; but this was no longer 'before'. There had been some kind of dramatic change, she could feel it; something had happened, here, in her house, under her nose, and she had missed it.

Soon they were walking along Barnov Street towards the opera house, to sit in the little park behind it. He loved this place; when he was little, he always used to beg her to sit on a bench there and eat ice cream. This time, too, they sat on a bench. Without ice cream, though. Christine was forced to acknowledge, with a crushing sense of melancholy, that the time of eating ice creams on empty benches was well and truly over, and with it Miqa's childhood.

'I think you know what I want to talk to you about. I would like to know what happened between you and Elene, and you know I'll be able to tell if you lie to me. If you tell me the truth, I promise you that, for my part, I won't judge either of you, and I will do the best I can to try to find a solution for your problem.' Christine took a fan from her handbag and started fanning herself. The air was stifling; it was muggy, and the sky above the city was heavily blanketed with cloud. The weather would probably break soon and a rain would chase away the heat.

Without looking at Miqa, she could sense his body relax beside her, his legs loosen, his hands emerge from his trouser pockets where he had hidden them. He began to shake his head in a sort of disbelief. Christine placed her hand over his, but he withdrew it, ashamed.

'She hates me,' he murmured, stirring up reddish dust with the tip of his shoe.

And suddenly it all came pouring out. He talked without drawing breath, waving his arms, shaking his head repeatedly. Beneath his bushy eyebrows, tears of indignation shone in his eyes. He told her about Elene's jealousy, which he had always sensed; about her caustic animosity, the way she cold-shouldered him at school, her condescending manner, and the more he tried to describe Elene as mean and spiteful, the more clearly his words painted a picture of a deeply insecure, lonely girl in desperate need of love, who had lost her way and was groping in the dark while lashing out around her, unaware of the damage she was doing. He told Christine about that afternoon, when he had knocked on her door, attracted by the music; ashamed and agitated, red-faced, he kept rubbing his sweaty hands on his trousers, unable to find the right words to describe what had happened next.

'And then I don't know what I did. Then I just did what she wanted me to. I forgot myself, Christine, I just didn't know what I was doing any more, but what was I supposed to do?'

'This is not good, this is not good at all, Miqa,' said Christine, when he abruptly stopped speaking. He flung his arms dramatically about her knees and buried his head in her lap, but Christine raised him up again and admonished him.

'Pull yourself together and sit up. Never show such weakness to anyone, ever. Do you understand me?'

'You don't believe me,' he began, sobbing, 'you don't believe me, do you?'

'I believe you, yes, I believe you. Nonetheless, we have a big problem, you and I, Miqa, and right now it's more important than anything else that we sort this problem out. You mustn't let yourself be carried along like that; you've got to defend yourself, Miqa! Why didn't you defend yourself?'

Christine sounded almost affronted. As if his behaviour could be attributed to a failure on her part.

'I don't know.'

He seemed to be thinking; he seemed to be asking himself the same question. It seemed to surprise him, too, but he couldn't come up with an answer.

Christine couldn't really gauge what the consequences might be — Elene seemed too unpredictable for that — but she knew that there would be consequences, in one form or another. Elene had taken her destructiveness too far; nonetheless, Kostya was still the head of this family, and if he should happen to find out about this *incident* he would, of course, protect his child. He would have no interest in hearing the other side; on the contrary, he would seize the opportunity finally to take action against the Eristavis. After having to restrain his hatred for Andro all these years, he would not pass up this opportunity: he would take out his anger on Andro's son.

'Will I be sent away? Will I have to go back to the village again?'

Miqa wiped away his tears with the pressed and folded handkerchief that she put in his breast pocket every other day. As if he had guessed what she was thinking.

'We must do everything we can to make sure that doesn't happen.'

'Do you believe me, Christine? Do you really believe me?'

'Yes, Miqa, I believe you. I know you.'

On the way home she had already decided to protect Miqa, to vouch for him, because unlike Elene he didn't have anyone else who would, and it seemed he could not do it for himself. Not yet, perhaps. Perhaps not ever.

She knew that this crazy, foolish incident would divide her family; even though it was inconceivable to her that she might wage war on her nephew, that other boy with whom she had eaten ice cream in the parks and gardens of the city, who had gazed at her with the same admiring, devoted eyes as Miqa did now. She had to remind herself that this little ice-cream-eating boy no longer existed in Kostya, had not existed for a long time, had disappeared forever; time and the war had killed this boy within him, whereas Miqa still had a chance of preserving and protecting the boy within, and thus, also, his childhood.

★

That night, Christine marched into Elene's room and dragged her out of bed. Elene, half-asleep, still hadn't quite worked out what was going on when Christine started firing words at her like a Kalashnikov.

'We didn't raise you to be such a monster! I want to know where this hatred has come from! I don't recognise you any more — my own flesh and blood, the child I carried in my arms, the child who used to dig in the garden with me ... No — I don't know who you are, how it could come to *this*. And I'm ashamed of you.'

Elene didn't say a word but clenched her fists in fury, pressed her lips firmly together, and looked away. There was just one thought crying out in her head: *it's not fair, it's not fair, it's not fair!* It couldn't be that she had lost, yet again, to this apathetic, passive intruder. It couldn't be that they gave him everything, showered him with everything Elene had pined for so desperately in those lonely years in Moscow. It couldn't be that his truth counted more than hers.

And at the same time another part of her was crying out for remorse, for a tearful confession, after which they would take her in their arms again and promise her that everything would be all right, would promise to love her for ever and ever — for who she was, and not for what she did.

For a moment these two thoughts seemed to explode in her head; she was on the verge of howling, of throwing her arms around Christine and clinging to her until she had made a clean breast of it, had rid herself of her jealousy and fear. But what words would suffice? What sentences could give a vivid illustration of her ordeals? How much time would be required? Hours, days, weeks? No: she couldn't do it. Perhaps she could have explained her discontent, listed her disappointments. But there was something else: ever since that afternoon there had been something else in her head, in her body, in her voice, a feeling she couldn't grasp, couldn't describe, a feeling worse than all her supposed hatred of Miqa. A feeling that frightened her, petrified her. But she couldn't admit to herself — it just wasn't possible — that what hurt her far more than his arrival in her kingdom and ascension to her throne was the memory that he had spurned her — that he had rejected her. And perhaps, if she had had a few more seconds, she really would have tried to make amends. But Christine's slap prevented her from doing so: it caught her full in the face, intervened, and made what had happened irreversible.

Christine's bony hand had hit Elene's right cheek. Dazed, and burning from the blow, she slid from her bed to the floor and threw up on the little rug.

Christine stared at Elene, hunched on the floor, looking up at her, her face contorted and smudged with tears; she kept shaking her head, as if she could see a dark future in the remains of Elene's food.

'What is it you want from me?' Elene was breathing heavily. 'What is it all of you want from me? Go to him, go on, go and give him your sympathy.'

'Have you had your period?' Christine's gaze was still fixed on the regurgitated food.

'Yes, I've had it since I was thirteen. What are you asking me that for?'

'I mean when was the last time you had it! My God!'

'No idea. A while ago. Leave me alone!'

'Please, no ... No, no, please, no ...'

Christine helped Elene to her feet, took her into the bathroom, and handed her a towel. Then she went to the kitchen and made herself the hot chocolate: she needed it now, before she decided what to do next. The situation was already cursed enough.

The next morning, after Miqa and Elene had left for school, Christine informed Nana that it was very likely her daughter was pregnant. This conjecture was to prove correct, and Elene was to stick to her version of the conception: she continued to accuse Miqa of using force and coercing her. Stasia was in a state of such distraction that she was not informed about the tragic events.

★

'Now what?' Christine asked Nana.

'My God, Christine, she's only fifteen; what are we supposed to do? My poor girl — how could he do that to her, how? And if Kostya finds out about it, I'll never see my daughter again. No, no, he can't; we can't allow that to happen.'

Nana's nerves were frayed. She hadn't been able to leave the house for days.

'He didn't do it. He didn't force her. Why won't you listen to me?'

'Because what you're saying is absolutely outrageous, and I will never allow you to assume that my daughter could ... No!'

'Either way, he has to be told.'

'You're insane! The whole lot of you here in this house, you're living in a parallel universe! Tell him? Him? The boy who brought this shame upon my child — I don't even want to think about what he did to her.' Nana started sobbing again. 'I don't want to see him again, I can't stand the sight of him any more; I can't guarantee anything, I feel like tearing him to pieces! Oh yes, *he has to be told*,' she said, imitating Christine. 'Don't make me laugh!'

'I don't think it's a decision for you or Kostya. The two of them must make a decision like that themselves. Elene and Miqa. Just them — no one else.' Christine spoke in a monotone, as if she were no longer even trying to persuade Nana of a different truth, as if she were already prepared for no one to believe her.

'That son of a bitch is going to leave this house — right now. And you can tell him I'd better not set eyes on him again, or else ...' Nana was rocking back and forth, distraught, like a mourner in a classical tragedy. 'I, for one, am not going to let that little bastard destroy my daughter's future.'

'But Nana —'

'I'll talk to my doctor. She's an excellent gynaecologist. She'll do it, off the record.'

'You can't let that happen — you can't make her do it. It'll have disastrous consequences.' Christine's voice was quiet now, feeble, as if she no longer believed her words could change anything.

'Disastrous consequences? We've got those already. Oh yes — serious, disastrous consequences. And we're going to remedy them before it's too late!' Nana seemed more composed now. She wiped her tears away with the corner of the tablecloth.

Christine stood. She wanted to go out, to get away from the impossibility of putting this right; she didn't want to see a sacrificial lamb slaughtered, she didn't want to weep for the wrong thing, she didn't want to go on participating in the sad power struggle Nana and Kostya's marriage had become, the indirect consequence of which was now in Elene's belly. But she didn't move. Something was holding her back; her legs felt like lead.

The image of a dumbstruck Kitty arose in her mind's eye. Kitty's young face, drained of life, when she rang her doorbell after all those days of uncertainty. Without her belly. Without her son. She rubbed her eyes. Miqa! He was what counted; she had to save him — from the wrong decisions, above all. She had to do something. She couldn't just watch and wait, again. She had to act.

The abortion was carried out one week later. One week was how long it took Nana to persuade her daughter that terminating the pregnancy was the only way for her to continue her carefree life and not become a social outcast, to finish school and hold on to the prospect of a secure future. One week, to impress upon her daughter that she could not breathe a word of this *incident* to her father. The first secret Nana was finally able to share with her daughter. Just her — mother and daughter, as she had always wanted it, without her husband muscling in.

★

Christine summoned Andro to Tbilisi. At the bus station, she took his arm, and instead of walking with him towards Vera Hill, as usual, she sat him down in the first snack bar they came to and explained the situation. Andro listened attentively, smoking his Kosmos cigarettes and scratching his head continually. His alcohol consumption had begun to show in his face: he looked puffy, and his cheeks were flecked with red.

Two years earlier, he had bribed the *kolkhoz* doctor to write him a certificate, and since then he had been categorised as unfit for the *kolkhoz* work he loathed; he now worked for a stonemason who made busts of Marx, Engels, and Lenin.

'I don't know what to say,' he said. He scratched his beard and drew on his cigarette.

'Then make a bit of an effort and help me resolve this situation to everyone's advantage.'

'To everyone's advantage? Are you joking, Christine?'

'They only have one more year of school ahead of them. It must be doable. But ...'

'He'll find out, anyway. It's like a bloody curse.'

'Kostya? No — he won't. Nobody wants that. Nana least of all, so she'll do everything she can to ensure he doesn't find out.'

'Things like that can't be kept secret.'

'Miqa will soon be of age. We just have to bridge this period. Then he can be independent, move into a boarding house or something ... Then he can take care of himself, stay here, study; I'll go on looking after him. It's just now, in this situation, it's too dangerous for them to stay under the same roof.'

'All my friends and relatives are dead, Christine. I'll take him with me. There's no alternative. He'll just have to go back to the village school.'

'I can't let him go just like that — it's only one year, for one year we'd have to —'

'I have nothing. I can't do anything. I'm grateful just to get these commissions and earn a few extra roubles when the master mason's too drunk and they let me do Marx or Engels instead. You make the most money with Lenin these days. Busts of Lenin fetch the best price. Now do you understand what my life is like?'

*

My mother only just managed to get her school-leaving diploma. Nana was so afraid of provoking Kostya's violent temper that she allowed him to believe Elene was doing marvellously well at school; he was delighted by his daughter's supposed ambition and cleverness. He also announced to the family the happy news that he had been gifted a large plot of land by the state in gratitude for services rendered. Like any Soviet citizen who was anyone, he too could now build himself a dacha.

The plot of land was just under an hour away by car, in a picturesque village northwest of the city, not far from a stud farm and an abandoned monastery. The land included the remains of an old, traditional country house dating back to the previous century, which had fallen into ruin, and which Kostya now wished to revive according to his own taste.

'My own home at last! I think we should all move there. It's not too far from the city to drive to work, but far enough to have some peace and quiet! I'm thinking of making the house more than just a dacha.'

He tasked his mother with organising the conversion and procuring the building materials. Stasia, who had entered her dreaded retirement, gladly accepted, in the belief that healing and a new beginning might indeed be possible in such a wondrous place.

So in the same year that, unbeknownst to Kostya and Miqa, a life had been prevented in the eternal kingdom of the women, construction began on the 'Green House', as your mother and I would later dub it, because by the time we were born it was already almost entirely overgrown with ivy. The house where Daria and I grew up.

What are our schools for if not indoctrination against Communism?

RICHARD NIXON

For Elene's sixteenth birthday, Kostya surprised his daughter with a brief visit and real French perfume, which was meant to show her that she could finally consider herself an adult. But the night before the big party Kostya wanted to throw in his daughter's honour, Elene disappeared and was nowhere to be found. Eventually they discovered a note, written in her pretty, girlish handwriting: *I've gone and I don't want you to look for me. I've permitted myself — and I apologise for that — to take two necklaces from Mama's jewellery box and a little money from Stasia's handbag. I am going to seek God. So don't worry and don't look for me. Your Elene.*

It took them almost a week to find her. Kostya made use of all his contacts and influence; she had indeed gone to a convent, near Kazbegi. Getting her out of there must have resembled a scene from a film: Nana told me later that Kostya threw his daughter over his shoulder like a rolled-up carpet, and she thrashed and screamed like a banshee. On the drive home, she prayed non-stop, threatening her parents with Hell and the Devil if they didn't take her back and leave her in peace.

Kostya was lenient and made allowances; he didn't reproach her, and he tried his very best to understand his child's dramatic transformation from supposedly model daughter to a God-seeking young woman uninterested in human society. He took a leave of absence, booked two rooms in a luxury sanatorium by the healing springs in Sochi, and flew there with Elene. He took her for meals in high-class restaurants and even allowed her to drink Crimean champagne; in the mornings, before the beaches got crowded, he went swimming with her in the violet-tinted sea; he took her on evening walks along the white promenades, and tried to guess what reasons for her rebellion could lie behind her silence. And it took days for the sea, the unasked questions, the reproaches not made, her father's undivided attention, the tranquillity, and the sense of security at his side finally to coax a smile out of Elene after all. Her stony expression softened; she even started telling him what she wanted to see or do on a particular day; and when she seemed to have forgotten her worries for a few moments (which wasn't often, but still), she was like the old Moscow Elene again, that cheerful soul bursting with energy, Kostya's disciplined, ambitious daughter. In moments like these, Kostya believed that what his wife had got wrong with his daughter could still be put right — by him, by his patience and devotion.

★

At that time, towards the end of summer, Vasili, whom all the Caucasian guests addressed in the Georgian manner as Vaso, was working as a lifeguard on the upmarket end of Sochi beach. He had just turned twenty, and dreamed of one day climbing into the hold of one of the passing ships, fleeing his origins and his Soviet predestination, for a western, preferably American, future. He had grown up fatherless; he had a mother who had worked all her life as a chambermaid in the spa sanatoriums, and an elder brother, a petty criminal currently serving five years imprisonment for car theft, from which, judging by his letters, he was highly likely to emerge a criminal mastermind.

But Vaso, who in addition to his Russian mother tongue also spoke Georgian, Armenian, Abkhazian, even a little German and Turkish, dreamed of something else: something big.

Ever since he was a little boy, he had watched guests going in and out of the sanatoriums, people who had better lives than he and his family did, who could afford to be served by people like him. He had always dreamed of being allowed, one day, to swap places with the guests. He could already see himself in those fluffy bathrobes, sipping Crimean champagne, his melancholy gaze fixed happily on the horizon, dressing up every evening for the various dances, accompanied by a beautiful woman with sparkling jewels dangling from her earlobes.

But all that his social standing, his opportunities, and his paternity as stated in his passport ('unknown') permitted him to do was to take a badly paid job as a waiter in one of the town's spa hotels, or to sign up aboard one of the filthy freighters that ploughed up and down the Black Sea and work transporting oranges and lemons on ships that never even went near the Atlantic. At best, he might secure a permanent position as a smart, slick-haired receptionist in one of the sanatoriums. None of this particularly appealed to Vaso. None of these prospects left any room for his dreams.

So he had decided to take the unusual but not unpleasant step of getting closer to those dreams and, in doing so, enjoying the advantages of a life Fate had not ordained for him. He was very good-looking; he had heard this ever since he was five years old, when he used to ride along the corridors of the sanatorium on his mother's cleaning trolley to cries of 'What a beautiful boy!' 'Look at those eyes!' 'What a pretty mouth, what a gorgeous head of hair!', from the female hotel guests in particular; until at some point, when he reached a certain age, these cries fell silent and he became aware instead of reddened cheeks, meaningful looks, and excited whispering whenever he appeared, equipped with gloves and hedge clippers, and started snipping away at the bushes around the sanatorium. His initial shyness and natural deference towards the hotel guests, which his mother had painstakingly inculcated into him, were quickly discarded. And as soon as it became clear to him that he was in no way worse or more stupid than the many guests lounging around or playing badminton, he grew bolder, permitted himself to exchange a few words with the female guests, became increasingly confident — and from there it was but a small step to win the ladies' favour for himself. He quickly realised that there was less in it for him with the young, shapely, sweet-smelling girls than with the older, less firm-skinned but more bored and daring women. Apart from their beautiful bodies, the girls had little to offer. They were entirely dependent on their fathers and mothers, fiancés and husbands. They, like him, were filled with longing; they too felt as if they were trapped in cages, albeit golden ones. It was quite different with the ladies over forty. Their dreams — fulfilled or unfulfilled — lay behind them; they had married, worked, had children, carried out their duties, experienced disappointments, and now, on reaching the high point of their lives, they felt drained and unloved. It was astonishing how many women spent their holidays alone because their husbands were either too busy or spending their time with younger, more attractive women.

Above all, though, these women were more generous. They had something to give in exchange for what he offered them. And since his initial seduction, at the age of fourteen, by a rich widow from Odessa who had introduced him to the art of love, Vaso had managed to amass quite a bit of money and other things of value. He had decided that one day he would buy himself a place on one of the international freighters. Then — Vaso was convinced of it — nothing would stand in the way of his American dream. But he never had enough money. It made no difference how long or how hard he worked or how many women he pleased, something always got in the way. Either it was his mother, whose health had suffered greatly with her advancing years; or his brother, who needed money to bribe people into reducing his sentence; or himself, having to invest in his career and needing new clothes. Easy come, easy go: he kept having to start all over again, but his American dream was stronger than any disappointment or hurdle he had to overcome.

With this dream at the back of his mind, he never tired of praising the supposed or actual beauty of all these lonely women, taking them to secret bays and remote beaches, singing them a few bawdy sailors' songs, and pleasuring them at night in their sanatorium and hotel beds. Tanned, with an athletic physique, his blond hair always waxed, perfumed perhaps a little too extravagantly, he was too obvious in his desperate desire to please, but attractive enough to rescue them, at least for the duration of their holiday, from their oppressive marriages, their boredom, and their fear of old age.

Vaso had adapted himself so superbly to older women, their desires and longings, that the attentions of a suntanned young girl late that summer must have rather taken him by surprise and been somewhat confusing.

My mother had noticed him on her very first day at the beach, where he was in charge of renting out wicker beach chairs and loungers, and from then on had not let him out of her sight. Again and again, she had used the time when Kostya was making work phone calls in his room to go to the beach alone and rent a beach chair; and Vaso, obligingly, and with rather more enthusiasm than strictly necessary, had led her to her selected spot, and had even fetched ice cubes for her drink.

Nor could Kostya fail to notice, to his disappointment, that Elene's smile possibly had less to do with him and his attentions than with the beau from the beach who glanced in Elene's direction more often than was proper and grinned from ear to ear whenever she walked past. At first, he considered suggesting to Elene that they change beaches, but then he decided to seize the opportunity and use the boy's infatuation for his own ends: because, unlike his wife, Kostya was convinced that he had everything under control. He started to leave the radiant couple alone from time to time, and stayed in the cafeteria or in his room more often. Then one evening, by which time the situation could not have been more obvious, he waited for Vaso after his shift and suggested that the boy take his daughter out to an exclusive restaurant. He, Kostya, would pick up the bill, so that his daughter's culinary requirements didn't prove an embarrassment. Yes — Kostya's plan was to let this lad play a not unimportant role in stabilising their father-daughter relationship. He would be the understanding, loving, open-minded father, would regain

Elene's favour in doing so, and would then convince her that the two of them deserved another chance, that the doors of all the faculties in Moscow would be open to her if she should consider returning after all.

But Elene was very far from the infatuated, highly strung, easily stressed girl her father thought he saw in her. Something inside her had broken off, like the handle from a pitcher, and, caught between self-loathing and the contempt she felt for her environment and her family, she was searching for other ways to smash the pitcher completely until it crumbled into dust and there was no longer any chance it would ever be mended.

Elene had done something terrible, of that she had no doubt; but the punishment had not come. On the contrary: the wrong person had been punished. She had wanted to seek God because if neither her family nor the state thought it necessary to punish her, God at least would have to. But God had not appeared to her. The fasting, the praying — none of it had worked. God was silent and elusive. In order for justice to prevail, she would have to inflict a suitable punishment on herself. She would keep searching until the punishment felt *suitable*.

I've always suspected that what lay behind Elene's unusually swift and confident decision to make Vaso her lover was a desire, whether conscious or unconscious, to give her womb a chance (yes, I know you're smiling at my choice of words here, Brilka; I can see you grinning in my mind's eye).

If I had asked her about it directly, she would, of course, have denied it, because all through our childhood she had tried to impress on my sister and me that we were the fruits of passionate love. But now I think that, for her, this summer affair was solely about proving to herself that her womb, and her whole body, was capable of conceiving *a love child*, not just *a dreadful consequence* or a fruit of *the terrible incident*.

As early as their second rendezvous (financed, again, by Kostya), she indicated to Vaso that she was definitely interested in other things as well, not just the tedious conversations that good form and appropriate, state-approved public etiquette permitted. Vaso was cautious. After all, he had long since realised whose daughter Elene Jashi was, and he didn't want to make a mistake that could end up costing him dearly.

I never met him, Brilka, and so I can't claim with any certainty that he was in love with your grandmother. A more likely assumption would, of course, be that he saw Elene as another opportunity to top up his savings. In any case, he feigned ignorance and naivety, and returned her punctually to the sanatorium after each meeting, at the time agreed with Kostya, conscientiously handing her over to her powerful father, who thanked him with a satisfied smile, shook his hand, and wished him a safe journey home.

But the will of a young, attractive woman — and, above all, of a certain Elene Jashi — can make an equally young, attractive man forget his principles. When they met for their third date, Elene persuaded Vaso that they shouldn't go to the boring restaurant again, but that he should show her Sochi's most beautiful hidden places instead.

First, they went for a walk along the quay, watched the ships in the distance, cast a great many stones into the sea, laughed and joked; then they went to a sailors' bar off the beaten track and tried a few different kinds of strong schnapps, wrinkling their noses as they did so; they kissed, leaning over the sticky counter, and eventually left the bar hand in hand to whizz along the promenade on his clapped-out moped. When Vaso turned to head back to her hotel, Elene started badgering him, begging him not to take her home yet; there was no need to be afraid of her father, she would explain it away herself if they were a little late, and besides, he had to be nice to her at the moment. Vaso had no alternative but to drive my mother to the other side of town and lie down beside her in a cool, stony bay.

It must have given Elene immense satisfaction; and he took what he needed for himself, too. Gentle and tender, keen to give her pleasure, although I don't know whether she was able to feel it (for my mother and sister's sakes, I hope so).

Time was short. After they had made love, and Elene had dipped her body in the salty, dark water to wash away the evidence, they dressed hurriedly — happy, sated, and laughing — and rode back to the sanatorium.

Your mother always thought of her conception as humiliating, Brilka. I tried to make it clear to her that hers must have been much more romantic than mine, but I could never convince her. We were always trying to outdo each other over whose genesis was the more undignified, as if it were a trophy worth fighting for.

Their leavetaking at the end of the summer was more sentimental than they had anticipated; apparently there was even a glint of a tear in Vaso's eyes when they embraced for the last time. Kostya, touched by the young man's heartfelt emotion, promised his daughter that he would invite him to Tbilisi if their love survived the separation and continued, as they had promised one another, in epistolary form.

Whether or not he was in love, Vasili was definitely impressed. Despite his many amorous adventures, in the course of his conquests he had never met a woman, young or old, who was happy to do without oaths and promises, without false hopes and illusory plans for the future, who demanded nothing of the kind. Who sought pleasure with such abandon, as if there were something she was trying to overcome by every means possible, with every inch of her body. But although he remained suspicious of Elene's permissiveness right till the last, at their parting he did whisper a few lover's oaths in her ear, to be on the safe side.

★

The boy had done his duty in exemplary fashion: Kostya was triumphant. When he suggested that she should consider her future, take some time, and look at a few institutes in Moscow, Elene offered no resistance, but agreed and went with him. Upon their arrival in Moscow, Elene let Lyuda cook for her, ate her beloved blinis with honey, went to the cinema, and actually did — largely out of boredom, and for fun — write long, yearning letters to Vasili. The idea of being in love amused her, and rather shook her contemptuous indifference towards both the world and herself. Vasili didn't lose much time, either: two weeks later, Elene received a reply. Perhaps their light-hearted summer affair really could turn into love, my mother must have thought; her reply was rather more passionate, more emotional than her first letter. But still it was a game, and because she wanted to escape her father's plans for her future in Moscow, she went on playing, more out of curiosity than conviction.

Vaso had revealed his American dream to her as they sat on the pier: he had stretched out his hand, pointed at the distant lights of ships, and said, with a sigh, that one day he would be there, *en route* to other lands and continents. So she hoped he would be true enough to himself not to abandon his course, even when he found out about her pregnancy.

The Moscow frosts had just begun to bite when Elene knocked on the door of Kostya's study, entered, and waited for him to set his work papers aside and look at her through his narrow reading glasses, before telling him that she was pregnant. According to her calculations, the child was due in May.

There was shouting; the papers on the desk flew through the air; there were threats, blunt insults, and coarse abuse, but at least there were no tears. It ended in dejected silence and a sort of resignation, and, later, rhetorical questions: how could it come to this, what has become of my wonderful girl, *et cetera*. At the end of the year, Kostya had no alternative but to invite the unsuspecting father to Moscow and inform him of his impending happiness.

*

The two men retired to Kostya's study. After a few delicacies and a litre of good Kindzmarauli, Vasili suddenly found that the future Kostya was sketching out for him didn't seem so bad after all. It would be a good and, above all, a solid alternative to his own risky, and as yet still unfinanced, American dream. He was even able to feign a degree of cheerfulness to Kostya regarding his role as a father.

He was told he would be able to study — 'Engineering would be good for your lively intellect and skilled hands, my boy; besides, the country will always need good engineers!' He and Elene would move into their own apartment in Moscow, would receive the greatest possible degree of support, and he would have a good time with the most generous and permissive girl he knew (naturally he didn't breathe a word of this last to his future father-in-law). Yes, that all sounded sensible; a bit less exciting, perhaps, than the voyage to America aboard the cargo ship, but much more tangible, much more real. Vasili dreamed himself into a sweet and carefree future, into a prosperity represented by this serious, decisive man who spoke to him so persuasively. And who left Vasili in no doubt that he would brook no contradiction.

*

The engagement was hastily celebrated. Nana and Vasili's mother were both flown to Moscow, and a small but *suitable* party was held. The guests smiled, toasted one another, and congratulated the young couple. Vasili was given a generous allowance so he could entertain his pregnant wife in the manner to which she was accustomed. He soon acquired a taste for his new life. Elene accepted all this with what was now her characteristic impenetrable indifference and turned all her attention to her belly, which was growing fuller and more prominent by the day. She was going to have a baby, she was going to be a mother, the best mother in the world, and she was going to do everything for her baby; she pictured how she would devote herself wholly to her new offspring to compensate for the other, dead, unwanted, unborn child.

One evening, the couple were leaving the Pushkin Museum hand in hand, talking excitedly about art, when Vasili stopped in the middle of the street, sat down on the pavement, and began to weep. Elene, overwhelmed by this unaccustomed sight and by her fiancé's sudden sorrow, sat down beside him and tentatively put her head on his shoulder. She didn't enquire about the reason for his sudden change of mood but waited until he had calmed down. Almost out of breath, gasping for air, he forced himself to describe to her his hatred of the country in which they lived; he told her about his childhood, the endless humiliations; he even gave her an unvarnished account of his romantic affairs. He talked about his mother, his brother; he bared his soul to her, as if all his life he had been waiting for this one confession. He spared her nothing, didn't gloss over his feelings, revealed to her even the smallest of his longings for revenge, the most secret of his desires.

They found a bench in a secluded street and sat down. He had talked himself into a frenzy; saliva had gathered in the corners of his mouth and he looked exhausted and empty. She put her arm around his shoulders and thought about what he had said.

'Aren't you surprised?' he asked, when he couldn't bear her silence any longer. 'Or disappointed?'

'I'm not disappointed, Vaso. I understand you, even. I understand you very well, at least I hope so. Sometimes I feel guilty; I didn't want it to be like this, and believe me, I didn't want you to suddenly be here, with me; that wasn't my plan. You shouldn't give up something that's so important to you for me, or for the baby.'

'But I want to be with you. This isn't because of you, Elene.'

'But more than being with me, you want to be somewhere else, don't you?'

'I don't know.'

'Aha. Well, there's one thing I definitely don't want: for you to become one of those pompous bastards who are always cheating on their wives and think they've got everything under control. You only have to look at my father. All that posturing — it disgusts me. I have worries of my own, you know. Don't think I don't. I just don't like talking about them.'

'I'll pull myself together. I promise I'll be stronger — for us, for you. I'll do better. It's just ... well, it's hard. And it all happened so suddenly, so unexpectedly.'

'I do understand. You know, I used to want to leave as well. I have an aunt in the West. She's a famous singer there.'

'Really?'

'Yes, but I'm not allowed to talk about her.'

'We could go together ...'

'Don't be childish. I don't want to. Your dreams aren't mine, Vaso. What would I do in the West? Where would I go? I belong here, with my family;

it doesn't matter how much I hate them, I still belong here. Perhaps I should have met you two years ago, in the summer. I was ... different then. Do you have anyone who could help you?'

'If I had enough money, yes. I know a couple of sailors who occasionally smuggle people onto the ships and —'

'Good. Very good. Listen. Papa wants us to get married before the baby comes. That means spring at the latest; recently, he's been talking about March. He'll give us money. For the wedding, our new life, and, you know, all that nonsense. He wants us to stay in Moscow; he doesn't want us to go to my mother's in Tbilisi. He thinks it's her fault. I used to think it was, too. That's not true. But it doesn't matter now. So we'll get the money and we'll act as if we're planning our wedding. Look for a place to hold the reception, make sure everything's stylish and expensive. That's how he wants it, so he can invite all his colleagues. On balance, he actually thinks it's good that you're a Russian. And we have to make an appointment with the registry office; and we should really do all this, too, because he checks up on everything; but we'll only ever pay people a deposit and say that the rest will follow on the day of the wedding. You'll get the rest. Go to Sochi; settle everything you need to settle there. And just before the wedding, you'll disappear. By the time they find out, you have to be gone. You *have* to be gone, Vaso, or you'll be finished. They won't spare you. My father least of all. It can't go wrong, otherwise you'll never see a window again without bars. Do you understand me?'

Vaso stared at his fiancée, wide-eyed, with a mixture of tremendous respect, fascination, and awe.

'When you're in Sochi, if you realise it's not going to work, come back and we'll have to get married. We can split up in a few years' time if you like; that's fine by me. If you doubt even for one second that you can make it — turn back.'

'You're talking like a pro.'

'A pro?'

'Yes; as if you had experience with this sort of thing.'

'I used to imagine it sometimes. That's all. The rest I know from my father. They all think I don't pick up on anything, but I pick up on everything, even things they don't pick up on themselves. I also know that my father covered for his sister when she left. But that doesn't matter now, either.'

'I don't know what to say.'

'Don't worry: the baby will have everything it needs. You know that. My father will do everything he can for us. And I'll do everything I can for the baby. I think it's going to be a girl.'

'What makes you think that?'

'No idea. I'll find a beautiful name for her. Haven't decided yet, though.'

'When I was little, there was a woman who lived in our neighbourhood. Some people said she was a witch. I think they were just jealous of her. Because she was different, and so special. She healed people with herbs, but no one trusted her an inch. She was a gypsy. Some people said she was a whore, but no one ever saw her with any men. Others said her family had been killed — deported, and so on — but no one really knew anything about her. She just turned up, overnight, in the place where we lived.

'When I was a child I often went to play in her garden. She lived in a converted garage, in the middle of a field. That was so romantic; it seemed so romantic to me. She was so ... different from everyone else I knew. I didn't know anything about her, either. But she knew how to sing, cook, and love. She really knew. She was always there for me. For me, and lots of other children who wandered around the neighbourhood not knowing what to do with themselves. She played with us; she was like a child herself, and she was always telling us stories.

'As I ... well, as I got older, I started to lust after her. One day I plucked up all my courage and went to see her. I mean, people had always claimed she did it with anyone for money. So I raided Mother's purse and went to see her. And when I explained to her what I wanted, she started to cry. It was so shocking to me that I just ran away. She just stood in front of me with the tears running down her cheeks. I couldn't even have imagined her ever crying at all. I saw how much I'd disappointed her. And I was so ashamed.

'Soon after that she was gone. From one day to the next — just as she had appeared. I never saw her again. She never came back. I don't even know if she's still alive. I think she was the only woman I've ever really loved. And the only one who didn't want to sleep with me. Ironic, isn't it?'

'What was her name?'

'Daria.'

And so it was that my sister got her name from a gypsy witch whom some took for a whore, but who, as far as my sister's unknown father was concerned, was the only saint he had ever met, back then, in his still-young life.

> We hear the command! In this brave time the people shall burn the past!
> With the proud flag we greet our eternal people, Georgia!
>
> PABLO IASHVILI

Daria, the sun child, came into this world in the stifling, sultry night of 4 June 1970, in a pastel-coloured room in a hospital reserved exclusively for Lubyanka personnel. People had started to call the Lubyanka building in Moscow 'Grown-Ups' World', after the big department store 'Children's World' was erected opposite it in 1957.

Kostya himself had driven his daughter to the hospital when she went into labour. He had rejected outright his wife's suggestion that she come to Moscow to support her daughter. He had paced up and down in the waiting room all night, and was the first person, after the midwife and Elene, to look into Daria's angelic face. He was also the one who registered his own surname on Daria's birth certificate. Naturally there was no question of giving his granddaughter the name of a deserter.

She was born during President Nixon's first term in office, one year after Neil Armstrong's landing on the moon, two years after Gagarin was killed in a mysterious plane crash, one year before Bernd Sievert was shot forty-three times and seriously wounded by East German border guards while attempting to escape over the Berlin Wall. The same year the Beatles announced they were splitting up, unleashing a flood of tears all around the world. Shortly before the *Easy Rider* wave washed over the eastern half of the globe and had every twenty-year-old praying that some blessed person would smuggle Harleys across every border. Shortly before Idi Amin seized power in Uganda; during the protest by the dissident Sakharov against sending members of the opposition to Soviet mental hospitals; and some months after the Nobel Prize was awarded to a certain Mr Beckett, who was still unknown in the East and, of course, nonetheless — or perhaps for that very reason — banned. Two years after the revolution that started in Paris — people still didn't know whether the history books would record it as failed or successful, or whether it could even be described as a revolution. Shortly after the publication of an article in *LIFE* magazine about the My Lai massacre in Vietnam, in which the American Task Force Barker unit raped, murdered, and wiped out an entire village. And exactly one month after the Green House was completed.

★

The Green House was, and still is, one of the most beautiful houses I've ever seen. Bordered by a thick forest of pine trees to the north, to the west encircled by a breathtaking gorge (the first thing Stasia did was erect a three-metre high fence in front of it), to the east, a narrow dirt path leading to the nearby village, and overlooking the barns of the stud farm to the south.

Construction was completed in what was, for Georgian workmen, a utopian timescale. Stasia had shown real talent as a building contractor: she had driven the workers the way an experienced shepherd drives his flock, had cooked them princely meals every evening, kept their schnapps bottles full, and had nonetheless managed to ensure that work began at seven each morning. This despite the fact that Soviet workmen were a breed apart, one that needed a vast amount of alcohol, food, and rest before they could so much as put one brick on top of another.

At the age of seventy she had not only achieved the impossible, but had also demonstrated good architectural taste. She had had the old wooden balconies restored, the curlicued ornaments and old banisters refurbished. Had the wooden floorboards typical of the region varnished dark red; had stone floors laid in the spacious kitchen and in all the bathrooms, as well as in the cellar; and even managed to resurrect the ruined fireplace in the guest bedroom.

There were eight rooms over two floors, and a huge terrace at the front of the house that was to become the main living space for the whole family, except in the winter months. And then there was the phenomenal piece of land the house was built upon, which, according to Stasia's plans, she and Christine were going to transform into an enchanting garden.

On the wide meadow that sloped up to the forest, she had a barn built, which — God knows why — she had the men paint lettuce-green. She claimed this barn for herself, and no one thought to ask what she intended to do in there, given that there was now plenty of room for everyone to have their own space in the magnificent house. They probably thought she wanted to use it for her gardening tools.

The Green House was an ideal place; it promised the world as it was meant to be. And the whole family was excited about moving in, looking forward to this new beginning and the arrival of a new family member. All except Christine.

She felt the loss of Miqa keenly: she was like a different person. She was seldom at home; no one knew where she went after work; they hardly ever heard her opera arias any more; her former passion — spending hours in the garden sowing seeds, weeding, trimming bushes, watering flowers — was extinguished. Added to the difficulty she had in coming to terms with her advancing age, and her perpetual resistance to retirement, was the disappointment of losing Miqa, whom she had raised with besotted love. The result was that Christine constantly gave the other women the feeling that they had done something wrong, that it was all their fault, because whenever she spoke to them now it was in a tone of condescension.

Any conversation about Miqa was stifled by Christine with icy vehemence. But what else could they have done, given the problems Miqa had caused? Stasia, newly returned from Prague, had been in no state to think about anything but her daughter. And ultimately they had had to make sure Miqa was safe from Kostya's anger; even Andro had been forced to acknowledge that. Stasia would not accept any reproach on this score. Sopio had whispered to her in a dream, all those years ago, that she should tell the boy stories of a good world, and this she had conscientiously done. Now the boy was almost a man, and he would have to learn to fend for himself. Stasia was too old to put rose-tinted spectacles on anyone's nose. She was too old to tell fairy tales. Besides, the boy — presumably it was in his nature — had made a terrible mistake, the consequences of which he, as well as her own biological grandchild, must bear. That was that — over and done with! She had done her duty; it was her right to take her well-earned, and above all peaceful, retirement and make the most of the opportunity the Green House offered them all.

But the more often Christine drove out to the house with her sister, to support her during its construction, the more her resistance to the plan intensified. It wasn't a new beginning for her, not here, not under these circumstances. She had allowed her beloved boy to be sent back like a parcel delivered to the wrong address. Neither her opportunistic sister nor her weak-willed daughter-in-law had tried to establish the truth; they had just stoked the girl's destructive fury and humiliated the boy in his defencelessness. And, although Christine respected her sister's great achievement and could see how meticulously she had worked, with such attention to detail, she nonetheless became increasingly convinced that this paradise on earth could never be her home. Miqa was not allowed to be here, the truth had no place here, and she would never find peace, not without the boy.

And when the next scandal surrounding Elene came along, and then the news reached Tbilisi that the Russian bastard Vasili had jilted his pregnant fiancée and sneakily, dishonourably, run off with the wedding money, Christine could not restrain herself. She remarked triumphantly that it was only logical that he had bolted before it was too late: sensible men didn't marry women who *coerced* them into things. Her *schadenfreude* was hard to comprehend; Nana responded with scorching fury, Stasia with bewilderment.

One month before the planned move to the Green House, Christine announced to her sister as they were washing up in the kitchen that she would not be going with them.

'What's that supposed to mean?' cried Stasia in astonishment, putting a plate back in the sink.

'What I just said: I'm staying here. This is my home.'

'Don't you see you're being childish? Of course this is your home. You don't have to move in straight away with all your worldly goods. As far as I'm concerned you can just come up for the weekends, while you're still working at the hospital —'

'I'm staying here. I've got nothing more to say on the subject. Besides, Miqa will apply to study in Tbilisi, and when he does I want him to live with me in *my* house.'

'All this time I didn't realise that this was *your* house, not *ours*! Elene will be here in two weeks. We'll help her with the baby, and we'll —'

'You and Nana will manage that without me.'

'He got my granddaughter pregnant, for goodness' sake, and we were considerate and didn't say anything to Kostya.'

'We brought Andro up, and when it mattered we failed to see what was going on. We let him make that terrible mistake; and why? Because back then our *own* children and their worries seemed more important, didn't they? I'm not going to make the same mistake with Miqa.'

Stasia had stepped aside and was lighting her filterless cigarette with one damp hand. 'Now you just listen to me. I've paid dearly enough for what he did — that's wicked, accusing me, saying I didn't do enough to —'

Goya came flapping into the kitchen. They could hear Nana shifting furniture upstairs; she was in a real moving frenzy.

'He didn't do it. You know he didn't. He gave in, he just gave in to your granddaughter. That was the full extent of his crime: he was just a boy, and he couldn't control himself with a half-naked girl.'

'Who had to pay the greater price? My poor girl, who had her womb scraped out at the age of fifteen, or Miqa, who had his fun and was sent back to his parents?' Stasia was screaming now; her eyes had narrowed to slits. 'It's a miracle she got pregnant again. Doesn't that count either, Christine?'

'I tried to prevent it.'

'And you didn't! And do you know why? Because we're not all-powerful, and we can't save *anyone*! When are you going to understand?'

> You will not succeed in leaving me:
> The door is open and your house — empty!
>
> MARINA TSVETAEVA

Driven by the growing strength of the women's movement, the mobilisation of the left and its increasingly insistent demands for a new kind of politics, a new way of life; whipped up by the people of '68 (who only became known as such years later), by Woodstock and the new music generation, by the public desire for demilitarisation which was growing increasingly vocal, at least in the West; driven by outrage over the murder of Martin Luther King, the world began to seek new weapons to carry its ideas.

There were the Hendrixes and the Joplins, of course, a new type of brilliant anarchist, but people also needed someone who could point the finger of blame at the world without recourse to heroin and marijuana. And then they happened upon my great-aunt Kitty, who had had a few hits, had even made it into the British charts, but was still living in her three-room flat in Soho; who dutifully paid her taxes, and could look back on an unusual political past. And what a past it was! But that only came to light when the photo was published. The photo from Wenceslas Square. The Magnum photo. It appeared in the papers, and exploded like a bomb.

Six months after the events in Prague, *The Guardian* published an article on the embarrassing failure of socialism. The main theme was, of course, the 'Prague Spring', so they went looking for interesting, as-yet-unpublished images. And found the photo of Kitty Jashi.

★

As was only to be expected, Amy had withdrawn from Kitty and left London without saying where she was going. Kitty heard that she had gone to her husband in Wales and, later, that she had left for Italy. It was months before she reappeared, again with no warning, and resumed her work with her protégée — in a much more businesslike and reserved way, but still. She asked no questions. The subject of Fred was, of course, taboo. She no longer invited Kitty to her home in King's Cross, nor did she take her to private functions, but she continued to arrange Kitty's radio and television appearances, planned her concerts, advised her in her dealings with the press, and went into overdrive trying to boost record sales with all kinds of advertising and marketing strategies. Kitty could hardly expect much more from her; the main thing was that Amy had kept her in her life, still believed in her music, and had put her organisational talents at her disposal.

Her call took Kitty by surprise. It was late, and it was a long time since Amy had rung at this hour: an evening call might appear overly intimate. She could tell from her voice that her manager (who no longer wanted to be her friend) was excited; layer by layer, the carefully cultivated formality stripped away from her vocal cords as she drenched Kitty in a torrent of words.

'Hang on a minute — what newspaper, did you say? I didn't understand a word of that. I'm at home, if you'd like ... No, I'm alone.'

Amy did in fact agree to come round in half an hour. 'We're only talking business,' she added, as if trying to legitimise her visit and under no circumstances allow the mood to become conciliatory. She was wearing a lurid green raincoat and a brightly coloured elastic band round her hair, which had gone completely wild and was falling in her eyes. She slammed the next day's edition of *The Guardian* down on the table in front of Kitty.

'And you don't tell me something like *this*!'

The big black-and-white photo of Kitty was splashed across the front page. Kitty had never seen it before. At first, she couldn't believe that the girl in the picture with the guitar was really her. Or was it a collage, just someone having a joke at her expense?

'So. What the bloody hell is this?' Amy flopped onto the sofa.

'I have no idea who took this photo, or how it ended up in here! I'm not even sure it's really me.'

'Are you insane? Who else would it be? The Pope?'

'I have no idea, Amy. Really I don't.'

'The real question should be: why are you in this picture at all? Why didn't you leave that bloody city the second that army of cut-throats marched in? Who, for God's sake, thinks of standing there and singing? You're a bit old for revolutions. I ought to thank you, really, for taking that madwoman away from me, but putting my source of income at risk, after I've spent years working my arse off for it — that's a bit much!'

'I'm sorry the first thing I thought of at the time wasn't your wallet!' Kitty answered sarcastically. Inwardly, though, she was triumphant. Amy seemed more than a little impressed; she had also broached that other unfortunate topic, which seemed to Kitty a very good sign.

'My God, that gang of terrorists could have arrested you and stuck you in a gulag somewhere,' ranted Amy, who only really took an interest in politics because it was fashionable, and whose impression of the Soviet Union could be summarised as follows: 'Dark. Grey. No clothes. Everyone in the same rubber boots. Cold. Slush. Cold again. Lots of old men. Bad music. Unhappy faces and no sex.' (Actually, she wasn't too far wrong on this last point, when you consider that in the land of my birth the established motto 'We don't have sex in the Soviet Union' was certainly not intended by the state as a joke.)

'Listen — you look hungry. I'll make us a little something to eat, and then we'll talk about everything, okay?' Kitty interrupted Amy's outraged monologue and strode into the kitchen.

Over supper she gave a detailed account of her stay in Prague, using vivid colours and big words to describe the street scenes she got caught up in, increasing Amy's respect still further; she answered her questions over and over again, but she omitted the encounter with her mother.

'This is all pretty crazy. And now that you've reassured me, I think perhaps it wasn't so stupid at all, darling — not stupid at all, what you did back there.'

'What are you getting at?'

'Well, read what it says here. They're hailing you as a minor heroine in the courageous fight against the evils of communism. I quote: "Miss Jashi raised her voice against oppression and totalitarianism." Blah blah blah. Come on, think — what am I getting at?'

'But ...'

'As of tomorrow, we can bank on getting interview requests. As of next week, you'll be in a BBC studio. I guarantee it. After that, the Americans will come. And they'll all want you to tell them how terrible it was, how you feared for your life, and how oppressed everyone is over there. Then you tell them about your terrible past and we can count on a European, maybe even an American, tour, after that maybe even a gold disc. That means: get started on a new album right away. This is the best publicity we could have dreamed of. You're the next big thing, darling.'

'I need time. I haven't written a single song since ...'

'Since ...? No, I don't want to hear it. Just a little piece of advice: the person you're thinking of is not necessarily the one who enhances your productivity, so I'd be a bit careful if I were you.'

Amy was like someone who'd been brought back to life: a new life, full of wonder, promises kept, and sweet recompense. She took out her pink notebook and scribbled in it avidly. Kitty covered her face with her hands and heaved a deep sigh.

'Oh, all right then, if you absolutely have to tell me. What's the matter? Oh, oh, oh, poor Kitty ... No, I can't actually imagine it, I mean, you're so bloody hetero, I don't understand it, my brain just refuses to process it. Although, if I think about it, she's capable of persuading even my husband to go to bed with her.'

'She's not well,' Kitty interrupted quietly. She started kneading her fingers. 'I sent her to a clinic last week. A detoxification programme in a clinic in Richmond. A new sort of clinic.'

'Detoxification programme? Has she been drinking too much again?'

'No. Worse.'

'How much worse?'

'Heroin.'

'Oh my God.' Amy's hand flew to her mouth. She jumped up, sat down again, wanted to say something, to object, respond in some way, but in the end she just sat there without speaking, staring at Kitty with frightened eyes.

'Yes, I didn't want to believe it either, but it's got bad, very bad. She almost died. I didn't dare ask you for help.'

'How long?'

'I don't know exactly. Since America, I think. When I got back from Prague, I found her half-unconscious, and all this paraphernalia in the bathroom. I completely freaked out. She hasn't painted anything for ages, let alone sold a picture. It was unbelievable, the amount of debt she'd run up. She wanted to call you, for money, but I ordered her not to. I thought —'

'You should have called me.'

'But I couldn't, and I didn't want to, Amy. Not like that. Not for this.'

'I'll pay for the clinic.'

'No, no, you don't have to do that. I can manage.'

'Yes, I do. Is she any better?'

'I don't know. She says she is, on the phone. The doctors strongly advised against visiting her in the first few weeks. I call her twice a week. She sounds better, but that doesn't necessarily mean anything. She's an incredible actress, as you know.'

'*As I know*. Yes. I certainly do.'

★

When Kitty paid the taxi driver, picked up Fred's little suitcase, and strode off towards Hyde Park to sit down on a secluded patch of grass, she already knew what she was letting herself in for. She had just collected Fred from the station. She was a bit thinner than usual; to Kitty's dismay, she had practically shaved her head; even her skin seemed whiter. With her green Ray-Bans balanced on her head she looked like a fourteen-year-old boy.

Kitty sensed that the battle was by no means won; that it had, in fact, only just begun. She tried not to let her shock at Fred's unkempt appearance show. However much she used to drink, looking good had always been important to her: perfect haircut, well-tailored clothes. Now, her trousers were torn at the knee, she smelled of stale sweat, and her hair appeared to have been sacrificed to lice or some other equally unappetising creatures.

Fred stretched out beside her on the damp grass. In the distance, a nursery school teacher was walking past with a gaggle of children.

'How could you do it?' Kitty began, struggling to control herself.

'I'm not going to justify myself,' Fred answered, indifferently.

'So as far as you're concerned I don't even deserve an explanation? You look terrible, by the way.'

'Sorry, I didn't have a chance to go and get my make-up done. As you know, I had to leave in an awful hurry.'

'And whose fault is that? I get a call from some hysterical nurse, who tells me they're throwing you out of the clinic for drugs and indecent behaviour. I mean, Fred ... *Indecent behaviour*!'

'I was practically dying, all I did was —'

'You probably seduced that nurse in the ladies' loo so she'd get you a fix.'

'I just wanted a little morphine, that's all. I was in pain.'

'Right. I'm going to make you an offer. I am only going to say this once. I will take you home, I will nurse you, I will cancel all my appointments, I will take time off, and I won't leave your side for three months, I will watch over you day and night so you finally escape this hell, and then ... you'll be clean. If you're not, if you try to mess me around or trick me, we'll never see each other again. But I will give you this one chance.'

'Hey, you're talking to me like I'm a baby.'

'Your intellectual level is not necessarily any higher, Fred. Right now, I'm making a commitment to you: that's the most important thing, that's what should be the most important thing for you.'

'I like it when you're furious. It makes you really sexy.'

'Don't change the subject. I'm waiting for an answer.'

'I don't know.'

'You don't know? Do you remember the first time we met? Do you remember how you came to me and said —'

'I'm not senile.'

'Good. Then you know what I'm talking about.'

'You never committed to me. I liked that. I always had to run after you. I liked that, too. And now you want to become like all the others?'

'You're an ungrateful bitch.'

'Yeah, go on, let it out. Finally an end to the nauseating do-gooder crap. Go ahead and spit out what's really going on inside. It'll do you good.'

'Shut up. Just shut the fuck up. You've ruined enough already. I'm not becoming like all the others. I'm doing something no one has ever done for you: giving you a chance to stay, and not keep on running.'

'Why? I'm not worth it, sweetie. I'm just a dried-up piece of shit. Go ahead, be angry with me.'

Fred fell silent. Scratched around in the earth with a little stone. Shifted her bottom back and forth. Picked at the hole in her trousers. Scratched her head, scratched her arms. Then she said quietly, almost inaudibly, 'Okay.'

'Okay what?'

'I'll try.'

So Kitty Jashi took her friend back to her flat and stayed there with her. Despite all Amy's threats and pleas for her to finally start work on the new album and respond to the interview requests — because of course Amy had been right, and the renewed interest in Kitty exceeded their wildest imaginings — Kitty stuck by her promise to save Fred from herself. And one June morning, when her guardian angel, her nameless friend, called to inform her that she had become the great-aunt of a healthy baby girl, Kitty was in the middle of holding a bowl to Fred's mouth as she vomited into it, cursing.

Creating the idea of an enemy for oneself releases a destructive power. Because it is not the enemy who creates mistrust, but mistrust that creates the enemy.

MERAB MAMARDASHVILI

When Daria asked Stasia why her eyes were different colours, Stasia answered her as follows: 'That, my sunshine, is because there are two animals who live inside you: a husky, the sled-dog with the piercing blue eyes, from whom you get your blue eye, and a hedgehog, small, shy, and prickly — you get your brown eye from him. Your husky is the brave part of you that's always running, that doggedly follows its path, on and on and on, that never shies away from any adventure, and the hedgehog is the part of you that needs protection and calm, security and lots of love, that fears the wide world of the husky and so is always trying to retreat.' Daria stuck to this story all her life, and would tell it whenever people commented, in amazement and wonder, on her eyes.

*

When I picture Daria as a little girl, I always see her dressed in her smart clothes, for which my grandmother was primarily responsible. She looked like a child from a pattern magazine, with stylish little patent-leather shoes and white socks, her curly blonde hair tied back in a ponytail. I see her purse her lips, holding sway over everyone and everything. A princess, whom our family was only sheltering temporarily, and who was therefore allowed to do anything, was entitled to anything she wanted.

Daria really did have the strangest, most beautiful eyes I've ever seen. And everything about her was beautiful and well-proportioned, practically perfect; only her deep voice, like that of a sulky boy, didn't really go with her angelic appearance. I can still hear the whispering whenever I think back to when we used to walk along the street holding Mother's hands: people speaking to one another in low voices, their glances lingering on her, circling her like wasps around a jam jar. Of course, I would be lying if I claimed I didn't suffer torments back then; I would be lying if I claimed I hadn't, some nights, wished a plague upon her. However, these torments were caused not so much by Daria or her beauty, but by our grandfather's idolisation of her. In his eyes, she had everything she needed to lead a brilliant life, everything he valued in the female sex: unparalleled beauty; the innate ability to smilingly, trippingly, get her own way; the sleepwalker's confidence that accompanies such beauty; and the obedience of a well-trained circus horse.

I've already said, Brilka, that despite all the many fights we had throughout our childhood, for me she was always the big sister I looked up to and wanted to emulate, in the certain knowledge that I would never succeed.

It seemed to be an unwritten law that Daria made everything she touched shine brightly, so it was no wonder that, later on, when the tables turned and the hedgehog inside her disappeared for ever, she also demonstrated the power to bring everything crashing down.

But I don't even exist yet; I haven't yet been born into our story. So I mustn't rely on my own memories; I must content myself with those of others that tally with my impression of how things were.

Before I let Daria's progenitor, whom our mother had helped to flee abroad, walk out of our story forever, I should perhaps mention that he really did get to America. Elene never talked about him. But one day, when the country we all came from had long since vanished from the maps of the world, she told me as she sat cracking walnuts that she'd always believed Vaso would make it. And indeed his criminal brother, who had gone on to become a 'businessman', had contacted her and told her that Vaso had died in Davenport, Iowa. At the time of his death, he was a gas-station attendant on his third marriage. An untreated obstruction of the bowel killed him; he hadn't been able to afford health insurance, and so hadn't gone to the doctor, despite the pain.

Even though his life had been anything but a classic example of the American dream, Elene — rather bitter and disappointed that her plan had come to so little and Vaso hadn't even made it to New York or LA but had fetched up as a lowly provincial gas-station attendant — said at the time that she didn't think it impossible that perhaps he had been able to wrest a bit more happiness from his life in the West. As far as I'm aware, his three American marriages were childless. He died without ever having seen or spoken to his only daughter.

★

Daria was destined to grow up fatherless. It was this that prompted my grandfather to bid farewell to the Moscow military arena and request a transfer to his homeland, even though for Kostya Jashi this relocation was tantamount to a demotion, as the Black Sea fleet had no military significance and was responsible solely for trade. A life without the sea, though, would only have been half a life for him. So he tested the waters at the Ministry of Internal Affairs and asked a few of his confidants in Georgia to enquire about a suitable position for him, because he knew that in Georgia — if he wanted it — all doors were open to him. After all, he had managed to survive in Russia, so he was more than good enough for Georgia. He could boast some triumphant successes on the secret council of the submarine fleet. Under the leadership of Admiral Gorshkov, his committee had managed, in a very short space of time, to build the best submarines in the world. With these, the Soviet fleet was not just numerically superior to the Americans', it had also broken all their records: for speed, for depth, for size. Kostya could look back on his career with pride. Certainly, many sacrifices had had to be made to achieve this rapid growth; certainly, they had had to suffer losses; but what Great Work was ever achieved without sacrifice?

Yes, he had found it hard to write the report on K-129, which sank in the middle of the Pacific. It had been no fun with K-8, either, in the Bay of Biscay, and as for K-19 — well, Kostya didn't even want to think about that.

The sea: yes, he had married the sea, and now he was thinking of exchanging his companion of many years for a small, soft girl with two different-coloured eyes.

He didn't want to go to Batumi or Poti to keep an eye on civilian merchant convoys, but the Black Sea offered him no alternative. Was it time to go ashore now? For good? To take care of his family; to care for Daria in a way that would make up for his failings with Elene? Would they manage to be a *normal* family at last?

Kostya felt the burden of age on his shoulders, its leaden weight like a heavy suit of armour. He was constantly checking himself in the mirror, counting the new wrinkles, cursing every annoying new nasal hair or little roll of fat around his waist. Although he still did callisthenics every morning like clockwork, placed great importance on looking elegant, and made considerable efforts to keep up with the fashion, he knew that soon he would no longer find it so easy to persuade these young, blonde, lavender-and-honey-scented women to be his companions. He knew the time would come when he would have to make do with the second- and third-eldest, fourth- and fifth-prettiest. And he feared it.

★

Then he was approached by an old friend from Tbilisi, who suggested that he might like to apply to sit as one of the thirty-two members of the National Council. They would welcome such an eminent, deserving man with open arms. And although it was hard for him to exchange the sea for the tedium of a desk job, he could see that this post was the best alternative for him in this situation. A council member was not inferior to a naval captain in terms either of remuneration or status. There, too, he would report to the MVD — familiar territory for Kostya. As a National Council member, he could ask for control of the harbour authority. They wouldn't be able to deny his request.

He contacted the relevant people and made his wishes known, which, as anticipated, were very warmly received. Yes, Kostya decided, he should indeed head home, even though Tbilisi had stopped being his home long ago. Yes, he must take command of the doomed ship that was his family and steer it into a safe harbour.

★

At the time of Kostya's return, people were already talking about a 'thaw'. Brezhnev's rise to power had marked the beginning of the era of the *eminences grises*. Fortunately, no one yet knew that he would remain in office for another eleven years, during more than half of which he would be seriously ill, and would lead the country into a state of stagnation. Brezhnev's greatest 'achievement' — along with the crushing of the Prague Spring — was the reintroduction of compulsory silence. Public criticism of the Generalissimus was strictly prohibited, and in that great empire, extending across eleven time zones, calm was maintained so scrupulously that the country imperceptibly fell into a coma.

Brezhnev's chest was decorated with an absurd number of medals; he was made a marshal, and declared, with satisfaction: 'The country is stable, peaceful, and in good condition. I am glad that everything here is proceeding normally.'

Yes, everything was *normal*. Because under his government there were no alcoholics, no sadists, no informers, and no creatures corroded by mistrust. After all, there was condensed milk, there was milk powder; there was even caviar, if you moved in the right circles, and complimentary dachas for the higher-ups; *kommunalkas* too, of course, infested with cockroaches; there was the *right idea*, for everyone to promote; there were fertile women; there were cheap cigarettes and comfortable Volgas, there was a lot of vodka and, *in extremis,* samogon, which never failed to do the trick — a few sips resulted in total blackout; and there were prisons for *bad* people, meaning those who didn't know how to appreciate this wonderful system. There were *proper*, state-approved methods for dealing with such vermin; and there were other means of repression.

The state informed its people which sanatorium they should recover in, gave them a profession, a place to live, and a purpose in life. Yes: everything was *normal*.

★

Kostya packed the expensive porcelain into cardboard boxes, gave away most of his furniture, sent the valuable tapestries and carpets to Tbilisi, and had everything transported to his hometown, along with his beloved cream-coloured GAZ-13 Chaika, the model known as 'The Seagull'.

He was received in Tbilisi in a manner befitting his status; endless tables were laid for him in a demonstration of sunny Georgia's excessive, manic hospitality. There was even an article about him in *The Communist*. A great hero had returned to his homeland. He was given an office in the Ministry of Internal Affairs on Chitadze Street, and a new driver.

And when he was offered the supervision of harbour dues along the Black Sea coast of the Georgian Soviet Socialist Republic, he accepted without discussion. In future he would commute between Tbilisi, Poti, Sokhumi, and Batumi, and the travelling suited him very well; it gave him the opportunity to live out his 'private life' undisturbed. For, despite his fear of ageing, at this point in time my grandfather had no intention whatsoever of completely renouncing his old way of life.

Corruption had long been rife in all areas of administration and government, but Kostya trusted that he would be able to cope with it. His years of working in the Soviet Union's toughest institutions had given him the necessary confidence for that. He had swum long enough in the immeasurable vastness of Russian seas; these Georgian ponds didn't scare him. What he did not consider, however, was that he had been living far away from Caucasian reality for too long, and was unable to muster sufficient understanding for his compatriots' *fluid* mentality. He was familiar with the strict rules of the game among the Russian elite; he was familiar with the authorities' covert corruption, which had been experiencing a veritable heyday since Brezhnev's inauguration, but he didn't see that Georgian corruption, Georgian greed, far exceeded that to which he was able to turn a blind eye. He failed to appreciate what a comfortable life the Georgian elite — including the intelligentsia — had established for themselves in their little piece of paradise during the decades of Bolshevik rule. How they had perfected the art of delusion. How good things were for them in their Russian trauma. How easy it actually was to live with the northern oppression that, off the record, they always professed to hate. In Russia, people believed in the power of the authorities, so they had never learned anything other than to live in constant fear of them. In Georgia, though, this fear was merely feigned: people here assumed on principle that those in power were dishonest and corrupt, and so would think in advance of ways to cheat, trick, or bribe them. They didn't believe in a system, or in any ideology; apart from, perhaps, the ideology of their own hedonism.

Once the initial fuss had died down, people had realised that the position their northern neighbour had assigned to them really wasn't all that bad. That it might well prove a mistake not to take advantage of this position. They could actually live in these conditions: one could be cultured, creative, musical, fond of drink, a little anarchic, yes, that, too, but only a little; beautiful and talkative, lazy and hot-tempered. What was wrong with that? These, after all, are the characteristics we Georgians are proud to cite as part of our national identity. Or were these actually Russian dreams that people had internalised to such a degree they had come to believe they were their own? So what? What was so bad about that? Yes, it could have been far worse. The whole vast empire was gazing enviously at this small, sunny piece of paradise! How many Soviet republics, how many autonomous regions, how many sister states would have liked to swap places with us, let alone all those oppressed, resettled minorities? Because as long as the shadow of our great countryman, the Generalissimus, kept watch over the people of Georgia, nothing could happen to us. Because nobody got past him. Not Russia, not the world.

It really was an impressively smart move by Mother Russia, Brilka: she decided always to encourage her small, rebellious, rather too unruly son Georgia in all his weaknesses, and to proclaim these weaknesses strengths, until the son began to delight in his role and believe he had tricked his mother, disempowered her, thereby failing to see the extent to which, in his eagerness to be loved and praised by his parent, he was prostituting himself for her love.

> How my soul yearned to catch butterflies!
> May it now find peace somewhere ...
> KONSTANTIN SLUCHEVSKY

There were ladybirds, the ones that had such pretty spots on their backs, and there were the smells of all the different family members to be noted and distinguished; there was the sun and the moon, and there was sleep, and the dreams Daria didn't usually remember after waking; there were stray dogs and cats, and there were comically patterned lizards; there were thousands of types of plant; there was the unfathomableness of all the different shades of light and earth, the nature of water, her mother's choice of blouse; there was Goya, claiming his new home.

Yes, there was plenty to sniff and touch, plenty to smell and taste; and she had things to learn — crawling, for instance, or the word '*Deda*'. Then there was the hilarity of being tickled by her grandfather's moustache when, with uncommon devotion, she threw her arms about him. The rural idyll around her, the horsewhispering from the stud farm, and the remoteness from the rest of the world protected her from all sorrow.

The only thing that could darken Daria's perfect horizon was her mother's sadness and lack of interest in her. For Elene had not been healed by her child, as she had hoped. It was too exhausting: the crying at night, the keeping to set feeding times, the post-natal hormonal swings. Her melancholy was too great, the pressure of being *obliged* to completely immerse herself in the joys of motherhood too stressful. And so, after enduring the first three months, Elene increasingly sidestepped her responsibilities and left her child more and more often with her own mother and grandmother, who seemed to have no problems whatsoever with the baby; on the contrary, they mastered every task very easily and with little effort, and even found it all delightful and exciting.

Initially, Elene was just as enthusiastic about the Green House as the rest of the family. But it wasn't long before she realised that she was lonely out there, cut off from everything. That neither her daughter nor her parents were capable of filling her inner emptiness. She had too much time to think. Too much time to mull things over. She imagined what it would have been like if Vasili had stayed with her, if she hadn't helped him to abandon her. Or if she had a place at university now and were living in Tbilisi, in a boarding house with others her own age; if she had made new friends, allies, kindred spirits. As it was, she felt permanently guilty, dirty, disorientated, and so full of anger: it was so stressful having to be Elene, Elene Jashi, having to carry this inheritance around with her, always having to be something special!

She prowled about, slept badly, was bad-tempered, bored. She found it hard to concentrate on anything for longer than an hour; nothing, it seemed, could rouse her interest, her curiosity. Sometimes she felt old, lethargic, and so alone that she asked herself whether she would ever be able to live like other people her age again. She didn't know what to do with herself. She crept out of her room at night, wandered about the garden, secretly smoking one of Stasia's cigarettes, biting her fingernails, staring at the night with restless eyes and searching for a way to be someone — anyone — other than herself. At what point had she failed to find herself? Where had she taken the wrong turning? When had she lost her way, and what way was it?

Her solitary walks took her further and further away from the Green House, away from Stasia and the child, away from her father and mother, who were both picked up early in the morning and brought back in the evening by Kostya's driver.

When she thought about her classmates in Moscow and Tbilisi, her old friends, she was filled with rage towards Daria. She was certain her friends didn't have swollen, aching breasts, or stretchmarks, didn't have to get up three times a night, and could go out, drink, party, study, travel, fall in and out of love, and live as their age and desires dictated.

Her walks grew longer. She got to know the surrounding villages and settlements. Visited the stud farm. She studied the lithe thoroughbred animals as they grazed. She watched the Arabs, Javakhians, and Kabardins. Imagined what it would be like to mount one and ride off into the unknown.

On one of these walks she met Miqail. I think it was his name that decided it. If he'd been called David, Seraphim, or Giorgi, perhaps she wouldn't have gone about things with such zeal and such readiness for self-sacrifice. He was a middle-aged man with a full beard and peculiar clothes. A simple cross hung around his neck. He was working at the stables for the summer.

Once she had overcome her initial mistrust, she grew more talkative;

this dour man seemed friendly, open, and interested in her troubles. Also, his speech betrayed his city origins: he was from Tbilisi.

Elene's walks became her main occupation. At around three o'clock, Miqail would take a break, and she would already be waiting outside the stable. She would bring a little picnic basket with her — Stasia's delicacies wrapped in aluminium foil, plus a little fruit and some vegetables — and if the opportunity presented itself she would pilfer a bottle of wine from Kostya's cellar. She liked Miqail's calmness, his self-control, and above all she liked the feeling that as a woman she didn't seem to interest him in the slightest. At first, she was almost offended, ascribing his lack of interest to her diminished attractiveness since the birth of Daria, but soon she found it liberating. This, she had to admit, was better and simpler.

He didn't ask stupid questions; he didn't seem the least bit surprised that she never once mentioned the father of her child; he wasn't interested in why such a young woman was living in such isolation and not pursuing an occupation, in line with socialist values, according to which no one in the Soviet Union was without work. He once asked her whether she believed in God. For some reason, Elene wasn't surprised by the question; it was as if she had been waiting for it. She didn't know, she answered; she would like to. Two years earlier she had even entered a convent, but it hadn't really done anything for her.

After this, Miqail began to supply Elene with Christian texts. He told her, later on, that his parents had fallen victim to state repression, so he had grown up with relatives and in children's homes. That his sister had killed herself after discovering that her own husband was spying on her. That, at the age of nineteen, he had ended up in Navtlukhi prison, and subsequently spent seven years in prison in Rostov. He had gone astray, as he put it. In prison he had found God, and now he propagated his own religion, a motley combination of Greek Orthodox ideology and Tolstoy's *A Confession* and *My Religion*.

After Rostov, he said, he had started roaming across the country, and was repeatedly arrested for refusing to work. He despised all forms of possession and lived by doing casual summer jobs in the countryside, because in Tbilisi a man like him would quickly become too conspicuous and wouldn't find any disciples for his ideology. And indeed, in the years of his peregrinations he did make a name for himself as a miracle healer (such things have always found fertile ground in the Caucasus), and away from the *kolkhozes* and tea plantations he found plenty of people to listen to the teachings he had cobbled together. It wasn't long before Elene, too, was counted among his followers.

He preached a life without possessions, a stateless system; he quoted the

Bible and Tolstoy, and kept supplying her with the *right* books.

Everything he said sounded so simple and so clever. As if all you had to do was follow his commandments and life would just be an endless orgy of happiness. But his commandments seemed impossible to put into practice. However hard Elene tried to forgive her parents, to not get annoyed with Daria, to never get worked up about her annoying family members, to be loving and forgiving, she would always come up against her own limits, run to Miqail, confess her 'sins' to him, and vent her frustration over the enforced harmony of daily life in the Green House.

'I can't stand it any more! And when I'm sitting on the terrace in the evening, I hear my father saying to my mother: "Look at the way she just wanders about, why doesn't she make something of herself, she's completely letting herself go, she has no interest in anything, it's just not normal, and then that stupid music, that music all the time, it's not healthy, what has she done to her hair, why doesn't she socialise with people her own age, why doesn't she come to Tbilisi with us, why's she always down in the village, where does she go there?" And so on. And Mother tries to calm him down, feeds him some lie or other, but she's just as disappointed in me. Sure, it'd be great for her if I were one of her students, then she could show off, she could say: "Look, this is my child, she may have been jilted by a deserter but she's got back on her feet, got her energy back, and now she's studying, and soon she'll find a strong Georgian guy who can be relied on not to walk out on her and will look after her properly. She'll be a good housewife to him, a sociable girl dancing through life, accompanying him on lovely summer holidays to Borjomi and skiing in Bakuriani in winter!" Honestly, it makes me want to throw up. What on earth should I do, Miqail? At night, when they're all asleep and Daria doesn't need feeding any more, I sneak up to the attic. It's the only place in the house where I can have my peace and quiet, where no one can find me. The extension isn't finished' — (it never would be, Brilka!) — 'and there's a balcony up there with no railing. I sit there, reading, smoking, thinking, and I can't come to a conclusion. No solution. Isn't that awful?'

But she didn't have the courage to speak of what she really wanted to confess. How she would have liked to confess to Miqail about that terrible afternoon; to admit that, ever since, all her actions, memories, and thoughts ended in this vague sense of deficiency, failure, and hopelessness. How much she would have liked to have told him about her squeaking bed, Miqa's confused, fearful expression, the terrible panic and destructive fury she had felt, which had so overwhelmed her, filling her with such fear, and which at times she still sensed in herself today. That although she felt remorse, there had also been a certain gratification, something deeply satisfying, because she had succeeded in driving him out and reconquering her rightful place, the throne she craved; except that this throne had turned out to be nothing like as desirable and comfortable as she had imagined.

She would have liked to ask Miqail what it was, this ball of emotions that time had failed to unravel, that still moved in her veins, in her blood vessels. Would so have liked to have known whether, beyond her anger, her jealousy of Miqa, there had been some other thing back then that had pierced her so deeply, so sharply, some thing capable of unleashing such destructive fury in her, a feeling that made everything else appear secondary. Why it was that, to this day, she became frantic with rage whenever she thought of how he hadn't defended himself, hadn't held her back.

★

Meanwhile, Brilka, your mother was learning to crawl, then walk. John Lennon released *Imagine*; Stasia gave up her trips to the city and any attempts to overcome the distance and contempt between herself and her sister; Kitty Jashi released her best and most popular album yet, *Replacement*, with the now-famous photo from Prague emblazoned on the cover. Bored by the New Testament, Elene read *Madame Bovary*, *Swann's Way*, *Scarlet and Black*, *Albert Savarus*, and *Lady Chatterley's Lover* (this last, of course, covertly); and some western journalist compiled a statistic according to which the average Soviet citizen spent around five-hundred and fifty-two hours a year queuing for food. He also claimed that one-third of the goods manufactured in the Soviet Union existed only on paper.

★

Withdrawal took precisely thirty-four days. Kitty left the flat only to buy necessities. The delirium and hallucinations, the outbursts of aggression, the vile insults, the pathetic begging and whimpering were followed by two fainting fits, during which Kitty had to call an ambulance, and utter hysteria that forced her to tie Fred's emaciated body to the bed. After many, many sleepless nights — and after Kitty had written five new songs — Fred Lieblich got out of bed at three o'clock one morning, showered, put on a clean shirt, came into Kitty's study, and looked at her friend, smiling as if nothing had happened.

When she saw Fred standing in front of her, wet-haired, smelling fresh, the feverish light of those recent days gone from her catlike eyes, Kitty's guitar slid to the floor; she put her hands over her mouth and started crying silently. Fred stood and smiled at her; neither woman trusted herself to go to the other. As if there were an invisible wall between them: impossible to transition straight from the role of nurse, or patient, to lover.

'Keep playing. Don't stop.'

Fred sat at Kitty's feet. Kitty took her guitar, played, and began to sing along with the chords.

As dawn was breaking, with Fred trailing her forefinger across Kitty's thigh, Kitty made her a proposition.

'I want to move to Vienna with you. I want you to go back there. I want us to make a home there for ourselves. There was a time when I wanted to go there with someone else. We never made it, and now he never will. But you and I could go. And I'd really like to. I'd really like to go back, too, but I can't. You can, and you should try. All of this here, all these people, they're not good for you. They don't see you, they don't know you, they don't understand you. Let's try it, you and I.'

> If man creates so much suffering, what right has he then
> to complain when he himself suffers?
>
> ROMAIN ROLLAND

Christine, wrapped in a spinach-green woollen coat, her face veiled in black tulle, strode along Rustaveli Boulevard. She had alighted from the tram at the opera house and was heading purposefully north.

People were walking up and down the boulevard. How strange it was, mused Christine, that you could rarely tell by looking at them what their stories were. Whether they had ever informed on someone to get a bigger apartment; whether their grandfather or grandmother had met their death in one of the many labour camps far away in the cold, white lands, or in a muddy ditch on the outskirts of the city; whether they had deceived others, cheated them, had believed in monsters; whether they had loved the wrong person; whether they had deserted someone, or would do so some day.

She stopped in front of the ochre-brick building and watched the students streaming out. She saw these loud young people laughing, pushing each other, or engaged in excited discussion; but she was looking for one particular student who, as usual, was taking his time.

She sat down on a bench diagonally across from the entrance and took out her crotchet work. It could be quite a while before the person she was waiting for appeared. She had a lot of things on her mind. How long would she be able to keep her house? Offended by her retreat, would Kostya continue to oppose it being turned into a residential community? After all, she was now all alone in that impressively large residence.

She turned her attention back to the present. Perhaps today she would manage it. Summon all her courage and speak to him. Perhaps today he would see her, notice her. Perhaps, though — as on so many other occasions — she would wait for him to come walking down the street, alone, head bowed, a tattered briefcase under his arm, only to pass her by, not even suspecting she was there. In fact, this was the likelier scenario.

She waited, listening to the heartbeat of this city in which she had spent almost her whole life — her whole, fractured life. Ramas had brought her here (her face lit up with an almost imperceptible smile at the thought) and talked to her for hours about Cézanne and Renoir. He'd taken her to Mushtaidi Park to see Buster Keaton's *The General* in the city's first open-air cinema. Was it really the acid that had killed her beauty, or the bullet with which he had shot himself in the Kojori forest? It seemed to her that a piece of the sky had broken off a long, long time ago, a thick blanket of clouds had dropped, and now it was raining splintered dreams. Perhaps Stasia was right, and one day the ghosts would crawl out from their hiding places. The false past had left its undead behind, and they all had last words to say. They couldn't accuse anyone else, only the living.

A snowflake landed on her coat. A couple of students started squealing and stretched out their palms to greet the first flakes. Why did he never laugh with these girls — why didn't he run out of the building as they did? The building that housed the State Institute for Film and Theatre, where Miqa had passed his entrance exam the previous year. He was always alone, so thoughtful, so morose.

She saw him coming down the steps. Past the old watchman, sitting absorbed in his *Pravda*; past the cafeteria, and the crowds of boys and girls who took no notice of him. She rose; he walked past her, didn't look at her, didn't look around, didn't raise his eyes from the pavement, as if a secret path were traced upon it that he was following unswervingly. She took a step back. Should she sit down again, or follow him? Then what? What would she say to him? He hadn't answered any of her letters, not one in eighteen months, until in the end she had stopped writing. Hastily, she stuffed her crotcheting into her handbag and took another step. He was hurrying down the road towards Lenin Square. Another step; and another. She walked behind him, maintaining a few metres' distance. But as they were passing the National Gallery, she couldn't stand it any more, and called his name. Miqa turned, startled, as if surprised that anyone should call him, that anyone knew him at all.

'May I invite you for coffee? Or tea? I don't even know whether you like coffee.'

She attempted a smile. He looked serious, far too serious for his age; a little neglected, but desperately touching in his efforts to conceal this neglect.

'I don't know.'

'Don't you have time? Do you need to be somewhere?'

'I don't like cafés.'

'As you wish. A little walk, perhaps? Or something to eat? I could do with some food, I can hear my stomach rumbling. There's a new restaurant in the Bath Quarter, apparently.'

'I don't know.'

'That's a yes, then?'

They walked along the boulevard slowly, hesitantly, until Christine took his arm and matched her pace to his. At first she thought he would pull away, but he let her hold his elbow and started to walk faster.

'My mother died three months ago,' he said suddenly, pressing Christine's arm more firmly to his side. She didn't know what to say: for the first time it occurred to her that she didn't know much about his mother. She had always declined to go with Andro whenever he came to collect Miqa.

'She had a heart condition. They should have put her on sick leave. She shouldn't have had to work so hard.'

'Oh God, Miqa, I'm so sorry ...'

They walked on in silence for a while. Little by little he started answering her questions: told her that his studies made him very happy, that he'd been very lucky because the group leader had put in a word for him, he wouldn't have had much chance otherwise; after all, it was a prestigious school for prestigious children from prestigious families, but he'd been lucky. Christine didn't interrupt the stream of words, nor did she tell him that this 'luck' was due to a great deal of lobbying on her part and the extra roubles she had slipped to the head of the examining board. He was living in a boarding house up in the Bagebi quarter, he told her. He didn't socialise much with his fellow students. One of them was the son of a famous Mosfilm actor, another the nephew of a well-known Tbilisi surgeon, this girl was the fiancée of the son of so-and-so, and so on and so forth.

He didn't often see his father; sometimes he would call the village post office or the neighbours and speak to him, but he hadn't been doing well since Miqa's mother's death.

They went into one of the restaurants along the river that served Georgian food. He looked so hungry; of course he was hungry, she'd known it the minute she set eyes on him. She ordered, ignoring his loud protests, happy that food provided the opportunity to keep him near her, at least for an hour. First, they brought bread, warm from the oven, with plum sauce, tomato sauce, pomegranate sauce. This was followed by a starter of bean soup, with warm corn bread and lots of coriander, just the way he liked it. Then she asked the waiter to serve spinach and aubergine dips with extra garlic. Greedily he fell on the food. When at last they brought *baẓhe* to the table his eyes sparkled. He dunked the bread in the various sauces, glancing at her gratefully as he did so.

'Forgive me, Miqa.'

She looked him straight in the eye. She reached for his hand. He still felt so familiar, so in need of protection. He glanced around, and seemed visibly uncomfortable to be touched by her in this way. But she didn't let go of him; she even moved her chair a little closer. He smelled her unmistakable scent: powder, and something he could never have put into words. He moved his face towards hers.

'What exactly should I forgive you for?'

'I left you on your own.'

He tensed, stared fixedly at his plate. Two women at a neighbouring table were looking over at them curiously.

'I've been coming to the Institute since September, hoping to speak to you. I've made a decision. I've chosen you. I took you into my home all those years ago, I swore that I'd be there for you, and it's unforgivable that, when it mattered, I wasn't able to fulfil my promise. I left you on your own. Give me a chance to make amends.'

Suddenly he leaned in and pressed his lips to hers. She turned her face away sharply: he tasted of tarragon and a broken childhood.

'I didn't mean it like that, Miqa,' she stammered.

'But I did.'

'I know this isn't how you see me, but I'm old, Miqa, I'm really old. Too old.'

'You're so beautiful.'

'You can live with me, move in with me; the house is empty, I'll be there for you and look after you.'

'Will you do me a favour?'

'Yes, of course, just say.'

'Show me your face. Show me the whole of your face. Please.'

She called for the bill.

★

The old house in the Vera quarter, in whose garden the dead loved to play their games of Patience, greeted the returnee with a familiarity that immediately made both of them sentimental, and therefore more conciliatory. Christine made coffee; they sat in the unlit kitchen until the whole house had been requisitioned by darkness.

Then she began to take the pins out of her hair, the fastenings of her protective shield; she let down her long, dyed tresses, she lined up the pins on the table like a miniature army, she took off the veil, laid it gently on the table, she turned her face towards him in the half-dark. She refused to turn on the light.

That night — this is how I always imagine it, Brilka — her age drained from her body; she brushed it from her skin like foam, so lightly, with a single sweep of her hand. Perhaps this was the last night in which Time permitted her to reclaim her place as undisputed beauty queen. Before age, which exacts an even higher price from the most beautiful among us, finally began to take its toll. He ran his fingers tentatively over her face, afraid that she might be made of glass, might shatter in his hands at any moment.

Hand in hand, they walked up the old, creaking, wooden staircase and down the narrow corridor to Christine's bedroom, which had once seemed to Miqa like the gateway to his one true home. She lay down, leaving the left side of the bed for him, as she used to when he was a little boy who would come creeping to her room during thunderstorms and climb into bed beside her. The boy she had always wanted to protect, and whom she'd had to abandon. He lay down beside her, straining to make out her features in the dark. She stroked his head and lent him her eyes, her images from the past, so he could see her as she had once been, as a nineteen-year-old girl of unearthly beauty, and happy — yes, she had been happy, she had managed to squeeze so much happiness out of life, and she wanted so much for him to understand that every happiness in life must be fought for, with all your might, by every means possible. She held him in her arms and felt the years fall away from her, felt herself grow younger at his side. She reached out and touched him through the darkness. He lay quietly on his side of the bed, and she stayed on hers; like two good schoolchildren they lay there, young and safe, in a cloak of timelessness, in a limitless world where anything seemed possible. There was just his hand that never tired of running over her skin. She smiled in the dark, and hoped that she would be able to banish Miqa's fear. That he would succeed in escaping the clutches of the day he was betrayed. She went on speaking quietly to him. The night was rough and overcast, the sky as if someone had poured milk over the clouds.

> The victors must and can be judged.
>
> GENERALISSIMUS

She pushed his hand away from her face, sat up suddenly in bed, and listened.

'I think I heard something.'

'What is it?' he asked drowsily, staring at Christine, wide-eyed.

'I think someone's in the house.'

'Who would be down there at this time of night? Who still has a key to your house?'

'I don't know. Perhaps ... He didn't give it back to me. Although he hasn't been here once since the move.'

'Who?'

'Kostya.'

As she spoke his name, she could already hear footsteps in the hall. She sprang up and hurried to the door, throwing a cardigan over her shoulders and signalling to Miqa to stay in bed. She peered out, stepped into the corridor, closed the door carefully behind her — and saw him running up the stairs. He was groping his way along the wall; apparently he hadn't found the light switch. Something had happened. He looked agitated. As she approached him she smelled the alcohol on his breath.

'What are you doing here?' she asked sternly, hoping she appeared reasonably composed.

'How could you?' he bellowed at her, at the top of his voice. His eyes were swollen, his cheeks red, beads of sweat were forming on his brow. 'Why are you covering for that monster?'

He recoiled, going down a couple of steps as Christine walked towards him. She had to get him downstairs, into the kitchen, away from the bedroom.

'Kostya, I don't understand what's wrong,' murmured Christine, although it was perfectly clear to her that the house of cards had finally collapsed.

'That bastard, that bastard ... What have you done to my girl? You're inhuman, you filthy ... you're all ...' He was obviously drunk.

Christine succeeded in manoeuvring him backwards into the kitchen. He staggered and sank onto a stool.

'You're liars, hypocrites, whores — nothing but cheap whores!' Suddenly he covered his face with his hands and started sobbing. Christine froze; her heart lurched, and she didn't know what to say. In a flash, he was her Kostya again, her little boy, her darling. When was the last time she had seen him cry? Had she ever seen him cry? Not even when Kitty ... not even when Mariam ... No, he hadn't cried then. What exactly had happened? What did he know, and who had told him?

'I trusted you with my child, my only daughter! I don't recognise her any more; it's as if her soul's been dashed to pieces. And I gave her everything, I tried ... What sort of women are you? What sort of people are you, to allow such a thing? Scum, that's what. My mad mother and my unprincipled wife, they think they know it all — but you — you, Christine? How could you defend him?' He was crying like a little boy now. 'I trusted you with my only child, and now this!'

'What did Elene say to you? Tell me, Kostya!'

'She's gone out — she's apathetic, lifeless. I don't recognise her any more. I thought, with the move, and if I came back ... But no — I didn't know about the surprise: it was all because of that bastard, that parasite! His family is the source of all our misery. We paid an inhuman price for those damned Eristavis, but no, nothing's ever enough for my mad mother, she still thinks we owe them something. But I swear to you, Christine, I'm going to find him and kill him and end this dreadful nightmare once and for all. I swear to you!'

'He didn't do it. Not the way Elene may have told you. It was a terrible misunderstanding, Kostya. You must listen to me —'

'A misunderstanding? A misunderstanding? What — you as well? He raped my daughter!'

'She was the one who made it happen. She was jealous; she felt neglected. She was angry with us — she thought we favoured him. She didn't know what she was doing. She seduced him ...'

★

Kostya's driver had brought him back to the Green House around seven that evening, as usual. As usual, they had wanted to have dinner, but Elene had not appeared at the appointed time; she wasn't back yet from her daily walk to the stud farm. Kostya was angry. After the meal, which they ate in preoccupied silence, he started drinking, out of concern or frustration. When Elene still wasn't home by eleven o'clock, Kostya drove down to the stud farm and round all the neighbouring villages, ringing his neighbours' doorbells, but nobody knew where his daughter might be. Daria, picking up on the general excitement, started howling and calling for Mama, something she very seldom did. Daria's tears fanned the flames of Kostya's anger, and by the time Elene reappeared at the Green House, after midnight and more than a little tipsy, escalation was inevitable.

Elene justified herself by saying she'd been out with friends and hadn't kept an eye on the time. Besides, she was an adult and had the right to come and go as she pleased. She lived here cut off from the outside world, it was enough to drive you mad, they should be glad she had managed to find any friends at all out here in the middle of nowhere.

'You're not even interested in your own child! This is not the kind of woman I raised my daughter to be!' bellowed Kostya, so loudly they could hear him all over the house.

'Oh yes it is! The two of you raised me to be exactly who I am!' replied Elene, in a voice dripping with scorn. Startled by her insolence, Kostya could think of no better response than to slap his daughter for the first time in her life. Elene staggered back, blood dripping from her nose. Nana screamed and ran to her daughter, who pushed her away.

'This can't go on!' Kostya groaned, and sat down at the table, where he knocked back another glass of red wine. 'And don't you go acting so innocent; you're the ones who ruined her, you spoiled her, you cured her of any discipline, any independence she —'

'And you waltz in here and want us to do everything your way. You may be someone important when you're with your fleet, but here you're just the same as everyone else!' Stasia had joined them; now she was the one doing the shouting.

'You're the ones who showed her how to live a life devoid of ambition. You're her role models! She has to start finally making something herself, she has to —'

'If you'd been raped, I'd like to see how you —' Stasia's sentence suddenly blew up in her face and immediately silenced the quarrel. She closed her eyes, hoping her son might not have heard, but of course it was too late.

Kostya got up from the table and walked, heavy-footed, towards his mother. She tried to evade him; she waved him away with her hand and went to leave the room, but Kostya, a whole head taller, was already standing in front of her and giving her a searching look.

'What did you just say?' he asked, calmly, with military alertness.

'Forget it, Kostya, I shouldn't have said it.' Stasia bowed her head and hoped Kostya would leave her in peace.

'Nana! Elene, come here, please!' he shouted, still barring his mother's path. Nana hurried into the room.

'What's going on?' she spat at him. 'All your shouting is just going to wake the child. You're bellowing as if we were in —' She had more to say, but stopped. Stasia's expression boded ill.

'Who?' Kostya hissed through his teeth.

'Who what?'

Nana glanced around, confused, hoping for some explanation from Stasia.

'Elene!' Kostya shouted again. His voice echoed alarmingly off the walls.

Finally, she appeared in the door. Her eyes were red, and she was holding a cloth full of ice cubes under her nose.

'Now what do you want?'

'Who did it to you? Who?'

Absolute horror spread across Elene's face. She immediately knew what her father was asking. 'What have you told him?' She turned to the others for an answer, her eyes filled with black, viscous fear.

'Tell me, for God's sake, tell me!' Kostya looked at them all, simultaneously incredulous, angry, beseeching. Stasia bowed her head; Nana cleared her throat; the heavy silence became unbearable.

Elene knew she had the choice not to betray him; to protect him, finally to put an end to her lie. But she didn't. She would tell. Yes — she would say his name, because the moment she shut her eyes she saw his in front of her. His eyes, above her. And the more time passed, the more she learned to live with her self-loathing, the more she reproached herself, the clearer it became to her that he had *sacrificed* her. It was his fault that that afternoon had ended with a trickle of blood on her thigh.

She didn't know what he had sacrificed her to or why; no, that she hadn't yet been able to understand. Whether it was the injustice she must inevitably personify in his eyes, or whether he had taken advantage of the situation — accepted it, submitted to it, borne it and not defended himself, not because he couldn't, but because he was hoping it would lead to something bigger. Something that might compensate him for all that would follow.

Yes, Elene wanted to know the truth. She wanted it very badly. But every time she thought she had identified it, it turned out to be a lie. Every time she thought she was getting an answer to her *why*, it turned out to be another question.

'Miqa.'

And at that very moment, as she spoke this evil name, this curse, out loud, a terrible fear overwhelmed her. She had destroyed something. She had smashed her hope with her own two hands. Now she was truly lost, and ... it felt good, it felt liberating.

Not to fulfil any expectations. Not to deserve any love. Not to hold out any prospect of rescue. Now she would perish with him. With him. Yes. If he didn't want what she had to offer, he would have to accept their shared misfortune. Yes. Amen. Hallelujah.

Perhaps there was a fraction of a second in which she could still have put her arms around her father's shoulders and explained it all to him, hugged him tight, wept before him, spoken out, and finally shed this terrible burden. But the moment passed, and was lost. What words would have sufficed to explain her whole life to him, the sum of all the things that constituted the essence of her up until that afternoon? And what words would have sufficed to cross Miqa's lies and her own and arrive at a common truth?

★

'You're very upset. I'll make you a cup of tea. We'll talk more tomorrow. First you need to calm down and sleep. I'll make up the bed for you.' Christine was frantically thinking how she could get Kostya to bed and Miqa out of the house. She struck a match to light the gas stove.

Her thoughts were interrupted by the sound of Miqa's hesitant voice. He was calling her, in the belief, or hope, that Kostya had gone.

'Who the hell —?'

Kostya immediately sat bolt upright and listened. He stared at his aunt in disbelief. Miqa called her name again. Before she could answer, Kostya ran out of the kitchen. She rushed after him. Miqa had been standing at the top of the stairs, half-asleep; Kostya had already grabbed him and knocked him down. First, he drove his fist into his solar plexus, and then, as the boy lay whimpering and writhing on the floor, he followed up by kicking him. When he tried to crawl away, Kostya grasped the nape of his neck as you might hold a savage dog back by the scruff, and yanked him to his feet. He punched him in the face. Miqa's lip split and blood ran down his chin, spattering his vest. Christine, who had come between them, heard her own voice screaming continuously; it seemed very far away, as if it didn't belong to her. But Kostya pushed her aside. She had to cling on to the banister so as not to lose her balance. Miqa slid along the wall, trying to get away, to run into the kitchen or out of the house, far, far away from this punishment he would never escape.

★

Punishment for what? Why was it that every time he tried to approach the essence of what had happened, everything coalesced in an impenetrable blackness? Who had betrayed whom, who had hurt whom? Another blow caught him, in the ribs this time. He slumped to the ground. It hurt like hell. His chest was spattered with blood, he could taste it on his tongue. Kostya's silhouette was blurred by the pain. He wanted to fight back, to squeeze all his strength into his fist and smash Kostya's face in, but he couldn't do it. Christine was watching him. Him: the one she had chosen. He had to live up to her expectations. She, the incomparable, the unparalleled.

He didn't care how old she was; he wanted her to need him as much as he needed her. He would not shrink away. He had to prove to her that she had made the right choice in renouncing her family for him. Her family, and above all her nephew! This furious sadist! Yes, she should watch, she should know Kostya's true face, because it had never really been about him and Elene, Elene was just the excuse; it had always been between him and this man who was now laying into him in such a frenzy.

And if he were to hit Kostya now, Christine would doubt him. She would never be able to love a violent man. The scars on her face alone would forbid it. For him, choosing Christine also meant that he had to remain a victim.

He could hardly hear Christine's screams any more; they sounded muffled. Would it perhaps be better to lie down, here, on this cold wooden floor, and never get up again? Would it be a heartrending sight for her? Another blow between the ribs. He couldn't breathe. He opened his mouth, gasping for oxygen; he mustn't lose consciousness, he had to control himself, mustn't oppose him, mustn't hit back.

Only when his face hit the floorboards did Kostya let him go, exhausted; he stepped back and looked at him with revulsion. But Miqa felt nothing now. Nothing mattered, because he knew that he had won. Christine was kneeling before him; now she would ease his pain, lay his head in her lap, wipe away his blood.

The sun rose. Cold, grey December light penetrated the hallway, making the scene appear even more hopeless than it already was. She felt her nephew's eyes on the back of her neck, and turned. 'Have you got what you wanted? Then you can go. I need to take him to hospital.'

Kostya's eyes were glazed. She wanted to pity him, to be able to forgive him, but felt only emptiness inside. She turned back to Miqa, supporting his head with her hand.

'If I see that bastard here one more time — if I catch him once more anywhere near you or Elene, I will personally see to it that he's locked up for the rest of his life.' Kostya marched back down to the kitchen.

Christine helped Miqa roll onto his back. He kept his eyes closed, but she knew that he was here, with her. And that was the most important thing.

'Don't move. I have to call a doctor,' she whispered in his ear.

'Will you stay with me?'

'Yes. I'm here. I'm staying here. I'll be right back.'

She heard the rushing of water in the kitchen. Laying his head carefully onto the floor, she got up and followed the sound. She had to call an ambulance. Kostya stood by the sink, holding his face in the jet of water.

'Now you listen to *me*, Kostya! I don't want you ever to go near that boy again, either. Do you understand? I am not letting him go. No — I'm not doing that again. He didn't do anything. Ask your daughter, interrogate her until she tells you what happened. I did not raise a rapist. But you have raised a liar. That's the truth for which you've broken his nose and ribs. And now you're going to put my key on the table and get out.'

She went to the phone and dialled the emergency number.

Kostya stood propped against the wall, exhausted, hurt, rejected — not a victor, just an old, sad, terribly lonely man.

'What are you talking about? You're my aunt — you're Christine, my Christine ...' he stammered, as she asked for the ambulance. 'You need someone to bring you to your senses. I should never have let you stay behind here on your own.'

He started to move towards Christine.

'Don't come any closer. Stay where you are.'

'Or what?'

He approached her. She stood her ground. She could bear it. She could bear to lose him. She loved him, her nephew; it was a love that had always challenged her, demanded too much of her, a love that would always have to be endured. But she had to think of the boy, the boy with the Eskimo ice cream who now lay half-unconscious on the floor, the boy she had to protect.

'He's not staying here, Christine. Not in my house.'

'This is still *my* house, may I remind you. My husband's house!'

'You were only able to keep it because I —'

'Go! Get out!'

She had never despised him as she did right now. Not even when he hit his sister; not even when he sent his fiancée to the scaffold. She had always had some understanding for him, always — until now.

'Don't take that risk, Christine!'

All she had to do was hold out her hand, to her nephew, who for so long she had worn so close to her heart, like a priceless amulet, and who at some point, without her realising, had cut the chain from which the amulet hung. But she stayed firm.

'Get out!'

When the ambulance arrived and she asked to ride with them, they asked her if the two of them were related. She replied in the affirmative and got into the back of the vehicle, holding Miqa's feeble hand in her own. On the way to the hospital she asked herself, again and again, why he hadn't tried, not even once, to defend himself.

> Life, I hold your reins in my hand
> Thus from your Hell I forge a Paradise.
>
> TABIDZE

The American bombing offensive in North Vietnam was followed by the food sack offensive, in which the US Air Force dropped sacks labelled 'Donated by the people of the United States' all over the devastated country. And Christine received a letter from the housing department. She was invited for an interview, where she was informed that, as a single woman, it was capitalist selfishness to claim such a large amount of living space. Christine, who had already prepared herself for the impending war with Kostya, and was under no illusion that she could win it, did not attempt to beg the officials not to throw her out of her own home. She was given the choice of handing over part of her living space to strangers, or accepting an apartment allocated to her by the state. She opted for the latter.

Luckily, those bastard officials didn't dare resettle her on the outskirts of the city: they offered her a two-room apartment in Vake. As a loyal state health-service employee of many years' standing, they said, she was entitled to live in the city centre.

It was a cruel break, an almost inhuman loss. She had spent practically her entire life in this house; this was where her story had been written, this was where it had all begun. Now that Kostya had declared war on her, though, her fear had vanished. It felt like a liberation: as if, all these years, the property had been keeping her from something essential. She could walk out, taking only the things that really mattered to her. And those weren't the old clothes and pictures, the furniture, all the stuff that had accumulated over the decades — they were the pictures she carried within herself, the memories she had stored in the photograph album of her mind. They were what mattered. No one could ever take them away from her. No government office. No commissariat. And no Kostya, either. She would take them all with her to her fifty-two-square-metre apartment. To her new life. Which, from now on, she alone would control.

Once Miqa's two broken ribs and split lip had healed, he helped her pack. They sold the silver cutlery and other household items, and he gave her enthusiastic advice about decorating the new apartment. Although neither of them said it out loud, both assumed he would move in to the new place with her. She installed a foldout sofa for him, and proudly showed him the sparsely furnished room he was to occupy from now on.

★

She cooked for him, did his laundry, and they would talk until late into the night, discussing everything that was on his mind. She spoiled him with little presents, like a pair of jeans bought for a horrendous sum from the illegal traders in Didube, which made Miqa shout for joy.

There was one thing, though, on which she would not relent. However much he clung to her, demanded her full attention, was jealous and possessive, she refused to get romantically involved with him. She managed their daily lives, provided him with what he needed, gave him security, and, little by little, cured him of his lack of confidence, encouraged him to take risks; but she never let herself get carried away by their former tenderness, she denied him the intimacy to which he so vehemently laid claim.

Instead, she convinced him to make friends with his peers, to connect with people his own age, and, although it broke her heart when she realised how hard this was for him, how alien he felt among his fellow students, she forced him to challenge himself. Ever since the nightmarish encounter with Kostya, she had been preoccupied by the shocking realisation that Miqa had never learned to defend himself, and for this she took the blame. Stasia had been right when she'd accused her of feeding him too many dreams and not letting him bite off enough tough reality.

She started telling him about her life. She didn't spare him; she guided him through the labyrinth of her thoughts and feelings, opened the doors on her fears and desires. She wanted him to understand that her body was shrivelled, her skin wrinkled and soft, that she walked more slowly than before. That all the memories and stories she spread out before him had come at a price, had not passed her by without leaving their mark. She wanted to shake him awake; she wanted him to rebel against her, but the more she talked about herself, the more words she excavated from her memory, the more she tried to restore him to reality, the more he clung to the dream he had of her.

★

It was only under duress that he accepted birthday invitations, or stayed behind with his fellow students in the cafeteria after lectures, or had a beer with them in Mushtaidi Park at the weekend. He started to bring home a few of his new acquaintances, more to impress her than anything else. Skinny, unkempt-looking young men with greasy hair who bit their fingernails. Later, the clique was joined by a girl with dark rings under her eyes and glasses that covered almost half her face. They would sit in his room, discussing the new generation of Soviet cinematographers and drinking cheap wine from teacups. For the most part, the girl just listened, leaning back on the couch with slightly exaggerated nonchalance and nibbling peanuts or sunflower seeds. Sometimes she would permit herself to make a comment: an ironic remark, or something funny, at any rate, that made everyone laugh. Christine had to admit that she had underestimated this girl at first, had thought she was just a decorative appendage for the boys. But the exact opposite was true: she was eloquent, quick-witted, had a sharp mind, and was impressively well-read. Lana, this girl with the cinnamon skin and the unspeakable glasses, wasn't even studying film or theatre with the boys. She was enrolled on an engineering degree at the Polytechnical Institute, but her keen interest in film meant that at some point she had come across this film studies course and got to know some of the students.

★

'Why don't you apply to study directing, Lana?' Christine asked her one day. 'You seem to know an awful lot about film, from what I can tell.' They were standing in her windowless kitchenette, where Lana was waiting for Christine to prepare tea so she could disappear with it back into Miqa's room.

'My father was a cobbler. He died of a stroke at fifty-three. My mother has worked as a secretary at a heating pipe manufacturer's for twenty-three years. We're Armenian. I can't risk it. I'd make a laughing-stock of myself the minute I walked out in front of those idiots on the examination board. A poor, ugly Armenian girl wants to be a director and make films, oh, how sweet! I really don't need that, Christine,' she answered, with her customary acerbity.

'You mustn't look at it like that, Lana. You've got talent. I may not know anything about the film business, but I see how the boys look up to you, and that, my dear, says a lot.'

'But Christine, you do know what they call us Armenians? Don't you? Please don't start telling me about the ancient friendship between our two nations; and I'd prefer not to have to hear anything about socialist equality, either. Yes, we Armenians are heartily welcome in this country, we have our own quarter and our own baths, we even have our own theatre, but the moment we feel like being something other than cobblers, goldsmiths, or pawnbrokers, we're swiftly called to heel. Also, we wear more gold necklaces. That's easily misunderstood, isn't it? Right? Come on, what is it they call Armenians in this country?'

'Lana, I think you're exaggerating somewhat with your racist classification.'

'The Jews of the Caucasus, Christine. That's what we're called. Any other questions?'

★

Perhaps it was Lana's wounded pride, the stigma that came with her background, that initially sparked her interest in Miqa. Perhaps she was just happy to have found someone who appreciated her talent and had no right to look down on her, because as the son of a traitor — a poor, banished alcoholic — he could count himself lucky that he was permitted to study at such an elite faculty. Or perhaps she thought that, through Miqa, she would get a chance to assist in the creation of something she was prohibited from doing herself. Resentful and ambitious as she was, though, this interest must very quickly have become a dogged determination that, on closer inspection, Christine found alarming.

Christine had spotted Lana's watchful eyes on Miqa, her feigned indifference; whenever he said anything, she would encourage him, and she made no secret of her hope that he would take her out to the cinema or theatre. At first, Christine thought that Lana's fearlessness, her talent for standing up for herself, would do Miqa good. But then she saw how easily Miqa could be manipulated, and how well Lana had mastered the art of manipulation, and from then on she steered clear, leaving it to Miqa to decide how far to take things with this quick-witted girl. To Christine, she seemed too grown-up for her age, too rational, too inscrutable and embittered. Not compassionate enough with Miqa's doubts and fears. Christine saw how she would steer every discussion the way she wanted it to go, how she always had to be right. Hidden behind her outsized glasses that made her eyes look like two little black dots was an impressive dose of scepticism and disappointment. But maybe Miqa needed a companion like this at his side? Someone so unwavering, so demanding? She would teach him to defend himself. Christine confined herself to her new role as hostess, and was happy to listen to the increasingly animated discussions in her apartment, which she seldom participated in but could follow clearly through the thin wall. She loved the *joie de vivre* the young people brought to the apartment, and she liked the contented smile on Miqa's face when she laid the table for his friends and invited them to sit and eat.

★

Until one afternoon she heard Miqa telling Lana about Sopio Eristavi. She turned off the radio and pricked up her ears.

'This is incredible. That's your story? We have to tell it; *you* have to.' Christine heard Lana's voice, urgent and insistent. 'That's a proper subject, not the cheap entertainment you normally see in our films. Do you realise what an amazing screenplay that would make? You could use her poems. You said your father kept them. You have to do it!'

'No one's going to fund this film. The Institute certainly won't. A screenplay like that wouldn't even make it past the board.'

'Of course not, Miqa, you silly boy; we'll have to trick them. We can't let any references to the actual person show through. No one will know her story, anyway. We have to let them think it's just a student film about the hard lot of an artist, all that nonsense. They'll think it's too ambitious; they'll smile at you condescendingly, but that's great, the best thing that can happen is for them to underestimate you. But we have to be careful. We'll write two screenplays. One will be presented to the board, and the actors will get the other. It's that simple. And when the film comes out, they can protest all they like, it won't matter, because it'll cause a stir and anyone with so much as a spark of honour in them will follow you. We could smuggle the film out of the country. My uncle works as a technician in a film studio, he has contacts, he can get us access to their editing room; we can work undisturbed, at night, when no one's there.'

★

Christine hoped Miqa would dismiss the idea as unworkable and make Lana stop talking about it. But the conversation kept recurring. The boys came less and less; more and more often Miqa and Lana retreated to his bedroom, and more and more often *her* name came up: Sopio Eristavi. Christine summoned all her courage and spoke to him about it. This time he was reticent, as if he had to keep a secret, and brushed her off with excuses. It was just an idea; what was wrong with him taking an interest in his ancestors' history; she was the one who'd encouraged him to seek out *like-minded people* and do things he wanted to do.

'I just want to be sure it's you who wants to do these things and not someone else,' she remarked pointedly, before going back to sit in front of the television.

Two months later, without telling Christine, he took Lana to the mountains to visit his father. Tidying his room after his return, Christine found the old, crumbling notebook containing Sopio's poems — poems that were banned before they even had a chance to find readers. She sat down on the edge of the sofa and started leafing through the pages, lost in thought. She immersed herself in individual poems, trying to resurrect the period they both celebrated and accused.

That evening, she opened the door to him with an icy expression, and later, as he was enthusiastically spooning up his soup, she placed the book on the table. He stared at the slim volume for a while, as if seeing it for the first time, then shrugged.

'Yes, I went and got it.'

'I don't like secrets, and you know it. What are you two planning?'

'We're going to make a film about my grandmother. We've already started writing a script. Lana has some amazing ideas.'

'Lana this, Lana that. Where are you in all this?' Christine surprised herself with her offended tone when asking the question.

'*You* wanted me to find someone *my own age*. Well, now I have.'

★

She spent weeks trying to dissuade him from his plan. It was too dangerous. Memories of his father's case were still too fresh. He shouldn't push his luck. There were things for which other people might be forgiven that he would not; they knew who his father was, after all, and this time she wouldn't be able to protect him if anything should happen. No, she had no one left whom she could ask for help. He should let it drop, he should find another subject, there were plenty. He was still too young to tackle Sopio's story, he understood too little of what it was he wanted to tell. But Miqa remained stubborn; he listened to her with an indifferent expression and insisted that he had already planned everything and thought it all through.

One morning, Christine found Lana sitting in the kitchen, poring over a great pile of notes and bits of paper. They'd been writing and discussing in Miqa's room the previous evening. Miqa, it seemed, was still asleep.

'You haven't been sitting here all night, have you? Why didn't you go and lie down?' asked Christine.

'I didn't want to offend you; the sofa bed is very narrow, after all,' murmured Lana, without looking up from the heap of papers.

'That's none of my business. I didn't even know you were —'

'We're not. Not yet. It's my mind he desires, not my body. I can't blame him. After all, I know who shaped his aesthetic ideals.'

Christine froze, coffee pot in hand. She didn't know whether to express outrage at the remark or ignore it.

'But he needs me,' Lana continued. 'And he knows it, and with time I'm sure he'll learn to lower his optical standards.'

'Oh, I'm sure you can get him to do that,' hissed Christine, through her teeth.

> Here am I floating round my tin can
> Far above the Moon
> Planet Earth is blue
> And there's nothing I can do.
>
> DAVID BOWIE

It continued to be a momentous period for the world: people were getting themselves in a state about the oil crisis, the Watergate scandal, Pinochet's seizure of power in Chile, but these historic events were so far removed from us that they might as well have been happening on a different planet. People in the Soviet Union had long since come to the conclusion that there was no point in thinking about the world's problems, because the world and its problems were nothing to do with them. The Soviet leader, the man with the bushy eyebrows, had already suffered several heart attacks and strokes; it was probably only with the greatest difficulty that he was able to function as leader of one half of the world. But that was no reason to get in a state, either. What difference would that make?

★

It was her grandparents, above all, who vied for Daria's attention, although it wasn't long before Nana realised her husband was way ahead in this discipline as well. No one else could make Daria beam as her grandfather did. No one could captivate her like him, or tickle her for so long, or become so absorbed in playing with her. In Kostya's eyes you could already see the dream of his granddaughter striding down the echoing corridors of an elite boarding school; you saw Daria as a medical student, then later with a model husband at her side, one who'd been toughened up by the hard regime of summer and sporting camps, a young *komsomolets* with a party membership card. His eyes were full of all the expectations that Elene refused to fulfil.

But how to deal with Elene? Pressure and threats had had little effect. Indifference seemed to get him nowhere. In some macabre way, since he had come to believe that that bastard Miqa Eristavi was the one responsible for all his child's misfortune, he had found it easier to deal with. It was the only plausible explanation as to why Elene had gone off the rails, which meant, furthermore, that he didn't have to reproach himself. Whenever Nana accompanied her husband to his colleagues' and subordinates' weddings and birthday parties, she saw the wistfulness in his face. How he envied these men their little virgins: the daughters and sisters, the fiancées and promised ones, moving so lightly and quietly through the decorated halls, down long tables decked with sumptuous feasts, always with lowered eyes, always a little intimidated by the masculine company of their fathers, brothers, fiancés, and husbands. Girls who would never dare to leave the house after dark, let along hang around with boys their own age, drink alcohol, and read depressing novels.

When his thoughts led him to a dead end he would confer with his wife. Their worries about Elene were the most consistent connection between them. Nana was just as disappointed, just as depressed as he was, which gave him reason to hope that his wife had not completely taken leave of her senses, unlike his mother — or, worse still, his aunt. Nana suggested to him that they force Elene into some form of education. If she wouldn't consider studying at the university, she should apply to a polytechnic. She needed an occupation; she needed something to do. Kostya, however, found it shameful to think of his child devoting herself to something lowly like agriculture or retail, and insisted that they wait a while longer. She would come to her senses eventually, when she had recovered from the sorrow of being jilted.

★

After the painful slap, Kostya had given his daughter an expensive present; he had wanted to put things right, to salve his guilty conscience. A brand-new VAZ-2103 Zhiguli, which had only just come onto the market. He himself taught her to drive, in an effort to win back her trust. And, to begin with, they all believed that, for Elene, the car represented the freedom to decide for herself when she felt like driving to Tbilisi. That with this gesture Kostya would be able, at least in part, to make amends. Elene was happy about the car. But she didn't go for drives in the countryside, as her mother suggested, nor did she want to drive to the university and look around; all she wanted to do was pick Miqail up and accompany him to his friends' place in Tbilisi.

He had taken her there a few times already. It was a small *kommunalka* on Plekhanov Street, where dissidents and rebels — that was how Miqail introduced them — would gather, listen to music, drink, and talk about God or politics. Their rebellion mostly consisted of smoking dope, and long, noisy kitchen debates. Nonetheless, to Elene they seemed brave and *different*. From the very first day she took a seat in this smoky gathering, she wanted to call these men her friends.

What puzzled Elene most was the realisation that almost all of these young men described themselves as religious, and that they considered the Orthodox faith a rebellion against the state. Elene had never really taken any interest in politics or the state. She was, of course, aware that she had been a privileged child, that certain things were open to her because her father's name was Kostya Jashi, but she had never agonised over class distinctions or Marxist doctrine. Politics was the preserve of men; her father was in politics, and that in itself was reason enough for her not to want anything to do with it.

To her, until now, being rebellious had primarily meant: doing her utmost not to fulfil her parents' expectations, listening to her aunt's records, sitting on the unfinished roof terrace staring dolefully at the sky, and perhaps reading de Sade, a heavily annotated edition that had passed through countless hands, a forbidden curio she had discovered in one of the old boxes in Christine's cellar. Although these rebels had a rather different understanding of their rebellion and thought of themselves as politically minded, God-fearing people, Elene soon realised from their conversations that both their rebellion and her own were about one thing and one thing only: dreaming of a world where rock music wasn't banned, where people wore blue jeans and went on demonstrations with home-made banners, a world where books and films — even really graphic ones — weren't censored; ultimately, the world where her vanished, taboo aunt was living. A world from which no one who fled to it ever returned. Yes: a *perfect, perfect world*. She soon felt at home in this society on the fringes of society, which fought its greatest battles in a fourteen-square-metre kitchen. It must feel so good — she thought initially, as she sat in the corner and listened, fascinated, to these leather-jackets — to have so many important reasons to oppose something. Of course, she was surprised by certain contradictions in their worldview; she couldn't make the connection between piety and hedonism, and she also found the chauvinistic and strictly regulated nature of their value system disconcerting. She found it hard to understand, for example, why it didn't seem contradictory to them, and above all to Miqail, their spiritual leader, that the majority of them had committed theft, got into a fight, or threatened someone with a knife, even though they considered themselves devout Christians. They justified this by saying that political violence against *the wrong people* was allowed, and that as a Soviet leftist you had to express yourself more brutally and convey your discontent more violently than, for example, in the West.

At that time, of course, she was still too naive. She didn't have the necessary distance or knowledge, or the awareness that, unlike the Russian underground, this profoundly Georgian form of revolt was limited to kitchen conversations, excessive alcohol consumption, and self-stylisation; or that, in rejecting the imperialist Slavic oppressor, it idealised all that was pre-Soviet — and therefore all that was bourgeois. And that, in doing this, they were not altogether averse to twisting historical facts and presenting things in whatever way best suited their own ideology.

All these boys, one after another, kissed Elene out of her long enchanted sleep. She let the warm sunbeams dance on her face. Where was she, who was she, where was she heading? How did this all fit together, and what was God's part in it? Was He even interested in earthly matters any more? With aching thoughts and painful, bright-eyed longing she gradually came back to life.

She had her thick chestnut hair bobbed again. She painted her fingernails. She used her mother's rouge. She went to a dressmaker and ordered some colourful summer clothes. She bought white high-heeled sandals in the Jewish Quarter, and used the French perfume her father had given her. She gave Daria noisy, smacking kisses on her plump pink cheeks, stepped on the gas, and whirled up clouds of dust on the unpaved country roads. She turned up the music. She giggled to herself. She even — albeit hesitantly — started to join in the heated discussions in the kitchen. Drank malt beer, and sometimes the bitter, homemade schnapps. She enjoyed the taste of pickled cabbage and gherkins. There was usually no shortage of female company, but they were mostly neighbourhood girls or friends who just wanted to smoke some hash, snog the boys and listen to the only Pink Floyd or Stones album for miles around.

Unlike these girls, Elene took an interest in the discussions: she debated and argued with the others. She earned their respect. She chewed gum and blew enormous bubbles. She danced to The Who with one of the boys in the *kommunalka*'s tiny kitchen. She kept puffing on a joint and enjoyed it when time slowed down around her.

During one such dance, in one of these slow-motion moments, she let Beqa kiss her. Beqa had the best leather jacket, was often the loudest in discussion, never seemed to sleep, and had the best taste in music of them all. She knew that he was twenty-four, and had spent two years in a juvenile detention colony for breaking into a government official's dacha. Although she wouldn't admit it to herself, she was impressed by this. She also knew that he had dropped out of his architecture degree, and that his jeans were — outrageously! — ripped at the knee, which was reason enough for the *militsiya* to stop him on the street and accuse him of wearing antisocial clothing.

And he's a fantastic kisser, too, thought Elene, snuggling even closer to him.

Two days later he asked her if she wanted to go to the House of Film with him to see a private screening of some horror flick called *The Exorcist*. He knew someone at the cinema, he could get his hands on tickets, and she didn't have to be afraid, because he would be there (this last sentence was what really captivated Elene).

They started going out together. Spring seduced them into holding hands and perfecting the art of kissing. They went to the cinema, again and again, because Beqa could get tickets for special screenings.

They watched Bruce Lee; Beqa gave her a bootleg album by Deep Purple, and they listened to *Made in Japan* together. Even the fact that other girls were after Beqa seemed to Elene to speak in his favour. Becoming a couple felt simple, easy, natural. No heart-rending declarations of love and that tiresome rigmarole. He took her hand in his, and that was it.

They didn't talk about their parents or home. They talked about Deep Purple and the films they saw. They felt weightless, like two cosmonauts in space. They didn't follow any rules. They didn't talk about an engagement, a wedding, children, a future together. They kissed openly on the street, in the car, in parks. And when their desire could no longer be satisfied with kisses and casual caresses, they drove up one evening to the Tbilisi Sea, waited for the café to close and the beach to empty, looked for some dense bushes, and laid down a blanket. They both felt that they were old enough, in their youth.

The nights by the lake were balmy; the stars were close. They didn't love each other. They just made love. And beckoned to me to come into the world.

> We were first in line,
> but those behind us are eating already!
>
> VLADIMIR VYSOTSKY

With her patience, tenacity, and single-mindedness, Lana too had succeeded in translating Miqa's ethereal, intellectualised yearning and fervour into the language of the body. She accepted what he offered her without a hint of reproach, hoping that beneath his unhappy reticence, his mute fatalism, there was much more to be found, much more to be had. After months of waiting and methodical preparation, Lana achieved her ultimate victory. The last of his defences fell. And even though his hands still didn't know quite what to do with her body, even though she was still slightly disappointed by his lack of passion, Lana was happy. She was also well aware that he was *rewarding* her: thanks to her ingenuity and the cleverly packaged half-truths in the second script, written for the commission, the screenplay had been approved. Miqa could make his film!

She knew, then, that for him this *act of love* was a sign of gratitude. But that didn't mean anything; soon this gratitude would become inevitability, then necessity, and he would find her body as indispensable as her survival strategies, her cleverness and support.

★

It was one of those dimly lit roadside restaurants in Mtskheta — wooden bungalows and booths with provisional-looking décor, and tired, drunken musicians always tootling the same tunes — that, contrary to expectations, serve the best Georgian food. Miqail and his Plekhanov Street friends, along with Beqa and Elene, had just enjoyed an excellent meal and were sitting outside, a little drunk now, making sentimental toasts, constantly hugging each other, and not thinking about politics for once.

The sixth-term film directing students from the State Institute for Film and Theatre were celebrating in the same restaurant. Naturally, Lana was also at this table. And the two parties would probably never have noticed each other, and the evening would have passed off without incident, if some of the students hadn't started singing.

The singing attracted the attention of Miqail's boys, and they sent the waiter over to the 'singing table' with a bottle of sparkling wine and a plate piled high with fruit. Whereupon a tipsy student came over, thanked them, and invited the group to join them. Tables were pushed together and they began switching seats. It was only when she had reached the other end of the terrace that Elene noticed Miqa. Concealing her agitation, she attempted a friendly smile, even venturing to greet him with a tentative kiss on the cheek. Everyone introduced themselves, shook hands, and clapped each other euphorically on the back or shoulder. Fresh jugs of wine were ordered; epic toasts were made.

The tension in Miqa's body, and Elene's frequent glances in his direction, did not escape Lana's notice, and she kept asking questions, wanting to know who this girl was. Christine's great-niece, he informed her, under duress. He excused himself, rose from the table, and marched over to the men's toilets. A few seconds later, Elene followed him. The door was half open and she peered in. Miqa was standing in front of the mirror, washing his hands.

'I'm happy to see you, even though it's strange ... Oh God, I don't know what I'm saying. How are you? Studying?'

'Yes.'

'Do you like it?'

'Yes, I do. And what are you doing now?'

He soaped his hands again, despite having just washed them, as if he were afraid of turning round, of having to look at Elene. She stared at his reflection.

'I feel so bad about the business with my father. I didn't mean —'

'Just forget it, okay?'

'I can't.'

'Let's go back. I expect they're waiting.'

'Why didn't you stop me? Why?'

She walked up to him. He left the water running and it dripped off his hands. He shook his wrists like an epileptic. Then, slowly, he turned round, avoiding her eyes, perhaps hoping to get past her. But she blocked his path, summoned all her courage, and stepped right up to him so that he had to look at her. And what she saw made her shudder. His eyes were filled with incandescent poison. Never had she seen a look of such corrosive, devastating hatred. She felt utterly disarmed. Utterly ignoble and worthless.

'What do you want from me? Huh?' he barked at her. 'Just get out of my life, will you. Stay out of it! Do you understand?'

His eyes had contracted to two small, dark dots, his mouth was twisted in an ugly, contemptuous line, the veins on his neck protruded in scarlet indignation.

'Why did you sleep with me?' There was a knot of iron stuck in her throat. Another second and she would start sobbing at the top of her voice, and she would never be able to stop, she would be stuck here, in this toilet that stank of urine, an appropriate location for the whole of her miserable existence.

'*Sleep?* I didn't sleep with you! I screwed, banged, fucked you!' He spat the words in her face. They burned. They were little blades slicing open her skin.

'Why would you say something like that?'

'You were the horny one. Totally driven by your urge to procreate! You had a real itch between your legs! That's how it was, wasn't it? The little whore who found her true vocation!'

Where were these words coming from? They sounded like a foreign language in his mouth. He'd never raised his voice, never contradicted anyone. Where was he finding such venom now, such blind, destructive fury? Had she turned him into this person who glared at her now with such malice in his eyes? Did he know the price she was paying? Did it show?

'What do you want from me? Shall I crawl to you on my knees? Can't you see I haven't forgiven myself? Is that what you need? Is it? Is that what you want, Miqa?'

She pressed her hand over her mouth to stop herself howling like a wolf.

'Yes, that's exactly what I want!' he retorted, and stepped to one side. He was going to leave; he was going to run away right then and leave her there in her misery. Yes, that was what would happen. No — she couldn't let it happen. She grabbed his wrist; he looked down, as if he couldn't believe she was daring to touch him, but he didn't wrench himself free, not yet. His eyes were unreadable. They frightened her. She didn't know whether it was pain or remorse, anger or disgust that gathered there. She hadn't known how to interpret his expression before, either.

She moved closer and flung her arms around him, clung to him, tried to capture his breath; perhaps his smell would make him seem familiar to her again.

'You enjoyed it. I know you enjoyed it, I looked into your eyes, I watched you the whole time; it gave you pleasure to see me lying underneath you. It gave you pleasure to see me suffer. Please tell me; say it and I'll kneel in front of you for all I care, I'll do whatever you tell me. Please, just admit it. I'll take all the blame, I'll beg my father to ask for your forgiveness, but do it, please!'

'You want me to do you a favour? Why? So you can feel less dirty, less bad? When it was you who couldn't keep your legs together!'

'Why won't you just admit it? Why can't we be honest with each other? Do you think I forgot it just like that, drew a line under it, that I simply moved on? Please!'

'Elene, that's not how it works. You can't expect me to absolve you so you can go on playing Miss Cheerful. You forced me into it, and no matter how you try to twist the facts, that's the way it'll always be!'

'Why don't you just say it? Why don't you say that you hate me?'

'Hate's far too big a word. That's another emotion you have to earn. What I feel for you is indifference, and how you deal with your pangs of conscience is your own affair. You should have thought about that before pulling up your dress.'

'You did it because you thought it was a way of denouncing me, exposing me in Christine's eyes. You slept with me so you could be alone with her. You hoped everything would be decided in your favour; you bet everything on that. It's true, isn't it? Are you surprised that I can see it?'

He didn't answer; instead, he tried to get away from her. Incapable of saying anything else, trapped inside her fear that he might escape her, abandon her to herself again, to the emptiness that held her so tightly in its arms, she stood on tiptoe and pressed her lips to his.

He wanted to grab her by the shoulders and push her away, but someone else got there first. Someone grabbed *his* shoulders and flung him to the damp floor of the toilet; already he could feel something connecting with his coccyx. Beqa had come looking for his girlfriend and found her kissing a strange man in the gents'. According to the male codex, when Georgian honour is violated, the only possible course of action is to punch one's rival to the ground.

Elene's screams brought everyone running from table to toilet, and the Plekhanov boys and the film students fell on each other in a savage brawl. Within seconds, a great scrum of male bodies had formed. They held their opponents' heads under their armpits, pressed them against the cold tiles, or slammed their fists into backs and knees, stomachs and faces.

Elene stood looking dumbly on, as if paralysed. She saw Lana throw herself between the men, in an attempt to shield Miqa, and get punched. Perhaps it was Elene's instinct that protected her, prevented her from joining in this orgy of flailing arms and legs; for although she didn't know it, at this point my mother was already pregnant with me, and perhaps I would not be here today if she had intervened in that fight.

Eventually the waiters, three other customers, and the burly restaurant owner pulled the men off each other and ended the punch-up. Elene was sitting on the pavement crying, her face in her hands, sobbing like her two-year-old daughter when she jerked awake in the night and cried out for her mother. Lana appeared beside her out of nowhere, with a torn blouse and a bloody scratch on her cheek, and glared down at her with loathing.

'Leave him alone.'

'It's not my fault. This time it's not my fault; I didn't want —'

'Just stay away from him, okay?'

Elene was surprised by the velvety voice of this woman who, just moments ago, had been defending Miqa without a thought for herself. Despite the harshness of her words, she sounded as if she sucked caramels every day to give her voice its soft and unctuous timbre.

'He didn't defend himself, again,' Elene murmured absently.

'What are you talking about?'

'He didn't defend himself!' Elene screamed.

★

Two weeks later, my mother found out about me, and accepted the news with calmness and equanimity, matter-of-factly, as if there were an inevitability to her getting pregnant, as if she existed only to offer up her body as a portal to all unborn children with an insatiable desire to enter the world.

Beqa, her rebellious boyfriend, received the news with less composure. He stared at her, stunned, scratched behind his ears, massaged his neck, cleared his throat, and tried to smile. Then he started doing everything in his power to persuade her. It was really difficult right now, he had no work, and not much prospect of any, either; he was living with his parents and certainly didn't want to sponge off them. And with her parents — no, there was absolutely no question of that, quite apart from the fact that Elene's father would never accept him as his new son-in-law; besides which, he was, as she knew, against the institution of marriage *per se*; of course he was happy that she was carrying the fruit of their love in her womb, it just wasn't the right time to be starting a family. So, hmm, er, perhaps this time, this one time, it would be possible to, er, well, hmm, 'get around' the problem.

My mother stood up without a word, tucked her handbag under her arm, and left Beqa.

★

When Kostya heard that he was to be a grandfather again, he hurled the pretty cup from which he was drinking his evening black tea, and its scalding contents, at the wall. It had been one of his wife's acquisitions; she was very keen on valuable household objects and was always asking someone with a travel permit to bring her back a Czech, German, or English tea set, of which she now had a sizeable collection. She screamed, shocked by his fury, as well as by the loss of the pretty cup, because what value was there in an incomplete tea set?

'Do you know what you are? Do you? A whore, a cheap, worthless whore, that's all,' he yelled at Elene. Coming from him, this vulgar word was like a dagger to her heart, because there was nothing Kostya hated more than people who screeched like fishwives, or vulgarity of any kind. His weapons were argument, contempt, coldness, rejection; never words like this.

Elene sank into a chair.

'Who said you could sit down? Huh? Who? That's my chair. And you will sit in it when I say you can. Because everything in this house was put here by me and my work — everything you can touch and see. The people who live here have worked. But you? You're a good-for-nothing — a freeloader and leech, on top of everything. The only thing you know how to do is trample on our nerves and our good name. That's your sole vocation in life!'

'Kostya, please,' Nana interjected, the shards of her Czech, German, or English teacup in her hand.

'What is it? What? Am I wrong? Enlighten me, then! She could have had it all, we gave her everything on a silver platter, and instead she trampled it all to bits with her slut's legs. She spits in our face, then laughs at us behind our backs with her criminal friends. Because that's what they are, my dear. That priest — don't make me laugh. He wants to prepare a path to God for me, does he? Are you familiar with his history? Did he tell you about his spell behind bars? Or did your John the Baptist neglect to mention that?'

'He's got nothing to do with it,' mumbled Elene.

'Oh, right, so it was an immaculate conception, was it?'

'He's not the father.'

'So much the better. Why don't you reveal to us the father of your child? Why don't you introduce him to us? Your honourable consort? It wasn't enough for you to get involved with a gigolo, a traitor, a deserter; no, something was still missing, you had to surpass yourself. Well, I can't wait to hear who it is this time. I'll never be able to wash the shame away now. This is the path you've chosen. So you will do as I tell you. Because as far as I can see you've got no one else who's in a position to help you. Apparently you can't even hang on to your criminal boyfriend. On Monday we will go to a doctor and he will carry out an abortion. Is that clear?'

Nana looked away from her daughter at the shards in her hand. Elene's chin began to tremble. Kostya stared defiantly out of the window at the sunlit landscape, into the free, clear day. And before another word could be uttered, Stasia entered the room, holding little Daria in one hand and her roll-up in the other. Daria laughed and ran to her mother.

'Something happened?' asked Stasia, and sat down at the table. Daria clambered onto Elene's lap as Elene struggled to control her chin.

'Leave Mama alone, Dariko. It's not your fault that she's a tart, my angel. Come to me,' said Kostya calmly, holding out his hand to Daria.

'I hate you!' screamed Elene, jumping up and setting Daria down on the floor.

'I'll just have to live with that. All I want to know is, are we agreed?'

'I'm going to keep the baby,' said Elene.

'Are you pregnant?' asked Stasia. She broke out in rasping laughter. Nana and Kostya shot her furious looks.

'Tart! Tart!' Daria shouted merrily, clearly delighted by the addition to her vocabulary.

★

I'm sure I would have been a wanted child, conceived in love, if Thekla had survived the era that was no longer hers, if Stasia had been allowed to follow Peter Vasilyev, if Ramas Iosebidze had prevented his wife from removing her mask at the New Year's ball, if Ida had conquered hope, if my grandfather had found the door between sea and horizon and opened it, if operating tables had not been used in schoolrooms, if Andro Eristavi had learned that, as a consequence of his mistaken beliefs, a child was ripped from Kitty's womb, if Kitty had kept Death at bay, if she had stayed, if the world had castrated the Little Big Men before they could sow their seed, if the ghosts had been allowed to finish singing their songs, and if hunger had not been stronger than love. Yes, everything would have been better then, the way we want it to be when we come into the world: loving parents, a free country with no Brezhnev, and Lou Reed for everyone.

> May there always be sunshine,
> May there always be blue skies,
> May there always be Mummy,
> May there always be me!
>
> PIONEER SONG

Because when I came into the world, Lou Reed was banned and Brezhnev — officially, at least — still firmly in place. As for loving parents: two months before my birth, my father managed to get himself sentenced to five years in prison for stealing a car, as if it had been his intention all along to avoid his responsibilities. They had managed to prove his involvement in other 'criminal intrigues' as well.

My mother paid a high price for preserving my life against Kostya's will. Throughout her pregnancy, she was forced to live like a prisoner, eat what was put in front of her, play with her daughter when her father ordered her to, watch the television programmes her father permitted her to see, get up when she was woken, and turn out her light when it was time to do so. Any form of religious reading material was taboo, as were 'lewd' romantic novels; she had to read them with a torch under the blanket. It was her punishment, which she accepted in silence; she smiled and nodded, was grateful, and applauded them for putting up with her.

Meanwhile, Miqail was arrested — with no warning, no indication whatsoever — by the *militsiya*, who detained him on charges of 'parasitism' and 'religious agitation'. And that was the end of Plekhanov Street for Elene. They started saying that she was putting the boys in danger, that her father was behind Miqail's sudden arrest. She couldn't throw her friends to the wolf that was her father. They had all done things that could easily put them behind bars; even if they hadn't, something would be found, if that was what Kostya wanted.

Nana and Stasia had fought alongside Elene for weeks to persuade Kostya that the child in his daughter's belly should not be aborted, no matter in what circumstances it had been conceived, or by whom. However, no sooner was it too late for an abortion than they started to side with Kostya again, making it clear to Elene that she had betrayed their hopes, too, and crushed their expectations. It was an excruciating time, but Elene decided to accept her martyrdom without protest. In order to give me life, she decided that God was greater than happiness and Heaven promised more than earthly existence. The daily battles with her father, the icy atmosphere in the house, a constant feeling of impotence, and, above all, the awareness of her own failure transformed Elene into a melancholy, scowling woman, usually sloppily dressed and, above all, very lonely. (We mustn't forget in all this how young she was. It's hard to believe, but she was only twenty-one when I was born.)

★

The heavier Kostya's losses on the domestic battlefield, the more powerful he seemed to become in office. And imperceptibly, as is usually the case, anaesthetised by the rural idyll he had created for himself and by good, expensive wine, fortified by the ocean of bureaucratic opportunities, by the freedom of the *nomenklatura* to do as they pleased, and by the political stagnation of the age, he didn't even notice that he was no longer giving a moment's thought to things that, in Russia, would have scandalised him and got people into serious trouble.

Everyone stole. Everyone cheated.

The butcher stole the best meat and sold it under the counter for three times the price. The *kolkhoz*es kept back part of the harvest and flogged it off elsewhere. Nurses pilfered gauze and bandages. The manager of the winery bribed representatives to smuggle crates of wine out of his own factory so he could use them to bribe other, more important people. Long-established thievery, practised until then in secret, was now the order of the day, and as everyone was doing it, no one had to be punished.

The *militsiya* acquitted people on charges of shoplifting and traffic offences; petty crimes were dealt with on the quiet. The public prosecutor's office sold acquittals for rape and murder. Teachers and professors handed out good grades in exchange for cream cakes, French perfumes, and fine chocolates. The building contractor helped himself to building materials. The doctor was twice as attentive when treating a patient if some cash had been slipped into the pocket of his white coat beforehand. Artists stole from one another. And the politicians didn't need to steal anything, because they already had the biggest share in all the other thievery.

People stole plaster of Paris, Rubin colour televisions, dressmaking patterns, cement, analgesics, Chinese thermos flasks decorated with red flowers, wool, condensed milk, spectacles, three-kopek school exercise books, talcum powder, beige polyester socks, furs, snowsuits (even in regions where it didn't snow), camera lenses, green plastic bowls, preserving jars, records (no matter whose), Kosmos or Astra cigarettes, and Hygiene aftershave.

And my grandfather participated in the general suppression of any consciousness of wrongdoing. Which required countless stays at spa resorts, business trips — all with female companions, of course — formal receptions, good Saperavi, and the perennial goodwill of his subjects.

That long black cloud is comin' down
I feel like I'm knockin' on heaven's door.

BOB DYLAN

I came into the world on a rainy autumn day, 8 November 1974, in a village hospital, after a labour that lasted precisely eight hours. The contractions started in the middle of a fight between my mother and her father. And the same day that my sister, as I've already said, concussed herself falling off a pony at the stud farm.

Apart from my birth, and my sister's fall, nothing special happened that day. Except, perhaps, for the fact that, on this day, my mother finally lost her patience in the eternal battle with her father and her eternal hope for the understanding of her female relatives, and started screaming.

'Are you a whore?' my grandfather is said to have yelled at her; and my mother, weeping, is said to have screamed back, 'I might as well be, the way you treat me!'

Two hours later, she went into labour.

Parties to the conflict: my domineering grandfather, my infantile grandmother, and my mother, increasingly losing control of her own life. Stasia was standing somewhere on the terrace, smoking one of her roll-ups. She had long since grown accustomed to this shouting, but that particular day something must have caused her to lose patience. Bursting into the living room, she snarled at her son: 'Tell me, have you completely lost your mind? Are you a sadist, or what? She's nine months pregnant! Perhaps you could let her give birth in peace first?'

For a moment an unaccustomed silence filled the room.

'You keep out of this, Stasia!' was Kostya's only comment.

'I'm to keep out of it, am I? You lunatic!'

It always astonished us how this delicate, sexless, ageless creature could, in seconds, fly into such a rage. Nana couldn't help smiling inside, but it didn't show on her face; her expression remained one of dismay and concern.

'Ugh!' shouted Kostya, probably referring to both his mother's choice of words and the general situation, and left the room.

He walked down the hill to the stud farm, with Daria, his golden girl, holding his hand, and stood with her admiring the Dagestani ponies. Then he sat her on one of them, and was holding her by the waist when the pony suddenly broke free and threw the little girl off. It happened so fast that my grandfather failed to catch her.

As my grandfather was throwing himself on his granddaughter in desperation, blaming the horse breeders and threatening to close 'the whole organisation' down, my mother started to groan. At the same moment that my mother, accompanied by her corpulent mother, was heading for the hospital in the village, my sister Daria, usually called Daro, Dari, or Dariko, was also being rushed to hospital, but in her case it was the best hospital in Tbilisi, not a ramshackle village clinic. It was announced that Daria had slight concussion. And a few hours later, a few kilometres north of the city, that I had come into the world.

'This child is a product of Elene's shamelessness and depravity, sealing my conclusive defeat in the battle for her honour, so I have absolutely no reason to be happy, or to celebrate anything at all. Even if it's not her fault, the girl is the embodiment of all the ills her mother has brought down upon us.' This was Kostya's only reaction to the happy news that he had become a grandfather for the second time.

And when I was finally brought to the Green House, the home that did not welcome me, my great-grandmother awoke from her somnambulistic state, looked at her great-granddaughter, and said: 'This is a different child. A special one. She needs a lot of protection and a lot of freedom.'

And everyone slapped their palms to their foreheads and groaned. The mad old lady had come back to life, and they weren't really sure whether this was a good thing or a disaster.

That same day, Stasia finally revealed to the members of her family the true purpose of her barn. It was to become her new rehearsal room. She planned to start dancing again, she said. At which everyone shook their heads in disbelief and mild embarrassment and presumably thought: *you must be joking!*

And I thought *what a wonderful world*, and laughed myself to sleep. Perhaps I saw them all, their heads bent over my cradle: Ida with her ringed fingers, fanning my cheeks; Thekla with her memorable scent of wilted flowers and powder; my great-great-grandfather, who smelled of chocolate, pensively shaking his head at the fact that, once again, I had to be given the surname Jashi. And then my sister Daria, who had easily and painlessly shaken off her concussion, came and bit my upper arm so hard that my screams frightened the horses in the field. Until my mother ran in, pulled Daria off me, and screamed at her in desperation, 'What are you doing? She's your sister, she's your little sister! You have to love her!'

★

The call came at dawn one day in May 1975. Kostya was still away on one of his business trips to Batumi. Elene, unable to sleep, was roaming the unfinished attic again. Nana was fast asleep and snoring. So Stasia dragged herself out of bed, looked for her slippers, and stumbled to the phone.

'Yes, damn it?' she panted into the receiver.
'Stasia?'
'Christine?'
'Are you well?'
'Yes, I'm all right, how are things with you?'
'I need your help.'
'Why, what's happened?'
'You have to help me.'
'Spit it out!'
'Miqa. Miqa.'
'What is it this time?'
'He was interrogated yesterday.'
'Interrogated?'
'Yes, the *militsiya* was here.'
'Those bastards. What's he done?'
'He made a film.'
'A film. What about?'
'About ... Sopio.'
'What?!'

A heavy pause followed, a pause that felt as if it were about to burst and spill its entrails.

'Yes, it was supposed to be his graduation film. He's been working on it for over a year now. It all seemed to be going well at first ...'
'Is it that bad?'
'Yes, I think so.'

'What do you want me to do?'

'Talk to him. To Kostya. I hate myself for having to ask you, but it's the only thing I can do for Miqa.'

There was a lump in Stasia's throat, something furry and nauseating; her words disintegrated in her mouth before she was able speak them. There was so much she wanted to say to her little sister; but where were they, the words, or at least the tears — why did her wretched tears so often forsake her?

'Stasia? Are you still there?'

'It's good to hear your voice, Christine.'

'You have to help me.'

'I'll speak to him when he gets back.'

Stasia went out into the cool, damp dawn, violet and marsh-green. There was nothing that lasted, nothing that was stronger than an echo, nothing that didn't run through your fingers, that didn't wither. Night after night she had placed her dreams under her pillow, hoping for a miracle, and the miracle had never come to pass.

And now there were worthless tears. Now there were fatherless daughters and motherless sons, now there were party badges on people's chests, now there were disorientated girls and boys behind bars, there was scorched earth; there were still *La Bayadère*s and *Petrushka*s, but for a long time now there had not been any parts in them for her.

Stasia was collapsing beneath the weight of her neutrality. What an effort it cost to absent yourself from the world.

She stood there in a threadbare nightdress, bare legs in filthy rubber boots, and looked out at the morning, at the dawn breaking over the land. The morning was infinitely, painfully beautiful. But the people who could have delighted in this beauty were wounded; they could not become one with it, were condemned to remain observers for all eternity.

Neutrality was an illusion.

A new day was breaking over Stasia.

Everything in the world is justified by history.

ANTON CHEKHOV

The film was called *The Story of A Careless Dream*. A rather pretentious title, admittedly, but certainly excusable in a young artist. For months he had worked on it like a man possessed. He had reconstructed his grandmother's life with tremendous dedication. And where he lacked money, he had used light and imagination, concentrating on the faces of his actors, deploying the tricks of the Surrealist filmmakers.

With the help of Lana's caramel-soft seductress voice, her dark eye of the disadvantaged, her fists of the oppressed, he had been able to win over a few fellow students — in particular, a promising young actress to play the lead. He had managed to convince them all of the necessity and significance of his film.

He had talked about it incessantly, like a madman: every image, every shot was important to him, he gave his cameraman a thousand instructions, storyboarded every scene with Lana, right down to the last detail. Again and again, he stressed that they couldn't afford to make mistakes, that any potential risks must be dealt with in advance.

Christine, wearily summoning all the strength her age permitted, had protested against it. She clung to the Cassandra role she had chosen, constantly speaking of the terrible future, yet never being believed; she never tired of warning Miqa about the dangers of the film. Every time she had a moment alone with him she would try to convince him to abandon his project, until he started to cut himself off from her, to come home later and later; until he shut her out of his secrets.

Their shared world, for which Christine had already paid such a high price, fell to pieces. And she felt that, in Miqa's world, she was like the scent a departed traveller leaves behind on objects and on clothes, a scent that grows fainter, more fleeting, day by day, until one day it vanishes completely.

★

They had already started editing the film when Lana realised she was pregnant.

She knew how sacred the film was to Miqa, and that any delay, any threat, any distraction could lead to a nervous breakdown. These past few months he had been so tense, so nervous, had even developed an almost pathological mistrust of his team, seeing spies and informers everywhere who might betray him. He shut himself off. Gave out no information about the current status of the project. He was unstable, full of doubts and fears. Lana had to support him; she had to go down this road with him right to the end. She had to pull herself together and keep the exciting news under wraps; she had to focus on him. She was his right hand and his left, and now, now of all times, when he was so insecure and eaten up by anxiety, those hands must not tremble.

She took a certain pride in how well she had mastered everything, how confidently and unerringly she had organised and coordinated the shoot, for months. And yes, she had always feared the moment when the film was finished, when it was sent out into the world, when he no longer needed her to steer his thoughts onto orderly paths and conquer his doubts. But now she had nothing more to fear: he would stay with her; she was carrying his child now, and that was far stronger, far more *definitive* than anything that had bound them before.

So she decided to keep the news to herself until the film was ready.

But then things started to happen very fast. One piece of carelessness led to another. Her uncle, who had made the film studio cutting room available to them for several nights, felt that he was getting out of his depth, and as he didn't want to risk losing his job he asked the two of them to look for another editing room to do the rest of the work. Now they were dependent on the film school. The whole team knew they mustn't let anything slip about the project, yet the walls inside the Institute were not leakproof. There were too many students going in and out, and rumours spread all too quickly, like the one that Miqa Eristavi was planning a minor cinematic insurrection in the editing suite. The rumours travelled up from floor to floor until at last they reached the directors' offices. A provocation? The commission began its investigation, summoned, questioned, harassed those involved, demanded information.

Lana had to act quickly. She spoke to the team again and again, used all her overwhelming powers of persuasion, made it clear to them how important it was that they kept their mouths shut, how important it was to shroud themselves in silence until the final cut of the film was released, to let nothing, absolutely nothing, leak out. She painted the film's glorious future in glittering colours: she spoke of invitations to foreign festivals, of prizes; she even let slip the illustrious term *resistance fighters*.

In all my life I have never met another woman who devoted as much energy as Lana to being an ideologist. For good or ill. Hers was a pure ideology of opposition. Permanently against something or someone. Never resting. Never achieving her aim. Never forgetting. Her fanaticism, it seems to me, was the mainstay of her identity. Not even pregnancy could stop her from plunging into this sea of intrigue, lies, and manipulation, just to guard Miqa's Holy Grail.

However, not everyone was prepared to risk as much. Not everyone was happy to see themselves in the role of resistance fighter, and this film was not so sacred to everyone that they were willing to get thrown out of the Institute, or worse: menacing warnings, punishments, being barred from their profession.

The camera assistant proved to be a man of weak disposition, and when he was summoned before the commission for the second time to confirm his initial statement — that it was just a harmless little film — he lost his nerve and admitted, shamefacedly, that he was not entirely sure the film really was in keeping with the Institute's philosophy, as everyone in the team had claimed. The following day, the entire group was summoned and subjected to detailed interrogation. The directorate ordered Miqa to hand over the reels of film to the board of examiners immediately.

Panic erupted. The actresses wept, the actors swore, the cameraman cursed the system, the sound engineer scratched his head, the lighting technician tried to sow seeds of hope — but everyone was agreed: Miqa had to hand the film over to the board. What was the worst that could happen? They might issue a ban and destroy the footage and they'd make a different, more *conformist* graduation film, but with a little remorse they'd all be out of danger. Surely he didn't mean to put the future of his fellow students on the line?

Miqa was lost for words, so Lana spoke up again. She berated them all for being cowards and fainthearted bureaucrats, incapable of fighting for an idea, incapable of taking risks, risks that came with the territory when you were an artist. She even called them feeble caricatures of artists. And before anyone could respond to or refute her accusations, she dragged Miqa, like a schoolboy, out of the cameraman's apartment where they were meeting to try to find a way out of the looming crisis.

Miqa was indignant. As they stepped out of the entrance hall onto the street, he started shouting at her, saying she had made him look ridiculous in the others' eyes, as if he had no voice of his own.

'Excuse me: you didn't say a thing! One moment longer and they would have convinced you to hand in the footage tomorrow, and draft an apology as well. That's right, isn't it, Miqa? I know you. I can read your thoughts and doubts before you're even aware of them.'

'I hate being treated like a child!'

'Oh, really?' She strode away and left him standing.

'I'm talking to you, Lana!'

'There's nothing to talk about. You're an artist — they're not.'

'What are you trying to say?' He hurried after her.

'You've put everything into this film — *we've* put everything into it, and I'm not going to let these cowards ruin it for us now. You knew people wouldn't applaud you for it. I told you there would be obstacles.'

'Obstacles? These aren't obstacles. We could all be slapped with an employment ban, and I —'

'What difference does it make, if you can't shoot the films you want to shoot, or if you're not allowed to shoot any at all? Would you care to explain?'

'I can't just turn them in like that. These people trusted me; they did what they could. Now it's up to me to protect them.'

'Oh, really? And what about me and your baby?'

'Baby?'

'Look, I wanted to tell you later, so you could edit in peace, and —'

'You're pregnant?'

'Yes. I'm pregnant, Miqa. We're having a baby. According to my calculations —'

'And you didn't tell me because you thought I should edit the film in peace first? Have I understood that right? Wait — stop, will you, you're practically running.'

'I don't want to stop. I don't want anything. I want to go through every contingency for tomorrow with you and then go home. I'm tired. It sickens me, constantly being surrounded by people who don't know how to make use of the opportunities they've been given. Who have everything and don't even value it. I'm sick of always wasting my time with these idiots. Is it too much to expect a bare minimum of professionalism?'

'Hey, Lana, Lana … Wait! What's got into you? Come here — let me look at you, at least.'

'The bus will be here any minute; come on, Miqa.'

He caught up with her and tried to grab her elbow, but she slipped away and carried on walking.

'Lana, you can't just tell me like that, in passing, that you're pregnant, and then not even stand still; my God, what's the matter with you?'

Suddenly she turned to him, her face contorted in a mask of disgust, contempt, and pain, and snarled, 'I don't want an idiot as a husband! And my child certainly doesn't deserve a coward as a father! I haven't turned my life upside down all these months, ignored my own interests and needs, plunged head first into this madness, and spent the whole time charming these brainless, talentless people for you just to throw in the towel now! Do you understand me, Miqa?'

She was seething with rage. He had never seen her in such a state. Lana, the model of composure and self-discipline, unbeatable in the art of self-control; Lana, far-sighted, patient, unerring, solution-orientated. He didn't understand where this ugly aggression, this blind fury, had come from all of a sudden, but it was obviously clouding her clear vision, making her incapable of understanding the seriousness of the situation.

'Tomorrow you turn up with a friendly smile, you put a brave face on it, you show how baffled you are by the hysteria around your little graduation film, and then you shrug your shoulders and claim the reels have disappeared. It's that simple. I've given them to my uncle for the time being; I told him to hold on to them for a few weeks, until all this has blown over. After that we'll find a way. That's what you're going to do; that's what we're going to do, Miqa.'

She had got herself under control again. On the last sentence her lips even parted in a contented smile.

'Come on, they're not going to lock you up over a film that nobody's seen. Hey, Miqa, don't look at me like that. We've got this far, we'll get through the last bit as well. And nothing'll happen to the others. *We* bear full responsibility.'

'Not *we*, Lana. *I* do.'

'You're very much mistaken about that.'

All of a sudden she looked as if all her determination, all her strength had left her. She bowed her head and stuck her hands in the pockets of her jacket, as if seeking protection.

'Aren't you even a little bit happy?' she mumbled sheepishly.

'What exactly do you mean?'

She moved her hands inside the jacket pockets to make her belly look round.

'What do you expect of me?'

'Nothing. I don't expect anything. I just wish you'd say yes.'

'Yes to what? To you? To the baby? To your plan?'

Now she looked at him. The uncertainty left her body in a flash, and her expression was impenetrable once more. He was ashamed: he would have liked to have given her a better answer, but he was still overwhelmed by her tone, her uncompromising demands, the furious insults she had heaped on his collective. But Lana was her old self again: indomitable, fortress-like, a woman without ghosts, the woman without mysteries. Effortlessly she swallowed the bitterness his words inevitably provoked in her, and set off for the bus stop.

'We'll have to get married now, won't we?' he asked her on the bus, taking her hand in his and pressing his forehead pensively against the dusty windowpane.

'The only thing you have to do is save this film! I've got through worse things than being jilted by a man while pregnant,' she replied, in her usual sarcastic tone, and pulled her hand away.

★

He got back from a state banquet in the early hours of the morning, weary but self-satisfied. He stank of wine and the invisible imprints of female attention bestowed upon him during the party. He wouldn't even have noticed her as he passed her on the terrace if she hadn't greeted him.

He stopped, puzzled. 'Why are you sitting out here at this time of night?'

'Sit with me, please. I'll make coffee for you as well.'

'Can't it wait? I'm dying of exhaustion.'

'No.'

He succumbed with a groan, and sat in the rocking chair with the sunflower cushions that it would take my sister and me many more years to destroy. Stasia served her son the promised coffee and sat down beside him.

'Miqa's made a film. A graduation film. About his grandmother. And now he's being interrogated. You have to sort it out.'

It wasn't a request. Kostya sipped at the hot coffee and took his time replying.

'Sort it out? Me?' he asked, as if he wanted to make sure he'd understood her correctly.

'Yes. You have to.'

He started laughing, as if his mother had just told him a malicious joke.

'You all think I'm omnipotent, don't you? Anyone in a hundred-kilometre radius who gets into some kind of trouble thinks they can come running with it to me?'

'He isn't *anyone*.'

'Exactly. Correct answer! He's the one responsible for my daughter's misfortune. And he can count himself lucky that I let him go on living! I think I've been generous enough.' He stood up abruptly and started heading towards the house. 'Oh yes, and tell Christine — because I know she asked you to do this — that she's made her decision, as I've made mine.'

'Kostya, wait ...'

He dismissed her with a wave of his hand and opened the front door. He went into the bathroom and stood in front of the mirror, saw the print on his cheek of a pair of red lips, shapely and wrinkle-free. He began to shave. He saw his clear face in the mirror. Carefully he sprinkled the shaving powder onto his palm, rubbed water into it, smeared the foam on his cheeks, applied the razor. A slight sting. Pomegranate-red liquid trickled down his left cheek.

He heard Daria chattering. She must just have woken up. The realisation elicited a smile; his lips parted between the white foam and dark-red blood. Somewhere a dog barked. A gentle breeze wafted through the corridors and rooms. There was an unforgivably tantalising smell of spring. Someone switched on the television. *Vremya* was on. News was being broadcast to the world. To each his own. It was a Saturday. Nana didn't have to go to work. Soon she would start ironing his shirts, Daria's clothes, the romper suits that belonged to his daughter's fatherless baby, Elene's trousers (always those scruffy trousers, never nice clothes in a feminine style!).

Soon Elene would force herself out of bed with the baby in her arms, would head for the breakfast table with the discontented expression that had become a permanent fixture on her face. Then she would wander apathetically around the grounds and gaze longingly down at the stud farm where her John the Baptist was no longer to be found. She would roam about, restless, compulsive, her trouser pockets full of years, her best years, to throw away.

The small cut on his face was throbbing. He ran some water into his hand and splashed a few drops on the bleeding wound.

Stasia's footsteps. She was bustling about the kitchen. Was she making jam, at this ungodly hour? The scent of peaches poured from the kitchen. Were there peaches already? Or were they plums? She would gaze at him reproachfully all day, he knew it. She would give him the silent treatment.

The baby wasn't silent, it was screaming. Kostya refused to speak my name. He found my name — as he had Daria's — idiotic. How did you come up with such a name? Why did Elene have to be different from everyone else, even when naming her children? And emphasise it, too. Why couldn't she give her children *normal* names? There were plenty of pretty girls' names. But no, she always had to thwart his plans; she, his daughter, who had become such a stranger to him.

He dabbed at the cut with the corner of a towel. The material soaked up the blood. A small scratch on his face. One more.

When had they all lost this ability — the ability to be happy? he asked himself, staring at the bloody corner of the towel.

The baby — I — was screaming. Why wasn't anyone dealing with her? His head ached. He'd drunk too much tonight. It had been a boozy dinner with colleagues from the Moscow MVD.

No, enough was enough. He didn't want to put anything right any more. Everyone was responsible for their own life. He didn't know why he suddenly found himself thinking of Giorgi Alania. What was he doing right now? The only male friend with whom he didn't have to pretend to be anything he wasn't. An effortless friendship. The only *relationship* in his life that hadn't ended in bed. What a relief.

What an enviable career Alania had had. What courage he had shown. What help he had given him. Had Kostya deserved it? He was so tired. What he would really have liked to do was lie down in the empty bathtub and go to sleep. But his thoughts pursued him. Restlessness. That must be Elene's fault. Her restlessness was infecting him, too. It seemed that, as ever, he was still receptive to her signals.

The faces of the starving people, when they broke through the Army Group North in those dark January days. Not again. Not Leningrad. Not these thoughts. He must pull himself together a little; it would come right again, all of it. He reeled slightly, sat down on the side of the bath.

'Everything all right?'

It was Nana, knocking on the door. His wife. When was the last time he had touched her? Why were they actually still together?

'Can't a man even shave in peace?'

'I didn't know, sorry.'

That submissive tone, that implicit reproach in every word she addressed to him. Why had she decided to stay with him? Was it easier that way?

Elene walked past the bathroom. He recognised her hurried steps; she was always in a rush, going somewhere, she herself didn't know where. What opportunities, what prospects she had thrown away, of her own volition, all for nothing. All that effort, all the years in Moscow, all the fights with Nana. For what? For this disgrace.

No, he mustn't soften. Why was he crying all of a sudden? Where was the sense in that? It must be the exhaustion. Work, the last few gruelling months, the birth of this fatherless child. He doubled up as if he had stomach-ache, wrapped his arms around his belly, drew in his head.

How was he supposed to put all of this right? How was he supposed to *compensate* all these people? For what exactly? For the things they had lost or forfeited *because of him?* Was that how it was? No, it wasn't his fault. He had had enough. It was time everyone started to make their own luck. He wiped his face with the towel.

Just this one thing, just this one last thing, then he would try to forget it all, would lie back and let things take their course. Yes: he had to settle it. He had to protect his family. He had to protect them from themselves. Perhaps this was his chance! He would put an end to Elene's suffering. He had to do it for Daria, for his little jewel. For her future, so she could grow up in peace, in a peaceful family, and not have to endure that mad restlessness in her mother's eyes.

He threw open the door, crept to his study, locked himself in, flicked through his address book, and called a number.

'Hello, Kostya here. Yes, yes, excellent, and yourself? Listen, I have a small request. I hope you can help me out. It's about a student, Film and Theatre Institute, yes, yes, here. Bit of a lowlife. Father a deserter, defected to the fascists back in the day. And as for him, well — looks like he's following in Papa's footsteps. No, not a criminal. An unremarkable sort of lad, really, but as they say, still waters ... That's right. Seems he's made some sort of film, yes, I think it's a graduation film. And from what I hear he's having some problems right now because of it. And I'd like it if these problems were not resolved all that quickly. You understand. What exactly ... Tell me, are you the *militsiya* man or am I? Of course you can drop in on him. In fact, you should. Yes, yes, of course. No, that's not the Education Ministry's responsibility. That's your responsibility, my friend. No, no one's going to hassle you about it. You should know by now that I keep my word. And you should also know that you'll be generously rewarded for your, hmm, support for a just cause. Excellent. That's what I like to hear, my friend. And yes, please keep me informed.'

> In the victory of Communism's immortal ideal,
> We see the future of our dear land.
> And to her fluttering scarlet banner,
> Selflessly true we always shall stand!
>
> SOVIET NATIONAL ANTHEM

The next morning, two *militsiya* officials appeared in the dean's office at the film faculty wanting to know how it was possible for a pathetic little student to permit himself the inexpressible effrontery of daring to do *a thing like this*.

'But, comrades, what film? There is no film.' The head of department tried to placate them. 'We questioned the student Eristavi yesterday and he assured us that the footage no longer exists …'

'And you believe him, my friend?' interrupted the stocky *militsiya* officer, the more abrupt of the two.

'No, of course not. But it does mean that he'll never be able to finish editing this film or show it anywhere, because we issued an immediate ban to this effect until we've seen the raw material ourselves. The student Eristavi is not a reactionary; he's more the sensitive type. I wouldn't worry about him.'

The dean was trying hard to get rid of the *militsiya* men so he could sort out the situation internally, without unpredictable outside interference.

'Comrade Eristavi won't get any stupid ideas. I assure you that this problem is not worth your time; I'm sure you have more important things to do than concern yourselves with such a harmless incident.'

'You can leave it to us to decide whether this matter is deserving of our attention or not, *Comrade!* And your students don't seem all that harmless. We've asked around: the whole institute is talking about this film.'

'But it doesn't exist. No one's ever seen it. Comrades, this is ridiculous!'

'Ridiculous? Ridiculous? You're calling us ridiculous? These anarchists hold nothing more sacred than trampling our values underfoot, laughing in our face, spitting on us — you're saying this is ridiculous? And these are the kind of people you're raising to be the artistic future of our country?'

'As long as there is no film, this boy can't be accused of anything. It's a lot of fuss about something trivial. Young people nowadays sometimes like to exaggerate. They all see themselves as rebels; you know how it is, comrades, we were all twenty once, and —'

'In that case, please inform your *harmless* student that we expect the reels to be in our possession by Wednesday. If after that he continues to maintain that all the footage has disappeared, he'll have to pay a visit to our headquarters.'

★

'They're trying to frighten you, can't you see? They're trying to frighten you, Miqa! Just hold your nerve. Stick to your story. You don't know where the reels are — that's actually true, in a way. You really don't know where *I've* taken the film. So there's no need for you to be afraid. I'm here with you. I'll be by your side.'

The non-existent film was threatening to have ever more serious consequences, and seemed to be sending Lana into absolute ecstasies.

'I swear they'll celebrate you as a hero. I'm telling you, the rumour mill in the Institute is already working overtime. They're going to envy you, they're going to worship you — yes, that's how a director should be, we should be like that, but no, we're just cowardly little idiots, mummy's boys and daddy's darlings — that's what they'll think. Yes, Miqa, they'll finally recognise you for what you are. Just imagine what it'll be like to tell our little one these stories: I'm sure it's going to be a boy, the spitting image of you, Miqa. Imagine how proud of us he'll be. When he sees *our* film, and we tell him this whole story. He'll look up to you, his brave Papa.'

'Stop it!' Miqa slammed his fist on the table. 'You're refusing to face the facts! Can't you see the trouble we're in? The *militsiya* are already on to my film; even if I get through this interrogation tomorrow I'll be thrown out.'

'Miqa, Miqa, my little one, come here ... you worry far too much!'

She got up and went over to him, snuggled against him, hopped onto his lap, and clasped his head in her hands.

'Do as I say. Then nothing will happen to you. Have I ever let you down? Have I ever given you a single reason to doubt my words? Miqa, please. We'll go there together. We'll clear this up. Please — leave the others out of it. Especially Christine. If she gets wind of it, she'll make an operatic scene to get you to give up and agree to hand over the film. Come on, give me your hand.

Look how swollen my breasts are; they're practically bursting at the seams.'

And she placed his hand on her breast, and planted a firm kiss on his lips.

*

The *militsiya* interrogation didn't last long. Miqa's attempts to stick to his version of events with the stolen film reels were dismissed in seconds as ludicrous. He was given an ultimatum and told he had to hand over the raw footage within the week. If he didn't, they told him with mischievously provocative smiles, the case would be passed on to the public prosecutor.

Sweating and gasping for breath, he reeled out onto the street. In that bare *militsiya* room he had suppressed all his fear, but now it erupted. Tears of humiliation and shame glittered in his eyes. Once he and Lana were far enough away from the *militsiya* station he started raging, right there in the middle of the street; saliva flew from his lips, he gesticulated wildly, stamped his feet, started saying something only to break off and begin again, until he stopped, exhausted, and, because he didn't know what else to do with himself, crouched down on his haunches.

She knelt beside him, put an arm round his shoulder, and spoke to him urgently, using all her powers of persuasion. Her calmness and confidence drove the consternation out of his body; again and again she stressed how proud their son would be of him now, what a great artist he was in her eyes, how valiantly he was fighting, that he had nothing to fear because they had no solid evidence against him.

'No one's seen this film. No one can bring charges against you over a blank, Miqa, a rumour, something that doesn't exist. No one can force you to do anything because of this. They're frightening you; they just want to intimidate you.'

He tried not to look at her, at her oily eyes behind the thick lenses of her glasses. He tried not to inhale her steadfast determination; because today, in this neutral, cold interrogation room, he had understood for the first time that the game had turned deadly serious. And that Lana, who had manoeuvred him into making the film, might have very different interests to him. He didn't want to look at her, so he wouldn't have to scream in her face that this was her fault; that it was him, not her, who was being subjected to this whole shameful process, that she had put not only him but all those involved, the people who had trusted him, in this terrible and absolutely unwarranted danger.

At the start of the interrogation, when he realised that these officials really were taking the whole thing very seriously, he was just about to admit that perhaps he had gone a bit far, and assure them that he would give the reels back the following morning. But then another thought had come to him, an absolutely irrational, incredible, yet almost logical thought. What if Kostya Jashi were behind all this? What if he had taken up arms against him again? Scarcely had the thought occurred to him, scarcely had he formulated it in his mind, than suddenly everything was as clear as day, consistent — and he felt he did have enough courage to go on defending his version of the truth. Because if Kostya Jashi was prepared to go this far, he was prepared to go farther. He wasn't going to be like Andro; he wasn't going to let Kostya Jashi break him.

And anyway, what was the problem? What was it about this film that was so forbidden? Was it really so very dangerous, as ground-breaking as Lana was trying to convince him it was? After all, it was only a graduation film. A somewhat provocative, daredevil, challenging look at a person's life, captured on celluloid with modest means and using narrative techniques borrowed from other films.

Lana had helped create a mythology around it, if only within the Institute. Perhaps this was actually a very different opportunity for him: because a film no one had seen, one that even the public prosecutor was after, could retain its promise of genius for as long as no one found it and no one saw it. Perhaps there really was no way out of this situation now, other than to keep it hidden. Perhaps he wouldn't gain his diploma, but with the right strategy he might instead gain an indestructible reputation. A reputation that in future would allow him to make the films he wanted to make, without Lana's help and support and all that these entailed.

So he would stick to Lana's plan: he would count on her to send the film into banishment somewhere it could not be found, and in doing so he would secure himself a future — one that involved some detours and crazy diversions, but which offered him exceptional prospects. Of course, it would be so much more bearable, so much *greater*, to believe that he was still engaged in a fight for his ideals, for Christine, for the things the world had denied him and he had snatched from its hands nonetheless, and that in doing so he was fearlessly overcoming all obstacles; a fight in which the roles of Good and Evil, Right and Wrong had already been assigned. Miqa Eristavi, avenger of his past, eternal lover, on one side; Kostya Jashi on the other.

Yes, he would follow this path, the path Lana had proposed. And he would allow her to go on believing that they were pursuing the same goals. But they weren't. This, too, became clear to him that day.

★

Later, he would ask himself whether it was the unhappy turn his and Christine's story had taken that had led him here. Was it in fact Christine's age that had driven him into this woman's arms? Would everything have been different if she had left the light on that night, when she took off her veil in front of him? Would he then finally have been cured of her? Instead, here he was, standing on the street in front of a woman, a stranger, who happened to be carrying his child. And it was then that he made the most momentous decision of his life.

'Agreed. Take the reels out of the city; hide them. Take them up to the village. Take them to my father. But do it when he's not there, otherwise he won't let you ... I'll tell you where to hide them. I'll go through with this, alone. I'll see it through to the end.'

'I knew I wasn't wrong about you.'

And Lana, brimming with happiness, ran her hand over his head and tousled his hair.

★

'He's refusing, Stasia. He says he doesn't have the film. I had a meeting with a lawyer today. She assumes there's some other reason for this peculiar business. I simply don't understand why they're making such a fuss about such a ridiculous issue. The lawyer suspects that *someone* is behind these interrogations. That's what she told me. You know I don't even want to contemplate —'

'Christine, please! What are you saying?'

Stasia pressed her hands to her back. She had spent the whole day giving orders to the workmen who were supposed to be covering the walls of her barn with mirrors. In a couple of days her dance hall would be finished, and then she would be ready to pass on Peter Vasilyev's legacy. There would be a few village girls with whom to practise her beloved pirouettes and *pas de chat*, *pas de basque*, and *pas de deux*. She leaned against the kitchen wall and stretched her spine.

'Could it be that Kostya is behind this whole —'

'Christine, what on earth makes you suspect such a terrible thing? The boy has only himself to blame. Why doesn't he just give them back the film, and then it'll all be over? Kostya? No, you mustn't even think it!'

'Miqa had to go to yet another interrogation, Stasia. It's not normal. I'm begging you, please find out.'

'And I'm telling you: stop this nonsense and get him to hand in the film.'

'At least consider for a moment the possibility that —'

'He's still your nephew. He adores you; you raised him, he's like your own flesh and blood. Fine: I'll talk to him again, all right? They can't do anything to the boy. He hasn't killed anyone. The times are different now ... and he isn't Andro.'

'His girlfriend is pregnant. He's going to be a father soon. They're having a baby, Stasia.'

★

She summoned all her courage, got into her Zhiguli, and, for the first time since my birth, she drove to the city. She had still never been to Christine's little apartment; she had been dreading this encounter all this time. But she had to face it now. If she did nothing, then one of these days she would burst, she would buckle beneath the weight of her own impotence.

Something was going on. She had sensed it immediately. The secret phone calls, and Stasia's whispering whenever she called Christine. Kostya's exaggerated show of activity. His uneasy expression. It was about Miqa, she was sure of it. She had pricked up her ears, and from the bits of information she was able to glean from scraps of her grandmother's and father's conversations she had soon put together a pretty accurate picture.

She had to intervene.

Christine flung open the door without asking who was there. She seemed to be expecting someone else. She froze, plucked at her black dress, which, as always, fitted her perfectly, and looked Elene up and down.

'What are you doing here?'

Of course she hadn't forgiven her. Of course not. It had been naive to hope for that.

'I heard ... about Miqa ... and I want to help. I thought if you could tell me exactly what's going on, I could talk to Papa and change his mind. Stasia won't be able to do it alone.'

'You — help? You've already *helped* enough. Oh, what the hell, come into my modest abode. I know you're accustomed to better things, but I can offer you tea as well.'

★

Christine did in fact tell her about the whole situation; more than this, she voiced her suspicion that Kostya was behind the state's excessive interest in

Miqa. Elene sat staring into the black tea in disbelief, her cheek propped on her fist, desperately racking her brains. But before she could say anything, they heard the front door open and Miqa's slow, heavy steps. He walked into the living room, where he paused for a moment in the doorway at the sight of Elene and gave Christine a quizzical look, as if considering beating a hasty retreat. She beckoned him over and he joined them at the table, but made no attempt to kiss Elene in greeting.

'Did you call the Jashis?' he called to Christine, who had gone to the kitchenette to warm up his lunch.

'No, I came of my own accord,' said Elene.

'Aha. You thought: poor Miqa, I have to see with my own eyes just how deep in the shit he is?'

'You have to give back the film,' she said, not responding to his hostility.

'Oh, and who asked for your opinion?'

A threatening 'Miqa!' came from the kitchen.

'What? Why should I follow *her* advice?'

'Because it isn't her advice, it's all our advice!'

Why couldn't she just say: 'Kostya has probably had my closest friends arrested, too. Kostya will take his revenge on you, and all because I was too much of a coward to distance myself from my false truth. A truth that — damn it, Miqa! — doesn't exist, or a truth that I don't know!' Why had she come here? For this! To warn him about her father. Perhaps this was what it had been about all along? All her eavesdropping and spying: she believed her father capable of the worst and expected him to take things to the limit. Knowing all the while that she had given him permission to do so. She had caused Kostya to neutralise Miqail, Beqa, and, yes, above all Miqa, the eternal thorn in his side, in the belief that doing so would mean she, Elene, was out of danger.

Elene had wanted to cut herself off from him, to bite through the umbilical cord with her teeth, an umbilical cord that had bound her not to her mother but to him, and still did.

Why couldn't she stand up and yell out what she was thinking so that the whole world could hear it: *Yes, I'm the gunpowder in Kostya's rifle. I am his right hand. I am the firing squad. I am his boss. I, I, I am his war, the war he is constantly fighting against the wrong enemy. It's me. Yes, I am being punished; for a long time I thought punishment had passed me by, but I am being punished, so hard, so suitably; yes, really, suitably. Because everything I say turns into a bullet, a bullet for him to load into his gun. Kostya will pursue you to the limit. Not because you did something to me, but because I wanted you to do something to me. I always thought*

I had to punish my whole family for letting you have the life at their side that should have been mine, but it's not true, it's completely untrue, I've understood that, Miqa, I know it now. It was never about that. I wanted to punish you because you drove me away. Because you didn't need me as I did you.

Because you didn't go sniffing like a hound for traces of me when you returned to the house after the holidays, the house I had to leave again when you arrived. Because you had no need of me. How I hated your vain, poetry-infected, gloomy self-sufficiency! How I hated your melancholic passions that had nothing to do with me, that never involved me at all!

No, no, it wasn't jealousy of the grown-ups that made me compete with you; it was jealousy of the grown-ups because they had you and I didn't. Because they were around you and I wasn't. Because you were here, and I was there.

I don't know you, I don't even know what kind of person you are. I don't know why you let people destroy your belief in the world so easily. I don't know whether you prefer raspberry or strawberry jam, Miqa, but I wanted to know that and many other things as well. But you always made it clear to me that I was unworthy of your dreams and wishes, that I didn't deserve your affection. Yet I put up with it all, I left everything to you, I left my whole world behind for you and went away.

Why wasn't it enough for you?

Why couldn't you at least have pretended to me, that wretched afternoon, that you liked me — a little, just a tiny little bit? Why did you have to display all your scorn, all your disgust, with such brutality? Why did you have to make it so blatantly obvious that even when I was offered up to you, gift-wrapped, I still wasn't worthy of your acceptance?

Tell me, admit it to me at last, yell it out: tell me how much you've hated me, all your life. How fervently you've wished me dead — totally, utterly annihilated! How hard you've tried all your life to suppress this hatred. To play the good, docile, perfect boy, the victim! Please, do me that favour, release me, say it to my face, do it, Miqa —

'I want my child to be able to be proud of me one day!'

Miqa was arguing with Christine. Elene, who had been lost in thought, was suddenly wide awake.

'Your child?'

'Yes, my child!' snapped Miqa defiantly.

'I didn't know ... I'm sorry,' she murmured.

'How would you have known?'

'Is it the woman from Mtskheta?'

Why did she feel so defenceless, so stupid? What had become of all her intentions?

'The woman from Mtskheta? Yes, that's the one. Her name's Lana, by the way!'

'Miqa, calm down, please. I won't have you using that tone!' Christine planted herself in front of him. His expression changed abruptly. Suddenly he was his old, obedient self, the melancholy, docile Miqa of his childhood. She put her arm around his shoulders, as if to remind him of who he was, what was at stake. What … Yes, this was precisely what was at stake. This round wooden table, where he had just sat down again, because she wanted him to; her butter biscuits, the black tea, not too hot, not too cold, with a slice of lemon. This life with her, this self-contained life with this old, veiled woman, stoically defying her age in her tight-fitting dress. Yes, this was what it came down to; but something had gone awry.

And once again Elene saw the absolute harmony between the two of them that had brought tears to her eyes all those years ago, in Christine's old house on Vera Hill, when she had sat on the branch of a tree and secretly spied into Christine's bedroom without being able, at the time, to understand what she saw. The way he had combed her hair, the way he had gazed at her, with such adoration. Wasn't she too old to receive such looks? How scandalous, how provocative this picture had seemed to her then. And it had been precisely this intimacy, the self-assurance with which she put her arm around his shoulders, the knowledge of something that could not, must not, be named, that had brought the tears to her eyes.

'I'm happy for you both.'

Elene's voice was barely audible. All of a sudden she wanted to get away, to flee; she didn't want to be at the mercy of these feelings any more, they were hardening into a lump in her throat. She didn't want to know anything any more, didn't want to look for any more answers. It would all be so much easier if she could accept the way things were and just carry on.

And yes, she should have said to him: 'Flee, drop everything and get out of here, stay away from me, stay away from Christine, stay away from all that reminds you of my family, start all over again, start your own story, go, run, forget your film and the past and that afternoon, and think of your child, a child with another woman who shielded you from blows for which I was responsible — don't ever look back again!' But could she say it to him?

No: she would let him walk, fall, into the abyss. Because it still felt so good to see him wrestle with himself, with his inability to become what he wanted to be. Yes, my friend, we'll walk this path to the end together, together, my Miqa! And all because it felt so good to see that he had not got what he wanted, either, when he ignored her pain and numbed his desires and pressed her body under his, and made clear to her with every second of it that she was not worth loving.

> Whoever wants to help the waverers must first stop wavering himself.
>
> VLADIMIR LENIN

In July, Miqa was arrested and charged. Just three days earlier, in a dark brown suit that was decidedly too warm, he had paid a visit to the Tbilisi registry office with Lana — wearing a smart, cream-coloured two-piece suit and a white rose in her hair — and two film school friends who still dared to act as witnesses, and had married the mother of his child.

The charge against him was 'misappropriation of state property', and he was also accused of 'anti-Soviet agitation and propaganda'. He was initially taken into custody in Ortachala. The trial date was set for the late autumn, and a special commission was set up to track down the film reels. Both Christine's apartment and Andro's house were searched. As the footage seemed to have vanished off the face of the earth, the lawyer gave neither Christine nor Lana any hope that Miqa would be released any time soon, because as long as the film reels were just a dangerous rumour, the state prosecutor could assume they did indeed contain something truly outrageous. He was also able to imply that the accused had shown an unwillingness to cooperate, which made his situation even worse.

When handing over a *peredacha* — the name given to packages smuggled to inmates by bribing the prison staff — the intermediary Christine had engaged was struck by the alarming state Miqa was in. The boy looked terrible, he said. Apparently he was having difficulty coping with life in jail; the other prisoners, most of them the worst sort of criminals, were giving him a very hard time; he was suffering from the unspeakable conditions: in short, the boy was not someone who could handle prison, and they had to get him out of there as fast as possible; he was at risk of both mental and physical breakdown.

★

'I think I made a mistake.' Lana didn't dare raise her eyes, didn't dare look at him directly. In the visitors' room the guard stood leaning against the wall, wheezing and trying to look as absent as possible. She leaned towards him across the scratched table.

'What are you trying to say?'

Even his voice had changed. As if it had renounced all interest in the outside world.

'You've got to get out of here! It's imperative, Miqa. Christine's right. You're not someone who can cope with a place like this.'

But before her lips could form another sentence, Miqa sat upright on his chair, shifted a little closer to her, and whispered: 'No way. Whatever happens, you will do *nothing*. Do you understand me? We're going to see this through to the end.'

'To the end? We're about to have a baby!'

'You knew that back then!'

'I don't want to take the blame for this.'

'Do as I tell you. That's all I want from you. I'd rather you told me what they think of me. Have you talked to the others? What are the lecturers saying?'

His face lit up for a moment. As if that was what mattered. As if none of this counted — his current state, his misery, his fear — only the opinion others had of him.

'They … they think you're a hero. They've even started a petition. The whole institute is up in arms. They've plastered your photo all over the building. They're planning to send an open letter to the public prosecutor's office. Even some of the lecturers are standing with the students and saying it's absurd to arrest you over a film that doesn't exist.'

She didn't know herself why she told him this. Perhaps because he wanted to hear it; it gave him the strength to endure it all. Because she was exaggerating: there were no photos of him, the petition had come to nothing, and the few lecturers who had initially supported him had been keeping their mouths shut since he'd been taken into custody. She had to keep this hope alive for him; but the more her belly swelled beneath her clothes, the more she despaired, the more senseless the whole undertaking seemed to her. The less she understood herself.

She'd tried to make contact with the film collective to get some moral support, but no one wanted to talk to her. People kept their distance, hung up when she called yet again. How could she ever have believed that his absence would be easier for her to bear than his lack of courage, his giving up? That she would rather have a director at her side than a father for her child?

★

Stasia had already laid the table and was waiting for her guests with great excitement.

'I've persuaded him. He's going to sit down with us. He'll hear you,' she whispered to her sister and Andro as they passed. *He'll hear you!* It took all of Christine's self-restraint to bite back a caustic remark. *He'll hear you!* As if he were the lord of the manor and they his serfs.

The table they sat at was laid as if for a feast. Nana had taken the children to Vake Park, and Elene was wandering around somewhere down in the village.

After about half an hour, Kostya appeared in his dressing gown with a thick scarf wound about his neck. He nodded absently to them both. No handshake, no embrace. Better that way, thought Christine. She patted Andro's hand under the table. Andro had come to town from the village at Christine's behest especially for this meeting. The sight of him filled Christine with alarm. He had gone bald, only his magnificent beard glowed white, and you couldn't miss the schnapps blotches on his cheeks. The hard skin on his hands was covered in boils — the price for his loyal devotion, for all the many heads of Marx, Engels, and Lenin.

'Apologies for my appearance. I can't seem to shake this flu; it's very annoying.' Kostya took a seat at the table. As if what he was wearing was the most important thing about this meeting.

The silence weighed heavily on them. Stasia's attempts at family small talk got nowhere. Andro pushed the food around his plate, and Christine seemed to have lost her appetite as well; she, too, held back while Stasia blathered something about the four village girls who had recently started coming to her for ballet lessons. Kostya sat stiffly at the end of the table, leaning back in his chair, like an observer of the scene who had been forbidden to contribute or intervene in any way. It was Christine who finally spoke up and began to voice her thoughts and suspicions about what had happened to Miqa.

The thin crust of civilised behaviour was soon scratched away and primitive energies released: an unimagined delight in destruction and relish for self-sabotage. They battered each other with words, fired sentences, wounded with revelations. And soon the forbidden name could no longer be avoided:

the ghost of Kitty was invoked, and a bonfire of memories lit in her honour. They vied for her love; they threw the scraps of all their memories into a magician's hat and mixed them together. And this feast of terrible memories would have been allowed to rage much longer if Kostya had not abandoned the path of conjecture and yelled out, in a threatening voice, one fact that massacred all others and turned Andro's grief for one son into a tragedy of two.

'You talk about her as if it were a logical consequence that my sister had to go away, that she couldn't go on living here! As if she made a free decision to leave us and her country! Have you ever thought about the life she would have had if you hadn't betrayed your homeland and she hadn't been carrying your son in her belly?'

Andro didn't understand. He had reached the limits of his physical capacity some time earlier, as no alcoholic drinks were on offer; he waggled his head like a Vanka Vstanka roly-poly toy, scratched his beard, and looked to Stasia for help. He searched for words, stammered. His ignorance was painful to behold. Kostya, coughing, also looked around him in surprise. Christine wondered whether he really was unaware that, after all these years, Andro still didn't know, was still groping in the dark, or whether he had planned this revenge. Would he pull the emergency brake and bring the train to a halt before it hurtled into the abyss? Seconds later, though, Kostya had shaken off his momentary puzzlement, and continued, undeterred.

'Andro — you must have wondered, didn't you?' He seemed to be making a huge effort to restrain himself, as words like 'parasite', 'traitor', 'bastard', and 'deserter' did not fall from his lips once that afternoon. He had opted for a crueller weapon: incontrovertible facts.

'You were irresponsible enough to believe the Nazis were our future. And that's why they abducted your beloved, and her child —'

'Kostya, please!'

Christine's voice was tentative, as if she weren't sure whether to stop her nephew or let him go on speaking. But while she was still grappling with her indecision, Kostya had already decided. He wanted finally to break his feeble yet tenacious enemy.

'They aborted the child — the child you planted in her womb with no thought of what it means to be a man, to bear responsibility for your wife and child, to protect them — even, if necessary, to protect them from yourself. Instead, you threw yourself so pitifully into the role of abused victim that others had no option but to bear that burden in your place!'

How skilfully Kostya placed every emphasis, every pause. As if he had been practising for this conversation all his life. An eerie silence fell, broken only by the ticking of the clock. You could practically hear the grass outside breathing.

*

Andro had followed Christine up to the Green House in the hope that Kostya would get his son out of the place he had sent him to. His life would surely have continued as imperceptibly as it had for years, indifferent, quiet, and brooding, leaving tracks he carefully obliterated behind him in the sure and certain belief that nothing in his life was worthy of preservation.

Perhaps he could not have prevented anything; could not, with his scabbed palms, have protected anything; perhaps he would not even have managed to convince his son that *his* life, at least, was worth preserving. But he would have tried — with what strength he had left he would have tried, if this atrocity, buried in a schoolyard long ago, had not robbed him of his last remaining shreds of empathy and the ability to battle through each day simply by continuing to exist.

Gradually, though, the ground split open. Time was combed the wrong way, the sequence of events shifted; misfortune was like a black bird's beating wing that momentarily brushed them all as it descended.

Christine knelt before him, pleaded with him, clasped his hands in hers, but he didn't want to stay, he didn't want to have to save or preserve anything any more. He went home, to his strong schnapps and the busts of Lenin. It was so good to be able to replace the present with the past.

Why hadn't she told him? Why hadn't she written to him? Why hadn't he known anything about her pregnancy?

He drank, and punched holes in the wall with his aching fists.

The nights carved bloody images on his chest.

He couldn't breathe.

He reached for a hammer and smashed it down on the big head of Lenin that the administration building had rejected three years earlier on the grounds that Lenin's nose was insufficiently distinguished.

He went on drinking.

The neighbours came running, knocked, and called out to him. He bolted the doors. He entrenched himself, and put his life on rewind.

> We won our peace,
> Clear days and dear.
> You're weeping? — I'm
> not worth a tear.
>
> ANNA AKHMATOVA

In another world, in another country, in another life, a woman woke from an uneasy sleep and sat up in bed. There was no getting back to sleep now, so she padded, barefoot, to the living room, took from her drinks cabinet the most expensive bottle of whisky she could find, and poured herself a glass. She didn't turn on the light. She was alone. She stood there staring into a darkness pierced by light from the streetlamps.

She felt a constriction in her chest, as if someone were holding her heart in their fist and squeezing it continuously. She watched as her pale, bare skin was illuminated by the play of light and shadow from the few cars driving past, their headlights sweeping across her windows.

She felt so tired all of a sudden. And then she remembered the dream that had woken her. She had dreamed of a young boy with curly blond hair. She saw Andro's face, an Andro as yet unscarred by the war, who carved wonderful angels out of wood. Andro, who had counted her eyelashes and smothered the palms of her hands with kisses, who had brushed locks of hair off her face and promised her that he would never change.

She knocked back the oily brown liquid in one gulp. For precisely seven nights now her mind had only been able to formulate one single thought: *I want to go home*. It was the only wish she had. The only one she was left with. *I want to go home* pulsed inside her like a gaping cut in her skin; *I want to go home* screamed inside her, scratched at her entrails, wanted to be shouted out, wanted to be fulfilled.

She had had so much happiness. She had been showered with such an outrageous amount of happiness, after unhappiness had smashed her into a thousand little pieces. Had she put herself back together again? Did she have a face again when she looked in the mirror?

All the cheering and applause, and all the songs, all the people who had believed in and supported her. She felt such gratitude — and incredulity, even now, after all the years of recognition. Incredulity that she had been given this chance, after the world had initially presented itself to her as a black and bottomless pit.

Was it her own life she was living? Were they really her songs? Or had she left her real life behind, surrendered it when she departed for a new world? She had snuck like a thief into someone else's life — the woman from Luxembourg, yes, the woman from Luxembourg, perhaps. *I want to go home!*

Or was another thought there, too? Was there something else? Yes: lurking behind every pulsating *I want to go home* were those four letters: *Fred.*

Fred, who had breathed new life into her, who had kissed her loins, had made her hips swing, who had wrapped her arms around her. Fred, who had promised to go with her to find old Vienna — 'I think it makes no sense whatsoever to go back to that Nazi stronghold, but fine, if you're absolutely set on it, we will.'

How nice it had been, making plans for a new beginning in the supposed certainty that she and Fred had been through hell and survived.

Leafing through property brochures. A lovely new apartment with a spacious studio for her friend. Fred telling her which of Vienna's districts were most attractive, and Kitty falling in love with them. How right it had felt, back then, this idea of a return to the future.

And then her American tour! Oh God, that had been good! Kitty smiled, poured herself some more whisky. The quiet grace with which Amy had come back into her life. That reception in New York! What a high they'd been on, after her first American concert, in that trendy factory loft in Brooklyn. Was it Brooklyn? What did it matter now?

Dancing with Amy in her dressing room. Amy — slightly annoyed — agreeing to Fred joining them on tour. The reunion at JFK; Fred's laughter. How captivating her beloved barfly had looked in that sea of people at the airport: crazy woman, egocentric ignoramus. How delicious the beer had been that they drank, later, in Greenwich Village. The walks in Central Park; the skyscrapers.

Her concerts had been well attended; always those crowds of people in the darkness, strafed by bright spotlights, singing along, fervent, quiet, and melancholy, then loud again and full of anger, singing against everything in their lives for which they had no songs. Amy sold the song rights; radio and television stations queued up for Kitty's sad Soviet story. 'The icon of the Left, the protest singer of Wenceslas Square!' Amy used to cry, guffawing with laughter, head thrown back, a silly plastic flower in her hair.

And as Kitty drained her second glass, she thought of the hotel rooms they had staggered back to, exhausted, after the concerts: Boston, Baltimore, Detroit, Miami, San Francisco, Las Vegas — yes, there too, in a little club that didn't really look the part in that city flooded with light and madness. Atlanta, Michigan, cities whose names she no longer recalled (too western for her ears, which gave everything an eastern accent), and, again and again, New York.

She had wanted her Vienna, and she had come to America. Her own, personal, western happiness. Had this happiness been a stolen one, too? Oh yes, those hotel rooms. Kitty shook her head. Images of the countless hotel beds, and her red-haired tightrope walker in them with her. The two of them had provoked the world too much with their happiness, had laughed in its face too long! How could the memory of their bodies between those high ceilings and plump pillows still be so clear? As if it were yesterday. That body, made of air and sorcery; the tiny red hairs in her armpit, her sharp knees, her skilled hands. The memory of desire was worst of all. Kitty's body seemed to have forgotten those caresses with such cruel ease, even as her mind still clung to them for all it was worth.

It was starting to grow light outside. A sunbeam cut like a dagger across the sky.

How could something feel so illicitly good, and then turn from one moment to the next into such unbearable pain? And how was it that now, when it was all over, when the only thought in her head was *I want to go home*, she recalled this happiness with such unflinching clarity? Without the woman who seemed to say to everyone, with unshakable confidence: I did it. I conquered death. Yes: I made it.

★

The pressure in her chest had eased. She looked out onto her balcony, which was crammed with plants. How often Amy had told her she should find herself a better flat, or even a townhouse; but this place was more than enough for her. The more space she had, the more rooms, the more she would have felt like a guest, a thief who had slipped into someone else's life.

She was a little cold, but too lethargic to get up and fetch herself a blanket.

She wanted to breathe. Just breathe quietly. Fred had never been faithful, she had just been loyal in her own way; and she'd known that, she had always known that. So why hadn't she been able to cope when confronted with the facts? Fred was inconsistent, she was reckless, she never walked on safe ground, she refused to justify her actions, she didn't want to be either healed or saved, she needed the intoxication that was her medicine.

And why couldn't all these countless postcards of happiness, filed away so neatly in her head, chase away the picture of that new-build flat in Camden? The flat she had spent more than four hours looking for because she hadn't had the exact address, one week before she completed the purchase of an apartment right on Vienna's Mariahilfer Strasse. Desire may not burn itself into the cells of the body, but the cells of her brain remembered every single second of the two or three minutes she had spent in that unfamiliar flat.

An unfurnished space, apparently still unoccupied, with a party in full swing; a place to which several phone calls had led her in search of Fred. She remembered — so precisely — every single line of the Stones' 'Hide Your Love', which was playing in the background. The people squatting on the floor, the smell of fresh paint, and smoke, and something else that seemed to her both familiar and utterly alien. Grinning people in hippie gear, stuck in the past; a bunch of good-for-nothings, spongers, the kind to which Fred had always been magically drawn.

Yes, her brain cells had registered it all so precisely: wandering through rooms full of bodies in search of her renegade, fickle, endangered girlfriend; repeatedly asking people high on themselves whether they had seen Fred Lieblich — then finding her, her very own Marlene Dietrich from *The Blue Angel*, and seeing, on her lap, one of those girls who seek out the laps of others: draped in Indian jewellery, uncombed hair down to her waist, ripped jeans, shimmying her small breasts in Fred's face.

Shrinking back; fighting her way through the throng, through the loud music that was suddenly a torment to her, and recognising in all those faces something far worse than the presence of the unknown girl, worse than Fred's arm round her waist, her glazed expression. Her delayed movements. It had taken only seconds for Kitty to recognise her brutal defeat in the battle with the yellow-brown liquid that flowed through the veins of her angel and the Indian hippie.

The next day, with Amy's help, she had packed Fred's things, rented a room for her near Lea Bridge, put the key in an envelope for her, and left it with the caretaker of the block. Then she changed the lock on her front door.

She stopped answering Fred's calls. Napkins covered in Fred's illegible handwriting appeared in her letterbox; she threw them in the bin without even glancing at them, and once, when Fred lay in wait for her and followed her down the street, she flagged down a taxi to escape her.

That was six months ago. Since then, Fred had vanished from her life, and even the otherwise well-informed Amy had no news of her.

She did not, of course, complete the purchase of the apartment in Vienna. Several concerts and radio performances were cancelled, and since that time she had not written a single song.

On Amy's advice, Kitty bought herself a cottage between Eastbourne and the magical Seven Sisters cliffs, and every day she planned to retreat there. But she couldn't even rouse herself to do that. The only thought that preoccupied her was *I want to go home.*

> Visit the Soviet Union, before it visits you.
>
> SOVIET IDIOM

Christine witnessed Miqa growing more uncommunicative, more absent with every visit, as if he were indifferent to his own fate. And in October, when I could already say seven words and Mirian Eristavi — known from the start as Miro — first saw the light of day, weighing in at 3,900 grams and fit as a fiddle, with variegated eyes, as if he couldn't decide on just one colour, Christine first saw on Miqa the marks of physical violence: a conspicuous blue-black bruise under his right eye and a leg he seemed to be dragging behind him. A stupid little fight with one of his cellmates, no more than that; she had nothing to fear, he told her. And with forced cheerfulness he asked after his son, wanting to know where Lana was going to live with the baby.

'It's very draughty in Lana's mother's apartment, and apparently there's mould in the bathroom; they'll stay with me for the time being, of course, until you get out. She has to finish her thesis this year, I'm sure she's told you. Her mother and I will help her. Her mother has diabetes, did you know that?'

Christine kept chattering mindlessly, anything to fill the silence. Miqa nodded at her, but his thoughts seemed to be elsewhere.

'Oh, the little boy is so gorgeous; you'll see him soon! He looks like you, but that might change, I'm telling you, you never really know with babies, they change from one hour to the next. The poor thing has colic at night, I'm afraid, and he cries a lot, but I —'

'I would have so liked to have children with you,' he said suddenly, with a glance at the guard, who was immersed in a newspaper. Since Christine had slipped him a few extra banknotes, he'd stopped being such a stickler about visiting times. Christine swallowed, breathed deeply, started nervously massaging her neck.

'You're talking nonsense, and I refuse to have such conversations.'

'I took the wrong path, Christine. I took the wrong path, in everything.

But I promise you I'm going to get out of here.'

There was no mistaking the anxiety in his voice, which he had hidden so well for so long.

'Tell me where to look! Tell me, and we'll get you out of here!' she whispered. 'I beg of you!'

But he just shook his head.

Two weeks later they were told that the prisoner was no longer in the cells: he'd been transferred to the adjoining prison hospital for a while because of 'kidney problems'.

★

'You two are going to drive there and fetch him. He doesn't reply to my letters, he won't answer the phone, he doesn't leave the house and won't open the door to anyone. I've got enough to worry about with Miqa: I have to try to get him transferred, I have to speak to the lawyer. He's locked up in there with a bunch of hardened criminals, he doesn't belong there, they know that, and they're taking their anger out on him! Go and bring him back to Tbilisi. Otherwise he's going to drink himself to death. I can't take care of everything.'

Lana stared sulkily at the wall, and Elene poked at the wooden floor with the toe of her shoe.

'Christine, I can drive there on my own ...' Lana tried to object.

'Elene's the one with the car, and you won't get him away from there on your own!' Christine's tone slipped. 'I'll look after Miro.'

Elene wasn't keen on spending six hours in a car with this woman in silence, but she didn't dare defy Christine, so the next day at dawn she parked outside the entrance to Christine's block and opened the car door for Lana, who settled herself in the passenger seat with a stony expression.

Autumn had already descended on the hills around Tbilisi, and they drove through thick fog as they left the city behind. Elene switched on the radio; it was tuned to some random station, and Lana tried to find something more suitable. Elene complained about the music until Lana was forced to make some comment about her own musical tastes. From favourite groups they moved on to favourite films; from favourite films they got onto childhood diseases and vaccinations; from vaccinations to their children and the challenges of being a new mother. By the time they got to Rekha the ice was broken, and when they stopped for a break and treated themselves to a meal in a rundown roadside café, at least Elene didn't feel threatened any more.

The steep, winding, partially unpaved roads continued to crawl upwards. They reached the mountain village as darkness fell. The place was unfamiliar to Elene, but Lana seemed to know her way around. They soon reached the little stone house, part of Miqa's late mother's dowry, a simple one-storey building with a squeaky gate. They called out to Andro and knocked, but there was no reply. As the door was locked, they decided to go back to the inn they had just driven past and wait there.

Later, when they returned to the house, it was already pitch dark. Only the white mountain peaks shone in the blackness, disguised as stars. No one answered this time, either. An old woman peered out of the house next door and asked what they wanted. Elene introduced Lana as Andro's daughter-in-law.

They should go in round the back, through the kitchen door, the old woman advised them. The man of the house was probably sleeping off his drink.

As they stepped over the threshold and into the kitchen they were hit by an overpowering stench of unwashed plates, rotting leftovers, and alcohol. They groped about in the dark for a bit until they found a light switch that worked. Filth everywhere: the rubbish hadn't been taken out for a long time, there were empty bottles in every corner, and dust lay over everything. Blocks of stone were piled up in the corridor, and broken stone noses and ears lay around on the floor; Lenin's mouth and Marx's distinctive beard were recognisable.

Mountains of clothes, more and more empty bottles, none of them labelled, piles of books, sacks of gypsum and metal. Suddenly Elene stopped. She was holding a small, framed picture in her hand.

'What's the matter?' asked Lana. Elene went on staring at the picture, spellbound. In the frame was a newspaper cutting, a black-and-white photograph.

'Who's that?'

Lana came and stood beside Elene.

'That's my aunt.'

'Your aunt? I didn't know you had an aunt.'

'Yes. My aunt lives in the West. She's a famous singer.'

Andro was lying in a room that looked as if it had once been a bedroom, snoring.

'He needs to sleep off the drink first, Elene — though he doesn't exactly look as if he's sleeping easily. Tomorrow morning we'll make him get in the car. Come on, help me! We're going to clear up!'

Resolutely, Lana set to work. She closed the bedroom door behind her, pushed Elene into the kitchen, turned on all the lights, and found a broom, some cloths, a bucket, and a piece of soap. Soon all the useless and filthy objects started piling up in the yard.

Afterwards, as they stood there in the darkened yard, Lana, hugging herself tightly, looked up at the sky. Millions of stars had suddenly appeared up there; they seemed so close, as if trying to form a diadem above their heads. As if the night were trying to bend a little lower over the Earth and listen to it.

'They're not here,' said Lana tonelessly.

'What aren't here?' asked Elene.

'I've turned the whole house upside down. Oh God, I have to find them. We have to find them!'

Elene stared at her incredulously. Then it dawned on her.

'Don't tell me the reels have been here all this time! Don't tell me you've known all along where they are!'

'They *were* —' Lana corrected her '— in a black box with "Miqa toys" on it. A black wooden box! Look for it!'

They crawled around the floor, looked under furniture, pushed wardrobes aside, inspected drawers. It was only after midnight that Elene heard a cry in the room next door and hurried in. Lana stood in the middle of the room with her back to her, gripping a small black box in both hands and trembling from head to foot; at first Elene couldn't tell whether it was with joy or despair. Lana turned to her and she saw her tear-streaked face.

And Elene couldn't help it: all of a sudden she felt incredibly close to this woman towards whom she had always felt a certain antipathy. She understood so well her despair, her guilt, her hatred, and her sense of rejection, too. Suddenly she felt compassion for this brusque woman who happened to have become pregnant by the man who had once made her, Elene, pregnant, as well. Seeing her like this, standing in the middle of the half-dark room with the box of film in her hand, trembling and crying, brought Elene an unimagined sense of relief. She had witnessed a dangerous disclosure, and any other vaguely clear-thinking person might have reproached Lana, said that she had acted selfishly, that she hadn't thought of saving her husband, that she had ruined his future. But Elene was incapable of putting even one such sentence to her.

Seeing Elene, Lana became aware of the shameful position she was in. She awoke from her trance, put the box down on the floor, and the two of them sat beside it.

'You won't be able to change anything now. It'll only make things worse. You won't be doing him a favour. And when it gets out that you knew where the film was, they'll treat you like a traitor. I don't know for sure what your reasons were for withholding this box, but I do know for sure that it won't make the slightest difference if you bring the film back now.' Elene spoke slowly and carefully, weighing every word.

'What are you talking about? He's being beaten. He's being subjected to harassment. He's suffering. He … First it was just the film, this bloody film, this ridiculous belief it could change something. Then it was the baby; I thought, our baby needs parents who are special. Then he was the one telling me I should stand firm. He'd fallen in love with this ridiculous idea. And I was so stupid — so intolerably stupid.'

Lana drew her arm right back and slapped herself, hard. But the slap didn't make anything right; it couldn't undo anything now.

'You have no idea …' Lana sobbed. She slapped her face over and over again. Elene didn't try to stop her. She wouldn't deprive her fellow sufferer of at least the illusion of relief.

There were countless versions of the truth, and as soon as you put them in your mouth they distorted themselves, crumbled like stale bread, leaving only an insipid taste on the tongue. In the end, Elene opted for what was probably the most incontestable truth when she told Lana, 'He doesn't love you. And he won't love you, no matter what you do.'

The next day they forced Andro into the car, still stupefied, and drove back to the city. The black box also went with them, though after that night Elene wasn't sure what Lana was planning to do with it.

It was a conundrum they were not given time to resolve. In Christine's apartment they found a note addressed to Elene. Miqa had been hospitalised in prison again; he needed to be transferred to a safer wing immediately; Elene must drive home and talk to her father. *Everything* was at stake.

Soviet Union — Staggering Success!

PRAVDA

'Hey, it's me. I think you've overdone it a bit …? What do you mean, it's no longer under your control? You're with the *militsiya*, of course you have control. What do you mean, *unconscious*? You should have taken care who you locked him up with. What I wanted? Did I ask you to beat him like a piece of meat? You disappoint me, my friend. It seems I'll have to deal with this *personally*. No, thank you. No, you've straightened out quite enough already. Why do I have to do all the thinking for everyone? What sort of rabble are you that you can't even add two and two together? Of course he can't defend himself; I mean, he didn't come from the delinquents' camp! You've got his file there in front of you. Fine; so tell your colleagues I don't want any further *proceedings*. Tell them to forget the whole thing. I don't want him to croak in there. When's the trial? Fine, so we'll wait out these three weeks and then … they'll let him go.'

Elene, leaning against her father's study door, overheard scraps of this phone conversation, but she couldn't even cry any more, although the tears were choking her.

★

He went up to the guards, showed his pass, and entered the grey hospital building with its barred windows. The big guard stared indifferently into space; two others were playing cards and smoking cheap Astras. When Kostya finally came out again, the darkness masked his face and it was hard to read his expression. He stopped in front of Christine.

'He's in a coma,' he said bluntly. 'There was a fight.'

'He was beaten into a coma?' Her mind refused to process this information.

'They … tried to strangle him.'

She hid her face in her hands.

'The doctors say they don't know how long his oxygen supply was cut off.'

'I want to go to him.'

'I don't think that's —'

'You're going to take me in there right now.'

'It'll take some time. I'll have to make a few calls first. He is a prisoner, after all.'

'A prisoner who was strangled without a single guard coming to his aid!'

★

Miqa spent five days in a coma before his ventilator was switched off. He looked as if he were asleep. The cuts and bruises had faded. Andro collapsed in the hospital corridor; Stasia rocked him back and forth as she had when he was little, as his mother had when she was still alive. Christine lay motionless, stretched over the dead body; she was admonished several times by the hospital staff, but no one dared forcibly drag her away from Miqa's corpse.

Only Lana screamed and kept slapping her hands against her thighs.

And when Stasia looked up, Sopio Eristavi was standing in the blue light in the middle of the hospital corridor. She stood there as if she had just dropped by to say hello, for no particular reason. A brief, casual visit. Stasia began to walk, on frail, unsteady legs, towards her eternally young friend.

'Now don't act as if you didn't expect to see me here,' said Sopio.

'I've made a mess of everything. Ever since you've been gone everything's just gone down the drain.' Stasia's lips were moving silently. 'He was only twenty-two, my God, just twenty-two. I haven't been able to hold on to anything, everything's trickled away, vanished, as if it fell through too coarse a sieve.'

'Oh, Tasiko, you incorrigible fatalist.'

'What should I have done? What?'

'Dance, Taso. You should have danced.'

'Who are you talking to, *Deda*?'

Kostya's voice echoed down the corridor, interrupting the ghostly dialogue. Stasia looked around. The corridor was empty. But her son had called her *Mother* again.

> Hearts of fire creates love desire
> High and higher to your place on the throne.
>
> EARTH, WIND & FIRE

Kitty was holding her breath. She couldn't believe it. She had done it. At last his voice was going to acquire a face. She could already hear him approaching. No, she wasn't ready to turn round just yet. *Breathe, breathe calmly, don't look*, she reminded herself. The footsteps came closer and closer, approaching the bench in Hyde Park where they'd agreed to have their first meeting — yes, it was unbelievable, their first meeting, after all these years!

She hadn't been able to breathe calmly all morning. Ever since she had tracked him down she'd been incapable of thinking about anything else. The possibility of putting a face to his voice had stopped her sleeping, thrown her thoughts into confusion, had even taken away her ability just to breathe quietly.

Even when — punctual as ever — he sat down beside her on the bench, she went on staring straight ahead; but out of the corner of her eye she caught a glimpse of his diminutive stature. She'd always imagined him to be tall — taller than her, anyway. A grey pinstripe suit — yes, this was more or less how she had pictured his taste in clothes — his glasses — had she imagined him wearing glasses? — his bald head — it had never even occurred to her that he might be bald.

'Kitty?'

Yes, it was his voice. Except that now it was right beside her. She felt cold sweat break out on her forehead. She must control herself. Turn her face towards him slowly, carefully. Nothing hasty or loud; nothing that would attract attention.

'Hello, Giorgi.'

Her voice let her down. She turned to him, taking great pains to conceal her excitement behind a smile. His face … his round, unprepossessing face seemed familiar. How could that be? Was his physical presence being coloured by his voice? This voice that had now acquired a body? Impossible! She was definitely seeing him for the first time.

'So, what now?'

He gave her a gentle, protective smile. A smile that matched the countless telephone conversations she had had with him over so many years. That soft, velvety baritone, its deep, soothing pitch, no scratches, no scars. And so familiar it sent shivers down her spine.

He smelled of aftershave lotion: citrus. It would take time for his real face to replace the phantoms of her imagination. She must imprint him on her memory now. Every single feature.

When she didn't reply he asked again, more seriously this time: 'How did you find me?'

'I hired a private detective. Yes — it was that simple, like in a *film noir*. That's exactly the kind of guy he was. He didn't have a raincoat, but he did wear a hat. And he assured me that anyone could be found, unless they didn't exist or were already dead. And I assured him that you existed. That you even lived in the same city as me. Yes, I knew that, Giorgi. I knew that right from the start. But it took him a long time. He said you were *a pro*.'

Now at last she was able to laugh, and the pressure, that terrible pressure in her chest, eased. 'And the last time, do you remember, Giorgi — oh God, I have to get used to that name. I'd never have guessed that name. There's still so much I have to get used to. And — well, I asked you to write me a letter, like in the good old days. Different phone box every time, he told me. So I had to ask you for this letter. And you didn't refuse. Luckily. And then my *film noir* hero somehow traced the letter back. And found you. I didn't want to know any more details. The only thing that mattered to me was your name. Then two days ago the call came: "I've found your man." That's what he said: *your man*. At first I thought he must have got mixed up. But then he said: "His name is Giorgi Alania. He works in the Soviet embassy in London, in the culture section." And suddenly it all made sense. The trip to Prague, and ... I knew then that it was you. And you know the rest. I just called up the embassy. I went to a phone box, incidentally, and called from there; I didn't dare call your number from my flat. And there really was an Alania in the culture section. And before you even said, "Can I help you?" I knew I'd found you. I've found you.'

'It's extremely dangerous, Kitty, what you did.'

'You have to understand! My life ... I had to find you. And I have to go home.'

It was only now that she noticed his hands were trembling. He was also avoiding looking at her directly. She shot him a casual, fleeting glance. He was wearing horn-rimmed spectacles, an unusual frame with ivory-coloured ornamentation. Behind the lenses, those sad-looking eyes. She wanted to touch him. The receding chin. The pallid skin. For a fraction of a second, he seemed to have no control over the situation, something that in all those years had never happened to him; it was as if he were somehow in need of protection. He, too, seemed to be longing for physical contact, for something that would push him to the limit, tear him out of his world.

'No one must find out that we've been in contact. It would put people in danger. Including people who are important to you.'

There was something about the way he was trying to maintain his image as her protector that made her sad.

'Visit me. Come to my flat. I want to see you. I want to get to know you!'

She jumped up from the bench, breathless. She couldn't bear his physical presence, this voice made flesh, any longer; she turned and walked away. Over the years she had stored up so many words for him, but was no longer capable of speaking a single one. She was sure, though, that now he had finally dared to emerge from his hiding place he wouldn't just disappear back into the darkness of anonymity. He would come to her. He had to!

She would ask him once, one last time, for a favour — no — for his help. She would convince him. Somehow. By any means at her disposal. What exactly those means were she didn't yet know; but he would not be able to deny her this one wish.

And when, five days later — it was late, already dark outside — there was a ring at her front door, she knew it was him. She hadn't left her flat since their meeting in Hyde Park. His helplessness when she had jumped up from the bench, his inability to stop her leaving, were sufficient indication to her that he would not be able to turn back. Just by agreeing to their meeting he had broken all of his rules. Now it was time to make new ones.

She took his coat. He polished his glasses nervously on his handkerchief. She fussed about, laid the little magazine table in the living room, rolled out the drinks trolley, forgot something, went to the kitchen, came back, sat down, jumped up again. He looked at the concert photos Amy had had framed and hung on the wall, despite Kitty's objections; he tapped on the glass with his fingertips, smoothed his trousers.

He declined the good whisky and asked for something non-alcoholic. She brought him elderflower cordial; he seemed pleased.

'I don't know where to start,' she said, finally sitting down opposite him on a low plush stool.

'Nor do I,' he said, and tried to smile. The familiar sound of his voice was reassuring, but it also worried her, because Kitty was all too aware that the person sitting before her was a stranger. She touched her lips to the whisky glass and fixed her gaze on Giorgi Alania.

★

At this point, Brilka, I have to jump back to the past, to the year 1942, after the Wehrmacht had invaded the Soviet Union and Giorgi Alania, a graduate of the Frunze Higher Naval School specialising in shipbuilding and engineering, was posted to the Amur Shipbuilding Plant at the farthest eastern tip of Russia, near the Sea of Japan. Thus Alania was lucky enough to avoid the war; he remained in the sub-zero temperatures of that inhospitable industrial town, surrounded by haggard, silent workers with furrowed faces who couldn't think of anything better to do with themselves at the end of the working day than to hurry back to their barracks to drink their home-brew.

He remained an outsider among his comrades. They were all either much older, or had different temperaments, different lives, and wanted different things to young Alania, who spent his free time keeping a close eye on news of the war, going for long walks beside stormy rivers, writing long, emotional letters to his best friend Kostya Jashi — in the first few years, at least — and, in the evenings, reading Jules Verne or Mayne Reid in his barracks by candlelight.

The work wasn't difficult for him. He had a quick and efficient mind. He always had a ready solution for every problem, and over time this won him a certain reputation. People didn't especially like him, but they treated him with respect. In addition to his daily tasks, he constantly occupied himself with new technical challenges, physical activity, reading, and cooking; nonetheless, here at the end of the world he felt cut off from everything, and alien. These feelings had been all too familiar to him as a child, but the intervening Leningrad years at Kostya's side had made him forget them. Now he had to get used to this sad state of affairs again, and his whole being rebelled against it.

He had always been an introvert, but the years in the shipyard, where communication with the outside world was reduced to a minimum and there were no like-minded people, made him an irascible, mistrustful man. He was aware of this insidious regression because he had been so different in Leningrad, with none of the doubts and complexes he'd thought he had overcome. In

Leningrad he had felt that Kostya's energy and confidence, his social ease, had rubbed off on him, encouraging him to be more audacious, to enjoy life, to trust people more. He really missed this friendship, which was perhaps the only effortless one in his life so far.

But in Komsomolsk-on-Amur Alania's self-doubt grew exponentially. He couldn't rid himself of the feeling that he was not worth loving. And the result of this assumption was disastrous failure in his dealings with the opposite sex.

Women seemed to look right through him. He had the most refined manners, could make the most elegant compliments, give the most beautiful presents — nothing helped. At best they rewarded him with a smile, thanked him coquettishly, and went on their way. A solitary date at the town's only 'Pioneer' cinema, with a schoolteacher he had struck up a conversation with on the harbour promenade, ended unhappily. When he put his hand on her shoulder at the climax of the film, the woman brushed it away so abruptly and with such revulsion that he couldn't help feeling disgust at himself.

After this rejection he never made any further attempt to win a woman's heart. But he was unlucky with prostitutes, too. He invited a notorious middle-aged woman with bleached blonde hair, bad teeth, darned stockings, and a strong Siberian accent to his house, and opened one of the better sparkling wines he saved for New Year. The woman got drunk, took off her clothes with absolutely no warning, then, with an expression of vacant indifference, grabbed him between the legs so hard that it hurt and he felt compelled to ask her to leave.

Since then he had felt only shame and mortification when the shipyard workers boasted of their amorous adventures. Over time, he realised that it was impossible for him to desire someone without at least the illusion of being desired and needed himself. That his longing was not for a woman's body, but for that body to need his. As the fatherless child of a single mother, he had been bullied in his village to the point of humiliation. At family gatherings his grandparents had treated him with contempt — no matter how good he was, in spite of all his achievements there was a perennial air of worthlessness, inadequacy, like bad breath, that he simply couldn't shake off. And he knew that this malady had its root in his dishonourable conception.

He became obsessed with this idea.

Perhaps he really was inferior — perhaps he owed his existence merely to an unfortunate *accident* — perhaps his mother really had acted disreputably? Why else was she so stubbornly silent about his progenitor? Why had she refused to pass on this knowledge to him, when it was surely the most natural thing in the world?

He wrote her a letter, formulating his question directly. He had a right to this knowledge, he said; she could not withhold it from him. He was old enough now to learn the truth of his conception. He didn't want to live with the stigma of *father unknown* any longer. He didn't want it branded on his face for all to see.

Months later, the answer reached him. Next time they saw each other, his mother promised, she would tell him everything, face to face; but not in writing, please, she mustn't do that. She promised him.

★

As is usual in stories like these, Brilka, in our story, too — or, in this case, to be precise, in Alania's — it all turned out quite differently. Shortly before the capture of Berlin, Alania received a visit from an elegantly dressed, pipe-smoking gentleman with a gold hammer-and-sickle insignia on the lapel of his black jacket. He had driven up to the shipyard building in a conspicuously large automobile — a rarity in the town — and asked for Giorgi Alania. They sat down in armchairs in the shipyard boss' office, facing each other. The distinguished gentleman introduced himself as an employee of the People's Commissariat for Internal Affairs, or NKVD. He talked for a while in a non-committal way about the importance of domestic political cooperation in these difficult times, the intensification of fighting on the counter-revolutionary fronts, the danger now posed by the capitalist region, and how important it was — more important than ever — to continue the socialist struggle. How watchful one now had to be in all respects — and here he gave Alania a searching look.

He asked questions: the gentleman wanted to know everything, from extremely personal matters to Alania's attitude towards his duty to the Motherland.

'Both the Frunze Higher Naval School and the Comrade Shipyard Director have given you outstanding recommendations. You were also, if I've ascertained this correctly, active in the Sokhumi Komsomol in your youth. Exemplary, really exemplary, Comrade Alania.'

Puffing on his pipe, the man nodded his bull-like head in approval.

'Excuse me, I don't quite understand … What can I do for you, if I might ask?' Alania was disconcerted.

'Well, the Party, of course, Comrade, the Party. Now, more than ever, the country needs good men, loyal to their homeland. Now that the war is won, the work begins in earnest. To think that the war is the end of everything would be a disastrous mistake. You're not in the union, which might be looked upon with disapproval in some quarters, but perhaps a good word can be put in for you nonetheless.'

Giorgi was baffled. How was it, then, that they had come looking for him, of all people? He was confused. He had been drifting; for the last four years, he had abandoned himself to his fate. He hadn't allowed himself to make any sort of plan. As the world went to rack and ruin, the only thing he wanted to understand was who he actually was. He had no time for the world any more; he was enough of a puzzle to himself. But why on earth had they specifically come looking for him?

He had no influential friends. The fulfilment of his duty to the Motherland consisted, to date, in his work for the shipyard. He might be a good learner, and quicker than many of his comrades, but he was certainly the last person anyone would think of when it came to bold adventures and daring secret operations. This man was not about to disclose anything, though, if indeed he knew. Far more likely that he was just carrying out an order, assessing and evaluating Alania on someone else's behalf.

In the half-hour he spent with the mysterious gentleman in the shipyard director's room, Alania mulled over a few things. Did this visit represent an opportunity to get out of this swamp? Regardless of what awaited him, regardless of where this visit might lead, it would certainly mean getting away from here, and back to the Giorgi he had wanted to be when he'd stood and saluted next to Kostya in their graduation parade.

'I'm at your service!' said Alania, uncertainly, but with visible relief; and he asked the NKVD man to explain his business in more detail.

★

In May 1945, Alania was summoned to Moscow and, at a secret session of the interior ministry, assigned to the newly established 'Repatriation' group. At that time there were almost five million Soviet citizens in Europe — primarily in western Europe. The group's job was to bring them home and protect them against enemy propaganda. The majority were prisoners-of-war and forced labourers; the Generalissimus himself had commanded that they be returned as a matter of urgency. After the war ended, the British and the Americans opened the camps and handed over around sixty thousand Soviet citizens. But there were still plenty more on western soil who had to be tracked down, lured with false promises, and brought back to the Soviet Union — by force, if necessary.

In many secret meetings at the NKVD, and in the Lubyanka, the talk was of the threat posed to exiled Soviet citizens in Europe. They were all being recruited by the capitalists, or by the Mensheviks, whose 'democratisation campaigns' were being financed by the Americans. The influential National Alliance of Russian Solidarists, or NTS for short — which was indeed financed by the Americans and collaborated with the exiled Mensheviks of the post-revolutionary era — was demonised incessantly.

In the post-war years, fighting these 'vermin' and repatriating 'endangered' Soviet citizens who fell victim to western propaganda became a top priority.

Now, Giorgi Alania was also to perform these tasks. In addition to his personal attributes and qualities, which had been so highly praised by someone or other, he needed special training, too: this would last three years, and would take place in Moscow.

He was shipped off to the capital of socialism, allocated an apartment on Tverskoy Boulevard that was reserved for the *nomenklatura*, and began his secret, specialist training. In addition to methods (with which I am unfortunately, or fortunately, not acquainted) for luring people back to the Soviet promised land, or abducting them and taking them there by force, this training also included learning the English language.

Everything changed for Alania in Moscow. He still wasn't all that popular with his co-workers, but he was serving a higher purpose; he was one of the chosen ones. People respected and valued him and, above all, his impressive aptitude for learning. He was living in a metropolis, even if it hadn't yet recovered from the apocalyptic war; and it was possible to find certain women here who were prepared, for a fee, or in return for other services, to simulate the passion he longed for and the desire he craved.

Alania no longer had time to spend on gloomy thoughts. He needed to become the best of the best. And his growing power — which until then he would never have dared to imagine, not even in his wildest dreams, and which had been granted so suddenly, so unexpectedly — meant he was able to do some good as well. He managed to track down his best friend, who had thankfully survived, and bring him to Moscow; he would heal his friend's wounds and help him become the man he surely would have become, had this terrible war not intervened.

★

In 1946, before Alania was able to undertake the journey home — he had repeatedly postponed it, as his comprehensive training left him no time — his mother died of a stroke. The news sent Alania into a state of shock that lasted for quite some time. He had missed his chance to hold his mother to her promise. The burning curiosity about his origins took possession of him once again, with unimagined intensity. He requested a leave of absence, and travelled back to the remote Abkhazian-Megrelian countryside.

After the funeral, he started to make determined enquiries. He questioned neighbours, his few detested relatives, his mother's colleagues; he was open, almost provocative, as his mother had nothing left to lose and he — well, he was not intending ever to come back.

Whether out of fear or ignorance, nobody had anything to tell him. Some swore by all that was holy that his mother had maintained a deathly silence all her life about the conception of her illegitimate child. Alania, however, was patient, he was meticulous, and his understanding of people was almost as good as his memory. His KGB identity card gained him access to the university archive in Kutaisi, where, among the countless files, he found the one bearing the name of the woman who had once had an entirely different future ahead of her, because she was the first and, for a long time, the only woman to be admitted to the faculty — a minor sensation. Until the only affair she had ever had in her life put an end to this prospective career before it could even begin.

According to his calculations, he must have been conceived while she was in Kutaisi, and so he persisted. He went through everything in his head once more. Then he examined it again. And suddenly it no longer seemed quite so logical to him that he had been conceived in this town. It was so unlike Gulo — his beloved Gulo, his 'little heart', whose heart they had torn out, whom they had forced to live like a leper — to let someone get her pregnant just days after taking up the university place she'd coveted for so long. It made so little sense that, on the one hand, she had decided that higher mathematics was her future, yet, on the other, she had chosen to bring him into the world. All her life she'd had nothing but contempt for the opposite sex, and if he stopped to think about it, he, her beloved son, had been the sole exception.

A terrible suspicion began to take shape in his mind, then suddenly came sharply into focus: absolutely logical, almost unavoidable, something that had been staring him in the face all along and which, for precisely this reason, he had failed to see. It wasn't Gulo's *fault*, as the whole village had claimed; it wasn't her recklessness, her supposedly sluttish capitalist ideology, that had destroyed her life and made a bastard of him; it wasn't her carelessness, it wasn't even pleasure, a lapse — no, it must quite simply have been something that was *done to her*.

It must have been rape! At first, the thought brought Alania a kind of relief, but then he felt a knot of anger forming. And this loathsome *deed*, of which he was the consequence, must have occurred shortly before her move to this town. She had wanted to study in Kutaisi, to start a new life; she would never have moved there, would never have fought so fiercely for her place at the university, if she'd known that she was expecting. Gulo had been, first and foremost, a pragmatic woman; she would have known that she wouldn't stand even the ghost of a chance with an illegitimate child. She must have already been pregnant when she came to the town and only found out once she was here. But if something so terrible had been done to her, why had she stayed so resolutely silent? Why hadn't she saved her honour? Then, too, he wouldn't have been regarded as just his stupid, reckless slut of a mother's mistake.

He went back to his home village and visited his mother's old school. He impressed the principal with his identity card, and finally received some useful information. The principal referred him to Gulo's old teacher, who was still alive and living in a neighbouring village. Alania paid a *kolkhoz* worker a few roubles to drive him to the village in his *droshky*. There he found the old teacher, who was now almost blind, though her mind still seemed to be sharp. It didn't take him long to explain whose son he was. She remembered Gulo quickly, and vividly. What a girl, what talent. She should have moved to the city, she hadn't been able to find happiness in the countryside, such a shame, such a shame. What he needed, though, were facts.

'Facts? What facts, my boy?'

The old woman pronounced the word as if something poisonous had just been put in her mouth. All of a sudden she seemed more alert, and started to shift in her seat.

'Who she was friends with before she went to university, for example. Who were her good —'

'Listen, I taught my pupils, I didn't make friends with them. I don't know about any of that, my son.'

But the manner, and the haste, with which the old lady blurted this out implied the opposite. Alania's work with the NKVD had taught him a great deal, had honed his mind into a kind of antenna that picked up everything, even things that went unsaid. He showed the woman his identification; she looked at it, straining her eyes, seemingly unable to decipher the writing.

'What's this, my boy?'

'You know exactly what this is.'

'And what do you want from me?'

She had dropped the 'my boy' this time. Her reedy voice was coloured with fear.

'You know something that I *have to* know. You remember something that means a great deal to me, and you don't want to tell me what it is, and although I would find it most distasteful, you're leaving me no choice but to —'

'Yes, yes, yes ... All right. I don't want any problems. My son is an upstanding socialist, he works for the tea plantation ...'

'I didn't threaten you. I just need some facts.'

'Fine. Your mother wasn't your typical sort of girl, even back then. Didn't gossip, didn't hang around with the shy village girls; she knew what she wanted, and she was very determined. I realised that early on, believe me. But funnily enough, she got on well with the Lezhava girl, although she was a blonde dolly-bird type, the opposite of Gulo. Pretty dresses and plunging necklines and driving the village boys crazy when she went out for her evening stroll. But she was the daughter of Comrade Lezhava, the *militsiya* commissar. The two of them got on well; the girl was good at reciting poems, and they became friends on the trip to Baku.'

'Baku? My mother was in Baku?'

'It was a trip for young Komosomol members. I remember it well; a nice trip, only the best students were allowed to go, and we took the Lezhava girl along because, well, because ... Four days we were there, maybe five. And ...' The woman paused; she seemed to be trying to find the right words, to put her memories in order, to turn back the clock.

'When — when exactly was that? When was this trip?'

'After graduation, in the summer. Special trips like those were only for the gold-medal graduates, so it must have been after they finished school.'

'What happened in Baku?'

'I don't know — my God, I'm an old woman, I wasn't with the girls every second ...'

Suddenly the woman's face seemed to convulse, as if she were warding off an unpleasant memory. Giorgi sensed that he was getting close to the truth.

'We met lots of people; they even put on a fancy reception for us.' Her face lit up briefly with something like pride.

'Who was at this reception?'

'Senior commissars, Party men, very important ones; we were promoting friendship between peoples.'

'Were they Azerbaijanis?'

'Yes, and there were Georgians, too.'

'And there was drinking?'

'I didn't let them drink.'

'And then?'

'Then? How should I know ... But nothing happened there; what are you getting at? I loved my girls and I protected them; and besides, they were honourable men, true communists, Party men, I told you!'

She was breathing heavily, and complained that she had high blood pressure. She called her son, told him to bring her her medicine. Alania got up. Of course she knew more, of course he could force her to tell him what she knew, but he suddenly felt despondent, he wanted to get out into the fresh air, out of this damp room that stank of medication.

'I won't trouble you any longer, but do you know what happened to the Lezhava girl? What was her first name, do you remember?'

'What was her name ... hmm ... no, I can't think of it. Ask in the village. Her family's been gone for years but people remember her — the men in particular remember her, I can tell you. As far as I know, she went to live in Batumi.'

★

Giorgi Alania stood there for a while on the dusty country road. As so often when he was nervous, his palms were damp, and his head hurt. The KGB card in his breast pocket felt like a bulletproof vest; it felt good. It made him feel that he would never have to ask anyone for anything ever again.

Alania went to Batumi, visited the local commissariat, showed them his card without comment, and waited until they provided him with information about the girl, Comrade Lezhava. In the past few days he had found on several occasions that the effect his KGB card had on others saved him a great deal of time and effort.

'*Our* Nelly?'

'*Our* Nelly?' asked Giorgi, perplexed. The man gave him a slightly crooked grin and raised his eyebrows meaningfully, as if to indicate to Alania that he was speaking of a particularly delightful person whom he could warmly recommend.

'She's a local character, you could say. A, er, very well-known lady. She lives in the big white house just behind the Archaeological Museum. And she can see into the future, too, so watch out, be on your guard …' Now the official was smiling maliciously.

'See into the future?'

'Yes, yes; she reads coffee grounds. And how!'

Alania interrupted what seemed to be turning into an uncomfortable conversation, thanked the official, and took the bus to the Green Cape along the shoreline of the dark, oily sea. It suddenly made him feel sentimental, evoking memories of his childhood, and made him miss his mother with an overwhelming, physical sensation.

You could hardly miss the house. It had been built at a time that recalled the hopeful era when the Rothschilds and Nobels were flirting with the Caucasus, when the Grand Hotels were being planned and the white ships from Europe could anchor in the local harbour without customs offices or any major hindrance. The house's old opulence had outlasted Bolshevik taste, but time had taken a serious toll on it. Slender-limbed bamboos shielded it from strangers' eyes. Alania stepped warily through the tall, rusty garden gate. Some little children were chasing a ball. He stopped the eldest boy and asked for Comrade Lezhava. The boy, annoyed at being called away from the game, just pointed upstairs.

Alania went in through the open wooden door, entered a marble-tiled hallway, and climbed the stairs. The stairwell was dilapidated; rainwater dripped from the ceiling, forming greyish puddles in various corners. When he reached the top he came to a green wooden door covered in peeling paint, and stopped. Should he turn round? Should he raise his hand and knock? Did she know the truth about him? What if this woman had nothing new to say to him? He knocked.

It was a little while before he heard a deep female voice: 'What the hell is it now? I haven't got any flour! I don't cook, and I don't have any onions either; and besides, I don't even live here, when are you finally going to understand that?' He knocked again and heard hurried footsteps on the other side of the door, which flew open at last, accompanied by a long stream of curses.

In front of him stood a … well, a vision. A tall, fleshy woman with an impressive bosom and beautiful, thick blonde hair that she had wound into a perfect bun. She was dressed in a lettuce-green slip, and was barefoot.

Her face suggested a life lived at full tilt; she was wearing crimson lipstick and had concealed the heavy, dark rings under her eyes with powder, which gave her a peculiar, doll-like appearance.

She looked surprised; presumably a strange young man had been the last person she was expecting.

And for the first time in Alania's life a miracle happened: her expression of irritation and surprise transformed into an irresistible smile. She plucked at her neckline, smoothed the slip over her hips, and in a catlike drawl breathed, 'What can I do for you?'

'I heard that you read coffee ...' murmured Giorgi Alania. He was now completely out of his depth and already breaking into a sweat. The woman opened the door a little more, peered down the stairs, then pulled him into the apartment by the sleeve of his jacket.

Like the rest of the house, the apartment had seen better days. What was left of the wallpaper clung to the wall rather than being glued there, and the tap, installed incongruously in the middle of the living room, dripped steadily. By contrast, the ceiling was adorned with an enormous chandelier that would have been more suited to a theatre than to this dark, damp abode, with its countless dusty souvenirs and the decorated hatboxes piled up in every corner.

'Who sent you to me?' she asked, and gestured to him to take a seat at a clothless round table heaped with objects.

'An acquaintance.'

'An acquaintance. Uh-huh. Normally I'd throw you out at once for that silly answer. But you don't look like one of *them*. I know who I can trust and who I can't. I can read faces like I read coffee grounds. But I hope you realise we could both get into a lot of trouble if you go around talking about my gifts. I'm here under a kind of house arrest; they keep an eye on me, they won't leave me alone. What have I done to them? Whose side am I a thorn in?'

Her whole body, her eyes, her mouth were flirting with him, radiating affection, they didn't recoil from his obvious lack of confidence, his shyness; no, they enticed him, encouraged him to look at them, to adore them. An unfamiliar sense of self-satisfaction warmed his belly. Inconceivable: his whole life until now without this affection, without this enchanting benevolence, this feeling.

She went over to a kitchen alcove, separated by a folding screen, and started to make coffee. The delicious scent filled the whole apartment, as if it were trying to accentuate Alania's happiness. When she returned with the coffee she was wearing slippers embroidered with flowers, which for some unaccountable reason filled him with delight. (She had dressed for him, had clothed her bare feet for him!)

'So what do you want to know?' she asked, sticking a filterless cigarette in the corner of her mouth.

Who raped my mother and got her pregnant! In his confusion, he almost blurted this out, but he managed to restrain himself in the nick of time, murmuring instead, 'About my professional career, and …'

'Let's have a look. What's your name?'

'Giorgi.'

'All right, Giorgi, *genacvale*. Drink all the coffee, then tip the cup upside down onto the saucer and let it stand, then turn it anticlockwise with your finger and ask your question, but not out loud, just concentrate on what it is you want to know. I alone can't do anything if your mind is blocked.'

'All right, of course, I understand.' Alania nodded like a first-grader being given his homework.

He tried to concentrate, but the only thing he could think of was the attention she was paying him, her sweet, rather weary scent that filled his nose. He brushed the coffee grounds with his finger, placed the cup on the saucer.

'What did you mean by house arrest?' he asked her, in an attempt to break the awkward silence that ensued, because the coffee grounds had to dry.

'Ha! What does it mean? That I've been a naughty girl and there are some men who are angry with me. I've fallen out of favour, as they would have said in my youth. Where are you from, Giorgi?' she asked, finally turning the cup over.

'From Kutaisi,' he lied.

'So where did you leave your accent?'

Alania sensed her mistrust.

'I live in Russia. I did my training in Leningrad, and now I work in Moscow.'

'Ah, that's excellent. An important man, then. What's brought you back to your old homeland?'

'My mother's death,' he blurted out.

'How terrible. My deepest sympathies. Always hard, when your own mother … Even though mine was cross with me all her life.'

She stared into the smeared cup as if she were reading a map there, a coded map.

'Well well, look at this! I see a lot of praise and recognition here. You're on the right path, Giorgi, *genacvale*, oh yes, you'll keep climbing your ladder; but rather desolate at heart, aren't you? Empty and sad. How's that, Giorgi? How can that be? So young — you should be enjoying life. Time never comes again; missed opportunities don't come round a second time. Instead, you're troubled. I see a long road here. You'll be going on a journey. A long journey, but a fruitful one. You will get there — oh yes, you'll get to where you want to be. But you must fill your heart, Giorgi, otherwise it will never be enough, no matter what comes, no matter what people say to you, no matter how many medals they pin to your breast; your heart is so terribly empty.'

'And my mother ...?'

'No; the grief for your mother, may she rest in peace, is not the only reason for your emptiness, is it, Giorgi?'

The way she said his name, as if her voice had been laced with honey, made him want her to go on speaking like that for ever, to keep talking to him and never stop. And she told him about many things that were supposedly troubling him, things he longed for and felt the lack of; she remained vague, lost herself in hints and allusions, yet he had the sense that she knew him, saw through him, even, as no one ever had before. He could no longer contain himself; something came over him, something bigger than himself, bigger even than his eternal question, the thread running through his entire life, and he started to weep, and at the same time was ashamed of his tears: all of a sudden, with no warning, tears were spilling from his eyes. She put her hand on his shoulder, stroked his head and repeated soothing words in her healing voice.

'It's all right; poor, poor Giorgi, oh God, such an empty heart, we have to do something about that right away, you have to do something about it, so alone, so lost, we have to do something about that, Giorgi, *genacvale*.'

We! This simple word sounded like a magic spell to him. At last he looked at her; something in the way she was comforting him gave him courage, and he dared to kiss her hand, which was resting on his shoulder. She stroked his head; he rose to his feet; he was a little shorter than her, but that didn't seem to bother her, either. Would she recoil if he went further? Broke through all his boundaries and gave her a kiss, right on her painted scarlet lips? Would she throw him out, would she curse him? She touched him; he had brought her hand to his lips; he simply had to finish what he had started. He laid his head on her collarbone; she did not recoil. He put his arms around her soft waist; she smiled at him, she was not ashamed of him. He kissed her and she returned his kiss.

Before long, they were lying on the wide bed with its sagging mattress, which was propped up on piles of heavy books. He pulled up her slip with a single movement of his hand, as if it were the most natural thing in the world, as if he had done it a thousand times before. No struggle, no agonies of embarrassment accompanied this attempt to disrobe, be close to, a woman's body. And so it was, that afternoon, that Giorgi Alania crossed into happiness with slow, deliberate movements, entirely without shame, sure of himself, with the unprecedented feeling of being truly desired. Of being longed for, wanted. Perhaps even — although it wasn't possible, he knew it, even at that moment

— anticipated. He was so happy to let somebody catch him. He felt free, as if he were floating, as if not even the laws of gravity could touch him; as if he could fly.

When he rose from this bed, late that evening, he was a new man: it was as if he had been reborn, confident, radiant, a whole head taller. Nelly, already back in her slip, was sitting at the round table, placing the cards. He dressed carefully, not taking his eyes off his new lover, still stunned by his good fortune.

'I just want to say, I'm under pretty close surveillance here. I've already had to give up the whole floor, apart from this room, to that pack of vermin. If they find me with a male visitor I'll lose this dump as well. So I think you should probably go now, Giorgi, *genacvale*.' She said it without raising her head from the cards.

'Yes, of course. I'd like to see you again, though.'

'I'm sure that can be arranged. It's just that I have to be a bit careful, you understand.'

'Yes, I understand. But if I can put in a good word for you at the commissariat ...'

'You'd do that?'

'I would, if I might come again.'

'Want to tell them how good I am at my job, eh?'

A bitter note had suddenly entered her voice. The honeyed sweetness was completely gone.

He didn't approach her again, didn't want to disturb her, even though he would have liked to have given her a kiss; he stood in the doorway, hesitating, dressed and ready to go, hoping she would see him out.

'When may I come again?'

'Next week, maybe.' She shrugged. 'But Giorgi, listen, I don't want to be rude, but the thing with the coffee grounds ... I have to live off something, you know. I like you, and there's no way I'd ask if these were different times, but ...'

He felt an icy cold take hold of his body. He would have given her everything, would have moved heaven and earth for her; he would have brought her to Moscow, yes, he'd even been thinking of it as she lay in his arms, but now ... not this! She couldn't ask him for money.

'Yes, of course, of course, I forgot.'

And he put all the money he had in his wallet on the little chest of drawers by the door.

★

If Alania had known that Nelly, this woman who had once dreamed of a career in theatre, had already bestowed this happiness on countless men, that her youth and her once-proud beauty were the price she had paid for never having to work in state employment, that she had once possessed beautiful diamonds, hats, and dresses, had had her own box at the theatre and an automobile, and in return would always wait until her men decided to leave their families for an hour or two in order to visit her. If he'd known that she had forgone a family of her own, had sought out solitude as her most loyal companion, and had repeatedly allowed herself to be thrown away like rubbish as soon as a man grew tired of her; that she had already had to endure countless words of abuse, torrents of hatred, and scornful looks; if he had known that for the past five years, after the death of her most long-standing and influential benefactor, the public prosecutor, she had survived by reading coffee grounds and doing embroidery; if he had known how willingly she would have forgotten all these injuries, exchanged them for other memories. If he had known that it was Nelly's drunkenness, her slipping and falling that night, that had led to his conception against his mother's will. Yes, if he had known all this, would he nonetheless have claimed her attention, her passion, her feigned comfort, and would he have stayed, in the intoxicating hope of being waited for, perhaps even loved? It's a question I will never be able to answer for us, Brilka.

The right to a failed life is inalienable.

AMÉLIE

Dawn was breaking; outside it began to drizzle. The sky had filled with clouds like a herd of animals. Kitty had talked a lot about herself, and in detail: about her feeling that she had become a figure with no umbilical cord, disconnected, without desires, floating freely through the air like an orphaned balloon that had slipped from someone's hand at a children's birthday party.

Before, he had talked a lot himself, an astonishing amount. It seemed to him that he hadn't talked as much in centuries. He felt weightless. Fearless.

He wanted time to stand still, just as it had all those years ago in Nelly's little attic apartment; Nelly, who might perhaps have been able to give him the liberating knowledge he sought, and instead had gifted him, for his journey through life, a disappointment that could never be healed.

It was so good to be able to see himself for a while through Kitty's eyes. And perhaps what she saw was actually true. Partly, anyway. Perhaps, in all the years of their long telephone calls, he had learned to be so much better than he was in real life. For her. For her voice. For her freedom, for the peace of her soul. Because she deserved it. He had never doubted that. She had not disappointed him.

Yes, of course he wanted to stay with her, to stop time. Still surprised that she had tracked him down. Unclear what the consequences of this encounter would be. Unsure how far he could let her into his life. And how he hated it, and had hated it all these years, that she thought it was fear of losing his position that held him back. How he would have loved to make clear to her that it wasn't about him, but her — her security.

And how he loved to look at her. Constantly, once he had overcome the shyness that had been building inside him for years, shyness of the body to which her voice belonged. The woman in front of him was made of flesh and blood; like that time, that one time long ago that she didn't even remember. Her mind had erased the image, the memory. The memory of that banal encounter in the sleepy little town near the steppe, in the empty station, when he gave her the package from her unhappy, lovelorn brother and asked her to stay with him until his train arrived and he could continue his journey home. But perhaps it was better that way. Better for her. He, however, had always had a phenomenal memory; this memory was precisely what had made him an irreplaceable secret agent. And this memory had retained, preserved forever, the image of the schoolgirl she had been back then, in this other life, in another era, in another world. This was the image he had recalled, this was the image he had pictured when he heard her voice, until her photos appeared in the press, until he even managed to see her in person, at one of her concerts, from the anonymity of the crowd.

He liked her way of gesticulating, her laughter lines, her expressions, her faint scent of baby cream, and the impression she gave of being slightly disorientated, out of place: even within her own four walls she seemed like a guest, as if she hadn't learned to accept this place, this language, these objects, even these clothes as her own.

He had talked about his work, even though he'd firmly intended not to. About all the shadows that pursued him, all the faces that had burned themselves into his skin like invisible tattoos. She had drunk whisky without speaking while he went on sipping at his glass of lemonade.

Later, he had talked about Leningrad, about the Naval School, and about Kostya. His voice always grew animated when he talked about this happy time. Even now, after so many years, all the things that had happened in between had not managed to dim this happiness.

Alania had never married, although, in the course of his life, he had had opportunities to do so. There had been women who had shown him that they were impressed by his prospects, his knowledge, his power, his quick wit, his subtle, refined, almost polite brutality. He could have deceived himself, could have interpreted these longings as love and settled down. But he had sworn loyalty to one woman, and he always kept his promise. That woman was now sitting in front of him. The brothels of London had provided him with what Kitty's voice was unable to give. It had always seemed the easiest way. He bought himself illusions, he bought himself a few hours' intimacy, and in time he learned to give himself over to these illusions. He sought out cultivated prostitutes. He entertained them; sometimes he went out with them, sometimes he bought them presents. They liked him, and he liked them, because they were good liars. Better than most respectable women.

And lies were an important part of his life. Throughout his years in

London, Giorgi Alania had located and personally repatriated so many people whom he lured with false promises, who followed him voluntarily or were forced to do so, that he now enjoyed a considerable reputation and a certain untouchability at headquarters in Moscow.

Yes, he had kept his promise, as he always kept his promises to Kitty. But in this instance he had done so with particular devotion, with particular conviction. Had risked everything for it. How often he had feared that it would all be exposed, that he wouldn't be able to protect her; how much willpower this promise had demanded of him. And yet how happy he had been to keep it. For her. The only saint in his life.

In the beginning, he had done it for Kostya, for his effortless love, but then he had had to admit to himself that Kostya no longer played such a crucial role in his desire to go on being there for this disembodied woman, for this voice. He had been a shadow for many years, but now they were sitting opposite each other, telling each other about their lives, expressing their most intimate thoughts and wishes, admitting things to one another as if they were two old friends who had celebrated birthdays and weddings together, had mourned people together, had spent their lives together.

He thought back to the day when he had realised she no longer needed his protection, that she was free: the day he heard her first song on the radio. He had done it; he had made her *untouchable*.

And now, for her, he had thrown all the rules out of the window, disregarded safety precautions, risked everything to protect what had seemed to him, for so many years, so immeasurably important. He had also allowed himself to be found by her, and it would be child's play for her to bring his house of cards tumbling down; he would have to fear for his life. But this, too, meant nothing to him in the light of her physical presence. Being caught, having his double life exposed, seemed laughably insignificant to him if he could have this face to go with this voice.

Night was now dangerously close to day. And the day that was dawning would be different from all the days of his life until now. Who would he be when he left this flat again?

Kitty took a deep breath and stretched on the sofa like a contented cat.

★

Elsewhere, in another world, a heavy, bloated body turned on its side. A bearded man, poisoned by alcohol and transgression, crippled by an unspeakable loss, battered by his own impotence, incapable of speech, let out an animal sound.

In the same world — in the same city, even — a thin, red-haired woman sat up on a mattress, beside a young woman whose name she did not recall, and bit her lip. The poison that consigned everything to oblivion had worn off; her head hurt, her body, too, but her mind was alert, and it raged and lamented, telling her that she had failed, she had lost someone and could not cope with this loss.

★

'You have to help me. If I don't go to Tbilisi, I'll lose my mind. This feeling is paralysing me, it's driving me mad. I can't think about anything else any more. I have to go back. I don't know what it is; for years I've been able to keep all these feelings and memories at bay, but I can't, not any more. I'm going to go. I have a British passport, but … Help me.'

Kitty spoke quietly, in a monotone, like a prayer to be recited over and over again.

'What do you hope will come of it?'

'I don't know, I just know I have to do it. It's the last thing I'll ask of you. I promise, Giorgi. Oh God, it's so strange to be saying your name.'

'I don't know if I want you never to ask me for anything again. But what you're asking lies outside my authority.'

The night melted down to a lump that stuck in the throat. They were like two acrobats who had fallen from their tightrope, circus people whose tents the wind had carried off in all directions.

His stomach clenched as if he were on a rollercoaster: with excitement and fear, at the thought of all that might happen. His legs were tingling. He knew the answer to the question she didn't dare ask him; he had carried it on the tip of his tongue all these years without realising. The answer to the question of why he had ensured, all this time, that she stayed alive, that she was still here. But he couldn't yet tell her that she was the longest — disembodied, but nonetheless the longest — and most constant relationship of his life.

A little chill ran down his spine. If she no longer needed him, if she were no longer dependent on his friendship, what else was there to give his life meaning? To stop the ice from filling his soul completely? No: he wanted her to ask him for help, wanted her to ask many more things of him.

'I was nineteen. Or maybe only eighteen. In any case, I was still in my first year at the Frunze Academy. I was taking the train to the Black Sea coast. Kostya had given me a parcel to take with me; I was to deliver it to his mother, or his aunt, and I was willing to make the detour because he told me that his sister ...'

Kitty, suddenly attentive, raised her head and stared at him incredulously, as if waking from long hibernation.

'... that she was at his grandfather's and maybe I could give her the parcel and she could send it on to Tbilisi. For some reason, he wanted this parcel to get there in a hurry. I remember it clearly: he put it together with such excitement. Anyway, I was happy to make the detour because I was so curious about Kostya's family, about his sister ...'

Kitty stared at him, dumbfounded. She knitted her brow, searching her memory for the missing pieces of the puzzle.

'It was right at the start of the war, the day I met you at the station.'

'Oh God — that was you,' whispered Kitty.

'I still remember it as if it were yesterday. That station entrance hall. I don't know why, but I was excited. I was going to meet Kostya's sister, I'd see a different side of him, find out more about him; I don't know what I was hoping for. I really don't. And then I saw you. You were wearing this awful school uniform, but without the pinafore. And your wild hair. It was falling over your face. When you arrived, you seemed to be in a rush, and so distracted, and I desperately wanted to talk to you. I was so curious. I wanted to know so much, to know how a man becomes like Kostya, and why, what sort of family he must come from ... And I got you. You were impatient; you said you had homework to do. I could scarcely hide my disappointment; I thought, I don't believe it, I've made such a detour, and for what, just these few minutes in this stupid hall to meet a schoolgirl who won't even look at me properly, and then ... I was annoyed. I didn't know what to say, and you took the parcel and left. I was so crushed; I thought, that's how it is, that's how it always is, people, especially women, they look through me, why would it be any different this time. But then you came back into the hall and gave me this huge smile. I was so happy and surprised and overwhelmed. Yes, it's true, I'm not exaggerating. Don't look at me like that. You were so full of life. I remembered how often Kostya had been exasperated with you, and said how rebellious you were. And all of a sudden I decided that was a marvellous thing.

'Later, you walked me to the train and waved me off. Yes: you waved me off. It was dark by then, and I pulled down the window and peered out, almost the whole of my upper body hanging out, and you stayed there, the whole time you stayed and waited, and for one brief moment I saw myself as a boy saying goodbye to his girlfriend. A boy in love, waving goodbye to a girl in love. That was enough. For a long time. A very long time.'

Kitty was silent. She stared thoughtfully into her empty glass, then down at the floor again, not daring to look him in the face. Then she turned to him, put her arms around his shoulders, and pressed her forehead to his.

Yes, from now on things would have to change, Alania knew that, after everything he had said. Decisively. Whether for better or worse he didn't know, but he would let them change, he would let them, because before him sat the only woman who loved him.

> Today I have so much to do:
> I must kill memory once and for all,
> I must turn soul to stone,
> I must learn to live again
>
> ANNA AKHMATOVA

It was a sullen, unsettled morning as the plane prepared for landing. It looked as if all the gloating ghosts had gathered on the clouds and were gleefully sticking out their tongues at the arriving passengers.

He had promised to pick her up. He would support her if she fell; he would stretch out a net of feathers for her to land softly, or simply spread his wings and fly away with her if she thought she were in a trap; if she suffocated, he would give her the kiss of life.

He had promised her all this in the long summer months in London, and in her house near Seven Sisters, which Kitty had finally visited, with him, in the sultry July heat.

Those had been days full of words regained. She felt safe; not safe in a physical sense, but in a much deeper one, as if before their meeting reality had been just one great threadbare backdrop, as if she had always been suspicious of this backdrop and had now finally learned to look behind it. A reality behind reality. Words behind which stood whole armies of other words. Sentences that drew countless others after them, and didn't trickle away into emptiness and insignificance.

Since that never-ending night, which went on long after the sun had risen, their first night without telephone or time limits, he had never spoken of his work again. The things he had to hide were ugly — the things he could not speak of, the things that frightened him — and she, too, was unwilling to jeopardise this fragile construct they both suddenly found themselves prepared to build. She just wanted him to stay. In her life. By her side. She sometimes wondered whether she would be prepared to receive all his secrets as the price for his years of loyalty. But she dreaded it; she didn't want to know what price he had paid in order to be able to support her. What worried her most of all, though, was — paradoxically — his decision to stay by her side. Why was he ignoring all his precautions, the agreements that governed his reality, and taking an inconceivable risk? Why wasn't he afraid that his double life might end in a prison cell? That his well-made play would be exposed as a farce?

She didn't ask him about it. Just welcomed him. Whenever he came to her; whenever he decided that it was time to come to her, and stay. Only formal, obligatory security measures were still maintained: the night became their day. They never left the flat together. They never met in public. They took different trains from the city to their cottage. Sometimes, as she watched him making her an omelette or flicking through her record collection, she would go rigid with fear. The thought that he might disappear again paralysed her. And thinking about the impossibility of a normal life together paralysed her, too. And sometimes, when he turned away from her, insisted on going for a walk alone, or skilfully, slickly, evaded a question, she thought it would be unbearable for her, impossible for her to live with, if ever she were compelled to despise him. For things he had done, for things he embodied, for things he concealed from her.

But then she consoled herself with the terrible thoughts that had haunted her all her life, the thoughts she had always tried so resolutely to suppress: the murder, Mariam, and the shadowy house on the Mtatsminda mountain. At moments like this, she meekly accepted that she was a murderess, and persuaded herself that she, a murderess, a traitor, had not the slightest reason to despise another, irrespective of what that person might have done.

They never touched. He seemed unused to physical contact: she was too overwhelming for him.

That was all right with her. She, too, needed to relearn how to be close to someone, if indeed she were ever to permit such a thing again. Their days on the English coast were filled with long, damp walks and the sound of the sea. Days full of sentences sucked like sweets. There, for the first time in ages, she was seized by the need to pick up her guitar and create something new. And when he set off for London, leaving her behind on her own, she unplugged the phone and sat down in the window seat, creating new melodies, teasing them out from deep within. She always kept some elderflower cordial ready for him in the fridge. She learned to hold back her memories of the red-haired woman and not let them ruin the atmosphere. Because things were good as they were.

And then one afternoon he travelled down from London, burst into the kitchen like an excited little boy who'd surpassed himself in his audacity, and planted himself in front of her, grinning.

'I think I've found a solution. At least, I hope I have.'

'What do you mean?' she asked, confused.

'I think I've found a way of getting you to Tbilisi.' He smiled his despondent smile, which for some reason always made her feel sad. 'I spoke to your manager. I explained to her that the authorities in Tbilisi would be interested in having you play a concert there, but that the request had to come from her. She seemed very surprised at first, but she responded well and said she was sure you'd be delighted to be able to travel back to your homeland. So I explained to her in detail whom she had to call and what she had to say, so there wouldn't be any suspicions, and afterwards she called our embassy and requested a concert in Tbilisi. As a sort of sign of peace on both sides. That was five days ago, and afterwards I had a meeting with the Culture Department that went on till midnight. I spoke to the ambassador, and he called Moscow. You should know you're famous in the Soviet Union; young people in particular listen to your songs. Since *Replacement* and the Prague photo you've been very popular there. So, anyway, they thought about it, and realised it wouldn't be such a stupid idea to take this opportunity and use it for their own purposes this time. Take a nice photo of you in your hometown, a gesture of reconciliation, so to speak, a sign that you have nothing against the Soviet Union, that what happened in Prague was a kind of silly misunderstanding. They need these gestures of reconciliation; for young people in particular, they need proof that we're not monsters.'

As he spoke, she stared at him in disbelief, incapable of processing there and then the information he was giving her, incapable of believing that her wish to go back could soon become reality.

'And what about you?' she asked later, over dinner.

'What about me?'

'Are you coming with me?'

'My plan is this: they won't give Amy an entry permit; she's far too British and capitalist, and she can't keep her mouth shut. If all goes smoothly, they'll assign me to take over Amy's job while you're in Georgia. And if that's approved, then for the two weeks they'll give you I'll be your official minder.'

'Ha! If they only knew you've been that for twenty years.'

★

Now the past was getting alarmingly close to the present, approaching at the speed of the Aeroflot plane.

Her legs were swollen. She had balled her hands into fists. Patches of sweat had formed under the arms of her white shirt. She squeezed her eyes shut and tried to get her breathing under control. Strangely enough, now, of all times, she found herself thinking of Fred. Now, when she was furthest away from her, and getting further with every kilometre. But she couldn't help imagining how Fred might find, experience, see the country that, after an absence of almost two decades, was unfamiliar to her as well. Where was Fred right now? What was she doing? Was someone protecting her, or had she already bartered all her guardian angels for the needle? She pressed her forehead against the seat in front. She had changed planes in Moscow and had had to endure endless checks, but the biggest test still lay ahead of her.

He was there, though. He had flown to his homeland ten days before her to organise everything on the ground. He would pick her up, and she would be able to breathe again. He would prevent her being buried entirely beneath the cascade of memories. She was sure he would.

★

The crowd began to cheer as soon as the plane doors opened and the stairway was brought over. They were all waving bunches of flowers, calmly and in time, as if carefully choreographed and synchronised; no one stepped out of line, no one screamed excessively, no one was insufficiently enthusiastic.

Even the journalists who did get a little out of line, running up to her and holding out their best wind-protected microphones, were polite and smiled at her encouragingly.

She allowed herself to be photographed, and responded politely to the vacuous questions their editorial departments had approved, as the crowd lapsed into reverential silence. She accepted the flowers, thanked people, and afterwards allowed herself to be led to the second floor of the airport building where a large group of editors, KGB agents, security men, and so-called programme directors, all in suits, were gathered around a long conference table. They gave ceremonial speeches, spoke of the significance of her concert, stressed her homeland's interest in her, the dangers of western propaganda and manipulation, and explained to her the programme she was to follow over the course of her two-week visit.

They were on the third speech before he entered the room. She recognised his footsteps even before he came in. He walked straight up to her and gave her a formal handshake. His gaze was calm, as if to convey to her that everything was going to be fine.

Once the official part of the reception was over, the delegation drove in several cars to an elegant banqueting hall somewhere in Krtsanisi, where they had laid on a lavish Georgian buffet and lots of Saperavi. The officious speeches continued in a slightly more relaxed tone. She was finding it hard to even swallow. Only Alania's knee, which kept brushing against hers beneath the floor-length tablecloth, gave her a sense of security. Yes, if she were to fall unconscious on the spot, he would revive her. Before her turn came to propose a toast thanking the minister for his speech, Kostya appeared in the doorway.

He was still tall, a formidable presence, moustachioed, uniform dripping with medals as he entered the room. She didn't dare stand up, rush over to him (did she want to? Was she allowed to?). She didn't know what was expected of her in this situation. But then people around her suddenly started clapping, and in the midst of this bombastic, artificial scenario her brother embraced his traitor of a sister whom he had lost to the evil imperialist world such a very, very long time ago, and for whom this almost biblical return of the prodigal daughter had been staged. All we need now is a marching band, she thought, and hugged Kostya tightly.

★

Kitty sat between Alania and her brother, eating delicious fresh river trout in pomegranate sauce and trying not to faint as people told her, with obvious pride, about the sold-out Philharmonia where both her concerts would take place, about the press interviews lined up for her, and the state banquet she was to attend along with a few other Soviet musicians. Three hours later, when she was finally allowed to leave the room at her brother's side and get into his Seagull — throwing Alania a look that was both grateful and a cry for help — she sank into the passenger seat and closed her eyes.

'You were very lucky. *He* managed it brilliantly. A very clever man,' said Kostya, when they had driven for a while in silence. She was incapable of saying anything in reply.

After they had crossed the city and were on the narrow, winding roads heading north, he told her there was some bad news as well.

'Is it Stasia?' she murmured. Her mouth was dry and cracked. Every word was painful.

'Oh, no; believe me, she'll outlive us all. It's about Eristavi.'

'Andro?'

'He's in hospital. His liver's about to give out; no wonder, given his passion for all things alcoholic. I mean, after the death of …'

'Of?'

'His son.'

'I didn't know he —'

'Drank? Drank is an understatement.'

★

Stasia wept, and had to sit down. Nana was so excited she dropped one of the cups from her most expensive Czech tea set. Daria laughed and performed a little dance for Kitty. I … I don't know what I did, probably nothing remarkable; a bit of prattling, a bit of tottering about. But what was most peculiar was Elene's reaction to Kitty's arrival. When she spotted her father's car on the drive she ran up the hill as fast as she could and hid.

Elene only returned to the house later that evening, when the tears had stopped rolling down Stasia's cheeks. Shamefaced, she slunk onto the terrace where the long table had been laid. The similarity was immediately apparent to all the family. It really was astonishing: the same thick hair, the same eyes, the same high cheekbones, even the same full lips; only Elene's body seemed slightly heavier and softer than Kitty's.

Kitty got to her feet and slowly approached her niece.

'It's all right, Elene.' She spoke in English. The girl was clearly intimidated, and she hoped the foreign language would make their meeting easier, as Kostya had told her Elene had learned English from her records. 'Where were you all this time? We've all been waiting for you.'

Elene finally raised her head; she seemed relieved. The girl with the two fatherless children looked so lost, so far removed from any notion Kitty had had of Kostya's daughter.

'I was afraid,' Elene said, also in English. The foreign language enabled her to be honest. No one else around the table would understand them.

'What of?' asked Kitty, shielding Elene's face with her body from her family's inquisitive looks.

'I don't know. That you might not be how I imagined.'

'How did you imagine me, then?'

'Different from all the others.'

'And are you disappointed?'

'No.'

'What are you two whispering about there, like a pair of schoolgirls? Elene, let Kitty come back to us — and will you come and sit down please, you're being rude!' called Kostya, irritated and disconcerted in equal measure.

'Andro has a photo of you in his house,' Elene continued, as if she hadn't heard her father. 'A photo from one of your concerts. But he's in hospital now. After Miqa's funeral, all he did was just keep drinking.'

Elene's eyes were wide open and locked on to Kitty as she spoke. As if the two of them were completely alone; as if the whole family weren't sitting a few metres away, keen to have a joyful celebration. Kitty's eyes widened. Miqa. Miqa. So that was the name of Andro's son. Now both his sons were dead, the born and the unborn.

'Elene's English is excellent!' Kitty called to the others, without turning round, without taking her horrified gaze off Elene.

'I wanted to tell you that before they serve up all the lies, and I know my father probably won't let me be alone with you. I wanted you to know. I wanted you to know that it's our fault, all of ours, that Miqa isn't with us any more. Mine above all. I don't know you, but I know a lot about you. They never told me anything, but I found out about you, as much as I could. You have to visit Andro. They'll follow you everywhere you go, but if you want we can try and shake them off. I drive to the hospital every day.'

'Thank you!'

Kitty cleared her throat. Then she put on the lightest and most carefree smile she possessed and turned to face the others.

★

Christine hadn't been able to bring herself to come to the Green House and welcome Kitty. She had visited the cemetery every day since Miqa's funeral. And she had looked after Andro, but had made no more attempts to stop him drinking. All too often he would drink himself unconscious, so that Christine had to call an ambulance, or he would end up in the drying-out cell for shouting abuse and breaching the peace.

Finally, two weeks before Kitty's return, Andro was admitted to the city hospital with advanced cirrhosis of the liver. As she sat beside his bed, Christine realised that in his death throes, bloated and no longer lucid, Andro actually seemed peaceful. Much more peaceful than before, when he had struggled with life instead of death. Lana and little Miro went back and forth between Christine's apartment and Lana's mother's place. The boy was sickly, morose, and highly strung, and Lana was finding it very hard to cope. In the past few weeks, Elene had been almost fanatically helpful. She had driven into town every day, gone shopping for Lana and Christine, taken Lana's little boy to the day nursery, picked him up again, and above all she had sat at Andro's bedside, held his hand, read to him, and told him all the latest gossip, even though he didn't really give the impression that he was listening or was able to understand what she said.

In those weeks, Elene made worrying about Lana her top priority. Lana was still stubbornly, desperately clinging to her pain, for fear of glimpsing the unforgivable fact that might lie beyond it: that she could have saved Miqa's life if she had given the film back in time. And that meant Elene could be certain she wouldn't have to encounter Lana's self-loathing, which would certainly be equal to her own. Because this, she was sure, would have pulled the already shaky ground from beneath her feet.

She let Lana play the role of grieving widow. Let her pain take centre stage. This, too, was a way of not having to deal with herself, with all that lay behind and before her. She joined forces with Lana in maintaining the bogus myth she clung to so persistently, the myth of the unwavering idealist who went forth to fight against the rotten, corrupt system, to drag its filth into the light, and had laid down his life for this great objective. In her own memory, Lana wanted to remain the brave fighter at his side, the custodian of his secret, the mother of his son, the woman to whom he had entrusted his heart and the most precious thing he ever owned: his film, his confession of faith. They both knew, of course, that they were lying to themselves, each in her own way. But this lie could be lived with, whereas the truth was uncertain, gave no clear answers, and left nothing but hatred and self-loathing. No — the truth paralysed; the lie liberated.

Kitty's return must have seemed to Elene like a sign from heaven. Bringing two lovers together: her last chance to make paltry atonement. She couldn't bring the dead back to life, but perhaps she could accomplish one small good deed; one small, sad, good deed. Andro's sickbed, and Kitty, a photograph personified.

Yes, perhaps this western resistance fighter, this anarchist, this goddess of music would find peace in Elene's stead, here at the deathbed of her childhood sweetheart. And she, Elene, would be able to watch her and learn how to accept things that came to nothing, that simply vanished into thin air. Things, feelings, hopes ... people.

'He doesn't love you.' That was what she had said to Lana, in Andro's house — but it was herself she had meant. And she had not prioritised Miqa's life over her inability to live with that fact. Now Miqa was dead. And Elene was still here. Just as godless as before. Just as alone. Just as confused.

> Peace, land, and bread!
>
> POSTER SLOGAN

Kitty had spotted Christine from the other end of the corridor. She had looked so old, and at the same time so childlike. The once-striking beauty had become an impoverished, eccentric, introverted figure. She held her aunt in her arms for a long time. Inhaled her scent, and remembered how, when she had returned from that village, from Hell, without her big belly and with burning stitches in her abdomen, she had run her fingers over Christine's wounds to draw her own map of survival.

The window of the hospital room looked out onto narrow-limbed, black-green cypresses, with tops that seemed to stab the clouds. Elene led Kitty into the room and explained to her that he came round intermittently, that when he did he even took a little food, but that he had not spoken since his arrival and Kitty shouldn't hope for too much. Then she offered her a chair, as if she, Elene, were the hostess at some happy event.

Another patient lay in the other corner of the room; he was conscious, and reading *Pravda*.

Cautiously, Kitty approached Andro's bed. He was lying slightly on his side, head turned towards the sunny window, one arm resting on top of the blanket. It took some time for her to see the old features in his face, which the intervening years had disfigured beyond all recognition. It wasn't easy to find the blond, curly-haired Andro, carver of angels, in this man with the matted beard.

How had he lived since she'd been gone? Who was the woman who had borne him a son? And what had his son been like? Did he resemble the son who had been denied the right to be born?

Elene told her that the doctors said he only had a few more weeks. Kitty stretched out her hand. She was shivering, although it was warm outside. Elene had gone over to the window and was looking down into the hospital garden with the tall cypresses and the white benches.

Neither of them saw the woman in a man's suit, with eyes like Andro's, who stood down there under the tallest cypress, looking up at them. Smiling patiently.

Dark veins were visible through his skin; skin rough and lined from the hard work to which he was so unsuited. From the busts of Lenin and the Generalissimus.

Kitty struggled for words.

'Andro, can you hear me?' she whispered, bringing her lips close to his ear. 'It's me, Kitty. I'm back. Here — my hand, can you feel it? I've come. To you, Andro.'

Only now did Kitty sit on the chair Elene had pulled up for her. Then she beckoned to Elene, who hurried over and sat on the edge of it, where Kitty had made space.

'Tell me about him. And about his son,' she said quietly, not taking her eyes off Andro's stony face.

As if she had waited centuries for this request, Elene began to talk. Cheerful and over-eager, the words and sentences gushed out of her such that even the *Pravda*-reading patient put down his paper for a moment and squinted over at them. She talked wildly, indiscriminately. About her childhood. About her time in Moscow. About Vasily and the Black Sea coast. Then the business with Miqa's film that no one had ever seen. Then about the night she and Lana had driven to the village in the mountains to fetch Andro. But mostly she talked about Miqa. She tried to tell the truth. She tried not to gloss over her own failure. But she couldn't do it: no matter what she said, no matter how long she went on talking, her words didn't create a unified picture, didn't make anything clear. There was no logic to her story, nothing made sense; the thread that could have led to Miqa's death was missing.

Elene kept glancing hopefully at Kitty, but gleaned no comfort from her features, no understanding, not even a reproach; it was as if Kitty's face were a mirror in which she saw only herself.

Suddenly, Kitty stood up and left the hospital room. Elene stared after her in dismay, incapable of connecting Kitty's exit to her report. Kitty walked past Christine into the orange-tiled hospital toilet, which stank of urine. The door swung shut behind her; immediately she leaned against it and stood there, motionless, for several minutes, trying to control her breathing. Then she walked over to the basin, which was yellowed with age, and turned on the tap. A brownish liquid flowed from it; recalling her mother's saying, 'Let the water run long enough and eventually it'll run clear,' she waited. Sure enough, the brown disappeared and the clear water came. She held her hands under it. She looked at herself in the scratched mirror. And screamed.

She sank to the wet floor, fell on her knees, still clinging to the basin with one hand. Her body was failing her. Her breath was failing her. People, too: all of them had failed her.

He would die. She would have to mourn him. He, too, would go.

There was so much she still wanted to say to him. She would have had to tell him the story of half her life. No — all of it. But differently: retold. The story he didn't know. Didn't understand. She wanted to puke up her silence, her impotence, into this miserable basin. To vomit with all she had and disgorge her fear, the fear of what was still to come. Yes: she was no longer interested in what might lie ahead. How could you live if you were constantly looking back?

★

She saw *him* again at the state banquet. Four days had passed since her arrival. Four days in the Green House, where a non-existent happiness was invoked and celebrated. There he stood, in the entrance to this stylish restaurant above the city, near the television tower. Between the white-clothed tables, under painfully garish lights, surrounded by frantic waiters and the suit-wearers who all dissolved into a grey mass in Kitty's eyes.

Kostya was originally supposed to accompany her to this reception, where she was to shake countless hands, give prepared answers to questions, and eat with people who inspected her with suspicion and, at the same time, were filled with envy; where she was to meet the musicians, painters, and writers who had been recognised and approved by the state and speak with them about the advantages of socialism. Where her every gesture and every word would be carefully weighed and she would be examined and judged on the degree of her capitalist depravity. Kostya, however, had caught the flu and stayed at home.

Instead, Kitty had brought her niece, who was wearing a bright yellow dress and was very excited. It seemed there was something she had to live with that she couldn't live with, and she was seeking in Kitty another life that Kitty — she was sure of it — would not be able to give her. Elene would end up being disappointed. This young woman looked so like her, yet was so unlike her in her passivity, her torpor, her inability to lead an autonomous life, while always longing for precisely that.

He greeted her, played the role of official chaperone so masterfully. He hadn't needed to rehearse this. Nor had she. He shook her hand. Not too firm, not too feeble.

Seated between Elene and a pianist, she kept glancing at him as she let the obligatory stilted speeches about friendship between peoples, art, homeland, socialism, the Georgian Communist Party and its impeccable leadership wash over her. And every time she looked at Alania she saw Andro's closed eyelids. The cracked lips, the feeble, cold hand, the ragged fingernails, the matted beard. And when she thought of him, she thought of the classroom and Mariam; she saw the blonde woman hidden behind the dark corner of a house, pulling her brother towards her. And then she saw the blood on the knife in the room on the Holy Mountain, and asked herself whether she had ever really left that room. And when she asked herself this, the next question was inevitable: after all that, how could she have bound anyone to her again, and how could she ever have believed a red-haired woman who, unlike her, was smart enough to know that concentration camp barracks and rooms with corpses are not places you ever leave?

★

Her rehearsals at the Philharmonia began the following day. They tried out the acoustics and the engineers did a sound check, under the eyes of Alania and two other men from the Georgian KGB. She hadn't performed for a very long time, particularly not in front of such a large audience. After her American tour, and then the split with Fred, she hadn't played any more big concerts.

She was to be accompanied on four songs from the album *Replacement* by a string quartet, and by a pianist for three more. They rehearsed together, and once they started playing she was actually able to forget Andro's face. Soon they were creating harmonies that drove the battle between socialism and capitalism out of her mind.

After rehearsals, Kitty would stroll around the streets of Tbilisi, accompanied by the three silent men. There was little she could do about the fact that she saw the city through the eyes of two people: the eyes of the red-haired junkie, Fred, and the eyes of the dying Andro.

The day of the concert was the only day Kitty didn't go to the hospital. Despite Alania's protests and the warnings of the security men, who refused to be shaken off, she had visited Andro in hospital every day, had stroked his hands and watched them artificially keep him alive; and once, unable to stop herself, she had lain on his chest and kissed his face over and over again. Elene had been outside, the *Pravda* patient asleep.

Now she was sitting alone in her dressing room at the Philharmonia, thinking of a particular hotel room in Baltimore. It had had heavy gold curtains, presumably from the Gilded Age. Fred had taken one of the curtains and wrapped the material round her body, draping it like a Victorian dress; she had put on Kitty's lipstick and posed as if singing an opera aria. Kitty had picked up Fred's newly purchased camera and taken a photo. A photo she'd never had developed, as the camera had disappeared along with the film and its owner.

Kitty hid her face in her hands for a moment, took a deep breath, rose to her feet, and stepped out on stage with her guitar. She would sing of her life of two halves. Here, on this stage, she could finally be who she was, and afterwards it would surely be harder for her to go back to the bad play in which she couldn't be who she wanted to be, couldn't say what she thought, couldn't mourn those she wanted to mourn. She was afraid the sentences she had learned by heart would run out, that she would lose control of her face, that her voice would crack. But she was buoyed up by the applause that broke out the moment she was caught in the spotlight, and the fear instantly vanished when she played the first chord on her guitar.

Who included me among the ranks of the human race?

JOSEPH BRODSKY

'I've got precisely twenty minutes. Then I have to go to some excruciating event, national children's dances or something. I wanted to have you to myself for a moment — you didn't come to the concert yesterday, and I thought ...'

Kitty was exhausted. She was sitting at the round table in Christine's living room, and her eyes had dark rings under them for lack of sleep.

Christine put her arms around her from behind and stood like that for a while. They listened to the old cuckoo clock ticking on the wall. Kitty closed her eyes. Leaned back against Christine's chest. Her body felt so weightless, like a bird you could hold in the palm of your hand.

'I don't know what's happened between you, but it seems unthinkable to me that you and *Deda* hardly see each other any more,' Kitty said wearily.

Christine moved away to fetch a carafe of cherry liqueur and two glasses. Then she sat down opposite her niece. Her gaze was full of warmth and comfort, as if she were laying a warm blanket round Kitty's shoulders.

'There are three men on the stairs outside my door. I assume they're here because of you.'

Christine poured the red liquid into the glasses.

'Yes, they follow me everywhere I go. Every second, every minute, they're there. Only when I'm with Kostya — then they leave us alone. Kostya's trustworthy enough for them. But I wanted to see you — all of you. Not this masquerade, Christine. I don't get to see you, *Deda* and Kostya are trying to turn my life into one long party, Andro isn't even conscious any more, and the rest, the rest is ... unbearable.'

Christine leaned across the table and pressed a kiss to Kitty's forehead. What Kitty really wanted to do was lie down on this table, right here and now, and ask her aunt to watch over her, to stroke her head as she had back then, during the worst time of her life; until her strength returned and she was healthy, raring to go and bursting with new songs. But at any minute they would knock on the door and remind her that this masquerade, in which, like it or not, she was playing the lead role, had to go on. She would go out to them, give them a friendly smile. They would warn her once again not to visit the dying deserter and traitor in hospital.

She got up and went to the bathroom. Since returning to her homeland she always seemed to be taking refuge in toilets and bathrooms, both public and private. They seemed to be the only places where she could assume she wouldn't be followed. It felt as if someone were squeezing her temples with forceps.

There was a knock on the apartment door. Kitty heard Christine open up. It was Alania. She recognised his footsteps. She heard him say something, and Christine invited him in. No — she couldn't go out yet. She let the water run.

★

'I'm sorry to disturb you, but they're waiting: I have to take Comrade Jashi away from you.' Alania was embarrassed. He felt inhibited and ugly before the once-beautiful Christine; he wanted to get out of this apartment again as quickly as possible. He thought of how Kostya had idolised this woman. This was the woman for whom he had delivered the parcel, an impotent attempt to comfort her after her tragedy. And it was the parcel he had to thank for his encounter with Kitty Jashi: it was because of Christine that he'd made that detour all those years ago. The detour that had lasted a lifetime.

She had opened the door to him, but now she stepped back in shock. Her lips parted as if she were going to cry out; then she closed them again and slowly backed away. She groped along the wall with one hand, feeling for something, found the switch and snapped on the overhead light. She stared at him as if she had seen something that scared her to death.

'Is everything all right?'

Alania raised his head and looked straight at her. Although it made him rather uneasy, he wanted to look at her properly, to impress her image on his mind. To seek the beauty behind the passage of time.

Christine had dyed her hair black and wore it swept into a stern, symmetrical bun at the nape of her neck. She wore a knee-length black dress and nylon stockings. One half of her face was veiled by a piece of dark-blue lace pinned to her hair. How many rumours had circulated about her, about the husband who had killed himself, about her lover? What strength must she have summoned, back then, to sacrifice her face for her honour, to preserve her dignity, to refrain from pumping her mind full of contempt.

Now she stepped a little closer to him. She slowly raised her right hand, as if she were about to touch him. Then lowered it again, and froze in that unnatural stance. He took a step towards her, afraid that she might fall, but she immediately folded both arms across her chest as if to protect herself from him.

'Who the hell are you? What are you doing in my apartment?' she asked quietly, almost hissing.

'Giorgi Alania — you must know my name, I'm an old friend of your nephew's. I trained with Kostya at the Frunze Higher Naval School in Leningrad, do you remember?'

He tried to speak in as calm and friendly a voice as possible.

'Giorgi Alania. Alania.' Christine repeated his name quizzically, as if it were very unusual, as if she were practising the correct pronunciation. Suddenly she shook her head, as if to dispel some fanciful thought; she seemed annoyed by her own irrational behaviour. 'I'm sorry; how silly of me. For a moment you reminded me of someone I used to know ... How stupid of me, that's just not possible, forgive me.'

Christine invited Alania into the living room.

'Kitty's in the bathroom. She'll be back in a minute.'

They sat down at the table, and Christine, clearly still agitated, reached for the glass of liqueur. She knocked it back and started scrutinising him again, studying his face. She kept shaking her head in disbelief, as if she were having an internal dialogue with herself. Then she laughed and slapped her forehead.

'Is there something the matter with my face?'

'No, no. It's just ...' she said, as if waking from a dream. 'It's just. I don't know how to say it.'

'Tell me what it is that's troubling you. I'd be more than happy to help.'

'You really do seem very familiar to me.'

Something about the way she said this made Alania prick up his ears.

'I think it's highly unlikely that we've met before. I would never have forgotten your face, never.'

'You are from Georgia, aren't you? Who are your parents?' she asked disarmingly, still absorbed in her examination of his features.

What was taking Kitty so long? Alania suddenly felt an urgent need to escape, not to be forced to continue this peculiar conversation.

'Yes, but you definitely won't know the village where my mother spent her whole life, I'm quite sure of that.' Alania continued to maintain an amiable and courteous tone.

'And your father?'

She wouldn't let it go. A question that was like a judgement. Alania cleared his throat. Lowered his head. Should he lie? Make up a father? A hardworking *kolkhoz* farmer, a patient teacher, a busy geologist, perhaps?

'There is no father.'

He gave the honest answer. Suddenly Christine stood up, walked over and stopped right in front of him; he smelled her slightly sweet, alcoholic breath as she bent down and touched his face. Goosebumps crept up his arm.

'Everyone has a father,' she said, almost inaudibly.

'I never had the chance to meet him. My mother died without explaining to me the precise circumstances of my … um, well, conception. I don't even know his name, and so I have no father.'

'It's quite remarkable … You're the spitting image of him. The same skin. Your voice is a little deeper, but it has the same timbre.'

'Who are you talking about?'

Alania was finding the situation increasingly uncomfortable. He tried to tell himself that she had, of course, mistaken him for someone else; but something about her manner refuted this. He wasn't prepared for it. Hoped that Kitty would come and save him.

'He was addicted to beautiful women. Preferably blonde, pale, tall, blue- or green-eyed. Was your mother blonde?'

She had listed these characteristics as if talking about a product that only rarely came onto the shelves at the grocer's. The alarm in her face had been replaced by a triumphant certainty.

'Yes, she was — and tall, too, but …'

'Or perhaps I'm entirely mistaken.'

She was about to go back to her chair, but he reflexively grabbed her hand and asked her to stop.

'Who are you talking about? Please, tell me.'

His voice wavered. He looked at her, appealing to her for help.

And then she spoke the name of the Little Big Man out loud. And as terrible and unlikely as this name seemed to him in the context of his own existence, at the same time it was like a key to the eternal puzzle of his origins. If he traced back the thread running through his life with this in mind, everything fitted together, completely logically. As if there could never have been any question of his having any other father. As if it were obvious that the Little Big Man had fathered him.

He had let go of her wrist. She, however, continued to look down at him.

His hands were trembling. He didn't have ultimate confirmation of this atrocity, but already the realisation was dripping into his consciousness like poison, paralysing his body.

Of course *it* had happened in Baku. The Little Big Man had studied there, he had lived there, had begun his stellar career there. And Gulo, little naive Gulo — what could she have said against him? The scales fell from his eyes. Of course his mother had had to remain silent. How could she have protected her offspring from his own progenitor?

Suddenly, he was paralysed by an appalling realisation. At some point *he* must have found out about his, Giorgi's, existence. Of course — he owed it all to the recommendation of his anonymous father: his admission to the naval academy that was open only to the best families in the country, the transfer to the Sea of Japan, his recruitment, and the move to Moscow! Beads of sweat broke out on Giorgi Alania's brow. He felt as if he were about to fall off his chair. The Amur shipyard, and the visit from the senior official just before the end of the war! Of course. His whole life had gone according to his invincible father's plan!

Yes, this woman was right. Everyone had a father.

He lost his composure: tears rolled down his cheeks. Christine didn't move. Nor was she looking at him any more. She had found what she had been searching for. Now she would be patient. She would wait. She had all the time in the world. She was the messenger. The black angel.

★

Even the security men had been invited to Kostya's table. They were all there: the madmen and the hypocrites, the parasites and the opportunists, the sympathisers, the servants and the commanders, the wives and the lovers, all sat there eating a celebratory dinner in Kitty's honour. Only Alania had not come. He had excused himself right at the beginning of the feast and disappeared. Kitty had waited for him in vain; she had hoped he would return and brush his knee against hers under the table, the assurance that everything was fine. But nothing was fine. She knew that, and so did he.

She found him on the hill, standing there in the dark. The terrifying abyss of the gorge fell away into infinite blackness. Crickets could be heard exchanging their secrets. The distant conviviality of the company around the table and the loud, long-winded toasts drifted up to where they stood, on the edge of the property, as snatches of echoes.

'What's going on? Why did you leave?' She saw that his eyes were red, swollen. He was shivering as if he were delirious. Without knowing why, she knelt before him.

'Giorgi? What's happened to you?'

'It can't be true, not now, not like this ...' he kept repeating.

For the first time, she saw terrible fear in his face. Now it was her turn to catch him, to offer him refuge, to spread her wings over him. He clasped her so tightly she could barely keep her balance. She took his hand and guided it to her neck. She nestled her head in his hand, she let his hand stroke her neck. She kissed him.

He ran his forefinger over his lips in disbelief, as if checking to see whether she had left her taste on them.

Sometimes it was lips that were the wings, sometimes just words, and sometimes treasured photos.

★

Andro died three days after Kitty's departure. He didn't regain consciousness, but my mother says the last time Kitty was there with him he clutched her hand. I don't know whether this was just the reflex of a dying man, or whether it could perhaps be construed as a gesture of reconciliation — which was my mother's interpretation.

BOOK VI

★

DARIA

> We're not the ones who invented this world,
> I'm not the one who invented this world.
> A world where you can do anything,
> But you'll never change a single thing.
>
> ALLA PUGACHEVA

For Daria and me, the Soviet Union meant: constant funeral marches and processions as aged gentlemen of the Communist Party were carried to their graves; carnations everywhere, macabre spectacles broadcast on all the television channels. For us, the Soviet Union meant: endless summer camps, Pioneer neckerchiefs. Tea plantations, apiaries, and *kolkhozes*. White knee-socks from China, tapestries of hunting scenes on the walls, Mishka Na Severe chocolates, and Lagidze's tarragon lemonade. Our grandfather's GAZ-13, the brightly coloured blocks of Plasticine with the frog on them, yellow Krya-Krya children's shampoo, Grandfather's Start shaving cream, the talcum powder in the bathroom cabinet with the cat's head on the pot, which we weren't allowed to use. Hygiene body lotion, and Stasia's Red Moscow perfume, which smelled of old people and was enough to give you a headache. The odourless brown bath-soap that was actually called 'Bath Soap'.

It was the brown school uniforms from Moscow — a symbol of prosperity — and the identical, but more coarsely cut, uniforms made in Tbilisi and worn by everyone whose parents were not company directors, professors, or commissars. It was the fat, white-aproned women sitting in canteens, grocery stores, cafés, hotel corridors, and beside the malt-beer tanks. The Cao Sao Vang Golden Star Aromatic Balm, also known as 'Vietnam ointment': tiger balm, which smelled appalling, and which you had rub on your chest if you had a cold coming on.

It was the triangular blue and white kefir cartons and milk in glass bottles, both of which could be bought in the city's *Gastronoms*, where the product range was otherwise pretty limited. The Soviet Union meant delicious condensed milk, which we would drink secretly straight from the can, and disgusting fish paste. The calendar that hung in every good socialist kitchen, with a daily recipe for socialist housewives, and all the important socialist holidays and biographies, and useful, but less socialist, tips for everyday life: 'Aloe vera can reduce inflammation, if you ...'

It was the red identity cards with the logo of Lenin's head for workers, pensioners, and Komsomol members; the games that were called things like 'The Thinker' or 'The Young Watchmaker', and especially the most coveted game 'The Young Chemist', over which Daria and I argued constantly. It was the man and the woman clutching, respectively, a hammer and a sickle, the identification for almost all socialist films (like MGM's roaring lion).

It was Cheburashka and Winnie the Pooh, which we pronounced 'Veeny da Puh', characters from socialist cartoons; it was the dreadful snowsuits our mother wrapped us up in every winter, which you had to take off completely if you wanted a wee, and the scratchy woollen socks. It was Misha the Bear with the medal belt, the mascot of the 1980 Moscow Olympics. (This bear lived on in almost every socialist household for many years after the Olympics in the form of every conceivable toy as well as on flags, plates, and cups.)

It was the yellow Zhigulis, the black Volgas, and the white Ladas. The red plastic stars you could stick to your chest, with a photo of Lenin as a baby or a child (age not really discernible). It was Melody records and Maxim cassettes, which didn't come cheap. Gulliver chocolate bars, and coffee-flavoured chewing gum, with a bitter taste no child in the world has ever found appealing. It was soft toys made of heavy, scratchy woollen material, predominantly dogs or bears (bears, always bears!), which only a very generous-minded person would describe as 'soft toys'. It was Friendship processed cheese and the Vanka-Vstanka roly-poly toy that looked like a hollow plastic Russian doll gone wrong. It was delicious Leningrad ice cream, solid oblongs wrapped in gold paper. It was the Russian Father Christmas with his red nose (minus the beer belly of the Coca-Cola Santa). It was heavy tin teapots and highly sought-after 8mm cameras. Brightly coloured underpants with pictures of happy sportsmen or the days of the week written on them. It was cheap pamphlets with titles like *The Truth About American Diplomats*. The grey and mostly out-of-order public phone-boxes. The grannies' net shopping-bags. (These are common to grannies all over the world, though; God knows where they get them from!)

It was buckwheat and meatballs. Rose jam. Indian instant coffee. Imitation jeans made by Mavin or Lae. Blue and beige school satchels; tooth powder; plastic dip pens; Kremlin-patterned vases; thin green exercise books with

'Exercise Book' written on them; Metro tokens stamped with an 'M'; table tennis and badminton in summer; bad haircuts; the Electronica 302 tape-recorder.

Astra brand cigarettes, which Stasia smoked, and Georgian Cosmos cigarettes (the first drag Daria and I took in the school toilets was on a Cosmos); electric clocks, for those who wanted to show off; abacuses in shops and at the market, at school and at work; dominoes in beautiful, slim boxes inlaid with mother-of-pearl.

It was plane tickets to Moscow for 36.50 roubles. (We did not avail ourselves of these.) It was *Illusion*, a programme shown every Saturday on the First Channel of the Georgian Public Broadcaster, which featured foreign films, sometimes censored, sometimes abridged. Classics like *Kind Hearts and Coronets*, at which Stasia always grew dewy-eyed, and *Some Like It Hot*, at which Kostya laughed wholeheartedly, but also *The Stunt Man* with Peter O'Toole and Barbara Hershey, who was a great favourite of Daria's and mine. It was the Bus Cinemas, busses that drove around the city's neighbourhoods, ringing bells like ice-cream vans; they would gather up an audience of mainly young people and show romantic films. The *Angélique* series from the 1960s was of course right at the top of the Bus Cinemas' top ten. Daria and I were always arguing about which was best, *Untameable Angélique* or *Angélique and the Sultan*. Next on the list came *The Count of Monte Cristo* and all the Bollywood movies.

It was cinemas, like the Apollo and the Kazbegi. It was *Ogonyok* magazine; it was illegally pedalled photos of foreign actors, which you could usually buy from gypsies in subways and outside Metro entrances. It was the musical-comedy films that came in patriotic, romantic, and pro-worker varieties, and were an insult to any level of intelligence. The polyester tracksuits and delicious Glace milkshakes: my favourite flavour — strawberry, Daria's — vanilla.

Later, it was Café Franzia, the Budapest restaurant, and the tea house opposite the university. It was secretly listening to Voice of America. It was the vending machines that looked like fridges, had 'Sparkling Water' written on them, and almost never worked. It was *Burda* magazine, which came from Germany and had to be bought on the black market, with its highly sought-after sewing patterns. It was the trolley buses, the hostile *militsiya* men, and the manuscripts of novels by dissidents and traitors, printed and distributed in secret.

We read the Russian and Georgian classics; Alexandre Dumas, of course; the French Romantics. Romain Rolland was very popular — he had sympathised with the communists, after all, and visited the Soviet Union. People could never agree on how to classify Joyce and Faulkner, but they weren't banned. The existentialists were difficult to get hold of. You could find plenty of Gorky though, and Krylov's fables. And Tolstoy, Henry James, Thackeray, and Twain, of course. Lermontov and Pushkin led the field. And, of course, *The Knight in the Panther's Skin* — Rustaveli's great Georgian epic — stood above them all.

The poets people read were mostly dead. But thanks to the *Literaturnaya Gazeta*, you might get lucky from time to time and find something by a living one.

Later still, for us, the Soviet Union meant saving up for black-market records, books, and videos. We bought the Stones, Pink Floyd, Led Zeppelin, and later Queen, too. In the 1980s it was Russian rock bands, Kino and DDT, who seemed not to give a damn whether or not the state approved of men having long hair.

It was the subversive poetry evenings in back courtyards, attics, basements. You had to be sufficiently 'anti' already to penetrate these illustrious circles. Your best bet was to be in trouble with the *militsiya*. In these back courtyards, attics, basements you'd find bottle-blondes with dark rings under their eyes who frequently jotted things down in notebooks decorated with dried flowers, and devoted most of their energy to looking pensive and unworldly. Boys who read out subversive poetry with great enthusiasm and spittle in the corners of their mouths, though nobody could say precisely what level of subversion you had to attain to become king of these courtyards, attics, basements. And bearded men over forty, who were also to be found in these courtyards, attics, basements — sometimes, albeit rarely, accompanied by women also over forty, who generally didn't colour their hair, who liked to talk about spirituality and believed the prophecies of Nostradamus; who had managed, in their youth, to hitchhike across the Northern Caucasus and still went camping in Svaneti.

It was the gypsy women who offered Marlboro Reds from a wicker basket, if you put enough money in the basket first. It was the lengths you had to go to in order to obtain a ticket for a private screening at the House of Film.

For me, the Soviet Union was the childhood I shared with my sister.

It was our grandfather's power. It was the innumerable compliments Daria received, like a rock star receiving the crowd's screams of wild devotion. It was fatherlessness. It was giggling every night under the bedclothes in the Green House. It was Stasia's ballet lessons in the barn, though for some reason I was the only one who did them; Daria didn't have to go. It was our fascination with Christine's veil, and the constant arguments between our mother and her father, or between me and Daria. It was shuttling back and forth between Mother's one-and-a-half-room pre-fab apartment and the Green House. It was

Kostya's all-forgiving love for Daria, and Stasia's grouchy but unconditional love for me. It was secretly tasting Stasia's liqueurs in the pantry. Hiding in the woods. It was being shouted at and grounded, the two constant companions of my misdeeds. The carnival costumes for school parties: rabbit ears, wolf tails, Red Riding Hood pinafores, Karlsson-on-the-Roof propellers, witches' talons, and even a skirt made of palm leaves (as Robinson Crusoe's Man Friday). The continual playground brawls, in which Daria took no part.

The Soviet Union was *Vremya* every evening, and the television announcer with the thick glasses who read all the news as if the world was going to end the following day. The Soviet Union was the red star atop the spruce that was put up on New Year's Eve. The Soviet Union was where international friendships and folk dances happened, where everyone was welcome, except those from 'abroad'. *They* were capitalists, and all over the world people were starving because other people were only interested in money, and let their fellow man sink into poverty so they could grow rich.

Abroad, no matter where, was Sodom and Gomorrah. Everyone there took drugs, and the governments took no interest in their citizens and let them die miserable deaths. Abroad, everyone did it with everyone else, and made babies no one was interested in and for whom there were no nursery places. Abroad was an evil place from which no Soviet citizen had ever returned. Abroad was full of wicked spies and human traffickers. They still had slaves, and they didn't know about things like friendship between nations and brotherliness. They were ruled entirely by the crude, brutal laws of money, or the illusion of a peaceful existence created by the lie of religion, which everyone knew was the opiate of the people.

You had to stay alert and help the countries that wanted to free themselves from the evil clutches of capitalism. The countries that had already freed themselves were our sisters, our friends, and we were allowed to travel to them. We could visit the Soviet Union (where in principle, of course, we already were); we could go to Mongolia, Yugoslavia, Albania, Bulgaria, Poland, Romania, the German Democratic Republic, Czechoslovakia, and Hungary; we could go to North Korea, China, Cuba, Guinea, South Yemen, Somalia, the Congo, Madagascar, Cambodia, Laos, Ethiopia, Angola, Mozambique, Benin, Grenada, Nicaragua, and Zimbabwe. And, just as I was starting school, we were also given permission to go to Vietnam. Soon after that we would also be allowed to go to Afghanistan.

So we had plenty of friends. And the countries ruled by the evil of capitalism — well, we didn't want to go to those places anyway. What did we want with decadent, warped western Europe, which was heading for collapse, to say nothing of the ultimate evil of America? What did we want with France, where they ate snails; or Italy, which was crawling with *mafiosi* and where people prayed to an old man in a white dress? What did we want with Latin America (with the exception of Cuba), where there were bugs and rainforests? What did we want with Japan, where they made women wear shoes that were much too small for them so their feet would stay small? What did we want with Scandinavia, where you couldn't even have a proper drinking session? What did we want with dangerous America, where drugs lay about on the street and everyone who wasn't rich got depressed and jumped out of windows one after another for lack of a motherly state to take care of them?

And yes, of course, people in the capitalist countries Abroad had some nice things, too: they had cool music and films; they didn't have to get married before they were allowed to have sex or get an apartment together; they had much better clothes. And you didn't have to spend weeks camping outside the Intourist office to get a visa for anywhere you wanted to go, and you didn't have to spend years on a waiting list for a car. But what did that matter? Freedom was, after all, just a matter of definition. They weren't allowed to go to Vietnam any more, and soon they wouldn't be allowed into Afghanistan. But we were.

For Daria and me, first and foremost the Soviet Union meant our family. Our family, and a famous aunt who lived abroad and who, as we believed for a long time, had been trafficked to the West by evil capitalists — why else would she have fled her homeland? The Soviet Union was our friends. Our streets. Our courtyards. Our parks. Our games. Our past. And, of course, the future. (What alternatives were there?)

For us, the Soviet Union was a privilege that both Daria and I enjoyed for many years, because we had our grandfather's surname.

★

Shortly after Kitty returned to London, Elene enrolled in the English language and literature preparatory course at the Institute of Foreign Languages and started studying for the entrance exam. Nana, beside herself with joy that her daughter had — hopefully — decided on a pedagogical career, advised, supported, and encouraged her. And Kostya, though he was suspicious of the English language, was also pleased that his daughter had finally come to her senses and wanted to make something of herself. Elene passed the entrance exam and embarked on her degree. It was too expensive to travel between the Green House and Tbilisi, and at first she stayed with a friend in Sololaki. She spent most of her time with Lana, though, who, after successfully submitting her diploma project, had found a position in the Centre for Engineering and Industrial Planning, which constructed large factories all over the Soviet Union. But Elene still avoided visiting Christine's apartment, where Christine was selflessly caring for little Miro.

Elene quickly grew bored with her fellow students, who were predominantly female and very conformist; instead, she made friends with people studying at the Academy of Art or the Institute of Film and Theatre, whom she had met through Lana. In doing so, Elene stayed true to form and followed her interests, or rather her lack of interest in the world: she mostly chose to be with young men who listened to rock music, smoked weed, attended those subversive poetry evenings, and talked a lot about spirituality. They weren't actually brave enough to stand up to the law, as Miqail, Beqa, and his friends had been, but in comparison with the good little foreign-language girls they were regular Che Guevaras.

At the start of her degree, Elene made several more attempts to emancipate herself from her family and above all from her father, with the approval of her friends, who objected to people using their family privileges for their own advantage (yet secretly did so themselves). But because nobody wanted to employ a privileged creature like Elene Jashi as a cleaning lady or security guard, Elene had to accept money from her father after all.

During the week, she stayed in the city. The weekends, she spent with us. Daria, the queen in Kostya's kingdom, was sent to a Tbilisi kindergarten, while I was left to my own devices, and to Stasia. Clad in white tights, I got to have ballet lessons and practise my ungainly leaps alongside a few girls from the village, while every morning Kostya's driver would take Daria into town and bring her and our grandparents home in the evening.

The mornings were a frenetic burst of activity (my first childhood memories): Kostya and Nana getting ready for work, the rushed breakfast, the search for Daria's clothes, and then the silence that descended when they had all gone off in the car and Stasia and I were left there alone. A wonderful, magical silence that harboured so many secrets. You just had to pay close attention and listen patiently for them. The crickets in summer, the doves in autumn, the forest in winter, the breeze that danced through the rocks in spring. The sweet melody of all these sounds was like an orchestra playing in perfect harmony, playing just for us, for Stasia and me.

The first thing Stasia and I would do was the gardening. In dirty rubber boots, armed with tools, we marched out into the rain, the sun, the wind, and took care of the flowers, fruit, and vegetables. Now and then, I would hear Stasia talking to her flowers, but I found nothing strange in that — it was a lovely, familiar ritual that made me feel safe and protected.

Later, we would gather up the leftovers from the previous day and put them in a tin bucket, which we took to the well in the middle of the village. We would distribute the contents of the bucket to the stray dogs there. Watching the lice-ridden creatures eating was one of my favourite pastimes in those days. Later still, Stasia would switch on the television, and we would watch *Skilful Hands*, with its tips for household chores and its grandmothers' remedies, like bringing down a fever with vinegar-soaked socks or curing a headache with lime blossom.

After lunch, we took our afternoon nap in Stasia's room, on the hard daybed where she preferred to sleep, which to me seemed the cosiest place in the world. When I woke up, Stasia would already be busy with dinner in the kitchen, and I would hear her clattering pots and pans about. The aroma of the spices she so loved would draw me to the kitchen. I would come running in, barefoot, wanting to help out right away. The radio was always playing in the background; she loved to listen to schmaltzy old songs as she prepared meals, and would sway along to certain melodies.

While dinner simmered in the pot or sizzled in the pan, we would go out onto the terrace and play a game of 'I Spy', during which I often accused her of pretending to be stupider than she was, because I always won. Some days, when she was especially pensive, she didn't want to play with me and instructed me to listen to the silence. She had told me once that only stupid children couldn't coax any sounds out of the silence, and because I didn't want to be a stupid child, I sat beside her wearing the most serious expression I could muster, pretending I was learning the secrets of the world.

Every Tuesday and Thursday, in the early evening, there was an activity I liked less: the ballet lessons. The farm girls would assemble promptly outside the barn. Stasia would begin to blossom, and I had to give it my all as well. In front of the makeshift mirrors, at the barre, which was too high for me, I had to pretend it was my greatest dream to become the next Maya Plisetskaya, the Bolshoi ballerina whom Stasia admired so much.

How she came alive during those lessons; how her eyes sparkled as she corrected our posture, as she tirelessly stretched alongside us; how reverently she would listen to the music as she choreographed silly little dances for us.

If I made a special effort, I would be richly rewarded after a successful ballet lesson with peeled pomegranates, sugared figs, and persimmons cut into tiny pieces. But for me the greatest reward was her stories. She started telling me tales from the past whenever she was pleased with my achievements. Stasia, who was otherwise so reticent, transformed into Scheherazade and introduced me to a hidden world painted in the most extraordinary colours. In flowery language, with dramatic climaxes and exciting twists, playing first one role and then another, putting on different voices, she brought the past into the present.

She constructed the house where she was born before my very eyes. Described her father, and the ever-present scent of chocolate that enveloped the house and attracted visitors. She spoke of the indomitable Kabardins and the steppe. She told me about the secret passages in the cave monastery. I could even feel the texture of her younger sister's clothes. (Stasia always spoke of little Christine in a particular tone, quiet, almost reverent, her eyes aglow.) I could touch Simon's uniform, could see her stepmother's jewellery sparkling.

She told me about the *Ballets Russes* and the grace of Anna Pavlova. She told me about the golden domes of the St Petersburg cathedrals. About the summer palace and Thekla's cellar storeroom. Quoted Sopio's poems to me, all of which she seemed to know by heart, and described her son's wheat-blond curls.

Her words were like magic spells, plunging me into another world, a world I didn't know, which lay somewhere long, long ago, in a place to which Stasia had the only key.

How I hated the days when she refused to tell me stories. How hard was the punishment when she was dissatisfied with my dancing. How deep my disappointment on the days when she decided I hadn't earned a tale. I would have danced until my feet bled or forced myself to do the splits hundreds of times over if only she would bring those enchanted times back to life for me. I loved her stories, but all the *arabesques* and *retirés* were foreign to me. My imagination grew fevered when her voice embarked on a story, not when I heard Tchaikovsky. I wanted to listen; I wanted to complete this other world in my head. I had fallen in love with this world, and the only reason I kept dancing was to have her tell me its stories.

If I was in luck and she kept telling stories until the others got back from the city, I could think of nothing else all evening, and even when I went to bed, I would refuse the bedtime fairy tale that Nana would read to Daria and me. I was so full of Stasia's memories that there was no more room inside me. Stasia's stories took possession of me; they filled me up. Without really understanding it myself, I dreamed of writing them down, transforming them into my own words. I wanted to turn them into my own story.

★

The whole of my childhood in the Green House — the time before I started asking questions, before anger and sadness could gather within me, before I broke open the beautiful puzzle that had been presented to me as our family history, before I began to peek behind the curtains that were drawn in my face — I spent with these stories, which were Stasia's memories. And so for me, my life begins right there, in the year 1900, in that bitterly cold winter when Stasia came into the world. I was born then, too, just as you were, Brilka. My childhood didn't start in 1974 — no, it began much earlier, it reaches much deeper. My childhood, when I thought myself free and happy, because I was so sure of Stasia's love, *is* these stories. Where they begin, I begin. All these places, towns, houses, people — they are all a part of my childhood. The Revolution as much as the War, the dead as much as the living. All these people, lives, places burned themselves so firmly into my brain, they were so present there, that I began to live with them. I still needed Stasia if I wanted to wander around in these times, to pass through them, dive into them. But soon, I hoped, I would be capable of telling the stories myself, telling them anew, completing them.

To Nana, Daria and I were children, to be chastised and educated. Children, who must be clearly shown what was good and what was bad. To Elene, we remained babies; babies who were aware of nothing beyond their own needs and pleasures, both of whom loved sweets and being taken to the zoo, who went to the circus or the puppet theatre on Sundays, and cried if they fell over or burned their fingers.

To Kostya, Daria was an angel and I was the bastard. Everything Daria did was enchanting, enthralling; it took his breath away. When she fell over, when her nose ran or she wet herself, it was heartrending or, at the very least, disarming.

I remained the foreign body in this little paradise Kostya had constructed for his princess. He avoided me. He didn't feel comfortable when — and this happened seldom enough — I was alone in the house with him, with no Nana, no Stasia, no Elene around to defend him from me.

Of course, I, too, would receive a present when Daria did, I got a kiss when he pressed one on Daria's cheek, and for lack of alternatives I, too, was taken for a walk or to the amusement park when he went out with Daria. It's just that certain things weren't expressed, not in words. Daria was the protective shield he held up against me. I had to learn to want what Daria wanted, to say what Daria said, to permit what Daria permitted, to refuse what Daria refused.

The evenings, when the adults and Daria brought the Green House back to life, were the most hated times of my childhood. In the evening, everything was entirely centred on Kostya and Daria. She was the sun in our galaxy. And we dying stars flared up every evening for the last time before collapsing and being extinguished in the universe, only to create ourselves anew the next morning as soon as they left the house.

At the weekends, just as I finally thought I had our mother all to myself, since Daria spent most of her time with Kostya, Daria would invariably get chicken pox or the flu, or fall over and hurt her knee, or simply whine and refuse to leave Elene's side for a second, and I would run to Stasia, filled with anger and disappointment, curl up on her lap, and cry my eyes out, until Mother finally extricated herself from Daria's arms, hurried over to me, and told me all sorts of nonsense, and in less than two minutes I would be forced to laugh.

But for some strange reason, I acknowledged Daria's rights and privileges. As if they were a law of nature, something self-evident. All the same, sometimes a blind rage rolled over me, something uncontrollable and irrational took possession of me, and I would run at Daria, ram my knee into her or throw her to the floor, give her a painful pinch in the belly or poke her backside with a pencil, which gave me a strange pleasure. Later, when I was at school, there was only one thing that could surpass this pleasure: testing my grandfather's patience. There was nothing in the world I loved more than making him lose his self-control, seeing his iron countenance transformed into a grimace of rage, causing his voice to waver. I knew if it got really bad, I could always run to Stasia, and she would shake her head and give me a sympathetic look and say, 'So, what have you done this time?'

★

Elene loved us in her chaotic, off-kilter way. She found it hard to watch her two children growing up without a father, to stay on top of her degree, and to swallow down the larger part of her self-hatred without anyone seeing, much as she wanted to be a woman who just sailed through all of this. Her inner turmoil was reflected in our behaviour. Sometimes we cried at night, our faces buried in our pillows, longing for our mother; sometimes we didn't want to see her at all. We would avoid her, and were shy and distant when she came to the Green House on Friday evenings.

Kostya constantly undermined her authority, made sarcastic comments about her parenting methods and largely ignored her wishes, to such a degree that we, too — unconsciously, of course — began siding with him, and refused to listen to her whenever our grandfather was around.

The times that made me saddest of all were when Elene wandered restlessly about the house and up to the attic like a hunted animal. I spied on her, tracking her, discovering her hiding places and watching in secret as, armed with a lamp, a blanket, a glass of wine or liqueur, and a book, she withdrew into a world to which we were denied access.

The only satisfaction I could glean from those days was the realisation that Elene showed Daria the same thoughtless indifference as she did me. It was a parity that united us in the battle for her attention. The equality of our efforts. For neither chickenpox nor tantrums could help Daria win Elene for herself; on such days, our mother remained as distant and unreachable for Daria as she was for me.

> Political power grows out of the barrel of a gun.
>
> CHAIRMAN MAO

Two funerals — the son and the father — in such close succession, Christine's total disappearance from his life, and his sister's surprise visit and the excitement surrounding it had taken more out of Kostya than he would have thought possible.

Unlike his mother and his aunt, who were both enjoying surprisingly good health at their advanced age — apart from a few rheumatic pains and low blood pressure (Stasia), and arthritis, varicose veins, and joint pain (Christine) — Kostya, who was now in his mid-fifties, was really feeling his age. Maybe it was just that he gave a lot more thought to his health than his mother or aunt did. He found it hard to admit that some of his female companions were now simply out of his league. But the thing that threw him most at that time was the news of Alania's transfer home.

His old friend had called and told him that, after more than twenty years in the field, he had been ordered back to headquarters and was returning to Moscow. Despite the untroubled tone Alania was so careful to maintain on the phone, my grandfather was not deaf to the tension and fear in his friend's voice. Something had gone wrong. Was it to do with Kitty? Had something come to light that should have remained buried? Of course, he couldn't permit himself such questions over the phone, but he sensed that he could not leave his friend alone now, could not abandon him to his fate. He promised to come to Moscow as soon as Alania's transfer had taken place.

★

Giorgi Alania had not been healed by the truth about his parentage. The thing he'd hoped for all his life had not happened. The paralysis remained. He couldn't talk to anyone about it, least of all Kitty. Letting Kitty in on the secret was out of the question.

After his return to London, he withdrew. He didn't get in touch with her, stopped visiting, wove a steel cocoon around himself. Kitty's attempts to help her friend and share in his troubles came to nothing. She felt cheated, useless, rejected. He blamed his withdrawal on the dangerous level of carelessness he had displayed over the past few months, and warned her about his colleagues, who could put an abrupt end to the friendship they had become increasingly open about. His behaviour had been stupid and naive, he said, when in fact everything was at stake.

'But now that we've been to Tbilisi together, now we know each other *officially*, so to speak, surely we don't have to hide from your people — surely there's nothing stopping us from seeing each other?' Kitty couldn't understand him.

'It's not appropriate for me to associate with a western singer. As much as we may have grown to like each other over those two weeks, the fundamental situation hasn't changed. Don't forget why I was sent to this country.'

He dashed her hopes. For the first time since he'd come into her life, she felt he had let her down. She was groping in the dark, unable to understand what had prompted his cold, distant demeanour, the unexpected way he had turned from her. She felt indignant that now, of all times, when she was so full of overwhelming and confusing feelings for him, he was leaving her on her own.

She didn't understand that he was ashamed, that he judged himself unworthy of her, that he was afraid of himself, of his heritage, of his own blood. That he had gone along with everything, had sent all those people home, using cunning, threats — and quite often violence. And what if none of it was true? What if all the hundreds of photos he had examined through a magnifying glass in the British Library, the old newspaper cuttings with portraits of a bald-headed little man with a pince-nez, a man who had so effortlessly taught the world to fear, were nothing to do with him at all? What if Ramas Iosebidze's unhappy widow had simply made a dreadful error?

Kitty was a silk thread that could be snapped with a flick of the wrist. Kitty had been the only thing worth dreaming about, as long as his dreams remained dreams. Kitty was the only bright, fragile, breakable thing for which it was worth heaping up these broken shards. What choice would he have, if she should want to link her future with his? He had no future. Not in the place where she was; and if there were to be a future for him — as unlikely as that seemed — he wasn't going to risk being spurned, rejected, or even despised by her.

He should never have stepped out of his own shadow. Never have become part of her life. Never have made plans with her. Never have travelled back into the past with her.

★

First, he missed one of their meetings. Just didn't turn up. Then he stopped calling. Kitty realised that something had been lost, something definitive had happened, and there was nothing she could do about it. She waited and waited. In vain. Then she called Amy.

'Finally! I thought you'd never get back in touch! I thought you'd got married back home and would be herding sheep in the Caucasus by now!' cried Amy indignantly, blowing a cloud of cigarette smoke into the receiver.

'I have twelve new songs. We can go into the studio next week, if you like. I'm ready. But I want to get out of London. As far away as I can.'

'Hallelujah! I'll sort everything out, and give you a call on Monday.' Amy went straight back to her no-nonsense managerial tone, and hung up.

The day Alania wrote his application for a transfer back to Moscow, Kitty went into the studio and recorded the first track for a new album with the simple title *Home*.

I remember it so well, Brilka: as you and I were driving across Greece, we talked about the first song on that album, the title track, and I remember you saying that the song wasn't about a place or a country, it was about a condition. You said you thought it was a song about childhood, and you asked me where people keep their childhood, and I remember telling you that we keep it hidden, between our ribs, in little liver spots and moles, in the roots of our hair, above our heart, in our ears or our laugh.

Home was released in 1976, five years after *Replacement*, the same year the whole of Vietnam became a socialist republic and Saigon ceased to exist and Ho Chi Minh City was born; when Mao Zedong died and China was visited by a devastating earthquake, as if the earth were joyfully shaking off the great dictator; the year Honecker was elected Chairman of the State Council of East Germany, and abortion was legalised in West Germany; the year Ulrike Meinhof was found hanged in her cell, and Fritz Lang died in LA and Agatha Christie in Winterbrook; the year of the great anti-apartheid uprising in Soweto; the year *Hotel California* was a hit and punk exploded into life— and the year Fred Lieblich embarked on her third and final stint in rehab.

★

'Girls, come with me,' whispered Elene.

I rubbed my eyes. I could only see her silhouette in the moonlight. Daria was already sitting on her bed, wearing her white pyjamas with the rocking horse print.

'Come on, Niza, wake up. We're going to do something exciting!'

Elene had been drinking, both Daria and I could smell it, and we braced ourselves for one of Mother's silly, playful, unpredictable moods.

It was the middle of the night, a Saturday. The previous day she hadn't come to the Green House as usual, and her absence had sent Kostya into an exhausting fit of rage. He spent hours ranting about his failure of a daughter and his wretched mother. He demanded that his wife convince Elene to move back into the Green House with her children. She should just go into the city every morning with the rest of them, with him, Nana, and Daria. Otherwise he would stop supporting her financially. Kostya demanded that Nana tell Elene all of this right now, this very minute. So Nana had no choice but to call the friend Elene still officially lived with and ask to speak to her daughter. The friend told her that Elene hadn't lived there for weeks; she had a new boyfriend and was presumably staying with him. Elene could not be found. Now, after her parents had spent two whole days searching for her, she had crept back into the house like a thief and was trying to kidnap us while we were half-asleep. Stuffing our clothes willy-nilly into a canvas bag, she warned us to be quiet. I had already jumped out of bed and was holding up my arms so she could pull a jumper over my head. Daria whined that she didn't want to get up, and wasn't at all excited about the promised adventure.

'Don't be a spoilsport!' Elene told her eldest daughter, forcing her into her clothes.

Soon we were tiptoeing out of the sleeping house to her car. There was a man at the wheel. We were bundled into the back, and the man stepped on the gas.

'This is my boyfriend, Aleko. So now you're finally getting to meet each other.' Elene turned to us from the front seat. 'Do you know what he does? He writes really brilliant things. Stories and poems and fairy tales — he can tell you stories that'll make your head spin. And he loves candyfloss, just like the two of you. He thinks we should go to Mushtaidi Park tomorrow and eat as much candyfloss as we like — what do you reckon?'

'I don't like candyfloss, Niza likes candyfloss. Grandfather says candyfloss gives you toothache. I prefer ice cream,' said Daria, interrupting our mother; but Elene seemed to have made up her mind that we were all going to be perfectly happy together, and refused to let it spoil her mood. The man was smiling at us, too, in the rear-view mirror. He seemed very tall: his head almost touched the car roof. He could have been Elene's father, not a 'boyfriend', or so I thought at the time; he looked much older than her, with his full beard and the big bags under his eyes.

When we arrived, my mother carried Daria up the stairs of their filthy apartment block while the tall, bearded man carried me. A grey dawn was already in the sky, and I was freezing. Elene unlocked a door and we entered a narrow hallway. The hall led straight into an uncarpeted room, the walls of which were covered with posters; there were two beanbags, a small hostess trolley that served as a table, and two oversized box speakers with dusty records piled up on them. A glass-panelled door with newspaper stuck over the space where the glass should have been led off into another, evidently smaller, room: the bedroom, presumably. The bed was a mattress on the floor, and clothes were draped everywhere, over the chairs and chests of drawers — there was no wardrobe. A large teddy bear with a missing ear sat on the mattress. Elene pointed at it and said it was a little welcome gift from her boyfriend.

She undressed us and laid us down on the mattress. I'd never shared a bed with Daria before. Luckily, she was too tired to protest.

Next morning, though, it started: 'This isn't a proper bed! I'm hungry. Where's Mama?' She immediately started complaining. I crept out of the room to find Elene. They had set up a much too narrow fold-out bed between the beanbags, and were lying asleep in each other's arms. They looked peaceful. A half-empty vodka bottle and a full ashtray stood beside the bed. I approached the sleeping couple and gently touched my mother's bare shoulder. It was March; spring was dragging its heels that year, and the air in the flat was icy. Elene woke instantly and sat up in bed, startled.

'Niza, my sunshine, how long have you been awake?'

'Daro's hungry,' I said firmly.

★

Later, we really did go to Mushtaidi Park. We went on all the carousels and ate candyfloss until we felt sick. (Daria ate it, too, as there were no ice creams on sale yet.)

Aleko, my mother's new boyfriend, plodded along behind us, resting a hand on our shoulders from time to time or giving us a tentative, rather awkward smile. Elene was beaming at us non-stop. This image of a perfect family seemed to make her happy.

That evening, Aleko cooked for us, and we were allowed to choose what went on our plates. Daria gradually overcame her initial shyness, blithely chatting away about horse breeding and boasting about her riding skills. At the end of the day we fell asleep exhausted and over-full, snuggled up together on our mattress. This time Daria didn't express indignation at having to sleep there.

The next few days followed the same pattern. We got up when we felt like it. Aleko made us pancakes. We were allowed to watch television for as long as we liked, eat what we liked, laze around, and make a racket. It was only on the fourth day that Daria asked when we would be going home to Grandfather. Elene started to explain that it wasn't normal for a mother to live apart from her children; that she missed us so much it was killing her; that she wanted to be with us, with us and Aleko; that we could all stay here and have a nice life together. But Daria refused to be content with this idea.

'Why can't we be with Grandfather? You can call him and he can come here!' she insisted.

'But Dariko, darling, that wouldn't work; we don't have enough room. Don't you like it here with Mama? Didn't you miss Mama at all?' Elene was visibly struggling to maintain her self-control.

'Yes, of course, but there aren't even any proper beds here!'

Daria sniffed disdainfully and I saw our mother's face flush with disappointment. Her father had long since won the battle for Daria's favour. Elene hunched over; she seemed to get smaller.

'I want to go home!' Now Daria's voice was loud and determined, and she stared at our mother with her different-coloured eyes.

'This *is* your home!' Elene's tone had grown sharper.

She was about to walk away and leave us to fret when Daria screamed with all her might, 'I want Grandfather! I want Grandfather!'

She started shouting and she didn't stop. She repeated the words again and again, until the bearded Aleko, who always looked slightly aggrieved, came into the room and planted himself between Daria and Elene.

'Daria, stop that right now!' Elene warned her; and I saw my mother turn back into the woman who paced up and down at night like a caged animal, unable to find peace, who looked right through you, who loved English songs, and could not forget a particular afternoon of forced love.

Daria demanded her rights, she didn't stop, didn't give in, she wanted what was her due, wanted security, wealth, privilege, not this horrible apartment, not this strange, scruffy man, and not — perhaps she suspected it already — this utterly chaotic, hopeless existence. And Elene raised her hand and gave her eldest daughter a burning slap that left her with a red mark.

> On the hills of Georgia lies the blanket of night …
>
> ALEXANDER PUSHKIN

'Have you completely lost your mind?'

Lana was agitated. She had taken off her glasses and was cleaning them nervously on a corner of her skirt, blinking continually as she did so in an effort to see her companion better. My mother was standing at the gas stove, making soup for us. Daria was asleep, and I was sitting in the corner, sorting nuts.

'Nana turned up at Christine's door yesterday. And Christine genuinely has no idea what's going on. Nana thinks she's covering for you. She's worried about where the children are. Surely you can't be that naive — you can't just kidnap the children from their beds like that!'

'Did you tell them anything?' my mother asked, calmly stirring the soup.

'I told them I would find you and take you back to your parents. I mean, your father's already started patrolling outside the university.'

'I'll get in touch with them.'

'But Elene, look around you. At this flat. Good Lord! You don't even have proper furniture.'

'Why does everyone keep going on about furniture? As if the meaning of life were to own as much furniture as possible!'

'I'm just trying to do you a favour, okay? Your children have been here for two weeks. You haven't shown your face at the institute. You've taken up with some guy old enough to be your father and —'

'My God! He's not *some guy*, and he's only thirty-seven!'

'To be perfectly honest, I think you're being silly. And egotistical. You've started a degree. You're getting the kind of support other mothers can only dream of, and what do you do? Force your children into some dirty hole and cook them vegetable soup and pretend you're a perfect family. Get off your backside and sort all this out with your father. As you might be aware, I'm no great friend of Kostya Jashi, but in your position —'

'And I thought you were my friend,' Elene interrupted her, offended.

'You think your friends are going to applaud you for this nonsense? I mean, what were you thinking? That your father would call and congratulate you on your new-found marital bliss?'

'Why are you being such a bitch? I thought you at least would understand. I'm going to start attending lectures again on Monday. I just needed some time for the girls. They have to get used to being here. Aleko and I are going to the registry office next month anyway — then my father will have to stop going on about his rights!'

'Just how crazy *are* you? Have you forgotten what your father's capable of? Surely you know him well enough by now. Please re-engage your brain.' Lana put her glasses back on and stopped blinking.

'I'm happy again, for the first time in ages. Aleko and I will get this right — this time, I'll get it right. And for God's sake, I *am* these children's mother.'

'A mother who won't be able to provide for these children. Who's taken up with a wannabe writer, who's going to spend the rest of her life in this dump and —'

'You don't even know him. Stop putting him down like that!' Elene raised her voice.

'Forgive me, but you haven't exactly hit the jackpot with your choice of men so far. My advice is: go home, and, most importantly, take your children back. I'm not going to keep covering for you.'

★

Three days later, there was a row at the Green House. Sparks flew, a glass door was broken, and Aleko stood in a corner like a New Year spruce that had been taken down and forgotten about. Kostya was beside himself. Elene screamed. Daria and I cried. Nana and Stasia tried to reconcile what was now irreconcilable.

Elene had informed her father that she was going to marry her new boyfriend. The thirty-seven-year-old sound technician (a sound technician who was still working as an assistant in the sound department at the state television station, although he was nearly forty!) and nascent writer (who was light years away from a writing career, who hadn't yet read at the Writers' Association, hadn't been approved or even joined). At this point, Aleko's only published work was a collection of short stories printed by one of the semi-legal private publishing houses, which he had distributed to friends and people he trusted.

He also had two sons with his ex-wife, though his meagre salary didn't really stretch to the maintenance payments; rather than plough his energy into his detested job, he preferred to spend his nights discussing 'the system' with his friends, watching pirated copies of banned films at closed private screenings, smoking weed, and drinking beer with vodka chasers.

Kostya swore, called Aleko a 'pansy', a 'failure', a 'scrounger', and a 'gigolo', and accused him of only wanting to marry his daughter in the hope that her father would guarantee them a secure income and a comfortable, prosperous life. But that was where he was wrong! Kostya yelled, his voice reverberating through the house. That was never going to happen: if his 'harlot' of a daughter dared to take such a shameful step and marry this 'parasite' without his consent, she would have to live with the consequences, one of which would most certainly be losing even weekly visiting rights with the children.

★

That August, Elene married Aleko, and Kostya's will was done: Daria and I stayed at the Green House. Elene took up her studies again and was at least allowed to come up and see us on Saturdays. But from that moment on, she was no longer permitted to stay overnight at the Green House. When I think back to this time, I remember all the jams, fruit baskets, bottles of liqueur, cakes, and biscuits wrapped in tinfoil that Nana and Stasia would smuggle into Elene's car before she set off back to Tbilisi in the evening.

★

I learned to read at four, and to write at five. I learned the Cyrillic and the Georgian alphabets, and when I presented Kostya with this fact by writing his name in both languages, he told me that Daria's calligraphy was better. When I drew a round Nana, a bent Stasia, a yellow Daria, a large Kostya, a red Elene, a black Aleko, and a tiny me, entitled the picture 'Our Family', and stuck it to the fridge door, Kostya disliked it so much that he tore it down and threw it in the bin.

I carried on dancing, in order to make Stasia's memories my own, and Daria rode the stud farm's beautiful bronze-coloured ponies. I liked vanilla ice cream; Daria liked chocolate ice cream. I liked the stray dogs in the village; Daria was afraid of them. I wore cut-off trousers as shorts and Daria wore brightly coloured skirts. I wore my hair short, while Daria's reached her waist.

I didn't like fairy tales, which for all their horror always had a happy ending (I mistrusted happy endings even as a child); Daria loved them.

We were both shielded by our ignorance, not just about our family, but the wider world, too. We didn't know that our grandfather was plagued by nightmares, all of which took place on a submarine, and featured an inferno, a tall woman with rings on her fingers, a man whittling wooden angels and his curly-haired son, who forced his love upon Kostya's daughter.

We didn't know that Stasia watched with fascination as Thekla and Sopio played Patience in our garden. We didn't know that, in far-off Moscow, Giorgi Alania was sliding into a deep depression. We didn't know that Elvis Aaron Presley had died at Graceland, bloated and estranged from the world. That our mother suffered two miscarriages before finally giving up on her desire to start a *proper* family, then began writing her degree dissertation (on Lady Macbeth, of all things). That Christine was doing everything in her power to confer on Miqa's son the happiness Miqa himself had lost. No one told us that Stasia's second-eldest sister, Meri, had died in Kutaisi, or that Lida had died a short while later, in the town where she was born — probably without fear, overjoyed to be entering the kingdom of heaven at last as a bride of Christ.

But perhaps we were already starting to suspect that the world resembled a tangle of threads, and that this was incredibly important in some complex, inexplicable way.

*

'Did you know that we've got different papas?' Daria said, out of the blue, without lifting her focused gaze from the artwork she was painting.

The summer was on its way; the world smelled lush, vital, as if life had begun to sweat. The noon light lent Daria's long ponytail a golden sheen. She was now eight years old, and attended the First Classical Gymnasium, the most elite school in Tbilisi, right on Rustaveli Boulevard, where her favourite subjects were Russian and Physical Culture. This was the term for PE at that time, as she would inform each of our guests, a little conceitedly, before accepting the adults' obligatory praise as if it was her due. And now she was telling me, casually, indifferently, that there was far more dividing than uniting us.

No, I hadn't known that. Hadn't even suspected. No one had told me. The word 'father' was as absent from Daria's lexicon as it was from mine. I shrank away from her and started shaking my head vigorously. No one spoke to us about it in the playground; it seemed that, given our grandfather's power, the parents had been coaching their children and had drummed into them the fact that this topic was not agreeable to the Jashis. It was the same in the Green House: the subject of fathers was never addressed. We thought of *Father* as someone who was far, far away, but who loved us and missed us and thought about us a lot. We were sure of it.

'Yes. So, your papa is in prison. And my papa is dead. He was a hero and he drowned trying to cross the big sea.'

Daria said it as if she were just telling me the time, in an off-hand tone and with an expression of extreme concentration on her face as she focused on finishing her picture.

'Why is my papa in prison?' I felt a bottomless well of disappointment open up inside me. My father, too, should be a hero who had tried to vanquish the sea.

'Because he's a criminal,' Daria replied nonchalantly.

'And why did your papa try and cross the sea? He must have known you can't do that; was he stupid or something?'

'*You're* stupid. Most people can't do it, but heroes can. That's why they're heroes,' she explained with disarming self-assurance.

I couldn't come up with any argument against that, and I had to confess that someone setting out to cross the big sea was a pretty impressive thing.

'Well, we've still got the same mother,' I said, to comfort myself.

I suddenly felt small, ugly, stupid, and powerless; I wanted to leave the room and find Stasia, demand that she explain why my father was a criminal and Daria's a hero, but I could feel something gathering inside me, an incredible rage that I couldn't put into words, couldn't articulate. I pounced on my sister from behind, grabbed her immensely long ponytail, which slid so gratefully into my hand, and pulled her to the floor, ignoring her cries and yelling in her face: 'At least *my* father's coming back one day — yours never will. Never!'

★

That same day, Aleko's short story was rejected by the *Literaturnaya Gazeta* again. Elene had submitted her final dissertation exactly one week earlier and wasn't sure whether she would pass. There was too much talk of power in it. The vodka bottle held the dregs from the previous evening, when Aleko and his friends had talked themselves hoarse about Visconti's *Rocco and His Brothers*. She poured what was left into a teacup and knocked back the fiery liquid. Elene felt tired, empty. Money was tight. Their prospects not that alluring. Her longing for her children gnawed at her, made her scratch her forearms raw, press her hands to her temples, blink; it parched her mouth.

The previous month, Beqa had been released from prison, and although this fact had given her no particular pleasure (after all, he hadn't written a single letter to her or his child in all those years), she still hoped he might want to meet me. Which meant that she had to apprise me of the less than romantic circumstances of my conception as quickly and gently as possible.

I guess you've found a better place.

KITTY JASHI

'They're bringing you your shirts perfectly ironed. You can relax.'

Amy was flitting about excitedly and blowing her cigarette smoke around the hotel suite. Kitty lay on the king-size bed, wrapped in the soft blankets, staring at the stucco on the high ceiling.

'Sold out, sold out, did you hear that, Kitty? We have to start the sound check tomorrow morning at eight o'clock sharp. You can go back to bed afterwards if you want. But we need to leave enough time for ... oh, never mind. Only Carnegie Hall could top this.'

She was striding up and down the room in her stripy corduroy trousers, a garish plastic flower in her hair, sucking dramatically on her cigarette.

The *Home* tour did seem to be surpassing all their expectations. Kitty had never had so much money in her account, never had such unanimous approval, never had so many young people in the audience, and had never felt so empty.

She made a huge effort to keep it together in public, then shut herself up for hours in the decadent, ostentatious hotel suites and dressing rooms, or secretly crept around the various European cities she visited, trying to fill her emptiness with fashionable distractions, trying to find something that could give her at least an illusion of joy. But every time she had to admit to herself that she had found nothing to fill the hole within. The only option she had left was to perfect the game she played with the public. To smile when she didn't feel like smiling, look interested when someone asked her a question, ignore the impulse to flee when it arose. And to give the over-excited Amy, so delighted by her success, the impression that everything was perfectly fine.

'How many pop stars can say they've sung at the Concertgebouw? I spoke to the cellist this afternoon, and she told me you have an incredibly large fan base in the Netherlands and that your old records are undergoing a kind of revival here.'

Amy went to the door; apparently the shirts had arrived. When she came back, she threw the radiant white shirts in their protective plastic sheaths onto Kitty's chest.

'Can you please stop this endless pseudo-meditation and join us back here on earth?' she said loudly, right into Kitty's ear.

'Can't I just be left in peace for ten minutes? I'm tired!' Kitty pulled the blanket over her head.

Then Amy's frenetic footsteps again, moving away from her bed, off to somewhere else.

★

Her solo concert in the Amsterdam Concertgebouw was scheduled for the following day. It was the climax of the tour, as the Concertgebouw was reserved for classical music, with very few exceptions. Kitty had spent a week with a string quartet rehearsing for this concert. A thirty-three-year-old producer Amy had conjured up from God knows where, who she claimed was the future of British music, wanted to record the concert and release it as a live album. In her last negotiations with him he had implied that Kitty's songs lacked the right *beat*, and that the age of purism Kitty represented was over once and for all. Despite the excitement of the past few weeks, the rehearsals that always lent her wings, getting to know the wonderful instrumentalists, who had given Kitty's songs their own memorable arrangements, something essential was missing: suddenly, she didn't seem to know who she was singing for, who her songs were directed at and addressed to. (Do you remember telling me, Brilka — in Berlin, I think it was — that in one interview Kitty said her songs were always letters written to particular people; that she found it impossible to sing without an addressee?)

This tour felt like her own personal Golgotha. She had never felt so old and worn out. So alienated. As if all spiritual nourishment had been withdrawn from her, and she had been reduced to purely biological functions.

'Then in December, we'll go to New York.' Amy's triumphant voice rang out from the next room. 'I mean, of course we'll take up *that* contract. You'll write for these people. You said yourself back then that composing under those circumstances might be more fun because you'd have some peace and quiet, so I don't want any objections. Anyway, I'm not going to pass up that much money just because you're going through one of your melancholy phases. You'll write the songs they want, and *voila*.'

'Have you heard any news of *her*?'

Kitty was standing in the doorway with the pillow in her hand.

'The last I heard she was in Wales, in a private hospital. I asked Magnus, he made enquiries; the hospital is supposed to be one of the best.'

'Did you pay for her treatment?'

'Yes. I did.'

Kitty was grateful to Amy for not trying to lie to her.

'The fact you sent her there doesn't necessarily mean she stayed.'

'I did what I could. The last time I saw her, she hardly had a good tooth left in her head. I get the sense she knows that this is her last chance.'

'I can't get her out of my head, Amy, especially when I have to perform — it always starts then, it's like a sickness, like a virus that infects me.'

'Would you take a look at the shirts and tell me which one you want to wear tomorrow? The concierge says they can have the best of the best delivered straight to the room. Do you want to try on some different styles?'

'Oh, spare me, please. They're white shirts. They all look the same.'

'Now that's where you're wrong!' Suddenly, Amy paused in her constant movement and studied Kitty. 'You've written some really wonderful songs. This album is your most mature work yet; you should enjoy it and be proud of yourself. I think it would be unforgivable if you didn't enjoy this success. If it sets your mind at rest, I'll call London and make some enquiries about her. Although as far as I'm concerned, for once, here and now, this is just about the two of us: you and me, and this thing we've created together. Do you get that? It's about *us*, not her.'

'She's as much a part of this *us* as we are, Amy; you know that.'

Kitty dropped the large, soft pillow on the floor. For a while they both stared at it, senselessly dropped, senselessly lying there, as if it was a proxy for someone or something else. Amy put her arms around Kitty's shoulders.

'This is not an easy thing for me to tell you, but when she looked at me, particularly in the last few months, and when she turned up at my door again not knowing what to do with herself, when she needed money or just a place to sleep, I knew she was looking at you, not me — that it was you she saw. Yes, Kitty: she stayed in my life because of you, as ridiculous as that sounds.'

★

The spotlight pierced her eyes. There was a mysterious quality to the silence. A breath held before the applause started; soon this silence would erupt into something phenomenal. The white shirt stuck to her exhausted body. She hadn't yet put down her guitar; she was standing at the front of the stage, looking into the darkened room where around two thousand people were sitting. She was still clutching the microphone. The string players rose from their seats and stepped towards the edge of the stage. Soon they would be judged and, ideally, rewarded for the two and a half hours they had spent giving their all, right to the end. The heat held her body in its grip, and she wiped her forehead with the handkerchief she always carried in her shirt pocket. The music was still ringing in her head. Her fingers still hurt from every single chord, remembered every single note they had played that evening.

During the first song, she had realised that the music was threatening to slip away from her, that her singing was unfocused, distracted, and mechanical, and she had forced herself to think of *her* face: of the red hair, of the photos they had taken together in America, of the words they had spoken and not spoken to each other — and the surrender, the longing, and above all the deep resentment came back into her voice. Eyes closed, she dedicated her songs to Fred, fervently hoping that she would return to herself. Not to Kitty, not to Amy, just to herself. And that evening she managed to keep the ghosts away from the stage. Fred Lieblich brought her songs back to life. Fred Lieblich was alive, and that evening she wanted to believe that she would stay that way.

Then, suddenly, the thunderous applause broke out; Kitty smiled through the sea of stage lights out into the darkness, bowed to her audience, turned round, beckoned her colleagues forward, and bowed again. The clapping was deafening.

> Let the trumpets loudly ring out
> And the cheerful drummers play!
> The song of friendship we will sing out
> Greeting this new golden day!
>
> PIONEER SONG

The autumn sun caressed my ankles as I ran down the hillside. I ran as fast as I could, lifting up the skirt of my school pinafore, racing the light breeze that pursued me from the woods.

I loved the places I thought of as mine: the woods, the clearing, the curve of the hillside. How often had I come up here after school and lain down in the grass. Neither rain nor wind, not even snow, could keep me from my walks. I would lie on the ground and look at the sky. It was a sight that helped me forget the most awful part of the day: the hours I spent at school. The boredom that overcame me there, the children I hated, the fist-fights, the people I fell out with, the insults, and, above all, Daria's coldness. She was two classes above me and refused to acknowledge me, didn't even come to my defence in the playground when someone threw a half-eaten apple at me, called me a swot, or pushed me over.

But that day I didn't want to stop, I didn't want to lie down. I wanted to run. I wanted everything that had happened that morning to be carried away by the wind.

'Niza is a nutcase, Niza is a nutcase!' They had all chanted it in chorus, then a stocky third-year boy had lunged at me and pulled my pinafore top down. There was a laugh of malicious glee from all sides. This encouraged the stork-like boy from 4a to yank my dress up over my head, at which everyone doubled up with laughter.

'Niza's got blue knickers, Niza's got blue knickers!' They were really bellowing now. I got away, made to run out of the playground, and then beautiful Anna from my class planted herself in my way. I clutched my skirt — the stork boy was trying to pull at it again from behind — clamped the hem between my legs and stood there like a toddler who had wet herself.

The others gathered round, joined hands, and formed a wall of bodies in front of me. I screwed up all my courage and tried to break through the barrier, but I couldn't; I fell flat on the ground. Again, they laughed. When I turned my head, I could see Daria standing on the other side of the playground, looking over and doing nothing. Just standing there with her friends, all of them pretty, with their spotless white knee-socks and flat patent-leather shoes, doing nothing, not even speaking. She stared over in my direction as if spellbound, as if she herself couldn't believe I was the one the other children were laughing at, pushing, humiliating, and insulting. She would have had the power to end my torment. But she didn't move.

She didn't move. Her brown eye seemed sad, ashamed, while her blue eye stared almost gleefully in my direction. My lips parted, I tried to say something, to call her name, but no sound came out. I was ashamed for her, ashamed on her behalf, because she couldn't admit her shame at having me for a sister. She was a victor, a winner, and a winner can't have a loser for a sister. A girl with tousled hair and scabby knees, her socks around her ankles. I couldn't hold back any longer; I started to cry. I was almost hysterical. I screamed so loudly and for so long that the teachers came rushing out of the building, chased away the swarm of children that had gathered round me, picked me up, and carried me into the school to phone my mother.

Now I wanted to forget it all. I wanted to erase these terrible images, these voices, from my head. I didn't want to think about sitting in the school sickbay while my mother conferred with my class teacher. As if I had committed some offence, as if she had to apologise for me. I wanted to shake off the unpleasant feeling that I was putting too much of a strain on my mother. This feeling hadn't left me for some time.

It was already starting to get dark. Elene hadn't stayed so long at the Green House in an eternity. Kostya and Nana would be home soon. It seemed she was waiting for her parents. For her father. Maybe she meant to tell him about my disgrace today. I ran faster, finding it hard to catch my breath, but I didn't want to stop. I prayed that she would just go home, that she wouldn't see Kostya, wouldn't tell him how they hated me and laughed at me. I was racing the wind. If I got down to the garden first, then it would all be over. The horror of school, the daily torment, Kostya's reproaches. And if the wind won, everything would stay as it was.

I stood at the garden gate and doubled up, gasping for breath. Had I won?

I couldn't feel the wind any more. I stretched out my palms and waited. I had outfoxed the wind. I was sure I'd won. Had I, had I?

The lights were already on in the house. I could hear muffled voices inside. I crept up to the terrace and sat on the creaking swing seat. Kostya and Nana were back — of course — and Elene's car was still in the driveway. My prayers had not been answered: she was talking to them about me.

Daria stepped outside. Eyed me with mistrust. Then she sat down hesitantly beside me.

'They told me to go outside. They're talking about you.'

I shuffled sideways a little, keeping my distance from her, to be on the safe side. There were brown plasters on both my knees, from the school sick-bay. Seeing the plasters made me think about that morning again, and I felt a cold, blind loathing come over me. I didn't want to stay next to my sister. I stood up, went to the door, and sat on the mat in front of it.

I could hear Kostya's trembling voice inside. Then I heard Elene fly into a rage.

'For God's sake, she's a really gifted child! When will you understand that? The teacher made it very clear again today. "Gifted", that was the word he used. It's not wishful thinking, not some kind of illusion. *Deda*, say something, won't you?' Elene was clearly appealing to Nana. 'You must have noticed, you must be able to see it! And you're telling me she's not making enough of an effort? Well, I salute you. I don't know anyone but you who would react to that news with those words! Any other grandfather would laugh with happiness, but no, not you, of course not. How could I forget: she's *my little bastard*, gifted or not!'

'Then find your children another grandfather,' Kostya retorted icily. 'Or better still, find yourself another father. You're old enough now. Find someone to pay for your children, for their education, their clothes, their future. Someone who can give them a good life!'

'This isn't about me, or you, or any of that crap — it's about Niza.'

I could hear in Elene's voice that she was close to tears.

'And what am I supposed to do now? What do you want from me? She's already at the best school in the city.'

'It's not about being at the best school. It's about how she needs to be treated, about the right methods, and above all the right environment. This month alone there've been three similar incidents, and she didn't even tell us. I mean, they're inflicting mental and physical cruelty on her, just because she's cleverer than the others.'

'And this teacher is qualified to make those judgements about the child, is he?'

'She's bored at school because she can do it all already, don't you understand? She's doing Daria's homework for her now! And she's only in the first year. Please!'

'Daria does her own homework,' retorted Kostya.

'Oh, stop it now!' Nana suddenly exclaimed.

'She needs a different kind of challenge. I don't know; the teacher thinks we should find out what other possibilities there are. Maybe a special school, or —'

'The child stays where she is. It's the best school in the city. And special treatment could hamper her development. She has to learn to fit in. After all, life isn't tailored to child prodigies. She has to learn to deal with it, and we have to toughen her up.'

'Toughen her up? To deal with what? Being punched and taunted?'

'Well, they won't have given her a shove because she's too clever, will they? She'll have been cheeky, or … I know what she's like!'

'A shove? You're out of your mind! *Deda*, say something, tell him how outrageous that is!'

Elene groaned. I fervently hoped she would manage to get to the end of the argument without crying. I wasn't sure why, but I didn't want her to cry in front of Kostya.

Daria pursed her lips as if she was about to whistle — it was what she did when she was embarrassed or wanted to cover something up. She gave the swing a nudge, then hauled herself into it. I got up from the doormat and went over to her.

'Shall I push you?'

She nodded to me like a landowner allowing a serf to kiss her hand. She probably thought this was a peace offering. Now and then I would help her with her homework; it looked as if she wanted my help again now, and that meant a reconciliation was necessary.

I pushed the swing with all my might. She cried out, but I carried on, swinging her higher and higher until she slipped off the seat and fell onto the hard ground. Her face was twisted in pain, but that pleased me. It gave me a moment of comfort before her voice rose in a soft, writhing, plaintive cry. In that moment, *I* was the winner. And it was a good feeling.

★

In the middle of the night, Stasia woke me and told me to follow her. Barefoot, I tiptoed slowly outside after her. Daria was sleeping in Kostya's bed, exhausted from crying, her ankle cooled by many ice packs. We went into the garden. It was a mild night with the warmth of the day still in it. Behind the lilac bushes, Stasia spread out a blanket, and we lay down together and looked up at the clear, starry sky. I snuggled up against her threadbare old towelling dressing gown. We lay like that for a while in silence.

'Shall I tell you a secret?' she said abruptly into the silence, pressing my head against her chest.

'Yes!' I whispered back excitedly. I loved her secrets no less than her stories.

'Do you see the cherry tree over there? Sometimes a friend of mine comes round. She sits under the cherry tree and smiles at me. Sometimes another friend comes as well, and they play cards. But they can't really be here at all. They've both been dead a long time.'

I pricked up my ears. I prepared myself for a ghost story, even if the beautiful clear night sky wasn't really the right setting for it.

'But that can't be true, *Bebo*.' I made an effort to bring some logic to the matter.

'Yes, well, I was coming to that.'

Stasia put her right hand inside her dressing gown, rustled around in her nightshirt, and paused.

'Sometimes we humans can't explain things, sometimes we don't understand things, but just because most people don't see these things and don't believe in them doesn't mean they don't exist.'

'And what don't most people see?'

'They don't see my friends standing under the cherry tree, and nor do they see how special you are.'

'Why am I special?'

'You can do things other people can't.'

'Like what?'

'You learn faster than the others. You have a different understanding of things. You have a feeling for people.'

'You mean I can tell if someone's been crying, even if they've already washed their face?'

'For example, yes.'

She took something out of her dressing gown and held it tightly in her hand.

'But why can't the others see your friends? Is one of them standing there now? Can I see her?'

'No, there's no one there just now. They probably have to sleep, too. I don't know if you would see them. Most people don't see them because they didn't know them, and they didn't love them enough.'

'What was your friend called?'

'Sopio.'

'And why did she die?'

'Because the world is a dung heap and most people are pieces of cow shit.'

'And me?' I giggled. I liked Stasia's choice of words.

'You're a diamond in the rough, and you have to learn to ignore the muck. Things aren't going to be easy for you at school, but you must learn to stand up for yourself. You must learn to get by without the others, if need be — even without your sister.'

'I didn't want to make her fall off the swing.' I didn't know why I was lying.

'It's all right to want it. But it was wrong of you to do it. She let you down. But don't hurt anybody just because they've hurt you: it'll come back like a boomerang. It won't lessen your own suffering. You need to understand that people don't hurt you because you're stupid or ugly; they hurt you because they're envious of you.'

'That's not true.' I didn't want to talk about that morning.

'No, it *is* true. Give me your hand; hold out your wrist, my eyesight's bad — yes, like that.'

She opened her fist and fastened something onto me. It felt cool and heavy.

'What's that?'

'It's a watch. An important person gave it to me. This watch is older than you, older than your mother, your grandfather, older than me, even. We'll hide this watch in your bedside cabinet — it'll be our little secret, all right? It'll wait there for you, until your wrist is big and strong enough for it. It will always protect you. It always protected me.'

'It's beautiful.'

'Yes, it is. It has magic powers, this watch. Oh, what's that sigh for; do you think I'm telling you fairy stories?'

'You tell me fairy stories all the time. How can your friend come here when she's dead? And why does she come?' I couldn't get the idea into my head. After all, I was a socialist child, and socialist children learn mistrust from an early age.

'I don't know, my sunshine, I don't know. Maybe there was something she left unfinished, a story she didn't finish telling.'

I nodded thoughtfully and tried to imagine the ghost of Stasia's dead friend. I had so many questions.

> The world is worn out like a coin,
> Now life is empty and quite dark,
> Don't be surprised if at this point
> I'm grateful for a little luck.
>
> GALAKTION TABIDZE

The whole country had celebrated the sixtieth anniversary of the Revolution, though the once gigantic Soviet empire now only existed on paper. Ministries, like those for Mechanical Engineering and Power Generation, were feeding off an economy that was no longer there. Meanwhile, alcoholism, theft, and absenteeism had become the norm. For the elite, though, those years were a golden age: everyone could help themselves without fear and could take away whatever there was to take. The General Secretary and head of state, a great lover of cars, owned an impressive fleet that included a Rolls-Royce and a ZiL armoured limousine. A passionate hunter, he promoted the master of his hunt, who flushed out wild boar for him, to the rank of general.

Diplomats, generals, ministers, directors — all these 'heroes of work' were having a seemingly endless party. And nobody in the country appeared to have any objection. There was only one mass demonstration under Brezhnev, during the Moscow Winter Olympics, when Vysotsky died and the actors of the Taganka Theatre took to the streets, until they were joined by tens of thousands of other people. Of course, the demonstration was crushed. Unrest at home was the last thing the head of the Party needed — he had been suffering from cerebral sclerosis for a decade. Just one year earlier, he had begun the invasion of Afghanistan 'in fulfilment of international socialist duties'. When the head of the Party was permanently released from his demanding work in November 1982, he was succeeded by the sixty-eight-year-old head of the KGB, a Mr Andropov, who had the irreproachable worldview of a secret service agent. The Party was now led by another seriously ill man who spent half his time in hospital before his kidneys gave out and his career came to an end after less than two years. He had no trouble ignoring the fact that Afghanistan was costing his empire millions it didn't have, and that the bodies of more and more fallen Soviet soldiers were having to be transported home. Andropov was succeeded by the seventy-two-year-old Chernenko, an unprepossessing Party bureaucrat who was already suffering from a serious lung condition when he took office. Chernenko managed to outdo his predecessor, spending even less time as General Secretary of the Central Committee before he died.

I might not have made any friends at school, but thanks to Stasia's watch, which was lying close at hand in my bedside cabinet (and did, unexpectedly, give me a certain security), or my own doggedness, I kept the violence and the mockery at bay. I began to develop the strategies that would help me survive the rest of my school years relatively unscathed. I had to be as normal and unproblematic as possible and, above all, not let the others see that the lessons didn't interest me in the slightest.

The one concession Kostya made was to allow me to skip the fifth year. In my new class I learned to act like the others, securing for myself a relatively peaceful coexistence with my classmates. I laughed at their jokes, and asked for help even when I didn't need it.

I knew it would pass. I knew I would soon be back at home with Stasia, where I could listen to her stories, walk in the woods, run around, work in the garden, and most importantly, in the late afternoon, go up to the roof terrace and be alone with my books. It would pass and I would be allowed to be myself again. Yes, it would pass, if I just trained myself to be patient.

Sometimes I brought Aleko's books or records back to the Green House, and there were always jealous outbursts from Daria. She wanted to know how I had spent the weekend, what exactly I'd been doing, and what new discoveries I'd made. She didn't want to feel excluded, and one day — she had just turned eleven — she announced that she wanted to spend the weekends with Elene and her husband as well. It was also Aleko who gave me one of the most beautiful gifts of my childhood: David, who was to become my Peter Vasilyev. David was an old school friend of Aleko's. He was one of the most brilliant minds of his generation and had been a promising physicist, but his fondness for banned political and philosophical writings had got him thrown out of the research institute, and he ended up teaching physics and mathematics at a school on the edge of the city. After his divorce, David had taken up residency in a little studio in the New Town, and the subject of his research had changed from atoms to life in general. Aleko had been reproaching my mother for not challenging me enough ever since I started school, and so one day he brought me to David and asked him to 'take a look' at me.

★

David was forty-two years old then, and looked at least ten years older. The social and scientific ostracism, the separation from his wife, who thought he was a loser, and the absence of his two sons, whom he missed terribly and did not see nearly enough, had all left their mark. He was not a tall man, and, like Stasia, he walked with a stoop. He had slender limbs, delicate features, beautiful, sunken, deep-green eyes, and an old-fashioned moustache. He made tea in a samovar and wore checked woollen slippers and beige or grey shirts. He always had cold hands, and he spoke slowly, as if his voice needed an eternity to come through to us.

He asked Aleko to leave the two of us alone, and set a small bowl of sweets down in front of me. Then he sat down opposite me in an armchair, fixed me with his green eyes, and said: 'I hear you're bored at school.'

I nodded shyly.

'So what does interest you?'

'Can people really see the dead?'

The question had been on my mind ever since my night-time conversation with Stasia. I'd never brought it up again with her, but every time I saw her sitting on her little stool in the garden and looking over at the cherry tree, I would try to make out the ghosts of her friends. I never could.

'I don't know,' he said.

I was very pleased with this answer. He seemed to be one of the few people who didn't react to my questions by pretending to be cleverer than they were.

He continued: 'I think if someone believes they can see a dead person, then perhaps they can.'

'But when you're dead, you're dead, and you're not there any more,' I insisted, pressing the point.

'I'm afraid we pretend to know a lot of things when we don't,' he said, confirming my suspicion. 'Do you know how big our universe is?'

I shook my head. Then he got out pens and paper, and started drawing the whole universe for me on a squared page from a school exercise book.

★

I could ask David what love tasted like. I could ask him why babies had a soft spot on the top of their heads that you weren't allowed to press, why tears were salty, and why whales had fountains on their heads; I could ask him what beauty was and why grandfathers loved some children and not others. I could ask him what suicide meant, I could ask him why butterflies lived such a short time and crows lived so long, I could ask him why we didn't fall over as the earth turned, and whether Led Zeppelin were worse than Pink Floyd. I could ask him if a child who didn't have a father really needed one. When I asked him if he believed in God, he said he was looking for Him and that, if he found Him, he would let me know and ask Him to grant me an audience. I was content with this answer.

I loved the fact that he didn't ruffle my hair or laugh at me indulgently, didn't shake his head or looked shocked. Even when I wanted to know if it was true that a man and a woman took off their clothes and lay on top of one another to make babies, he got out a medical book and explained the process of human biology that leads to conception, which seemed far more plausible to me than my mother's or Stasia's silly explanations involving storks or bees.

He painted the world for me. And the world aroused a pathological interest in me. It wasn't the limited world of school, or Kostya's clearly structured world, or my mother and Aleko's world, plagued by day-to-day worries, or Daria's rose-tinted world, or the raw and ethereal world of Stasia. It was a world I felt at home in. It was a large, unfathomable world, in which not every question had an answer. And, above all, a world in which nothing was *normal*.

Twice a week, I was allowed to visit him after school. They were the happiest two days of the week. I would leave David's studio floating on air. I danced my way onto the trolley-bus. I looked about me and laughed. Ran up the stairs to Mother's flat.

Thanks to David, I learned to live with the cracks that surrounded me. I learned to look at myself in the mirror: my dark face, my skinny, shapeless body, my short stature, my dark eyes, so dark you couldn't make out the iris in them, my curly, untameable hair that refused to be coaxed into any style, the hooked nose, and the duck's beak that was my mouth, and I learned not to compare any of this with Daria. I had David, so what did it matter that Daria had Kostya? She was welcome to him, I thought.

★

Although my father was alive and Daria's was dead, mine was in no particular hurry to get to know me. I saw him once, briefly, when I was nine or ten, before he went back to prison for another four years (a break-in at a university dean's house). And so I wondered which of us had been luckier, Daria or me. We met — Elene, Beqa, and I — in the café with the sweet fizzy drinks, where I had tarragon lemonade. He was a broken, chain-smoking, heavy-set man, who looked around nervously and had even less idea of what to say to me than other people did.

It seemed incomprehensible that my mother could ever have loved this man. Eventually, though, he asked her whether I shouldn't take his surname. 'Can't have people calling her a bastard,' he added, eyeing me with visible dissatisfaction. It seemed I was neither pretty nor charming enough for him to love me straight away, but he would deign to give me his name, the only thing he had to give me.

Elene replied tersely that I already had a name and didn't need a new one. What I *could* use was a father who took some interest in me, but it looked like we'd have to keep searching for one of those, didn't it? Elene put her arm round my shoulders, and soon after that we left the café. Of course, at that time I couldn't have known what it was like to spend five years in a Soviet prison. But whether that would have excused his behaviour, his lack of interest, his inability to start a conversation with me, I don't know. As Elene and I stepped out onto Rustaveli Boulevard, I saw tears running down her face. She clasped my hand tightly and dragged me along behind her. I wasn't particularly sad. I'd never had a father, and wasn't expecting one — but Elene was.

I wanted to comfort her. But she walked so quickly I had trouble keeping up with her.

We walked and walked. And then we stopped at the entrance to a dark, old staircase in the middle of Vake. I had never been there before.

'Where are we?' I asked my mother as we started up the dilapidated stairs.

'We're going to see your great-great-aunt,' she replied, pulling me after her.

When I look back on this first meeting with my father, I always think of the tarragon lemonade, and then of Miro. Not the man who fathered me. I don't think of Rustaveli Boulevard and the café where the three of us sat, but of Christine's small, cosy apartment. Because on the day when I should have got to know my father and found myself sitting opposite a stranger instead, I met Miro. The plan hadn't worked: my father had not come back into our lives. The first father, the father of the child who was never born, was dead — a miserable death in a prison hospital. Elene had helped the second flee to another continent. The third had now turned from a would-be revolutionary into a criminal; and the fourth, a man who loved her as she loved him, but who couldn't make anything of himself and drowned his untold stories in alcohol, was someone with whom she was unable to have children.

Christine's hands were covered in flour. She opened the door without asking who was there. Maybe she was expecting someone else. She was wearing a veil that covered half her face. If it hadn't been for the flour on her hands, you might have thought she was a character from a film; there was an air of unreality about her.

'Now I know!' I burst out, before the two adults could speak to each other. 'You're Christine, Stasia's sister. I've seen photos of you!'

'And you must be Niza.'

The one visible side of her mouth curled into the suggestion of a gentle smile. Christine made a welcoming gesture and we went inside.

We sat at a round table decorated with a crocheted cloth similar to the one Stasia had put on our living room table at home, and ate Christine's bean soup. I was hypnotised by the old cuckoo clock on the wall: I couldn't wait for the hour to strike and the bird to hop out.

My eyes were also drawn to this mysterious lady who was apparently my beloved Stasia's sister. I found it difficult to connect the two. Stasia's rubber boots, her brash manner, the vulgar language she sometimes used — it seemed impossible to reconcile all that with this striking, elegant person. Everything about her was so considered; there was an affected quality to her language, and this strange curtain over her face put me in mind of a fancy-dress ball. Elene's tension, the hesitant way she moved, didn't escape me either. I must have sensed then that a kind of wall had been erected between these women, and my mother was trying to shake it.

'What's going on?' Christine asked her great-niece, after finally taking a seat between us at the little table.

'It's all so bloody difficult!' my mother burst out, as if she'd just been waiting for this question.

'Come on, then, tell me about it,' Christine prompted her. My mother had come here to be comforted, I thought then, but this woman had difficulty comforting her. Something was holding her back; at one point she raised her hand as if to touch Elene's shoulder, but then had second thoughts about it. They both acted as if I was invisible. That annoyed me, because I didn't really know how I was supposed to behave. But I decided to stay quiet and eat my soup. There was something going on between these two people that had nothing to do with me.

'It's all so unbearable.'

At once, Elene started to sob. I hated it when she got like this. When she gave free rein to her tears. I knew then that things were bad, that she couldn't *pull herself together* any more, one of the main tasks of her day-to-day life.

'I think about him every day. Every day I see his face in my mind. I don't know how I'm supposed to forget him. And everything's been going wrong since … since he …'

Christine's face darkened. Her expression reminded me of Stasia's when she stopped in the garden and looked over at the cherry tree. Did this woman see the dead, too? Was that the only connection between the two sisters? The ability to see ghosts?

My mother sobbed and complained, bemoaning her life and the way she had failed herself, her father, her husband. She complained of the drab hopelessness of her existence and her fatherless children. The impossibility of offering her girls a good life. And one name came up again and again: Miqa. I'd never heard it before. Eventually she started talking about how 'gifted' I was. (She always used this word, though she spoke it as if it were some kind of illness, a terrible fate I was suffering.) How I hated it!

She probably would have kept on like this for hours, and Christine would have let her, but then the doorbell rang and Christine, her eyes still on Elene, got up, slowly, reluctantly, and went to open the door.

★

There was no telling from Lana's face whether she was pleased to see my mother or whether she was uncomfortable with the impromptu visit. Miro, however, expressed his delight quite openly. He looked me up and down, ran around the table three times, pulled my hair, laughed loudly, and was told several times to behave himself, but still he didn't stop dancing for joy. Later, he was told to sit next to me and eagerly tucked into the bean soup. He kept pulling faces, and even his mother's raised voice didn't have the desired effect; on the contrary, it made him giggle wildly. But he had achieved something incredible: Elene was smiling again.

Miro was lively and funny. He seemed to have assumed the role of the clown at an early age, and played it with tremendous gusto. He wasn't much taller than me at the time (this certainly changed later on), and he had wild curls that danced around his forehead and black eyes with calf-like eyelashes. But that afternoon, I remember very clearly, it was his speed that impressed me most: how quickly he thought, spoke, moved. As if he were constantly afraid of missing something and was always trying to do at least three things at once. When he was eating, he couldn't sit still; when he was speaking, he couldn't stand still; when he moved, he couldn't hold his tongue. I immediately liked the gap in his teeth, too. Whenever he grinned — which he did often, from ear to ear — he revealed the space between his front teeth, which gave him a very comical aspect, as if this gap were also there purely to make you laugh.

After the meal, he asked me if I wanted to go to the playground out in the rear courtyard. Uncertainly, I agreed. I was surprised by his invitation; I wasn't used to such gestures, especially from a boy. The rear courtyard proved to be an endless labyrinth of little passages and alleyways through which he directed me to the playground. To my great delight, it was deserted.

He fooled around, showing off all that he could do: how high he could climb, how high he could swing, and how fast he could run. That afternoon, he made it his mission to amuse me. And I liked it.

At his side, for the first time in ages, I felt like a child again. A child like any other.

> If we do not stay in control of the literature process, it will look like there was not a single bright day in the 70 years of Soviet power.
>
> VIKTOR CHEBRIKOV

We always went to the circus. Whether on a school trip, as a kind of fulfilment of cultural duty, or for fun with the family. Although Kostya had little time for acrobatics and performing animals, for some inexplicable reason he thought it important to induct us children into the circus world.

I was not a particular fan of this world of illusion. I may have been impressed by a few of the trapeze artists, or by some of the ladies with feathers who rode their horses so skilfully. But the clowns saddened me, as did the tigers that had to jump through a burning tyre. These performances seemed so unnatural. I didn't understand why old men in make-up and red noses were pretending to be stupider than they were, or what was so great about wild animals wearing humiliating little bow-ties and skirts and doing things that went against their nature. What saddened me most of all was the ostentatiously funny dwarves — perhaps because I myself was very short, and there was no way I wanted to be exhibited and stared at like that.

Daria loved the circus more than anything. When we went to see a show at the state circus, she would run like the wind up the endless steps we had to climb to get into the building, looking back again and again to make absolutely sure we were still behind her. Each time we went, she would beg for a lolly or a homemade toy from the gypsy women who stood in the grounds with their budgies on their shoulders, touting their cheap wares. It was part of the ritual for Daria, and that, to her, was sacred.

But on this particular Sunday — it must have been in 1985 — something special happened. Something I would never have expected.

It was the long-awaited performance by Moscow's most famous circus. Daria had talked of nothing else for days. I had armed myself for the long afternoon with a book covered in white paper — I wasn't officially allowed to read *grown-up books* yet, though they were what I loved most, and what I usually read in order to spare myself a few hours of torment at school. Stasia's years as a librarian had taught her some useful things about illegal literature, and she knew all the techniques for smuggling and disguising it. The neutral book-cover idea was one of hers; they were usually plain white wrappers, which I then covered with drawings. Happy stick-men and brightly coloured butterflies aroused the least suspicion.

While the others laughed at the Russian clowns and applauded the animals' tricks, I turned the pages of my book. It was dark in the auditorium, something I hadn't considered. (The last time, when our class had watched *Red Riding Hood* in the Theatre for Children and Young People, there had been more light.) But just the texture of the pages reassured me. And then suddenly a young girl in a blue jersey and white tights stepped into the ring. Daria sighed with disappointment: the girl looked too normal, as if she'd come from a local gymnastics club. Then she was hoisted up to a tightrope at a dizzying height, and the audience fell silent.

I put the book back in my bag and started watching the acrobat. I was spellbound. She could fly. As if on invisible wings that carried her up to tremendous heights. She spun and tumbled, fell and caught herself, danced on the tightrope as if weightless. I had never seen anyone with such elegance, grace, and physical perfection. Her long plait, which flew along with her, looked like a third arm for her to hold on with.

When I glanced over at Daria, her mouth was hanging open and her eyes shone like two glow-worms in the dark. She was as incredulous at the sight as I was. How could this girl make all the people here hold their breath? How could she be so unafraid? How did you learn to fly?

Daria's hand left the armrest of her seat and made its way over to me. She gripped my wrist and squeezed. Then she leaned over in her seat and pressed herself against me. Why me? Why wasn't she sharing her fascination with the grandfather she idolised? I craned my neck, looked at Kostya, and understood: he was leaning back, his body showing none of the excitement that had gripped Daria and me. Kostya was seeing things differently to Daria. For the first time. And this realisation had probably frightened her and made her reach for my hand.

'Isn't it incredible?' my beautiful sister whispered in my ear, clutching my hand more tightly.

I nodded enthusiastically, caught between confusion and gratitude.

'I want to do that, too,' she decided, at that moment, with complete conviction.

'You'd have to train an awful lot, though.'

I thought my objection would disappoint her, but instead she asked eagerly where you could do that.

'I don't know, but they must do acrobatics courses at the Palace of Sport. Mustn't they?'

'Can you find out for me, please?'

She was begging me. She, Daria, was begging *me*! I couldn't believe it.

Daria didn't have the patience to really get to grips with anything. If things didn't reveal themselves to her in the blink of an eye, she lost interest. This impatience had even made her give up riding, which she had loved so much as a little girl; she lacked the endurance for the stud-farm horses, which were difficult to control, and instead she had turned her attention to her friends. So I was all the more amazed at her enthusiasm for such a physically demanding activity.

All Kostya's attempts to get her to stick with one of the usual extra-curricular groups had failed. Be it Georgian folk-dance, piano lessons, or craft courses, Daria would attend them for a few weeks, then come home one day in floods of tears, saying that the other children there were stupid, or the teacher wasn't treating her well and — horror of horrors — wasn't paying her any attention. The next day, Kostya would go with her and, following a formal complaint to the management, Daria would be removed from the group and would return home content and beaming from ear to ear. Her feverish determination that afternoon was something completely new and unexpected.

'I'd give anything to be able to do that.'

Daria wouldn't let it go. Then Kostya leant over to us and asked what all this excited chatter was about. Daria's succinct answer was no less astounding to me than her determination.

'Nothing,' she said.

This *nothing* was the first secret my sister decided to share with me alone.

And, just two weeks after the trip to the circus, Elene signed her eldest daughter up for a gymnastics course at the Sport Institute. David had told me about the Sport Institute, and I had passed the tip on to my mother. As if Daria already suspected that our grandfather wouldn't necessarily approve of her newfound passion, she kept the news a secret from him, and the day Elene took her to the course for the first time she just told Kostya that she wanted to stay in the city and spend two or three days with her mother.

★

The sea at the Seven Sisters was furious. The waves bashed their heads against the rough cliffs with impressive force, as if they had been battling each other for years. The sky was grey, shot through with a yellowish glow. The beach was damp, cold, and deserted. She looked at her footprints in the wet sand; she smelled the salt; she closed her eyes and wrapped the oversized woollen shawl around her shoulders. She was always amazed at the synchronicity with which the sea and the air composed their own unique music.

She relished the solitude after the tour. The peace. The phone off the hook. The unopened post. The anonymity she enjoyed in this place. The ever-busy Amy had departed just a few days ago and left her to her thoughts. Amy made such an effort not to surrender to the ageing process. All the creams she had laid out in the bathroom; all the bright clothes, their garish colours designed to mask her body's flaws. How moved Kitty was by these attempts to resist the inevitable: the headbands, the turbans, the diets, the refusal to wear reading glasses.

Her gaze travelled to the rim of the horizon, where the sea cut across the sky. She breathed deeply.

★

'Look, look, the sea!'

I gave a loud cry and leapt out of the car. We had left the winding roads behind us, traversed the jagged hills, and now the great, endless blue stretched out before us. Kostya was driving himself — a rare sight — and Daria and I were in the back of his official car. He had stopped especially for us, so we could give proper voice to our excitement over the sea, and we bounded exuberantly across the field beside the road, squealing with delight. My joy had less to do with the sea than with the fact that, this time, our grandfather had brought me along on the trip, not just Daria. We were driving to Gagra, in Abkhazia, where we would stay for a week. A lovely long week in March, a trip for which we were even being allowed to miss school. The previous evening, he had come back to the Green House thoroughly merry, and had instructed Nana to pack our things as well as his: he was going to Abkhazia the next day and would take the girls with him. He didn't say Daria, or Daro, but *the girls*.

I lay awake half the night, glancing over at Daria every couple of hours, afraid that it had just been a joke and he and Daria would already have left without me; but Daria was sleeping peacefully in her bed.

I knew that Kostya's invitation to accompany him on his trip was first and foremost a peace offering for Daria. He had found her out, and her acrobatic dreams had caused the first real argument between grandfather and favourite grandchild. However, when he saw that she was absolutely serious about it, he tried to turn the situation to his advantage, and quickly found out all he could about the course and the other opportunities Daria could take advantage of as she made her way into the top league of acrobats.

We stopped off in Batumi. He had been invited to dinner at the house of a good friend and colleague, and intended to combine business with pleasure. We would drive on the next morning, he said.

It was a small, neat house on Queen Tamar Promenade. Newly renovated and smelling of fresh paint, its large garden planted with slender apple trees. A wooden table was laid and waiting for us in the garden, and a lot of unfamiliar faces turned towards us with curiosity as we strolled through the black gate. The host, a stocky, well-fed, balding man whom I had often seen at dinner parties in the Green House, hurried up to Kostya, greeted him with a hearty handshake, and slapped him on the shoulder several times. Daria and I received moist kisses on both cheeks, and were shown to the table.

The eager hostess, who was constantly running back and forth between kitchen and garden, embraced us and filled our plates with all sorts of delicious food. Kostya instantly made himself the centre of attention and began to entertain the party with an array of affected, heavy-handed anecdotes about his work life, all of which were followed by gales of laughter.

Later the host, who was also the *tamada*, the toastmaster, took it in turns with Kostya to make speeches, and they gave increasingly hearty toasts, with increasingly glowing cheeks and increasingly hoarse voices, all of which bored me and most of which I already knew off by heart.

Just when I had given up hope of ever escaping this orgy of food and drink, a fine-boned young woman appeared out of nowhere, as if wafted into the garden by chance on an imperceptible evening breeze, and sat down next to the host. She leaned her head against his chest; she could only be his daughter. She was received warmly by the other guests, dispensed friendly greetings and hugs, and greeted Kostya, too, with a coy nod.

She was wearing a beautiful striped summer dress that exposed her shoulders — it was a little too light for the season — and her hair was tied back in a thick, high ponytail that hung down her back. I gathered from the conversation that she was studying law in Tbilisi. Her father called on her to make a toast to the guests, which she did in a slightly insincere and excessively friendly manner. However, a tremulous unease shimmered through her show of friendliness. She kept kneading her fingers, playing with her rings, and jiggling her feet in their pumps. When she had drained her wine glass, she stood up unexpectedly, excused herself, and disappeared as quickly as she had arrived.

Looking for the toilet, I strayed into the rear courtyard and saw the young woman sitting there at a little garden table, drinking wine. She was dropping dice onto the backgammon board, over and over again, as if the sound reassured her. The table stood in darkness, lit only by a small candle that had to contend with the draft.

'Sorry!' I muttered. 'I'm looking for the toilet.'

She got up at once, flashed her insincere smile at me, and took me there. When I came out, she was leaning against the wall of the house, as if waiting for me.

'You're the younger one, aren't you? So you must be Niza.'

I nodded, surprised that she knew my name. I had never seen her before.

'I'm Rusa. I live in Tbilisi, too,' she told me, looking at the sky. She had a soft, sugar-sweet voice that sounded as if it had been dipped in caramel.

'Would you like a glass of grape juice?' she asked me. And, without waiting for my reply, she went back to the little table and poured me a glass of dark red juice from a carafe. I took a seat opposite her on a low stool and, without really thinking about it, started placing the backgammon pieces on their starting positions.

'You play backgammon? Not really a children's game, is it?'

But then, as if rousing herself from a long absence, she suddenly gave me a look that was full of enthusiasm.

'Well then — shall we?' She rubbed her hands in eager expectation. 'Did your grandfather teach you?' She tried to make the question sound casual.

'No, my stepfather,' I answered, just as casually.

We began to play. She was wholly committed to the game, which I liked. She played with great concentration and — I noticed this at once — she didn't pretend to be more stupid than she was. We threw the dice again and again.

'Why are you here, why don't you go back to the others?' I asked, finally, because the question was nagging at me. She shrugged.

'They're not my friends. They're Papa's friends. I'm only here for a week, anyway. I ought to be preparing for my exams. I've got my finals very soon, but for some reason I'm so distracted this evening. I just can't concentrate.'

She sighed.

'We're only away for a week as well. We're driving on to Gagra tomorrow.'

'I know,' she said with a tired nod, and once again I wondered how she knew. I was growing to like her, though. Her delicate appearance was deceptive; the sugar-sweet mask hid great strength and energy, which, for some reason I couldn't fathom, she was doing her utmost to restrain. She was talkative, too, with a quick wit, and during the game she kept making me laugh. She did impressions of some of the guests — Kostya's colleagues, most of whom I also knew from the Green House — and usually she was spot on. She had a deep understanding of people, it seemed, and an impressive talent for mimicking them.

'You've all made a hash of it again, can't you do *anything* right, I'm telling you, you'd all be *done for* if I wasn't here!' I had joined in her game and was imitating Kostya's voice. 'Well, who am I?' I cried delightedly.

Suddenly Rusa's face darkened and she gripped the dice in her fist, lost in thought.

'You do a good impression of him,' she said at last, sounding more sad than amused, and dropped the dice loudly onto the board. At that moment we heard footsteps, and my grandfather appeared behind me. He was clearly a little intoxicated by the fresh sea air and the wine.

'So this is where you are! You can't just wander off like that, Niza, it's rude.'

'I talked her into playing with me. You can blame me,' said Rusa, coming to my aid.

Kostya was forced to nod his assent. 'Yes, she's mad about that game. I'm almost afraid she's going to get us into real trouble one day with her playing.'

I was annoyed at him for saying that. I hadn't wanted to before, but at that moment I decided to become a professional player and get him into real trouble.

'Really, she plays tremendously well,' Rusa protested.

I didn't like most of Kostya's friends and colleagues. They were all loud, and liked to show off, and were terrifically busy. They liked to drink, and their bejewelled wives sparkled like Christmas trees and spoke to us children as if we had been lobotomised or were forever two years old. But Rusa was different. She was young, fresh, witty, curious. She didn't ask me stupid questions, like did I prefer mummy or daddy, or which was my favourite subject at school, nor did she require some humiliating performance of me, like reciting a poem or doing the splits. And for some obscure reason I wanted her to like me.

Kostya suddenly went over to the other side of the table and laid an arm around Rusa's bare shoulders. Her body tensed visibly; she sat up a little straighter and lowered her eyes.

'Well then, you'll have a pastime in common for the coming week,' he said, and disappeared back into the darkness. We continued our game in silence. I mulled over his final words.

'Are you going to Gagra, too?' I finally dared to ask. She nodded, avoiding my eyes. 'Then we can play tomorrow as well, in the car!' I concluded enthusiastically.

'I'm afraid we can't do that; I'm taking the train. Besides, it's our little secret, and we mustn't tell the others, all right?' she explained to me in a whisper.

I won the game. But I wasn't happy about it at all.

★

Kitty stretched. She had been struggling with back pain for a while now. She bent forwards, let her arms dangle, raised them again, and stopped stiffly where she was. Instinctively, she took a step back, feeling for the key in her coat pocket. She was standing at the gate of her cottage, and she could see a figure pacing back and forth outside her front door.

The light from the streetlamp was too weak; she couldn't make out who it was. Only that the visitor was male. Maybe it was one of the villagers — but why would he be waiting at her door, and what was that by his feet? Could it be a suitcase?

A persistent fan who had tracked her down? A dangerous madman? For a moment, she considered vanishing into the darkness again, heading for the village's only pub, or contacting the police. She took a step forwards. Her eyes weren't what they used to be, and reading glasses didn't help much, either. All at once, she felt her knees go weak, felt a shudder run down her spine, felt the sweat on her palms. Yes, maybe her head was playing a nasty trick on her and she was seeing ghosts. Maybe it was time to go back to London; maybe she had simply spent too long alone with her memories.

But the figure went on standing there, it was alive, it was *real*, and the closer she looked, the more expectant joy prevailed over consternation, and she quickened her pace.

'Giorgi!'

She called his name, and he turned round. A moment later, she felt his arms around her. The familiarity was there, even without his voice: he hadn't yet uttered a word; he didn't even seem to have the strength to say her name. Without having taken a proper look at him, she reached for his hand and dragged him into the house. She didn't want to lose a second. She wanted to be led by her joy.

'Forgive me, please, forgive me, Kitty, forgive me …' he murmured, over and over, but she didn't want any questions, any answers, she wanted to stay in the here and now, without hurrying ahead or looking back. She helped him out of his coat and pressed him to her again and again, kissing his cheeks, his forehead, his mouth.

Outside, a man brushed past the fence. A man with curly hair, who stopped for a moment to catch his breath, and shot the pair of them a dark glance before going on his way towards the sea, towards the water's edge. To the furthest edge, and much further. Searching for Vienna. But Kitty and Alania were standing where he could no longer see them, in the darkness of the cold hallway, like two supplicants. They didn't let each other go. Kitty rested her forehead against his and stayed there.

'I'm not worthy of you. I ruined everything. I ran away. I ran away from myself. You're the only good deed of my life, Kitty. The hangman's blood flows in me …'

He said the words as if he had practised them over and over for a long time. He was incoherent. Kitty didn't understand, but it was all the same to her. She never would have dared to imagine that the sudden appearance of this tired, sad figure would make her so hungry for life. No, she didn't want to be an old woman who took lonely walks on the beach. She wanted to live — even if the price for that was having to fling open the doors to all her ghosts and let them in.

'Don't go away again. I love you,' she said, and was astonished at these words that burst out of her mouth with such apparent ease. He released himself from her arms, took hold of her elbows, and stared at her through the darkness, as if searching for confirmation of these words in her face. As if he had never heard these words before in his life. He kissed her, and Kitty was back in the little park with the green-painted benches, in a southern town that might once have become the Nice of the Caucasus.

She was astonished at the strength in his arms, those slender arms she had looked at so often, committing every part of his body to memory, after years of the disembodied voice on the telephone.

She followed him as he outran himself, left himself behind. She wanted to follow him to where she could be another person, too. But when he touched her, all the American hotel rooms came back to her. And the whirling figure of Fred Lieblich. He is not her, thought Kitty, as she helped him shed his clothes. How old must he be? Nearly sixty? Over sixty? Oh God, were they really so old already? Were there really so many years between them and the park, between them and Andro, between them and the classroom? No, no, no, not again, she told herself, and clutched his collar, buried her face in his neck.

The floor was cold, but they took pleasure in their youthful recklessness, their obliviousness to the world around them, the abandonment of all reason. She wanted to stay in the hallway, in this narrow, dark hallway on the cold floor. She wanted to let out a full-throated trill. She wanted to bake the world a welcome cake. He loved her like a hungry boy, and she wanted to love him like a hungry girl. And with every caress she wanted to cheat time, roll back a year, two, three, ten, more, be the Kitty she was before the ghosts started hammering at her door. Go back to the time when she didn't want to roll back time because everything was still ahead of her. Including the possibilities there had been in that one brief meeting in a cheerless, deserted railway station.

She forgot her backache, forgot her bad eyes, forgot the eternal loneliness.

The idea of being with this man — not the boy with the blond curls and the wooden angels, not in Vienna, but perhaps in London or Moscow — was seductive and, at the same time, impossible. If there had been even the slightest possibility of that, if things had been ever so slightly different, would Andro still be alive, would she still have her womb? Would Mariam be her brother's wife? And would she have children? One child, two, even three? Then she would have sung in secret under the shower, and thousands of people would never have sung along to all her songs — but would that be so terrible? So unimaginable? If she had never seen all those cities, never composed all those songs, never ... met Fred?

She closed her eyes. She saw Andro's face looming over her. She closed her eyes. She saw Fred smiling at her. She closed her eyes. She saw Mariam cradling her head in the sunny barn. She closed her eyes. She saw the blonde woman lit up by a naked bulb. She closed her eyes. No, it never stopped. She saw Giorgi Alania covering her body in kisses. And she held him tight with all her strength. She wanted to vanish. To shrink, to dissolve, become air.

> A man, a people — without an ideal — is born blind.
>
> MAXIM GORKY

They were sitting on the bed, fully clothed. She was moaning softly and digging her red-painted fingernails into his back; his face was buried in her neck, and I couldn't see what he was feeling. I didn't know if he was whispering something in her ear or if it was his hand, which had disappeared under her dress, that was making her moan. Her lips parted, she opened her eyes wide, raised her right hand as if she wanted to stop him touching her, but then thought better of it and pulled his head down towards her. I pressed myself against the wall, unable to tear myself away from the scene. I held my breath.

Daria was asleep in the next room. We were staying in a large house belonging to one of Kostya's colleagues, who had let him have it as a favour for the whole week of our holiday. We were occupying the second floor. We had a sea view. The sound of the waves had woken me. I'd got up to take a look at the sea, to make sure it was still there.

I'd even briefly considered waking Daria, but she was exhausted from our games on the shingle beach. The water was still too cold for swimming, but we'd paddled, collected stones and mussels, and romped about until we fell into bed, dog-tired.

Kostya had been cheerful that day as well, even giving me a kiss on the forehead.

I'd been so happy I would have liked to stay on this beach forever. With my sister and my grandfather, who I'd discovered could be so easy-going and so kind-hearted. And with this witty, charming Rusa, who was staying in the house with us, who cooked for us and made us laugh, who looked after us when Kostya went about his business, and with whom I so loved to play backgammon.

Daria eyed her mistrustfully, and didn't seem to appreciate having to vie with a grown woman for Kostya's favour, but I was delighted with her and wanted her as my friend.

She had the guest room on the top floor. Kostya was in the room next to ours. And I was about to go out onto the balcony, to look at the sea, when a soft moan made me pause. Rusa's beautiful, inviting voice. I padded back into the hall, to Kostya's room, since that was clearly where her voice was coming from. The door was slightly ajar, and a little table lamp was burning on the chest of drawers by the bed.

What I saw made me freeze.

I was ashamed. It was the sea's fault. This sight was not meant for my eyes. The forbidden nature of the image was clear to me, even though I'd never laid eyes on such a scene before. But still it was strange, and illogical: Kostya was much too old for such a young woman — wasn't he too old to be doing *that sort of thing* at all? And Rusa was clearly too young; or was I mistaken? Now I was standing stock still, fascinated by this forbidden sight, and I was afraid for her. The power he seemed to have over her frightened me. To me, it felt dangerous, seeing her at his mercy like that. As she fell back onto the bed, I prised myself away from the wall and hurried back to the room I shared with Daria.

Kostya left for Sukhumi in the car early the next morning, and Daria, Rusa, and I went to the beach and paddled.

She made us omelettes for breakfast, and gave us some bread and jam. We took a rubber dinghy out to a remote dam and collected the mussels that clung to the dam walls. For lunch she cooked the mussels in tomato sauce, and I couldn't get enough of them, though Daria wrinkled her nose in disgust. Together we drew brightly coloured landscapes in chalk on the asphalt outside the house. She made funny hats for us out of the *Komsomolskaya Pravda*. We ate Bird's Milk chocolates until we felt sick. She had slender ankles and soft hips. She let me plait her hair. I liked myself as I was in her eyes, the way she looked at me when she combed my hair. So kind, so affectionate. We talked about books, and I told her the secret of the fake book covers. She laughed and clapped her hands in delight. We sunbathed, and in the evening we went out for a trout dinner with Kostya. On the way there he let me sit on his shoulders. I was beside myself with happiness. He laughed a lot when she told him stories. I didn't know he could laugh so much.

I wanted time to stand still. I was fearful of the journey home. I was already pained by the very idea of having to go back to school. I was pained by the thought of Rusa being gone, and with her Kostya's good mood and his leniency with me. I tried to cling tight to every single moment, and I thought of her face, contorted with the frightening, painful knowledge that soon she would have to let him go.

★

The next evening, he didn't come back at seven, as he'd promised. We were supposed to be having dinner together. Rusa had made rissoles, at Daria's request. She'd gone to a lot of trouble, even putting on an apron that had been hanging up in the kitchen. She had uncorked a bottle of wine. Had laid the table with great care, and bought cut flowers, which she'd arranged in vases on the table. She had put on make-up and stuck a flower in her hair.

But he didn't come. The three of us ate together. We ate quickly. Afterwards, Daria felt sick; the food hadn't agreed with her, and Rusa had to look after her. She gave her some valerian and put her to bed. When Daria fell asleep at about ten, and Kostya still wasn't there, Rusa took off her make-up and disappointment spread across her face. The two of us sat on the balcony. I offered to play a game with her, but she didn't want to. She brought out the wine and drank it straight from the bottle.

'He must have work to do. He's always got a lot of work to do. He'll be here soon,' I said, and was glad that, contrary to my expectations and despite the disappointment mounting within her, she didn't cry. She beckoned me over and clasped me tightly in her arms.

'You're such a great girl, Niza. Your mama must be incredibly proud of you,' she said, kissing my parting.

'I think you're a great girl, too, and you shouldn't be sad because of Kostya,' I told her, sitting on the arm of her chair.

'He's never going to change,' she murmured.

'Do you want to be with him?'

'Oh, Niza.'

'But he's much too old,' I said, in the honest hope that she might rethink her love. In my heart of hearts, I thought she was far too great for him.

'I'd like things to have been different. Believe me, if someone had told me three years ago that this would happen, I'd have laughed at them. My parents …'

'What about them?'

'They'd kill me if they knew that …'

'But they'll never know. I won't tell anybody.'

She tried to smile, but couldn't quite manage it. She drank and drank, as if the wine were juice, and told me about her life. I suddenly began to feel more grown-up than her, and I brought her some water, as Nana always did when Kostya drank too much.

Rusa told me about her father's birthday party, when she had met Kostya for the first time. How charming he was, how different from all her father's other friends, how sensitive and profound he had been. And then they had bumped into each other outside the university. She'd very nearly walked past him, but then she had stopped and allowed him to invite her for coffee. Afterwards, he had his driver take her back to her aunt's house, where she was living while she studied in Tbilisi. She'd stood in the courtyard for a long time after he left. She knew she wanted to see him again, even if she sensed it was a terribly stupid idea.

After weeks of trying to get this man out of her head, she had phoned him at his office. It had been going on for a year now. The surreptitiousness, as she called it, was what she found hardest to bear. This game of hide-and-seek. The indignity of sneaking around. The secret places where they met. The lies. And, above all, the terrible suspicion that she wasn't the only one he met in secret.

Her tongue grew steadily heavier, and the pauses between her words lengthened. Finally she added, in a chillingly cynical and pitiless tone, that she wanted to become a judge and pass judgement on injustices, yet here she was, doing such a monstrous injustice to herself.

I racked my brains, searching for a way out for Rusa. For a moment, I even considered pairing her off with David — he would be much more interesting for her, or so I thought at the time — and then I could have both of them around permanently, and everyone would be happy.

It was well after midnight, and Kostya still wasn't back. I went up to her room with her, as she'd already started to sway. I helped her out of her clothes. She fell onto the bed in her underwear and lay there motionless. I left the room. I decided to summon all my courage, wait for Kostya, and explain to him how much she loved him, and how important it was that he never make her wait again. But then I heard water running in the bathroom. I remembered that Mother always knocked on the bathroom door when Aleko went into the bathroom drunk, and I decided to do the same. I felt responsible for her, at least until Kostya was back. I knocked tentatively, timidly, but there was no response. Then I leaned against the door and it fell open: she hadn't locked it.

She was sitting on the floor, both arms in a bucket of water on her lap. The water was full of blood. There was no bathtub, so she'd had to improvise. Her eyes were closed. I didn't know what you were supposed to do when someone had slit their wrists. I didn't know if it was bad that the cuts were horizontal, if vertical ones would have been better, but I lunged towards her, overturning the bucket as I did so. The bloody water stained the floor red. I shook her, begged her to look at me. Her breathing was laboured. I didn't know what number to dial, or if there was even a telephone in the house. I laid her on the floor and she let out a barely audible groan. I tried to focus. Biology lessons, my conversations with David. Useful knowledge. It occurred to me that with deep cuts the crucial thing was to stop the bleeding. I took some towels and a floor cloth and knotted them tightly round her arms. I thought about waking Daria, screaming at the top of my lungs until she woke up, but decided against it. Daria had a terrible fear of blood. Then I ran downstairs, searching for a telephone — and at that moment I saw headlights illuminating the garden.

I ran outside, thunderstruck.

'Kostya, Kostya!' I screamed at the top of my voice, running towards him. I wanted to hit him when I saw him frown, as if he were going to tell me off for being up so late, but before he could say anything I grabbed his sleeve and dragged him up the stairs.

★

He slapped her a few times, then he took her in his arms and picked her up. He was trembling. He told me not to wake Daria, he told me to wait here for them, he told me everything was going to be fine, but I screamed and kept saying I wanted to go with them, I wouldn't leave her alone. He didn't have the time or the energy to discuss it, so he let me get in the back of the car with her and hold her head as he drove, cursing, trembling.

At the hospital, several people came running. She was put on a trolley and wheeled away. Kostya and I were left sitting in the cold light of an empty waiting room. He put his hands over his face and fell silent. I paced up and down, trying to swallow my tears. Then I sat down beside him, exhausted.

'You were very brave, Niza,' he said without looking at me. 'You were very courageous. She's lost a lot of blood, but the doctors will help her. It was unforgivable of me to leave you alone. You should never have had to go through something like that.'

He still wasn't looking at me. Kept his face buried in his hands.

'She wants you to be with her,' I said.

He hesitated, turned to me. 'Did she tell you that?'

'Yes.'

'She's very young, and at that age, people are just very ... emotional.'

'But it's not right.'

'What isn't right?'

'That you made her wait. Is it true you have other girlfriends besides her?'

'Did she tell you that, too?'

'Yes.'

'I ... no, I was just ... I had to work.'

'Until now?'

It was all too much for him. He wanted to comfort me, he wanted to play the grandfather, and he didn't want to be taken to task by a schoolgirl. He wasn't prepared for that. (Kostya Jashi was accountable to no one; that was the life he had constructed for himself, starting, perhaps, on the day he went into the water to mourn the woman whose death had taken his conscience along with it.)

'You often hurt other people.'

I didn't know why I said it. I wasn't thinking. Usually, I always thought before saying a word to Kostya. I was sobbing. I felt undone. I wanted Rusa to live, to take her exams and become a judge. I wanted her to go on playing backgammon with me. He put his arms around me. I couldn't let myself go, my body was too tense. I had so many questions for him. And so many fears. I knew that the intimacy of recent days was not built on firm ground.

'Is that what you think?' he asked tentatively.

'Yes. You hurt Mama, too. She often cries because of you. And Stasia, though she never says anything. And ... and me.'

He looked at me, and I didn't know if he was horrified or just surprised. I didn't care now whether he would ever love me again. I just wanted her to live.

'I love your mother,' he said suddenly, and leant back in his chair. In the reception area, a few paramedics and nurses were huddled around a little television set; something exciting was happening on it. They seemed upset. One of the nurses was making coffee on a little electric hotplate while staring spellbound at the screen.

'Some things just don't turn out the way we want them to,' he said.

I waited for him to go on, but then he got up and went over to the reception desk to see what was happening — and froze.

How could he watch television now! Even if the world was ending, how could he walk away without giving me an answer? The answer I needed. The honesty I needed so that Rusa would live.

He beckoned to me. I hesitated. I walked slowly over to the television. The head of state, Chernenko, had died. It didn't interest me, it left me cold. I didn't care if a Mr Chernenko was alive or dead, I just wanted Rusa to live.

I lowered my eyes and stared at my sandals and the dirty tiled floor. It was so bleak, this place. Someone as beautiful and clever as Rusa didn't deserve to die in a place like this.

Chernenko died. Rusa survived, but something inside her died as well.

Kostya and I drove home at daybreak. In silence. He didn't say anything else. We took the coast road. It was getting light. Less than a decade later this town would be destroyed by tanks, bombs, fire and thousands of bullets, but fortunately I didn't know that yet.

When we arrived, Daria was still fast asleep, unaware of all that had happened.

That night, I learned that heads of state are always more important than everyone else.

I learned that ghosts aren't necessarily dead people.

I learned that the sea doesn't accept anything that hasn't already been washed clean.

I learned that love, however light and hopeful it might once have been, can end with unexpected suddenness in a bleak hospital.

★

After seven decades, the Soviet Union had served its time. It was already devouring itself from within, using up all its energy and resources; it had swallowed itself, but was not yet able to vomit. For this, it needed a new Party leader, who at the unprecedentedly young age of fifty-four was a regular whippersnapper in Party terms, and who — against all expectations — did in fact come to power in 1985. Comrade Gorbachev was to inherit the world of 'socialist peace', which encompassed thirty-four per cent of the global population. And in the cause of spreading this peace, on taking office he received the gift of wars in Angola, Mozambique, Ethiopia, Nicaragua, El Salvador, and Afghanistan.

I became an adult in 1985, in a single moment, the night Chernenko died and Rusa survived.

> It was a palace:
> pink as the blush of a winter morning
> large as the world, old as the wind.
> We were daughters almost of a tsar,
> almost a tsar's daughters ...
>
> MARINA TSVETAEVA

Giorgi Alania was able spend precisely two days with Kitty Jashi without getting into difficulties.

Over the past few years, since he'd returned to Moscow, he had been working for the ministry as an 'escort' for international cultural and sporting exchanges, meaning that every few months he accompanied Cossack choirs or ballet companies on their tours, or took young chess players to their competitions abroad, and observed them. He now answered directly to the Lubyanka.

One such trip had taken him to London, with a gymnastics team from the Youth Sports Palace in Moscow, whom he was accompanying to an international junior gymnastics competition. Never in his wildest dreams had he imagined that he would be sent to London again after his transfer request. And he *had* dreamed about it over the last few years, manically, constantly, cursing himself, unable to believe he had so callously abandoned the only girlfriend — the only woman — whom he hadn't paid for a kiss.

His decision had resulted from an impulse, a cruel mood, which was ultimately the consequence of his meeting with Christine. He had fled blindly. He'd believed he was protecting Kitty, but after a few months back in Moscow he had begun to reflect on his decision, had begun to harbour doubts, and had come to the conclusion that he'd made a terrible mistake and destroyed the only glimmer of light in his life.

On top of this came the fact that, after such a long time in London, Alania was no longer accustomed to life under socialism. The strict surveillance, the constant mistrust, the discontent among his colleagues, the dreariness of daily life soon started to weigh on him. His personality regained the familiar choleric tendency that Kitty Jashi had so effortlessly made him forget. He made himself unpopular with his subordinates. He was irritable, dissatisfied, hostile. He vehemently rejected any possibility of a personal relationship or any kind of intimacy with his colleagues. He might have been an outsider before, but now he was open about the fact, emphasising it with every word, every gesture.

The longing was the worst thing. The urge just to run away and go to Kitty's flat that came over him so often and so suddenly, as if his desires refused to accept his reality. The sense of joyful anticipation he had known in London, when he was going to see Kitty that same evening, now started to take possession of him in Moscow — always followed by the painful realisation that it wasn't going to happen. The dreams that all revolved around her, which so often woke him with a start in the night. To escape them, Alania started doing something he hadn't done since he was a young man: drinking. Wine at first, in small quantities, to help him relax in the evening; then, later, harder drinks, to forget. The next morning, he wouldn't remember going to sleep; sometimes he would wake up in the most unlikely places in his apartment: in the bathroom, on the rug, even on the little balcony that he usually only used for hanging out his washing.

And perhaps he really would have succeeded, would have drunk himself into an oblivion where there were no memories of Kitty and London, no father, and no hopes that only ever led to disappointment — but then Fate played into his hands and gave him the opportunity to travel to England.

★

Her effusive emotions, her heartfelt welcome, the caresses, and the intimacy, this incredible intimacy he was granted once he had found her. He couldn't believe it; he found it hard to accept her words, her joy at his arrival.

Even if, in the hours that remained to them, they didn't fall into each other's arms again, didn't give themselves to each other with such abandon, even if there were no more kisses and passionate caresses, this one memory would be enough for a lifetime, and he would never complain, never expect anything again — but he could still hope, or maybe it was only now that he could start hoping. She had forgiven him even before he could beg her forgiveness, and this happiness was more than he had dared to expect: she didn't want to hear any explanation or justification.

And when he tried to tell her his story anyway, in the kitchen the following morning, she interrupted him and asked him to let sleeping dogs lie. She knew him, she trusted him, and she assumed there had been pressing reasons for him to do what he had done, but she didn't want to know; they were irrelevant now. She wanted to enjoy the present, she said, the limited time they had together, and she didn't want to hurry into the future or be forced to look back.

His second attempt at this conversation, during a good long walk by the sea, was also unsuccessful. She didn't want to know. She didn't want to talk. Instead, she took his hand in hers and pulled him along the damp sand.

The evening before his return to London, he told her that she had given him the greatest, most wholehearted happiness he had ever felt. That he was afraid of his life in Moscow. That she had been the ground beneath his feet, all these years — all his life, it seemed to him, from the moment he first met her in the deserted station. But she didn't respond to this confession, either. She poured him some more whisky, her face giving nothing away, and he couldn't tell whether his words pleased or troubled her. She looked at him as if he were describing an entirely banal event, as if he were speaking of some very ordinary matter.

And he didn't understand how it was possible for her to overwhelm him with her love one night, and the next day refuse to know or hear anything more about this love. As if her own behaviour had scared her, made her inhibited. But what more could he expect? Wasn't that already far more than he had hoped for, before coming here?

Looking back, his whole life seemed to lead up to him coming here — *having* to come here — to say all that he had to say to her, to forget everything else. It had all led to them finding each other at last, in their old age, whatever label, whatever name they gave it. Driving out each other's demons, making themselves a fresh pot of tea, going for walks. Or was it presumptuous to think there could be a new beginning for him?

Before they went to bed — he wished she would invite him into her bedroom, but she didn't — as she pressed a tentative kiss onto his lips, he gathered all his courage, took hold of her wrist, and forced her to look at him. Then he said he would try to find a way never to leave her side again. She smiled, but the smile was weak, and she stroked his cheek gently, but without much feeling.

'Go to bed now, Giorgi,' she said.

'What's wrong?' he asked. 'Tell me what you're thinking. I don't want to sleep. I don't want to squander another minute. Stay with me, talk to me. I want to listen to you as long as necessary. If you don't want to listen to me, then at least let me listen to you. Please.' He was begging her.

'We don't need any more words, Giorgi, and that's all right. There's simply nothing more to say.'

'But of course there is, there's so much to say: so much that thinking about it sometimes makes me dizzy. It's all the same to me whether I'm arrested or released; I don't have anything to worry about any more. I'm more sure of myself now than I ever have been.'

'What exactly do you want to discuss? Yes, I used to cling to the illusion that words could change things, that if everything was said, everything expressed, then it would be easier; but that was a fallacy. The reason you became so essential to me wasn't because you kept me alive; it was the fact that you knew all about me, and still stayed with me. That with every phone call, every word, everything you did to help, you forgave me a little. And that was what enabled me to live, what made it all possible, the path I took, the songs, the people I met, the travel, the happiness — yes, that too. Even the happiness I found with other people.

'But a murderess is still a murderess, Giorgi, and no matter how often and how much I sing, no matter how many words I say, no matter how much happiness I am granted, I will never be able to forget that. No — quite the opposite: with each year of my life the memory grows clearer. Doubt, abhorrence — they'll keep on growing, and I'm starting to understand that, to accept it, and I feel better for it; yes, it's incredible but it's true. I'm not afraid any more; I feel certain, clear. Because this way at least I can retain the good — and there has been so much good in my life, so much unforeseeable good, so many wonderful things along my path. This way, at least all the wonderful things that have happened to me aren't instantly tainted by the horror. This way I don't have to tell myself I haven't earned it, this happiness, these people, these possibilities. I can accept them as well.'

These words surprised him so much that it took him a few minutes to compose an answer. Thoughts raced around his head, aimless, disorientated. He felt as if the world had been turned upside down.

'Kitty, Kitty, wait, wait, what are you talking about? You mustn't think like that. You're not a ...' He couldn't make the word pass his lips, not in connection with her. 'You didn't kill anyone. The reason I couldn't talk to you, that I had to flee, was that I was the one who —'

But she interrupted him again: 'I know who you are. I know what you might have done. I know what the price was for keeping me alive. I'm not blind, Giorgi. And I also know that only a murderer is in a position to forgive a murderess. Or a dead man. Nobody else. I know it, Giorgi.'

But where did these thoughts come from? Where had the fatal, monstrous finality of her self-analysis come from? How could she think such a thing? This woman who was so bright and kind, who was worshipped and desired by thousands of people, who was so modest and emphatic? This woman he had adored his whole life! A cold shudder ran down his spine. He wanted to seize her and hold her as tightly as she had held him in the first seconds of their reunion, drive all this gloom and horror out of her, but he felt paralysed. He was still gripping her by the elbow, but his grip loosened, his strength vanished. Her words, her frightening composure, her calm had left him frozen rigid.

He let go of her elbow and put both arms around her. She made no attempt to free herself from his embrace. She laid her head on his shoulder. They stayed like that, motionless.

'I'll come back. For good,' he said quietly.

'You can't do that.'

'You know I'm good at making the impossible possible,' he said, trying to sound light-hearted.

'Yes, you are.'

'You mustn't think like that.' His words sounded ridiculous and impotent to him, but he didn't know how else to say it.

'Don't worry. I told you already, things are good now, Giorgi. Things are really good.'

★

'Do me a favour, Kitty, please,' he said at dawn, before setting off for the station.

'I'd gladly do you any favour in the world, if I only could. You know that.'

She seemed unusually cheerful that morning.

'Don't forget the words you said to me. Don't do anything to invalidate them. Preserve them for me. Because I'm going to hold on tight to them. You love many people, and many people love you, but I ... You're all I have.'

He was amazed at how easy it was to speak these words, to formulate his plea, which sounded so self-evident, so logical to him.

She smiled and nodded.

★

She had felt a strange premonition all morning. As if this day would bring her something. Something new, confusing, and disturbing all at once. She had gone down to the kiosk to get a newspaper, and had come back up to the flat. The frenetic pace of London life felt unfamiliar. She missed the peace of the Seven Sisters, the seclusion. She had enjoyed being alone, and had asked Amy to give her a few days off before she had to think about studios and producers again.

In the paper, she had read that a Comrade Gorbachev had been made General Secretary of the Communist Party of the Soviet Union. The news, which surprised everyone, left her cold. She was used to them coming and going without anything changing. She folded the newspaper again and sat down on the balcony with her plants.

Amy kept telling her to buy a bigger flat, or a house; after all, she had the money. But what for, she wondered. Why swap a flat that held such lovely memories for a new, empty one that had yet to be filled with life?

And when the doorbell rang, she knew her morning's apprehension had not been unfounded.

'I have a studio again. I'm working again. I'm even teaching a drawing class, can you imagine?' she said, still standing in the doorway. She clearly had new teeth; she was still unhealthily gaunt, but there was some colour in her cheeks again, and the red hair, with a few white strands mixed in, had regained its shine.

Kitty didn't invite her guest into the flat. And Fred didn't seem to expect it.

'I've got an exhibition coming up soon, and I want you to come to the opening,' she added. And then, quietly: 'Maybe you'd like to sing a couple of songs for me?'

'Why should I?' asked Kitty sceptically.

'I'm clean,' she replied, as if Kitty's singing were a logical reward for completing rehab.

'I'm too old for new beginnings,' said Kitty, not knowing herself why she was saying it.

'I don't believe in new beginnings, have you forgotten? But I believe in you. And in your voice.'

She smiled. Her cat's eyes shone. Yes, she was alive. Fred had survived, and now she was standing in front of Kitty, asking her to sing. To celebrate her survival. Yes, maybe she should do that, sing life's praises. Life, as it was. Life, with its murderers, its classrooms, the cheated, the left-behind, the words that had no meaning any more, life with its miracles and coincidences, its kisses and revulsion. Oh, to hell with it, thought Kitty. Maybe Fred had been right all along when she said the heart was not a chamber that could be locked from the inside.

'I'll think about it,' she said, and a smile lit up her face before she shut the door again.

Three days later, Kitty Jashi saw Andro Eristavi. She was in a taxi on her way to an interview in town, and as she looked out of the car window, she saw him with a striking clarity and *alive*, standing on the other side of the street. She yelled at the taxi driver to stop immediately. Leaped out of the car and ran across the road without looking left or right. But he had already disappeared, and she knew there was no sense in looking for him. He would come back when it was time: of that she was certain.

★

'Excuse me. I don't mean to bother you, I just ...'

An older man in corduroy trousers and a flowery shirt had stopped Daria and me on the street. We had just left school; in a minute, Daria would have to get the trolleybus to her acrobatics class, and I had to take the Metro to David's studio. So the last thing we needed was old men in corduroy trousers wanting to admire my sister's different-coloured eyes.

'I'm sorry, we're in a bit of a rush ...' I cut in.

'Just two minutes, I beg you. I'm a screenwriter. I work for Kote Latsabidze. He's working on a new film at the moment, and he's still looking for an actress who ... Please come to a casting at the studio tomorrow.'

He hastily wrote an address on a page of his notebook and pressed it into my sister's hand.

'You're exactly what he's looking for!' he said in parting, and disappeared.

We stopped on the street and stared at the note. Kote Latsabidze was well known; Aleko and his friends mentioned his name a lot. He was a very promising director who had made two short films and one feature, which had been the subject of much discussion, as it had somehow managed to evade the censors and had gained considerable recognition abroad. But at that point, I still hadn't seen any of his films.

Daria's face lit up with curiosity, while I regarded the slip of paper with a degree of mistrust. Why approach someone on the street? There were enough actresses in the country, weren't there? Daria put the note in her school bag with a shrug of her shoulders; it was impossible to tell if she was pleased with the offer or indifferent to it. At the bus stop, I tried to talk to her about it again, but still she just shrugged, so I let it drop.

The next day, when Kostya's driver came to collect us and Daria was nowhere to be found, it all came back to me. Had she really gone to the casting on her own?

Of course, I kept quiet about this at home, and gave them some excuse about her making a last-minute decision to go over to a friend's house and cram for her controlled assessments.

That evening, she phoned and said it was already late; she was going to stay with Elene and Aleko and go to school from there in the morning. Kostya's displeasure permeated the whole house. Daria had started her periods, and small breasts had become apparent under her tops, so Kostya's surveillance had increased significantly. After all, everyone knew that almost all her male classmates were in love with her. After the phone call, I was certain she had been to the studio. The next morning at school, I dragged her into the girls' toilets and demanded information.

'I covered for you, so you owe me an explanation!' I hissed at her.

'Yes, I went. And guess what — they've asked me to go back this afternoon. Latsabidze was there, too, and he was smiling at me all the way through. But this time they want me to bring a parent with me.'

She looked at me expectantly. Even now I couldn't tell if she was genuinely excited by this business, or if she was just going through with it out of curiosity, to see how far she would get. She'd shown no desire to be an actress before. Well — my sister was full of surprises.

'What exactly did you have to do?' I asked.

'Read some lines. Look at the camera and imagine something.'

'Imagine what?'

'That my boyfriend had been put in jail.'

'What's the film about, then?'

'It's about this guy who wants to make a film, but he's not allowed; some political thing.'

'Uh huh. And what does Mama say?'

'She thinks it's not entirely kosher; she wants to visit the studio herself first, without me, to see what it's all about. But this guy's a genius, everyone says so, and Aleko said that this was a once-in-a-lifetime opportunity.'

'And Kostya?'

'What about Kostya?'

The bell rang shrilly in the playground; she was already heading for the door.

'Don't act so naive. "What about Kostya?"' I mimicked her.

'Oh my God, don't be such a spoilsport — I'll win him over somehow. I'm going to wear beautiful clothes; they'll do my make-up, shoot me in a nice light, I'll get my own dressing room, and I might even have to kiss a boy,' she giggled, already imagining her friends' faces pale with envy, before rushing out of the toilets.

★

After school, I went to Mother's, where I found Elene agitated and Aleko no less ruffled. She didn't want to have to pick a quarrel with her father again, and he was trying to convince her at least to give the thing a chance.

Finally, the two of them set off for the studio together. I was gripped by a strange excitement, too, and waited impatiently for their return.

Latsabidze explained to our mother that his film was set in the Tbilisi Film Institute; it contained a degree of criticism of the system, but that was all *packaged* in such a way that it wasn't going to be banned. He'd been inspired by a former film student there, who had made a film, and had disappeared, and had died in prison for his ideals. The screenplay would be far enough removed from the real story, but those in the know would pick up enough references to understand what it was about. Officially, his film was a story about a filmmaker going through an artistic crisis. His family and friends played a large role. And his muse. That was the part he had in mind for Daria.

Elene crumpled. 'The student ... do you mean Miqa Eristavi?'

Latsabidze nodded. 'Yes, Miqa Eristavi; do you know the story? The whole of Tbilisi heard about it at the time. And everyone kept quiet instead of running out onto the streets. That's the way we always are, the communists and the conformists.'

'And why my daughter? Why not an actress? Daria's too young, and she has no experience at all,' she asked Latsabidze, trying to pull herself together.

'Believe me, I've looked at a lot of actresses; we've done talent searches in various cities. All of the main parts will of course be played by professionals' — he reeled off a few famous names — 'but for the role of Anna I need someone very special. A young woman who looks like she's stepped out of a dream. My colleague alerted me to your daughter; he said her beauty would render me speechless, and I thought, well, we'll see about that, but when she walked in, everyone in the room was convinced she was the one we were looking for. And after working with her for two hours, I have to tell you, she's not just very beautiful, she's also extraordinarily gifted. And incredibly photogenic.'

And he carried on persuading Elene, assuring her that they would only need Daria on set during the winter holidays, and that of course they would always have a chaperone for her.

'We'll make sure your daughter is well prepared. I'll rehearse the lines with her, there'll be no great demands on you. You know, I have a daughter myself, and I know what girls Daria's age are like: they need a lot of attention.'

Elene was struck dumb. Her knees gave way, and Aleko had to support her as they left the studio. They found a bench on the street. Aleko looked at her in bewilderment, tried to comfort her, asked what was going on, why she had reacted so strangely. But she just shook her head in disbelief and put her hands over her mouth, as if she were trying to stop herself from screaming. She asked Aleko to leave her alone; she would come home later. She took a bus to the New Town. She got out at the Institute of Engineering and Planning, entered the large building, and took the lift to the tenth floor.

Lana was sitting with three other women, leaning over a huge architectural plan and chewing on a pencil. Her big glasses dangled on her chest at the end of a chain, and her face was red with tension. It took a moment for her to notice Elene.

'Well, well, what a surprise. To what do I owe this honour?' She turned to Elene with the usual note of irony in her voice and gave her colleagues a ten-minute break. She put on her glasses, tidied her hair, opened the window, and started making coffee.

'What's up? You look kind of ... pale?' she said.

'I need to talk to you.'

'I'm all ears.'

And Elene told her what had just happened, talked — she was still upset — about Latsabidze, his film, and Daria, how she and Aleko had gone there without a clue and only then discovered what the film was actually about: Miqa, his film, the scandal. And now the absurd coincidence of them wanting her teenage daughter to play the muse!

There was no reaction from Lana. She didn't interrupt, didn't contradict her, didn't nod, just went on calmly making the coffee.

'I remember now: Latsabidze contacted me a few months ago as well, wanting to interview me, wanting my "personal recollections of Miqa" — that was how he put it. At that point, I didn't think anything would come of it. But it looks as if the boy got his way. I'd never have thought it!'

She started pouring the coffee into two small cups.

'Is that all you've got to say?'

'Yes; why, did you think I'd be against it? Would that change anything? If they want to remember my husband, let them. I hope it doesn't land them behind bars as well. It's all the same to me. Do you think it's over just because I buried him? You weren't his wife, Elene. You didn't have a child with him. And he deserves to be talked about, to be remembered ...'

Now Elene regretted having come here. What had she been hoping for? What did Lana mean by that: *You weren't his wife?* What exactly did she want? Revenge? Some kind of reparation? To see justice done? Sometimes she managed to go for weeks without thinking about him; about the scenes from their childhood that often appeared out of nowhere in her mind's eye, about the fight in Mtskheta, his funeral. The trip to the mountains with Lana, the miserable ending. Sometimes, though, the memories came back, marching through her head like immense armies, stamping their feet, accompanied by an ominous hum that almost always turned into a headache.

'My mother is seriously ill. I have to go to the hospital,' said Lana, jolting her out of her thoughts.

'I'm sorry, I didn't know — why didn't you ... I can look after Miro, if you ...'

'Christine's helping out. He spends most of his time at hers, anyway. He idolises her. And you should eat more fruit — you really do look very pale, you need more vitamins and some sun,' Lana called after her as Elene left her office.

★

Daria begged, Daria cried, Daria hugged Elene, implored her, Daria promised to work harder at school, Daria was desperate to do this film. Aleko backed her up, tried to persuade Elene. Latsabidze was a good guy, he said; he knew plenty of people in the film business, and Daria would be looked after. Even with everything that had happened, this was an important undertaking that they had to support; it had nothing to do with Eristavi, the man she remembered; it was art, not a documentary. This back-and-forth went on for two days. Aleko promised her that, if necessary, he would speak to Kostya, so that Kostya's rage wouldn't fall on Elene alone. Through all of this, I sat in a corner, spooning up the rice pudding I hated, marvelling at Daria's powers of persuasion.

★

No one had ever heard Kitty Jashi sing like that. As if she were caressing the blood in her own veins, delighting in death, revelling in the fact she no longer had to accept frontiers of any kind.

She had arrived at the gallery in a black dress, and spent a long time standing in silence in front of Fred's new pictures. Then she got up onto the little stage that had been erected for her and took the microphone. The fact that she wasn't wearing her usual uniform of white shirt and black trousers was taken by those in the know as a sign that they were going to hear a new interpretation of her songs.

She congratulated the painter, spoke of the hard-won strength that shone out of the paintings, and then started to sing songs from the *Home* album.

Kitty — and you know this better than I do, Brilka — was a rather reserved singer when she performed in public, for which she had often been criticised, particularly by musicians of the younger generation. She was too controlled on stage, they said, she never went into ecstasies, never forgot herself, her voice was too composed, she let her lyrics and melodies take precedence over her personality, hid herself behind the songs.

But that evening something wholly unexpected happened. (Best described in the interview Amy gave to *Rolling Stone* in 1988, the issue with Kitty Jashi on the cover and a seven-page feature on her inside.) According to Amy, the audience in the gallery were treated to a 'strip show of the soul'. After a few minutes, the guests, reticent at first, then increasingly astonished, began to move as if joining in a wild circle dance, shaking their heads and limbs, while others, more than a few of them, sang along with tears in their eyes. How naked Kitty was before them; it made them want to undress as well, to shed their protection and their shells and absorb her songs in all their purity. Everyone in the room, Amy said, knew they were witnessing something unique.

The photographers, who had only come to see Miss Jashi, rather than for the once so promising and now forgotten Austrian painter, whipped out their cameras, and Kitty screamed into a lightning storm of flashes, uninhibited, revelling in the idolatry, as if the cameras were spurring her on to greater unpredictability.

When she stopped singing, according to Amy, the room fell silent for over a minute before a roar of applause broke over them all.

Bathed in sweat, she stumbled off the little stage, down the clapping, cheering aisle through her audience and out of the room. There, Amy caught her, and Kitty just smiled at her and said she had seen *him*; he had come back for her, and that evening she had sung for Fred and for him. Amy, of course, had no idea what she was talking about, but left it at that for the time being and let the champagne flow.

★

Daria had never been any good at lying, especially not to Kostya, so she decided to stay with Mother for a few days after they had signed the contract, even though she detested the little flat and was reluctant to give up the comfort she was used to at home. She told Kostya she had a particularly hard week of training coming up in her acrobatics course, and she wanted to spare herself the long car journeys and give herself time to prepare.

It was unusual for me to be the only child at the Green House. For a week it felt as if Daria and I had swapped roles. I was usually the one who stayed in Tbilisi, not the other way round. After I had overcome my initial uneasiness, though, I started to enjoy it. Now I was allowed to sit in front of the television with Kostya late into the evening, even choosing what we watched, and at breakfast my eggs were cooked for exactly three minutes, not five, which was how Daria preferred them.

Kostya, who had begun to suspect something was amiss, interrogated me. He started innocuously, with questions about Mother's and Aleko's daily routines, then moved on to how things were going at school, before asking about Daria's friends. Since the incident that night in Gagra, since the morning he had collected Rusa from the hospital with her arms bandaged and taken her to the station, I hadn't been alone with him. Our conversations had not strayed beyond banalities, and although I understood only too well why he hadn't approached me again before that week, I was enjoying it. I enjoyed the attention he bestowed on me, the way he treated me like a grown-up, almost as an equal, and I enjoyed the vague sense that he was dependent on me: on me and what I knew.

★

That morning, he had not been feeling well; he had a cold, and decided to stay at home. It was only after he had dismissed his driver that it occurred to him I still had to go to school — but before he could think about how I was going to get to Tbilisi, I offered to miss a day of school and stay there with him, saying I could look after him. Nana had already gone to work, and Stasia had disappeared into her barn.

Unexpectedly, he agreed and went back to bed, having listed all the things I was to bring him. I found the lemons and made some hot tea, got the thermometer from the medicine cabinet, and sat down beside him on his bed. He didn't seem to object to that, either.

We watched *Animal World* on television. We drank strong tea, he wrapped in a blanket and me in my pyjamas. The programme was about sea mammals, and to my great surprise he started telling me about the ocean and the dolphins he had seen on his travels. From dolphins he moved on to ships, and from there he went on to talk about Leningrad and his student days. I listened, spellbound; I could have listened to his stories for hours, letting him lead me into unfamiliar worlds, if the telephone hadn't kept ringing. I had to get up and bring it to him. Since he made no move to send me out of the room, I stayed there on his bed, watching the sea creatures.

He didn't say much. He just asked a few questions, kept repeating 'Hm, hm' and 'Yes, I understand', before finally hanging up. The expression on his face was one of unease. He lay still for a moment, then heaved himself up and threw a dressing gown round his shoulders.

'Is everything all right?' I asked.

'I take one day off, and they can't manage without me.'

'Do you have to go in?' I could feel disappointment spreading through me.

'No, but someone's coming here. They didn't want to tell me who. They're just sending him up here, like it's a bordello!' he said indignantly, and started searching his wardrobe for a suitable outfit.

'Put some proper clothes on, it's an official visit. And tell your great-grandmother to take off her smock and those awful rubber boots.' Reluctantly, I did what was asked of me and put on my school uniform, the most official thing I could find, though I left off the cuffs that Stasia washed every day, and the lace collar, as well as the silly white pinafore apron.

Less than half an hour later, a black Volga pulled into the drive. Kostya, wearing a well-fitting pin-striped suit that I had never seen before, came down the steps and stood at the entrance to the garden. I was up on the terrace, watching with great curiosity. Two *militsiya* officers got out first, then a man in a long raincoat, whom I had seen visiting Kostya at the Green House from time to time. He spoke to Kostya alone for a while, and my grandfather just nodded, though I didn't get the sense that he really understood what was expected of him. Finally, Kostya, who was clearly annoyed at being bothered by business matters when he was off sick, brushed the raincoat man aside, went over to the Volga, and opened the passenger door.

The first thing I saw was a metal stick, then a woman's hand gripping Kostya's wrist, then a pair of high-heeled shoes, testing the ground beneath them. Only then did the woman get out, in an elegant suit of dark-blue bouclé and a white headscarf. She looked like an actress from a *film noir* movie, hurtling along the Monte Carlo coast in a convertible, pursued by a sinister man. As she turned to Kostya with some hesitation and I spotted the huge black glasses, I realised that the visitor was blind.

The scarf and glasses masked her face, making it difficult to tell how old she was. She might have been Kostya's age, or a lot younger. Kostya was just as surprised as I was. It seemed to be the first time he'd met the woman: they shook hands formally, and after Kostya had exchanged a few words with the raincoat man, he led her up to the house. She used her stick expertly and didn't take the arm that Kostya proffered.

When they reached the terrace where I was standing, uncertain whether to make myself known, she asked who was present apart from the two of them. Slightly taken aback, Kostya introduced me. She came up to me and held out her hand, inclining her head a little and smiling gently.

'So you're Niza, are you. Hello, I'm Ida.'

The woman spoke a strange-sounding Russian. Her name made Kostya twitch nervously, but he said nothing. The sound of his footsteps showed her the way to the front door; then he led her into his study. I was tasked with bringing her a glass of water — she had declined tea or coffee.

Something about her fascinated me. I wasn't sure whether it was her disability or something else. She seemed so clear and self-assured, as if she could somehow *see through us*. Driven by my curiosity, I tiptoed to the study door, which had been left slightly ajar, in the hope of overhearing a few scraps of their conversation.

'Comrade Yvania said you were in Georgia on private business and wanted to see me,' said Kostya, since the lady seemed in no hurry to reveal the purpose of her visit.

'Yes. I've just come from Leningrad. After all these years, I was finally allowed to give a concert in my home country,' she told him in her peculiar Russian.

I was trying to figure out where she came from, but I hadn't met many foreigners in the course of my short life, and soon abandoned the attempt.

'I'm sorry to say that nobody informed me of your visit, otherwise I would have arranged a more fitting reception. Although culture doesn't really fall within my remit.'

'As I said, I'm here in a private capacity,' the lady interrupted him. 'To see you. I requested a degree of anonymity from your colleagues at the ministry, and I apologise if I am keeping you from other things. This is a purely personal matter. I wasn't aware that you — well, that you held such an important position. I had imagined it would be rather less complicated.'

What kind of *purely personal matter* could this be? If I knew Kostya, he would give his colleagues short shrift later for sending a complete stranger to his house.

'No, no, please, I just feel a little — well, how shall I put it — embarrassed to be receiving you with so little preparation.'

Kostya was still groping in the dark. But she put an end to this exchange of polite, empty words by announcing in a much more abrupt tone:

'Forty years I've been waiting for this opportunity. I've been looking for you for forty years.'

There was an oppressive pause. Kostya was completely at a loss, not knowing whether to respond or wait for what was coming next.

'I've been living in West Germany since 1955. No, let me correct myself: I managed to track down your address many years ago, when you were in Moscow. But at that time I wasn't able to make contact with you directly, and I was reluctant to go through the official channels. What I have to tell you, I could only tell you in person. So I had to wait.'

I could hear Kostya breathing heavily, but he didn't ask any questions.

'As I mentioned, I come from Leningrad. I know you know the city: you went to the academy there, you lived there.'

She seemed to be searching for words. Was what she had to say so grave or so momentous that forty years had not been long enough to find the right words for it?

'So I know that you worked for the Road, and were there throughout the blockade. I was there, too. I lived through the blockade. Lost most of my family and ... my eyesight. The fact that I am sitting here with you, that I survived, that I was able to pursue my passion for the piano, start a family, have a life, is all thanks to one person, and that person is also the reason I came looking for you. I assume you know now who I'm talking about?'

Again, the oppressive silence. Kostya murmured something, but I couldn't catch the words.

'She loved you very much,' the woman said suddenly.

For some reason these were the words that surprised me most. As if I had been expecting a terrible event, an awful deed, but not love. I found these words so difficult to associate with Kostya. Inconceivable, I thought, that this woman had searched for and found him after forty years to tell him that he had been loved.

'She didn't know if you were still alive, but I think the hope that you were kept her going through the years of the blockade. You were her most treasured memory, and that helped her to endure the horror. You were the only person she wanted to remember. It was very important to her that you should know this. That's why I searched for you, and it's why I'm here. Because I have her to thank for *everything*: for all that I am and all that I have.'

Ida E. sat opposite my grandfather in the Green House, a meeting delayed by decades, and gave him her memories of *his* Ida.

Of course, at the time I understood nothing of all this. I didn't know what a blockade was, or which woman they were talking about, but I guessed from Kostya's bearing when he emerged from the room afterwards, a changed man, that it was serious. And without realising what was happening to me as I eavesdropped on these strange stories through the crack in the door, I was certainly aware that this moment would have consequences for me, too. Perhaps that was the day I realised that so many other stories were already written into that of my own short, ordinary life, and had their place alongside the thoughts and memories I was gathering for myself, which helped me to grow. Perhaps it was when I realised that the stories I so loved to tease out of Stasia were no fairy tales, whisking me off to a different age; they formed the very ingredients of my life. Crouching outside Kostya's study door, holding my breath and clenching my fists in concentration, it became clear to me that, more than anything else in life, I wanted to do what this woman, blind and yet so far-sighted, was doing right then: I wanted to bring together the things that had fallen apart. Assemble other people's memories, which only reveal their connections when a whole is created from a host of individual parts. All of us, whether we know it or not, perform our own dance within this overall picture, following a mysterious choreography. (Yes, Brilka, you were right: we do all dance!)

Ida E. spent more than an hour in my grandfather's study, telling her story. In that hour, Kostya barely said a word; but the woman didn't seem to expect him to. Before she pushed back her chair and headed for the door, I heard her place something on the table and say: 'This is my autobiography. It was published in Germany a few years ago, and has been translated into other languages, too. Not Russian, unfortunately. But I had a translation done anyway, for private use — for you, I mean. I thought you deserved to hear about it all in more detail. The book is dedicated to Ida.'

I heard my grandfather murmur a mournful, crushed 'Thank you', before opening the door and bidding her farewell: 'Thank you, from the bottom of my heart. Thank you.'

I had never heard the phrase 'from the bottom of my heart' from Kostya's lips.

He watched the car drive away, and stood there for a long time afterwards, staring into the emptiness the car had left behind. Then suddenly he turned on his heel and called out to me to fetch a bottle of wine from the cellar.

When I came back, he was lying on his bed with his legs pulled up, sobbing like a little child. Seeing him lying there, looking so desperate, I wanted to turn round and creep straight out again, certain that he wouldn't tolerate my presence in his moment of weakness. But he motioned me to stay where I was and give him the bottle. His hands were trembling so much he couldn't get the cork out. I was unable to move; I stared at him in bewilderment, my heart clenching with pity. I could never have dreamed that one day I would feel pity for my powerful, despotic grandfather, the man who made my life so difficult. But the way he looked made me so sad I was on the point of crying myself, and I took the bottle and ran down to the kitchen, where I uncorked it after several attempts. Just then, I spotted a clean milk bottle on the draining board — like so many Soviet housewives, Stasia saved them for some inexplicable reason. It had a wider opening than the wine bottle, and I poured the wine into it. I went back to the bedroom and, as you might with an orphaned deer or calf, I held it to his mouth, which was sticky with tears. He began to suckle gratefully, then to swallow down greedy gulps of the red liquid.

I put a blanket over him. Then I lay down beside him and waited until his tears had dried up. What wouldn't I have given at one time to see my grandfather weak and in need of help, vulnerable and fragile — but now it had actually happened, I couldn't bear it.

I kicked off my shoes and they clattered onto the wooden floor. I slid over to him tentatively, placing a timid hand on his side, and touched his wrist so lightly he would hardly have felt it.

At that moment, I was closer to him than to anyone else in the world. Mother's, Nana's or Daria's tears, even my own, had never had such an effect on me. Nor had the sight of Rusa's opened veins; nothing could have unsettled me like this did. After a little while, I gave free rein to my own tears as well. I was crying for the closeness that could have existed between us.

He lay rigid on the bed for some time, staring at the blank ceiling, then he sat up, sniffing, and took a swig from the bottle, this time without my help.

'Was she your girlfriend?' I whispered, exhausted. I was finding it hard even to talk.

'I was there, I was close by, I could have ...' he murmured. I didn't know what he meant.

'Do you still love her?'

'She's dead. She's been dead for a very long time.'

'Stasia says there are ghosts.'

'Stasia talks a lot of nonsense. You shouldn't believe everything she says.' He looked at the bottle in his hand in amazement, and asked me how the decent wine had got into a milk bottle.

'The neck of the wine bottle was too narrow. You would have spilled it.'

'Thank you ... I didn't know she had stayed in Leningrad. She should have been evacuated long before. I ...'

He kept the final sentence to himself. He had retreated into his thoughts again.

'You must have been much nicer then,' I said, after a minute or two of trying to imagine my grandfather as a young man. He looked down at me and couldn't suppress a smile.

'So you don't think I'm nice now?'

'Not usually, no.'

'And why are you so eager for me to be nice?'

'Well, you want other people to be nice to you too, don't you?'

He seemed nonplussed by my frankness. He looked as though he were searching for a response befitting the situation, but instead he smiled, shook his head, reached out, and pinched my cheek, eliciting a loud cry of protest from me.

We lay there in the semi-darkness of the room, and he listened to me. He didn't interrupt, didn't tell me off, didn't reproach me, didn't correct me; he let me say everything I had to say. I talked about a whole jumble of things. There was no chronology; I just said everything that came into my head. I spoke with him as I had seldom spoken with anyone, apart from David, and as I did so, I was not the wilful little girl, not the secretive girl with the gloomy expression and the pathological curiosity, the one everyone was always worrying about. I was just me. And it was such a relief not to have to make an effort; and he simply sat there, sipping at his milk bottle and listening to me, smiling now and then or shaking his head as if in agreement, frowning, smacking his lips — and Brilka, he was the best, most attentive listener in the world.

He was there, with me, for me. I was grateful to Ida for this afternoon with the person whose love I had wanted above everyone else's, ever since I was born. And in that moment of weakness I broke the rules that I had trained myself so rigorously to observe with him; I softened, became garrulous; I took off my protective armour and inducted him into my secrets. I told him about Mother's money worries and Aleko's problems; I told him about David, about Daria, about the audition.

I spent the whole afternoon in his room, on his bed, and, naive as I was, I believed that words could be a substitute for love and remembering could make amends for the past.

I was wrong. Of course I was wrong.

I believe dangers await only those who do not react to life.

MIKHAIL GORBACHEV

The reaction was delayed, but all the more terrible for that. And, for the first time, it fell on Daria. Kostya's rage was characteristically elemental and uncompromising — something so familiar to me, and so alien to my sister.

After Ida E.'s visit, Kostya spent a whole week at home. He and I went on watching television in his bedroom, breakfasting on Nana's pancakes and talking about this and that, but this everyday chit-chat had nothing in common with the naked intensity of that afternoon.

Exactly one week later, he called for his driver, and, after dropping me off at school, went to the ministry. He told me he would collect me and Daria later. And with that, I knew that my temporary reign in the Green House had come to an end. I looked for Daria at school, but even during the long break there was no sign of her in the playground. Eventually, I found her, puffy-eyed and red-nosed, sitting on a bench behind the school building. She was alone — an unusual sight. I sat down beside her. When I tried to put my arms around her, she pushed me away harshly and I ended up on the ground.

'You've ruined everything! I hate you!' she yelled, before running off.

I finally managed to call Elene's apartment from a payphone. Aleko's subdued voice gave me an intimation of the trouble I'd caused. Kostya had phoned them the previous evening, threatened his daughter and her husband with never being allowed to see Daria again, and told them he would see the whole film studio smashed to smithereens if they didn't stop this nonsense right away, terminate the contract immediately, and send Daria straight back to his care. Elene was lying in bed, the picture of misery, Aleko told me, and despite his cautious manner I could hear the reproach in his voice.

I was a traitor! I had betrayed my mother, Aleko, and above all my sister, for the sake of a little intimacy with Kostya, a little affection. Now everything was ruined, and I was to blame.

The war between Elene and Kostya, which these past few years had been more of a tacit ceasefire, was raging again with a destructive force it had never previously possessed, and this time everyone would be drawn in; this time, victory and defeat would be absolute.

Kostya's mood was at a low point for another reason, too: Gorbachev had assumed the leadership of the Communist Party and announced reforms for the 27th Party Congress, which was to take place the following spring. Kostya kept shaking his head every time he saw the leader's face in the newspaper and exclaiming that this 'cowardly opportunist' would wreck the country. Gorbachev had voiced criticism of the authorities and their corruption, which the masses had greeted more with confusion than delight.

I tried to make amends — not knowing what for exactly, or, more importantly, where to begin.

Kostya's surveillance increased to absurd levels: Daria was not allowed to go for a stroll after school with her friends, or to the ice-cream parlour, or to spend more than two minutes on the phone. She was driven to school and the sports institute, and collected again, with excessive punctuality. He didn't permit her a single second of freedom. She had to turn down birthday party invitations and come up with ridiculous excuses for not going. But the thing that really broke my heart was the lack of fight in her, the way she accepted all this as if she deserved nothing better, as if the punishment were inevitable, as if she felt terribly guilty for having gone behind Kostya's back and deceived him.

The real magnitude of my defeat only became clear to me when, a few weeks later, David called Aleko. After beating about the bush for a long time, he admitted to his old friend that he had a 'delicate matter' to discuss with him, and asked Aleko to visit him the following day.

Aleko returned crushed. He waited for Elene to leave for a lesson with one of her private pupils, then called me into the kitchen. He had to smoke two cigarettes before he was ready to outline the full extent of the catastrophe I had set in motion with my openness, and into which I had now also dragged David. As soon as he said David's name, before he had even mentioned the problem, I knew that something had been irrevocably destroyed, and I fought back the tears with all my might.

'He doesn't want to see me any more, does he?' I blurted out, and the tears began to flow.

'It's not that he doesn't want to; he can't. He's not allowed to.'

'Because of Kostya?' I whimpered. Aleko nodded mutely. 'Did ... did he go and visit him? But ... what ... what bad things did he tell David about me?'

'It's not about you, Niza. Kostya seems to have got a look at David's file and brought to light a few secrets that David would rather had remained hidden.'

'But ... what kind of ... secrets?' I simply couldn't imagine that my caring mentor had anything to hide.

'I don't know, Niza. He didn't want to tell me, and that's his right, after all — that's why it's a secret, because he doesn't want to talk about it. But he said Kostya had threatened to make this secret public if he went on *teaching* you.'

'But he doesn't teach me. We ... All we do is talk!'

'I know, Niziko, but he teaches other people. That's how he earns his living, and if your grandfather has something up his sleeve that could damage his reputation, he won't be able to make ends meet, and that would be a disaster: do you understand me?'

'But David hasn't done anything — not him, not David ... I want to go and see him, please, please, Aleko, drive me there, I have to ...'

'Hey, little one, we can't do that now. He says you can phone him any time if you need to, but visiting ... well, that's not such a good idea at the moment. I'm sorry, Niza; I don't know what Kostya found out that would make him keep you away from David. And I do know what he means to you.'

That night, I hurled myself against the walls, banged my head against the cupboard, and cut my school uniform to ribbons, and at dawn I decided to go to war with Kostya. I had nothing left to lose. He had razed everything I held dear, had callously exploited all the things that might break my heart, and everything in me was crying out for revenge.

But before that, I had to find out what he had on David. The following evening, I marched straight into my grandfather's study and confronted him. Angry that I hadn't knocked, he got up from his seat, pushed his reading glasses up onto his head, and looked at me disapprovingly.

'How often must I tell you that when doors are closed, they may not simply be opened?'

'You lied to me, you used me, you've ruined everything! You're a mean person, I hate you!' I shouted in his face. Completely taken aback by how loud I was, he took a step backwards and sat down again heavily in his office chair.

'You just watch what you're saying, young lady!' He always adopted this slightly overbearing, teacherly tone when he was momentarily at a loss for words.

'What did you say to him? How could you ...'

I was trying my hardest not to burst into tears in front of him, even if the tears were starting to choke me again. My voice wavered, and I had to hold on to the edge of his desk with one hand in order to stay upright. Fear mingled with my despair, rendering me defenceless, impulsive, uncontrollable, and I knew that this state could quickly become a trap for me.

'Ah, now I understand. You mean your *pedagogue*, am I right?'

'I love him, and he hasn't done anything and he helps me and he — I want him back!' I screamed.

'It doesn't surprise me that your stepfather is friends with such freaks of nature, but the fact that your mother didn't think to check who she was sending her own child to every week is unforgivable, even by her standards. And she teaches children herself!'

'What did you say to him? I want you to call him right away and apologise — you don't know him, you don't know how …'

'Now, Niza, please calm down and listen. I won't allow you to speak to me in that tone of voice. I only did what any thinking, responsible person, and a grandfather, above all, would do for his granddaughter.'

'I don't want to calm down, I want you to call him and —'

Suddenly he slammed his fist down, and the whole table shook. I shrank back instinctively, but didn't let go of the table edge.

'Listen to me, and stop interrupting! I just wanted to find out what sort of teacher they were sending you to. You're still young, easily influenced, and as the person in charge of your education, Niza, it's important for me to know who I am allowing to influence and shape my little girl. I had no intention of harming your teacher. I just looked up some information about him, and what did I discover but that my granddaughter was sitting under the roof of a pervert; that a pervert was explaining the world to her.'

'He's not sick, what are you talking about?' I didn't know what to say. I didn't understand any of this. 'He's really good at physics and philosophy, and he can do higher mathematics too, and he taught himself four languages and —'

'Yes, I'm sure you're right. But I have to ask myself why your good-for-nothing stepfather didn't take the trouble to find out why this genius had abandoned his career and taken to brainwashing little children in his own apartment instead.'

'He's always had different views …'

'Views. Exactly, Niza, different *views*,' Kostya interrupted me, smirking and leaning back in his chair. 'I have protected you from something he might have inflicted on you. I did what I had to do, what any normal father —'

'But you're not my father!'

I was raising my voice again, which displeased him so much that he suddenly leapt up, came over, and planted himself right in front of me. He looked down and hissed in my face: 'Mark you: your teacher is a sick man. He's a danger to society, and to children in particular, and that is why you will never go back there again, do you understand me? You'll have to be content with this explanation for the time being. And now I would like you to get out of my room and never come in here without knocking again.'

Seeing his face so close to mine, smelling his breath, the confidence in his eyes intimidated me. I wanted to rush out of the room at once, but the will to see David again was greater than my impulse to flee. I looked him in the eye and said quietly, but firmly: 'He's not sick. *You're* sick. You, not him!'

I watched him lose control of his features, saw rage take possession of him — the only thing we had in common just then — but I had resolved not to weaken, whatever the cost.

'He's a *pederast*. Your wonderful teacher is a sick bastard. Is that reason enough for you now?'

'A what?'

'A man who loves little boys and —'

'But I'm not a boy!' was the best I could come up with.

'A man who does things with them that an adult should not do with children.'

'Like the things you did with Rusa, you mean?'

My grandfather's slap had so much weight behind it that I lost my balance and almost fell to the floor, before steadying myself, thinking for a moment I had gone deaf in my left ear. He stared at his hand in shock, as if it might hold a plausible explanation for his behaviour.

'You shouldn't have pushed me that far …' he muttered.

★

I lay awake the whole night thinking. David had only done things with me that made me happy. What part of giving me joy, protecting me, was supposed to be sick? At the same time, my grandfather had sounded so threatening as he uttered those strange words, and the vivid recollection of that burning slap kept me from dialling David's number.

The thought that from now on I would have to forgo seeing David had me paralysed with fear. I would have nowhere to offload my questions, to get the anger and frustration off my chest. How would I manage without his library and, above all, his understanding? As I couldn't come to terms with the idea, I decided to seek out the only person who wasn't constantly reminding me of my betrayal and ask him for help once again. I described my confrontation with Kostya in detail to Aleko, explained the questions and concerns I had about the term *pederast*, and asked him to tell David that I would do everything in my power to be allowed to carry on visiting him. I didn't expect the reaction my words elicited from Aleko. Even before he gave full vent to his rage, I knew I'd made another mistake.

For the first time, he took Kostya's side, and actually insulted David, using terrible words, calling him a 'dissembler' and a 'lecher'. I stood in the corner, horrified, letting the tide of insults wash over me. What had I set in motion? Why did that blind woman have to turn up at our house and make me soft and affectionate with her sad story? What on earth had I been thinking when I triggered this chain reaction, which, once started, I just couldn't stop?

'Now I know why his wife doesn't let the children see him any more, and why his former colleagues speak so badly of him. And there I was, thinking he was my friend. The lying bastard, I'll give him what for. You should be grateful to your grandfather, Niza!'

Aleko's eyes were bloodshot, the spittle flew from his lips, and my attempts to mollify him didn't help at all.

When Elene came back, he stormed past her, saying he had to take care of something, and disappeared out of the door. I could tell another calamity was approaching. But should I tell Elene? It felt too risky. She was already angry with me; every time she looked at me it was with a hurt, reproachful expression; and in any case I still didn't know exactly what a *pederast* was.

The week wore on and still there was no imminent prospect of seeing David. I couldn't stand it any longer; I skipped the last two lessons at school and took the trolleybus to David's apartment.

I had to ring several times before he answered the door. He had bruises under his eyes and a bandage round his head. He stepped back in alarm, and after reassuring himself that I was alone, he let me into the hallway, though he didn't invite me any further into his studio. We stood together in semi-darkness. This time I made no effort to hold back my tears. And he made no move to comfort me.

'I didn't mean to,' I wailed.

'I know, I know, Niza.' His tone was cold and distant.

'Who did that?' I stammered, pointing at the bandage.

'It's not important now. I'm afraid we can't see each other any longer.'

'But I want to stay with you.'

A cautious smile flitted across his face.

'I know, but we can't always do the things we want to do.'

'But you ... you said we should always fight for the things that are important to us. You're important to me.'

'In some situations, learning to live with things is more worthwhile than fighting them.'

These were the first words David had uttered that I didn't agree with. Now I was sobbing again, breathlessly, uncontrollably.

'Give it a few years, Niza, and you'll be old enough to decide for yourself whom you want to be friends with and whom you don't.'

'But I'm old enough now. Are you really a *pederast*?' I wiped my nose on the sleeve of my coat.

'No, I'm not.'

'What does *pederast* mean, David?'

'It's when older men are attracted to children or teenage boys.'

'So what are you, then?'

'I'm homosexual.'

'What does that mean?'

'I'm attracted to adult men.'

'And are you attracted to me, too?'

He smiled to himself again, this time in a more relaxed way.

'Yes, Niza; I feel attracted to you, yes, but not in the way I meant it just now. *Attracted* in that sense also has a sexual component. And happily that component doesn't exist between us.'

'But why do the others say you're a *pederast* when you're not?'

'Because most people here use the term wrongly. They call all homosexuals *pederasts* because it's an insult, and they class homosexuals as sick people, too — not only *pederasts*.'

'But then we can carry on seeing each other, can't we, if you're not a *pederast*? We just have to explain to them that you like adult men and not children, and anyway I'm not a man. They'll understand that, won't they?'

'No, I'm afraid they won't, and we can't do that. I hope that one day you'll understand why I can't ignore this ban, not under any circumstances: it's not within my power. You'll always be a friend of mine. But you have to go now, Niza. I'm sorry, but you must.'

★

The next day — it was a grey November afternoon — I went straight to the State Film Studio after school and asked to see Kote Latsabidze. He wasn't there, but when I insisted and told the secretary it was a matter of vital importance, they called him.

Two hours later, he arrived, a bald-headed man in jogging bottoms and a military jacket. I thought he looked more like a hardened criminal than an artist, but then I remembered Aleko's friends, who had exactly the same look, and decided not to give the matter any further consideration. I introduced myself and explained the situation to him in detail. He asked me twice if this was really *the* Kostya Jashi I was talking about.

Finally, I gave him a thorough explanation of my plan. As I was speaking, he kept opening his mouth as if to make some objection, then closing it again. From time to time, he smiled to himself, though I couldn't be sure if it was because my plan amused him, or if it was a sense of relief at having come a step closer to getting the actress he wanted.

'Daria's little sister. Well I never. Daria's little sister ...' he murmured, as if he couldn't make the connection between Daria and me at all.

'And you don't think your grandfather will get wind of this and land us in a great deal of trouble? Your grandfather is a powerful man, kiddo, he could endanger the whole project. In any case, I can't use her without consent from a guardian: your sister is underage.'

'What do you mean? You've got my mother's consent, haven't you? It's just a matter of playing for time. It's a matter of keeping Kostya away while you make the film.'

He stared at me in disbelief, then let out a laugh. I was annoyed; the fact that he found it so hard to take me seriously really rubbed me up the wrong way.

Suddenly a terrible thought made me flinch. 'You've found someone else, haven't you?'

Unexpectedly, he shook his head. 'There are a few contenders, but I haven't been able to decide on anyone yet. Your sister is still my first choice.'

'Please!' I begged him. 'She won't disappoint you. Daria wants to do it so much. Come on — please. We can do this. It's a good plan. Believe me.'

'How old are you exactly?' he asked me, getting up from his chair.

'Eleven,' I said, hoping the number would sound serious and grown-up to his ears, but not sure that it had.

He left the room for a few minutes. When he came back, he had a cigarette in his mouth, and he paced restlessly up and down. Then, suddenly, he stopped in the middle of the room and winked at me.

'All right, kiddo, we'll do it your way. It's not bad, this plan you've cooked up. I mean that. I'll have my secretary dig out the contract and I'll wait for your call. Deal?'

He gave me a mischievous grin. I leapt up delightedly and shook his hand, then ran out of the room, through the high-ceilinged studios, and out onto the street, relieved and happy.

★

'Wake up, I need to talk to you.'

I sat on my sister's bed and shook her awake. She grumbled at me, turned to face the wall, and pulled the covers over her head.

'It's important. Come on, Daria, you have to listen to me. You can do your film. I went to see Latsabidze today.'

The blanket loosened, she poked her nose out, then pulled the covers down below her chin and turned onto her back.

'And how's that going to work? They'll have found someone else by now.'

'No, there's no one else. He wants you.'

The words took effect. She sat up suddenly. 'Can you please just talk like a normal person and tell me what on earth you're going on about?' she snapped.

'All right. But only on condition that it stays between us. Just you and me. You can't tell Mama or Kostya, you can't even say anything to Stasia, let alone your friends.'

'Yes, now come on, tell me!'

'At school, there's a poster on the notice board. The Komsomol Youth is offering pupils a three-week skiing course in Bakuriani. The whole thing's being staffed by students from the Institute of Education. Three weeks, no parents, with only students in charge. Think about it. Latsabidze says he's quite sure he can film all your scenes in those three weeks.'

'You mean ...'

'Yes, I signed us up for the course yesterday.'

'But that's total madness! The minute I don't turn up, they'll phone home!'

'Yes, and that's why I have a plan. We'll spend weeks going on at Kostya about how happy it would make us to learn to ski, along with the other children. Then we'll get on the coach with everyone else outside the school. We drive off, waving to him from the window like good little girls, and once we've left the city, you start whimpering. Ow, ow, ow — it seems you can act, so you can pretend to have appendicitis. Someone told me that's really bad, and it means you have to have an operation right away. So they'll stop the bus and try to contact our parents. That's where I come in. I'll say, you know what, Daria's dad can get here much quicker than Grandfather or Mother could; he works near here. And then I'll give them Latsabidze's number.

'They're students, they have nothing to do with the school, they don't know us, they don't know who our father and mother are, let alone our grandfather. He'll say he's your dad. And he'll drive out to where the coach is. As soon as you see him, throw your arms around his neck, or whatever, and that'll be that.

'You go off and do the film. Every now and then, you call Kostya and go on about how much you're enjoying Bakuriani. And if he should decide to call the camp himself, I'll think of something. You're out skiing, or asleep, or whatever. And when we come back, we just give Kostya the wrong arrival time. So Latsabidze can come to collect me, with you in tow; then later on we call Kostya or Mama and say whoops, we got back a bit earlier than expected.'

Daria was listening very closely. Her whole body seemed to vibrate with tension. We hadn't switched the light on, and the moonlight falling through the open curtains gave our faces a blueish hue. Slowly, my words filtered through to her. She seemed already to be seeing the images of my plan in her mind's eye. All at once, her face lit up, her eyebrows returned to their normal position, her lips parted, and she giggled to herself.

'You're completely bonkers, do you know that? Why are you so keen to help me all of a sudden, when you're the one who told on me?'

'I just want you to believe me. I didn't see any of this coming. It's not what I wanted.'

'Do you really think we can pull this off?'

'If you stick to the plan, and above all don't breathe a word to anyone, then yes.'

'All right, all right, I can do that. Oh God, does he really not have anyone? He still hasn't cast the role?'

'Yes, that's what I've been saying.'

'I can't believe it … But you hate sports! How will you cope with three weeks up there?'

'Well, I made a mess of things, so it's up to me to pay for it. I hope you realise you'll owe me, though, if I survive three weeks of exercise in Bakuriani.'

'It's the craziest plan I've ever heard, but it might just work.'

★

And the plan did work. Kostya agreed. Fresh air, sport, the Komsomol Youth — it all sounded good to him. Not long after the New Year celebrations, we took the coach to Bakuriani. As I'd suspected, the staff were a bunch of students who liked to drink and party, and who didn't have the slightest suspicion when Daria was fished off the coach by a film director ham-acting the role of our father.

For me, though, it was a difficult time: sharing a room in the spartan, unrenovated facilities of the Youth and Sport House with four other chattering girls was absolutely unbearable, as were the tasteless porridge for breakfast and the burnt hamburgers for supper, and being constantly harried out into the cold by eager sports students, particularly as I could find no pleasure at all in hurtling through the snow on skis that were much too long and much too old. I would rather have spent my time with *Wuthering Heights*, the book I was reading just then. But I offered up my sacrifice patiently, constantly reminding myself why I was doing it. Twice I had to save the day, when Kostya phoned unannounced, demanding to speak to Daria, and tried to send me up from the camp's filthy lobby to fetch her from her room. Both times I managed to give him convincing excuses, and he allowed himself to be fobbed off. Both times I reached Daria on Latsabidze's private number, which he had given me for emergencies like these, and she called Kostya back with only a slight delay. He didn't suspect a thing.

At the end of the second week, I was delivered from a circle of screeching, spotty, crude boys with their latent hysteria and their constant stream of obscene jokes. For there, unexpectedly coming towards me across the piste, was Miro. He was in Bakuriani with another sports group; an enthusiastic skier ever since he was little, he was training for some upcoming junior competition. At first, he didn't recognise me; he was in the company of other spotty, crude boys telling obscene jokes. When he finally realised who I was, a smile as bright as the snow surrounding us spread over his dark face.

'What are *you* doing here?'

'The same as you, I imagine,' I replied, and the boys standing round him sniggered.

Miro flashed them a warning glance, and they instantly fell silent. It looked like he held some sway with them. He was staying in the other block, where girls weren't allowed, but he and a few of his buddies still managed to sneak into our block every evening. There was a real holiday camp atmosphere. Although I didn't find his buddies even remotely entertaining, I joined their group, took part in the nightly fun and the pyjama parties, tried to appear as nonchalant and carefree as them, and was as daring as I could manage to be.

Once, we peeled off from the rest of the group during training and stomped through the blinding white on our skis. At his side — he was always pulling faces and telling me silly anecdotes — I felt both light and safe. Not long after this, there was a communal lunch in a mountain cabin for both our camps, and he caught me reading Emily Brontë. He swiped a leftover bowl of stewed peaches for us, sat down beside me, and asked what I was reading.

'I can't be bothered with reading; I always look at the end of the book first,' he said shyly, as I put the book down. 'But I love it when someone reads to me. I'm a good listener. Christine reads to me a lot, but she always chooses such boring stuff.'

'So what sort of books *do* you like?'

'Well, I thought *The Three Musketeers* was great.'

I nodded. 'Shall I read you something?'

'Yes, oh yes.'

I hadn't expected such enthusiasm — I'd thought he would agree just to be polite. We arranged to meet that evening: I would leave the ground-floor window open and he would climb in.

He really did arrive at the time we'd agreed, and we tiptoed into the television room, which was empty, as the television had long since given up the ghost. In the room's cold, comfortless light we sat down on the battered sofa, and I started to read the novel to him. He listened attentively; his body tensed during particularly emotional scenes, he clenched his fists and even pinched my arm once because he couldn't bear the tension. When he climbed out of the window in the dawn light, I inwardly thanked my sister for being so desperate to do that film.

★

I met her three days before our departure. She was standing by a lift in a red ski-suit, with two other young women in attractive outfits carrying skis and poles under their arms. I stopped in my tracks and concentrated on the red of her ski-suit. I could feel my heart beginning to thud louder and louder. I felt as if ten horses were galloping through my veins. I had so often pictured what it would be like to meet her. I had so much to say to her; I had secretly composed the sentences I would use. But I couldn't move. I watched her from a distance before taking a few steps towards her. She saw me.

Rusa! I wanted to shout, but my voice failed me. She took a step towards me, then stopped. We were both fearful. And when I finally managed to approach her, I could sense her shrinking back, as if afraid to be hugged by me. Her eyes were clouded. She wanted to say something, but seemed not to know what or how. I was so eager to know what she was doing, how she was. And now I was standing in front of her, not speaking, ashamed, as if I had a reason to be ashamed in front of her. Her face had changed. Her smile was no longer carefree; it was stoic, defying the world and all its obstacles, as if she found it an effort to smile at all.

'Are you here with your grandfather?' was the first thing she asked me.

'No, with the Komsomol Youth. Are you well?' I asked her tentatively.

She shrugged. 'I have to be, don't I? I just have to work out how to get my life back on track, Niza. But I haven't forgotten you.'

She said this, and I felt nothing. I just wanted to get away. I nodded politely and turned around. I had taken a few steps when I heard her calling my name, but I didn't look back. I just kept walking towards a flushed, grinning Miro, who was speeding in my direction.

★

The last bit of the plan worked, too. Latsabidze came to meet me from the bus; waving and enfolding me in his arms, he acted the part of my father. I let him play his role. Later, we called Mother and lied to her that we had got the arrival time wrong and were already in the city.

At home, my sister whispered to me that making films was the only thing she wanted to do from then on. Acrobatics was history; acting was her new passion. She spoke of the great talent that Latsabidze and his whole team had told her she possessed, of the praise from experienced colleagues, of the atmosphere on set, the interesting people, the way they all kept talking about her photogenic face. She told me that as soon as she finished school, she was going to study acting. Finally, she added a brief 'Thank you'. I leaned back with a contented smile.

> Our magazines are practically vying as to who
> can spit at the Soviet Union the best.
>
> VIKTOR CHEBRIKOV

She participated in fundraising galas and performed at various benefit concerts along with other rock and pop stars. She made a huge number of television appearances and gave countless interviews. She took up offers of various guest spots alongside famous colleagues. The *Herald Tribune* called her the British Patti Smith.

Kitty transformed herself, rejected her age. Gave interviews, spoke about her past, criticised the Soviet Union, criticised her homeland, criticised the USA, criticised politics, made herself vulnerable. Her album sales soared; Amy rejoiced. Young people were rediscovering her old albums. But as much as she refused to acknowledge her age, her body was increasingly showing signs of it: tiredness and indifference had taken hold. She could blank them out as long as she surrounded herself with loud music, fun, crowds of people, and alcohol. With gratitude, she accepted all those things that had previously been distasteful to her. With ease, she opened up to everything that had been so foreign to her nature all these years. She could be joyful, euphoric, she could let herself go, leave herself behind, outsmart herself. A little more each time. Shifting a little further away from herself each time.

Like a phoenix, she could rise from the ashes every evening and transform herself beneath the hot stage lights. She could be what she was not. For an hour, or two, or three, sometimes even seven hours, or the whole night, she could pretend to be a woman who had the world at her feet and knew how to deal with it. But she wasn't writing any more. She hadn't written a single new song. There was nothing more she wanted to say.

And afterwards, at night, if she was left on her own, if she came home to her bed, she tried not to think about the man who had a drawn her a map for survival, and what he was doing now, or about the woman who had wanted so desperately to obliterate this map. She wished the man well, even though he was living in a world that had become foreign to him. Wished for the woman to survive, and for galleries to welcome her in.

But Andro was coming more often; she saw him in the audience. When she looked down from the stage into the dark crowd, she would see him standing in the front row, with his shining curls. She saw him when she looked out onto the street in the morning, standing under her window, looking up at her. She saw him when she was hurrying across the road to Amy's house, from where they would drive to the studio or to an interview. Or in one of the noisy, smoke-filled clubs she went to with friends and acquaintances, where she would sit and listen to people tell her again how 'great' or 'cool' or 'epoch-making' she was. She saw him smiling at her in the mirror when she retreated to the toilets and put her face under the running water. He stayed. He was there. He would never leave. He was waiting for her. Of that, she was certain. He didn't press her; he had all the time in the world.

Once, during a party at the luxurious house of a patron of the arts overlooking Waterlow Park, she took her glass of champagne out into the garden to get some fresh air and have a moment alone. She saw him standing there under a sycamore tree. She froze, thinking he would quickly vanish again, but when he showed no signs of going, she strode confidently over and stood shoulder to shoulder with him, making no attempt to touch him.

'I just wanted to live, to survive — is that really so terrible? Is that why you're here? Why does everything keep starting over, Andro, like a merry-go-round, again and again? Perhaps that's just how the world works. But when you stand there in silence, it makes me think you're trying to tell me something — that I should have done things differently, perhaps. He would have been a grown man now. I think about him every day. I promised him I would keep him: here, here, everywhere in me.

'But I'm talking nonsense. I know, I can't believe I'm really asking you all this. I just want to sing, water my hydrangeas, and have a glass of good whisky now and then. Is that too much to ask? Please, do something; help me, Andro!'

Suddenly, she collapsed; the glass fell onto the wet ground, she caught herself on the rough bark of the tree, scratched her hand to pieces, dirtied her black trousers, knelt on the slimy earth of the garden, then sat down, legs bent, her back against the tree. Andro had vanished. There was nobody there now. Only the distant lights from the house and a buzz of animated voices — but they had nothing more to say to her, nor she to them.

She got up. Brushed the soil from her trousers, leaned against the tree. Life was flaking away from her, and she was what was left. She had never yet managed to come to terms with that, not since she had run away. Which was exactly thirty-five years ago.

★

Starting on 25 February 1986, the 27th Party Congress of the Communist Party of the Soviet Union, under the leadership of their new General Secretary Gorbachev, passed radical reforms to stimulate the economy and extend freedom of speech and of the press, and called for *glasnost*.

Later that year, Gorbachev allowed the nuclear physicist Sakharov to return from exile, which many people saw as the first step towards real reform. The new General Secretary pushed for an 'acceleration of social and economic development', even if those plans threatened to founder when they encountered reality. Within a mere six months of taking office, he had replaced seventy per cent of the Politburo.

However, the economy had long been stagnating, and nepotism and corruption had reached unprecedented levels. The wave of privatisation, and the withdrawal of state control over companies, met with great resistance. And this resistance came in part from my grandfather, Konstantin Jashi, who was of the opinion that the country needed stricter controls, not another revolution: everything had been left to decay for long enough, and was now threatening to fall apart.

In sunny Georgia, people were caught between euphoria over the upcoming reforms, and worry at the indecision of the reformer. Freedom of the press and publishers meant that many previously banned manuscripts, translations, essays, and articles finally saw the light of day. Increasingly, groups of people gathered in university and school buildings to debate the future, though they were still very cautious. You could read more and more criticism between the lines of poems and songs.

'If you want changes, you can't make them dependent on everyone being in favour of them,' Kostya grumbled as he sat in front of the television in the evening, watching the news. 'Otherwise they're doomed to failure from the outset. But this would-be reformer wants everyone to love him. The communists *and* the capitalists. He'll kill himself trying.'

At the time, I paid no attention to his words or his concerns. I had no interest in watching *Vremya*, either. After our great falling-out, I had lost all interest in my grandfather, or at least I hoped I had. I didn't want anything more to do with his problems.

Instead, I enjoyed the sweet fruits my little revenge plot was bearing: Daria's undivided attention and blind trust. She no longer avoided me in the playground — quite the opposite: she invited me into her clique and introduced me to all her friends, which filled me with pride. I had done more than just outsmart Kostya. I had also managed to prove to my sister that my love for her was more steadfast than that of the grandfather she so admired. I had proved to her that it was worth sticking with me. It was entirely gratifying.

Even Latsabidze shook my hand when I accompanied Daria to the studio on her last day for some pick-up shots, and thanked me for my support. The film was called *The Way*, he told me, and would be released soon. I wanted to share my triumph with someone, so one afternoon I took the trolleybus to Vake and rang Christine's doorbell. I followed her into the shady sitting room, which smelled of freshly made jam. She didn't ask what I was doing there; she just served me a delicious dumpling soup. After I'd eaten, she asked me if I was there to see Miro.

'Yes, I am,' I said.

'He told me about the lovely time you had in Bakuriani.' She eyed me approvingly. 'And Stasia says you're a very clever girl.'

She poured a small measure of liqueur from a carafe into a glass. I had already moved on to a piece of cake and was trying to eat it without dropping crumbs.

'You used to live with us, didn't you?' Once again, I was having trouble reining in my curiosity.

'No, that's not strictly true. They all used to live with me. I had a big house then, a beautiful house. Your grandfather and your great-aunt grew up there. We had a lovely garden, with a fountain, and ... well. Times have changed.'

Then she told me that Miro had gone to a go-kart race at Mziuri Park with some friends. But she would let him know I had dropped by.

'Come again, whenever you like,' she said, as she saw me to the door. I was overjoyed at the offer.

The atmosphere in Elene's apartment had been sepulchral for some time. My mother was always complaining of headaches, so Aleko had moved his drinking sessions out of the house — which only ended up causing more arguments when he came home late and drunk. So I decided to go to Mziuri Park, which wasn't far from Christine's flat, and look for Miro.

Down at the far end of the park, where it bordered on Tbilisi Zoo, I eventually found a small track and a crowd of adolescent boys in leather jackets and lumberjack shirts, standing around smoking cigarettes and cheering on the drivers. I sensed their eyes appraising me as I marched through the group, asking for Miro. Eventually I spotted him sitting on a folding chair, sorting out some slips of paper with another boy. When I appeared in front of him, he leaped up from the chair in surprise and alarm.

'What are *you* doing here?' he cried.

'I was at Christine's, and she told me I'd find you here. I thought I'd stop by.'

'Yes, great, that's really good of you. But you can't tell anyone about this, okay? You have to be sixteen to drive. They make an exception for me,' he said, grinning from ear to ear.

'Can you drive, then?'

'Yup. But right now I'm taking the bets.'

'Bets?'

He took me to one side, laid an arm meaningfully around my shoulders, and whispered in my ear that this was technically an illegal activity, but the boys were just making a bit of pocket money, and it was no big deal. To be on the safe side, he added that I mustn't tell anyone.

'But if *I* just caught you here with these bits of paper, how easy do you think it's going to be for the *militsiya* to cotton on to you and your bets?' I pressed him.

He scratched his ear, giving the question some thought. This didn't seem to have crossed his mind before.

'You need to organise this whole thing better, be smarter about it. That's what I think, anyway,' I explained.

'You think? How?' He bent his head down to me; a curl dropped over his forehead and tickled my cheek.

'Well, I could always do it for you.'

I didn't know the first thing about go-kart racing, and I was intimidated by all the boys. But the idea came to me as I was thinking how nice it would be to see Miro more often.

'You? But you don't have a clue what you're doing.'

'I've got lots of free time after school. My mother doesn't really check up on me, and I'm a fast learner.'

He thought for a minute, then hurried over to the others and conferred with them. He came back to me looking very pleased.

'They think it's a clever idea. We'll explain everything to you; nobody'll suspect a girl. You need to be here at two tomorrow, The Shark'll be here then, he's the boss.'

'The Shark?'

'Yeah, The Shark. He's nineteen,' he said reverentially, as if there were some great merit in being nineteen.

I would have to skip the last period of geography the following day to get to the park on time, but that was doable.

★

It was simple: just after sunset, when everyone had left the park, the little go-kart track opened for the teenagers and their adult leader. They bribed the attendants to turn a blind eye. Officially, these were training sessions; unofficially, a pastime for cool kids and a way of making some fast pocket money. The races took place in the dark. Before the race, you could write the name of your favourite on a slip of paper and drop it into a bucket, like a tombola. You had to give your money to The Shark beforehand — there was a different rate for each race — and afterwards it was shared out among the winners. From now on, I was to manage the finances.

The Shark — a skinny chain-smoker with bad skin and greasy hair, who wore genuine Levis that seemed permanently moulded to his body — was sceptical at first, but I convinced him. I calculated quickly, refused to enter into discussions, and kept the money in my tights — a very safe hiding-place. The only challenge consisted in telling my mother that I was taking a course in 'Literary Appreciation' at the Youth Palace and so would be late home three nights a week. But she soon acquiesced, and sometimes I even managed to avoid trekking all the way home first by going to Christine's and eating there, before walking to the track with Miro. Christine had discussed it with Elene; it made no difference to her whether she was feeding one mouth or two, and most of the time Lana wasn't there — she was always working, or away at architecture conventions in various Soviet cities.

Despite my initial shyness, I soon found it easy to spend time in the company of the go-karting boys; I actually felt more comfortable around them than with the girls at school. I didn't have to be pretty, I didn't have to think about my clothes, I just had to sip from a beer bottle from time to time, then belch, or take a drag on a cigarette — that was enough for them to accept me as part of their community.

During the races, in which I took little interest, I read my books. The boys sometimes made idiotic jokes about my *love stories*, but I hit back by saying that it was a good job at least one of us could read and write. These kinds of remarks gradually earned me respect. The Shark's initial fear that I was too much of a *girl* for the job proved unfounded. I quickly learned to laugh at dirty jokes, and not to immediately class lewd comments as a sign of intellectual backwardness. I learned to spit a long way, and to run as fast as I could when someone told us the 'pigs' were about.

At that time, Miro was precisely at the interface between *Wuthering Heights* and 'Fuck your mum', and it was still unclear which side he would eventually come down on. His need for everyone to like him, and to make everyone laugh, sometimes got on my nerves, but he always managed to overcome my annoyance by taking things one step further, carrying on until I was forced to laugh. But when he no longer needed to clown around, in those quiet moments when he would sit down beside me and I would read aloud to him, I felt needed and right, in this place with this permanently grinning boy at my side.

★

I knew it was getting late. I was already thinking up excuses for Elene. There had been an argument between The Shark and the other boys over the outcome of a race, which had remained unresolved, so I'd had to hang on to the money. I was tired, and it was already after ten, and I would probably have had to wait ages for the trolleybus, so Miro and I trudged back to Christine's on foot, and Christine called my mother. Then she gave me the phone.

'I'm sorry, *Deda*. I was chatting to Miro and I lost track of time.'

'I can't come and collect you now; Aleko's taken the car. You can stay at Christine's tonight. And tomorrow you need to come straight home after school. Kostya's going to pick you both up after Daria's gymnastics class, is that clear?'

We played cards and giggled over what had happened that day. Miro did impressions of the boys from the track. Lana was at a week-long conference in Rostov, and we had his room to ourselves. There was a camp bed set up for me beside his bed. After the light had been turned out, he switched on a torch, hopped in beside me, and pressed a book into my hands.

'What's that?' I whispered.

'*Amphibian Man* by Belyaev. I'm on page one-hundred and nineteen already. Would you go on reading?'

I refrained from making any comment and started reading the science fiction novel to him.

'Can you smell that?' I asked him after a while. The digital alarm clock Miro was so proud of, a gift his mother had brought back from Dresden, read 02:45. The smell was so intense that for a moment I felt quite peculiar. Miro sat up and sniffed as well, picking up the scent like a hungry animal.

'What *is* it?' I asked. I had never smelled anything so delicious in my life.

'It smells like chocolate. Christine must be baking a chocolate cake. Right?'

'Yes, let's go and look ...'

We both leapt up at the same time, I shoved my feet into his slippers, which were at least four sizes too big, and we ran into the next room.

Christine was sitting in front of the television — there was no picture, just the coloured stripes signalling that programmes had finished — spooning a black liquid out of a teacup. She didn't notice us at first, and went on eating in slow motion.

Puzzled, we stared first at her, then the television, then her again. Miro crept over and hugged her from behind. She gave a start, as if someone had jolted her out of a dream, then planted a kiss on his forehead.

'What are you two doing out here? Why aren't you asleep?'

'What is that crazy stuff you're eating?'

He stared at her cup. She put a hand over it.

'Nothing. I mean: it's not for children.'

'But we're not children any more,' Miro retorted cheekily.

'Oh yes you are. Go away. You've got school tomorrow, had you forgotten?'

'But Christy' — he called her Christy, affectionately — 'we want to try it too. It smells so delicious. What is it?'

'No!'

She almost shouted the word, and leapt up from her chair. For a moment, we stood facing each other, like big cats circling their territory. Then Miro ran into the kitchen and came back carrying a little metal jug, which looked like a Turkish coffee pot. He was already dipping his forefinger into the jug and licking it. He closed his eyes appreciatively and made a strange movement with his head.

'No!' Christine cried out again, before falling back into her armchair in front of the television.

But now Miro was putting his forefinger, covered in thick, gooey chocolate, into my mouth. I felt goosebumps on my arms, and something tightened inside me. It was a little piece of paradise on earth. It was the most wonderful flavour I had ever tasted. We scraped out what little remained, our fingers reaching into the pot, into our mouths, and back again. Christine sat rigid in her chair, neither looking at us nor making any further attempt to stop us.

'Oh my God, Christy!' Miro lowered himself onto the arm of her chair and put an arm round her shoulders. 'Why have you never made that for us? It's so delicious.'

'My sister was right. She was always right,' she whispered.

With the heavenly flavour of the chocolate still in my mouth, I sensed an aftertaste of sadness. Something about this flavour had made me fearful. It left so many questions on my tongue.

★

The next morning at school, we heard that there had been an explosion in a Ukrainian nuclear power plant called Chernobyl, and we were probably all now going to mutate and ultimately die a painful death.

'But the Ukraine is miles away,' a boy in the eighth class said in the playground.

'Not far enough, though. Anyway, it doesn't matter how far away you are. We won't be able to eat or drink anything: everything's contaminated, and we'll all get hydrocephaly,' a particularly bright boy in the top form retorted.

'And will the trees turn pink, and the earth go blue? I read that's what happened in Hiroshima.'

'This is much worse than Hiroshima. The whole world will be contaminated now. Even America,' insisted the older boy, who seemed to be a follower of conspiracy theories.

'Maybe the Yanks provoked it? On purpose, so that —'

'They must have. People here would never allow such a thing to happen, they're more careful than that,' said a shocked girl in John Lennon glasses.

'We're all going to turn into zombies,' another girl was wailing as I hurried out of the playground.

That evening, on the way home with Daria in Kostya's car, I asked what it would really mean. Kostya asked the driver to pull over. He got into the back with us and put his arms around Daria and me. I flinched, not having touched him since our afternoon on his bed.

'Everything will be all right. Nothing's going to happen to you. Not to you.'

★

Kostya hardly left his bedroom any more. When he sat down in front of the television, unshaven, in his dressing gown, he did nothing but rant about 'weaklings', 'thieves', and 'enemies of the state', and insist that this country needed an iron hand to get it back on its feet. Some days, he drank wine straight after breakfast.

Now and again, gloomy-eyed men from the ministry pulled up at the Green House in their Volgas, Kostya would take them into his study, and we would hear indignant exclamations through the wall. The gentlemen often hurried out looking shocked and left the house. At the end of May, he finally went back to work. When he came home that evening, the first thing he did was smash every last piece of Nana's Czech tea set against the wall. In a rage, he shouted that he was going to show those swine: he was the one responsible for getting them those posts in the first place, for them having any work at all; he would show them who it was they were dealing with.

'Are you out of your mind?' Nana shouted. Kostya had smashed one of her special editions to smithereens.

Daria and I sat, petrified, on the swing seat, which was on the point of falling apart. Daria had met Latsabidze a few days previously. The film had been edited, but the premiere had been postponed for the time being because of Chernobyl. First, there would be a private screening in the House of Film, to which he had invited her. And Daria, flushed and excited, had asked me if I wanted to go with her. Since then, all she could think about was what she was going to wear. I realised with some discomfort that she had started mentioning one particular name a lot, and every time she did, she had this stupid, dreamy look on her face.

'Who *is* this Lasha you keep talking about?'

'Our head cameraman.'

'What's going on with him?'

'What do you mean, going on?'

'You're always talking about him.'

'He's picked me up from school twice now.'

Kostya's loud, distorted voice could still be heard from inside the house.

'What do you mean, picked you up? Did you arrange to meet him?'

'He asked me out to the cinema, on Friday.'

'But what kind of guy is he?' I asked.

'He's lovely. And so handsome. He always wears such great clothes, and he's been to America: he's seen New York, and he's even met some of the stars.'

'And how old is he?'

'Thirty-three.'

'That's seriously old.'

'Rubbish. Anyway, I prefer mature men.'

I was astonished: up to now, Daria hadn't preferred any kind of men, or she simply hadn't had the time to think about them, being too preoccupied with herself. But now she seemed to have come out of hibernation.

'The devil take your old tea set — they're trying to throw me out of the ministry, they want me to take up some crummy post in the MVD. They even had the cheek to tell me to my face that there were irregularities in the accounts — under my leadership! Brainless idiots!'

As background music to Kostya's tirade, we could hear Mozart's *Magic Flute* wafting from the barn. Stasia had been in there all day.

'They're trying to throw Grandfather out?' Daria was suddenly all ears. I started listening as well.

'These namby-pambies — I'll show them. I'll sack the lot of them, get them all out. You can't trust anyone any more — anyone, do you hear me? No one has a single spark of humanity in them in this day and age, let alone decency or morality. They should open up their *own* accounts, then we'll see who's got a clean record!'

'But Kostya ... Tell me that's not true. Is it? Are there really irregularities in your accounts?' Nana asked anxiously.

'Irregularities? Irregularities? The whole country is one big irregularity. What do you think you live on, hmm? The summer health spas and your little tea parties with your friends. How do you think I paid for your best friend's operation, with the best doctor in the country? What or who do you think gave us all this? Your salary, and mine? Do you honestly believe that?'

Daria's bottom lip began to quiver. She grasped my hand.

'They all steal and lie, they all want backhanders, no one lifts a finger otherwise. That's what this rotten country is. But you wanted me to come back. To come back to this rat-hole. This would never have happened in the navy. Being a man *means* something there. Do you know what sort of lowlifes I've had to waste my time on all these years? Do you think I enjoyed it? I didn't invent the system. I just ended up in this rat-hole, because of you and your oh-so-clever daughter. Who's now settled for an alcoholic. The accounts — don't make me laugh. The accounts. I'd like to see anyone in any state institution open up his accounts!'

'Kostya!' Nana sounded frightened, unnerved. 'I'm asking you, are there any irregularities in your accounting?'

'There *is* no accounting — you still don't get it, do you? There's nothing that's still sacred to these people, and you want to know why? Because they let this weakling take power, this would-be revolutionary who's afraid to stand up in front of his people. And how long has this been going on? And what about where you are? What's it like in your sacred university? How much would I have to pay them to let me study law? How much would I have to shell out to become a doctor? How do things work there? Or is syntax so exciting that you've stopped paying attention to the world around you? You *wanted* to live like this. You all wanted to live like this.'

'Kostya, for pity's sake, what are you talking about?'

'You wanted the health spas and the driver and you wanted *crêpe de chine* from Italy and Opium from France; you wanted to be the envy of your friends, to show them how good you had it, that you'd hit the jackpot, as it were. I had to play along, Nana, or I'd have been thrown out long ago,' he shouted, then abruptly fell silent.

Daria had stood up and was looking at me wide-eyed. I didn't know what to say; I didn't dare move. Mozart, too, abruptly fell silent.

> How this state has mocked us!
>
> ANATOLY RYBAKOV

It was raining in Moscow. At Sheremetyevo, Kostya hailed a taxi. He would have liked to have let his friend know he was coming so Alania could pick him up from the airport, but he hadn't been able to reach him. He'd been trying for over a week, but Alania remained elusive. Kostya hadn't let that put him off, though. He still had enough friends in the Lubyanka; he would find him.

He had taken a room in the Hotel Mir, and on the way there he felt all the pressure of the past week, the discontent, the anger, ebbing away. As always when he approached this city, he felt safe. The city seemed to welcome him. And unlike Leningrad, no nightmares bound him to Moscow. This was where he had reached the pinnacle of his career. Achieved fame and respect. Those had been better times; times that he loved to recall.

After putting his luggage in his room, he had the taxi take him straight to the Sovietsky, the legendary restaurant you had to earn the right to eat in.

He ordered Crimean champagne, caviar blinis, fish in beetroot sauce. For a while, he let all his troubles fall away. Here, he was his old self: the powerful, generous Kostya who had everything under his control. To finish, he treated himself to a birch vodka, then headed off for Kutuzovsky Prospect — the most recent address he had for Alania.

He would talk to him; Alania, his good old friend, would back him up; he'd get everything straightened out. He would show these lickspittles who it was they were dealing with. If the worst came to the worst, Alania could write him a transfer letter, talk to the right people. And if there were no other way round it, Kostya would move back to Moscow. He would take Daria with him. She would have her school-leaving certificate soon, and she would get a decent university place here. He would rent a nice apartment near Sadovaya, an area he had always been particularly fond of.

He felt strong and full of vigour. It was the city that gave him this good feeling. He would make a fresh start. Leave that Georgian rabble behind and start dealing with professionals and honourable men at long last.

And he still had a few numbers in his address book. Of course, some of his former companions might now be wives and mothers, but others would still be happy to revive the good old days.

If his countryman Shevardnadze had risen to become First Secretary of the Georgian SSR and then Soviet Foreign Minister, then he, Kostya Jashi, could rise to similar heights. He just had to get in front of the right people.

From the back seat of the taxi, he looked out at the familiar streets and squares, the boulevards and buildings. Yes, here he had been happy, here everything had been all right. Elene had been here with him, and her love had belonged to him alone. He leaned back. The rain had eased off and the sky was clearing. The streetlamps were starting to come on.

He got out in front of a tower block. A new building that wasn't familiar to him. Why had his friend come back, anyway? He soon found the nameplate. An old woman was just coming out of the block; he quickly slipped through the main door and took the lift to the ninth floor. He rang the bell. No one answered. Then he started knocking. Somehow he knew Alania was there. He knocked and called out:

'It's me, Kostya! Giorgi, are you there? I think you are. Come on, it's me. I flew to Moscow, I have to see you.'

Suddenly he heard footsteps behind the door, and slowly the handle turned. A bald head appeared. Alania had aged a great deal. His cheeks were sunken; he had obviously lost weight, and it made him look even slighter and more frail than before. His lips were dry and cracked. And he was unkempt, although he had always placed such value on his appearance.

The flat was in disarray. Hasn't been cleaned in a long time, thought Kostya. There were piles of unwashed crockery in the kitchen. The place smelled of alcohol and stale air. Alania fixed Kostya with his small eyes and tried to smile. Then he opened his thin arms and embraced his old friend.

'I've been trying to reach you for over a week. Nobody could tell me anything. I didn't know how else to get hold of you. I flew here to talk to you. I was sure I'd find you. Come on, you old bastard, give me another hug!'

Alania fetched a vodka bottle and, without asking, poured them both a glass of the clear liquid. 'Vodka? You?'

Kostya tried to appear cheerful and ignore the mess.

'Three more days. Then I'm gone. Forever,' said Alania with a smile, raising his glass to Kostya.

'What do you mean, gone? Gone where?'

'A chess tournament in Holland. And then I'll disappear. London.'

'What are you talking about? You're going AWOL?'

'It's all over, Kostya. All of it. I'm going back to London; nothing else matters now.' He poured himself another glass.

'Now then, Alania, I don't like the sound of this at all — what are you going on about?'

'If they catch me, they catch me. I don't care.'

'Hey, look at me. What on earth has got into you? Yes, of course I know things aren't exactly going well for us — I mean, no wonder, just look at the scoundrels they've got on the Central Committee now — but that's no reason to …'

'It's over, can't you see? It's over.'

'Then retire, but stop talking such nonsense, my friend.'

'We failed, Kostya. All of us. It was all for nothing.'

'Hey, Gio, I really don't like the sound of this. And why are you drinking, all of a sudden? You've never been a drinker!'

'I sent people back. I forced hundreds of them onto boats and planes; I lied to them and made false promises. Some of them would die, I knew that, and I carried on all the same. It was my job. Some went straight to the camps. Most went to the camps. I did that. I sent people to their deaths, do you understand?'

'Listen! They were deserters, enemies of the state, and traitors of the worst kind. What else could you have done but your duty? You served your country, Giorgi; you did nothing wrong! You acted out of loyalty and devotion to your country! And now you're sitting in this pigsty feeling sorry for yourself!'

'Do you remember when we were in Leningrad? How wonderful that was. We believed in what we were doing. We had so many plans.' Alania suddenly slumped back in his chair, put down his glass, and stared out of the grimy window into the night. 'It was all just lies, illusions. And that's what we devoted our lives to. Don't you understand, Kostya?'

The telephone started to ring. Alania didn't move, as if he couldn't hear it.

'Gio, you should answer that.'

'Like hell I will.' His voice suddenly sounded angry. He shook his head and reached for the vodka bottle again. 'This whole farce. Why aren't you sick of it yet, why don't you give it up? It's a mystery to me.'

He poured himself another glass.

'You shouldn't drink so much.'

'Drink? I shouldn't drink so much? I should drink myself to death. I thought I was doing something meaningful by serving my country, I thought I … I'm not even worth spitting on. And you. Look at you. You …'

'Now just you calm down!'

'I don't want to calm down. I'm going. I'm going to her.'

'Her?'

'Your sister.'

'I don't believe it… Don't tell me, at your age, you … Oh dear God, not Kitty, please!'

'She's the only person who —'

'You're not going anywhere. You'll turn down the trip. You'll be off sick. I won't allow you to make a fool of yourself. I mean: you, one of the KGB's finest, getting caught somewhere in the West, trying to escape? I won't allow it!'

'Kostya, why won't you understand? It's finished; it's over. There's no mercy for our kind, one way or the other. And soon none of this is going to exist! Look around you!'

'Alania, you're being sentimental. You need to pull yourself together and get a grip on your life again. We'll get through this together, we've survived worse things.'

'And why are you here? To get me back on track?' Alania suddenly snapped at him. 'Do you want an interview at the Lubyanka? Things got a bit tricky for you at home, have they? Has the ground already started to shake in our homeland? You're clutching at the wrong straw, my friend.'

'Has something been going on all these years between you and Kitty?'

Kostya emptied his glass in one gulp. Something had to be done; this business was completely outrageous. Alania, Giorgi Alania, with his exemplary career, Kostya's personal hero!

'Was something going on? What do you think was going on? This shitty game of hide-and-seek, that's what was going on. And I was blind enough not to understand that she was my only anchor. I'm going to seize my last chance — and you, you should, too.'

They must have entered into some kind of relationship, he and Kitty; it had been bound to happen after he'd spent so many years protecting her. Kostya might have known. His western, liberal sister must have put the idea in Alania's head. Suddenly, a thought came to him: he shouldn't stay here; he should take Alania to Tbilisi with him instead. Moscow had never been Alania's city the way it had been Kostya's. Alania was too unprepossessing, too quiet for the city; he challenged it too little. He was more suited to the south, with his sentimentality and the Georgian sing-song in his voice. Yes, he would take Alania with him and save him from himself.

'You're going to take a week or two off, and we're going to fly to Tbilisi. I'll take care of it tomorrow. This place isn't doing you any good. Can't you afford a better flat? No wonder you're fading away here.'

'Kostya, Kostya: steadfast and incorrigible, hmm? Have you heard about Afghanistan?' Alania said. 'A total disaster. You don't want to know how many were killed — I mean the real number, not the official one. They're going to pull our troops out in the next couple of years, because there's nothing they can do there. The arms industry will be reduced to a minimum. Your fabulous nuclear submarines will be scrapped. They haven't realised that their well-intentioned "good deeds" are just going to make everything worse. They can't see that the criticism they've suddenly begun to allow will bring the whole house of cards tumbling down.' He spoke thoughtfully, his face turned towards the window. 'They're still using these reforms to try to score points with the population, but they're overestimating themselves. If you're sitting on a dung heap, you shouldn't let people go poking about in it. The road ahead is not going to be a peaceful one. As soon as they loosen their grip, everyone will start clamouring for their own piece of the pie and holding their hand out, but unfortunately there won't be much left of the pie by then, Kostya. And if you don't open your eyes soon, you're going to be stuck inside this house of cards when it falls in on you. The West will applaud when the "evil empire" turns out not to be so evil, after all, and shows itself ready to cooperate. They'll cry hurrah, because they aren't sending tanks onto the streets. But the fucking tanks will be there, all right, it's just that they won't be sent out in the name of the Communist Party any more, and that's the only thing the West cares about. The feeling that they were right all along, that they were tough and patient enough to wait until our glorious homeland drove itself into the ground. So, look around and open your eyes, my friend! Take some good advice from a friend. And, by the way, men like you, Kostya, are the worst at dealing with failure.'

Alania was speaking quietly again now, calmly. Kostya lowered his head, trying to focus on his goal, and not attribute any great significance to Alania's words. He had to stop him; he had to save Alania, as Alania had once saved him. Alania would insist on his truth, and ruin himself. Kostya couldn't allow that.

★

At about seven the next morning, when Alania had finally fallen into a drunken sleep, Kostya crept out of the flat and drove to the Lubyanka. His pass gained him access to the building, but he was sent to the waiting room and instructed to take a seat until the director arrived. Kostya tried not to show how offended he was. No one would have dared to make him wait in the old days. Well, his friend was right about one thing: the old days were no more. Another age had dawned.

It was only at around nine that Alania's director appeared and ushered him into his office. Kostya introduced himself and told him that Alania was sick and in urgent need of a rest cure, and for this reason was unable to travel with the chess team. The stout young man with the rosy cheeks jotted something down in his notebook and nodded in agreement. Kostya mentioned that he had missed being in Moscow, in the hope that the man would ask where he had come from. And he did, but just as Kostya was getting into his stride and was about to tell him about his career and his history, the man — who was many years his junior — interrupted and excused himself, saying that he was very busy.

At the hotel, he dropped wearily onto the bed. Yes, times had definitely changed. No, not for the better, not for the better, he thought to himself, before falling into a deep sleep.

★

'How could you?' There was despair in Alania's voice. 'You were my best, my only friend.'

The ringing had jolted Kostya awake, and he crawled to the telephone. How had Alania found him, he wondered: he had left no address. Well — he was a man of great *intelligence*.

'You were about to ruin your life. You should be thanking me for saving your neck.'

'You haven't saved anything, you've destroyed it all! I don't have any more foreign postings this year. She'll ... she'll never forgive me.'

It was dark in the room. What time was it? How long had he slept? This business with Alania was starting to get on his nerves. He switched on the bedside lamp.

'Now listen here, Giorgi. Shut up and listen to me! You're behaving like a sixteen-year-old. Wake up! You were about to throw everything away, and I stopped you. You'll thank me for this one day! You need peace and quiet and good people who'll take care of you. You need good food and fresh air. The day after tomorrow we're flying to Tbilisi, and you can stay there for as long as you need to get back to your old self.'

Alania didn't turn up at the airport. Kostya also missed the flight: he went back to Alania's flat, but the door remained locked, and his incessant ringing, knocking, and shouting went unanswered.

The next day, Kostya boarded the plane to Tbilisi alone. Embittered, disappointed, brooding.

★

She hadn't left the flat for two weeks. She'd even had her food delivered. Nor did she answer the phone, and even when Amy started a riot under her window and nearly got into a fistfight with the paparazzi lurking there, Kitty didn't open the door.

That evening, she had a gig at a private club in Notting Hill, to raise funds for people infected with HIV. She had to go out. She had to force herself out. She had been standing in front of the wardrobe for half an hour, unable even to take out the necessary clothes and get dressed. A chauffeur was picking her up soon, in a limousine with blacked-out windows, to drive her to the club. That was good; she was sure she could have a little whisky in the car.

She had been reading the papers and thinking about the fact that the world was in the process of turning the page. That evening she would send her backing singers away and take to the stage alone, just her and her guitar. She wanted to be alone.

In the past two weeks she had spoken with Andro a lot. He was there all the time. Even when she couldn't see him, she could sense him. But he hadn't turned up since yesterday. Neither under her window nor in her head.

She found a black blazer and put it on over her bare skin. She tried to apply some lipstick, but her hand was trembling and she couldn't draw a straight line. Not much longer now and she could get in the car and allow herself a drink. Another hour or two and she would have got through the evening. Just three songs to sing. Three songs she wanted to sing alone.

As they drove past Ladbroke Gardens she held her face out to the breeze, stuck her head out of the open window, felt the bitter, warming taste of whisky on her tongue. She leaned back. She knew she was losing her mind. In the last few days, she had even heard Mariam whispering in her ear. Heard her mother calling to her. And the previous night she had been woken by a tantalising scent. The smell of her grandfather's hot chocolate.

'Damn it all, I nearly died of worry. I didn't even know if you were going to turn up today. What on earth is up with you? Were you ill? Why didn't you open the door to me, or answer the phone? Those bloody photographers have been skulking around outside your house twenty-four hours a day. I almost lost it. Oh god, I'm so relieved you're here.'

Amy, in a sparkling jumpsuit and too much make-up, came running up to her, put an arm around her shoulder, and steered her through the backstage area. Kitty wanted to sing Amy a hymn of gratitude. Wanted to kiss her hands and weep with emotion when she saw the stage prepared perfectly for her and the cough sweets Amy had placed ready in a bowl in the wings. But she didn't have the strength. She would be lucky if she had enough strength for three songs.

At least there were no cameras this evening. It was a private event. She wondered how much they had already collected. For a good cause. Who even knew what a good cause was?

She clutched her guitar. Her most secure anchor in life. The lights dimmed. The sophisticated, wealthy audience regarded her with curiosity as she stepped into the cone of light on stage. She spoke a few words of greeting that Amy had asked her to say into the mic. Yes, donate, please, please donate! Then she closed her eyes. She sensed her. She was there. Fred Lieblich had come. She was standing down there somewhere, looking at her with her cat's eyes. The woman who had come back to life — but life was much too restless: it hadn't waited for her, for either of them.

She sang, and in the last song she raised her voice, higher and higher, until it cracked and a deep, beautiful silence took possession of her. She felt as if she were about to faint. It was so easy to disappear when so many eyes were on you. For the length of a song, it was possible to forget. Carried by the applause, she swam off stage, sank into a swivel chair in the dressing room, and laid her head on the make-up table. Amy fussed over her. Laughed; was delighted. Kitty didn't listen to her. She looked at herself in the mirror. In the pitiless light of the make-up mirror. The wrinkles, the exhaustion, her attempt to outrun time. The bewilderment in her eyes. Luckily, Amy vanished from the dressing room again, to 'do some networking', as she called it, and left her there alone.

'You're not doing so well. Let's get out of here.'

Fred was standing in the doorway. What a beautiful person, Kitty thought to herself, looking at her in the mirror, and what a waste.

'I'm fine.' Kitty straightened up.

'You're lying. I've got a car, and I'm sober. Let's run away.'

'Where to?'

'Wherever you want.'

'There's nowhere I want to go.'

'There's always the sea.'

'That's too far.'

'Doesn't matter. Come on, I'm not going to gobble you up. You need some fresh air. Come on!'

They crept out the back way. Fred had parked an old van not far from the stage door. Amy must have got her a backstage pass; she would hardly have got into the club otherwise. In the van, Kitty was suddenly overcome by an incredible tiredness, and closed her eyes. She had brought only her guitar and a small handbag. She'd even left her coat behind.

'You need to head for Eastbourne. I'll tell you where to turn off,' she told Fred, before falling asleep.

The journey of almost two hours completely passed her by. She hadn't slept so well and so deeply for a long time, without nightmares jolting her awake.

'So this provincial backwater is where Madame Jashi is making a home for her old age?'

Kitty slowly opened her eyes and heard Fred laughing.

'Go left here; it's the second turn-off on the right.'

She switched the light on. How long was it since she had last been here? When her sad friend had come to find her, arriving out of the blue and promising to return.

The house seemed lost in a sleeping-beauty slumber. The night was clear and warm. They could hear the sea. Kitty instantly felt better. Fred lit a cigarette and stood outside the door.

'Let's go down to the water. I've got big torches and blankets. There are some dried peaches left, and some good Scotch.'

Fred agreed enthusiastically.

They made their way to the sea with the torches. It took them a while to walk the narrow path along the steep cliffs and down to the beach, where they spread the blankets on the damp sand and stretched out. It was so frighteningly peaceful and quiet. The sharp sickle of the crescent moon bathed the water in a yellowish light.

Fred touched her, her hand wandering up Kitty's spine. Then she took

Kitty in her arms. Kissed her face. Stroked her skin. Kitty let it happen. It felt good. It felt like coming home. The stars were sprinkled across the sky like tiny freckles. They lay together. They brushed the hair from each other's foreheads. Kitty took Fred's face in her hands and looked at her, committing her to memory.

'It's my turn now,' said Fred Lieblich.

A few metres away, at the foot of the cliff, Kitty saw Andro standing; she rubbed her eyes, tried to concentrate on Fred's face, but he was still there. He had returned. She sensed his presence with every fibre of her body.

'What is it?' asked Fred, grasping her wrist. 'Are you cold?'

'No, it's fine.'

'I want to know what's wrong. I want to be there. For you. Please, let me.'

'Let's just be here, you and me, that's all.'

'Yes.'

'Yes what?'

'We can go to Vienna.'

'Vienna.'

'I could show you some beautiful places, if they're still there, and we can drink the best hot chocolate in the world.'

'I doubt that.'

Fred laid her head in Kitty's lap and dreamed herself away, to the Vienna of her childhood. Before she learned what it sounds like when you cut a body down from a rope. She sipped the good Scotch Kitty had brought. Later, she couldn't remember when exactly she had fallen asleep.

★

Kitty took off her clothes. She wanted to be naked. Free. She folded her underwear. Neatly, as her mother had taught her when she was a little girl. Andro was standing behind her, watching. Then she stepped tentatively into the cold water. The waves pounded against her skin, made her suppress the cries she wanted to let out; she dived under. The water carried her out. In the distance she could still see the light of the torches, the blanket, the woman lying on it, until everything fused together into a tiny bright dot.

Andro was swimming behind her. Kitty swallowed water. The waves were high; they rocked her to and fro, tossed her out and back again. She was afraid, but only briefly, only until Andro's face appeared before her again. Darkness lay over the water; she couldn't see anything in front of her and she was disorientated. Even the light vanished into the distance. Then, suddenly, something gleamed beneath her feet. Little fish, a shoal of little fish was circling her. It made her laugh out loud.

This is happiness, thought Kitty: happiness. Like afternoon sweat on our skin after we made love, back then, the first time. The last song tonight, and the gratitude in Amy's eyes. The loneliness of Giorgi Alania, which I ended for one second of his life when I held him. The bus journeys across America. These fish beneath my feet, this moon above me, these cliffs, these waves, and the fear, vanishing.

She circled her arms in the emptiness. There was no shore any more. No earth. Just nothingness, and the little fish, swimming with her, and the endless water.

Kostya's laughter, when she managed to make him laugh. Andro's soft kisses on her lips. Cherries, which always gave her a stomach ache. Her mother's worry lines, at the exact centre of her forehead. The songs. The concert in Amsterdam, the incredible excitement that had greeted her. Had she earned it, this happiness? If all these people knew what she had done, would they go on buying her records and singing her songs?

She went under; she could feel her strength leaving her.

'Mariam?' She reached out her hand. 'Did it hurt? What was it like? Does it hurt?'

They stood me against the wall. Then the first shot came. And then another. I think there were three; they do it to make sure. It was quick. I didn't feel much. Don't worry.

Mariam's voice echoed in her head.

'I don't want you to hate me, Mariam.'

How could I hate you, Kitty? Don't you remember how good things were when we were together?

'It wasn't good. It was hell on earth.'

Don't talk nonsense. Remember. We lived, Kitty. We were there.

Kitty couldn't reply. Her lungs were already filling with water. But the fish swam around her and shone with a fantastic green light.

★

Her body was pulled from the water three hours after Fred Lieblich alerted the coastguard. She hadn't drifted very far. She'd never been a good swimmer, and it hadn't taken long for her strength and breath to fail her.

I'll swap the government for a kilo of macaroni!

PLACARD AT A DEMONSTRATION

The film was released in cinemas and caused the expected furore. First and foremost, Brilka, I have to tell you that I really was bowled over by my sister and the way she played her role. I sat in the House of Film during the unofficial premiere and watched Daria change into another person. I couldn't believe that Daria could play a role so convincingly, that she was so capable of transforming herself. The film was good, and it moved me.

At the end, the whole auditorium rose to its feet, and, amid lengthy applause, the actors, including my beautiful sister in a strappy silver dress, were invited onto the stage. The lovely cameraman, Lasha, stood beside her with his arm around her shoulders.

There was something narcissistic about him. He was fashionably dressed and had fine features, but his eyes were cold, as if they could only perceive the world through the viewfinder of a camera — the world, and people. People, with the exception of my sister. He practically devoured her with his eyes. But I thought he was too old for her, and in any case he already had a wife, who had come with him that evening to the screening and hung on his arm throughout for all to see. A woman just as chic as he was, and perhaps as superficial.

What did Daria see in this man, I kept asking myself at the premiere party afterwards, which was held in a restaurant by the river.

Daria would be invited to all the official receptions from then on, so at some point we would have to reveal our secret. It was only four weeks until the film would be released in cinemas, provided the censor didn't step in before then. But it had been kept very symbolic, its references were more general than direct, and people were fortified by the new wind blowing from Moscow, so the assumption was that everything would go ahead as planned.

That same evening, I convinced Daria to confess everything to Elene and Aleko, reassuring her we could deal with Kostya later.

'In about two weeks, Daria is going to become a kind of rising star in the acting firmament. I just wanted you to know beforehand, and I want you to support us — I mean her. Daria.'

We were in the kitchen. My mother was washing dishes and Aleko was reading the paper. Daria had locked herself in the bathroom, fearing that a storm was about to break over her.

'What are you talking about?' Elene asked, off-hand, still occupied with the dirty dishes.

One thing at a time, in a calm, considered manner, I explained our scheme to her: the trip to Bakuriani without Daria, Latsabidze's support — right up to the private screening that evening.

'We weren't at a birthday party. We've just been to the preview of the film, and Daria really is bloody good!'

They stared at me uncomprehendingly. Aleko's mouth hung open. I thought he would praise me, pat me on the back; he'd always praised me for being what my mother called 'an annoying clever-clogs' at times. This time, though, I seemed to have completely confounded him, and there was no support from his side.

'How could the two of you *do* something like this? Do you have any idea what you've done?! After everything I've had to go through with your grandfather!' Elene screamed at me. Her face was twisted with pain. 'And do you know what will happen because of this? You lied to me! You led us all up the garden path! My own child, my daughter!'

I was surprised, and unprepared for her rage to be directed at me.

'But *Deda*, it's turned out to be a great film: everyone loved it, and —'

'Oh, bravo, Niza! Do you actually know how old you are? Do you know? How grown-up do you think you are?'

'It was what I wanted. Niza was just trying to make amends.' At last Daria had come out of the bathroom to support me.

Elene fell silent for a moment. Then she sat down and buried her face in her hands. For a while we all stood around in silence, waiting for her to look at us again.

'Make amends? You wanted to make amends ... You can't *make amends* for anything, that's just a bloody lie, remember that!' she said, suddenly quiet.

'Elene, please,' said Aleko, trying to calm things down.

'What? "Elene, please" what? She's landed us all in a bloody awful situation. And if she thinks she's so clever, she can come up with another plan as to how we're going to make amends for *this* — and how I can stop my father denying me access to the house my daughters live in. Because I'll be the one who'll end up paying for all this again.'

'I think you could give her just a tiny bit of recognition. I mean, at her age ... well. You could be the future leader of the Communist Party if you carry on like this, kiddo.'

But Elene looked at him scornfully and went on shaking her head.

'She lies. She lies all the time. I wonder when it started. What we missed. She plays truant, she sneaks around, she hangs out with Lana's lazy son — it seems her grades have gone down as well. She could be top of the class with no effort, but apparently that's too much to ask from this little madam. She's got better things to do.'

'He's not lazy,' I said, in a small voice, in Miro's defence.

★

The new General Secretary published an article in *Pravda* that spoke of 'class interests' and 'general human values', and was regarded by conservatives in the country as the ultimate renunciation of Lenin's legacy. The gradual withdrawal of Soviet troops from Afghanistan and the summits with Reagan, the nuclear disarmament treaties being discussed, were further signs of the Soviet Union drawing closer to the West.

There was unrest in the Lubyanka, too. By coincidence, Alania returned to work that day, after his long absence. He only went to the press department that morning in search of a colleague who might be able to tell him about upcoming cultural visits to Europe. He had to get a foothold in the ministry again quickly, so he could apply for another trip as soon as possible. A gentleman and a lady in a mohair jumper were sitting hunched over some newspapers, scanning the foreign press. They went about their work with aggressive boredom — the enthusiasm for this task, which had once been so coveted (you had all the major foreign newspapers at your disposal, an incredible privilege), seemed to have disappeared. Alania even harboured the suspicion that the material they filtered out didn't even end up in the thick files on their superiors' desks any longer, because these days no one was interested in what people in other countries were writing about. The threat had shifted: it no longer came from outside the borders of the Soviet Union, but from within.

In passing, Alania's eye fell on an edition of *The Guardian* lying on a table. During his time in London he had been a regular reader of the paper, and now a sentimental urge made him reach for it.

'Comrade Alania? Can we help you?' the woman asked, unwrapping the tinfoil from a sandwich.

'I'm looking for Comrade …' Alania fell silent, holding the paper in front of his nose as if he were being remote-controlled. 'Excuse me, but …'

The lady rose from her seat, but Alania stopped her with a very firm gesture.

'When was this paper printed?' he asked in an authoritative tone.

'Last month sometime. Three weeks ago. Look, it'll say on the … oh, right, the front page is missing. What is it, Comrade Alania? Is something wrong?'

Without replying, Giorgi Alania marched out of the room with the newspaper in his hand and went out into the street.

The international music scene is mourning the singer Kitty Jashi. Miss Jashi, who gained enormous popularity in the 1960s with her catchy, heartfelt songs and her political activism …

Alania sat down on the pavement. His legs were shaking. He tried to make some connection between this shocking news and Kitty, the woman who kept him alive, and to whom he had promised to return. His mind started calculating feverishly, he reckoned up the days, the dates, and the single burning question that formed in his head was whether he would have reached her in time if Kostya Jashi hadn't stopped him. Whether she would still have been alive today.

★

The call came just as Elene had finally plucked up her courage and gone up to the Green House, with Daria and me in tow.

The day before, she had informed her father over the phone that she had something to discuss with him, and now the four of us were sitting in the living room. We could hear Stasia humming in the garden and Nana making dinner in the kitchen. Elene had revealed to him, as calmly and collectedly as she could, that he would soon be seeing his beloved granddaughter on cinema posters, and, more importantly, on a number of screens, and that unfortunately this was a matter of fact and there was now nothing to be done about it.

Kostya drank his strong black tea without saying a word, and nothing in his body language, his outward appearance, showed that he had taken in what Elene had just told him. We could hear the clock on the wall ticking; Daria shuffled restlessly in her chair and kept looking over at our grandfather.

I chewed my fingernails, waiting for the lightning that would strike at any minute, and the thunder that would come with it. This was between Kostya and me — I knew that, even before he got up and came towards me with his hand raised threateningly.

'So *you* thought this up, did you, you little bitch?'

Elene rose from her chair; it was pure maternal instinct. Then Daria lunged towards him: 'It's what I wanted — *I* wanted it, Grandfather!'

But in the middle of Daria's shouting, Nana burst into the room. She was stony-faced, and her plump cheeks were flushed. She was holding a saucepan lid in her hand, and her lips were parted.

'Telephone!' she stammered, but Kostya didn't turn round — he kept his eyes fixed on me.

'Not now!' he shouted.

'Yes, now!' Nana's voice quivered.

'I said not now!'

'For god's sake, go to the telephone!' she cried, and fell limply into the chair her husband had just vacated. Kostya moved slowly, suspiciously, towards the door.

'Who is it?' he asked, erring on the side of caution.

'Alania. He'll tell you himself,' whispered Nana, and let the lid fall from her hand.

'Mama? Is everything all right?' asked Elene.

'It's just …'

'Go outside!' said Elene, turning to Daria and me, as if she'd just remembered that we were there.

Before we left the room, I heard Grandmother say Kitty's name.

> They cry that I stole the moon, and that it was theirs.
>
> VLADIMIR VYSOTSKY

They decided to keep the news from Stasia. Even Daria and I had to promise not to tell her anything.

Two weeks after the phone call, when Stasia and I were digging manure into the garden, she suddenly stopped and asked me to bring her the little stool she used when she needed to take a breather. She sat down on it, and suddenly froze. Then she lowered her head, and I could see tears rolling down her cheeks. I crept over and hugged her from behind, incapable of looking her in the eye. If she asked me whether her daughter was dead, I wouldn't be able to lie to her.

Eventually, she got up and carried on with her work. We didn't say a word. A few birds twittered. A car drove by in the distance.

'Is it the ghosts again?' I said, breaking the silence.

She looked at me and gave me a wise smile. 'Yes, my sunshine, it's the ghosts again.'

'Are they over there by the cherry tree? Can you see them?'

It was an eerie thought that two dead women, invisible to me, were playing cards not fifty metres away.

'Yes, I can see them.'

'Are the two of them playing cards again?'

'Three of them. There are three of them playing,' she said; and I didn't dare ask who the third was.

★

Kitty Jashi was laid to rest in London. The police were forced to erect barriers to cope with the onslaught of mourners and rubberneckers. Amy and Fred walked behind the coffin. Fred had hardly said a word since the night she called the coastguard.

Two months after the funeral, Alania called Fred Lieblich. They met in a pub on Leicester Square. He felt terrible. He had a nasty cold, he was chilled to the bone, and his face was covered in red pustules. There was something uncanny, hard, in her eyes. They were eyes from which all trace of empathy had gone.

Fred took a drag on her cigarette. She looked at him as if he were an object, something lifeless. She probably wouldn't feel anything even if he were to drop dead right in front of her, he thought to himself. But he told her the most incredible story she had ever heard in her life. In his soft, upper-class English he told her the story of Kitty Jashi and Giorgi Alania. Of the day he saw her for the first time on a station platform in a small Georgian town, up to her escape from Tbilisi. Of Mariam and Kostya, of her child, and of Andro. She hadn't known all the facts; Kitty had only mentioned some of the people, some of the names to her. But this sickly-looking man revealed to her the whole panorama of Kitty's life, which was so inextricably interwoven with her own.

The way he told his story was clear and straightforward, and yet she felt she needed another four ears, a second or third brain to comprehend it all, to take it all in and make sense of it. His story had a mantra-like quality, and even though most of what he said sounded so dire, so final, it gave her comfort. Something like grace, a kind of meaning within the absolute senselessness of her death.

He told her about Kitty's escape from Prague, and her years in London, and how he had feared for her safety every day. He told her how Kitty had increasingly become part of his life, perhaps the most important part. He spoke of their phone calls, and she remembered how Kitty would retreat behind closed doors in her flat to speak on the phone. And now his words carried her along, spread out a carpet before her, a carpet in which there seemed to be a logic to everything, a cruel logic.

And when he told her about their last meeting in the house by the sea, about that night and their desperate lovemaking on the cold hall floor, yes, the details too, it seemed almost harmonious to her, that night, the end of his and her story, and despite a passing flash of childish jealousy, she understood the point of departure for Kitty's final journey, and didn't know what to say. Her words seemed helpless against his. And although he wanted her to, she couldn't tell him about her final hours with Kitty. She simply wasn't capable. He would be the first person she told, she said, one day; she would seek him out.

For a while, he looked crestfallen. Then he nodded politely, understandingly, and blew his nose in a handkerchief that she thought looked like a relic from another age.

She asked him how he had come to be to London, and what he was planning to do.

'I fled. I don't know yet. I won't be going back, in any case. I can't go back now.'

'But you can't just stay here, I assume; it's not that simple?' she asked, lighting another cigarette.

'No,' he said, and made an effort to smile, to alleviate the danger emanating from this 'no'.

'What do you want to do now?'

'I'll think of something.'

'Why did she never tell me anything about you?'

He shrugged. 'I assume she wanted to put some distance between you and her past.'

'She was my heart. My black heart.' She wondered why she had said that, but it felt honest. 'Amy will take care of her estate. Amazingly, there was a will: Kitty wanted to start a foundation for young musicians. And I get the Seven Sisters house. I'll probably sell it. I can't bear this city, this country. I just need to get away. Marry me,' she said suddenly.

'What do you mean by that?'

'Well, exactly what I said. Marry me, then you can stay. I'm going to move away in any case. You can have the house, or move elsewhere; either way, you'll get leave to remain in this country. Then you'll be a free man.'

He lowered his head. She didn't know whether the offer had overwhelmed or frightened him.

'But don't expect me to become your best friend and go and visit her grave with you. I'd just be glad if I could help you in some way.'

He stared at his hands, apparently still not knowing how to react.

'You can think it all over. You've got my number. But don't take longer than a week. First, because I'm an old bat, and secondly, I don't want to put off my move for too long.'

She got up. Before she left the pub, he asked her where she was planning to go.

'Vienna,' she said.

At that, he told her that he would gratefully accept her offer.

★

Kostya holed himself up in the Green House. He sat in his study for hours, drank wine, stared goggle-eyed at the television, and started emitting tirades of abuse at the *Vremya* evening news once more. His compulsory retirement had cut him off from the outside world at a stroke. As if someone had clipped his wings, he had lost the will to live overnight.

At first, visitors still came to see him on a regular basis: colleagues and subordinates who worked for the MVD or the port customs authority. But these visits grew less and less frequent, and the tables laid for them by Nana and Stasia ever smaller.

Daria, on the other hand, was fêted. Her platform was no longer just the school and the playground; now the whole city admired her, and soon, perhaps, the whole country. Impossible, people said, not to like 'that damned pretty girl' from the film. People recognised her in the street, asked for autographs; directors phoned. Even the teachers — this time without Kostya's intervention — turned a blind eye when marking her work, so she didn't do at all badly in her school-leaving exams, although with all her public engagements she barely had any time for revision.

Daria was still part of family life in the Green House, but nothing there was the same as before, and both she and Kostya knew it, felt it, and were equally pained by it. Kostya hadn't been able to hold on to her. She had slipped away from him, achieved a success that he had not set in motion. This knowledge made the ground beneath his feet quake. This knowledge made his mind, which was already ailing, wander restlessly through the gloomiest and blackest of realms.

The more her relationship with Kostya hardened, though, the closer she and I became. We talked every day. I was inducted into her secrets, hugged, and pampered; she took me out with her; people admired me for being her sister; I was permitted to share in her fame.

For me, life in the Green House was becoming increasingly unbearable. I couldn't endure Kostya's disdain. Every day I expected him to lose control, to shout at me. I slept badly, crept around my own home on tiptoe. And I could no longer count on Stasia. She was too old, too fragile, and ever since her two dead visitors had become three, I knew that the unreality which had always existed for her had taken over. After Kitty's death — which no one ever told her about — there was no more Tchaikovsky and Mozart to be heard from the barn. And there were no more pupils, either. Within a short time, her body seemed to have lost all its strength. She complained constantly about her infirmity and often spent the whole day in bed. The garden, too, began to run wild. No matter how hard I tried to maintain order in her plant kingdom, this patch of earth now looked like a wilderness that suddenly refused to be tamed.

A few days after her eighteenth birthday, Daria got an offer from a Ukrainian director to play a role in a film that would be shot in Kiev. At first, she hesitated, unsure whether she would make it through six weeks alone in a foreign country, but when she heard that the lovely Lasha was going to be behind the camera, she immediately said yes.

I remained unconvinced by him. His self-satisfied smirk made it clear to others that he was aware of his superiority, his good looks. But no matter how often I tried to persuade Daria, my arguments failed to convince her, and I was powerless against the fact that she worshipped him. Her admiration may still have been a childish, naive crush, but soon, I suspected, she would want more.

And when Daria told me that she and Lasha were soulmates, and he would give anything just to be able to look at her for a single hour each day, I knew that the battle was lost. I wasn't skilled in matters of the heart. I never was, Brilka, and I'm still not, to this day.

I didn't want to make the same mistake twice and let Elene or someone else in on Daria's secret, but I had to stop her, protect her. I had a bad feeling about this; a very bad feeling.

One afternoon at the go-kart track, I took Miro aside and told him I needed his advice. I told him it was about a 'friend' and outlined Daria's situation to him. Miro gave me the impression that he was considerably more experienced in this sort of thing than I was.

By this time, the go-kart track in Mziuri Park had its own regular crowd of spectators. And they weren't just teenagers and schoolboys wanting to be part of the action. Grown men, petrol-heads and would-be racing drivers, swarmed around the track, staging races or betting on the victor.

They'd given me the nickname 'Einstein', and the name had spread so quickly that sometimes I myself forgot that I answered to another name elsewhere. Naturally I would have preferred another nickname: 'Bardot', for example, which was what they called a busty blonde who was always among the spectators; or 'Claudia', The Shark's brunette girlfriend who supposedly looked like Claudia Cardinale; or 'Alla', the girl they'd named after Russia's national singer Alla Pugacheva because of her funny poodle perm. 'Einstein' meant you were clever first and foremost, and although I was flattered by it, it meant first and foremost that no one would ever press his lips to mine as we danced to 'Take My Breath Away', wrapped in each other's arms.

'I think the guy's a bastard, and he either has to leave his wife or your friend should stop seeing him. It's that simple,' Miro pronounced, confident as always, after listening to my concerns. He scratched the back of his ear and turned his attention to the track, checking that everything was taking its usual course. What he had told me was in fact a simple, indisputable truth; but I doubted that these words, which I wanted to repeat to my sister with the same emphasis, would have the same enlightening effect on her as they did on me, or that they would get everything back on the rails.

'And what about you?' he suddenly asked me.

'What about me?'

'Do you have someone, too?'

'Are you taking the piss?'

That was the only answer I could think of. He didn't say anything, but I thought I saw a little smile flash at the corners of his mouth. And then he slid closer to me and hugged me tightly, something he often did. This time, though, the gesture felt unfamiliar, unexpected, and I tensed. I had always found physical intimacy difficult. And Miro was very physical. He was always there with a peck on the cheek or a smacking kiss, a hug or a shove, as if he needed this constant physical contact in order to be sure of himself.

'And you?' I whispered softly, without turning towards him, in the hope that he might not hear my question.

'Yes. There is someone.'

Of course. How stupid of me! In a split second I was plunged into misery. 'Who?'

'You.'

He fell silent and stared at the ground again. I couldn't believe it. I asked again, and he repeated that meagre 'you'. I looked at him and saw the boy who only revealed himself when we were left alone together: the boy whose eyes misted up when I read to him from the romantic novels he loved so much, though he would never admit it in front of his friends, the boy who didn't seem to care that I was a head shorter than him, too scrawny, too flat-chested, that I had bony knees and a long nose, that I had bluish circles under my eyes, that my hair could never be teased into a pretty bun or a symmetrical plait, that my eyes were so black you couldn't see the pupils in them. A boy who preferred me to all these Bardots and Claudias at the go-kart track.

'You and I are a good fit, though, don't you think?' He spoke the words very fast, as if he had a hot potato in his mouth or wanted to get the whole thing over with quickly. 'I'll love you forever.'

It sounded like a line from one of the many books and films I had read or watched. But you didn't usually find a line like that in good books and films. In good books and films people didn't say what they meant; they suffered, failed, and regretted. It was only in bad books and films that people said things like that, and there was no way I wanted us to be two characters from a bad book or film.

I stood there, rooted to the spot, incapable of saying anything in reply. He took my face in his trembling hands, looked at me, and gave me a kiss on the lips. I didn't know how to kiss, I didn't know how to be beautiful, I didn't know how to desire. I knew how other people did it — but I didn't yet have my own language for talking about my feelings. That didn't seem to bother him; he pressed his lips to mine a few more times before we were interrupted by The Shark calling for us, and Miro walked off, hesitantly, though also looking proud and content.

During my last year at school, I moved in permanently with Elene, in the city. I was surprised at how hard it was to turn my back on the Green House so definitively, only seeing Stasia at the weekends, missing Nana's pancakes and the *Illusioni* and *Animal World* programmes on television, as well as the garden, the freedom, the woods, and the whispering of the horses — the most constant music of my childhood — but I knew that otherwise the sepulchral mood would tip me into a deep black hole.

*

The same year I finished school, protests flared up once more in Czechoslovakia on the twenty-first anniversary of the Soviet invasion. A degree of unrest was felt in Georgia, too; new national demands were made and numerous discussion circles founded.

Georgian students were suddenly daring to write letters of protest to magazines. People started new clubs and accepted former dissidents as members. It was the year they started talking about an 'awakening'; the year Latsabidze's film *The Way* achieved cult status — after it had been screened at Cannes and awarded a special prize, and the filmmakers themselves had not been granted exit visas to attend. It was the year Madonna sang 'Like a Prayer'. The year Fred Lieblich finally moved to Vienna. The year terms like 'national interests' and 'territorial integrity' first started circulating. The year when clubs suddenly turned into political parties. It was the year Hungary opened its border with Austria and an uncontrollable flood of refugees from East Germany washed into the West. The year of mass demonstrations on both sides of the Berlin Wall. The year six communist dictatorships in Eastern Europe crumbled into dust, and Ceaușescu and his wife Elena were executed by his people.

The year people in my homeland began to discuss the 'Soviet occupation'.
The year the Berlin Wall fell.
The year of the first free elections in Georgia since 1921.
It was the year of the 9th of April in Tbilisi.

> The meeting that never took place
> Still sobs round the corner
>
> ANNA AKHMATOVA

There was a hunger strike outside the Central Committee's main building; the people's most important demand seemed to be a change to the constitution that would allow the SSR states to ask to leave the USSR. Tents were erected in the middle of Rustaveli Boulevard, an unheard-of, unprecedented occurrence.

The escalation in the clashes between the Communist and National Parties, and the constant unrest in the city, meant that school-leaving exams were brought forward to March.

School was finally over. At the leavers' ball, I sat on the steps of the great hall, smoked a cigarette, and waited for Miro, who was supposed to be coming to pick me up. For the first time in my life I was wearing a smart dress (I think it might have been the first time I'd worn a dress at all); it was one of Daria's that my mother had taken in for me, and I felt like a scarecrow.

I was planning to apply to the university's history faculty. Actually, though, I had no idea what to do with my life. I was interested in so many things that it was agony having to decide on a particular direction, and I would have liked just to carry on with things the way they were: with Miro and the other boys from Mziuri Park, holding our races, hanging around and living aimlessly, living in the moment.

Miro didn't know what he wanted, either. His mother was urging him to study architecture, as he was good at drawing, but he greeted her suggestions with cold indifference. Lana had tried everything she could to keep him away from the go-kart track, but in the end she had failed.

'And now?' Miro had arrived in a shabby denim jacket and white trousers, and sat down beside me on the steps. Loud music was coming from the hall, and everyone was dancing. I snuggled up to him. 'Don't you want to go in?'

'No.'

'Is there really no one in there you want to see, Einstein?'
'No. Now let's get out of here.'
'But you look interesting, in your dress.'
'Stop lying, I look stupid. But at least I've got it over with.'
'So where do you want to go?'
'Let's just go for a walk.'

And I slipped my arm through his and we went down the steps three at a time, putting our old life behind us as quickly as possible and careening into the new one.

On the river bank we saw the street lamps reflected in the river. We walked past brightly coloured houses, across the hill, past the sulphur baths, and carried on up the cobbled streets through the Armenian and the Jewish quarters which, people said, were growing emptier and emptier now that so many people were emigrating. We strolled into Lenin Square and both of us felt the strange silence there, the windswept disquiet, the unfamiliar darkness surrounding us. Although it was the weekend and not yet all that late, the streets were almost deserted. Most of the restaurants along the river promenade were closed. Most of the windows were shut. I pressed myself closer to him. Hardly anyone coming towards us. Hardly any cars passing by. Darkness, the dim light of the streetlamps, and a menacing silence.

Of course, we were too young for reality that night. Of course, dreams tasted better than the past and the future. Of course, hope was more attractive than the present. Of course, we were infatuated with each other and with revelling in our idea of love. Of course, we were the first and last lovers on the planet. Of course, the threat that hung in the air was a mere trifle compared to the turmoil we felt inside. Of course, that night we were wiser and more cunning than life itself.

★

The Abkhazians started demanding constitutional changes for the Abkhazian SSR, too. Among other things, they wanted to restore the 1921 constitution, which designated Abkhazia a republic of the Union rather than a constituent part of the Georgian republic. The Abkhazian elite were angered by the undertone of nationalism prevalent in the Georgian media at the time.

As I travelled around the city, I kept hearing people call out, 'Down with the Russian Empire!'

I spent the days that followed my leavers' ball in a delirium. I stopped going to the go-kart track and asked Miro to run my 'book' for me. I went to the Green House and shut myself up in the room that used to be mine and Daria's.

There was a Queen poster on the wall, which Daria had torn out of a foreign pop magazine. Our beds were perfectly made; Nana still kept the house in good order. I could hear the television in the living room; Kostya was sitting there, unshaven, in a stained dressing gown, and didn't even bother to greet me as I walked past him. Stasia was having problems with her blood pressure and spent a lot of time in bed.

It was rainy, cold, and damp. I wanted to cry. The room looked so deserted without Daria, without our shared past. I stretched out on the bed and stared at the ceiling. Nana had folded the clothes that Daria hadn't taken with her neatly and piled them on a chair. Everything was so clean and so tidy, and that made it so dead, and so much sadder. The life had gone out of the room, out of the whole house.

My brain felt sore. I was making no progress. I didn't know what to do with myself and my life. I could feel fissures and fractures around me; I sensed that the ground I trod on was made of glass; I wanted to do something, but I didn't know where to start. I was looking for a place where I belonged, and this house was no longer that place. I felt like a third wheel at Elene and Aleko's. Miro and I had nowhere to escape the watchful eye of Lana or Christine, and Mziuri Park, with the boys I called my friends, was starting to bore me. I felt as if I were made up of a random collection of clichés. My head was one big ragbag of uselessness and distraction.

'They'll shed blood yet, you'll see. Those pigs! Those Nazis! They'll trample the people underfoot! And this dunderheaded opportunist in charge of the CP is going to let them massacre us!'

Kostya was ranting in the living room again. I crept over to him cautiously and shifted uneasily from one foot to the other, hoping he would speak to me — but, as if I were one of Stasia's translucent ghosts, he didn't. On the screen I could see angry people talking to the camera, bellowing, spitting.

'What's happened?' I finally ventured to ask.

'Our Central Committee must have sent some kind of telegram to Moscow asking for help, because they can't handle the demonstrations here. They're panicking because of the nationalists and they're already showing that they're helpless and overwhelmed by the situation. And now, of course, Moscow will come marching in; finally they have a perfectly good, official reason to come and give us a good smack in the chops. And the Georgian Central Committee will come out of it looking good, because they won't be the ones who got their hands dirty and brought the wrath of the Russians down on their own people.'

'What does that mean?'

'Think about it! What's that prodigious brain of yours for, eh? You can still use it, can't you?'

'Will it —'

'Yes, if the government doesn't take the right steps, there will be bloodshed. They say, "Yes, but look at the Poles or the Czechs, look at the Baltic" — but they're too stupid to understand that we're not the Poles or the Baltic. *They're* practically in the West — they're just a stone's throw from West Germany or Finland — but we're here at the feet of the giant, miles away from anyone, and for all those years we enjoyed being the giant's favourite child. Now those idiots are saying they want to stand on their own two feet. But they've never stood on their own two feet. Not for two hundred years. And this gang of dissidents, people who've been shut out and spat on, who are trying to take advantage of all this — well, you've got all sorts in that mob: fanatical nationalists, the red intelligentsia, the esoteric fanatics, fatalistic mystics, criminals and cutthroats. A right old mixture. They're all looking for their pot of gold. But it was a good thing, it was a *good* thing that the giant was holding them in his fist.'

'But every person —'

'Every person, every person! Most people are bloodsuckers; they're like ticks. They want to do nothing and fill their bellies just the same. They don't want to work, but they want to be rich. Most of them want a roof over their heads, sausage in the fridge, a woman's warm arse in their bed to cuddle up to, and children who are no better than them.'

'And what do you want? What did you want for Elene? What do you want for Daria?'

Then he did look at me again, with that look that was reserved just for me. As if he despised and pitied me at the same time.

'You can't let it go, can you? Have you made it your life's work to make my life difficult?'

'I just want to understand you.'

'Ah, you want to understand me? If you'd understood me, you wouldn't have driven your sister to this disgrace, single-handedly sent her off into this depraved world. You would have made an effort at school and done well in your exams.' (How did he know about my poor grades?) 'If you'd understood me, you wouldn't have started hanging around with that Eristavi bastard, and

—' (How did he know about Miro and me?) 'And ... Oh, never mind.'

'All people are bastards to you. Everyone is weak and stupid. Everyone who doesn't live like you.'

'Be quiet. Watch television if you want to, and be grateful I still tolerate your presence here at all.'

'All those people out there want a different life; they want to be treated like human beings. All those students demonstrating and starving out there aren't going to be content with sausage in the fridge, a warm arse in bed, and holding their tongues about everything else. They want to decide for themselves what they have in the fridge, whose arse they have next to them, and what they think and say.'

'Well then, go out there, sit down and starve with them. You'll be a student yourself soon: be like them, and when someone points a Kalashnikov at you, don't say I didn't warn you.'

'A lot of Union republics have just been through all this, and so far —'

'None of those poxy Union republics is Georgia!' He sounded almost desperate.

I didn't know how to respond, and marched out of the room indignantly.

And Russia did come, first in the guise of General Kochetov, who was the representative of the Soviet defence minister at the time, and had previously served in the Caucasus. He hadn't even left the airport before he was asking the Georgian Communist Party representatives what the government was planning to do to normalise the situation. But this so-called government was already so divided, its members so at odds with each other, so disunited on what they wanted, that they just stood around looking bewildered and babbling vaguely. On April 5th, Daria returned from the shoot. Beaming, beautiful, her eyes sparkling. She brought presents and souvenirs for everyone. She was wearing a brown leather jacket, which made her look like a real film star and most certainly did not come from a Moscow department store. Elene, Aleko, and I went to pick her up. Several people stopped her on her way out and asked for her autograph. She handled the scene with impressive ease.

The lovely Lasha's wife was also waiting at the airport. She ran to him and covered him in kisses. I saw how Daria turned away from their meeting with raised eyebrows and put on her enchanting smile for us.

We wanted to go straight from the airport to the Green House together, to give Kostya, Nana, and Stasia a nice surprise. We bought fresh fruit and vegetables at the market, and meat to make shashlik, and drove out to the house.

Kostya's bottom lip began to tremble when he caught sight of Daria, and even though he tried to maintain the iron countenance of a man who would not be moved, he still folded her in his arms and hugged her with all his might. I could see that something in her had changed, something was happening to her. She chattered incessantly about the exciting shoot, the fantastic screenplay, her helpful colleagues, and despite her best efforts she couldn't stop herself mentioning Lasha, too. His name cropped up in every second sentence.

'Daria, please tell me it's not true. Please tell me you haven't got yourself involved with that conceited prig!' I whispered to her as we went into the kitchen to slice tomatoes for the salad.

'Yes!' she breathed, almost with relief. 'We're together. He loves me, and he's going to leave his wife.'

★

On 7 April, I went back to the city to meet Miro. We wanted to watch *The Evil Dead*; The Shark had got hold of a VHS copy and commended it to us as a real hair-raiser. When I met Miro at the bus stop, I could see the dejection on his face from a long way off. The Russians were on their way into the city, he told me in a whisper. Order was to be restored and the right to demonstrate and assemble might be revoked completely for weeks to come.

The Shark was ill, and cancelled our video evening. We wandered aimlessly around the streets. Miro suggested going to the park and taking a couple of karts round the track. I didn't want to drive, so we found a quiet spot and lay down in the cool grass. He spread his denim jacket out under my bottom. I'd brought *Moby-Dick* with me and I read to him for a while, but he seemed distracted and wasn't really listening. I, too, found it hard to concentrate. A lot of things were going through my head.

I ran my fingers through his hair. He stroked my belly. I knew he wanted to find something in my body that would indicate the future, but I denied him his wish. I knew he was mistaken; for today, at least, he was mistaken. Perhaps it would be different tomorrow. I wanted to spend always and forever in this twilight, in this silence, lying on the damp grass with him. But at the same time I couldn't suppress the turmoil inside me any longer. I ran my hand over the old edition of Melville and closed my eyes.

'I'm going to write, too. I'm going to write books,' I told him, expecting him to question me or at least express his surprise. But he didn't; he just nodded, as if he'd been expecting me to say those words all this time, and gave me a kiss.

'Yes, you should. You should do that — write books, I mean,' he said later, after he had walked me back to Elene's flat. 'I'll pick you up tomorrow evening,' he promised as he left.

When I phoned Christine's apartment on 8 April, nobody answered. Usually, Christine was always there. Miro didn't turn up. Aleko wasn't home. Mother said she was going to her tutorial and wouldn't be back until late. She told me to stay at home: unrest was expected.

But I went out all the same, and headed towards Rustaveli Boulevard. I saw countless people on the streets, and *militsiya* cars going by. At that point I didn't know that several divisions from Moscow and the Northern Caucasus had already arrived in Tbilisi. I didn't know there were tanks rolling into the city, or that the 345th Regiment was on its way to Georgia, the soldiers who would later be deployed as 'peacekeeping' troops in the Caucasian civil wars.

I didn't know that the nationalists, who by this point had been informed that the military was on its way, still weren't telling people to go home. On the contrary: the crowd was growing from one minute to the next; people were swarming like ants in the streets, the whole city seemed to be on its feet.

I managed to get to Vake on an over-crowded trolleybus, but I didn't find anyone at home. I spent several minutes knocking and ringing the bell. Then I walked back — there were no more trolleybuses. I called the Green House from a phone box. Stasia picked up.

'Sunshine, where are you? Are you all right? Kostya says things are probably going to escalate if they don't manage to send people home. Daria has gone into the city — we begged her to stay, but she was adamant that she was going to the demonstration with her friends. I hope you're at your mother's?'

'Friends' in this case was synonymous with the lovely Lasha. I hadn't had him down as a patriot.

'If Daria isn't home soon, Kostya's going to go into the city and look for her,' she told me. I heard her dry lips touch the end of a cigarette.

'It's all right, I'll find her, and we'll come home together tonight. We'll take a taxi. Tell Kostya to have some cash ready, I don't have much on me. And tell Mama that Daria and I are coming out to yours tonight, so that she doesn't worry.'

'Niza, wait, listen, where are you ...'

I hung up.

If Daria was already there, I could assume that Miro had gone to the demonstration as well. I started to walk quickly. I was walking alongside people waving the Georgian flag and shouting slogans. I didn't pay much attention to their words. It was dark, and the streetlights were on. Sweating, I left Rustaveli station behind me, ran past the Filmmakers' Union and on towards the Opera and the National Film School. I reached Qashveti Church, went through the underpass, caught sight of my school, and plunged into the crowd.

The secretary of the Georgian Central Committee appeared before the throng, supporting the Patriarch of the Georgian Orthodox Church. The Patriarch was supposed to tell people to return home, because the secretary knew that nobody would take any notice of what he said now. The nationalists called on the people to keep the peace, whatever that meant. I searched and searched. I called Daria's name, I called Miro's. I bumped into a few pupils from my school — the fact that so many young people were here came as a huge surprise to me.

'They came to me and told me to expect danger. We have only a matter of minutes to avert this danger ... Let us go into the Qashveti Church and pray,' said the Patriarch.

Why wasn't he telling people to go home, if the situation was really that serious? How was a church supposed to offer protection to so many people?

The Russian commander and his men were already on their way to the House of Government. And I went on looking for the people I loved. I was forced into the crush, people squeezed past me, and it took me forever to forge a path through the mass of demonstrators. Suddenly, I heard a murmur run through the crowd. I hopped up and down — I was too small, I couldn't see what was happening, all the heads, backs, and necks blocked my view — but then I heard a strange, dull, heavy sound followed by the noise of several engines. My ears were well-schooled when it came to engines, and I didn't need to crane my neck to know that a whole army of military vehicles was rolling towards us along the two parallel streets that passed the House of Government, followed by swamp-green tanks. I had never seen a tank before, and the sight — the crowd had begun to part — made me stop in my tracks, fascinated.

The panic that now broke out seemed to me like an uncontrollable virus, airborne and infecting everyone, but giving each of them different symptoms. It crippled me. I felt myself go cold, beads of cold sweat forming on my forehead. What was I doing here? What was I demonstrating for or against? What sort of country did I want to live in? I had never given these questions much thought before. Some of the demonstrators were running up the steps to the House of Government, others were falling back towards my old school, but the convoys were already there, no one could escape them.

I climbed onto a podium that had been constructed for the speeches, and from there up to the great pillars of the colonnade; then, suddenly, I saw her. I saw her standing in the front courtyard of the school, as if she had suddenly been abandoned by everyone on this planet, looking about her, helpless and confused.

'Christine!' I yelled at the top of my voice. But how was she supposed to hear me? Thousands of people were screaming and shouting to each other. Some were using megaphones. Luckily, I was able to keep sight of her. She stood there as if entranced, looking out for someone or something. At first I thought she had come because of Miro, and that gave me hope — it meant he was nearby, and I would find him — but when I looked closer it occurred to me that there was something very determined about the way she was standing there, straight and tall, as if she had her own aim, some purpose that had brought her here and which she was steadfastly pursuing.

She was wearing a tight, knee-length dress, which looked colourless in the bluish light of the streetlamps, and high heels. From a distance, she could have passed for thirty; you couldn't see her veil, just her coal-black hair contrasting sharply with the white of her face. Her posture was faultless, her shoulders straight, her lovely, slender ankles encased in sheer black stockings. She was wearing a little hat with a feather on it. I hurriedly climbed down again. Pushed people aside, barged my way through the panicking crowd. I snaked my way around hundreds of bodies, hiding behind them as I went. I tried to keep Christine in view; she mustn't get away, I had to reach her. I crept down the steps, made my way through a corridor of people, and left the grounds of the government building. Then I was able to run. I reached the comparatively empty playground in seconds. Its wide expanse offered little protection, so not many people had sought refuge there. Christine was standing in the middle of it, staring at something. By the time I reached the playground, the military had enclosed the whole avenue from all sides. There was no escape. Here and there, a few Georgian *militsiya* officers were dotted among the people, but they were completely overwhelmed, and instead of creating order, their frightening shouts were just driving people together even more.

Someone fell over in front of me, but I didn't stop; I kept running towards this woman who seemed to have stepped out of a different reality, and I fled towards this reality, because the one surrounding me was terrible and frightened me.

She suddenly turned, about to head towards the House of Government, and at that very moment I touched her shoulder. She gave a start, and immediately backed off a little, but then she recognised me and let out a sigh of relief.

And then it was my turn to stumble backwards. She really wasn't wearing a veil, and an awful, grotesque visage stared out at me from the left half of her face. I didn't know how I could bear it without showing my horror, so I looked at the ground. At that, she took a step forward and was about to walk away again when I called out: 'It's me, Christine — Niza! What are you doing here? We have to get out, we have to get out of here fast!'

My cry was hysterical. I didn't dare look at the street now. I could hear a sound that was muffled and at the same time very sharp, and I didn't want to turn around, didn't want to prepare myself for might happen next or was already happening. And she smiled. This smile was no less frightening to me than the massive military presence. I tried to concentrate on the right side of her face to stop myself from screaming. Then Christine turned to me and said, resolutely: 'We have to stop them. The Bolsheviks can't be allowed to march in here again. We have to stop the Red Army. Otherwise it'll start all over again, and *he*'ll come back. He'll take charge again, and Ramas —'

'Who? Who are you talking about? That's not the Red Army, Christine.'

She gave me a baffled look, then waved a hand in front of my face as if trying to dispel my doubts, and shook her head.

'You don't understand, little one ...'

'It's 1989, Christine.'

'But we have to stop them. Otherwise *he*'ll be back. And Ramas can't go through all that again. You have to tell your friends that they're coming back, and what that means; you have to explain to them that it's starting all over again. But you'll help me, won't you? You're a clever girl! I have to stop them. I never tried before. I have to try now. Do you understand?'

'Christine, you're confused, we have to get you home. Where's Miro?'

The yelling behind me was now deafeningly loud. I felt my knees go weak. I heard someone screaming that they had spades. I didn't understand what he meant. What spades? I had to get this confused woman out of here, to say nothing of myself. I took her by the elbow and pulled her after me. Without turning round, without looking towards the avenue, I made for the school building.

Of course: I should have thought of it earlier. The school! My old school — never in my wildest dreams could I have imagined being so pleased to see it. I just had to get inside the building somehow, and then out to the playground at the back — and from there we could get to the Mtatsminda, the Holy Mountain, and escape. The school doors were locked. The only option was to break a window on the ground floor, climb in, and open one of the doors from the inside for

Christine. She wouldn't be able to climb into the building in her current state. I could see a small group of people rushing into the front yard. I quickened my pace, but Christine was stubborn; she kept stopping, shouting, trying to make me stand still. I was pulling her by the arm with all my strength, but her feet kept turning over: her shoes weren't exactly designed for fleeing armed conflict.

She slipped away from me a number of times, and I had to stop, collect her, urge her on. The crowd was steadily growing around us, retreating, moving towards the school building, looking for an escape route. There were soldiers in the school grounds as well. They were running and shouting, holding their guns in front of them like shields. Suddenly I heard a dull thud and something sprayed across my cheek. Sickened, I looked around and saw a body slump to the ground. A soldier was hitting a young man with a spade, and he was doubled up with pain.

I wanted to vomit, but fear drove me on; I summoned all my strength, grabbed Christine, and dragged her after me. We managed to escape the crowd, which was rolling towards us like an unstoppable wave. There was no one outside the west wing of the school, though; no people or soldiers had reached the dark alleyway. I ducked down and made Christine take off her shoe, then smashed a windowpane with the heel.

'Wait here. I'll come and get you, okay?'

I yelled the words in her ear several times, then set about removing shards of glass from the frame. Christine, however, insisted on going back to the demonstration.

'Christine, it's not the Red Army,' I kept repeating.

'Of course it is, little one! Who else would it be? Of course it's the Bolsheviks!'

I couldn't waste any more time on pointless explanations. I pulled a big shard of glass out of the window frame, and it sliced into my thumb. I cried out. The blood ran down my hand. Christine stared at my wound in fascination before starting all over again:

'We have to do something. I've told Miqa we have to build barricades. He's here somewhere — I know him, he won't be able to sit still as long as I'm here.'

I heaved myself up onto the windowsill and got one leg through the window. I could do it. The opening might be large enough for me, but I would never get this confused old woman through it and into the school. How was I going to look for a door and at the same time make sure she stayed put and waited for me?

Once inside, I reached out to her, and suddenly she took my hand of her own accord. We stood there, holding hands, me inside and her outside, looking at each other. I looked her in the eye. I tried to imagine her face without the terrible chemical burns. To see how she had once looked. Before the Reds came. I impressed on her that she had to stay right there and not take a single step towards the main entrance, and suddenly her face lit up, as if something incredibly amusing had struck her, and she started to laugh. The carefree laugh of a child. I, meanwhile, was close to tears. I begged her; I told her again and again to calm down, to stay where she was, to stop laughing, but the more I tried to persuade her, the funnier she found it, and the louder and wilder her laughter became. Until, from one moment to the next, she calmed down and brought her face close to mine.

And then she told me the most macabre joke I have ever heard: macabre not because of its content, but because of the context. I was paralysed, powerless, fascinated by her madness, and I stayed at the window and listened. I will tell you this joke in the course of our story, Brilka, but not now. I can't tell it yet. That awful night isn't over yet. I'm still standing there, in that dark school corridor, not knowing how I'm going to manage to save my own life and at the same time preserve hers.

Because she was already victorious; she had outwitted time, separated herself from the laws of the world, but I have not. I still have to stick to the facts. To my memories, which are constantly playing nasty tricks on me. To the images that populate my head. I can't repeat it to you yet, but soon — soon I will. I promise you. Once I've reached you, once I've got past all the things that stopped me coming to you, then I'll do it.

When she had told her joke and made sure I had understood the punchline, she let go of my hand, whipped round, and before I could grab her dress or her arm through the opening, she ran off.

I tried to climb back out of the window, called her name over and over, but by the time I was halfway out again I could no longer see her and I knew it was pointless to go on looking. She had disappeared into the still-growing throng, become part of it, sunk into it, had sought and found refuge in the epicentre of the activity.

An animal sound, completely alien to me, escaped my throat. For a few moments, I stood frozen in the dark corridor, not knowing what to do. As I crouched on the cold floor of my school, trembling all over, I heard screams outside, bodies hitting the ground, people crying for help, and again and again the dull sound of spades hitting a body, a head, a life.

I was expecting shots to ring out at any second, but there were none. That made the whole thing even more unbearable: the fact that no shots had been fired left room for hope that we might get out of this alive, that we might escape this hell. Then I heard the strange word: 'Gas!' I couldn't make sense of it at first, until I realised it was tear gas being used on the crowd. I struggled to my feet and walked slowly down the unlit corridor, creeping through the ghostly darkness of the empty school building I had hated for so many years, and which now was saving me from the sight of things I couldn't bear. I climbed the stairs. My shoes made strange creaking sounds on the wood. Various poets and philosophers watched me from the walls, and in their midst was Uncle Lenin, beckoning to me still.

Suddenly, I started to run: of course, there was a telephone in the staffroom, I should call Mother, or ask Kostya for help, so someone would come and get me out of there. At the same time, though, I knew it was impossible. It didn't matter which member of my family it was, they would inevitably get caught up in this inhuman scenario. They would be threatened by spades and Kalashnikovs, tanks and gas. No, that was unthinkable. That option no longer existed.

I went upstairs to my former classroom, the door of which was open, and sat down at the desk that had had to withstand years of my hatred for the school and for my fellow pupils. Into which I had carved numerous words and pictures. Cries for help, threats. Even in the dark I could decipher them, and for some reason they pleased me. They seemed like a fixed point to cling to, a sign that the world as I had known it had once existed and wasn't just a product of my imagination. I clung to 'Lenin + Marx = bullshit', to, 'The maths teacher is a dork', and to '124 more days and I'm out of here'. I tried to recall the days and times when I had scratched these words into the solid wood of the desk. Some I could remember; others had vanished from my mind. I lay down on the bench, clutched it with both hands; I listened out for shots, or someone calling out the conclusive word 'dead', but I heard nothing. I could still hope.

I had lost all sense of time. I concentrated on my own heartbeat. I can't remember how long I lay there, waiting to be rescued or killed. Eventually, when the noise from outside was no longer quite so deafening, I got up and went back downstairs. I was surprised that nobody had hit on the idea of taking refuge in the school, and at the same time I felt guilty for not having thrown open the doors and beckoned people in.

I went to the back exit and rattled the door. It was locked from inside. I went to the toilets and found a window in the boys' that could be opened. Then

I looked out — the back of the school was deserted. I could just hear some shouting from a side street. It was only when I was outside again, standing on the asphalt, that I noticed: all this time I'd been holding something in the hand I hadn't cut, and my fingers were already cramped from gripping it. I looked down: it was Christine's plain black shoe. To this day, something about this image still makes me seize up with fright. I pressed the shoe to my chest and started sobbing, hard, and at the same time I set off, running. I climbed a fence, got past two military vehicles, and finally escaped, up through the windswept streets of the Holy Mountain.

It was only when I reached the hidden back alleys of Vera that I stood and caught my breath. I had run all the way there without stopping. I had fallen down, picked myself up, and carried on running. The hubbub and the screams had vanished. This sleepy old neighbourhood looked peaceful, as if a few kilometres away people weren't laying into other people with spades. The houses were sunk in a deep sleep. Out of breath, I sat down on the kerb. My home city had never seemed so big, and so lonely. And so divided.

With no strength left, I hammered on Christine's door. I can't remember how I got there; I just know that I avoided the main roads and kept walking, going slower and slower, but not stopping until I reached Christine's apartment. It was the first place I thought of going. In my state of mind at the time I doubt I could have had other, more altruistic, reasons; I doubt I was worrying about Christine's or Miro's wellbeing. I just didn't have the strength to walk any further.

*

Miro opened the door. He told me he'd been looking for me: they were all worried out of their minds, and Christine had disappeared without a trace. Elena and Aleko had been round. Everyone was half-dead with worry. When he noticed the blood on my clothes and face, he winced, but I let him know it was nothing serious with a little shake of my head — I didn't have the energy to do more than that. Luckily, I didn't need to ask him to call home, to give them the all clear, let them know I was still alive. 'What about Daria?' I asked. He reassured me that she had been on Rustaveli with the lovely Lasha in the early evening, but when the atmosphere got too tense for him he'd taken her back to the Green House, managing to leave just in time before things escalated. Without getting undressed or washing, I fell onto Miro's bed and was asleep in seconds.

It was already morning when I was woken by Miro's hand on my cheek. He had buttered some slices of bread for me and made tea, which he held under my nose. I sat up and fell on the food — I'd had no idea I was so hungry.

Lana was in Baku at a building design conference; she was calling regularly to check in. Elene would pick me up that afternoon, Miro told me cautiously. A state of emergency had been declared in the city and a curfew was in place.

Christine was still missing, and I told him about our encounter the previous night. I didn't mention her mental state, though: I didn't know how he would react. I needed to stick to the facts, to rock-solid facts, *normal* things, familiar things. The time. Miro's face. The smell of his bedsheets. The stains on my clothes. The eucalyptus on Miro's windowsill. The poster of the racing car on the wall. These were things I could comprehend, things I knew; they didn't overwhelm me. Everything else was too much, too huge, demanded too much strength from me.

Miro watched me open-mouthed, murmuring to himself, rather shyly, asking what exactly I was doing. But I didn't let him put me off as I carefully laid my clothes on the floor. Folded my shirt, my trousers. I didn't wear a bra; with my flat chest, it would have been completely pointless. Finally, I took off my knickers as well and walked past him, as God had made me, to the tiny shower cubicle in the bathroom, which was right beside the front door.

A few minutes later he came into the bathroom and stopped in front of the shower curtain.

I opened the curtain. I wanted him to look at me. I wanted him to see everything. Everything that had written itself onto my body the previous night, and for which I had no words.

I reached out to him as the hot, healing water rained down on me. He took my hand and stood there for a while, wordlessly, eyes on the floor, as if thinking about what to do next. Then he stuck his head into the shower and gave me a kiss. I put my arms round his neck and pulled him in.

Later, he carried me into his bedroom, wrapped in a towel and slung over his shoulder like a rolled-up carpet, threw me onto the unmade bed, and lay down beside me. We had already pulled off his wet clothes in the shower.

For the first time, we were naked. For the first time, I didn't care whether I was desirable or beautiful enough for him. For the first time, I wanted him to read my body like a story. I drew him down towards me. Folded him in my arms. His fingertips trembled, his lips were cold, his skin was rough and his muscles tense, his eyes shone. I could feel how reluctant, how unprepared he was to be with me like this, now of all times. Now, as our worlds were falling apart.

There, in his childhood bed, in Christine's abandoned apartment.

I clung to him, my heart racing. As my hands explored his belly, touched his nipples, brushed his Adam's apple, I could see the soldier swinging his spade, the body of the young man falling to the ground. I could see Christine's chemical burns as Miro smelled my skin and kissed my breasts, as he lifted me up and laid me on top of him, all the while looking at me and brushing my unruly, wet hair out of my face. And I thought I was back in the dark, empty corridor in my school, hearing the screams of the people outside, trampling each other and calling for help. I clung to him, as if his body could undo these images, these sounds. If I just held on tight enough, if I loved him fiercely enough, if I dug my knees into the mattress, put my hands on his chest to support myself, if I took him inside me, could I offer him a refuge, even though I hadn't managed to take Christine and all those other people into my hiding place?

I turned my head away, not wanting him to be infected with my images, because he was so close to me, closer than ever before.

My dirty denim jacket from the previous day was lying on the floor, and out of the pocket stuck the tip of Christine's black shoe.

> 72 years — on the road to nowhere!
>
> DEMONSTRATION PLACARD

The military took control of the whole city centre.

The search for Christine took a long time; it was only at the end of the following day that her body was identified in one of the city hospitals. The official cause of death was cardiac arrest. Engulfed by the crowd, she had fallen to the ground. Hadn't got up again. Unofficially, though, it was the return of the past and her inability to halt it.

The military's attack on the demonstration, which had seemed like an eternity to me, had apparently lasted just thirty minutes. Thirty minutes that had cost twenty-one people their lives, among them my great-great-aunt Christine. Thirty minutes, twenty-one dead, and hundreds injured. My family assumed that Christine had lost her veil in the mêlée, and I didn't disillusion them.

We were sitting in the cold hallway of the hospital basement, outside the pathology department. The waiting room was full. People sat there, some crying, others letting out a laugh of relief when the body was not that of the person they were looking for. Stasia went first; she went in alone. She didn't want any of us there. Kostya was sitting apart from us, at the other end of the room. When Stasia came back and nodded to us all, letting us know that it really was Christine, he just shook his head. Stasia's face gave nothing away: no horror, no pain, just a heavy emptiness. One hand was pressed to her side — she seemed to have an ache there.

★

Unfortunately, Kostya was right: nothing much changed after 9 April. There was a general sense of helplessness, and the population was split by the realisation of how powerless it was. One half felt spurred on to more radical action by the military's brutal attack; the other half felt resigned. Even the anticipated protests from the West against Gorbachev's bloodthirsty politics proved to be a false hope: everyone soon realised that the West wanted to go on seeing Gorbachev as a reformer and liberator. Even *Le Monde* described the events of 9 April as 'a Georgian coup, and an act of provocation'.

The First Secretary of the Georgian Communist Party was hastily voted out of office and Moscow's candidate, Shevardnadze, was placed at its head. When a Moscow news team asked him whether there was a general anti-Russian feeling in Georgia at the time, he replied: 'We have no evidence to support this conclusion.' Shevardnadze, the Soviet foreign minister and, at that moment, the most powerful Georgian in the Kremlin, flew to Tbilisi and spoke of a wound that should be healed as quickly as possible. The Red intelligentsia tried not to burn any more bridges with Moscow and started openly criticising the nationalists, calling them fanatics.

Kostya was to meddle in his beloved granddaughter's life one last time. He accosted the lovely Lasha on the street and issued him with an ultimatum: either he swiftly separate from his wife and marry Daria, if he couldn't leave her alone; or else he should see to it that within forty-eight hours he had not only vanished from her life, but preferably from the city as well. It was only when I discovered that the lovely Lasha came from a respected Tbilisi family of doctors, and that his grandfather had been a Party functionary, that I understood why Kostya had done it. He would never have looked favourably on the match otherwise.

And the unexpected actually happened: the following week, the lovely Lasha filed for divorce. The paperwork was rushed through, and everything was arranged for his civil wedding to Daria.

Now that nothing stood in the way of her marrying the man she had chosen, her happiness seemed complete. Daria was already talking about the challenge of juggling her career and married life, while Miro and I stumbled through those months with no orientation, searching for a foothold. We got into the works of Machiavelli, which were enjoying a resurgence in popularity at the time; we anaesthetised ourselves with kissing and sex and cheap schnapps; we accepted the constant clashes with Lana and Elene, who had now formed a close alliance based on the conviction that we were no good for each other; we hung around the now practically deserted go-kart track and tried to keep the dismal present at bay.

Miro had suddenly started dreaming of a career as a filmmaker (he wanted to finish what his father had started — though he had never used the word 'father' before in all the time I'd known him).

'You'll write, I'll direct. Isn't it a brilliant idea?'

'But I don't write.'

'No, but you will.'

'I don't know, Miro. I don't think I'm good enough.'

'Don't talk nonsense. You just have to do it. Just make a start.'

When I sat beside him, lay, laughed, or talked with him, I wasn't afraid of the aggressive voices on the radio or television. I had the confidence, the illusion, that no one could hurt us if we just stuck together. We were always able to comfort each other by making love. We perfected the art of banishing the images from our heads while clinging to one another like two wild little animals. We wanted to intoxicate each other, hold back tomorrow, and outwit the present. We made love in dark stairwells, at night, behind the go-kart track, on the back seats and bonnets of various cars, in his childhood bed when Lana was out, and once even in the attic of the Green House. When I slept with him, I was thoughtless, I was free. Freed from the crippling expectations I placed on myself; freed of my own inadequacies.

But as the end of May approached and Miro still hadn't submitted his application to the Film Institute, I pressed him to tell me why. For my part, I had finally started making a few sketches and notes to start work on my first novel. Irritated, he replied that he couldn't get the necessary documents together this year, and, for that reason, largely at his mother's behest, he had applied for the Polytechnic Institute, where he would sit the entrance exam for the engineering course.

What followed was our first argument, during which it became clear to me that Miro was a dreamer, someone for whom having dreams was more important than realising them, and that, by contrast, I was a person for whom the dreams stopped at the precise moment when you decided they were just dreams and entrusted them to a distant, uncertain future or the vagaries of fate. Unexpectedly, this insight gave me the strength to put my own doubts aside and start writing. I overcame my inhibitions, retreated to the Green House, and wrote like a woman possessed for a whole week. I wanted to tell my — our — story. But I didn't yet have a beginning or an end. I let myself be guided by disordered sentences and unfinished characters. I tried to sharpen my memory, to bring scenes and faces back to life. I wanted to prove to myself, but, above all, to Miro, that it could be done, that we could become what we wanted to become, slowly, one step at a time.

I sat in the attic and wrote until my fingers couldn't take any more. I used a thick leather-bound notebook that had been a present from David, and which I had saved for a special occasion.

★

Finally, Kostya got the wedding he had once wanted for his daughter. Finally, everything was going according to his plan; it was just his country that wasn't playing along any more.

Countless people were invited and came to the grand hall in Ortachala. Daria glittered and sparkled in her white dress. The managing director of the wine factory, the chief consultant in cardiac surgery, the singer (and recipient of the Order of Lenin), the former colleagues from the ministry, the trade union heads and the Komsomol leaders, along with numerous directors, actors, and musicians, all lent their lustre to the celebration. All the people to whom Kostya wanted to show what a pearl, what a rising star in the firmament of beauties he had raised. And even if his pearl had selected a very dubious line of work, even if the bridegroom was a few years older than her, they were still the model couple.

The celebratory mood also meant people could quickly and easily forget what was happening on the streets, the shaky footing on which this country stood, the country most of those present had served with unwavering loyalty all their lives. With a few glasses of the best Kakheti wine they could forget the fear in their bones. The fear of the day when the system would chew them up and spit them out. You could forget a lot on such an evening.

The images of Daria's wedding are so clear in my mind, Brilka, even now; it's as if I have a photo album in my head that I can leaf through at will. My sister's happy face, her shining eyes, the little bunch of white roses in her hand, the newlyweds' tentative kiss, her euphoria, the knowledge that she was indestructible, beautiful — and the arrogance inherent in such beauty.

And I often think, when I see these images in my mind's eye, of the moment I found Daria in the toilets, where she was reapplying her lipstick, and looked at her in the mirror. How she turned to me then and wrapped her arms around me. How she whispered in my ear that she loved me ('I love you so much, you little weirdo') and how she planted a red kiss on my cheek, which was sweaty from dancing with Miro. And how she then flew off like the wind and left me standing there, bewildered and overwhelmed; how I put my hand to my cheek to hold on to her kiss, in the hope its impression would stay there forever.

> The old clock keeps good time.
>
> JOSEPH BRODSKY

The following year, I took up my place in the history faculty at the university, and argued constantly with the professors and my fellow students. These long-winded debates wore me down. Final dissertations were often returned on the grounds that the work contained too much 'Soviet propaganda' and too little 'nationalism'.

Outside, tanks rolled past. There were curfews, and incessant demonstrations. Young men suddenly started carrying weapons in public. It was frightening how quickly we got used to this martial sight, as if it were the most normal thing in the world to walk around the city in broad daylight with a rifle over your shoulder.

One by one, the statues of our socialist fathers were torn down. The largest, the statue of Lenin on Lenin Square, was the last to fall, amid a bombardment of eggs and tomatoes.

I had to get used to endless walking: the streets were blocked by people's assemblies and rallies, and public transport was irregular.

The go-kart track was closed because The Shark and a few of the boys from his clique had joined the newly founded 'Mkhedrioni', a private army, and the others didn't have time to drive around for fun now, either — everyone wanted to help write his country's future! Now, with guns on their hips, they felt important, thought themselves untouchable, and met conspiratorially in the former Chess Palace to discuss the *new national values* and get drunk without anyone trying to stop them.

Daria and the lovely Lasha moved into a flat near Vake Park that his parents had bought for their son's second marriage. Daria's clothes had become strikingly fashionable, and now that she was married she was always busy. Since the wedding, she was like a different person. She seemed incredibly capable and was clearly making an effort to appear more grown-up and self-aware than she was. She accepted an offer to appear in a three-part historical television drama, this time in Leningrad. Lasha wasn't involved in the production, but he went with her anyway; they were away all summer.

And at the Green House, unimaginable things were happening. One Saturday morning, woken by the noise, I discovered workmen in overalls in the living room, packing up our three-piece suite under Nana's watchful eye. When I asked what was going to happen to our beautiful furniture — that was Kostya's favourite sofa, after all — Nana said she was afraid we could no longer afford to have favourite pieces of furniture. That evening, I went into the kitchen and put two hundred and thirty roubles on the table in front of Nana: all the money I had earned at the go-kart track, which I had been planning to use to finally get myself a pair of genuine Levis and a number of banned books. She looked taken aback, and refused to accept the money. Things weren't bad enough for us to start letting our children support us, she said. ('Give it to your mother instead.')

My mother was always complaining that people no longer had the money to give their children private tuition. She would shout at Aleko that she didn't know how she was supposed to earn anything now, and Aleko would take her in his arms and promise her it would be all right. I gave up my dream of genuine Levis and slipped the cash I'd saved up into my mother's bag. Instead of thanks, I earned a scolding, and had to give an account of where the money had come from. I was then told I had been wasting my time with the wrong friends. Once again, I ran out of the flat and slammed the door behind me.

In all this time, my longing to see David hadn't diminished in the least. Quite the opposite, in fact: it had transformed into a burning in my chest that made me think of him every day; and I realised that the burning wouldn't stop until I found a replacement for him. But there could only be one replacement: David himself. I had been over to his studio a few times, and hung around on the street in the hope that he might appear around a corner. Day by day, I ventured closer to the door of his apartment building, but for a long time I didn't dare ring the bell.

Then one afternoon, after a heated discussion with one of my professors that led nowhere, I couldn't stand it any longer and rang his doorbell. It was a while before I heard his footsteps. When he opened the door, he was holding a ruler. His glasses dangled on a chain against his chest; he seemed smaller than I remembered him, but his deep-set eyes were just as alert as they had been when I was lucky enough to enjoy his company twice a week. He studied me for a while, unsure who it was standing in front of him, and then his face lit up.

'Niza!' he murmured, and I saw his marsh-green eyes grow moist. I took a tentative step towards him, opened my arms, and wrapped them around him with all my strength. He let himself be hugged — stiffly at first, then relaxing and relenting in my arms. At that moment, I realised that we had never touched. It was thoughts and words that had made us close, and this intimacy didn't need to be proven by physical contact.

'I hoped you would come back one day,' he said, and, as usual, as if years had not passed since we'd last met, he started to heat up his samovar. The familiarity of the room took away all my fear and uncertainty.

I spoke in a chaotic flood of words; I couldn't stop. As if I had to vomit everything out. As usual he didn't interrupt; he listened with a look of concentration on his face and kept pouring us more tea.

'I feel like I'm suffocating — I want to do so much and I'm so inhibited. I'm constantly disappointing people. I try to do everything right, but I don't even know what right *is*. I don't know why I'm studying what I'm studying. The only thing I know is that I want to write and to be with Miro. But it's not enough. *I'm* not enough. Nothing is helping Miro to get on and do what he wants to do.'

Everything I had held back for so long had broken out of me in a torrent. David thought for a long time, with a searching look in his eyes.

'You can't live for anyone else, Niza, and nobody can live for you. And it would be terrible if you could. *You* become what *you* want to be, and leave other people alone.'

'But I don't know what I want to be, David, that's the thing!'

'Do what you're best at. I can't give you any answers. I never have answered a question for you. I always just listened and gave you time to find the answer for yourself.'

'Can I ... can I come and visit you?'

'I take it nobody else is going to come round and threaten to have me locked up?'

'I'm so ashamed. I hate my family. I hate *him*.'

'It's all right. It was nothing new for me. It just hurt to let you go. At the start of my career, I fell in love with a man, six years younger than me — he was my research assistant. I was married at the time and my wife was pregnant with our second son. Rumours started going around, and a colleague denounced me to the head of the institute. But that's all over now.'

'That shouldn't have happened to you.'

'You're old enough: come and visit me whenever you like. Besides, I can't infect you now; you already like men!'

We both laughed. A tortured laugh, perhaps, but one that made everything that had happened disappear.

'And if you don't know who you are, then look at all the possible versions of you, find the most impossible one, and become that,' he said, before giving me a goodbye hug. I walked home slowly, past the dwindling displays in the grocery shops, past the city's new pawnbrokers.

★

Daria was laying the table. Luckily her husband was in the next room, watching a Dinamo game. I hadn't visited my sister very often recently; the lovely Lasha never left her side, and he watched her like a guard dog. I don't think we'd had a single conversation since the wedding without him there.

Daria was rehearsing Katherine in *The Taming of the Shrew* at the Marjanishvili — to the great chagrin of her fellow students, as it was virtually impossible for a student to bag a leading role at such a renowned theatre.

The telephone rang. She disappeared from the kitchen for a moment. When she came back, she was followed by Lasha, whom I was no longer allowed to call 'the lovely Lasha' because it annoyed Daria.

'Who was that?' he asked.

'The assistant director. About rehearsals tomorrow. Please don't start this again,' she whispered, and turned her back to him. To my disappointment, however, he still sat down at the table with us.

'And what did he want from you?'

'What do you think he wanted? I've already told you: he wanted to discuss the timing of the rehearsals.'

'What is there to discuss?'

'Please, Lasha. Niza and I wanted a moment to ourselves ...'

'Perhaps he wanted to discuss how low your neckline should be?'

'Seriously, Lasha, you're being paranoid!'

'Oh, I'm paranoid, am I?'

'Hey, what's that supposed to mean?' I intervened.

'What does it mean? That's exactly what I'm asking your sister, but she hasn't given me an answer. I left my wife for her — and my wife idolised me! Idolised! And where's my thanks? She flirts with all these losers, she's forever wiggling her backside at them, and she thinks I'm an idiot.'

Suddenly I heard something shatter. Daria had broken a plate in the sink.

She whirled round, her face streaming with tears.

'Why are you doing this to me? She's my little sister. Why are you doing this to me now? I can't go on like this. I don't understand what's happened to you. Why you do this to me. You were never like this before, you weren't like this, I know it.'

'I'm doing it to you, am I? To you? I'm not doing anything to you! I just want a decent wife by my side. You only got where you are now because I shot you from the right angle. And now you're playing the big star and I'm not good enough for you any more, huh? You think you're better than me now because you get offers of work and I'm sitting around here unemployed? Do you know all the things I've done, all the people I've worked with, you ungrateful slut!'

That was too much for me. I leaped up and shouted at him to shut his filthy mouth.

Daria tried to come between us, clearly ashamed in front of me, and he snorted disdainfully, shouted something insulting in my face and left the kitchen.

*

Three days later, I intercepted Daria as she was leaving her rehearsal, and forced her to go for a walk with me.

'What's going on?'

'Not you, too, Niza. I'll deal with it. He's just a bit jealous,' she said in a subdued murmur, and stared rummaging for something in her bag.

'A bit jealous? He called you an ungrateful slut — sorry, but —'

'He's a man; it's hard for him to deal with this whole situation. Plus he has hardly any offers of work. The broadcasters are only interested in politics now; the film subsidies have been cut. We're thinking about going to Russia. He has good contacts there. I love him, I love Lasha, and I don't want him to feel like this because of me.'

'Are you kidding? So now it's your fault that he's being an arsehole as well?'

'No, I don't mean it like that, but it's difficult for him. I worry about him.'

'Maybe you should be worrying about yourself.'

'I do. But this is between me and him, Niza. I don't expect you to understand, but please be charitable, okay? And I don't want Mama or Kostya to hear about it. He just lost his temper and —'

'Lost his temper. Seems like he loses his temper quite a lot.'

'I'm not a maximalist like you, Niza.'

'Maximalist? What are you talking about? It's completely normal to object to being called a slut, especially when you're practically drooling over the guy doing the name-calling.'

'You're a fine one to tell me what's normal.'

'Don't start that again. Not like this. We've put all that behind us.'

'Just take a look at yourself before you start hauling me over the coals. What kind of life are you living? What are you doing with all your talent? You're always hanging around with those losers; you don't even have any female friends. That's not normal. A girl needs female friends.'

'I thought *you* were my friend.'

She didn't seem to have been expecting this response — her expression changed suddenly, she took a step towards me, and something like guilt flashed in her brown eye.

'But I'm your sister, Niza,' she said softly.

'Yes, it sounds like you're *just* my sister,' I replied, turned and ran off. From one second to the next it had begun to pour with rain.

> 'Her silence flouts me, and I'll be revenged!'
>
> THE TAMING OF THE SHREW

'God, this whole thing is some kind of nationwide psychosis!' Miro slapped his hand against his forehead. Neither of us could tear our eyes away from the television screen. The Russian hypnotist and miracle healer Kashpirovsky, who had been performing mass hypnosis on television for quite some time, leading his huge audience into delusion and stupidity, had come to our city. In Tbilisi, too, thousands of people had made the pilgrimage to the Philharmonic Hall where he was doing his show, hoping to be healed. Outside the Philharmonic Hall, a little band of upright citizens was holding a pathetic demonstration, their placards warning of 'Satanism'; telling people to save their souls and leave the 'heretical show' post-haste. But that didn't seem to bother the 'devil worshippers' as crowds of them streamed into the hall. Many fell into ecstatic swoons or burst into tears, gasping for air and struggling for words.

Lana was on another of her trips, and Miro and I shut ourselves up in his room for hours.

'So we're on the verge of economic collapse; in a month or two there will be a hundred parties fighting for power; the National Movement has fallen out with just about everyone and they're starting to tear each other apart; the communists are trying to save their arses; the Mkhedrioni Army is bullying the population; the Abkhazians and Ossetians are clamouring for autonomy; there are warnings of impending inflation, and what do we do? We invite a hypnotist over from Russia to "heal" everyone?'

I doubled up with laughter, then leaped off the bed and ran around his room, laughing hysterically and taking my clothes off as I went, while in the background Kashpirovsky drove the demons out of the Georgian people, until Miro finally caught me, threw me onto the bed, and landed heavily beside me. At times like these, the world and all its miracle healers, reformers, nationalists, and fanatics could go hang as far as we were concerned.

★

In March 1990, the law of 'national sovereignty' was passed. Other Union republics followed Georgia's example, and even if that didn't mean then that they would leave the USSR, everyone knew that sooner or later that was what would happen. After the fall of the Berlin Wall, the political situation had changed across the world. Gorbachev — however friendly he appeared to the West — reacted harshly and imposed economic sanctions on all Union republics that had claimed national sovereignty; but against all of them together, including those that followed, he was powerless. He couldn't employ the same punitive measures on all fronts; it would be too dangerous for Russia. And so this development was interpreted and accepted as an unpleasant but unavoidable consequence of his great reforms.

In Georgia, a party other than the Communist Party won an election for the first time since 1921. The 'Round Table–Free Georgia' nationalist union came to power, under the leadership of writer's son and former dissident Gamsakhurdia.

When I asked Aleko what sort of person he was, and why he always spoke like a man possessed, as if someone were after him or he was afraid he wouldn't be able to finish expressing his thoughts, he summarised in a resigned tone: 'Well, yes, maybe he really is scared someone's going to cut him off. Even as a schoolboy, he was arrested for anti-communist activities. Then later he had to spend two years in exile for founding the "Action Group for the Defence of Human Rights". But this is the first time anyone's really listened to him, so he has to roar like a lion to get everything out that he wasn't allowed to say for all those years. Actually, though, they say he has a penchant for mysticism, for this — what's it called again, some kind of new religion or something, it's all the rage at the moment: anthro ... something. In any case, esotericism and politics, it's a terrible combination. And I'm telling you, the people who are left over, who didn't get into Gamsakhurdia's party, the nationalists and the camp followers he didn't choose as friends, the people he left behind and didn't offer high positions to — they'll band together, even if they all hate each other, and they'll wage war on him,' He started to leaf through the daily paper, the front page of which carried a picture of a demonstration, as usual. I was too lazy to ask what they were demonstrating about this time.

★

Miro had always found it easy to distract himself. I, on the other hand, was increasingly beset by doubt when I was left alone: how were we ever supposed to find a way back out of this chaos? Where should we go? Where were you even supposed to begin? And what sort of life would it be then? Or should I somehow do it myself and not place any expectations on him, as David had advised me — should I start with myself? But how? How could I expect *nothing* from him? When you loved someone — you *had* to expect something, didn't you?

Unfortunately, I wasn't a book that I could read and understand. I could only understand by *experiencing* myself, by living, and life always seemed to be one step ahead of me, as though I would never be able to catch up with it. Eventually, this contradiction was carried over into my relationship with Miro. More and more often he seemed annoyed, left me waiting, turned up with his boys without telling me in advance, was out of sorts and difficult to satisfy, and accused me of controlling him. I felt shabby, sure that a lot of the brittle emotions that left me feeling helpless didn't have much to do with him at all, that they were caused by my own inadequacy. I was jealous of the new friends he was making at university. The thing I had so loved about him I now hated with a passion. I couldn't bear it when he clowned around in front of his new friends and played the entertainer at every party and get-together.

I was also disconcerted by the fact that he had suddenly started to think his degree wasn't all that bad. He had told me he was made for something else, and now he seemed content with the meagre prospects afforded by his institute. I was afraid I would come to despise him, and then myself as well, now that he suddenly appeared so conformist, so comfortable, and so conciliatory. Now that he had suddenly started to dismiss art as the luxury of our age. To accuse me of being gloomy, depressing, unkind, even argumentative.

The more our words failed, the more misunderstandings they caused, the better our bodies spoke to each other at night. As if they were glad that our thoughts, our feelings were playing tricks on us. But by day we began to argue: first a little, then constantly. I told him that the life he was always talking about wasn't just going to fall into his lap. He said defensively that he wasn't prepared to do the things my *complicated little head* thought up. I said I was reclaiming a life that had meaning. He retorted that the two of us, our relationship, was meaning enough for him. I was focusing on things that lay outside this blissful, all-healing love.

There were days when more than anything else I wished I were normal and wanted the things that most people my age wanted. When I wished I could wake up with an unconditional Yes inside me, shout it out, run to Miro, tell him we should go to the registry office and get an official stamp on our love and an official bed. Days when I wanted to prove to everyone around me that I wasn't as complicated as people told me I was; that I wanted the same things as other people. A little rented flat with an old gas cooker, baking an apple cake in the oven, a washing line strung across the living room with Miro's underwear hung out to dry. No: I would inevitably start hating him, punishing him for not daring to do things with me, for the fact that we hadn't overcome our fears and limitations, that we had remained prisoners of ourselves. I'd accuse him of stopping me from becoming what I might have become.

★

Even as she opened the door to me, I knew I would take revenge on him. And in a strange way, the realisation pleased me.

Her institute had called. She hadn't turned up there for weeks and they couldn't get hold of her by phone. Elene had asked me to look in on Daria; she suspected her daughter was in bed with the flu. I already suspected something quite different, but I didn't want to worry Mother.

'What happened?' I asked, getting straight to the point.

'I got a cold, and —'

'Am I not even allowed to come in? Do we have to stand around out here?'

'Listen, I don't want you to catch my cold, and anyway, he's asleep, and —'

'Oh, the *pasha* is asleep. Of course, we mustn't disturb his rest. Pardon me, I forgot.'

'Niza, don't start.'

I put my foot in the door and pushed past her into the flat. As she shrank back I saw the violet bloom below her left eye, and then her swollen lower lip. I didn't know whether it was disgust or pity I was feeling.

'Daria! I don't believe this ...'

She tried to hold me back, but I ran into the bedroom where Lasha was lying on his back, fully clothed and snoring. I pounced, straddled him, and before he could wake up and defend himself, I had already punched him in the stomach. He howled with pain, grabbed me, and hurled me off the bed.

Daria screamed, but everything was happening so quickly and I was in such a rage that I snatched up the nearest chair and began waving it around, while my brother-in-law struggled to his feet and came towards me, roaring. I swung the chair back and cracked him on the knee with it before he could get out of the way. The roar turned into a pitiful whine.

Before I could say anything, Daria grabbed me from behind with both arms and dragged me, together with the chair, which I refused to put down, out into the hall.

'Have you completely lost your mind?' she hissed at me.

'And now you're going to tell me he really loves you, and jealousy just made his hand slip. How are you meant to go on stage with a face like a boxer?'

'He's not doing so well.'

'What about you? How are you doing?'

'I told you not to get involved! Just stay out of it!'

I dropped the chair and staggered back a little way.

'Daria, Daro ... What on earth is wrong with you?'

She jerked her head towards the door, and as I slowly and reluctantly shuffled out into the stairwell, she slammed it in my face.

★

Over the next three days, I called her repeatedly; the telephone rang at least a hundred times in her flat, but no one picked up. Then I decided to go to The Shark. I marched right into the Chess Palace, where they still had their headquarters, and asked for him. The uniformed, armed Mkhedrioni soldiers at the entrance glanced at me with disdain and giggled like two schoolgirls, but at least they didn't send me away. One of them backed slowly into the building, keeping his eyes on me, while the other blew gum bubbles in my face. A few minutes later, the first soldier came back, this time at a brisk pace — the silly grin had vanished, too — and told me to follow him inside.

In a smoke-filled backroom that smelled of alcohol, I found The Shark sitting with two other uniformed soldiers, cleaning his gun. I had never seen a rifle up close before, and my eyes were drawn to it in fascination. The Shark jumped up and wrapped his huge paws around me, lifting me up with a laugh.

'Our Einstein is here! Hey, you morons, this girl's got more brains than all of you put together! Come and meet her! She's got guts, I tell you! And whenever she comes here, you treat her like a lady, okay?' he called out.

The men glanced over at me with a degree of respect in their eyes.

'So, what's up, kiddo? How's our little friend Miro?'

'He's fine. He's not the reason I'm here. I need your help.'

I looked over hesitantly at the two soldiers.

'Don't worry, Einstein, go ahead, these guys are my brothers. So, who's been stupid enough to mess with you?' The Shark laughed, showing me to a chair.

'Not me. It's my sister.'

'Oh, man, she's hot. She's so hot — I just saw her on television and ... Hey, you guys, do you know who her sister is? You're not going to believe this: Daria Jashi! Isn't that amazing? So what's wrong, Einstein?'

I gave him a brief outline of the problem.

'He's a total mug if he's screwed things up with that angel. You'd have to be an idiot not to pander to every whim of a woman like that.'

The two others nodded in agreement.

'Will you help me?'

'Of course. You're like a little sister to me. We've been through a lot together, haven't we?'

★

Two days later, The Shark and his friends accosted Lasha outside the door of his apartment block and 'had a chat' with him. He sustained two broken ribs and a concussion, and ended up in hospital, where his doctor parents looked after him. Daria confronted me. One of the neighbours had recognised The Shark, which was how she had made the connection with me. She was not very understanding of my sisterly attempt to help. She screamed at me hysterically; full of hatred, and with a little *schadenfreude*, too, she told me she loved him more than anything else in the world and there was nothing I could do to change that. She would keep her mouth shut this time, because she was ashamed for me — ashamed that I, her little sister, was capable of something so awful — but if I or any of my criminal friends ever thought about doing anything to her husband again, there would be dire consequences for me. She added that she was glad to be moving out of this 'bloody country full of peasants and criminals' as soon as Lasha was out of hospital.

'Where are you going?' I murmured, avoiding her gaze.

'To Moscow. A month from now we'll be out of this hole. Lasha's best friend is building up his own *business*,' — she said the word in English — 'and —'

'He's building what?'

'Learn some English!' she snarled. 'They're going to start their own *business* and earn a lot of money, and then Lasha can decide which films he wants to work on and which he doesn't, and we'll be off out of this shitty country. To a place where people won't beat him up on his own doorstep in broad daylight!'

'And what about your studies?'

'I can finish my degree in Moscow and act there! Everything is so backward here, anyway. People here don't even know the meaning of the word *professional*.'

'He's hit you once, and he'll do it again!'

'You're not God, Niza. When are you going to understand that?'

'What's this got to do with God?'

'You try to control everything, but that's not how things work. It's my life and I'll live it how I want, with whomever I want.'

★

The first free presidential elections in Russian history took place in June 1991. Daria moved to Moscow with her lovely Lasha, and Kostya was surprisingly acquiescent; he still believed that *over there* all was not yet lost, whereas our country had been sliding towards the abyss for a long time.

Lasha's parents had advanced him some start-up capital so he could buy into his friend's *business* — something to do with banking and loans or credit or something like that, as Daria vaguely described it shortly before they left. What she didn't tell us at that dinner was that she had also contributed some jewellery from her dowry.

★

Georgia declared its independence and reinstated the old constitution of 1918. The Georgian flag flew over the House of Government — newly renamed the Parliament Building — and we got a new national anthem of our own. So now we were free, though no one really seemed to know what 'freedom' meant. The peace lasted just six months, then demonstrations, riots, political tensions, and heated debates in parliament finally culminated in a coup against Gamsakhurdia, led by the National Guard and the Mkhedrioni Army. Attacks on party offices, shootings in the street, break-ins, beatings, injuries, arrests, yelling in parliament, yes, yelling everywhere, wild insults, aggression, and finally bankruptcy were everyday occurrences.

During that time, everything of value disappeared from the Green House: the beautiful furniture, the porcelain vases and mother-of-pearl caskets, all the silver cutlery, Nana's jewellery and even her tea set collection. All the German, Czech, and Chinese tea sets assembled with such love and effort found their way out of the cabinet in the living room and onto the black market on the 'Dry Bridge'.

All non-Georgian ethnicities are multiplying here at a catastrophic speed.

ZVIAD GAMSAKHURDIA

'This is all taking on a shape strongly reminiscent of a dictatorship ... I am resigning. Let it be my contribution — my protest, if you will — against the coming dictatorship.' So said the Soviet foreign minister, our countryman Shevardnadze, as he left his position. Gorbachev, he claimed, was supporting the protests by Ossetian and Abkhazian separatists, who were complaining about Gamsakhurdia's strict nationalist policies, portraying themselves as victims of these policies, and heightening the anti-Georgian feeling already prevalent in the Russian media.

As Gorbachev was booed at the May parade outside the Kremlin, Kostya, wearing his obligatory towelling dressing-gown and baggy pyjamas, stared glassy-eyed at the television screen, shaking his head like a nodding dog.

'It's official: his reforms have made him the biggest laughing stock in Soviet history. My hearty congratulations!'

As he stirred his tea, I realised that recently his hands had started to shake.

'And he claims to be a *humanist*? Him? That's a joke! The man who allowed these bloodbaths to take place in Tbilisi and Baku? But why am I complaining about him when we have our own little fascist right here: Gamsakhurdia,' he grumbled to himself.

I had taken up residence in the Green House again for a few weeks; more and more of my lectures were being cancelled, and I had decided to devote more time to my writing. To talk to Stasia, check on a few facts from her stories. I had borrowed a stack of books about the revolutionary period from the university library and set out to work my way through them. It was painfully obvious now that things were missing; that there was so much we lacked. It wasn't just the furniture and the vases, it was something else, something bigger, that we had all mislaid, and which, at the time, I was unable to put into words.

When I discovered that Kostya had even sold his greatest treasure, the

GAZ-13, the extent of our privations finally became clear to me. We couldn't keep acting as though nothing had changed. I was saddened by the fact that Kostya and Nana accepted the small amount of money Daria sent them from Moscow every few weeks. At the same time, I knew it would only make everything worse if we admitted that, like ninety per cent of the Georgian population, we were facing total bankruptcy. We had to preserve the illusion that everything was as it used to be and keep going about our day-to-day business, so that the ground didn't completely open up beneath our feet. Because we already knew how unstable this ground was. Pensions arrived late or not at all, and they didn't stretch nearly far enough. Elene's earnings were irregular. The fruit and vegetables from our garden were a blessing for us; food shortages and the other constrictions of daily life were not felt as harshly in the countryside as they were in the city.

When Elene was paid, in order to avoid any long discussions with me, or hurting my pride, she would tuck a few notes into my coat pocket. They would last me a while, for trolleybus or metro tickets.

Lana's building institute fell victim to the cuts and was closed down. Miro was forced to look for a job, which was anything but easy in those days. As he was good with cars, he started helping out in a garage run by a friend's father, who tuned up car engines to make them perform better. Most of the garage's customers were Mkhedrionists, the only people at that time who could still afford such luxuries. People in uniform and men with guns met in the backroom of this garage, where they waited for their cars to be brought up to the desired horsepower and passed the time playing cards.

I often visited Miro there, so I had plenty of opportunities to watch them. The games fascinated me, and gradually I started to understand the tactics they used, and when it was sensible to fold. Above all, I was fascinated by the sums of money that changed hands. One day, one of the men in uniform asked me if I played poker; they were a player short. I knew the rules from Aleko and his friends, but had little experience myself. When I saw the heap of notes on the little wooden crate that served as their card table, I told them I was a good poker player. I won the very first hand (which to this day I believe was pure luck, and nothing to do with my own abilities) and left the garage with a few notes in my pocket.

Back home, I made Aleko sit down with me and spend a whole night teaching me the tricks and subtleties of poker playing. This was draw poker, and Aleko and his friends usually played five-card stud, so he had to get himself up to speed as well, and called a friend who explained the details to him over the phone. He sat there on the phone like a schoolboy, with a pen, writing in an old exercise book.

'Why are you so desperate to know all this?' he asked, a little suspicious of my sudden enthusiasm for the game. 'I hope you're not planning to do anything illegal?'

'I'm playing with some guys from university for a few kopeks.'

'I know how obsessed you get with games, and I'd advise you to be careful. I'm all too aware of how addictive these things can be, so just make sure you don't get in over your head. And not a word to your mother!'

'Not a word, I promise!'

And I gave him a big kiss on his stubbly cheek.

Over the weeks that followed, I was able to demonstrate what I'd learned. I went to the garage, withdrew to the back room with the Mkhedrionists, and played for all I was worth. My poverty and my absolute will to win spurred me on to incredible audacity; I bluffed and took huge risks. I'd lied to them, claiming my father had been a professional player (and had therefore spent a fair amount of time behind bars, which was actually the truth). And once they had convinced themselves of my loyalty, they started inviting me back to their headquarters, where they drank their home-brew and played with greater obsession and fewer inhibitions.

Poker took me to a huge variety of places: former factory buildings, empty schools, and abandoned printing works, filled with bored, mainly drunk Mkhedrionists, oblivious to their surroundings as they played. (They all considered themselves nationalists, so they drank *chacha* and not vodka during these binges, to rule out any sympathy for Russia from the start.) I remained calm and collected, played my cards close to my chest (literally), and soon acquired something of a reputation. And, as I was aware of the fragility of a player's luck, I tried to bid high as long as Fate was on my side. Driven by my ambition, I played every hand, and frequently left the table with my pockets full. On my way back, I would think about who I could slip the money to at home, the food shopping I could do, and to whom I could bring a little joy with it.

Miro very quickly got wind of my activities, which were officially strictly illegal, and made a scene, saying it was dangerous to have anything to do with these cutthroats. But I stood my ground and told him there was nothing dangerous about it; I was just on an incredible winning streak that I wanted to exploit to the full. For a few days after the argument we weren't on speaking terms, but I was sure he, too, would soon see the advantages of my new 'work'.

They tolerated me because I proved myself equal to them as a player, and above all because I was a woman and they thought I posed no threat. But after I had scored a few wins, a man I had never seen before turned up at the old print works one afternoon, took three bottles of *chacha* out of a plastic bag, and set them down on the card table. He greeted everyone individually with a military handshake and was enthusiastically welcomed. Last of all, he came up to me, gave me his hand, and said, with a roguish expression on his face, 'So you're the legendary Einstein everyone's been telling me about. Well then, let's see just how smart you are.'

I wanted to crawl off into a corner. One thing was clear: the other players had set me up. This guy may have been small — only a little taller than me, and gangly in a way that made his uniform hang off him, but he had a large tattoo on his neck (a tiger, winding itself round his throat), a shaved head that gave him a brutish aspect, and under his camouflage shirt his arms were muscular. The most striking thing about him, however, was a scar that split his right eyebrow in two. I disliked him on sight. Unlike most of the other players, who had probably joined the Mkhedrioni out of an excess of pent-up energy and a lack of other prospects, there was something fanatical about him, as if he had given over his whole life to the pursuit of a rock-solid conviction.

He was nervous; he cracked his knuckles, scratched his hairless head, or chewed on a match. His Makarov (I could now tell one make of gun from another) was always at his side, and the pistol on his belt made me feel uneasy.

So this was the man I was to play: Cello. He was really good. He was a brilliant manipulator, and that only increased my sense of unease. He looked like he wasn't a good loser — a fact that might cause me problems — but it was too late to pull out. He won the first round, but in the second I had a wonderful hand and won by a mile; in the third, a split pot eventually went my way. He congratulated me with an extravagant high-five and called out to the group, 'Well then, lads, you weren't exaggerating. It's nice to play someone who's my equal!'

We received an enthusiastic round of applause.

★

For a while, I regained a degree of inner stability. My writing gave me a clear structure to my day, and the guilt I felt about living at my family's expense was eased by my poker winnings (although since that afternoon I had been a little more circumspect with my visits). I even felt something like self-satisfaction. As inflation was now in full swing, the Georgian coupon, the transition currency, was worth nothing. The Mkhedrionists had switched to dollars — God knows where they got them. Little by little, I amassed the incredible sum of two hundred and fifty dollars. I meant to spend it on a used car to make Kostya, who was stuck in his Green House, mobile again. Miro helped me with the purchase, and I become the proud owner of a black Zhiguli. I drove up to the Green House, grinning from ear to ear, and enticed Kostya out of his lethargy and into the driveway by sounding the horn loudly.

'What on earth are you doing?' he snapped at me.

'*Voilà*: it's a present for you!' I announced, pointing to the car.

'You don't have a driving licence — you can't drive a car! How did you get here?' He still didn't seem to understand.

'I can drive perfectly well; Aleko taught me. But that's not the point. This is a present for you. It's not a beautiful Chaika, but it'll get you into town.'

'You always were good at surprises, I'll give you that. And what would you do if the *militsiya* stopped you?'

'The *militsiya* is called the police now, and I'd slip them a hundred-thousand coupon, and it would be fine.'

'How many roubles is that?'

'At the current rate of inflation, about three.'

'That's how much they're fining people now for traffic offences?'

'It's not a traffic offence, Kostya.'

'What is it then, driving around without a licence and putting other people in danger? In Moscow they would never —'

'Ask Daria, when you speak to her: apparently in Moscow the police turn a blind eye to much worse things if you show them a few notes. But don't you even want to take a look at my present?'

'Where did you get the money?'

'I saved it up. I got a bursary,' I lied.

He was still keeping his distance and eyeing me and the car with a mixture of uncertainty and interest, which he was trying hide under a cloak of severity.

'Well then, let's see if you really can handle a car.'

'And how shall I prove that to you?'

'Drive me into town.'

'You really want me to drive you?'

'Yes.'

I waited ten minutes while he got changed, then we took the Zhiguli into the city. On the drive, we heard on the radio that South Ossetia, too, had declared its autonomy. Kostya stared out of the window all the way, as if seeing the roads for the first time.

'So, where are we going?' I asked.

'To Vera cemetery.'

I didn't ask questions. When we got there, I knew he wanted to visit Christine's grave. At the graveside, Kostya rolled up his sleeves and started pulling up the weeds that were already growing over the stone. He cleared them like a man possessed. I tried to help him, but I couldn't keep up. Then, as if waking from a dream, he sat down on the ground, exhausted. On the way he had bought a bunch of white roses, which now lay on the grave. The place was windswept and inhospitable. I sat down beside him.

'Almost a whole century lies buried here. Isn't that remarkable?' he said, and the way he said it gave me a start.

'I can't visit my sister's grave. You live your whole life for the state, serving it to the best of your ability, and then that! Yes; that's how it is when ...'

He didn't finish his sentence, and I didn't dare prompt him. I wanted to take his hand in mine, but I didn't dare do that, either.

Later, he thanked me for thinking of the car, but said that he didn't need it, not any more. There was no longer any reason for him to go anywhere. I was welcome to play his chauffeur, should he decide he did want to go into the city after all: I had certainly proved I was safe on the roads. But I should take a driving test all the same, he said, before getting out of the car again outside the Green House.

★

It was around this time that I met Severin. I was wandering along the 'Dry Bridge', on the lookout for old books that might help me as I wrote down Stasia's stories (books that weren't just propaganda, like most of what was in the library). Severin was kneeling on the ground in front of an old blanket piled high with second-hand books, lost in thought as he leafed through one of them. His haircut and the style of his clothes told me he wasn't from Georgia.

He was young — we must have been about the same age — tall and well-built. He looked strikingly healthy, and exuded something you rarely find in Georgian men: calm. I decided to talk to him. My curiosity about foreigners was hard to rein in. In German-accented Russian he told me he came from West Germany; he had been living in Berlin for a few years now, and was travelling around current and former Soviet countries for his father's antique furniture shop, on the hunt for rare pieces to take back to Germany. You could do good business in the East, he said: people would sometimes sell fabulous things for a few groschen, and even though he found the task abhorrent, he had no other choice.

Smiling, he went on to explain that his real passion was history, with a focus on Eastern Europe. He loved the Russian language dearly, had been learning it since he was a boy, had trained as a restorer to please his father, and was now here pursuing his passion. How exciting it was to be here at such a time, under these circumstances! At the epicentre of the action, he said. Two years ago he wouldn't even have dared to dream of it. Everything had changed overnight: no more Wall, no more East Germany, and soon the whole Soviet Union would be gone, too. He had been to many cities in Russia, and had always wanted to visit *golden Colchis*.

'And now here I am!'

'Yes, well — as you can see, there isn't much of golden Colchis left here. Not even anything from the Bronze Age.'

He smiled his mischievous smile again.

'And have you struck it lucky? Have you managed to discover a rare item yet?'

'Listen, don't get me wrong. I'm doing it for my father's business. Personally, I don't like to see people, especially old people, having to sell their most valuable possessions for so little money.'

'So you feel guilty?'

'Sorry.'

'*Sorry*. That sounds so easy. You're the first person I've heard say that word. Not counting in films.'

He smiled, this time a little more sadly. He was probably the only person smiling at all in this part of town, I thought to myself. It seemed to me like a very pleasant change.

'And what are you reading?' I asked.

'I'm interested in political power structures. I'm teaching myself about Soviet history.'

'You won't find much about power structures in the Russian books. It'll be all brotherliness and equality there.'

We had interests in common. I questioned him about his western life; he wanted to hear all about my eastern life. We strolled through the deserted, windy streets and didn't notice evening falling. I suggested finding one of the few cafés still open in the Old Town, and Severin followed me to Leselidze Street. We drank cheap, lukewarm beer (there was no electricity in the bar) and went on chatting for hours by candlelight. He was staying in a private house with a Georgian family who kept their heads above water by subletting rooms. He had been in the city two weeks and wanted to stay as long as he could. I even told him about my attempts at writing, and complained about the lack of good secondary literature. He offered to provide me with the right books — but most of the books he had with him were in German. When he saw my disappointment, he said we could make a deal: I would teach him Georgian, and in return he would teach me German.

We quickly became friends. We found it easy to like each other. We had similar taste in writing, though he made me realise that there was a huge gap in my reading when it came to contemporary literature, because it was impossible to get hold of the books. He was far better versed in contemporary art as well. We both liked films, and aimless walks on the riverbank. He was restless, searching, and that soon made him feel very familiar to me. The only thing about him that left me almost embarrassingly confused was the fact that he flirted with socialism and was always quoting Marx. I simply couldn't comprehend someone who came from the West and could afford to travel to Paris, Rome, New York, or Tokyo journeying through the rubble of the Soviet Union, taking in the exotic adventure of the East, searching out rare antiques for the capitalist market, and at the same time talking about the advantages of a system that had long been heading towards its demise.

We started meeting regularly. We drilled each other on vocabulary over tea or beer in his accommodation. He told me about West Berlin, Europe, a world I knew only vaguely from books and films. I asked one question after another. There was something slightly lost about his light-heartedness. As if he were constantly wanting to be surprised, swept away from himself, from everything that seemed familiar and certain to him. As if the unknown were the only thing that counted. When I asked him why he didn't just study history and philosophy, if he was already so obsessed by it, he smiled again in his rakish, ambiguous way and told me that the years of doing battle with his father had worn him out. That several times already he had run away, only to return to the shelter of his family when everything had gone wrong.

'My father is a great businessman, you have to give him that. He moved us all to Berlin a few years ago because he could already smell that history was about to be written, and he wasn't wrong. He's made a fortune with old GDR lamps and wallpaper. Westerners are prepared to pay through the nose for simple, factory-made crockery and curtains from the Soviet Union.'

English tasted like sea air and like an autumn sunset on a northern coast; it smelled slightly of fish shops, a little of rain. I thought French, which I had never learned, must dissolve like apricot jam on the tongue and taste of dry white wine. Russian tasted of an endless plain, of wheat fields, of loneliness and illusions. But Georgian tasted dusty, full — almost over-full — and sometimes also like a game of hide-and-seek in the woods. By contrast, the German that Severin taught me tasted icy and bitter at first; then the flavour changed and transformed into the taste of algae, of dark green moss; then it became pungent again, but more pleasant; and later, much later, German was like ripe chestnuts in my mouth, and heights, yes, dizzying heights.

He learned the thirty-three letters of the Georgian alphabet. I learned the German words for 'shitty country', 'exploiter', 'genocide', and 'Cold War'. Sentences like 'How are you?' and 'Do you come from the West or the East?' Later, I learned the words for things like 'house', 'child', 'girl'. And then his silly, perpetual 'okay'.

'*Das Mädchen* — why is 'girl' neuter, not feminine? I don't understand it,' I grumbled.

'Because Germans are so incredibly tactful, you know? They don't want to disadvantage anyone.'

'Who's going to feel disadvantaged? I think it's stupid that I'm a neuter *das* while you're quite clearly a masculine *der*.'

We laughed until he was red-faced, with tears in his eyes — something that didn't otherwise feel natural for a person like Severin: he walked around as though he had a sticker on his forehead reading: 'There's nothing that can rattle me or throw me off balance'.

'Okay, people who are neither one nor the other, they might feel disadvantaged. Me, for example,' he explained.

'You're a *der*. How does being a *der* disadvantage you, if you please?'

'Well, I like boys.'

'Oh, right, I see. But that makes you a double-*der*, doesn't it?'

And once again he shook with laughter.

'That's the kind of logic that might just help me make my sexual orientation comprehensible to my parents.'

'You'd get locked up for that in the Soviet Union,' I added contemplatively, with David's story on my mind.

'Thanks for the tip. That's a huge comfort. In Germany, they castrate you. Nice life, huh?'

'Really?'

'Yes, and they take a hot iron and brand the word "poof" on your chest.'

'Oh my God — maybe you really are better off staying here.'

He laughed again, slapping the flat of his hand against his thigh.

'No, it's not that bad! It's okay in Germany, actually. But listen, if my father had his way, that's exactly what would happen.'

'Well, either way, I just want you to teach me German for as long as possible, and I want to keep your books a while longer,' I said, lighting a cigarette.

'Okay, sure thing.'

From then on, I went with him on his long marches, looking at rugs, armchairs, silver cutlery, crockery, and all kinds of lampshades. We were invited into various apartments and houses where there was something Severin wanted to see. I acted as interpreter, but when I saw a war veteran selling his medals I told him the whole thing made me so sad it might be better if he did his father's job alone.

On 19 August, while Gorbachev was on holiday in the Crimea, the Communist Party of the Soviet Union and other reactionary and conservative forces made a final attempt to halt *perestroika*. They declared a state of emergency, mobilised against the new Union Treaty, declared that any relaxation of the communist system effectively meant the end of that system, and asked the KGB for support (its head was one of the coup's central figures). The coup failed, and three Party functionaries committed suicide, but from then on Gorbachev's days seemed to be numbered as well. It was no use now that he agreed to the abolition or — as it later turned out — restructuring of the KGB, or that as a final demonstration of his own power he had the leaders of the coup arrested. Yeltsin seized his chance, proclaimed a country-wide ban on the Communist Party, and had its property confiscated. On paper, Gorbachev may still have been president of the Russian Republic, but by 24 August the tricolour Russian flag was already hanging over the seat of government in Moscow.

The Soviet Union, the country in which I was born and grew up, no longer existed.

★

When the Gulf War broke out, I was lying in bed with Miro, thinking about how I was going to survive the winter without losing my mind. Electricity blackouts were occurring with increasing regularity. We had to get by with old kerosene lamps. The central heating had stopped working, too. So we had to make other preparations for winter. We got hold of firewood and stinking petrol stoves, which would provide a little heat. We had more things to worry about than keeping up with history.

> Only the gods are not afraid of gifts.
> Try to meet a god.
>
> MARINA TSVETAEVA

They said a civil war had broken out in Tbilisi. The city lay in darkness. Everyone was against everyone: the opposition — though by that time nobody knew who was actually in it — was against Gamsakhurdia; the Communist Party was for itself; the private army was for more power; the partisans for anarchy; criminals for justice; the intelligentsia for Shevardnadze; and the rest of the people somewhere in between. Shots were fired with increasing frequency; a curfew was imposed. Barricades were erected everywhere they could be, and voices amplified by megaphones became part of the everyday background noise.

Despite all this, Severin didn't want to leave. I was annoyed by his excitement and interest in these tragic developments. I suggested that the only reason he saw any good in the destructive potential of what was happening here was that the world he came from was still in one piece. Lectures were cancelled. Demonstrations weren't. We were always hearing about people who had been physically attacked or held up and robbed.

I wrote, and froze. The poker games were temporarily put on hold. The boys had more important things to do. Everywhere stank of petrol. Everywhere was cold. Everywhere people looked about them fearfully and flinched if something was dropped on the floor.

We wanted to spend New Year's Eve 1991 all together at the Green House because shots kept being fired in Tbilisi and bullets had shattered our neighbours' windows. There was a worried phone call from Daria every week, but she had stopped sending money to Kostya and Nana. I suspected something was wrong, but I put the thought to the back of my mind. I had enough worries of my own.

With the civil war, something else entered the country: heroin. The staircases of apartment blocks were increasingly littered with needles. There were more and more glassy eyes on the metro, more and more absent expressions.

We sold and sold. My mother even pawned her wedding ring. When there was nothing left to sell, and the money I had saved from the poker games was gone as well, Stasia announced that there was only one way for us to survive. That night, a delicious aroma spread through the house. We wandered sleepily into the kitchen in nightshirts and pyjamas, and discovered our ninety-one-year-old Stasia at the kitchen table — with a chocolate torte in front of her.

'What on earth is that?' I cried out. I wanted to stick a finger into the wonderful cake then and there, but Nana stopped me, and Stasia explained that she had made it using her father's old recipe. She wanted us to take it into town and sell it to one of the small, newly-opened kiosks that offered cakes and pancakes.

At first everyone thought it was a crazy idea, but then Elene told us excitedly that she knew someone in Tbilisi who sold confectionary in his shop, and she would try taking the cake to this man in the morning.

I drove her into the city the next day, and together we took the cake to the little basement shop Elene had mentioned. The corpulent and excessively hairy owner took the cake with some reluctance, and of course for much less money than we had originally asked, saying he would see how it sold. He thought individual slices would do better; at the moment the Mkhedrioni were probably the only ones who could afford a whole cake.

But by the next day the cake had sold, and he ordered three more from Elene. In two weeks, we sold a total of ten cakes. Stasia refused to accept help from other members of the family, and insisted on keeping the family recipe a secret. I was the only one she would countenance as an assistant in this difficult task.

'Only Niza. No one else. She's the only one in this house who can withstand the curse!'

My mother and Nana exchanged meaningful looks. Initially, I was far from delighted at having the honour of assisting her. I hated any kind of kitchen job, and baking in particular had never been one of my strengths. But Stasia was adamant and wouldn't be persuaded otherwise. I told myself that at least this was a good opportunity to spend more time with the increasingly frail Stasia and finish collecting my stories.

The first night, as I watched her make the chocolate, I remembered the delicious aroma in Christine's apartment that had enticed Miro and me out of our beds and into the kitchen. And as she stirred the dark mass, I heard, for the first time, the story of the chocolate-maker's hot chocolate, and the curse that, according to Stasia, went with it.

'You should never have been allowed to taste it, and now you have. My sister, may she rest in peace, never believed me. She used it to put the Little Big Man in his grave, and even after that she still doubted. But you — you must promise me faithfully: two dessert spoons of the mixture are all you need for a cake. You must never make it in its pure form for someone you love. Swear it to me.'

The scent melted me along with the chocolate as I watched her mixing the ingredients with hands that were old but still nimble, cautiously, carefully tasting, and measuring everything several times as if it were a medicine, a poison, and not this heavenly chocolate. And of course I didn't believe a word she said. Chocolate was there to be eaten, after all, and I just wanted to dive into this dark mass and lick it all up. But she watched over me, sternly ensuring that not one of my fingers found its way into the pan; tasting to check the flavour was all that was allowed. Stasia's cakes got us through the winter, and spring, too, and when Boris Yeltsin was elected as Russia's first president in June 1991 our cake business really took off. Our world was sinking, and people wanted to stuff themselves with cake until they felt sick.

'When times are bad, business is good for confectioners — that's what my father always said.'

Stasia repeated these words like a mantra as I stood beside her in the kitchen, stirring the black mass by candlelight.

★

She was thinner now; her cheeks seemed sunken and her eyes gleamed. Her dress no longer clung sleekly to her hips, but hung loose on her body. Her hair was tied back in a hurried ponytail and her make-up had been carelessly applied. Nonetheless, she was recognised at the airport, and although people didn't ask for her autograph — which in any case wouldn't have been practical in the semi-darkness of the complete electricity blackout in the arrivals hall— they stared as she passed and whispered to one another.

We hugged for a long time.

'So where's your husband?' I asked my sister.

'He stayed in Moscow.'

'That's nice for us: we'll all have a bit more of you. The Green House is expecting you. We've cooked your favourite things.'

'I'm so glad to be home,' said Daria, before falling asleep in the back seat of the car.

Kostya had put on some decent clothes for once, in honour of Daria's visit, and was wearing a white shirt and pressed suit trousers. We had a late supper, and Daria told us about Moscow, about the chaos there, the extreme food shortages. The one good thing was that she had been able to get a part in a play, and had work. When Elene asked her about Lasha's business, she prevaricated and changed the subject. Three days later, she went to their empty apartment to 'take care of a few things' and disappeared for days. The telephone was cut off, so I drove to her building and rang the bell for a long time. Even on the stairs I could hear loud music and a hubbub of voices coming from her apartment. I was surprised that she had visitors and hadn't thought it necessary to tell me. The whole apartment was full of people I didn't know. I could only see a few of her old friends. People were standing around drinking vodka by the light of kerosene lamps, which stank to high heaven, playing guitar and singing. The flat was untidy, as if she hadn't made any attempt to clean it since she'd got back. When someone pressed a vodka glass into my hand, I knocked back the bitter liquid in one go and listened with irritation to these people's drunken nonsense, all the while keeping my eyes on my sister. I had never seen her like this: she was hysterical, loud, forward, almost vulgar; her skirt was hitched up and her make-up had run. She danced around, told Russian jokes, kept throwing her arms around her friends' necks, and eventually ended up on the lap of one of these strangers, who in his drunken state instantly started feeling her up — but not even this seemed to bother her.

When she went to the toilet, I followed her and locked the door behind us.

'What's wrong with you?'

'Spare me your moralising. I've been away for a long time — I missed them all so much, and my friends —'

'Your friends? I'm pretty sure you've never met most of these people before. Come on, please. There's something wrong. Please, Daria — I don't want to stop you doing anything, I just want to know you're all right, and I haven't seen you for so long — I really missed you, and I thought —'

Suddenly, she threw her arms around me and started to cry.

'It's all going wrong. I don't know what to do. He ... he ... Lasha's in real trouble.'

In short order she told me that his business hadn't gone well from the start; he was dependent on help from his parents, but wanted to maintain his standard of living, and was increasingly losing himself in the whirlwind of Moscow life. She told me he had been injecting heroin for quite a while, and sometimes he would disappear without trace for days on end. She kept saying how much she loved him, though, as if she were afraid I would tell her to leave him. But before I could say anything, she wiped her face, put on a smile, and, beaming once more, hurried back into the living room where she was loudly welcomed.

Daria had always known what place in the world was her due, what she could expect from life; she hadn't doubted things, she hadn't questioned herself or the world around her. She had just chosen the wrong person to love, and she herself had granted him permission to knock her world off kilter. She had practically laughed in his face and said, 'You love me — you may do it; take everything you need, take everything, as long as it makes you happy.'

And he had.

She stood before me, with those sunken cheeks and dark shadows under her eyes. Her blue eye was glassy; her brown eye was dull. She had lost her equilibrium.

And as I watched her, as she danced in the arms of some idiot, I had a frightening realisation: Lasha had managed to turn her into his nightmare version of her. He had projected all his fears, complexes, and manias onto her. And she had let it happen. He had managed to transform her love into a dull, dirty, swampy mass, so that he could finally accept it. I watched her dancing and felt nauseous.

Where was my wonderful, unbroken, self-sufficient Daria, the beautiful queen of Kostya's realm? And where was Kostya's realm now, anyway? Where were we all living?

★

Three days later, I met Aleko. He was distraught. He told me that David had been stopped in the street by some men who'd tried to mug him. When they discovered there was nothing in his purse, they wanted his gold chain, but he defended himself. (I tried to remember a chain around his neck. Had I ever noticed? No.)

'Is he dead?' I asked Aleko, marvelling at my own composure.

'Yes. Nine stab wounds. Probably some kind of criminal gang or friends of the Mkhedrioni.'

'For a chain?'

'For a chain.'

I shut myself in the bathroom and stayed there for hours. I held the world tightly in my fist but still it ran through my fingers as if it were made of sand.

I lay down in the empty bathtub. The water had been cut off again.

Time seemed to shatter against the backs of my knees. I was eight, I was ten, and I was in David's apartment. I saw the drawings and pictures on his walls, I tasted the scalding tea on my tongue, I heard his voice. Would he play cards with the other ghosts now, too? He didn't like cards. If he played anything, it would have to be backgammon.

I tried to cry. I had never been good at it. I had no tears. I hated this country, I hated these people, I hated this bathtub, I hated myself and my powerlessness. Why had he done it? Refusing to give up a chain, for God's sake? Why had he done that to me? I thought about the blood in the bathroom, at the seaside that time; about beautiful Rusa and how she had pretended to be carefree in the snow, so many months later.

I laid my face against the cold edge of the bath.

I went under. Even though there was no water.

Christine's halved face, the screeching human mass of 9 April, the cold of the last two winters, the darkness on the streets, David's words, our last meeting, the strong tea, my desperate sister's glassy eyes, Miro's laugh, the pervasive hopelessness of these days, the pages I had filled (with what, exactly?), my mother's despondent expression, the smell of the hot chocolate ... At that moment, everything merged together in my mind.

How long would I be able to lie there? And what would it change? This useless grief.

I gave myself a slap. I wanted to feel something. I wanted it to hurt. I wanted to be closer to David. I wanted to hold on to him: in my unspoken words to him, in my vision of the afternoons and evenings I could have spent with him. In the next room, my mother put on Kitty Jashi's album *Home*, and perhaps that was the first time I consciously listened to her music. And perhaps it was Kitty's music that enticed me out of the bath, out of the house again after those endless, empty hours, Brilka.

★

'Do you know why everyone, even his former allies, wants to get rid of Gamsakhurdia now? Do you know why they're all railing against him?' Kostya was getting worked up over supper again, as we sat around the kitchen table by candlelight during a blackout, listening to the battery-operated radio. 'Because people are starting to realise that in return for the *sovereignty* they so desperately wanted, they'll have to change their lifestyle. No more quick flights to Moscow, with its restaurants and its Russian women; no more Caucasian swagger, no more privileges, no more *sunny Georgia*. And now they realise that's not what they wanted at all.'

Uprisings were still happening all over the country. If you wanted bread, you had to start queuing in the middle of the night. The National Guard and the Mkhedrioni refused to enter into cooperation with the Ministry for the Interior. They had long since abandoned the rule of law — if anyone was actually still abiding by it — and were making laws of their own. No authority was going to tell them what they should and shouldn't do any more. At the end of the year, when Gamsakhurdia had all Russian television channels blocked in an effort to keep negative Russian propaganda away from Georgia, general dissatisfaction was aroused once more. Those average citizens who, a few months previously, had fervently shouted 'freedom' and 'sovereignty' at the demonstrations were now upset at being denied Russian 'culture'.

'Yes, I suppose it's true: we are a nation that looks at itself through others' eyes. I'm afraid I can't remember who said that,' Stasia commented that evening, agreeing with her son for once.

★

We made chocolate cakes to the recipe of a long-dead confectioner who was trained in Budapest and Vienna, using flour and powdered milk with USAID printed on the packets, and cocoa powder adorned with a red star. Meanwhile, the National Guard, working with the Mkhedrioni, occupied all the city's central buildings and set up posts outside them. Once again, people thronged Rustaveli Boulevard. And once again, shots were fired; once again, people were killed and wounded. What surprised me most of all was the general indifference of the city's population to these warlike acts. Flame-throwers kept causing fires, the sound of Kalashnikovs was constant, yet most people still went calmly about their daily business.

The metro was running; cinemas were open; passers-by stopped in the street and watched with cold expressions, their faces motionless as the soldiers loaded their guns.

After Severin got caught up in it, too (he was attacked and robbed), he handed all his books over to me and left, promising to come back as soon as he'd taken care of some stuff in Berlin. The day before his departure I invited him up to the Green House, and we ate polenta and cheese in silence. I'd got very used to him; I had learned to love our intimacy, and the German words that I promised to go on memorising in his absence. I could see that the thought of returning to order after all this chaos troubled him, too.

'You should go to Europe, Niza,' he told me, this time in German.

'Europe, yes, Europe. Remember when you said you wanted to be at the epicentre of history?'

'Yes, well, maybe I've changed, or maybe I just got tired. Tired of this fear. I was never afraid before — I wasn't afraid when I came here. It's different now.'

Before I drove him back into town, we went up to the attic, took a candle out onto the unfinished roof terrace, smoked a cigarette, and looked at the clear, starry sky. Piles of old books and my notes lay in the corner. This had been my kingdom, my retreat for so many years. Despite the chaos of those days, I vowed to try to leave enough space within me that I wouldn't forget him. At that time, I didn't think I would ever see him again.

> Within Russia, take as much sovereignty as you can swallow.
>
> BORIS YELTSIN

On 7 January, the battles were declared to be over, and the Mkhedrioni uncorked the champagne outside the Parliament Building. Gamsakhurdia had been forced to flee, and after being denied residency in Armenia, he ended up in Chechnya. The demonstrations continued; Gamsakhurdia's followers tried again to set up shop all over Tbilisi, but the Mkhedrionists and the National Guard opened fire on them. Southern Georgia, especially Samegrelo, the region with the most presidential supporters, was up in arms.

People demanded Shevardnadze's return to Georgian politics. It had started to dawn on everyone that dissidents and criminals would not be able to bring this chaos to an end. And there were increasing signs of a power struggle between the Mkhedrioni and the National Guard.

Shortly after Shevardnadze's return in March 1992, my sister also came to Tbilisi for a few weeks. She withdrew to our childhood bedroom, announcing that she and the lovely Lasha had had 'a falling out'; he had even greater 'financial problems', and she wasn't sure how long she would be staying with us. She firmly blocked all of Kostya's attempts to get any more out of her; however, she had more colour in her cheeks than the previous year, when she had spent two weeks doing nothing but partying. But her gaze was absent, her demeanour restless and jumpy, and even her normally soothing smile had something artificial and contrived about it. The happiness she had always radiated so majestically, the satisfaction at being at the centre of everything, the confidence that she could reach out and grasp anything she wanted — all the things she used to display so openly — seemed to have been snuffed out, as if her main impetus, the sole engine for all these characteristics, had been switched off.

It made me sad to sense her emptiness, and I decided to spend more time with her, support her, tease out her secrets, and show her at long last that it was time to tell her lovely Lasha to go to hell. But she was slippery as a fish, eluding anything that might come too close for comfort; she was an expert at manipulating every conversation. I found it difficult to figure her out, something I used to be able to do so well. But between then and now lay her love, her marriage, Moscow, and the countless moments and emotions I had not shared with her, the experiences she'd had without me.

Just two weeks later, Lasha suddenly turned up at the front door. He had grown thin, and his face had an unhealthy, yellowish hue. His appearance at once brought Daria back to life. She turned her attention to him, patting his cheeks all the time, preparing his favourite food. She stopped complaining about the blackouts and how cold the house was; she snuggled up to him, showered him with tender gestures, and seemed to completely ignore his snubs and his lack of interest in her. As if she didn't even notice that he wasn't returning her kisses and shunned her tenderness. I couldn't watch. I turned my eyes away from her. Couldn't get the images out of my head. This man had done something terrible to my sister; he had taken something precious from her, something important had changed in her, and I wouldn't and couldn't come to terms with it. Once again, I decided to interfere in someone else's life. This time, though, I wouldn't be able to win the fight alone. Perhaps Kostya — as difficult as this was for me — would become my ally. Perhaps he would summon his dwindling energy, pour his pent-up frustration and rage over Lasha's head and make him stay away from Daria. For that reason, I was more than grateful to Kostya for persuading the two of them to stay in the Green House rather than going to their apartment. It was more difficult to get provisions in the city, he told them, and, above all, it was more dangerous there. I had given over our old bedroom to them, and was sleeping in Stasia's room. We had all started huddling together: it was cold, and there wasn't enough petrol and wood to heat all the rooms.

Over the days we spent living together, Daria's arguments with Lasha began to escalate. He had done all this for a 'little two-bit whore', I heard him shouting, from the other side of the door. He was an 'ungrateful pig, a rotten bastard, a nothing', Daria retorted. And my suspicion from the last party was increasingly confirmed: she was doing all she could to prove to herself that he was right, that she really did correspond to his image of her, that she deserved to be mistreated. And if Daria finally succumbed to this image her husband had created of her, her life would be ruined — of that I was also certain. 'All or nothing at all' had always been her motto. Once her appetite was piqued, she couldn't stop eating. If she was beautiful, she had to be the most beautiful. If she was an actress, she would play only leading roles. If her interest in someone or something was aroused, she couldn't stop until she possessed the object of her desire. If she fell in love, she had to get married. Once she was in love, it had to be forever. If they had a fight, she would let herself be beaten and insulted in the most despicable way. I was certain that if ever she were to start hating herself, it would end in complete self-destruction.

One night, I was lying in bed and heard Daria's footsteps in the corridor. She passed my door and started climbing the stairs to the attic. I quickly threw on a jumper and hurried after her. She had lit a small candle and was sitting beside my pile of dust-covered books with her knees drawn up to her chest. When she heard my footsteps, she looked round in alarm.

'Oh, it's you ...' she said, with a note of disappointment in her voice, as if she'd been hoping someone else had followed her.

'Yes, it's *only* me.'

'Do you want to have a cigarette with me?'

'Sure.'

'Funny that in all these years we still haven't managed to put up a railing,' she said thoughtfully.

'I like it the way it is.'

'It's pretty high, isn't it?'

'Yes, it is. Do you remember how much we loved coming up here as children?'

'I was always afraid of heights — I only did it because of you, so you wouldn't think I was a coward.'

'A fear of heights doesn't exactly go with being a trapeze artist, does it?'

'I've always done things that scared me.'

'Uh-huh ... And are you scared of your husband, too, Daria?'

'I don't want to talk about him. Just drop it, please.'

'He's a filthy swine. All those things he says are just his warped imagination.'

She looked at me in shock.

'Have you been eavesdropping?'

'Even without hearing his wonderful words, you can tell how much he *loves* you just by looking at him.'

'That's not true. He does, even if you can't see it.'

'When? When he hits you, you mean, or when he can't get it up to have his way with you?'

'You're going too far. It's got nothing to do with you!'

'You're my sister, for God's sake, and I won't let this bastard break you.'

'He's ill. Try to understand that. You have to be lenient with him. He has so many problems, and there's so little I can do to help him ... You live in your world. You don't know what it's like to love a person so desperately.'

Our cigarette ends burned in the dark like two amorous glow-worms.

'All you're doing is living up to his twisted ideas, Daria.'

At these words, she looked at me thoughtfully. As if this one sentence had really got through to her.

'I just can't do it,' she said in a weak voice, and buried her head between her knees.

I couldn't hold back any longer: I wrapped my arms around her with all my strength. She tried to shake me off and get up, but I clung on tightly. I wanted to hold her, I wanted to save her.

I wanted her to be mean to me again, and so beautiful that you would forgive her anything; I wanted her to drive me into a white-hot rage, to be catty and capricious — anything but this, this hunched back, this sluggishness and submissiveness, this guilt, this disappointment. I let out a laugh.

'You're crazy,' she cried. She freed herself from my embrace and fell back, exhausted. I crawled over to her and laid my head on her belly. Hesitantly, she brushed a strand of hair from my forehead.

'You had my husband beaten up by your criminal friends, Niza. That doesn't help.'

'But he —'

'*That* doesn't help!'

'I won't do it again. I promise. I'll do anything you want. But don't go back. You have to start acting again.'

'Who's interested in films or theatre these days?'

'It won't be like this forever.'

'Oh, Niza.'

She hugged me to her and rubbed my back. Then she got up and brushed the dust from her nightshirt.

'I have to go back down. He can't sleep without me.'

★

The fighting continued in southern Georgia between Gamsakhurdia's followers and the new government, but Shevardnadze's return did seem to have brought a glimmer of hope to the conflict with the Abkhazians. His desire 'to forget all the quarrels of the past' gave the Abkhazians hope that their demands for sovereignty would be met with a more open mind. But when words did not lead to deeds, and the Georgian State Council made an attempt to convert the port of Ochamchira in Abkhazia into a base for Georgian naval forces, this hope was quickly extinguished. In Tbilisi, too, people began to speculate as to whether Shevardnadze would really manage to avoid more bloodshed. At the centre of these disagreements was Abkhazia's future status within or outside Georgia's borders. And when, in July 1992, the Abkhazian parliament suspended the 1978 constitution of the Abkhazian ASSR and reintroduced the constitution of 1925, the Georgian defence minister and head of the National Guard ordered Georgian troops to march into Abkhazia. He justified this as a 'measure necessary to defend territorial integrity against the separatist efforts of the Abkhazian parliament'.

That was how the war started.

Daria went back to Moscow with Lasha. A few months after her departure, she called the Green House and screamed down the phone. It was only after Nana had made several attempts to calm her down that Daria was able to get a clear sentence out: her husband had been shot by debt collectors of some kind, and was now in intensive care. The bullet had grazed his spine.

Only at the end of the phone call did she mention, almost in passing and completely unable to cope, that she was expecting a baby.

> Patriotism is slavery.
>
> TOLSTOY

Daria held out longer and better than we had feared. Your mother was impressively brave. Right up to your birth, Brilka, she showed incredible strength, and managed to protect you and keep you away from all dangers and from the horror that surrounded her. She held out as long as she could. You have to understand that, Brilka.

I was astounded by her steely discipline, her unbroken will, and above all her love for this person who rewarded her only with his contempt, with verbal and physical torture and endless complaining. I don't know where she found the strength to do it all. Anyone who offers themselves up as a sacrifice with open arms — I thought at the time — anyone who gives all they have will sooner or later be empty. After two complicated operations, which his parents even sold their apartment to fund (the procedures were carried out in Israel), Lasha was brought back to Tbilisi and the Green House for a long period of rehabilitation. The apartment on Vake Park had also been sold to pay off his debts. Paralysed from the waist down, he was in a lot of pain and dependent on expensive drugs. The doctors had not given up hope that one day he would walk again, provided the patient was strong-willed and had access to the latest medical techniques and a capable physiotherapist. But even if the two families had been able to drum up more money for treatment abroad, and had engaged the best physiotherapist in the country, you couldn't have called this particular patient strong-willed.

I kept escaping to the city, to the library, or to Miro's narrow bed. I was fleeing from myself, from the grim news that arrived every day from Abkhazia, from the images we had to reconcile ourselves to, would have to get used to from now on, the streams of refugees and the constantly rising death toll. The eyes of crying children and the charred ruins of houses. The women who had been raped. The bombed-out buildings. The calm sea; again and again, the calm sea. The evil Abkhazians, the good Georgians. The evil Georgians, the good Abkhazians. And the Russians; again and again, the Russians: the *peacekeeping troops*, the *mediators* — who were also the biggest provider of arms and training to the Abkhazians. The sixteen- or seventeen-year-olds brought in to fight by the Mkhedrioni and the National Guard, lured by fantastic promises of vague heroism, by weed — and, if that didn't do it, heroin. The poor training and organisation of the Georgian army. Pushing forward and being forced back. The fire; fire, again and again: cars, houses, people burning. And the sea; again and again, the sea, calmly looking on as the horror unfolded.

We, who lived far from the battlefields and were only concerned with getting through the next day; we who were without work, without any prospects, any answers; we who had to worry every day about where we were going to get firewood, kerosene, candles, flour, sugar, butter, milk powder, learned to live with these images of the war, to repress them. We got used to the muffled shouts, a strange mixture of joy and rage, when the electricity came back on; we got used to it going off again and a muffled but unmistakeable groan running through the house; to hearing the government disparaged in ever-clearer terms in the city. But we also got used to the idea that the blue helmets, the UN troops, NATO, and the West, were not going to come and save us and defend us against evil Russia. Got used to the fatalistic thought that we Georgians would not succeed in pulling ourselves out of this swamp, either. No; we didn't really believe that.

In this city of millions, everyone was soon acquainted with everyone else, because who knew: maybe they would come in useful for some kind of errand or purchase. Skinny hens, anchored with string, ran up and down the balconies of tower blocks. The street dogs multiplied at a rate of knots and roamed the streets at night in search of a little sustenance, howling like a pack of wolves.

We got used to everything.

We played dominoes, cards, board games, we told jokes, listened to one another in dark kitchens, living rooms, bedrooms, where we sat wrapped in thick blankets and clutching hot water bottles, in a silence that descended over the city like a bell jar as darkness fell. We remembered old stories, and rejoiced as never before when the winter was finally over and spring came, bringing warmth, lighter days, and a few less worries. We could eke out a box of matches forever, bake cakes with maize flour, and make ten different varieties of bean soup. And we could laugh at ourselves and our improvised solutions: at the Komsomol membership book with its Lenin's head that was plugging a hole in the window, or the teapot that we wrapped in a woollen blanket to keep the tea warm for longer. We stopped listening to news of fresh robberies, break-ins, and murders. We were glad when the day was over and we were still alive. No, we didn't want to think about the war raging in another part of our country, tearing our fathers, brothers, husbands, friends, neighbours, and acquaintances away from us and bringing them back maimed and traumatised or even in wooden coffins.

Everyone was afraid for someone. Everyone was missing a family member, a friend. And so we tiptoed around the war, closed our eyes. And when we had electricity, we watched the images of the war in Yugoslavia on television. It was strange: we took an interest in this foreign war; for a moment we were even grateful because it gave us a chance to forget our own.

We were living in a timeless time.

*

Daria's belly started to show quite early on. The pregnancy didn't make her blossom; she looked weary and haggard, as if she were saving up the last of her strength for the birth, after which she could finally submit to a process of decline that could no longer be staved off. Elene was worried about her. Kostya was worried about her. Nana, Stasia, Aleko — everyone was watching her, whispering and conferring behind her back. Nobody wanted this fate for her, but nobody dared to tell her that it might be time to think about a divorce, time to hand Lasha over to a hospital or at least to the ministrations of his parents.

The intoxicating aroma of hot chocolate woke me again in the night, and I went into the kitchen, where Stasia had baked three cake bases with the help of a gas canister and was sitting at the table smoking, when the raised voices of marital conflict started up again in Daria's bedroom. Stasia stared into the distance, pretending not to hear what was going on in the other room. I contemplated just marching in there and suffocating my brother-in-law with a pillow. But I never went into the bedroom. No one did. We all looked through him as if he were a ghost.

Some days, I retired to the attic with my typewriter and wrote until the letters began to swim in front of my eyes. It didn't matter now how well I wrote, or what I was writing; the main thing was to do it, to stop myself losing my mind, to forget, to transport myself to far-off times and other lives simply in order to escape my own.

My most important essay, which I had written by weak candlelight, was not accepted. I had probably paid too little attention to nationalist propaganda when I wrote my piece on 'The Generalissimus — a Georgian'. My professor even thought it 'tended towards treason'.

'You must lack all conscience, Jashi!' he reproached me. 'To write like this in times like these, as if we didn't have enough pressure from Russia. You're studying history — my goodness, take a look around you! Look at the state your country is in. And you? You pour out this filth, now of all times, when the country is at war, when these Abkhazian and Ossetian traitors are crawling before the Russians, you can think of nothing better to do than pen this libellous piece of filth about your homeland? This doesn't just insult me, as someone trying to educate you to be an objective person with an analytical mind — it insults all those young people risking their lives for your freedom —'

'This war shouldn't have been allowed to happen. It's our refusal to engage frankly with ourselves as a nation, with what we are, that led to it. It was this total capriciousness, an unprincipled approach, a lack of diplomatic skill, a kind of thinking based on nothing but pure instinct, and blind patriotism that got us into this situation, if you ask me. And all I was trying to do in my essay was to understand why we're stuck in this mess, and why nobody has thought to question these things!'

'You have dared to call into question the fact that Russia —'

'Russia, Russia. I hear this word all the time. Or America, or Europe, or whatever. When are we going to stop viewing ourselves through the eyes of a patron? When will we finally start looking in the mirror, without false sentimentality or pity, without this disgusting patriotism based on nothing but myths?'

'Jashi, you've overstepped the mark!'

'I'm just trying to expose how certain things are connected. Aren't you sick of these endless glorifications and perpetual conspiracy theories as well?'

'Audacity is not necessarily a quality to be proud of, Jashi! Imagine what would happen if an essay like this were to fall into the hands of someone in Moscow; what joy it would bring them to read that yes, we Georgians are traitors, we're unprincipled, we're —'

'Perhaps we're not entirely blameless in this whole mess, have you ever considered that?'

'Well, it seems *you* have, and what glorious conclusions you have drawn. Bravo, Jashi! Bravo! You should apply for the Russian secret service.'

'Russia, again; the KGB, again. You see, that's exactly what I mean.'

'You want the truth? The truth, do you? Why don't you just go to Sokhumi and see with your own eyes what's going on there. Go to Abkhazia and then report back — objectively, critically, instructively! If you don't, I shall expect a complete rewrite of this essay.'

I was so filled with anger at my professor that I immediately decided to go to Abkhazia. I wanted to prove to this nationalistic idiot that I was right. I knew that I could never tell Miro what I had in mind, so I decided to search for a way to get there on my own. My plan seemed to me at once absurd and elitist, but I was stubborn. I would go there and see for myself how helpless our troops were, see the Russian 'peacekeepers' who were bringing tanks and munitions into the country by boat, the brutality of the Abkhazians, the brutality of the Georgians, the brutality of the Russians. I would see the indescribable conditions in which Georgian refugees were trekking on foot through the Svaneti mountains. Yes, I would stop closing my eyes to the apocalypse on the Black Sea. I would go there. I would write about it. The war was already everywhere. It was just a question of perspective: whether you encountered it with your eyes open or shut, I thought.

How stupid I was.

I set out for the Chess Palace, the headquarters where I had once gone to find The Shark. I found only a few Mkhedrioni still there. They had nothing left to drink, and the looks they gave me weren't as self-assured and piercing as they had been before. When I asked after The Shark, one of the guards cleared his throat, scratched his head, and eventually said that The Shark had been killed last month in Gagra.

'How?'

I don't know why I wanted to know that.

'Shot in the head. They didn't have trenches.'

The man lowered his eyes.

I tried to imagine The Shark dead. What he had felt as he was hit. I couldn't do it. The only thing I could think of was that beautiful house in Gagra, my games of backgammon with Rusa, and her blood in the bathroom. The sea; again and again, the dark, whispering sea that had no interest in whether we were at war or at peace. Half of the territory in Abkhazia was already in Abkhazian — and therefore in Russian — hands. The border with Russia was open. It was just Sokhumi left now. In December, the day before the arrival of 1994, Gamsakhurdia died in the mountains of Samegrelo, where he had been hiding with his followers. His wife confirmed that it was suicide, but for many years half the population maintained that he had died a hero's death fighting the Mkhedrioni. And then, before I could go to the war, the war came to me.

I decided to find Cello. According to Miro, he had been turning up at the garage quite often recently, which meant he was in Tbilisi and not fighting. He could help me get to Abkhazia. Sure enough, people at the print works, which was still one of the Mkhedrioni's bases, confirmed that he was in the city and would be there the following day. The next evening, I used the last of my petrol to drive to the print works, where I found a few familiar faces from the poker games. They all greeted me effusively. Cello, however, just shook my hand rather than hugging me like the rest of them. He offered me a chair and sat down opposite me.

'The boys say you want to talk to me about something?'

His probing gaze made me just as uncomfortable as it had before, and I tried to appear as neutral as possible.

'Well, yes. I thought you might be able to help me get to Abkhazia.'

'Abkhazia? You?' he asked in disbelief. 'That's a place you flee from; you don't want to go there of your own free will, believe me.'

'I know, but ... I want to write about it, about everything that's going on there, and I thought ...'

'So you write, do you? Any more hidden talents, Einstein?'

'Well, I want to try.'

'No, the boys are right: there's no figuring you out.'

'Can you help me?' I asked, looking him in the eye this time. He paused for what seemed an eternity, scratched his bald head, and ran his tongue over his unnaturally red lips.

'Can I help you. Hmm ... I don't know, Einstein. You never looked like someone who needed help.'

'Everyone needs help sometimes.'

I was annoyed with myself for my submissive answer, but at that moment I couldn't think of anything better to say.

'I would have liked it if you'd needed something before. In the days when we used to play cards here, remember?'

'Of course I remember. It was fun, wasn't it?'

'Fun. Hmm, fun. I don't know. Depends who for, doesn't it?'

I knew it. I'd known it at the time: he was a bad loser.

'So ...?'

'So. Well, thinking about it, I could help you; sure I could. I have my ways. I could get you a press pass. Fifty dollars and you've got yourself a deal. But I need to have my fun as well, right? I need to get something out of this as well, don't you agree?'

'Come on, what do you want?'

'Well, we could play a game. I've got a hundred dollar note on me. That must be enough of an incentive for you, right? I haven't played in a long time, and the boys are itching for a game as well. The ones who are left, that is. So, boys: a game of poker?' he yelled out, not taking his eyes off me. An enthusiastic murmur came back in response.

'I don't have any money.'

'Oh, we won't let that stop us. Like I said, I've got a hundred.'

'But what if I lose?'

'Oh, come on, you *never* lose. You don't need to worry about that.'

'Yes I do. So, what if I lose?'

'Then I get a kiss, and I get to stroke your left breast, with no material in the way, if you get my meaning.'

I don't know which took me aback more: the cold precision of his idea, or the fact that he even had such a fantasy about me.

'One kiss, and one touch of my breast?' I asked.

'That's right.'

'And then you'll sort out the press pass for me?'

'That's right.'

'And what if I win?'

'Then you get a hundred dollars and the press pass as well.'

'Agreed.'

'I knew my offer wouldn't scare you away. That's why you're Einstein, and not just some random girl, right?'

'Then find some cards and get the boys over here.'

It was a nerve-wracking game. From somewhere they produced a full bottle of *chacha*, and I was so nervous that for once I joined in the drinking. Everyone emptied their pockets and laid notes and coins on the makeshift card table. Everyone except me. Even as we were playing I had a creeping sense of doubt about how serious his offer was, and it also quickly became clear to me that my lucky streak had run out that day. Stubborn as I was, though, I kept playing, spurred on by the idea of getting to the battlefield and bagging myself a hundred dollars to boot.

We played as if possessed. With the utmost concentration, and literally everything at stake. But there was nothing I could do with the cards I was dealt. I tried to escape unscathed, but even the best bluffs didn't help me win a hand.

Of course I lost. Of course he won.

I still clung to the idea that he was just going to grope my almost non-existent breast and stick his tongue down my throat. I'd been through worse. Fortunately, he didn't celebrate his luck in the game as ostentatiously as he had before, on the odd occasions when he managed to outsmart me. He didn't make a big deal of it; he just stood up at the end and asked the boys to leave us alone, saying we had something to take care of. I wasn't happy about this; we could just have gone into one of the other rooms.

Before long, they had all said their goodbyes, slapping me on the shoulder and hugging me, and Cello and I were alone together. He carried on drinking. Suddenly I thought of Miro. What would he say about this absurd and humiliating scheme? I felt ashamed. But a player always pays his debts. One way or another. I tried to look calm and composed.

When the bottle was empty, he turned his probing eyes on me and asked if we should make good on the promise. I got up and planted myself in front of him, unbuttoned my shirt, doing everything with deliberate, mechanical movements, and stood there topless before him. He bent down and pressed his full, blood-red lips to my mouth. He tasted bitter, of alcohol and something else that at the time I couldn't put into words, but would now call *brutality*. Even though the whole thing seemed incredible and repulsive to me and I couldn't get Miro's face out of my head; even though I now saw myself as stupid and naive to want to travel to the heart of a nightmare and assume I could find some form of truth there; even though I was already cursing my professor and realising that I would never voluntarily go to a warzone, that I was grateful not to be among the hundreds of thousands of Georgians forced to flee over the Caucasian mountain passes, risking their lives in the freezing cold — despite all this, at that point I still wasn't frightened. Not of this cold, emotionless man mechanically kissing me, this man who thought he was humiliating me by putting me in this situation, taking his revenge for the fact that he had lost to me so often in the past. At that point, I still thought I would soon be able to leave the room and hurry back to Miro, confess my absurd plan to him, and apologise for being arrogant and over-estimating myself. But then he grasped my other breast as well and squeezed it so hard I flinched with pain. What if he didn't keep his promise? We were alone. It was late. The print works were in the basement of an old, empty newspaper building. I tensed and tried not to let him feel the fear that was rising within me.

'Right, then. I kept my word,' I said, turning my face away. But he grabbed me by the waist and pulled me towards him.

'Didn't I say you had many talents …'

Now his voice sounded excited. The arrogance had left his face. I tore myself away, took a step back, and buttoned my shirt again. But as I did so he planted himself in front of me and grabbed a handful of my tousled hair. In seconds he had pulled my head towards him and was looking right into my eyes. Still, yes, even then, I was sure I would manage to escape, to forget this horribly stupid, unforgivably idiotic idea of mine and never see this man again.

'You're a good player, Einstein,' he whispered in my ear, before licking my neck.

I tried to put up as little resistance as possible, saving my strength for the crucial battle. Because there would be one — of this I was now sure.

'That's enough, Cello. You've had your fun — and, come on, I'm sure a guy like you wants bigger breasts than mine.'

I don't know why I said that to him. Whatever I was trying to achieve, I achieved the exact opposite. He pulled harder at my hair and made me cry out in shock and pain.

'You think you're better than me, do you?' he yelled. 'You think I'm not worthy of you? Well, we'll see, won't we, we'll see about that ...'

He shoved his hand between my legs. I bent forward and pushed him away with both hands. He still had hold of my hair, and dragged me with him. I tried digging my fingernails into his hand to free myself, but he didn't loosen his grip.

'You think you're so superior, don't you? You little slut!' he yelled, and spittle flew from his lips and hit the tip of my nose. How I hated this word. Slut! It reminded me of Lasha. Reminded me of my sister's powerlessness. Of the sacrifices she offered up to her executioner. I summoned all my strength, and despite the pain in my head I managed to free myself from him and punch him in the stomach. I wanted to hit lower down, to lay him out, but he dodged, stooped, went red in the face, and tried to grab me again.

No, it really wasn't my day. My lucky streak had completely run out.

I started running. Knocked over empty glasses and two chairs. I was heading for the exit, but he barred my way and made a grab for me. He caught my sleeve, pulled me towards him; I slipped away, tried to get my hands on something I could cling to, but failed. He seized me by the waist again, spun me round, encircled my throat with one hand, choked the air out of me, threw me to the floor. I crawled away, coughing, gasping for breath. I pulled myself up on an old printing machine, but already he was standing behind me, I could smell his breath; he pressed himself against my backside and started unbuttoning my trousers. Something rammed into my stomach; the pain was crippling. It was a metal handle, and I tried to wriggle away from it while simultaneously resisting him, moving my hips from side to side so he couldn't get at the buttons on my trousers.

But as soon as he managed to grab the first button, he ripped the rest off (why did even my buttons let me down, why did they put up no resistance, why did they give in so quickly?!) and my trousers slipped down of their own accord, as if they were conspiring against me.

I remember him holding both my hands behind my back with one of his. I remember that as he penetrated me I felt as if I had to throw up. I remember him whispering in my ear the whole time. Panting, breathing heavily. But I don't remember what he said. I just recall this 'Good, good', every letter of which he pronounced as if he were saying the word for the first time and had to get used to the sound. I remember that for some reason, as he bore down on my pelvis with the whole of his weight, bending me further and further over, I thought I had to try and remember some poem, some story, and concentrate on it — something I liked, something familiar, to distract me from his mechanical movements, his muttering and panting. But I couldn't think of a story strong enough to block out this wretched, painful reality. Instead, a song suddenly came to me. I tried to follow the melody until it crystallised clearly enough in my head. It was Edith Piaf. *'La Foule'*. It's a song I've always loved, and suddenly I could hear a whole orchestra in my head, and then the shimmering voice of Piaf piercing through it all, and even though I didn't recognise or understand individual words, I clung to her scratchy R, her hard L, listened to the accordion in the background and tried to imagine a dark stage, on which — far, far away from here, I was sure, in a place where I had never been, and more importantly a place where he had never been either — the little sparrow stood, illuminated by a single spotlight, singing her song just for me, just to me. It was a beautiful idea, and for a few seconds it succeeded in taking me away from this place and blocking out his clumsy, brutal thrusts.

I remember that he had difficulty, kept stopping, trying to find a more comfortable position for himself, all the time twisting my hands up my back. I remember that once or twice he even let out a cry of annoyance, as if he were dissatisfied with his own qualities as a lover; but of course he took out his frustration on me and abused my body all the more ruthlessly.

I remember that — when Edith had stopped singing, although she had already sung me an extended, much slower version of her trademark song — I wondered why he didn't stop, why he wasn't finished with me, with himself, with his urge. Why did it keep on starting all over again? How many hours, days, weeks was this going to last? When had time stopped, and above all, who had stopped it?

I remember that I didn't scream. That I stood there mutely waiting for time to start up again, for the hands of the clock to resume their movement.

And then he turned me round, furious that he was unable to ejaculate and get his triumphant satisfaction. He threw me to the floor and fell on me, pushing my legs apart with his knee. Now he upped the tempo, and his breathing became unexpectedly calmer, more regular, as if he were feeling really good now, not having to rush or make an effort. I turned my face away. I didn't want to look at him. And then I saw the *chacha* bottle we had emptied together. It was lying there, an abandoned, now useless object that one of us had knocked over in flight or pursuit — rolling gently back and forth, as if trying to keep time with him. I remember that I had seldom in my life been so glad to see anything as this empty bottle.

I had to free my hand in order to reach it. I had to be quick. I wouldn't get a second attempt; not with my current run of bad luck.

I slowly released my arm, which was trapped under his chest. In order not to draw his attention to my movement, I put it around his neck. As if I had finally come to terms with having to give him pleasure. He registered it with a brief groan. Then I raised my arm cautiously, laid it on the floor, stretched out my fingers and finally — the first bit of luck I'd had that evening — touched the cold surface of the bottle. Now I had to shatter it with one blow and hit him with the bottleneck. His panting was growing louder as I swung it back and smashed it on the floor with all my might. The noise gave him a start, but he was too close to his ultimate pleasure to be able to pause, let alone stop altogether. And that didn't matter now: the bottle — the only friend I had in this room, after even my buttons had let me down — was broken, the neck ending in jagged shards. And it would do. It would serve its purpose. As he finally looked up, overcome with convulsions, the bottle in my hand hit his waist and cut into his skin.

He let out a howl, no longer capable of putting the brakes on his pleasure, despite the pain, and rolled sideways. The next time, I struck harder. The glass pierced his arm, and blood began to run onto my stomach. He curled up in pain and let go of me completely. But he still seemed to be in a haze, he still didn't comprehend the full extent of my hatred.

In a flash, I was back on my feet, bending over him, my trembling hand holding the sharp bottleneck in front of his face. I looked at him properly for the first time. The scar that split his eyebrow in two. For some reason, I imagined that another woman who had once been in my position, who had held another broken bottle, had left this scar behind. Something about this improbable idea was very satisfying. I held the bottleneck out towards him and waved it in his face. But suddenly he convulsed, his eyes widened as he kept looking into mine, he stretched out his bleeding arm, his mouth twisted into a contented smile, and he ejaculated, letting out a loud, almost joyful laugh as he did so.

I remember everything, but I don't remember what I felt through it all.

> Wherever we had been in Russia ...
> the magical name of Georgia came up constantly.
> People who had never been there, and who possibly never could go there,
> spoke of Georgia ... as a kind of second heaven.
>
> JOHN STEINBECK

The worst thing was not my inability to weep over it, or that I told nobody. Nor was it the fact that I could hardly bear to touch Miro any more, couldn't explain anything to him, punished him vicariously for something he couldn't have the slightest idea about. And it wasn't that my anger and my hatred were directed inwards more than towards the person who had done this to me. The worst thing was the numbness inside. The huge emptiness. My self-control in dealing with everyday things. The emotionless continuation of business as usual. Carrying on silently as if nothing had happened. Not letting anything show, just being disciplined and capable after that unspeakable experience.

The days were like waking dreams that followed the night. Stasia's voice at my bedside. The images in my head and the attempts to replace them with Edith Piaf.

The aroma of chocolate came at night, as always: powerful, irresistible. Lasha's fits of rage, Daria's groaning, Elene's whispers, Nana's cautious footsteps, and Kostya's oppressive silence. Waking dreams in which, little by little, Stasia brought the past closer to me. Waking dreams from which you couldn't rouse yourself. My failure. My powerlessness, which I thought I had smashed with a broken bottle. How very wrong I had been about that.

By the end of July 1993, everyone knew that Georgia didn't stand a chance in Abkhazia. With the exception of Sokhumi, all the centres in Abkhazia were occupied by Abkhazian, Russian, and 'hired' military forces from Caucasian republics. On 27 July, with Russian mediation, an agreement was signed for the immediate withdrawal of the Georgian military from Abkhazian territory. The contract also ruled that all Abkhazian troops were to be overseen by Russian 'peacekeeping forces'. That summer, some of the Abkhazian refugees returned to their ruined villages and towns. The authorities said all of Abkhazia's schools and universities would reopen on 1 September.

Daria's belly was round and her resistance fragile. She looked weakened. It seemed to be only a matter of time until the dams broke. And they broke. They broke at the same time as the Georgian-Abkhazian-Russian agreement. They broke on the day the Sokhumi massacre began.

On 16 September, Abkhazian troops stormed the city. The offensive had been planned beforehand at the headquarters of the Russian 'peacekeeping troops'. And these troops were not permitted to intervene. However, they took up key positions on the border, so that the Georgian troops who were left in Sokhumi couldn't hope for any more reinforcements.

The number of civilian victims, who were driven out of their houses and shot in the street, ran to five thousand. Later, more than one thousand cases of rape were registered. Torture victims were never counted.

All those who had survived the offensive had to flee to the mountains again, hoping for a second time that they would reach the valleys alive.

Daria's desperate, near-hysterical voice woke me with a start.

'No, it's not your baby; is that what you want to hear? It isn't. I whored around like you told me to, to get hold of your fucking drugs. I did everything, yes, everything you imagine in your sick fantasies, and much more. Satisfied? Yes? Do you want the details, you cripple?'

This word changed something. It was an evil curse that should never have been said out loud. A sinister magic spell. But it was the way she said it, much more than the word itself, that frightened me. Behind the obvious and provocative contempt, her voice concealed a deep wound. As if she were directing the word at herself. As if she wanted to hurt herself with it.

He said something I couldn't make out, though his tone was calm, almost submissive; then I heard the door open and slam shut again. I looked out of the window and saw Daria, barefoot, walking through the garden. I saw her cross the vegetable plot and head towards the hill. She carried her belly in front of her like a shield, swollen, leaning back slightly as she struggled up the slope. I was already pulling my plimsolls on to run after her, but I stopped in the doorway. I could feel that there was no strength left in me. Not a single word of comfort, not a shred of emotion that could have been a crutch to her bottomless sadness.

When Daria returned from her night-time escape, she announced to her family at the breakfast table that from now on she didn't care what happened to Lasha. She wanted nothing more to do with him, and she was about to call his parents and tell them to come and collect him, or what was left of him. No one asked what had caused her sudden change of heart; no one probed, no one took sides. Then Daria disappeared. Nobody knew where she was; I even had to go and search for her in the woods. Not even when Lasha and his wheelchair were loaded into a minibus by his parents, who had sacrificed everything they owned for their only son, did she make an appearance. It seemed by then she didn't have enough love left to say goodbye.

★

In November, just three days before my birthday, Daria's waters broke, and I drove to Tbilisi, ignoring all the speed limits, flying through that year's unexpected early snow. When we pulled up at the hospital, the whole place lay in darkness. The electricity was off again, and I had to light the way for the groaning Daria with a torch, up the stairs to the maternity ward — and persuade you, Brilka, in your mother's belly, to give us a few more minutes to find our way to reception.

I spent a long time thinking about how I should introduce you to this story when you finally came into the world. This story, which is being told only in order to reach you. To reach you and, with you, the beginning. The whole purpose of writing this story is for you to come into the world again and have the chance to start everything differently, anew.

And I came to the conclusion that, at this point, I can't go on writing if that *you* exists twice over. I've decided to make you *my* Brilka to start with, so that I can carry on with my story, can reach you at long last: you, the true, the actual Brilka, whom in any case I won't be able to describe, not with all the words in the world — you, who could offer me the only *you* that I couldn't transform into a *she*.

But as long as I am still forging a path towards you, I have to borrow your essence, your image, and invent you afresh. Differently; in my own way. The way I saw you, the way I found and lost you. I have to invent you, Brilka, until one day you become real again. You, Brilka, came into the world and your name, *Anastasia Jashi*, was entered into the birth register, and you brought us all something like happiness for the first time in a long while, something we had almost forgotten existed. 'Jashi. Full stop. Anastasia is going to be a Jashi.' Daria, married or not, remained adamant. 'The name was good enough for the two of us, after all.'

Jashi, then. Anastasia Jashi. But Daria didn't want it shortened to Stasia. 'It's so *Russian*. Ani, maybe?' She was not to be called Ani. Brilka would give herself her own name. A name as wayward and unique as she herself was wayward and unique. But for the time being she was tiny, with a mass of black hair. Her eyes, too, were black on black, and her skin was shrivelled and wrinkled, as if she had been born with a hundred years of wisdom. She didn't cry; she was impressively calm and looked intently at the world and the people in it with her piercing black-black eyes, as if she had already seen through us all.

I wanted to look at her constantly, wanted her to see through me. I wanted to lay her on my stomach, to feel her warmth. I was an aunt. I was her aunt. This tiny creature gave me a function. Gave me a purpose. I could leave the bed and the room I had barricaded myself into for weeks.

Sokhumi fell in December. The end of the war was proclaimed, but in our bodies and heads it continued. We still felt the emptiness that the last few years had excavated inside us with huge shovels. Only the sea remained unscathed, lapping in its usual rhythm against the pebbles and the dark sand.

*

'I can't stand this any longer. You're as mute as a fish with me. I don't know what you're thinking any more. Sometimes I even wonder whether I still know you at all. You don't answer the phone when I call, you're absent, and when you do condescend to come out somewhere with me you stare into space. You don't even want to read any more. I really don't know what's wrong with you. And I don't want our only connection to be this bed. These little visits you make here. You come, you get into bed with me, we sleep together, then we have a cup of tea, smoke a cigarette, and I walk you to your car. And then you're gone. As if we were having a secret affair. What are these doubts you're plagued by? Is it still because of David? Is it your family problems? But the guy's gone now, isn't he? Your sister split up with him. Things can only get better. Come on, talk to me. And your eyes, the way you look at me. I'm going crazy. Seriously. You're always assessing me somehow. You're putting me through these secret tests I know nothing about. Tests I can't even consciously take.'

Miro had been invited to a birthday party that he had been talking about for days. I was supposed to be going with him. Lana had been out of the house all day; I'd come over early, and we had spent the whole morning in bed. When the time came to get ready, when he got up and started to put his clothes on, I turned over and curled up like a tired old cat. I didn't want to get up. I didn't want to leave this bed. I wanted him to stay with me. Just to hold me, without saying anything. That was all I wanted. The idea of being among people, of relaxing and chatting and drinking, laughing at jokes and singing along to songs, even having to dance, was abhorrent to me. It caused me physical discomfort.

He tried to persuade me, threw my clothes onto the blanket. Then he lost his patience and started talking, louder and louder, increasingly uncertain and helpless, until his despair turned into blind rage and he pulled the covers off me, grabbed my wrists, yanked me upright, twisted my hand, and I began to scream.

He let go. But I didn't stop screaming. I screamed like a banshee, distraught, flailing my arms around, fending him off, preventing him from getting close to me. Then I stopped screaming and began to cry. The tears ran down my cheeks without a sound. I slid along the wall and flopped onto the bed. Half naked, I hugged myself with both arms and rocked back and forth. He sat down beside me, but made no attempt to touch me.

'I want to go, and if you don't want to come with me, that's up to you.'

It seemed his stock of sympathy was just as exhausted as my will to explain. He got up and started combing his hair in front of the mirror. I wanted him to leave me in peace, but at the same time I couldn't bear the idea that he was about to go and leave me to myself.

I went over to him. I clung to him. I tried to keep hold of him. He released himself from my arms and went on with his preparations. I was so desperate to tell him everything, to explain it all, describe it all. But I didn't know how. I wanted so badly to keep hold of him; it felt like a matter of life and death that he should stay with me, that he was there for me that night. Yes, I wanted him to save me from myself. Was that too much to ask? Was that so impossible?

'You always want everything at once. And the minute someone can't offer you that, you turn away from them. Do you think I'm happy? Do you think I like things the way they are? Do you think this shitty country doesn't get on my nerves? Rezo — you know, from my course — he offered to get me a job at his father's construction company,' he added quietly. He pulled on a black suit over a white shirt carefully ironed by Lana. I could never iron anything so perfectly.

'A new company — only got its licence this year. His father has brought in investors, and once it's up and running he wants to leave things to Rezo and me. The investors are Turks, but we're hoping to get into the European market as well in a few years. When the situation here has stabilised, the property business is going to boom. Like it has in lots of post-Soviet countries. I'm going to start with building permits, and then later I can do something more creative —'

'Building permits?'

The words jolted me out of my spiral of thoughts. I stopped in front of him and gave him a puzzled look.

'Yes, building permits. What's so strange about that?'

'I don't know. You and building permits. That *is* strange.'

'Jesus — I thought you'd be pleased if I didn't have to tart up cars for fat cats in that filthy garage any more. It's a proper job, something fun, something that's more me, professionally, and —'

'Building permits? Oh, right, they're *much* more you.'

'Don't get sarcastic with me. I'm not going to let you spoil my evening, or my future. Today's already been demanding enough.'

'I didn't know being intimate with me was demanding for you.'

'It's not intimacy, Niza. *This* isn't intimacy any more. At least be honest with yourself.'

Christine's old television set was on in the next room, and I could hear a bad Mexican actress in a bad Mexican soap, underscored with bad, kitschy Mexican music, telling a bad Mexican actor that she would love him forever and wait for him forever on their favourite *hacienda*, but she had to marry José Gilberto, because she had no other choice.

'What about the film?'

I knew that asking that question just then would make him angrier still, but I had to ask it all the same.

'The film, the film! Who's going to be interested in a film right now? Take a look around you, Niza — wake up!'

'But we were going to —'

'Come on, get your shoes on. I have to go. Everyone's waiting for me.'

I was angry at him. At the compromise he was about to enter into, at his way of adapting and accepting everything, but above all I was angry with him because he had not managed to change me. To make me normal. To tame me. I cursed my earlier loyalty to myself and my irrationality, my stupidity, my contradictions, my hopes, and the idea that I could make a difference. An idea that had been taken from me in the space of a few minutes by a sadist, with my trousers down, pressed up against an old printing machine, hands twisted behind my back.

How could it be that the person I loved so obsessively, the person who occupied most of my thoughts, hopes, and ideas, had not been able to do what a cruel stranger had managed so effortlessly? To break me. To drive all hope out of my body. All sense of resistance. All sense of stubbornness. And how could it be that, despite the assumption I would be better off without these hopes, I was skating through life without them as if on sheet ice, as if tied to a sled that I couldn't steer — and now Miro couldn't stop this bloody sled, either? How could it be that I was drowning in my own depths and he was unable to reach out the hand that could pull me up?

But even in my anger, I understood how stupid it was. How unfair. He could only perceive the invisible consequences of that night. The bruises had long since vanished. And everything else that had been given to me in the print works as a permanent reminder of that night was not just invisible but unspeakable. How could I expect him to see the invisible and speak the unspeakable for me? It was impossible. Of course he was failing me. Just as I was failing myself, my daily life, my stories, my non-existent future, my aspirations, my fellow human beings, my country, my time, and now him as well.

Why couldn't he just see through me the way my sister's little baby did? Why did he find it so difficult? This laughing, gentle, playful boy who, over the years, had taught me what it was to dream life, and who in his untroubled way had introduced me to love. Who had taken me up and given me a home within him. But now that he was about to finish his degree and would soon be occupied with boring building permits, now that he was dreaming dreams he could be sure would come true, now that he wanted to go to parties and drink toasts to levity, I had become too heavy, too intransigent, too black, and too bitter.

Why had he not revealed to me when we were first together that our love wasn't meant to withstand wars, poverty, cold, electricity blackouts, disappointments, and above all a single night: a night in an empty print works that was now used for something very different from the spreading of news — yes, something very different. Why had he not shielded me from this love? When he constantly reproached me for not committing to him, how could I convince him that he was wrong? I committed to him all those years ago in the television room of the youth centre, where I read *Wuthering Heights* to him and travelled with him through time and worlds, and felt that anything that could be thought and described was possible. Yes, I had committed to him. It was my own self I had never committed to. It was my life, which I always kept at arm's length, incapable of settling on one of the billions of versions of ME and standing by it, pursuing it. 'Of all the possible versions of yourself, find the most impossible one,' David had advised me, and maybe I had done just that. Maybe I myself was the impossibility.

I couldn't let him go, let him leave the room, but nor could I go with him. I clung to his neck, literally begged him to stay, tugged at his jacket. He was annoyed, thought I was being silly, refused to believe that staying could seem like such a life-and-death matter to me. First, he tried gently to convince me to pull myself together. When his persuasion had no effect, he kept shaking me off, pushing me back, and when that didn't help, either, he took hold of me, lifted me up, and flung me away. I banged my head against the wall, slid down it, and sat on the floor. My head hurt, and I pressed my hand to where I had hit it. He looked down at me for a while, breathing heavily, not knowing what to think, then gave a reproachful shake of his head and stormed out of the room.

★

A month after Anastasia's birth, Daria's milk dried up. Daria started sleepwalking, getting up in the night and wandering around the house, sometimes even into the garden. She stomped through the snow barefoot, dressed only in a long, thin nightshirt, her shadow passing across the winter landscape with a striking elegance, like a wanton version of Ophelia on her way to the brook. Motherhood gave her back the beauty that had been crushed beneath the weight of her marriage; the baby lent her an alarming magnificence. Her straw-blonde hair had grown to waist-length again, covering her back. Her skin had regained its ivory colour. We had to lure her back into the house, carefully, cautiously. In the morning she would have no memory of the previous night. Elene and I started to take turns keeping watch. Daria had become a tightrope walker again.

Twice, Daria took her daughter into the city to show the baby to Lasha. She said that both times he cried when he held little Anastasia in his arms. She told me this with a degree of gratification in her voice. But after he heard that Daria had given his daughter her own surname, he refused any further contact. Daria stopped mentioning Lasha's name. She stopped talking about him. Overnight, it was if this person had never existed for her. And we all played her game, too, banishing Lasha's memory from the house.

One morning, a few days before New Year, Daria came into the kitchen — Elene and I were just packing up Stasia's cakes — and said she wanted to come into town with us. She couldn't stand being in this 'palace' a moment longer;

she needed people around her. Mother was pleased, and agreed. Daria's cheeks glowed as she gazed out at the snowy landscape from the back seat of the car. And I too was glad to see her showing some emotion again. I hoped the storm clouds had passed. We dropped Daria off somewhere on Lenin Square, which was now called Freedom Square. One of the rusty advertising hoardings displayed an old circus poster with a clown's face grinning idiotically. It had gained a few bullet holes during the civil war. I felt sorry for the poor clown. They had taken out their frustration on his red nose. Then we delivered the cakes to the basement shop and I drove on to the university.

As I was leaving the university building, I spotted Lasha's ex-wife at the bus stop, having an animated conversation with two other women. Luckily she didn't recognise me, and my curiosity made me sidle closer to the little group. They were talking about Lasha. She was telling her friends about his physiotherapy, the progress he was making, and the hope that one day he would be able to walk again. She announced with evident pride that she was about to move him into her flat, so that she wouldn't have to keep going to his parents' house to look after him.

'And what about his wife?' one of the friends asked.

'That little tramp? It was lucky he realised in time what it was he'd let himself in for. All those debts were down to her: he had to maintain her standard of living, because Madame Jashi was used to the best of the best. He told me how she shamed and made a fool of him in Moscow. That when he didn't bring home any money she wouldn't speak to him for days — can you imagine? The poor man had tears in his eyes when he told me that. I knew right from the start she would bring him nothing but misery. I mean, she doesn't even know the meaning of love; she just wanted to prove that she could have him, prove she could make him leave me. But I knew he'd come to his senses one day. And in that respect, something good did come out of this *tragedy* that befell him ...'

I wanted to run at her, wrap her hair round my hand, and throw her to the ground, to give her the loudest, hardest slap I was capable of, but I felt paralysed, unable even to summon up the strength to make myself known or give her a retort. Instead, ashamed and empty, I stood by and watched as the women got on the trolleybus and left.

★

We spent four days looking for Daria. For four days we phoned everyone she knew. My mother was trembling all over, and Kostya's hands could barely hold the receiver. On the fourth day, one of her former friends finally gave me an address where she 'might possibly be staying'. It was a building in the new town that housed some artists' studios. A guy who looked like he'd just stepped out of a boxing ring opened the door. Without telling him who I was or what I was doing there I ran past him, through the tiny front courtyard and into a smoky room with a high ceiling supported by pillars. The boxer strode after me. There were a few unfinished sculptures standing about, Janis Joplin was blaring from the huge speakers, and it stank of marijuana.

Some girls in short skirts were lounging on a battered sofa, while a long-haired joker told some wisecrack to make them laugh. Daria was sitting on the arm of the sofa, leaning against the wall and laughing with them. She was drunk. I dragged her outside and bundled her into the car. But not before I had persuaded the boxer to lend me some money, as the search for Daria had emptied my petrol tank and I didn't have a cent left to my name.

> Can you picture what will be
> So limitless and free
> Desperately in need of some stranger's hand
> In a desperate land
>
> THE DOORS

'Who do you think you are? Are you trying to set yourself up as my keeper again? Leave me alone! If I want to get drunk, I'll get drunk. I can do whatever I want. And you — with your choice of friends, you can't exactly turn your nose up at mine.'

'And where do you think it's going to get you, staying out, getting stoned out of your mind in that artists' colony? Who are these people, anyway? Where on earth did you pick them up? You're not like them.'

'Oh yeah? What am I then? A great actress?'

'Yes, you are, but you need to start doing something about that again. This country is going to the dogs; you're not the only one having a hard time, Daro.'

'You think you know better than me. You think you've hooked yourself a great guy who's going to love you forever and have intellectual conversations with you, who'll support you and fulfil your every wish. That's what you think, isn't it? Miro will cheat on you the first chance he gets. He'll leave you lying on the floor, step over you, and carry right on walking. They're all like that. Yeah, yeah — our poor gifted girl still thinks she has to change the world.'

'I have no reason to assume Miro will leave me at the first opportunity. They're *not* all like that, Daria.'

She laughed in my face.

'Oh, the poor little gifted girl doesn't believe me. She only sees the good in people, right? No, all your friends are noble. They're all little heroes, just like you.'

'Stop it, Daria. Stop being so horrible. You're not like this.'

'Oh yes, I forgot: you're above everything and everyone. But a few more disappointments, a few heroic deeds that don't work out, a few more wounds, and a real, deep insight into the mind of your sweet-natured boyfriend and you'll stop seeing the good in people, Niza.'

'Do you think I've never been disappointed in my life? Would it make you feel better if I told you what —'

'Oh please, keep your suffering to yourself. I've got enough of my own.'

'Your suffering! As if everything else were irrelevant compared to your unhappy marriage! Well I'm sorry to disappoint you, but not everyone is as much of a pig as your beloved husband.'

'Oh, you're wrong; your saintly Miro is no better. Want to bet on it?'

Something about the way she said it, the devilish look on her face, the *schadenfreude*, shocked me and made me shudder. I left the room without saying another word. On the terrace, I could hear big Stasia singing little Anastasia a lullaby.

★

Even though I was so angry with her that I decided I would never go looking for her again, would never heave her, drunk and staggering, into the car and drive her home, I never held out for more than twenty-four hours. I would go to the studios or wherever else she was and pick her up. Even Stasia warned me to leave her be, and Aleko advised me to let her 'get it out of her system', get over her heartache, but I just couldn't. It made me sick to think of her drinking herself into forgetfulness, into irresponsibility. But I now know that focusing entirely on Daria's troubles wasn't a selfless mission; it made it easier to distract myself from my own. The unfamiliar places I entered on my searches for her kept me from revisiting the place I didn't want to return to. I could go for several hours at a time without thinking about the print works or the images that had invaded and occupied my head. When I was thinking about Daria, I didn't have to think about the problems Miro and I were having. Since our last argument, it felt as if he had been deliberately avoiding me. He always pretended to be busy, was always inventing some excuse as to why he had no time for me.

★

One morning — when, at Kostya's entreaty, Daria had spent three days in a row at the Green House — I found her on the roof terrace, wrapped in a blanket, staring glassy-eyed into the distance as the tears ran down her cheeks.

It was a long time before she came out with it: she had heard from Lasha's parents that his ex-wife had rented them an apartment, moved Lasha in, and arranged a carer to look after him. Her father, who worked at the Ministry for Energy and Infrastructure, could afford to support his daughter financially. And, she added, still staring fixedly into the distance, Lasha had asked for a divorce. The ex-wife didn't want to remain an ex-wife for very much longer.

That same evening, Daria vanished from the house while we were all sleeping, and the next morning I had an indignant ex-wife on the phone. She told me to kindly come and collect my drunken tramp of a sister. Daria had turned up in the middle of the night outside the new flat she shared with Lasha (she didn't forget to mention this piece of news) and woken all the neighbours, shouting his name all over the courtyard. When she had found the right staircase, she had hammered incessantly on the door and shouted for him. She had whined that she loved him and that she'd made a mistake. She had pulled up her jumper and screamed that Lasha should take a look at what he was missing. At this I had to press my hand to my lips to suppress an urge to vomit. It tore me apart inside. Something in me exploded. I didn't know if it was the humiliation that Daria had brought on me with her senseless, absurd behaviour, or my own powerlessness to do anything about it, to *heal* her.

Over the weeks that followed, I had to collect my sister from a lot of different apartments. I got to know the farthest-flung corners of the city, the suburbs and the surrounding countryside. Most frequently, though, I found her in the sculptors' studio in the new town. That was the most constant and significant den of her rebellion. By this time, I knew most of the people there: would-be artists, former Mkhedrioni, heroin addicts, peaceful students who had sold or pawned all their possessions and now owned nothing, wanted nothing, were capable of nothing except killing time with a few others who shared their fate. The parties seemed to provide the only confirmation that they were still alive.

Elene was shrivelling up with worry, losing weight, and looking like a shadow of her former self; when she wasn't delivering cakes and giving private tuition, she tore herself apart for Daria. She kept taking her to see doctors and herbal healers; she even brought a clairvoyant to the apartment. Daria dutifully submitted to examinations and talked to a therapist — then slipped out of the house at night.

Only now and then, when she held her daughter in her arms and whispered to her, did my sister's mood lighten a little. When she saw her laughing, or fed her with a little red plastic spoon. That gave me hope — some assurance that the state she was in wasn't permanent, that it would soon be over. At moments like these, I believed that Daria could be herself again. Full of playful frivolity, full of verve, full of trust.

But these moments vanished as quickly and unexpectedly as they arrived. Elene and I were both forced to confess that we couldn't pin her down, and we decided to change tactics. I took it upon myself to win back Daria's trust by going to parties and getting drunk as well. If I went everywhere with her, I would be better able to keep an eye on her and prevent any further disasters.

This was the time when our mother's yearning for God was reignited. Forced to admit to herself that she had failed and was powerless where Daria was concerned, she was in such despair that there was nothing a doctor or herbalist could do to help. Only something greater could steady her. Yes, God had to come back. First, she started fasting, which to me seemed an extraordinary provocation in view of the food shortages at that time. Then I found her with her nose buried in the Bible. Then people kept telling me she was at church. The living room wall gradually became an icon shrine. If no human being was capable of helping her and her daughter, then maybe God would do it.

And the time seemed to be ripe for it, as well: the Orthodox Church and its elders gained a tremendous following in that period. Seventy years of persistent repression and persecution was made up for ten times over: crowds flocked to the churches, old and new. More and more people were putting up icons at home; more and more unemployed ex-soldiers and Mkhedrioni found their new calling, put on black cassocks, and started to preach. Neither Aleko, who seemed dismayed by his wife's newfound piety, nor the committed atheist and communist Kostya, could do anything about it.

★

It was March or April, I can't remember exactly, when Miro came to the studios for the first time. He had just bought himself an old Honda and was proud of his new purchase. Work seemed to be bolstering his self-esteem, which had been chipped away over the years. He was earning money, he was respected, he was making plans and was already starting to look like a little patriarch. Even the style of his clothes had changed. He was seeing less and less of his old friends from go-karting days, and more and more well-dressed young men I didn't know, every one of whom smacked of *business*.

On the phone he had told me that he'd just been paid and wanted to take me out to the Metekhi Hotel's chic restaurant. I told him he would do better not to throw away his hard-earned money, but inwardly I was glad because he sounded light and cheerful. A terrible longing for him took hold of me. So we arranged to meet that evening. Later, though, Elene called and asked me to bring my sister home. That morning Daria had thrown a tantrum, smashing crockery in front of her and Aleko, and had then vanished. I swore and cursed her. I didn't want to let Daria's moods spoil my lovely, quiet evening with Miro. But Elene begged me, and I gave in.

In the car, I explained the situation to Miro and asked him to help me get Daria back to Elene's before we went ahead with our plans — even though I had no wish to take him to this accursed place. To my surprise, he agreed at once, adding that he had long been curious about where I was hanging out. He drove me to the studio. The party people were sitting round a long wooden table, eating soup that Daria had made. She was wearing an apron, her eyes sparkled, and her hair was pinned up with a pencil. That evening she was playing the role of perfect hostess, and I sensed immediately how happy it made her. She hugged me tightly and put an arm round Miro, introducing him to every one of her friends.

For a moment I cursed Elene and her panic. Daria seemed neither out of control nor aggressive. Quite the reverse: it was a long time since I had seen her looking so at ease. She was wearing a knee-length blue dress that made her pale eye glow, and she had even put on lipstick. She had herself under control; she was fine. I could allow myself a nice evening with Miro. I put my arm through his, said goodbye to everyone, and pulled him towards the exit. But he stayed where he was, whispering in my ear that it was nice here, and the people were all so welcoming and interesting. Daria was sure to be disappointed if we didn't try her soup. I couldn't understand it: I finally had a chance to leave this place, and now the person I spent most of my time longing for wanted to stay.

'That's a really stupid idea, Miro. Let's get out of here!'

'But why? I like it. Come on, we can go to the restaurant another time — come on, Niza. I think it would be rude to just up and leave now.'

Daria was already at his side; she took his hand and led him to the table. I had no choice but to accept the situation. Of all the things I could have imagined, the possibility of Miro feeling at home in this place had never even crossed my mind.

But when he took a seat at the table, started eating, quickly connected with the others, laughed easily, joked and played the charmer, the reason for his sudden sympathy with these people became clear to me. He missed his old friends. He missed the relaxed atmosphere of those days in Mziuri Park. Missed the lack of responsibility, how untroubled they had been, missed his rough, lively friends who, while they couldn't talk about building projects, had plenty to say on the subjects of beautiful women and fast cars. He missed this carefree time, this intoxicating joy, and I decided to quickly curb my disappointment and relive the old days with him.

He kept pace with the drinking, told his jokes, amused the group, and enjoyed their unreserved attention. Daria, too, was clearly taken with his easy manner and sat close to him. She had never really been interested in him before: he'd been too unremarkable for her in her glittering world. Songs were sung. People made silly toasts. I was happy to see the old Miro again. I laughed at his jokes, threw my arms round his neck, drank toasts to brotherhood, giggled and bantered with him and the other guests. It felt so good to forget everything, to relinquish control for once and just enjoy myself. I danced with Daria, with the boxer, with Miro. And in the early morning, when the three of us were in the back seat of a taxi riding through a city still half in darkness, I felt alive again for the first time in ages. I rested my head on Miro's shoulder and held Daria's hand tightly in mine.

★

Over the days that followed, Miro kept pestering me to take him to the studios again. I tried to explain to him that he had caught one of the better evenings there; it wasn't usually that relaxed. More often than not the guests took things too far, and Daria certainly wasn't always as docile and affectionate as she had been that evening. But he wouldn't hear any of it. I kept coming up with excuses for why we couldn't go, and for that reason I stayed away from the studios for a while myself. But he went back. Again and again. After a while, I didn't even need to ask him what his plan for the evening was; the answer was clear. Sometimes I let him go to the studios alone; I stayed at the Green House and made tentative efforts to start writing again. I sat on the roof terrace. Dangled my legs over the drop. I watched Anastasia as she slept. I read, or stared at the stars. I tried to stop up the yawning emptiness inside me, with letters and words, sentences and stories. But that only worked for a little while — just until the next day began to dawn.

I missed David. I held conversations with him in my head. I followed the scent of chocolate into the kitchen and assisted Stasia and her arthritic fingers with the baking. I helped my mother take the cakes into the city. I said nothing, and on the drive into town I had to make a tremendous effort not to yell at her to *shut up* when she started talking again about the importance of faith and the church and the purifying power of fasting.

I dragged myself in to university. I just had to get through this last year. Just a few more months. I boycotted the lectures by the professor who had suggested I go to Abkhazia, not knowing that I would find my Abkhazia in a print works in the new town. At the studios, I pretended to be someone without a care in the world, let Miro kiss me and massage my shoulders, drank cheap vodka. Let the boxer and his friends talk me into dancing a drunken *sirtaki*.

Either the world was turning at double speed, or it had stopped turning altogether. I no longer knew or cared. There was nothing I was able to prevent, and nothing I was able to preserve. I wasn't even able to control anything, except my car.

Miro changed. He let himself go. He neglected his work. He smashed his new car into a telegraph pole because he was always driving home drunk. He grabbed my hand and dragged me to the toilet with him, where he tugged at my clothes and kissed my neck. I had no strength to put up any resistance; I just let it happen. I had become indifferent to something I once loved so much.

★

April brought a heatwave to the city. The air became unbreathable. The exhaust fumes of cars — mostly western models outlawed in their home countries and sold on to the East — made it even worse. But the heatwave didn't stop the party people from partying even harder. The music was turned up. The doors and windows were thrown open. The skirts and dresses got shorter. The consumption of alcohol and drugs more unrestrained. And I — I could feel my strength dwindling. My final exams were coming up in June, and I hadn't lifted a finger for them. Essays that still had to be written were repeatedly put off. And the person whose shoulder I could have cried on had become a source of worry himself. I stopped intervening when people locked horns at the studios, paid no attention when someone collapsed in the toilet again, ignored the boxer lifting up my sister's dress. Sat silently in a corner reading or withdrew to the bathroom when the noise level and the heat became unbearable, and put my hands over my ears until the worst was over.

And now, when I look back on those hot spring days, when I try — over and over — to reconstruct that one night, I can't help thinking that I allowed things to reach that point. That in some cursed, vaguely intuitive way I foresaw it and didn't want to stop it happening. Maybe inwardly I was almost hoping, longing for it. Maybe I was searching for a compelling reason to finally give up the role of chaperone. I couldn't go and I couldn't stay; I was caught between her laughter and her torment, which always began at daybreak. Between my *no* and her *yes*. Between my longing for something whole and her destructive drive. Caught between her addiction to burning herself out and my desire to hold her back. When I think about that night, I realise that I wanted to let go, that I deliberately walked into it. Yes, Brilka: I did.

★

I had been irritated all evening. I wanted to go home. I wanted to sleep. Instead, I was hanging around in this hellhole, occupied with anything but myself and my own problems. Luckily Miro wasn't there that evening. One less thing to worry about, I thought, and decided that if I couldn't get away I was going to drink. Daria and the others were playing Super Mario, the most exciting invention since the video recorder. I felt the bitter liquid burn my throat.

Eventually I tugged at Daria's shirtsleeve and asked her to come home with me in the car. She waved me off, engrossed in her game. When she continued to ignore me, I found an empty bottle in the kitchen, filled it with cold water, and poured it over her head. Shocked, she leaped to her feet, yelled at me — what was I thinking, had I gone mad — and told me to get out. I didn't know what else to do but grab Daria by the wrists and push her to the floor. Then I jumped on her, as I had so often when we were little, pinned her arms to the ground, and shouted in her face that she had to come with me right now.

The boxer grabbed me by the shoulders and pulled me off my sister. I swore, flailed my arms, snarled at him; I was beside myself. Finally, he managed to throw me out of the studio and slammed the door in my face. I sat in the car, started the engine, switched it off again. I didn't feel capable of driving. I got out again and started running. I didn't know where I was running to, but I knew I didn't want to stand still. I zigzagged around. Having raced for miles I sat down on a bench somewhere, dripping with sweat. It was already late; the metro had stopped running. It was eerie. I decided to go back and drive home: I was never going to get to Elene's on foot. I was too exhausted.

It took maybe an hour to get back to the car. By this time, I had sobered up and regretted doing what I had done. I had to be sensible. Had to make another attempt to take Daria home.

When I got to my car, I was confused: Miro's car was now parked outside the building as well. The door was open, and I got in without any trouble. Head held high, I marched past the boxer, ignored startled comments from a few female guests, and went looking for Daria. But she was nowhere to be seen. No trace of her. Or of Miro. I asked a drunk girl who was sitting in the kitchen, absentmindedly eating sunflower seeds, but she didn't know where my sister was. I was about to go out again when I found a narrow door in the hallway. I wrenched it open. It was a staircase leading down to the cellar. I went down into the darkness, clinging on to the wall as I couldn't find a light switch. I heard rustling, then a giggle. I recognised Daria's voice, and peered curiously into the cramped cellar room.

I saw them standing in a corner. I squeezed my eyes shut in the hope that I had imagined it, but when I opened them again, I saw Daria with one arm round his neck, her fingers buried in his hair. His hands were all over her body. She looked composed, as if she were a stranger to passion, while he was obviously lost in the moment. I knew him so well. I knew exactly what he was feeling. He was kissing her in a way he had not kissed me for a long time.

I felt my knees go weak, and suddenly my mouth was filled with the bitterest taste I had ever known. I didn't realise it was the taste of betrayal. A soft whimper escaped my lips. Miro quickly let go of her and looked round. It made no sense to stay hidden; I took a step into the darkness of the room. Daria stayed where she was, motionless, looking me coldly straight in the eye, while Miro muttered something to himself and struck his forehead with the palm of his hand.

After what felt like an eternity, she said in a trembling, cracking voice, 'And now? Now will you finally leave me in peace?' Miro glanced at her uncertainly; he had no idea what was going on, he seemed to consist entirely of his own shame. He stared at the floor, then gathered all his courage and took a step towards me, but I motioned him to stop. Strangely, I felt sorry for him just then. All my anger was directed at her. I wished she had never existed, I wished I had never given her my love. I wished I had never followed her here. I wished I had never enabled her to do that film. I turned and ran up the stairs.

It was only the next morning, when I came into the kitchen and found Elene there, dissolved in tears, with Nana rocking her back and forth like a baby, that I discovered Lasha had died of an overdose the previous night. Daria had known it all along. Daria had known it when she was playing Super Mario; when I threw her to the floor; when she went down the cellar stairs with Miro.

★

Over the weeks that followed, I didn't leave the Green House. When Miro phoned, he was told that I didn't want to see him, and the one time he turned up on the driveway I asked Kostya to go out and let him know he wasn't welcome. Elene and Aleko finally brought Daria home after two weeks of solid drinking. Locked her in. Elene stayed with us in the Green House and kept watch over her daughter. She fed her, banned all alcohol from the house, fetched a doctor who prescribed some kind of sedative.

Lasha's death was the beginning of her end. And no matter how hard the others tried to hold on to her, she kept striding purposefully towards it. I knew it, I could see it, but I couldn't and wouldn't do anything more to stop her. If she managed to go a few days without alcohol, if she regained her appetite and paid attention to her daughter, a dramatic relapse would follow, as if pre-programmed. She stole money from Elene's bag, slipped out to the only corner shop in the village, and bought vodka. When we made the corner shop owner swear not to sell her any more alcohol, she found a farmer who would give her home-brewed *chacha*.

One night, sleepless as usual and sitting on the roof terrace again, I watched as she crept out onto the drive. I could see a silhouette there. A man I didn't know. He handed her something wrapped in paper, which rustled pleasantly in her hand. It didn't take long to work out what the present was.

★

That August was sweltering. I was forever putting cold compresses on my face: there were now no working ventilators in the house and the attic was like a furnace. I drifted listlessly around the house. I couldn't sleep. In the kitchen I found unwashed bowls and pans. Stasia had been baking. Her age made her increasingly careless: she had left the remains of the hot chocolate in a little bowl on the gas cooker. I couldn't resist. I snatched the bowl and went up to the roof terrace.

When I got there, I saw a candle burning. I found Daria sitting in my usual spot, dangling her legs and eating a slice of watermelon. I was about to turn round but she asked me to stay. I went over to her and sat a little way off, on the edge.

I put the bowl down beside me. The aroma was irresistible: it even woke her from her torpor. Unable to resist the temptation any longer, I stuck a finger into the bowl.

'Is that Stasia's chocolate that we must never taste?' she asked, smiling at me.

I wondered when I had last seen her smile. 'Yes.'

'Can I try it?'

I shrugged and set the bowl down between us. She leaned over and put her forefinger into the black mass.

'Stasia thinks it's cursed,' I said, shaking my head.

'It's heavenly!' she groaned.

Greedily, we licked the bowl clean.

'What about you?' she asked. 'Is that what you think?'

'That it's cursed? To be honest, I think we're already so cursed that we can withstand this as well. And unlike all the other curses, at least this one tastes divine!'

She laughed.

'I want Anastasia to be different. I want her to have as little of me in her as possible.'

'All of this will pass. The curses, and all the rest of it.'

'You know, that's always driven me crazy. I've always hated that about you — I hated it so much, Niza …'

'What do you mean?'

'The way you … You always try to make everything right. The fact that you're even sitting here talking to me. Why don't you still hate me?'

'Who says I don't?'

'Oh, come on. I've never understood how you do it. They'd kick you, and you'd get right back up again like a roly-poly doll; you got up and carried on. But surely even you must weaken eventually. No one can bear it. Always finding a way to carry on, keep going; never stopping, always being prepared. For the worst.'

'You've got the wrong impression of me.'

'No, I haven't. I hope you know exactly why I did it. It was nothing to do with him.'

I felt sweat break out on my forehead. I didn't want to talk about it. I wasn't ready for it. But I nodded.

We sat like that until dawn, in our favourite place, the only place we still had in common, and spoke briefly about what had happened that night, but nothing more. We were both aware of our inadequacies, our failures, our cruelties. We were each so frighteningly knowledgeable about the other.

The sky was an indescribable colour, one that existed only in that place. If I could have invented this colour anew and given it a name, I would have made that sky the colour of a broken world. Broken and beautiful.

'No. It won't happen to you. Never,' she said suddenly.

'What? What won't ever happen to me?'
'You'll never weaken.'

★

Nine sunrises later, my sister was dead. On the night of her death, her secret visitor had brought her another bottle, and she had got drunk on the roof terrace. A little breeze had risen and blown away the exhausting heat. I was in bed: that particular night, I wasn't there for her.

She finished the bottle of vodka and fell from the top floor, her temple smashing into the hard, dry August ground. She fell from our terrace, which had never been finished, never been fitted with a railing. From the attic that had provided our mother, Daria, and me with so many hiding places, where we pursued our dreams, licked our wounds, where we shook off our anger. Where we had always enjoyed the unique sky, which seemed so close to this enchanted place that you only had to reach out your hand to touch it.

Stasia found her in the early hours of the morning, lying with her face on the earth. Her arms were spread wide, as if she were trying to learn to fly as she fell. As if she were balancing on an invisible tightrope.

Stasia knocked on my window from the outside, waking me with a start. I had slept more soundly than I had in months. Yawning, I stretched towards the sun, walked out into the garden, unsuspecting — but even before I saw her body lying there, Stasia's face had already told me everything. She knelt down beside the motionless body, Daria's head in her lap, hugging her shoulders and rocking back and forth. Her lips formed soundless words; her face had disappeared behind a veil of deepest grief. She kept putting her lips to Daria's forehead, kissing her hands, stroking her hair.

I remember that, before I had even realised what had happened, the first thought that came to my mind was that I had to somehow keep Kostya away from this sunlit spot. That I had to destroy this image. Prevent Kostya and Elene from ever setting eyes on it. Pull Stasia away from Daria's body. Cover Daria up, take her inside, order her to get up. Yes: she must just be unconscious — it was the alcohol that had rendered her motionless, and Stasia simply hadn't realised that she was just sleeping off her binge.

I knelt down by my sister and started pummelling her. Get up, I told her. Come on, you stupid cow, get up, you're scaring us, I whimpered, but Stasia pressed my head against her breast.

'No, Niza, no, she's not going to get up, she can't get up, let her go, Niza, let her go, my sunshine.'

Her words came like a litany: monotonous, calm. But I didn't let go of Daria; finally, I turned her face towards me and saw the blood on her temple, saw the finality written into her features, her bluish lips, her eyelids, the sun beating down on them so mercilessly. Even then I refused to acknowledge her death. I shook her. I tried to get her on her feet. Until Stasia gave me a slap and forced me to look at her.

'She's dead, my sunshine, she's dead. There's nothing more we can do.'

'How do you know? Are you a doctor? We have to get her to the hospital, we have to —'

'I know the dead, Niza. I know them,' she said; and I froze. Then I leaned to one side and vomited. Stasia instructed me to stay there and not do anything, and went into the house to phone Aleko. I don't know how much time passed before he arrived. Luckily no one else was awake yet; luckily it was still too early to mourn a death. Stasia and I spent minutes or hours sitting hunched over Daria's body, shielding it with our own from the burning sun.

And I remember showing enough presence of mind to go to Aleko as he got out of the car and put my hand over his mouth so that he didn't cry out.

'You have to help me get her to her room. While Mama and Kostya are still asleep, right now. You have to help me!'

I'll never forget his look. Never. He looked at me and I knew that at that moment he was asking himself how, in the face of what had happened, I managed to say these words and not break down, how I managed to think about Elene and Kostya. He was wondering what kind of person I was.

> In this life there's nothing new in dying,
> But nor, of course, is living any newer.
>
> SERGEI YESENIN

Death laid itself over our eyelids, over our skin, like a layer of dust. We were all its prisoners. I smelled and felt it everywhere. I wondered whether the line between life and death even still existed in our house, or if we, the house's inhabitants, were all dead already and simply didn't know it.

I felt Daria's death spread like an incurable disease that had infected us all. It was just that each of us displayed different symptoms. Each of us was sick in our own way.

While the sight of Daria's shattered temple shredded the last remnants of Stasia's energy, while Nana threatened to collapse under her own weight and the weight of Daria's death, while Aleko crept around the house on tiptoe, and little Anastasia, who had been an unusually good-tempered baby, now screamed almost constantly, my mother froze.

She was like an oracle from a classical play, giving dire predictions. Her movements were imperceptible and noiseless, and when she touched us it was mechanical. Her face was suddenly old and hard, her eyes frightening. She wouldn't put the little girl down. She screamed at us the minute we approached her and offered to take over the night shift. She talked to herself. She prayed for hours. She kept the candles burning and stayed in her black mourning clothes. She warned us of God's anger and told us to say an Our Father three times a day for Daria's soul.

But as the days streamed past and we did our utmost to seal shut the doors to Death again, pressing the weight of our weakened bodies against them, my grandfather Konstantin Jashi was summoning Death with all the strength he had left. He spent whole days at Daria's gravestone, which had been erected next to Christine's. He looked through us, at Daria. In these moments, when he was oblivious to everything around him, he started to smile, and I knew he could see Daria, that he was recalling Daria's first steps, remembering how he had straightened her plait, feeling her warm hands on the back of his neck. Hearing her laugh.

It was almost impossible to tear him away from these memories; he swore at us and refused to return to the present, which tasted to him of deadly poison, while the past still retained the taste and the smell of Daria's rosy cheeks.

His grey beard hung raggedly from his chin; his cheekbones protruded like the ribs of a gulag prisoner. His hands wouldn't stop trembling, and he couldn't finish a drink without spilling it over his knee. He couldn't sleep; if he ate, he had to vomit afterwards. Drank himself so senseless that sometimes he just fell over and lay there on the floor, or even wet himself. All of the will to love and to live that he had left after Ida was taken by Daria when she went. I suspected he would seize the first opportunity to follow her. And he didn't have long to wait.

★

In October 1994, two months after Daria's death, he was diagnosed with acute myeloid leukaemia. The inferno during the submarine test run and the sickness he thought he had beaten in an Austrian clinic had returned to his body. He refused chemotherapy; he refused medication.

At lunch one day he calmly explained to us where this illness had come from, and how he had been treated before. He reminded Elene of the time he'd had to leave her alone. Tears ran down Nana's cheeks, and Stasia got up from her seat, trembling, and dropped her plate on the way to the sink. Kostya spoke of the catastrophe, of the dead sailors, of the official secrets document.

Just five weeks later, he was bed-ridden. All attempts by his mother, wife, daughter, and granddaughter to persuade him to go to hospital failed.

At the end of November, I went into his bedroom and lay down beside him. I took his hand in mine and remembered those twenty-four hours I had spent with him in this bed, collecting his tears, holding out the wine to him, sharing our secrets. It was another life. A life in which Daria had been alive.

We said nothing, and I listened to the ticking of the old wall clock. I laid my head on his sunken chest; I closed my eyes to avoid seeing his sickly pallor and the blemishes on his skin.

'Do you know what I've been thinking about all this time?' I heard him say, his weary voice sounding as if it came from a long way off.

'No, what?'

'All those years, all those decades, there were millions, billions, of busts and statues and pictures here. Where've they all gone?'

'What statues and pictures?' I asked.

'You know, of Lenin, Marx, and Engels, the Generalissimus — all those men!' He seemed to be giving it serious thought.

'They've gone.'

'But they can't all just disappear, just like that!'

'Apparently they can. Everything disappears sooner or later.'

'Nothing disappears. Nothing, Niza!' He laid his hand on mine.

'You mean, everything is hidden somewhere, waiting to be found again?' I tried to bring myself to smile.

'Everything is waiting to come back.' Lost in his own thoughts, he squeezed my hand more tightly.

I listened to his breathing. I listened to his heartbeat. I thought about how much I loved him and about all the things I would have done and given to have him return my love, ever since I was born. And suddenly I started to think it wasn't so bad that he never had.

I forgave him in light of the love he had given to someone else: my sister. I forgave him, because at that moment I understood that this was the connection I had been looking for all this time, perhaps our most profound connection: our love for the same woman, who was now no longer with us. I forgave him for his coldness and his domineering nature, I forgave him his tyranny, I forgave him for overlooking me so often. I forgave him for letting me spend so many nights weeping alone in my bed; I forgave him for deceiving so many people and making them unhappy, for betraying so many.

The object of our love had gone. And nothing else mattered any more. We had lost the person whose love we had fought over. There was nothing more worth arguing about.

I curled myself around him, laid my head in the crook of his neck, and stayed there until he fell asleep. Then I wove my thoughts and the words that I had never said to him and never would, all my feelings about him, into his dreams.

Kostya died in December. Absurdly, or logically, the official cause of death was cardiac arrest. His heart had pre-empted his illness.

The night after his funeral I saw Stasia go into the barn for the first time in years, and I followed her. She put on *Tosca*. She stood at the window with her eyes closed, listening to Puccini. I approached cautiously, my face swollen.

'What are you doing here?' I asked her.

'It's what Christine wanted. I put it on for Christine,' she replied.

'Why Christine?'

'Well, she came to fetch him. She was here today. She came for Kostya,' she said, as if it were the most obvious thing in the world: one dead person had come to fetch another.

'So Christine fetched Grandfather?'

'Yes; Christine and another woman, a stranger.'

'A stranger? What kind of stranger?'

'I've never seen her before in my life.'

'What did she look like, Stasia?'

'Tall, thin — too thin for my liking — with a lot of rings on her fingers. Beautiful rings.'

I didn't know now which of us was mad.

'And where did you see them?'

'Where I always see them. In the garden. They stood there for quite a while, a little way off, where the fig tree used to be before we cut it down, do you remember?'

'So you saw Christine and this woman fetch Kostya?'

'No, I didn't see Kostya. They were here for him, I know that. But it takes time.'

'And Daria? Did somebody fetch her?'

Even as I asked the question I was ashamed, but at the same time I envied her this madness, this gift or paranoia. I would have liked to share her certainty that somebody had come to get Daria; that she hadn't just *disappeared*.

'Kitty ...' she said, and her mouth twisted out of shape. Tosca launched into 'Vissi d'arte'.

'What about Kitty?' I felt something clench in my stomach.

'She was there under the cherry tree so often in the days before what happened with Daria. She and Thekla were always sitting there ...'

'But Kitty ...'

'Oh, I know. Of course I do. You all think I'm too old to notice when my own daughter dies, do you?' Her voice was suddenly filled with contempt.

'And you say Kitty's there sometimes, too?'

'Yes. My little girl, my beautiful Kitty.'

'And you believe that Kitty ... um, came to fetch Daria?'

'I have outlived both of my children and my great-granddaughter. Now I hope it won't be long before they all come together, to fetch me.'

I lowered my head. 'If Kitty came for her, then maybe she's looking after Daria now.'

I clung to these words, not at all convinced of what I was saying — but it was such a comforting thought, such a lovely idea.

'Sometimes one is much stronger when one is weaker, Niza.'

She surfaced suddenly from Tosca's lament and looked at me for a moment, only to sink back immediately into her thoughts. And when, reaching the climax of her despair, Tosca asked her God why he punished her so, I began to dance.

Stasia watched me. She seemed unsettled at first, then something like a smile began to spread across her face. I performed all those movements she had taught me as a child and which my body could still remember. I spun around, leaped through the air, pulled in my legs, stretched them out; I flew through the empty room. I danced my best dance. A dance of death for Stasia and her ghosts.

When I left the barn, drenched in sweat, I saw Miro coming towards me. Without a word, I went to him, hooked my arm through his, and started up the path towards the woods. It was dark and cold, but I was hot. He seemed grateful that I was touching him again. He didn't ask what was wrong with me, and I was glad of it. We trudged through the dry leaves and came to a halt under a large fir tree.

The night was clear, and the stars were especially bright. He started to cry. I let him, without pretending I was able to offer him any comfort.

'I have to go away,' I said.

'What do you mean, away? Away where?'

'I don't know yet. But far enough away from here. I can't live here any more. Every day I struggle to keep from collapsing on the spot. Will you come with me?'

'But where to? How will that work?' he asked, wiping away the tears on the sleeve of his jacket.

'It will work somehow. Just come with me. I'll sort it out. To Europe, somewhere, just a long way away.'

'You can't do that, Niza. These things don't just happen. You have to —'

'I'm going, Miro. One way or another.'

'But what about us?'

'I'm not sure if there still is an us, Miro, and if there is, I don't want this us any more. I want a new us.'

'I can't cope with that, I ... What would we do?'

'I didn't think I could cope with *this*, either.'

'You can't go, Niza. No, you can't do that to me.'

'Miro. Please.'

He pressed me up against the fir tree and showered me with kisses; he held me tight, dried his salty face on mine, kissed my hands, and whispered words of love in my ear. He assured me that everything would be fine, that he would be with me, that it was over now, we could make a new start. He kept telling me we belonged together, there was nothing that could change that, he begged me to stay, and scattered his kisses all over my face and body, like little trophies he seemed to be awarding me for having survived. But I couldn't accept them now. There was no going back, and every fibre of my body seemed to know that. I knew that a part of me would always remain behind in this place, but this part was no longer capable of living.

★

A week after Kostya's funeral I called Severin in Berlin and asked him if he wanted to marry me.

'Excuse me?' he asked in disbelief.

'You heard me right. Would you marry me?'

'And what would be the point of that?'

'Then I can finally leave this accursed country.'

'You know I won't be able to fulfil my marital duties.'

'Good! I have no intention of asking you to.'

'Fine. I'll marry you.'

'Perfect. Then send me an invitation so that I can apply for a visa. And please, hurry!'

★

Before my departure, I wrote an open letter to the university, in which I explained my reasons for not wanting to take any exams there, or hand in my dissertation. I recounted the dialogue between my professor and me, and on the pages that followed I described the narrow, corrupt, nationalistic, and — in part — pro-Soviet attitude at the university. To this day I don't know whether this letter was ever published or even read by anyone.

After that, I went to the Green House, gathered up all my exercise books, notes, and above all the stories I had typed out on the typewriter — mountains of pages had accumulated there over the last few years — and carried everything down to a large tin bucket in the garden. Then I started a fire and watched as all my hopes, plans, and ideas went up in flames. But I regretted nothing. I felt nothing.

I bought the plane ticket to Berlin with the money I got for Thekla's gold watch — the watch Stasia had once given me as a protective amulet, to shield me from the laughter of my fellow pupils, from the hostility and lovelessness of the normal people of this world, from loneliness, Kostya's indifference, Daria's ignorance, evil looks, and God knows what else. When she gave it to me, I'd had no idea that much worse was still to come: things from which neither the watch nor Stasia herself would be able to protect me.

The night before my departure, Stasia came into my room and wordlessly pressed an old, leather-bound notebook into my hands. It contained my great-great-grandfather's recipes, written with a scratchy fountain pen. And, on the very last page, the precise formula for the hot chocolate.

When I asked her what I was supposed to do with it, she just shrugged her shoulders, gave me a tentative kiss on the temple, and walked out. And, on 24 January 1995, I left Georgia, that once sunny land, now storm-tossed, cold, and sunk in darkness. I took a plane to Istanbul, and from there I crossed the now invisible border into the West for the first time.

★

Two years after Kostya, Nana died of a stroke. I didn't go back. Elene and Aleko sold their little apartment to make ends meet. They moved into the Green House. Elene devoted herself exclusively to her granddaughter, whom she raised with a firm hand. Aleko carried on drinking beer and vodka, playing backgammon, and philosophising about life with those of his friends who were still alive. And he argued with his wife, because she prayed too much for his liking and he was finding it harder and harder to compete with her love for God.

Stasia died at the age of ninety-nine. She just went to sleep and didn't wake up again. In her final years she was almost blind and talked to almost no one but herself. She lived to be one year younger than the century.

I didn't go back. Nor do I know who came to fetch her. But I imagined them all coming for her that morning, just as she had wished: Thekla in her dressing-gown; her White-Red Lieutenant; beautiful Christine and her husband; sharp-tongued Sopio; Kitty; Mariam; the angel-carving Andro, and his curly-headed son Miqa. (Or maybe even two sons?) Kostya and Nana; perhaps even Ida, hovering somewhere in the background. And, first and foremost, my sister Daria, with the different-coloured eyes.

A year after my departure, Anastasia began to call herself 'Bri', and refused to respond when someone addressed her by her given name. It took another three years for Anastasia to vanish completely, leaving only Brilka.

I didn't go back.

BOOK VII

★

NIZA

> What you hide away is lost;
> What you give away is yours.
>
> SHOTA RUSTAVELI

Severin occupied a pre-war apartment in Wedding, Berlin, with a tiled stove and high, stuccoed ceilings. He still worked at his father's shop, whose customers were now almost all of the seriously wealthy kind and no longer so eager for the rare finds from the East that Severin had once obtained. The trend was moving towards Asia, as he explained to me not long after my arrival.

He wore white trainers, summer and winter. Every other day he would cook spaghetti in a mushy tomato sauce, and he had recently fallen in love with a boy called Gerrit, though Gerrit didn't want a serious relationship. He had an impressive video collection, which proved very helpful for my integration. He lived for the weekends, when he could go out, drink, and dance without feeling guilty. (The idea that you could only let go on a Friday or a Saturday had a logic that was completely impenetrable to me.)

His friends looked on me as one of the curiosities he brought back from his numerous trips. Every one of them was a left-wing liberal, and they were all active in some organisation or other, everything from animal protection to asylum-seekers' rights. Severin said I should tell them if their curiosity and their questions were getting on my nerves, but I didn't dare: I always felt compelled to dispense information about my country and my life with all the drama and emotion I could muster. Afterwards, I usually felt terrible and locked myself in the bathroom. Severin was understanding about my moods, for a completely illogical reason that just sent me into a greater fury. He called my condition the 'Eastern Blues', and claimed to be very familiar with it.

He refused to countenance living in separate apartments; he kept saying the two of us were going to be great flatmates. He didn't even want to let me get a job for the first few months, thinking it might overtax me, which wouldn't be good for my state of mind. I did as I was told: he signed me up for a language course, and I parked myself in a classroom with people of every possible nationality, from countries I had only encountered in my old children's book of *World Folk Tales*. I put on a friendly smile and said, in German, 'Hello, my name is Niza and I come from Georgia. Georgia is a small country in the Caucasus, and ...' One of my fellow pupils then asked if Georgia wasn't part of Russia, which forced me into a digression on the brief history of the Soviet Union, still making an effort to maintain the friendly smile, and this tired me out so much that I spent the rest of the lesson in a semi-conscious daze, wondering what I was doing here and what on earth was to become of my life.

Severin showed me the city. He enjoyed playing host. He was finally able to put his historical knowledge to good use, and gave me detailed lectures about some building or other, some street or other, some former or current resident.

In March, just before my tourist visa ran out, we trooped down to the registry office and applied for a marriage licence. After jumping through numerous bureaucratic hoops and obtaining all kinds of documents, we were able to marry.

I bought a dress in a second-hand shop — until then I hadn't owned any dresses — and he borrowed a suit. And when the registrar called upon us to do so, we kissed very passionately by our standards, then spent the whole evening laughing about it. He didn't invite his parents to our wedding.

'They'd only put the kibosh on the whole thing. I wouldn't even put it past my father to tell the registrar it was a sham marriage. I don't want to put you in danger,' he explained to me.

Later, we went to a fast food stand, stood under a red and white umbrella with dancing pandas on it, and ate currywurst until we felt sick.

★

For the first few months, I suffered from broken sleep and panic attacks; nightmarish images would wake me with a start. I spent whole nights sitting on the window seat, staring out into the darkness, smoking and wondering what to do with all the time that lay ahead of me. I had no motivation. No will. No joy. But there was something liberating about this state. For the first time in what felt like an eternity I sensed an almost masochistic pleasure in this inner emptiness. I suppressed all thoughts of home, limited myself to brief phone calls in which I summarised and prettified things, and told them about non-existent plans.

I wrote more honest letters to Miro, but never sent them. And every time he called — which was regularly, to begin with, then less and less frequently — I felt a fat lump in my throat, which left a rusty taste behind on my tongue.

Slowly, I felt my way back into the language and began timidly exploring Severin's bookshelves, taking out one book after another and negotiating them with the help of a dictionary. Starved and hollow as I was, every line, even the most hackneyed sentence, had the capacity to send me into a genuine paroxysm of joy.

I took great delight in our summertime visits to the little arthouse cinema, the walks along the Spree, the delicious ice cream in the Italian *gelateria*, and the Turkish kebabs. When I had no idea what to do with my day, I accompanied Severin's friends to their university lectures and sat there doing my best to be invisible.

The idea of studying, of working towards something, scared me at first. But I was much more afraid of doing nothing. I took casual jobs, working as a kitchen porter in a Russian restaurant, walking dogs, doing the night shift in a twenty-four-hour off-licence, even working in an upmarket shoe shop, although I knew absolutely nothing about shoes. I never lasted more than four weeks in any of them. My boredom was becoming increasingly unbearable, and the panic attacks had finally subsided, so I pulled myself together and enrolled on a degree course in modern history and politics at the Humboldt University. Severin strengthened my resolve, saying I could chuck it in at any time if it got too much for me.

I slipped into my new and truly monotonous student life very quickly. And I kept working: I had discovered a garage in the Neukölln district calling itself 'The Shed', which was run by a lesbian couple who only employed women. They were looking for someone to work the till. After a trial day, they hired me, and I sensed I would stay there longer than the usual four weeks.

Caro and Maggie, the couple who owned the garage, seemed to like me, too. After a while they even started letting me into the workshop, where I was allowed to lend a hand.

For the first time since I had come to Berlin, I felt something like joy in this place. I loved being able to distract myself from my thoughts with physical activity — even if Severin shook his head when I came home with dirty hair, covered in streaks of oil.

Now, I remember very little about my first two years in Berlin. All I have are a few images, and a recollection of the strange, semi-conscious state in which I was trapped. When I think back to this time, it's this 'not' state I always think of. All I remember is not wanting, not being able, not feeling. As if I were attached to an invisible device, my only life source, which made me get up every morning, do the things I had to do, put my time to some sort of meaningful use.

But I also remember the feeling of being constantly short of time. My fear of free time that I might have to spend alone with myself — time when I would have to think, feel something, remember something — made me create an almost impossible schedule, stuffing the day so full that in the evening I had no choice but to collapse into bed half-dead and fall asleep in seconds.

I ran. I cycled. I walked. I fled. I had no time to miss anyone or anything; I had no time to grieve, no time to laugh, no time for regret, remorse, reflection. No time to be lovesick, no time to live. I functioned, and I did that splendidly.

And when, in those few moments when I could no longer hide from myself, the images and memories flooded over me, I would press my face into a cushion, a book, even a shoe or a plate so hard that my eyes could see nothing but a pattern of colours, and then I would hurry back to my tasks.

I needed two mute, introverted years to replace my own words with foreign ones. I needed new faces in order to forget the old. I needed new shoes and jackets, new poets and philosophers; I needed time to catch up on time, to become young again, to cement the walls around me.

To my great relief, Severin, who initially made a huge effort to integrate me into his circle of friends, began to leave me in peace. He asked less and less often how I was doing, and managed to stay out of my way for days at a time. He organised our life together with little notes on the fridge, which were never about anything more than the need to buy milk or toilet paper. When it was his birthday or New Year, when I was forced to join in and dance, to share in the general happiness, I fulfilled this duty without objection, along with the countless other duties in my life that had to be fulfilled.

During one of the few arguments we had —I didn't usually have the energy for an argument — he called me a robot and accused me of having forfeited all my likeable qualities. But when I then suggested that I find my own place to live, he refused, saying he didn't want to give up on our 'marriage' just like that. And in fact I sometimes wished I could have gone to his room, sat on his bed, and howled out everything that had been building up inside me: how catastrophically I had failed myself and the world, how suddenly I had given up my family, my homeland, the world I had thought was mine. I wanted to hold someone responsible for my paralysis, implicate him in my state of not-being. But I knew it was pointless, that my situation would only become even more unbearable after such a desperate confession. I didn't want sympathy. I didn't want to hear: 'But you couldn't have changed anything' — and I didn't want to be convinced of the opposite. Without my self-hatred, what would I have had left? What could I then have used to keep hold of the past? With what emotions could I then have faced the world, and, above all, what motivation would I have had to go on living?

One day, Severin brought home a cat and informed me that she was our new housemate. I had a fit of rage. I myself didn't understand what made me overreact like that, screaming that I couldn't do it, that I didn't want to feel responsible. For anyone. Not even for an animal. He looked at me sadly, not knowing what to do. It wasn't just his annoyance that I had lost my spontaneity, my easy-going manner, my sense of humour — everything that had bound the two of us together in those dark, cold days in Tbilisi. There was a deeper sadness in his eyes, too, and that might have been something new: a degree of understanding. Understanding for the effort it took me not to think about the stories, my stories and those of others that I had borrowed and assimilated over the years, in the hope that I would be able to go on writing them one day.

The cat was returned.

★

After one of my rare phone calls with Miro, which was peppered with sarcastic comments from him and ended in an argument, I left the house in a rage, went to a club, and spent so long smiling at some lanky guy that he couldn't help but notice and take a seat at the bar with me. After just three sentences I had my tongue in his mouth. He took me back to his apartment in Kreuzberg, which he shared with his girlfriend, who was away, and I lay down in their bed. For the first time my body tried to love someone who wasn't Miro. For the first time I feigned desire for a complete stranger.

When he had fallen asleep, I crept out of the apartment, hailed a taxi, and went out drinking. Severin found me the next morning, asleep on the living-room floor. He sat down beside me, lifted my head into his lap, ran his fingers through my hair, and talked to me as if he were saying a prayer: 'Niza, you have to talk. You have to talk to someone. Otherwise you'll eat yourself up inside. I can see it, you know. And if you don't want to talk to me, then go to a therapist, get some help.'

But I didn't want to know; I just kept pinching my arms and thighs, my cheeks and belly until he was forced to take hold of my hands and rock me to sleep like a baby.

I'd just wanted to feel something again.

★

My history professor kept me behind after a seminar, wanting to talk about an essay I had just submitted. She fixed her eyes on me from behind her large glasses.

'I would venture to say that you have a great gift, Miss Jashi.'

I held my breath. This word belonged in my old life, it mustn't turn up again here, not here, not now and never again, anywhere.

'Not that I know of.' I tried to sidestep.

'You are, perhaps, aware that there is support available for nurturing special gifts?'

'Listen, I'm not gifted!'

'Well, let's see. You write better German now than your native-speaker classmates. You absorb information at an incredible speed, but on the other hand you are surprisingly bad at making use of it in a purposeful way. You have problems with attribution. Then again, you have a store of knowledge that is, how shall I put it, remarkable. You are highly focused when something interests you, but incredibly lax when you already know something. The fact that you rarely associate with people your own age also suggests that you're not being stretched enough. You are uncommunicative, awkward, and stubborn. And you aren't always scrupulous with the truth …'

'So? Are those all signs of being gifted, then? Don't you think that's a little — well, clichéd?'

'It would be a cliché to assume that what you have is a deficiency, not a gift. The cliché is your fear of confessing to your own talents and making proper use of them. I don't know who taught you not to use these talents. It was most certainly a mistake.'

'I like it here. I don't want anything to change. Please.'

'I'm your professor, not your mother. As your professor, I would advise you to apply for a research grant. I further recommend that you apply for a post as an assistant at one of our research centres. If you make a little effort, you can finish your degree ahead of time. You could do so much more, Miss Jashi. And if I were your mother, I would advise you to start facing up to your talents at once, and dealing with your absurd reluctance to use them.'

It was the first time since coming to Berlin that I had cried in front of anyone.

★

Caro was a trained car mechanic with strikingly long legs, tattoos on her arms, and one of a lizard around her ear. She idolised her girlfriend, a DJ who played many of the city's clubs and belonged to a feminist performance-art group. She loved fast cars, but above all she loved to play cards.

The first time she asked me whether I played, I said no. When she pressed me again, saying that she didn't believe me, given how curious I had always been whenever she talked about her poker games, I replied that I had given up. And when she finally persuaded me and took me to a game with her, I had to go to the bathroom after the first hand and throw up. Caro declared that I had professional qualities, and took me to a game in the backstreets of Pankow, where we played a very serious-looking group for money in a strange building that was more like a warehouse than anything else. I won some cash that evening, and deliberately left it on the seat in the U-Bahn. I handed my next win over to Caro. It was only on the third occasion that, as I raked in the cash, I managed not to immediately think of that hundred-dollar note that had made me stay at the print works and eventually, with trousers round my ankles and aching limbs, ram the neck of a broken bottle into a man's skin.

By that winter, I had so much money that at Christmas I was able to send home a considerable sum, get myself an old Volvo 760, and buy Severin some special edition trainers he had been drooling over for months.

'Where did you get the cash?' he asked suspiciously.

'I play cards,' I confessed in a neutral tone.

'You do *what*? You play cards? Where?'

'Private games.'

'You know you could get yourself in trouble doing that?'

'Oh, don't start, okay? I love capitalism — just let me love it! I lived under socialism for long enough! Come on, Severin!'

That made us both laugh.

★

In the Christmas holidays I got into my dark blue Volvo, took what remained of my winnings, and set off. I didn't know where I was going; I just drove through snowy landscapes and along icy roads. On the move, on my way somewhere, the feeble sun at my back, I felt something homely, something familiar, something that allowed me to breathe easy. I stopped at service stations, slept in cheap motels, ate bad food, and felt good. I crossed the whole of Germany. I drove to Paris. The borders had disappeared, and I wondered where they had gone. In Paris, I took a seat in a café and ate a slice of almond gateau. I watched the passers-by; I watched snowflakes falling onto the Seine. I drifted. I tried to take in the scent of the city. I was happy that no one knew me there, that I knew no one. I thought about my childhood and tried to reconstruct the pictures that had been in my mind as I'd read Hugo, Balzac, Flaubert, Proust, Colette and Miller, Voltaire and Diderot, Genet, Duras.

I thought about the French films I had so enjoyed watching with Aleko, Daria, and later Miro. The discussions afterwards.

I sat on a bench, looking out at the passing tourist boats, and wondered whether the city would have disappointed Stasia, whether it would have held its own against her idea of it, whether it would have welcomed her and, most importantly, let her dance. I saw Stasia behind my closed eyelids, and watched her dance for me.

I drove on from Paris to Lyon, then to Geneva and Turin. I crossed Switzerland, I crossed Italy and sang along to an old song on the radio and thought about my sister's different-coloured eyes. I exchanged my language for the songs on the car radio. I exchanged my native language for all the languages I borrowed for a few days, like the pretty hair slides I had once borrowed from Daria.

I crossed Europe, which had once been so far away and which now melted together beneath my tyres. I visited Rome and held back my tears at the thought that my sister would never be able to set her different-coloured eyes on all this beauty.

> Imagine me; I shall not exist if you do not imagine me.
>
> VLADIMIR NABOKOV

In April 1998, Miro called. He would be travelling to Amsterdam in the next few days and wanted to see me again. He seemed to have been drinking, and was very tearful on the phone. He murmured something about a ferocious longing for me. I agreed.

After hanging up, I spent a while looking silently at my reflection in the window. I saw a very small woman whose age and sex seemed somehow of secondary importance. I saw the short, untidy hair, which could never be tamed, saw the flat chest, the sloping shoulders, the sharp cheekbones, and the long, hooked nose. Saw the tired circles under my eyes, the duck lips, the dark eyes that looked so cagey, so inexpressive, and wondered what he might say about it all, whether he would recognise me, what we would have to say to each other after all this time. I wondered whether we would be able to smell, taste, feel on each other everything that had happened in between, the other people there had been in the last few years. And whether that would mean anything.

I got off the train in Amsterdam and went straight to the hotel where he was staying. I had forbidden him from meeting me on the platform. In my unsettled state I couldn't handle any sentimental scenes.

I knocked, and he immediately flung open the door. We looked at each other. I put my little overnight bag down on the floor. He was more grown-up, more imposing, more self-assured. The playfulness had gone from his face. He was wearing suit trousers, which for some reason made me feel completely overwhelmed.

He took my hand and pulled me into the room. He threw me onto the bed, and before I knew what was happening we were both undressed and wresting the memories from each other, the memories of what we once had been and what we had believed we would remain forever.

We didn't say a word. We struggled in silence, each of us trying to expand our ribcages to let the other one in, trying to scratch off the layers of time that stuck to our skins like a crust. It seemed so easy to be an *us* again. Our intimacy was so effortlessly restored. I could love him so effortlessly, like no one else in the world.

It was dark in the room; we hadn't turned a light on. We listened to each other breathing.

'Let's try again,' I said to him. 'Let's do it. We'll make it work, if you want it to. I have so little to keep me here, yet there's so little calling me back. But if I had you again, if I could bring you back into my life, then ...'

He hesitated, laid his head on my chest, stretched, sighed, said I was right, that he didn't want to forget me, that he was sure we would make it work. That he had to think about coming to Europe. That we had a future, a future together. That we should go to Berlin, the very next day.

And I believed him, unquestioningly.

Holding hands, we marched to the station the next morning. Holding hands, we bought our tickets. Holding hands, we got on the train. Our carriage was very full, so I asked him to wait while I found an emptier one. He stayed in his seat. When I came back, he wasn't in his seat any more. The train was still stationary. I thought he had gone to the toilet, but then I saw that his little suitcase was gone as well. I didn't want to think the worst. Maybe he was scared of thieves, or wanted to have a quick shave in the train toilet, I told myself. He hadn't had time for a shave that morning, and had complained about it. I forced myself to sit down. The train was about to leave. I stared at my watch; I stared at the empty seat in front of me. I didn't dare ask the other passengers about him: I already knew the answer and didn't want to believe it.

As the train began to move, I leaped up from my seat and ran to the door. I wanted to get off, but it was too late, and I had no choice but to take my leave of him from the window as the train pulled away and I saw him, the collar of his coat turned up, his gaze fixed on the ground, hurrying along the platform as if he were escaping from something. Wordlessly, with a deep horror and a sense of devastating finality lying heavy on my limbs, I watched as he vanished into the crowd.

★

Ignoring what my professor had said, I took the usual amount of time to complete my degree. I didn't intend to hurry; I had nothing to hurry towards. Even when, over the months that followed, she kept talking to me about the research post, I declined the offer and avoided the subject. I did, however, play regular games of poker, and sent the money to Georgia. When my mother asked where I was getting so much money from as a student, I told her something about a generous grant. I don't know whether she believed me. Or whether it even mattered to her. Mostly, when we spoke on the phone, she talked about God, Jesus, and the Church, and when she wasn't talking about this trio, it was about Anastasia, whom everyone now called Brilka, and who was apparently not as keen on becoming a pious, God-fearing child as Elene wished.

I kept working at the garage, and when everything got too much for me, when I was sick of the city and day-to-day life, I got in my car and drove all over Europe. Sometimes with Severin; sometimes without him. Vienna was the only place I gave a wide berth. I associated the city with other people's dreams.

My professor, who had a real bee in her bonnet about me, insisted that after my finals I should write a thesis. She introduced me to a colleague of hers, an expert on Eastern Europe, who had just got funding for a project researching the Cold War and was looking for a *capable* assistant, as she informed me with a satisfied grin. The Eastern Europe expert turned out to be a thoroughly charming, eloquent, and quick-witted man, who assailed me with countless questions and had already read my final dissertation. In the past few years I had done my best to steer clear of Eastern Europe. My reaction to being forced to consider it again was one of extreme aversion. However, as I had no real alternative, and no idea what to make of my life, I said I was prepared to do it. And so I became a research assistant, writing my thesis as part of a project which was to culminate in the publication of a wide-ranging book.

I kept running. I didn't stop. I didn't pause for breath.

★

Four years after my arrival in Berlin, Elene called me and told me Stasia had died. I pulled out my old suitcase, which was gathering dust under my bed, and found the recipe book Stasia had bequeathed me. I read through the recipes, but most importantly I tried to memorise the mixture of ingredients for the hot chocolate. In the morning I bought everything I needed and made my great-great-grandfather's hot chocolate.

Mechanically spooning up the dark liquid, I wept for my great storyteller, the spirit-seeing great-grandmother who was woven into my dreams. And along with her, I wept for the fact that I had not yet learned how so many of the stories ended, had not yet understood the connections between so many events, and that she would never again be able to help me understand.

★

I remember this dream as well as if it had all really happened. I remember his face so well, imperceptibly different from the photo I had found as a child among the old pictures in the living room cabinet. I dreamed of this man, Kostya's friend, who had helped Kitty Jashi across the border. In the dream I didn't remember his name, but I knew that at the Green House I had seen an old photo of him in which he was wearing a naval uniform and standing beside my grandfather, smiling into the lens. In my dream, he visited me in Berlin and brought me a bunch of violets, beautiful dark-blue violets, like the ones from the garden of my childhood. And he smiled at me. In my dream, he was young, just as he was in the photo from St Petersburg. I invited him into my apartment, we drank tea, and he showed me a suitcase — but I woke up before I could find out what was in it.

Three days later, I couldn't stand it any longer, and phoned home. I had trouble getting my mother to remember who I was talking about: after all, I didn't know his name. I just knew that he had travelled with Kitty when she returned to Tbilisi, and that he was the one who had brought my grandfather the news of his sister's death.

'You mean Giorgi Alania. What made you think of him?'

'I don't know. He just came to mind for some reason. Do you know where he is — whether he's still alive? And if so, where I might find him?'

'What do you want with him?'

'It's to do with my thesis. I'm researching Soviet prisoners, and I thought —'

For the first time since I left home, I wasn't telling my mother a pack of lies.

'I've no idea what became of him. But yes, he was Kostya's best friend.'

'Can you think who I could ask about him?'

'Some of Kostya's old colleagues are still around; they must remember him.'

In fact, just a few days later my mother got me the phone number of one of Kostya's old colleagues. And when I heard his name, and then his voice, I knew who it was. It was Rusa's father, who had been such a good host to us in Batumi, never guessing that his friend was having an affair with his daughter.

'Oh, so you research depressing things like that these days, do you? I'm sure your grandfather would be proud of you,' he said, after hearing me out.

'Guess who's on the phone!' he suddenly called out to someone. 'Kostya Jashi's granddaughter, who's living in Germany. The *wunderkind*, do you remember?'

Then I heard footsteps in the background, and suddenly there was a female voice on the line.

'Niza?'

I recognised her at once. The velvet-soft voice hadn't changed.

'Rusa?'

I tried to picture her face. The delicate face from before I found her in the bathroom. The face from before I met her in the snow. The face of a carefree woman in love, who simply wanted too much, and who was so good at backgammon. She was very affectionate, wanted to know all about me, and told me she was working as a lawyer now; she was married and had two sons. I was a little taken aback by so much openness and warmth. She seemed to have nothing in common with the woman in the red snow suit from Bakuriani. Before she handed the receiver back to her father, she murmured softly into the mouthpiece, 'I'm so sorry about Kostya. I was too afraid to come to his funeral; I just couldn't. I wanted to keep him alive in my memory.'

'I understand.'

'Niza?'

'Yes?'

'Thank you.'

I didn't say anything else.

Of course you could save a person. I just hadn't managed to save my sister. With the people I loved, I hadn't managed it. Or with myself. At least there's her, I thought. At least I managed to save her.

Rusa's father told me that Alania had been living in London for more than ten years. He had asked to be transferred there at the start of *perestroika*, and since then Rusa's father had heard nothing more from him, which meant he had no contact details, either. I thanked him and hung up, thinking I would just drop this naive idea and go back to my books. But the next day Rusa called me: she had so wanted to do me a good turn that she'd pestered her father until he called someone in Moscow, who knew someone, who ... and so on and so on, until she had finally tracked down an English postal address. I noted down the address and thanked her. A place near the very lyrically named Seven Sisters.

I flew to London and took the train down to Sussex. I had a taxi take me to the address I'd been given. It was a pretty, rather out-of-the-way cottage with a lovely rose garden, ringed with elder trees. Nobody answered the door. Until that point I hadn't doubted that my plan would work. Unsure what to do next,

I sat down on a small wooden bench, lit a cigarette, and let the distant sound of the sea envelop me. I considered taking a room for the night somewhere nearby and getting the train back to London the following morning. I was annoyed at my own naivety: how could I have hoped that this stranger would be here to welcome me, sitting in his rocking chair wrapped in a woollen blanket, smoking a pipe, ready to tell me stories about his past? What had I come here for in the first place? Did my visit really have anything to do with my research, or was I actually looking for answers for myself, which I pretended not to need? After I had smoked my third cigarette and cursed myself for now having to trudge back through this no man's land in the windswept darkness, I heard footsteps.

On the narrow dirt path that led up to the cottage, I made out the silhouette of a man carrying a stick and a torch. I leaped up and approached him cautiously. I called out that I was part of a research project on the history of the Soviet Union and needed information. It was only when I had spoken the words that I realised I'd said them in Georgian.

He shone his torch in my direction. Stopped, but then carried on moving towards me. When he shone the torch in my face I had to narrow my eyes, but despite the bright light I knew that I had found him. An unexpected wave of euphoria rolled over me.

He walked with a stoop, and evidently with some difficulty, always leaning on his stick. He simply passed me by without a word, unlocked the door, and disappeared, slamming the door in my face. Shocked, I stayed where I was, then started to knock tentatively, explaining my request again in as friendly a tone as possible. But there was no response to my knocking. I was angry, and about to turn and leave, but then I stopped and shouted through the door: 'I'm Kostya's granddaughter. I'm here because of Kostya. Because of him and Kitty. And I'm here because of you. I'm here because of my great-grandmother and my grandmother, and I'm here because of my sister, and I ...'

I could hear my heart hammering. I was afraid. I was afraid of rejection and of what he would have to say to me, in equal measure. It was only when he tentatively opened the door and switched on the light that I realised my whole body was trembling. As I stood before him, he raised his liver-spotted hands to my cheeks, took hold of my face, and stared at me, wide-eyed, for a long time.

'You're Kostya's *little girl?*' he asked in Georgian.

'I think you're mistaking me for my sister. I'm the younger one. My sister ... she's dead.'

He let go of my face and took a little step back.

'The beautiful girl?'
'Yes, the beautiful girl.'
'Good God. How? What happened?'
He invited me in.

★

I stayed in the Seven Sisters house for four whole days. Since I had left Tbilisi, this frail old man was the first person with whom I could speak about my past. He convinced me to stay with him; when I learned that the house had once belonged to my great-aunt, I accepted his offer. And he willingly answered my questions. For every one of my stories, he gave me one of his. Stories about the many photos that adorned most of the walls in the house. The photos of a woman I didn't know, who had been my great-aunt.

Every day, a red-haired carer came to help him with everyday tasks, and to lay out his medication for him.

'What's wrong with you?' I asked him.

'A better question would be what isn't wrong with me,' he replied.

We ate potato soup. He showed me the bay where Kitty Jashi had taken her own life. He stayed up on the cliff: his legs hurt. I climbed down the steep path to the beach alone, looking for the last traces of her, but found only the sea.

He told me things about people I'd assumed I had known, and after hearing these stories, I could no longer assume that I did. He opened himself to me like a book and let me read him. He made me a pudding with shaking hands and veiled eyes.

'You said you came here because of your grandfather and because of Kitty. Because of your great-grandmother and grandmother. And to ask me questions. But you didn't say: I'm here for my own sake. Why?'

His question surprised me. I didn't know what to say, but he gave me a smile that was like an embrace. Perhaps finally the meaning of it all would be revealed here; perhaps I was close to making a connection. But my fear didn't vanish; it grew with every story. All the ghosts gathered in my head as he went on weaving the carpet before my eyes. I watched him do it, never able to recognise my own thread amid all the confusing patterns.

I went down to the rough, stony beach. I sat down on the wet sand. I let the wind whip my face. I stretched out towards the sea. I let myself go.

Of course Stasia had been right: of course they were still there. And they stayed. I screamed. I didn't want to keep listening out for them across time. I didn't want to chase after them any more. I didn't want card-playing ghosts in my garden, and yet here I was, sitting with Alania, filled to bursting with all these words, all these things that had happened, all these stories which, clearer in his words than they had been in Stasia's, showered down upon me with incredible force, burying me under their weight.

For me, there had always been something magical about Stasia's stories; they were fables and fairy-tales from another world. The things Alania told me were facts, real and brutal.

I had wanted to lead a life. My life. I had wanted a history I could use, a history that could have provided anecdotes in sentimental sepia for evenings with my Berlin friends, for instance, or at least for a few solution-orientated therapy sessions. Yes, that was the life I should have been leading. Wasn't that why I had crossed the border from East to West, the border from Then to Now?

I dug myself into the wet sand. I hadn't come to the sea for it to remind me of all the things that hadn't happened in my life. No; I wanted to know what was still possible. And here, looking out at its grey expanse, I understood that too many stories were already gathered within me, blocking the view ahead, and the temptation just to keep looking back, like Orpheus, at what lay behind me was too great.

I climbed the steep path up the cliff. I asked him to go on talking. I asked him to answer only the questions that were important for my research project. Nothing else of a personal nature. Not a single familiar name, nothing about my own flesh and blood — please.

He looked at me quizzically, poured us some elderflower lemonade. He put a record on the old record player. He closed his eyes.

'This voice — her voice. That remains. Always,' he said. 'Yes, ask me. Go ahead and ask me what you want to know. But go to London. Do it soon. Find Amy. She spent years trying to track down someone from your family. Only, back then, when she had the strength for it, the Iron Curtain was still in place and nobody got through. And I stayed out of it; after I moved, I didn't want to take a single step backwards ... Go and visit her.'

'I don't know how relevant that would be.'

'You know, it's really fascinating,' he went on, as if he hadn't heard me. 'I knew that one day someone would come; that someone would come looking for *all that*.'

'I really just want to write my thesis. That's all.'

'You shouldn't separate your history from history in general; you shouldn't try to amputate yourself from it. No matter what you do with it all, this isn't the way to do it.'

'It's for a piece of academic research, not a romantic novel.'

'Go to London. Or to Vienna. Fred Lieblich, talk to Fred Lieblich, I can give you her address. Who knows how much longer these traces of the past will still be visible.'

I didn't reply.

★

I didn't go to London, or to Vienna.

And I didn't go back, either.

I didn't write.

Not a single line.

I forbade myself from thinking about words that might have a meaning, a meaning that went beyond the banalities of everyday life. Words that described more than I was ready to remember. I forbade myself from using more words than were strictly necessary to deal with day-to-day life. I forbade myself from creating my own sentences, finding an independent form for my thoughts. Yes; in fact, I forbade myself from thinking anything at all.

I didn't finish my thesis. I refused. I didn't want to possess any abilities beyond those necessary for everyday tasks. For the monotonous research work, for other people's lives, for the hours I spent in the workshop, and for playing cards. I went through the motions of doing research and assisted the project leader, who was constantly urging me to get on and do something with my material. In our work together I proved stubborn and uninsightful, but he didn't drop me from the project.

The promised publication came out in 2002 and caused some controversy. Although I was a contributor, I stayed out of it, and brusquely declined when the Eastern Europe expert offered to take me along to his conferences. The project was over, and I hoped that this was one duty I had now escaped — but then I was recommended to the Otto Suhr Institute for Political Science, which offered me a guest lectureship. I accepted on the spur of the moment, because we had just been caught playing poker in the back room of a restaurant and were only able to avoid prosecution by paying a horrendous amount in compensation to the landlord.

I wanted to carry on sending money to Georgia, and there was my divorce from Severin to pay for, and Severin and Gerrit were going to live together, which meant I had to find an apartment of my own. I agreed to lecture on the Cold War. I learned others' sentences off by heart, others' theses and experiences, and reeled them off day after day in the lecture hall. Every day I expected complaints from the students to reach the dean's office about my inability to teach them anything, or at least my lack of enthusiasm. But they didn't complain; they accepted me, just as I accepted everything, as my life turned into a dull progression. A path that led nowhere.

I found a recently-renovated apartment in an old building in Motzstraße, and, after a boozy farewell party in our old place, I moved out and cleared the way for Severin's long-desired happiness. Once in a while, I would go out with men who usually had a wife or a girlfriend and didn't want that to change. I went on driving across Europe in the hope of eventually arriving somewhere. I didn't read newspapers, didn't watch television, only used the internet to write emails and stay in touch with the university. I lost interest in the world, both the eastern and the western parts of it.

I called Mother and Aleko, and heard Brilka growing up in the background. Brilka was too strong-willed, too taciturn to speak to me on the phone. She fobbed me off and quickly passed the receiver back to the adults.

I received postcards from England written in a barely legible hand. If I responded at all, my replies were very polite and distant; I didn't react to his pleas and insistence, which I found intrusive.

I had found peace, the golden centre of my existence, more rust-red than golden, but that didn't matter to me, and I kept looking straight ahead: as time went on, it no longer took as much effort.

Twice, Elene and Aleko came to visit me in Berlin, and I played the uncomplicated daughter. They didn't bring Brilka; they said she was staying with Lasha's parents. They told me she was growing up to be a keen dancer, and I thought of Stasia. Stasia — wherever she was — was watching contentedly, while at the same time keeping a strict eye on her steps.

★

Once, Severin, Gerrit, and I were sitting in a pub, our eyes fixed on the television positioned above the bar, when we saw Shevardnadze being carried away from his lectern by security personnel. A tall man rushed forward carrying a rose, followed by a jeering throng, and we witnessed the overthrow that was to herald a new revolution and a new era in Georgia. I recognised the parliament building, saw my old school and Rustaveli Boulevard. But these places seemed so distant, so far removed, that I had trouble connecting them with me. Meanwhile, Severin was almost frantic in his jubilation over the new, young revolutionary and probable future president. Like the whole of the West, he seemed to be rejoicing along with the Georgian people, who were hoping for a better life, an end to corruption, a more open attitude to the West, a putative democracy.

Severin looked at me curiously, wanting to see my joy as well, but I had already turned my eyes away and was just muttering to myself that this was the third Georgian Messiah since 1989 and neither of the previous ones had managed to carry out his mission. I, at least, had no interest in another saviour.

'Get us another beer. In four years, at most, we'll know which of us was right,' was all I said.

Gerrit, too, was fired up by the images of the peaceful revolution and the symbolic rose, and called me a fatalist. 'Here, nobody comes out and complains about anything. Nobody bothers to get off their backside. So everyone's doing okay here, are they? At least there is still a sense of possibility in Georgia: be glad that people there aren't indifferent to their country and their future! At least they've got that!'

There was a strange longing in his eyes as he went on staring at the television. And once again I marvelled at the western yearning for chaos.

In scarf, with hand before my eyes,
I'll shout outdoors and ask the kids:
Oh tell me, dear ones, if you please,
Just what millennium this is?

BORIS PASTERNAK

2006

At the moment when Aman Baron, whom most people knew as 'the Baron', was confessing that he loved me — with heartbreaking intensity and unbearable lightness, but a love that was unhealthy, enfeebled, disillusioned — my twelve-year-old niece Brilka was leaving her hotel in Amsterdam on her way to the train station. She had with her a small bag, hardly any money, and a tuna sandwich. She was heading for Vienna, and bought herself a cheap weekend ticket, valid only on local trains. A handwritten note left at reception said she did not intend to return to her homeland with the dance troupe and that there was no point in looking for her.

At this precise moment, I was lighting a cigarette and succumbing to a coughing fit, partly because I was overwhelmed by what I was hearing, and partly because the smoke went down the wrong way. Aman (whom I personally never called 'the Baron') immediately came over, slapped me on the back so hard I couldn't breathe, and stared at me in bewilderment. He was only four years younger than me, but I felt decades older; besides, at this point I was well on my way to becoming a tragic figure — without anyone really noticing, because by now I was a master of deception.

I read the disappointment in his face. My reaction to his confession was not what he'd anticipated. Especially after he'd invited me to accompany him on tour in two weeks' time.

Outside, a light rain began to fall. It was June, a warm evening with weightless clouds that decorated the sky like little balls of cotton wool.

When I had recovered from my coughing fit, and Brilka had boarded the first train of her odyssey, I flung open the balcony door and collapsed on the sofa. I felt as if I were suffocating.

After sitting on the sofa and putting my face in my hands, after rubbing my eyes and avoiding Aman's gaze for as long as possible, I knew I would have to weep again, but not now, not at this moment, while Brilka was watching old, new Europe slipping past her outside the train window and smiling for the first time since her arrival on this continent of indifference. I don't know what she saw that made her smile as she left the city of miniature bridges, but that doesn't matter any more. The main thing is, she was smiling.

At that moment, I was thinking that I would have to weep. In order not to, I turned, went into the bedroom, and lay down. I didn't have to wait long for Aman. Grief like his is very quickly healed if you offer to heal it with your body, especially when the patient is twenty-eight years old.

I kissed myself out of my enchanted sleep.

As Aman laid his head on my belly, my twelve-year-old niece was leaving the Netherlands, crossing the German border in her compartment that stank of beer and loneliness, while several hundred kilometres away her unsuspecting aunt feigned love with a twenty-eight-year-old shadow. All the way across Germany she travelled, in the hope it would get her somewhere.

★

I met Aman in a little bar near my apartment. He was performing there with his band, a trio who called themselves 'The Barons'. He played his own interpretation of 'Cry Me a River' in a drunken endless loop, and I realised that, after an eternity, I was actually feeling something; that, as he played, something had taken hold of me and wasn't letting go. So much so that when he finished, I had to go up and talk to him, find out where he was performing next. He was nice, tipsy, and talkative. The bar had been half-empty, and most people disappeared quite quickly after the gig; we seemed to be the only ones left. It turned into a long conversation. Since his fellow band members had also gone, and by the time we finished talking he was so drunk he couldn't find his way home, I decided to take him with me. And so he ended up on my sofa. The next morning, he was gone, having left without a word, and then, four days later, at two in the morning, he rang my doorbell again. I let him in, asked no questions, and once more gave him a blanket and pillows. So it went on for a few weeks. He came, slept, and disappeared early the next day.

One February evening — his visits had become a kind of normality for me and I had started leaving the sofa-bed unfolded — he arrived sober for once, sat down, and asked me if he could have a cup of tea. I made him one. Then I went to bed, but it wasn't long before I was woken by the singing of his saxophone. I wandered into the living room in my old nightshirt. He was sitting there playing, oblivious to everything around him. I watched him and wanted to cry, but crying was something I had unlearned, so I just stood there. Eventually he looked at me, and we looked at each other for a long time and admitted the desolation we carried within us. It was a very honest moment. A moment that overwhelmed us both.

Then I disappeared back to bed, and he went on playing. After a while, he fell silent, and I waited for him to start again. I heard him taking a shower, I heard him in the kitchen, getting something from the fridge, and then suddenly he was standing before me, naked. I looked at him steadily. He lay down beside me and said I reminded him of someone, it made him so terribly sad, he was so infinitely sad, oh God how sad, so very sad, and without ceasing this talk of sadness, he embraced me, and I, still a little speechless, his melody still in my ears, finally gave in and opened my arms.

In bed, he told me his story. He told me that his mother now lived in Israel, that his father had left them when he was three and had broken off contact. He told me that he had dropped out of school and had passed the music-school entrance exam at seventeen and then quit that, too, that he didn't have anywhere to live right now, that he hadn't been able to fall in love for many years. And so on and so on.

The next day, he disappeared again. I woke up and he simply wasn't there. But that was fine by me. The best thing about him was that he didn't expect anything. That he came and went. That he made no demands. That he was content with a cup of tea, a shot of whisky, some chicken soup. That he was free. Free of wishes.

It went on like this for almost a year. We never went out, never went to the cinema, we did none of the things that people who like each other do. We didn't arrange anything, we made no plans. Sometimes when I came home he would be sitting on the staircase. I never knew what he did when he wasn't spending the night in my apartment, and he knew just as little about me.

★

After Aman fell asleep, I got up, went to the bathroom, sat on the edge of the bath, and started to cry. I wept a century's worth of tears over the feigning of love, the longing to believe in words that once defined my life. I went into the kitchen, smoked a cigarette, stared out of the window. It had stopped raining, and somehow I knew that it was happening, something had been set in motion, something beyond this apartment with the high ceilings and the orphaned books; with the many lamps I had collected so eagerly, a substitute for the sky, an illusion of true light.

★

The following evening, I received a call from my mother, who was always threatening to die if I didn't return soon to the homeland I had fled all those years ago. Her voice trembled as she informed me that 'the child' had disappeared. It took me a while to work out which child she was talking about, and what it all had to do with me.

'So tell me again: where exactly was she?'

'In Amsterdam, for goodness' sake, what's the matter with you? Aren't you listening to me? She ran away yesterday and left a message. I got a call from the group leader. They've looked everywhere for her, and —'

'Wait, wait, wait. How can an eleven-year-old girl disappear from a hotel, especially if she —'

'She's twelve. She turned twelve in November. You forgot, of course. But that was only to be expected.'

I took a deep drag on my cigarette and prepared myself for the impending disaster. Because if my mother's voice was anything to go by, it would be no easy matter just to wash my hands of this and disappear: my favourite pastime in recent years. I armed myself for the obligatory reproaches, all of them intended to make clear to me what a bad daughter and failed human being I was. Things I was only too well aware of without my mother's intervention.

'Okay, she turned twelve, and I forgot, but that won't get us anywhere right now. Have they informed the police?'

'Yes, what do you think? They're looking for her.'

'Then they'll find her. She's a spoilt little girl with a tourist visa, I presume, and she —'

'Do you have even a spark of humanity left in you?'

'Sorry. I'm just trying to think aloud.'

'So much the worse, if those are your thoughts.'

'Mama!'

'They're going to call me. In an hour at most, they said, and I'm praying that they find her, and find her fast. And then I want you to go to wherever she is — she won't have got all that far — and I want you to fetch her.'

'I —'

'She's your sister's daughter. And you will fetch her. Promise me!'

'But —'

'Do it!'

'Oh god. All right, fine.'

'And don't take the Lord's name in vain.'

'Aren't I even allowed to say "Oh god" now?'

'You're going to fetch her and bring her back with you. And then you'll put her on the plane.'

They found her that same night, in a small town just outside Vienna, waiting for a connecting train. She was picked up by the Austrian police and taken to the police station. My mother woke me and told me I had to go to Mödling.

As I threw on some clothes, Aman stared at me wide-eyed, not understanding the world around him any more. Perhaps he never had understood it.

'What niece, and where the hell is Mödling?'

'I'll be on the first plane at six o'clock. I'll pick her up. Then I'll get the flight back from Vienna at four and be here in the evening. The day after tomorrow I'll put her on a plane to Tbilisi, and then we can talk properly, okay?'

'I could come with you, I could —'

'No. I have to sort this out on my own. Please don't be cross, it really isn't a big deal. She's just an adolescent runaway. I need to make sure I bring her to her senses.'

★

By midday, I had reached the little railway station in the provincial Austrian town. She was sitting there in the empty waiting room with a police officer and a station employee. I signed some form or other, apologised several times for the situation, and took charge of my niece.

I hadn't seen a recent photo of her and was amazed at how tall she was. She didn't look like any of us. She had a buzz cut and John Lennon glasses, and was wearing an oversized lumberjack shirt and ripped jeans. The only thing I recognised about her straight away were the black-on-black eyes that were still just as they had been when she was born. She had long, thick lashes, a very light complexion that reminded me of Daria, and rosy cheeks. Her face had a highly focused, serious look, as if she had never smiled in her life. Her drooping shoulders, awkward body language, and the restlessness in her limbs were the only things that gave away her age.

'What do we do now?' she asked me as we left the station building and I lit a cigarette.

'What do you think? If I don't put you on a plane soon and send you home, your grandmother is going to kill me.'

'I'm not getting on a plane. I'm scared of flying.'

'How did you get to Amsterdam? On a horse?' This was going to be fun.

'I can only fly if I have at least three people I know with me.'

'What are you talking about?'

'That's just how it is. If I don't stick to the rule, we'll crash,' she said, as if it were an undisputed fact.

'Are you taking the mickey? Because if so, you've chosen the wrong person. I don't like it when people take the mickey.'

'I'm telling you how it is. I always stick to the rules.'

'Fine, but your rules are not my rules, and since I'm *in loco parentis* right now, I make the rules.'

'I don't want to go home,' she said suddenly, in a soft voice, turning her eyes away.

I looked at her, disconcerted. She had a very particular way of speaking that I found slightly unnerving. I was already feeling overwhelmed and I wondered how I was going to deal with the next few hours in her company.

'First, we're going to fly to Berlin, and then —'

'But I've already said I don't fly. Not unless there are at least three people with me who know me.'

'And *I* said this isn't up for debate.'

'You're even more awful than I thought,' she yelled at me, looking me in the eye with a piercing gaze. She started drawing invisible circles on the paving stones with the tip of her dirty trainer.

'And you're an ill-mannered, troublesome little girl who is really getting on my nerves right now.'

She shrugged and turned her back on me.

'I'm hungry,' she announced, and started rummaging in her rucksack.

'You'll get everything you want if you get on that plane.'

'No.'

'But I can't possibly take you to Berlin by train, it'll take forever and I have to ... I've got things to do.'

'You fly, and I'll follow on the train. I got here by myself, didn't I, so I can get back as well. By myself!'

I decided to change tack and be a little more sympathetic. I tried to persuade her, to convince her of the advantages of flying, promised to keep her in Berlin for two or three days, to explore the city with her. But she remained stubborn, gave me the cold shoulder, and wouldn't hear another word about planes. Should I call Elene and ask her about the best way to deal with her? I could hardly drag her onto a plane; she was almost two heads taller than me.

I left her alone for a moment, took a few steps away, and fished out my mobile, which I hardly used. The battery symbol was always flashing because I never thought to charge it. I called my mother.

'What is wrong with this child?' I complained to her. 'She's crazy. She refuses to fly. I don't have time to pander to her whims. I'm going to hand her the phone, and you need to make it clear to her that she's getting on a plane to Berlin with me and —'

'Oh, thank the Lord, I'm so glad you found her.' I heard Elene exhale. 'Yes, she can be very peculiar, Niza. She has her methods, and —'

'Methods? What methods? I don't have time for methods. I have to work. I have to get back to Berlin, and if she doesn't do as I say right now I'm going to tie her up and —'

'Oh, Niza, come on — think of yourself; what do you think you were like at her age? You drove me to distraction. In some ways, she's very like you.'

'She is not like me. She's spoilt!' I snapped at Elene, but before she could reply I heard a beep and the phone gave up the ghost. I swore and walked back over to my niece.

I decided to outwit her. At least she wasn't refusing to get on a train.

We travelled to Vienna.

On the train, she bit her fingernails constantly, shuffled about in her seat, walked up and down the aisle, sat down again, then pulled a large notebook and an old Walkman out of her rucksack, put the headphones on, and started writing. I didn't even make the effort to start a conversation. My brain was working overtime, planning how I could trick her into getting on the plane. In

Vienna I found the closest café to the station and we had a meal. And there was another surprise in store for me. She proved to be a fussy eater, and explained that she only ate food by colour, and certain colours weren't part of her diet. I bit my lip to stop myself screaming at her to shut up and eat what was put in front of her.

I steered her into a taxi, on the pretext of taking a look around the city, but she quickly cottoned on to my intention of going to the airport, screamed blue murder, and shouted at me and the taxi driver in such a way that he pulled over. She jumped out and stormed off, taking great, angry strides, bent forward under the weight of her large rucksack. After I had paid the taxi fare I had to run to catch up and make sure I didn't lose her; then I placated her and gave her my solemn promise that we would take the train.

The sleeper from Vienna to Berlin didn't leave until ten o'clock that night, so we had a few hours to kill. We went and sat in a station café. She drank three Fantas, one after another.

'That's terrible stuff — don't you want a proper juice?'

She scorned my suggestion with a black look. After that, I decided to spare my nerves and leave her in peace. When I had got her safely back to Tbilisi, I would confront my mother and ask her what she was thinking, letting the girl turn into such a brat.

I bought some newspapers and immersed myself in them. When I glanced up, she wasn't at the table any more. I panicked. The sleeper was leaving in half an hour. I searched the crowd for her gangly figure, her round glasses, her drooping shoulders. I called her name and swore like a trooper.

Finally, I found her in the ladies' toilets. I went mad, screamed at her, what was she thinking, what did she think she was doing there — she could forget about playing her little games with me. She regarded me with indifference and went to the sink to wash her hands, entirely ignoring my rage. I stood behind her and stared at her in the mirror.

'For god's sake, what is *wrong* with you? Your behaviour is outrageous. Why did you want to come here, anyway? What did you want to do in Vienna? What was this whole escapade about, and why are you testing my nerves?'

She looked at me in the mirror for a while, calmly washed her hands, and said, as she walked past me, '*You* have a real problem, you know that?'

On the sleeper, she tucked herself away on the top bunk with her Walkman. I couldn't suppress a smile; it felt like an eternity since I had seen anyone with a Walkman. I woke up every two hours and checked that she was still there.

When we arrived in Berlin, we took a taxi back to my apartment. She missed out every second stair on the staircase; it seemed she had an irrational rule about that, too. I refrained from asking why. I was too tired from the trip and too worked up for any more surprises.

I was glad that we didn't see Aman. That spared me any further explanations. I got everything I had out of the fridge and prepared breakfast for her. Again, she began to sort through the food. I paid closer attention this time: she seemed to love everything yellow or orange. Fanta. Egg yolk. Oranges. She rejected dark green entirely. White appeared to be acceptable. Red was not touched, so the packet of salami was pushed to the edge of the table.

Watching her eat, I tried desperately to recall everything my mother had told me about her. She adored dancing. She hated it when people called her Anastasia. She wasn't particularly academic. But she liked to read. She loved animals. Had some kind of allergy, but I couldn't remember to what. She loved cartoons. She liked horses, 'Like her mother!' She didn't get on with girls her own age. She was scared of thunder and lightning. That was the limit of my knowledge; I had to admit that I didn't know her, that I couldn't connect these facts, that I had no insight into her thoughts and feelings. We were strangers, and it seemed she was trying to emphasise this with every word she spoke to me, with every look and every gesture.

But why hadn't Elene told me about the neuroses and phobias she seemed to have so many of? They were enough to drive you to distraction!

'So what do we do now?' I asked her, once she had managed to sit opposite me for a full thirty minutes, chewing and sorting, without giving me any more unpleasant surprises. She shrugged again in her ignorant way, and again I felt the urge to shake her. I tried to follow my mother's advice and remember what Daria and I were like at that age, but nothing comparable came to mind. This was a long way outside my experience.

'Shrugging isn't going to get us anywhere. We have to agree on something, and in any case your grandparents are waiting for you, and worrying.'

'Why? I mean, you're their daughter. They know I'm in good hands.'

She chopped up a cucumber and painstakingly cut off the skin.

'Why do you do that?'

'What?'

'This thing with your food?'

'If I mix red and green, I'll die,' she said nonchalantly.

'What on earth would make you think that?'

'And what on earth would make you never visit us, not even once?'

The question floored me. I didn't know what to say.

I went into the living room and made up the sofa-bed for her. I put a clean towel in the bathroom and a new toothbrush on the edge of the basin. I opened the balcony door and sat down at the little table with a cigarette. I urgently needed to think of a solution. Cunning and false promises weren't going to work. She would refuse point blank to come to the airport. And even if I could convince her to get on a plane with me, there was no way I could fly to Georgia. The semester in Berlin was not yet over, and then I still had some things to work up for the Eastern Europe specialist, and thirdly, and fourthly, and so on. I wanted to pull the covers over my head and wait for things to sort themselves out.

Suddenly, she was standing barefoot in front of me on the balcony, complaining that there wasn't even a television in the apartment.

'There's more to life than sitting in front of the box all day,' I retorted, annoyed.

'Such as?'

'Going for walks. Reading. Thinking. Or working out how Madame is going to get home.'

'I told you I don't want to go home. At least, not right now.'

'Okay, fine. So what *do* you want to do?'

'I have to go to Vienna.'

'Vienna. I see. And what does Madame intend to do in Vienna?'

'I have to meet someone there.'

'Who on earth do you want to meet in Vienna?'

'A woman. You don't know her.'

'Listen, Brilka ... Why such an odd name, anyway? Brilka. Why do you call yourself that? Your real name is so much prettier.'

'I can call myself what I like. It's nobody else's business, least of all yours.'

Unfortunately, she was right. I hadn't shown any interest in her for twelve years, and to demand any kind of rights now would be overstepping the mark.

'Listen, Brilka. I have a life here, I have obligations. Your grandmother instructed me to get you back to Georgia as quickly as possible. As you may have noticed, this whole business has taken me rather by surprise, and just so you know, this isn't particularly convenient for me, either. I can't just drop everything and get on a plane with you. You're not going to Vienna. At least, not now, and I won't be able to look after you, either. So find another option.'

'It wouldn't be enough for you to get on a plane with me, in any case. There have to be at least three people I know. I've explained this to you.'

'Now just stop this ridiculous nonsense.'

'It's not nonsense!' She was suddenly shouting — then she turned her back on me and walked into the living room.

When I came in from the balcony, she wasn't in the apartment. Her things were still there, but she herself had disappeared. I went downstairs and looked for her on the street, on the surrounding streets, went to Nollendorfplatz, looked for her in the U-Bahn station. My nerves were in tatters. I went back and called my mother again. I complained to her, accused her of not having brought the girl up properly, and demanded that she talk to Brilka and persuade her to go to the airport with me.

'She's behaving like a lunatic. I don't know what to do with her.'

'Well, then make a bit more of an effort, Niza. I'm afraid I don't have an instruction manual to give you.'

'But *Deda*, no, you can't do this to me. Talk to her. Do something! You brought her up, you must know how to deal with her.'

'Maybe you can convince her to go back to Amsterdam. She might listen, and then she can travel home with the group.'

'I don't understand why you let her get away with all this. You were so much stricter with us!'

'Yes, but *you* had a mother.'

The words made me flinch. I decided not to say any more. I clung feverishly to the suggestion she had made about Amsterdam; that might be a solution. But it was already starting to get dark, and I still didn't know where she was. I decided to go out again, but as I was putting my shoes on the doorbell rang, and she marched up the stairs as if nothing had happened and walked past me into the apartment. I could already hear her calling from the kitchen that she was hungry.

I wanted to protest, to bring her to her senses, but I realised I didn't have the energy for it, and went into the kitchen. Since there was nothing left in the fridge, I suggested we go shopping. Suddenly she seemed excited by this — very banal — idea, and even smiled at me.

'And can I choose what we buy?' she asked excitedly, as if we were talking about her Christmas list, not groceries.

I admitted defeat.

The previous year, I had bought a turquoise 1969 Ami 8 Citroën, with a wonderful leather interior and a dual carburettor. It was my pride and joy, and I had even risked playing in another anonymous poker game in Schöneberg to afford the restoration work, which wasn't exactly cheap. I went out to the car with her. Going for a little drive would kill some time; plus she would find it difficult to escape once we were in it.

She seemed to like the car. She touched every button and knob, and wanted to feel the steering wheel. What seemed to delight her most of all, though, was the old cassette player. Without asking if I wanted to listen to her music, she took the tape out of her Walkman and put it in. The songs were poor quality recordings taken from the radio, which broke off in the middle or faded out in certain places. But I had to admit that, for her age, her taste in music was well-developed and quite good. When I started to turn into the supermarket car park, she murmured plaintively that it was a shame we were there already.

'You like driving, then?'

'Yes.'

At least that was one thing we had in common.

'Do you want to keep going?'

'Yes.'

I accelerated again. She wound down the window and put her hand out into the warm airstream. I looked over at her tentatively. All at once there was something young, naive, girlish in her face. Something about the sight of her moved me, and I was ashamed of my inability to deal with her.

'Is the old cherry tree still standing, in the garden?'

I don't know why I thought of the cherry tree, of all things, but an image of her suddenly came into my mind, playing in the garden, running round the cherry tree, in the same spot where Stasia's ghosts played cards, and I liked the idea.

'Yes. It's still there. But it doesn't really flower any more. Elene and Aleko aren't very good with plants. Stasia used to do all that.'

'Do you remember her?'

'Of course.'

'But you were still very young then.'

'She smoked filterless cigarettes and talked to ghosts. She wore green boots and dungarees. Her hands shook, and when she was younger she wanted to be a great ballet dancer.' She was watching the street, the passers-by, the passing cars, and humming along to her songs. When a song came on that she particularly liked, she rewound the cassette and listened to it again.

'What else do you remember?'

'Everything,' she said confidently, and once again I was at a loss for words. Something about the way she said it gave me the sense that she was right, even if I didn't know what this *everything* covered. The certainty in her voice piqued my interest.

'You mean *absolutely everything*?'

'Yes, but I don't remember you,' she said, snippy again.

'Well, that's not exactly surprising. Shall we go back? I mean, the supermarkets will be closing soon.'

'No, keep driving.'

We drove around aimlessly. Into the balmy summer night. Gradually, my tension eased. I stopped feeling so overwhelmed and harassed.

'So, what do you remember?'

Brilka put her head out of the window and shut her eyes.

'I don't really like remembering.'

'Why not?'

'Maybe I just don't enjoy it.'

'Well, there are a lot of things I don't enjoy, either, but I do them anyway.'

Once again, I was taken aback by her precocious manner. For a moment I wished she were a docile little girl who loved dolls, wore frilly dresses, and stuck pony posters on her wall. 'What don't you enjoy? Give me an example,' I said.

'Well, the fact that you fetched me back, for example. I mean, I knew Elene would phone you, and that you'd come and get me. I was just hoping I would make it before you found me, that I'd make it to Vienna. I don't enjoy going to school, I don't enjoy going to church with Elene, I don't enjoy having to invite a load of schoolfriends to my birthday every year so Elene doesn't worry about me. I don't enjoy listening to stupid music, either. I don't enjoy dancing the girls' parts in our dance troupe. I don't enjoy it when people answer my questions by saying: that all happened a long time ago, it's of no interest to you.'

'Aha. And what are the questions people give you that answer to?'

'Most of them.'

'For example?'

'For example, whether my mother killed herself or whether it was an accident when she fell off the roof terrace.'

Luckily, we had stopped at a red light, otherwise that would have made me slam my foot down on the brake.

'What would make you think that?' I asked her, still looking straight ahead. 'I mean, that she wanted to kill herself?'

'Well, you don't fall off a roof terrace just like that, do you?'

'Did Elene tell you that? That she fell off the terrace?'

'No, someone at school told me. Elene just said she'd had an accident. But my mother was the most beautiful actress in the whole of Georgia, did you know that?' As she said it, her face lit up and her tone softened.

'It was an accident. She didn't want to kill herself.'

Somebody sounded their horn behind us. The lights had been green for some time.

Later, we went to a kebab shop, and I waited almost half an hour for her to start eating, because first everything had to be neatly separated and sorted into colours on her plate. Red cabbage and meat were immediately placed on a side plate and pushed away.

When she had finally fallen asleep on the sofa-bed, I crept into the living room and studied her soft face. Only my sister had slept so peacefully, so blissfully.

> The sun is in mourning
> The springtime glitters
> We have slept away wakefulness forever
>
> STANISLAV POPLAVSKY

I couldn't get hold of anyone in Amsterdam; they had already moved on. The next morning, when Brilka went for a shower, I snuck a look at her passport. Her tourist visa was valid for another two weeks.

After breakfast, which took her an eternity, as I'd expected, she sat out on the balcony with her Walkman and her notebook and wrote.

I trusted her, left her alone, and went to my lecture. Aman hadn't reappeared, and I didn't know whether this was a good or a bad sign. He had to prepare for the tour, and would have less time now.

In the early evening, I persuaded her to go for a walk with me. She kept her headphones on and trudged along behind me with an air of boredom. The next evening, I took her to the cinema. She seemed to have a pretty fair grasp of English, and we watched a Hollywood blockbuster in the original language. I had been on the internet, researching other ways of getting her home safely. But the huge distance meant that a plane was really the only option. When I explained to her that her visa would soon run out and she couldn't stay in Germany any longer, she shrugged again and retorted in her usual insolent manner that I was clever enough to come up with something.

In her regular phone calls with Elene, she talked about me and Berlin with exuberance, laughing repeatedly, as if her stay here were an entertaining holiday. She told her about her discoveries and the things we had done together with an enthusiasm she never displayed to me. She merely accepted all my suggestions, everything I showed or told her, with a nonchalant indifference, as if nothing in the world could impress her.

★

'You can't hang around here forever. You have to go back, go to school or your dance classes, or whatever,' I said, making another attempt to persuade her over breakfast, a week after she had arrived in my apartment.

She peeled a radish until the red skin had disappeared entirely, then calmly popped it into her mouth. Completely ignored what I had said. I snatched the plate from her hand and stood over her, forcing her to look at me.

'Listen when I'm talking to you.'

'I don't want to go home. I have to go to Vienna. And you either have to drive me there or let me go by myself. I'll come back, don't worry.'

'How likely do you think that is? I can't let you go to Vienna by yourself. And I can't go with you, either. Nor do I want to have to look after you the whole time. As you may have realised, I'm not that keen on children.'

'I'm not a child.'

'Of course, you think you're all grown up. Besides, I promised your grandmother I'd get you back in one piece.'

'You always say "your grandmother", you never say "my mother".'

'What does that have to do with anything? Are you even listening to me?'

'I don't have school. It's the school holidays in Georgia and my dance troupe is still travelling. I'm free.'

'But *I'm* not, for crying out loud!'

I slammed the plate back down on the table and left the kitchen.

When I came back to the apartment that evening, I found Aman on the stairs, his saxophone case beside him. He was reading one of the free advertising papers that had been lying around on the staircase, and he looked exhausted: the last few nights, which he had obviously drunk his way through, were etched into his face. I was sorry for him. I felt unkind.

'What are you doing here?'

'There's a kid in there.'

'Yes, I expect you're right. It's my mad niece, who doesn't want to go back home.'

'I was hoping you'd get in touch.'

'Where've you been sleeping all this time? You really need an apartment, Aman.'

'I thought I had one.'

I was annoyed; I got my key out and opened the door. He placed his saxophone case carefully on the hall floor. Brilka was sitting on the balcony with a plate of peeled apples, her eyes closed as she listened to her music. She hadn't heard us come in and thought she was alone. She was swaying rhythmically back and forth, her bare feet tapping on the floor to the same beat. In ripped shorts, her long, thin legs looked like they belonged to a grasshopper. Her hair was standing up in tufts. Her deliberate effort at relaxation was almost moving.

I went into the kitchen with Aman, made him some tea, and sat down opposite him. It was a humid evening and our clothes were sticking to us. I wanted to take him in my arms, ask him to play me something, get drunk on the sight of him or on his music, fall asleep wrapped in each other's arms with no promises, no plans, no admissions on my part.

'I'm a bit overwhelmed by the whole thing,' I said, when I had explained the situation. 'I have to get her home somehow and I don't know how to do it. But whatever happens, I won't be able to come on tour with you.'

'Bring her along.'

How I hated this naivety. Everything was so simple: he had a solution for everything.

'She's only twelve, Aman. Come on, I can't just take her on tour!'

'This isn't because of her. It's you,' he said, taking a sip of his tea.

'Aman, this is too quick for me, all this.'

'Too quick? Too quick? How long have we known each other? How long has this thing been going on between us, Niza?'

'That doesn't mean anything. How long you've known someone. That's something else.'

'You're a coward. You're just a coward.'

He lowered his eyes ruefully. The way he admitted defeat so quickly was something else I couldn't stand about him. This maxim that he hadn't come into the world to change anything, but to make the best of it.

'But we were fine. We had a good thing going.'

'No; I wasn't fine with it.'

'My God, Aman. I always valued the fact that you spared me all this sentimental crap, and now you go and do just what people always do.'

He turned his oily eyes on me. I hated this look. This sad, all-accepting look.

Suddenly, Brilka was standing over us. She eyed Aman uncertainly, then strode up to him and put out her hand in a very grown-up way. She introduced herself in English. Aman seemed amused; he took her hand and shook it and said his own name as well. She went to the fridge and got out one of her bottles of Fanta, which I had bought in bulk and lugged up to the apartment. She drank from the bottle, scratching her knee with her left foot as she did so. She looked like a yogi practising a Fanta meditation. I couldn't suppress a smile.

'Is that your saxophone in the hall?' she asked.

'How do you know it's a saxophone? Did you look inside?' I snapped at her in Georgian. But Aman had already gone out, and came back with the saxophone. He beckoned her over and showed her some of the fingering. Then he let her blow into it. I took my chance and escaped into the bathroom; I needed to be alone, to stand under the shower. I was grateful to her for coming into the kitchen just then and ending that unpleasant conversation.

When I came back out, still damp, the two of them were standing by the door ready to leave.

'What's going on? Where are you off to?'

'Down to Nollendorfplatz. We're going to make some money,' Brilka announced proudly.

'What? What are you going to do there?'

I cast an admonishing glance at Aman.

'She dances like a second Mata Hari, she says, so we're going to see if that's true. I'll play, she'll dance, and if we're good then people will throw piles of money at us. And then your niece can buy cassettes and ice cream. That's the deal.'

They were out of the door before I had a chance to object.

For a brief moment, I felt something like jealousy of Aman. It had taken him just a few minutes to make a connection with my niece, while she put me to the test every day, stretching my patience and strength to the limit. I got dressed, initially decided to stay in the apartment and sulk, but didn't hold out for long and went down to Nollendorfplatz. I stopped at the corner, where they couldn't see me, and watched from a distance. They had positioned themselves outside the entrance to the U-Bahn. He was sitting on a step, playing with such abandon that it inevitably drew me in, swept me along, as he always did, even when I was listening to him not in a large concert hall but in a dingy bar that stank of urine. At first, Brilka stood off to one side, looking nervously at the passers-by. Gradually she ventured closer to Aman. When he started up something rhythmical, she finally stepped in front of him and began to dance. Initially she was tentative and uncertain, a little self-conscious and bashful, but soon her tension vanished and she too was in her element, just like Aman.

Of course, what she performed wasn't rehearsed choreography. She was reacting to his music with her body, becoming lighter and lighter, as if she might start to float, becoming freer, more uninhibited, until something like happiness spread across her face. Captivated by the unusual sight, I stood motionless, spellbound as I watched this ecstatic, oblivious pair, wishing I had the same means at my disposal for forgetting the world around me.

People stopped, applauded, threw their coins into Aman's case. There was an intimacy about them, as if they had been in tune with each other for decades, their light-footed tightrope act floating between two worlds.

What did she want, what should I be seeing, recognising — guessing, even? What was she hoping to find in Vienna? What would this answer mean for me?

Thinking about it today, I can't fathom why I didn't see the fundamental, obvious thing here; why I asked her only the wrong questions. The question I should have asked wasn't what she hoped to find in Vienna. The question was why she was *here*. With me.

Watching her, I tried with my whole body to stem the flood of images. I didn't want any comparisons, parallels, overlaps. The longer I watched her, the closer the others moved towards me again. The dead and the living. And I stood somewhere in between, still not knowing to whom I belonged.

★

Later, the three of us strolled through the streets as she ate an ice cream, coins jangling in her pocket. She kept putting her hand to them, clearly proud of her haul. She walked a little way behind us, hopping over potholes, missing paving stones or kerbs. In Genthiner Strasse she caught up with us, walked beside Aman, and hooked her arm through his. He took a bite of her ice cream. She squealed in delight and pulled it away from him. She spent the whole evening trying to convince him to take their 'show', as she called their joint performance, to other parts of the city where there were more people. I didn't want to spoil the peaceable atmosphere, and relied on Aman to take an adult approach. But he was already suggesting other U-Bahn stations that might be good for playing and dancing. Maybe they could test the waters with a little gig at the club where he usually played, he said; the audience there was open to anything, and his band were sure to be just as keen on the idea, and seeing as it was a Friday, they could go there right away. Of course, she was immediately full of enthusiasm.

My attempt to intervene failed before I could even begin. I didn't stand a chance. I protested half-heartedly, explained that there were things called child protection laws and it was too late at night to drag a twelve-year-old girl out to some smoky dive. But she was already hanging on his arm and following him around like a faithful dog. I had no choice but to pack my things and trudge after them. It was the club where I had first met Aman, where he and his band played regularly. The other band members were clearly enamoured with this cheeky creature who immediately took over the stage, working out how big it was, and wanting to see the lights. In short, The Barons agreed to the idea and kicked off their gig. The boys opened with 'Every Time We Say Goodbye'. I thought I could see a touch of fear in Brilka's face, but she very quickly found her own rhythm, adjusted her body to the band's beat and transformed the melody into pure joy. She was a good improviser. People clapped and shouted bravo. She bowed coquettishly and gave Aman a kiss on the cheek before leaving the stage. We went out to get some fresh air. Side by side, we stood at the door and listened to the boys for another few minutes; they'd got into their stride and were fired up by the crowd.

'You're really good,' I said.

'I know.'

'Modesty doesn't seem to be one of your strengths, though.'

'Aman's cool. He's much cooler than you.'

'Thanks a lot.'

'You shouldn't send him away.'

'So you're an expert on personal relationships as well, are you?'

She looked at me through narrowed eyes and puffed air out of her mouth.

'Why are you grinning?' she asked.

'You remind me of someone.'

'Who?'

'Your mother.'

'Really?'

Her pupils widened. Her powerful reaction surprised me.

'Yes, you do,' I told her, feeling more lenient.

'I made these shorts from Mama's old jeans. But Elene always says I'm like you.' She gave me a probing look.

'Does she?'

'Yes, that's what she says.'

★

Aman asked if he could 'borrow' Brilka for a few performances. She went down really well — she could come on tour with him as well. 'As a kind of support act,' he said with a laugh. Brilka had already fallen asleep, and I didn't think any of this was a laughing matter. The feeling that my life had been turned upside down overnight was too powerful for that, and I had no idea how to undo it all; I was hardly getting any work done. I started to wash up. I didn't want him looking at me with his pleading puppy-dog eyes any more. I never wanted to feel so cruel again.

'Do you really find it so difficult to say what it is you want?' He didn't let up.

'Come on, you can see I've got this kid on my hands. I can't just drop everything and —'

'On your hands? You should be glad she wants to be here with you.'

'She doesn't want to be here with me. She wants to go to Vienna, for God's sake, and only she knows what it is she wants to do there.'

'She says it's to do with some songs. She wants the rights for them. It all sounded very plausible, quite a mature plan.'

I leaned on the sink, unable to decide who I should be more angry with — him, her, or myself.

'You could talk to her about it. You do speak the same language, after all. She'll explain it to you,' he went on. 'Of course she wanted to come to you, Niza. She was hoping you'd help her.'

'Okay, have you lost your mind as well now? What am I supposed to help her with?'

'Well, maybe you should ask her that yourself!'

Just then, I heard the front door click shut, and ran into the next room in a panic. The sofa was empty and her rucksack was gone, as were the trainers in the hall. I shoved my feet into a pair of sandals and ran out into the street in just the baggy t-shirt I slept in. Luckily she hadn't got very far: I caught up with her near the U-Bahn station and took hold of her.

'Where are you going?'

And as she turned to face me, I suddenly let her go. Her face was streaming with tears and her chin was quivering. I wondered whether she could have picked up on what Aman and I were talking about, despite her lack of German.

'Brilka, what's wrong?' My voice cracked.

'I'm going to the station. I'll get the train home. I don't want to do this any more,' she mumbled.

'You can't get the train home. That's ridiculous; you have to fly, Brilka.'

'I thought …'

She tried to walk on, but I blocked her path. 'What did you think?'

'I hoped you … you would keep me here with you.'

'Keep you, how?'

'Oh, forget it.'

'No, wait, please. Don't go. Wait. I'm just … I'm not used to this. I'm overwhelmed. The job and Aman and —'

'Maybe you should find another job if you're so unhappy,' she said, reverting to her usual condescending tone. She wiped her nose on the hem of her shirt and lowered her head, seemingly unsure whether to stay or go.

'Why are you so desperate to get to Vienna?'

'Because I want to secure the rights to Kitty's songs for my choreography.'

'Kitty's? Kitty Jashi's?'

'Yes, who else?'

'Okay. Kitty's songs, then. Why Kitty?'

'Because I'm her biggest fan on this earth!'

She shook her head incredulously, as if she couldn't believe I had never noticed this. And no, I hadn't noticed.

'Okay. Okay. I didn't know. Her songs, then. You want the rights to her songs?'

'Yes, I want to be the only one to choreograph dances to her music. I've already written out all the individual parts.'

I took a step closer to her. She shrank back. Still undecided as to whether or not she could trust me.

'Written them out?'

'Yes — in my head it's all finished, and I wrote it in my book, too, so I wouldn't forget anything.'

'But why Vienna?'

'That's where Fred Lieblich lives.'

'Fred Lieblich?'

I remembered Alania — he had mentioned Fred Lieblich.

'Yes. She knew Kitty really well, and she knows the head of the foundation in London as well, Amy something, who owns the song rights and —'

'How do you know all this?'

Alania had mentioned Amy and London as well.

'Er, hello? Are you actually listening to me?' She rolled her eyes.

'Okay. Okay.'

'What does okay mean? Are you going to drive me there?'

'You remember, in Mödling, you said you knew I'd come to get you? You said you knew Elene would phone me. What did you mean by that?'

'What do you think I meant? I knew you'd come and get me and that then I'd be here …'

'Here?'

'Yes.'

'So you wanted to come to Berlin?'

'Everyone says you're so clever. I thought you'd sort it out — the song rights, I mean. You could help me, if you only wanted to.'

Three days and several visits to the authorities later, her visa had been extended.

★

I tried to smile kindly when Aman and Brilka went out in the evenings 'to earn some money'; I tried to keep to myself the comments about streets and smoky bars being no place for a child. I wasn't one of her official guardians, and she made that abundantly clear to me, just as Aman made it clear that I had no right to tell him what to do when I still hadn't decided whether to be with him or not. But I didn't want to decide. I wanted to be carried along on the banal tide of everyday events, to walk with regular, calm steps alongside everyone else. To keep my regular rhythm, not let myself be thrown off balance.

I let her go. I provided food for her. I went on buying Fanta. I extended my route home, took detours, sat in a café for a while to read a newspaper and stay out of their way for as long as possible. Them and their expectations of me.

Brilka had been with me for two weeks when Aman packed up his belongings. She threw her arms round his neck and didn't want to let go. When I went to kiss him, he shrank back.

'I'm away for three months. The schedule for the whole tour is on the kitchen table. If you don't show up, I'll take that as your answer.'

He gave Brilka a bear hug, then went out, slamming the door behind him.

Again, I sensed my annoyance with him. What was the point of this unromantic ultimatum, what was this sentimental nonsense? Why did he expect something like this from me — didn't he know that our bond was fundamentally non-binding, and that that was the only certainty to which we could lay claim?

'Do you love him the same way you loved Miro Eristavi?' Brilka asked me abruptly. She slid down the wall in the corridor and dropped to the floor, her eyes still on the door as if she hoped Aman might come back at any second.

Miro? What was all this? How did she know? Without giving her a reply, I stumbled back into the kitchen. She followed me.

'Miro came to visit us once. He brought me sweets — I was still little. Elene told me you loved him once. But Aman is better.'

She took a bottle of Fanta from the fridge and went back to her sofa.

There has been war here for two thousand years.

A war without reason or sense.

War is a thing of youth.

A medicine for wrinkles.

ZOI

I began to feel overwhelmed to an unimagined degree. Sleep had abandoned me. My head felt as though boiling lava had taken the place of my brain. During lectures I kept losing my thread and starting to stutter. The ground beneath my feet trembled as if I were in the middle of an earthquake. I couldn't hold myself together any longer. The worst thing was the evenings I spent with her, now on my own. How lost she looked from behind, when I came into the apartment and saw her sitting on the little stool on the balcony, how out of place, her bare legs on the railings, the food sorted by colour on her plate, the bulging notebook on her lap, the muffled music from her headphones, the way she swayed in her seat and the closed-off, engrossed, waiting, demanding, provoking look in her black-on-black eyes. I couldn't bear the fact that I was gradually learning to decipher her gestures and expressions, that I recognised the longing in her tone of voice. That I could see the tears coming before they appeared in her eyes.

I tried to ward off the sense of familiarity that was growing inside me. I withdrew whenever she started to get too close. Left her to her desperate dreams and demanding thoughts. Her ever more direct, abrupt questions. They were mostly about the time before she was born. She was mostly interested in a past to which she had always been denied access. Above all, I was daunted by the questions about her mother: what Daria was like, her preferences, her dreams, the exact sequence of events in the days before her death. Then there were questions about her father, questions about me. Questions about happiness, both general and specific; why no one in our family had been able to hold on to this happiness for any length of time. Why I hadn't been home, not even once. My replies were brief, matter-of-fact, and only masqueraded as answers; in reality, they weren't answers at all. And then there were her remarkable questions about death. A topic she seemed to be truly obsessed with.

At night, when she was calmer, she started asking about the present. Why I had gone away, why I didn't want to tell her anything about her mother, why I didn't live with Aman, or worse still: why I had never wanted to meet her.

It was a daily challenge for me to make her see who I was, to make her see the bridges that existed between us and those that did not. To explain why she hadn't been given signposts and directions for certain things along her path. Why she had no mother and no father; why her only aunt wanted nothing to do with her.

Her whole life seemed to consist of one big *why*. As if she had come into the world without an umbilical cord and her greatest aim was to find it, a frantic search I was unable to help her with. More to the point, one I was unwilling to help her with.

I would retreat into the bathroom and run the water so as not to hear anything. I would try to read a book. Stay locked in there until she went to bed and left me in peace. I turned up the music in my bedroom, unable to shake the feeling that she would pursue me all the way into sleep. Three times I fled the apartment in the middle of the night. Without leaving her a note, a message. Left her there asleep and got drunk with Severin or Caro. I couldn't bear being exposed to her fears and longings any more. I was ashamed of my behaviour, and couldn't stop worrying, even as I was pouring vodka or wine down my throat to anaesthetise myself, to still something that would not, could not, be quieted.

There came a point when even my night-time escapes were no longer an option, since I couldn't stop thinking about her, couldn't outwit her any longer, couldn't escape her questions even by putting some distance between us. One evening, when she had retreated to the living room earlier than usual and gone to bed, I decided to dig out the old hot chocolate recipe and make myself a cup. I hoped its taste would allow me to forget everything, at least for a few hours. I set to work.

I recalled the candlelit kitchen of the Green House, and Stasia with her arthritic fingers, bent over the black, bubbling mass, keeping all the house's other inhabitants away from her magic drink, fearful that its curse might strike them, hoping that I would be strong enough to withstand all the curses in the world.

Of course she was woken by the scent of the chocolate. Just as, years earlier, Miro and I had been lured into Christine's living room by the irresistible aroma, she came running into the kitchen and watched me wide-eyed as I greedily devoured the black mass. She immediately wanted to know what I was eating. The taste had actually dulled my senses, and I sat there in an ecstatic apathy, spooning up the last remnants of the chocolate. But for some reason, at that moment I wanted to believe Stasia's grim prophecies. For the first time, I considered the possibility that my great-grandmother might have been right. As irrational as it seemed, just then I was entirely convinced that I should keep Brilka away from the chocolate; it was as if Stasia were standing behind me and I was heeding her warning. I was convinced it was my duty to make sure the curse didn't touch her.

I leaped up as if I'd been stung by a wasp, clutching the cup with the remains of the chocolate in it, holding it above my head for fear she might snatch it out of my hand. Brilka's eyes betrayed her incomprehension.

'What's that?' she asked, confused.

'It's Stasia's chocolate. Or to be more precise, her father's. But the chocolate is cursed.'

I couldn't believe I had actually uttered these words. For a moment she eyed me with mistrust, as if trying to work out whether I was pulling her leg. My expression, and the terror she could see in my face, prompted by the memory of that evening in the attic, must have convinced her, because she approached me and said, in her deliberately indifferent tone, 'I don't eat anything brown, in any case.'

These words disarmed me. I lowered my hand and let out a laugh of relief. Of course: she didn't eat brown food. Her conviction made her immune to the cursed state of complete abandon that came with tasting the chocolate. All at once I felt incredibly silly. I put the cup back down on the table.

'Anyway, even if it's true, for every curse there's a spell that makes it harmless,' she added, completely sure of herself. She picked up the cup, took it to the sink, and tipped the remnants of the chocolate away.

I was overcome with relief. How reasonable, how almost logical her idea sounded. Yes, she was right, she must be right. For every curse — so the legends would have it, in any case — there was a spell that suspended its effects, made its power vanish. Why had Stasia never considered this possibility?

Brilka turned on the tap and watched the clear water dissolve the thick, brown liquid, until it was no more than a thin, pale line circling its way to the plughole. Then she looked at me, her face relaxed, her lips spreading into an understanding smile, as if trying to signal that I needn't be afraid; she was here with me to face down any curse in the world.

★

She was sitting tight. I could sense it. She was waiting for my resistance to break, for the moment when the last threads of my patience would snap and I would be swept away into a maelstrom of events that had slipped out of my control. She was waiting for me to say something, to make confessions and promises. In her own way, she hoped she was proceeding with more skill and cunning than Aman, who had not managed to force me into making an admission.

Maybe she wanted to prove to me that my old life felt like a blank space; she seemed to be waiting for me to need her, to become reliant on her presence, her devotion, her trust. She was waiting for my rejection to prove weaker than my longing. She probably thought that if she persevered, remained absolute, stayed strong, she could cure me of my paralysis.

She came dangerously close to me and my nightmares. She worked me into a white-hot rage. She made me hate Aman for giving me a stupid ultimatum and leaving me alone with her. For demanding more from me than I was ready to give just then. I hated the tug on my heartstrings when, before I left the apartment in the morning, I found her headband with the little stars on it on the edge of the bath; hated the sight of her lonely trainers in the hall, which made me sad. I hated the fact that she had started to make coffee for me in the mornings, and pretended this was the result of a misunderstanding; I hated the fact that she fetched the post from the pigeonhole downstairs and weeded out the junk mail.

I got to know her many tics: she had to avoid stepping on patterned paving stones, and always had to step in puddles. As soon as a traffic light changed from red to amber she would count to three, and was happy if it turned green just then, precisely then. She hummed a song whenever it started to rain. She put her hands over her ears when someone rang the doorbell. She did three press-ups when she was frightened of something and didn't want to admit it.

But I had now recognised the rational pattern behind her seemingly irrational actions: these little tricks, which helped her to deal with day-to-day life, protected her from a permanent or imagined threat — and this threat was nothing less than Death. She believed she could protect herself from him, outwit him with these small actions. The doorbell might mean bad news. The traffic lights changing too quickly or too slowly might cause an accident. The colour red in food might provoke a calamity. Rain might lead to a storm and someone could be struck by lightning, and so on and so on. I didn't *want* to rack my brains over why a twelve-year-old girl should be living in permanent fear of death. But I was already doing it.

With all her neuroses, how she got through a school day with children her own age was a mystery to me. She never mentioned any friends, classmates, neighbours' children she had any connection with, or whom she was missing. I was taken aback by her disarming honesty and simultaneously overwhelmed by her strong value judgements, these highly developed structures in her head. The grown-up way she had of seeing things in definite terms. Dividing them into a clear yes or no. There was never a maybe with her. Never any indecision or hesitation. What she wanted and what she didn't always seemed crystal clear. As if she had an infallible plan, invisible to others, which she had to follow with meek compliance. A vision, a mission in life. Only when she danced, when she moved, were all these compulsions, all these bad omens, rituals, and preventative measures forgotten. Then she didn't care that it might rain, or that she might fall over and hurt herself; she wasn't interested in whether a calamity had been set in motion, whether death was lying in wait for her. She was free, relaxed. She was herself, without her fears and compulsions. When she danced, she was the sole ruler in a realm of open spaces and possibilities.

★

There was a thunderstorm outside. I couldn't sleep. I kept turning from one side to the other. I missed Aman, and admitting it required no less of an effort than finding sleep. I got up, threw the window open, let in the rain-soaked air, lay down again. I remembered his hands, his way of looking at me as if there were no tomorrow, as if we were the last survivors of the whole human race. I remembered the quiet, tender months when he first arrived and stayed. How good and peaceful it had been, before he decided to present me with crazy decisions, knowing full well that I wouldn't be capable of making them, that it would mean a hopeless ending.

I gave a start when I saw her standing in the doorway, wearing an old t-shirt of mine with a picture of two kangaroos on it. I hadn't heard her come into my room; she usually knocked when she wanted something. She looked frightened and pressed herself against the door. Her eyes were wide, she had her hands over her ears, and her chin was quivering — as it always did when she was about to burst into tears. I leaped up, switched on the little table lamp, and went over to her.

'Brilka, what's wrong?'

'The thunder ...' she whispered.

For the first time, she allowed me to put my arms around her. I led her back to my bed and lay down beside her. She pressed herself to me. It seemed that none of her secret rituals were any use against thunder.

'What are you frightened of? Nothing's going to happen to you. We're safe here.'

'But you're frightened, too.'

'Frightened? Of the lightning?'

'No, not the lightning. Other things.'

'Of course; sometimes I get scared, too.'

'Of what?'

'Of things not working out the way I planned. That people who are important to me are unhappy. That someone might hurt me. That something will be out of my control.'

'Have I hurt you?'

'No, you haven't hurt me.'

She clung to me with all her might.

'Did my mother hurt you?'

'We hurt each other. I'm afraid it's bound to hurt a bit, when you live with someone.'

'And does it hurt now?'

'No.'

'But why? You're still alive, aren't you?'

'Not really, it would seem.'

She fell asleep with her head under the covers, her arm across my stomach. I watched over her all night.

★

We set out for home again when it began to get dark. I had taken Brilka to a summer party thrown by Caro and her new flame out in Brandenburg, but I wasn't keen to spend the night. Brilka had clearly felt at ease there, speaking English all afternoon, and was now dozing beside me. I was taking the back roads, as there had been reports of congestion on the motorway, and suddenly there it was, standing in front of me. A deer in the middle of the road. I braked, I sounded the horn, but it stayed there, rooted to the spot, blinded by my headlights. It stared at us unwaveringly, as if trying to warn us about something.

We came closer and closer; I resisted my impulse to suddenly wrench the steering wheel round and stepped even harder on the brake. Brilka didn't make a sound; like me, she was staring in fascination at the deer. I had the feeling that everything was happening in slow motion. The deer was beautiful. Lithe and wheat-coloured. It must still have been very young; its ears were beautifully shaped and unusually large. Its brown eyes with their long lashes made me feel humble.

I wondered what it must be thinking as I clutched the steering wheel and hoped to come to a stop in time without hurting the animal. In that moment its safe getaway seemed to me an existential thing. As if its survival also determined my own. And at that moment, as we came to a halt with a final, violent jerk that flung us both forwards, it bounded away and vanished into the darkness of the field.

My knees were trembling as I staggered out of the car. Brilka was still sitting motionless, not making a sound. I looked at the spot where the deer had vanished, but it was impossible to see anything in the darkness. I leaned on the bonnet and lit a cigarette. In an instant, it broke over me: I was overcome by a convulsive fit of weeping, there was no holding it back. I was choking, and there was nothing I could do about it. I just heard the car door opening and Brilka's hurried footsteps; I felt her arms enfolding me. I felt that I was no longer capable of resisting her. I gave in, sank into her slender arms, pressed myself to her with all my despair, buried my head in the crook of her neck. We sat down at the side of the road, and she took my hand in hers and waited until I was able to think again, to drive, to live.

'Fine. I'll drive you. I'll take you to Tbilisi. I can't go on like this! You, you … you make me … We'll go to Vienna first, and from there to Georgia. We'll drive the whole bloody way! That's fine with me! It has to stop. I don't want this. I can't do it any more!'

That was what I promised her, once I had pulled myself together a little and got behind the wheel again. If I had been expecting to hear a cry of delight from her, a little thank you at least, I was deceiving myself. She said nothing for the rest of the journey; it felt as if she was almost disappointed.

*

On a humid, sticky day in July we packed everything into the car and set off.

I had spent two days studying the maps with her, and now she was desperate to prove to me that she could be a good navigator. The day before we left, I fought my desire to call Aman. I saw on the tour plan that they would just have arrived in Bern. But what was I supposed to say to him? That I missed him, that I was sleeping in his ragged vest, that I was drinking from his teacup, that I was about to take the most ludicrous trip of my life, that I hated nothing more than having to make promises, that I hoped to find another, better ending for Brilka.

I didn't call.

The first stop was to be Vienna. I felt strangely transparent and excited at the same time. I was looking forward to the journey, but not to getting there. On the way, Brilka talked incessantly about Kitty Jashi, describing her music to me, telling me about her life. She analysed her albums, played me her songs, pointed out particular nuances and details of the composition. On the way to Vienna there was an apocalyptic rainstorm and many hours on the motorway. There were Kitty Jashi's albums and Brilka's euphoric voice. There were plans and speculation about the days to come. We stopped at service stations that stank of greasy food, argued about the length of our breaks and about my desire to smoke one more cigarette. We played silly word games. In between, we sat in silence, or she fell into a restless sleep, and I had to keep looking at her out of the corner of my eye to reassure myself that, even in sleep, there wasn't anything she needed. There was us, and there was the past I was driving back to — though perhaps it held a future for Brilka, too.

There were the two of us, and with every kilometre I put behind us everything else disappeared, shearing off from me as if it had never existed. As if it had been my destiny to become her driver, driving her into the life she was pointing to with her long forefinger.

We reached Vienna. The city gave me the impression that it had witnessed something terrible and had been holding its breath in terror ever since, letting no fresh air into its lungs.

Brilka's euphoria grew ever greater. We left the car outside the little hotel we had chosen and took the tram into the centre. She danced and hopped along in front of me, rubbing her hands, preparing herself for reaching her great goal, hardly believing that she'd really done it, that her plan was really going to come off. As the two of us searched the city map for Fred Lieblich's address, I asked her in passing where she'd got it from. She had just called the foundation, she replied. In London. She had told them several times who she was and what she wanted. She had written, too, letters and emails. And eventually they had passed one of her letters or emails on to Vienna and Fred Lieblich had replied to her. With an envelope containing only a slip of paper with the address. 'That was all. She didn't write anything else. Can you imagine? She wanted me to come!' And with that, Brilka knew she had to go to Vienna.

I concealed from her the fact that her doggedness, her persistence, and the determination with which she had acted were qualities that thoroughly impressed me.

She jumped over every second paving stone, her rucksack bouncing from side to side on her back, a tortoise whose shell had grown too big. Her hair had grown and no longer stood up from her head in hedgehog spikes. She was wearing my flip-flops, and her long, grass-stalk legs moved purposefully; unlike her upper body, they seemed to have a solid anchor, as if they always knew where they had to carry their owner. I couldn't get enough of watching her. I walked a little way behind her, to keep her in my line of vision.

We had arrived at the Naschmarkt. She checked every street sign against her map, wanting to be sure that she would find the right house, that she would soon reach her destination. The nearer we came to her goal, the more taciturn, pensive, edgy she became. I followed her, trusting that she would find what she was looking for. We stopped outside an apartment building with balconies supported by muscular Titans' arms. She read the nameplates with concentration, and her face lit up. She pressed the buzzer.

The door opened at once, as if our arrival was expected, and we walked up a marble staircase. On the top floor a broad wooden door stood open, awaiting us. We went in cautiously, Brilka letting me go first. As we entered the apartment, I was hit by the smell of fresh paint.

'Hello?' I called into the empty rooms, and heard my voice echo back from several sides at once. The parquet floor was freshly polished, the walls newly painted; the apartment must have just been completely refurbished. An elegant middle-aged woman wearing a dark blue suit and a pearl necklace appeared in the doorway, but her artificial smile soon turned to confusion.

'Oh! I thought Mr and Mrs Lambert were due now. I must have made some sort of mistake with my appointments. I take it you're here to view the apartment?'

Even though Brilka spoke no German and couldn't understand the estate agent, she grasped the situation at once, and I could literally see the disappointment spread across her face. It was as if she were shrinking, pulling her shoulders further and further in. She started to slide her feet back and forth on the polished parquet beside me.

'Oh, I'm sorry to disturb you — we're actually here to see Frau Lieblich. We thought ...' I broke off, let my eyes wander searchingly around the apartment's light, spacious rooms.

'Frau Lieblich died just over a month ago. I am sorry. I've been brought in to show the apartment to interested parties. I'm the estate agent.' And she handed me a business card, as if trying to interest me in taking a closer look at the place. 'We're selling, not letting it,' she added, with her artificial sales smile.

Brilka had understood the news of the death, and immediately turned and left the room. I didn't know what to say, but the estate agent jumped in first: 'Were you related to Frau Lieblich?'

'No. At least, not directly.'

'A very headstrong lady. Over eighty, but so young in her mind, and —' she had to search for the right word for a long time '— right to the end, how can I put it, very sharp-tongued: really, she had a mouth on her, you might say. But I was glad to have her as a customer, even if she could be very, well, headstrong.'

'Had she always lived in this apartment?'

'Since she moved here from London, yes. I sold her this apartment all those years ago. She had very particular ideas about what she wanted, and she wasn't disappointed when she came here. She saw the place and stayed. And up there, you see the stairs there, it's a kind of maisonette, she had her studio up there. But she hardly used it in the final years of her life. Her joints were too bad.'

'Did she have relatives? Did someone take care of her?'

'No, no relatives. She didn't like anyone getting too close to her, anyway. She didn't have much contact with the neighbours, either. But she certainly wasn't lonely. No, people like her know exactly what to do with their time.'

'What about the proceeds?'

She eyed me mistrustfully for a moment, but when I pointed out the probable absence of relatives, she decided to answer me after all.

'Her will says the proceeds from the sale of the apartment are to go to a particular organisation, the Kitty Jashi Foundation. A well-known singer in the sixties and seventies, and a friend of Frau Lieblich. She killed herself, but that was a long time ago now,' she explained in a conspiratorial tone, as if the fact of her suicide were the crucial thing about Kitty's life and work.

'A foundation, you say?'

'For musically gifted children. The head office is in London. Very nice people. But may I ask you who you are, and —'

But before I was faced with the embarrassment of having to tell her the story of our family and our journey to Vienna, the doorbell rang and her next client released me from the awkward situation.

I started looking for Brilka, but she was no longer in the apartment. Before leaving, I asked the estate agent exactly when Fred Lieblich had died, and worked out the dates. It had been three days after I had arrived in Mödling and forced Brilka to go with me to Berlin. I ran down the stairs, almost colliding with the Lamberts, and found Brilka sitting on the pavement a few metres from the front door, her head in her hands. It was unpleasant watching her cry, but I had no choice but to sit down beside her. I made no attempt to put my arms round her or whisper useless words of comfort. I waited for her to look up of her own accord, to look at me and ask me one of her questions. A vague sense of failure was growing inside me; I felt disappointment with myself welling up: why hadn't I brought her straight here, a month ago, when we were in Vienna?

'She's dead, isn't she?' she asked, without lifting her head.

I gave her my silence in reply at first, then pulled myself together and said, 'She died last winter. I asked the estate agent. So we shouldn't reproach ourselves. We wouldn't have got to meet her in any case.'

Seldom in my life have I been so disgusted with myself as at that moment, when I sold her this shameless lie as the truth.

> A feeling that lifts your heart,
> Swimming free through the flood.
>
> MIKHAIL LERMONTOV

Once we had crossed the Italian border, it wasn't just the colour of the sun and the scent of the air that changed, but Brilka's expression. She had barely said a word to me since Vienna, and didn't want to share her music with me any more, either, sealing herself off with her headphones as if to punish me for the disappointment our belated visit to Fred Lieblich's apartment had caused her. When we took a break, she separated her food even more manically than usual and gave me only brief replies. She wrote frantically in her notebook, resting on her knee. Conversation was impossible. She did things she had not done in Berlin, like crossing herself three times when we drove past the site of an accident, or drawing five stars on the back of her hand with a biro every time we drove over a national border.

To cheer her up I stopped off in Florence, booking a nice hotel *en route*. Italy seemed to do her good. Maybe because she had no goal in this country that she could fail to reach; because she expected nothing here but sunshine and beauty. We looked round the city, and I showed her a few hidden places I'd discovered on my first trip to Italy. But the fire seemed to have gone out of her, and although she did reply whenever I asked her a question, and her appetite seemed to have returned, she didn't want to take the initiative any more. Neither an Italian ice cream nor the night-time view from the Piazzale Michelangelo of the city bathed in coloured lights awakened her passion.

Only once, as we were listening to a busker playing the violin in the Piazza della Repubblica, did she thaw for a moment and begin to move slowly to his melody. I stopped and watched her: as she had done with Aman, she lost herself in her own secret world, which fascinated and drew in the other watchers along with me: a happy twelve-year-old girl, reaching for life with both hands. In Berlin, the sight had filled me with pride and admiration, but now I had a bitter taste in my mouth, the taste of regret, for not having helped her, led her to her goal; for having lied to and disappointed her.

On the way back to the hotel I couldn't stand it any more: I seized her by the elbows and shouted at her that it wasn't my fault, she should stop punishing me. I repeated my lie that Fred Lieblich had been dead for several months; I held on to it, wanted to believe it myself. But not even my fit of rage seemed to make any difference to her. She listened, batted her thick eyelashes a few times, then walked on towards the hotel in silence.

When I woke the next morning she had already gone down to the breakfast room, leaving her bulging notebook on the bed. I hesitated, but, spurred on by her refusal to talk to me, curiosity finally made me reach for the book. I opened it in the middle, leafed further on, and found the pages she had written in Berlin. Most of the entries were about me. I appeared in almost every note she had made since her arrival. The things I saw there about myself did not make for pleasant reading. Sometimes she was really sharp-tongued — sarcastic, even — and I found it hard to believe that the entries had been written by a twelve-year-old. But through these notes, which described her emotional state in very precise terms, though they hardly ever extended to more than half a page, there shone a frighteningly deep sadness.

I went on reading; I couldn't stop. As though it were a secret book I had spent years searching for and had finally discovered. A book of revelations. I flicked obsessively back to the start. There, the tone seemed different, more objective and less emotional. Descriptions of everyday events, notes for her choreography, though the precision of her descriptions was no less impressive here.

And then I came to a page from last winter. It contained only incoherent isolated sentences, which had probably been written over the course of a month. *I hate it all. I hate her.* Two days later: *I won't pray until Elene can prove to me that Mama is with God.* Then: *Aleko made me go back to school today. I couldn't think of any more excuses for staying at home. I can't tell him, I can't tell him what they did to me in the toilets last week, or he'll tell Elene, and then she'll cry or pray even more.* The page ended with: *I got her letter today.* (*Her* was underlined three times and followed by several exclamation marks.) *A letter from F. L. I know it: from now on everything will be fine. Everything will be different.* A few pages later, I found the following note: *If I run up and down the stairs three times this evening, there definitely won't be a thunderstorm.* And: *If Elene makes rissoles for me tonight, they won't throw stuff at me at school again tomorrow.*

She must have made the following entry just before her journey to Vienna: *And then, when I have the rights, I'll call her and ask her to come and pick me up, if*

Elene hasn't told her already. That depends on what time they realise I'm not at the hotel. I found a cheap ticket on the internet today. Then we'll go to her house, and then, once we've spent a little time together, that's when I'll ask her. I don't know how yet, exactly, but I'll ask her. Maybe like this: Do you want to write the story for my dance? But maybe I'll think of something better before then.

I'm so happy. Soon, soon, yes, soon.

The last note I was able to read before my eyes began to swim with tears was this: *If I make it to V., if Elene calls her and she comes to pick me up, if she takes me with her — then I won't die.*

How could I have been so blind? How could I so consistently overlook what was right in front of me? How could I have ignored Brilka's existence so completely all these years? How could I, paralysed and caught up in my own helplessness, have spent years acting as if she didn't exist? The girl who had set out, undaunted, to look for a new, better story for herself and her ghosts?

That time in the car on the country road, when we managed to stop just in time and not run over that beautiful animal, I should have explained to her that my tears, my breakdown, weren't the fruit of fear, of having come within a whisker of killing an animal, but of the sudden realisation that I still had the ability to love.

To love her.

Why had I not told her that it was easier to live with the empty space behind my ribs than with the permanent, annihilating fear that this feeling sparked in me? Why had I not had the courage to explain that the love that threatened me, through her, put my life in danger? That I knew only too well the hatred it could leave behind once it was gone; and how easily, how suddenly it could become a destructive force when the person it belonged to was no longer there, or no longer able to return the feeling. How it then started to destroy; this emptiness.

And at the same time, I wondered how I could resist her. How could I withstand the flood she brought with her? How could I stop the army that would invade my life with her? Stop my sister's face with the different-coloured eyes coming through the door along with her; Stasia and her card-playing ghosts; Kostya and his poisoned grief; his sister, Kitty, unknown to me, with her eerie songs; her old friend from the English coast; Christine, bare-faced in the final hours I saw her alive. David and his chain. My mother, dead-eyed after weeping for her favourite child. Cello and his naked loins, pressed against my backside in the abandoned print works. I would be overrun by an army against which I would be powerless.

How could I make her understand what life tasted like once I had seen Daria lying motionless after her fall from the attic? How my fear tasted, the fear of going back and finding nothing left of what I once regarded as part of myself? Finding nothing to welcome me, embrace me, be my home? Having nothing left to remind me of myself before the world, my world, our world, the world we used to live in, broke apart and left behind nothing but dust, graves and dead dreams? Was life *really* like a carpet whose pattern you had to learn to read? And if so, why had I not yet learned?

★

We drove along the Adriatic coast. We cut the time into slices. We didn't believe in it any more, we had our own time. We were following our memories, it was just that we weren't yet ready to share them with each other. We stopped and went swimming off small, remote beaches. She was nervous of the water, but gradually she learned to trust me. We swam out. We watched the sun caress us beneath the surface.

On a beach near Bari she put her headphones on me and convinced me to dance. She encouraged me, corrected my posture: she, the master of her art, and I, the obedient pupil. I started drinking Fanta, and let her give me directions. We took the ferry from Brindisi and watched the high waves rebelling against the rain.

When we arrived in Greece, we got back in the car and drove across the country, sleeping in little hotels and B&Bs. There, her lightness and joy finally returned. We reached Thessaloniki and stayed in the city for three days. We ate ice cream, white or yellow. Although here she dared to try a scoop of raspberry — until now, red had been taboo. I felt proud as I watched her overcome her fear.

In Turkey, she started asking questions again. This time I gave her more honest answers; her questions didn't frighten me any more.

As we reached the Black Sea coast she suddenly burst into tears, and I had to pull up at a petrol station. She ran away, shut herself in the toilet, and made me wait for over an hour.

I left her to her sorrow. Her sorrow over the borders that could be felt once again, over the dark hue of the Black Sea. I left her to her sorrow over the fact that we would soon reach our destination, which, as I now knew, had not been her destination when she left her hotel in Amsterdam.

The landscape changed outside our windows. The water changed. The bays, the roads, the people were different. The houses and the smells. We changed, without being able to put it into words. From Hopa we crossed the Georgian border and wound our way along the mountain passes, lost ourselves in the gorges, reappeared, drove down roads lined with bamboo and pine trees, and finally reached Batumi. When we arrived, we took a room and strolled down to the beach in the sickly yellow moonlight. To my surprise, not a soul was there. We sat down and started throwing pebbles into the water. We were too scared to admit that the end of our journey made us afraid.

'So, what's it like?' she asked me after a while.

'What's what like?'

'Being back. Do you feel anything?'

'Give me a while longer, I still don't have the sense of this place.'

'How far do we have to drive tomorrow?'

'If we set off in good time we'll be there late afternoon, early evening.'

'And how long will you stay?'

'I don't know yet. I need to …'

I fell silent. I knew she knew just as well as I did that there was nothing else I *needed* to do. That all the *needing* had drained away from me since I got in the car with her. That my life was in the here and now, with her at my side, in my car, on these roads. But, as ever, I fell silent this time, too. I couldn't do it. My fear of what she had awakened in me was still too great.

In the early evening of the next day we reached Tbilisi.

> In vain I sought my loved one's grave;
> Despair plunged me in deepest woe.
> Scarce holding back the sobs I cried:
> O where art thou, my Suliko?
>
> AKAKI TSERETELI

I stayed at the Green House for two weeks. I let my mother take care of me and played backgammon with Aleko. I walked up and down the hill. I searched for the ghosts under the cherry tree. But I never went up to the attic, the stairs to which were now blocked by a door that was permanently locked. I drove into the city, sat in newly opened cafes and restaurants, wandered aimlessly around the streets. All the city had to say to me were things I no longer wanted to hear, and all I wanted to confess to it, I kept to myself. I asked after the people I used to know. I looked around hesitantly. I didn't allow myself to get involved in any more political debates with Aleko, who thought that the country was on the road to improvement, that the new president had western values, and that his young cabinet had what it took to prise Georgia away from Russia once and for all and take it into Europe.

I passed the places I used to pass every day, looked for streets and buildings that had been familiar and were familiar no more.

Only in the hours I spent with Brilka, the evenings when she danced for me, when we ate together, when she showed me something that was important to her, when she woke me in the morning and chattered away to me — only then did I feel at home.

★

One evening, I dialled the number I still had in my head, and recognised Lana's voice at once. It took her a while to understand who was calling. Then she started telling me how much she had missed me and how good it was to hear my voice again. Apparently I no longer represented a danger to her son. The kilometres and the years that lay between us were probably security enough for her. When I finally asked after Miro, she began talking about how busy he was, but then she gave me his mobile number all the same and invited me to dinner, which I politely declined. Of course it was easy to love me from a distance. I called him and we arranged to meet in a café in the Old Town the following day.

He was aloof from the beginning; he fiddled self-importantly with his car keys and smelled of an unfamiliar aftershave. From the very first second, he talked of nothing but his work. He was the head of a small building firm which was doing fantastically well as the real estate market was booming. He told me about his travels and his life, which was wholly dedicated to work and seemed to include everything except life itself. He asked me no questions, as if afraid I might say something that would throw him off balance. Something that might challenge this image of the happy, imperturbable man. But eventually, when I could bear the whole act no longer, I touched his hand tentatively and asked him how he was.

'But I've just been telling you how I am,' he replied with a nervous laugh.

'What, you mean all that nonsense? I asked how you are, Miro. You can try as hard as you like to be a stranger, but it's never going to feel that way to me.'

'I'm not trying —'

'I thought I had a thousand questions for you, but now it feels like I don't have any at all.'

'Well, that's fine with me.'

'I just wanted to see you, to know how you are. I'm not here to reproach you.'

'And what should you be reproaching me for?'

'Maybe for kissing my mentally unstable sister? Maybe for leaving me alone on the train we were supposed to be getting together? Maybe for hurting me very badly?'

'And here we go again with the reproaches ... Let's change the subject.'

'Where did you *go*, Miro, after you got off the train?'

For a moment he looked straight at me with his big eyes; for a moment I thought I saw a flash of something familiar after all, but then his face resumed its neutral, impassive look and I lowered my gaze.

'What about the film?' I asked, before getting up from the table.

'What film?'

'What film?' I repeated in disbelief.

'Oh right, the film. Good grief, Niza, what decade are you living in?'

'I'd like an answer, please!'

'It turned out the material had been damaged in storage. Apparently it was too damp where it was. Most of it was irreparably destroyed.'

★

Two days before my departure, I took Brilka to visit the graves of Christine, Stasia, Kostya, and Daria. We sat in the shadow of an oak tree, looking at the gravestones. I had a cold beer and Brilka sucked at a bottle of Fanta. The place was hot, empty, and quiet.

'I don't want to stay here,' she said suddenly, pulling at a blade of grass.

'But you have to go back to school, and carry on with your dancing, too, and —'

'Take me back with you.'

Although by now I knew the right answer, the one that should have followed her request, I said nothing.

'I'll find a way to get hold of Kitty's rights.'

She was wrestling with herself, with her pride, with her fear of another disappointment, and yet she kept going, because, unlike me, she was brave.

'Will you write me a story?'

'What kind of story?'

I played the innocent. I couldn't admit to having read her notebook. I couldn't expose myself to an even greater risk of her hating me.

'About Kitty and all that. Then I'll use it for my choreography.'

'I can't.'

'Sometimes I hate you!' she cried, springing to her feet. 'Then go away. Get out of here! I wish you'd all leave me in peace!'

From one second to the next she had started shrieking hysterically.

'Brilka, you need people to look after you; you need structure and a secure life, and those are things I can't give you. I've got enough problems of my own. Come on, you've seen how I live. Brilka, please, look at me!'

'Just say it, say it! Admit it! Stop lying to me, like you lie to everyone — Aman and your mother and Aleko, and the whole world and yourself as well — and probably my mother, too!' she snarled angrily in my face.

'Say what? Admit what, Brilka?'

'That you don't want me. You're no better than them. You're worse than all the others, even. Much worse. At least tell me that you don't want me, you never wanted me!'

'But Brilka, that's not true ... Stop, wait!'

She started running through the graves. I ran after her.

'You're lying again! Just leave me alone. Piss off. Go away. Everything I wanted has already gone wrong!'

'Brilka, stop!'

She wanted to hide her tears from me. I couldn't bear her weeping. Or my lies. I wanted so much to be able to give her something other than my devastating answers. But I was so terribly afraid of being brought to life by her — without realising that she had done it long ago.

★

On the day I went to the airport — I left the car for Aleko; it wouldn't have survived the long journey back — Brilka was nowhere to be found. I didn't say goodbye to her.

> What we love we shall grow to resemble.
>
> BARNARD OF CLAIRVAUX

Back in Berlin, I spent ten whole days trying to go back to my old life. Then, when I realised with a painful clarity how pointless the attempt was, I stopped trying.

I gave notice to my employer. I gave notice on my apartment. I said goodbye to the garage. I rented a cellar storage room and put all my possessions in it. I asked Severin to put me up for a few weeks. I wrote Aman an email, begging his forgiveness and promising to explain everything to him, as soon as I was able. Everything that prevented me from making and keeping a promise. I went to the bars, warehouses, and private apartments where people played poker, and gathered money. By early October, I had scraped together enough to fly to England, and make a start.

★

'I knew you'd come back,' Giorgi Alania said as he opened the door to me.

'Tell me everything, everything you remember, everything about you and my family. If you don't object, I'll leave this Dictaphone running.'

That was how I greeted him.

He did as I asked. And I stayed with him for over a week.

After that, I went to London and arranged to meet Amy in a retirement home in Notting Hill. Alania had put us in touch.

She came with me to the office of Kitty's foundation. I outlined my request to her and to the foundation's employees. With Alania's and Amy's help, and of course because Brilka was one of Kitty Jashi's few living relatives, I quickly got an agreement. The legal issues were cleared up, and the contracts were handed over: from now on, Brilka Jashi was permitted to use all of Kitty Jashi's songs in dance performances and choreography, and also had the exclusive rights to do this.

Then I travelled to Vienna, rented a little room, and began to write. When my money ran out, I sought out the places where people played poker. I stayed in Vienna for a few months, then packed my things and flew to St Petersburg. There too, I rented a room. I wrote and played.

Nobody knew where I was. I never called anyone, never gave out my address, formed no close ties, and went only to those places relevant to the story I had to tell.

I didn't contact Brilka, either.

From St Petersburg, I took the train to Moscow, and continued the story on the eighth floor of a dilapidated high-rise. Giorgi Alania proved a great help with my research in Moscow, too. He put me in touch with former colleagues and friends, who filled in the gaps, helped me search for my answers, opened up their archives to me.

From Moscow it was back to Berlin, where I met the Eastern Europe specialist, told him about my project, and asked him to give me access to his personal archive. He agreed.

Then I went to Prague. From Prague, I flew back to Moscow. And from Moscow back to London.

My journey took a little over a year. For a year I thought about Brilka every day. For a year I talked with her incessantly in my mind. For a year I wrote day and night and lived through the words and out of my suitcase, splitting these days and nights between the poker table and the writing table, swapping one unfamiliar room for another. Gradually a kind of peace settled over me. As I wrote, I was forced to discover how to feel again. Like people who learn to walk or talk again after a serious accident.

A little over a year after crossing the Georgian border with Brilka, I finished my book. Brilka's book. Just before I travelled back to Berlin with the finished manuscript in my hand, the news of Alania's death reached me. Amy had written me a letter. His last wish was to be cremated. His ashes were to be given over to the wind, in the bay where Kitty Jashi had swum out, never to return. I travelled to the Seven Sisters. There, standing on the beach between the cliffs, for the first time in years I felt something like confidence.

★

I went to the Berlin jazz club where The Barons still performed. I listened to their jam session with closed eyes. In the dim stage lights, Aman's cheeks looked less sunken than they had before, and his eyes, too, seemed to have stopped their aimless roaming.

After his performance, I caught up with him at the back door; I knew his habits. As he stepped out and put a cigarette in his mouth, I held a lighter to it.

'I'll be back soon,' I said.

'What do you mean, you'll be back soon? You're standing right in front of me.'

'I'm leaving again in three days, but after that I'll be back, to stay.'

'You're looking good, Niza.'

'I'm feeling good. You're looking good, too. So tell me, is it serious?'

'How do you mean?'

'Well, your shirt and your eau de Cologne … There's somebody behind that. So, is it serious? Hey, come on, I didn't expect you to stay faithful to me.'

'Is that important to you, then — if it's serious?'

'You never answered my email.'

'And you never answered me.'

'Yes, you're right. I didn't answer you. But I haven't answered anyone.'

'I'm pleased to see you,' he murmured, putting an arm around me.

I pressed my head against his chin, and we stayed like that for a while.

'I still owe you an answer. Come and visit me when I'm back.'

I wrote my new address in Friedrichshain on his cigarette packet and gave it back to him. He took it hesitantly. Suddenly, he burst out laughing and shook his head.

'Yes, there's a lot you still owe me.'

'I always pay my debts.'

I smiled at him and began walking backwards, away from him.

'Hey, where are you off to?'

'I told you, I'll be back.'

'When?'

'Soon.'

'I know that "soon"; last time it was over a year. I might be gone by then …'

'Well, I'll probably have to take that risk this time as well.'

2007

I arrived in Tbilisi at dawn on 7 November. Brilka had turned fourteen two days earlier. I took a taxi to the Green House. No one was expecting me; no one knew I was coming. I went up the steps to the house and sat on the veranda. It was still cold, but I didn't mind. I waited for the house and its occupants to wake up, watching the gloomy November day slowly get lighter.

Shortly after eight, I heard Elene's footsteps inside and knocked. She cried out when she saw me, then threw her arms round my neck and called out to Aleko. I hardly dared ask after Brilka, but Elene soon told me she was staying with Lasha's parents as it was expected to snow. She had to stay there during the week because of the long journey to school. ('Oh my goodness, she'll go crazy when she finds out you're here. She talks about you a lot, Niza. She's so tall now, you won't believe it. But as precocious and cheeky as ever!') As Elene made coffee and I cuddled up to Aleko, she asked where I had been all this time, and why I hadn't been in touch. Had I buried myself in my work again?

'Yes, but this time it was a different sort of work. I'll drive into town in a bit and pick Brilka up from school. Is the car still roadworthy?'

'Yes, it's still holding out. I fixed it up myself,' said Aleko, whose beard was now snow-white.

'You need to take care in the city, Niza, the elections are coming up and there are demonstrations every day, all over the city,' Elene said, interrupting him.

'Demonstrations? Against what?'

'Against the government, the president, who do you think?' Elene rolled her eyes at my apparently stupid question.

'Really? I thought he was the great white hope ...'

'Yes, that's what we all thought. Only there's no effective opposition in this country any more. Unemployment hasn't fallen one bit. Yes, there were reforms and restructuring, but the money keeps on flowing into the pockets of individuals — it makes you wonder who it was all for. This country still isn't at peace, Niziko!'

'I'm just going to drive into town, pick her up, and come back here. I don't intend to go to the demonstration.'

'There's going to be a big police presence. They're worried it might escalate.'

'Everything was still very quiet on the way here. I got through fine,' I objected.

'People are still sleeping. You know as well as I do: in this country people need a lie-in before they start a revolution. We don't do demonstrations or coups without a good night's sleep,' Aleko remarked, putting an arm round my shoulders.

We drank Elene's strong coffee. I listened to Aleko voice his dissatisfaction with the state, the president, the authoritarian leadership, and Georgia's tragic inability to take the right path, then I got in my car, the car Brilka and I had crossed the continent in. I drove along the winding roads back into the city, to Brilka's school. When I got there, I went straight in and looked for her classroom. The teacher told me she hadn't shown up for lessons that day. And her absences were becoming more frequent.

I left the school and drove to Lasha's parents' house in Didube.

The two old doctors offered me coffee and cake. Time had stood still in their apartment. You could see that their pension didn't stretch nearly far enough for their needs. In a long, narrow room I discovered traces of Brilka: yellow bedsheets, a few posters of dancers on the walls, some of Kitty's old records, and three pairs of headphones. My heart started pounding. But she herself wasn't there. She had set off for school with her satchel on her back as usual. I phoned the Green House and asked about her friends, the address of her dance school, anywhere she might be hanging out and killing time. I spent the whole day looking for her and calling phone numbers Elene had given me. Nobody knew anything; most seemed not to have a very close relationship with her.

Aleko came into town in a neighbour's car. On the phone he had suggested quietly — not wanting Elene to overhear — that Brilka might have gone to the demonstration. That would be just like her, he said, to go despite all his warnings. There were two big protest marches that day; I should go to one, and he would look for her at the other. I should go to Rustaveli Boulevard, he said: the first demonstration was due to take place outside the parliament building.

He would go to Heroes Square, to the state broadcaster's main building.

Once again, time stood still for me. Once again, I had to go back — but this time, it was in order to move forward.

The streets were starting to fill up. I could hear sirens, and police vehicles raced by at a rate of one a minute. Once again, I saw the crowd of people, marching with placards and banners and chanting slogans. I heard them roaring. And I was stuck in a traffic jam. I swore. My concern for Brilka was overwhelming. I managed to park the car in a side street, got out, and continued on foot.

I marched towards Rustaveli Boulevard, to the parliament building and my former school. Once again I was walking there alone. Police officers and security personnel were moving among the crowd in ever greater numbers. I saw their batons dangling against their legs. I saw the rubber coshes in their hands, and the tear-gas masks on their belts. It started to rain. Someone yelled that the police had stormed the broadcaster that favoured the opposition and had chased the journalists out with batons. The crowd started running like wild animals. I began to move faster, keeping a lookout for Brilka, calling her name. I dived into the crowd, surfaced again, tore myself away, let them push me back. I had to find her. Nothing else mattered.

★

I searched for you with all my senses, Brilka. With all my senses I wanted to find you. Because I had come back and I had your songs with me and I had written your book.

I didn't know whether you would be ready for all these stories at your young age — that was something I asked myself so often that year — but I had no choice: I had to be as mercilessly honest with you as you had been with me. I know, Brilka, that anything else would have been unforgivable. I made that demand of you. You shouldn't have to be afraid any more, not of thunder and lightning or of accidents or of death. I wrote for you, and against the curse. I tried to clear your way of all stumbling blocks and traps. You will stumble anyway, you will fall, but I will be there, I will help as best I can, to get you back on your feet. I will be there from now on, for the rest of my life. That is the only promise I can give to anyone. And I'm giving it to you.

I rushed to you, Brilka. I didn't know where you were, but I sensed you would be close by, and tear gas, coshes, and guns could not stop me searching for you.

I knew I would find you, Brilka. I owed you the question: do you want to come with me, to Vienna, to Berlin, it doesn't matter where, the important thing is *with me*. Do you still need my help? Do you still want to dance through life, telling the story of another life? I'm here to ask you if you can forgive me for not wanting or being able to offer you a home before, when you needed it most.

I couldn't keep you with me, I failed, I led you to a false goal. I couldn't gather up your loneliness, couldn't give you the confidence that you would find what you were looking for. I didn't tell you that, to me, you're the most special girl in the world.

Yes, Brilka, I searched for you in order to say all this, to ask all this.

I owe these lines to a century that cheated and deceived everyone, all those who hoped. I owe these lines to an enduring betrayal that settled over my family like a curse. I owe these lines to my sister, whom I could never forgive for flying away that night without wings; to my grandfather, whose heart my sister tore out; to my great-grandmother, who danced a *pas de deux* with me at the age of eighty-three; to my mother, who went off in search of God ... I owe these lines to Miro, who infected me with love as if it were poison; I owe these lines to my father, whom I never really got to know; I owe these lines to a chocolate-maker and a White-Red Lieutenant; to a prison cell; to an operating table in the middle of a classroom; to a book I would never have written, if ... I owe these lines to an infinite number of fallen tears; I owe these lines to myself, a woman who left home to find herself and gradually lost herself instead; but, above all, I owe these lines to you, Brilka.

I owe them to you because you deserve the eighth life. Because they say the number eight represents infinity, constant recurrence. I am giving my eight to you.

A century connects us. A red century. Forever and eight. Your turn, Brilka. I've adopted your heart. I've cast mine away. Accept my eight.

*

Screams around me. I saw policemen pouncing on a shouting demonstrator. I could already smell the tear gas, and again I found myself outside my old school. Again I saw blood spraying, a young man sinking to the ground, and black-hooded, armed men leaping on him. But my eyes didn't retain the image; they were looking out for you alone, and no one else.

And suddenly I stopped in my tracks. I recalled the joke, the joke that wasn't really a joke, which Christine told me on the day I saw her alive for the last time, eighteen years ago. I promised I would tell it to you, when the time came. The time has come.

Dante is walking through Purgatory. Criminals and violent men are burning in agony on a mighty bonfire; some are drowning in a sea of blood. In the distance, Dante sees a man who is only up to his knees in blood. He approaches, recognises Lavrenti Beria, and asks him: 'Why is it so shallow where you are, Lavrenti?' And Beria replies with a malicious grin: 'I'm standing on the shoulders of Joseph Stalin, sir!' And even though the joke really wasn't a joke, Brilka, at that moment I couldn't help but laugh at it. All those years ago, when I was standing with one leg inside the school building, trying to hold on to Christine, I couldn't laugh at it. But now I did.

★

I stood there, laughing like a crazy person, just as hysterically as Christine had laughed at it back then; because I also felt, as she had done, the decades being churned together. I saw Christine run past me without her veil; I saw Kostya waving to me in the distance; I even saw The Shark, proudly cleaning his gun and preparing to go to war, a war that was not won, ever, anywhere. I saw Kitty standing on Wenceslas Square in Prague and heard her singing. I saw my great-grandmother dance. I saw Miro's scabby knees in short trousers on a deserted playground. I saw myself running down the slope towards the Green House. In this crowd of people, I saw a flash of Thekla's dressing gown and heard Sopio Eristavi's footsteps behind me. I thought I saw Ramas ahead of me, in the midst of the yelling throng; Giorgi Alania must be here, too, maybe Ida as well, Mariam certainly, and I thought I smelled the aroma of hot chocolate, but this time I knew that it would fail to have its supposedly sinister effect. For I had found the antidote to the magic formula: you, Brilka. And I was sure that you too would find your own antidote that would render all curses harmless. I thought I could feel one of Andro Eristavi's wooden angels in my coat pocket. I heard Miqa Eristavi running after the crowd. Yes, I was sure Daria was here, too. Here, somewhere nearby.

I had left Rustaveli Boulevard behind and was standing on Freedom Square, where the statue of Lenin had once stood and where St George was now displayed atop a pillar. The crowd filled the square, pushing like an unstoppable current in every direction.

I didn't stop. I was looking for you.

★

And when I reached the city hall, there, in the corner, I finally saw you, too, Brilka. I saw you standing there motionless, watching the crowd, as if you were viewing a fantastic film. Finally, I saw you, Brilka, and I called out to you through the crowd. It didn't matter whether you could hear me or not; I had found you and I would manage to forge a path through the last few metres to you.

Eighteen years previously, I had hidden, in a school, trembling, filled with fear and hopelessness — but you, Brilka, stood there calmly, watching it all with your black-on-black eyes. You knew you would stand firm, you wouldn't fall, you would continue unwaveringly along your path, however the tide might turn or the wind might blow. And I knew in that moment, more surely than ever, that you are the miracle child. You are. Break through heaven and chaos, break through us all, break through these lines, break through the ghost world and the real world, break through the inversion of love, of faith, shorten the centimetres that always separated us from happiness, break through the destiny that never was.

Break through me and you.

Live through all wars. Cross all borders. To you I dedicate all gods and all rosaries, all burnings, all decapitated hopes, all stories. Break through them. Because you have the means to do it, Brilka. The eight — remember it. All of us will always be interwoven in this number and will always be able to listen to each other, down through the centuries.

You can do it.

Be everything we were and were not. Be a lieutenant, a tightrope walker, a sailor, an actress, a film-maker, a pianist, a lover, a mother, a nurse, a writer; be red and white, or blue; be chaos and heaven; and be them and me, and don't be any of it. Above all, dance countless *pas de deux*.

I have written down for you all the words that I possessed.

★

And suddenly your eyes found me. You recognised my face in the crowd. You squeezed your eyes tight shut, as if you were seeing a mirage, but I was still there when you opened them again. You took a step forwards, out of your enchanted world, into this ugly reality. Towards me. Because of me. So I could still hope. I couldn't tell exactly what your face showed, but for now that step you took was enough for me.

Just a few more metres, a few minutes — but what did that matter, what were they, when we had travelled through an entire century together? Your lips formed my name, and I nodded: yes, yes, here I am. In a moment I'll be with you. And I saw you smile, raise your hand, and reach out to me from a distance.

Watching all this, I thought that I had already dreamed this life, somewhere, sometime.

Just a few more moments, and we'll find each other.

BOOK VIII

★

BRILKA

Here ends Nino Haratischwili's
The Eighth Life (for Brilka).

The first edition of this book was printed
and bound at Transcontinental Printing
in Beauceville, Quebec, in February 2026.

A NOTE ON THE TYPE

The text of this novel was set in Fournier, a serif typeface released by Monotype Corporation in 1924. It was based on the typeface of the same name created by French typefounder and typographic theoretician Pierre-Simon Fournier around 1742. With its strong contrast between thin and thick strokes and sparse serif bracketing, Fournier was a "transitional" style of typeface, and anticipated the more severe modern fonts that would debut later in the 18th century. Its light, clean design presents well on the page, making it a popular choice for printed matte.

HarperVia

An imprint dedicated to publishing international voices, offering readers a chance to encounter other lives and other points of view via the language of the imagination.